Conan the Barbarian: born on a battlefield in Cimmeria, his life was spent wandering the world of the legendary Hyborian Age. From boy-thief to pirate, mercenary and outlaw, ultimately becoming King of Aquilona, Conan carved a red swathe through lost cities and unexplored jungles, facing hideous horrors or supernatural menaces with nothing more than a sharp sword in his hand and a beautiful woman by his side.

Collected together here in the chronological order they were first published are Robert E. Howard's definitive stories of Conan, exactly as he wrote them, as fresh, atmospheric and vibrant today as they were when they originally appeared in the pulp magazines of more than seventy years ago.

'Howard's writing seems so highly charged with energy that it nearly gives off sparks' Stephen King

'A hero of mythic proportion, fashioned by a storyteller who helped define what modern fantasy should be' Raymond E. Feist

'The most popular hero in epic fantasy . . . This is Conan exactly as Robert E. Howard presented him' Karl Edward Wagner

'My, can Howard tell a story!' Starlog

'Conan is the barbarian hero to end all barbarian heroes; his later imitations seem pallid by comparison' L. Sprague de Camp

'Pure adventure yarns with a touch of weirdness' H.P. Lovecraft

'Howard had a great love for all that was lost and strange and faraway' Leigh Brackett

'The bloodiest hero in all fantasy fiction' Brian Lumley

'It is writing which is so concrete, kinetic, manifest, that it seems not to have been cogitated into words' John Clute

'No one has ever done it quite like Howard' *Dreamwatch*

'There has never been another hero quite like Conan' *Science Fiction Chronicle*

ALSO BY ROBERT E. HOWARD

Novels

Conan the Conqueror (1950)
Almuric (1964)
The Hour of the Dragon (1977)
Post Oaks and Sand Roughs (1990)

Short Story Collections

A Gent from Bear Creek (1937)
The Hyborian Age (1938)
Skull-Face and Others (1946)
The Sword of Conan (1952)
King Conan (1953)
The Coming of Conan (1953)
The Challenge from Beyond (1954) with C.L. Moore, A. Merritt, H.P. Lovecraft and Frank Belknap Long, Jr
Conan the Barbarian (1954)
Tales of Conan (1955) with L. Sprague de Camp
The Dark Man and Others (1963)
The Pride of Bear Creek (1966)
Conan the Adventurer (1966) with L. Sprague de Camp
Conan the Warrior (1967) with L. Sprague de Camp
Conan the Usurper (1967) with L. Sprague de Camp
King Kull (1967) with Lin Carter
Conan (1967) with L. Sprague de Camp and Lin Carter
Wolfshead (1968)
Red Shadows (1968)
Conan the Freebooter (1968) with L. Sprague de Camp
Conan the Wanderer (1968) with L. Sprague de Camp and Lin Carter
Conan of Cimmeria (1969) with L. Sprague de Camp and Lin Carter
Bran Mak Morn (1969)
The Moon of Skulls (1969)
The Hand of Kane (1970)
Solomon Kane (1971)
Red Blades of Black Cathay (1971) with Tevis Clyde Smith
Marchers of Valhalla (1972)
The Sowers of the Thunder (1973)
The Vultures (1973)
The Lost Valley of Iskander (1974)
The People of the Black Circle (1974)
Tigers of the Sea (1974)
The Incredible Adventures of Dennis Dorgan (1974)
The Swords of Shahrazar (1975)
A Witch Shall Be Born (1975)
Red Nails (1975)
The Tower of the Elephant (1975)
The Devil in Iron (1976)
Rogues in the House (1976)
The Book of Robert E. Howard (1976)
Black Vulmea's Vengeance (and Other Tales of Pirates) (1976)
The Second Book of Robert E. Howard (1976)
The Grim Land and Others (1976)
The Iron Man and Other Tales of the Ring (1976)
The Return of Skull-Face (1977) with Richard A. Lupoff
Son of the White Wolf (1977)
The Pride of Bear Creek (1977)
Three-Bladed Doom (1977)
The Sword Woman (1977)
The People of the Black Circle (1977)
Red Nails (1977)
The Robert E. Howard Omnibus (1977)
Skull-Face (1978)
Kull (1978)
Queen of the Black Coast (1978)
Black Canaan (1978)
The Last Ride (1978)
Solomon Kane: Skulls in the Stars (1978) with J. Ramsey Campbell
Solomon Kane: The Hills of the Dead (1979) with J. Ramsey Campbell
Black Colossus (1979)
The Jewels of Gwahlur (1979)
Hawks of Outremer (1979) with Richard L. Tierney

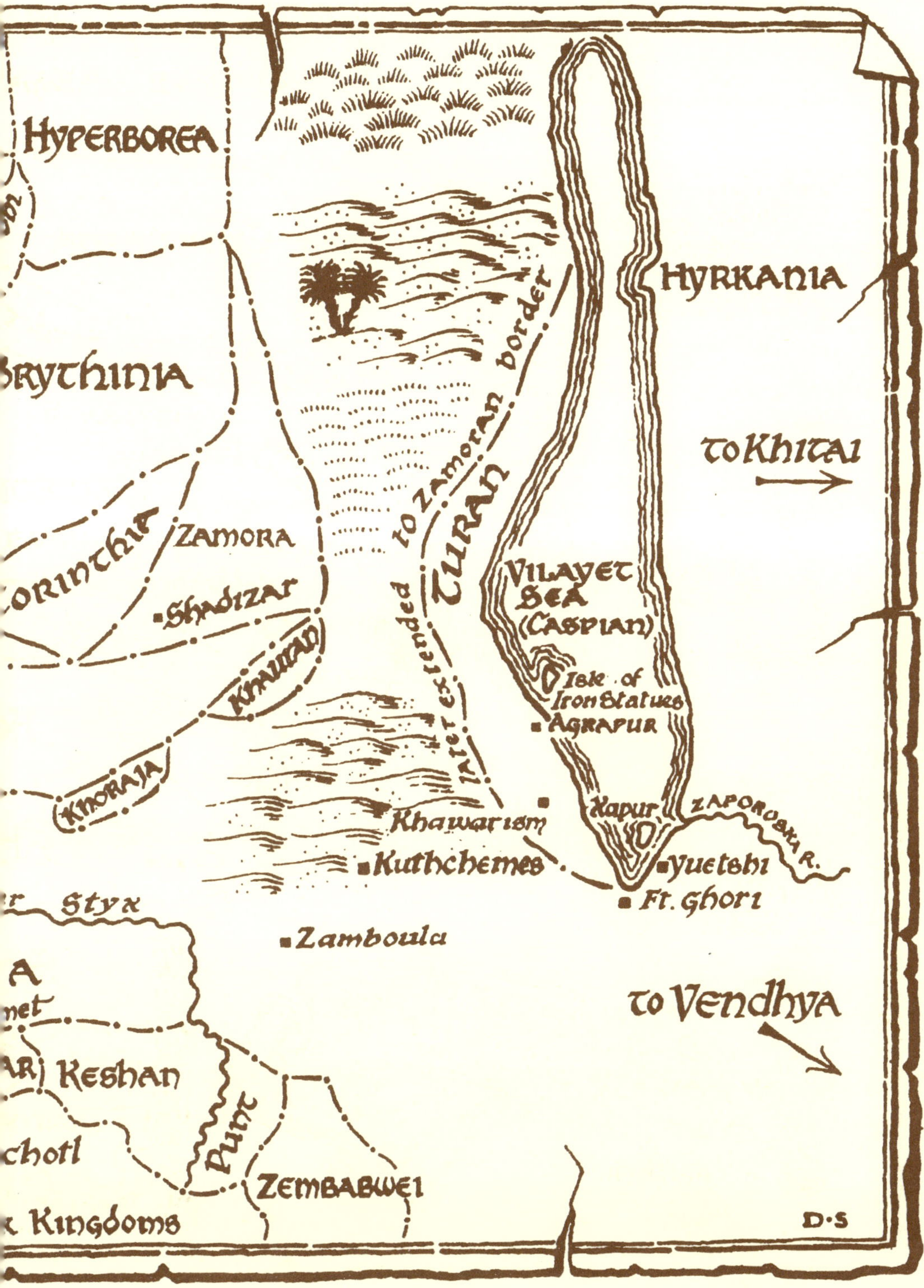

HYPERBOREA

BRYTHINIA

CORINTHIA ZAMORA
• Shadizar

KHAURAN

KHORAJA

to Zamoran border
TURAN

HYRKANIA

to Khitai →

VILAYET
SEA
(CASPIAN)

Isle of
Iron Statues
• Agrapur

• Khawarism
• Kuthchemes

Styx

• Zamboula

• Xapur ZAPOROSKA R.
• Yuetshi
• Ft. Ghori

to Vendhya →

KESHAN

chotl

Puntt

Kingdoms ZEMBABWEI

D·S

The Road of Azrael (1979)
The Gods of Bal-Sagoth (1979)
Pigeons from Hell (1979)
Mayhem on Bear Creek (1979)
Lord of the Dead (1981)
The Pool of the Black One (1986)
Cthulhu: The Mythos and Kindred Horrors (1987)
Robert E. Howard's World of Heroes (1989)
The Conan Chronicles (1989) with L. Sprague de Camp and Lin Carter
The Conan Chronicles 2 (1989) with L. Sprague de Camp and Lin Carter
Eons of the Night (1996)
Trails in Darkness (1996)
Beyond the Borders (1996)
Ghor Kin-Slayer: The Saga of Genseric's Fifth-Born Son (1997) with Divers Hands
The Essential Conan (1998)
The Savage Tales of Solomon Kane (1998)
The Ultimate Triumph (2000)
The Conan Chronicles Volume 1: The People of the Black Circle (2000)
The Conan Chronicles Volume 2: The Hour of the Dragon (2001)
Bran Mak Morn: The Last King (2001)
Nameless Cults: The Cthulhu Mythos Fiction of Robert E. Howard (2001)
Robert E. Howard: The Power of the Writing Mind (2003)
Robert E. Howard's Complete Conan of Cimmeria, Volume One (2003)
Waterfront Fists and Others: The Collected Fight Stories of Robert E. Howard (2003)
Graveyard Rats and Others (2003)
Complete Action Stories (2003)
The Coming of Conan the Cimmerian (2003)
Gates of Empire and Other Tales of the Crusades (2004)
Robert E. Howard's Complete Conan of Cimmeria, Volume Two (2004)
Treasures of Tartary and Other Heroic Tales (2004)
The Bloody Crown of Conan (2004)
Shadow Kingdoms: The Weird Works of Robert E. Howard, Volume 1 (2004)
Moon of Skulls: The Weird Works of Robert E. Howard, Volume 2 (2005)
The Black Stranger and Other American Tales (2005)
Lord of Samarcand and Other Adventure Tales of the Old Orient (2005)
The End of the Trail: Western Stories (2005)
Boxing Stories (2005)
The Riot at Bucksnort and Other Western Tales (2005)
Blood of the Gods and Other Stories (2005)
The Conquering Sword of Conan (2005)

Poetry

Always Comes Evening (1957)
Etchings in Ivory (Poems in Prose) (1968)
Singers in the Shadows (1970)
Echoes from an Iron Harp (1972)
Rhymes of Death (1975)
Verses in Ebony (1975)
The Grim Land and Others (1976)
Night Images (1977)
The Ghost Ocean: Poems of Horror and Supernatural (1982)
Shadows of Dreams (1989)

THE COMPLETE CHRONICLES OF
CONAN

CENTENARY EDITION

ROBERT E. HOWARD

Edited and with an Afterword by
STEPHEN JONES

Illustrated by
LES EDWARDS

GOLLANCZ
LONDON

Copyright © Robert E. Howard
All rights reserved

The right of Robert E. Howard to be identified as
the author of this work, and the right of Stephen Jones to be
identified as the author of the afterword, has been asserted by them
in accordance with the Copyright, Designs and Patents Act 1988.

First published in Great Britain in 2006 by
Gollancz
An imprint of the Orion Publishing Group
Orion House, 5 Upper St Martin's Lane, London WC2H 9EA

A CIP catalogue record for this book is available
from the British Library

ISBN 978-0-575-07766-9 (cased)
ISBN 978-0-575-07780-5 (trade paperback)

20 19 18 17 16 15 14 13 12

Typeset by Deltatype Ltd, Birkenhead, Merseyside
Printed in Great Britain by
Clays Ltd, St Ives plc

www.orionbooks.co.uk

ACKNOWLEDGEMENTS

Grateful acknowledgement is made to the following individuals for their help and inspiration in the compiling of this very special centenary edition: Jo Fletcher, Malcolm Edwards, Danny Baror, Val and Les Edwards, Terry Allen, Danny Street, Rusty Burke, Patrice Louinet, Karl Edward Wagner, Glenn Lord, Novalyn Price Ellis, Joe Marek, Scott F. Wyatt, Robert Weinberg, Randy Broecker, Lew Cabos, Stefan Dziemianowicz, Kent Butler, Alistair Durie, Larry Richter, Erik Arthur and L. Sprague de Camp.

All excerpts from the letters of Robert E. Howard are quoted by permission of Conan Properties, Inc.

Map of The Hyborian Age copyright © 2000 by Dave Senior, from a map prepared by Robert E. Howard.

'The Hyborian Age' copyright © 1936 by Donald A. Wollheim for *The Phantagrah*, February, August and October-November 1936, and copyright © 1938 by the Los Angeles-New York Cooperative Publications for *The Hyborian Age*. Reprinted by permission of Conan Properties, Inc.

'Cimmeria' (verse) copyright © 1965 by Glenn Lord for *The Howard Collector*, Winter 1965. Reprinted by permission of Conan Properties, Inc.

'The Phoenix on the Sword' copyright © 1932 by the Popular Fiction Publishing Company. Originally published in *Weird Tales*, December 1932. Reprinted by permission of Conan Properties, Inc.

'The Scarlet Citadel' copyright © 1932 by the Popular Fiction Publishing Company. Originally published in *Weird Tales*, January 1933. Reprinted by permission of Conan Properties, Inc.

'The Tower of the Elephant' copyright © 1933 by the Popular Fiction Publishing Company. Originally published in *Weird Tales*, March 1933. Reprinted by permission of Conan Properties, Inc.

'Black Colossus' copyright © 1933 by the Popular Fiction Publishing Company. Originally published in *Weird Tales*, June 1933. Reprinted by permission of Conan Properties, Inc.

'The Slithering Shadow' copyright © 1933 by the Popular Fiction Publishing Company. Originally published in *Weird Tales*, September 1933. Reprinted by permission of Conan Properties, Inc.

'The Pool of the Black One' copyright © 1933 by the Popular Fiction Publishing Company. Originally published in *Weird Tales*, October 1933. Reprinted by permission of Conan Properties, Inc.

'Rogues in the House' copyright © 1934 by the Popular Fiction Publishing Company. Originally published in *Weird Tales*, January 1934. Reprinted by permission of Conan Properties, Inc.

'Shadows in the Moonlight' copyright © 1934 by the Popular Fiction Publishing Company. Originally published in *Weird Tales*, April 1934. Reprinted by permission of Conan Properties, Inc.

'Queen of the Black Coast' copyright © 1934 by the Popular Fiction Publishing Company. Originally published in *Weird Tales*, May 1934. Reprinted by permission of Conan Properties, Inc.

'The Devil in Iron' copyright © 1934 by the Popular Fiction Publishing Company. Originally published in *Weird Tales*, August 1934. Reprinted by permission of Conan Properties, Inc.

'The People of the Black Circle' copyright © 1934 by the Popular Fiction Publishing Company. Originally published in *Weird Tales*, September, October and November 1934. Reprinted by permission of Conan Properties, Inc.

'A Witch Shall Be Born' copyright © 1934 by the Popular Fiction Publishing Company. Originally published in *Weird Tales*, December 1934. Reprinted by permission of Conan Properties, Inc.

'Jewels of Gwahlur' copyright © 1935 by the Popular Fiction Publishing Company. Originally published in *Weird Tales*, March 1935. Reprinted by permission of Conan Properties, Inc.

'Beyond the Black River' copyright © 1935 by the Popular Fiction Publishing Company. Originally published in *Weird Tales*, May and June 1935. Reprinted by permission of Conan Properties, Inc.

'Shadows in Zamboula' copyright © 1935 by the Popular Fiction Publishing Company. Originally published in *Weird Tales*, November 1935. Reprinted by permission of Conan Properties, Inc.

'Red Nails' copyright © 1936 by the Popular Fiction Publishing Company. Originally published in *Weird Tales*, July, August-September and October 1936. Reprinted by permission of Conan Properties, Inc.

'The Hour of the Dragon' (verse) copyright © 1969 by Glenn Lord for *The Howard Collector*, Spring 1969. Reprinted by permission of Conan Properties, Inc.

'The Hour of the Dragon' copyright © 1935 and 1936 by the Popular Fiction Publishing Company. Originally published in *Weird Tales*, December 1935, January, February, March and April 1936. Reprinted by permission of Conan Properties, Inc.

'The God in the Bowl' copyright © 1952 by Space Publications, Inc. Originally published in a somewhat different version in *Super Science Fiction*, September 1952. This version copyright © 1975 by Glenn Lord. Originally published in *The Tower of the Elephant*. Reprinted by permission of Conan Properties, Inc.

'The Black Stranger' copyright © 1953 by Future Publications, Inc. Originally published in a somewhat different version in *Fantasy Magazine*, February-March 1953. This version copyright © 1987 by Conan Properties, Inc. Originally published in *Echoes of Valor*. Reprinted by permission of Conan Properties, Inc.

'The Frost-Giant's Daughter' copyright © 1953 by Future Publications, Inc. Originally published in a somewhat different version in *Fantasy Fiction*, August 1953. This version copyright © 1976 by Glenn Lord. Originally published in *Rogues in the House*. Reprinted by permission of Conan Properties, Inc.

'Drums of Tombalku' copyright © 1966 by L. Sprague de Camp. Originally published in a somewhat different version in *Conan the Adventurer*. This version copyright © 1986 by Conan Properties, Inc. Originally published in *The Pool of the Black One*. Reprinted by permission of Conan Properties, Inc.

'The Vale of Lost Women' copyright © 1967 by Health Knowledge, Inc. Originally published in *Magazine of Horror*, Spring 1967 (whole number 15). Reprinted by permission of Conan Properties, Inc.

'Wolves Beyond the Border' (draft) copyright © 1967 by L. Sprague de Camp. Originally published in a somewhat different version in *Conan the Usurper*. This version copyright © 2000 by Conan Properties, Inc.

'The Snout in the Dark' (draft) copyright © 1969 by L. Sprague de Camp. Originally published in a somewhat different version in *Conan of Cimmeria*. This version copyright © 1979 by Conan Properties, Inc. Originally published in *Jewels of Gwahlur*. Reprinted by permission of Conan Properties, Inc.

'The Hall of the Dead' (synopsis) copyright © 1976 by Glenn Lord. Originally published in *The Last Celt: A Bio-Bibliography of Robert Ervin Howard*. Reprinted by permission of Conan Properties, Inc.

'The Hand of Nergal' (fragment) copyright © 1976 by Glenn Lord. Originally published in *The Last Celt: A Bio-Bibliography of Robert Ervin Howard*. Reprinted by permission of Conan Properties, Inc.

'Notes on Various Peoples of the Hyborian Age' originally published by The Robert E. Howard United Press Association (REHupa). Reprinted in *A Gazeteer of the Hyborian World of Conan and an Ethnogeographical Dictionary of Principal Peoples of the Era*, compiled by Lee N. Falconer. Copyright © 1977 by Starmont House. Reprinted by permission of Conan Properties, Inc.

'Afterword: Robert E. Howard and Conan' copyright © 2000, 2006 by Stephen Jones.

In memory of
KARL EDWARD WAGNER
*who began this project
more than a quarter of a century ago,
and*
L. SPRAGUE DE CAMP
*for keeping the
Hyborian Age alive.*

CONTENTS

The Hyborian Age	1
Cimmeria (verse)	21
The Phoenix on the Sword	23
The Scarlet Citadel	44
The Tower of the Elephant	79
Black Colossus	101
The Slithering Shadow	134
The Pool of the Black One	163
Rogues in the House	188
Shadows in the Moonlight	209
Queen of the Black Coast	236
The Devil in Iron	262
The People of the Black Circle	289
A Witch Shall Be Born	356
Jewels of Gwahlur	393
Beyond the Black River	431
Shadows in Zamboula	478
Red Nails	505
The Hour of the Dragon (verse)	574
The Hour of the Dragon	575
The God in the Bowl	733
The Black Stranger	751
The Frost-Giant's Daughter	818
Drums of Tombalku (draft)	826
The Vale of Lost Women	847
Wolves Beyond the Border (draft)	862
The Snout in the Dark (draft)	880
The Hall of the Dead (synopsis)	888
The Hand of Nergal (fragment)	890
Notes on Various Peoples of the Hyborian Age	893
Afterword: Robert E. Howard and Conan by Stephen Jones	897

THE HYBORIAN AGE

(Nothing in this article is to be considered as an attempt to advance any theory in opposition to accepted history. It is simply a fictional background for a series of fiction-stories. When I began writing the Conan stories a few years ago, I prepared this 'history' of his age and the peoples of that age, in order to lend him and his sagas a greater aspect of realness. And I found that by adhering to the 'facts' and spirit of that history, in writing the stories, it was easier to visualize (and therefore to present) him as a real flesh-and-blood character rather than a ready-made product. In writing about him and his adventures in the various kingdoms of his Age, I have never violated the 'facts' or spirit of the 'history' here set down, but have followed the lines of that history as closely as the writer of actual historical-fiction follows the lines of actual history. I have used this 'history' as a guide in all the stories in this series that I have written.)

Of that epoch known by the Nemedian chroniclers as the Pre-Cataclysmic Age, little is known except the latter part, and that is veiled in the mists of legendry. Known history begins with the waning of the Pre-Cataclysmic civilization, dominated by the kingdoms of Kamelia, Valusia, Verulia, Grondar, Thule and Commoria. These peoples spoke a similar language, arguing a common origin. There were other kingdoms, equally civilized, but inhabited by different, and apparently older races.

The barbarians of that age were the Picts, who lived on islands far out on the western ocean; the Atlanteans, who dwelt on a small continent between the Pictish Islands and the main, or Thurian Continent; and the Lemurians, who inhabited a chain of large islands in the eastern hemisphere.

There were vast regions of unexplored land. The civilized kingdoms, though enormous in extent, occupied a comparatively small portion of the whole planet. Valusia was the western-most kingdom of the Thurian Continent; Grondar the eastern-most. East of Grondar, whose people were less highly cultured than those of their kindred kingdoms, stretched a wild and barren expanse of deserts. Among the less arid stretches of desert, in the jungles, and among the mountains, lived scattered clans and tribes of primitive savages. Far to the south there was a mysterious civilization, unconnected with the Thurian culture, and apparently pre-human in its nature. On the far-eastern shores of the Continent there lived another race, human, but mysterious and non-Thurian, with which the Lemurians from time to time came in contact. They apparently came from a shadowy and nameless continent lying somewhere east of the Lemurian Islands.

The Thurian civilization was crumbling; their armies were composed largely of barbarian mercenaries. Picts, Atlanteans and Lemurians were their generals, their statesmen, often their kings. Of the bickerings of the kingdoms, and the wars between Valusia and Commoria, as well as the conquests by which the Atlanteans founded a kingdom on the mainland, there were more legends than accurate history.

Then the Cataclysm rocked the world. Atlantis and Lemuria sank, and the Pictish Islands were heaved up to form the mountain peaks of a new continent. Sections of the Thurian Continent vanished under the waves, or sinking, formed great inland lakes and seas. Volcanoes broke forth and terrific earthquakes shook down the shining cities of the empires. Whole nations were blotted out.

The barbarians fared a little better than the civilized races. The inhabitants of the Pictish Islands were destroyed, but a great colony of them, settled among the mountains of Valusia's southern frontier, to serve as a buffer against foreign invasion, was untouched. The Continental kingdom of the Atlanteans likewise escaped the common ruin, and to it came thousands of their tribesmen in ships from the sinking land. Many Lemurians escaped to the eastern coast of the Thurian Continent, which was comparatively untouched. There they were enslaved by the ancient race which already dwelt there, and their history, for thousands of years, is a history of brutal servitude.

In the western part of the Continent, changing conditions created strange forms of plant and animal life. Thick jungles covered the plains, great rivers cut their roads to the sea, wild mountains were heaved up, and lakes covered the ruins of old cities in fertile valleys. To the Continental kingdom of the Atlanteans, from sunken areas, swarmed myriads of beasts and savages – ape-men and apes. Forced to battle continually for their lives, they yet managed to retain vestiges of their former state of highly advanced barbarism. Robbed of metals and ores, they became workers in stone like their distant ancestors, and had attained a real artistic level, when their struggling culture came into contact with the powerful Pictish nation. The Picts had also reverted to flint, but had advanced more rapidly in the matter of population and war-science. They had none of the Atlanteans' artistic nature; they were a ruder, more practical, more prolific race. They left no pictures painted or carved on ivory, as did their enemies, but they left remarkably efficient flint weapons in plenty.

These stone-age kingdoms clashed, and in a series of bloody wars, the outnumbered Atlanteans were hurled back into a state of savagery, and the evolution of the Picts was halted. Five hundred years after the Cataclysm the barbaric kingdoms have vanished. It is now a nation of savages – the Picts – carrying on continual warfare with tribes of savages – the Atlanteans. The Picts had the advantage of numbers and unity, whereas the Atlanteans had fallen into loosely knit clans. That was the west of that day.

In the distant east, cut off from the rest of the world by the heaving up of gigantic mountains and the forming of a chain of vast lakes, the Lemurians are toiling as slaves of their ancient masters. The far south is still veiled in mystery. Untouched by the Cataclysm, its destiny is still pre-human. Of the civilized races of the Thurian Continent, a remnant of one of the non-Valusian nations dwells among the low mountains of the southeast – the Zhemri. Here and there about the world are scattered clans of apish savages, entirely ignorant of the rise and fall of the great civilizations. But in the far north another people are slowly coming into existence.

At the time of the Cataclysm, a band of savages, whose development was not much above that of the Neanderthal, fled to the north to escape destruction. They found the snow-countries inhabited only by a species of ferocious snow-apes – huge shaggy white animals, apparently native to that climate. These they fought and drove beyond the Arctic circle, to perish, as the savages thought. The latter, then, adapted themselves to their hardy new environment and throve.

After the Pictish–Atlantean wars had destroyed the beginnings of what might have been a new culture, another, lesser cataclysm further altered the appearance of the original continent, left a great inland sea where the chain of lakes had been, to further separate west from east, and the attendant earthquakes, floods and volcanoes completed the ruin of the barbarians which their tribal wars had begun.

A thousand years after the lesser cataclysm, the western world is seen to be a wild country of jungles and lakes and torrential rivers. Among the forest-covered hills of the northwest exist wandering bands of ape-men, without human speech, or the knowledge of fire or the use of implements. They are the descendants of the Atlanteans, sunk back into the squalling chaos of jungle-bestiality from which ages ago their ancestors so laboriously crawled. To the southwest dwell scattered clans of degraded, cave-dwelling savages, whose speech is of the most primitive form, yet who still retain the name of Picts, which has come to mean merely a term designating men – themselves, to distinguish them from the true beasts with which they contend for life and food. It is their only link with their former stage. Neither the squalid Picts nor the apish Atlanteans have any contact with other tribes or peoples.

Far to the east, the Lemurians, levelled almost to a bestial plane themselves by the brutishness of their slavery, have risen and destroyed their masters. They are savages stalking among the ruins of a strange civilization. The survivors of that civilization, who have escaped the fury of their slaves, have come westward. They fall upon that mysterious pre-human kingdom of the south and overthrow it, substituting their own culture, modified by contact with the older one. The newer kingdom is called Stygia, and remnants of the older nation seemed to have survived, and even been worshipped, after the race as a whole had been destroyed.

Here and there in the world small groups of savages are showing signs of an upward trend; these are scattered and unclassified. But in the north, the tribes are growing. These people are called Hyborians, or Hybori; their god was Bori – some great chief, whom legend made even more ancient as the king who led them into the north, in the days of the great Cataclysm, which the tribes remember only in distorted folklore.

They have spread over the north, and are pushing southward in leisurely treks. So far they have not come in contact with any other races; their wars have been with one another. Fifteen hundred years in the north country have made them a tall, tawny-haired, grey-eyed race, vigorous and warlike, and already exhibiting a well-defined artistry and poetism of nature. They still live mostly by the hunt, but the southern tribes have been raising cattle for some centuries. There is one exception in their so far complete isolation from other races: a wanderer into the far north returned with the news that the supposedly deserted ice wastes were inhabited by an extensive tribe of ape-like men, descended, he swore, from the beasts driven out of the more habitable land by the ancestors of the Hyborians. He urged that a large war-party be sent beyond the arctic circle to exterminate these beasts, whom he swore were evolving into true men. He was jeered at; a small band of adventurous young warriors followed him into the north, but none returned.

But tribes of the Hyborians were drifting south, and as the population increased this movement became extensive. The following age was an epoch of wandering and conquest. Across the history of the world tribes and drifts of tribes move and shift in an everchanging panorama.

Look at the world five hundred years later. Tribes of tawny-haired Hyborians have moved southward and westward, conquering and destroying many of the small unclassified clans. Absorbing the blood of conquered races, already the descendants of the older drifts have begun to show modified racial traits, and these mixed races are attacked fiercely by new, purer-blooded drifts, and swept before them, as a broom sweeps debris impartially, to become even more mixed and mingled in the tangled debris of races and tag-ends of races.

As yet the conquerors have not come in contact with the older races. To the southeast the descendants of the Zhemri, given impetus by new blood resulting from admixture with some unclassified tribe, are beginning to seek to revive some faint shadow of their ancient culture. To the west the apish Atlanteans are beginning the long climb upward. They have completed the cycle of existence; they have long forgotten their former existence as men; unaware of any other former state, they are starting the climb unhelped and unhindered by human memories. To the south of them the Picts remain savages, apparently defying the laws of Nature by neither progressing nor retrogressing. Far to the south dreams the ancient mysterious kingdom of Stygia. On its eastern borders wander clans of nomadic savages, already known as the Sons of Shem.

Next to the Picts, in the broad valley of Zingg, protected by great mountains, a nameless band of primitives, tentatively classified as akin to the Shemites, has evolved an advanced agricultural system and existence.

Another factor has added to the impetus of Hyborian drift. A tribe of that race has discovered the use of stone in building, and the first Hyborian kingdom has come into being – the rude and barbaric kingdom of Hyperborea, which had its beginning in a crude fortress of boulders heaped to repel tribal attack. The people of this tribe soon abandoned their horse-hide tents for stone houses, crudely but mightily built, and thus protected, they grew strong. There are few more dramatic events in history than the rise of the rude, fierce kingdom of Hyperborea, whose people turned abruptly from their nomadic life to rear dwellings of naked stone, surrounded by cyclopean walls – a race scarcely emerged from the polished stone age, who had by a freak of chance, learned the first rude principles of architecture.

The rise of this kingdom drove forth many other tribes, for, defeated in the war, or refusing to become tributary to their castle-dwelling kinsmen, many clans set forth on long treks that took them halfway around the world. And already the more northern tribes are beginning to be harried by gigantic blond savages, not much more advanced than ape-men.

The tale of the next thousand years is the tale of the rise of the Hyborians, whose warlike tribes dominate the western world. Rude kingdoms are taking shape. The tawny-haired invaders have encountered the Picts, driving them into the barren lands of the west. To the northwest, the descendants of the Atlanteans, climbing unaided from apedom into primitive savagery, have not yet met the conquerors. Far to the east the Lemurians are evolving a strange semi-civilization of their own. To the south the Hyborians have founded the kingdom of Koth, on the borders of those pastoral countries known as the Lands of Shem, and the savages of those lands, partly through contact with the Hyborians, partly through contact with the Stygians who have ravaged them for centuries, are emerging from barbarism. The blond savages of the far north have grown in power and numbers so that the northern Hyborian tribes move southward, driving their kindred clans before them. The ancient kingdom of Hyperborea is overthrown by one of these northern tribes, which, however, retains the old name. Southeast of Hyperborea a kingdom of the Zhemri has come into being, under the name of Zamora. To the southwest, a tribe of Picts have invaded the fertile valley of Zingg, conquered the agricultural people there, and settled among them. This mixed race was in turn conquered later by a roving tribe of Hybori, and from these mingled elements came the kingdom of Zingara.

Five hundred years later the kingdoms of the world are clearly defined. The kingdoms of the Hyborians – Aquilonia, Nemedia, Brythunia, Hyperborea, Koth, Ophir, Argos, Corinthia, and one known as the Border Kingdom – dominate the western world. Zamora lies to the east, and Zingara to the southwest of these kingdoms – people alike in darkness of complexion and exotic habits, but otherwise unrelated. Far to the south sleeps Stygia, untouched by foreign invasion, but the peoples of Shem have exchanged the Stygian yoke for the less galling one of Koth. The dusky masters have been driven south of the great river Styx, Nilus, or Nile, which, flowing north from the shadowy hinterlands, turns almost at right angles and flows almost due west through the pastoral meadowlands of Shem, to empty into the great sea. North of Aquilonia, the western-most Hyborian kingdom, are the Cimmerians, ferocious savages, untamed by the invaders, but advancing rapidly because of contact with them; they are the descendants of the Atlanteans, now progressing more steadily than their old enemies the Picts, who dwell in the wilderness west of Aquilonia.

Another five centuries and the Hybori peoples are the possessors of a civilization so virile that contact with it virtually snatched out of the wallow of savagery such tribes as it touched. The most powerful kingdom is Aquilonia, but others vie with it in strength and mixed race; the nearest to the ancient root-stock are the Gundermen of Gunderland, a northern province of Aquilonia. But this mixing has not weakened the race. They are supreme in the western world, though the barbarians of the wastelands are growing in strength.

In the north, golden-haired, blue-eyed barbarians, descendants of the blond arctic savages, have driven the remaining Hyborian tribes out of the snow countries, except the ancient kingdom of Hyperborea, which resists their onslaught. Their country is called Nordheim, and they are divided into the red-haired Vanir of Vanaheim, and the yellow-haired Æsir of Asgard.

Now the Lemurians enter history again as Hyrkanians. Through the centuries they have pushed steadily westward, and now a tribe skirts the southern end of the great inland sea – Vilayet – and establishes the kingdom of Turan on the southwestern shore. Between the inland sea and the eastern borders of the native kingdoms lie vast expanses of steppes and in the extreme north and extreme south, deserts. The non-Hyrkanian dwellers of these territories are scattered and pastoral, unclassified in the north, Shemitish in the south, aboriginal, with a thin strain of Hyborian blood from wandering conquerors. Toward the latter part of the period other Hyrkanian clans push westward, around the northern extremity of the inland sea, and clash with the eastern outposts of the Hyperboreans.

Glance briefly at the peoples of that age. The dominant of Hyborians are no longer uniformly tawny-haired and grey-eyed. They have mixed with other races. There is a strong Shemitish, even a Stygian strain among the peoples of Koth, and to a lesser extent, of Argos, while in the case of the latter, admixture with the Zingarans has been more extensive than with the Shemites. The eastern Brythunians have intermarried with the dark-skinned Zamorians, and the people of southern Aquilonia have mixed with the brown Zingarans until black hair and brown eyes are the dominant type in Poitain, the southernmost province. The ancient kingdom of Hyperborea is more aloof than the others, yet there is alien blood in plenty in its veins, from the capture of foreign women – Hyrkanians, Æsir and Zamorians. Only in the province of Gunderland, where the people keep no slaves, is the pure Hyborian stock found unblemished. But the barbarians have kept their bloodstream pure; the Cimmerians are tall and powerful, with dark hair and blue or grey eyes. The people of Nordheim are of similar build, but with white skins, blue eyes and golden or red hair.

The Picts are of the same type as they always were – short, very dark, with black eyes and hair. The Hyrkanians are dark and generally tall and slender, though a squat slant-eyed type is more and more common among them, resulting from mixture with a curious race of intelligent, though stunted, aborigines, conquered by them among the mountains east of Vilayet, on their westward drift. The Shemites are generally of medium height, though sometimes when mixed with Stygian blood, gigantic, broadly and strongly built, with hook noses, dark eyes and blue-black hair. The Stygians are tall and well made, dusky, straight-featured – at least the ruling classes are of that type. The lower classes are a down-trodden, mongrel horde, a mixture of negroid, Stygian, Shemitish, even Hyborian bloods. South of Stygia are the vast black kingdoms of the Amazons, the Kushites, the Atlaians and the hybrid empire of Zembabwe.

Between Aquilonia and the Pictish wilderness lie the Bossonian marches, peopled by descendants of an aboriginal race, conquered by a tribe of Hyborians, early in the first ages of the Hyborian drift. This mixed people never attained the civilization of the purer Hyborians, and was pushed by them to the very fringe of the civilized world. The Bossonians are of medium height and complexion, their eyes brown or grey, and they are mesocephalic. They live mainly by agriculture, in large walled villages, and are part of the Aquilonian kingdom. Their marches extend from the Border Kingdom in the north to Zingara in the southwest, forming a bulwark for Aquilonia against both the Cimmerians and the Picts. They are stubborn defensive fighters, and centuries of warfare against northern and western barbarians have caused them to evolve a type of defense almost impregnable against direct attack.

Five hundred years laters the Hyborian civilization was swept away. Its fall was unique in that it was not brought about by internal decay, but by the growing power of the barbarian nations and the Hyrkanians. The Hyborian peoples were overthrown while their vigorous culture was in its prime.

Yet it was Aquilonia's greed which brought about that overthrow, though indirectly. Wishing to extend their empire, her kings made war on their neighbors. Zingara, Argos and Ophir were annexed outright, with the western cities of Shem, which had, with their more eastern kindred, recently thrown off the yoke of Koth. Koth itself, with Corinthia and the eastern Shemitish tribes, was forced to pay Aquilonia tribute and lend aid in wars. An ancient feud had existed between Aquilonia and Hyperborea, and the latter now marched to meet the armies of her western rival. The plains of the Border Kingdom were the scene of a great and savage battle, in which the northern hosts were utterly defeated, and retreated into their snowy fastnesses, whither the victorious Aquilonians did not pursue them. Nemedia, which had successfully resisted the western kingdom for centuries, now drew Brythunia and Zamora, and secretly, Koth, into an alliance which bade fair to crush the rising empire. But before their armies could join battle, a new enemy appeared in the east, as the Hyrkanians made their first real thrust at the western world. Reinforced by adventurers from east of Vilayet, the riders of Turan swept over Zamora, devastated eastern Corinthia, and were met on the plains of Brythunia by the Aquilonians who defeated them and hurled them flying eastward. But the back of the alliance was broken, and Nemedia took the defensive in future wars, aided occasionally by Brythunia and Hyperborea, and, secretly, as usual, by Koth. This defeat of the Hyrkanians showed the nations the real power of the western kingdom, whose splendid armies were augmented by mercenaries, many of them recruited among the alien Zingarans, and the barbaric Picts and Shemites. Zamora was reconquered from the Hyrkanians, but the people discovered that they had merely exchanged an eastern master for a western master. Aquilonian soldiers were quartered there, not only to protect the ravaged country, but also to keep the people in subjection. The Hyrkanians were not convinced; three more invasions burst upon the Zamorian borders, and the Lands of Shem, and were hurled back by the Aquilonians, though the Turanian armies grew larger as hordes of steel-clad riders rode out of the east, skirting the southern extremity of the inland sea.

But it was in the west that a power was growing destined to throw down the kings of Aquilonia from their high places. In the north there was incessant bickering along the Cimmerian borders between the black-haired warriors and the Nordheimir; and the Æsir, between wars with the Vanir, assailed Hyperborea and pushed back the frontier, destroying city after city. The Cimmerians also fought the Picts and Bossonians impartially, and several times raided into Aquilonia itself, but their wars were less invasions than mere plundering forays.

But the Picts were growing amazingly in population and power. By a strange twist of fate, it was largely due to the efforts of one man, and he an alien, that they set their feet upon the ways that led to eventual empire. This man was Arus, a Nemedian priest, a natural-born reformer. What turned his mind toward the Picts is not certain, but this much is history – he determined to go into the western wilderness and modify the rude ways of the heathen by the introduction of the gentle worship of Mitra. He was not daunted by the grisly tales of what had happened to traders and explorers before him, and by some whim of fate he came among the people he sought, alone and unarmed, and was not instantly speared.

The Picts had benefited by contact with Hyborian civilization, but they had always fiercely resisted that contact. That is to say, they had learned to work crudely in copper and tin, which were found scantily in their country, and for which latter metal they raided into the mountains of Zingara, or traded hides, whale's teeth, walrus tusks and such few things as savages have to trade. They no longer lived in caves and tree-shelters, but built tents of hides, and crude huts, copied from those of the Bossonians. They still lived mainly by the chase, since their wilds swarmed with game of all sorts, and the rivers and sea with fish, but they had learned how to plant grain, which they did sketchily, preferring to steal it from their neighbors the Bossonians and Zingarans. They dwelt in clans which were generally at feud with each other, and their simple customs were blood-thirsty and utterly inexplicable to a civilized man, such as Arus of Nemedia. They had no direct contact with the Hyborians, since the Bossonians acted as a buffer between them. But Arus maintained that they were capable of progress, and events proved the truth of his assertion – though scarcely in the way he meant.

Arus was fortunate in being thrown in with a chief of more than usual intelligence – Gorm by name. Gorm cannot be explained, any more than Genghis Khan, Othman, Attila, or any of those individuals, who, born in naked lands among untutored barbarians, yet possess the instinct for conquest and empire-building. In a sort of bastard-Bossonian, the priest made the chief understand his purpose, and though extremely puzzled, Gorm gave him permission to remain among his tribe unbutchered – a case unique in the history of the race. Having learned the language Arus set himself to work to eliminate the more unpleasant phases of Pictish life – such as human sacrifice, blood-feud, and the burning alive of captives. He harangued Gorm at length, whom he found to be an interested, if unresponsive listener. Imagination reconstructs the scene – the black-haired chief, in his tiger-skins and necklace of human teeth, squatting on the dirt floor of the wattle hut, listening intently to the eloquence of the priest, who probably sat on a carven, skin-covered block of mahogany provided in his honor – clad in the silken robes of a Nemedian priest, gesturing with his slender white hands as he expounded the eternal rights and justices which were the truths of Mitra. Doubtless he pointed with repugnance at the rows of skulls which adorned the walls of the hut and urged Gorm to forgive his enemies instead of putting their bleached remnants to such use. Arus was the highest product of an innately artistic race, refined by centuries of civilization; Gorm had behind him a heritage of a hundred thousand years of screaming savagery – the pad of the tiger was in his stealthy step, the grip of the gorilla in his black-nailed hands, the fire that burns in a leopard's eyes burned in his.

Arus was a practical man. He appealed to the savage's sense of material gain; he pointed out the power and splendor of the Hyborian kingdoms, as an example of the power of Mitra, whose teachings and works had lifted them up to their high places. And he spoke of cities, and fertile plains, marble walls and iron chariots, jeweled towers, and horsemen in their glittering armor riding to battle. And Gorm, with the unerring instinct of the barbarian, passed over his words regarding gods and their teachings, and fixed on the material powers thus vividly described. There in that mud-floored wattle hut, with the silk-robed priest on the mahogany block, and the dark-skinned chief crouching in his tiger-hides, was laid the foundations of empire.

As has been said, Arus was a practical man. He dwelt among the Picts and found much that an intelligent man could do to aid humanity, even when that humanity was cloaked in tiger-skins and wore necklaces of human teeth. Like all priests of Mitra, he was instructed in many things. He found that there were vast deposits of iron ore in the Pictish hills, and he taught the natives to mine, smelt and work it into implements – agricultural implements, as he fondly believed. He instituted other reforms, but these were the most important things he did: he instilled in Gorm a desire to see the civilized lands of the world; he taught the Picts how to work in iron; and he established contact between them and the civilized world. At the chief's request he conducted him and some of his warriors through the Bossonian marches, where the honest villagers stared in amazement, into the glittering outer world.

Arus no doubt thought that he was making converts right and left, because the Picts listened to him, and refrained from smiting him with their copper axes. But the Pict was little calculated to seriously regard teachings which bade him forgive his enemy and abandon the warpath for the ways of honest drudgery. It has been said that he lacked artistic sense; his whole nature led to war and slaughter. When the priest talked of the glories of the civilized nations, his dark-skinned listeners were intent, not on the ideals of his religion, but on the loot which he unconsciously described in the narration of rich cities and shining lands. When he told how Mitra aided certain kings to overcome their enemies, they paid scant heed to the miracles of Mitra, but they hung on the description of battle-lines, mounted knights, and maneuvers of archers and spearmen. They harkened with keen dark eyes and inscrutable countenances, and they went their ways without comment, and heeded with flattering intentness his instructions as to the working of iron, and kindred arts.

Before his coming they had filched steel weapons and armor from the Bossonians and Zingarans, or had hammered out their own crude arms from copper and bronze. Now a new world opened to them, and the clang of sledges re-echoed throughout the land. And Gorm, by virtue of this new craft, began to assert his dominance over other clans, partly by war, partly by craft and diplomacy, in which latter art he excelled all other barbarians.

Picts now came and went freely into Aquilonia, under safe-conduct, and they returned with more information as to armor-forging and sword-making. More, they entered Aquilonia's mercenary armies, to the unspeakable disgust of the sturdy Bossonians. Aquilonia's kings toyed with the idea of playing the Picts against the Cimmerians, and possibly thus destroying both menaces, but they were too busy with their policies of aggression in the south and east to pay much heed to the vaguely known lands of the west, from which more and more stocky warriors swarmed to take service among the mercenaries.

These warriors, their service completed, went back to their wilderness with good ideas of civilized warfare, and that contempt for civilization which arises from familiarity with it. Drums began to beat in the hills, gathering-fires smoked on the heights, and savage sword-makers hammered their steel on a thousand anvils. By intrigues and forays too numerous and devious to enumerate, Gorm became chief of chiefs, the nearest approach to a king the Picts had had in thousands of years. He had waited long; he was past middle age. But now he moved against the frontiers, not in trade, but in war.

Arus saw his mistake too late; he had not touched the soul of the pagan, in which lurked the hard fierceness of all the ages. His persuasive eloquence had not caused a ripple in the Pictish conscience. Gorm wore a corselet of silvered mail now, instead of the tiger-skin, but underneath he was unchanged – the everlasting barbarian, unmoved by theology or philosophy, his instincts fixed unerringly on rapine and plunder.

The Picts burst on the Bossonian frontiers with fire and sword, not clad in tiger-skins and brandishing copper axes as of yore, but in scale-mail, wielding weapons of keen steel. As for Arus, he was brained by a drunken Pict, while making a last effort to undo the work he had unwittingly done. Gorm was not without gratitude; he caused the skull of the slayer to be set on the top of the priest's cairn. And it is one of the grim ironies of the universe that the stones which covered Arus's body should have been adorned with that last touch of barbarity – above a man to whom violence and blood-vengeance were revolting.

But the newer weapons and mail were not enough to break the lines. For years the superior armaments and sturdy courage of the Bossonians held the invaders at bay, aided, when necessary, by imperial Aquilonian troops. During this time the Hyrkanians came and went, and Zamora was added to the empire.

Then treachery from an unexpected source broke the Bossonian lines. Before chronicling this treachery, it might be well to glance briefly at the Aquilonian empire. Always a rich kingdom, untold wealth had been rolled in by conquest, and sumptuous splendor had taken the place of simple and hardy living. But degeneracy had not yet sapped the kings and the people; though clad in silks and cloth-of-gold, they were still a vital, virile race. But arrogance was supplanting their former simplicity. They treated less powerful people with growing contempt, levying more and more tributes on the conquered. Argos, Zingara, Ophir, Zamora and the Shemite countries were treated as subjugated provinces, which was especially galling to the proud Zingarans, who often revolted, despite savage retaliations.

Koth was practically tributary, being under Aquilonia's 'protection' against the Hyrkanians. But Nemedia the western empire had never been able to subdue, although the latter's triumphs were of the defensive sort, and were generally attained with the aid of Hyperborean armies. During this period Aquilonia's only defeats were: her failure to annex Nemedia; the rout of an army sent into Cimmeria; and the almost complete destruction of an army by the Æsir. Just as the Hyrkanians found themselves unable to withstand the heavy cavalry charges of the Aquilonians, so the latter, invading the snow-countries, were overwhelmed by the ferocious hand-to-hand fighting of the Nordics. But Aquilonia's conquests were pushed to the Nilus, where a Stygian army was defeated with great slaughter, and the king of Stygia sent tribute – once at least – to divert invasion of his kingdom. Brythunia was reduced in a series of whirlwind wars, and preparations were made to subjugate the ancient rival at last – Nemedia.

With their glittering hosts greatly increased by mercenaries, the Aquilonians moved against their old-time foe, and it seemed as if the thrust were destined to crush the last shadow of Nemedian independence. But contentions arose between the Aquilonians and their Bossonian auxilliaries.

As the inevitable result of imperial expansion, the Aquilonians had become haughty and intolerant. They derided the ruder, unsophisticated Bossonians, and hard feeling grew between them – the Aquilonians despising the Bossonians and the latter resenting the attitude of their masters – who now boldly called themselves such, and treated the Bossonians like conquered subjects, taxing them exorbitantly, and conscripting them for their wars of territorial expansion – wars the profits of which the Bossonians shared little. Scarcely enough men were left in the marches to guard the frontier, and hearing of Pictish outrages in their homelands, whole Bossonian regiments quit the Nemedian campaign and marched to the western frontier, where they defeated the dark-skinned invaders in a great battle.

This desertion, however, was the direct cause of Aquilonia's defeat by the desperate Nemedians, and brought down on the Bossonians the cruel wrath of the imperialists – intolerant and short-sighted as imperialists invariably are. Aquilonian regiments were secretly brought to the borders of the marches, the Bossonian chiefs were invited to attend a great conclave, and, in the guise of an expedition against the Picts, bands of savage Shemitish soldiers were quartered among the unsuspecting villagers. The unarmed chiefs were massacred, the Shemites turned on their stunned hosts with torch and sword, and the armored imperial hosts were hurled ruthlessly on the unsuspecting people. From north to south the marches were ravaged and the Aquilonian armies marched back from the borders, leaving a ruined and devastated land behind them.

And then the Pictish invasion burst in full power along those borders. It was no mere raid, but the concerted rush of a whole nation, led by chiefs who had served in Aquilonian armies, and planned and directed by Gorm – an old man now, but with the fire of his fierce ambition undimmed. This time there were no strong walled villages in their path, manned by sturdy archers, to hold back the rush until the imperial troops could be brought up. The remnants of the Bossonians were swept out of existence, and the blood-mad barbarians swarmed into Aquilonia, looting and burning, before the legions, warring again with the Nemedians, could be marched into the west. Zingara seized this opportunity to throw off the yoke, which example was followed by Corinthia and the Shemites. Whole regiments of mercenaries and vassals mutinied and marched back to their own countries, looting and burning as they went. The Picts surged irresistibly eastward, and host after host was trampled beneath their feet. Without their Bossonian archers the Aquilonians found themselves unable to cope with the terrible arrow-fire of the barbarians. From all parts of the empire legions were recalled to resist the onrush, while from the wilderness horde after horde swarmed forth, in apparently inexhaustible supply. And in the midst of this chaos, the Cimmerians swept down from their hills, completing the ruin. They looted cities, devastated the country, and retired into the hills with their plunder, but the Picts occupied the land they had over-run. And the Aquilonian empire went down in fire and blood.

Then again the Hyrkanians rode from the blue east. The withdrawal of the imperial legions from Zamora was their incitement. Zamora fell easy prey to their thrusts, and the Hyrkanian king established his capital in the largest city of the country. This invasion was from the ancient Hyrkanian kingdom of Turan, on the shores of the inland sea, but another, more savage Hyrkanian thrust came from the north. Hosts of steel-clad riders galloped around the northern extremity of the inland sea, traversed the icy deserts, entered the steppes, driving the aborigines before them, and launched themselves against the western kingdoms. These newcomers were not at first allies with the Turanians, but skirmished with them as with the Hyborians; new drifts of eastern warriors bickered and fought, until all were united under a great chief, who came riding from the very shores of the eastern ocean. With no Aquilonian armies to oppose them, they were invincible. They swept over and subjugated Brythunia, and devastated southern Hyperborea, and Corinthia. They swept into the Cimmerian hills, driving the black-haired barbarians before them, but among the hills, where cavalry was less effectual, the Cimmerians turned on them, and only a disorderly retreat, at the end of a whole day of bloody fighting, saved the Hyrkanian hosts from complete annihilation.

While these events had been transpiring, the kingdoms of Shem had conquered their ancient master, Koth, and had been defeated in an attempted invasion of Stygia. But scarcely had they completed their degradation of Koth, when they were over-run by the Hyrkanians, and found themselves subjugated by sterner masters than the Hyborians had ever been. Meanwhile the Picts had made themselves complete masters of Aquilonia, practically blotting out the inhabitants. They had broken over the borders of Zingara, and thousands of Zingarans, fleeing the slaughter into Argos, threw themselves on the mercy of the westward-sweeping Hyrkanians, who settled them in Zamora as subjects. Behind them as they fled, Argos was enveloped in the flame and slaughter of Pictish conquest, and the slayers swept into Ophir and clashed with the westward-riding Hyrkanians. The latter, after their conquest of Shem, had overthrown a Stygian army at the Nilus and over-run the country as far south as the black kingdom of Amazon, of whose people they brought back thousands as captives, settling them among the Shemites. Possibly they would have completed their conquests in Stygia, adding it to their widening empire, but for the fierce thrusts of the Picts against their western conquests.

Nemedia, unconquerable by Hyborians, reeled between the riders of the east and the swordsmen of the west, when a tribe of Æsir, wandering down from their snowy lands, came into the kingdom, and were engaged as mercenaries; they proved such able warriors that they not only beat off the Hyrkanians, but halted the eastward advance of the Picts.

The world at that time presents some such picture: a vast Pictish empire, wild, rude and barbaric, stretches from the coasts of Vanaheim in the north to the southern-most shores of Zingara. It stretches east to include all Aquilonia except Gunderland, the northern-most province, which, as a separate kingdom in the hills, survived the fall of the empire, and still maintains its independence. The Pictish empire also includes Argos, Ophir, the western part of Koth, and the western-most lands of Shem. Opposed to this barbaric empire is the empire of the Hyrkanians, of which the northern boundaries are the ravaged lines of Hyperborea, and the southern, the deserts south of the lands of Shem. Zamora, Brythunia, the Border Kingdom, Corinthia, most of Koth, and all the eastern lands of Shem are included in this empire. The borders of Cimmeria are intact; neither Pict nor Hyrkanian has been able to subdue these warlike barbarians. Nemedia, dominated by the Æsir mercenaries, resists all invasions. In the north Nordheim, Cimmeria and Nemedia separate the conquering races, but in the south, Koth has become a battle-ground where Picts and Hyrkanians war incessantly. Sometimes the eastern warriors expel the barbarians from the kingdom entirely; again the plains and cities are in the hands of the western invaders. In the far south, Stygia, shaken by the Hyrkanian invasion, is being encroached upon by the great black kingdoms. And in the far north, the Nordic tribes are restless, warring continually with the Cimmerians, and sweeping the Hyperborean frontiers.

Gorm was slain by Hialmar, a chief of the Nemedian Æsir. He was a very old man, nearly a hundred years old. In the seventy-five years which had elapsed since he first heard the tale of empires from the lips of Arus – a long time in the life of a man, but a brief space in the tale of nations – he had welded an empire from straying savage clans, he had overthrown a civilization. He who had been born in a mud-walled, wattle-roofed hut, in his old age sat on golden thrones, and gnawed joints of beef presented to him on golden dishes by naked slave-girls who were the daughters of kings. Conquest and the acquiring of wealth altered not the Pict; out of the ruins of the crushed civilization no new culture arose phoenix-like. The dark hands which shattered the artistic glories of the conquered never tried to copy them. Though he sat among the glittering ruins of shattered palaces and clad his hard body in the silks of vanquished kings, the Pict remained the eternal barbarian, ferocious, elemental, interested only in the naked primal principles of life, unchanging, unerring in his instincts which were all for war and plunder, and in which arts and the cultured progress of humanity had no place. Not so with the Æsir who settled in Nemedia. These soon adopted many of the ways of their civilized allies, modified powerfully, however, by their own intensely virile and alien culture.

For a short age Pict and Hyrkanian snarled at each other over the ruins of the world they had conquered. Then began the glacier ages, and the great Nordic drift. Before the southward moving ice-fields the northern tribes drifted, driving kindred clans before them. The Æsir blotted out the ancient kingdom of Hyperborea, and across its ruins came to grips with the Hyrkanians. Nemedia had already become a Nordic kingdom, ruled by the descendants of the Æsir mercenaries. Driven before the onrushing tides of Nordic invasion, the Cimmerians were on the march, and neither army nor city stood before them. They surged across and completely destroyed the kingdom of Gunderland, and marched across ancient Aquilonia, hewing their irresistible way through the Pictish hosts. They defeated the Nordic-Nemedians and sacked some of their cities, but did not halt. They continued eastward, overthrowing a Hyrkanian army on the borders of Brythunia.

Behind them hordes of Æsir and Vanir swarmed into the lands, and the Pictish empire reeled beneath their strokes. Nemedia was overthrown, and the half-civilized Nordics fled before their wilder kinsmen, leaving the cities of Nemedia ruined and deserted. These fleeing Nordics, who had adopted the name of the older kingdom, and to whom the term Nemedian henceforth refers, came into the ancient land of Koth, expelled both Picts and Hyrkanians, and aided the people of Shem to throw off the Hyrkanian yoke. All over the western world, the Picts and Hyrkanians were staggering before this younger, fiercer people. A band of Æsir drove the eastern riders from Brythunia and settled there themselves, adopting the name for themselves. The Nordics who had conquered Hyperborea assailed their eastern enemies so savagely that the dark-skinned descendants of the Lemurians retreated into the steppes, pushed irresistibly back toward Vilayet.

Meanwhile the Cimmerians, wandering southeastward, destroyed the ancient Hyrkanian kingdom of Turan, and settled on the southwestern shores of the inland sea. The power of the eastern conquerors was broken. Before the attacks of the Nordheimr and the Cimmerians, they destroyed all their cities, butchered such captives as were not fit to make the long march, and then, herding thousands of slaves before them, rode back into the mysterious east, skirting the northern edge of the sea, and vanishing from western history, until they rode out of the east again, thousands of years later, as Huns, Mongols, Tatars and Turks. With them in their retreat went thousands of Zamorians and Zingarans, who were settled together far to the east, formed a mixed race, and emerged ages afterward as gypsies.

Meanwhile, also, a tribe of Vanir adventurers had passed along the Pictish coast southward, ravaged ancient Zingara, and come into Stygia, which, oppressed by a cruel aristocratic ruling class, was staggering under the thrusts of the black kingdoms to the south. The red-haired Vanir led the slaves in a general revolt, overthrew the reigning class, and set themselves up as a caste of conquerors. They subjugated the northern-most black kingdoms, and built a vast southern empire, which they called Egypt. From these red-haired conquerors the earlier Pharaohs boasted descent.

The western world was now dominated by Nordic barbarians. The Picts still held Aquilonia and part of Zingara, and the western coast of the continent. But east to Vilayet, and from the Arctic circle to the lands of Shem, the only inhabitants were roving tribes of Nordheimr, excepting the Cimmerians, settled in the old Turanian kingdom. There were no cities anywhere, except in Stygia and the lands of Shem; the invading tides of Picts, Hyrkanians, Cimmerians and Nordics had levelled them in ruins, and the once dominant Hyborians had vanished from the earth, leaving scarcely a trace of their blood in the veins of their conquerors. Only a few names of lands, tribes and cities remained in the languages of the barbarians, to come down through the centuries connected with distorted legend and fable, until the whole history of the Hyborian age was lost sight of in a cloud of myths and fantasies. Thus in the speech of the gypsies lingered the terms Zingara and Zamora; the Æsir who dominated Nemedia were called Nemedians, and later figured in Irish history, and the Nordics who settled in Brythunia were known as Brythunians, Brythons or Britons.

There was no such thing, at that time, as a consolidated Nordic empire. As always, the tribes had each its own chief or king, and they fought savagely among themselves. What their destiny might have been will not be known, because another terrific convulsion of the earth, carving out the lands as they are known to moderns, hurled all into chaos again. Great strips of the western coast sank; Vanaheim and western Asgard – uninhabited and glacier-haunted wastes for a hundred years – vanished beneath the waves. The ocean flowed around the mountains of western Cimmeria to form the North Sea; these mountains became the islands later known as England, Scotland and Ireland, and the waves rolled over what had been the Pictish wilderness and the Bossonian marches. In the north the Baltic Sea was formed, cutting Asgard into the peninsulas later known as Norway, Sweden and Denmark, and far to the south the Stygian continent was broken away from the rest of the world, on the line of cleavage formed by the river Nilus in its westward trend. Over Argos, western Koth and the western lands of Shem, washed the blue ocean men later called the Mediterranean. But where land sank elsewhere, a vast expanse west of Stygia rose out of the waves, forming the whole western half of the continent of Africa.

The buckling of the land thrust up great mountain ranges in the central part of the northern continent. Whole Nordic tribes were blotted out, and the rest retreated eastward. The territory about the slowly drying inland sea was not affected, and there, on the western shores, the Nordic tribes began a pastoral existence, living in more or less peace with the Cimmerians, and gradually mixing with them. In the west the remnants of the Picts, reduced by the cataclysm once more to the status of stone-age savages, began, with the incredible virility of their race, once more to possess the land, until, at a later age, they were overthrown by the westward drift of the Cimmerians and Nordics. This was so long after the breaking-up of the continent that only meaningless legends told of former empires.

This drift comes within the reach of modern history and need not be repeated. It resulted from a growing population which thronged the steppes west of the inland sea – which still later, much reduced in size, was known as the Caspian – to such an extent that migration became an economic necessity. The tribes moved southward, northward and westward, into those lands now known as India, Asia Minor and central and western Europe.

They came into these countries as Aryans. But there were variations among these primitive Aryans, some of which are still recognized today, others which have long been forgotten. The blond Achaians, Gauls and Britons, for instance, were descendants of pure-blooded Æsir. The Nemedians of Irish legendry were the Nemedian Æsir. The Danes were descendants of pure-blooded Vanir; the Goths – ancestors of the other Scandinavian and Germanic tribes, including the Anglo-Saxons – were descendants of a mixed race whose elements contained Vanir, Æsir and Cimmerian strains. The Gaels, ancestors of the Irish and Highland Scotch, descended from pure-blooded Cimmerian clans. The Cymric tribes of Britain were a mixed Nordic–Cimmerian race which preceded the purely Nordic Britons into the isles, and thus gave rise to a legend of Gaelic priority. The Cimbri who fought Rome were of the same blood, as well as the Gimmerai of the Assyrians and Grecians, and Gomer of the Hebrews. Other clans of the Cimmerians adventured east of the drying inland sea, and a few centuries later mixed with Hyrkanian blood, returned westward as Scythians. The original ancestors of the Gaels gave their name to modern Crimea.

The ancient Sumerians had no connection with the western race. They were a mixed people, of Hyrkanian and Shemitish bloods, who were not taken with the conquerors in their retreat. Many tribes of Shem escaped that captivity, and from pure-blooded Shemites, or Shemites mixed with Hyborian or Nordic blood, were descended the Arabs, Israelites, and other straighter-featured Semites. The Canaanites, or Alpine Semites, traced their descent from Shemitish ancestors mixed with the Kushites settled among them by their Hyrkanian masters; the Elamites were a typical race of this type. The short, thick-limbed

Etruscans, base of the Roman race, were descendants of a people of mixed Stygian, Hyrkanian and Pictish strains, and originally lived in the ancient kingdom of Koth. The Hyrkanians, retreating to the eastern shores of the continent, evolved into the tribes later known as Tatars, Huns, Mongols and Turks.

The origins of other races of the modern world may be similarly traced; in almost every case, older far than they realize, their history stretches back into the mists of the forgotten Hyborian age . . .

CIMMERIA

I remember

The dark woods, masking slopes of sombre hills;
The gray clouds' leaden everlasting arch;
The dusky streams that flowed without a sound,
And the lone winds that whispered down the passes.

Vista on vista marching, hills on hills,
Slope beyond slope, each dark with sullen trees,
Our gaunt land lay. So when a man climbed up
A rugged peak and gazed, his shaded eye
Saw but the endless vista – hill on hill,
Slope beyond slope, each hooded like its brothers.

It was a gloomy land that seemed to hold
All winds and clouds and dreams that shun the sun,
With bare boughs rattling in the lonesome winds,
And the dark woodlands brooding over all,
Not even lightened by the rare dim sun
Which made squat shadows out of men; they called it
Cimmeria, land of Darkness and deep Night.

It was so long ago and far away
I have forgot the very name men called me.
The ax and flint-tipped spear are like a dream,
And hunts and wars are shadows. I recall
Only the stillness of that somber land;
The clouds that piled forever on the hills,

The dimness of the everlasting woods.
Cimmeria, land of Darkness and the Night.

Oh, soul of mine, born out of shadowed hills,
To clouds and winds and ghosts that shun the sun,
How many deaths shall serve to break at last
This heritage which wraps me in the gray
Apparel of ghosts? I search my heart and find
Cimmeria, land of Darkness and the Night.

THE PHOENIX ON THE SWORD

'Know, oh prince, that between the years when the oceans drank Atlantis and the gleaming cities, and the years of the rise of the Sons of Aryas, there was an Age undreamed of, when shining kingdoms lay spread across the world like blue mantles beneath the stars – Nemedia, Ophir, Brythunia, Hyperborea, Zamora with its dark-haired women and towers of spider-haunted mystery, Zingara with its chivalry, Koth that bordered on the pastoral lands of Shem, Stygia with its shadow-guarded tombs, Hyrkania whose riders wore steel and silk and gold. But the proudest kingdom of the world was Aquilonia, reigning supreme in the dreaming west. Hither came Conan, the Cimmerian, black-haired, sullen-eyed, sword in hand, a thief, a reaver, a slayer, with gigantic melancholies and gigantic mirth, to tread the jeweled thrones of the Earth under his sandaled feet.'

THE NEMEDIAN CHRONICLES

1

OVER SHADOWY SPIRES AND gleaming towers lay the ghostly darkness and silence that runs before dawn. Into a dim alley, one of a veritable labyrinth of mysterious winding ways, four masked figures came hurriedly from a door which a dusky hand furtively opened. They spoke not but went swiftly into the gloom, cloaks wrapped closely about them; as silently as the ghosts of murdered men they disappeared in the darkness. Behind them a sardonic countenance was framed in the partly opened door; a pair of evil eyes glittered malevolently in the gloom.

'Go into the night, creatures of the night,' a voice mocked. 'Oh, fools, your doom hounds your heels like a blind dog, and you know it not.'

The speaker closed the door and bolted it, then turned and went up the corridor, candle in hand. He was a somber giant, whose dusky skin revealed his Stygian blood. He came into an inner chamber, where a tall, lean man in worn velvet lounged like a great lazy cat on a silken couch, sipping wine from a huge golden goblet.

'Well, Ascalante,' said the Stygian, setting down the candle, 'your dupes have slunk into the streets like rats from their burrows. You work with strange tools.'

'Tools?' replied Ascalante. 'Why, they consider *me* that. For months now, ever since the Rebel Four summoned me from the southern desert, I have been living in the very heart of my enemies, hiding by day in this obscure house, skulking through dark alleys and darker corridors at night. And I have accomplished what those rebellious nobles could not. Working through them, and through other agents, many of whom have never seen my face, I have honeycombed the empire with sedition and unrest. In short I, working in the shadows, have paved the downfall of the king who sits throned in the sun. By Mitra, I was a statesman before I was an outlaw.'

'And these dupes who deem themselves your masters?'

'They will continue to think that I serve them, until our present task is completed. Who are they to match wits with Ascalante? Volmana, the dwarfish count of Karaban; Gromel, the giant commander of the Black Legion; Dion, the fat baron of Attalus; Rinaldo, the hare-brained minstrel. I am the force which has welded together the steel in each, and by the clay in each, I will crush them when the time comes. But that lies in the future; tonight the king dies.'

'Days ago I saw the imperial squadrons ride from the city,' said the Stygian.

'They rode to the frontier which the heathen Picts assail – thanks to the strong liquor which I've smuggled over the borders to madden them. Dion's great wealth made *that* possible. And Volmana made it possible to dispose of the rest of the imperial troops which remained in the city. Through his princely kin in Nemedia, it was easy to persuade King Numa to request the presence of Count Trocero of Poitain, seneschal of Aquilonia; and of course, to do him honor, he'll be accompanied by an imperial escort, as well as his own troops, and Prospero, King Conan's right-hand man. That leaves only the king's personal bodyguard in the city – besides the Black Legion. Through Gromel I've corrupted a spendthrift officer of that guard, and bribed him to lead his men away from the king's door at midnight.

'Then, with sixteen desperate rogues of mine, we enter the palace by a secret tunnel. After the deed is done, even if the people do not rise to welcome us, Gromel's Black Legion will be sufficient to hold the city and the crown.'

'And Dion thinks that crown will be given to him?'

'Yes. The fat fool claims it by reason of a trace of royal blood. Conan makes a bad mistake in letting men live who still boast descent from the old dynasty, from which he tore the crown of Aquilonia.

'Volmana wishes to be reinstated in royal favor as he was under the old regime, so that he may lift his poverty-ridden estates to their former grandeur. Gromel hates Pallantides, commander of the Black Dragons, and desires the command of the whole army, with all the stubbornness of the Bossonian. Alone of us all, Rinaldo has no personal ambition. He sees in Conan a red-handed, rough-footed barbarian who came out of the north to plunder a civilized land. He idealizes the king whom Conan killed to get the crown, remembering only that he occasionally patronized the arts, and forgetting the evils of his reign, and he is making the people forget. Already they openly sing *The Lament for the King* in which Rinaldo lauds the sainted villain and denounces Conan as "that black-hearted savage from the abyss." Conan laughs, but the people snarl.'

'Why does he hate Conan?'

'Poets always hate those in power. To them perfection is always just behind the last corner, or beyond the next. They escape the present in dreams of the past and future. Rinaldo is a flaming torch of idealism, rising, as he thinks, to overthrow a tyrant and liberate the people. As for me – well, a few months ago I had lost all ambition but to raid the caravans for the rest of my life; now old dreams stir. Conan will die; Dion will mount the throne. Then he, too, will die. One by one, all who oppose me will die – by fire, or steel, or those deadly wines you know so well how to brew. Ascalante, king of Aquilonia! How like you the sound of it?'

The Stygian shrugged his broad shoulders.

'There was a time,' he said with unconcealed bitterness, 'when I, too, had my ambitions, beside which yours seem tawdry and childish. To what a state I have fallen! My old-time peers and rivals would stare indeed could they see Thoth-Amon of the Ring serving as the slave of an outlander, and an outlaw at that; and aiding in the petty ambitions of barons and kings!'

'You laid your trust in magic and mummery,' answered Ascalante carelessly. 'I trust my wits and my sword.'

'Wits and swords are as straws against the wisdom of the Darkness,' growled the Stygian, his dark eyes flickering with menacing lights and shadows. 'Had I not lost the Ring, our positions might be reversed.'

'Nevertheless,' answered the outlaw impatiently, 'you wear the stripes of my whip on your back, and are likely to continue to wear them.'

'Be not so sure!' the fiendish hatred of the Stygian glittered for an instant redly in his eyes. 'Some day, somehow, I will find the Ring again, and when I do, by the serpent-fangs of Set, you shall pay—'

The hot-tempered Aquilonian started up and struck him heavily across the mouth. Thoth reeled back, blood starting from his lips.

'You grow over-bold, dog,' growled the outlaw. 'Have a care; I am still your master who knows your dark secret. Go upon the housetops and shout that Ascalante is in the city plotting against the king – if you dare.'

'I dare not,' muttered the Stygian, wiping the blood from his lips.

'No, you do not dare,' Ascalante grinned bleakly. 'For if I die by your stealth or treachery, a hermit priest in the southern desert will know of it, and will break the seal of a manuscript I left in his hands. And having read, a word will be whispered in Stygia, and a wind will creep up from the south by midnight. And where will you hide your head, Thoth-Amon?'

The slave shuddered and his dusky face went ashen.

'Enough!' Ascalante changed his tone peremptorily. 'I have work for you. I do not trust Dion. I bade him ride to his country estate and remain there until the work tonight is done. The fat fool could never conceal his nervousness before the king today. Ride after him, and if you do not overtake him on the road, proceed to his estate and remain with him until we send for him. Don't let him out of your sight. He is mazed with fear, and might bolt – might even rush to Conan in a panic, and reveal the whole plot, hoping thus to save his own hide. Go!'

The slave bowed, hiding the hate in his eyes, and did as he was bidden. Ascalante turned again to his wine. Over the jeweled spires was rising a dawn crimson as blood.

2

When I was a fighting-man, the kettle-drums they beat;
The people scattered gold-dust before my horse's feet;
But now I am a great king, the people hound my track
With poison in my wine-cup, and daggers at my back.
                                            THE ROAD OF KINGS

The room was large and ornate, with rich tapestries on the polished panelled walls, deep rugs on the ivory floor, and with the lofty ceiling adorned with intricate carvings and silver scrollwork. Behind an ivory, gold-inlaid writing-table sat a man whose broad shoulders and sun-browned skin seemed out of place among those luxuriant surroundings. He seemed more a part of the sun and winds and high places of the outlands. His slightest movement spoke of steel-spring muscles knit to a keen brain with the co-ordination of a born fighting-man. There was nothing deliberate or measured about his actions. Either he was perfectly at rest – still as a bronze statue – or else he was in motion, not with the jerky quickness of over-tense nerves, but with a catlike speed that blurred the sight which tried to follow him.

His garments were of rich fabric, but simply made. He wore no ring or ornaments, and his square-cut black mane was confined merely by a cloth-of-silver band about his head.

Now he laid down the golden stylus with which he had been laboriously scrawling on waxed papyrus, rested his chin on his fist, and fixed his smoldering blue eyes enviously on the man who stood before him. This person was occupied in his own affairs at the moment, for he was taking up the laces of his gold-chased armor, and abstractedly whistling – a rather unconventional performance, considering that he was in the presence of a king.

'Prospero,' said the man at the table, 'these matters of statecraft weary me as all the fighting I have done never did.'

'All part of the game, Conan,' answered the dark-eyed Poitanian. 'You are king – you must play the part.'

'I wish I might ride with you to Nemedia,' said Conan enviously. 'It seems ages since I had a horse between my knees – but Publius says that affairs in the city require my presence. Curse him!

'When I overthrew the old dynasty,' he continued, speaking with the easy familiarity which existed only between the Poitanian and himself, 'it was easy enough, though it seemed bitter hard at the time. Looking back now over the wild path I followed, all those days of toil, intrigue, slaughter and tribulation seem like a dream.

'I did not dream far enough, Prospero. When King Namedides lay dead at my feet and I tore the crown from his gory head and set it on my own, I had reached the ultimate border of my dreams. I had prepared myself to take the crown, not to hold it. In the old free days all I wanted was a sharp sword and a straight path to my enemies. Now no paths are straight and my sword is useless.

'When I overthrew Namedides, *then* I was the Liberator – now they spit at my shadow. They have put a statue of that swine in the temple of Mitra, and people go and wail before it, hailing it as the holy effigy of a saintly monarch who was done to death by a red-handed barbarian. When I led her armies to victory as a mercenary, Aquilonia overlooked the fact that I was a foreigner, but now she can not forgive me.

'Now in Mitra's temple there come to burn incense to Namedides' memory, men whom his hangmen maimed and blinded, men whose sons died in his dungeons, whose wives and daughters were dragged into his seraglio. The fickle fools!'

'Rinaldo is largely responsible,' answered Prospero, drawing up his sword-belt another notch. 'He sings songs that make men mad. Hang him in his jester's garb to the highest tower in the city. Let him make rimes for the vultures.'

Conan shook his lion head. 'No, Prospero, he's beyond my reach. A great poet is greater than any king. His songs are mightier than my scepter; for he has near ripped the heart from my breast when he chose to sing for me. I shall die and be forgotten, but Rinaldo's songs will live for ever.

'No, Prospero,' the king continued, a somber look of doubt shadowing his eyes, 'there is something hidden, some undercurrent of which we are not aware. I sense it as in my youth I sensed the tiger hidden in the tall grass. There is a nameless unrest throughout the kingdom. I am like a hunter who crouches by his small fire amid the forest, and hears stealthy feet padding in the darkness, and almost sees the glimmer of burning eyes. If I could but come to grips with something tangible, that I could cleave with my sword! I tell you, it's not by chance that the Picts have of late so fiercely assailed the frontiers, so that the Bossonians have called for aid to beat them back. I should have ridden with the troops.'

'Publius feared a plot to trap and slay you beyond the frontier,' replied Prospero, smoothing his silken surcoat over his shining mail, and admiring his tall lithe figure in a silver mirror. 'That's why he urged you to remain in the city. These doubts are born of your barbarian instincts. Let the people snarl! The mercenaries are ours, and the Black Dragons, and every rogue in Poitain swears by you. Your only danger is assassination, and that's impossible, with men of the imperial troops guarding you day and night. What are you working at there?'

'A map,' Conan answered with pride. 'The maps of the court show well the countries of south, east and west, but in the north they are vague and faulty. I am adding the northern lands myself. Here is Cimmeria, where I was born. And—'

'Asgard and Vanaheim,' Prospero scanned the map. 'By Mitra, I had almost believed those countries to have been fabulous.'

Conan grinned savagely, involuntarily touching the scars on his dark face. 'You had known otherwise, had you spent your youth on the northern frontiers of Cimmeria! Asgard lies to the north, and Vanaheim to the northwest of Cimmeria, and there is continual war along the borders.'

'What manner of men are these northern folk?' asked Prospero.

'Tall and fair and blue-eyed. Their god is Ymir, the frost-giant, and each tribe has its own king. They are wayward and fierce. They fight all day and drink ale and roar their wild songs all night.'

'Then I think you are like them,' laughed Prospero. 'You laugh greatly, drink deep and bellow good songs; though I never saw another Cimmerian who drank aught but water, or who ever laughed, or ever sang save to chant dismal dirges.'

'Perhaps it's the land they live in,' answered the king. 'A gloomier land never was – all of hills, darkly wooded, under skies nearly always gray, with winds moaning drearily down the valleys.'

'Little wonder men grow moody there,' quoth Prospero with a shrug of his shoulders, thinking of the smiling sun-washed plains and blue lazy rivers of Poitain, Aquilonia's southernmost province.

'They have no hope here or hereafter,' answered Conan. 'Their gods are Crom and his dark race, who rule over a sunless place of everlasting mist, which is the world of the dead. Mitra! The ways of the Æsir were more to my liking.'

'Well,' grinned Prospero, 'the dark hills of Cimmeria are far behind you. And now I go. I'll quaff a goblet of white Nemedian wine for you at Numa's court.'

'Good,' grunted the king, 'but kiss Numa's dancing-girls for yourself only, lest you involve the states!'

His gusty laughter followed Prospero out of the chamber.

3

Under the caverned pyramids great Set coils asleep;
Among the shadows of the tombs his dusky people creep.
I speak the Word from the hidden gulfs that never knew the sun—
Send me a servant for my hate, oh scaled and shining One!

The sun was setting, etching the green and hazy blue of the forest in brief gold. The waning beams glinted on the thick golden chain which Dion of Attalus twisted continually in his pudgy hand as he sat in the flaming riot of blossoms and flower-trees which was his garden. He shifted his fat body on his marble seat and glanced furtively about, as if in quest of a lurking enemy. He sat within a circular grove of slender trees, whose interlapping branches cast a thick shade over him.

Near at hand a fountain tinkled silverly, and other unseen fountains in various parts of the great garden whispered an everlasting symphony.

Dion was alone except for the great dusky figure which lounged on a marble bench close at hand, watching the baron with deep somber eyes. Dion gave little thought to Thoth-Amon. He vaguely knew that he was a slave in whom Ascalante reposed much trust, but like so many rich men, Dion paid scant heed to men below his own station in life.

'You need not be so nervous,' said Thoth. 'The plot can not fail.'

'Ascalante can make mistakes as well as another,' snapped Dion, sweating at the mere thought of failure.

'Not he,' grinned the Stygian savagely, 'else I had not been his slave, but his master.'

'What talk is this?' peevishly returned Dion, with only half a mind on the conversation.

Thoth-Amon's eyes narrowed. For all his iron self-control, he was near bursting with long pent-up shame, hate and rage, ready to take any sort of a desperate chance. What he did not reckon on was the fact that Dion saw him, not as a human being with a brain and a wit, but simply a slave, and as such, a creature beneath notice.

'Listen to me,' said Thoth. 'You will be king. But you little know the mind of Ascalante. You can not trust him, once Conan is slain. I can help you. If you will protect me when you come to power, I will aid you.

'Listen, my lord. I was a great sorcerer in the south. Men spoke of Thoth-Amon as they spoke of Rammon. King Ctesphon of Stygia gave me great honor, casting down the magicians from the high places to exalt me above them. They hated me, but they feared me, for I controlled beings from *outside* which came at my call and did my bidding. By Set, mine enemy knew not the hour when he might awake at midnight to feel the taloned fingers of a nameless horror at his throat! I did dark and terrible magic with the Serpent Ring of Set, which I found in a nighted tomb a league beneath the earth, forgotten before the first man crawled out of the slimy sea.

'But a thief stole the Ring and my power was broken. The magicians rose up to slay me, and I fled. Disguised as a camel-driver, I was traveling in a caravan in the land of Koth, when Ascalante's reavers fell upon us. All in the caravan were slain except myself; I saved my life by revealing my identity to Ascalante and swearing to serve him. Bitter has been that bondage!

'To hold me fast, he wrote of me in a manuscript, and sealed it and gave it into the hands of a hermit who dwells on the southern borders of Koth. I dare not strike a dagger into him while he sleeps, or betray him to his enemies, for then the hermit would open the manuscript and read – thus Ascalante instructed him. And he would speak a word in Stygia—'

Again Thoth shuddered and an ashen hue tinged his dusky skin.

'Men knew me not in Aquilonia,' he said. 'But should my enemies in Stygia learn my whereabouts, not the width of half a world between us would suffice to save me from such a doom as would blast the soul of a bronze statue. Only a king with castles and hosts of swordsmen could protect me. So I have told you my secret, and urge that you make a pact with me. I can aid you with my wisdom, and you can protect me. And some day I will find the Ring—'

'Ring? Ring?' Thoth had underestimated the man's utter egoism. Dion had not even been listening to the slave's words, so completely engrossed was he in his own thoughts, but the final word stirred a ripple in his self-centeredness.

'Ring?' he repeated. 'That makes me remember – my ring of good fortune. I had it from a Shemitish thief who swore he stole it from a wizard far to the south, and that it would bring me luck. I paid him enough, Mitra knows. By the gods, I need all the luck I can have, what with Volmana and Ascalante dragging me into their bloody plots – I'll see to the ring.'

Thoth sprang up, blood mounting darkly to his face, while his eyes flamed with the stunned fury of a man who suddenly realizes the full depths of a fool's swinish stupidity. Dion never heeded him. Lifting a secret lid in the marble seat, he fumbled for a moment among a heap of gewgaws of various kinds – barbaric charms, bits of bones, pieces of tawdry jewelry – luck-pieces and conjures which the man's superstitious nature had prompted him to collect.

'Ah, here it is!' He triumphantly lifted a ring of curious make. It was of a metal like copper, and was made in the form of a scaled serpent, coiled in three loops, with its tail in its mouth. Its eyes were yellow gems which glittered balefully. Thoth-Amon cried out as if he had been struck, and Dion wheeled and gaped, his face suddenly bloodless. The slave's eyes were blazing, his mouth wide, his huge dusky hands outstretched like talons.

'The Ring! By Set! The Ring!' he shrieked. 'My Ring – stolen from me—'

Steel glittered in the Stygian's hand and with a heave of his great dusky shoulders he drove the dagger into the baron's fat body. Dion's high thin squeal broke in a strangled gurgle and his whole flabby frame collapsed like melted butter. A fool to the end, he died in mad terror, not knowing why. Flinging aside the crumpled corpse, already forgetful of it, Thoth grasped the ring in both hands, his dark eyes blazing with a fearful avidness.

'My Ring!' he whispered in terrible exultation. 'My power!'

How long he crouched over the baleful thing, motionless as a statue, drinking the evil aura of it into his dark soul, not even the Stygian knew. When he shook himself from his revery and drew back his mind from the nighted abysses where it had been questing, the moon was rising, casting long shadows across the smooth marble back of the garden-seat, at the foot of which sprawled the darker shadow which had been the lord of Attalus.

'No more, Ascalante, no more!' whispered the Stygian, and his eyes burned red as a vampire's in the gloom. Stooping, he cupped a handful of congealing blood from the sluggish pool in which his victim sprawled, and rubbed it in the copper serpent's eyes until the yellow sparks were covered by a crimson mask.

'Blind your eyes, mystic serpent,' he chanted in a blood-freezing whisper. 'Blind your eyes to the moonlight and open them on darker gulfs! What do you see, oh serpent of Set. Whom do you call from the gulfs of the Night. Whose shadow falls on the waning Light? Call him to me, oh serpent of Set!'

Stroking the scales with a peculiar circular motion of his fingers a motion which always carried the fingers back to their starting place, his voice sank still lower as he whispered dark names and grisly incantations forgotten the world over save in the grim hinterlands of dark Stygia, where monstrous shapes move in the dusk of the tombs.

There was a movement in the air about him, such a swirl as is made in water when some creature rises to the surface. A nameless, freezing wind blew on him briefly, as if from an opened Door. Thoth felt a presence at his back, but he did not look about. He kept his eyes fixed on the moonlit space of marble, on which a tenuous shadow hovered. As he continued his whispered incantations, this shadow grew in size and clarity, until it stood out distinct and horrific. Its outline was not unlike that of a gigantic baboon, but no such baboon ever walked the earth, not even in Stygia. Still Thoth did not look, but drawing from his girdle a sandal of his master – always carried in the dim hope that he might be able to put it to such use – he cast it behind him.

'Know it well, slave of the Ring!' he exclaimed. 'Find him who wore it and destroy him! Look into his eyes and blast his soul, before you tear out his throat! Kill him! Aye,' in a blind burst of passion, 'and all with him!'

Etched on the moonlit wall Thoth saw the horror lower its misshapen head and take the scent like some hideous hound. Then the grisly head was thrown back and the thing wheeled and was gone like a wind through the trees. The Stygian flung up his arms in maddened exultation, and his teeth and eyes gleamed in the moonlight.

A soldier on guard without the walls yelled in startled horror as a great loping black shadow with flaming eyes cleared the wall and swept by him with a swirling rush of wind. But it was gone so swiftly that the bewildered warrior was left wondering whether it had been a dream or a hallucination.

4

When the world was young and men were weak,
   and the fiends of the night walked free,
I strove with Set by fire and steel and the
   juice of the upas-tree;
Now that I sleep in the mount's black heart,
   and the ages take their toll,
Forget ye him who fought with the Snake to
   save the human soul?

Alone in the great sleeping-chamber with its high golden dome King Conan slumbered and dreamed. Through swirling gray mists he heard a curious call, faint and far, and though he did not understand it, it seemed not within his power to ignore it. Sword in hand he went through the gray mist, as a man might walk through clouds, and the voice grew more distinct as he proceeded until he understood the word it spoke – it was his own name that was being called across the gulfs of Space or Time.

Now the mists grew lighter and he saw that he was in a great dark corridor that seemed to be cut in solid black stone. It was unlighted, but by some magic he could see plainly. The floor, ceiling and walls were highly polished and gleamed dully, and they were carved with the figures of ancient heroes and half-forgotten gods. He shuddered to see the vast shadowy outlines of the Nameless Old Ones, and he knew somehow that mortal feet had not traversed the corridor for centuries.

He came upon a wide stair carved in the solid rock, and the sides of the shaft were adorned with esoteric symbols so ancient and horrific that King Conan's skin crawled. The steps were carven each with the abhorrent figure of the Old Serpent, Set, so that at each step he planted his heel on the head of the Snake, as it was intended from old times. But he was none the less at ease for all that.

But the voice called him on, and at last, in darkness that would have been impenetrable to his material eyes, he came into a strange crypt, and saw a vague white-bearded figure sitting on a tomb. Conan's hair rose up and he grasped his sword, but the figure spoke in sepulchral tones.

'Oh man, do you know me?'

'Not I, by Crom!' swore the king.

'Man,' said the ancient, 'I am Epemitreus.'

'But Epemitreus the Sage has been dead for fifteen hundred years!' stammered Conan.

'Harken!' spoke the other commandingly. 'As a pebble cast into a dark lake sends ripples to the further shores, happenings in the Unseen World have broken like waves on my slumber. I have marked you well, Conan of Cimmeria, and the stamp of mighty happenings and great deeds is upon you. But dooms are loose in the land, against which your sword can not aid you.'

'You speak in riddles,' said Conan uneasily. 'Let me see my foe and I'll cleave his skull to the teeth.'

'Loose your barbarian fury against your foes of flesh and blood,' answered the ancient. 'It is not against men I must shield you. There are dark worlds barely guessed by man, wherein formless monsters stalk – fiends which may be drawn from the Outer Voids to take material shape and rend and devour at the bidding of evil magicians. There is a serpent in your house, oh king – an adder in your kingdom, come up from Stygia, with the dark wisdom of the shadows in his murky soul. As a sleeping man dreams of the serpent which crawls near him, I have felt the foul presence of Set's neophyte. He is drunk with terrible power, and the blows he strikes at his enemy may well bring down the kingdom. I have called you to me, to give you a weapon against him and his hell-hound pack.'

'But why?' bewilderedly asked Conan. 'Men say you sleep in the black heart of Golamira, whence you send forth your ghost on unseen wings to aid Aquilonia in times of need, but I – I am an outlander and a barbarian.'

'Peace!' the ghostly tones reverberated through the great shadowy cavern. 'Your destiny is one with Aquilonia. Gigantic happenings are forming in the web and the womb of Fate, and a blood-mad sorcerer shall not stand in the path of imperial destiny. Ages ago Set coiled about the world like a python about its prey. All my life, which was as the lives of three common men, I fought him. I drove him into the shadows of the mysterious south, but in dark Stygia men still worship him who to us is the arch-demon. As I fought Set, I fight his worshippers and his votaries and his acolytes. Hold out your sword.'

Wondering, Conan did so, and on the great blade, close to the heavy silver guard, the ancient traced with a bony finger a strange symbol that glowed like white fire in the shadows. And on the instant crypt, tomb and ancient vanished, and Conan, bewildered, sprang from his couch in the great golden-domed chamber. And as he stood, bewildered at the strangeness of his dream, he realized that he was gripping his sword in his hand. And his hair prickled at the nape of his neck, for on the broad blade was carven a symbol – the outline of a phoenix. And he remembered that on the tomb in the crypt he had seen what he had thought to be a similar figure, carven of stone. Now he wondered if it had been but a stone figure, and his skin crawled at the strangeness of it all.

Then as he stood, a stealthy sound in the corridor outside brought him to life, and without stopping to investigate, he began to don his armor; again he was the barbarian, suspicious and alert as a gray wolf at bay.

5

What do I know of cultured ways, the gilt, the craft and the lie?
I, who was born in a naked land and bred in the open sky.
The subtle tongue, the sophist guile, they fail when the broadswords sing;
Rush in and die, dogs – I was a man before I was a king.

THE ROAD OF KINGS

Through the silence which shrouded the corridor of the royal palace stole twenty furtive figures. Their stealthy feet, bare or cased in soft leather, made no sound either on thick carpet or bare marble tile. The torches which stood in niches along the halls gleamed red on dagger, sword and keen-edged ax.

'Easy all!' hissed Ascalante. 'Stop that cursed loud breathing, whoever it is! The officer of the night-guard has removed most of the sentries from these halls and made the rest drunk, but we must be careful, just the same. Back! Here comes the guard!'

They crowded back behind a cluster of carven pillars, and almost immediately ten giants in black armor swung by at a measured pace. Their faces showed doubt as they glanced at the officer who was leading them away from their post of duty. This officer was rather pale; as the guard passed the hiding-places of the conspirators, he was seen to wipe the sweat from his brow with a shaky hand. He was young, and this betrayal of a king did not come easy to him. He mentally cursed the vain-glorious extravagance which had put him in debt to the money-lenders and made him a pawn of scheming politicians.

The guardsmen clanked by and disappeared up the corridor.

'Good!' grinned Ascalante. 'Conan sleeps unguarded. Haste! If they catch us killing him, we're undone – but few men will espouse the cause of a dead king.'

'Aye, haste!' cried Rinaldo, his blue eyes matching the gleam of the sword he swung above his head. 'My blade is thirsty! I hear the gathering of the vultures! On!'

They hurried down the corridor with reckless speed and stopped before a gilded door which bore the royal dragon symbol of Aquilonia.

'Gromel!' snapped Ascalante. 'Break me this door open!'

The giant drew a deep breath and launched his mighty frame against the panels, which groaned and bent at the impact. Again he crouched and plunged. With a snapping of bolts and a rending crash of wood, the door splintered and burst inward.

'In!' roared Ascalante, on fire with the spirit of the deed.

'In!' yelled Rinaldo. 'Death to the tyrant!'

They stopped short. Conan faced them, not a naked man roused mazed and unarmed out of a deep sleep to be butchered like a sheep, but a barbarian wide-awake and at bay, partly armored, and with his long sword in his hand.

For an instant the tableau held – the four rebel noblemen in the broken door, and the horde of wild hairy faces crowding behind them – all held momentarily frozen by the sight of the blazing-eyed giant standing sword in hand in the middle of the candle-lighted chamber. In that instant Ascalante beheld, on a small table near the royal couch, the silver scepter and the slender gold circlet which was the crown of Aquilonia, and the sight maddened him with desire.

'In rogues!' yelled the outlaw. 'He is one to twenty and he has no helmet!'

True; there had been lack of time to don the heavy plumed casque, or to lace in place the side-plates of the cuirass, nor was there now time to snatch the great shield from the wall. Still, Conan was better protected than any of his foes except Volmana and Gromel, who were in full armor.

The king glared, puzzled as to their identity. Ascalante he did not know; he could not see through the closed vizors of the armored conspirators, and Rinaldo had pulled his slouch cap down above his eyes. But there was no time for surmise. With a yell that rang to the roof, the killers flooded into the room, Gromel first. He came like a charging bull, head down, sword low for the disembowelling thrust. Conan sprang to meet him, and all his tigerish strength went into the arm that swung the sword. In a whistling arc the great blade flashed through the air and crashed on the Bossonian's helmet. Blade and casque shivered together and Gromel rolled lifeless on the floor. Conan bounded back, still gripping the broken hilt.

'Gromel!' he spat, his eyes blazing in amazement, as the shattered helmet disclosed the shattered head; then the rest of the pack were upon him. A dagger point raked along his ribs between breastplate and backplate, a sword-edge flashed before his eyes. He flung aside the dagger-wielder with his left arm, and smashed his broken hilt like a cestus into the swordsman's temple. The man's brains spattered in his face.

'Watch the door, five of you!' screamed Ascalante, dancing about the edge of the singing steel whirlpool, for he feared that Conan might smash through their midst and escape. The rogues drew back momentarily, as their leader seized several and thrust them toward the single door, and in that brief respite Conan leaped to the wall and tore therefrom an ancient battle-ax which, untouched by time, had hung there for half a century.

With his back to the wall he faced the closing ring for a flashing instant, then leaped into the thick of them. He was no defensive fighter; even in the teeth of overwhelming odds he always carried the war to the enemy. Any other man would have already died there, and Conan himself did not hope to survive, but he did ferociously wish to inflict as much damage as he could before he fell. His barbaric soul was ablaze, and the chants of old heroes were singing in his ears.

As he sprang from the wall his ax dropped an outlaw with a severed shoulder, and the terrible back-hand return crushed the skull of another. Swords whined venomously about him, but death passed him by breathless margins. The Cimmerian moved in a blur of blinding speed. He was like a tiger among baboons as he leaped, side-stepped and spun, offering an ever-moving target, while his ax wove a shining wheel of death about him.

For a brief space the assassins crowded him fiercely, raining blows blindly and hampered by their own numbers; then they gave back suddenly – two corpses on the floor gave mute evidence of the king's fury, though Conan himself was bleeding from wounds on arm, neck and legs.

'Knaves!' screamed Rinaldo, dashing off his feathered cap, his wild eyes glaring. 'Do ye shrink from the combat? Shall the despot live? Out on it!'

He rushed in, hacking madly, but Conan, recognizing him, shattered his sword with a short terrific chop and with a powerful push of his open hand sent him reeling to the floor. The king took Ascalante's point in his left arm, and the outlaw barely saved his life by ducking and springing backward from the swinging ax. Again the wolves swirled in and Conan's ax sang and crushed. A hairy rascal stooped beneath its stroke and dived at the king's legs, but after wrestling for a brief instant at what seemed a solid iron tower, glanced up in time to see the ax falling, but not in time to avoid it. In the interim one of his comrades lifted a broadsword with both hands and hewed through the king's left shoulder-plate, wounding the shoulder beneath. In an instant Conan's cuirass was full of blood.

Volmana, flinging the attackers right and left in his savage impatience, came plowing through and hacked murderously at Conan's unprotected head. The king ducked deeply and the sword shaved off a lock of his black hair as it whistled above him. Conan pivoted on his heel and struck in from the side. The ax crunched through the steel cuirass and Volmana crumpled with his whole left side caved in.

'Volmana!' gasped Conan breathlessly. 'I'll know that dwarf in Hell—'

He straightened to meet the maddened rush of Rinaldo, who charged in wild and wide open, armed only with a dagger. Conan leaped back, lifting his ax.

'Rinaldo!' his voice was strident with desperate urgency. 'Back! I would not slay you—'

'Die, tyrant!' screamed the mad minstrel, hurling himself headlong on the king. Conan delayed the blow he was loth to deliver, until it was too late. Only when he felt the bite of the steel in his unprotected side did he strike, in a frenzy of blind desperation.

Rinaldo dropped with his skull shattered, and Conan reeled back against the wall, blood spurting from between the fingers which gripped his wound.

'In, now, and slay him!' yelled Ascalante.

Conan put his back against the wall and lifted his ax. He stood like an image of the unconquerable primordial – legs braced far apart, head thrust forward, one hand clutching the wall for support, the other gripping the ax on high, with the great corded muscles standing out in iron ridges, and his features frozen in a death snarl of fury – his eyes blazing terriby through the mist of blood which veiled them. The men faltered – wild, criminal and dissolute though they were, yet they came of a breed men called civilized, with a civilized background; here was the barbarian – the natural killer. They shrank back – the dying tiger could still deal death.

Conan sensed their uncertainty and grinned mirthlessly and ferociously.

'Who dies first?' he mumbled through smashed and bloody lips.

Ascalante leaped like a wolf, halted almost in midair with incredible quickness and fell prostrate to avoid the death which was hissing toward him. He frantically whirled his feet out of the way and rolled clear as Conan recovered from his missed blow and struck again. This time the ax sank inches deep into the polished floor close to Ascalante's revolving legs.

Another misguided desperado chose this instant to charge, followed half-heartedly by his fellows. He intended killing Conan before the Cimmerian could wrench his ax from the floor, but his judgment was faulty. The red ax lurched up and crashed down and a crimson caricature of a man catapulted back against the legs of the attackers.

At that instant a fearful scream burst from the rogues at the door as a black misshapen shadow fell across the wall. All but Ascalante wheeled at the cry, and then, howling like dogs, they burst blindly through the door in a raving, blaspheming mob, and scattered through the corridors in screaming flight.

Ascalante did not look toward the door; he had eyes only for the wounded king. He supposed the noise of the fray had at last roused the palace, and that the loyal guards were upon him, though even in that moment it seemed strange that his hardened rogues should scream so terribly in their flight. Conan did not look toward the door because he was watching the outlaw with the burning eyes of a dying wolf. In this extremity Ascalante's cynical philosophy did not desert him.

'All seems to be lost, particularly honor,' he murmured. 'However, the king is dying on his feet – and—' Whatever other cogitation might have passed through his mind is not to be known; for, leaving the sentence uncompleted, he ran lightly at Conan just as the Cimmerian was perforce employing his ax-arm to wipe the blood from his blind eyes.

But even as he began his charge, there was a strange rushing in the air and a heavy weight struck terrifically between his shoulders. He was dashed headlong and great talons sank agonizingly in his flesh. Writhing desperately beneath his attacker, he twisted his head about and stared into the face of Nightmare and lunacy. Upon him crouched a great black thing which he knew was born in no sane or human world. Its slavering black fangs were near his throat and the glare of its yellow eyes shriveled his limbs as a killing wind shrivels young corn.

The hideousness of its face transcended mere bestiality. It might have been the face of an ancient, evil mummy, quickened with demoniac life. In those abhorrent features the outlaw's dilated eyes seemed to see, like a shadow in the madness that enveloped him, a faint and terrible resemblance to the slave Thoth-Amon. Then Ascalante's cynical and all-sufficient philosophy deserted him, and with a ghastly cry he gave up the ghost before those slavering fangs touched him.

Conan, shaking the blood-drops from his eyes, stared frozen. At first he thought it was a great black hound which stood above Ascalante's distorted body; then as his sight cleared he saw that it was neither a hound nor a baboon.

With a cry that was like an echo of Ascalante's death-shriek, he reeled away from the wall and met the leaping horror with a cast of his ax that had behind it all the desperate power of his electrified nerves. The flying weapon glanced singing from the slanting skull it should have crushed, and the king was hurled halfway across the chamber by the impact of the giant body.

The slavering jaws closed on the arm Conan flung up to guard his throat, but the monster made no effort to secure a death-grip. Over his mangled arm it glared fiendishly into the king's eyes, in which there began to be mirrored a likeness of the horror which stared from the dead eyes of Ascalante. Conan felt his soul shrivel and begin to be drawn out of his body, to drown in the yellow wells of cosmic horror which glimmered spectrally in the formless chaos that was growing about him and engulfing all life and sanity. Those eyes grew and became gigantic, and in them the Cimmerian glimpsed the reality of all the abysmal and blasphemous horrors that lurk in the outer darkness of formless voids and nighted gulfs. He opened his bloody lips to shriek his hate and loathing, but only a dry rattle burst from his throat.

But the horror that paralysed and destroyed Ascalante roused in the Cimmerian a frenzied fury akin to madness. With a volcanic wrench of his whole body he plunged backward, heedless of the agony of his torn arm, dragging the monster bodily with him. And his out-flung hand struck something his dazed fighting-brain recognized as the hilt of his broken sword. Instinctively he gripped it and struck with all the power of nerve and thew, as a man stabs with a dagger. The broken blade sank deep and Conan's arm was released as the abhorrent mouth gaped as in agony. The king was hurled violently aside, and lifting himself on one hand he saw, as one mazed, the terrible convulsions of the monster from which thick blood was gushing through the great wound his broken blade had torn. And as he watched, its struggles ceased and it lay jerking spasmodically, staring upward with its grisly dead eyes. Conan blinked and shook the blood from his own eyes; it seemed to him that the thing was melting and disintegrating into a slimy unstable mass.

Then a medley of voices reached his ears, and the room was thronged with the finally roused people of the court – knights, peers, ladies, men-at-arms, councillors – all babbling and shouting and getting in one another's way. The Black Dragons were on hand, wild with rage, swearing and ruffling, with their hands on their hilts and foreign oaths in their teeth. Of the young officer of the door-guard nothing was seen, nor was he found then or later, though earnestly sought after.

'Gromel! Volmana! Rinaldo!' exclaimed Publius, the high councillor, wringing his fat hands among the corpses. 'Black treachery! Some one shall dance for this! Call the guard.'

'The guard is here, you old fool!' cavalierly snapped Pallantides, commander of the Black Dragons, forgetting Publius' rank in the stress of the moment. 'Best stop your caterwauling and aid us to bind the king's wounds. He's like to bleed to death.'

'Yes, yes!' cried Publius, who was a man of plans rather than action. 'We must bind his wounds. Send for every leech of the court! Oh, my lord, what a black shame on the city! Are you entirely slain?'

'Wine!' gasped the king from the couch where they had lain him. They put a goblet to his bloody lips and he drank like a man half dead of thirst.

'Good!' he grunted, falling back. 'Slaying is cursed dry work.'

They had staunched the flow of blood, and the innate vitality of the barbarian was asserting itself.

'See first to the dagger-wound in my side,' he bade the court physicians. 'Rinaldo wrote me a deathly song there, and keen was the stylus.'

'We should have hanged him long ago,' gibbered Publius. 'No good can come of poets – who is this?'

He nervously touched Ascalante's body with his sandalled toe.

'By Mitra!' ejaculated the commander. 'It is Ascalante, once count of Thune! What devil's work brought *him* up from his desert haunts?'

'But why does he stare so?' whispered Publius, drawing away, his own eyes wide and a peculiar prickling among the short hairs at the back of his fat neck. The others fell silent as they gazed at the dead outlaw.

'Had you seen what he and I saw,' growled the king, sitting up despite the protests of the leeches, 'you had not wondered. Blast your own gaze by looking at—' He stopped short, his mouth gaping, his finger pointing fruitlessly. Where the monster had died, only the bare floor met his eyes.

'Crom!' he swore. 'The thing's melted back into the foulness which bore it!'

'The king is delirious,' whispered a noble. Conan heard and swore, with barbaric oaths.

'By Badb, Morrigan, Macha and Nemain!' he concluded wrathfully. 'I am sane! It was like a cross between a Stygian mummy and a baboon. It came through the door, and Ascalante's rogues fled before it. It slew Ascalante, who was about to run me through. Then it came upon me and I slew it – how I know not, for my ax glanced from it as from a rock. But I think that the Sage Epemitreus had a hand in it—'

'Hark how he names Epemitreus, dead for fifteen hundred years!" they whispered to each other.

'By Ymir!' thundered the king. 'This night I talked with Epemitreus! He called to me in my dreams, and I walked down a black stone corridor carved with old gods, to a stone stair on the steps of which were the outlines of Set, until I came to a crypt, and a tomb with a phoenix carved on it—'

'In Mitra's name, lord king, be silent!' It was the high-priest of Mitra who cried out, and his countenance was ashen.

Conan threw up his head like a lion tossing back its mane, and his voice was thick with the growl of the angry lion.

'Am I slave, to shut my mouth at your command?'

'Nay, nay, my lord!' The high-priest was trembling, but not through fear of the royal wrath. 'I meant no offense.' He bent his head close to the king and spoke in a whisper that carried only to Conan's ears.

'My lord, this is a matter beyond human understanding. Only the inner circle of the priestcraft know of the black stone corridor carved in the black heart of Mount Golamira, by unknown hands, or of the phoenix-guarded tomb where Epemitreus was laid to rest fifteen hundred years ago. And since that time no living man has entered it, for his chosen priests, after placing the Sage in the crypt, blocked up the outer entrance of the corridor so that no man could find it, and today not even the high-priests know where it is. Only by word of mouth, handed down by the high-priests to the chosen few, and jealously guarded, does the inner circle of Mitra's acolytes know of the resting-place of Epemitreus in the black heart of Golamira. It is one of the Mysteries, on which Mitra's cult stands.'

'I can not say by what magic Epemitreus brought me to him,' answered Conan. 'But I talked with him, and he made a mark on my sword. Why that mark made it deadly to demons, or what magic lay behind the mark, I know not; but though the blade broke on Gromel's helmet, yet the fragment was long enough to kill the horror.'

'Let me see your sword,' whispered the high-priest from a throat gone suddenly dry.

Conan held out the broken weapon and the high-priest cried out and fell to his knees.

'Mitra guard us against the powers of darkness!' he gasped. 'The king has indeed talked with Epemitreus this night! And there on the sword – it is the secret sign none might make but him – the emblem of the immortal phoenix which broods for ever over his tomb! A candle, quick! Look again at the spot where the king said the goblin died!'

It lay in the shade of a broken screen. They threw the screen aside and bathed the floor in a flood of candle-light. And a shuddering silence fell over the people as they looked. Then some fell on their knees calling on Mitra, and some fled screaming from the chamber.

There on the floor where the monster had died, there lay, like a tangible shadow, a broad dark stain that could not be washed out; the thing had left its outline clearly etched in its blood, and that outline was of no being of a sane and normal world. Grim and horrific it brooded there, like the shadow cast by one of the apish gods that squat on the shadowy altars of dim temples in the dark land of Stygia.

THE SCARLET CITADEL

They trapped the Lion on Shamu's plain;
They weighted his limbs with an iron chain;
They cried aloud in the trumpet-blast,
They cried, 'The Lion is caged at last!'
Woe to the cities of river and plain
If ever the Lion stalks again!

OLD BALLAD

1

THE ROAR OF THE battle had died away; the shout of victory mingled with the cries of the dying. Like gay-hued leaves after an autumn storm, the fallen littered the plain; the sinking sun shimmered on burnished helmets, gilt-worked mail, silver breastplates, broken swords, and the heavy regal folds of silken standards, overthrown in pools of curdling crimson. In silent heaps lay war-horses and their steel-clad riders, flowing manes and blowing plumes stained alike in the red tide. About them and among them, like the drift of a storm, were strewn slashed and trampled bodies in steel caps and leather jerkins – archers and pikemen.

The oliphants sounded a fanfare of triumph all over the plain, and the hoofs of the victors crunched in the breasts of the vanquished as all the straggling, shining lines converged inward like the spokes of a glittering wheel, to the spot where the last survivor still waged unequal strife.

That day Conan, king of Aquilonia, had seen the pick of his chivalry cut to pieces, smashed and hammered to bits, and swept into eternity. With five thousand knights he had crossed the southeastern border of

Aquilonia and ridden into the grassy meadowlands of Ophir, to find his former ally, King Amalrus of Ophir, drawn up against him with the hosts of Strabonus, king of Koth. Too late he had seen the trap. All that a man might do he had done with his five thousand cavalrymen against the thirty thousand knights, archers and spearmen of the conspirators.

Without bowmen or infantry, he had hurled his armored horsemen against the oncoming host, had seen the knights of his foes in their shining mail go down before his lances, had torn the opposing center to bits, driving the riven ranks headlong before him, only to find himself caught in a vise as the untouched wings closed in. Strabonus' Shemitish bowmen had wrought havoc among his knights, feathering them with shafts that found every crevice in their armor, shooting down the horses, the Kothian pikemen rushing in to spear the fallen riders. The mailed lancers of the routed center had re-formed, reinforced by the riders from the wings, and had charged again and again, sweeping the field by sheer weight of numbers.

The Aquilonians had not fled; they had died on the field, and of the five thousand knights who had followed Conan southward, not one left the plain of Shamu alive. And now the king himself stood at bay among the slashed bodies of his house-troops, his back against a heap of dead horses and men. Ophirean knights in gilded mail leaped their horses over mounds of corpses to slash at the solitary figure; squat Shemites with blue-black beards, and dark-faced Kothian knights ringed him on foot. The clangor of steel rose deafeningly; the blackmailed figure of the western king loomed among his swarming foes, dealing blows like a butcher wielding a great cleaver. Riderless horses raced down the field; about his iron-clad feet grew a ring of mangled corpses. His attackers drew back from his desperate savagery, panting and livid.

Now through the yelling, cursing lines rode the lords of the conquerors – Strabonus, with his broad dark face and crafty eyes; Amalrus, slender, fastidious, treacherous, dangerous as a cobra; and the lean vulture Tsotha-lanti, clad only in silken robes, his great black eyes glittering from a face that was like that of a bird of prey. Of this Kothian wizard dark tales were told; tousle-headed women in northern and western villages frightened children with his name, and rebellious slaves were brought to abased submission quicker than by the lash, with the threat of being sold to him. Men said that he had a whole library of dark works bound in skin flayed from living human victims, and that in nameless pits below the hill whereon his palace sat, he trafficked with the powers of darkness, trading screaming girl slaves for unholy secrets. He was the real ruler of Koth.

Now he grinned bleakly as the kings reined back a safe distance from the grim iron-clad figure looming among the dead. Before the savage blue eyes blazing murderously from beneath the crested, dented helmet, the boldest shrank. Conan's dark scarred face was darker yet with passion; his black armor was hacked to tatters and splashed with blood; his great sword red to the cross-piece. In this stress all the veneer of civilization had faded; it was a barbarian who faced his conquerors. Conan was a Cimmerian by birth, one of those fierce moody hillmen who dwelt in their gloomy, cloudy land in the north. His saga, which had led him to the throne of Aquilonia, was the basis of a whole cycle of hero-tales.

So now the kings kept their distance, and Strabonus called on his Shemitish archers to loose their arrows at his foe from a distance; his captains had fallen like ripe grain before the Cimmerian's broadsword, and Strabonus, penurious of his knights as of his coins, was frothing with fury. But Tsotha shook his head.

'Take him alive.'

'Easy to say!' snarled Strabonus, uneasy lest in some way the black-mailed giant might hew a path to them through the spears. 'Who can take a man-eating tiger alive? By Ishtar, his heel is on the necks of my finest swordsmen! It took seven years and stacks of gold to train each, and there they lie, so much kite's meat. Arrows, I say!'

'Again, nay!' snapped Tsotha, swinging down from his horse. He laughed coldly. 'Have you not learned by this time that my brain is mightier than my sword?'

He passed through the lines of the pikemen, and the giants in their steel caps and mail brigandines shrank back fearfully, lest they so much as touch the skirts of his robe. Nor were the plumed knights slower in making room for him. He stepped over the corpses and came face to face with the grim king. The hosts watched in tense silence, holding their breath. The black-armored figure loomed in terrible menace over the lean, silk-robed shape, the notched, dripping sword hovering on high.

'I offer you life, Conan,' said Tsotha, a cruel mirth bubbling at the back of his voice.

'I give you death, wizard,' snarled the king, and backed by iron muscles and ferocious hate the great sword swung in a stroke meant to shear Tsotha's lean torso in half. But even as the host cried out, the wizard stepped in, too quick for the eye to follow, and apparently merely laid an open hand on Conan's left forearm, from the rigid muscles of which the mail had been hacked away. The whistling blade veered from its arc and the mailed giant crashed heavily to earth, to lie motionless. Tsotha laughed silently.

'Take him up and fear not; the lion's fangs are drawn.'

The kings reined in and gazed in awe at the fallen lion. Conan lay stiffly, like a dead man, but his eyes glared up at them, wide open, and blazing with helpless fury.

'What have you done to him?' asked Amalrus uneasily.

Tsotha displayed a broad ring of curious design on his finger. He pressed his fingers together and on the inner side of the ring a tiny steel fang darted out like a snake's tongue.

'It is steeped in the juice of the purple lotus which grows in the ghost-haunted swamps of southern Stygia,' said the magician. 'Its touch produces temporary paralysis. Put him in chains and lay him in a chariot. The sun sets and it is time we were on the road for Khorshemish.'

Strabonus turned to his general Arbanus.

'We return to Khorshemish with the wounded. Only a troop of the royal cavalry will accompany us. Your orders are to march at dawn to the Aquilonian border, and invest the city of Shamar. The Ophireans will supply you with food along the march. We will rejoin you as soon as possible, with reinforcements.'

So the host, with its steel-sheathed knights, its pikemen and archers and camp-servants, went into camp in the meadowlands near the battlefield. And through the starry night the two kings and the sorcerer who was greater than any king rode to the capital of Strabonus, in the midst of the glittering palace troop, and accompanied by a long line of chariots, loaded with the wounded. In one of these chariots lay Conan, king of Aquilonia, weighted with chains, the tang of defeat in his mouth, the blind fury of a trapped tiger in his soul.

The poison which had frozen his mighty limbs to helplessness had not paralysed his brain. As the chariot in which he lay rumbled over the meadowlands, his mind revolved maddeningly about his defeat. Amalrus had sent an emissary imploring aid against Strabonus, who, he said, was ravaging his western domain, which lay like a tapering wedge between the border of Aquilonia and the vast southern kingdom of Koth. He asked only a thousand horsemen and the presence of Conan, to hearten his demoralized subjects. Conan now blasphemed mentally. In his generosity he had come with five times the number the treacherous monarch had asked. In good faith he had ridden into Ophir, and had been confronted by the supposed rivals allied against him. It spoke significantly of his prowess that they had brought up a whole host to trap him and his five thousand.

A red cloud veiled his vision; his veins swelled with fury and in his temples a pulse throbbed maddeningly. In all his life he had never known greater and more helpless wrath. In swift-moving scenes the pageant of his life passed fleetingly before his mental eye – a panorama wherein moved shadowy figures which were himself, in many guises and conditions – a skin-clad barbarian; a mercenary swordsman in horned helmet and scale-mail corselet; a corsair in a dragon-prowed galley that trailed a crimson wake of blood and pillage along southern coasts; a captain of hosts in burnished steel, on a rearing black charger; a king on a golden throne with the lion banner flowing above, and throngs of gay-hued courtiers and ladies on their knees. But always the jouncing and rumbling of the chariot brought his thoughts back to revolve with maddening monotony about the treachery of Amalrus and the sorcery of Tsotha. The veins nearly burst in his temples and the cries of the wounded in the chariots filled him with ferocious satisfaction.

Before midnight they crossed the Ophirean border and at dawn the spires of Khorshemish stood up gleaming and rose-tinted on the southeastern horizon, the slim towers overawed by the grim scarlet citadel that at a distance was like a splash of bright blood in the sky. That was the castle of Tsotha. Only one narrow street, paved with marble and guarded by heavy iron gates, led up to it, where it crowned the hill dominating the city. The sides of that hill were too sheer to be climbed elsewhere. From the walls of the citadel one could look down on the broad white streets of the city, on minaretted mosques, shops, temples, mansions, and markets. One could look down, too, on the palaces of the king, set in broad gardens, high-walled, luxurious riots of fruit trees and blossoms, through which artificial streams murmured, and silvery fountains rippled incessantly. Over all brooded the citadel, like a condor stooping above its prey, intent on its own dark meditations.

The mighty gates between the huge towers of the outer wall clanged open, and the king rode into his capital between lines of glittering spearmen, while fifty trumpets pealed salute. But no throngs swarmed the white-paved streets to fling roses before the conqueror's hoofs. Strabonus had raced ahead of news of the battle, and the people, just rousing to the occupations of the day, gaped to see their king returning with a small retinue, and were in doubt as to whether it portended victory or defeat.

Conan, life sluggishly moving in his veins again, craned his neck from the chariot floor to view the wonders of this city which men called the Queen of the South. He had thought to ride some day through these golden-chased gates at the head of his steel-clad squadrons, with the great lion banner flowing over his helmeted head. Instead he entered in chains, stripped of his armor, and thrown like a captive slave on the bronze floor of his conqueror's chariot. A wayward devilish mirth of mockery rose above his fury, but to the nervous soldiers who drove the chariot his laughter sounded like the muttering of a rousing lion.

2

Gleaming shell of an outworn lie; fable of Right divine—
You gained your crowns by heritage, but Blood
  was the price of mine.
The throne that I won by blood and sweat, by
  Crom, I will not sell
For promise of valleys filled with gold, or threat
  of the Halls of Hell!
                    THE ROAD OF KINGS

In the citadel, in a chamber with a domed ceiling of carven jet, and the fretted arches of doorways glimmering with strange dark jewels, a strange conclave came to pass. Conan of Aquilonia, blood from unbandaged wounds caking his huge limbs, faced his captors. On either side of him stood a dozen black giants, grasping their long-shafted axes. In front of him stood Tsotha, and on divans lounged Strabonus and Amalrus in their silks and gold, gleaming with jewels, naked slave-boys beside them pouring wine into cups carved of a single sapphire. In strong contrast stood Conan, grim, blood-stained, naked but for a loin-cloth, shackles on his mighty limbs, his blue eyes blazing beneath the tangled black mane that fell over his low broad forehead. He dominated the scene, turning to tinsel the pomp of the conquerors by the sheer vitality of his elemental personality, and the kings in their pride and splendor were aware of it each in his secret heart, and were not at ease. Only Tsotha was not disturbed.

'Our desires are quickly spoken, king of Aquilonia,' said Tsotha. 'It is our wish to extend our empire.'

'And so you want to swine my kingdom,' rasped Conan.

'What are you but an adventurer, seizing a crown to which you had no more claim than any other wandering barbarian?' parried Amalrus. 'We are prepared to offer you suitable compensation—'

'Compensation?' It was a gust of deep laughter from Conan's mighty chest. 'The price of infamy and treachery! I am a barbarian, so I shall sell my kingdom and its people for life and your filthy gold? Ha! How did you come to your crown, you and that black-faced pig beside you? Your fathers did the fighting and the suffering, and handed their crowns to you on golden platters. What you inherited without lifting a finger – except to poison a few brothers – I fought for.

'You sit on satin and guzzle wine the people sweat for, and talk of divine rights of sovereignty – bah! I climbed out of the abyss of naked barbarism to the throne and in that climb I spilt my blood as freely as I spilt that of others. If either of us has the right to rule men, by Crom, it is I! How have you proved yourself my superior?

'I found Aquilonia in the grip of a pig like you – one who traced his genealogy for a thousand years. The land was torn with the wars of the barons, and the people cried out under suppression and taxation. Today no Aquilonian noble dares maltreat the humblest of my subjects, and the taxes of the people are lighter than anywhere else in the world.

'What of you? Your brother, Amalrus, holds the eastern half of your kingdom and defies you. And you, Strabonus, your soldiers are even now besieging castles of a dozen or more rebellious barons. The people of both your kingdoms are crushed into the earth by tyrannous taxes and levies. And you would loot mine – ha! Free my hands and I'll varnish this floor with your brains!'

Tsotha grinned bleakly to see the rage of his kingly companions.

'All this, truthful though it be, is beside the point. Our plans are no concern of yours. Your responsibility is at an end when you sign this parchment, which is an abdication in favor of Prince Arpello of Pellia. We will give you arms and horse, and five thousand golden lunas, and escort you to the eastern frontiers.'

'Setting me adrift where I was when I rode into Aquilonia to take service in her armies, except with the added burden of a traitor's name!' Conan's laugh was like the deep short bark of a timber wolf. 'Arpello, eh? I've had suspicions of that butcher of Pellia. Can you not even steal and pillage frankly and honestly, but you must have an excuse, however thin? Arpello claims a trace of royal blood; so you use him as an excuse for theft, and a satrap to rule through! I'll see you in hell first.'

'You're a fool!' exclaimed Amalrus. 'You are in our hands, and we can take both crown and life at our pleasure!'

Conan's answer was neither kingly nor dignified, but characteristically instinctive in the man, whose barbaric nature had never been submerged in his adopted culture. He spat full in Amalrus' eyes. The king of Ophir leaped up with a scream of outraged fury, groping for his slender sword. Drawing it, he rushed at the Cimmerian, but Tsotha intervened.

'Wait, your majesty; this man is *my* prisoner.'

'Aside, wizard!' shrieked Amalrus, maddened by the glare in the Cimmerian's blue eyes.

'Back, I say!' roared Tsotha, roused to awesome wrath. His lean hand came from his sleeve and cast a shower of dust into the Ophirean's contorted face. Amalrus cried out and staggered back, clutching at his eyes, the sword falling from his hand. He dropped limply on the divan, while the Kothian guards looked on stolidly and King Strabonus hurriedly gulped another goblet of wine, holding it with hands that trembled. Amalrus lowered his hands and shook his head violently, intelligence slowly sifting back into his gray eyes.

'I went blind,' he growled. 'What did you do to me, wizard?'

'Merely a gesture to convince you who was the real master,' snapped Tsotha, the mask of his formal pretense dropped, revealing the naked evil personality of the man. 'Strabonus has learned his lesson – let you learn yours. It was but a dust I found in a Stygian tomb which I flung into your eyes – if I brush out their sight again, I will leave you to grope in darkness for the rest of your life.'

Amalrus shrugged his shoulders, smiled whimsically and reached for a goblet, dissembling his fear and fury. A polished diplomat, he was quick to regain his poise. Tsotha turned to Conan, who had stood imperturbably during the episode. At the wizard's gesture, the blacks laid hold of their prisoner and marched him behind Tsotha, who led the way out of the chamber through an arched doorway into a winding corridor, whose floor was of many-hued mosaics, whose walls were inlaid with gold tissue and silver chasing, and from whose fretted arched ceiling swung golden censers, filling the corridor with dreamy perfumed clouds. They turned down a smaller corridor, done in jet and black jade, gloomy and awful, which ended at a brass door, over whose arch a human skull grinned horrifically. At this door stood a fat repellent figure, dangling a bunch of keys – Tsotha's chief eunuch, Shukeli, of whom grisly tales were whispered – a man with whom a bestial lust for torture took the place of normal human passions.

The brass door let onto a narrow stair that seemed to wind down into the very bowels of the hill on which the citadel stood. Down these stairs went the band, to halt at last at an iron door, the strength of which seemed unnecessary. Evidently it did not open on outer air, yet it was built as if to withstand the battering of mangonels and rams. Shukeli opened it, and as he swung back the ponderous portal, Conan noted the evident uneasiness among the black giants who guarded him; nor did Shukeli seem altogether devoid of nervousness as he peered into the darkness beyond. Inside the great door there was a second barrier, composed of great steel bars. It was fastened by an ingenious bolt which had no lock and could be worked only from the outside; this bolt shot back, the grille slid into the wall. They passed through, into a broad corridor, the floor, walls and arched ceiling of which seemed to be cut out of solid stone. Conan knew he was far underground, even below the hill itself. The darkness pressed in on the guardsmen's torches like a sentient, animate thing.

They made the king fast to a ring in the stone wall. Above his head in a niche in the wall they placed a torch, so that he stood in a dim semicircle of light. The blacks were anxious to be gone; they muttered among themselves, and cast fearful glances at the darkness. Tsotha motioned them out, and they filed through the door in stumbling haste, as if fearing the darkness might take tangible form and spring upon their backs. Tsotha turned toward Conan, and the king noticed uneasily that the wizard's eyes shone in the semi-darkness, and that his teeth much resembled the fangs of a wolf, gleaming whitely in the shadows.

'And so, farewell, barbarian,' mocked the sorcerer. 'I must ride to Shamar, and the siege. In ten days I will be in your palace in Tamar, with my warriors. What word from you shall I say to your women, before I flay their dainty skins for scrolls whereon to chronicle the triumphs of Tsotha-lanti?'

Conan answered with a searing Cimmerian curse that would have burst the very eardrums of an ordinary man, and Tsotha laughed thinly and withdrew. Conan had a glimpse of his vulture-like figure through the thick-set bars, as he slid home the grate; then the heavy outer door clanged, and silence fell like a pall.

3

> *The Lion strode through the halls of Hell;*
> *Across his path grim shadows fell*
> *Of many a mowing, nameless shape—*
> *Monsters with dripping jaws agape.*
> *The darkness shuddered with scream and yell*
> *When the Lion stalked through the halls of Hell.*
>   OLD BALLAD

King Conan tested the ring in the wall and the chain that bound him. His limbs were free, but he knew that his shackles were beyond even his iron strength. The links of the chain were as thick as his thumb and were fastened to a band of steel about his waist, a band broad as his hand and half an inch thick. The sheer weight of his shackles would have slain a lesser man with exhaustion. The locks that held band and chain were massive affairs that a sledge-hammer could hardly have dinted. As for the ring, evidently it went clear through the wall and was clinched on the other side.

Conan cursed and panic surged through him as he glared into the darkness that pressed against the half-circle of light. All the superstitious dread of the barbarian slept in his soul, untouched by civilized logic. His primitive imagination peopled the subterranean darkness with grisly shapes. Besides, his reason told him that he had not been placed there merely for confinement. His captors had no reason to spare him. He had been placed in these pits for a definite doom. He cursed himself for his refusal of their offer, even while his stubborn manhood revolted at the thought, and he knew that were he taken forth and given another chance, his reply would be the same. He would not sell his subjects to the butcher. And yet it had been with no thought of any one's gain but his own that he had seized the kingdom originally. Thus subtly does the instinct of sovereign responsibility enter even a red-handed plunderer sometimes.

Conan thought of Tsotha's last abominable threat, and groaned in sick fury, knowing it was no idle boast. Men and women were to the wizard no more than the writhing insect is to the scientist. Soft white hands that had caressed him, red lips that had been pressed to his, dainty white bosoms that had quivered to his hot fierce kisses, to be stripped of their delicate skin, white as ivory and pink as young petals – from Conan's lips burst a yell so frightful and inhuman in its mad fury that a listener would have started in horror to know that it came from a human throat.

The shuddering echoes made him start and brought back his own situation vividly to the king. He glared fearsomely at the outer gloom, and thought of all the grisly tales he had heard of Tsotha's necromantic cruelty, and it was with an icy sensation down his spine that he realized that these must be the very Halls of Horror named in shuddering legendry, the tunnels and dungeons wherein Tsotha performed horrible experiments with beings human, bestial, and, it was whispered, demoniac, tampering blasphemously with the naked basic elements of life itself. Rumor said that the mad poet Rinaldo had visited these pits, and been shown horrors by the wizard, and that the nameless monstrosities of which he hinted in his awful poem, *The Song of the Pit*, were no mere fantasies of a disordered brain. That brain had crashed to dust beneath Conan's battle-ax on the night the king had fought for his life with the assassins the mad rimer had led into the betrayed palace, but the shuddersome words of that grisly song still rang in the king's ears as he stood there in his chains.

Even with the thought the Cimmerian was frozen by a soft rustling sound, blood-freezing in its implication. He tensed in an attitude of listening, painful in its intensity. An icy hand stroked his spine. It was the unmistakable sound of pliant scales slithering softly over stone. Cold sweat beaded his skin, as beyond the ring of dim light he saw a vague and colossal form, awful even in its indistinctness. It reared upright, swaying slightly, and yellow eyes burned icily on him from the shadows. Slowly a huge, hideous, wedge-shaped head took form before his dilated eyes, and from the darkness oozed, in flowing scaly coils, the ultimate horror of reptilian development.

It was a snake that dwarfed all Conan's previous ideas of snakes. Eighty feet it stretched from its pointed tail to its triangular head, which was bigger than that of a horse. In the dim light its scales glistened coldly, white as hoar-frost. Surely this reptile was one born and grown in darkness, yet its eyes were full of evil and sure sight. It looped its titan coils in front of the captive, and the great head on the arching neck swayed a matter of inches from his face. Its forked tongue almost brushed his lips as it darted in and out, and its fetid odor made his senses reel with nausea. The great yellow eyes burned into his, and Conan gave back the glare of a trapped wolf. He fought frenziedly against the mad impulse to grasp the great arching neck in his tearing hands. Strong beyond the comprehension of civilized man, he had broken the neck of a python in a fiendish battle on the Stygian coast, in his corsair days. But this reptile was venomous; he saw the great fangs, a foot long, curved like scimitars. From them dripped a colorless liquid that he instinctively knew was death. He might conceivably crush that wedge-shaped skull with a desperate clenched fist, but he knew that at his first hint of movement, the monster would strike like lightning.

It was not because of any logical reasoning process that Conan remained motionless, since reason might have told him – since he was doomed anyway – to goad the snake into striking and get it over with; it was the blind black instinct of self-preservation that held him rigid as a statue blasted out of iron. Now the great barrel reared up and the head was poised high above his own, as the monster investigated the torch. A drop of venom fell on his naked thigh, and the feel of it was like a white-hot dagger driven into his flesh. Red jets of agony shot through Conan's brain, yet he held himself immovable; not by the twitching of a muscle or the flicker of any eyelash did he betray the pain of the hurt that left a scar he bore to the day of his death.

The serpent swayed over him, as if seeking to ascertain whether there were in truth life in this figure which stood so death-like still. Then suddenly, unexpectedly, the outer door, all but invisible in the shadows, clanged stridently. The serpent, suspicious as all its kind, whipped about with a quickness incredible for its bulk, and vanished with a long-drawn slithering down the corridor. The door swung open and remained open. The grille was withdrawn and a huge dark figure was framed in the glow of torches outside. The figure glided in, pulling the grille partly to behind it, leaving the bolt poised. As it moved into the light of the torch over Conan's head, the king saw that it was a gigantic black man, stark naked, bearing in one hand a huge sword and in the other a bunch of keys. The black spoke in a sea-coast dialect, and Conan replied; he had learned the jargon while a corsair on the coasts of Kush.

'Long have I wished to meet you, Amra,' the black gave Conan the name by which the Cimmerian had been known to the Kushites in his piratical days – Amra, the Lion. The slave's woolly skull split in an animal-like grin, showing white tusks, but his eyes glinted redly in the torchlight. 'I have dared much for this meeting. Look! The keys to your chains! I stole them from Shukeli. What will you give me for them?'

He dangled the keys in front of Conan's eyes.

'Ten thousand golden lunas,' answered the king quickly, new hope surging fiercely in his breast.

'Not enough!' cried the black, a ferocious exultation shining on his ebon countenance. 'Not enough for the risks I take. Tsotha's pets might come out of the dark and eat me, and if Shukeli finds out I stole his keys, he'll hang me up by my— well, what will you give me?'

'Fifteen thousand lunas and a palace in Poitain,' offered the king.

The black yelled and stamped in a frenzy of barbaric gratification.

'More!' he cried. 'Offer me more! What will you give me?'

'You black dog!' a red mist of fury swept across Conan's eyes. 'Were I free I'd give you a broken back! Did Shukeli send you here to mock me?'

'Shukeli knows nothing of my coming, white man,' answered the black, craning his thick neck to peer into Conan's savage eyes. 'I know you from of old, since the days when I was a chief among a free people, before the Stygians took me and sold me into the north. Do you not remember the sack of Abombi, when your sea-wolves swarmed in? Before the palace of King Ajaga you slew a chief and a chief fled from you. It was my brother who died; it was I who fled. I demand of you a blood-price, Amra!'

'Free me and I'll pay you your weight in gold pieces,' growled Conan.

The red eyes glittered, the white teeth flashed wolfishly in the torchlight.

'Aye, you white dog, you are like all your race; but to a black man gold can never pay for blood. The price I ask is – your head!'

The word was a maniacal shriek that sent the echoes shivering. Conan tensed, unconsciously straining against his shackles in his abhorrence of dying like a sheep; then he was frozen by a great horror. Over the black's shoulder he saw a vague horrific form swaying in the darkness.

'Tsotha will never know!' laughed the black fiendishly, too engrossed in his gloating triumph to take heed of anything else, too drunk with hate to know that Death swayed behind his shoulder. 'He will not come into the vaults until the demons have torn your bones from their chains. I will have your head, Amra!'

He braced his knotted legs like ebon columns and swung up the massive sword in both hands, his great black muscles rolling and cracking in the torchlight. And at that instant the titanic shadow behind him darted down and out, and the wedge-shaped head smote with an impact that re-echoed down the tunnels. Not a sound came from the thick blubbery lips that flew wide in fleeting agony. With the thud of the stroke, Conan saw the life go out of the wide black eyes with the suddenness of a candle blown out. The blow knocked the great black body clear across the corridor, and horribly the gigantic sinuous shape whipped around it in glistening coils that hid it from view, and the snap and splintering of bones came plainly to Conan's ears. Then something made his heart leap madly. The sword and the keys had flown from the black's hands to crash and jangle on the stone – and the keys lay almost at the king's feet.

He tried to bend to them, but the chain was too short; almost suffocated by the mad pounding of his heart, he slipped one foot from its sandal, and gripped them with his toes; drawing his foot up, he grasped them fiercely, barely stifling the yell of ferocious exultation that rose instinctively to his lips.

An instant's fumbling with the huge locks and he was free. He caught up the fallen sword and glared about. Only empty darkness met his eyes, into which the serpent had dragged a mangled, tattered object that only faintly resembled a human body. Conan turned to the open door. A few quick strides brought him to the threshold – a squeal of high-pitched laughter shrilled through the vaults, and the grille shot home under his very fingers, the bolt crashed down. Through the bars peered a face like a fiendishly mocking carven gargoyle – Shukeli the eunuch, who had followed his stolen keys. Surely he did not, in his gloating, see the sword in the prisoner's hand. With a terrible curse Conan struck as a cobra strikes; the great blade hissed between the bars and Shukeli's laughter broke in a death-scream. The fat eunuch bent at the middle, as if bowing to his killer, and crumpled like tallow, his pudgy hands clutching vainly at his spilling entrails.

Conan snarled in satisfaction; but he was still a prisoner. His keys were futile against the bolt which could be worked only from the outside. His experienced touch told him the bars were hard as the sword; an attempt to hew his way to freedom would only splinter his one weapon. Yet he found dents on those adamantine bars, like the marks of incredible fangs, and wondered with an involuntary shudder what nameless monsters had assailed the barriers so terribly. Regardless, there was but one thing for him to do, and that was to seek some other outlet. Taking the torch from the niche, he set off down the corridor, sword in hand. He saw no sign of the serpent or its victim, only a great smear of blood on the stone floor.

Darkness stalked on noiseless feet about him, scarcely driven back by his flickering torch. On either hand he saw dark openings, but he kept to the main corridor, watching the floor ahead of him carefully, lest he fall into some pit. And suddenly he heard the sound of a woman, weeping piteously. Another of Tsotha's victims, he thought, cursing the wizard anew, and turning aside, followed the sound down a smaller tunnel, dank and damp.

The weeping grew nearer as he advanced and lifting his torch, he made out a vague shape in the shadows. Stepping closer, he halted in sudden horror at the anthropomorphic bulk which sprawled before him. Its unstable outlines somewhat suggested an octopus, but its malformed tentacles were too short for its size, and its substance was a quaking, jelly-like stuff which made him physically sick to look at. From among this loathsome gelid mass reared up a frog-like head, and he was frozen with nauseated horror to realize that the sound of weeping was coming from those obscene blubbery lips. The noise changed to an abominable high-pitched tittering as the great unstable eyes of the monstrosity rested on him, and it hitched its quaking bulk toward him. He backed away and fled up the tunnel, not trusting his sword. The creature might be composed of terrestrial matter, but it shook his very soul to look upon it, and he doubted the power of man-made weapons to harm it. For a short distance he heard it flopping and floundering after him, screaming with horrible laughter. The unmistakably human note in its mirth almost staggered his reason. It was exactly such laughter as he had heard bubble obscenely from the fat lips of the salacious women of Shadizar, City of Wickedness, when captive girls were stripped naked on the public auction block. By what hellish arts had Tsotha brought this unnatural being into life? Conan felt vaguely that he had looked on blasphemy against the eternal laws of nature.

He ran toward the main corridor, but before he reached it he crossed a sort of small square chamber, where two tunnels crossed. As he reached this chamber, he was flashingly aware of some small squat bulk on the floor ahead of him; then before he could check his flight or swerve aside, his foot struck something yielding that squalled shrilly, and he was precipitated headlong, the torch flying from his hand and being extinguished as it struck the stone floor. Half stunned by his fall, Conan rose and groped in the darkness. His sense of direction was confused, and he was unable to decide in which direction lay the main corridor. He did not look for the torch, as he had no means of rekindling it. His groping hands found the openings of the tunnels, and he chose one at random. How long he traversed it in utter darkness, he never knew, but suddenly his barbarian's instinct of near peril halted him short.

He had the same feeling he had had when standing on the brink of great precipices in the darkness. Dropping to all fours, he edged forward, and presently his outflung hand encountered the edge of a well, into which the tunnel floor apparently dropped abruptly. As far down as he could reach the sides fell away sheerly, dank and slimy to his touch. He stretched out an arm in the darkness and could barely touch the opposite edge with the point of his sword. He could leap across it then, but there was no point in that. He had taken the wrong tunnel and the main corridor lay somewhere behind him.

Even as he thought this, he felt a faint movement of air; a shadowy wind, rising from the well, stirred his black mane. Conan's skin crawled. He tried to tell himself that this well connected somehow with the outer world, but his instincts told him it was a thing unnatural. He was not merely inside the hill; he was below it, far below the level of the city streets. How then could an outer wind find its way into the pits and blow up from *below*? A faint throbbing pulsed on that ghostly wind, like drums beating far, far below. A strong shudder shook the king of Aquilonia.

He rose to his feet and backed away, and as he did *something* floated up out of the well. What it was, Conan did not know. He could see nothing in the darkness, but he distinctly felt a presence – an invisible, intangible intelligence which hovered malignly near him. Turning, he fled the way he had come. Far ahead he saw a tiny red spark. He headed for it, and long before he thought to have reached it, he caromed headlong into a solid wall and saw the spark at his feet. It was his torch, the flame extinguished, but the end a glowing coal. Carefully he took it up and blew upon it, fanning it into flame again. He gave a sigh as the tiny blaze leaped up. He was back in the chamber where the tunnels crossed, and his sense of direction came back.

He located the tunnel by which he had left the main corridor, and even as he started toward it, his torch-flame flickered wildly as if blown upon by unseen lips. Again he felt a presence, and he lifted his torch, glaring about.

He saw nothing; yet he sensed, somehow, an invisible, bodiless thing that hovered in the air, dripping slimily and mouthing obscenities that he could not hear but was in some instinctive way aware of. He swung viciously with his sword and it felt as if he were cleaving cobwebs. A cold horror shook him then, and he fled down the tunnel, feeling a foul burning breath on his naked back as he ran.

But when he came out into the broad corridor, he was no longer aware of any presence, visible or invisible. Down it he went, momentarily expecting fanged and taloned fiends to leap at him from the darkness. The tunnels were not silent. From the bowels of the earth in all directions came sounds that did not belong in a sane world. There were titterings, squeals of demoniac mirth, long shuddering howls, and once the unmistakable squalling laughter of a hyena ended awfully in human words of shrieking blasphemy. He heard the pad of stealthy feet, and in the mouths of the tunnels caught glimpses of shadowy forms, monstrous and abnormal in outline.

It was as if he had wandered into hell – a hell of Tsotha-lanti's making. But the shadowy things did not come into the corridor, though he distinctly heard the greedy sucking-in of slavering lips, and felt the burning glare of hungry eyes. And presently he knew why. A slithering sound behind him electrified him, and he leaped to the darkness of a near-by tunnel, shaking out his torch. Down the corridor he heard the great serpent crawling, sluggish from its recent grisly meal. From his very side something whimpered in fear and shrunk away in the darkness. Evidently the main corridor was the great snake's hunting-ground, and the other monsters gave it room.

To Conan the serpent was the least horror of them; he almost felt a kinship with it when he remembered the weeping, tittering obscenity, and the dripping, mouthing thing that came out of the well. At least it was of earthly matter; it was a crawling death, but it threatened only physical extinction, whereas these other horrors menaced mind and soul as well.

After it had passed on down the corridor, he followed, at what he hoped was a safe distance, blowing his torch into flame again. He had not gone far when he heard a low moan that seemed to emanate from the black entrance of a tunnel near by. Caution warned him off, but curiosity drove him to the tunnel, holding high the torch that was now little more than a stump. He was braced for the sight of anything, yet what he saw was what he had least expected. He was looking into a broad cell, and a space of this was caged off with closely set bars extending from floor to ceiling, set firmly in the stone. Within these bars lay a figure, which, as he approached, he saw was either a man, or the exact likeness of a man, twined and bound about with the tendrils of a thick vine which seemed to grow through the solid stone of the floor. It was covered with strangely pointed leaves and crimson blossoms – not the satiny red of natural petals, but a livid, unnatural crimson, like a perversity of flower-life. Its clinging, pliant branches wound about the man's naked body and limbs, seeming to caress his shrinking flesh with lustful avid kisses. One great blossom hovered exactly over his mouth. A low bestial moaning drooled from the loose lips; the head rolled as if in unbearable agony, and the eyes looked full at Conan. But there was no light of intelligence in them; they were blank, glassy, the eyes of an idiot.

Now the great crimson blossom dipped and pressed its petals over the writhing lips. The limbs of the wretch twisted in anguish; the tendrils of the plant quivered as if in ecstasy, vibrating their full snaky lengths. Waves of changing hues surged over them; their color grew deeper, more venomous.

Conan did not understand what he saw, but he knew that he looked on Horror of some kind. Man or demon, the suffering of the captive touched Conan's wayward and impulsive heart. He sought for entrance and found a grille-like door in the bars, fastened with a heavy lock, for which he found a key among the keys he carried, and entered. Instantly the petals of the livid blossoms spread like the hood of a cobra, the tendrils reared menacingly and the whole plant shook and swayed toward him. Here was no blind growth of natural vegetation. Conan sensed a strange, malignant intelligence; the plant could see him, and he felt its hate emanate from it in almost tangible waves. Stepping warily nearer, he marked the root-stem, a repulsively supple stalk thicker than his thigh, and even as the long tendrils arched toward him with a rattle of leaves and hiss, he swung his sword and cut through the stem with a single stroke.

Instantly the wretch in its clutches was thrown violently aside as the great vine lashed and knotted like a beheaded serpent, rolling into a huge irregular ball. The tendrils thrashed and writhed, the leaves shook and rattled like castanets, and petals opened and closed convulsively; then the whole length straightened out limply, the vivid colors paled and dimmed, a reeking white liquid oozed from the severed stump.

Conan stared, spellbound; then a sound brought him round, sword lifted. The freed man was on his feet, surveying him. Conan gaped in wonder. No longer were the eyes in the worn face expressionless. Dark and meditative, they were alive with intelligence, and the expression of imbecility had dropped from the face like a mask. The head was narrow and well-formed, with a high splendid forehead. The whole build of the man was aristocratic, evident no less in his tall slender frame than in his small trim feet and hands. His first words were strange and startling.

'What year is this?' he asked, speaking in Kothian.

'Today is the tenth of the month Yuluk, of the year of the Gazelle,' answered Conan.

'Yagkoolan Ishtar!' murmured the stranger. 'Ten years!' he drew a hand across his brow, shaking his head as if to clear his brain from cobwebs. 'All is dim yet. After a ten-year emptiness, the mind can not be expected to begin functioning clearly at once. Who are you?'

'Conan, once of Cimmeria. Now king of Aquilonia.'

The other's eyes showed surprise.

'Indeed? And Namedides?'

'I strangled him on his throne the night I took the royal city,' answered Conan.

A certain naïveté in the king's reply twitched the stranger's lips.

'Pardon, your majesty. I should have thanked you for the service you have done me. I am like a man woken suddenly from sleep deeper than death and shot with nightmares of agony more fierce than hell, but I understand that you delivered me. Tell me – why did you cut the stem of the plant Yothga instead of tearing it up by the roots?'

'Because I learned long ago to avoid touching with my flesh that which I do not understand,' answered the Cimmerian.

'Well for you,' said the stranger. 'Had you been able to tear it up, you might have found things clinging to the roots against which not even your sword would prevail. Yothga's roots are set in hell.'

'But who are you?' demanded Conan.

'Men call me Pelias.'

'What!' cried the king. 'Pelias the sorcerer, Tsotha-lanti's rival, who vanished from the earth ten years ago?'

'Not entirely from the earth,' answered Pelias with a wry smile. 'Tsotha preferred to keep me alive, in shackles more grim than rusted iron. He pent me in here with this devil flower whose seeds drifted down through the black cosmos from Yag the Accursed, and found fertile field only in the maggot-writhing corruption that seethes on the floors of hell.

'I could not remember my sorcery and the words and symbols of my power, with that cursed thing gripping me and drinking my soul with its loathsome caresses. It sucked the contents of my mind day and night, leaving my brain as empty as a broken wine-jug. Ten years! Ishtar preserve us!'

Conan found no reply, but stood holding the stump of the torch, and trailing his great sword. Surely the man was mad – yet there was no madness in the strange dark eyes that rested so calmly on him.

'Tell me, is the black wizard in Khorshemish? But no – you need not reply. My powers begin to wake, and I sense in your mind a great battle and a king trapped by treachery. And I see Tsotha-lanti riding hard for the Tybor with Strabonus and the king of Ophir. So much the better. My art is too frail from the long slumber to face Tsotha yet. I need time to recruit my strength, to assemble my powers. Let us go forth from these pits.'

Conan jangled his keys discouragedly.

'The grille to the outer door is made fast by a bolt which can only be worked from outside. Is there no other exit from these tunnels?'

'Only one which neither of us would care to use, seeing that it goes down and not up,' laughed Pelias. 'But no matter. Let us see to the grille.'

He moved toward the corridor with uncertain steps, as of long-unused limbs, which gradually became more sure. As he followed, Conan said uneasily, 'There is a cursed big snake creeping about this tunnel. Let us be wary lest we step into his mouth.'

'I remember him of old,' answered Pelias grimly, 'the more as I was forced to watch while ten of my acolytes were fed to him. He is Satha, the Old One, chiefest of Tsotha's pets.'

'Did Tsotha dig these pits for no other reason than to house his cursed monstrosities?' asked Conan.

'He did not dig them. When the city was founded three thousand years ago there were ruins of an earlier city on and about this hill. King Khossus V, the founder, built his palace on the hill, and digging cellars beneath it, came upon a walled-up doorway, which he broke into and discovered the pits, which were about as we see them now. But his grand vizier came to such a grisly end in them that Khossus in a fright walled up the entrance again. He said the vizier fell into a well – but he had the cellars filled in, and later abandoned the palace itself, and built himself another in the suburbs, from which he fled in panic on discovering some black mold scattered on the marble floor of his chamber one morning.

'He then departed with his whole court to the eastern corner of the kingdom and built a new city. The palace on the hill was not used and fell into ruins. When Akkutho I revived the lost glories of Khorshemish, he built a fortress there. It remained for Tsotha-lanti to rear the scarlet citadel and open the way to the pits again. Whatever fate overtook the grand vizier of Khossus, Tsotha avoided it. He fell into no well, though he did descend into a well he found, and came out with a strange expression which has not since left his eyes.

'I have seen that well, but I do not care to seek in it for wisdom. I am a sorcerer, and older than men reckon, but I am human. As for Tsotha

– men say that a dancing-girl of Shadizar slept too near the pre-human ruins on Dagoth Hill and woke in the grip of a black demon; from that unholy ruin was spawned an accursed hybrid men call Tsotha-lanti—'

Conan cried out sharply and recoiled, thrusting his companion back. Before them rose the great shimmering white form of Satha, an ageless hate in its eyes. Conan tensed himself for one mad berserker onslaught – to thrust the glowing fagot into that fiendish countenance and throw his life into the ripping sword-stroke. But the snake was not looking at him. It was glaring over his shoulder at the man called Pelias, who stood with his arms folded, smiling. And in the great cold yellow eyes slowly the hate died out in a glitter of pure fear – the only time Conan ever saw such an expression in a reptile's eyes. With a swirling rush like the sweep of a strong wind, the great snake was gone.

'What did he see to frighten him?' asked Conan, eyeing his companion uneasily.

'The scaled people see what escapes the mortal eye,' answered Pelias cryptically. 'You see my fleshly guise; he saw my naked soul.'

An icy trickle disturbed Conan's spine, and he wondered if, after all, Pelias were a man, or merely another demon of the pits in the mask of humanity. He contemplated the advisability of driving his sword through his companion's back without further hesitation. But while he pondered, they came to the steel grille, etched blackly in the torches beyond, and the body of Shukeli, still slumped against the bars in a curdled welter of crimson.

Pelias laughed, and his laugh was not pleasant to hear.

'By the ivory hips of Ishtar, who is our doorman? Lo, it is no less than the noble Shukeli himself, who hanged my young men by their feet and skinned them with squeals of laughter! Do you sleep, Shukeli? Why do you lie so stiffly, with your fat belly sunk in like a dressed pig's?'

'He is dead,' muttered Conan, ill at ease to hear these wild words.

'Dead or alive,' laughed Pelias, 'he shall open the door for us.'

He clapped his hands sharply and cried, 'Rise, Shukeli! Rise from hell and rise from the bloody floor and open the door for your masters! Rise, I say!'

An awful groan reverberated through the vaults. Conan's hair stood on end and he felt clammy sweat bead his hide. For the body of Shukeli stirred and moved, with infantile gropings of the fat hands. The laughter of Pelias was merciless as a flint hatchet, as the form of the eunuch reeled upright, clutching at the bars of the grille. Conan, glaring at him, felt his blood turn to ice, and the marrow of his bones to water; for Shukeli's wide-open eyes were glassy and empty, and from the great gash in his belly his entrails hung limply to the floor. The eunuch's feet stumbled among his entrails as he worked the bolt, moving like a brainless automaton. When he had first stirred, Conan had thought that by some incredible chance the eunuch was alive; but the man was dead – had been dead for hours.

Pelias sauntered through the opened grille, and Conan crowded through behind him, sweat pouring from his body, shrinking away from the awful shape that slumped on sagging legs against the grate it held open. Pelias passed on without a backward glance, and Conan followed him, in the grip of nightmare and nausea. He had not taken half a dozen strides when a sodden thud brought him round. Shukeli's corpse lay limply at the foot of the grille.

'His task is done, and hell gapes for him again,' remarked Pelias pleasantly, politely affecting not to notice the strong shudder which shook Conan's mighty frame.

He led the way up the long stairs, and through the brass skull-crowned door at the top. Conan gripped his sword, expecting a rush of slaves, but silence gripped the citadel. They passed through the black corridor and came into that in which the censers swung, billowing forth their everlasting incense. Still they saw no one.

'The slaves and soldiers are quartered in another part of the citadel,' remarked Pelias. 'Tonight, their master being away, they doubtless lie drunk on wine or lotus-juice.'

Conan glanced through an arched, golden-silled window that let out upon a broad balcony, and swore in surprise to see the dark-blue star-flecked sky. It had been shortly after sunrise when he was thrown into the pits. Now it was past midnight. He could scarcely realize he had been so long underground. He was suddenly aware of thirst and a ravenous appetite. Pelias led the way into a golden-domed chamber, floored with silver, its lapis-lazuli walls pierced by the fretted arches of many doors.

With a sigh Pelias sank onto a silken divan.

'Silks and gold again,' he sighed. 'Tsotha affects to be above the pleasures of the flesh, but he is half devil. I am human, despite my black arts. I love ease and good cheer – that's how Tsotha trapped me. He caught me helpless with drink. Wine is a curse – by the ivory bosom of Ishtar, even as I speak of it, the traitor is here! Friend, please pour me a goblet – hold! I forgot you are a king. I will pour.'

'The devil with that,' growled Conan, filling a crystal goblet and proffering it to Pelias. Then, lifting the jug, he drank deeply from the mouth, echoing Pelias' sigh of satisfaction.

'The dog knows good wine,' said Conan, wiping his mouth with the back of his hand. 'But by Crom, Pelias, are we to sit here until his soldiers awake and cut our throats?'

'No fear,' answered Pelias. 'Would you like to see how fortune holds with Strabonus?'

Blue fire burned in Conan's eyes and he gripped his sword until his knuckles showed blue. 'Oh, to be at sword-points with him!' he rumbled.

Pelias lifted a great shimmering globe from an ebony table.

'Tsotha's crystal. A childish toy, but useful when there is lack of time for higher science. Look in, your majesty.'

He laid it on the table before Conan's eyes. The king looked into cloudy depths which deepened and expanded. Slowly images crystalized out of mist and shadows. He was looking on a familiar landscape. Broad plains ran to a wide winding river, beyond which the level lands ran up quickly into a maze of low hills. On the northern bank of the river stood a walled town, guarded by a moat connected at each end with the river.

'By Crom!' ejaculated Conan. 'It's Shamar! The dogs besiege it!'

The invaders had crossed the river; their pavilions stood in the narrow plain between the city and the hills. Their warriors swarmed about the walls, their mail gleaming palely under the moon. Arrows and stones rained on them from the towers and they staggered back, but came on again.

Even as Conan cursed, the scene changed. Tall spires and gleaming domes stood up in the mist, and he looked on his own capital of Tamar, where all was confusion. He saw the steel-clad knights of Poitain, his staunchest supporters, whom he had left in charge of the city, riding out of the gate, hooted and hissed by the multitude which swarmed the streets. He saw looting and rioting, and men-at-arms whose shields bore the insignia of Pellia, manning the towers and swaggering through the markets. Over all, like a fantasmal picture, he saw the dark, triumphant face of Prince Arpello of Pellia. The images faded.

'So!' cursed Conan, 'My people turn on me the moment my back is turned—'

'Not entirely,' broke in Pelias. 'They have heard that you are dead. There is no one to protect them from outer enemies and civil war, they think. Naturally, they turn to the strongest noble, to avoid the horrors of anarchy. They do not trust the Poitanians, remembering former wars. But Arpello is on hand, and the strongest prince of the central realm.'

'When I come to Aquilonia again he will be but a headless corpse rotting on Traitor's Common,' Conan ground his teeth.

'Yet before you can reach your capital,' reminded Pelias, 'Strabonus may be before you. At least his riders will be ravaging your kingdom.'

'True!' Conan paced the chamber like a caged lion. 'With the fastest horse I could not reach Shamar before midday. Even there I could do no good except to die with the people, when the town falls – as fall it will in a few days at most. From Shamar to Tamar is five days' ride, even if you kill your horses on the road. Before I could reach my capital and raise an army, Strabonus would be hammering at the gates; because raising an army is going to be hell – all my damnable nobles will have scattered to their own cursed fiefs at the word of my death. And since the people have driven out Trocero of Poitain, there's none to keep Arpello's greedy hands off the crown – and the crown-treasure. He'll hand the country over to Strabonus, in return for a mock-throne – and as soon as Strabonus' back is turned, he'll stir up revolt. But the nobles won't support him, and it will only give Strabonus excuse for annexing the kingdom openly. Oh Crom, Ymir, and Set! If I had but wings to fly like lightning to Tamar!'

Pelias, who sat tapping the jade table-top with his finger-nails, halted suddenly, and rose as with a definite purpose, beckoning Conan to follow. The king complied, sunk in moody thoughts, and Pelias led the way out of the chamber and up a flight of marble, gold-worked stairs that let out on the pinnacle of the citadel, the roof of the tallest tower. It was night, and a strong wind was blowing through the star-filled skies, stirring Conan's black mane. Far below them twinkled the lights of Khorshemish, seemingly farther away than the stars above them. Pelias seemed withdrawn and aloof here, one in cold unhuman greatness with the company of the stars.

'There are creatures,' said Pelias, 'not alone of earth and sea, but of air and the far reaches of the skies as well, dwelling apart, unguessed of men. Yet to him who holds the Master-words and Signs and the Knowledge underlying all, they are not malignant nor inaccessible. Watch, and fear not.'

He lifted his hands to the skies and sounded a long weird call that seemed to shudder endlessly out into space, dwindling and fading, yet never dying out, only receding farther and farther into some unreckoned cosmos. In the silence that followed, Conan heard a sudden beat of wings in the stars, and recoiled as a huge bat-like creature alighted beside him. He saw its great calm eyes regarding him in the starlight; he saw the forty-foot spread of its giant wings. And he saw it was neither bat nor bird.

'Mount and ride,' said Pelias. 'By dawn it will bring you to Tamar.'

'By Crom!' muttered Conan. 'Is this all a nightmare from which I shall presently awaken in my palace at Tamar? What of you? I would not leave you alone among your enemies.'

'Be at ease regarding me,' answered Pelias. 'At dawn the people of Khorshemish will know they have a new master. Doubt not what the gods have sent you. I will meet you in the plain by Shamar.'

Doubtfully Conan clambered upon the ridged back, gripping the arched neck, still convinced that he was in the grasp of a fantastic nightmare. With a great rush and thunder of titan wings, the creature took the air, and the king grew dizzy as he saw the lights of the city dwindle far below him.

4

'The sword that slays the king cuts the cords of the empire.'
AQUILONIAN PROVERB

The streets of Tamar swarmed with howling mobs, shaking fists and rusty pikes. It was the hour before dawn of the second day after the battle of Shamar, and events had occurred so swiftly as to daze the mind. By means known only to Tsotha-lanti, word had reached Tamar of the king's death, within half a dozen hours after the battle. Chaos had resulted. The barons had deserted the royal capital, galloping away to secure their castles against marauding neighbors. The well-knit kingdom Conan had built up seemed tottering on the edge of dissolution, and commoners and merchants trembled at the imminence of a return of the feudalistic regime. The people howled for a king to protect them against their own aristocracy no less than foreign foes. Count Trocero, left by Conan in charge of the city, tried to reassure them, but in their unreasoning terror, they remembered old civil wars, and how this same count had besieged Tamar fifteen years before. It was shouted in the streets that Trocero had betrayed the king; that he planned to plunder the city. The mercenaries began looting the quarters, dragging forth screaming merchants and terrified women.

Trocero swept down on the looters, littered the streets with their corpses, drove them back into their quarter in confusion, and arrested their leaders. Still the people rushed wildly about, with brainless squawks, screaming that the count had incited the riot for his own purposes.

Prince Arpello came before the distracted council and announced himself ready to take over the government of the city until a new king could be decided upon, Conan having no son. While they debated, his agents stole subtly among the people, who snatched at a shred of royalty. The council heard the storm outside the palace windows, where the multitude roared for Arpello the Rescuer. The council surrendered.

Trocero at first refused the order to give up his baton of authority, but the people swarmed about him, hissing and howling, hurling stones and offal at his knights. Seeing the futility of a pitched battle in the streets with Arpello's retainers, under such conditions, Trocero hurled the baton in his rival's face, hanged the leaders of the mercenaries in the market-square as his last official act, and rode out of the southern gate at the head of his fifteen hundred steel-clad knights. The gates slammed behind him and Arpello's suave mask fell away to reveal the grim visage of the hungry wolf.

With the mercenaries cut to pieces or hiding in their barracks, his were the only soldiers in Tamar. Sitting his war-horse in the great square, Arpello proclaimed himself king of Aquilonia, amid the clamor of the deluded multitude.

Publius the Chancellor, who opposed this move, was thrown into prison. The merchants, who had greeted the proclamation of a king with relief, now found with consternation that the new monarch's first act was to levy a staggering tax on them. Six rich merchants, sent as a delegation of protest, were seized and their heads slashed off without ceremony. A shocked and stunned silence followed this execution. The merchants, as is the habit of merchants when confronted by a power they can not control with money, fell on their fat bellies and licked their oppressor's boots.

The common people were not perturbed at the fate of the merchants, but they began to murmur when they found that the swaggering Pellian soldiery, pretending to maintain order, were as bad as Turanian bandits. Complaints of extortion, murder and rape poured in to Arpello, who had taken up his quarters in Publius' palace, because the desperate councillors, doomed by his order, were holding the royal palace against his soldiers. He had taken possession of the pleasure-palace, however, and Conan's girls were dragged to his quarters. The people muttered at the sight of the royal beauties writhing in the brutal hands of the iron-clad retainers – dark-eyed damsels of Poitain, slim black-haired wenches from Zamora, Zingara and Hyrkania, Brythunian girls with tousled yellow heads, all weeping with fright and shame, unused to brutality.

Night fell on a city of bewilderment and turmoil, and before midnight word spread mysteriously in the street that the Kothians had followed up their victory and were hammering at the walls of Shamar. Somebody in Tsotha's mysterious secret-service had babbled. Fear shook the people like an earthquake, and they did not even pause to wonder at the witchcraft by which the news had been so swiftly transmitted. They stormed at Arpello's doors, demanding that he march southward and drive the enemy back over the Tybor. He might have subtly pointed out that his force was not sufficient, and that he could not raise an army until the barons recognized his claim to the crown. But he was drunk with power, and laughed in their faces.

A young student, Athemides, mounted a column in the market, and with burning words accused Arpello of being a cats-paw for Strabonus, painting a vivid picture of existence under Kothian rule, with Arpello as satrap. Before he finished, the multitude was screaming with fear and howling with rage. Arpello sent his soldiers to arrest the youth, but the people caught him up and fled with him, deluging the pursuing retainers with stones and dead cats. A volley of crossbow quarrels routed the mob, and a charge of horsemen littered the market with bodies, but Athemides was smuggled out of the city to plead with Trocero to retake Tamar, and march to aid Shamar.

Athemides found Trocero breaking his camp outside the walls, ready to march to Poitain, in the far southwestern corner of the kingdom. To the youth's urgent pleas he answered that he had neither the force necessary to storm Tamar, even with the aid of the mob inside, nor to face Strabonus. Besides, avaricious nobles would plunder Poitain behind his back, while he was fighting the Kothians. With the king dead, each man must protect his own. He was riding to Poitain, there to defend it as best he might against Arpello and his foreign allies.

While Athemides pleaded with Trocero, the mob still raved in the city with helpless fury. Under the great tower beside the royal palace the people swirled and milled, screaming their hate at Arpello, who stood on the turrets and laughed down at them while his archers ranged the parapets, bolts drawn and fingers on the triggers of their arbalests.

The prince of Pellia was a broad-built man of medium height, with a dark stern face. He was an intriguer, but he was also a fighter. Under his silken jupon with its gilt-braided skirts and jagged sleeves, glimmered burnished steel. His long black hair was curled and scented, and bound back with a cloth-of-silver band, but at his hip hung a broadsword the jeweled hilt of which was worn with battles and campaigns.

'Fools! Howl as you will! Conan is dead and Arpello is king!'

What if all Aquilonia were leagued against him? He had men enough to hold the mighty walls until Strabonus came up. But Aquilonia was divided against itself. Already the barons were girding themselves each to seize his neighbor's treasure. Arpello had only the helpless mob to deal with. Strabonus would carve through the loose lines of the warring barons as a galley-ram through foam, and until his coming, Arpello had only to hold the royal capital.

'Fools! Arpello is king!'

The sun was rising over the eastern towers. Out of the crimson dawn came a flying speck that grew to a bat, then to an eagle. Then all who saw screamed in amazement, for over the walls of Tamar swooped a shape such as men knew only in half-forgotten legends, and from between its titan-wings sprang a human form as it roared over the great tower. Then with a deafening thunder of wings it was gone, and the folk blinked, wondering if they dreamed. But on the turret stood a wild barbaric figure, half naked, blood-stained, brandishing a great sword. And from the multitude rose a roar that rocked the very towers, 'The king! It is the king!'

Arpello stood transfixed; then with a cry he drew and leaped at Conan. With a lion-like roar the Cimmerian parried the whistling blade, then dropped his own sword, gripped the prince and heaved him high above his head by crotch and neck.

'Take your plots to hell with you!' he roared, and like a sack of salt, he hurled the prince of Pellia far out, to fall through empty space for a hundred and fifty feet. The people gave back as the body came hurtling down, to smash on the marble pave, spattering blood and brains, and lie crushed in its splintered armor, like a mangled beetle.

The archers on the tower shrank back, their nerve broken. They fled, and the beleaguered councilmen sallied from the palace and hewed into them with joyous abandon. Pellian knights and men-at-arms sought safety in the streets and the crowd tore them to pieces. In the streets the fighting milled and eddied, plumed helmets and steel caps tossed among the tousled heads and then vanished; swords hacked madly in a heaving forest of pikes, and over all rose the roar of the mob, shouts of acclaim mingling with screams of blood-lust and howls of agony. And high above all, the naked figure of the king rocked and swayed on the dizzy battlements, mighty arms brandished, roaring with gargantuan laughter that mocked all mobs and princes, even himself.

5

*A long bow and a strong bow, and let the sky
  grow dark!
The cord to the nock, the shaft to the ear, and the
  king of Koth for a mark!*
            SONG OF THE BOSSONIAN ARCHERS

The midafternoon sun glinted on the placid waters of the Tybor, washing the southern bastions of Shamar. The haggard defenders knew that few of them would see that sun rise again. The pavilions of the besiegers dotted the plain. The people of Shamar had not been able successfully to dispute the crossing of the river, outnumbered as they were. Barges, chained together, made a bridge over which the invader poured his hordes. Strabonus had not dared march on into Aquilonia with Shamar, unsubdued, at his back. He had sent his light riders, his spahis, inland to ravage the country, and had reared up his siege engines in the plain. He had anchored a flotilla of boats, furnished him by Amalrus, in the middle of the stream, over against the river-wall. Some of these boats had been sunk by stones from the city's ballistas, which crashed through their decks and ripped out their planking, but the rest held their places and from their bows and mast-heads, protected by mantlets, archers raked the riverward turrets. These were Shemites, born with bows in their hands, not to be matched by Aquilonian bowmen.

On the landward side mangonels rained boulders and tree-trunks among the defenders, shattering through roofs and crushing humans like beetles; rams pounded incessantly at the stones; sappers burrowed like moles in the earth, sinking their mines beneath the towers. The moat had been dammed at the upper end, and emptied of its water, had been filled up with boulders, earth and dead horses and men. Under the walls the mailed figures swarmed, battering at the gates, rearing up scaling-ladders, pushing storming-towers, thronged with spearmen, against the turrets.

Hope had been abandoned in the city, where a bare fifteen hundred men resisted forty thousand warriors. No word had come from the kingdom whose outpost the city was. Conan was dead, so the invaders shouted exultantly. Only the strong walls and the desperate courage of the defenders had kept them so long at bay, and that could not suffice for ever. The western wall was a mass of rubbish on which the defenders stumbled in hand-to-hand conflict with the invaders. The other walls were buckling from the mines beneath them, the towers leaning drunkenly.

Now the attackers were massing for a storm. The oliphants sounded, the steel-clad ranks drew up on the plain. The storming-towers, covered with raw bull-hides, rumbled forward. The people of Shamar saw the banners of Koth and Ophir, flying side by side, in the center, and made out, among their gleaming knights, the slim lethal figure of the golden-mailed Amalrus, and the squat black-armored form of Strabonus. And between them was a shape that made the bravest blench with horror – a lean vulture figure in a filmy robe. The pikemen moved forward, flowing over the ground like the glinting waves of a river of molten steel; the knights cantered forward, lances lifted, guidons streaming. The warriors on the wall drew a long breath, consigned their souls to Mitra, and gripped their notched and red-stained weapons.

Then without warning, a bugle-call cut the din. A drum of hoofs rose above the rumble of the approaching host. North of the plain across which the army moved, rose ranges of low hills, mounting northward and westward like giant stair-steps. Now down out of these hills, like spume blown before a storm shot the spahis who had been laying waste the countryside, riding low and spurring hard, and behind them the sun shimmering on moving ranks of steel. They moved into full view, out of the defiles – mailed horsemen, the great lion banner of Aquilonia floating over them.

From the electrified watchers on the towers a great shout rent the skies. In ecstasy warriors clashed their notched swords on their riven shields, and the people of the town, ragged beggars and rich merchants, harlots in red kirtles and dames in silks and satins, fell to their knees and cried out for joy to Mitra, tears of gratitude streaming down their faces.

Strabonus, frantically shouting orders, with Arbanus, who would wheel around the ponderous lines to meet this unexpected menace, grunted, 'We still outnumber them, unless they have reserves hidden in the hills. The men on the battle-towers can mask any sorties from the city. These are Poitanians – we might have guessed Trocero would try some such mad gallantry.'

Amalrus cried out in unbelief.

'I see Trocero and his captain Prospero – *but who rides between them?*'

'Ishtar preserve us!' shrieked Strabonus, paling. 'It is King Conan!'

'You are mad!' squalled Tsotha, starting convulsively. 'Conan has been in Satha's belly for days!' He stopped short, glaring wildly at the host which was dropping down, file by file, into the plain. He could not mistake the giant figure in black, gild-worked armor on the great black stallion, riding beneath the billowing silken folds of the great banner. A scream of feline fury burst from Tsotha's lips, flecking his beard with foam. For the first time in his life, Strabonus saw the wizard completely upset, and shrank from the sight.

'Here is sorcery!' screamed Tsotha, clawing madly at his beard. 'How could he have escaped and reached his kingdom in time to return with an army so quickly? This is the work of Pelias, curse him! I feel his hand in this! May I be cursed for not killing him when I had the power!'

The kings gaped at the mention of a man they believed ten years dead, and panic, emanating from the leaders, shook the host. All recognized the rider on the black stallion. Tsotha felt the superstitious dread of his men, and fury made a hellish mask of his face.

'Strike home!' he screamed, brandishing his lean arms madly. 'We are still the stronger! Charge and crush these dogs! We shall yet feast in the ruins of Shamar tonight! Oh Set!' he lifted his hands and invoked the serpent-god to even Strabonus' horror, 'grant us victory and I swear I will offer up to thee five hundred virgins of Shamar, writhing in their blood!'

Meanwhile the opposing host had debouched onto the plain. With the knights came what seemed a second, irregular army on tough swift ponies. These dismounted and formed their ranks on foot – stolid Bossonian archers, and keen pikemen from Gunderland, their tawny locks blowing from under their steel caps.

It was a motley army Conan had assembled, in the wild hours following his return to his capital. He had beaten the frothing mob away from the Pellian soldiers who held the outer walls of Tamar, and impressed them into his service. He had sent a swift rider after Trocero to bring him back. With these as nucleus of an army he had raced southward, sweeping the countryside for recruits and for mounts. Nobles of Tamar and the surrounding countryside had augmented his forces, and he had levied recruits from every village and castle along his road. Yet it was but a paltry force he had gathered to dash against the invading hosts, though of the quality of tempered steel.

Nineteen hundred armored horsemen followed him, the main bulk of which consisted of the Poitanian knights. The remnants of the mercenaries and professional soldiers in the trains of loyal noblemen made up his infantry – five thousand archers and four thousand pikemen. This host now came on in good order – first the archers, then the pikemen, behind them the knights, moving at a walk.

Over against them Arbanus ordered his lines, and the allied army moved forward like a shimmering ocean of steel. The watchers on the city walls shook to see that vast host, which overshadowed the powers of the rescuers. First marched the Shemitish archers, then the Kothian spearmen, then the mailed knights of Strabonus and Amalrus. Arbanus' intent was obvious – to employ his footmen to sweep away the infantry of Conan, and open the way for an overpowering charge of his heavy cavalry.

The Shemites opened fire at five hundred yards, and arrows flew like hail between the hosts, darkening the sun. The western archers, trained by a thousand years of merciless warfare with the Pictish savages, came stolidly on, closing their ranks as their comrades fell. They were far outnumbered, and the Shemitish bow had the longer range, but in accuracy the Bossonians were equal to their foes, and they balanced sheer skill in archery by superiority in morale, and in excellence of armor. Within good range they loosed, and the Shemites went down by whole ranks. The blue-bearded warriors in their light mail shirts could not endure punishment as could the heavier-armored Bossonians. They broke, throwing away their bows, and their flight disordered the ranks of the Kothian spearmen behind them.

Without the support of the archers, these men-at-arms fell by the hundreds before the shafts of the Bossonians, and charging in madly to close quarters, they were met by the spears of the pikemen. No infantry was a match for the wild Gundermen, whose homeland, the northernmost province of Aquilonia was but a day's ride across the Bossonian marches from the borders of Cimmeria, and who, born and bred to battle, were the purest blood of all the Hyborian peoples. The Kothian spearmen, dazed by their losses from arrows, were cut to pieces and fell back in disorder.

Strabonus roared in fury as he saw his infantry repulsed, and shouted for a general charge. Arbanus demurred, pointing out the Bossonians re-forming in good order before the Aquilonian knights, who had sat their steeds motionless during the mêlée. The general advised a temporary retirement, to draw the western knights out of the cover of the bows, but Strabonus was mad with rage. He looked at the long shimmering ranks of his knights, he glared at the handful of mailed figures over against him, and he commanded Arbanus to give the order to charge.

The general commended his soul to Ishtar and sounded the golden oliphant. With a thunderous roar the forest of lances dipped, and the great host rolled across the plain, gaining momentum as it came. The whole plain shook to the rumbling avalanche of hoofs, and the shimmer of gold and steel dazzled the watchers on the towers of Shamar.

The squadrons clave the loose ranks of the spearmen, riding down friend and foe alike, and rushed into the teeth of a blast of arrows from the Bossonians. Across the plain they thundered, grimly riding the storm that scattered their way with gleaming knights like autumn leaves.

Another hundred paces and they would ride among the Bossonians and cut them down like corn; but flesh and blood could not endure the rain of death that now ripped and howled among them. Shoulder to shoulder, feet braced wide, stood the archers, drawing shaft to ear and loosing as one man, with deep short shouts.

The whole front rank of the knights melted away, and over the pin-cushioned corpses of horses and riders, their comrades stumbled and fell headlong. Arbanus was down, an arrow through his throat, his skull smashed by the hoofs of his dying war-horse, and confusion ran through the disordered host. Strabonus was screaming an order, Amalrus another, and through all ran the superstitious dread the sight of Conan had awakened.

And while the gleaming ranks milled in confusion, the trumpets of Conan sounded, and through the opening ranks of the archers crashed home the terrible charge of the Aquilonian knights.

The hosts met with a shock like that of an earthquake, that shook the tottering towers of Shamar. The disordered squadrons of the invaders could not withstand the solid steel wedge, bristling with spears, that rushed like a thunder-bolt against them. The long lances of the attackers ripped their ranks to pieces, and into the heart of their host rode the knights of Poitain, swinging their terrible two-handed swords.

The clash and clangor of steel was as that of a million sledges on as many anvils. The watchers on the walls were stunned and deafened by the thunder as they gripped the battlements and watched the steel maelstrom swirl and eddy, where plumes tossed high among the flashing swords, and standards dipped and reeled.

Amalrus went down, dying beneath the trampling hoofs, his shoulderbone hewn in twain by Prospero's two-handed sword. The invaders' numbers had engulfed the nineteen hundred knights of Conan, but about this compact wedge, which hewed deeper and deeper into the looser formation of their foes, the knights of Koth and Ophir swirled and smote in vain. They could not break the wedge.

Archers and pikemen, having disposed of the Kothian infantry which was strewn in disorderly flight across the plain, came to the edges of the fight, loosing their arrows point-blank, running in to slash at girths and horses' bellies with their knives, thrusting upward to spit the riders on their long pikes.

At the tip of the steel wedge Conan roared his heathen battle-cry and swung his great sword in glittering arcs of death that made naught of steel burganet or mail haburgeon. Straight through a thundering waste of steel-sheathed foes he rode, and the knights of Koth closed in behind him, cutting him off from his warriors. As a thunderbolt strikes, Conan struck, hurtling through the ranks by sheer power and velocity, until he came to Strabonus, livid, among his palace troops. Now here the battle hung in balance, for with his superior numbers, Strabonus still had opportunity to pluck victory from the knees of the gods.

But he screamed when he saw his arch-foe within arm's length at last, and lashed out wildly with his ax. It clanged on Conan's helmet, striking fire, and the Cimmerian reeled and struck back. The five-foot blade crushed Strabonus' casque and skull, and the king's charger reeled screaming, hurling a limp and sprawling corpse from the saddle. A great cry went up from the host, which faltered and gave back. Trocero and his house troops, hewing desperately, cut their way to Conan's side, and the great banner of Koth went down. Then behind the dazed and stricken invaders went up a mighty clamor and the blaze of a huge conflagration. The defenders of Shamar had made a desperate sortie, cut down the men masking the gates, and were raging among the tents of the besiegers, cutting down the camp followers, burning the pavilions, and destroying the siege engines. It was the last straw. The gleaming army melted away in flight and the furious conquerors cut them down as they ran.

The fugitives raced for the river, but the men on the flotilla, harried sorely by the stones and shafts of the revived citizens, cast loose and pulled for the southern shore, leaving their comrades to their fate. Of these many gained the shore, racing across the barges that served as a bridge, until the men of Shamar cut these adrift and severed them from the shore. Then the fight became a slaughter. Driven into the river to drown in their armor, or hacked down along the bank, the invaders perished by thousands. No quarter they had promised; no quarter they got.

From the foot of the low hills to the shores of the Tybor, the plain was littered with corpses, and the river whose tide ran red, floated thick with the dead. Of the nineteen hundred knights who had ridden south with Conan, scarcely five hundred lived to boast of their scars, and the slaughter among the archers and pikemen was ghastly. But the great shining host of Strabonus and Amalrus was hacked out of existence, and those that fled were less than those that died.

While the slaughter yet went on along the river, the final act of a grim drama was being played out in the meadowland beyond. Among those who had crossed the barge-bridge before it was destroyed was Tsotha, riding like the wind on a gaunt weird-looking steed whose stride no natural horse could match. Ruthlessly riding down friend and foe, he gained the southern bank, and then a glance backward showed him a grim figure on a great black stallion in mad pursuit. The lashings had already been cut, and the barges were drifting apart, but Conan came recklessly on, leaping his steed from boat to boat as a man might leap from one cake of floating ice to another. Tsotha screamed a curse, but the great stallion took the last leap with a straining groan, and gained the southern bank. Then the wizard fled away into the empty meadowland, and on his trail came the king, riding madly and silently, swinging the great sword that spattered his trail with crimson drips.

On they fled, the hunted and the hunter, and not a foot could the black stallion gain, though he strained each nerve and thew. Through a sunset land of dim light and illusive shadows they fled, till sight and sound of the slaughter died out behind them. Then in the sky appeared a dot, that grew into a huge eagle as it approached. Swooping down from the sky, it drove at the head of Tsotha's steed, which screamed and reared, throwing his rider.

Old Tsotha rose and faced his pursuer, his eyes those of a maddened serpent, his face an inhuman mask of awful fury. In each hand he held something that shimmered, and Conan knew he held death there.

The king dismounted and strode toward his foe, his armor clanking, his great sword gripped high.

'Again we meet, wizard!' he grinned savagely.

'Keep off!' screamed Tsotha like a blood-mad jackal. 'I'll blast the flesh from your bones! You can not conquer me – if you hack me in pieces, the bits of flesh and bone will reunite and haunt you to your doom! I see the hand of Pelias in this, but I defy ye both! I am Tsotha, son of—'

Conan rushed, sword gleaming, eyes slits of wariness. Tsotha's right hand came back and forward, and the king ducked quickly. Something passed by his helmeted head and exploded behind him, searing the very sands with a flash of hellish fire. Before Tsotha could toss the globe in his left hand, Conan's sword sheared through his lean neck. The wizard's head shot from his shoulders on an arching fount of blood, and the robed figure staggered and crumpled drunkenly. Yet the mad black eyes glared up at Conan with no dimming of their feral light, the lips writhed awfully, and the hands groped hideously, as if searching for the severed head. Then with a swift rush of wings, something swooped from the sky – the eagle which had attacked Tsotha's horse. In its mighty talons it snatched up the dripping head and soared skyward, and Conan stood struck dumb, for from the eagle's throat boomed human laughter, in the voice of Pelias the sorcerer.

Then a hideous thing came to pass, for the headless body reared up from the sand, and staggered away in awful flight on stiffening legs, hands outstretched blindly toward the dot speeding and dwindling in the dusky sky. Conan stood like one turned to stone, watching until the swift reeling figure faded in the dusk that purpled the meadows.

'Crom!' his mighty shoulders twitched. 'A murrain on these wizardly feuds! Pelias has dealt well with me, but I care not if I see him no more. Give me a clean sword and a clean foe to flesh it in. Damnation! What would I not give for a flagon of wine!'

THE TOWER OF THE ELEPHANT

1

TORCHES FLARED MURKILY ON the revels in the Maul, where the thieves of the east held carnival by night. In the Maul they could carouse and roar as they liked, for honest people shunned the quarter, and watchmen, well paid with stained coins, did not interfere with their sport. Along the crooked, unpaved streets with their heaps of refuse and sloppy puddles, drunken roisterers staggered, roaring. Steel glinted in the shadows where wolf preyed on wolf, and from the darkness rose the shrill laughter of women, and the sounds of scufflings and strugglings. Torchlight licked luridly from broken windows and wide-thrown doors, and out of these doors, stale smells of wine and rank sweaty bodies, clamor of drinking-jacks and fists hammered on rough tables, snatches of obscene songs, rushed like a blow in the face.

In one of these dens merriment thundered to the low smoke-stained roof, where rascals gathered in every stage of rags and tatters – furtive cut-purses, leering kidnappers, quick-fingered thieves, swaggering bravoes with their wenches, strident-voiced women clad in tawdry finery. Native rogues were the dominant element – dark-skinned, dark-eyed Zamorians, with daggers at their girdles and guile in their hearts. But there were wolves of half a dozen outland nations there as well. There was a giant Hyperborean renegade, taciturn, dangerous, with a broadsword strapped to his great gaunt frame – for men wore steel openly in the Maul. There was a Shemitish counterfeiter, with his hook nose and curled blue-black beard. There was a bold-eyed Brythunian wench, sitting on the knee of a tawny-haired Gunderman – a wandering mercenary soldier, a deserter from some defeated army. And the fat gross rogue whose bawdy jests were causing all the shouts of mirth was a professional kidnapper come up from distant Koth to teach woman-stealing to Zamorians who were born with more knowledge of the art than he could ever attain.

This man halted in his description of an intended victim's charms, and thrust his muzzle into a huge tankard of frothing ale. Then blowing the foam from his fat lips, he said, 'By Bel, god of all thieves, I'll show them how to steal wenches: I'll have her over the Zamorian border before dawn, and there'll be a caravan waiting to receive her. Three hundred pieces of silver, a count of Ophir promised me for a sleek young Brythunian of the better class. It took me weeks, wandering among the border cities as a beggar, to find one I knew would suit. And is she a pretty baggage!'

He blew a slobbery kiss in the air.

'I know lords in Shem who would trade the secret of the Elephant Tower for her,' he said, returning to his ale.

A touch on his tunic sleeve made him turn his head, scowling at the interruption. He saw a tall, strongly made youth standing beside him. This person was as much out of place in that den as a gray wolf among mangy rats of the gutters. His cheap tunic could not conceal the hard, rangy lines of his powerful frame, the broad heavy shoulders, the massive chest, lean waist and heavy arms. His skin was brown from outland suns, his eyes blue and smoldering; a shock of tousled black hair crowned his broad forehead. From his girdle hung a sword in a worn leather scabbard.

The Kothian involuntarily drew back; for the man was not one of any civilized race he knew.

'You spoke of the Elephant Tower,' said the stranger, speaking Zamorian with an alien accent. 'I've heard much of this tower; what is its secret?'

The fellow's attitude did not seem threatening, and the Kothian's courage was bolstered up by the ale, and the evident approval of his audience. He swelled with self-importance.

'The secret of the Elephant Tower?' he exclaimed. 'Why, any fool knows that Yara the priest dwells there with the great jewel men call the Elephant's Heart, that is the secret of his magic.'

The barbarian digested this for a space.

'I have seen this tower,' he said. 'It is set in a great garden above the level of the city, surrounded by high walls. I have seen no guards. The walls would be easy to climb. Why has not somebody stolen this secret gem?'

The Kothian stared wide-mouthed at the other's simplicity, then burst into a roar of derisive mirth, in which the others joined.

'Harken to this heathen!' he bellowed. 'He would steal the jewel of

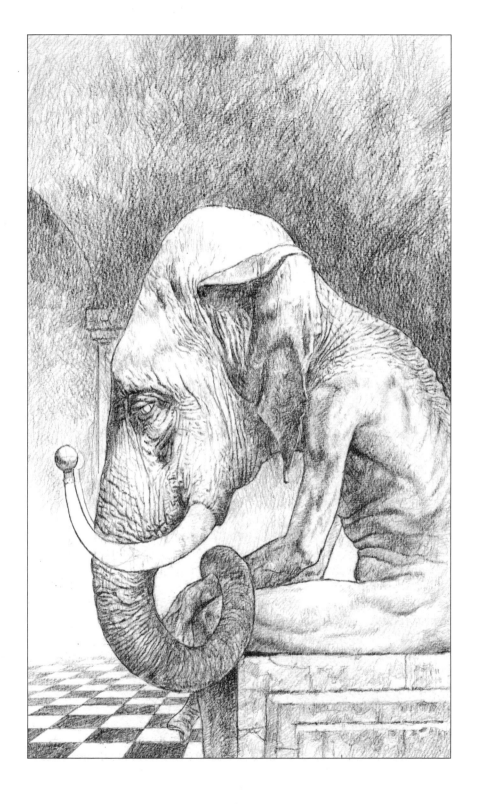

Yara! – Harken, fellow,' he said, turning portentously to the other, 'I suppose you are some sort of a northern barbarian—'

'I am a Cimmerian,' the outlander answered, in no friendly tone. The reply and the manner of it meant little to the Kothian; of a kingdom that lay far to the south, on the borders of Shem, he knew only vaguely of the northern races.

'Then give ear and learn wisdom, fellow,' said he, pointing his drinking-jack at the discomfited youth. 'Know that in Zamora, and more especially in this city, there are more bold thieves than anywhere else in the world, even Koth. If mortal man could have stolen the gem, be sure it would have been filched long ago. You speak of climbing the walls, but once having climbed, you would quickly wish yourself back again. There are no guards in the gardens at night for a very good reason – that is, no human guards. But in the watch-chamber, in the lower part of the tower, are armed men, and even if you passed those who roam the gardens by night, you must still pass through the soldiers, for the gem is kept somewhere in the tower above.'

'But if a man *could* pass through the gardens,' argued the Cimmerian, 'why could he not come at the gem through the upper part of the tower and thus avoid the soldiers?'

Again the Kothian gaped at him.

'Listen to him!' he shouted jeeringly. 'The barbarian is an eagle who would fly to the jeweled rim of the tower, which is only a hundred and fifty feet above the earth, with rounded sides slicker than polished glass!'

The Cimmerian glared about, embarrassed at the roar of mocking laughter that greeted this remark. He saw no particular humor in it, and was too new to civilization to understand its discourtesies. Civilized men are more discourteous than savages because they know they can be impolite without having their skulls split, as a general thing. He was bewildered and chagrined, and doubtless would have slunk away, abashed, but the Kothian chose to goad him further.

'Come, come!' he shouted. 'Tell these poor fellows, who have only been thieves since before you were spawned, tell them how you would steal the gem!'

'There is always a way, if the desire be coupled with courage,' answered the Cimmerian shortly, nettled.

The Kothian chose to take this as a personal slur. His face grew purple with anger.

'What!' he roared. 'You dare tell us our business, and intimate that we are cowards? Get along; get out of my sight!' And he pushed the Cimmerian violently.

'Will you mock me and then lay hands on me?' grated the barbarian, his quick rage leaping up; and he returned the push with an open-handed blow that knocked his tormentor back against the rude-hewn table. Ale splashed over the jack's lip, and the Kothian roared in fury, dragging at his sword.

'Heathen dog!' he bellowed. 'I'll have your heart for that!'

Steel flashed and the throng surged wildly back out of the way. In their flight they knocked over the single candle and the den was plunged in darkness, broken by the crash of upset benches, drum of flying feet, shouts, oaths of people tumbling over one another, and a single strident yell of agony that cut the din like a knife. When a candle was relighted, most of the guests had gone out by doors and broken windows, and the rest huddled behind stacks of wine-kegs and under tables. The barbarian was gone; the center of the room was deserted except for the gashed body of the Kothian. The Cimmerian, with the unerring instinct of the barbarian, had killed his man in the darkness and confusion.

2

The lurid lights and drunken revelry fell away behind the Cimmerian. He had discarded his torn tunic, and walked through the night naked except for a loin-cloth and his high-strapped sandals. He moved with the supple ease of a great tiger, his steely muscles rippling under his brown skin.

He had entered the part of the city reserved for the temples. On all sides of him they glittered white in the starlight – snowy marble pillars and golden domes and silver arches, shrines of Zamora's myriad strange gods. He did not trouble his head about them; he knew that Zamora's religion, like all things of a civilized, long-settled people, was intricate and complex, and had lost most of the pristine essence in a maze of formulas and rituals. He had squatted for hours in the courtyard of the philosophers, listening to the arguments of theologians and teachers, and come away in a haze of bewilderment, sure of only one thing, and that, that they were all touched in the head.

His gods were simple and understandable; Crom was their chief, and he lived on a great mountain, whence he sent forth dooms and death. It was useless to call on Crom, because he was a gloomy, savage god, and he hated weaklings. But he gave a man courage at birth, and the will and might to kill his enemies, which, in the Cimmerian's mind, was all any god should be expected to do.

His sandalled feet made no sound on the gleaming pave. No watchmen passed, for even the thieves of the Maul shunned the temples, where strange dooms had been known to fall on violators. Ahead of him he saw, looming against the sky, the Tower of the Elephant. He mused, wondering why it was so named. No one seemed to know. He had never seen an elephant, but he vaguely understood that it was a monstrous animal, with a tail in front as well as behind. This a wandering Shemite had told him, swearing that he had seen such beasts by the thousands in the country of the Hyrkanians; but all men knew what liars were the men of Shem. At any rate, there were no elephants in Zamora.

The shimmering shaft of the tower rose frostily in the stars. In the sunlight it shone so dazzlingly that few could bear its glare, and men said it was built of silver. It was round, a slim perfect cylinder, a hundred and fifty feet in height, and its rim glittered in the starlight with the great jewels which crusted it. The tower stood among the waving exotic trees of a garden raised high above the general level of the city. A high wall enclosed this garden, and outside the wall was a lower level, likewise enclosed by a wall. No lights shone forth; there seemed to be no windows in the tower – at least not above the level of the inner wall. Only the gems high above sparkled frostily in the starlight.

Shrubbery grew thick outside the lower, or outer wall. The Cimmerian crept close and stood beside the barrier, measuring it with his eyes. It was high, but he could leap and catch the coping with his fingers. Then it would be child's play to swing himself up and over, and he did not doubt that he could pass the inner wall in the same manner. But he hesitated at the thought of the strange perils which were said to await within. These people were strange and mysterious to him; they were not of his kind – not even of the same blood as the more westerly Brythunians, Nemedians, Kothians and Aquilonians, whose civilized mysteries had awed him in times past. The people of Zamora were very ancient, and, from what he had seen of them, very evil.

He thought of Yara, the high priest, who worked strange dooms from this jeweled tower, and the Cimmerian's hair prickled as he remembered a tale told by a drunken page of the court – how Yara had laughed in the face of a hostile prince, and held up a glowing, evil gem before him, and how rays shot blindingly from that unholy jewel, to envelop the prince, who screamed and fell down, and shrank to a withered blackened lump that changed to a black spider which scampered wildly about the chamber until Yara set his heel upon it.

Yara came not often from his tower of magic, and always to work evil on some man or some nation. The king of Zamora feared him more than he feared death, and kept himself drunk all the time because that fear was more than he could endure sober. Yara was very old – centuries old, men said, and added that he would live for ever because of the magic of his gem, which men called the Heart of the Elephant, for no better reason than they named his hold the Elephant's Tower.

The Cimmerian, engrossed in these thoughts, shrank quickly against the wall. Within the garden someone was passing, who walked with a measured stride. The listener heard the clink of steel. So after all a guard did pace those gardens. The Cimmerian waited, expected to hear him pass again, on the next round, but silence rested over the mysterious gardens.

At last curiosity overcame him. Leaping lightly he grasped the wall and swung himself up to the top with one arm. Lying flat on the broad coping, he looked down into the wide space between the walls. No shrubbery grew near him, though he saw some carefully trimmed bushes near the inner wall. The starlight fell on the even sward and somewhere a fountain tinkled.

The Cimmerian cautiously lowered himself down on the inside and drew his sword, staring about him. He was shaken by the nervousness of the wild at standing thus unprotected in the naked starlight, and he moved lightly around the curve of the wall, hugging its shadow, until he was even with the shrubbery he had noticed. Then he ran quickly toward it, crouching low, and almost tripped over a form that lay crumpled near the edges of the bushes.

A quick look to right and left showed him no enemy in sight at least, and he bent close to investigate. His keen eyes, even in the dim starlight, showed him a strongly built man in the silvered armor and crested helmet of the Zamorian royal guard. A shield and a spear lay near him, and it took but an instant's examination to show that he had been strangled. The barbarian glanced about uneasily. He knew that this man must be the guard he had heard pass his hiding-place by the wall. Only a short time had passed, yet in that interval nameless hands had reached out of the dark and choked out the soldier's life.

Straining his eyes in the gloom, he saw a hint of motion through the shrubs near the wall. Thither he glided, gripping his sword. He made no more noise than a panther stealing through the night, yet the man he was stalking heard. The Cimmerian had a dim glimpse of a huge bulk close to the wall, felt relief that it was at least human; then the fellow wheeled quickly with a gasp that sounded like panic, made the first motion of a forward plunge, hands clutching, then recoiled as the Cimmerian's blade caught the starlight. For a tense instant neither spoke, standing ready for anything.

'You are no soldier,' hissed the stranger at last. 'You are a thief like myself.'

'And who are you?' asked the Cimmerian in a suspicious whisper.
'Taurus of Nemedia.'
The Cimmerian lowered his sword.
'I've heard of you. Men call you a prince of thieves.'
A low laugh answered him. Taurus was tall as the Cimmerian, and heavier; he was big-bellied and fat, but his every movement betokened a subtle dynamic magnetism, which was reflected in the keen eyes that glinted vitally, even in the starlight. He was barefooted and carried a coil of what looked like a thin, strong rope, knotted at regular intervals.
'Who are you?' he whispered.
'Conan, a Cimmerian,' answered the other. 'I came seeking a way to steal Yara's jewel, that men call the Elephant's Heart.'
Conan sensed the man's great belly shaking in laughter, but it was not derisive.
'By Bel, god of thieves!' hissed Taurus. 'I had thought only myself had courage to attempt *that* poaching. These Zamorians call themselves thieves – bah! Conan, I like your grit. I never shared an adventure with anyone, but by Bel, we'll attempt this together if you're willing.'
'Then you are after the gem, too?'
'What else? I've had my plans laid for months, but you, I think, have acted on a sudden impulse, my friend.'
'You killed the soldier?'
'Of course. I slid over the wall when he was on the other side of the garden. I hid in the bushes; he heard me, or thought he heard something. When he came blundering over, it was no trick at all to get behind him and suddenly grip his neck and choke out his fool's life. He was like most men, half blind in the dark. A good thief should have eyes like a cat.'
'You made one mistake,' said Conan.
Taurus's eyes flashed angrily.
'I? I, a mistake? Impossible!'
'You should have dragged the body into the bushes.'
'Said the novice to the master of the art. They will not change the guard until past midnight. Should any come searching for him now, and find his body, they would flee at once to Yara, bellowing the news, and give us time to escape. Were they not to find it, they'd go on beating up the bushes and catch us like rats in a trap.'
'You are right,' agreed Conan.
'So. Now attend. We waste time in this cursed discussion. There are no guards in the inner garden – human guards, I mean, though there are sentinels even more deadly. It was their presence which baffled me for so long, but I finally discovered a way to circumvent them.'

'What of the soldiers in the lower part of the tower?'

'Old Yara dwells in the chambers above. By that route we will come – and go, I hope. Never mind asking me how. I have arranged a way. We'll steal down through the top of the tower and strangle old Yara before he can cast any of his accursed spells on us. At least we'll try; it's the chance of being turned into a spider or a toad, against the wealth and power of the world. All good thieves must know how to take risks.'

'I'll go as far as any man,' said Conan, slipping off his sandals.

'Then follow me.' And turning, Taurus leaped up, caught the wall and drew himself up. The man's suppleness was amazing, considering his bulk; he seemed almost to glide up over the edge of the coping. Conan followed him, and lying flat on the broad top, they spoke in wary whispers.

'I see no light,' Conan muttered. The lower part of the tower seemed much like that portion visible from outside the garden – a perfect, gleaming cylinder, with no apparent openings.

'There are cleverly constructed doors and windows,' answered Taurus, 'but they are closed. The soldiers breathe air that comes from above.'

The garden was a vague pool of shadows, where feathery bushes and low spreading trees waved darkly in the starlight. Conan's wary soul felt the aura of waiting menace that brooded over it. He felt the burning glare of unseen eyes, and he caught a subtle scent that made the short hairs on his neck instinctively bristle as a hunting dog bristles at the scent of an ancient enemy.

'Follow me,' whispered Taurus, 'keep behind me, as you value your life.'

Taking what looked like a copper tube from his girdle, the Nemedian dropped lightly to the sward inside the wall. Conan was close behind him, sword ready, but Taurus pushed him back, close to the wall, and showed no indication to advance, himself. His whole attitude was of tense expectancy, and his gaze, like Conan's, was fixed on the shadowy mass of shrubbery a few yards away. This shrubbery was shaken, although the breeze had died down. Then two great eyes blazed from the waving shadows, and behind them other sparks of fire glinted in the darkness.

'Lions!' muttered Conan.

'Aye. By day they are kept in subterranean caverns below the tower. That's why there are no guards in this garden.'

Conan counted the eyes rapidly.

'Five in sight; maybe more back in the bushes. They'll charge in a moment—'

'Be silent!' hissed Taurus, and he moved out from the wall, cautiously as if treading on razors, lifting the slender tube. Low rumblings rose from the shadows and the blazing eyes moved forward. Conan could sense the great slavering jaws, the tufted tails lashing tawny sides. The air grew tense – the Cimmerian gripped his sword, expecting the charge and the irresistible hurtling of giant bodies. Then Taurus brought the mouth of the tube to his lips and blew powerfully. A long jet of yellowish powder shot from the other end of the tube and billowed out instantly in a thick green-yellow cloud that settled over the shrubbery, blotting out the glaring eyes.

Taurus ran back hastily to the wall. Conan glared without understanding. The thick cloud hid the shrubbery, and from it no sound came.

'What is that mist?' the Cimmerian asked uneasily.

'Death!' hissed the Nemedian. 'If a wind springs up and blows it back upon us, we must flee over the wall. But no, the wind is still, and now it is dissipating. Wait until it vanishes entirely. To breathe it is death.'

Presently only yellowish shreds hung ghostily in the air; then they were gone, and Taurus motioned his companion forward. They stole toward the bushes, and Conan gasped. Stretched out in the shadows lay five great tawny shapes, the fire of their grim eyes dimmed for ever. A sweetish cloying scent lingered in the atmosphere.

'They died without a sound!' muttered the Cimmerian. 'Taurus, what was that powder?'

'It was made from the black lotus, whose blossoms wave in the lost jungles of Khitai, where only the yellow-skulled priests of Yun dwell. Those blossoms strike dead any who smell of them.'

Conan knelt beside the great forms, assuring himself that they were indeed beyond power of harm. He shook his head; the magic of the exotic lands was mysterious and terrible to the barbarians of the north.

'Why can you not slay the soldiers in the tower in the same way?' he asked.

'Because that was all the powder I possessed. The obtaining of it was a feat which in itself was enough to make me famous among the thieves of the world. I stole it out of a caravan bound for Stygia, and I lifted it, in its cloth-of-gold bag, out of the coils of the great serpent which guarded it, without awaking him. But come, in Bel's name! Are we to waste the night in discussion?'

They glided through the shrubbery to the gleaming foot of the tower, and there, with a motion enjoining silence, Taurus unwound his knotted cord, on one end of which was a strong steel hook. Conan saw his plan, and asked no questions as the Nemedian gripped the line a short distance below the hook, and began to swing it about his head. Conan laid his ear to the smooth wall and listened, but could hear nothing. Evidently the soldiers within did not suspect the presence of intruders, who had made no more sound than the night wind blowing through the trees. But a strange nervousness was on the barbarian; perhaps it was the lion-smell which was over everything.

Taurus threw the line with a smooth, ripping motion of his mighty arm. The hook curved upward and inward in a peculiar manner, hard to describe, and vanished over the jeweled rim. It apparently caught firmly, for cautious jerking and then hard pulling did not result in any slipping or giving.

'Luck the first cast,' murmured Taurus. 'I—'

It was Conan's savage instinct which made him wheel suddenly; for the death that was upon them made no sound. A fleeting glimpse showed the Cimmerian the giant tawny shape, rearing upright against the stars, towering over him for the death-stroke. No civilized man could have moved half so quickly as the barbarian moved. His sword flashed frostily in the starlight with every ounce of desperate nerve and thew behind it, and man and beast went down together.

Cursing incoherently beneath his breath, Taurus bent above the mass, and saw his companion's limbs move as he strove to drag himself from under the great weight that lay limply upon him. A glance showed the startled Nemedian that the lion was dead, its slanting skull split in half. He laid hold of the carcass, and by his aid, Conan thrust it aside and clambered up, still gripping his dripping sword.

'Are you hurt, man?' gasped Taurus, still bewildered by the stunning swiftness of that touch-and-go episode.

'No, by Crom!' answered the barbarian. 'But that was as close a call as I've had in a life noways tame. Why did not the cursed beast roar as he charged?'

'All things are strange in this garden,' said Taurus. 'The lions strike silently – and so do other deaths. But come – little sound was made in that slaying, but the soldiers might have heard, if they are not asleep or drunk. That beast was in some other part of the garden and escaped the death of the flowers, but surely there are no more. We must climb this cord – little need to ask a Cimmerian if he can.'

'If it will bear my weight,' grunted Conan, cleansing his sword on the grass.

'It will bear thrice my own,' answered Taurus. 'It was woven from the tresses of dead women, which I took from their tombs at midnight, and steeped in the deadly wine of the upas tree, to give it strength. I will go first – then follow me closely.'

The Nemedian gripped the rope and, crooking a knee about it, began the ascent; he went up like a cat, belying the apparent clumsiness of his bulk. The Cimmerian followed. The cord swayed and turned on itself, but the climbers were not hindered; both had made more difficult climbs before. The jeweled rim glittered high above them, jutting out from the perpendicular – a fact which added greatly to the ease of the ascent.

Up and up they went, silently, the lights of the city spreading out further and further to their sight as they climbed, the stars above them more and more dimmed by the glitter of the jewels along the rim. Now Taurus reached up a hand and gripped the rim itself, pulling himself up and over. Conan paused a moment on the very edge, fascinated by the great frosty jewels whose gleams dazzled his eyes – diamonds, rubies, emeralds, sapphires, turquoises, moonstones, set thick as stars in the shimmering silver. At a distance their different gleams had seemed to merge into a pulsing white glare; but now, at close range, they shimmered with a million rainbow tints and lights, hypnotizing him with their scintillations.

'There is a fabulous fortune here, Taurus,' he whispered; but the Nemedian answered impatiently. 'Come on! If we secure the Heart, these and all other things shall be ours.'

Conan climbed over the sparkling rim. The level of the tower's top was some feet below the gemmed ledge. It was flat, composed of some dark blue substance, set with gold that caught the starlight, so that the whole looked like a wide sapphire flecked with shining gold-dust. Across from the point where they had entered there seemed to be a sort of chamber, built upon the roof. It was of the same silvery material as the walls of the tower, adorned with designs worked in smaller gems; its single door was of gold, its surface cut in scales, and crusted with jewels that gleamed like ice.

Conan cast a glance at the pulsing ocean of lights which spread far below them, then glanced at Taurus. The Nemedian was drawing up his cord and coiling it. He showed Conan where the hook had caught – a fraction of an inch of the point had sunk under a great blazing jewel on the inner side of the rim.

'Luck was with us again,' he muttered. 'One would think that our combined weight would have torn that stone out. Follow me; the real risks of the venture begin now. We are in the serpent's lair, and we know not where he lies hidden.'

Like stalking tigers they crept across the darkly gleaming floor and halted outside the sparkling door. With a deft and cautious hand Taurus tried it. It gave without resistance, and the companions looked in, tensed for anything. Over the Nemedian's shoulder Conan had a glimpse of a glittering chamber, the walls, ceiling and floor of which were crusted with great white jewels which lighted it brightly, and which seemed its only illumination. It seemed empty of life.

'Before we cut off our last retreat,' hissed Taurus, 'go you to the rim and look over on all sides; if you see any soldiers moving in the gardens, or anything suspicious, return and tell me. I will await you within this chamber.'

Conan saw scant reason in this, and a faint suspicion of his companion touched his wary soul, but he did as Taurus requested. As he turned away, the Nemedian slipt inside the door and drew it shut behind him. Conan crept about the rim of the tower, returning to his starting-point without having seen any suspicious movement in the vaguely waving sea of leaves below. He turned toward the door – suddenly from within the chamber there sounded a strangled cry.

The Cimmerian leaped forward, electrified – the gleaming door swung open and Taurus stood framed in the cold blaze behind him. He swayed and his lips parted, but only a dry rattle burst from his throat. Catching at the golden door for support, he lurched out upon the roof, then fell headlong, clutching at his throat. The door swung to behind him.

Conan, crouching like a panther at bay, saw nothing in the room behind the stricken Nemedian, in the brief instant the door was partly open – unless it was not a trick of the light which made it seem as if a shadow darted across the gleaming door. Nothing followed Taurus out on the roof, and Conan bent above the man.

The Nemedian stared up with dilated, glazing eyes, that somehow held a terrible bewilderment. His hands clawed at his throat, his lips slobbered and gurgled; then suddenly he stiffened, and the astounded Cimmerian knew that he was dead. And he felt that Taurus had died without knowing what manner of death had stricken him. Conan glared bewilderedly at the cryptic golden door. In that empty room, with its glittering jeweled walls, death had come to the prince of thieves as swiftly and mysteriously as he had dealt doom to the lions in the gardens below.

Gingerly the barbarian ran his hands over the man's half-naked body, seeking a wound. But the only marks of violence were between his shoulders, high up near the base of his bull-neck – three small wounds, which looked as if three nails had been driven deep in the flesh and withdrawn. The edges of these wounds were black, and a faint smell as of putrefaction was evident. Poisoned darts? thought Conan – but in that case the missiles should be still in the wounds.

Cautiously he stole toward the golden door, pushed it open, and looked inside. The chamber lay empty, bathed in the cold, pulsing glow of the myriad jewels. In the very center of the ceiling he idly noted a curious design – a black eight-sided pattern, in the center of which four gems glittered with a red flame unlike the white blaze of the other jewels. Across the room there was another door, like the one in which he stood, except that it was not carved in the scale pattern. Was it from that door that death had come? – and having struck down its victim, had it retreated by the same way?

Closing the door behind him, the Cimmerian advanced into the chamber. His bare feet made no sound on the crystal floor. There were no chairs or tables in the chamber, only three or four silken couches, embroidered with gold and worked in strange serpentine designs, and several silver-bound mahogany chests. Some were sealed with heavy golden locks; others lay open, their carven lids thrown back, revealing heaps of jewels in a careless riot of splendor to the Cimmerian's astounded eyes. Conan swore beneath his breath; already he had looked upon more wealth that night than he had ever dreamed existed in all the world, and he grew dizzy thinking of what must be the value of the jewel he sought.

He was in the center of the room now, going stooped forward, head thrust out warily, sword advanced, when again death struck at him soundlessly. A flying shadow that swept across the gleaming floor was his only warning, and his instinctive sidelong leap all that saved his life. He had a flashing glimpse of a hairy black horror that swung past him with a clashing of frothing fangs, and something splashed on his bare shoulder that burned like drops of liquid hellfire. Springing back, sword high, he saw the horror strike the floor, wheel and scuttle toward him with appalling speed – a gigantic black spider, such as men see only in nightmare dreams.

It was as large as a pig, and its eight thick hairy legs drove its ogreish body over the floor at headlong pace; its four evilly gleaming eyes shone with a horrible intelligence, and its fangs dripped venom that Conan knew, from the burning of his shoulder where only a few drops had splashed as the thing struck and missed, was laden with swift death. This was the killer that had dropped from its perch in the middle of the ceiling on a strand of its web, on the neck of the Nemedian. Fools that they were not to have suspected that the upper chambers would be guarded as well as the lower!

These thoughts flashed briefly through Conan's mind as the monster rushed. He leaped high, and it passed beneath him, wheeled and charged back. This time he evaded its rush with a sidewise leap, and struck back like a cat. His sword severed one of the hairy legs, and again he barely saved himself as the monstrosity swerved at him, fangs clicking fiendishly. But the creature did not press the pursuit; turning, it scuttled across the crystal floor and ran up the wall to the ceiling, where it crouched for an instant, glaring down at him with its fiendish red eyes. Then without warning it launched itself through space, trailing a strand of slimy grayish stuff.

Conan stepped back to avoid the hurtling body – then ducked frantically, just in time to escape being snared by the flying web-rope. He saw the monster's intent and sprang toward the door, but it was quicker, and a sticky strand cast across the door made him a prisoner. He dared not try to cut it with his sword; he knew the stuff would cling to the blade, and before he could shake it loose, the fiend would be sinking its fangs into his back.

Then began a desperate game, the wits and quickness of the man matched against the fiendish craft and speed of the giant spider. It no longer scuttled across the floor in a direct charge, or swung its body through the air at him. It raced about the ceiling and the walls, seeking to snare him in the long loops of sticky gray web-strands, which it flung with a devilish accuracy. These strands were thick as ropes, and Conan knew that once they were coiled about him, his desperate strength would not be enough to tear him free before the monster struck.

All over the chamber went on that devil's game, in utter silence except for the quick breathing of the man, the low scuff of his bare feet on the shining floor, the castanet rattle of the monstrosity's fangs. The gray strands lay in coils on the floor; they were looped along the walls; they overlaid the jewel-chests and silken couches, and hung in dusky festoons from the jeweled ceiling. Conan's steel-trap quickness of eye and muscle had kept him untouched, though the sticky loops had passed him so close they rasped his naked hide. He knew he could not always avoid them; he not only had to watch the strands swinging from the ceiling, but to keep his eye on the floor, lest he trip in the coils that lay there. Sooner or later a gummy loop would writhe about him, python-like, and then, wrapped like a cocoon, he would lie at the monster's mercy.

The spider raced across the chamber floor, the gray rope waving out behind it. Conan leaped high, clearing a couch – with a quick wheel the fiend ran up the wall, and the strand, leaping off the floor like a live thing, whipped about the Cimmerian's ankle. He caught himself on his hands as he fell, jerking frantically at the web which held him like a pliant vise, or the coil of a python. The hairy devil was racing down the wall to complete its capture. Stung to frenzy, Conan caught up a jewel chest and hurled it with all his strength. It was a move the monster was not expecting. Full in the midst of the branching black legs the massive missile struck, smashing against the wall with a muffled sickening crunch. Blood and greenish slime spattered, and the shattered mass fell with the burst gem-chest to the floor. The crushed black body lay among the flaming riot of jewels that spilled over it; the hairy legs moved aimlessly, the dying eyes glittered redly among the twinkling gems.

Conan glared about, but no other horror appeared, and he set himself to working free of the web. The substance clung tenaciously to his ankle and his hands, but at last he was free, and taking up his sword, he picked his way among the gray coils and loops to the inner door. What horrors lay within he did not know. The Cimmerian's blood was up, and since he had come so far, and overcome so much peril, he was determined to go through to the grim finish of the adventure, whatever that might be. And he felt that the jewel he sought was not among the many so carelessly strewn about the gleaming chamber.

Stripping off the loops that fouled the inner door, he found that it, like the other, was not locked. He wondered if the soldiers below were still unaware of his presence. Well, he was high above their heads, and if tales were to be believed, they were used to strange noises in the tower above them – sinister sounds, and screams of agony and horror.

Yara was on his mind, and he was not altogether comfortable as he opened the golden door. But he saw only a flight of silver steps leading down, dimly lighted by what means he could not ascertain. Down these he went silently, gripping his sword. He heard no sound, and came presently to an ivory door, set with blood-stones. He listened, but no sound came from within; only thin wisps of smoke drifted lazily from beneath the door, bearing a curious exotic odor unfamiliar to the Cimmerian. Below him the silver stair wound down to vanish in the dimness, and up that shadowy well no sound floated; he had an eery feeling that he was alone in a tower occupied only by ghosts and phantoms.

3

Cautiously he pressed against the ivory door and it swung silently inward. On the shimmering threshold Conan stared like a wolf in strange surroundings, ready to fight or flee on the instant. He was looking into a large chamber with a domed golden ceiling; the walls were of green jade, the floor of ivory, partly covered by thick rugs. Smoke and exotic scent of incense floated up from a brazier on a golden tripod, and behind it sat an idol on a sort of marble couch. Conan stared aghast; the image had the body of a man, naked, and green in color; but the head was one of nightmare and madness. Too large for the human body, it had no attributes of humanity. Conan stared at the wide flaring ears, the curling proboscis, on either side of which stood white tusks tipped with round golden balls. The eyes were closed, as if in sleep.

This then, was the reason for the name, the Tower of the Elephant, for the head of the thing was much like that of the beasts described by the Shemitish wanderer. This was Yara's god; where then should the gem be, but concealed in the idol, since the stone was called the Elephant's Heart?

As Conan came forward, his eyes fixed on the motionless idol, the eyes of the thing opened suddenly! The Cimmerian froze in his tracks. It was no image – it was a living thing, and he was trapped in its chamber!

That he did not instantly explode in a burst of murderous frenzy is a fact that measures his horror, which paralyzed him where he stood. A civilized man in his position would have sought doubtful refuge in the conclusion that he was insane; it did not occur to the Cimmerian to doubt his senses. He knew he was face to face with a demon of the Elder World, and the realization robbed him of all his faculties except sight.

The trunk of the horror was lifted and quested about, the topaz eyes stared unseeingly, and Conan knew the monster was blind. With the thought came a thawing of his frozen nerves, and he began to back silently toward the door. But the creature heard. The sensitive trunk stretched toward him, and Conan's horror froze him again when the being spoke, in a strange, stammering voice that never changed its key or timbre. The Cimmerian knew that those jaws were never built or intended for human speech.

'Who is here? Have you come to torture me again, Yara? Will you never be done? Oh, Yag-kosha, is there no end to agony?'

Tears rolled from the sightless eyes, and Conan's gaze strayed to the limbs stretched on the marble couch. And he knew the monster would not rise to attack him. He knew the marks of the rack, and the searing brand of the flame, and tough-souled as he was, he stood aghast at the ruined deformities which his reason told him had once been limbs as comely as his own. And suddenly all fear and repulsion went from him, to be replaced by a great pity. What this monster was, Conan could not know, but the evidences of its sufferings were so terrible and pathetic that a strange aching sadness came over the Cimmerian, he knew not why. He only felt that he was looking upon a cosmic tragedy, and he shrank with shame, as if the guilt of a whole race were laid upon him.

'I am not Yara,' he said. 'I am only a thief. I will not harm you.'

'Come near that I may touch you,' the creature faltered, and Conan came near unfearingly, his sword hanging forgotten in his hand. The sensitive trunk came out and groped over his face and shoulders, as a blind man gropes, and its touch was light as a girl's hand.

'You are not of Yara's race of devils,' sighed the creature. 'The clean, lean fierceness of the wastelands marks you. I know your people from of old, whom I knew by another name in the long, long ago when another world lifted its jeweled spires to the stars. There is blood on your fingers.'

'A spider in the chamber above and a lion in the garden,' muttered Conan.

'You have slain a man too, this night,' answered the other. 'And there is death in the tower above. I feel; I know.'

'Aye,' muttered Conan. 'The prince of all thieves lies there dead from the bite of a vermin.'

'So – and so!' The strange inhuman voice rose in a sort of low chant. 'A slaying in the tavern and a slaying on the road – I know; I feel. And the third will make the magic of which not even Yara dreams – oh, magic of deliverance, green gods of Yag!'

Again tears fell as the tortured body was rocked to and fro in the grip of varied emotions. Conan looked on, bewildered.

Then the convulsions ceased; the soft, sightless eyes were turned toward the Cimmerian, the trunk beckoned.

'Oh man, listen,' said the strange being. 'I am foul and monstrous to you, am I not? Nay, do not answer; I know. But you would seem as strange to me, could I see you. There are many worlds besides this earth, and life takes many shapes. I am neither god nor demon, but flesh and blood like yourself, though the substance differ in part, and the form be cast in a different mold.

'I am very old, oh man of the waste countries; long and long ago I came to this planet with others of my world, from the green planet Yag, which circles for ever in the outer fringe of this universe. We swept through space on mighty wings that drove us through the cosmos quicker than light, because we had warred with the kings of Yag and were defeated and outcast. But we could never return, for on earth our wings withered from our shoulders. Here we abode apart from earthly life. We fought the strange and terrible forms of life which then walked the earth, so that we became feared, and were not molested in the dim jungles of the east, where we had our abode.

'We saw men grow from the ape and build the shining cities of Valusia, Kamelia, Commoria and their sisters. We saw them reel before the thrusts of the heathen Atlanteans and Picts and Lemurians. We saw the oceans rise and engulf Atlantis and Lemuria, and the isles of the Picts, and shining cities of civilization. We saw the survivors of Pictdom and Atlantis build their stone-age empires, and go down to ruin, locked in bloody wars. We saw the Picts sink into abysmal savagery, the Atlanteans into apedom again. We saw new savages drift southward in conquering waves from the Arctic circle to build a new civilization, with new kingdoms called Nemedia, and Koth, and Aquilonia and their sisters. We saw your people rise under a new name from the jungles of the apes that had been Atlanteans. We saw the descendants of the Lemurians who had survived the cataclysm, rise again through savagery and ride westward as Hyrkanians. And we saw this race of devils, survivors of the ancient civilization that was before Atlantis sank, come once more into culture and power – this accursed kingdom of Zamora.

'All this we saw, neither aiding nor hindering the immutable cosmic law, and one by one we died; for we of Yag are not immortal, though our lives are as the lives of planets and constellations. At last I alone was left, dreaming of old times among the ruined temples of jungle-lost Khitai, worshipped as a god by an ancient yellow-skinned race. Then came Yara, versed in dark knowledge handed down through the days of barbarism, since before Atlantis sank.

'First he sat at my feet and learned wisdom. But he was not satisfied with what I taught him, for it was white magic, and he wished evil lore, to enslave kings and glut a fiendish ambition. I would teach him none of the black secrets I had gained, through no wish of mine, through the eons.

'But his wisdom was deeper than I had guessed; with guile gotten among the dusky tombs of dark Stygia, he trapped me into divulging a secret I had not intended to bare; and turning my own power upon me, he enslaved me. Ah, gods of Yag, my cup has been bitter since that hour!

'He brought me up from the lost jungles of Khitai where the gray apes danced to the pipes of the yellow priests, and offerings of fruit and wine heaped my broken altars. No more was I a god to kindly jungle-folk – I was slave to a devil in human form.'

Again tears stole from the unseeing eyes.

'He pent me in this tower which at his command I built for him in a single night. By fire and rack he mastered me, and by strange unearthly tortures you would not understand. In agony I would long ago have taken my own life, if I could. But he kept me alive – mangled, blinded, and broken – to do his foul bidding. And for three hundred years I have done his bidding, from this marble couch, blackening my soul with cosmic sins, and staining my wisdom with crimes, because I had no other choice. Yet not all my ancient secrets has he wrested from me, and my last gift shall be the sorcery of the Blood and the Jewel.

'For I feel the end of time draw near. You are the hand of Fate. I beg of you, take the gem you will find on yonder altar.'

Conan turned to the gold and ivory altar indicated, and took up a great round jewel, clear as crimson crystal; and he knew that this was the Heart of the Elephant.

'Now for the great magic, the mighty magic, such as earth has not seen before, and shall not see again, through a million million of millenniums. By my life-blood I conjure it, by blood born on the green breast of Yag, dreaming far-poised in the great blue vastness of Space.

'Take your sword, man, and cut out my heart; then squeeze it so that the blood will flow over the red stone. Then go you down these stairs and enter the ebony chamber where Yara sits wrapped in lotus-dreams of evil. Speak his name and he will awaken. Then lay this gem before him, and say "Yag-kosha gives you a last gift and a last enchantment". Then get you from the tower quickly; fear not, your way shall be made clear. The life of man is not the life of Yag, nor is human death the death of Yag. Let me be free of this cage of broken blind flesh, and I will once more be Yogah of Yag, morning-crowned and shining, with wings to fly, and feet to dance, and eyes to see, and hands to break.'

Uncertainly Conan approached, and Yag-kosha, or Yogah, as if sensing his uncertainty, indicated where he should strike. Conan set his teeth and drove the sword deep. Blood streamed over the blade and his hand, and the monster started convulsively, then lay back quite still. Sure that life had fled, at least life as he understood it, Conan set to work on his grisly task and quickly brought forth something that he felt must be the strange being's heart, though it differed curiously from any he had ever seen. Holding the pulsing organ over the blazing jewel, he pressed it with both hands, and a rain of blood fell on the stone. To his surprise, it did not run off, but soaked into the gem, as water is absorbed by a sponge.

Holding the jewel gingerly, he went out of the fantastic chamber and came upon the silver steps. He did not look back; he instinctively felt that some transmutation was taking place in the body on the marble couch, and he further felt that it was of a sort not to be witnessed by human eyes.

He closed the ivory door behind him and without hesitation descended the silver steps. It did not occur to him to ignore the instructions given him. He halted at an ebony door, in the center of which was a grinning silver skull, and pushed it open. He looked into a chamber of ebony and jet, and saw, on a black silken couch, a tall, spare form reclining. Yara the priest and sorcerer lay before him, his eyes open and dilated with the fumes of the yellow lotus, far-staring, as if fixed on gulfs and nighted abysses beyond human ken.

'Yara!' said Conan, like a judge pronouncing doom. 'Awaken!'

The eyes cleared instantly and became cold and cruel as a vulture's. The tall silken-clad form lifted erect, and towered gauntly above the Cimmerian.

'Dog!' His hiss was like the voice of a cobra. 'What do you here?'

Conan laid the jewel on the ebony table.

'He who sent this gem bade me say "Yag-kosha gives you a last gift and a last enchantment".'

Yara recoiled, his dark face ashy. The jewel was no longer crystal-clear; its murky depths pulsed and throbbed, and curious smoky waves of changing color passed over its smooth surface. As if drawn hypnotically, Yara bent over the table and gripped the gem in his hands, staring into its shadowed depths, as if it were a magnet to draw the shuddering soul from his body. And as Conan looked, he thought that his eyes must be playing him tricks. For when Yara had risen up from his couch, the priest had seemed gigantically tall; yet now he saw that Yara's head would scarcely come to his shoulder. He blinked, puzzled, and for the first time that night, doubted his own senses. Then with a shock he realized that the priest was shrinking in stature – was growing smaller before his very gaze.

With a detached feeling he watched, as a man might watch a play; immersed in a feeling of overpowering unreality, the Cimmerian was no longer sure of his own identity; he only knew that he was looking upon the external evidence of the unseen play of vast Outer forces, beyond his understanding.

Now Yara was no bigger than a child; now like an infant he sprawled on the table, still grasping the jewel. And now the sorcerer suddenly realized his fate, and he sprang up, releasing the gem. But still he dwindled, and Conan saw a tiny, pygmy figure rushing wildly about the ebony table-top, waving tiny arms and shrieking in a voice that was like the squeak of an insect.

Now he had shrunk until the great jewel towered above him like a hill, and Conan saw him cover his eyes with his hands, as if to shield them from the glare, as he staggered about like a madman. Conan sensed that some unseen magnetic force was pulling Yara to the gem. Thrice he raced wildly about it in a narrowing circle, thrice he strove to turn and run out across the table; then with a scream that echoed faintly in the ears of the watcher, the priest threw up his arms and ran straight toward the blazing globe.

Bending close, Conan saw Yara clamber up the smooth, curving surface, impossibly, like a man climbing a glass mountain. Now the priest stood on the top, still with tossing arms, invoking what grisly names only the gods know. And suddenly he sank into the very heart of the jewel, as a man sinks into a sea, and Conan saw the smoky waves close over his head. Now he saw him in the crimson heart of the jewel, once more crystal-clear, as a man sees a scene far away, tiny with great distance. And into the heart came a green, shining winged figure with the body of a man and the head of an elephant – no longer blind or crippled. Yara threw up his arms and fled as a madman flees, and on his heels came the avenger. Then, like the bursting of a bubble, the great jewel vanished in a rainbow burst of iridescent gleams, and the ebony table-top lay bare and deserted – as bare, Conan somehow knew, as the marble couch in the chamber above, where the body of that strange transcosmic being called Yag-kosha and Yogah had lain.

The Cimmerian turned and fled from the chamber, down the silver stairs. So mazed was he that it did not occur to him to escape from the tower by the way he had entered it. Down that winding, shadowy silver well he ran, and came into a large chamber at the foot of the gleaming stairs. There he halted for an instant; he had come into the room of soldiers. He saw the glitter of their silver corselets, the sheen of their jeweled sword-hilts. They sat slumped at the banquet board, their dusky plumes waving somberly above their drooping helmeted heads; they lay among their dice and fallen goblets on the wine-stained lapis-lazuli floor. And he knew that they were dead. The promise had been made, the word kept; whether sorcery or magic or the falling shadow of great green wings had stilled the revelry, Conan could not know, but his way had been made clear. And a silver door stood open, framed in the whiteness of dawn.

Into the waving green gardens came the Cimmerian, and as the dawn wind blew upon him with the cool fragrance of luxuriant growths, he started like a man waking from a dream. He turned back uncertainly, to stare at the cryptic tower he had just left. Was he bewitched and enchanted? Had he dreamed all that had seemed to have passed? As he looked he saw the gleaming tower sway against the crimson dawn, its jewel-crusted rim sparkling in the growing light, and crash into shining shards.

BLACK COLOSSUS

'The Night of Power, when Fate stalked through the corridors of the world like a colossus just risen from an age-old throne of granite—'
E. HOFFMAN PRICE: THE GIRL FROM SAMARKAND

1

ONLY THE AGE-OLD SILENCE brooded over the mysterious ruins of Kuthchemes, but Fear was there; Fear quivered in the mind of Shevatas, the thief, driving his breath quick and sharp against his clenched teeth.

He stood, the one atom of life amidst the colossal monuments of desolation and decay. Not even a vulture hung like a black dot in the vast blue vault of the sky that the sun glazed with its heat. On every hand rose the grim relics of another, forgotten age: huge broken pillars, thrusting up their jagged pinnacles into the sky; long wavering lines of crumbling walls; fallen cyclopean blocks of stone; shattered images, whose horrific features the corroding winds and dust-storms had half erased. From horizon to horizon no sign of life: only the sheer breathtaking sweep of the naked desert, bisected by the wandering line of a long-dry river course; in the midst of that vastness the glimmering fangs of the ruins, the columns standing up like broken masts of sunken ships – all dominated by the towering ivory dome before which Shevatas stood trembling.

The base of this dome was a gigantic pedestal of marble rising from what had once been a terraced eminence on the banks of the ancient river. Broad steps led up to a great bronze door in the dome, which rested on its base like the half of some titanic egg. The dome itself was of pure ivory, which shone as if unknown hands kept it polished.

Likewise shone the spired gold cap of the pinnacle, and the inscription which sprawled about the curve of the dome in golden hieroglyphics yards long. No man on earth could read those characters, but Shevatas shuddered at the dim conjectures they raised. For he came of a very old race, whose myths ran back to shapes undreamed of by contemporary tribes.

Shevatas was wiry and lithe, as became a master-thief of Zamora. His small round head was shaven, his only garment a loin-cloth of scarlet silk. Like all his race, he was very dark, his narrow vulture-like face set off by his keen black eyes. His long, slender and tapering fingers were quick and nervous as the wings of a moth. From a gold-scaled girdle hung a short, narrow, jewel-hilted sword in a sheath of ornamented leather. Shevatas handled the weapon with apparently exaggerated care. He even seemed to flinch away from the contact of the sheath with his naked thigh. Nor was his care without reason.

This was Shevatas, a thief among thieves, whose name was spoken with awe in the dives of the Maul and the dim shadowy recesses beneath the temples of Bel, and who lived in songs and myths for a thousand years. Yet fear ate at the heart of Shevatas as he stood before the ivory dome of Kuthchemes. Any fool could see there was something unnatural about the structure; the winds and suns of three thousand years had lashed it, yet its gold and ivory rose bright and glistening as the day it was reared by nameless hands on the bank of the nameless river.

This unnaturalness was in keeping with the general aura of these devil-haunted ruins. This desert was the mysterious expanse lying southeast of the lands of Shem. A few days' ride on camel-back to the southwest, as Shevatas knew, would bring the traveller within sight of the great river Styx at the point where it turned at right angles with its former course, and flowed westward to empty at last into the distant sea. At the point of its bend began the land of Stygia, the dark-bosomed mistress of the south, whose domains, watered by the great river, rose sheer out of the surrounding desert.

Eastward, Shevatas knew, the desert shaded into steppes stretching to the Hyrkanian kingdom of Turan, rising in barbaric splendor on the shores of the great inland sea. A week's ride northward the desert ran into a tangle of barren hills, beyond which lay the fertile uplands of Koth, the southernmost realm of the Hyborian races. Westward the desert merged into the meadowlands of Shem, which stretched away to the ocean.

All this Shevatas knew without being particularly conscious of the knowledge, as a man knows the streets of his town. He was a far traveller and had looted the treasures of many kingdoms. But now he

hesitated and shuddered before the highest adventure and the mightiest treasure of all.

In that ivory dome lay the bones of Thugra Khotan, the dark sorcerer who had reigned in Kuthchemes three thousand years ago, when the kingdoms of Stygia stretched far northward of the great river, over the meadows of Shem, and into the uplands. Then the great drift of the Hyborians swept southward from the cradle-land of their race near the northern pole. It was a titanic drift, extending over centuries and ages. But in the reign of Thugra Khotan, the last magician of Kuthchemes, gray-eyed, tawny-haired barbarians in wolfskins and scale-mail had ridden from the north into the rich uplands to carve out the kingdom of Koth with their iron swords. They had stormed over Kuthchemes like a tidal wave, washing the marble towers in blood, and the northern Stygian kingdom had gone down in fire and ruin.

But while they were shattering the streets of his city and cutting down his archers like ripe corn, Thugra Khotan had swallowed a strange terrible poison, and his masked priests had locked him into the tomb he himself had prepared. His devotees died about that tomb in a crimson holocaust, but the barbarians could not burst the door, nor ever mar the structure by maul or fire. So they rode away, leaving the great city in ruins, and in his ivory-domed sepulcher great Thugra Khotan slept unmolested, while the lizards of desolation gnawed at the crumbling pillars, and the very river that watered his land in old times sank into the sands and ran dry.

Many a thief sought to gain the treasure which fables said lay heaped about the moldering bones inside the dome. And many a thief died at the door of the tomb, and many another was harried by monstrous dreams to die at last with the froth of madness on his lips.

So Shevatas shuddered as he faced the tomb, nor was his shudder altogether occasioned by the legend of the serpent said to guard the sorcerer's bones. Over all myths of Thugra Khotan hung horror and death like a pall. From where the thief stood he could see the ruins of the great hall wherein chained captives had knelt by the hundreds during festivals to have their heads hacked off by the priest-king in honor of Set, the Serpent-god of Stygia. Somewhere near by had been the pit, dark and awful, wherein screaming victims were fed to a nameless amorphous monstrosity which came up out of a deeper, more hellish cavern. Legend made Thugra Khotan more than human; his worship yet lingered in a mongrel degraded cult, whose votaries stamped his likeness on coins to pay the way of their dead over the great river of darkness of which the Styx was but the material shadow. Shevatas had seen this likeness, on coins stolen from under the tongues of the dead, and its image was etched indelibly in his brain.

But he put aside his fears and mounted to the bronze door, whose smooth surface offered no bolt or catch. Not for naught had he gained access into darksome cults, had harkened to the grisly whispers of the votaries of Skelos under midnight trees, and read the forbidden iron-bound books of Vathelos the Blind.

Kneeling before the portal, he searched the sill with nimble fingers; their sensitive tips found projections too small for the eye to detect, or for less-skilled fingers to discover. These he pressed carefully and according to a peculiar system, muttering a long-forgotten incantation as he did so. As he pressed the last projection, he sprang up with frantic haste and struck the exact center of the door a quick sharp blow with his open hand.

There was no rasp of spring or hinge, but the door retreated inward, and the breath hissed explosively from Shevatas's clenched teeth. A short narrow corridor was disclosed. Down this the door had slid, and was now in place at the other end. The floor, ceiling and sides of the tunnel-like aperture were of ivory, and now from an opening on one side came a silent writhing horror that reared up and glared on the intruder with awful luminous eyes; a serpent twenty feet long, with shimmering, iridescent scales.

The thief did not waste time in conjecturing what night-black pits lying below the dome had given sustenance to the monster. Gingerly he drew the sword, and from it dripped a greenish liquid exactly like that which slavered from the scimitar-fangs of the reptile. The blade was steeped in the poison of the snake's own kind, and the obtaining of that venom from the fiend-haunted swamps of Zingara would have made a saga in itself.

Shevatas advanced warily on the balls of his feet, knees bent slightly, ready to spring either way like a flash of light. And he needed all his co-ordinate speed when the snake arched its neck and struck, shooting out its full length like a stroke of lightning. For all his quickness of nerve and eye, Shevatas had died then but for chance. His well-laid plans of leaping aside and striking down on the outstretched neck were put at naught by the blinding speed of the reptile's attack. The thief had but time to extend the sword in front of him, involuntarily closing his eyes and crying out. Then the sword was wrenched from his hand and the corridor was filled with a horrible thrashing and lashing.

Opening his eyes, amazed to find himself still alive, Shevatas saw the monster heaving and twisting its slimy form in fantastic contortions, the sword transfixing its giant jaws. Sheer chance had hurled it full against the point he had held out blindly. A few moments later the serpent sank into shining, scarcely quivering coils, as the poison on the blade struck home.

Gingerly stepping over it, the thief thrust against the door, which this time slid aside, revealing the interior of the dome. Shevatas cried out; instead of utter darkness he had come into a crimson light that throbbed and pulsed almost beyond the endurance of mortal eyes. It came from a gigantic red jewel high up in the vaulted arch of the dome. Shevatas gaped, inured though he was to the sight of riches. The treasure was there, heaped in staggering profusion – piles of diamonds, sapphires, rubies, turquoises, opals, emeralds; zikkurats of jade, jet and lapis lazuli; pyramids of gold wedges; teocallis of silver ingots; jewel-hilted swords in cloth-of-gold sheaths; golden helmets with colored horsehair crests, or black and scarlet plumes; silver-scaled corselets; gem-crusted harness worn by warrior-kings three thousand years in their tombs; goblets carven of single jewels; skulls plated with gold, with moonstones for eyes; necklaces of human teeth set with jewels. The ivory floor was covered inches deep with gold dust that sparkled and shimmered under the crimson glow with a million scintillant lights. The thief stood in a wonderland of magic and splendor, treading stars under his sandalled feet.

But his eyes were focussed on the dais of crystal which rose in the midst of the shimmering array, directly under the red jewel, and on which should be lying the moldering bones, turning to dust with the crawling of the centuries. And as Shevatas looked, the blood drained from his dark features; his marrow turned to ice, and the skin of his back crawled and wrinkled with horror, while his lips worked soundlessly. But suddenly he found his voice in one awful scream that rang hideously under the arching dome. Then again the silence of the ages lay among the ruins of mysterious Kuthchemes.

2

Rumors drifted up through the meadowlands, into the cities of the Hyborians. The word ran along the caravans, the long camel-trains plodding through the sands, herded by lean, hawk-eyed men in white kaftans. It was passed on by the hook-nosed herdsmen of the grasslands, from the dwellers in tents to the dwellers in the squat stone cities where kings with curled blue-black beards worshipped round-bellied gods with curious rites. The word passed up through the fringe of hills where gaunt tribesmen took toll of the caravans. The rumors came into the fertile uplands where stately cities rose above blue lakes and rivers: the rumors marched along the broad white roads thronged with ox-wains, with lowing herds, with rich merchants, knights in steel, archers and priests.

They were rumors from the desert that lies east of Stygia, far south of the Kothian hills. A new prophet had risen among the nomads. Men spoke of tribal war, of a gathering of vultures in the southeast, and a terrible leader who led his swiftly increasing hordes to victory. The Stygians, ever a menace to the northern nations, were apparently not connected with this movement; for they were massing armies on their eastern borders and their priests were making magic to fight that of the desert sorcerer, whom men called Natohk, the Veiled One; for his features were always masked.

But the tide swept northwestward, and the blue-bearded kings died before the altars of their pot-bellied gods, and their squat-walled cities were drenched in blood. Men said that the uplands of the Hyborians were the goal of Natohk and his chanting votaries.

Raids from the desert were not uncommon, but this latest movement seemed to promise more than a raid. Rumor said Natohk had welded thirty nomadic tribes and fifteen cities into his following, and that a rebellious Stygian prince had joined him. This latter lent the affair an aspect of real war.

Characteristically, most of the Hyborian nations were prone to ignore the growing menace. But in Khoraja, carved out of Shemite lands by the swords of Kothic adventurers, heed was given. Lying southeast of Koth, it would bear the brunt of the invasion. And its young king was captive to the treacherous king of Ophir, who hesitated between restoring him for a huge ransom, or handing him over to his enemy, the penurious king of Koth, who offered no gold, but an advantageous treaty. Meanwhile, the rule of the struggling kingdom was in the white hands of young princess Yasmela, the king's sister.

Minstrels sang her beauty throughout the western world, and the pride of a kingly dynasty was hers. But on that night her pride was dropped from her like a cloak. In her chamber whose ceiling was a lapis lazuli dome, whose marble floor was littered with rare furs, and whose walls were lavish with golden frieze-work, ten girls, daughters of nobles, their slender limbs weighted with gem-crusted armlets and anklets, slumbered on velvet couches about the royal bed with its golden dais and silken canopy. But princess Yasmela lolled not on that silken bed. She lay naked on her supple belly upon the bare marble like the most abased suppliant, her dark hair streaming over her white shoulders, her slender fingers intertwined. She lay and writhed in pure horror that froze the blood in her lithe limbs and dilated her beautiful eyes, that pricked the roots of her dark hair and made goose-flesh rise along her supple spine.

Above her, in the darkest corner of the marble chamber, lurked a vast shapeless shadow. It was no living thing of form or flesh and blood. It was a clot of darkness, a blur in the sight, a monstrous night-born incubus that might have been deemed a figment of a sleep-drugged brain, but for the points of blazing yellow fire that glimmered like two eyes from the blackness.

Moreover, a voice issued from it – a low subtle inhuman sibilance that was more like the soft abominable hissing of a serpent than anything else, and that apparently could not emanate from anything with human lips. Its sound as well as its import filled Yasmela with a shuddering horror so intolerable that she writhed and twisted her slender body as if beneath a lash, as though to rid her mind of its insinuating vileness by physical contortion.

'You are marked for mine, princess,' came the gloating whisper. 'Before I wakened from the long sleep I had marked you, and yearned for you, but I was held fast by the ancient spell by which I escaped mine enemies. I am the soul of Natohk, the Veiled One! Look well upon me, princess! Soon you shall behold me in my bodily guise, and shall love me!'

The ghostly hissing dwindled off in lustful titterings, and Yasmela moaned and beat the marble tiles with her small fists in her ecstasy of terror.

'I sleep in the palace chamber of Akbatana,' the sibilances continued. 'There my body lies in its frame of bones and flesh. But it is but an empty shell from which the spirit has flown for a brief space. Could you gaze from that palace casement you would realize the futility of resistance. The desert is a rose-garden beneath the moon, where blossom the fires of a hundred thousand warriors. As an avalanche sweeps onward, gathering bulk and momentum, I will sweep into the lands of mine ancient enemies. Their kings shall furnish me skulls for goblets, their women and children shall be slaves of my slaves' slaves. I have grown strong in the long years of dreaming . . .

'But thou shalt be my queen, oh princess! I will teach thee the ancient forgotten ways of pleasure. We—' Before the stream of cosmic obscenity which poured from the shadowy colossus, Yasmela cringed and writhed as if from a whip that flayed her dainty bare flesh.

'Remember!' whispered the horror. 'The days will not be many before I come to claim mine own!'

Yasmela, pressing her face against the tiles and stopping her pink ears with her dainty fingers, yet seemed to hear a strange sweeping noise, like the beat of bat wings. Then, looking fearfully up, she saw only the moon that shone through the window with a beam that rested like a silver sword across the spot where the phantom had lurked.

Trembling in every limb, she rose and staggered to a satin couch, where she threw herself down, weeping hysterically. The girls slept on, but one, who roused, yawned, stretched her slender figure and blinked about. Instantly she was on her knees beside the couch, her arms about Yasmela's supple waist.

'Was it – was it—?' Her dark eyes were wide with fright. Yasmela caught her in a convulsive grasp.

'Oh, Vateesa. *It* came again! I saw It – heard It speak! It spoke Its name – Natohk! It is Natohk! It is not a nightmare – it towered over me while the girls slept like drugged ones. What – oh, *what* shall I do?'

Vateesa twisted a golden bracelet about her rounded arm in meditation.

'Oh, princess,' she said, 'it is evident that no mortal power can deal with It, and the charm is useless that the priests of Ishtar gave you. Therefore seek you the forgotten oracle of Mitra.'

In spite of her recent fright, Yasmela shuddered. The gods of yesterday become the devils of tomorrow. The Kothians had long since abandoned the worship of Mitra, forgetting the attributes of the universal Hyborian god. Yasmela had a vague idea that, being very ancient, it followed that the deity was very terrible. Ishtar was much to be feared, and all the gods of Koth. Kothian culture and religion had suffered from a subtle admixture of Shemite and Stygian strains. The simple ways of the Hyborians had become modified to a large extent by the sensual, luxurious, yet despotic habits of the East.

'Will Mitra aid me?' Yasmela caught Vateesa's wrist in her eagerness. 'We have worshipped Ishtar so long—'

'To be sure he will!' Vateesa was the daughter of an Ophirean priest who had brought his customs with him when he fled from political enemies to Khoraja. 'Seek the shrine! I will go with you.'

'I will!' Yasmela rose, but objected when Vateesa prepared to dress her. 'It is not fitting that I come before the shrine clad in silk. I will go naked, on my knees, as befits a suppliant, lest Mitra deem I lack humility.'

'Nonsense!' Vateesa had scant respect for the ways of what she deemed a false cult. 'Mitra would have folks stand upright before him – not crawling on their bellies like worms, or spilling blood of animals all over his altars.'

Thus objurgated, Yasmela allowed the girl to garb her in the light sleeveless silk shirt, over which was slipped a silken tunic, bound at the waist by a wide velvet girdle. Satin slippers were put upon her slender feet, and a few deft touches of Vateesa's pink fingers arranged her dark wavy tresses. Then the princess followed the girl, who drew aside a heavy gilt-worked tapestry and threw the golden bolt of the door it concealed. This let into a narrow winding corridor, and down this the two girls went swiftly, through another door and into a broad hallway. Here stood a guardsman in crested gilt helmet, silvered cuirass and gold-chased greaves, with a long-shafted battle-ax in his hands.

A motion from Yasmela checked his exclamation and, saluting, he took his stand again beside the doorway, motionless as a brazen image. The girls traversed the hallway, which seemed immense and eery in the light of the cressets along the lofty walls, and went down a stairway where Yasmela shivered at the blots of shadows which hung in the angles of the walls. Three levels down they halted at last in a narrow corridor whose arched ceiling was crusted with jewels, whose floor was set with blocks of crystal, and whose walls were decorated with golden frieze-work. Down this shining way they stole, holding each other's hands, to a wide portal of gilt.

Vateesa thrust open the door, revealing a shrine long forgotten except by a faithful few, and royal visitors to Khoraja's court, mainly for whose benefit the fane was maintained. Yasmela had never entered it before, though she was born in the palace. Plain and unadorned in comparison to the lavish display of Ishtar's shrines, there was about it a simplicity of dignity and beauty characteristic of the Mitran religion.

The ceiling was lofty, but it was not domed, and was of plain white marble, as were the walls and floor, the former with a narrow gold frieze running about them. Behind an altar of clear green jade, unstained with sacrifice, stood the pedestal whereon sat the material manifestation of the deity. Yasmela looked in awe at the sweep of the magnificent shoulders, the clear-cut features – the wide straight eyes, the patriarchal beard, the thick curls of the hair, confined by a simple band about the temples. This, though she did not know it, was art in its highest form – the free, uncramped artistic expression of a highly esthetic race, unhampered by conventional symbolism.

She fell on her knees and thence prostrate, regardless of Vateesa's admonition, and Vateesa, to be on the safe side, followed her example; for after all, she was only a girl, and it was very awesome in Mitra's shrine. But even so she could not refrain from whispering in Yasmela's ear.

'This is but the emblem of the god. None pretends to know what Mitra looks like. This but represents him in idealized human form, as near perfection as the human mind can conceive. He does not inhabit this cold stone, as your priests tell you Ishtar does. He is everywhere – above us, and about us, and he dreams betimes in the high places among the stars. But here his being focusses. Therefore call upon him.'

'What shall I say?' whispered Yasmela in stammering terror.

'Before you can speak, Mitra knows the contents of your mind—' began Vateesa. Then both girls started violently as a voice began in the air above them. The deep, calm, bell-like tones emanated no more from the image than from anywhere else in the chamber. Again Yasmela trembled before a bodiless voice speaking to her, but this time it was not from horror or repulsion.

'Speak not, my daughter, for I know your need,' came the intonations like deep musical waves beating rhythmically along a golden beach. 'In one manner may you save your kingdom, and saving it, save all the world from the fangs of the serpent which has crawled up out of the darkness of the ages. Go forth upon the streets alone, and place your kingdom in the hands of the first man you meet there.'

The unechoing tones ceased, and the girls stared at each other. Then, rising, they stole forth, nor did they speak until they stood once more in Yasmela's chamber. The princess stared out of the gold-barred windows. The moon had set. It was long past midnight. Sounds of revelry had died away in the gardens and on the roofs of the city. Khoraja slumbered beneath the stars, which seemed to be reflected in the cressets that twinkled among the gardens and along the streets and on the flat roofs of houses where folk slept.

'What will you do?' whispered Vateesa, all a-tremble.

'Give me my cloak,' answered Yasmela, setting her teeth.

'But alone, in the streets, at this hour!' expostulated Vateesa.

'Mitra has spoken,' replied the princess. 'It might have been the voice of the god, or a trick of a priest. No matter. I will go!'

Wrapping a voluminous silken cloak about her lithe figure and donning a velvet cap from which depended a filmy veil, she passed hurriedly through the corridors and approached a bronze door where a dozen spearmen gaped at her as she passed through. This was in a wing of the palace which let directly onto the street; on all other sides it was surrounded by broad gardens, bordered by a high wall. She emerged into the street, lighted by cressets placed at regular intervals.

She hesitated; then, before her resolution could falter, she closed the door behind her. A slight shudder shook her as she glanced up and down the street, which lay silent and bare. This daughter of aristocrats had never before ventured unattended outside her ancestral palace. Then, steeling herself, she went swiftly up the street. Her satin-slippered feet fell lightly on the pave, but their soft sound brought her heart into her throat. She imagined their fall echoing thunderously through the cavernous city, rousing ragged rat-eyed figures in hidden lairs among the sewers. Every shadow seemed to hide a lurking assassin, every blank doorway to mask the slinking hounds of darkness.

Then she started violently. Ahead of her a figure appeared on the eery street. She drew quickly into a clump of shadows, which now seemed like a haven of refuge, her pulse pounding. The approaching figure went not furtively, like a thief, or timidly, like a fearful traveller. He strode down the nighted street as one who has no need or desire to walk softly. An unconscious swagger was in his stride, and his footfalls resounded on the pave. As he passed near a cresset she saw him plainly – a tall man, in the chain-mail hauberk of a mercenary. She braced herself, then darted from the shadow, holding her cloak close about her.

'Sa-ha!' his sword flashed half out of his sheath. It halted when he saw it was only a woman that stood before him, but his quick glance went over her head, seeking the shadows for possible confederates.

He stood facing her, his hand on the long hilt that jutted forward from beneath the scarlet cloak which flowed carelessly from his mailed shoulders. The torchlight glinted dully on the polished blue steel of his greaves and basinet. A more baleful fire glittered bluely in his eyes. At first glance she saw he was no Kothian; when he spoke she knew he was no Hyborian. He was clad like a captain of the mercenaries, and in that desperate command there were men of many lands, barbarians as well as civilized foreigners. There was a wolfishness about this warrior that marked the barbarian. The eyes of no civilized man, however wild or criminal, ever blazed with such a fire. Wine scented his breath, but he neither staggered nor stammered.

'Have they shut you into the street?' he asked in barbarous Kothic, reaching for her. His fingers closed lightly about her rounded wrist, but she felt that he could splinter its bones without effort. 'I've but come from the last wine-shop open – Ishtar's curse on these white-livered reformers who close the grog-houses! "Let men sleep rather than guzzle," they say – aye, so they can work and fight better for their masters! Soft-gutted eunuchs, I call them. When I served with the mercenaries of Corinthia we swilled and wenched all night and fought all day – aye, blood ran down the channels of our swords. But what of you, my girl? Take off that cursed mask—'

She avoided his clutch with a lithe twist of her body, trying not to appear to repulse him. She realized her danger, alone with a drunken barbarian. If she revealed her identity, he might laugh at her, or take himself off. She was not sure he would not cut her throat. Barbaric men did strange inexplicable things. She fought a rising fear.

'Not here,' she laughed. 'Come with me—'

'Where?' His wild blood was up, but he was wary as a wolf. 'Are you taking me to some den of robbers?'

'No, no, I swear it!' She was hard put to avoid the hand which was again fumbling at her veil.

'Devil bite you, hussy!' he growled disgustedly. 'You're as bad as a Hyrkanian woman, with your damnable veil. Here – let me look at your figure, anyway.'

Before she could prevent it, he wrenched the cloak from her, and she heard his breath hiss between his teeth. He stood holding the cloak, eyeing her as if the sight of her rich garments had somewhat sobered him. She saw suspicion flicker sullenly in his eyes.

'Who the devil are you?' he muttered. 'You're no street-waif – unless your leman robbed the king's seraglio for your clothes.'

'Never mind.' She dared to lay her white hand on his massive iron-clad arm. 'Come with me off the street.'

He hesitated, then shrugged his mighty shoulders. She saw that he half believed her to be some noble lady, who, weary of polite lovers, was taking this means of amusing herself. He allowed her to don the cloak again, and followed her. From the corner of her eye she watched him as they went down the street together. His mail could not conceal his hard lines of tigerish strength. Everything about him was tigerish, elemental, untamed. He was alien as the jungle to her in his difference from the debonair courtiers to whom she was accustomed. She feared him, told herself she loathed his raw brute strength and unashamed barbarism, yet something breathless and perilous inside her leaned toward him; the hidden primitive chord that lurks in every woman's soul was sounded and responded. She had felt his hardened hand on her arm, and something deep in her tingled to the memory of that contact. Many men had knelt before Yasmela. Here was one she felt had never knelt before any one. Her sensations were those of one leading an unchained tiger; she was frightened, and fascinated by her fright.

She halted at the palace door and thrust lightly against it. Furtively watching her companion, she saw no suspicion in his eyes.

'Palace, eh?' he rumbled. 'So you're a maid-in-waiting?'

She found herself wondering, with a strange jealousy, if any of her maids had ever led this war-eagle into her palace. The guards made no sign as she led him between them, but he eyed them as a fierce dog might eye a strange pack. She led him through a curtained doorway into an inner chamber, where he stood, naïvely scanning the tapestries, until he saw a crystal jar of wine on an ebony table. This he took up with a gratified sigh, tilting it toward his lips. Vateesa ran from an inner room, crying breathlessly, 'Oh my princess—'

'*Princess!*'

The wine-jar crashed to the floor. With a motion too quick for sight to follow, the mercenary snatched off Yasmela's veil, glaring. He recoiled with a curse, his sword leaping into his hand with a broad shimmer of blue steel. His eyes blazed like a trapped tiger's. The air was supercharged with tension that was like the pause before the bursting of a storm. Vateesa sank to the floor, speechless with terror, but Yasmela faced the infuriated barbarian without flinching. She realized her very life hung in the balance: maddened with suspicion and unreasoning panic, he was ready to deal death at the slightest provocation. But she experienced a certain breathless exhilaration in the crisis.

'Do not be afraid,' she said. 'I am Yasmela, but there is no reason to fear me.'

'Why did you lead me here?' he snarled, his blazing eyes darting all about the chamber. 'What manner of trap is this?'

'There is no trickery,' she answered. 'I brought you here because you can aid me. I called on the gods – on Mitra – and he bade me go into the streets and ask aid of the first man I met.'

This was something he could understand. The barbarians had their oracles. He lowered his sword, though he did not sheathe it.

'Well, if you're Yasmela, you need aid,' he grunted. 'Your kingdom's in a devil of a mess. But how can I aid you? If you want a throat cut, of course—'

'Sit down,' she requested. 'Vateesa, bring him wine.'

He complied, taking care, she noticed, to sit with his back against a solid wall, where he could watch the whole chamber. He laid his naked sword across his mail-sheathed knees. She glanced at it in fascination. Its dull blue glimmer seemed to reflect tales of bloodshed and rapine; she doubted her ability to lift it, yet she knew that the mercenary could wield it with one hand as lightly as she could wield a riding-whip. She noted the breadth and power of his hands; they were not the stubby undeveloped paws of a troglodyte. With a guilty start she found herself imagining those strong fingers locked in her dark hair.

He seemed reassured when she deposited herself on a satin divan opposite him. He lifted off his basinet and laid it on the table, and drew back his coif, letting the mail folds fall upon his massive shoulders. She saw more fully now his unlikeness to the Hyborian races. In his dark, scarred face there was a suggestion of moodiness; and without being marked by depravity, or definitely evil, there was more than a suggestion of the sinister about his features, set off by his smoldering blue eyes. A low broad forehead was topped by a square-cut tousled mane as black as a raven's wing.

'Who are you?' she asked abruptly.

'Conan, a captain of the mercenary spearmen,' he answered, emptying the wine-cup at a gulp and holding it out for more. 'I was born in Cimmeria.'

The name meant little to her. She only knew vaguely that it was a wild grim hill-country which lay far to the north, beyond the last outposts of the Hyborian nations, and was peopled by a fierce moody race. She had never before seen one of them.

Resting her chin on her hands, she gazed at him with the deep dark eyes that had enslaved many a heart.

'Conan of Cimmeria,' she said, 'you said I needed aid. Why?'

'Well,' he answered, 'any man can see that. Here is the king your brother in an Ophirean prison; here is Koth plotting to enslave you; here is this sorcerer screaming hell-fire and destruction down in Shem – and what's worse, here are your soldiers deserting every day.'

She did not at once reply; it was a new experience for a man to speak so forthrightly to her, his words not couched in courtier phrases.

'Why are my soldiers deserting, Conan?' she asked.

'Some are being hired away by Koth,' he replied, pulling at the wine-jar with relish. 'Many think Khoraja is doomed as an independent state. Many are frightened by tales of this dog Natohk.'

'Will the mercenaries stand?' she asked anxiously.

'As long as you pay us well,' he answered frankly. 'Your politics are nothing to us. You can trust Amalric, our general, but the rest of us are only common men who love loot. If you pay the ransom Ophir asks, men say you'll be unable to pay us. In that case we might go over to the king of Koth, though that cursed miser is no friend of mine. Or we might loot this city. In a civil war the plunder is always plentiful.'

'Why would you not go over to Natohk?' she inquired.

'What could he pay us?' he snorted. 'With fat-bellied brass idols he looted from the Shemite cities? As long as you're fighting Natohk, you may trust us.'

'Would your comrades follow you?' she asked abruptly.

'What do you mean?'

'I mean,' she answered deliberately, 'that I am going to make you commander of the armies of Khoraja!'

He stopped short, the goblet at his lips, which curved in a broad grin. His eyes blazed with a new light.

'Commander? Crom! But what will your perfumed nobles say?'

'They will obey me!' She clasped her hands to summon a slave, who entered, bowing deeply. 'Have Count Thespides come to me at once, and the chancellor Taurus, lord Amalric, and the Agha Shupras.

'I place my trust in Mitra,' she said, bending her gaze on Conan, who was now devouring the food placed before him by the trembling Vateesa. 'You have seen much war?'

'I was born in the midst of a battle,' he answered, tearing a chunk of meat from a huge joint with his strong teeth. 'The first sound my ears heard was the clang of swords and the yells of the slaying. I have fought in blood-feuds, tribal wars, and imperial campaigns.'

'But can you lead men and arrange battle-lines?'

'Well, I can try,' he returned imperturbably. 'It's no more than sword-play on a larger scale. You draw his guard, then – stab, slash! And either his head is off, or yours.'

The slave entered again, announcing the arrival of the men sent for, and Yasmela went into the outer chamber, drawing the velvet curtains behind her. The nobles bent the knee, in evident surprize at her summons at such an hour.

'I have summoned you to tell you of my decision,' said Yasmela. 'The kingdom is in peril—'

'Right enough, my princess.' It was Count Thespides who spoke – a tall man, whose black locks were curled and scented. With one white hand he smoothed his pointed mustache, and with the other he held a velvet chaperon with a scarlet feather fastened by a golden clasp. His pointed shoes were satin, his cote-hardie of gold-broidered velvet. His manner was slightly affected, but the thews under his silks were steely. 'It were well to offer Ophir more gold for your royal brother's release.'

'I strongly disagree,' broke in Taurus the chancellor, an elderly man in an ermine-fringed robe, whose features were lined with the cares of his long service. 'We have already offered what will beggar the kingdom to pay. To offer more would further excite Ophir's cupidity. My princess, I say as I have said before: Ophir will not move until we have met this invading horde. If we lose, he will give king Khossus to Koth; if we win, he will doubtless restore his majesty to us on payment of the ransom.'

'And in the meantime,' broke in Amalric, 'the soldiers desert daily, and the mercenaries are restless to know why we dally.' He was a Nemedian, a large man with a lion-like yellow mane. 'We must move swiftly, if at all—'

'Tomorrow we march southward,' she answered. 'And there is the man who shall lead you!'

Jerking aside the velvet curtains she dramatically indicated the Cimmerian. It was perhaps not an entirely happy moment for the disclosure. Conan was sprawled in his chair, his feet propped on the ebony table, busily engaged in gnawing a beef-bone which he gripped firmly in both hands. He glanced casually at the astounded nobles, grinned faintly at Amalric, and went on munching with undisguised relish.

'Mitra protect us!' exploded Amalric. 'That's Conan the northron, the most turbulent of all my rogues! I'd have hanged him long ago, were he not the best swordsman that ever donned hauberk—'

'Your highness is pleased to jest!' cried Thespides, his aristocratic features darkening. 'This man is a savage – a fellow of no culture or breeding! It is an insult to ask gentlemen to serve under him! I—'

'Count Thespides,' said Yasmela, 'you have my glove under your baldric. Please give it to me, and then go.'

'Go?' he cried, starting. 'Go where?'

'To Koth or to Hades!' she answered. 'If you will not serve me as I wish, you shall not serve me at all.'

'You wrong me, princess,' he answered, bowing low, deeply hurt. 'I would not forsake you. For your sake I will even put my sword at the disposal of this savage.'

'And you, my lord Amalric?'

Amalric swore beneath his breath, then grinned. True soldier of fortune, no shift of fortune, however outrageous, surprized him much.

'I'll serve under him. A short life and a merry one, say I – and with Conan the Throat-slitter in command, life is likely to be both merry and short. Mitra! If the dog ever commanded more than a company of cut-throats before, I'll eat him, harness and all!'

'And you, my Agha?' she turned to Shupras.

He shrugged his shoulders resignedly. He was typical of the race evolved along Koth's southern borders – tall and gaunt, with features leaner and more hawk-like than his purer-blooded desert kin.

'Ishtar gives, princess.' The fatalism of his ancestors spoke for him.

'Wait here,' she commanded, and while Thespides fumed and gnawed his velvet cap, Taurus muttered wearily under his breath, and Amalric strode back and forth, tugging at his yellow beard and grinning like a hungry lion, Yasmela disappeared again through the curtains and clapped her hands for her slaves.

At her command they brought harness to replace Conan's chain-mail – gorget, sollerets, cuirass, pauldrons, jambes, cuisses and sallet. When Yasmela again drew the curtains, a Conan in burnished steel stood before his audience. Clad in the plate-armor, vizor lifted and dark face shadowed by the black plumes that nodded above his helmet, there was a grim impressiveness about him that even Thespides grudgingly noted. A jest died suddenly on Amalric's lips.

'By Mitra,' said he slowly, 'I never expected to see you cased in coat-armor, but you do not put it to shame. By my finger-bones, Conan, I have seen kings who wore their harness less regally than you!'

Conan was silent. A vague shadow crossed his mind like a prophecy. In years to come he was to remember Amalric's words, when the dream became the reality.

3

In the early haze of dawn the streets of Khoraja were thronged by crowds of people who watched the hosts riding from the southern gate. The army was on the move at last. There were the knights, gleaming in richly wrought plate-armor, colored plumes waving above their burnished sallets. Their steeds, caparisoned with silk, lacquered leather and gold buckles, caracoled and curvetted as their riders put them through their paces. The early light struck glints from lance-points that rose like a forest above the array, their pennons flowing in the breeze. Each knight wore a lady's token, a glove, scarf or rose, bound to his helmet or fastened to his sword-belt. They were the chivalry of Khoraja, five hundred strong, led by Count Thespides, who, men said, aspired to the hand of Yasmela herself.

They were followed by the light cavalry on rangy steeds. The riders were typical hillmen, lean and hawk-faced; peaked steel caps were on their heads and chain-mail glinted under their flowing kaftans. Their main weapon was the terrible Shemitish bow, which could send a shaft five hundred paces. There were five thousand of these, and Shupras rode at their head, his lean face moody beneath his spired helmet.

Close on their heels marched the Khoraja spearmen, always comparatively few in any Hyborian state, where men thought cavalry the only honorable branch of service. These, like the knights, were of ancient Kothic blood – sons of ruined families, broken men, penniless youths, who could not afford horses and plate-armor, five hundred of them.

The mercenaries brought up the rear, a thousand horsemen, two thousand spearmen. The tall horses of the cavalry seemed hard and savage as their riders; they made no curvets or gambades. There was a grimly business-like aspect to these professional killers, veterans of bloody campaigns. Clad from head to foot in chain-mail, they wore their vizorless head-pieces over linked coifs. Their shields were unadorned, their long lances without guidons. At their saddle-bows hung battle-axes or steel maces, and each man wore at his hip a long broadsword. The spearmen were armed in much the same manner, though they bore pikes instead of cavalry lances.

They were men of many races and many crimes. There were tall Hyperboreans, gaunt, big-boned, of slow speech and violent natures; tawny-haired Gundermen from the hills of the northwest; swaggering Corinthian renegades; swarthy Zingarians, with bristling black mustaches and fiery tempers; Aquilonians from the distant west. But all, except the Zingarians, were Hyborians.

Behind all came a camel in rich housings, led by a knight on a great war-horse, and surrounded by a clump of picked fighters from the royal house-troops. Its rider, under the silken canopy of the seat, was a slim, silk-clad figure, at the sight of which the populace, always mindful of royalty, threw up its leather cap and cheered wildly.

Conan the Cimmerian, restless in his plate-armor, stared at the bedecked camel with no great approval, and spoke to Amalric, who rode beside him, resplendent in chain-mail threaded with gold, golden breastplate and helmet with flowing horsehair crest.

'The princess would go with us. She's supple, but too soft for this work. Anyway, she'll have to get out of these robes.'

Amalric twisted his yellow mustache to hide a grin. Evidently Conan supposed Yasmela intended to strap on a sword and take part in the actual fighting, as the barbarian women often fought.

'The women of the Hyborians do not fight like your Cimmerian women, Conan,' he said. 'Yasmela rides with us to watch the battle. Anyway,' he shifted in his saddle and lowered his voice, 'between you and me, I have an idea that the princess dares not remain behind. She fears something—'

'An uprising? Maybe we'd better hang a few citizens before we start—'

'No. One of her maids talked – babbled about *Something* that came into the palace by night and frightened Yasmela half out of her wits. It's some of Natohk's deviltry, I doubt not. Conan, it's more than flesh and blood we fight!'

'Well,' grunted the Cimmerian, 'it's better to go meet an enemy than to wait for him.'

He glanced at the long line of wagons and camp-followers, gathered the reins in his mailed hand, and spoke from habit the phrase of the marching mercenaries, 'Hell or plunder, comrades – march!'

Behind the long train the ponderous gates of Khoraja closed. Eager heads lined the battlements. The citizens well knew they were watching life or death go forth. If the host was overthrown, the future of Khoraja would be written in blood. In the hordes swarming up from the savage south, mercy was a quality unknown.

All day the columns marched, through grassy rolling meadowlands, cut by small rivers, the terrain gradually beginning to slope upward. Ahead of them lay a range of low hills, sweeping in an unbroken rampart from east to west. They camped that night on the northern slopes of those hills, and hook-nosed, fiery-eyed men of the hill tribes came in scores to squat about the fires and repeat news that had come up out of the mysterious desert. Through their tales ran the name of Natohk like a crawling serpent. At his bidding the demons of the air brought thunder and wind and fog, the fiends of the underworld shook the earth with awful roaring. He brought fire out of the air and consumed the gates of walled cities, and burnt armored men to bits of charred bone. His warriors covered the desert with their numbers, and he had five thousand Stygian troops in war-chariots under the rebel prince Kutamun.

Conan listened unperturbed. War was his trade. Life was a continual battle, or series of battles, since his birth. Death had been a constant companion. It stalked horrifically at his side; stood at his shoulder beside the gaming-tables; its bony fingers rattled the wine-cups. It loomed above him, a hooded and monstrous shadow, when he lay down to sleep. He minded its presence no more than a king minds the presence of his cup-bearer. Some day its bony grasp would close; that was all. It was enough that he lived through the present.

However, others were less careless of fear than he. Striding back from the sentry lines, Conan halted as a slender cloaked figure stayed him with an outstretched hand.

'Princess! You should be in your tent.'

'I could not sleep.' Her dark eyes were haunted in the shadow. 'Conan, I am afraid!'

'Are there men in the host you fear?' His hand locked on his hilt.

'No man,' she shuddered. 'Conan, is there anything you fear?'

He considered, tugging at his chin. 'Aye,' he admitted at last, 'the curse of the gods.'

Again she shuddered. 'I am cursed. A fiend from the abysses has set his mark upon me. Night after night he lurks in the shadows, whispering awful secrets to me. He will drag me down to be his queen in hell. I dare not sleep – he will come to me in my pavilion as he came in the palace. Conan, you are strong – keep me with you! I am afraid!'

She was no longer a princess, but only a terrified girl. Her pride had fallen from her, leaving her unashamed in her nakedness. In her frantic fear she had come to him who seemed strongest. The ruthless power that had repelled her, drew her now.

For answer he drew off his scarlet cloak and wrapped it about her, roughly, as if tenderness of any kind were impossible to him. His iron hand rested for an instant on her slender shoulder, and she shivered again, but not with fear. Like an electric shock a surge of animal vitality swept over her at his mere touch, as if some of his superabundant strength had been imparted to her.

'Lie here.' He indicated a clean-swept space close to a small flickering fire. He saw no incongruity in a princess lying down on the naked ground beside a campfire, wrapped in a warrior's cloak. But she obeyed without question.

He seated himself near her on a boulder, his broadsword across his knees. With the firelight glinting from his blue steel armor, he seemed like an image of steel – dynamic power for the moment quiescent; not resting, but motionless for the instant, awaiting the signal to plunge again into terrific action. The firelight played on his features, making them seem as if carved out of substance shadowy yet hard as steel. They were immobile, but his eyes smoldered with fierce life. He was not merely a wild man; he was part of the wild, one with the untameable elements of life; in his veins ran the blood of the wolf-pack; in his brain lurked the brooding depths of the northern night; his heart throbbed with the fire of blazing forests.

So, half meditating, half dreaming, Yasmela dropped off to sleep, wrapped in a sense of delicious security. Somehow she knew that no flame-eyed shadow would bend over her in the darkness, with this grim figure from the outlands standing guard above her. Yet once again she wakened, to shudder in cosmic fear, though not because of anything she saw.

It was a low mutter of voices that roused her. Opening her eyes, she saw that the fire was burning low. A feeling of dawn was in the air. She could dimly see that Conan still sat on the boulder; she glimpsed the long blue glimmer of his blade. Close beside him crouched another figure, on which the dying fire cast a faint glow. Yasmela drowsily made out a hooked beak of a nose, a glittering bead of an eye, under a white turban. The man was speaking rapidly in a Shemite dialect she found hard to understand.

'Let Bel wither my arm! I speak truth! By Derketo, Conan, I am a prince of liars, but I do not lie to an old comrade. I swear by the days when we were thieves together in the land of Zamora, before you donned hauberk!

'I saw Natohk; with the others I knelt before him when he made incantations to Set. But I did not thrust my nose in the sand as the rest did. I am a thief of Shumir, and my sight is keener than a weasel's. I squinted up and saw his veil blowing in the wind. It blew aside, and I saw – I saw – Bel aid me, Conan, I say I *saw*! My blood froze in my veins and my hair stood up. What I had seen burned my soul like a red-hot iron. I could not rest until I had made sure.

'I journeyed to the ruins of Kuthchemes. The door of the ivory dome stood open; in the doorway lay a great serpent, transfixed by a sword. Within the dome lay the body of a man, so shrivelled and distorted I could scarce make it out at first – it was Shevatas, the Zamorian, the only thief in the world I acknowledged as my superior. The treasure was untouched; it lay in shimmering heaps about the corpse. That was all.'

'There were no bones—' began Conan.

'There was nothing!' broke in the Shemite passionately. 'Nothing! Only the *one* corpse!'

Silence reigned an instant, and Yasmela shrank with a crawling nameless horror.

'Whence came Natohk?' rose the Shemite's vibrant whisper. 'Out of the desert on a night when the world was blind and wild with mad clouds driven in frenzied flight across the shuddering stars, and the howling of the wind was mingled with the shrieking of the spirits of the wastes. Vampires were abroad that night, witches rode naked on the wind, and werewolves howled across the wilderness. On a black camel he came, riding like the wind, and an unholy fire played about him; the cloven tracks of the camel glowed in the darkness. When Natohk dismounted before Set's shrine by the oasis of Aphaka, the beast swept into the night and vanished. And I have talked with tribesmen who swore that it suddenly spread gigantic wings and rushed upwards into the clouds, leaving a trail of fire behind it. No man has seen that camel since that night, but a black brutish man-like shape shambles to Natohk's tent and gibbers to him in the blackness before dawn. I will tell you, Conan, Natohk is – look, I will show you an image of what I saw that day by Shushan when the wind blew aside his veil!'

Yasmela saw the glint of gold in the Shemite's hand, as the men bent closely over something. She heard Conan grunt; and suddenly blackness rolled over her. For the first time in her life, princess Yasmela had fainted.

4

Dawn was still a hint of whiteness in the east when the army was again on the march. Tribesmen had raced into camp, their steeds reeling from the long ride, to report the desert horde encamped at the Well of Altaku. So through the hills the soldiers pushed hastily, leaving the wagon trains to follow. Yasmela rode with them; her eyes were haunted. The nameless horror had been taking even more awful shape, since she had recognized the coin in the Shemite's hand the night before – one of those secretly molded by the degraded Zugite cult, bearing the features of a man dead three thousand years.

The way wound between ragged cliffs and gaunt crags towering over narrow valleys. Here and there villages perched, huddles of stone huts, plastered with mud. The tribesmen swarmed out to join their kin, so that before they had traversed the hills, the host had been swelled by some three thousand wild archers.

Abruptly they came out of the hills and caught their breath at the vast expanse that swept away to the south. On the southern side the hills fell away sheerly, marking a distinct geographical division between the Kothian uplands and the southern desert. The hills were the rim of the uplands, stretching in an almost unbroken wall. Here they were bare and desolate, inhabited only by the Zaheemi clan, whose duty it was to guard the caravan road. Beyond the hills the desert stretched bare, dusty, lifeless. Yet beyond its horizon lay the Well of Altaku, and the horde of Natohk.

The army looked down on the Pass of Shamla, through which flowed the wealth of the north and the south, and through which had marched the armies of Koth, Khoraja, Shem, Turan and Stygia. Here the sheer wall of the rampart was broken. Promontories ran out into the desert, forming barren valleys, all but one of which were closed on the northern extremity by rugged cliffs. This one was the Pass. It was much like a great hand extended from the hills; two fingers, parted, formed a fan-shaped valley. The fingers were represented by a broad ridge on either hand, the outer sides sheer, the inner, steep slopes. The vale pitched upward as it narrowed, to come out on a plateau, flanked by gully-torn slopes. A well was there, and a cluster of stone towers, occupied by the Zaheemis.

There Conan halted, swinging off his horse. He had discarded the plate-armor for the more familiar chain-mail. Thespides reined in and demanded, 'Why do you halt?'

'We'll await them here,' answered Conan.

''T'were more knightly to ride out and meet them,' snapped the count.

'They'd smother us with numbers,' answered the Cimmerian. 'Besides, there's no water out there. We'll camp on the plateau—'

'My knights and I camp in the valley,' retorted Thespides angrily. 'We are the vanguard, and *we*, at least, do not fear a ragged desert swarm.'

Conan shrugged his shoulders and the angry nobleman rode away. Amalric halted in his bellowing order, to watch the glittering company riding down the slope into the valley.

'The fools! Their canteens will soon be empty, and they'll have to ride back up to the well to water their horses.'

'Let them be,' replied Conan. 'It goes hard for them to take orders from me. Tell the dog-brothers to ease their harness and rest. We've marched hard and fast. Water the horses and let the men munch.'

No need to send out scouts. The desert lay bare to the gaze, though just now this view was limited by low-lying clouds which rested in whitish masses on the southern horizon. The monotony was broken only by a jutting tangle of stone ruins, some miles out on the desert, reputedly the remnants of an ancient Stygian temple. Conan dismounted the archers and ranged them along the ridges, with the wild tribesmen. He stationed the mercenaries and the Khoraji spearmen on the plateau about the well. Farther back, in the angle where the hill road debouched on the plateau, was pitched Yasmela's pavilion.

With no enemy in sight, the warriors relaxed. Basinets were doffed, coifs thrown back on mailed shoulders, belts let out. Rude jests flew back and forth as the fighting-men gnawed beef and thrust their muzzles deep into ale-jugs. Along the slopes the hillmen made themselves at ease, nibbling dates and olives. Amalric strode up to where Conan sat bareheaded on a boulder.

'Conan, have you heard what the tribesmen say about Natohk? They say – Mitra, it's too mad even to repeat. What do you think?'

'Seeds rest in the ground for centuries without rotting, sometimes,' answered Conan. 'But surely Natohk is a man.'

'I am not sure,' grunted Amalric. 'At any rate, you've arranged your lines as well as a seasoned general could have done. It's certain Natohk's devils can't fall on us unawares. Mitra, what a fog!'

'I thought it was clouds at first,' answered Conan. 'See how it rolls!'

What had seemed clouds was a thick mist moving northward like a great unstable ocean, rapidly hiding the desert from view. Soon it engulfed the Stygian ruins, and still it rolled onward. The army watched in amazement. It was a thing unprecedented – unnatural and inexplicable.

'No use sending out scouts,' said Amalric disgustedly. 'They couldn't see anything. Its edges are near the outer flanges of the ridges. Soon the whole Pass and these hills will be masked—'

Conan, who had been watching the rolling mist with growing nervousness, bent suddenly and laid his ear to the earth. He sprang up with frantic haste, swearing.

'Horses and chariots, thousands of them! The ground vibrates to their tread! Ho, there!' His voice thundered out across the valley to electrify the lounging men. 'Burganets and pikes, you dogs! Stand to your ranks!'

At that, as the warriors scrambled into their lines, hastily donning head-pieces and thrusting arms through shield-straps, the mist rolled away, as something no longer useful. It did not slowly lift and fade like a natural fog; it simply vanished, like a blown-out flame. One moment the whole desert was hidden with the rolling fleecy billows, piled mountainously, stratum above stratum; the next, the sun shone from a cloudless sky on a naked desert – no longer empty, but thronged with the living pageantry of war. A great shout shook the hills.

At first glance the amazed watchers seemed to be looking down upon a glittering sparkling sea of bronze and gold, where steel points twinkled like a myriad stars. With the lifting of the fog the invaders had halted as if frozen, in long serried lines, flaming in the sun.

First was a long line of chariots, drawn by the great fierce horses of Stygia, with plumes on their heads – snorting and rearing as each naked driver leaned back, bracing his powerful legs, his dusky arms knotted with muscles. The fighting-men in the chariots were tall figures, their hawk-like faces set off by bronze helmets crested with a crescent supporting a golden ball. Heavy bows were in their hands. No common archers these, but nobles of the South, bred to war and the hunt, who were accustomed to bringing down lions with their arrows.

Behind these came a motley array of wild men on half-wild horses – the warriors of Kush, the first of the great black kingdoms of the grasslands south of Stygia. They were shining ebony, supple and lithe, riding stark naked and without saddle or bridle.

After these rolled a horde that seemed to encompass all the desert. Thousands on thousands of the war-like Sons of Shem: ranks of horsemen in scale-mail corselets and cylindrical helmets – the *asshuri* of Nippr, Shumir and Eruk and their sister cities; wild white-robed hordes – the nomad clans.

Now the ranks began to mill and eddy. The chariots drew off to one side while the main host came uncertainly onward. Down in the valley the knights had mounted, and now Count Thespides galloped up the slope to where Conan stood. He did not deign to dismount but spoke abruptly from the saddle.

'The lifting of the mist has confused them! Now is the time to charge! The Kushites have no bows and they mask the whole advance. A charge of my knights will crush them back into the ranks of the Shemites, disrupting their formation. Follow me! We will win this battle with one stroke!'

Conan shook his head. 'Were we fighting a natural foe, I would agree. But this confusion is more feigned than real, as if to draw us into a charge. I fear a trap.'

'Then you refuse to move?' cried Thespides, his face dark with passion.

'Be reasonable,' expostulated Conan. 'We have the advantage of position—'

With a furious oath Thespides wheeled and galloped back down the valley where his knights waited impatiently.

Amalric shook his head. 'You should not have let him return, Conan. I – look there!'

Conan sprang up with a curse. Thespides had swept in beside his men. They could hear his impassioned voice faintly, but his gesture toward the approaching horde was significant enough. In another instant five hundred lances dipped and the steel-clad company was thundering down the valley.

A young page came running from Yasmela's pavilion, crying to Conan in a shrill, eager voice. 'My Lord, the princess asks why you do not follow and support Count Thespides?'

'Because I am not so great a fool as he,' grunted Conan, reseating himself on the boulder and beginning to gnaw a huge beef-bone.

'You grow sober with authority,' quoth Amalric. 'Such madness as that was always your particular joy.'

'Aye, when I had only my own life to consider,' answered Conan. 'Now – what in hell—'

The horde had halted. From the extreme wing rushed a chariot, the naked charioteer lashing the steeds like a madman; the other occupant was a tall figure whose robe floated spectrally on the wind. He held in his arms a great vessel of gold and from it poured a thin stream that sparkled in the sunlight. Across the whole front of the desert horde the chariot swept, and behind its thundering wheels was left, like the wake behind a ship, a long thin powdery line that glittered in the sands like the phosphorescent track of a serpent.

'That's Natohk!' swore Amalric. 'What hellish seed is he sowing?'

The charging knights had not checked their headlong pace. Another fifty paces and they would crash into the uneven Kushite ranks, which stood motionless, spears lifted. Now the foremost knights had reached the thin line that glittered across the sands. They did not heed that crawling menace. But as the steel-shod hoofs of the horses struck it, it was as when steel strikes flint – but with more terrible result. A terrific explosion rocked the desert, which seemed to split apart along the strewn line with an awful burst of white flame.

In that instant the whole foremost line of the knights was seen enveloped in that flame, horses and steel-clad riders withering in the glare like insects in an open blaze. The next instant the rear ranks were piling up on their charred bodies. Unable to check their headlong velocity, rank after rank crashed into the ruins. With appalling suddenness the charge had turned into a shambles where armored figures died amid screaming, mangled horses.

Now the illusion of confusion vanished as the horde settled into orderly lines. The wild Kushites rushed into the shambles, spearing the wounded, bursting the helmets of the knights with stones and iron hammers. It was all over so quickly that the watchers on the slopes stood dazed; and again the horde moved forward, splitting to avoid the charred waste of corpses. From the hills went up a cry: 'We fight not men but devils!'

On either ridge the hillmen wavered. One rushed toward the plateau, froth dripping from his beard.

'Flee, flee!' he slobbered. 'Who can fight Natohk's magic?'

With a snarl Conan bounded from his boulder and smote him with the beef-bone; he dropped, blood starting from nose and mouth. Conan drew his sword, his eyes slits of blue bale-fire.

'Back to your posts!' he yelled. 'Let another take a backward step and I'll shear off his head! Fight, damn you!'

The rout halted as quickly as it had begun. Conan's fierce personality was like a dash of ice-water in their whirling blaze of terror.

'Take your places,' he directed quickly. 'And stand to it! Neither man nor devil comes up Shamla Pass this day!'

Where the plateau rim broke to the valley slope the mercenaries braced their belts and gripped their spears. Behind them the lancers sat their steeds, and to one side were stationed the Khoraja spearmen as reserves. To Yasmela, standing white and speechless at the door of her tent, the host seemed a pitiful handful in comparison to the thronging desert horde.

Conan stood among the spearmen. He knew the invaders would not try to drive a chariot charge up the Pass in the teeth of the archers, but he grunted with surprize to see the riders dismounting. These wild men had no supply trains. Canteens and pouches hung at their saddle-peaks. Now they drank the last of their water and threw the canteens away.

'This is the death-grip,' he muttered as the lines formed on foot. 'I'd rather have had a cavalry charge; wounded horses bolt and ruin formations.'

The horde had formed into a huge wedge, of which the tip was the Stygians and the body, the mailed *asshuri*, flanked by the nomads. In close formation, shields lifted, they rolled onward, while behind them a tall figure in a motionless chariot lifted wide-robed arms in grisly invocation.

As the horde entered the wide valley mouth the hillmen loosed their shafts. In spite of the protective formation, men dropped by dozens. The Stygians had discarded their bows; helmeted heads bent to the blast, dark eyes glaring over the rims of their shields, they came on in an inexorable surge, striding over their fallen comrades. But the Shemites gave back the fire, and the clouds of arrows darkened the skies. Conan gazed over the billowing waves of spears and wondered what new horror the sorcerer would invoke. Somehow he felt that Natohk, like all his kind, was more terrible in defense than in attack; to take the offensive against him invited disaster.

But surely it was magic that drove the horde on in the teeth of death. Conan caught his breath at the havoc wrought in the onsweeping ranks. The edges of the wedge seemed to be melting away, and already the valley was strewn with dead men. Yet the survivors came on like madmen unaware of death. By the very numbers of their bows, they began to swamp the archers on the cliffs. Clouds of shafts sped upward, driving the hillmen to cover. Panic struck at their hearts at that unwavering advance, and they plied their bows madly, eyes glaring like trapped wolves.

As the horde neared the narrower neck of the Pass, boulders thundered down, crushing men by the scores, but the charge did not waver. Conan's wolves braced themselves for the inevitable concussion. In their close formation and superior armor, they took little hurt from the arrows. It was the impact of the charge Conan feared, when the huge wedge should crash against his thin ranks. And he realized now there was no breaking of that onslaught. He gripped the shoulder of a Zaheemi who stood near.

'Is there any way by which mounted men can get down into the blind valley beyond that western ridge?'

'Aye, a steep, perilous path, secret and eternally guarded. But—'

Conan was dragging him along to where Amalric sat upon his great war-horse.

'Amalric!' he snapped. 'Follow this man! He'll lead you into yon outer valley. Ride down it, circle the end of the ridge, and strike the horde from the rear. Speak not, but go! I know it's madness, but we're doomed anyway; we'll do all the damage we can before we die! Haste!'

Amalric's mustache bristled in a fierce grin, and a few moments later his lancers were following the guide into a tangle of gorges leading off from the plateau. Conan ran back to the pikemen, sword in hand.

He was not too soon. On either ridge Shupras's hillmen, mad with anticipation of defeat, rained down their shafts desperately. Men died like flies in the valley and along the slopes – and with a roar and an irresistible upward surge the Stygians crashed against the mercenaries.

In a hurricane of thundering steel, the lines twisted and swayed. It was war-bred noble against professional soldier. Shields crashed against shields, and between them spears drove in and blood spurted.

Conan saw the mighty form of prince Kutamun across the sea of swords, but the press held him hard, breast to breast with dark shapes that gasped and slashed. Behind the Stygians the *asshuri* were surging and yelling.

On either hand the nomads climbed the cliffs and came to handgrips with their mountain kin. All along the crests of the ridges the combat raged in blind, gasping ferocity. Tooth and nail, frothing mad with fanaticism and ancient feuds, the tribesmen rent and slew and died. Wild hair flying, the naked Kushites ran howling into the fray.

It seemed to Conan that his sweat-blinded eyes looked down into a rising ocean of steel that seethed and eddied, filling the valley from ridge to ridge. The fight was at a bloody deadlock. The hillmen held the ridges, and the mercenaries, gripping their dipping pikes, bracing their feet in the bloody earth, held the Pass. Superior position and armor for a space balanced the advantage of overwhelming numbers. But it could not endure. Wave after wave of glaring faces and flashing spears surged up the slope, the *asshuri* filling the gaps in the Stygian ranks.

Conan looked to see Amalric's lancers rounding the western ridge, but they did not come, and the pikemen began to reel back under the shocks. And Conan abandoned all hope of victory and of life. Yelling a command to his gasping captains, he broke away and raced across the plateau to the Khoraja reserves who stood trembling with eagerness. He did not glance toward Yasmela's pavilion. He had forgotten the princess; his one thought was the wild beast instinct to slay before he died.

'This day you become knights!' he laughed fiercely, pointing with his dripping sword toward the hillmen's horses, herded nearby. 'Mount and follow me to hell!'

The hill steed reared wildly under the unfamiliar clash of the Kothic armor, and Conan's gusty laugh rose above the din as he led them to where the eastern ridge branched away from the plateau. Five hundred footmen – pauper patricians, younger sons, black sheep – on half-wild Shemite horses, charging an army, down a slope where no cavalry had ever dared charge before!

Past the battle-choked mouth of the Pass they thundered, out onto the corpse-littered ridge. Down the steep slope they rushed, and a score lost their footing and rolled under the hoofs of their comrades. Below them men screamed and threw up their arms – and the thundering charge ripped through them as an avalanche cuts through a forest of saplings. On through the close-packed throngs the Khorajis hurtled, leaving a crushed-down carpet of dead.

And then, as the horde writhed and coiled upon itself, Amalric's lancers, having cut through a cordon of horsemen encountered in the outer valley, swept around the extremity of the western ridge and smote the host in a steel-tipped wedge, splitting it asunder. His attack carried all the dazing demoralization of a surprize on the rear. Thinking themselves flanked by a superior force and frenzied at the fear of being cut off from the desert, swarms of nomads broke and stampeded, working havoc in the ranks of their more steadfast comrades. These staggered and the horsemen rode through them. Up on the ridges the desert fighters wavered, and the hillmen fell on them with renewed fury, driving them down the slopes.

Stunned by surprize, the horde broke before they had time to see it was but a handful which assailed them. And once broken, not even a magician could weld such a horde again. Across the sea of heads and spears Conan's madmen saw Amalric's riders forging steadily through the rout, to the rise and fall of axes and maces, and a mad joy of victory exalted each man's heart and made his arm steel.

Bracing their feet in the wallowing sea of blood whose crimson waves lapped about their ankles, the pikemen in the Pass mouth drove forward, crushing strongly against the milling ranks before them. The Stygians held, but behind them the press of the *asshuri* melted; and over the bodies of the nobles of the South who died in their tracks to a man, the mercenaries rolled, to split and crumple the wavering mass behind.

Up on the cliffs old Shupras lay with an arrow through his heart; Amalric was down, swearing like a pirate, a spear through his mailed thigh. Of Conan's mounted infantry, scarce a hundred and fifty remained in the saddle. But the horde was shattered. Nomads and mailed spearmen broke away, fleeing to their camp where their horses were, and the hillmen swarmed down the slopes, stabbing the fugitives in the back, cutting the throats of the wounded.

In the swirling red chaos a terrible apparition suddenly appeared before Conan's rearing steed. It was prince Kutamun, naked but for a loin-cloth, his harness hacked away, his crested helmet dented, his limbs splashed with blood. With a terrible shout he hurled his broken hilt full into Conan's face, and leaping, seized the stallion's bridle. The Cimmerian reeled in his saddle, half stunned, and with awful strength the dark-skinned giant forced the screaming steed upward and backward, until it lost its footing and crashed into the muck of bloody sand and writhing bodies.

Conan sprang clear as the horse fell, and with a roar Kutamun was on him. In that mad nightmare of battle, the barbarian never exactly knew how he killed his man. He only knew that a stone in the Stygian's hand crashed again and again on his basinet, filling his sight with flashing sparks, as Conan drove his dagger again and again into his foe's body, without apparent effect on the prince's terrible vitality. The world was swimming to Conan's sight, when with a convulsive shudder the frame that strained against his stiffened and then went limp.

Reeling up, blood streaming down his face from under his dented helmet, Conan glared dizzily at the profusion of destruction which spread before him. From crest to crest the dead lay strewn, a red carpet that choked the valley. It was like a red sea, with each wave a straggling line of corpses. They choked the neck of the Pass, they littered the slopes. And down in the desert the slaughter continued, where the survivors of the horde had reached their horses and streamed out across the waste, pursued by the weary victors – and Conan stood appalled as he noted how few of these were left to pursue.

Then an awful scream rent the clamor. Up the valley a chariot came flying, making nothing of the heaped corpses. No horses drew it, but a great black creature that was like a camel. In the chariot stood Natohk, his robes flying; and gripping the reins and lashing like mad, crouched a black anthropomorphic being that might have been a monster ape.

With a rush of burning wind the chariot swept up the corpse-littered slope, straight toward the pavilion where Yasmela stood alone, deserted by her guards in the frenzy of pursuit. Conan, standing frozen, heard her frenzied scream as Natohk's long arm swept her up into the chariot. Then the grisly steed wheeled and came racing back down the valley, and no man dared speed arrow or spear lest he strike Yasmela, who writhed in Natohk's arms.

With an inhuman cry Conan caught up his fallen sword and leaped into the path of the hurtling horror. But even as his sword went up, the forefeet of the black beast smote him like a thunderbolt and sent him hurtling a score feet away, dazed and bruised. Yasmela's cry came hauntingly to his stunned ears as the chariot roared by.

A yell that had nothing of the human in its timbre rang from his lips as Conan rebounded from the bloody earth and seized the rein of a riderless horse that raced past him, throwing himself into the saddle without bringing the charger to a halt. With mad abandon he raced after the rapidly receding chariot. He struck the levels flying, and passed like a whirlwind through the Shemite camp. Into the desert he fled, passing clumps of his own riders, and hard-spurring desert horsemen.

On flew the chariot, and on raced Conan, though his horse began to reel beneath him. Now the open desert lay all about them, bathed in the lurid desolate splendor of sunset. Before him rose up the ancient ruins, and with a shriek that froze the blood in Conan's veins, the unhuman charioteer cast Natohk and the girl from him. They rolled on the sand, and to Conan's dazed gaze, the chariot and its steed altered awfully. Great wings spread from a black horror that in no way resembled a camel, and it rushed upward into the sky, bearing in its wake a shape of blinding flame, in which a black man-like shape gibbered in ghastly triumph. So quickly it passed, that it was like the rush of a nightmare through a horror-haunted dream.

Natohk sprang up, cast a swift look at his grim pursuer, who had not halted but came riding hard, with sword swinging low and spattering red drops; and the sorcerer caught up the fainting girl and ran with her into the ruins.

Conan leaped from his horse and plunged after them. He came into a room that glowed with unholy radiance, though outside the dusk was falling swiftly. On a black jade altar lay Yasmela, her naked body gleaming like ivory in the weird light. Her garments lay strewn on the floor, as if ripped from her in brutal haste. Natohk faced the Cimmerian – inhumanly tall and lean, clad in shimmering green silk. He tossed back his veil, and Conan looked into the features he had seen depicted on the Zugite coin.

'Aye, blench, dog!' The voice was like the hiss of a giant serpent. 'I am Thugra Khotan! Long I lay in my tomb, awaiting the day of awakening and release. The arts which saved me from the barbarians long ago likewise imprisoned me, but I knew one would come in time – and he came, to fulfill his destiny, and to die as no man has died in three thousand years!

'Fool, do you think you have conquered because my people are scattered? Because I have been betrayed and deserted by the demon I enslaved? I am Thugra Khotan, who shall rule the world despite your paltry gods! The desert is filled with my people; the demons of the earth shall do my bidding, as the reptiles of the earth obey me. Lust for a woman weakened my sorcery. Now the woman is mine, and feasting on her soul, I shall be unconquerable! Back, fool! You have not conquered Thugra Khotan!'

He cast his staff and it fell at the feet of Conan, who recoiled with an involuntary cry. For as it fell it altered horribly; its outline melted and writhed, and a hooded cobra reared up hissing before the horrified Cimmerian. With a furious oath Conan struck, and his sword sheared the horrid shape in half. And there at his feet lay only the two pieces of a severed ebon staff. Thugra Khotan laughed awfully, and wheeling, caught up something that crawled loathsomely in the dust of the floor.

In his extended hand something alive writhed and slavered. No tricks of shadows this time. In his naked hand Thugra Khotan gripped a black scorpion, more than a foot in length, the deadliest creature of the desert, the stroke of whose spiked tail was instant death. Thugra Khotan's skull-like countenance split in a mummy-like grin. Conan hesitated; then without warning he threw his sword.

Caught off guard, Thugra Khotan had no time to avoid the cast. The point struck beneath his heart and stood out a foot behind his shoulders. He went down, crushing the poisonous monster in his grasp as he fell.

Conan strode to the altar, lifting Yasmela in his blood-stained arms. She threw her white arms convulsively about his mailed neck, sobbing hysterically, and would not let him go.

'Crom's devils, girl!' he grunted. 'Loose me! Fifty thousand men have perished today, and there is work for me to do—'

'No!' she gasped, clinging with convulsive strength, as barbaric for the instant as he in her fear and passion. 'I will not let you go! I am yours, by fire and steel and blood! You are mine! Back there, I belong to others – here I am mine – and yours! You shall not go!'

He hesitated, his own brain reeling with the fierce upsurging of his violent passions. The lurid unearthly glow still hovered in the shadowy chamber, lighting ghostlily the dead face of Thugra Khotan, which seemed to grin mirthlessly and cavernously at them. Out on the desert, in the hills among the oceans of dead, men were dying, were howling with wounds and thirst and madness, and kingdoms were staggering. Then all was swept away by the crimson tide that rode madly in Conan's soul, as he crushed fiercely in his iron arms the slim white body that shimmered like a witch-fire of madness before him.

THE SLITHERING SHADOW

1

THE DESERT SHIMMERED IN the heat waves. Conan the Cimmerian stared out over the aching desolation and involuntarily drew the back of his powerful hand over his blackened lips. He stood like a bronze image in the sand, apparently impervious to the murderous sun, though his only garment was a silk loin-cloth, girdled by a wide gold-buckled belt from which hung a saber and a broad-bladed poniard. On his clean-cut limbs were evidences of scarcely healed wounds.

At his feet rested a girl, one white arm clasping his knee, against which her blond head drooped. Her white skin contrasted with his hard bronzed limbs; her short silken tunic, low-necked and sleeveless, girdled at the waist, emphasized rather than concealed her lithe figure.

Conan shook his head, blinking. The sun's glare half blinded him. He lifted a small canteen from his belt and shook it, scowling at the faint splashing within.

The girl moved wearily, whimpering.

'Oh, Conan, we shall die here! I am so thirsty!'

The Cimmerian growled wordlessly, glaring truculently at the surrounding waste, with outthrust jaw, and blue eyes smoldering savagely from under his black tousled mane, as if the desert were a tangible enemy.

He stooped and put the canteen to the girl's lips.

'Drink till I tell you to stop, Natala,' he commanded.

She drank with little panting gasps, and he did not check her. Only when the canteen was empty did she realize that he had deliberately allowed her to drink all their water supply, little enough that it was.

Tears sprang to her eyes. 'Oh, Conan,' she wailed, wringing her hands, 'why did you let me drink it all? I did not know – now there is none for you!'

'Hush,' he growled. 'Don't waste your strength in weeping.'

Straightening, he threw the canteen from him.

'Why did you do that?' she whispered.

He did not reply, standing motionless and immobile, his fingers closing slowly about the hilt of his saber. He was not looking at the girl; his fierce eyes seemed to plumb the mysterious purple hazes of the distance.

Endowed with all the barbarian's ferocious love of life and instinct to live, Conan the Cimmerian yet knew that he had reached the end of his trail. He had not come to the limits of his endurance, but he knew another day under the merciless sun in those waterless wastes would bring him down. As for the girl, she had suffered enough. Better a quick painless sword-stroke than the lingering agony that faced him. Her thirst was temporarily quenched; it was a false mercy to let her suffer until delirium and death brought relief. Slowly he slid the saber from its sheath.

He halted suddenly, stiffening. Far out on the desert to the south, something glimmered through the heat waves.

At first he thought it was a phantom, one of the mirages which had mocked and maddened him in that accursed desert. Shading his sun-dazzled eyes, he made out spires and minarets, and gleaming walls. He watched it grimly, waiting for it to fade and vanish. Natala had ceased to sob; she struggled to her knees and followed his gaze.

'Is it a city, Conan?' she whispered, too fearful to hope. 'Or is it but a shadow?'

The Cimmerian did not reply for a space. He closed and opened his eyes several times; he looked away, then back. The city remained where he had first seen it.

'The devil knows,' he grunted. 'It's worth a try, though.'

He thrust the saber back in its sheath. Stooping, he lifted Natala in his mighty arms as though she had been an infant. She resisted weakly.

'Don't waste your strength carrying me, Conan,' she pleaded. 'I can walk.'

'The ground gets rockier here,' he answered. 'You would soon wear your sandals to shreds,' glancing at her soft green foot-wear. 'Besides, if we are to reach that city at all, we must do it quickly, and I can make better time this way.'

The chance for life had lent fresh vigor and resilience to the Cimmerian's steely thews. He strode out across the sandy waste as if he had just begun the journey. A barbarian of barbarians, the vitality and endurance of the wild were his, granting him survival where civilized men would have perished.

He and the girl were, so far as he knew, the sole survivors of Prince Almuric's army, that mad motley horde which, following the defeated rebel prince of Koth, swept through the Lands of Shem like a devastating sandstorm and drenched the outlands of Stygia with blood. With a Stygian host on its heels, it had cut its way through the black kingdom of Kush, only to be annihilated on the edge of the southern desert. Conan likened it in his mind to a great torrent, dwindling gradually as it rushed southward, to run dry at last in the sands of the naked desert. The bones of its members – mercenaries, outcasts, broken men, outlaws – lay strewn from the Kothic uplands to the dunes of the wilderness.

From that final slaughter, when the Stygians and the Kushites closed in on the trapped remnants, Conan had cut his way clear and fled on a camel with the girl. Behind them the land swarmed with enemies; the only way open to them was the desert to the south. Into those menacing depths they had plunged.

The girl was Brythunian, whom Conan had found in the slave-market of a stormed Shemite city, and appropriated. She had had nothing to say in the matter, but her new position was so far superior to the lot of any Hyborian woman in a Shemitish seraglio, that she accepted it thankfully. So she had shared in the adventures of Almuric's damned horde.

For days they had fled into the desert, pursued so far by Stygian horsemen that when they shook off the pursuit, they dared not turn back. They pushed on, seeking water, until the camel died. Then they went on foot. For the past few days their suffering had been intense. Conan had shielded Natala all he could, and the rough life of the camp had given her more stamina and strength than the average woman possesses; but even so, she was not far from collapse.

The sun beat fiercely on Conan's tangled black mane. Waves of dizziness and nausea rose in his brain, but he set his teeth and strode on unwaveringly. He was convinced that the city was a reality and not a mirage. What they would find there he had no idea. The inhabitants might be hostile. Nevertheless it was a fighting chance, and that was as much as he had ever asked.

The sun was nigh to setting when they halted in front of the massive gate, grateful for the shade. Conan stood Natala on her feet, and stretched his aching arms. Above them the walls towered some thirty feet in height, composed of a smooth greenish substance that shone almost like glass. Conan scanned the parapets, expecting to be challenged, but saw no one. Impatiently he shouted, and banged on the gate with his saber-hilt, but only the hollow echoes mocked him. Natala cringed close to him, frightened by the silence. Conan tried the portal, and stepped back, drawing his saber, as it swung silently inward. Natala stifled a cry.

'Oh, look, Conan!'

Just inside the gate lay a human body. Conan glared at it narrowly, then looked beyond it. He saw a wide open expanse, like a court, bordered by the arched doorways of houses composed of the same greenish material as the outer walls. These edifices were lofty and imposing, pinnacled with shining domes and minarets. There was no sign of life among them. In the center of the court rose the square curb of a well, and the sight stung Conan, whose mouth felt caked with dry dust. Taking Natala's wrist he drew her through the gate, and closed it behind them.

'Is he dead?' she whispered, shrinkingly indicating the man who lay limply before the gate. The body was that of a tall powerful individual, apparently in his prime; the skin was yellow, the eyes slightly slanted; otherwise the man differed little from the Hyborian type. He was clad in high-strapped sandals and a tunic of purple silk, and a short sword in a cloth-of-gold scabbard hung from his girdle. Conan felt his flesh. It was cold. There was no sign of life in the body.

'Not a wound on him,' grunted the Cimmerian, 'but he's dead as Almuric with forty Stygian arrows in him. In Crom's name, let's see to the well! If there's water in it, we'll drink, dead men or no.'

There was water in the well, but they did not drink of it. Its level was a good fifty feet below the curb, and there was nothing to draw it up with. Conan cursed blackly, maddened by the sight of the stuff just out of his reach, and turned to look for some means of obtaining it. Then a scream from Natala brought him about.

The supposedly dead man was rushing upon him, eyes blazing with indisputable life, his short sword gleaming in his hand. Conan cursed amazedly, but wasted no time in conjecture. He met the hurtling attacker with a slashing cut of his saber that sheared through flesh and bone. The fellow's head thudded on the flags; the body staggered drunkenly, an arch of blood jetting from the severed jugular; then it fell heavily.

Conan glared down, swearing softly.

'This fellow is no deader now than he was a few minutes agone. Into what madhouse have we strayed?'

Natala, who had covered her eyes with her hands at the sight, peeked between her fingers and shook with fear.

'Oh, Conan, will the people of the city not kill us, because of this?'

'Well,' he growled, 'this creature would have killed us if I hadn't lopped off his head.'

He glanced at the archways that gaped blankly from the green walls above them. He saw no hint of movement, heard no sound.

'I don't think any one saw us,' he muttered. 'I'll hide the evidence—'

He lifted the limp carcass by its swordbelt with one hand, and grasping the head by its long hair in the other, he half carried, half dragged the ghastly remains over to the well.

'Since we can't drink this water,' he gritted vindictively, 'I'll see that nobody else enjoys drinking it. Curse such a well, anyway!' He heaved the body over the curb and let it drop, tossing the head after it. A dull splash sounded far beneath.

'There's blood on the stones,' whispered Natala.

'There'll be more unless I find water soon,' growled the Cimmerian, his short store of patience about exhausted. The girl had almost forgotten her thirst and hunger in her fear, but not Conan.

'We'll go into one of these doors,' he said. 'Surely we'll find people after awhile.'

'Oh, Conan!' she wailed, snuggling up as close to him as she could. 'I'm afraid! This is a city of ghosts and dead men! Let us go back into the desert! Better to die there, than to face these terrors!'

'We'll go into the desert when they throw us off the walls,' he snarled. 'There's water somewhere in this city, and I'll find it, if I have to kill every man in it.'

'But what if they come to life again?' she whispered.

'Then I'll keep killing them until they stay dead!' he snapped. 'Come on! That doorway is as good as another! Stay behind me, but don't run unless I tell you to.'

She murmured a faint assent and followed him so closely that she stepped on his heels, to his irritation. Dusk had fallen, filling the strange city with purple shadows. They entered the open doorway, and found themselves in a wide chamber, the walls of which were hung with velvet tapestries, worked in curious designs. Floor, walls and ceiling were of the green glassy stone, the walls decorated with gold frieze-work. Furs and satin cushions littered the floor. Several doorways let into other rooms. They passed through, and traversed several chambers, counterparts of the first. They saw no one, but the Cimmerian grunted suspiciously.

'Some one was here not long ago. This couch is still warm from contact with a human body. That silk cushion bears the imprint of some one's hips. Then there's a faint scent of perfume lingering in the air.'

A weird unreal atmosphere hung over all. Traversing this dim silent palace was like an opium dream. Some of the chambers were unlighted, and these they avoided. Others were bathed in a soft weird light that seemed to emanate from jewels set in the walls in fantastic designs. Suddenly, as they passed into one of these illumined chambers, Natala cried out and clutched her companion's arm. With a curse he wheeled, glaring for an enemy, bewildered because he saw none.

'What's the matter?' he snarled. 'If you ever grab my sword-arm again, I'll skin you. Do you want me to get my throat cut? What were you yelling about?'

'Look there,' she quavered, pointing.

Conan grunted. On a table of polished ebony stood golden vessels, apparently containing food and drink. The room was unoccupied.

'Well, whoever this feast is prepared for,' he growled, 'he'll have to look elsewhere tonight.'

'Dare we eat it, Conan?' ventured the girl nervously. 'The people might come upon us, and—'

'*Lir an mannanan mac lir!*' he swore, grabbing her by the nape of her neck and thrusting her into a gilded chair at the end of the table with no great ceremony. 'We starve and you make objections! Eat!'

He took the chair at the other end, and seizing a jade goblet, emptied it at a gulp. It contained a crimson wine-like liquor of a peculiar tang, unfamiliar to him, but it was like nectar to his parched gullet. His thirst allayed, he attacked the food before him with rare gusto. It too was strange to him: exotic fruits and unknown meats. The vessels were of exquisite workmanship, and there were golden knives and forks as well. These Conan ignored, grasping the meat-joints in his fingers and tearing them with his strong teeth. The Cimmerian's table manners were rather wolfish at any time. His civilized companion ate more daintily, but just as ravenously. It occurred to Conan that the food might be poisoned, but the thought did not lessen his appetite; he preferred to die of poisoning rather than starvation.

His hunger satisfied, he leaned back with a deep sigh of relief. That there were humans in that silent city was evidenced by the fresh food, and perhaps every dark corner concealed a lurking enemy. But he felt no apprehension on that score, having a large confidence in his own fighting ability. He began to feel sleepy, and considered the idea of stretching himself on a near-by couch for a nap.

Not so Natala. She was no longer hungry and thirsty, but she felt no desire to sleep. Her lovely eyes were very wide indeed as she timidly glanced at the doorways, boundaries of the unknown. The silence and mystery of the strange place preyed on her. The chamber seemed larger, the table longer than she had first noticed, and she realized that she was farther from her grim protector than she wished to be. Rising quickly, she went around the table and seated herself on his knee, glancing nervously at the arched doorways. Some were lighted and some were not, and it was at the unlighted ones she gazed longest.

'We have eaten, drunk and rested,' she urged. 'Let us leave this place, Conan. It's evil. I can feel it.'

'Well, we haven't been harmed so far,' he began, when a soft but sinister rustling brought him about. Thrusting the girl off his knee he rose with the quick ease of a panther, drawing his saber, facing the doorway from which the sound had seemed to come. It was not repeated, and he stole forward noiselessly, Natala following with her heart in her mouth. She knew he suspected peril. His outthrust head was sunk between his giant shoulders, he glided forward in a half crouch, like a stalking tiger. He made no more noise than a tiger would have made.

At the doorway he halted, Natala peering fearfully from behind him. There was no light in the room, but it was partially illuminated by the radiance behind them, which streamed across it into yet another chamber. And in this chamber a man lay on a raised dais. The soft light bathed him, and they saw he was a counterpart of the man Conan had killed before the outer gate, except that his garments were richer, and ornamented with jewels which twinkled in the uncanny light. Was he dead, or merely sleeping? Again came that faint sinister sound, as if some one had thrust aside a hanging. Conan drew back, drawing the clinging Natala with him. He clapped his hand over her mouth just in time to check her shriek.

From where they now stood, they could no longer see the dais, but they could see the shadow it cast on the wall behind it. And now another shadow moved across the wall: a huge shapeless black blot. Conan felt his hair prickle curiously as he watched. Distorted though it might be, he felt that he had never seen a man or beast which cast such a shadow. He was consumed with curiosity, but some instinct held him frozen in his tracks. He heard Natala's quick panting gasps as she stared with dilated eyes. No other sound disturbed the tense stillness. The great shadow engulfed that of the dais. For a long instant only its black bulk was thrown on the smooth wall. Then slowly it receded, and once more the dais was etched darkly against the wall. But the sleeper was no longer upon it.

An hysterical gurgle rose in Natala's throat, and Conan gave her an admonitory shake. He was aware of an iciness in his own veins. Human foes he did not fear; anything understandable, however grisly, caused no tremors in his broad breast. But this was beyond his ken.

After a while, however, his curiosity conquered his uneasiness, and he moved out into the unlighted chamber again, ready for anything. Looking into the other room, he saw it was empty. The dais stood as he had first seen it, except that no bejeweled human lay thereon. Only on its silken covering shone a single drop of blood, like a great crimson gem. Natala saw it and gave a low choking cry, for which Conan did not punish her. Again he felt the icy hand of fear. On that dais a man had lain; *something* had crept into the chamber and carried him away. What that something was, Conan had no idea, but an aura of unnatural horror hung over those dim-lit chambers.

He was ready to depart. Taking Natala's hand, he turned back, then hesitated. Somewhere back among the chambers they had traversed, he heard the sound of a footfall. A human foot, bare or softly shod, had made that sound, and Conan, with the wariness of a wolf, turned quickly aside. He believed he could come again into the outer court, and yet avoid the room from which the sound had appeared to come.

But they had not crossed the first chamber on their new route, when the rustle of a silken hanging brought them about suddenly. Before a curtained alcove stood a man eyeing them intently.

He was exactly like the others they had encountered: tall, well made, clad in purple garments, with a jeweled girdle. There was neither surprize nor hostility in his amber eyes. They were dreamy as a lotus-eater's. He did not draw the short sword at his side. After a tense moment he spoke, in a far-away detached tone, and a language his hearers did not understand.

On a venture Conan replied in Stygian, and the stranger answered in the same tongue: 'Who are you?'

'I am Conan, a Cimmerian,' answered the barbarian. 'This is Natala, of Brythunia. What city is this?'

The man did not at once reply. His dreamy sensuous gaze rested on Natala, and he drawled, 'Of all my rich visions, this is the strangest! Oh, girl of the golden locks, from what far dreamland do you come? From Andarra, or Tothra, or Kuth of the star-girdle?'

'What madness is this?' growled the Cimmerian harshly, not relishing the man's words or manner.

The other did not heed him.

'I have dreamed more gorgeous beauties,' he murmured; 'lithe women with hair dusky as night, and dark eyes of unfathomed mystery. But your skin is white as milk, your eyes as clear as dawn, and there is about you a freshness and daintiness alluring as honey. Come to my couch, little dream-girl!'

He advanced and reached for her, and Conan struck aside his hand with a force that might have broken his arm. The man reeled back, clutching the numbed member, his eyes clouding.

'What rebellion of ghosts is this?' he muttered. 'Barbarian, I command ye – begone! Fade! Dissipate! Fade! Vanish!'

'I'll vanish your head from your shoulders!' snarled the infuriated Cimmerian, his saber gleaming in his hand. 'Is this the welcome you give strangers? By Crom, I'll drench these hangings in blood!'

The dreaminess had faded from the other's eyes, to be replaced by a look of bewilderment.

'Thog!' he ejaculated. 'You are real! Whence come you? Who are you? What do you in Xuthal?'

'We came from the desert,' Conan growled. 'We wandered into the city at dusk, famishing. We found a feast set for some one, and we ate it. I have no money to pay for it. In my country, no starving man is denied food, but you civilized people must have your recompense – if you are like all I ever met. We have done no harm and we were just leaving. By Crom, I do not like this place, where dead men rise, and sleeping men vanish into the bellies of shadows!'

The man started violently at the last comment, his yellow face turning ashy.

'What do you say? Shadows? Into the bellies of shadows?'

'Well,' answered the Cimmerian cautiously, 'whatever it is that takes a man from a sleeping-dais and leaves only a spot of blood.'

'You have seen? You have *seen*?' The man was shaking like a leaf; his voice cracked on the high-pitched note.

'Only a man sleeping on a dais, and a shadow that engulfed him,' answered Conan.

The effect of his words on the other was horrifying. With an awful scream the man turned and rushed from the chamber. In his blind haste he caromed from the side of the door, righted himself, and fled through the adjoining chambers, still screaming at the top of his voice. Amazed, Conan stared after him, the girl trembling as she clutched the giant's arm. They could no longer see the flying figure, but they still heard his frightful screams, dwindling in the distance, and echoing as from vaulted roofs. Suddenly one cry, louder than the others, rose and broke short, followed by blank silence.

'Crom!'

Conan wiped the perspiration from his forehead with a hand that was not entirely steady.

'Surely this is a city of the mad! Let's get out of here, before we meet other madmen!'

'It is all a nightmare!' whimpered Natala. 'We are dead and damned! We died out on the desert and are in hell! We are disembodied spirits – *ow*!' Her yelp was induced by a resounding spank from Conan's open hand.

'You're no spirit when a pat makes you yell like that,' he commented, with the grim humor which frequently manifested itself at inopportune times. 'We are alive, though we may not be if we loiter in this devil-haunted pile. Come!'

They had traversed but a single chamber when again they stopped short. Some one or something was approaching. They faced the doorway whence the sounds came, waiting for they knew not what. Conan's nostrils widened, and his eyes narrowed. He caught the faint scent of the perfume he had noticed earlier in the night. A figure framed itself in the doorway. Conan swore under his breath; Natala's red lips opened wide.

It was a woman who stood there staring at them in wonder. She was tall, lithe, shaped like a goddess; clad in a narrow girdle crusted with jewels. A burnished mass of night-black hair set off the whiteness of her ivory body. Her dark eyes, shaded by long dusky lashes, were deep with sensuous mystery. Conan caught his breath at her beauty, and Natala stared with dilated eyes. The Cimmerian had never seen such a woman; her facial outline was Stygian, but she was not dusky-skinned like the Stygian women he had known; her limbs were like alabaster.

But when she spoke, in a deep rich musical voice, it was in the Stygian tongue.

'Who are you? What do you in Xuthal? Who is that girl?'

'Who are you?' bluntly countered Conan, who quickly wearied of answering questions.

'I am Thalis the Stygian,' she replied. 'Are you mad, to come here?'

'I've been thinking I must be,' he growled. 'By Crom, if I am sane, I'm out of place here, because these people are all maniacs. We stagger in from the desert, dying of thirst and hunger, and we come upon a dead man who tries to stab me in the back. We enter a palace rich and luxuriant, yet apparently empty. We find a meal set, but with no feasters. Then we see a shadow devour a sleeping man—' He watched her narrowly and saw her change color slightly. 'Well?'

'Well what?' she demanded, apparently regaining control of herself.

'I was just waiting for you to run through the rooms howling like a wild woman,' he answered. 'The man I told about the shadow did.'

She shrugged her slim ivory shoulders. 'That was the screams I heard, then. Well, to every man his fate, and it's foolish to squeal like a rat in a trap. When Thog wants me, he will come for me.'

'Who is Thog?' demanded Conan suspiciously.

She gave him a long appraising stare that brought color to Natala's face and made her bite her small red lip.

'Sit down on that divan and I will tell you,' she said. 'But first tell me your names.'

'I am Conan, a Cimmerian, and this is Natala, a daughter of Brythunia,' he answered. 'We are refugees of an army destroyed on the borders of Kush. But I am not desirous of sitting down, where black shadows might steal up on my back.'

With a light musical laugh, she seated herself, stretching out her supple limbs with studied abandon.

'Be at ease,' she advised. 'If Thog wishes you, he will take you, wherever you are. That man you mentioned, who screamed and ran – did you not hear him give one great cry, and then fall silent? In his frenzy, he must have run full into that which he sought to escape. No man can avoid his fate.'

Conan grunted non-committally, but he sat down on the edge of a couch, his saber across his knees, his eyes wandering suspiciously about the chamber. Natala nestled against him, clutching him jealously, her legs tucked up under her. She eyed the stranger woman with suspicion and resentment. She felt small and dust-stained and insignificant before this glamorous beauty, and she could not mistake the look in the dark eyes which feasted on every detail of the bronzed giant's physique.

'What is this place, and who are these people?' demanded Conan.

'This city is called Xuthal; it is very ancient. It is built over an oasis, which the founders of Xuthal found in their wanderings. They came from the east, so long ago that not even their descendants remember the age.'

'Surely there are not many of them; these palaces seem empty.'

'No; and yet more than you might think. The city is really one great palace, with every building inside the walls closely connected with the others. You might walk among these chambers for hours and see no one. At other times, you would meet hundreds of the inhabitants.'

'How is that?' Conan inquired uneasily; this savored too strongly of sorcery for comfort.

'Much of the time these people lie in sleep. Their dream-life is as important – and to them as real – as their waking life. You have heard of the black lotus? In certain pits of the city it grows. Through the ages they have cultivated it, until, instead of death, its juice induces dreams, gorgeous and fantastic. In these dreams they spend most of their time. Their lives are vague, erratic, and without plan. They dream, they wake, drink, love, eat and dream again. They seldom finish anything they begin, but leave it half completed and sink back again into the slumber of the black lotus. That meal you found – doubtless one awoke, felt the urge of hunger, prepared the meal for himself, then forgot about it and wandered away to dream again.'

'Where do they get their food?' interrupted Conan. 'I saw no fields or vineyards outside the city. Have they orchards and cattle-pens within the walls?'

She shook her head. 'They manufacture their own food out of the primal elements. They are wonderful scientists, when they are not drugged with their dream-flower. Their ancestors were mental giants, who built this marvelous city in the desert, and though the race became slaves to their curious passions, some of their wonderful knowledge still remains. Have you wondered about these lights? They are jewels, fused with radium. You rub them with your thumb to make them glow, and rub them again, the opposite way, to extinguish them. That is but a single example of their science. But much they have forgotten. They take little interest in waking life, choosing to lie most of the time in death-like sleep.'

'Then the dead man at the gate—' began Conan.

'Was doubtless slumbering. Sleepers of the lotus are like the dead. Animation is apparently suspended. It is impossible to detect the slightest sign of life. The spirit has left the body and is roaming at will through other, exotic worlds. The man at the gate was a good example of the irresponsibility of these people's lives. He was guarding the gate, where custom decrees a watch be kept, though no enemy has ever advanced across the desert. In other parts of the city you would find other guards, generally sleeping as soundly as the man at the gate.'

Conan mulled over this for a space.

'Where are the people now?'

'Scattered in different parts of the city; lying on couches, on silken divans, in cushion-littered alcoves, on fur-covered daises; all wrapt in the shining veil of dreams.'

Conan felt the skin twitch between his massive shoulders. It was not soothing to think of hundreds of people lying cold and still throughout the tapestried palaces, their glassy eyes turned unseeingly upward. He remembered something else.

'What of the thing that stole through the chambers and carried away the man on the dais?'

A shudder twitched her ivory limbs.

'That was Thog, the Ancient, the god of Xuthal, who dwells in the sunken dome in the center of the city. He has always dwelt in Xuthal. Whether he came here with the ancient founders, or was here when they built the city, none knows. But the people of Xuthal worship him. Mostly he sleeps below the city, but sometimes at irregular intervals he grows hungry, and then he steals through the secret corridors and the dim-lit chambers, seeking prey. Then none is safe.'

Natala moaned with terror and clasped Conan's mighty neck as if to resist an effort to drag her from her protector's side.

'Crom!' he ejaculated aghast. 'You mean to tell me these people lie down calmly and sleep, with this demon crawling among them?'

'It is only occasionally that he is hungry,' she repeated. 'A god must have his sacrifices. When I was a child in Stygia the people lived under the shadow of the priests. None ever knew when he or she would be seized and dragged to the altar. What difference whether the priests give a victim to the gods, or the god comes for his own victim?'

'Such is not the custom of my people,' Conan growled, 'nor of Natala's either. The Hyborians do not sacrifice humans to their god, Mitra, and as for my people – by Crom, I'd like to see a priest try to drag a Cimmerian to the altar! There'd be blood spilt, but not as the priest intended.'

'You are a barbarian,' laughed Thalis, but with a glow in her luminous eyes. 'Thog is very ancient and very terrible.'

'These folk must be either fools or heroes,' grunted Conan, 'to lie down and dream their idiotic dreams, knowing they might awaken in his belly.'

She laughed. 'They know nothing else. For untold generations Thog has preyed on them. He has been one of the factors which have reduced their numbers from thousands to hundreds. A few more generations and they will be extinct, and Thog must either fare forth into the world for new prey, or retire to the underworld whence he came so long ago.

'They realize their ultimate doom, but they are fatalists, incapable of resistance or escape. Not one of the present generation has been out of sight of these walls. There is an oasis a day's march to the south – I have seen it on the old maps their ancestors drew on parchment – but no man of Xuthal has visited it for three generations, much less made any attempt to explore the fertile grasslands which the maps show lying another day's march beyond it. They are a fast-fading race, drowned in lotus-dreams, stimulating their waking hours by means of the golden wine which heals wounds, prolongs life, and invigorates the most sated debauchee.

'Yet they cling to life, and fear the deity they worship. You saw how one went mad at the knowledge that Thog was roving the palaces. I have seen the whole city screaming and tearing its hair, and running frenziedly out of the gates, to cower outside the walls and draw lots to see which would be bound and flung back through the arched doorways to satisfy Thog's lust and hunger. Were they not all slumbering now, the word of his coming would send them raving and shrieking again through the outer gates.'

'Oh, Conan!' begged Natala hysterically. 'Let us flee!'

'In good time,' muttered Conan, his eyes burning on Thalis' ivory limbs. 'What are you, a Stygian woman, doing here?'

'I came here when a young girl,' she answered, leaning lithely back against the velvet divan, and intertwining her slender fingers behind her dusky head. 'I am the daughter of a king, no common woman, as you can see by my skin, which is as white as that of your little blond there. I was abducted by a rebel prince, who, with an army of Kushite bowmen, pushed southward into the wilderness, searching for a land he could make his own. He and all his warriors perished in the desert, but one, before he died, placed me on a camel and walked beside it until he dropped and died in his tracks. The beast wandered on, and I finally passed into delirium from thirst and hunger, and awakened in this city. They told me I had been seen from the walls, early in the dawn, lying senseless beside a dead camel. They went forth and brought me in and revived me with their wonderful golden wine. And only the sight of a woman would have led them to have ventured that far from their walls.

'They were naturally much interested in me, especially the men. As I could not speak their language, they learned to speak mine. They are very quick and able of intellect; they learned my language long before I learned theirs. But they were more interested in me than in my language. I have been, and am, the only thing for which a man of them will forgo his lotus-dreams for a space.'

She laughed wickedly, flashing her audacious eyes meaningly at Conan.

'Of course the women are jealous of me,' she continued tranquilly. 'They are handsome enough in their yellow-skinned way, but they are dreamy and uncertain as the men, and these latter like me not only for my beauty, but for my reality. I am no dream! Though I have dreamed the dreams of the lotus, I am a normal woman, with earthly emotions and desires. With such these moon-eyed yellow women can not compare.

'That is why it would be better for you to cut that girl's throat with your saber, before the men of Xuthal waken and catch her. They will put her through paces she never dreamed of! She is too soft to endure what I have thrived on. I am a daughter of Luxur, and before I had known fifteen summers I had been led through the temples of Derketo, the dusky goddess, and had been initiated into the mysteries. Not that my first years in Xuthal were years of unmodified pleasure! The people of Xuthal have forgotten more than the priestesses of Derketo ever dreamed. They live only for sensual joys. Dreaming or waking, their lives are filled with exotic ecstasies, beyond the ken of ordinary men.'

'Damned degenerates!' growled Conan.

'It is all in the point of view,' smiled Thalis lazily.

'Well,' he decided, 'we're merely wasting time. I can see this is no place for ordinary mortals. We'll be gone before your morons awake, or Thog comes to devour us. I think the desert would be kinder.'

Natala, whose blood had curdled in her veins at Thalis's words, fervently agreed. She could speak Stygian only brokenly, but she understood it well enough. Conan stood up, drawing her up beside him.

'If you'll show us the nearest way out of this city,' he grunted, 'we'll take ourselves off.' But his gaze lingered on the Stygian's sleek limbs and ivory breasts.

She did not miss his look, and she smiled enigmatically as she rose with the lithe ease of a great lazy cat.

'Follow me,' she directed and led the way, conscious of Conan's eyes fixed on her supple figure and perfectly poised carriage. She did not go the way they had come, but before Conan's suspicions could be roused, she halted in a wide ivory-cased chamber, and pointed to a tiny fountain which gurgled in the center of the ivory floor.

'Don't you want to wash your face, child?' she asked Natala. 'It is stained with dust, and there is dust in your hair.'

Natala colored resentfully at the suggestion of malice in the Stygian's faintly mocking tone, but she complied, wondering miserably just how much havoc the desert sun and wind had wrought on her complexion – a feature for which women of her race were justly noted. She knelt beside the fountain, shook back her hair, slipped her tunic down to her waist, and began to lave not only her face, but her white arms and shoulders as well.

'By Crom!' grumbled Conan. 'A woman will stop to consider her beauty, if the devil himself were on her heels. Haste, girl; you'll be dusty again before we've got out of sight of this city. And Thalis, I'd take it kindly if you'd furnish us with a bit of food and drink.'

For answer Thalis leaned herself against him, slipping one white arm about his bronzed shoulders. Her sleek naked flank pressed against his thigh and the perfume of her foamy hair was in his nostrils.

'Why dare the desert?' she whispered urgently. 'Stay here! I will teach you the ways of Xuthal. I will protect you. I will love you! You are a real man: I am sick of these moon-calves who sigh and dream and wake, and dream again. I am hungry for the hard, clean passion of a man from the earth. The blaze of your dynamic eyes makes my heart pound in my bosom, and the touch of your iron-thewed arm maddens me.

'Stay here! I will make you king of Xuthal! I will show you all the ancient mysteries, and the exotic ways of pleasure! I—' She had thrown both arms about his neck and was standing on tiptoe, her vibrant body shivering against his. Over her ivory shoulder he saw Natala, throwing back her damp tousled hair, stop short, her lovely eyes dilating, her red lips parting in a shocked O. With an embarrassed grunt, Conan disengaged Thalis's clinging arms and put her aside with one massive arm. She threw a swift glance at the Brythunian girl and smiled enigmatically, seeming to nod her splendid head in mysterious cogitation.

Natala rose and jerked up her tunic, her eyes blazing, her lips pouting sulkily. Conan swore under his breath. He was no more monogamous in his nature than the average soldier of fortune, but there was an innate decency about him that was Natala's best protection.

Thalis did not press her suit. Beckoning them with her slender hand to follow, she turned and walked across the chamber. There, close to the tapestried wall, she halted suddenly. Conan, watching her, wondered if she had heard the sounds that might be made by a nameless monster stealing through the midnight chambers, and his skin crawled at the thought.

'What do you hear?' he demanded.

'Watch that doorway,' she replied, pointing.

He wheeled, sword ready. Only the empty arch of the entrance met his gaze. Then behind him sounded a quick faint scuffling noise, a half-choked gasp. He whirled. Thalis and Natala had vanished. The tapestry was settling back in place, as if it had been lifted away from the wall. As he gaped bewilderedly, from behind that tapestried wall rang a muffled scream in the voice of the Brythunian girl.

2

When Conan turned, in compliance with Thalis's request, to glare at the doorway opposite, Natala had been standing just behind him, close to the side of the Stygian. The instant the Cimmerian's back was turned, Thalis, with a pantherish quickness almost incredible, clapped her hand over Natala's mouth, stifling the cry she tried to give. Simultaneously the Stygian's other arm was passed about the blond girl's supple waist, and she was jerked back against the wall, which seemed to give way as Thalis' shoulder pressed against it. A section of the wall swung inward, and through a slit that opened in the tapestry Thalis slid with her captive, just as Conan wheeled back.

Inside was utter blackness as the secret door swung to again. Thalis paused to fumble at it for an instant, apparently sliding home a bolt, and as she took her hand from Natala's mouth to perform this act, the Brythunian girl began to scream at the top of her voice. Thalis's laugh was like poisoned honey in the darkness.

'Scream if you will, little fool. It will only shorten your life.'

At that Natala ceased suddenly, and cowered shaking in every limb.

'Why did you do this?' she begged. 'What are you going to do?'

'I am going to take you down this corridor for a short distance,' answered Thalis, 'and leave you for one who will sooner or later come for you.'

'Ohhhhhh!' Natala's voice broke in a sob of terror. 'Why should you harm me? I have never injured you!'

'I want your warrior. You stand in my way. He desires me – I could read the look in his eyes. But for you, he would be willing to stay here and be my king. When you are out of the way, he will follow me.'

'He will cut your throat,' answered Natala with conviction, knowing Conan better than Thalis did.

'We shall see,' answered the Stygian coolly from the confidence of her power over men. 'At any rate, you will not know whether he stabs or kisses me, because you will be the bride of him who dwells in darkness. Come!'

Half mad with terror, Natala fought like a wild thing, but it availed her nothing. With a lithe strength she would not have believed possible in a woman, Thalis picked her up and carried her down the black corridor as if she had been a child. Natala did not scream again, remembering the Stygian's sinister words; the only sounds were her desperate quick panting and Thalis' soft taunting lascivious laughter. Then the Brythunian's fluttering hand closed on something in the dark – a jeweled dagger-hilt jutting from Thalis's gem-crusted girdle. Natala jerked it forth and struck blindly and with all her girlish power.

A scream burst from Thalis's lips, feline in its pain and fury. She reeled, and Natala slipped from her relaxing grasp, to bruise her tender limbs on the smooth stone floor. Rising, she scurried to the nearest wall and stood there panting and trembling, flattening herself against the stones. She could not see Thalis, but she could hear her. The Stygian was quite certainly not dead. She was cursing in a steady stream, and her fury was so concentrated and deadly that Natala felt her bones turn to wax, her blood to ice.

'Where are you, you little she-devil?' gasped Thalis. 'Let me get my fingers on you again, and I'll—' Natala grew physically sick as Thalis described the bodily injuries she intended to inflict on her rival. The Stygian's choice of language would have shamed the toughest courtezan in Aquilonia.

Natala heard her groping in the dark, and then a light sprang up. Evidently whatever fear Thalis felt of the black corridor was submerged in her anger. The light came from one of the radium gems which adorned the walls of Xuthal. This Thalis had rubbed, and now she stood bathed in its reddish glow: a light different from that which the others had emitted. One hand was pressed to her side and blood trickled between the fingers. But she did not seem weakened or badly hurt, and her eyes blazed fiendishly. What little courage remained to Natala ebbed away at sight of the Stygian standing limned in that weird glow, her beautiful face contorted with a passion that was no less than hellish. She now advanced with a pantherish tread, drawing her hand away from her wounded side, and shaking the blood drops impatiently from her fingers. Natala saw that she had not badly harmed her rival. The blade had glanced from the jewels of Thalis's girdle and inflicted only a very superficial flesh-wound, only enough to rouse the Stygian's unbridled fury.

'Give me that dagger, you fool!' she gritted, striding up to the cowering girl.

Natala knew she ought to fight while she had the chance, but she simply could not summon up the courage. Never much of a fighter, the darkness, violence and horror of her adventure had left her limp, mentally and physically. Thalis snatched the dagger from her lax fingers and threw it contemptuously aside.

'You little slut!' she ground between her teeth, slapping the girl viciously with either hand. 'Before I drag you down the corridor and throw you into Thog's jaws I'll have a little of your blood myself! You would dare to knife me – well, for that audacity you shall pay!'

Seizing her by the hair, Thalis dragged her down the corridor a short distance, to the edge of the circle of light. A metal ring showed in the wall, above the level of a man's head. From it depended a silken cord. As in a nightmare Natala felt her tunic being stripped from her, and the next instant Thalis had jerked up her wrists and bound them to the ring, where she hung, naked as the day she was born, her feet barely touching the floor. Twisting her head, Natala saw Thalis unhook a jewel-handled whip from where it hung on the wall, near the ring. The lashes consisted of seven round silk cords, harder yet more pliant than leather thongs.

With a hiss of vindictive gratification, Thalis drew back her arm, and Natala shrieked as the cords curled across her loins. The tortured girl writhed, twisted and tore agonizedly at the thongs which imprisoned her wrists. She had forgotten the lurking menace her cries might summon, and so apparently had Thalis. Every stroke evoked screams of anguish. The whippings Natala had received in the Shemite slave-markets paled to insignificance before this. She had never guessed the punishing power of hard-woven silk cords. Their caress was more exquisitely painful than any birch twigs or leather thongs. They whistled venomously as they cut the air.

Then, as Natala twisted her tear-stained face over her shoulder to shriek for mercy, something froze her cries. Agony gave place to paralyzing horror in her beautiful eyes.

Struck by her expression, Thalis checked her lifted hand and whirled quick as a cat. Too late! An awful cry rang from her lips as she swayed back, her arms upflung. Natala saw her for an instant, a white figure of fear etched against a great black shapeless mass that towered over her; then the white figure was whipped off its feet, the shadow receded with it, and in the circle of dim light Natala hung alone, half fainting with terror.

From the black shadows came sounds, incomprehensible and blood-freezing. She heard Thalis's voice pleading frenziedly, but no voice answered. There was no sound except the Stygian's panting voice, which suddenly rose to screams of agony, and then broke in hysterical laughter, mingled with sobs. This dwindled to a convulsive panting, and presently this too ceased, and a silence more terrible hovered over the secret corridor.

Nauseated with horror, Natala twisted about and dared to look fearfully in the direction the black shape had carried Thalis. She saw nothing, but she sensed an unseen peril, more grisly than she could understand. She fought against a rising tide of hysteria. Her bruised wrists, her smarting body were forgotten in the teeth of this menace which she dimly felt threatened not only her body, but her soul as well.

She strained her eyes into the blackness beyond the rim of the dim light, tense with fear of what she might see. A whimpering gasp escaped her lips. The darkness was taking form. Something huge and bulky grew up out of the void. She saw a great misshapen head emerging into the light. At least she took it for a head, though it was not the member of any sane or normal creature. She saw a great toad-like face, the features of which were as dim and unstable as those of a specter seen in a mirror of nightmare. Great pools of light that might have been eyes blinked at her, and she shook at the cosmic lust reflected there. She could tell nothing about the creature's body. Its outline seemed to waver and alter subtly even as she looked at it; yet its substance was apparently solid enough. There was nothing misty or ghostly about it.

As it came toward her, she could not tell whether it walked, wriggled, flew or crept. Its method of locomotion was absolutely beyond her comprehension. When it had emerged from the shadows she was still uncertain as to its nature. The light from the radium gem did not illumine it as it would have illumined an ordinary creature. Impossible as it seemed, the being seemed almost impervious to the light. Its details were still obscure and indistinct, even when it halted so near that it almost touched her shrinking flesh. Only the blinking toad-like face stood out with any distinctness. The thing was a blur in the sight, a black blot of shadow that normal radiance would neither dissipate nor illuminate.

She decided she was mad, because she could not tell whether the being looked up at her or towered above her. She was unable to say whether the dim repulsive face blinked up at her from the shadows at her feet, or looked down at her from an immense height. But if her sight convinced her that whatever its mutable qualities, it was yet composed of solid substance, her sense of feel further assured her of that fact. A dark tentacle-like member slid about her body, and she screamed at the touch of it on her naked flesh. It was neither warm nor cold, rough nor smooth; it was like nothing that had ever touched her before, and at its caress she knew such fear and shame as she had never dreamed of. All the obscenity and salacious infamy spawned in the muck of the abysmal pits of Life seemed to drown her in seas of cosmic filth. And in that instant she knew that whatever form of life this thing represented it was not a beast.

She began to scream uncontrollably, the monster tugged at her as if to tear her from the ring by sheer brutality; then something crashed above their heads, and a form hurtled down through the air to strike the stone floor.

3

When Conan wheeled to see the tapestry settling back in place and to hear Natala's muffled cry, he hurled himself against the wall with a maddened roar. Rebounding from the impact that would have splintered the bones of a lesser man, he ripped away the tapestry revealing what appeared to be a blank wall. Beside himself with fury he lifted his saber as though to hew through the marble, when a sudden sound brought him about, eyes blazing.

A score of figures faced him, yellow men in purple tunics, with short swords in their hands. As he turned they surged in on him with hostile cries. He made no attempt to conciliate them. Maddened at the disappearance of his sweetheart, the barbarian reverted to type.

A snarl of bloodthirsty gratification hummed in his bull-throat as he leaped, and the first attacker, his short sword overreached by the whistling saber, went down with his brains gushing from his split skull. Wheeling like a cat, Conan caught a descending wrist on his edge, and the hand gripping the short sword flew into the air scattering a shower of red drops. But Conan had not paused or hesitated. A pantherish twist and shift of his body avoided the blundering rush of two yellow swordsmen, and the blade of one missing its objective, was sheathed in the breast of the other.

A yell of dismay went up at this mischance, and Conan allowed himself a short bark of laughter as he bounded aside from a whistling cut and slashed under the guard of yet another man of Xuthal. A long spurt of crimson followed his singing edge and the man crumpled screaming, his belly-muscles cut through.

The warriors of Xuthal howled like mad wolves. Unaccustomed to battle, they were ridiculously slow and clumsy compared to the tigerish barbarian whose motions were blurs of quickness possible only to steel thews knit to a perfect fighting-brain. They floundered and stumbled, hindered by their own numbers; they struck too quick or too soon, and cut only empty air. He was never motionless or in the same place an instant; springing, side-stepping, whirling, twisting, he offered a constantly shifting target for their swords, while his own curved blade sang death about their ears.

But whatever their faults, the men of Xuthal did not lack courage. They swarmed about him yelling and hacking, and through the arched doorways rushed others, awakened from their slumbers by the unwonted clamor.

Conan, bleeding from a cut on the temple, cleared a space for an instant with a devastating sweep of his dripping saber, and cast a quick glance about for an avenue of escape. At that instant he saw the tapestry on one of the walls drawn aside, disclosing a narrow stairway. On this stood a man in rich robes, vague-eyed and blinking, as if he had just awakened and had not yet shaken the dusts of slumber from his brain. Conan's sight and action were simultaneous.

A tigerish leap carried him untouched through the hemming ring of swords, and he bounded toward the stair with the pack giving tongue behind him. Three men confronted him at the foot of the marble steps, and he struck them with a deafening crash of steel. There was a frenzied instant when the blades flamed like summer lightning; then the group fell apart and Conan sprang up the stair. The oncoming horde tripped over three writhing forms at its foot: one lay face-down in a sickening welter of blood and brains; another propped himself on his hands, blood spurting blackly from his severed throat veins; the other howled like a dying dog as he clawed at the crimson stump that had been an arm.

As Conan rushed up the marble stair, the man above shook himself from his stupor and drew a sword that sparkled frostily in the radium light. He thrust downward as the barbarian surged upon him. But as the point sang toward his throat, Conan ducked deeply. The blade slit the skin of his back, and Conan straightened, driving his saber upward as a man might wield a butcher-knife, with all the power of his mighty shoulders.

So terrific was his headlong drive that the sinking of the saber to the hilt into the belly of his enemy did not check him. He caromed against the wretch's body, knocking it sideways. The impact sent Conan crashing against the wall; the other, the saber torn through his body, fell headlong down the stair, ripped open to the spine from groin to broken breastbone. In a ghastly mess of streaming entrails the body tumbled against the men rushing up the stairs, bearing them back with it.

Half stunned, Conan leaned against the wall an instant, glaring down upon them; then with a defiant shake of his dripping saber, he bounded up the steps.

Coming into an upper chamber, he halted only long enough to see that it was empty. Behind him the horde was yelling with such intensified horror and rage, that he knew he had killed some notable man there on the stair, probably the king of that fantastic city.

He ran at random, without plan. He desperately wished to find and succor Natala, who he was sure needed aid badly; but harried as he was by all the warriors in Xuthal, he could only run on, trusting to luck to elude them and find her. Among those dark or dimly lighted upper chambers he quickly lost all sense of direction, and it was not strange that he eventually blundered into a chamber into which his foes were just pouring.

They yelled vengefully and rushed for him, and with a snarl of disgust he turned and fled back the way he had come. At least he thought it was the way he had come. But presently, racing into a particularly ornate chamber, he was aware of his mistake. All the chambers he had traversed since mounting the stair had been empty. This chamber had an occupant, who rose up with a cry as he charged in.

Conan saw a yellow-skinned woman, loaded with jeweled ornaments but otherwise nude, staring at him with wide eyes. So much he glimpsed as she raised her hand and jerked a silken rope hanging from the wall. Then the floor dropped from under him, and all his steel-trap coordination could not save him from the plunge into the black depths that opened beneath him.

He did not fall any great distance, though it was far enough to have snapped the leg bones of a man not built of steel springs and whalebone.

He hit cat-like on his feet and one hand, instinctively retaining his grasp on his saber hilt. A familiar cry rang in his ears as he rebounded on his feet as a lynx rebounds with snarling bared fangs. So Conan, glaring from under his tousled mane, saw the white naked figure of Natala writhing in the lustful grasp of a black nightmare shape that could have only been bred in the lost pits of hell.

The sight of that awful shape alone might have frozen the Cimmerian with fear. In juxtaposition to his girl, the sight sent a red wave of murderous fury through Conan's brain. In a crimson mist he smote the monster.

It dropped the girl, wheeling toward its attacker, and the maddened Cimmerian's saber, shrilling through the air, sheared clear through the black viscous bulk and rang on the stone floor, showering blue sparks. Conan went to his knees from the fury of the blow; the edge had not encountered the resistance he had expected. As he bounded up, the thing was upon him.

It towered above him like a clinging black cloud. It seemed to flow about him in almost liquid waves, to envelop and engulf him. His madly slashing saber sheared through it again and again, his ripping poniard tore and rent it; he was deluged with a slimy liquid that must have been its sluggish blood. Yet its fury was nowise abated.

He could not tell whether he was slashing off its members or whether he was cleaving its bulk, which knit behind the slicing blade. He was tossed to and fro in the violence of that awful battle, and had a dazed feeling that he was fighting not one, but an aggregation of lethal creatures. The thing seemed to be biting, clawing, crushing and clubbing him all at the same time. He felt fangs and talons rend his flesh; flabby cables that were yet hard as iron encircled his limbs and body, and worse than all, something like a whip of scorpions fell again and again across his shoulders, back and breast, tearing the skin and filling his veins with a poison that was like liquid fire.

They had rolled beyond the circle of light, and it was in utter blackness that the Cimmerian battled. Once he sank his teeth, beast-like, into the flabby substance of his foe, revolting as the stuff writhed and squirmed like living rubber from between his iron jaws.

In that hurricane of battle they were rolling over and over, farther and farther down the tunnel. Conan's brain reeled with the punishment he was taking. His breath came in whistling gasps between his teeth. High above him he saw a great toad-like face, dimly limned in an eery glow that seemed to emanate from it. And with a panting cry that was half curse, half gasp of straining agony, he lunged toward it, thrusting with all his waning power. Hilt-deep the saber sank, somewhere below the grisly face, and a convulsive shudder heaved the vast bulk that half enveloped the Cimmerian. With a volcanic burst of contraction and expansion, it tumbled backward, rolling now with frantic haste down the corridor. Conan went with it, bruised, battered, invincible, hanging on like a bulldog to the hilt of his saber which he could not withdraw, tearing and ripping at the shuddering bulk with the poniard in his left hand, goring it to ribbons.

The thing glowed all over now with a weird phosphorous radiance, and this glow was in Conan's eyes, blinding him, as suddenly the heaving billowing mass fell away from beneath him, the saber tearing loose and remaining in his locked hand. This hand and arm hung down into space, and far below him the glowing body of the monster was rushing downward like a meteor. Conan dazedly realized that he lay on the brink of a great round well, the edge of which was slimy stone. He lay there watching the hurtling glow dwindling and dwindling until it vanished into a dark shining surface that seemed to surge upward to meet it. For an instant a dimming witchfire glimmered in those dusky depths; then it disappeared and Conan lay staring down into the blackness of the ultimate abyss from which no sound came.

4

Straining vainly at the silk cords which cut into her wrists, Natala sought to pierce the darkness beyond the radiant circle. Her tongue seemed frozen to the roof of her mouth. Into that blackness she had seen Conan vanish, locked in mortal combat with the unknown demon, and the only sounds that had come to her straining ears had been the panting gasps of the barbarian, the impact of struggling bodies, and the thud and rip of savage blows. These ceased, and Natala swayed dizzily on her cords, half fainting.

A footstep roused her out of her apathy of horror, to see Conan emerging from the darkness. At the sight she found her voice in a shriek which echoed down the vaulted tunnel. The manhandling the Cimmerian had received was appalling to behold. At every step he dripped blood. His face was skinned and bruised as if he had been beaten with a bludgeon. His lips were pulped, and blood oozed down his face from a wound in his scalp. There were deep gashes in his thighs, calves and forearms, and great bruises showed on his limbs and body from impacts against the stone floor. But his shoulders, back and upper-breast muscles had suffered most. The flesh was bruised, swollen and lacerated, the skin hanging in loose strips, as if he had been lashed with wire whips.

'Oh, Conan!' she sobbed. 'What has happened to you?'

He had no breath for conversation, but his smashed lips writhed in what might have been grim humor as he approached her. His hairy breast, glistening with sweat and blood, heaved with his panting. Slowly and laboriously he reached up and cut her cords, then fell back against the wall and leaned there, his trembling legs braced wide. She scrambled up from where she had fallen and caught him in a frenzied embrace, sobbing hysterically.

'Oh, Conan, you are wounded unto death! Oh, what shall we do?'

'Well,' he panted, 'you can't fight a devil out of hell and come off with a whole skin!'

'Where is it?' she whispered. 'Did you kill it?'

'I don't know. It fell into a pit. It was hanging in bloody shreds, but whether it can be killed by steel I know not.'

'Oh, your poor back!' she wailed, wringing her hands.

'It lashed me with a tentacle,' he grimaced, swearing as he moved. 'It cut like wire and burned like poison. But it was its damnable squeezing that got my wind. It was worse than a python. If half my guts are not mashed out of place, I'm much mistaken.'

'What shall we do?' she whimpered.

He glanced up. The trap was closed. No sound came from above.

'We can't go back through the secret door,' he muttered. 'That room is full of dead men, and doubtless warriors keep watch there. They must have thought my doom sealed when I plunged through the floor above, or else they dare not follow me into this tunnel. – Twist that radium gem off the wall. – As I groped my way back up the corridor I felt arches opening into other tunnels. We'll follow the first we come to. It may lead to another pit, or to the open air. We must chance it. We can't stay here and rot.'

Natala obeyed, and holding the tiny point of light in his left hand and his bloody saber in his right, Conan started down the corridor. He went slowly, stiffly, only his animal vitality keeping him on his feet. There was a blank glare in his bloodshot eyes, and Natala saw him involuntarily lick his battered lips from time to time. She knew his suffering was ghastly, but with the stoicism of the wilds he made no complaint.

Presently the dim light shone on a black arch, and into this Conan turned. Natala cringed at what she might see, but the light revealed only a tunnel similar to that they had just left.

*

How far they went she had no idea, before they mounted a long stair and came upon a stone door, fastened with a golden bolt.

She hesitated, glancing at Conan. The barbarian was swaying on his feet, the light in his unsteady hand flinging fantastic shadows back and forth along the wall.

'Open the door, girl,' he muttered thickly. 'The men of Xuthal will be waiting for us, and I would not disappoint them. By Crom, the city has not seen such a sacrifice as I will make!'

She knew he was half delirious. No sound came from beyond the door. Taking the radium gem from his blood-stained hand, she threw the bolt and drew the panel inward. The inner side of a cloth-of-gold tapestry met her gaze and she drew it aside and peeked through, her heart in her mouth. She was looking into an empty chamber in the center of which a silvery fountain tinkled.

Conan's hand fell heavily on her naked shoulder.

'Stand aside, girl,' he mumbled. 'Now is the feasting of swords.'

'There is no one in the chamber,' she answered. 'But there is water—'

'I hear it,' he licked his blackened lips. 'We will drink before we die.'

He seemed blinded. She took his darkly stained hand and led him through the stone door. She went on tiptoe, expecting a rush of yellow figures through the arches at any instant.

'Drink while I keep watch,' he muttered.

'No, I am not thirsty. Lie down beside the fountain and I will bathe your wounds.'

'What of the swords of Xuthal?' He continually raked his arm across his eyes as if to clear his blurred sight.

'I hear no one. All is silent.'

He sank down gropingly and plunged his face into the crystal jet, drinking as if he could not get enough. When he raised his head there was sanity in his bloodshot eyes and he stretched his massive limbs out on the marble floor as she requested, though he kept his saber in his hand, and his eyes continually roved toward the archways. She bathed his torn flesh and bandaged the deeper wounds with strips torn from a silk hanging. She shuddered at the appearance of his back; the flesh was discolored, mottled and spotted black and blue and a sickly yellow, where it was not raw. As she worked she sought frantically for a solution to their problem. If they stayed where they were, they would eventually be discovered. Whether the men of Xuthal were searching the palaces for them, or had returned to their dreams, she could not know.

As she finished her task, she froze. Under the hanging that partly concealed an alcove, she saw a hand's breadth of yellow flesh.

Saying nothing to Conan, she rose and crossed the chamber softly, grasping his poniard. Her heart pounded suffocatingly as she cautiously drew aside the hanging. On the dais lay a young yellow woman, naked and apparently lifeless. At her hand stood a jade jar nearly full of peculiar golden-colored liquid. Natala believed it to be the elixir described by Thalis, which lent vigor and vitality to the degenerate Xuthal. She leaned across the supine form and grasped the vessel, her poniard poised over the girl's bosom. The latter did not wake.

With the jar in her possession, Natala hesitated, realizing it would be the safer course to put the sleeping girl beyond the power of waking and raising an alarm. But she could not bring herself to plunge the Cimmerian poniard into that still bosom, and at last she drew back the hanging and returned to Conan, who lay where she had left him, seemingly only partly conscious.

She bent and placed the jar to his lips. He drank, mechanically at first, then with a suddenly roused interest. To her amazement he sat up and took the vessel from her hands. When he lifted his face, his eyes were clear and normal. Much of the drawn haggard look had gone from his features, and his voice was not the mumble of delirium.

'Crom! Where did you get this?'

She pointed. 'From that alcove, where a yellow hussy is sleeping.'

He thrust his muzzle again into the golden liquid.

'By Crom,' he said with a deep sigh, 'I feel new life and power rush like wildfire through my veins. Surely this is the very elixir of Life!'

'We had best go back into the corridor,' Natala ventured nervously. 'We shall be discovered if we stay here long. We can hide there until your wounds heal—'

'Not I,' he grunted. 'We are not rats, to hide in dark burrows. We leave this devil-city now, and let none seek to stop us.'

'But your wounds!' she wailed.

'I do not feel them,' he answered. 'It may be a false strength this liquor has given me, but I swear I am aware of neither pain nor weakness.'

With sudden purpose he crossed the chamber to a window she had not noticed. Over his shoulder she looked out. A cool breeze tossed her tousled locks. Above was the dark velvet sky, clustered with stars. Below them stretched a vague expanse of sand.

'Thalis said the city was one great palace,' said Conan. 'Evidently some of the chambers are built like towers on the wall. This one is. Chance has led us well.'

'What do you mean?' she asked, glancing apprehensively over her shoulder.

'There is a crystal jar on that ivory table,' he answered. 'Fill it with water and tie a strip of that torn hanging about its neck for a handle while I rip up this tapestry.'

She obeyed without question, and when she turned from her task she saw Conan rapidly tying together the long tough strips of silk to make a rope, one end of which he fastened to the leg of the massive ivory table.

'We'll take our chance with the desert,' said he. 'Thalis spoke of an oasis a day's march to the south, and grasslands beyond that. If we reach the oasis we can rest until my wounds heal. This wine is like sorcery. A little while ago I was little more than a dead man; now I am ready for anything. Here is enough silk left for you to make a garment of.'

Natala had forgotten her nudity. The mere fact caused her no qualms, but her delicate skin would need protection from the desert sun. As she knotted the silk length about her supple body, Conan turned to the window and with a contemptuous wrench tore away the soft gold bars that guarded it. Then, looping the loose end of his silk rope about Natala's hips, and cautioning her to hold on with both hands, he lifted her through the window and lowered her the thirty-odd feet to the earth. She stepped out of the loop, and drawing it back up, he made fast the vessels of water and wine, and lowered them to her. He followed them, sliding down swiftly, hand over hand.

As he reached her side, Natala gave a sigh of relief. They stood alone at the foot of the great wall, the paling stars overhead and the naked desert about them. What perils yet confronted them she could not know, but her heart sang with joy because they were out of that ghostly, unreal city.

'They may find the rope,' grunted Conan, slinging the precious jars across his shoulders, wincing at the contact with his mangled flesh. 'They may even pursue us, but from what Thalis said, I doubt it. That way is south,' a bronze muscular arm indicated their course; 'so somewhere in that direction lies the oasis. Come!'

Taking her hand with a thoughtfulness unusual for him, Conan strode out across the sands, suiting his stride to the shorter legs of his companion. He did not glance back at the silent city, brooding dreamily and ghostlily behind them.

'Conan,' Natala ventured finally, 'when you fought the monster, and later, as you came up the corridor, did you see anything of – of Thalis?'

He shook his head. 'It was dark in the corridor; but it was empty.'

She shuddered. 'She tortured me – yet I pity her.'

'It was a hot welcome we got in that accursed city,' he snarled. Then his grim humor returned. 'Well, they'll remember our visit long enough, I'll wager. There are brains and guts and blood to be cleaned off the marble tiles, and if their god still lives, he carries more wounds than I. We got off light, after all: we have wine and water and a good chance of reaching a habitable country, though I look as if I've gone through a meat-grinder, and you have a sore—'

'It's all your fault,' she interrupted. 'If you had not looked so long and admiringly at that Stygian cat—'

'Crom and his devils!' he swore. 'When the oceans drown the world, women will take time for jealousy. Devil take their conceit! Did I tell the Stygian to fall in love with me? After all, she was only human!'

THE POOL OF THE BLACK ONE

Into the west, unknown of man,
Ships have sailed since the world began.
Read, if you dare, what Skelos wrote,
With dead hands fumbling his silken coat;
And follow the ships through the wind-blown wrack—
Follow the ships that come not back.

1

SANCHA, ONCE OF KORDAVA, yawned daintily, stretched her supple limbs luxuriously, and composed herself more comfortably on the ermine-fringed silk spread on the carack's poop-deck. That the crew watched her with burning interest from waist and forecastle she was lazily aware, just as she was also aware that her short silk kirtle veiled little of her voluptuous contours from their eager eyes. Wherefore she smiled insolently and prepared to snatch a few more winks before the sun, which was just thrusting his golden disk above the ocean, should dazzle her eyes.

But at that instant a sound reached her ears unlike the creaking of timbers, thrum of cordage and lap of waves. She sat up, her gaze fixed on the rail, over which, to her amazement, a dripping figure clambered. Her dark eyes opened wide, her red lips parted in an O of surprize. The intruder was a stranger to her. Water ran in rivulets from his great shoulders and down his heavy arms. His single garment – a pair of bright crimson silk breeks – was soaking wet, as was his broad gold-buckled girdle and the sheathed sword it supported. As he stood at the rail, the rising sun etched him like a great bronze statue. He ran his fingers through his streaming black mane, and his blue eyes lit as they rested on the girl.

'Who are you?' she demanded. 'Whence did you come?'

He made a gesture toward the sea that took in a whole quarter of the compass, while his eyes did not leave her supple figure.

'Are you a merman, that you rise up out of the sea?' she asked, confused by the candor of his gaze, though she was accustomed to admiration.

Before he could reply, a quick step sounded on the boards, and the master of the carack was glaring at the stranger, fingers twitching at sword-hilt.

'Who the devil are you, sirrah?' this one demanded in no friendly tone.

'I am Conan,' the other answered imperturbably. Sancha pricked up her ears anew; she had never heard Zingaran spoken with such an accent as the stranger spoke it.

'And how did you get aboard my ship?' The voice grated with suspicion.

'I swam.'

'Swam!' exclaimed the master angrily. 'Dog, would you jest with me? We are far beyond sight of land. Whence do you come?'

Conan pointed with a muscular brown arm toward the east, banded in dazzling gold by the lifting sun.

'I came from the Islands.'

'Oh!' The other regarded him with increased interest. Black brows drew down over scowling eyes, and the thin lip lifted unpleasantly.

'So you are one of those dogs of the Barachans.'

A faint smile touched Conan's lips.

'And do you know who I am?' his questioner demanded.

'This ship is the *Wastrel*; so you must be Zaporavo.'

'Aye!' It touched the captain's grim vanity that the man should know him. He was a tall man, tall as Conan, though of leaner build. Framed in his steel morion his face was dark, saturnine and hawk-like, wherefore men called him the Hawk. His armor and garments were rich and ornate, after the fashion of a Zingaran grandee. His hand was never far from his sword-hilt.

There was little favor in the gaze he bent on Conan. Little love was lost between Zingaran renegades and the outlaws who infested the Baracha Islands off the southern coast of Zingara. These men were mostly sailors from Argos, with a sprinkling of other nationalities. They raided the shipping, and harried the Zingaran coast towns, just as the Zingaran buccaneers did, but these dignified their profession by calling themselves Freebooters, while they dubbed the Barachans pirates. They were neither the first nor the last to gild the name of thief.

Some of these thoughts passed through Zaporavo's mind as he toyed with his sword-hilt and scowled at his uninvited guest. Conan gave no hint of what his own thoughts might be. He stood with folded arms as placidly as if upon his own deck; his lips smiled and his eyes were untroubled.

'What are you doing here?' the Freebooter demanded abruptly.

'I found it necessary to leave the rendezvous at Tortage before moonrise last night,' answered Conan. 'I departed in a leaky boat, and rowed and bailed all night. Just at dawn I saw your topsails, and left the miserable tub to sink, while I made better speed in the water.'

'There are sharks in these waters,' growled Zaporavo, and was vaguely irritated by the answering shrug of the mighty shoulders. A glance toward the waist showed a screen of eager faces staring upward. A word would send them leaping up on the poop in a storm of swords that would overwhelm even such a fighting-man as the stranger looked to be.

'Why should I burden myself with every nameless vagabond that the sea casts up?' snarled Zaporavo, his look and manner more insulting than his words.

'A ship can always use another good sailor,' answered the other without resentment. Zaporavo scowled, knowing the truth of that assertion. He hesitated, and doing so, lost his ship, his command, his girl, and his life. But of course he could not see into the future, and to him Conan was only another wastrel, cast up, as he put it, by the sea. He did not like the man; yet the fellow had given him no provocation. His manner was not insolent, though rather more confident than Zaporavo liked to see.

'You'll work for your keep,' snarled the Hawk. 'Get off the poop. And remember, the only law here is my will.'

The smile seemed to broaden on Conan's thin lips. Without hesitation but without haste he turned and descended into the waist. He did not look again at Sancha, who, during the brief conversation, had watched eagerly, all eyes and ears.

As he came into the waist the crew thronged about him – Zingarans, all of them, half naked, their gaudy silk garments splashed with tar, jewels glinting in ear-rings and dagger-hilts. They were eager for the time-honored sport of baiting the stranger. Here he would be tested, and his future status in the crew decided. Up on the poop Zaporavo had apparently already forgotten the stranger's existence, but Sancha watched, tense with interest. She had become familiar with such scenes, and knew the baiting would be brutal and probably bloody.

But her familiarity with such matters was scanty compared to that of Conan. He smiled faintly as he came into the waist and saw the menacing figures pressing truculently about him. He paused and eyed the ring inscrutably, his composure unshaken. There was a certain code about these things. If he had attacked the captain, the whole crew would have been at his throat, but they would give him a fair chance against the one selected to push the brawl.

The man chosen for this duty thrust himself forward – a wiry brute, with a crimson sash knotted about his head like a turban. His lean chin jutted out, his scarred face was evil beyond belief. Every glance, each swaggering movement was an affront. His way of beginning the baiting was as primitive, raw and crude as himself.

'Baracha, eh?' he sneered. 'That's where they raise dogs for men. We of the Fellowship spit on 'em – like this!'

He spat in Conan's face and snatched at his own sword.

The Barachan's movement was too quick for the eye to follow. His sledge-like fist crunched with a terrible impact against his tormentor's jaw, and the Zingaran catapulted through the air and fell in a crumpled heap by the rail.

Conan turned towards the others. But for a slumbering glitter in his eyes, his bearing was unchanged. But the baiting was over as suddenly as it had begun. The seamen lifted their companion; his broken jaw hung slack, his head lolled unnaturally.

'By Mitra, his neck's broken!' swore a black-bearded sea-rogue.

'You Freebooters are a weak-boned race,' laughed the pirate. 'On the Barachas we take no account of such taps as that. Will you play at sword-strokes, now, any of you? No? Then all's well, and we're friends, eh?'

There were plenty of tongues to assure him that he spoke truth. Brawny arms swung the dead man over the rail, and a dozen fins cut the water as he sank. Conan laughed and spread his mighty arms as a great cat might stretch itself, and his gaze sought the deck above. Sancha leaned over the rail, red lips parted, dark eyes aglow with interest. The sun behind her outlined her lithe figure through the light kirtle which its glow made transparent. Then across her fell Zaporavo's scowling shadow and a heavy hand fell possessively on her slim shoulder. There were menace and meaning in the glare he bent on the man in the waist; Conan grinned back, as if at a jest none knew but himself.

Zaporavo made the mistake so many autocrats make; alone in somber grandeur on the poop, he underestimated the man below him. He had his opportunity to kill Conan, and he let it pass, engrossed in his own gloomy ruminations. He did not find it easy to think any of the dogs beneath his feet constituted a menace to him. He had stood in the high places so long, and had ground so many foes underfoot, that he unconsciously assumed himself to be above the machinations of inferior rivals.

Conan, indeed, gave him no provocation. He mixed with the crew, lived and made merry as they did. He proved himself a skilled sailor, and by far the strongest man any of them had seen. He did the work of three men, and was always first to spring to any heavy or dangerous task. His mates began to rely upon him. He did not quarrel with them, and they were careful not to quarrel with him. He gambled with them, putting up his girdle and sheath for a stake, won their money and weapons, and gave them back with a laugh. The crew instinctively looked toward him as the leader of the forecastle. He vouchsafed no information as to what had caused him to flee the Barachas, but the knowledge that he was capable of a deed bloody enough to have exiled him from that wild band increased the respect felt toward him by the fierce Freebooters. Toward Zaporavo and the mates he was imperturbably courteous, never insolent or servile.

The dullest was struck by the contrast between the harsh, taciturn, gloomy commander, and the pirate whose laugh was gusty and ready, who roared ribald songs in a dozen languages, guzzled ale like a toper, and – apparently – had no thought for the morrow.

Had Zaporavo known he was being compared, even though unconsciously, with a man before the mast, he would have been speechless with amazed anger. But he was engrossed with his broodings, which had become blacker and grimmer as the years crawled by, and with his vague grandiose dreams; and with the girl whose possession was a bitter pleasure, just as all his pleasures were.

And she looked more and more at the black-maned giant who towered among his mates at work or play. He never spoke to her, but there was no mistaking the candor of his gaze. She did not mistake it, and she wondered if she dared the perilous game of leading him on.

No great length of time lay between her and the palaces of Kordava, but it was as if a world of change separated her from the life she had lived before Zaporavo tore her screaming from the flaming caravel his wolves had plundered. She, who had been the spoiled and petted daughter of the Duke of Kordava, learned what it was to be a buccaneer's plaything, and because she was supple enough to bend without breaking, she lived where other women had died, and because she was young and vibrant with life, she came to find pleasure in the existence.

The life was uncertain, dream-like, with sharp contrasts of battle, pillage, murder, and flight. Zaporavo's red visions made it even more uncertain than that of the average Freebooter. No one knew what he planned next. Now they had left all charted coasts behind and were plunging further and further into that unknown billowy waste ordinarily shunned by seafarers, and into which, since the beginnings of Time, ships had ventured, only to vanish from the sight of man for ever. All known lands lay behind them, and day upon day the blue surging immensity lay empty to their sight. Here there was no loot – no towns to sack nor ships to burn. The men murmured, though they did not let their murmurings reach the ears of their implacable master, who tramped the poop day and night in gloomy majesty, or pored over ancient charts and time-yellowed maps, reading in tomes that were crumbling masses of worm-eaten parchment. At times he talked to Sancha, wildly it seemed to her, of lost continents, and fabulous isles dreaming unguessed amidst the blue foam of nameless gulfs, where horned dragons guarded treasures gathered by pre-human kings, long, long ago.

Sancha listened, uncomprehending, hugging her slim knees, her thoughts constantly roving away from the words of her grim companion back to a clean-limbed bronze giant whose laughter was gusty and elemental as the sea wind.

So, after many weary weeks, they raised land to westward, and at dawn dropped anchor in a shallow bay, and saw a beach which was like a white band bordering an expanse of gently grassy slopes, masked by green trees. The wind brought scents of fresh vegetation and spices, and Sancha clapped her hands with glee at the prospect of adventuring ashore. But her eagerness turned to sulkiness when Zaporavo ordered her to remain aboard until he sent for her. He never gave any explanation for his commands; so she never knew his reason, unless it was the lurking devil in him that frequently made him hurt her without cause.

So she lounged sulkily on the poop and watched the men row ashore through the calm water that sparkled like liquid jade in the morning sunlight. She saw them bunch together on the sands, suspicious, weapons ready, while several scattered out through the trees that fringed the beach. Among these, she noted, was Conan. There was no mistaking that tall brown figure with its springy step. Men said he was no civilized man at all, but a Cimmerian, one of those barbaric tribesmen who dwelt in the gray hills of the far North, and whose raids struck terror in their southern neighbors. At least, she knew that there was something about him, some super-vitality or barbarism that set him apart from his wild mates.

Voices echoed along the shore, as the silence reassured the buccaneers. The clusters broke up, as men scattered along the beach in search of fruit. She saw them climbing and plucking among the trees, and her pretty mouth watered. She stamped a little foot and swore with a proficiency acquired by association with her blasphemous companions.

The men on shore had indeed found fruit, and were gorging on it, finding one unknown golden-skinned variety especially luscious. But Zaporavo did not seek or eat fruit. His scouts having found nothing indicating men or beasts in the neighborhood, he stood staring inland, at the long reaches of grassy slopes melting into one another. Then, with a brief word, he shifted his sword-belt and strode in under the trees. His mate expostulated with him against going alone, and was rewarded by a savage blow in the mouth. Zaporavo had his reasons for wishing to go alone. He desired to learn if this island were indeed that mentioned in the mysterious *Book of Skelos*, whereon, nameless sages aver, strange monsters guard crypts filled with hieroglyph-carven gold. Nor, for murky reasons of his own, did he wish to share his knowledge, if it were true, with any one, much less his own crew.

Sancha, watching eagerly from the poop, saw him vanish into the leafy fastness. Presently she saw Conan, the Barachan, turn, glance briefly at the men scattered up and down the beach; then the pirate went quickly in the direction taken by Zaporavo, and likewise vanished among the trees.

Sancha's curiosity was piqued. She waited for them to reappear, but they did not. The seamen still moved aimlessly up and down the beach, and some had wandered inland. Many had lain down in the shade to sleep. Time passed and she fidgeted about restlessly. The sun began to beat down hotly, in spite of the canopy above the poop-deck. Here it was warm, silent, draggingly monotonous; a few yards away across a band of blue shallow water, the cool shady mystery of tree-fringed beach and woodland-dotted meadow beckoned her. Moreover, the mystery concerning Zaporavo and Conan tempted her.

She well knew the penalty for disobeying her merciless master, and she sat for some time, squirming with indecision. At last she decided that it was worth even one of Zaporavo's whippings to play truant, and with no more ado she kicked off her soft leather sandals, slipped out of her kirtle and stood up on the deck naked as Eve. Clambering over the rail and down the chains, she slid into the water and swam ashore. She stood on the beach a few moments, squirming as the sands tickled her small toes, while she looked for the crew. She saw only a few, at some distance up or down the beach. Many were fast asleep under the trees, bits of golden fruit still clutched in their fingers. She wondered why they should sleep so soundly, so early in the day.

None hailed her as she crossed the white girdle of sand and entered the shade of the woodland. The trees, she found, grew in irregular clusters, and between these groves stretched rolling expanses of meadow-like slopes. As she progressed inland, in the direction taken by Zaporavo, she was entranced by the green vistas that unfolded gently before her, soft slope beyond slope, carpeted with green sward and dotted with groves. Between the slopes lay gentle declivities, likewise swarded. The scenery seemed to melt into itself, or each scene into the other; the view was singular, at once broad and restricted. Over all a dreamy silence lay like an enchantment.

Then she came suddenly onto the level summit of a slope, circled with tall trees, and the dreamily faery-like sensation vanished abruptly at the sight of what lay on the reddened and trampled grass. Sancha involuntarily cried out and recoiled, then stole forward, wide-eyed, trembling in every limb.

It was Zaporavo who lay there on the sward, staring sightlessly upward, a gaping wound in his breast. His sword lay near his nerveless hand. The Hawk had made his last swoop.

It is not to be said that Sancha gazed on the corpse of her lord without emotion. She had no cause to love him, yet she felt at least the sensation any girl might feel when looking on the body of the man who was first to possess her. She did not weep or feel any need of weeping, but she was seized by a strong trembling, her blood seemed to congeal briefly, and she resisted a wave of hysteria.

She looked about her for the man she expected to see. Nothing met her eyes but the ring of tall, thickly leafed forest giants, and the blue slopes beyond them. Had the Freebooter's slayer dragged himself away, mortally wounded? No bloody tracks led away from the body.

Puzzled, she swept the surrounding trees, stiffening as she caught a rustle in the emerald leaves that seemed not to be of the wind. She went toward the trees, staring into the leafy depths.

'Conan?' Her call was inquiring; her voice sounded strange and small in the vastness of silence that had grown suddenly tense.

Her knees began to tremble as a nameless panic swept over her.

'Conan!' she cried desperately. 'It is I – Sancha! Where are you? Please, Conan—' Her voice faltered away. Unbelieving horror dilated her brown eyes. Her red lips parted to an inarticulate scream. Paralysis gripped her limbs; where she had such desperate need of swift flight, she could not move. She could only shriek wordlessly.

2

When Conan saw Zaporavo stalk alone into the woodland, he felt that the chance he had watched for had come. He had eaten no fruit, nor joined in the horse-play of his mates; all his faculties were occupied with watching the buccaneer chief. Accustomed to Zaporavo's moods, his men were not particularly surprised that their captain should choose to explore an unknown and probably hostile isle alone. They turned to their own amusement, and did not notice Conan when he glided like a stalking panther after the chieftain.

Conan did not underrate his dominance of the crew. But he had not gained the right, through battle and foray, to challenge the captain to a duel to the death. In these empty seas there had been no opportunity for him to prove himself according to Freebooter law. The crew would stand solidly against him if he attacked the chieftain openly. But he knew that if he killed Zaporavo without their knowledge, the leaderless crew would not be likely to be swayed by loyalty to a dead man. In such wolf-packs only the living counted.

So he followed Zaporavo with sword in hand and eagerness in his heart, until he came out onto a level summit, circled with tall trees, between whose trunks he saw the green vistas of the slopes melting into the blue distance. In the midst of the glade Zaporavo, sensing pursuit, turned, hand on hilt.

The buccaneer swore.

'Dog, why do you follow me?'

'Are you mad, to ask?' laughed Conan, coming swiftly toward his erstwhile chief. His lips smiled, and in his blue eyes danced a wild gleam.

Zaporavo ripped out his sword with a black curse, and steel clashed against steel as the Barachan came in recklessly and wide open, his blade singing a wheel of blue flame about his head.

Zaporavo was the veteran of a thousand fights by sea and by land. There was no man in the world more deeply and thoroughly versed than he in the lore of swordcraft. But he had never been pitted against a blade wielded by thews bred in the wild lands beyond the borders of civilization. Against his fighting-craft was matched blinding speed and strength impossible to a civilized man. Conan's manner of fighting was unorthodox, but instinctive and natural as that of a timber wolf. The intricacies of the sword were as useless against his primitive fury as a human boxer's skill against the onslaughts of a panther.

Fighting as he had never fought before, straining every last ounce of effort to parry the blade that flickered like lightning about his head, Zaporavo in desperation caught a full stroke near his hilt, and felt his whole arm go numb beneath the terrific impact. That stroke was instantly followed by a thrust with such terrible drive behind it that the sharp point ripped through chain-mail and ribs like paper, to transfix the heart beneath. Zaporavo's lips writhed in brief agony, but, grim to the last, he made no sound. He was dead before his body relaxed on the trampled grass, where blood drops glittered like spilt rubies in the sun.

Conan shook the red drops from his sword, grinned with unaffected pleasure, stretched like a huge cat – and abruptly stiffened, the expression of satisfaction on his face being replaced by a stare of bewilderment. He stood like a statue, his sword trailing in his hand.

As he lifted his eyes from his vanquished foe, they had absently rested on the surrounding trees, and the vistas beyond. And he had seen a fantastic thing – a thing incredible and inexplicable. Over the soft rounded green shoulder of a distant slope had loped a tall black naked figure, bearing on its shoulder an equally naked white form. The apparition vanished as suddenly as it had appeared, leaving the watcher gasping in surprize.

The pirate stared about him, glanced uncertainly back the way he had come, and swore. He was nonplussed – a bit upset, if the term might be applied to one of such steely nerves as his. In the midst of realistic, if exotic surroundings, a vagrant image of fantasy and nightmare had been introduced. Conan doubted neither his eyesight nor his sanity. He had seen something alien and uncanny, he knew; the mere fact of a black figure racing across the landscape carrying a white captive was bizarre enough, but this black figure had been unnaturally tall.

Shaking his head doubtfully, Conan started off in the direction in which he had seen the thing. He did not argue the wisdom of his move; with his curiosity so piqued, he had no choice but to follow its promptings.

Slope after slope he traversed, each with its even sward and clustered groves. The general trend was always upward, though he ascended and descended the gentle inclines with monotonous regularity. The array of rounded shoulders and shallow declivities was bewildering and apparently endless. But at last he advanced up what he believed was the highest summit on the island, and halted at the sight of green shining walls and towers, which, until he had reached the spot on which he then stood, had merged so perfectly with the green landscape as to be invisible, even to his keen sight.

He hesitated, fingered his sword, then went forward, bitten by the worm of curiosity. He saw no one as he approached a tall archway in the curving wall. There was no door. Peering warily through, he saw what seemed to be a broad open court, grass-carpeted, surrounded by a circular wall of the green semi-translucent substance. Various arches opened from it. Advancing on the balls of his bare feet, sword ready, he chose one of these arches at random, and passed into another similar court. Over an inner wall he saw the pinnacles of strangely shaped tower-like structures. One of these towers was built in, or projected into the court in which he found himself, and a broad stair led up to it, along the side of the wall. Up this he went, wondering if it were all real, or if he were not in the midst of a black lotus dream.

At the head of the stair he found himself on a walled ledge, or balcony, he was not sure which. He could now make out more details of the towers, but they were meaningless to him. He realized uneasily that no ordinary human beings could have built them. There was symmetry about their architecture, and system, but it was a mad symmetry, a system alien to human sanity. As for the plan of the whole town, castle, or whatever it was intended for, he could see just enough to get the impression of a great number of courts, mostly circular, each surrounded by its own wall, and connected with the others by open arches, and all, apparently, grouped about the cluster of fantastic towers in the center.

Turning in the other direction from these towers, he got a fearful shock, and crouched down suddenly behind the parapet of the balcony, glaring amazedly.

The balcony or ledge was higher than the opposite wall, and he was looking over that wall into another swarded court. The inner curve of the further wall of that court differed from the others he had seen, in that, instead of being smooth, it seemed to be banded with long lines or ledges, crowded with small objects the nature of which he could not determine.

However, he gave little heed to the wall at the time. His attention was centered on the band of beings that squatted about a dark green pool in the midst of the court. These creatures were black and naked, made like men, but the least of them, standing upright, would have towered head and shoulders above the tall pirate. They were rangy rather than massive, but were finely formed, with no suggestion of deformity or abnormality, save as their great height was abnormal. But even at that distance Conan sensed the basic diabolism of their features.

In their midst, cringing and naked, stood a youth that Conan recognized as the youngest sailor aboard the *Wastrel*. He, then, had been the captive the pirate had seen borne across the grass-covered slope. Conan had heard no sound of fighting – saw no blood-stains or wounds on the sleek ebon limbs of the giants. Evidently the lad had wandered inland away from his companions and been snatched up by a black man lurking in ambush. Conan mentally termed the creatures black men, for lack of a better term; instinctively he knew that these tall ebony beings were not men, as he understood the term.

No sound came to him. The blacks nodded and gestured to one another, but they did not seem to speak – vocally, at least. One, squatting on his haunches before the cringing boy, held a pipe-like thing in his hand. This he set to his lips, and apparently blew, though Conan heard no sound. But the Zingaran youth heard or felt, and cringed.

He quivered and writhed as if in agony; a regularity became evident in the twitching of his limbs, which quickly became rhythmic. The twitching became a violent jerking, the jerking regular movements. The youth began to dance, as cobras dance by compulsion to the tune of the faquir's fife. There was naught of zest or joyful abandon in that dance. There was, indeed, abandon that was awful to see, but it was not joyful. It was as if the mute tune of the pipes grasped the boy's inmost soul with salacious fingers and with brutal torture wrung from it every involuntary expression of secret passion. It was a convulsion of obscenity, a spasm of lasciviousness – an exudation of secret hungers framed by compulsion: desire without pleasure, pain mated awfully to lust. It was like watching a soul stripped naked, and all its dark and unmentionable secrets laid bare.

Conan glared frozen with repulsion and shaken with nausea. Himself as cleanly elemental as a timber wolf, he was yet not ignorant of the perverse secrets of rotting civilizations. He had roamed the cities of Zamora, and known the women of Shadizar the Wicked. But he sensed here a cosmic vileness transcending mere human degeneracy – a perverse branch on the tree of Life, developed along lines outside human comprehension. It was not at the agonized contortions and posturing of the wretched boy that he was shocked, but at the cosmic obscenity of these beings which could drag to light the abysmal secrets that sleep in the unfathomed darkness of the human soul, and find pleasure in the brazen flaunting of such things as should not be hinted at, even in restless nightmares.

Suddenly the black torturer laid down the pipes and rose, towering over the writhing white figure. Brutally grasping the boy by neck and haunch, the giant up-ended him and thrust him head-first into the green pool. Conan saw the white glimmer of his naked body amid the green water, as the black giant held his captive deep under the surface. Then there was a restless movement among the other blacks, and Conan ducked quickly below the balcony wall, not daring to raise his head lest he be seen.

After a while his curiosity got the better of him, and he cautiously peered out again. The blacks were filing out of an archway into another court. One of them was just placing something on a ledge of the further wall, and Conan saw it was the one who had tortured the boy. He was taller than the others, and wore a jeweled head-band. Of the Zingaran boy there was no trace. The giant followed his fellows, and presently Conan saw them emerge from the archway by which he had gained access to that castle of horror, and file away across the green slopes, in the direction from which he had come. They bore no arms, yet he felt that they planned further aggression against the Freebooters.

But before he went to warn the unsuspecting buccaneers, he wished to investigate the fate of the boy. No sound disturbed the quiet. The pirate believed that the towers and courts were deserted save for himself.

He went swiftly down the stair, crossed the court and passed through an arch into the court the blacks had just quitted. Now he saw the nature of the striated wall. It was banded by narrow ledges, apparently cut out of the solid stone, and ranged along these ledges or shelves were thousands of tiny figures, mostly grayish in color. These figures, not much longer than a man's hand, represented men, and so cleverly were they made that Conan recognized various racial characteristics in the different idols, features typical of Zingarans, Argoseans, Ophireans and Kushite corsairs. These last were black in color, just as their models were black in reality. Conan was aware of a vague uneasiness as he stared at the dumb sightless figures. There was a mimicry of reality about them that was somehow disturbing. He felt of them gingerly and could not decide of what material they were made. It felt like petrified bone; but he could not imagine petrified substance being found in the locality in such abundance as to be used so lavishly.

He noticed that the images representing types with which he was familiar were all on the higher ledges. The lower ledges were occupied by figures the features of which were strange to him. They either embodied merely the artists' imagination, or typified racial types long vanished and forgotten.

Shaking his head impatiently, Conan turned toward the pool. The circular court offered no place of concealment; as the body of the boy was nowhere in sight, it must be lying at the bottom of the pool.

Approaching the placid green disk, he stared into the glimmering surface. It was like looking through a thick green glass, unclouded, yet strangely illusory. Of no great dimensions, the pool was round as a well, bordered by a rim of green jade. Looking down he could see the rounded bottom – how far below the surface he could not decide. But the pool seemed incredibly deep – he was aware of a dizziness as he looked down, much as if he were looking into an abyss. He was puzzled by his ability to see the bottom; but it lay beneath his gaze, impossibly remote, illusive, shadowy, yet visible. At times he thought a faint luminosity was apparent deep in the jade-colored depth, but he could not be sure. Yet he was sure that the pool was empty except for the shimmering water.

Then where in the name of Crom was the boy whom he had seen brutally drowned in that pool? Rising, Conan fingered his sword, and gazed around the court again. His gaze focussed on a spot on one of the higher ledges. There he had seen the tall black place something

– cold sweat broke suddenly out on Conan's brown hide.

Hesitantly, yet as if drawn by a magnet, the pirate approached the shimmering wall. Dazed by a suspicion too monstrous to voice, he glared up at the last figure on that ledge. A horrible familiarity made itself evident. Stony, immobile, dwarfish, yet unmistakable, the features of the Zingaran boy stared unseeingly at him. Conan recoiled, shaken to his soul's foundations. His sword trailed in his paralyzed hand as he glared, open-mouthed, stunned by the realization which was too abysmal and awful for the mind to grasp.

Yet the fact was indisputable; the secret of the dwarfish figures was revealed, though behind that secret lay the darker and more cryptic secret of their being.

3

How long Conan stood drowned in dizzy cogitation, he never knew. A voice shook him out of his gaze, a feminine voice that shrieked more and more loudly, as if the owner of the voice were being borne nearer. Conan recognized that voice, and his paralysis vanished instantly.

A quick bound carried him high up on the narrow ledges, where he clung, kicking aside the clustering images to obtain room for his feet. Another spring and a scramble, and he was clinging to the rim of the wall, glaring over it. It was an outer wall; he was looking into the green meadow that surrounded the castle.

Across the grassy level a giant black was striding, carrying a squirming captive under one arm as a man might carry a rebellious child. It was Sancha, her black hair falling in disheveled rippling waves, her olive skin contrasting abruptly with the glossy ebony of her captor. He gave no heed to her wrigglings and cries as he made for the outer archway.

As he vanished within, Conan sprang recklessly down the wall and glided into the arch that opened into the further court. Crouching there, he saw the giant enter the court of the pool, carrying his writhing captive. Now he was able to make out the creature's details.

The superb symmetry of body and limbs was more impressive at close range. Under the ebon skin long, rounded muscles rippled, and Conan did not doubt that the monster could rend an ordinary man limb from limb. The nails of the fingers provided further weapons, for they were grown like the talons of a wild beast. The face was a carven ebony mask. The eyes were tawny, a vibrant gold that glowed and glittered. But the face was inhuman; each line, each feature was stamped with evil – evil transcending the mere evil of humanity. The thing was not a human – it could not be; it was a growth of Life from the pits of blasphemous creation – a perversion of evolutionary development.

The giant cast Sancha down on the sward, where she grovelled, crying with pain and terror. He cast a glance about as if uncertain, and his tawny eyes narrowed as they rested on the images overturned and knocked from the wall. Then he stooped, grasped his captive by her neck and crotch, and strode purposefully toward the green pool. And Conan glided from his archway, and raced like a wind of death across the sward.

The giant wheeled, and his eyes flared as he saw the bronzed avenger rushing toward him. In the instant of surprize his cruel grip relaxed and Sancha wriggled from his hands and fell to the grass. The taloned hands spread and clutched, but Conan ducked beneath their swoop and drove his sword through the giant's groin. The black went down like a felled tree, gushing blood, and the next instant Conan was seized in a frantic grasp as Sancha sprang up and threw her arms around him in a frenzy of terror and hysterical relief.

He cursed as he disengaged himself, but his foe was already dead; the tawny eyes were glazed, the long ebony limbs had ceased to twitch.

'Oh, Conan,' Sancha was sobbing, clinging tenaciously to him, 'what will become of us? What are these monsters? Oh, surely this is hell and that was the devil—'

'Then hell needs a new devil.' The Barachan grinned fiercely. 'But how did he get hold of you? Have they taken the ship?'

'I don't know.' She tried to wipe away her tears, fumbled for her skirt, and then remembered that she wore none. 'I came ashore. I saw you follow Zaporavo, and I followed you both. I found Zaporavo – was – was it you who—'

'Who else?' he grunted. 'What then?'

'I saw a movement in the trees,' she shuddered. 'I thought it was you. I called – then I saw that – that black *thing* squatting like an ape among the branches, leering down at me. It was like a nightmare; I couldn't run. All I could do was squeal. Then it dropped from the tree and seized me – oh, oh, oh!' She hid her face in her hands, and was shaken anew at the memory of the horror.

'Well, we've got to get out of here,' he growled, catching her wrist. 'Come on; we've got to get to the crew—'

'Most of them were asleep on the beach as I entered the woods,' she said.

'Asleep?' he exclaimed profanely. 'What in the seven devils of hell's fire and damnation—'

'Listen!' She froze, a white quivering image of fright.

'I heard it!' he snapped. 'A moaning cry! Wait!'

He bounded up the ledges again and, glaring over the wall, swore with a concentrated fury that made even Sancha gasp. The black men were returning, but they came not alone or empty-handed. Each bore a limp human form; some bore two. Their captives were the Freebooters; they hung slackly in their captors' arms, and but for an occasional vague movement or twitching, Conan would have believed them dead. They had been disarmed but not stripped; one of the blacks bore their sheathed swords, a great armload of bristling steel. From time to time one of the seamen voiced a vague cry, like a drunkard calling out in sottish sleep.

Like a trapped wolf Conan glared about him. Three arches led out of the court of the pool. Through the eastern arch the blacks had left the court, and through it they would presumably return. He had entered by the southern arch. In the western arch he had hidden, and had not had time to notice what lay beyond it. Regardless of his ignorance of the plan of the castle, he was forced to make his decision promptly.

Springing down the wall, he replaced the images with frantic haste, dragged the corpse of his victim to the pool and cast it in. It sank instantly and, as he looked, he distinctly saw an appalling contraction – a shrinking, a hardening. He hastily turned away, shuddering. Then he seized his companion's arm and led her hastily toward the southern archway, while she begged to be told what was happening.

'They've bagged the crew,' he answered hastily. 'I haven't any plan, but we'll hide somewhere and watch. If they don't look in the pool, they may not suspect our presence.'

'But they'll see the blood on the grass!'

'Maybe they'll think one of their own devils spilled it,' he answered. 'Anyway, we'll have to take the chance.'

They were in the court from which he had watched the torture of the boy, and he led her hastily up the stair that mounted the southern wall, and forced her into a crouching position behind the balustrade of the balcony; it was poor concealment, but the best they could do.

Scarcely had they settled themselves, when the blacks filed into the court. There was a resounding clash at the foot of the stairs, and Conan stiffened, grasping his sword. But the blacks passed through an archway on the southwestern side, and they heard a series of thuds and groans. The giants were casting their victims down on the sward. An hysterical giggle rose to Sancha's lips, and Conan quickly clapped his hand over her mouth, stifling the sound before it could betray them.

After a while they heard the padding of many feet on the sward below, and then silence reigned. Conan peered over the wall. The court was empty. The blacks were once more gathered about the pool in the adjoining court, squatting on their haunches. They seemed to pay no heed to the great smears of blood on the sward and the jade rim of the pool. Evidently blood stains were nothing unusual. Nor were they looking into the pool. They were engrossed in some inexplicable conclave of their own; the tall black was playing again on his golden pipes, and his companions listened like ebony statues.

Taking Sancha's hand, Conan glided down the stair, stooping so that his head would not be visible above the wall. The cringing girl followed perforce, staring fearfully at the arch that let into the court of the pool, but through which, at that angle, neither the pool nor its grim throng were visible. At the foot of the stair lay the swords of the Zingarans. The clash they had heard had been the casting down of the captured weapons.

Conan drew Sancha toward the southwestern arch, and they silently crossed the sward and entered the court beyond. There the Freebooters lay in careless heaps, mustaches bristling, ear-rings glinting. Here and there one stirred or groaned restlessly. Conan bent down to them, and Sancha knelt beside him, leaning forward with her hands on her thighs.

'What is that sweet cloying smell?' she asked nervously. 'It's on all their breaths.'

'It's that damned fruit they were eating,' he answered softly. 'I remember the smell of it. It must have been like the black lotus, that makes men sleep. By Crom, they are beginning to awake – but they're unarmed, and I have an idea that those black devils won't wait long before they begin their magic on them. What chance will the lads have, unarmed and stupid with slumber?'

He brooded for an instant, scowling with the intentness of his thoughts; then seized Sancha's olive shoulder in a grip that made her wince.

'Listen! I'll draw those black swine into another part of the castle and keep them busy for a while. Meanwhile you shake these fools awake, and bring their swords to them – it's a fighting chance. Can you do it?'

'I – I – don't know!' she stammered, shaking with terror, and hardly knowing what she was saying.

With a curse, Conan caught her thick tresses near her head and shook her until the walls danced to her dizzy sight.

'You *must* do it!' he hissed at her. 'It's our only chance!'

'I'll do my best!' she gasped, and with a grunt of commendation and an encouraging slap on the back that nearly knocked her down, he glided away.

A few moments later he was crouching at the arch that opened into the court of the pool, glaring upon his enemies. They still sat about the pool, but were beginning to show evidences of an evil impatience. From the court where lay the rousing buccaneers he heard their groans growing louder, beginning to be mingled with incoherent curses. He tensed his muscles and sank into a pantherish crouch, breathing easily between his teeth.

The jeweled giant rose, taking his pipes from his lips – and at that instant Conan was among the startled blacks with a tigerish bound. And as a tiger leaps and strikes among his prey, Conan leaped and struck: thrice his blade flickered before any could lift a hand in defense; then he bounded from among them and raced across the sward. Behind him sprawled three black figures, their skulls split.

But though the unexpected fury of his surprize had caught the giants off guard, the survivors recovered quickly enough. They were at his heels as he ran through the western arch, their long legs sweeping them over the ground at headlong speed. However, he felt confident of his ability to outfoot them at will; but that was not his purpose. He intended leading them on a long chase, in order to give Sancha time to rouse and arm the Zingarans.

And as he raced into the court beyond the western arch, he swore. This court differed from the others he had seen. Instead of being round, it was octagonal, and the arch by which he had entered was the only entrance or exit.

Wheeling, he saw that the entire band had followed him in; a group clustered in the arch, and the rest spread out in a wide line as they approached. He faced them, backing slowly toward the northern wall. The line bent into a semicircle, spreading out to hem him in. He continued to move backward, but more and more slowly, noting the spaces widening between the pursuers. They feared lest he should try to dart around a horn of the crescent, and lengthened their line to prevent it.

He watched with the calm alertness of a wolf, and when he struck it was with the devastating suddenness of a thunderbolt – full at the center of the crescent. The giant who barred his way went down cloven to the middle of the breast-bone, and the pirate was outside their closing ring before the blacks to right and left could come to their stricken comrade's aid. The group at the gate prepared to receive his onslaught, but Conan did not charge them. He had turned and was watching his hunters without apparent emotion, and certainly without fear.

This time they did not spread out in a thin line. They had learned that it was fatal to divide their forces against such an incarnation of clawing, rending fury. They bunched up in a compact mass, and advanced on him without undue haste, maintaining their formation.

Conan knew that if he fell foul of that mass of taloned muscle and bone, there could be but one culmination. Once let them drag him down among them where they could reach him with their talons and use their greater body-weight to advantage, even his primitive ferocity would not prevail. He glanced around the wall and saw a ledge-like projection above a corner on the western side. What it was he did not know, but it would serve his purpose. He began backing toward that corner, and the giants advanced more rapidly. They evidently thought that they were herding him into the corner themselves, and Conan found time to reflect that they probably looked on him as a member of a lower order, mentally inferior to themselves. So much the better. Nothing is more disastrous than underestimating one's antagonist.

Now he was only a few yards from the wall, and the blacks were closing in rapidly, evidently thinking to pin him in the corner before he realized his situation. The group at the gate had deserted their post and were hastening to join their fellows. The giants half-crouched, eyes blazing like golden hell-fire, teeth glistening whitely, taloned hands lifted as if to fend off attack. They expected an abrupt and violent move on the part of their prey, but when it came, it took them by surprize.

Conan lifted his sword, took a step toward them, then wheeled and raced to the wall. With a fleeting coil and release of steel muscles, he shot high in the air, and his straining arm hooked its fingers over the projection. Instantly there was a rending crash and the jutting ledge gave way, precipitating the pirate back into the court.

He hit on his back, which for all its springy sinews would have broken but for the cushioning of the sward, and rebounding like a great cat, he faced his foes. The dancing recklessness was gone from his eyes. They blazed like blue bale-fire; his mane bristled, his thin lips snarled. In an instant the affair had changed from a daring game to a battle of life and death, and Conan's savage nature responded with all the fury of the wild.

The blacks, halted an instant by the swiftness of the episode, now made to sweep on him and drag him down. But in that instant a shout broke the stillness. Wheeling, the giants saw a disreputable throng crowding the arch. The buccaneers weaved drunkenly, they swore incoherently; they were addled and bewildered, but they grasped their swords and advanced with a ferocity not dimmed in the slightest by the fact that they did not understand what it was all about.

As the blacks glared in amazement, Conan yelled stridently and struck them like a razor-edged thunderbolt. They fell like ripe grains beneath his blade, and the Zingarans, shouting with muddled fury, ran groggily across the court and fell on their gigantic foes with bloodthirsty zeal.

They were still dazed; emerging hazily from drugged slumber, they had felt Sancha frantically shaking them and shoving swords into their fists, and had vaguely heard her urging them to some sort of action. They had not understood all she said, but the sight of strangers, and blood streaming, was enough for them.

In an instant the court was turned into a battle-ground which soon resembled a slaughter-house. The Zingarans weaved and rocked on their feet, but they wielded their swords with power and effect, swearing prodigiously, and quite oblivious to all wounds except those instantly fatal. They far outnumbered the blacks, but these proved themselves no mean antagonists. Towering above their assailants, the giants wrought havoc with talons and teeth, tearing out men's throats, and dealing blows with clenched fists that crushed in skulls. Mixed and mingled in that mêlée, the buccaneers could not use their superior agility to the best advantage, and many were too stupid from their drugged sleep to avoid blows aimed at them. They fought with a blind wild-beast ferocity, too intent on dealing death to evade it. The sound of the hacking swords was like that of butchers' cleavers, and the shrieks, yells and curses were appalling.

Sancha, shrinking in the archway, was stunned by the noise and fury; she got a dazed impression of a whirling chaos in which steel flashed and hacked, arms tossed, snarling faces appeared and vanished, and straining bodies collided, rebounded, locked and mingled in a devil's dance of madness.

Details stood out briefly, like black etchings on a background of blood. She saw a Zingaran sailor, blinded by a great flap of scalp torn loose and hanging over his eyes, brace his straddling legs and drive his sword to the hilt in a black belly. She distinctly heard the buccaneer grunt as he struck, and saw the victim's tawny eyes roll up in sudden agony; blood and entrails gushed out over the driven blade. The dying black caught the blade with his naked hands, and the sailor tugged blindly and stupidly; then a black arm hooked about the Zingaran's head, a black knee was planted with cruel force in the middle of his back. His head was jerked back at a terrible angle, and something cracked above the noise of the fray, like the breaking of a thick branch. The conqueror dashed his victim's body to the earth – and as he did, something like a beam of blue light flashed across his shoulders from behind, from right to left. He staggered, his head toppled forward on his breast, and thence, hideously, to the earth.

Sancha turned sick. She gagged and wished to vomit. She made abortive efforts to turn and flee from the spectacle, but her legs would not work. Nor could she close her eyes. In fact, she opened them wider. Revolted, repelled, nauseated, yet she felt the awful fascination she had always experienced at sight of blood. Yet this battle transcended anything she had ever seen fought out between human beings in port raids or sea battles. Then she saw Conan.

Separated from his mates by the whole mass of the enemy, Conan had been enveloped in a black wave of arms and bodies, and dragged down. Then they would quickly have stamped the life out of him, but he had pulled down one of them with him, and the black's body protected that of the pirate beneath him. They kicked and tore at the Barachan and dragged at their writhing comrade, but Conan's teeth were set desperately in his throat, and the pirate clung tenaciously to his dying shield.

An onslaught of Zingarans caused a slackening of the press, and Conan threw aside the corpse and rose, blood-smeared and terrible. The giants towered above him like great black shadows, clutching, buffeting the air with terrible blows. But he was as hard to hit or grapple as a blood-mad panther, and at every turn or flash of his blade, blood jetted. He had already taken punishment enough to kill three ordinary men, but his bull-like vitality was undiminished.

His war cry rose above the medley of the carnage, and the bewildered but furious Zingarans took fresh heart and redoubled their strokes, until the rending of flesh and the crunching of bone beneath the swords almost drowned the howls of pain and wrath.

The blacks wavered, and broke for the gate, and Sancha squealed at their coming and scurried out of the way. They jammed in the narrow archway, and the Zingarans stabbed and hacked at their straining backs with strident yelps of glee. The gate was a shambles before the survivors broke through and scattered, each for himself.

The battle became a chase. Across grassy courts, up shimmering stairs, over the slanting roofs of fantastic towers, even along the broad coping of the walls, the giants fled, dripping blood at each step, harried by their merciless pursuers as by wolves. Cornered, some of them turned at bay and men died. But the ultimate result was always the same – a mangled black body twitching on the sward, or hurled writhing and twisting from parapet or tower roof.

Sancha had taken refuge in the court of the pool, where she crouched, shaking with terror. Outside rose a fierce yelling, feet pounded the sward, and through the arch burst a black, red-stained figure. It was the giant who wore the gemmed headband. A squat pursuer was close behind, and the black turned, at the very brink of the pool. In his extremity he had picked up a sword dropped by a dying sailor, and as the Zingaran rushed recklessly at him, he struck with the unfamiliar weapon. The buccaneer dropped with his skull crushed, but so awkwardly the blow was dealt, the blade shivered in the giant's hand.

He hurled the hilt at the figures which thronged the arch, and bounded toward the pool, his face a convulsed mask of hate. Conan burst through the men at the gate, and his feet spurned the sward in his headlong charge.

But the giant threw his great arms wide and from his lips rang an inhuman cry – the only sound made by a black during the entire fight. It screamed to the sky its awful hate; it was like a voice howling from the pits. At the sound the Zingarans faltered and hesitated. But Conan did not pause. Silently and murderously he drove at the ebon figure poised on the brink of the pool.

But even as his dripping sword gleamed in the air, the black wheeled and bounded high. For a flash of an instant they saw him poised in midair above the pool; then with an earth-shaking roar, the green waters rose and rushed up to meet him, enveloping him in a green volcano.

Conan checked his headlong rush just in time to keep from toppling into the pool, and he sprang back, thrusting his men behind him with mighty swings of his arms. The green pool was like a geyser now, the noise rising to deafening volume as the great column of water reared and reared, blossoming at the crest with a great crown of foam.

Conan was driving his men to the gate, herding them ahead of him, beating them with the flat of his sword; the roar of the water-spout seemed to have robbed them of their faculties. Seeing Sancha standing paralyzed, staring with wide-eyed terror at the seething pillar, he accosted her with a bellow that cut through the thunder of the water and made her jump out of her daze. She ran to him, arms outstretched, and he caught her up under one arm and raced out of the court.

In the court which opened on the outer world, the survivors had gathered, weary, tattered, wounded and blood-stained, and stood gaping dumbly at the great unstable pillar that towered momentarily nearer the blue vault of the sky. Its green trunk was laced with white; its foaming crown was thrice the circumference of its base. Momentarily it threatened to burst and fall in an engulfing torrent, yet it continued to jet skyward.

Conan's eyes swept the bloody, naked group, and he cursed to see only a score. In the stress of the moment he grasped a corsair by the neck and shook him so violently that blood from the man's wounds spattered all near them.

'Where are the rest?' he bellowed in his victim's ear.

'That's all!' the other yelled back, above the roar of the geyser. 'The others were all killed by those black—'

'Well, get out of here!' roared Conan, giving him a thrust that sent him staggering headlong toward the outer archway. 'That fountain is going to burst in a moment—'

'We'll all be drowned!' squawked a Freebooter, limping toward the arch.

'Drowned, hell!' yelled Conan. 'We'll be turned to pieces of petrified bone! Get out, blast you!'

He ran to the outer archway, one eye on the green roaring tower that loomed so awfully above him, the other on stragglers. Dazed with blood-lust, fighting, and the thunderous noise, some of the Zingarans moved like men in a trance. Conan hurried them up; his method was simple. He grasped loiterers by the scruff of the neck, impelled them violently through the gate, added impetus with a lusty kick in the rear, spicing his urgings for haste with pungent comments on the victim's ancestry. Sancha showed an inclination to remain with him, but he jerked away her twining arms, blaspheming luridly, and accelerated her movements with a tremendous slap on the posterior that sent her scurrying across the plateau.

Conan did not leave the gate until he was sure all his men who yet lived were out of the castle and started across the level meadow. Then he glanced again at the roaring pillar looming against the sky, dwarfing the towers, and he too fled that castle of nameless horrors.

The Zingarans had already crossed the rim of the plateau and were fleeing down the slopes. Sancha waited for him at the crest of the first slope beyond the rim, and there he paused for an instant to look back at the castle. It was as if a gigantic green-stemmed and white-blossomed flower swayed above the towers; the roar filled the sky. Then the jade-green and snowy pillar broke with a noise like the rending of the skies, and walls and towers were blotted out in a thunderous torrent.

Conan caught the girl's hand, and fled. Slope after slope rose and fell before them, and behind sounded the rushing of a river. A glance over his straining shoulder showed a broad green ribbon rising and falling as it swept over the slopes. The torrent had not spread out and dissipated; like a giant serpent it flowed over the depressions and the rounded crests. It held a consistent course – *it was following them.*

The realization roused Conan to a greater pitch of endurance. Sancha stumbled and went to her knees with a moaning cry of despair and exhaustion. Catching her up, Conan tossed her over his giant shoulder and ran on. His breast heaved, his knees trembled; his breath tore in great gasps through his teeth. He reeled in his gait. Ahead of him he saw the sailors toiling, spurred on by the terror that gripped them.

The ocean burst suddenly on his view, and in his swimming gaze floated the *Wastrel*, unharmed. Men tumbled into the boats helter-skelter. Sancha fell into the bottom and lay there in a crumpled heap.

Conan, though the blood thundered in his ears and the world swam red to his gaze, took an oar with the panting sailors.

With hearts ready to burst from exhaustion, they pulled for the ship. The green river burst through the fringe of trees. Those trees fell as if their stems had been cut away, and as they sank into the jade-colored flood, they vanished. The tide flowed out over the beach, lapped at the ocean, and the waves turned a deeper, more sinister green.

Unreasoning, instinctive fear held the buccaneers, making them urge their agonized bodies and reeling brains to greater effort; what they feared they knew not, but they did know that in that abominable smooth green ribbon was a menace to body and to soul. Conan knew, and as he saw the broad line slip into the waves and stream through the water toward them, without altering its shape or course, he called up his last ounce of reserve strength so fiercely that the oar snapped in his hands.

But their prows bumped against the timbers of the *Wastrel*, and the sailors staggered up the chains, leaving the boats to drift as they would. Sancha went up on Conan's broad shoulder, hanging limp as a corpse, to be dumped unceremoniously on to the deck as the Barachan took the wheel, gasping orders to his skeleton of a crew. Throughout the affair, he had taken the lead without question, and they had instinctively followed him. They reeled about like drunken men, fumbling mechanically at ropes and braces. The anchor chain, unshackled, splashed into the water, the sails unfurled and bellied in a rising wind. The *Wastrel* quivered and shook herself, and swung majestically seaward. Conan glared shoreward; like a tongue of emerald flame, a ribbon licked out on the water futilely, an oar's length from the *Wastrel*'s keel. It advanced no further. From that end of the tongue, his gaze followed an unbroken stream of lambent green, across the white beach, and over the slopes, until it faded in the blue distance.

The Barachan, regaining his wind, grinned at the panting crew. Sancha was standing near him, hysterical tears coursing down her cheeks. Conan's breeks hung in blood-stained tatters; his girdle and sheath were gone, his sword, driven upright into the deck beside him, was notched and crusted with red. Blood thickly clotted his black mane, and one ear had been half torn from his head. His arms, legs, breast and shoulders were bitten and clawed as if by panthers. But he grinned as he braced his powerful legs, and swung on the wheel in sheer exuberance of muscular might.

'What now?' faltered the girl.

'The plunder of the seas!' he laughed. 'A paltry crew, and that chewed and clawed to pieces, but they can work the ship, and crews can always be found. Come here, girl, and give me a kiss.'

'A kiss?' she cried hysterically. 'You think of kisses at a time like this?'

His laughter boomed above the snap and thunder of the sails, as he caught her up off her feet in the crook of one mighty arm, and smacked her red lips with resounding relish.

'I think of Life!' he roared. 'The dead are dead, and what has passed is done! I have a ship and a fighting crew and a girl with lips like wine, and that's all I ever asked. Lick your wounds, bullies, and break out a cask of ale. You're going to work ship as she never was worked before. Dance and sing while you buckle to it, damn you! To the devil with empty seas! We're bound for waters where the seaports are fat, and the merchant ships are crammed with plunder!'

ROGUES IN THE HOUSE

'One fled, one dead, one sleeping in a golden bed'
OLD RIME

1

AT A COURT FESTIVAL, Nabonidus, the Red Priest, who was the real ruler of the city, touched Murilo, the young aristocrat, courteously on the arm. Murilo turned to meet the priest's enigmatic gaze, and to wonder at the hidden meaning therein. No words passed between them, but Nabonidus bowed and handed Murilo a small gold cask. The young nobleman, knowing that Nabonidus did nothing without reason, excused himself at the first opportunity and returned hastily to his chamber. There he opened the cask and found within a human ear, which he recognized by a peculiar scar upon it. He broke into a profuse sweat, and was no longer in doubt about the meaning in the Red Priest's glance.

But Murilo, for all his scented black curls and foppish apparel, was no weakling to bend his neck to the knife without a struggle. He did not know whether Nabonidus was merely playing with him, or giving him a chance to go into voluntary exile, but the fact that he was still alive and at liberty proved that he was to be given at least a few hours, probably for meditation. But he needed no meditation for decision; what he needed was a tool. And Fate furnished that tool, working among the dives and brothels of the squalid quarters even while the young nobleman shivered and pondered in the part of the city occupied by the purple-towered marble and ivory palaces of the aristocracy.

There was a priest of Anu whose temple, rising at the fringe of the slum district, was the scene of more than devotions. The priest was fat and full-fed, and he was at once a fence for stolen articles and a spy for the police. He worked a thriving trade both ways, because the district on which he bordered was The Maze, a tangle of muddy winding alleys and sordid dens, frequented by the boldest thieves in the kingdom. Daring above all were a Gunderman deserter from the mercenaries and a barbaric Cimmerian. Because of the priest of Anu, the Gunderman was taken and hanged in the market-square. But the Cimmerian fled, and learning in devious ways of the priest's treachery, he entered the temple of Anu by night, and cut off the priest's head. There followed a great turmoil in the city, but search for the killer proved fruitless until his punk betrayed him to the authorities, and led a captain of the guard and his squad to the hidden chamber where the barbarian lay drunk.

Waking to stupefied but ferocious life when they seized him, he disemboweled the captain, burst through his assailants and would have escaped, but for the liquor that still clouded his senses. Bewildered and half blinded, he missed the open door in his headlong flight, and dashed his head against the stone wall so terrifically that he knocked himself senseless. When he came to, he was in the strongest dungeon in the city, shackled to the wall with chains not even his barbaric thews could break.

To this cell came Murilo, masked and wrapped in a wide black cloak. The Cimmerian surveyed him with interest, thinking him the executioner sent to dispatch him. Murilo set him at rights, and regarded him with no less interest. Even in the dim light of the dungeon, with his limbs loaded with chains, the primitive power of the man was evident. His mighty body and thick-muscled limbs combined the strength of a grizzly with the quickness of a panther. Under his tangled black mane his blue eyes blazed with unquenchable savagery.

'Would you like to live?' asked Murilo. The barbarian grunted, new interest glinting in his eyes.

'If I arrange for your escape will you do a favor for me?' the aristocrat asked.

The Cimmerian did not speak, but the intentness of his gaze answered for him.

'I want you to kill a man for me.'

'Whom?'

Murilo's voice sank to a whisper. 'Nabonidus, the king's priest!'

The Cimmerian showed no sign of surprise or perturbation. He had none of the fear or reverence for authority that civilization instills in men. King or beggar, it was all one to him. Nor did he ask why Murilo had come to him, when the quarters were full of cutthroats outside prisons.

'When am I to escape?' he demanded.

'Within the hour. There is but one guard in this part of the dungeon at night. He can be bribed; he *has* been bribed. See, here are the keys to your chains. I'll remove them, and after I have been gone an hour, the guard, Athicus, will unlock the door to your cell. You will bind him with strips torn from your tunic; so when he is found, the authorities will think you were rescued from the outside, and will not suspect him. Go at once to the house of the Red Priest, and kill him. Then go to the Rats' Den, where a man will meet you and give you a pouch of gold and a horse. With those you can escape from the city and flee the country.'

'Take off these cursed chains now,' demanded the Cimmerian. 'And have the guard bring me food. By Crom, I have lived on moldy bread and water for a whole day and I am nigh to famishing.'

'It shall be done; but remember – you are not to escape until I have had time to reach my house.'

Freed of his chains, the barbarian stood up and stretched his heavy arms, enormous in the gloom of the dungeon. Murilo again felt that if any man in the world could accomplish the task he had set, this Cimmerian could. With a few repeated instructions he left the prison, first directing Athicus to take a platter of beef and ale in to the prisoner. He knew he could trust the guard, not only because of the money he had paid, but also because of certain information he possessed regarding the man.

When he returned to his chamber, Murilo was in full control of his fears. Nabonidus would strike through the king – of that he was certain. And since the royal guardsmen were not knocking at his door, it was as certain that the priest had said nothing to the king, so far. Tomorrow he would speak, beyond a doubt – if he lived to see tomorrow.

Murilo believed the Cimmerian would keep faith with him. Whether the man would be able to carry out his purpose remained to be seen. Men had attempted to assassinate the Red Priest before, and they had died in hideous and nameless ways. But they had been products of the cities of men, lacking the wolfish instincts of the barbarian. The instant that Murilo, turning the gold cask with its severed ear in his hands, had learned through his secret channels that the Cimmerian had been captured, he had seen a solution of his problem.

In his chamber again, he drank a toast to the man, whose name was Conan, and to his success that night. And while he was drinking, one of his spies brought him the news that Athicus had been arrested and thrown into prison. The Cimmerian had not escaped.

Murilo felt his blood turn to ice again. He could see in this twist of fate only the sinister hand of Nabonidus, and an eery obsession began to grow on him that the Red Priest was more than human – a sorcerer who read the minds of his victims and pulled strings on which they danced like puppets. With despair came desperation. Girding a sword beneath his black cloak, he left his house by a hidden way, and hurried through the deserted streets. It was just at midnight when he came to the house of Nabonidus, looming blackly among the walled gardens that separated it from the surrounding estates.

The wall was high but not impossible to negotiate. Nabonidus did not put his trust in mere barriers of stone. It was what was inside the wall that was to be feared. What these things were Murilo did not know precisely. He knew there was at least a huge savage dog that roamed the gardens and had on occasion torn an intruder to pieces as a hound rends a rabbit. What else there might be he did not care to conjecture. Men who had been allowed to enter the house on brief, legitimate business, reported that Nabonidus dwelt among rich furnishings, yet simply, attended by a surprisingly small number of servants. Indeed, they mentioned only one as having been visible – a tall silent man called Joka. Someone else, presumably a slave, had been heard moving about in the recesses of the house, but this person no one had ever seen. The greatest mystery of that mysterious house was Nabonidus himself, whose power of intrigue and grasp on international politics had made him the strongest man in the kingdom. People, chancellor and king moved puppet-like on the strings he worked.

Murilo scaled the wall and dropped down into the gardens, which were expanses of shadow, darkened by clumps of shrubbery and waving foliage. No light shone in the windows of the house which loomed so blackly among the trees. The young nobleman stole stealthily yet swiftly through the shrubs. Momentarily he expected to hear the baying of the great dog, and to see its giant body hurtle through the shadows. He doubted the effectiveness of his sword against such an attack, but he did not hesitate. As well die beneath the fangs of a beast as the ax of the headsman.

He stumbled over something bulky and yielding. Bending close in the dim starlight, he made out a limp shape on the ground. It was the dog that guarded the gardens, and it was dead. Its neck was broken and it bore what seemed to be the marks of great fangs. Murilo felt that no human being had done this. The beast had met a monster more savage than itself. Murilo glared nervously at the cryptic masses of bush and shrub; then with a shrug of his shoulders, he approached the silent house.

The first door he tried proved to be unlocked. He entered warily, sword in hand, and found himself in a long shadowy hallway dimly illumined by a light that gleamed through the hangings at the other end. Complete silence hung over the whole house. Murilo glided along the hall and halted to peer through the hangings. He looked into a lighted room, over the windows of which velvet curtains were drawn so closely as to allow no beam to shine through. The room was empty, in so far as human life was concerned, but it had a grisly occupant, nevertheless. In the midst of a wreckage of furniture and torn hangings that told of a fearful struggle, lay the body of a man. The form lay on its belly, but the head was twisted about so that the chin rested behind a shoulder. The features, contorted into an awful grin, seemed to leer at the horrified nobleman.

For the first time that night, Murilo's resolution wavered. He cast an uncertain glance back the way he had come. Then the memory of the headsman's block and ax steeled him, and he crossed the room, swerving to avoid the grinning horror sprawled in its midst. Though he had never seen the man before, he knew from former descriptions that it was Joka, Nabonidus's saturnine servant.

He peered through a curtained door into a broad circular chamber, banded by a gallery halfway between the polished floor and the lofty ceiling. This chamber was furnished as if for a king. In the midst of it stood an ornate mahogany table, loaded with vessels of wine and rich viands. And Murilo stiffened. In a great chair whose broad back was toward him, he saw a figure whose habiliments were familiar. He glimpsed an arm in a red sleeve resting on the arm of the chair; the head, clad in the familiar scarlet hood of the gown, was bent forward as if in meditation. Just so had Murilo seen Nabonidus sit a hundred times in the royal court.

Cursing the pounding of his own heart, the young nobleman stole across the chamber, sword extended, his whole frame poised for the thrust. His prey did not move, nor seem to hear his cautious advance. Was the Red Priest asleep, or was it a corpse which slumped in that great chair? The length of a single stride separated Murilo from his enemy, when suddenly the man in the chair rose and faced him.

The blood went suddenly from Murilo's features. His sword fell from his fingers and rang on the polished floor. A terrible cry broke from his livid lips; it was followed by the thud of a falling body. Then once more silence reigned over the house of the Red Priest.

2

Shortly after Murilo left the dungeon where Conan the Cimmerian was confined, Athicus brought the prisoner a platter of food which included, among other things, a huge joint of beef and a tankard of ale.

Conan fell to voraciously, and Athicus made a final round of the cells, to see that all was in order, and that none should witness the pretended prison-break. It was while he was so occupied that a squad of guardsmen marched into the prison and placed him under arrest. Murilo had been mistaken when he assumed this arrest denoted discovery of Conan's planned escape. It was another matter; Athicus had become careless in his dealings with the underworld, and one of his past sins had caught up with him.

Another jailer took his place, a stolid, dependable creature whom no amount of bribery could have shaken from his duty. He was unimaginative, but he had an exalted idea of the importance of his job.

After Athicus had been marched away to be formally arraigned before a magistrate, this jailer made the rounds of the cells as a matter of routine. As he passed that of Conan, his sense of propriety was shocked and outraged to see the prisoner free of his chains, and in the act of gnawing the last shreds of meat from a huge beef-bone. The jailer was so upset that he made the mistake of entering the cell alone, without calling guards from other parts of the prison. It was his first mistake in the line of duty, and his last. Conan brained him with the beef-bone, took his poniard and his keys, and made a leisurely departure. As Murilo had said, only one guard was on duty there at night. The Cimmerian passed himself outside the walls by means of the keys he had taken, and presently emerged into the outer air, as free as if Murilo's plan had been successful.

In the shadows of the prison walls, Conan paused to decide his next course of action. It occurred to him that since he had escaped through his own actions, he owed nothing to Murilo; yet it had been the young nobleman who had removed his chains and had the food sent to him, without either of which his escape would have been impossible. Conan decided that he was indebted to Murilo, and, since he was a man who discharged his obligations eventually, he determined to carry out his promise to the young aristocrat. But first he had some business of his own to attend to.

He discarded his ragged tunic and moved off through the night naked but for a loin-cloth. As he went he fingered the poniard he had captured – a murderous weapon with a broad double-edged blade nineteen inches long. He slunk along alleys and shadowed plazas until he came to the district which was his destination – The Maze. Along its labyrinthian ways he went with the certainty of familiarity. It was indeed a maze of black alleys and enclosed courts and devious ways; of furtive sounds, and stenches. There was no paving on the streets; mud and filth mingled in an unsavory mess. Sewers were unknown; refuse was dumped into the alleys to form reeking heaps and puddles. Unless a man walked with care he was likely to lose his footing and plunge waist-deep into nauseous pools. Nor was it uncommon to stumble over a corpse lying with its throat cut or its head knocked in, in the mud. Honest folk shunned The Maze with good reason.

Conan reached his destination without being seen, just as one he wished fervently to meet was leaving it. As the Cimmerian slunk into the courtyard below, the girl who had sold him to the police was taking leave of her new lover in a chamber one flight up. This young thug, her door closed behind him, groped his way down a creaking flight of stairs, intent on his own meditations, which, like those of most of the denizens of The Maze, had to do with the unlawful acquirement of property. Part-way down the stairs, he halted suddenly, his hair standing up. A vague bulk crouched in the darkness before him, a pair of eyes blazed like the eyes of a hunting beast. A beast-like snarl was the last thing he heard in life; as the monster lurched against him, a keen blade ripped through his belly. He gave one gasping cry, and slumped down limply on the stairway.

The barbarian loomed above him for an instant, ghoul-like, his eyes burning in the gloom. He knew the sound was heard, but the people in The Maze were careful to attend to their own business. A death-cry on darkened stairs was nothing unusual. Later, some one would venture to investigate, but only after a reasonable lapse of time.

Conan went up the stairs and halted at the door he knew well of old. It was fastened within, but his blade passed between the door and the jamb and lifted the bar. He stepped inside, closing the door after him, and faced the girl who had betrayed him to the police.

The wench was sitting cross-legged in her shift on her unkempt bed. She turned white and stared at him as if at a ghost. She had heard the cry from the stairs, and she saw the red stain on the poniard in his hand. But she was too filled with terror on her own account to waste any time lamenting the evident fate of her lover. She began to beg for her life, almost incoherent with terror. Conan did not reply; he merely stood and glared at her with his burning eyes, testing the edge of his poniard with a calloused thumb.

At last he crossed the chamber, while she cowered back against the wall, sobbing frantic pleas for mercy. Grasping her yellow locks with no gentle hand, he dragged her off the bed. Thrusting his blade back in its sheath, he tucked his squirming captive under his left arm, and strode to the window. Like most houses of that type, a ledge encircled each story, caused by the continuance of the window-ledges. Conan kicked the window open and stepped out on that narrow band. If any had been near or awake, they would have witnessed the bizarre sight of a man moving carefully along the ledge, carrying a kicking, half-naked wench under his arm. They would have been no more puzzled than the girl.

Reaching the spot he sought, Conan halted, gripping the wall with his free hand. Inside the building rose a sudden clamor, showing that the body had at last been discovered. His captive whimpered and twisted, renewing her importunities. Conan glanced down into the muck and slime of the alleys below; he listened briefly to the clamor inside and the pleas of the wench; then he dropped her with great accuracy into a cesspool. He enjoyed her kickings and flounderings and the concentrated venom of her profanity for a few seconds, and even allowed himself a low rumble of laughter. Then he lifted his head, listened to the growing tumult within the building, and decided it was time for him to kill Nabonidus.

3

It was a reverberating clang of metal that roused Murilo. He groaned and struggled dazedly to a sitting posture. About him all was silence and darkness, and for an instant he was sickened with the fear that he was blind. Then he remembered what had gone before, and his flesh crawled. By the sense of touch he found that he was lying on a floor of evenly joined stone slabs. Further groping discovered a wall of the same material. He rose and leaned against it, trying in vain to orient himself. That he was in some sort of a prison seemed certain, but where and how long he was unable to guess. He remembered dimly a clashing noise, and wondered if it had been the iron door of his dungeon closing on him, or if it betokened the entrance of an executioner.

At this thought he shuddered profoundly and began to feel his way along the wall. Momentarily he expected to encounter the limits of his prison, but after a while he came to the conclusion that he was travelling down a corridor. He kept to the wall, fearful of pits or other traps, and was presently aware of something near him in the blackness. He could see nothing, but either his ears had caught a stealthy sound, or some subconscious sense warned him. He stopped short, his hair standing on end; as surely as he lived, he felt the presence of some living creature crouching in the darkness in front of him.

He thought his heart would stop when a voice hissed in a barbaric accent: 'Murilo! Is it you?'

'Conan!' Limp from the reaction, the young nobleman groped in the darkness and his hands encountered a pair of great naked shoulders.

'A good thing I recognized you,' grunted the barbarian. 'I was about to stick you like a fattened pig.'

'Where are we, in Mitra's name?'

'In the pits under the Red Priest's house; but why—'

'What is the time?'

'Not long after midnight.'

Murilo shook his head, trying to assemble his scattered wits.

'What are you doing here?' demanded the Cimmerian.

'I came to kill Nabonidus. I heard they had changed the guard at your prison—'

'They did,' growled Conan. 'I broke the new jailer's head and walked out. I would have been here hours agone, but I had some personal business to attend to. Well, shall we hunt for Nabonidus?'

Murilo shuddered. 'Conan, we are in the house of the archfiend! I came seeking a human enemy; I found a hairy devil out of hell!'

Conan grunted uncertainly; fearless as a wounded tiger as far as human foes were concerned, he had all the superstitious dreads of the primitive.

'I gained access to the house,' whispered Murilo, as if the darkness were full of listening ears. 'In the outer gardens I found Nabonidus's dog mauled to death. Within the house I came upon Joka, the servant. His neck had been broken. Then I saw Nabonidus himself seated in his chair, clad in his accustomed garb. At first I thought he too was dead. I stole up to stab him. He rose and faced me. God!' The memory of that horror struck the young nobleman momentarily speechless as he relived that awful instant.

'Conan,' he whispered, 'it was no *man* that stood before me! In body and posture it was not unlike a man, but from the scarlet hood of the priest grinned a face of madness and nightmare! It was covered with black hair, from which small pig-like eyes glared redly; its nose was flat, with great flaring nostrils; its loose lips writhed back, disclosing huge yellow fangs, like the teeth of a dog. The hands that hung from the scarlet sleeves were misshapen and likewise covered with black hair. All this I saw in one glance, and then I was overcome with horror; my senses left me and I swooned.'

'What then?' muttered the Cimmerian uneasily.

'I recovered consciousness only a short time ago; the monster must have thrown me into these pits. Conan, I have suspected that Nabonidus was not wholly human! He is a demon – a were-thing! By day he moves among humanity in the guise of men, and by night he takes on his true aspect.'

'That's evident,' answered Conan. 'Everyone knows there are men who take the form of wolves at will. But why did he kill his servants?'

'Who can delve the mind of a devil?' replied Murilo. 'Our present interest is in getting out of this place. Human weapons can not harm a were-man. How did you get in here?'

'Through the sewer. I reckoned on the gardens being guarded. The sewers connect with a tunnel that lets into these pits. I thought to find some door leading up into the house unbolted.'

'Then let us escape by the way you came!' exclaimed Murilo. 'To the devil with it! Once out of this snake-den, we'll take our chance with the king's guardsmen, and risk a flight from the city. Lead on!'

'Useless,' grunted the Cimmerian. 'The way to the sewers is barred. As I entered the tunnel an iron grille crashed down from the roof. If I had not moved quicker than a flash of lightning, its spear-heads would have pinned me to the floor like a worm. When I tried to lift it, it wouldn't move. An elephant couldn't shake it. Nor could anything bigger than a rabbit squirm between the bars.'

Murilo cursed, an icy hand playing up and down his spine. He might have known Nabonidus would not leave any entrance into his house unguarded. Had Conan not possessed the steel-spring quickness of a wild thing, that falling portcullis would have skewered him. Doubtless his walking through the tunnel had sprung some hidden catch that released it from the roof. As it was, both were trapped living.

'There's but one thing to do,' said Murilo, sweating profusely. 'That's to search for some other exit; doubtless they're all set with traps, but we have no other choice.'

The barbarian grunted agreement, and the companions began groping their way at random down the corridor. Even at that moment, something occurred to Murilo.

'How did you recognize me in this blackness?' he demanded.

'I smelled the perfume you put on your hair, when you came to my cell,' answered Conan. 'I smelled it again a while ago, when I was crouching in the dark and preparing to rip you open.'

Murilo put a lock of his black hair to his nostrils; even so the scent was barely apparent to his civilized senses, and he realized how keen must be the organs of the barbarian.

Instinctively his hand went to his scabbard as they groped onward, and he cursed to find it empty. At that moment a faint glow became apparent ahead of them, and presently they came to a sharp bend in the corridor, about which the light filtered grayly. Together they peered around the corner, and Murilo, leaning against his companion, felt his huge frame stiffen. The young nobleman had also seen it – the body of a man, half naked, lying limply in the corridor beyond the bend, vaguely illuminated by a radiance which seemed to emanate from a broad silver disk on the farther wall. A strange familiarity about the recumbent figure, which lay face down, stirred Murilo with inexplicable and monstrous conjectures. Motioning the Cimmerian to follow him, he stole forward and bent above the body. Overcoming a certain repugnance, he grasped it and turned it on its back. An incredulous oath escaped him; the Cimmerian grunted explosively.

'Nabonidus! The Red Priest!' ejaculated Murilo, his brain a dizzy vortex of whirling amazement. 'Then who – what—?'

The priest groaned and stirred. With cat-like quickness Conan bent over him, poniard poised above his heart. Murilo caught his wrist.

'Wait! Don't kill him yet—'

'Why not?' demanded the Cimmerian. 'He has cast off his wereguise, and sleeps. Will you awaken him to tear us to pieces?'

'No, wait!' urged Murilo, trying to collect his jumbled wits. 'Look! He is not sleeping – see that great blue welt on his shaven temple? He has been knocked senseless. He may have been lying here for hours.'

'I thought you swore you saw him in beastly shape in the house above,' said Conan.

'I did! Or else – he's coming to! Keep back your blade, Conan; there is a mystery here even darker than I thought. I must have words with this priest, before we kill him.'

Nabonidus lifted a hand vaguely to his bruised temple, mumbled, and opened his eyes. For an instant they were blank and empty of intelligence; then life came back to them with a jerk, and he sat up, staring at the companions. Whatever terrific jolt had temporarily addled his razor-keen brain, it was functioning with its accustomed vigor again. His eyes shot swiftly about him, then came back to rest on Murilo's face.

'You honor my poor house, young sir,' he laughed coolly, glancing at the great figure that loomed behind the young nobleman's shoulder. 'You have brought a bravo, I see. Was your sword not sufficient to sever the life of my humble self?'

'Enough of this,' impatiently returned Murilo. 'How long have you lain here?'

'A peculiar question to put to a man recovering consciousness,' answered the priest. 'I do not know what time it now is. But it lacked an hour or so of midnight when I was set upon.'

'Then who is it that masquerades in your own gown in the house above?' demanded Murilo.

'That will be Thak,' answered Nabonidus, ruefully fingering his bruises. 'Yes, that will be Thak. And in my gown? The dog!'

Conan, who comprehended none of this, stirred restlessly, and growled something in his own tongue. Nabonidus glanced at him whimsically.

'Your bully's knife yearns for my heart, Murilo,' he said. 'I thought you might be wise enough to take my warning and leave the city.'

'How was I to know that was to be granted me?' returned Murilo. 'At any rate, my interests are here.'

'You are in good company with that cutthroat,' murmured Nabonidus. 'I had suspected you for some time. That was why I caused that pallid court secretary to disappear. Before he died he told me many things, among others the name of the young nobleman who bribed him to filch state secrets, which the nobleman in turn sold to rival powers. Are you not ashamed of yourself, Murilo, you white-handed thief?'

'I have no more cause for shame than you, you vulture-hearted plunderer,' answered Murilo promptly. 'You exploit a whole kingdom for your personal greed, and under the guise of disinterested statesmanship, you swindle the king, beggar the rich, oppress the poor, and sacrifice the whole future of the nation for your ruthless ambition. You are no more than a fat hog with his snout in the trough. You are a greater thief than I am. This Cimmerian is the most honest man of the three of us, because he steals and murders openly.'

'Well, then, we are all rogues together,' agreed Nabonidus equably. 'And what now? My life?'

'When I saw the ear of the secretary that had disappeared, I knew I was doomed,' said Murilo abruptly, 'and I believed you would invoke the authority of the king. Was I right?'

'Quite so,' answered the priest. 'A court secretary is easy to do away with, but you are a bit too prominent. I had intended telling the king a jest about you in the morning.'

'A jest that would have cost me my head,' muttered Murilo. 'Then the king is unaware of my foreign enterprises?'

'As yet,' sighed Nabonidus. 'And now, since I see your companion has his knife, I fear that jest will never be told.'

'You should know how to get out of these rat-dens,' said Murilo. 'Suppose I agree to spare your life. Will you help us to escape, and swear to keep silent about my thievery?'

'When did a priest keep an oath?' complained Conan, comprehending the trend of the conversation. 'Let me cut his throat; I want to see what color his blood is. They say in The Maze that his heart is black, so his blood must be black too—'

'Be quiet,' whispered Murilo. 'If he does not show us the way out of these pits, we may rot here. Well, Nabonidus, what do you say?'

'What does a wolf with his leg in the trap say?' laughed the priest. 'I am in your power and if we are to escape, we must aid one another. I swear, if we survive this adventure, to forget all your shifty dealings. I swear by the soul of Mitra!'

'I am satisfied,' muttered Murilo. 'Even the Red Priest would not break that oath. Now to get out of here. My friend here entered by way of the tunnel, but a grille fell behind him and blocked the way. Can you cause it to be lifted?'

'Not from these pits,' answered the priest. 'The control lever is in the chamber above the tunnel. There is only one other way out of these pits, which I will show you. But tell me, how did you come here?'

Murilo told him in a few words, and Nabonidus nodded, rising stiffly. He limped down the corridor, which here widened into a sort of vast chamber, and approached the distant silver disk. As they advanced the light increased, though it never became anything but a dim shadowy radiance. Near the disk they saw a narrow stair leading upward.

'That is the other exit,' said Nabonidus. 'And I strongly doubt if the door at the head is bolted. But I have an idea that he who would go through that door had better cut his own throat first. Look into the disk.'

What had seemed a silver plate was in reality a great mirror set in the wall. A confusing system of copper-like tubes jutted out from the wall about it, bending down toward it at right angles. Glancing into these tubes, Murilo saw a bewildering array of smaller mirrors. He turned his attention to the larger mirror in the wall, and ejaculated in amazement. Peering over his shoulder, Conan grunted.

They seemed to be looking through a broad window into a well-lighted chamber. There were broad mirrors on the walls, with velvet hangings between; there were silken couches, chairs of ebony and ivory, and curtained doorways leading off from the chamber. And before one doorway which was not curtained, sat a bulky black object that contrasted grotesquely with the richness of the chamber.

Murilo felt his blood freeze again as he looked at the horror which seemed to be staring directly into his eyes. Involuntarily he recoiled from the mirror, while Conan thrust his head truculently forward, till his jaws almost touched the surface, growling some threat or defiance in his own barbaric tongue.

'In Mitra's name, Nabonidus,' gasped Murilo, shaken, 'what is it?'

'That is Thak,' answered the priest, caressing his temple. 'Some would call him an ape, but he is almost as different from a real ape as he is different from a real man. His people dwell far to the east, in the mountains that fringe the eastern frontiers of Zamora. There are not many of them, but if they are not exterminated, I believe they will become human beings, in perhaps a hundred thousand years. They are in the formative stage; they are neither apes, as their remote ancestors were, nor men, as their remote descendants may be. They dwell in the high crags of well-nigh inaccessible mountains, knowing nothing of fire or the making of shelter or garments, or the use of weapons. Yet they have a language of a sort, consisting mainly of grunts and clicks.

'I took Thak when he was a cub, and he learned what I taught him much more swiftly and thoroughly than any true animal could have done. He was at once bodyguard and servant. But I forgot that being partly a man, he could not be submerged into a mere shadow of myself, like a true animal. Apparently his semi-brain retained impressions of hate, resentment, and some sort of bestial ambition of its own.

'At any rate, he struck when I least expected it. Last night he appeared to go suddenly mad. His actions had all the appearance of bestial insanity, yet I know that they must have been the result of long and careful planning.

'I heard a sound of fighting in the garden, and going to investigate – for I believed it was yourself, being dragged down by my watch-dog – I saw Thak emerge from the shrubbery dripping with blood. Before I was aware of his intention, he sprang at me with an awful scream and struck me senseless. I remember no more, but can only surmise that, following some whim of his semi-human brain, he stripped me of my gown and cast me still living into the pit – for which reason, only the gods can guess. He must have killed the dog when he came from the garden, and after he struck me down, he evidently killed Joka, as you saw the man lying dead in the house. Joka would have come to my aid, even against Thak, whom he always hated.'

Murilo stared at the mirror at the creature which sat with such monstrous patience before the closed door. He shuddered at the sight of the great black hands, thickly grown with hair that was almost fur-like. The body was thick, broad and stooped. The unnaturally wide shoulders had burst the scarlet gown, and on these shoulders Murilo noted the same thick growth of black hair. The face peering from the scarlet hood was utterly bestial, and yet Murilo realized that Nabonidus spoke truth when he said that Thak was not wholly a beast. There was something in the red murky eyes, something in the creature's clumsy posture, something in the whole appearance of the thing that set it apart from the truly animal. That monstrous body housed a brain and soul that were just budding awfully into something vaguely human. Murilo stood aghast as he recognized a faint and hideous kinship between his kind and that squatting monstrosity, and he was nauseated by a fleeting realization of the abysses of bellowing bestiality up through which humanity had painfully toiled.

'Surely he sees us,' muttered Conan. 'Why does he not charge us? He could break this window with ease.'

Murilo realized that Conan supposed the mirror to be a window through which they were looking.

'He does not see us,' answered the priest. 'We are looking into the chamber above us. That door that Thak is guarding is the one at the head of these stairs. It is simply an arrangement of mirrors. Do you see those mirrors on the walls? They transmit the reflection of the room into these tubes, down which other mirrors carry it to reflect it at last on an enlarged scale in this great mirror.'

Murilo realized that the priest must be centuries ahead of his generation, to perfect such an invention; but Conan put it down to witchcraft, and troubled his head no more about it.

'I constructed these pits for a place of refuge as well as a dungeon,' the priest was saying. 'There are times when I have taken refuge here, and through these mirrors, watched doom fall upon those who sought me with ill intent.'

'But why is Thak watching that door?' demanded Murilo.

'He must have heard the falling of the grating in the tunnel. It is connected with bells in the chambers above. He knows someone is in the pits, and he is waiting for him to come up the stairs. Oh, he has learned well the lessons I taught him. He has seen what happened to men who come through that door, when I tugged at the rope that hangs on yonder wall, and he waits to mimic me.'

'And while he waits, what are we to do?' demanded Murilo.

'There is naught we can do, except watch him. As long as he is in that chamber, we dare not ascend the stairs. He has the strength of a true gorilla, and could easily tear us all to pieces. But he does not need to exert his muscles; if we open that door he has but to tug that rope, and blast us into eternity.'

'How?'

'I bargained to help you escape,' answered the priest; 'not to betray my secrets.'

Murilo started to reply, then stiffened suddenly. A stealthy hand had parted the curtains of one of the doorways. Between them appeared a dark face whose glittering eyes fixed menacingly on the squat form in the scarlet robe.

'Petreus!' hissed Nabonidus. 'Mitra, what a gathering of vultures this night is!'

The face remained framed between the parted curtains. Over the intruder's shoulder other faces peered – dark, thin faces, alight with sinister eagerness.

'What do they here?' muttered Murilo, unconsciously lowering his voice, although he knew they could not hear him.

'Why, what would Petreus and his ardent young nationalists be doing in the house of the Red Priest?' laughed Nabonidus. 'Look how eagerly they glare at the figure they think is their arch-enemy. They have fallen into your error; it should be amusing to watch their expressions when they are disillusioned.'

Murilo did not reply. The whole affair had a distinctly unreal atmosphere. He felt as if he were watching the play of puppets, or as a disembodied ghost himself, impersonally viewing the actions of the living, his presence unseen and unsuspected.

He saw Petreus put his finger warningly to his lips, and nod to his fellow-conspirators. The young nobleman could not tell if Thak were aware of the intruders. The apeman's position had not changed, as he sat with his back toward the door through which the men were gliding.

'They had the same idea you had,' Nabonidus was muttering at his ear. 'Only their reasons were patriotic rather than selfish. Easy to gain access to my house, now that the dog is dead. Oh, what a chance to rid myself of their menace once and for all! If I were sitting where Thak sits – a leap to the wall – a tug on that rope—'

Petreus had placed one foot lightly over the threshold of the chamber; his fellows were at his heels, their daggers glinting dully. Suddenly Thak rose and wheeled toward him. The unexpected horror of his appearance, where they had thought to behold the hated but familiar countenance of Nabonidus, wrought havoc with their nerves, as the same spectacle had wrought upon Murilo. With a shriek Petreus recoiled, carrying his companions backward with him. They stumbled and floundered over each other, and in that instant Thak, covering the distance in one prodigious, grotesque leap, caught and jerked powerfully at a thick velvet rope which hung near the doorway.

Instantly the curtains whipped back on either hand, leaving the door clear, and down across it something flashed with a peculiar silvery blur.

'He remembered!' Nabonidus was exulting. 'The beast is half a man! He had seen the doom performed, and he remembered! Watch, now! Watch! Watch!'

Murilo saw that it was a panel of heavy glass that had fallen across the doorway. Through it he saw the pallid faces of the conspirators. Petreus, throwing out his hands as if to ward off a charge from Thak, encountered the transparent barrier, and from his gestures, said something to his companions. Now that the curtains were drawn back, the men in the pits could see all that took place in the chamber that contained the nationalists. Completely unnerved, these ran across the chamber toward the door by which they had apparently entered, only to halt suddenly, as if stopped by an invisible wall.

'The jerk of the rope sealed that chamber,' laughed Nabonidus. 'It is simple; the glass panels work in grooves in the doorways. Jerking the rope trips the spring that holds them. They slide down and lock in place, and can only be worked from outside. The glass is unbreakable; a man with a mallet could not shatter it. Ah!'

The trapped men were in a hysteria of fright; they ran wildly from one door to another, beating vainly at the crystal walls, shaking their fists wildly at the implacable black shape which squatted outside. Then one threw back his head, glared upward, and began to scream, to judge from the working of his lips, while he pointed toward the ceiling.

'The fall of the panels released the clouds of doom,' said the Red Priest with a wild laugh. 'The dust of the gray lotus, from the Swamps of the Dead, beyond the land of Khitai.'

In the middle of the ceiling hung a cluster of gold buds; these had opened like the petals of a great carven rose, and from them billowed a gray mist that swiftly filled the chamber. Instantly the scene changed from one of hysteria to one of madness and horror. The trapped men began to stagger; they ran in drunken circles. Froth dripped from their lips, which twisted as in awful laughter. Raging, they fell upon one another with daggers and teeth, slashing, tearing, slaying in a holocaust of madness. Murilo turned sick as he watched, and was glad that he could not hear the screams and howls with which that doomed chamber must be ringing. Like pictures thrown on a screen, it was silent.

Outside the chamber of horror Thak was leaping up and down in brutish glee, tossing his long hairy arms on high. At Murilo's shoulder Nabonidus was laughing like a fiend.

'Ah, a good stroke, Petreus! That fairly disemboweled him! Now one for you, my patriotic friend! So! They are all down, and the living tear the flesh of the dead with their slavering teeth.'

Murilo shuddered. Behind him the Cimmerian swore softly in his uncouth tongue. Only death was to be seen in the chamber of the gray mist; torn, gashed and mangled, the conspirators lay in a red heap, gaping mouths and blood-dabbled faces staring blankly upward through the slowly swirling eddies of gray.

Thak, stooping like a giant gnome, approached the wall where the rope hung, and gave it a peculiar sidewise pull.

'He is opening the farther door,' said Nabonidus. 'By Mitra, he is more human than even I had guessed! See, the mist swirls out of the chamber, and is dissipated. He waits, to be safe. Now he raises the other panel. He is cautious – he knows the doom of the gray lotus, which brings madness and death. By Mitra!'

Murilo jerked about at the electric quality of the exclamation.

'Our one chance!' exclaimed Nabonidus. 'If he leaves the chamber above for a few minutes, we will risk a dash up those stairs.'

Suddenly tense, they watched the monster waddle through the

doorway and vanish. With the lifting of the glass panel, the curtains had fallen again, hiding the chamber of death.

'We must chance it!' gasped Nabonidus, and Murilo saw perspiration break out on his face. 'Perhaps he will be disposing of the bodies as he has seen me do. Quick! Follow me up those stairs!'

He ran toward the steps and up them with an agility that amazed Murilo. The young nobleman and the barbarian were close at his heels, and they heard his gusty sigh of relief as he threw open the door at the top of the stairs. They burst into the broad chamber they had seen mirrored below. Thak was nowhere to be seen.

'He's in that chamber with the corpses!' exclaimed Murilo. 'Why not trap him there as he trapped them?'

'No, no!' gasped Nabonidus, an unaccustomed pallor tingeing his features. 'We do not know that he is in there. He might emerge before we could reach the trap-rope, anyway! Follow me into the corridor; I must reach my chamber and obtain weapons which will destroy him. This corridor is the only one opening from this chamber which is not set with a trap of some kind.'

They followed him swiftly through a curtained doorway opposite the door of the death-chamber, and came into a corridor, into which various chambers opened. With fumbling haste Nabonidus began to try the doors on each side. They were locked, as was the door at the other end of the corridor.

'My God!' The Red Priest leaned against the wall, his skin ashen. 'The doors are locked, and Thak took my keys from me. We are trapped, after all.'

Murilo stared appalled to see the man in such a state of nerves, and Nabonidus pulled himself together with an effort.

'That beast has me in a panic,' he said. 'If you had seen him tear men as I have seen – well, Mitra aid us, but we must fight him now with what the gods have given us. Come!'

He led them back to the curtained doorway, and peered into the great chamber in time to see Thak emerge from the opposite doorway. It was apparent that the beast-man had suspected something. His small, close-set ears twitched; he glared angrily about him, and approaching the nearest doorway, tore aside the curtains to look behind them.

Nabonidus drew back, shaking like a leaf. He gripped Conan's shoulder. 'Man, do you dare pit your knife against his fangs?'

The Cimmerian's eyes blazed in answer.

'Quick!' the Red Priest whispered, thrusting him behind the curtains, close against the wall. 'As he will find us soon enough, we will draw him to us. As he rushes past you, sink your blade in his back if you can.

You Murilo, show yourself to him, and then flee up the corridor. Mitra knows, we have no chance with him in hand-to-hand combat, but we are doomed anyway when he finds us.'

Murilo felt his blood congeal in his veins, but he steeled himself, and stepped outside the doorway. Instantly Thak, on the other side of the chamber, wheeled, glared, and charged with a thunderous roar. His scarlet hood had fallen back, revealing his black misshapen head; his black hands and red robe were splashed with a brighter red. He was like a crimson and black nightmare as he rushed across the chamber, fangs bared, his bowed legs hurtling his enormous body along at a terrifying gait.

Murilo turned and ran back into the corridor, and quick as he was, the shaggy horror was almost at his heels. Then as the monster rushed past the curtains, from among them catapulted a great form that struck full on the apeman's shoulders, at the same instant driving the poniard into the brutish back. Thak screamed horribly as the impact knocked him off his feet, and the combatants hit the floor together. Instantly there began a whirl and thrash of limbs, the tearing and rending of a fiendish battle.

Murilo saw that the barbarian had locked his legs about the apeman's torso, and was striving to maintain his position on the monster's back, while he butchered it with his poniard. Thak, on the other hand, was striving to dislodge his clinging foe, to drag him around within reach of the giant fangs that gaped for his flesh. In a whirlwind of blows and scarlet tatters they rolled along the corridor, revolving so swiftly that Murilo dared not use the chair he had caught up, lest he strike the Cimmerian. And he saw that in spite of the handicap of Conan's first hold, and the voluminous robe that lashed and wrapped about the apeman's limbs and body, Thak's giant strength was swiftly prevailing. Inexorably he was dragging the Cimmerian around in front of him. The apeman had taken punishment enough to have killed a dozen men. Conan's poniard had sunk again and again into his torso, shoulders and bull-like neck; he was streaming blood from a score of wounds, but unless the blade quickly reached some absolutely vital spot, Thak's inhuman vitality would survive to finish the Cimmerian, and after him, Conan's companions.

Conan was fighting like a wild beast himself, in silence except for his gasps of effort. The black talons of the monster and the awful grasp of those misshapen hands ripped and tore at him, the grinning jaws gaped for his throat. Then Murilo, seeing an opening, sprang and swung the chair with all his power, and with force enough to have brained a human being. The chair glanced from Thak's slanted black skull; but the stunned monster momentarily relaxed his rending grasp, and in that instant Conan, gasping and streaming blood, plunged forward and sank his poniard to the hilt in the apeman's heart.

With a convulsive shudder the beastman started from the floor, then sank limply back. His fierce eyes set and glazed, his thick limbs quivered and became rigid.

Conan staggered dizzily up, shaking the sweat and blood out of his eyes. Blood dripped from his poniard and fingers, and trickled in rivulets down his thighs, arms and breast. Murilo caught at him to support him, but the barbarian shook him off impatiently.

'When I cannot stand alone, it will be time to die,' he mumbled, through mashed lips. 'But I'd like a flagon of wine.'

Nabonidus was staring down at the still figure as if he could not believe his own eyes. Black, hairy, abhorrent, the monster lay, grotesque in the tatters of the scarlet robe; yet more human than bestial, even so, and possessed somehow of a vague and terrible pathos.

Even the Cimmerian sensed this, for he panted: 'I have slain a *man* tonight, not a *beast*. I will count him among the chiefs whose souls I've sent into the dark, and my women will sing of him.'

Nabonidus stooped and picked up a bunch of keys on a golden chain. They had fallen from the apeman's girdle during the battle. Motioning his companions to follow him, he led them to a chamber, unlocked the door, and led the way inside. It was illumined like the others. The Red Priest took a vessel of wine from a table and filled crystal beakers. As his companions drank thirstily, he murmured: 'What a night! It is nearly dawn, now. What of you, my friends?'

'I'll dress Conan's hurts, if you will fetch me bandages and the like,' said Murilo, and Nabonidus nodded, and moved toward the door that led into the corridor. Something about his bowed head caused Murilo to watch him sharply. At the door the Red Priest wheeled suddenly. His face had undergone a transformation. His eyes gleamed with his old fire, his lips laughed soundlessly.

'Rogues together!' his voice rang with its accustomed mockery. 'But not fools together. You are the fool, Murilo!'

'What do you mean?' the young nobleman started forward.

'Back!' Nabonidus's voice cracked like a whip. 'Another step and I will blast you!'

Murilo's blood turned cold as he saw that the Red Priest's hand grasped a thick velvet rope which hung among the curtains just outside the door.

'What treachery is this?' cried Murilo. 'You swore—'

'I swore I would not tell the king a jest concerning you! I did not swear not to take matters into my own hands if I could. Do you think I would pass up such an opportunity? Under ordinary circumstances I would not dare kill you myself, without sanction of the king, but now none will ever know. You will go into the acid-vats along with Thak and the nationalist fools, and none will be the wiser. What a night this has been for me! If I have lost some valuable servants, I have nevertheless rid myself of various dangerous enemies. Stand back! I am over the threshold, and you cannot possibly reach me before I tug this cord and send you to hell. Not the gray lotus, this time, but something just as effective. Nearly every chamber in my house is a trap. And so, Murilo, fool that you are—'

Too quickly for the sight to follow, Conan caught up a stool and hurled it. Nabonidus instinctively threw up his arm with a cry, but not in time. The missile crunched against his head, and the Red Priest swayed and fell face-down in a slowly widening pool of dark crimson.

'His blood was red, after all,' grunted Conan.

Murilo raked back his sweat-plastered hair with a shaky hand as he leaned against the table, weak from the reaction of relief.

'It is dawn,' he said. 'Let us get out of here, before we fall afoul of some other doom. If we can climb the outer wall without being seen, we won't be connected with this night's work. Let the police write their own explanation.'

He glanced at the body of the Red Priest where it lay etched in crimson, and shrugged his shoulders.

'He was the fool, after all; had he not paused to taunt us, he could have trapped us easily.'

'Well,' said the Cimmerian tranquilly, 'he's travelled the road all rogues must walk at last. I'd like to loot the house, but I suppose we'd best go.'

As they emerged from the dimness of the dawn-whitened garden, Murilo said: 'The Red Priest has gone into the dark, so my road is clear in the city, and I have nothing to fear. But what of you? There is still the matter of that priest in The Maze, and—'

'I'm tired of this city anyway,' grinned the Cimmerian. 'You mentioned a horse waiting at the Rats' Den. I'm curious to see how fast that horse can carry me into another kingdom. There's many a highway I want to travel before I walk the road Nabonidus walked this night.'

SHADOWS IN THE MOONLIGHT

1

A SWIFT CRASHING OF horses through the tall reeds; a heavy fall, a despairing cry. From the dying steed there staggered up its rider, a slender girl in sandals and girdled tunic. Her dark hair fell over her white shoulders, her eyes were those of a trapped animal. She did not look at the jungle of reeds that hemmed in the little clearing, nor at the blue waters that lapped the low shore behind her. Her wide-eyed gaze was fixed in agonized intensity on the horseman who pushed through the reedy screen and dismounted before her.

He was a tall man, slender, but hard as steel. From head to heel he was clad in light silvered mesh-mail that fitted his supple form like a glove. From under the dome-shaped, gold-chased helmet his brown eyes regarded her mockingly.

'Stand back!' her voice shrilled with terror. 'Touch me not, Shah Amurath, or I will throw myself into the water and drown!'

He laughed, and his laughter was like the purr of a sword sliding from a silken sheath.

'No, you will not drown, Olivia, daughter of confusion, for the marge is too shallow, and I can catch you before you can reach the deeps. You gave me a merry chase, by the gods, and all my men are far behind us. But there is no horse west of Vilayet that can distance Irem for long.' He nodded at the tall, slender-legged desert stallion behind him.

'Let me go!' begged the girl, tears of despair staining her face. 'Have I not suffered enough? Is there any humiliation, pain or degradation you have not heaped on me? How long must my torment last?'

'As long as I find pleasure in your whimperings, your pleas, tears and writhings,' he answered with a smile that would have seemed gentle to a stranger. 'You are strangely virile, Olivia. I wonder if I shall ever weary of you, as I have always wearied of women before. You are ever fresh and unsullied, in spite of me. Each new day with you brings a new delight.

'But come – let us return to Akif, where the people are still feting the conqueror of the miserable *kozaki*; while he, the conqueror, is engaged in recapturing a wretched fugitive, a foolish, lovely, idiotic runaway!'

'No!' She recoiled, turning toward the waters lapping bluely among the reeds.

'Yes!' His flash of open anger was like a spark struck from flint. With a quickness her tender limbs could not approximate, he caught her wrist, twisting it in pure wanton cruelty until she screamed and sank to her knees.

'Slut! I should drag you back to Akif at my horse's tail, but I will be merciful and carry you on my saddle-bow, for which favor you shall humbly thank me, while—'

He released her with a startled oath and sprang back, his saber flashing out, as a terrible apparition burst from the reedy jungle sounding an inarticulate cry of hate.

Olivia, staring up from the ground, saw what she took to be either a savage or a madman advancing on Shah Amurath in an attitude of deadly menace. He was powerfully built, naked but for a girdled loincloth, which was stained with blood and crusted with dried mire. His black mane was matted with mud and clotted blood; there were streaks of dried blood on his chest and limbs, dried blood on the long straight sword he gripped in his right hand. From under the tangle of his locks, bloodshot eyes glared like coals of blue fire.

'You Hyrkanian dog!' mouthed this apparition in a barbarous accent. 'The devils of vengeance have brought you here!'

'*Kozak!*' ejaculated Shah Amurath, recoiling. 'I did not know a dog of you escaped! I thought you all lay stiff on the steppe, by Ilbars River.'

'All but me, damn you!' cried the other. 'Oh, I've dreamed of such a meeting as this, while I crawled on my belly through the brambles, or lay under rocks while the ants gnawed my flesh, or crouched in the mire up to my mouth – I dreamed, but never hoped it would come to pass. Oh, gods of Hell, how I have yearned for this!'

The stranger's bloodthirsty joy was terrible to behold. His jaws champed spasmodically, froth appeared on his blackened lips.

'Keep back!' ordered Shah Amurath, watching him narrowly.

'Ha!' It was like the bark of a timber wolf. 'Shah Amurath, the great Lord of Akif! Oh, damn you, how I love the sight of you – you, who fed my comrades to the vultures, who tore them between wild horses, blinded and maimed and mutilated them – *ai*, you dog, you filthy dog!' His voice rose to a maddened scream, and he charged.

In spite of the terror of his wild appearance, Olivia looked to see him fall at the first crossing of the blades. Madman or savage, what could he do, naked, against the mailed chief of Akif?'

There was an instant when the blades flamed and licked, seeming barely to touch each other and leap apart; then the broadsword flashed past the saber and descended terrifically on Shah Amurath's shoulder. Olivia cried out at the fury of that stroke. Above the crunch of the rending mail, she distinctly heard the snap of the shoulder-bone. The Hyrkanian reeled back, suddenly ashen, blood spurting over the links of his hauberk; his saber slipped from his nerveless fingers.

'Quarter!' he gasped.

'Quarter?' There was a quiver of frenzy in the stranger's voice. 'Quarter such as you gave us, you swine!'

Olivia closed her eyes. This was no longer battle, but butchery, frantic, bloody, impelled by an hysteria of fury and hate, in which culminated the sufferings of battle, massacre, torture, and fear-ridden, thirst-maddened, hunger-haunted flight. Though Olivia knew that Shah Amurath deserved no mercy or pity from any living creature, yet she closed her eyes and pressed her hands over her ears, to shut out the sight of that dripping sword that rose and fell with the sound of a butcher's cleaver, and the gurgling cries that dwindled away and ceased.

She opened her eyes, to see the stranger turning away from a gory travesty that only vaguely resembled a human being. The man's breast heaved with exhaustion or passion; his brow was beaded with sweat; his right hand was splashed with blood.

He did not speak to her, or even glance toward her. She saw him stride through the reeds that grew at the water's edge, stoop, and tug at something. A boat wallowed out of its hiding-place among the stalks. Then she divined his intention, and was galvanized into action.

'Oh, wait!' she wailed, staggering up and running toward him. 'Do not leave me! Take me with you!'

He wheeled and stared at her. There was a difference in his bearing. His bloodshot eyes were sane. It was as if the blood he had just shed had quenched the fire of his frenzy.

'Who are you?' he demanded.

'I am called Olivia. I was *his* captive. I ran away. He followed me. That's why he came here. Oh, do not leave me here! His warriors are not far behind him. They will find his corpse – they will find me near it – oh!' She moaned in her terror and wrung her white hands.

He stared at her in perplexity.

'Would you be better off with me?' he demanded. 'I am a barbarian, and I know from your looks that you fear me.'

'Yes, I fear you,' she replied, too distracted to dissemble. 'My flesh crawls at the horror of your aspect. But I fear the Hyrkanians more. Oh, let me go with you! They will put me to the torture if they find me beside their dead lord.'

'Come, then.' He drew aside, and she stepped quickly into the boat, shrinking from contact with him. She seated herself in the bow, and he stepped into the boat, pushed off with an oar, and using it as a paddle, worked his way tortuously among the tall stalks until they glided out into open water. Then he set to work with both oars, rowing with great, smooth, even strokes, the heavy muscles of arms and shoulders and back rippling in rhythm to his exertions.

There was silence for some time, the girl crouching in the bows, the man tugging at the oars. She watched him with timorous fascination. It was evident that he was not an Hyrkanian, and he did not resemble the Hyborian races. There was a wolfish hardness about him that marked the barbarian. His features, allowing for the strains and stains of battle and his hiding in the marshes, reflected that same untamed wildness, but they were neither evil nor degenerate.

'Who are you?' she asked. 'Shah Amurath called you a *kozak*; were you of that band?'

'I am Conan, of Cimmeria,' he grunted. 'I was with the *kozaki*, as the Hyrkanian dogs called us.'

She knew vaguely that the land he named lay far to the northwest, beyond the farthest boundaries of the different kingdoms of her race.

'I am a daughter of the King of Ophir,' she said. 'My father sold me to a Shemite chief, because I would not marry a prince of Koth.'

The Cimmerian grunted in surprize.

Her lips twisted in a bitter smile. 'Aye, civilized men sell their children as slaves to savages, sometimes. They call your race barbaric, Conan of Cimmeria.'

'We do not sell our children,' he growled, his chin jutting truculently.

'Well – I was sold. But the desert man did not misuse me. He wished to buy the good will of Shah Amurath, and I was among the gifts he brought to Akif of the purple gardens. Then—' She shuddered and hid her face in her hands.

'I should be lost to all shame,' she said presently. 'Yet each memory stings me like a slaver's whip. I abode in Shah Amurath's palace, until some weeks agone he rode out with his hosts to do battle with a band of invaders who were ravaging the borders of Turan. Yesterday he returned in triumph, and a great fete was made to honor him. In the drunkenness and rejoicing, I found an opportunity to steal out of the city on a stolen horse. I had thought to escape – but he followed, and about midday came up with me. I outran his vassals, but him I could not escape. Then you came.'

'I was lying hid in the reeds,' grunted the barbarian. 'I was one of those dissolute rogues, the Free Companions, who burned and looted along the borders. There were five thousand of us, from a score of races and tribes. We had been serving as mercenaries for a rebel prince in eastern Koth, most of us, and when he made peace with his cursed sovereign, we were out of employment; so we took to plundering the outlying dominions of Koth, Zamora and Turan impartially. A week ago Shah Amurath trapped us near the banks of Ilbars with fifteen thousand men. Mitra! The skies were black with vultures. When the lines broke, after a whole day of fighting, some tried to break through to the north, some to the west. I doubt if any escaped. The steppes were covered with horsemen riding down the fugitives. I broke for the east, and finally reached the edge of the marshes that border this part of Vilayet.

'I've been hiding in the morasses ever since. Only the day before yesterday the riders ceased beating up the reed-brakes, searching for just such fugitives as I. I've squirmed and burrowed and hidden like a snake, feasting on musk-rats I caught and ate raw, for lack of fire to cook them. This dawn I found this boat hidden among the reeds. I hadn't intended going out on the sea until night, but after I killed Shah Amurath, I knew his mailed dogs would be close at hand.'

'And what now?'

'We shall doubtless be pursued. If they fail to see the marks left by the boat, which I covered as well as I could, they'll guess anyway that we took to sea, after they fail to find us among the marshes. But we have a start, and I'm going to haul at these oars until we reach a safe place.'

'Where shall we find that?' she asked hopelessly. 'Vilayet is an Hyrkanian pond.'

'Some folk don't think so,' grinned Conan grimly; 'notably the slaves that have escaped from galleys and become pirates.'

'But what are your plans?'

'The southwestern shore is held by the Hyrkanians for hundreds of miles. We still have a long way to go before we pass beyond their northern boundaries. I intend to go northward until I think we have passed them. Then we'll turn westward, and try to land on the shore bordered by the uninhabited steppes.'

'Suppose we meet pirates, or a storm?' she asked. 'And we shall starve on the steppes.'

'Well,' he reminded her, 'I didn't ask you to come with me.'

'I am sorry.' She bowed her shapely dark head. 'Pirates, storms, starvation – they are all kinder than the people of Turan.'

'Aye.' His dark face grew somber. 'I haven't done with them yet. Be at ease, girl. Storms are rare on Vilayet at this time of year. If we make the steppes, we shall not starve. I was reared in a naked land. It was those cursed marshes, with their stench and stinging flies, that nigh unmanned me. I am at home in the high lands. As for pirates—' He grinned enigmatically, and bent to the oars.

The sun sank like a dull-glowing copper ball into a lake of fire. The blue of the sea merged with the blue of the sky, and both turned to soft dark velvet, clustered with stars and the mirrors of stars. Olivia reclined in the bows of the gently rocking boat, in a state dreamy and unreal. She experienced an illusion that she was floating in midair, stars beneath her as well as above. Her silent companion was etched vaguely against the softer darkness. There was no break or falter in the rhythm of his oars; he might have been a fantasmal oarsman, rowing her across the dark lake of Death. But the edge of her fear was dulled, and, lulled by the monotony of motion, she passed into a quiet slumber.

Dawn was in her eyes when she awakened, aware of a ravenous hunger. It was a change in the motion of the boat that had roused her; Conan was resting on his oars, gazing beyond her. She realized that he had rowed all night without pause, and marvelled at his iron endurance. She twisted about to follow his stare, and saw a green wall of trees and shrubbery rising from the water's edge and sweeping away in a wide curve, enclosing a small bay whose waters lay still as blue glass.

'This is one of the many islands that dot this inland sea,' said Conan. 'They are supposed to be uninhabited. I've heard the Hyrkanians seldom visit them. Besides, they generally hug the shores in their galleys, and we have come a long way. Before sunset we were out of sight of the mainland.'

With a few strokes he brought the boat in to shore and made the painter fast to the arching root of a tree which rose from the water's edge. Stepping ashore, he reached out a hand to help Olivia. She took it, wincing slightly at the bloodstains upon it, feeling a hint of the dynamic strength that lurked in the barbarian's thews.

A dreamy quiet lay over the woods that bordered the blue bay. Then somewhere, far back among the trees, a bird lifted its morning song. A breeze whispered through the leaves, and set them to murmuring. Olivia found herself listening intently for something, she knew not what. What might be lurking amid those nameless woodlands?

As she peered timidly into the shadows between the trees, something swept into the sunlight with a swift whirl of wings: a great parrot which dropped on to a leafy branch and swayed there, a gleaming image of jade and crimson. It turned its crested head sidewise and regarded the invaders with glittering eyes of jet.

'Crom!' muttered the Cimmerian. 'Here is the grandfather of all parrots. He must be a thousand years old! Look at the evil wisdom of his eyes. What mysteries do you guard, Wise Devil?'

Abruptly the bird spread its flaming wings and, soaring from its perch, cried out harshly: '*Yagkoolan yok tha, xuthalla!*' and with a wild screech of horribly human laughter, rushed away through the trees to vanish in the opalescent shadows.

Olivia stared after it, feeling the cold hand of nameless foreboding touch her supple spine.

'What did it say?' she whispered.

'Human words, I'll swear,' answered Conan; 'but in what tongue I can't say.'

'Nor I,' returned the girl. 'Yet it must have learned them from human lips. Human, or—' she gazed into the leafy fastness and shuddered slightly, without knowing why.

'Crom, I'm hungry!' grunted the Cimmerian. 'I could eat a whole buffalo. We'll look for fruit; but first I'm going to cleanse myself of this dried mud and blood. Hiding in marshes is foul business.'

So saying, he laid aside his sword, and wading out shoulder-deep into the blue water, went about his ablutions. When he emerged, his clean-cut bronze limbs shone, his streaming black mane was no longer matted. His blue eyes, though they smoldered with unquenchable fire, were no longer murky or bloodshot. But the tigerish suppleness of limb and the dangerous aspect of feature were not altered.

Strapping on his sword once more, he motioned the girl to follow him, and they left the shore, passing under the leafy arches of the great branches. Underfoot lay a short green sward which cushioned their tread. Between the trunks of the trees they caught glimpses of faerylike vistas.

Presently Conan grunted in pleasure at the sight of golden and russet globes hanging in clusters among the leaves. Indicating that the girl should seat herself on a fallen tree, he filled her lap with the exotic delicacies, and then himself fell to with unconcealed gusto.

'Ishtar!' said he, between mouthfuls. 'Since Ilbars I have lived on rats, and roots I dug out of the stinking mud. This is sweet to the palate, though not very filling. Still, it will serve if we eat enough.'

Olivia was too busy to reply. The sharp edge of the Cimmerian's hunger blunted, he began to gaze at his fair companion with more interest than previously, noting the lustrous clusters of her dark hair, the peach-bloom tints of her dainty skin, and the rounded contours of her lithe figure which the scanty silk tunic displayed to full advantage.

Finishing her meal, the object of his scrutiny looked up, and meeting his burning, slit-eyed gaze, she changed color and the remnants of the fruit slipped from her fingers.

Without comment, he indicated with a gesture that they should continue their explorations, and rising, she followed him out of the trees and into a glade, the farther end of which was bounded by a dense thicket. As they stepped into the open there was a ripping crash in this thicket, and Conan, bounding aside and carrying the girl with him, narrowly saved them from something that rushed through the air and struck a tree-trunk with a thunderous impact.

Whipping out his sword, Conan bounded across the glade and plunged into the thicket. Silence ensued, while Olivia crouched on the sward, terrified and bewildered. Presently Conan emerged, a puzzled scowl on his face.

'Nothing in that thicket,' he growled. 'But there was something—'

He studied the missile that had so narrowly missed them, and grunted incredulously, as if unable to credit his own senses. It was a huge block of greenish stone which lay on the sward at the foot of the tree, whose wood its impact had splintered.

'A strange stone to find on an uninhabited island,' growled Conan.

Olivia's lovely eyes dilated in wonder. The stone was a symmetrical block, indisputably cut and shaped by human hands. And it was astonishingly massive. The Cimmerian grasped it with both hands, and with legs braced and the muscles standing out on his arms and back in straining knots, he heaved it above his head and cast it from him, exerting every ounce of nerve and sinew. It fell a few feet in front of him. Conan swore.

'No man living could throw that rock across this glade. It's a task for siege engines. Yet here there are no mangonels or ballistas.'

'Perhaps it was thrown by some such engine from afar,' she suggested.

He shook his head. 'It didn't fall from above. It came from yonder thicket. See how the twigs are broken? It was thrown as a man might throw a pebble. But who? What? Come!'

She hesitantly followed him into the thicket. Inside the outer ring of leafy brush, the undergrowth was less dense. Utter silence brooded over all. The springy sward gave no sign of footprint. Yet from this mysterious thicket had hurtled that boulder, swift and deadly. Conan bent closer to the sward, where the grass was crushed down here and there. He shook his head angrily. Even to his keen eyes it gave no clue as to what had stood or trodden there. His gaze roved to the green roof above their heads, a solid ceiling of thick leaves and interwoven arches. And he froze suddenly.

Then rising, sword in hand, he began to back away, thrusting Olivia behind him.

'Out of here, quick!' he urged in a whisper that congealed the girl's blood.

'What is it? What do you see?'

'Nothing,' he answered guardedly, not halting his wary retreat.

'But what is it, then? What lurks in this thicket?'

'Death!' he answered, his gaze still fixed on the brooding jade arches that shut out the sky.

Once out of the thicket, he took her hand and led her swiftly through the thinning trees, until they mounted a grassy slope, sparsely treed, and emerged upon a low plateau, where the grass grew taller and the trees were few and scattered. And in the midst of that plateau rose a long broad structure of crumbling greenish stone.

They gazed in wonder. No legends named such a building on any island of Vilayet. They approached it warily, seeing that moss and lichen crawled over the stones, and the broken roof gaped to the sky. On all sides lay bits and shards of masonry, half hidden in the waving grass, giving the impression that once many buildings rose there, perhaps a whole town. But now only the long hall-like structure rose against the sky, and its walls leaned drunkenly among the crawling vines.

Whatever doors had once guarded its portals had long rotted away. Conan and his companion stood in the broad entrance and stared inside. Sunlight streamed in through gaps in the walls and roof, making the interior a dim weave of light and shadow. Grasping his sword firmly, Conan entered, with the slouching gait of a hunting panther, sunken head and noiseless feet. Olivia tiptoed after him.

Once within, Conan grunted in surprize, and Olivia stifled a scream.

'Look! Oh, look!'

'I see,' he answered. 'Nothing to fear. They are statues.'

'But how life-like – and how evil!' she whispered, drawing close to him.

They stood in a great hall, whose floor was of polished stone, littered with dust and broken stones, which had fallen from the ceiling. Vines, growing between the stones, masked the apertures. The lofty roof, flat and undomed, was upheld by thick columns, marching in rows down the sides of the walls. And in each space between these columns stood a strange figure.

They were statues, apparently of iron, black and shining as if continually polished. They were life-sized, depicting tall, lithely powerful men, with cruel hawk-like faces. They were naked, and every swell, depression and contour of joint and sinew was represented with incredible realism. But the most life-like feature was their proud, intolerant faces. These features were not cast in the same mold. Each face possessed its own individual characteristics, though there was a tribal likeness between them all. There was none of the monotonous uniformity of decorative art, in the faces at least.

'They seem to be listening – and waiting!' whispered the girl uneasily.

Conan rang his hilt against one of the images.

'Iron,' he pronounced. 'But Crom! In what molds were they cast?'

He shook his head and shrugged his massive shoulders in puzzlement.

Olivia glanced timidly about the great silent hall. Only the ivy-grown stones, the tendril-clasped pillars, with the dark figures brooding between them, met her gaze. She shifted uneasily and wished to be gone, but the images held a strange fascination for her companion. He examined them in detail, and barbarian-like, tried to break off their limbs. But their material resisted his best efforts. He could neither disfigure nor dislodge from its niche a single image. At last he desisted, swearing in his wonder.

'What manner of men were these copied from?' he inquired of the world at large. 'These figures are black, yet they are not like negroes. I have never seen their like.'

'Let us go into the sunlight,' urged Olivia, and he nodded, with a baffled glance at the brooding shapes along the walls.

So they passed out of the dusky hall into the clear blaze of the summer sun. She was surprized to note its position in the sky; they had spent more time in the ruins than she had guessed.

'Let us take to the boat again,' she suggested. 'I am afraid here. It is a strange evil place. We do not know when we may be attacked by whatever cast the rock.'

'I think we're safe as long as we're not under the trees,' he answered. 'Come.'

The plateau, whose sides fell away toward the wooded shores on the east, west and south, sloped upward toward the north to abut on a tangle of rocky cliffs, the highest point of the island. Thither Conan took his way, suiting his long stride to his companion's gait. From time to time his glance rested inscrutably upon her, and she was aware of it.

They reached the northern extremity of the plateau, and stood gazing up the steep pitch of the cliffs. Trees grew thickly along the rim of the plateau east and west of the cliffs, and clung to the precipitous incline. Conan glanced at these trees suspiciously, but he began the ascent, helping his companion on the climb. The slope was not sheer, and was broken by ledges and boulders. The Cimmerian, born in a hill country, could have run up it like a cat, but Olivia found the going difficult. Again and again she felt herself lifted lightly off her feet and over some obstacle that would have taxed her strength to surmount, and her wonder grew at the sheer physical power of the man. She no longer found his touch repugnant. There was a promise of protection in his iron clasp.

At last they stood on the ultimate pinnacle, their hair stirring in the sea wind. From their feet the cliffs fell away sheerly three or four hundred feet to a narrow tangle of woodlands bordering the beach. Looking southward they saw the whole island lying like a great oval mirror, its bevelled edges sloping down swiftly into a rim of green, except where it broke in the pitch of the cliffs. As far as they could see, on all sides stretched the blue waters, still, placid, fading into dreamy hazes of distance.

'The sea is still,' sighed Olivia. 'Why should we not take up our journey again?'

Conan, poised like a bronze statue on the cliffs, pointed northward. Straining her eyes, Olivia saw a white fleck that seemed to hang suspended in the aching haze.

'What is it?'

'A sail.'

'Hyrkanians?'

'Who can tell, at this distance?'

'They will anchor here – search the island for us!' she cried in quick panic.

'I doubt it. They come from the north, so they can not be searching for us. They may stop for some other reason, in which case we'll have to hide as best we can. But I believe it's either pirate, or an Hyrkanian galley returning from some northern raid. In the latter case they are not likely to anchor here. But we can't put to sea until they've gone out of sight, for they're coming from the direction in which we must go. Doubtless they'll pass the island tonight, and at dawn we can go on our way.'

'Then we must spend the night here?' she shivered.

'It's safest.'

'Then let us sleep here, on the crags,' she urged.

He shook his head, glancing at the stunted trees, at the marching woods below, a green mass which seemed to send out tendrils straggling up the sides of the cliffs.

'Here are too many trees. We'll sleep in the ruins.'

She cried out in protest.

'Nothing will harm you there,' he soothed. 'Whatever threw the stone at us did not follow us out of the woods. There was nothing to show that any wild thing lairs in the ruins. Besides, you are soft-skinned, and used to shelter and dainties. I could sleep naked in the snow and feel no discomfort, but the dew would give you cramps, were we to sleep in the open.'

Olivia helplessly acquiesced, and they descended the cliffs, crossed the plateau and once more approached the gloomy, age-haunted ruins. By this time the sun was sinking below the plateau rim. They had found fruit in the trees near the cliffs, and these formed their supper, both food and drink.

The southern night swept down quickly, littering the dark blue sky with great white stars, and Conan entered the shadowy ruins, drawing the reluctant Olivia after him. She shivered at the sight of those tense black shadows in their niches along the walls. In the darkness that the starlight only faintly touched, she could not make out their outlines; she could only sense their attitude of waiting – waiting as they had waited for untold centuries.

Conan had brought a great armful of tender branches, well leafed. These he heaped to make a couch for her, and she lay upon it, with a curious sensation as of one lying down to sleep in a serpent's lair.

Whatever her forebodings, Conan did not share them. The Cimmerian sat down near her, his back against a pillar, his sword across his knees. His eyes gleamed like a panther's in the dusk.

'Sleep, girl,' said he. 'My slumber is light as a wolf's. Nothing can enter this hall without awaking me.'

Olivia did not reply. From her bed of leaves she watched the immobile figure, indistinct in the soft darkness. How strange, to move in fellowship with a barbarian, to be cared for and protected by one of a race, tales of which had frightened her as a child! He came of a people bloody, grim and ferocious. His kinship to the wild was apparent in his every action; it burned in his smoldering eyes. Yet he had not harmed her, and her worst oppressor had been a man the world called civilized. As a delicious languor stole over her relaxing limbs and she sank into foamy billows of slumber, her last waking thought was a drowsy recollection of the firm touch of Conan's fingers on her soft flesh.

2

Olivia dreamed, and through her dreams crawled a suggestion of lurking evil, like a black serpent writhing through flower gardens. Her dreams were fragmentary and colorful, exotic shards of a broken, unknown pattern, until they crystalized into a scene of horror and madness, etched against a background of cyclopean stones and pillars.

She saw a great hall, whose lofty ceiling was upheld by stone columns marching in even rows along the massive walls. Among these pillars fluttered great green and scarlet parrots, and the hall was thronged with black-skinned, hawk-faced warriors. They were not negroes. Neither they nor their garments nor weapons resembled anything of the world the dreamer knew.

They were pressing about one bound to a pillar: a slender white-skinned youth, with a cluster of golden curls about his alabaster brow. His beauty was not altogether human – like the dream of a god, chiseled out of living marble.

The black warriors laughed at him, jeered and taunted in a strange tongue. The lithe naked form writhed beneath their cruel hands. Blood trickled down the ivory thighs to spatter on the polished floor. The screams of the victim echoed through the hall; then lifting his head toward the ceiling and the skies beyond, he cried out a name in an awful voice. A dagger in an ebon hand cut short his cry, and the golden head rolled on the ivory breast.

As if in answer to that desperate cry, there was a rolling thunder as of celestial chariot-wheels, and a figure stood before the slayers, as if materialized out of empty air. The form was of a man, but no mortal man ever wore such an aspect of inhuman beauty. There was an unmistakable resemblance between him and the youth who dropped lifeless in his chains, but the alloy of humanity that softened the godliness of the youth was lacking in the features of the stranger, awful and immobile in their beauty.

The blacks shrank back before him, their eyes slits of fire. Lifting a hand, he spoke, and his tones echoed through the silent halls in deep rich waves of sound. Like men in a trance the black warriors fell back until they were ranged along the walls in regular lines. Then from the stranger's chiseled lips rang a terrible invocation and command: '*Yagkoolan yok tha, xuthalla!*'

At the blast of that awful cry, the black figures stiffened and froze. Over their limbs crept a curious rigidity, an unnatural petrification. The stranger touched the limp body of the youth, and the chains fell away from it. He lifted the corpse in his arms; then ere he turned away, his tranquil gaze swept again over the silent rows of ebony figures, and he pointed to the moon, which gleamed in through the casements. And they understood, those tense, waiting statues that had been men . . .

Olivia awoke, starting up on her couch of branches, a cold sweat beading her skin. Her heart pounded loud in the silence. She glanced wildly about. Conan slept against his pillar, his head fallen upon his massive breast. The silvery radiance of the late moon crept through the gaping roof, throwing long white lines along the dusty floor. She could see the images dimly, black, tense – waiting. Fighting down a rising hysteria, she saw the moonbeams rest lightly on the pillars and the shapes between.

What was that? A tremor among the shadows where the moonlight fell. A paralysis of horror gripped her, for where there should have been the immobility of death, there was movement: a slow twitching, a flexing and writhing of ebon limbs – an awful scream burst from her lips as she broke the bonds that held her mute and motionless. At her shriek Conan shot erect, teeth gleaming, sword lifted.

'The statues! The statues! – *Oh my God, the statues are coming to life!*'

And with the cry she sprang through a crevice in the wall, burst madly through the hindering vines, and ran, ran, ran – blind, screaming, witless – until a grasp on her arm brought her up short and she shrieked and fought against the arms that caught her, until a familiar voice penetrated the mists of her terror, and she saw Conan's face, a mask of bewilderment in the moonlight.

'What in Crom's name, girl? Did you have a nightmare?' His voice sounded strange and far away. With a sobbing gasp she threw her arms about his thick neck and clung to him convulsively, crying in panting catches.

'Where are they? Did they follow us?'

'Nobody followed us,' he answered.

She sat up, still clinging to him, and looked fearfully about. Her blind flight had carried her to the southern edge of the plateau. Just below them was the slope, its foot masked in the thick shadows of the woods. Behind them she saw the ruins looming in the high-swinging moon.

'Did you not see them? – The statues, moving, lifting their hands, their eyes glaring in the shadows?'

'I saw nothing,' answered the barbarian uneasily. 'I slept more soundly than usual, because it has been so long since I have slumbered the night through; yet I don't think anything could have entered the hall without waking me.'

'Nothing entered,' a laugh of hysteria escaped her. 'It was something there already. Ah, Mitra, we lay down to sleep among them, like sheep making their bed in the shambles!'

'What are you talking about?' he demanded. 'I woke at your cry, but before I had time to look about me, I saw you rush out through the crack in the wall. I pursued you, lest you come to harm. I thought you had a nightmare.'

'So I did!' she shivered. 'But the reality was more grisly than the dream. 'Listen!' And she narrated all that she had dreamed and thought to see.

Conan listened attentively. The natural skepticism of the sophisticated man was not his. His mythology contained ghouls, goblins, and necromancers. After she had finished, he sat silent, absently toying with his sword.

'The youth they tortured was like the tall man who came?' he asked at last.

'As like as son to father,' she answered, and hesitantly: 'If the mind could conceive of the offspring of a union of divinity with humanity, it would picture that youth. The gods of old times mated sometimes with mortal women, our legends tell us.'

'What gods?' he muttered.

'The nameless, forgotten ones. Who knows? They have gone back into the still waters of the lakes, the quiet hearts of the hills, the gulfs beyond the stars. Gods are no more stable than men.'

'But if these shapes were men, blasted into iron images by some god or devil, how can they come to life?'

'There is witchcraft in the moon,' she shuddered. '*He* pointed at the moon; while the moon shines on them, they live. So I believe.'

'But we were not pursued,' muttered Conan, glancing toward the brooding ruins. 'You might have dreamed they moved. I am of a mind to return and see.'

'No, no!' she cried, clutching him desperately. 'Perhaps the spell upon them holds them in the hall. Do not go back! They will rend you limb from limb! Oh, Conan, let us go into our boat and flee this awful island! Surely the Hyrkanian ship has passed us now! Let us go!'

So frantic was her pleading that Conan was impressed. His curiosity in regard to the images was balanced by his superstition. Foes of flesh and blood he did not fear, however great the odds, but any hint of the supernatural roused all the dim monstrous instincts of fear that are the heritage of the barbarian.

He took the girl's hand and they went down the slope and plunged into the dense woods, where the leaves whispered, and nameless night-birds murmured drowsily. Under the trees the shadows clustered thick, and Conan swerved to avoid the denser patches. His eyes roved continuously from side to side, and often flitted into the branches above them. He went quickly yet warily, his arm girdling the girl's waist so strongly that she felt as if she were being carried rather than guided. Neither spoke. The only sound was the girl's quick nervous panting, the rustle of her small feet in the grass. So they came through the trees to the edge of the water, shimmering like molten silver in the moonlight.

'We should have brought fruit for food,' muttered Conan; 'but doubtless we'll find other islands. As well leave now as later; it's but a few hours till dawn—'

His voice trailed away. The painter was still made fast to the looping root. But at the other end was only a smashed and shattered ruin, half submerged in the shallow water.

A stifled cry escaped Olivia. Conan wheeled and faced the dense shadows, a crouching image of menace. The noise of the night-birds was suddenly silent. A brooding stillness reigned over the woods. No breeze moved the branches, yet somewhere the leaves stirred faintly.

Quick as a great cat Conan caught up Olivia and ran. Through the shadows he raced like a phantom, while somewhere above and behind them sounded a curious rushing among the leaves, that implacably drew closer and closer. Then the moonlight burst full upon their faces, and they were speeding up the slope of the plateau.

At the crest Conan laid Olivia down, and turned to glare back at the gulf of shadows they had just quitted. The leaves shook in a sudden breeze; that was all. He shook his mane with an angry growl. Olivia crept to his feet like a frightened child. Her eyes looked up at him, dark wells of horror.

'What are we to do, Conan?' she whispered.

He looked at the ruins, stared again into the woods below.

'We'll go to the cliffs,' he declared, lifting her to her feet. 'Tomorrow I'll make a raft, and we'll trust our luck to the sea again.'

'It was not – not *they* that destroyed our boat?' It was half question, half assertion.

He shook his head, grimly taciturn.

Every step of the way across that moon-haunted plateau was a sweating terror for Olivia, but no black shapes stole subtly from the looming ruins, and at last they reached the foot of the crags, which rose stark and gloomily majestic above them. There Conan halted in some uncertainty, at last selecting a place sheltered by a broad ledge, nowhere near any trees.

'Lie down and sleep if you can, Olivia,' he said. 'I'll keep watch.'

But no sleep came to Olivia, and she lay watching the distant ruins and the wooded rim until the stars paled, the east whitened, and dawn in rose and gold struck fire from the dew on the grass-blades.

She rose stiffly, her mind reverting to all the happenings of the night. In the morning light some of its terrors seemed like figments of an overwrought imagination. Conan strode over to her, and his words electrified her.

'Just before dawn I heard the creak of timbers and the rasp and clack of cordage and oars. A ship has put in and anchored at the beach not far away – probably the ship whose sail we saw yesterday. We'll go up the cliffs and spy on her.'

Up they went, and lying on their bellies among the boulders, saw a painted mast jutting up beyond the trees to the west.

'An Hyrkanian craft, from the cut of her rigging,' muttered Conan. 'I wonder if the crew—'

A distant medley of voices reached their ears, and creeping to the southern edge of the cliffs, they saw a motly horde emerge from the fringe of trees along the western rim of the plateau, and stand there a space in debate. There was much flourishing of arms, brandishing of swords, and loud rough argument. Then the whole band started across the plateau toward the ruins, at a slant that would take them close by the foot of the cliffs.

'Pirates!' whispered Conan, a grim smile on his thin lips. 'It's an Hyrkanian galley they've captured. Here – crawl among these rocks.

'Don't show yourself unless I call to you,' he instructed, having secreted her to his satisfaction among a tangle of boulders along the crest of the cliffs. 'I'm going to meet these dogs. If I succeed in my plan, all will be well, and we'll sail away with them. If I don't succeed – well, hide yourself in the rocks until they're gone, for no devils on this island are as cruel as these sea-wolves.'

And tearing himself from her reluctant grasp, he swung quickly down the cliffs.

Looking fearfully from her eyrie, Olivia saw the band had neared the foot of the cliffs. Even as she looked, Conan stepped out from among the boulders and faced them, sword in hand. They gave back with yells of menace and surprize; then halted uncertainly to glare at this figure which had appeared so suddenly from the rocks. There were some seventy of them, a wild horde made up of men from many nations: Kothians, Zamorians, Brythunians, Corinthians, Shemites. Their features reflected the wildness of their natures. Many bore the scars of the lash or the branding-iron. There were cropped ears, slit noses, gaping eye-sockets, stumps of wrists – marks of the hangman as well as scars of battle. Most of them were half naked, but the garments they wore were fine; gold-braided jackets, satin girdles, silken breeches, tattered, stained with tar and blood, vied with pieces of silver-chased armor. Jewels glittered in nose-rings and ear-rings, and in the hilts of their daggers.

Over against this bizarre mob stood the tall Cimmerian in strong contrast with his hard bronzed limbs and clean-cut vital features.

'Who are you?' they roared.

'Conan the Cimmerian!' His voice was like the deep challenge of a lion. 'One of the Free Companions. I mean to try my luck with the

Red Brotherhood. Who's your chief?'

'I, by Ishtar!' bellowed a bull-like voice, as a huge figure swaggered forward: a giant, naked to the waist, where his capacious belly was girdled by a wide sash that upheld voluminous silken pantaloons. His head was shaven except for a scalp-lock, his mustaches dropped over a rat-trap mouth. Green Shemitish slippers with upturned toes were on his feet, a long straight sword in his hand.

Conan stared and glared.

'Sergius of Khrosha, by Crom!'

'Aye, by Ishtar!' boomed the giant, his small black eyes glittering with hate. 'Did you think I had forgot? Ha! Sergius never forgets an enemy. Now I'll hang you up by the heels and skin you alive. At him, lads!'

'Aye, send your dogs at me, big-belly,' sneered Conan with bitter scorn. 'You were always a coward, you Kothic cur.'

'Coward! To me?' The broad face turned black with passion. 'On guard, you northern dog! I'll cut out your heart!'

In an instant the pirates had formed a circle about the rivals, their eyes blazing, their breath sucking between their teeth in bloodthirsty enjoyment. High up among the crags Olivia watched, sinking her nails into her palms in her painful excitement.

Without formality the combatants engaged, Sergius coming in with a rush, quick on his feet as a giant cat, for all his bulk. Curses hissed between his clenched teeth as he lustily swung and parried. Conan fought in silence, his eyes slits of blue bale-fire.

The Kothian ceased his oaths to save his breath. The only sounds were the quick scuff of feet on the sward, the panting of the pirate, the ring and clash of steel. The swords flashed like white fire in the early sun, wheeling and circling. They seemed to recoil from each other's contact, then leap together again instantly. Sergius was giving back; only his superlative skill had saved him thus far from the blinding speed of the Cimmerian's onslaught. A louder clash of steel, a sliding rasp, a choking cry – from the pirate horde a fierce yell split the morning as Conan's sword plunged through their captain's massive body. The point quivered an instant from between Sergius's shoulders, a hand's breadth of white fire in the sunlight; then the Cimmerian wrenched back his steel and the pirate chief fell heavily, face down, and lay in a widening pool of blood, his broad hands twitching for an instant.

Conan wheeled toward the gaping corsairs.

'Well, you dogs!' he roared. 'I've sent your chief to hell. What says the law of the Red Brotherhood?'

Before any could answer, a rat-faced Brythunian, standing behind his fellows, whirled a sling swiftly and deadly. Straight as an arrow sped the stone to its mark, and Conan reeled and fell as a tall tree falls to the woodsman's ax. Up on the cliff Olivia caught at the boulders for support. The scene swam dizzily before her eyes; all she could see was the Cimmerian lying limply on the sward, blood oozing from his head.

The rat-faced one yelped in triumph and ran to stab the prostrate man, but a lean Corinthian thrust him back.

'What, Aratus, would you break the law of the Brotherhood, you dog?'

'No law is broken,' snarled the Brythunian.

'No law? Why, you dog, this man you have just struck down is by just rights our captain!'

'Nay!' shouted Aratus. 'He was not of our band, but an outsider. He had not been admitted to fellowship. Slaying Sergius does not make him captain, as would have been the case had one of us killed him.'

'But he wished to join us,' retorted the Corinthian. 'He said so.'

At that a great clamor arose, some siding with Aratus, some with the Corinthian, whom they called Ivanos. Oaths flew thick, challenges were passed, hands fumbled at sword-hilts.

At last a Shemite spoke up above the clamor: 'Why do you argue over a dead man?'

'He's not dead,' answered the Corinthian, rising from beside the prostrate Cimmerian. 'It was a glancing blow; he's only stunned.'

At that the clamor rose anew, Aratus trying to get at the senseless man and Ivanos finally bestriding him, sword in hand, and defying all and sundry. Olivia sensed that it was not so much in defense of Conan that the Corinthian took his stand, but in opposition to Aratus. Evidently these men had been Sergius's lieutenants, and there was no love lost between them. After more arguments, it was decided to bind Conan and take him along with them, his fate to be voted on later.

The Cimmerian, who was beginning to regain consciousness, was bound with leather girdles, and then four pirates lifted him, and with many complaints and curses, carried him along with the band, which took up its journey across the plateau once more. The body of Sergius was left where it had fallen; a sprawling, unlovely shape on the sun-washed sward.

Up among the rocks, Olivia lay stunned by the disaster. She was incapable of speech or action, and could only lie there and stare with horrified eyes as the brutal horde dragged her protector away.

How long she lay there, she did not know. Across the plateau she saw the pirates reach the ruins and enter, dragging their captive. She saw them swarming in and out of the doors and crevices, prodding into the heaps of debris, and clambering about the walls. After awhile a score of them came back across the plateau and vanished among the trees on the western rim, dragging the body of Sergius after them, presumably to cast into the sea. About the ruins the others were cutting down trees and securing material for a fire. Olivia heard their shouts, unintelligible in the distance, and she heard the voices of those who had gone into the woods, echoing among the trees. Presently they came back into sight, bearing casks of liquor and leathern sacks of food. They headed for the ruins, cursing lustily under their burdens.

Of all this Olivia was but mechanically cognizant. Her overwrought brain was almost ready to collapse. Left alone and unprotected, she realized how much the protection of the Cimmerian had meant to her. There intruded vaguely a wonderment at the mad pranks of Fate, that could make the daughter of a king the companion of a red-handed barbarian. With it came a revulsion toward her own kind. Her father, and Shah Amurath, they were civilized men. And from them she had had only suffering. She had never encountered any civilized man who treated her with kindness unless there was an ulterior motive behind his actions. Conan had shielded her, protected her, and – so far – demanded nothing in return. Laying her head in her rounded arms she wept, until distant shouts of ribald revelry roused her to her own danger.

She glanced from the dark ruins about which the fantastic figures, small in the distance, weaved and staggered, to the dusky depths of the green forest. Even if her terrors in the ruins the night before had been only dreams, the menace that lurked in those green leafy depths below was no figment of nightmare. Were Conan slain or carried away captive, her only choice would lie between giving herself up to the human wolves of the sea, or remaining alone on that devil-haunted island.

As the full horror of her situation swept over her, she fell forward in a swoon.

3

The sun was hanging low when Olivia regained her senses. A faint wind wafted to her ears distant shouts and snatches of ribald song. Rising cautiously, she looked out across the plateau. She saw the pirates clustered about a great fire outside the ruins, and her heart leaped as a group emerged from the interior dragging some object she knew was Conan. They propped him against the wall, still evidently bound fast, and there ensued a long discussion, with much brandishing of weapons. At last they dragged him back into the hall, and took up anew the business of ale-guzzling. Olivia sighed; at least she knew that the Cimmerian still lived. Fresh determination steeled her. As soon as night fell, she would steal to those grim ruins and free him or be taken herself in the attempt. And she knew it was not selfish interest alone which prompted her decision.

With this in mind she ventured to creep from her refuge to pluck and eat nuts which grew sparsely near at hand. She had not eaten since the day before. It was while so occupied that she was troubled by a sensation of being watched. She scanned the rocks nervously, then, with a shuddering suspicion, crept to the north edge of the cliff and gazed down into the waving green mass below, already dusky with the sunset. She saw nothing; it was impossible that she could be seen, when not on the cliff's edge, by anything lurking in those woods. Yet she distinctly felt the glare of hidden eyes, and felt that *something* animate and sentient was aware of her presence and her hiding-place.

Stealing back to her rocky eyrie, she lay watching the distant ruins until the dusk of night masked them, and she marked their position by the flickering flames about which black figures leaped and cavorted groggily.

Then she rose. It was time to make her attempt. But first she stole back to the northern edge of the cliffs, and looked down into the woods that bordered the beach. And as she strained her eyes in the dim starlight, she stiffened, and an icy hand touched her heart.

Far below her something moved. It was as if a black shadow detached itself from the gulf of shadows below her. It moved slowly up the sheer face of the cliff – a vague bulk, shapeless in the semi-darkness. Panic caught Olivia by the throat, and she struggled with the scream that tugged at her lips. Turning, she fled down the southern slope.

That flight down the shadowed cliffs was a nightmare in which she slid and scrambled, catching at jagged rocks with cold fingers. As she tore her tender skin and bruised her soft limbs on the rugged boulders over which Conan had so lightly lifted her, she realized again her dependence on the iron-thewed barbarian. But this thought was but one in a fluttering maelstrom of dizzy fright.

The descent seemed endless, but at last her feet struck the grassy levels, and in a very frenzy of eagerness she sped away toward the fire that burned like the red heart of night. Behind her, as she fled, she heard a shower of stones rattle down the steep slope, and the sound lent wings to her heels. What grisly climber dislodged those stones she dared not try to think.

Strenuous physical action dissipated her blind terror somewhat and before she had reached the ruin, her mind was clear, her reasoning faculties alert, though her limbs trembled from her efforts.

She dropped to the sward and wriggled along on her belly until, from behind a small tree that had escaped the axes of the pirates, she watched her enemies. They had completed their supper, but were still drinking, dipping pewter mugs or jewelled goblets into the broken heads of the wine-casks. Some were already snoring drunkenly on the grass, while others had staggered into the ruins. Of Conan she saw nothing. She lay there, while the dew formed on the grass about her and the leaves overhead, and the men about the fire cursed, gambled and argued. There were only a few about the fire; most of them had gone into the ruins to sleep.

She lay watching them, her nerves taut with the strain of waiting, the flesh crawling between her shoulders at the thought of what might be watching her in turn – of what might be stealing up behind her. Time dragged on leaden feet. One by one the revellers sank down in drunken slumber, until all were stretched senseless beside the dying fire.

Olivia hesitated – then was galvanized by a distant glow rising through the trees. The moon was rising!

With a gasp she rose and hurried toward the ruins. Her flesh crawled as she tiptoed among the drunken shapes that sprawled beside the gaping portal. Inside were many more; they shifted and mumbled in their besotted dreams, but none awakened as she glided among them. A sob of joy rose to her lips as she saw Conan. The Cimmerian was wide awake, bound upright to a pillar, his eyes gleaming in the faint reflection of the waning fire outside.

Picking her way among the sleepers, she approached him. Lightly as she had come, he had heard her; had seen her when first framed in the portal. A faint grin touched his hard lips.

She reached him and clung to him an instant. He felt the quick beating of her heart against his breast. Through a broad crevice in the wall stole a beam of moonlight, and the air was instantly supercharged with subtle tension. Conan felt it and stiffened. Olivia felt it and gasped. The sleepers snored on. Bending quickly, she drew a dagger from its senseless owner's belt, and set to work on Conan's bonds. They were sail cords, thick and heavy, and tied with the craft of a sailor. She toiled desperately, while the tide of moonlight crept slowly across the floor toward the feet of the crouching black figures between the pillars.

Her breath came in gasps; Conan's wrists were free, but his elbows and legs were still bound fast. She glanced fleetingly at the figures along the walls – waiting, waiting. They seemed to watch her with the awful patience of the undead. The drunkards beneath her feet began to stir and groan in their sleep. The moonlight crept down the hall, touching the black feet. The cords fell from Conan's arms, and taking the dagger from her, he ripped the bonds from his legs with a single quick slash. He stepped out from the pillar, flexing his limbs, stoically enduring the agony of returning circulation. Olivia crouched against him, shaking like a leaf. Was it some trick of the moonlight that touched the eyes of the black figures with fire, so that they glimmered redly in the shadows?

Conan moved with the abruptness of a jungle cat. Catching up his sword from where it lay in a stack of weapons near by, he lifted Olivia lightly from her feet and glided through an opening that gaped in the ivy-grown wall.

No word passed between them. Lifting her in his arms he set off swiftly across the moon-bathed sward. Her arms about his iron neck, the Ophirean closed her eyes, cradling her dark curly head against his massive shoulder. A delicious sense of security stole over her.

In spite of his burden, the Cimmerian crossed the plateau swiftly, and Olivia, opening her eyes, saw that they were passing under the shadow of the cliffs.

'Something climbed the cliffs,' she whispered. 'I heard it scrambling behind me as I came down.'

'We'll have to chance it,' he grunted.

'I am not afraid – now,' she sighed.

'You were not afraid when you came to free me, either,' he answered. 'Crom, what a day it has been! Such haggling and wrangling I never heard. I'm nearly deaf. Aratus wished to cut out my heart, and Ivanos refused, to spite Aratus, whom he hates. All day long they snarled and spat at one another, and the crew quickly grew too drunk to vote either way—'

He halted suddenly, an image of bronze in the moonlight. With a quick gesture he tossed the girl lightly to one side and behind him. Rising to her knees on the soft sward, she screamed at what she saw.

Out of the shadows of the cliffs moved a monstrous shambling bulk – an anthropomorphic horror, a grotesque travesty of creation.

In general outline it was not unlike a man. But its face, limned in the bright moonlight, was bestial, with close-set ears, flaring nostrils, and a great flabby-lipped mouth in which gleamed white tusk-like fangs. It was covered with shaggy grayish hair, shot with silver which shone in the moonlight, and its great misshapen paws hung nearly to the earth. Its bulk was tremendous; as it stood on its short bowed legs, its bullet-head rose above that of the man who faced it; the sweep of the hairy breast and giant shoulders was breathtaking; the huge arms were like knotted trees.

The moonlight scene swam, to Olivia's sight. This, then, was the end of the trail – for what human being could withstand the fury of that hairy mountain of thews and ferocity? Yet as she stared in wide-eyed horror at the bronzed figure facing the monster, she sensed a kinship in the antagonists that was almost appalling. This was less a struggle between man and beast than a conflict between two creatures of the wild, equally merciless and ferocious. With a flash of white tusks, the monster charged.

The mighty arms spread wide as the beast plunged, stupefyingly quick for all his vast bulk and stunted legs.

Conan's action was a blur of speed Olivia's eye could not follow. She only saw that he evaded that deadly grasp, and his sword, flashing like a jet of white lightning, sheared through one of those massive arms between shoulder and elbow. A great spout of blood deluged the sward as the severed member fell, twitching horribly, but even as the sword bit through, the other malformed hand locked in Conan's black mane.

Only the iron neck-muscles of the Cimmerian saved him from a broken neck that instant. His left hand darted out to clamp on the beast's squat throat, his left knee was jammed hard against the brute's hairy belly. Then began a terrific struggle, which lasted only seconds, but which seemed like ages to the paralyzed girl.

The ape maintained his grasp in Conan's hair, dragging him toward the tusks that glistened in the moonlight. The Cimmerian resisted this effort, with his left arm rigid as iron, while the sword in his right hand, wielded like a butcher-knife, sank again and again into the groin, breast and belly of his captor. The beast took its punishment in awful silence, apparently unweakened by the blood that gushed from its ghastly wounds. Swiftly the terrible strength of the anthropoid overcame the leverage of braced arm and knee. Inexorably Conan's arm bent under the strain; nearer and nearer he was drawn to the slavering jaws that gaped for his life. Now the blazing eyes of the barbarian glared into the bloodshot eyes of the ape. But as Conan tugged vainly at his sword, wedged deep in the hairy body, the frothing jaws snapped spasmodically shut, an inch from the Cimmerian's face, and he was hurled to the sward by the dying convulsions of the monster.

Olivia, half fainting, saw the ape heaving, thrashing and writhing, gripping, man-like, the hilt that jutted from its body. A sickening instant of this, then the great bulk quivered and lay still.

Conan rose and limped over to the corpse. The Cimmerian breathed heavily, and walked like a man whose joints and muscles have been wrenched and twisted almost to their limit of endurance. He felt his bloody scalp and swore at the sight of the long black red-stained strands still grasped in the monster's shaggy hand.

'Crom!' he panted. 'I feel as if I'd been racked! I'd rather fight a dozen men. Another instant and he'd have bitten off my head. Blast him, he's torn a handful of my hair out by the roots.'

Gripping his hilt with both hands he tugged and worked it free. Olivia stole close to clasp his arm and stare down wide-eyed at the sprawling monster.

'What – what is it?' she whispered.

'A gray man-ape,' he grunted. 'Dumb, and man-eating. They dwell in the hills that border the eastern shore of this sea. How this one got to this island, I can't say. Maybe he floated here on driftwood, blown out from the mainland in a storm.'

'And it was he that threw the stone?'

'Yes; I suspected what it was when we stood in the thicket and I saw the boughs bending over our heads. These creatures always lurk in the deepest woods they can find, and seldom emerge. What brought him into the open, I can't say, but it was lucky for us; I'd have had no chance with him among the trees.'

'It followed me,' she shivered. 'I saw it climbing the cliffs.'

'And following his instinct, he lurked in the shadow of the cliff, instead of following you out across the plateau. His kind are creatures of darkness and the silent places, haters of sun and moon.'

'Do you suppose there are others?'

'No, else the pirates had been attacked when they went through the woods. The gray ape is wary, for all his strength, as shown by his hesitancy in falling upon us in the thicket. His lust for you must have been great, to have driven him to attack us finally in the open. What—'

He started and wheeled back toward the way they had come. The night had been split by an awful scream. It came from the ruins.

Instantly there followed a mad medley of yells, shrieks and cries of blasphemous agony. Though accompanied by a ringing of steel, the sounds were of massacre rather than battle.

Conan stood frozen, the girl clinging to him in a frenzy of terror. The clamor rose to a crescendo of madness, and then the Cimmerian turned and went swiftly toward the rim of the plateau, with its fringe of moon-limned trees. Olivia's legs were trembling so that she could not walk; so he carried her, and her heart calmed its frantic pounding as she nestled into his cradling arms.

They passed under the shadowy forest, but the clusters of blackness held no terrors, the rifts of silver discovered no grisly shape. Night-birds murmured slumberously. The yells of slaughter dwindled behind them, masked in the distance to a confused jumble of sound. Somewhere a parrot called, like an eery echo: *'Yagkoolan yok tha, xuthalla!'* So they came to the tree-fringed water's edge and saw the galley lying at anchor, her sail shining white in the moonlight. Already the stars were paling for dawn.

4

In the ghastly whiteness of dawn a handful of tattered, blood-stained figures staggered through the trees and out on to the narrow beach. There were forty-four of them, and they were a cowed and demoralized band. With panting haste they plunged into the water and began to wade toward the galley, when a stern challenge brought them up standing.

Etched against the whitening sky they saw Conan the Cimmerian standing in the bows, sword in hand, his black mane tossing in the dawn wind.

'Stand!' he ordered. 'Come no nearer. What would you have, dogs?'

'Let us come aboard!' croaked a hairy rogue fingering a bloody stump of ear. 'We'd be gone from this devil's island.'

'The first man who tries to climb over the side, I'll split his skull,' promised Conan.

They were forty-four to one, but he held the whip-hand. The fight had been hammered out of them.

'Let us come aboard, good Conan,' whined a red-sashed Zamorian, glancing fearfully over his shoulder at the silent woods. 'We have been so mauled, bitten, scratched and rended, and are so weary from fighting and running, that not one of us can lift a sword.'

'Where is that dog Aratus?' demanded Conan.

'Dead, with the others! It was devils fell upon us! They were rending us to pieces before we could awake – a dozen good rovers died in their sleep. The ruins were full of flame-eyed shadows, with tearing fangs and sharp talons.'

'Aye! put in another corsair. 'They were the demons of the isle, which took the forms of molten images, to befool us. Ishtar! We lay down to sleep among them. We are no cowards. We fought them as long as mortal man may strive against the powers of darkness. Then we broke away and left them tearing at the corpses like jackals. But surely they'll pursue us.'

'Aye, let us come aboard!' clamored a lean Shemite. 'Let us come in peace, or we must come sword in hand, and though we be so weary you will doubtless slay many of us, yet you can not prevail against us many.'

'Then I'll knock a hole in the planks and sink her,' answered Conan grimly. A frantic chorus of expostulation rose, which Conan silenced with a lion-like roar.

'Dogs! Must I aid my enemies? Shall I let you come aboard and cut out my heart?'

'Nay, nay!' they cried eagerly. 'Friends – friends, Conan . We are thy comrades! We be all lusty rogues together. We hate the king of Turan, not each other.'

Their gaze hung on his brown, frowning face.

'Then if I am one of the Brotherhood,' he grunted, 'the laws of the Trade apply to me; and since I killed your chief in fair fight, then I am your captain!'

There was no dissent. The pirates were too cowed and battered to have any thought except a desire to get away from that island of fear. Conan's gaze sought out the blood-stained figure of the Corinthian.

'How, Ivanos!' he challenged. 'You took my part, once. Will you uphold my claims again?'

'Aye, by Mitra!' The pirate, sensing the trend of feeling, was eager to ingratiate himself with the Cimmerian. 'He is right, lads; he is our lawful captain!'

A medley of acquiescence rose, lacking enthusiasm perhaps, but with sincerity accentuated by the feel of the silent woods behind them which might mask creeping ebony devils with red eyes and dripping talons.

'Swear by the hilt,' Conan demanded.

Forty-four sword-hilts were lifted toward him, and forty-four voices blended in the corsair's oath of allegiance.

Conan grinned and sheathed his sword. 'Come aboard, my bold swashbucklers, and take the oars.'

He turned and lifted Olivia to her feet, from where she had crouched shielded by the gunwales.

'And what of me, sir?' she asked.

'What would you?' he countered, watching her narrowly.

'To go with you, wherever your path may lie!' she cried, throwing her white arms about his bronzed neck.

The pirates, clambering over the rail, gasped in amazement.

'To sail a road of blood and slaughter?' he questioned. 'This keel will stain the blue waves crimson wherever it plows.'

'Aye, to sail with you on blue seas or red,' she answered passionately. 'You are a barbarian, and I am an outcast, denied by my people. We are both pariahs, wanderers of earth. Oh, take me with you!'

With a gusty laugh he lifted her to his fierce lips.

'I'll make you Queen of the Blue Sea! Cast off there, dogs! We'll scorch King Yildiz's pantaloons yet, by Crom!'

QUEEN OF THE BLACK COAST

1 Conan Joins the Pirates

Believe green buds awaken in the spring,
  That autumn paints the leaves with somber fire;
Believe I held my heart inviolate
  To lavish on one man my hot desire.
                                    THE SONG OF BÊLIT

Hoofs drummed down the street that sloped to the wharfs. The folk that yelled and scattered had only a fleeting glimpse of a mailed figure on a black stallion, a wide scarlet cloak flowing out on the wind. Far up the street came the shout and clatter of pursuit, but the horseman did not look back. He swept out onto the wharfs and jerked the plunging stallion back on its haunches at the very lip of the pier. Seamen gaped up at him, as they stood to the sweep and striped sail of a high-prowed, broad-waisted galley. The master, sturdy and black-bearded, stood in the bows, easing her away from the piles with a boat-hook. He yelled angrily as the horseman sprang from the saddle and with a long leap landed squarely on the mid-deck.

'Who invited you aboard?'

'Get under way!' roared the intruder with a fierce gesture that spattered red drops from his broadsword.

'But we're bound for the coasts of Kush!' expostulated the master.

'Then I'm for Kush! Push off, I tell you!' The other cast a quick glance up the street, along which a squad of horsemen were galloping; far behind them toiled a group of archers, crossbows on their shoulders.

'Can you pay for your passage?' demanded the master.

'I pay my way with steel!' roared the man in armor, brandishing the great sword that glittered bluely in the sun. 'By Crom, man, if you don't get under way, I'll drench this galley in the blood of its crew!'

The shipmaster was a good judge of men. One glance at the dark scarred face of the swordsman, hardened with passion, and he shouted a quick order, thrusting strongly against the piles. The galley wallowed out into clear water, the oars began to clack rhythmically; then a puff of wind filled the shimmering sail, the light ship heeled to the gust, then took her course like a swan, gathering headway as she skimmed along.

On the wharfs the riders were shaking their swords and shouting threats and commands that the ship put about, and yelling for the bowmen to hasten before the craft was out of arbalest range.

'Let them rave,' grinned the swordsman hardily. 'Do you keep her on her course, master steersman.'

The master descended from the small deck between the bows, made his way between the rows of oarsmen, and mounted the mid-deck. The stranger stood there with his back to the mast, eyes narrowed alertly, sword ready. The shipman eyed him steadily, careful not to make any move toward the long knife in his belt. He saw a tall powerfully built figure in a black scale-mail hauberk, burnished greaves and a blue-steel helmet from which jutted bull's horns highly polished. From the mailed shoulders fell the scarlet cloak, blowing in the sea-wind. A broad shagreen belt with a golden buckle held the scabbard of the broadsword he bore. Under the horned helmet a square-cut black mane contrasted with smoldering blue eyes.

'If we must travel together,' said the master, 'we may as well be at peace with each other. My name is Tito, licensed master-shipman of the ports of Argos. I am bound for Kush, to trade beads and silks and sugar and brass-hilted swords to the black kings for ivory, copra, copper ore, slaves and pearls.'

The swordsman glanced back at the rapidly receding docks, where the figures still gesticulated helplessly, evidently having trouble in finding a boat swift enough to overhaul the fast-sailing galley.

'I am Conan, a Cimmerian,' he answered. 'I came into Argos seeking employment, but with no wars forward, there was nothing to which I might turn my hand.'

'Why do the guardsman pursue you?' asked Tito. 'Not that it's any of my business, but I thought perhaps—'

'I've nothing to conceal,' replied the Cimmerian. 'By Crom, though I've spent considerable time among you civilized peoples, your ways are still beyond my comprehension.

'Well, last night in a tavern, a captain in the king's guard offered violence to the sweetheart of a young soldier, who naturally ran him through. But it seems there is some cursed law against killing guardsmen, and the boy and his girl fled away. It was bruited about that I was seen with them, and so today I was haled into court, and a judge asked me where the lad had gone. I replied that since he was a friend of mine, I could not betray him. Then the court waxed wrath, and the judge talked a great deal about my duty to the state, and society, and other things I did not understand, and bade me tell where my friend had flown. By this time I was becoming wrathful myself, for I had explained my position.

'But I choked my ire and held my peace, and the judge squalled that I had shown contempt for the court, and that I should be hurled into a dungeon to rot until I betrayed my friend. So then, seeing they were all mad, I drew my sword and cleft the judge's skull; then I cut my way out of the court, and seeing the high constable's stallion tied near by, I rode for the wharfs, where I thought to find a ship bound for foreign parts.'

'Well,' said Tito hardily, 'the courts have fleeced me too often in suits with rich merchants for me to owe them any love. I'll have questions to answer if I ever anchor in that port again, but I can prove I acted under compulsion. You may as well put up your sword. We're peaceable sailors, and have nothing against you. Besides, it's as well to have a fighting-man like yourself on board. Come up to the poop-deck and we'll have a tankard of ale.'

'Good enough,' readily responded the Cimmerian, sheathing his sword.

The *Argus* was a small sturdy ship, typical of those trading-craft which ply between the ports of Zingara and Argos and the southern coasts, hugging the shoreline and seldom venturing far into the open ocean. It was high of stern, with a tall curving prow; broad in the waist, sloping beautifully to stem and stern. It was guided by the long sweep from the poop, and propulsion was furnished mainly by the broad striped silk sail, aided by a jibsail. The oars were for use in tacking out of creeks and bays, and during calms. There were ten to the side, five fore and five aft of the small mid-deck. The most precious part of the cargo was lashed under this deck, and under the fore-deck. The men slept on deck or between the rowers' benches, protected in bad weather by canopies. With twenty men at the oars, three at the sweep, and the shipmaster, the crew was complete.

So the *Argus* pushed steadily southward, with consistently fair weather. The sun beat down from day to day with fiercer heat, and the canopies were run up – striped silken cloths that matched the shimmering sail and the shining goldwork on the prow and along the gunwales.

They sighted the coast of Shem – long rolling meadowlands with the white crowns of the towers of cities in the distance, and horsemen with blue-black beards and hooked noses, who sat their steeds along the shore and eyed the galley with suspicion. She did not put in; there was scant profit in trade with the sons of Shem.

Nor did master Tito pull into the broad bay where the Styx river emptied its gigantic flood into the ocean, and the massive black castles of Khemi loomed over the blue waters. Ships did not put unasked into this port, where dusky sorcerers wove awful spells in the murk of sacrificial smoke mounting eternally from blood-stained altars where naked women screamed, and where Set, the Old Serpent, arch-demon of the Hyborians but god of the Stygians, was said to writhe his shining coils among his worshippers.

Master Tito gave that dreamy glass-floored bay a wide berth, even when a serpent-prowed gondola shot from behind a castellated point of land, and naked dusky women, with great red blossoms in their hair, stood and called to his sailors, and posed and postured brazenly.

Now no more shining towers rose inland. They had passed the southern borders of Stygia and were cruising along the coasts of Kush. The sea and the ways of the sea were never-ending mysteries to Conan, whose homeland was among the high hills of the northern uplands. The wanderer was no less of interest to the sturdy seamen, few of whom had ever seen one of his race.

They were characteristic Argosean sailors, short and stockily built. Conan towered above them, and no two of them could match his strength. They were hardy and robust, but his was the endurance and vitality of a wolf, his thews steeled and his nerves whetted by the hardness of his life in the world's wastelands. He was quick to laugh, quick and terrible in his wrath. He was a valiant trencherman, and strong drink was a passion and a weakness with him. Naïve as a child in many ways, unfamiliar with the sophistry of civilization, he was naturally intelligent, jealous of his rights, and dangerous as a hungry tiger. Young in years, he was hardened in warfare and wandering, and his sojourns in many lands were evident in his apparel. His horned helmet was such as was worn by the golden-haired Æsir of Nordheim; his hauberk and greaves were of the finest workmanship of Koth; the fine ring-mail which sheathed his arms and legs was of Nemedia; the blade at his girdle was a great Aquilonian broadsword; and his gorgeous scarlet cloak could have been spun nowhere but in Ophir.

So they beat southward, and master Tito began to look for the high-walled villages of the black people. But they found only smoking ruins on the shore of a bay, littered with naked black bodies. Tito swore.

'I had good trade here, aforetime. This is the work of pirates.'

'And if we meet them?' Conan loosened his great blade in its scabbard.

'Mine is no warship. We run, not fight. Yet if it came to a pinch, we have beaten off reavers before, and might do it again; unless it were Bêlit's *Tigress*.'

'Who is Bêlit?'

'The wildest she-devil unhanged. Unless I read the signs a-wrong, it was her butchers who destroyed that village on the bay. May I some day see her dangling from the yard-arm! She is called the queen of the black coast. She is a Shemite woman, who leads black raiders. They harry the shipping and have sent many a good tradesman to the bottom.'

From under the poop-deck Tito brought out quilted jerkins, steel caps, bows and arrows.

'Little use to resist if we're run down,' he grunted. 'But it rasps the soul to give up life without a struggle.'

It was just at sunrise when the lookout shouted a warning. Around the long point of an island off the starboard bow glided a long lethal shape, a slender serpentine galley, with a raised deck that ran from stem to stern. Forty oars on each side drove her swiftly through the water, and the low rail swarmed with naked blacks that chanted and clashed spears on oval shields. From the masthead floated a long crimson pennon.

'Bêlit!' yelled Tito, paling. 'Yare! Put her about! Into that creek-mouth! If we can beach her before they run us down, we have a chance to escape with our lives!'

So, veering sharply, the *Argus* ran for the line of surf that boomed along the palm-fringed shore, Tito striding back and forth, exhorting the panting rowers to greater efforts. The master's black beard bristled, his eyes glared.

'Give me a bow,' requested Conan. 'It's not my idea of a manly weapon, but I learned archery among the Hyrkanians, and it will go hard if I can't feather a man or so on yonder deck.'

Standing on the poop, he watched the serpent-like ship skimming lightly over the waters, and landsman though he was, it was evident to him that the *Argus* would never win that race. Already arrows, arching from the pirate's deck, were falling with a hiss into the sea, not twenty paces astern.

'We'd best stand to it,' growled the Cimmerian; 'else we'll all die with shafts in our backs, and not a blow dealt.'

'Bend to it, dogs!' roared Tito with a passionate gesture of his brawny fist. The bearded rowers grunted, heaved at the oars, while their muscles coiled and knotted, and sweat started out on their hides. The timbers of the stout little galley creaked and groaned as the men fairly ripped her through the water. The wind had fallen; the sail hung limp. Nearer crept the inexorable raiders, and they were still a good mile from the surf when one of the steersmen fell gagging across a sweep, a long arrow through his neck. Tito sprang to take his place, and Conan, bracing his feet wide on the heaving poop-deck, lifted his bow. He could see the details of the pirate plainly now. The rowers were protected by a line of raised mantelets along the sides, but the warriors dancing on the narrow deck were in full view. These were painted and plumed, and mostly naked, brandishing spears and spotted shields.

On the raised platform in the bows stood a slim figure whose white skin glistened in dazzling contrast to the glossy ebon hides about it. Bêlit, without a doubt. Conan drew the shaft to his ear – then some whim or qualm stayed his hand and sent the arrow through the body of a tall plumed spearman beside her.

Hand over hand the pirate galley was overhauling the lighter ship. Arrows fell in a rain about the *Argus*, and men cried out. All the steersmen were down, pincushioned, and Tito was handling the massive sweep alone, gasping black curses, his braced legs knots of straining thews. Then with a sob he sank down, a long shaft quivering in his sturdy heart. The *Argus* lost headway and rolled in the swell. The men shouted in confusion, and Conan took command in characteristic fashion.

'Up, lads!' he roared, loosing with a vicious twang of cord. 'Grab your steel and give these dogs a few knocks before they cut our throats! Useless to bend your backs any more: they'll board us ere we can row another fifty paces!'

In desperation the sailors abandoned their oars and snatched up their weapons. It was valiant, but useless. They had time for one flight of arrows before the pirate was upon them. With no one at the sweep, the *Argus* rolled broadside, and the steel-baked prow of the raider crashed into her amidships. Grappling-irons crunched into the side. From the lofty gunwales, the black pirates drove down a volley of shafts that tore through the quilted jackets of the doomed sailormen, then sprang down spear in hand to complete the slaughter. On the deck of the pirate lay half a dozen bodies, an earnest of Conan's archery.

The fight on the *Argus* was short and bloody. The stocky sailors, no match for the tall barbarians, were cut down to a man. Elsewhere the battle had taken a peculiar turn. Conan, on the high-pitched poop, was on a level with the pirate's deck. As the steel prow slashed into the *Argus*, he braced himself and kept his feet under the shock, casting away his bow. A tall corsair, bounding over the rail, was met in midair by the Cimmerian's great sword, which sheared him cleanly through the torso, so that his body fell one way and his legs another. Then, with a burst of fury that left a heap of mangled corpses along the gunwales, Conan was over the rail and on the deck of the *Tigress*.

In an instant he was the center of a hurricane of stabbing spears and lashing clubs. But he moved in a blinding blur of steel. Spears bent on his armor or swished empty air, and his sword sang its death-song. The fighting-madness of his race was upon him, and with a red mist of unreasoning fury wavering before his blazing eyes, he cleft skulls, smashed breasts, severed limbs, ripped out entrails, and littered the deck like a shambles with a ghastly harvest of brains and blood.

Invulnerable in his armor, his back against the mast, he heaped mangled corpses at his feet until his enemies gave back panting in rage and fear. Then as they lifted their spears to cast them, and he tensed himself to leap and die in the midst of them, a shrill cry froze the lifted arms. They stood like statues, the black giants poised for the spear-casts, the mailed swordsman with his dripping blade.

Bêlit sprang before the blacks, beating down their spears. She turned toward Conan, her bosom heaving, her eyes flashing. Fierce fingers of wonder caught at his heart. She was slender, yet formed like a goddess: at once lithe and voluptuous. Her only garment was a broad silken girdle. Her white ivory limbs and the ivory globes of her breasts drove a beat of fierce passion through the Cimmerian's pulse, even in the panting fury of battle. Her rich black hair, black as a Stygian night, fell in rippling burnished clusters down her supple back. Her dark eyes burned on the Cimmerian.

She was untamed as a desert wind, supple and dangerous as a she-panther. She came close to him, heedless of his great blade, dripping with blood of her warriors. Her supple thigh brushed against it, so close she came to the tall warrior. Her red lips parted as she stared up into his somber menacing eyes.

'Who are you?' she demanded. 'By Ishtar, I have never seen your like, though I have ranged the sea from the coasts of Zingara to the fires of the ultimate south. Whence come you?'

'From Argos,' he answered shortly, alert for treachery. Let her slim hand move toward the jeweled dagger in her girdle, and a buffet of his open hand would stretch her senseless on the deck. Yet in his heart he did not fear; he had held too many women, civilized or barbaric, in his iron-thewed arms, not to recognize the light that burned in the eyes of this one.

'You are no soft Hyborian!' she exclaimed. 'You are fierce and hard as a gray wolf. Those eyes were never dimmed by city lights; those thews were never softened by life amid marble walls.'

'I am Conan, a Cimmerian,' he answered.

To the people of the exotic climes, the north was a mazy half-mythical realm, peopled with ferocious blue-eyed giants who occasionally descended from their icy fastnesses with torch and sword. Their raids had never taken them as far south as Shem, and this daughter of Shem made no distinction between Æsir, Vanir or Cimmerian. With the unerring instinct of the elemental feminine, she knew she had found her lover, and his race meant naught, save as it invested him with the glamor of far lands.

'And I am Bêlit,' she cried, as one might say, 'I am queen.'

'Look at me, Conan!' She threw wide her arms. 'I am Bêlit, queen of the black coast. Oh, tiger of the North, you are cold as the snowy mountains which bred you. Take me and crush me with your fierce love! Go with me to the ends of the earth and the ends of the sea! I am a queen by fire and steel and slaughter – be thou my king!'

His eyes swept the blood-stained ranks, seeking expressions of wrath or jealousy. He saw none. The fury was gone from the ebon faces. He realized that to these men Bêlit was more than a woman: a goddess whose will was unquestioned. He glanced at the *Argus*, wallowing in the crimson sea-wash, heeling far over, her decks awash, held up by the grappling-irons. He glanced at the blue-fringed shore, at the far green hazes of the ocean, at the vibrant figure which stood before him; and his barbaric soul stirred within him. To quest these shining blue realms with that white-skinned young tiger-cat – to love, laugh, wander and pillage—

'I'll sail with you,' he grunted, shaking the red drops from his blade.

'Ho, N'Yaga!' her voice twanged like a bowstring. 'Fetch herbs and dress your master's wounds! The rest of you bring aboard the plunder and cast off.'

As Conan sat with his back against the poop-rail, while the old shaman attended to the cuts on his hands and limbs, the cargo of the ill-fated *Argus* was quickly shifted aboard the *Tigress* and stored in small cabins below deck. Bodies of the crew and of fallen pirates were cast overboard to the swarming sharks, while wounded blacks were laid in the waist to be bandaged. Then the grappling-irons were cast off, and as the *Argus* sank silently into the blood-flecked waters, the *Tigress* moved off southward to the rhythmic clack of the oars.

As they moved out over the glassy blue deep, Bêlit came to the poop. Her eyes were burning like those of a she-panther in the dark as she tore off her ornaments, her sandals and her silken girdle and cast them at his feet. Rising on tiptoe, arms stretched upward, a quivering line of naked white, she cried to the desperate horde: 'Wolves of the blue sea, behold ye now the dance – the mating-dance of Bêlit, whose fathers were kings of Askalon!'

And she danced, like the spin of a desert whirlwind, like the leaping of a quenchless flame, like the urge of creation and the urge of death. Her white feet spurned the blood-stained deck and dying men forgot death as they gazed frozen at her. Then, as the white stars glimmered through the blue velvet dusk, making her whirling body a blur of ivory fire, with a wild cry she threw herself at Conan's feet, and the blind flood of the Cimmerian's desire swept all else away as he crushed her panting form against the black plates of his corseleted breast.

2 The Black Lotus

In that dead citadel of crumbling stone
Her eyes were snared by that unholy sheen,
And curious madness took me by the throat,
As of a rival lover thrust between.

THE SONG OF BÊLIT

The *Tigress* ranged the sea, and the black villages shuddered. Tomtoms beat in the night, with a tale that the she-devil of the sea had found a mate, an iron man whose wrath was as that of a wounded lion. And survivors of butchered Stygian ships named Bêlit with curses, and a white warrior with fierce blue eyes; so the Stygian princes remembered this man long and long, and their memory was a bitter tree which bore crimson fruit in the years to come.

But heedless as a vagrant wind, the *Tigress* cruised the southern coasts, until she anchored at the mouth of a broad sullen river, whose banks were jungle-clouded walls of mystery.

'This is the river Zarkheba, which is Death,' said Bêlit. 'Its waters are poisonous. See how dark and murky they run? Only venomous reptiles live in that river. The black people shun it. Once a Stygian galley, fleeing from me, fled up the river and vanished. I anchored in this very spot, and days later, the galley came floating down the dark waters, its decks blood-stained and deserted. Only one man was on board, and he was mad and died gibbering. The cargo was intact, but the crew had vanished into silence and mystery.

'My lover, I believe there is a city somewhere on that river. I have heard tales of giant towers and walls glimpsed afar off by sailors who dared go part-way up the river. We fear nothing: Conan, let us go and sack that city!'

Conan agreed. He generally agreed to her plans. Hers was the mind that directed their raids, his the arm that carried out her ideas. It mattered little to him where they sailed or whom they fought, so long as they sailed and fought. He found the life good.

Battle and raid had thinned their crew; only some eighty spearmen remained, scarcely enough to work the long galley. But Bêlit would not take the time to make the long cruise southward to the island kingdoms where she recruited her buccaneers. She was afire with eagerness for her latest venture; so the *Tigress* swung into the river mouth, the oarsmen pulling strongly as she breasted the broad current.

They rounded the mysterious bend that shut out the sight of the sea, and sunset found them forging steadily against the sluggish flow, avoiding sandbars where strange reptiles coiled. Not even a crocodile did they see, nor any four-legged beast or winged bird coming down to the water's edge to drink. On through the blackness that preceded moonrise they drove, between banks that were solid palisades of darkness, whence came mysterious rustlings and stealthy footfalls, and the gleam of grim eyes. And once an inhuman voice was lifted in awful mockery – the cry of an ape, Bêlit said, adding that the souls of evil men were imprisoned in these man-like animals as punishment for past crimes. But Conan doubted, for once, in a gold-barred cage in an Hyrkanian city, he had seen an abysmal sad-eyed beast which men told him was an ape, and there had been about it naught of the demoniac malevolence which vibrated in the shrieking laughter that echoed from the black jungle.

Then the moon rose, a splash of blood, ebony-barred, and the jungle awoke in horrific bedlam to greet it. Roars and howls and yells set the black warriors to trembling, but all this noise, Conan noted, came from farther back in the jungle, as if the beasts no less than men shunned the black waters of Zarkheba.

Rising above the black denseness of the trees and above the waving fronds, the moon silvered the river, and their wake became a rippling scintillation of phosphorescent bubbles that widened like a shining road of bursting jewels. The oars dipped into the shining water and came up sheathed in frosty silver. The plumes on the warrior's headpiece nodded in the wind, and the gems on sword-hilts and harness sparkled frostily.

The cold light struck icy fire from the jewels in Bêlit's clustered black locks as she stretched her lithe figure on a leopardskin thrown on the deck. Supported on her elbows, her chin resting on her slim hands, she gazed up into the face of Conan, who lounged beside her, his black mane stirring in the faint breeze. Bêlit's eyes were dark jewels burning in the moonlight.

'Mystery and terror are about us, Conan, and we glide into the realm of horror and death,' she said. 'Are you afraid?'

A shrug of his mailed shoulders was his only answer.

'I am not afraid either,' she said meditatively. 'I was never afraid. I have looked into the naked fangs of Death too often. Conan, do you fear the gods?'

'I would not tread on their shadow,' answered the barbarian conservatively. 'Some gods are strong to harm, others, to aid; at least so say their priests. Mitra of the Hyborians must be a strong god, because his people have built their cities over the world. But even the Hyborians fear Set. And Bel, god of thieves, is a good god. When I was a thief in Zamora I learned of him.'

'What of your own gods? I have never heard you call on them.'

'Their chief is Crom. He dwells on a great mountain. What use to call on him? Little he cares if men live or die. Better to be silent than to call his attention to you; he will send you dooms, not fortune! He is grim and loveless, but at birth he breathes power to strive and slay into a man's soul. What else shall men ask of the gods?'

'But what of the worlds beyond the river of death?' she persisted.

'There is no hope here or hereafter in the cult of my people,' answered Conan. 'In this world men struggle and suffer vainly, finding pleasure only in the bright madness of battle; dying, their souls enter a gray misty realm of clouds and icy winds, to wander cheerlessly throughout eternity.'

Bêlit shuddered. 'Life, bad as it is, is better than such a destiny. What do you believe, Conan?'

He shrugged his shoulders. 'I have known many gods. He who denies them is as blind as he who trusts them too deeply. I seek not beyond death. It may be the blackness averred by the Nemedian skeptics, or Crom's realm of ice and cloud, or the snowy plains and vaulted halls of the Nordheimer's Valhalla. I know not, nor do I care. Let me live deep while I live; let me know the rich juices of red meat and stinging wine on my palate, the hot embrace of white arms, the mad exultation of battle when the blue blades flame and crimson, and I am content. Let teachers and priests and philosophers brood over questions of reality and illusion. I know this: if life is illusion, then I am no less an illusion, and being thus, the illusion is real to me. I live, I burn with life, I love, I slay, and am content.'

'But the gods are real,' she said, pursuing her own line of thought.

'And above all are the gods of the Shemites – Ishtar and Ashtoreth and Derketo and Adonis. Bel, too, is Shemitish, for he was born in ancient Shumir, long, long ago and went forth laughing, with curled beard and impish wise eyes, to steal the gems of the kings of old times.

'There is life beyond death, I know, and I know this, too, Conan of Cimmeria –' she rose lithely to her knees and caught him in a pantherish embrace – 'my love is stronger than any death! I have lain in your arms, panting with the violence of our love; you have held and crushed and conquered me, drawing my soul to your lips with the fierceness of your bruising kisses. My heart is welded to your heart, my soul is part of your soul! Were I still in death and you fighting for life, I would come back from the abyss to aid you – aye, whether my spirit floated with the purple sails on the crystal sea of paradise, or writhed in the molten flames of hell! I am yours, and all the gods and all their eternities shall not sever us!'

A scream rang from the lookout in the bows. Thrusting Bêlit aside, Conan bounded up, his sword a long silver glitter in the moonlight, his hair bristling at what he saw. The black warrior dangled above the deck, supported by what seemed a dark pliant tree trunk arching over the rail. Then he realized that it was a gigantic serpent which had writhed its glistening length up the side of the bow and gripped the luckless warrior in its jaws. Its dripping scales shone leprously in the moonlight as it reared its form high above the deck, while the stricken man screamed and writhed like a mouse in the fangs of a python. Conan rushed into the bows, and swinging his great sword, hewed nearly through the giant trunk, which was thicker than a man's body. Blood drenched the rails as the dying monster swayed far out, still gripping its victim, and sank into the river, coil by coil, lashing the water to bloody foam, in which man and reptile vanished together.

Thereafter Conan kept the lookout watch himself, but no other horror came crawling up from the murky depths, and as dawn whitened over the jungle, he sighted the black fangs of towers jutting up among the trees. He called Bêlit, who slept on the deck, wrapped in his scarlet cloak; and she sprang to his side, eyes blazing. Her lips were parted to call orders to her warriors to take up bow and spears; then her lovely eyes widened.

It was but the ghost of a city on which they looked when they cleared a jutting jungle-clad point and swung in toward the in-curving shore. Weeds and rank river grass grew between the stones of broken piers and shattered paves that had once been streets and spacious plazas and broad courts. From all sides except that toward the river, the jungle crept in, masking fallen columns and crumbling mounds with poisonous green. Here and there buckling towers reeled drunkenly against the morning sky, and broken pillars jutted up among the decaying walls. In the center space a marble pyramid was spired by a slim column, and on its pinnacle sat or squatted something that Conan supposed to be an image until his keen eyes detected life in it.

'It is a great bird,' said one of the warriors, standing in the bows.

'It is a monster bat,' insisted another.

'It is an ape,' said Bêlit.

Just then the creature spread broad wings and flapped off into the jungle.

'A winged ape,' said old N'Yaga uneasily. 'Better we had cut our throats than come to this place. It is haunted.'

Bêlit mocked at his superstitions and ordered the galley run inshore and tied to the crumbling wharfs. She was the first to spring ashore, closely followed by Conan, and after them trooped the ebon-skinned pirates, white plumes waving in the morning wind, spears ready, eyes rolling dubiously at the surrounding jungle.

Over all brooded a silence as sinister as that of a sleeping serpent. Bêlit posed picturesquely among the ruins, the vibrant life in her lithe figure contrasting strangely with the desolation and decay about her. The sun flamed up slowly, sullenly, above the jungle, flooding the towers with a dull gold that left shadows lurking beneath the tottering walls. Bêlit pointed to a slim round tower that reeled on its rotting base. A broad expanse of cracked, grass-grown slabs led up to it, flanked by fallen columns, and before it stood a massive altar. Bêlit went swiftly along the ancient floor and stood before it.

'This was the temple of the old ones,' she said. 'Look – you can see the channels for the blood along the sides of the altar, and the rains of ten thousand years have not washed the dark stains from them. The walls have all fallen away, but this stone block defies time and the elements.'

'But who were these old ones?' demanded Conan.

She spread her slim hands helplessly. 'Not even in legendary is this city mentioned. But look at the handholes at either end of the altar! Priests often conceal their treasures beneath their altars. Four of you lay hold and see if you can lift it.'

She stepped back to make room for them, glancing up at the tower which loomed drunkenly above them. Three of the strongest blacks had gripped the handholes cut into the stone – curiously unsuited to human hands – when Bêlit sprang back with a sharp cry. They froze in their places, and Conan, bending to aid them, wheeled with a startled curse.

'A snake in the grass,' she said, backing away. 'Come and slay it; the rest of you bend your backs to the stone.'

Conan came quickly toward her, another taking his place. As he impatiently scanned the grass for the reptile, the giant blacks braced their feet, grunted and heaved with their huge muscles coiling and straining under their ebon skin. The altar did not come off the ground, but it revolved suddenly on its side. And simultaneously there was a grinding rumble above and the tower came crashing down, covering the four black men with broken masonry.

A cry of horror rose from their comrades. Bêlit's slim fingers dug into Conan's arm-muscles. 'There was no serpent,' she whispered. 'It was but a ruse to call you away. I feared; the old ones guarded their treasure well. Let us clear away the stones.'

With herculean labor they did so, and lifted out the mangled bodies of the four men. And under them, stained with their blood, the pirates found a crypt carved in the solid stone. The altar, hinged curiously with stone rods and sockets on one side, had served as its lid. And at first glance the crypt seemed brimming with liquid fire, catching the early light with a million blazing facets. Undreamable wealth lay before the eyes of the gaping pirates; diamonds, rubies, bloodstones, sapphires, turquoises, moonstones, opals, emeralds, amethysts, unknown gems that shone like the eyes of evil women. The crypt was filled to the brim with bright stones that the morning sun struck into lambent flame.

With a cry Bêlit dropped to her knees among the blood-stained rubble on the brink and thrust her white arms shoulder-deep into that pool of splendor. She withdrew them, clutching something that brought another cry to her lips – a long string of crimson stones that were like clots of frozen blood strung on a thick gold wire. In their glow the golden sunlight changed to bloody haze.

Bêlit's eyes were like a woman's in a trance. The Shemite soul finds a bright drunkenness in riches and material splendor, and the sight of this treasure might have shaken the soul of a sated emperor of Shushan.

'Take up the jewels, dogs!' her voice was shrill with her emotions.

'Look!' a muscular black arm stabbed toward the *Tigress*, and Bêlit wheeled, her crimson lips a-snarl, as if she expected to see a rival corsair sweeping in to despoil her of her plunder. But from the gunwales of the ship a dark shape rose, soaring away over the jungle.

'The devil-ape has been investigating the ship,' muttered the blacks uneasily.

'What matter?' cried Bêlit with a curse, raking back a rebellious lock with an impatient hand. 'Make a litter of spears and mantles to bear these jewels – where the devil are you going?'

'To look to the galley,' grunted Conan. 'That bat-thing might have knocked a hole in the bottom, for all we know.'

He ran swiftly down the cracked wharf and sprang aboard. A moment's swift examination below decks, and he swore heartily, casting a clouded glance in the direction the bat-being had vanished. He returned hastily to Bêlit, superintending the plundering of the crypt. She had looped the necklace about her neck, and on her naked white bosom the red clots glimmered darkly. A huge naked black stood crotch-deep in the jewel-brimming crypt, scooping up great handfuls of splendor to pass them to eager hands above. Strings of frozen iridescence hung between his dusky fingers; drops of red fire dripped from his hands, piled high with starlight and rainbow. It was as if a black titan stood straddle-legged in the bright pits of hell, his lifted hands full of stars.

'That flying devil has staved in the water-casks,' said Conan. 'If we hadn't been so dazed by these stones we'd have heard the noise. We were fools not to have left a man on guard. We can't drink this river water. I'll take twenty men and search for fresh water in the jungle.'

She looked at him vaguely, in her eyes the blank blaze of her strange passion, her fingers working at the gems on her breast.

'Very well,' she said absently, hardly heeding him. 'I'll get the loot aboard.'

The jungle closed quickly about them, changing the light from gold to gray. From the arching green branches creepers dangled like pythons. The warriors fell into single file, creeping through the primordial twilights like black phantoms following a white ghost.

Underbrush was not so thick as Conan had anticipated. The ground was spongy but not slushy. Away from the river, it sloped gradually upward. Deeper and deeper they plunged into the green waving depths, and still there was no sign of water, either running stream or stagnant pool. Conan halted suddenly, his warriors freezing into basaltic statues. In the tense silence that followed, the Cimmerian shook his head irritably.

'Go ahead,' he grunted to a sub-chief, N'Gora. 'March straight on until you can no longer see me; then stop and wait for me. I believe we're being followed. I heard something.'

The blacks shuffled their feet uneasily, but did as they were told. As they swung onward, Conan stepped quickly behind a great tree, glaring back along the way they had come. From that leafy fastness anything might emerge. Nothing occurred; the faint sounds of the marching spearmen faded in the distance. Conan suddenly realized that the air was impregnated with an alien and exotic scent. Something gently brushed his temple. He turned quickly. From a cluster of green, curiously leafed stalks, great black blossoms nodded at him. One of these had touched him. They seemed to beckon him, to arch their pliant stems toward him. They spread and rustled, though no wind blew.

He recoiled, recognizing the black lotus, whose juice was death, and whose scent brought dream-haunted slumber. But already he felt a subtle lethargy stealing over him. He sought to lift his sword, to hew down the serpentine stalks, but his arm hung lifeless at his side. He opened his mouth to shout to his warriors, but only a faint rattle issued. The next instant, with appalling suddenness, the jungle waved and dimmed out before his eyes; he did not hear the screams that burst out awfully not far away, as his knees collapsed, letting him pitch limply to the earth. Above his prostrate form the great black blossoms nodded in the windless air.

3 The Horror in the Jungle

Was it a dream the nighted lotus brought?
 Then curst the dream that bought my sluggish life;
And curst each laggard hour that does not see
 Hot blood drip blackly from the crimsoned knife.
THE SONG OF BÊLIT

First there was the blackness of an utter void, with the cold winds of cosmic space blowing through it. Then shapes, vague, monstrous and evanescent, rolled in dim panorama through the expanse of nothingness, as if the darkness were taking material form. The winds blew and a vortex formed, a whirling pyramid of roaring blackness. From it grew Shape and Dimension; then suddenly, like clouds dispersing, the darkness rolled away on either hand and a huge city of dark green stone rose on the bank of a wide river, flowing through an illimitable plain. Through this city moved beings of alien configuration.

Cast in the mold of humanity, they were distinctly not men. They were winged and of heroic proportions; not a branch on the mysterious stalk of evolution that culminated in man, but the ripe blossom on an alien tree, separate and apart from that stalk. Aside from their wings, in physical appearance they resembled man only as man in his highest form resembles the great apes. In spiritual, esthetic and intellectual development they were superior to man as man is superior to the gorilla. But when they reared their colossal city, man's primal ancestors had not yet risen from the slime of the primordial seas.

These beings were mortal, as are all things built of flesh and blood.

They lived, loved and died, though the individual span of life was enormous. Then, after uncounted millions of years, the Change began. The vista shimmered and wavered, like a picture thrown on a windblown curtain. Over the city and the land the ages flowed as waves flow over a beach, and each wave brought alterations. Somewhere on the planet the magnetic centers were shifting; the great glaciers and ice-fields were withdrawing toward the new poles.

The littoral of the great river altered. Plains turned into swamps that stank with reptilian life. Where fertile meadows had rolled, forests reared up, growing into dank jungles. The changing ages wrought on the inhabitants of the city as well. They did not migrate to fresher lands. Reasons inexplicable to humanity held them to the ancient city and their doom. And as that once rich and mighty land sank deeper and deeper into the black mire of the sunless jungle, so into the chaos of squalling jungle life sank the people of the city. Terrific convulsions shook the earth; the nights were lurid with spouting volcanoes that fringed the dark horizons with red pillars.

After an earthquake that shook down the outer walls and highest towers of the city, and caused the river to run black for days with some lethal substance spewed up from the subterranean depths, a frightful chemical change became apparent in the waters the folk had drunk for millenniums uncountable.

Many died who drank of it; and in those who lived, the drinking wrought change, subtle, gradual and grisly. In adapting themselves to the changing conditions, they had sunk far below their original level. But the lethal waters altered them even more horribly, from generation to more bestial generation. They who had been winged gods became pinioned demons, with all that remained of their ancestors' vast knowledge distorted and perverted and twisted into ghastly paths. As they had risen higher than mankind might dream, so they sank lower than man's maddest nightmares reach. They died fast, by cannibalism, and horrible feuds fought out in the murk of the midnight jungle. And at last among the lichen-grown ruins of their city only a single shape lurked, a stunted abhorrent perversion of nature.

Then for the first time humans appeared: dark-skinned, hawk-faced men in copper and leather harness, bearing bows – the warriors of prehistoric Stygia. There were only fifty of them, and they were haggard and gaunt with starvation and prolonged effort, stained and scratched with jungle-wandering, with blood-crusted bandages that told of fierce fighting. In their minds was a tale of warfare and defeat, and flight before a stronger tribe which drove them ever southward, until they lost themselves in the green ocean of jungle and river.

Exhausted they lay down among the ruins where red blossoms that bloom but once in a century waved in the full moon, and sleep fell upon them. And as they slept, a hideous shape crept red-eyed from the shadows and performed weird and awful rites about and above each sleeper. The moon hung in the shadowy sky, painting the jungle red and black; above the sleepers glimmered the crimson blossoms, like splashes of blood. Then the moon went down and the eyes of the necromancer were red jewels set in the ebony of night.

When dawn spread its white veil over the river, there were no men to be seen: only a hairy winged horror that squatted in the center of a ring of fifty great spotted hyenas that pointed quivering muzzles to the ghastly sky and howled like souls in hell.

Then scene followed scene so swiftly that each tripped over the heels of its predecessor. There was a confusion of movement, a writhing and melting of lights and shadows, against a background of black jungle, green stone ruins and murky river. Black men came up the river in long boats with skulls grinning on the prows, or stole stooping through the trees, spear in hand. They fled screaming through the dark from red eyes and slavering fangs. Howls of dying men shook the shadows; stealthy feet padded through the gloom, vampire eyes blazed redly. There were grisly feasts beneath the moon, across whose red disk a bat-like shadow incessantly swept.

Then abruptly, etched clearly in contrast to these impressionistic glimpses, around the jungled point in the whitening dawn swept a long galley, thronged with shining ebon figures, and in the bows stood a white-skinned ghost in blue steel.

It was at this point that Conan first realized that he was dreaming. Until that instant he had had no consciousness of individual existence. But as he saw himself treading the boards of the *Tigress*, he recognized both the existence and the dream, although he did not awaken.

Even as he wondered, the scene shifted abruptly to a jungle glade where N'Gora and nineteen black spearmen stood, as if awaiting someone. Even as he realized that it was he for whom they waited, a horror swooped down from the skies and their stolidity was broken by yells of fear. Like men maddened by terror, they threw away their weapons and raced wildly through the jungle, pressed close by the slavering monstrosity that flapped its wings above them.

Chaos and confusion followed this vision, during which Conan feebly struggled to awake. Dimly he seemed to see himself lying under a nodding cluster of black blossoms, while from the bushes a hideous shape crept toward him. With a savage effort he broke the unseen bonds which held him to his dreams, and started upright.

Bewilderment was in the glare he cast about him. Near him swayed the dusky lotus, and he hastened to draw away from it.

In the spongy soil near by there was a track as if an animal had put out a foot, preparatory to emerging from the bushes, then had withdrawn it. It looked like the spoor of an unbelievably large hyena.

He yelled for N'Gora. Primordial silence brooded over the jungle, in which his yells sounded brittle and hollow as mockery. He could not see the sun, but his wilderness-trained instinct told him the day was near its end. A panic rose in him at the thought that he had lain senseless for hours. He hastily followed the tracks of the spearmen, which lay plain in the damp loam before him. They ran in single file, and he soon emerged into a glade – to stop short, the skin crawling between his shoulders as he recognized it as the glade he had seen in his lotus-drugged dream. Shields and spears lay scattered about as if dropped in headlong flight.

And from the tracks which led out of the glade and deeper into the fastnesses, Conan knew that the spearmen had fled, wildly. The footprints overlay one another; they weaved blindly among the trees. And with startling suddenness the hastening Cimmerian came out of the jungle onto a hill-like rock which sloped steeply, to break off abruptly in a sheer precipice forty feet high. And something crouched on the brink.

At first Conan thought it to be a great black gorilla. Then he saw that it was a giant black man that crouched ape-like, long arms dangling, froth dripping from the loose lips. It was not until, with a sobbing cry, the creature lifted huge hands and rushed towards him, that Conan recognized N'Gora. The black man gave no heed to Conan's shout as he charged, eyes rolled up to display the whites, teeth gleaming, face an inhuman mask.

With his skin crawling with the horror that madness always instils in the sane, Conan passed his sword through the black man's body; then, avoiding the hooked hands that clawed at him as N'Gora sank down, he strode to the edge of the cliff.

For an instant he stood looking down into the jagged rocks below, where lay N'Gora's spearmen, in limp, distorted attitudes that told of crushed limbs and splintered bones. Not one moved. A cloud of huge black flies buzzed loudly above the blood-splashed stones; the ants had already begun to gnaw at the corpses. On the trees about sat birds of prey, and a jackal, looking up and seeing the man on the cliff, slunk furtively away.

For a little space Conan stood motionless. Then he wheeled and ran back the way he had come, flinging himself with reckless haste through the tall grass and bushes, hurdling creepers that sprawled snake-like across his path. His sword swung low in his right hand, and an unaccustomed pallor tinged his dark face.

The silence that reigned in the jungle was not broken. The sun had set and great shadows rushed upward from the slime of the black earth. Through the gigantic shades of lurking death and grim desolation Conan was a speeding glimmer of scarlet and blue steel. No sound in all the solitude was heard except his own quick panting as he burst from the shadows into the dim twilight of the river-shore.

He saw the galley shouldering the rotten wharf, the ruins reeling drunkenly in the gray half-light.

And here and there among the stones were spots of raw bright color, as if a careless hand had splashed with a crimson brush.

Again Conan looked on death and destruction. Before him lay his spearmen, nor did they rise to salute him. From the jungle-edge to the riverbank, among the rotting pillars and along the broken piers they lay, torn and mangled and half devoured, chewed travesties of men.

All about the bodies and pieces of bodies were swarms of huge footprints, like those of hyenas.

Conan came silently upon the pier, approaching the galley above whose deck was suspended something that glimmered ivory-white in the faint twilight. Speechless, the Cimmerian looked on the Queen of the Black Coast as she hung from the yard-arm of her own galley. Between the yard and her white throat stretched a line of crimson clots that shone like blood in the gray light.

4 The Attack from the Air

The shadows were black around him,
The dripping jaws gaped wide,
Thicker than rain the red drops fell;
But my love was fiercer than Death's black spell,
Nor all the iron walls of hell
Could keep me from his side.

THE SONG OF BÊLIT

The jungle was a black colossus that locked the ruin-littered glade in ebon arms. The moon had not risen; the stars were flecks of hot amber in a breathless sky that reeked of death. On the pyramid among the fallen towers sat Conan the Cimmerian like an iron statue, chin propped on massive fists. Out in the black shadows stealthy feet padded and red eyes glimmered. The dead lay as they had fallen. But on the deck of the *Tigress*, on a pyre of broken benches, spear-shafts and leopardskins, lay the Queen of the Black Coast in her last sleep, wrapped in Conan's scarlet cloak. Like a true queen she lay, with her plunder heaped high about her: silks, cloth-of-gold, silver braid, casks of gems and golden coins, silver ingots, jeweled daggers and teocallis of gold wedges.

But of the plunder of the accursed city, only the sullen waters of Zarkheba could tell where Conan had thrown it with a heathen curse. Now he sat grimly on the pyramid, waiting for his unseen foes. The black fury in his soul drove out all fear. What shapes would emerge from the blackness he knew not, nor did he care.

He no longer doubted the visions of the black lotus. He understood that while waiting for him in the glade, N'Gora and his comrades had been terror-stricken by the winged monster swooping upon them from the sky, and fleeing in blind panic, had fallen over the cliff, all except their chief, who had somehow escaped their fate, though not madness. Meanwhile, or immediately after, or perhaps before, the destruction of those on the riverbank had been accomplished. Conan did not doubt that the slaughter along the river had been massacre rather than battle. Already unmanned by their superstitious fears, the blacks might well have died without striking a blow in their own defense when attacked by their inhuman foes.

Why he had been spared so long, he did not understand, unless the malign entity which ruled the river meant to keep him alive to torture him with grief and fear. All pointed to a human or superhuman intelligence – the breaking of the water-casks to divide the forces, the driving of the blacks over the cliff, and last and greatest, the grim jest of the crimson necklace knotted like a hangman's noose about Bêlit's white neck.

Having apparently saved the Cimmerian for the choicest victim, and extracted the last ounce of exquisite mental torture, it was likely that the unknown enemy would conclude the drama by sending him after the other victims. No smile bent Conan's grim lips at the thought, but his eyes were lit with iron laughter.

The moon rose, striking fire from the Cimmerian's horned helmet. No call awoke the echoes; yet suddenly the night grew tense and the jungle held its breath. Instinctively Conan loosened the great sword in its sheath. The pyramid on which he rested was four-sided, one – the side toward the jungle – carved in broad steps. In his hand was a Shemite bow, such as Bêlit had taught her pirates to use. A heap of arrows lay at his feet, feathered ends towards him, as he rested on one knee.

Something moved in the blackness under the trees. Etched abruptly in the rising moon, Conan saw a darkly blocked-out head and shoulders, brutish in outline. And now from the shadows dark shapes came silently, swiftly, running low – twenty great spotted hyenas. Their slavering fangs flashed in the moonlight, their eyes blazed as no true beast's eyes ever blazed.

Twenty: then the spears of the pirates had taken toll of the pack, after all. Even as he thought this, Conan drew nock to ear, and at the twang of the string a flame-eyed shadow bounded high and fell writhing. The rest did not falter; on they came, and like a rain of death among them fell the arrows of the Cimmerian, driven with all the force and accuracy of steely thews backed by a hate hot as the slag-heaps of hell.

In his berserk fury he did not miss; the air was filled with feathered destruction. The havoc wrought among the onrushing pack was breathtaking. Less than half of them reached the foot of the pyramid. Others dropped upon the broad steps. Glaring down into the blazing eyes, Conan knew these creatures were not beasts; it was not merely in their unnatural size that he sensed a blasphemous difference. They exuded an aura tangible as the black mist rising from a corpse-littered swamp. By what godless alchemy these beings had been brought into existence, he could not guess; but he knew he faced diabolism blacker than the Well of Skelos.

Springing to his feet, he bent his bow powerfully and drove his last shaft point blank at a great hairy shape that soared up at his throat. The arrow was a flying beam of moonlight that flashed onward with but a blur in its course, but the were-beast plunged convulsively in midair and crashed headlong, shot through and through.

Then the rest were on him, in a nightmare rush of blazing eyes and dripping fangs. His fiercely driven sword shore the first asunder; then the desperate impact of the others bore him down. He crushed a narrow skull with the pommel of his hilt, feeling the bone splinter and blood and brains gush over his hand; then, dropping the sword, useless at such deadly close quarters, he caught at the throats of the two horrors which were ripping and tearing at him in silent fury. A foul acrid scent almost stifled him, his own sweat blinded him. Only his mail saved him from being ripped to ribbons in an instant. The next, his naked right hand locked on a hairy throat and tore it open. His left hand, missing the throat of the other beast, caught and broke its foreleg. A short yelp, the only cry in that grim battle, and hideously human-like, burst from the maimed beast. At the sick horror of that cry from a bestial throat, Conan involuntarily relaxed his grip.

One, blood gushing from its torn jugular, lunged at him in a last spasm of ferocity, and fastened its fangs on his throat – to fall back dead, even as Conan felt the tearing agony of its grip.

The other, springing forward on three legs, was slashing at his belly as a wolf slashes, actually rending the links of his mail. Flinging aside the dying beast, Conan grappled the crippled horror and, with a muscular effort that brought a groan from his blood-flecked lips, he heaved upright, gripping the struggling, tearing fiend in his arms. An instant he reeled off balance, its fetid breath hot on his nostrils; its jaws snapping at his neck; then he hurled it from him, to crash with bone-splintering force down the marble steps.

As he reeled on wide-braced legs, sobbing for breath, the jungle and the moon swimming bloodily to his sight, the thrash of bat-wings was loud in his ears. Stooping, he groped for his sword, and swaying upright, braced his feet drunkenly and heaved the great blade above his head with both hands, shaking the blood from his eyes as he sought the air above him for his foe.

Instead of attack from the air, the pyramid staggered suddenly and awfully beneath his feet. He heard a rumbling crackle and saw the tall column above him wave like a wand. Stung to galvanized life, he bounded far out; his feet hit a step, halfway down, which rocked beneath him, and his next desperate leap carried him clear. But even as his heels hit the earth, with a shattering crash like a breaking mountain the pyramid crumpled, the column came thundering down in bursting fragments. For a blind cataclysmic instant the sky seemed to rain shards of marble. Then a rubble of shattered stone lay whitely under the moon.

Conan stirred, throwing off the splinters that half covered him. A glancing blow had knocked off his helmet and momentarily stunned him. Across his legs lay a great piece of the column, pinning him down. He was not sure that his legs were unbroken. His black locks were plastered with sweat; blood trickled from the wounds in his throat and hands. He hitched up on one arm, struggling with the debris that prisoned him.

Then something swept down across the stars and struck the sward near him. Twisting about, he saw it – *the winged one!*

With fearful speed it was rushing upon him, and in that instant Conan had only a confused impression of a gigantic man-like shape hurtling along on bowed and stunted legs; of huge hairy arms outstretching misshapen black-nailed paws; of a malformed head, in whose broad face the only features recognizable as such were a pair of blood-red eyes. It was a thing neither man, beast, nor devil, imbued with characteristics subhuman as well as characteristics superhuman.

But Conan had no time for conscious consecutive thought. He threw himself toward his fallen sword, and his clawing fingers missed it by inches. Desperately he grasped the shard which pinned his legs, and the veins swelled in his temples as he strove to thrust it off him. It gave slowly, but he knew that before he could free himself the monster would be upon him, and he knew that those black-taloned hands were death.

The headlong rush of the winged one had not wavered. It towered over the prostrate Cimmerian like a black shadow, arms thrown wide – a glimmer of white flashed between it and its victim.

In one mad instant she was there – a tense white shape, vibrant with love fierce as a she-panther's. The dazed Cimmerian saw between him and the onrushing death, her lithe figure, shimmering like ivory beneath the moon; he saw the blaze of her dark eyes, the thick cluster of her burnished hair; her bosom heaved, her red lips were parted, she cried out sharp and ringing at the ring of steel as she thrust at the winged monster's breast.

'*Bêlit!*' screamed Conan. She flashed a quick glance at him, and in her dark eyes he saw her love flaming, a naked elemental thing of raw fire and molten lava. Then she was gone, and the Cimmerian saw only the winged fiend which had staggered back in unwonted fear, arms lifted as if to fend off attack. And he knew that Bêlit in truth lay on her pyre on the *Tigress*'s deck. In his ears rang her passionate cry: 'Were I still in death and you fighting for life I would come back from the abyss—'

With a terrible cry he heaved upward hurling the stone aside. The winged one came on again, and Conan sprang to meet it, his veins on fire with madness. The thews started out like cords on his forearms as he swung his great sword, pivoting on his heel with the force of the sweeping arc. Just above the hips it caught the hurtling shape, and the knotted legs fell one way, the torso another as the blade sheared clear through its hairy body.

Conan stood in the moonlit silence, the dripping sword sagging in his hand, staring down at the remnants of his enemy. The red eyes glared up at him with awful life, then glazed and set; the great hands knotted spasmodically and stiffened. And the oldest race in the world was extinct.

Conan lifted his head, mechanically searching for the beast-things that had been its slaves and executioners. None met his gaze. The bodies he saw littering the moon-splashed grass were of men, not beasts: hawk-faced, dark-skinned men, naked, transfixed by arrows or mangled by sword-strokes. And they were crumbling into dust before his eyes.

Why had not the winged master come to the aid of its slaves when he struggled with them? Had it feared to come within reach of fangs that might turn and rend it? Craft and caution had lurked in that misshapen skull, but had not availed in the end.

Turning on his heel, the Cimmerian strode down the rotting wharfs and stepped aboard the galley. A few strokes of his sword cut her adrift, and he went to the sweep-head. The *Tigress* rocked slowly in the sullen water, sliding out sluggishly toward the middle of the river, until the broad current caught her. Conan leaned on the sweep, his somber gaze fixed on the cloak-wrapped shape that lay in state on the pyre the richness of which was equal to the ransom of an empress.

5 The Funeral Pyre

Now we are done with roaming, evermore;
   No more the oars, the windy harp's refrain;
Nor crimson pennon frights the dusky shore;
   Blue girdle of the world, receive again
Her whom thou gavest me.
THE SONG OF BÊLIT

Again dawn tinged the ocean. A redder glow lit the river-mouth. Conan of Cimmeria leaned on his great sword upon the white beach, watching the *Tigress* swinging out on her last voyage. There was no light in his eyes that contemplated the glassy swells. Out of the rolling blue wastes all glory and wonder had gone. A fierce revulsion shook him as he gazed at the green surges that deepened into purple hazes of mystery.

Bêlit had been of the sea; she had lent it splendor and allure. Without her it rolled a barren, dreary and desolate waste from pole to pole. She belonged to the sea; to its everlasting mystery he returned her. He could do no more. For himself, its glittering blue splendor was more repellent than the leafy fronds which rustled and whispered behind him of vast mysterious wilds beyond them, and into which he must plunge.

No hand was at the sweep of the *Tigress*, no oars drove her through the green water. But a clean tanging wind bellied her silken sail, and as a wild swan cleaves the sky to her nest, she sped seaward, flames mounting higher and higher from her deck to lick at the mast and envelop the figure that lay lapped in scarlet on the shining pyre.

So passed the Queen of the Black Coast, and leaning on his

red-stained sword, Conan stood silently until the red glow had faded far out in the blue hazes and dawn splashed its rose and gold over the ocean.

THE DEVIL IN IRON

1

THE FISHERMAN LOOSENED HIS knife in its scabbard. The gesture was instinctive, for what he feared was nothing a knife could slay, not even the saw-edged crescent blade of the Yuetshi that could disembowel a man with an upward stroke. Neither man nor beast threatened him in the solitude which brooded over the castellated isle of Xapur.

He had climbed the cliffs, passed through the jungle that bordered them, and now stood surrounded by evidences of a vanished state. Broken columns glimmered among the trees, the straggling lines of crumbling walls meandered off into the shadows, and under his feet were broad paves, cracked and bowed by roots growing beneath.

The fisherman was typical of his race, that strange people whose origin is lost in the gray dawn of the past, and who have dwelt in their rude fishing huts along the southern shore of the Sea of Vilayet since time immemorial. He was broadly built, with long apish arms and a mighty chest, but with lean loins and thin bandy legs. His face was broad, his forehead low and retreating, his hair thick and tangled. A belt for a knife and a rag for a loin-cloth were all he wore in the way of clothing.

That he was where he was proved that he was less dully incurious than most of his people. Men seldom visited Xapur. It was uninhabited, all but forgotten, merely one among the myriad isles which dotted the great inland sea. Men called it Xapur, the Fortified, because of its ruins, remnants of some prehistoric kingdom, lost and forgotten before the conquering Hyborians had ridden southward. None knew who reared those stones, though dim legends lingered among the Yuetshi which half intelligibly suggested a connection of immeasurable antiquity between the fishers and the unknown island kingdom.

But it had been a thousand years since any Yuetshi had understood the import of these tales; they repeated them now as a meaningless formula, a gibberish framed by their lips by custom. No Yuetshi had come to Xapur for a century. The adjacent coast of the mainland was uninhabited, a reedy marsh given over to the grim beasts that haunted it. The fisher's village lay some distance to the south, on the mainland. A storm had blown his frail fishing craft far from his accustomed haunts, and wrecked it in a night of flaring lightning and roaring waters on the towering cliffs of the isle. Now in the dawn the sky shone blue and clear, the rising sun made jewels of the dripping leaves. He had climbed the cliffs to which he had clung through the night because, in the midst of the storm, he had seen an appalling lance of lightning fork out of the black heavens, and the concussion of its stroke, which had shaken the whole island, had been accompanied by a cataclysmic crash that he doubted could have resulted from a riven tree.

A dull curiosity had caused him to investigate; and now he had found what he sought and an animal-like uneasiness possessed him, a sense of lurking peril.

Among the trees reared a broken dome-like structure, built of gigantic blocks of the peculiar iron-like green stone found only on the islands of Vilayet. It seemed incredible that human hands could have shaped and placed them, and certainly it was beyond human power to have overthrown the structure they formed. But the thunderbolt had splintered the ton-heavy blocks like so much glass, reduced others to green dust, and ripped away the whole arch of the dome.

The fisherman climbed over the debris and peered in, and what he saw brought a grunt from him. Within the ruined dome, surrounded by stone-dust and bits of broken masonry, lay a man on the golden block. He was clad in a sort of skirt and a shagreen girdle. His black hair, which fell in a square mane to his massive shoulders, was confined about his temples by a narrow gold band. On his bare, muscular breast lay a curious dagger with a jeweled pommel, shagreen-bound hilt, and a broad crescent blade. It was much like the knife the fisherman wore at his hip, but it lacked the serrated edge, and was made with infinitely greater skill.

The fisherman lusted for the weapon. The man, of course, was dead; had been dead for many centuries. This dome was his tomb. The fisherman did not wonder by what art the ancients had preserved the body in such a vivid likeness of life, which kept the muscular limbs full and unshrunken, the dark flesh vital. The dull brain of the Yuetshi had room only for his desire for the knife with its delicate waving lines along the dully gleaming blade.

Scrambling down into the dome, he lifted the weapon from the man's breast. And as he did so, a strange and terrible thing came to pass. The muscular dark hands knotted convulsively, the lids flared open, revealing great dark magnetic eyes whose stare struck the startled fisherman like a physical blow. He recoiled, dropping the jeweled dagger in his perturbation. The man on the dais heaved up to a sitting position, and the fisherman gaped at the full extent of his size, thus revealed. His narrowed eyes held the Yuetshi and in those slitted orbs he read neither friendliness nor gratitude; he saw only a fire as alien and hostile as that which burns in the eyes of a tiger.

Suddenly the man rose and towered above him, menace in his every aspect. There was no room in the fisherman's dull brain for fear, at least for such fear as might grip a man who has just seen the fundamental laws of nature defied. As the great hands fell to his shoulders, he drew his saw-edged knife and struck upward with the same motion. The blade splintered against the stranger's corded belly as against a steel column, and then the fisherman's thick neck broke like a rotten twig in the giant hands.

2

Jehungir Agha, lord of Khawarizm and keeper of the coastal border, scanned once more the ornate parchment scroll with its peacock seal, and laughed shortly and sardonically.

'Well?' bluntly demanded his counsellor Ghaznavi.

Jehungir shrugged his shoulders. He was a handsome man, with the merciless pride of birth and accomplishment.

'The king grows short of patience,' said he. 'In his own hand he complains bitterly of what he calls my failure to guard the frontier. By Tarim, if I can not deal a blow to these robbers of the steppes, Khawarizm may own a new lord.'

Ghaznavi tugged his gray-shot beard in meditation. Yezdigerd, king of Turan, was the mightiest monarch in the world. In his palace in the great port city of Aghrapur was heaped the plunder of empires. His fleets of purple-sailed war galleys had made Vilayet an Hyrkanian lake. The dark-skinned people of Zamora paid him tribute, as did the eastern provinces of Koth. The Shemites bowed to his rule as far west as Shushan. His armies ravaged the borders of Stygia in the south and the snowy lands of the Hyperboreans in the north. His riders bore torch and sword westward into Brythunia and Ophir and Corinthia, even to the borders of Nemedia. His gilt-helmeted swordsmen had trampled hosts under their horses' hoofs, and walled cities went up in flames at his command. In the glutted slave markets of Aghrapur, Sultanapur, Khawarizm, Shahpur and Khorusun, women were sold for three small silver coins – blond Brythunians, tawny Stygians, dark-haired Zamorians, ebon Kushites, olive-skinned Shemites.

Yet, while his swift horsemen overthrew armies far from his frontiers, at his very borders an audacious foe plucked his beard with a red-dripping and smoke-stained hand.

On the broad steppes between the Sea of Vilayet and the borders of the easternmost Hyborian kingdoms, a new race had sprung up in the past half-century, formed originally of fleeing criminals, broken men, escaped slaves, and deserting soldiers. They were men of many crimes and countries, some born on the steppes, some fleeing from the kingdoms in the west. They were called *kozak*, which means wastrel.

Dwelling on the wild, open steppes, owning no law but their own peculiar code, they had become a people capable of defying the Grand Monarch. Ceaselessly they raided the Turanian frontier, retiring in the steppes when defeated; with the pirates of Vilayet, men of much the same breed, they harried the coast, preying off the merchant ships which plied between the Hyrkanian ports.

'How am I to crush these wolves?' demanded Jehungir. 'If I follow them into the steppes, I run the risk either of being cut off and destroyed, or having them elude me entirely and burn the city in my absence. Of late they have been more daring than ever.'

'That is because of the new chief who has risen among them,' answered Ghaznavi. 'You know whom I mean.'

'Aye!' replied Jehungir feelingly. 'It is that devil Conan; he is even wilder than the *kozaks*, yet he is crafty as a mountain lion.'

'It is more through wild animal instinct than through intelligence,' answered Ghaznavi. 'The other *kozaks* are at least descendants of civilized men. He is a barbarian. But to dispose of him would be to deal them a crippling blow.'

'But how?' demanded Jehungir. 'He has repeatedly cut his way out of spots that seemed certain death for him. And, by instinct or cunning, he has avoided or escaped every trap set for him.'

'For every beast and for every man there is a trap he will not escape,' quoth Ghaznavi. 'When we have parleyed with the *kozaks* for the ransom of captives, I have observed this man Conan. He has a keen relish for women and strong drink. Have your captive Octavia fetched here.'

Jehungir clapped his hands, and an impassive Kushite eunuch, an image of shining ebony in silken pantaloons, bowed before him and went to do his bidding. Presently he returned, leading by the wrist a tall handsome girl, whose yellow hair, clear eyes and fair skin identified her as a pure-blooded member of her race. Her scanty silk tunic, girded at the waist, displayed the marvelous contours of her magnificent figure. Her fine eyes flashed with resentment and her red lips were sulky, but submission had been taught her during her captivity. She stood with hanging head before her master until her motioned her to a seat on the divan beside him. Then he looked inquiringly at Ghaznavi.

'We must lure Conan away from the *kozaks*,' said the counsellor abruptly. 'Their war camp is at present pitched somewhere on the lower reaches of the Zaporoska River – which, as you well know, is a wilderness of reeds, a swampy jungle in which our last expedition was cut to pieces by those masterless devils.'

'I am not likely to forget that,' said Jehungir wryly.

'There is an uninhabited island near the mainland,' said Ghaznavi, 'known as Xapur, the Fortified, because of some ancient ruins upon it. There is a peculiarity about it which makes it perfect for our purpose. It has no shore-line, but rises sheer out of the sea in cliffs a hundred and fifty feet tall. Not even an ape could negotiate them. The only place where a man can go up or down is a narrow path on the western side that has the appearance of a worn stair, carved into the solid rock of the cliffs.

'If we could trap Conan on that island, alone, we could hunt him down at our leisure, with bows, as men hunt a lion.'

'As well wish for the moon,' said Jehungir impatiently. 'Shall we send him a messenger, bidding him climb the cliffs and await our coming?'

'In effect, yes!' Seeing Jehungir's look of amazement, Ghaznavi continued: 'We will ask for a parley with the *kozaks* in regard to prisoners, at the edge of the steppes by Fort Ghori. As usual, we will go with a force and encamp outside the castle. They will come, with an equal force, and the parley will go forward with the usual distrust and suspicion. But this time we will take with us, as if by casual chance, your beautiful captive.' Octavia changed color and listened with intensified interest as the counsellor nodded toward her. 'She will use all her wiles to attract Conan's attention. That should not be difficult. To that wild reaver she should appear a dazzling vision of loveliness. Her vitality and substantial figure should appeal to him more vividly than would one of the doll-like beauties of your seraglio.'

Octavia sprang up, her white fists clenched, her eyes blazing and her figure quivering with outraged anger.

'You would force me to play the trollop with this barbarian?' she exclaimed. 'I will not! I am no market-block slut to smirk and ogle at a steppes-robber. I am the daughter of a Nemedian lord—'

'You were of the Nemedian nobility before my riders carried you off,' returned Jehungir cynically. 'Now you are merely a slave who will do as she is bid.'

'I will not!' she raged.

'On the contrary,' rejoined Jehungir with studied cruelty, 'you will. I like Ghaznavi's plan. Continue, prince among counsellors.'

'Conan will probably wish to buy her. You will refuse to sell her, of course, or to exchange her for Hyrkanian prisoners. He may then try to steal her, or take her by force – though I do not think even he would break the parley-truce. Anyway, we must be prepared for whatever he might attempt.

'Then, shortly after the parley, before he has time to forget all about her, we will send a messenger to him, under a flag of truce, accusing him of stealing the girl, and demanding her return. He may kill the messenger, but at least he will think that she has escaped.

'Then we will send a spy – a Yuetshi fisherman will do – to the *kozak* camp, who will tell Conan that Octavia is hiding on Xapur. If I know my man, he will go straight to that place.'

'But we do not know that he will go alone,' Jehungir argued.

'Does a man take a band of warriors with him, when going to a rendezvous with a woman he desires?' retorted Ghaznavi. 'The chances are all that he *will* go alone. But we will take care of the other alternative. We will not await him on the island, where we might be trapped ourselves, but among the reeds of a marshy point which juts out to within a thousand yards of Xapur. If he brings a large force, we'll beat a retreat and think up another plot. If he comes alone or with a small party, we will have him. Depend upon it, he will come, remembering your charming slave's smiles and meaning glances.'

'I will never descend to such shame!' Octavia was wild with fury and humiliation. 'I will die first!'

'You will not die, my rebellious beauty,' said Jehungir, 'but you will be subjected to a very painful and humiliating experience.'

He clapped his hands, and Octavia paled. This time it was not the Kushite who entered, but a Shemite, a heavily muscled man of medium height with a short, curled, blue-black beard.

'Here is work for you, Gilzan,' said Jehungir. 'Take this fool, and play with her awhile. Yet be careful not to spoil her beauty.'

With an inarticulate grunt the Shemite seized Octavia's wrist, and at the grasp of his iron fingers, all the defiance went out of her. With a piteous cry she tore away and threw herself on her knees before her implacable master, sobbing incoherently for mercy.

Jehungir dismissed the disappointed torturer with a gesture, and said to Ghaznavi: 'If your plan succeeds, I will fill your lap with gold.'

3

In the darkness before dawn an unaccustomed sound disturbed the solitude that slumbered over the reedy marshes and the misty waters of the coast. It was not a drowsy water-fowl nor a waking beast. It was a human who struggled through the thick reeds, which were taller than a man's head.

It was a woman, had there been anyone to see, tall and yellow-haired, her splendid limbs molded by her draggled tunic. Octavia had escaped in good earnest, every outraged fiber of her still tingling from her experience in a captivity that had become unendurable.

Jehungir's mastery of her had been bad enough; but with deliberate fiendishness Jehungir had given her to a nobleman whose name was a byword for degeneracy even in Khawarizm.

Octavia's resilient flesh crawled and quivered at her memories. Desperation had nerved her climb from Jelal Khan's castle on a rope made of strips from torn tapestries, and chance had led her to a picketed horse. She had ridden all night, and dawn found her with a foundered steed on the swampy shores of the sea. Quivering with the abhorrence of being dragged back to the revolting destiny planned for her by Jelal Khan, she plunged into the morass, seeking a hiding-place from the pursuit she expected. When the reeds grew thinner around her and the water rose about her thighs, she saw the dim loom of an island ahead of her. A broad span of water lay between, but she did not hesitate. She waded out until the low waves were lapping about her waist; then she struck out strongly, swimming with a vigor that promised unusual endurance.

As she neared the island, she saw that it rose sheer from the water in castle-like cliffs. She reached them at last, but found neither ledge to stand on below the water, not to cling to above. She swam on, following the curve of the cliffs, the strain of her long flight beginning to weight her limbs. Her hands fluttered along the sheer stone, and suddenly they found a depression. With a sobbing gasp of relief, she pulled herself out of the water and clung there, a dripping white goddess in the dim starlight.

She had come upon what seemed to be steps carved in the cliff. Up them she went, flattening herself against the stone as she caught the faint clack of muffled oars. She strained her eyes and thought she made out a vague bulk moving toward the reedy point she had just quitted. But it was too far away for her to be sure, in the darkness, and presently the faint sound ceased, and she continued her climb. If it were her pursuers, she knew of no better course than to hide on the island. She knew that most of the islands off that marshy coast were uninhabited. This might be a pirate's lair, but even pirates would be preferable to the beast she had escaped.

A vagrant thought crossed her mind as she climbed, in which she mentally compared her former master with the *kozak* chief with whom – by compulsion – she had shamelessly flirted in the pavilions of the camp by Fort Ghori, where the Hyrkanian lords had parleyed with the warriors of the steppes. His burning gaze had frightened and humiliated her, but his cleanly elemental fierceness set him above Jelal Khan, a monster such as only an overly opulent civilization can produce.

She scrambled up over the cliff edge and looked timidly at the dense shadows which confronted her. The trees grew close to the cliffs, presenting a solid mass of blackness. Something whirred above her head and she cowered, even though realizing it was only a bat.

She did not like the look of those ebony shadows, but she set her teeth and went toward them, trying not to think of snakes. Her bare feet made no sound in the spongy loam under the trees. Once among them, the darkness closed frighteningly about her. She had not taken a dozen steps when she was no longer able to look back and see the cliffs and the sea beyond. A few steps more and she became hopelessly confused and lost her sense of direction. Through the tangled branches not even a star peered. She groped and floundered on, blindly, and then came to a sudden halt.

Somewhere ahead there began the rhythmical booming of a drum. It was not such a sound as she would have expected to hear in that time and place. Then she forgot it as she was aware of a presence near her. She could not see, but she knew that something was standing beside her in the darkness.

With a stifled cry she shrank back, and as she did so, something that even in her panic she recognized as a human arm curved about her waist. She screamed and threw all her supple young strength into a wild lunge for freedom, but her captor caught her up like a child, crushing her frantic resistance with ease. The silence with which her frenzied pleas and protests were received added to her terror as she felt herself being carried through the darkness toward the distant drum which still pulsed and muttered.

4

As the first tinge of dawn reddened the sea, a small boat with a solitary occupant approached the cliffs. The man in the boat was a picturesque figure. A crimson scarf was knotted about his head; his wide silk breeches, of flaming hue, were upheld by a broad sash which likewise supported a scimitar in a shagreen scabbard. His gilt-worked leather boots suggested the horseman rather than the seaman, but he handled his boat with skill. Through his widely open white silk shirt showed his broad muscular breast, burned brown by the sun.

The muscles of his heavy bronzed arms rippled as he pulled the oars with an almost feline ease of motion. A fierce vitality that was evident in each feature and motion set him apart from common men; yet his expression was neither savage nor somber, though the smoldering blue eyes hinted at ferocity easily wakened. This was Conan, who had wandered into the armed camps of the *kozaks* with no other possession than his wits and his sword, and who had carved his way to leadership among them.

He paddled to the carven stair as one familiar with his environs, and moored the boat to a projection of the rock. Then he went up the worn steps without hesitation. He was keenly alert, not because he consciously suspected hidden danger, but because alertness was a part of him, whetted by the wild existence he followed.

What Ghaznavi had considered animal intuition or some sixth sense was merely the razor-edge faculties and savage wit of the barbarian. Conan had no instinct to tell him that men were watching him from a covert among the reeds of the mainland.

As he climbed the cliff, one of these men breathed deeply and stealthily lifted a bow. Jehungir caught his wrist and hissed an oath into his ear. 'Fool! Will you betray us? Don't you realize he is out of range? Let him get upon the island. He will go looking for the girl. We will stay here awhile. He *may* have sensed our presence or guessed our plot. He may have warriors hidden somewhere. We will wait. In an hour, if nothing suspicious occurs, we'll row up to the foot of the stair and await him there. If he does not return in a reasonable time, some of us will go upon the island and hunt him down. But I do not wish to do that if it can be helped. Some of us are sure to die if we have to go into the bush after him. I had rather catch him descending the stair, where we can feather him with arrows from a safe distance.'

Meanwhile the unsuspecting *kozak* had plunged into the forest. He went silently in his soft leather boots, his gaze sifting every shadow in eagerness to catch sight of the splendid tawny-haired beauty of whom he had dreamed ever since he had seen her in the pavilion of Jehungir Agha by Fort Ghori. He would have desired her even if she had displayed repugnance toward him. But her cryptic smiles and glances had fired his blood, and with all the lawless violence which was his heritage he desired that white-skinned golden-haired woman of civilization.

He had been on Xapur before. Less than a month ago he had held a secret conclave here with a pirate crew. He knew that he was approaching a point where he could see the mysterious ruins which gave the island its name, and he wondered if he would find the girl hiding among them. Even with the thought he stopped as though struck dead.

Ahead of him, among the trees, rose something that his reason told him was not possible. *It was a great dark green wall, with towers rearing beyond the battlements.*

Conan stood paralyzed in the disruption of the faculties which demoralizes anyone who is confronted by an impossible negation of sanity. He doubted neither his sight nor his reason, but something was monstrously out of joint. Less than a month ago only broken ruins had showed among the trees. What human hands could rear such a mammoth pile as now met his eyes, in the few weeks which had elapsed? Besides, the buccaneers who roamed Vilayet ceaselessly would have learned of any work going on on such a stupendous scale, and would have informed the *kozaks*.

There was no explaining this thing, but it was so. He was on Xapur and that fantastic heap of towering masonry was on Xapur, and all was madness and paradox; yet it was all true.

He wheeled back through the jungle, down the carven stair and across the blue waters to the distant camp at the mouth of the Zaporoska. In that moment of unreasoning panic even the thought of halting so near the inland sea was repugnant. He would leave it behind him, would quit the armed camps and the steppes, and put a thousand miles between him and the blue mysterious East where the most basic laws of nature could be set at naught, by what diabolism he could not guess.

For an instant the future fate of kingdoms that hinged on this gayclad barbarian hung in the balance. It was a small thing that tipped the scales – merely a shred of silk hanging on a bush that caught his uneasy glance. He leaned to it, his nostrils expanding, his nerves quivering to a subtle stimulant. On that bit of torn cloth, so faint that it was less with his physical faculties than by some obscure instinctive sense that he recognized it, lingered the tantalizing perfume that he connected with the sweet firm flesh of the woman he had seen in Jehungir's pavilion. The fisherman had not lied, then; she *was* here! Then in the soil he saw a single track of a bare foot, long and slender, but a man's not a woman's, and sunk deeper than was natural. The conclusion was obvious; the man who made that track was carrying a burden, and what should it be but the girl the *kozak* was seeking?

He stood silently facing the dark towers that loomed through the trees, his eyes slits of blue bale-fire. Desire for the yellow-haired woman vied with a sullen primordial rage at whoever had taken her. His human passion fought down his ultra-human fears, and dropping into the stalking crouch of a hunting panther, he glided toward the walls, taking advantage of the dense foliage to escape detection from the battlements.

As he approached he saw that the walls were composed of the same green stone that had formed the ruins, and he was haunted by a vague sense of familiarity. It was as if he looked upon something he had never seen before, but had dreamed of, or pictured mentally. At last he recognized the sensation. The walls and towers followed the plan of the ruins. It was as if the crumbling lines had grown back into the structures they originally were.

No sound disturbed the morning quiet as Conan stole to the foot of the wall which rose sheer from the luxuriant growth. On the southern reaches of the inland sea the vegetation was almost tropical. He saw no one on the battlements, heard no sounds within. He saw a massive gate a short distance to his left, and had had no reason to suppose that it was not locked and guarded. But he believed that the woman he sought was somewhere beyond that wall, and the course he took was characteristically reckless.

Above him vine-festooned branches reached out toward the battlements. He went up a great tree like a cat, and reaching a point above the parapet, he gripped a thick limb with both hands, swung back and forth at arm's length until he had gained momentum, and then let go and catapulted through the air, landing cat-like on the battlements. Crouching there he stared down into the streets of a city.

The circumference of the wall was not great, but the number of green stone buildings it contained was surprising. They were three or four stories in height, mainly flat-roofed, reflecting a fine architectural style. The streets converged like the spokes of a wheel into an octagon-shaped court in the center of the town which gave upon a lofty edifice, which, with its domes and towers, dominated the whole city. He saw no one moving in the streets or looking out of the windows, though the sun was already coming up. The silence that reigned there might have been that of a dead and deserted city. A narrow stone stair ascended the wall near him; down this he went.

Houses shouldered so closely to the wall that halfway down the stair he found himself within arm's length of a window, and halted to peer in. There were no bars, and the silk curtains were caught back with satin cords. He looked into a chamber whose walls were hidden by dark velvet tapestries. The floor was covered with thick rugs, and there were benches of polished ebony, and an ivory dais heaped with furs.

He was about to continue his descent, when he heard the sound of someone approaching in the street below. Before the unknown person could come round a corner and see him on the stair, he stepped quickly across the intervening space and dropped lightly into the room, drawing his scimitar. He stood for an instant statue-like; then as nothing happened he was moving across the rugs toward an arched doorway when a hanging was drawn aside, revealing a cushioned alcove from which a slender, dark-haired girl regarded him with languid eyes.

Conan glared at her tensely, expecting her momentarily to start screaming. But she merely smothered a yawn with a dainty hand, rose from the alcove and leaned negligently against the hanging which she held with one hand.

She was undoubtedly a member of a white race, though her skin was very dark. Her square-cut hair was black as midnight, her only garment a wisp of silk about her supple hips.

Presently she spoke, but the tongue was unfamiliar to him, and he shook his head. She yawned again, stretched lithely, and without any show of fear or surprize, shifted to a language he did understand, a dialect of Yuetshi which sounded strangely archaic.

'Are you looking for someone?' she asked, as indifferently as if the invasion of her chamber by an armed stranger were the most common thing imaginable.

'Who are you?' he demanded.

'I am Yateli,' she answered languidly. 'I must have feasted late last night, I am so sleepy now. Who are you?'

'I am Conan, a *hetman* among the *kozaks*,' he answered, watching her narrowly. He believed her attitude to be a pose, and expected her to try to escape from the chamber or rouse the house. But, though a velvet rope that might be a signal cord hung near her, she did not reach for it.

'Conan,' she repeated drowsily. 'You are not a Dagonian. I suppose you are a mercenary. Have you cut the heads off many Yuetshi?'

'I do not war on water rats!' he snorted.

'But they are very terrible,' she murmured. 'I remember when they were our slaves. But they revolted and burned and slew. Only the magic of Khosatral Khel has kept them from the walls—' She paused, a puzzled look struggling with the sleepiness of her expression. 'I forgot,' she muttered. 'They *did* climb the walls, last night. There was shouting and fire, and people calling in vain on Khosatral.' She shook her head as if to clear it. 'But that can not be,' she murmured, 'because I am alive, and I thought I was dead. Oh, to the devil with it!'

She came across the chamber, and taking Conan's hand, drew him to the dais. He yielded in bewilderment and uncertainty. The girl smiled at him like a sleepy child; her long silky lashes drooped over dusky, clouded eyes. She ran her fingers through his thick black locks as if to assure herself of his reality.

'It was a dream,' she yawned. 'Perhaps it's all a dream. I feel like a dream now. I don't care. I can't remember something – I have forgotten – there is something I can not understand, but I grow so sleepy when I try to think. Anyway, it doesn't matter.'

'What do you mean?' he asked uneasily. 'You said they climbed the walls last night? Who?'

'The Yuetshi. I thought so, anyway. A cloud of smoke hid everything, but a naked, blood-stained devil caught me by the throat and drove his knife into my breast. Oh, it hurt! But it was a dream, because see, there is no scar.' She idly inspected her smooth bosom, and then sank upon Conan's lap and passed her supple arms around his massive neck. 'I can not remember,' she murmured, nestling her dark head against his mighty breast. 'Everything is dim and misty. It does not matter. You are no dream. You are strong. Let us live while we can. Love me!'

He cradled the girl's glossy head in the bend of his heavy arm, and kissed her full red lips with unfeigned relish.

'You are strong,' she repeated, her voice waning. 'Love me – love—' The sleepy murmur faded away; the dusky eyes closed, the long lashes drooping over the sensuous cheeks; the supple body relaxed in Conan's arms.

He scowled down at her. She seemed to partake of the illusion that haunted this whole city, but the firm resilience of her limbs under his questing fingers convinced him that he had a living human girl in his arms, and not the shadow of a dream. No less disturbed, he hastily laid her on the furs upon the dais. Her sleep was too deep to be natural. He decided that she must be an addict of some drug, perhaps like the black lotus of Xuthal.

Then he found something else to make him wonder. Among the furs on the dais was a gorgeous spotted skin, whose predominant hue was golden. It was not a clever copy, but the skin of an actual beast. And that beast, Conan knew, had been extinct for at least a thousand years; it was the great golden leopard which figures so predominantly in Hyborian legendry, and which the ancient artists delighted to portray in pigments and marble.

Shaking his head in bewilderment, Conan passed through the archway into a winding corridor. Silence hung over the house, but outside he heard a sound which his keen ears recognized as something ascending the stair on the wall from which he had entered the building. An instant later he was startled to hear something land with a soft but weighty thud on the floor of the chamber he had just quitted. Turning quickly away, he hurried along the twisting hallway until something on the floor before him brought him to a halt.

It was a human figure, which lay half in the hall and half in an opening that obviously was normally concealed by a door which was a duplicate of the panels of the wall. It was a man, dark and lean, clad only in a silk loin-cloth, with a shaven head and cruel features, and he lay as if death had struck him just as he was emerging from the panel. Conan bent above him, seeking the cause of his death, and discovered him to be merely sunk in the same deep sleep as the girl in the chamber.

But why should he select such a place for his slumbers? While meditating on the matter, Conan was galvanized by a sound behind him. Something was moving up the corridor in his direction. A quick glance down it showed that it ended in a great door which might be locked. Conan jerked the supine body out of the panel-entrance and stepped through, pulling the panel shut after him. A click told him it was locked in place. Standing in utter darkness, he heard a shuffling tread halt just outside the door, and a faint chill trickled along his spine. That was no human step, nor that of any beast he had ever encountered.

There was an instant of silence, then a faint creak of wood and metal. Putting out his hand he felt the door straining and bending inward, as if a great weight were being steadily borne against it from the outside. As he reached for his sword, this ceased and he heard a strange slobbering mouthing that prickled the short hairs on his scalp. Scimitar in hand he began backing away, and his heels felt steps, down which he nearly tumbled. He was in a narrow staircase leading downward.

He groped his way down in the blackness, feeling for, but not finding, some other opening in the walls. Just as he decided that he was no longer in the house, but deep in the earth under it, the steps ceased in a level tunnel.

5

Along the black silent tunnel Conan groped, momentarily dreading a fall into some unseen pit; but at last his feet struck steps again, and he went up them until he came to a door on which his fumbling fingers found a metal catch. He came out into a dim and lofty room of enormous proportions. Fantastic columns marched around the mottled walls, upholding a ceiling, which, at once translucent and dusky, seemed like a cloudy midnight sky, giving an illusion of impossible height. If any light filtered in from the outside it was curiously altered.

In a brooding twilight Conan moved across the bare green floor. The great room was circular, pierced on one side by the great bronze valves of a giant door. Opposite this, on a dais against the wall, up to which led broad curving steps, there stood a throne of copper, and when Conan saw what was coiled on this throne, he retreated hastily, lifting his scimitar.

Then, as the thing did not move, he scanned it more closely, and presently mounted the glass steps and stared down at it. It was a gigantic snake, apparently carved in some jade-like substance. Each scale stood out as distinctly as in real life, and the iridescent colors were vividly reproduced. The great wedge-shaped head was half submerged in the folds of its trunk; so neither the eyes nor jaws were visible. Recognition stirred in his mind. This snake was evidently meant to represent one of those grim monsters of the marsh which in past ages had haunted the reedy edges of Vilayet's southern shores. But, like the golden leopard, they had been extinct for hundreds of years. Conan had seen rude images of them, in miniature, among the idol-huts of the Yuetshi, and there was a description of them in the *Book of Skelos*, which drew on prehistoric sources.

Conan admired the scaly torso, thick as his thigh and obviously of great length, and he reached out and laid a curious hand on the thing. And as he did so, his heart nearly stopped. An icy chill congealed the blood in his veins and lifted the short hair on his scalp. Under his hand there was not the smooth, brittle surface of glass or metal or stone, but the yielding, fibrous mass of a *living* thing. He felt cold, sluggish life flowing under his fingers.

His hand jerked back in instinctive repulsion. Sword shaking in his grasp, horror and revulsion and fear almost choking him, he backed away and down the glass steps with painful care, glaring in awful fascination at the grisly thing that slumbered on the copper throne. It did not move.

He reached the bronze door and tried it, with his heart in his teeth, sweating with fear that he should find himself locked in with that slimy horror. But the valves yielded to his touch, and he glided through and closed them behind him.

He found himself in a wide hallway with lofty tapestried walls, where the light was the same twilight gloom. It made distant objects indistinct and that made him uneasy, rousing thoughts of serpents gliding unseen through the dimness. A door at the other end seemed miles away in the illusive light. Nearer at hand the tapestry hung in such a way as to suggest an opening behind it, and lifting it cautiously he discovered a narrow stair leading up.

While he hesitated he heard in the great room he had just left, the same shuffling tread he had heard outside the locked panel. Had he been followed through the tunnel? He went up the stair hastily, dropping the tapestry in place behind him.

Emerging presently into a twisting corridor, he took the first doorway he came to. He had a twofold purpose in his apparently aimless prowling: to escape from the building and its mysteries, and to find the Nemedian girl who, he felt, was imprisoned somewhere in this palace, temple, or whatever it was. He believed it was the great domed edifice in the center of the city, and it was likely that here dwelt the ruler of the town, to whom a captive woman would doubtless be brought.

He found himself in a chamber, not another corridor, and was about to retrace his steps, when he heard a voice which came from behind one of the walls. There was no door in that wall, but he leaned close and heard distinctly. And an icy chill crawled slowly along his spine. The tongue was Nemedian, but the voice was not human. There was a terrifying resonance about it, like a bell tolling at midnight.

'There was no life in the Abyss, save that which was incorporated in me,' it tolled. 'Nor was there light, nor motion, nor any sound. Only the urge behind and beyond life guided and impelled me on my upward journey, blind, insensate, inexorable. Through ages upon ages, and the changeless strata of darkness I climbed—'

Ensorcelled by that belling resonance, Conan crouched forgetful of all else, until its hypnotic power caused a strange replacement of faculties and perception, and sound created the illusion of sight. Conan was no longer aware of the voice, save as far-off rhythmical waves of sound. Transported beyond his age and his own individuality, he was seeing the transmutation of the being men called Khosatral Khel which crawled up from Night and the Abyss ages ago to clothe itself in the substance of the material universe.

But human flesh was too frail, too paltry to hold the terrific essence that was Khosatral Khel. So he stood up in the shape and aspect of a man, but his flesh was not flesh, nor the bone, bone, nor blood, blood. He became a blasphemy against all nature, for he caused to live and think and act a basic substance that before had never known the pulse and stir of animate being.

He stalked through the world like a god, for no earthly weapon could harm him, and to him a century was like an hour. In his wanderings he came upon a primitive people inhabiting the island of Dagonia, and it pleased him to give this race culture and civilization, and by his aid they built the city of Dagon and they abode there and worshipped him. Strange and grisly were his servants, called from the dark corners of the planet where grim survivals of forgotten ages yet lurked. His house in Dagon was connected with every other house by tunnels through which his shaven-headed priests bore victims for the sacrifice.

But after many ages a fierce and brutish people appeared on the shores of the sea. They called themselves Yuetshi, and after a fierce battle they were defeated and enslaved, and for nearly a generation they died on the altars of Khosatral.

His sorcery kept them in bonds. Then their priest, a strange gaunt man of unknown race, plunged into the wilderness, and when he returned he bore a knife that was of no earthly substance. It was forged of a meteor which flashed through the sky like a flaming arrow and fell in a far valley. The slaves rose. Their saw-edged crescents cut down the men of Dagon like sheep, and against that unearthly knife the magic of Khosatral was impotent. While carnage and slaughter bellowed through the red smoke that choked the streets, the grimmest act of that grim drama was played in the cryptic dome behind the great daised chamber with its copper throne and its walls mottled like the skin of serpents.

From that dome the Yuetshi priest emerged alone. He had not slain his foe, because he wished to hold the threat of his loosing over the heads of his own rebellious subjects. He had left Khosatral lying upon the golden dais with the mystic knife across his breast for a spell to hold him senseless and inanimate until doomsday.

But the ages passed and the priest died, the towers of deserted Dagon crumbled, the tales became dim, and the Yuetshi were reduced by plagues and famines and war to scattered remnants, dwelling in squalor along the seashore.

Only the cryptic dome resisted the rot of time, until a chance thunderbolt and the curiosity of a fisherman lifted from the breast of the god the magic knife and broke the spell. Khosatral Khel rose and lived and waxed mighty once more. It pleased him to restore the city as it was in the days before its fall. By his necromancy he lifted the towers from the dust of forgotten millenniums, and the folk which had been dust for ages moved in life again.

But folk who have tasted death are only partly alive. In the dark corners of their souls and minds death still lurks unconquered. By night the people of Dagon moved and loved, hated and feasted, and remembered the fall of Dagon and their own slaughter only as a dim dream; they moved in an enchanted mist of illusion, feeling the strangeness of their existence but not inquiring the reasons therefor. With the coming of day they sank into deep sleep, to be roused again only by the coming of night, which is akin to death.

All this rolled in a terrible panorama before Conan's consciousness as he crouched beside the tapestried wall. His reason staggered. All certainty and sanity were swept away, leaving a shadowy universe through which stole hooded figures of grisly potentialities. Through the belling of the voice which was like a tolling of triumph over the ordered laws of a sane planet, a human sound anchored Conan's mind from its flight through spheres of madness. It was the hysterical sobbing of a woman.

Involuntarily he sprang up.

6

Jehungir Agha waited with growing impatience in his boat among the reeds. More than an hour passed, and Conan had not reappeared. Doubtless he was still searching the island for the girl he thought to be hidden there. But another surmise occurred to the Agha. Suppose the *hetman* had left his warriors near by, and that they should grow suspicious and come to investigate his long absence? Jehungir spoke to the oarsmen, and the long boat slid from among the reeds and glided toward the carven stairs.

Leaving half a dozen men in the boat, he took the rest, ten mighty archers of Khawarizm, in spired helmets and tiger-skin cloaks. Like hunters invading the retreat of the lion, they stole forward under the trees, arrows on string. Silence reigned over the forest except when a great green thing that might have been a parrot swirled over their heads with a low thunder of broad wings, and then sped off through the trees. With a sudden gesture Jehungir halted his party, and they stared incredulously at the towers that showed through the verdure in the distance.

'Tarim!' muttered Jehungir. 'The pirates have rebuilt the ruins! Doubtless Conan is there. We must investigate this. A fortified town this close to the mainland! – Come!'

With renewed caution they glided through the trees. The game had altered; from pursuers and hunters they had become spies.

And as they crept through the tangled growth, the man they sought was in peril more deadly than their filigreed arrows.

Conan realized with a crawling of his skin that beyond the wall the belling voice had ceased. He stood motionless as a statue, his gaze fixed on a curtained door through which he knew that a culminating horror would presently appear.

It was dim and misty in the chamber, and Conan's hair began to lift on his scalp as he looked. He saw a head and a pair of gigantic shoulders grow out of the twilight gloom. There was no sound of footsteps, but the great dusky form grew more distinct until Conan recognized the figure of a man. He was clad in sandals, a skirt and a broad shagreen girdle. His square-cut mane was confined by a circlet of gold. Conan stared at the sweep of the monstrous shoulders, the breadth of the swelling breast, the bands and ridges and clusters of muscles on torso and limbs. The face was without weakness and without mercy. The eyes were balls of dark fire. And Conan knew that this was Khosatral Khel, the ancient from the Abyss, the god of Dagonia.

No word was spoken. No word was necessary. Khosatral spread his great arms, and Conan, crouching beneath them, slashed at the giant's belly. Then he bounded back, eyes blazing with surprise. The keen edge had rung on the mighty body as on an anvil, rebounding without cutting. Then Khosatral came upon him in an irresistible surge.

There was a fleeting concussion, a fierce writhing and intertwining of limbs and bodies, and then Conan sprang clear, every thew quivering from the violence of his efforts; blood started where the grazing fingers had torn the skin. In that instant of contact he had experienced the ultimate madness of blasphemed nature; no human flesh had bruised his, but *metal* animated and sentient; it was a body of living iron which opposed his.

Khosatral loomed above the warrior in the gloom. Once let those great fingers lock and they would not loosen until the human body hung limp in their grasp. In that twilit chamber it was as if a man fought with a dream-monster in a nightmare.

Flinging down his useless sword, Conan caught up a heavy bench and hurled it with all his power. It was such a missile as few men could even lift. On Khosatral's mighty breast it smashed into shreds and splinters. It did not even shake the giant on his braced legs. His face lost something of its human aspect, a nimbus of fire played about his awesome head, and like a moving tower he came on.

With a desperate wrench Conan ripped a whole section of tapestry from the wall and whirling it, with a muscular effort greater than that required for throwing the bench, he flung it over the giant's head. For an instant Khosatral floundered, smothered and blinded by the clinging stuff that resisted his strength as wood or steel could not have done, and in that instant Conan caught up his scimitar and shot out into the corridor. Without checking his speed he hurled himself through the door of the adjoining chamber, slammed the door and shot the bolt.

Then as he wheeled he stopped short, all the blood in him seeming to surge to his head. Crouching on a heap of silk cushions, golden hair streaming over her naked shoulders, eyes blank with terror, was the woman for whom he had dared so much. He almost forgot the horror at his heels until a splintering crash behind him brought him to his senses. He caught up the girl and sprang for the opposite door. She was too helpless with fright either to resist or to aid him. A faint whimper was the only sound of which she seemed capable.

Conan wasted no time trying the door. A shattering stroke of his scimitar hewed the lock asunder, and as he sprang through to the stair that loomed beyond it, he saw the head and shoulders of Khosatral crash through the other door. The colossus was splintering the massive panels as if they were of cardboard.

Conan raced up the stair, carrying the big girl over one shoulder as easily as if she had been a child. Where he was going he had no idea, but the stair ended at the door of a round, domed chamber. Khosatral was coming up the stair behind them, silently as a wind of death, and as swiftly.

The chamber's walls were of solid steel, and so was the door. Conan shut it and dropped in place the great bars with which it was furnished. The thought struck him that this was Khosatral's chamber, where he locked himself in to sleep securely from the monsters he had loosed from the Pits to do his bidding.

Hardly were the bolts in place when the great door shook and trembled to the giant's assault. Conan shrugged his shoulders. This was the end of the trail. There was no other door in the chamber, nor any window. Air, and the strange misty light, evidently came from interstices in the dome. He tested the nickel edge of his scimitar, quite cool now that he was at bay. He had done his volcanic best to escape; when the giant came crashing through that door he would explode in another savage onslaught with his useless sword, not because he expected it to do any good, but because it was his nature to die fighting. For the moment there was no course of action to take, and his calmness was not forced or feigned.

The gaze he turned on his fair companion was as admiring and intense as if he had a hundred years to live. He had dumped her unceremoniously on the floor when he turned to close the door, and she had risen to her knees, mechanically arranging her streaming locks and her scanty garment. Conan's fierce eyes glowed with approval as they devoured her thick golden hair, her clear wide eyes, her milky skin, sleek with exuberant health, the firm swell of her breasts, the contours of her splendid hips.

A low cry escaped her as the door shook and a bolt gave way with a groan.

Conan did not look around. He knew the door would hold a little while longer.

'They told me you had escaped,' he said. 'A Yuetshi fisher told me you were hiding here. What is your name?'

'Octavia,' she gasped mechanically. Then words came in a rush. She caught at him with desperate fingers. 'Oh Mitra! what nightmare is this? The people – the dark-skinned people – one of them caught me in the forest and brought me here. They carried me to – to that – that *thing*. He told me – he said – am I mad? Is this a dream?'

He glanced at the door which bulged inward as if from the impact of a battering-ram.

'No,' he said, 'it's no dream. That hinge is giving way. Strange that a devil has to break down a door like a common man; but after all, his strength itself is a diabolism.'

'Can you not kill him?' she panted. 'You are strong.'

Conan was too honest to lie. 'If a mortal man could kill him, he'd be dead now,' he answered. 'I nicked my blade on his belly.'

Her eyes dulled. 'Then you must die, and I must – oh Mitra!' she screamed in sudden frenzy, and Conan caught her hands, fearing that she would harm herself. 'He told me what he was going to do to me!' she panted. 'Kill me! Kill me with your sword before he bursts the door!'

Conan looked at her, and shook his head.

'I'll do what I can,' he said. 'That won't be much, but it'll give you a chance to get past him down the stair. Then run for the cliffs. I have a boat tied at the foot of the steps. If you can get out of the palace you may escape him yet. The people of this city are all asleep.'

She dropped her head in her hands. Conan took up his scimitar and moved over to stand before the echoing door. One watching him would have realized that he was waiting for a death he regarded as inevitable. His eyes smoldered more vividly; his muscular hand knotted harder on his hilt; that was all.

The hinges had given under the giant's terrible assault and the door rocked crazily, held only by the bolts. And these solid steel bars were buckling, bending, bulging out of their sockets. Conan watched in an almost impersonal fascination, envying the monster his inhuman strength.

Then without warning the bombardment ceased. In the stillness Conan heard other noises on the landing outside – the beat of wings, and a muttering voice that was like the whining of wind through midnight branches. Then presently there was silence, but there was a new *feel* in the air. Only the whetted instincts of barbarism could have sensed it, but Conan knew, without seeing or hearing him leave, that the master of Dagon no longer stood outside the door.

He glared through a crack that had been started in the steel of the portal. The landing was empty. He drew the warped bolts and cautiously pulled aside the sagging door. Khosatral was not on the stair, but far below he heard the clang of a metal door. He did not know whether the giant was plotting new devilries or had been summoned away by that muttering voice, but he wasted no time in conjectures.

He called to Octavia, and the new note in his voice brought her up to her feet and to his side almost without her conscious volition.

'What is it?' she gasped.

'Don't stop to talk!' He caught her wrist. 'Come on!' The chance for action had transformed him; his eyes blazed, his voice crackled. 'The knife!' he muttered, while almost dragging the girl down the stair in his fierce haste. 'The magic Yuetshi blade! He left it in the dome! I—' his voice died suddenly as a clear mental picture sprang up before him. The dome adjoined the great room where stood the copper throne – sweat started out on his body. The only way to that dome was through that room with its copper throne and the foul thing that slumbered in it.

But he did not hesitate. Swiftly they descended the stair, crossed the chamber, descended the next stair, and came into the great dim hall with its mysterious hangings. They had seen no sign of the colossus. Halting before the great bronze-valved door, Conan caught Octavia by her shoulders and shook her in his intensity.

'Listen!' he snapped. 'I'm going into that room and fasten the door. Stand here and listen; if Khosatral comes, call to me. If you hear me cry for you to go, run as though the devil were on your heels – which he probably will be. Make for that door at the other end of the hall, because I'll be past helping you. I'm going for the Yuetshi knife!'

Before she could voice the protest her lips were framing, he had slid through the valves and shut them behind him. He lowered the bolt cautiously, not noticing that it could be worked from the outside. In the dim twilight his gaze sought that grim copper throne; yes, the scaly brute was still there, filling the throne with its loathsome coils. He saw a door behind the throne and knew that it led into the dome. But to reach it he must mount the dais, a few feet from the throne itself.

A wind blowing across the green floor would have made more noise than Conan's slinking feet. Eyes glued on the sleeping reptile he reached the dais and mounted the glass steps. The snake had not moved. He was reaching for the door . . .

The bolt on the bronze portal clanged and Conan stifled an awful oath as he saw Octavia come into the room. She stared about, uncertain in the deeper gloom, and he stood frozen, not daring to shout a warning. Then she saw his shadowy figure and ran toward the dais, crying: 'I want to go with you! I'm afraid to stay alone – *oh!*' She threw up her hands with a terrible scream as for the first time she saw the occupant of the throne. The wedge-shaped head had lifted from its coils and thrust out toward her on a yard of shining neck.

Conan cleared the space between him and the throne with a desperate bound, his scimitar swinging with all his power. And with such blinding speed did the serpent move that it whipped about and met him in full midair, lapping his limbs and body with half a dozen coils. His half-checked stroke fell futilely as he crashed down on the dais, gashing the scaly trunk but not severing it.

Then he was writhing on the glass steps with fold after slimy fold knotting about him, twisting, crushing, killing him. His right arm was still free, but he could get no purchase to strike a killing blow, and he knew one blow must suffice. With a groaning convulsion of muscular expansion that bulged his veins almost to bursting on his temples and tied his muscles in quivering, tortured knots, he heaved up on his feet, lifting almost the full weight of that forty-foot devil.

An instant he reeled on wide-braced legs, feeling his ribs caving in on his vitals and his sight growing dark, while his scimitar gleamed above his head. Then it fell, shearing through the scales and flesh and vertebrae. And where there had been one huge writhing cable, now there were horribly two, lashing and flopping in the death throes. Conan staggered away from their blind strokes. He was sick and dizzy, and blood oozed from his nose. Groping in a dark mist he clutched Octavia and shook her until she gasped for breath.

'Next time I tell you to stay somewhere,' he gasped, 'you stay!'

He was too dizzy even to know whether she replied. Taking her wrist like a truant schoolgirl, he led her around the hideous stumps that still looped and knotted on the floor. Somewhere, in the distance, he thought he heard men yelling, but his ears were still roaring so that he could not be sure.

The door gave to his efforts. If Khosatral had placed the snake there to guard the thing he feared, evidently he considered it ample precaution. Conan half expected some other monstrosity to leap at him with the opening of the door, but in the dimmer light he saw only the vague sweep of the arch above, a dully gleaming block of gold, and a half-moon glimmer on the stone.

With a gasp of gratification he scooped it up, and did not linger for further exploration. He turned and fled across the room and down the great hall toward the distant door that he felt led to the outer air. He was correct. A few minutes later he emerged into the silent streets, half carrying, half guiding his companion. There was no one to be seen, but beyond the western wall there sounded cries and moaning wails that made Octavia tremble. He led her to the southwestern wall, and without difficulty found a stone stair that mounted the rampart. He had appropriated a thick tapestry rope in the great hall, and now, having reached the parapet, he looped the soft strong cord about the girl's hips and lowered her to the earth. Then, making one end fast to a merlon, he slid down after her. There was but one way of escape from the island – the stair on the western cliffs. In that direction he hurried, swinging wide around the spot from which had come the cries and the sound of terrible blows.

Octavia sensed that grim peril lurked in those leafy fastnesses. Her breath came pantingly and she pressed close to her protector. But the forest was silent now, and they saw no shape of menace until they emerged from the trees and glimpsed a figure standing on the edge of the cliffs.

Jehungir Agha had escaped the doom that had overtaken his warriors when an iron giant sallied suddenly from the gate and battered and crushed them into bits of shredded flesh and splintered bone. When he saw the swords of his archers break on that man-like juggernaut, he had known it was no human foe they faced, and he had fled, hiding in the deep woods until the sounds of slaughter ceased. Then he crept back to the stair, but his boatmen were not waiting for him.

They had heard the screams, and presently, waiting nervously, had seen, on the cliff above them, a blood-smeared monster waving gigantic arms in awful triumph. They had waited for no more. When Jehungir came upon the cliffs they were just vanishing among the reeds beyond ear-shot. Khosatral was gone – had either returned to the city or was prowling the forest in search of the man who had escaped him outside the walls.

Jehungir was just preparing to descend the stairs and depart in Conan's boat, when he saw the *hetman* and the girl emerge from the trees. The experience which had congealed his blood and almost blasted his reason had not altered Jehungir's intentions toward the *kozak* chief. The sight of the man he had come to kill filled him with gratification. He was astonished to see the girl he had given to Jelal Khan, but he wasted no time on her. Lifting his bow he drew the shaft to its head and loosed. Conan crouched and the arrow splintered on a tree, and Conan laughed.

'Dog!' he taunted. 'You can't hit me! I was not born to die on Hyrkanian steel! Try again, pig of Turan!'

Jehungir did not try again. That was his last arrow. He drew his scimitar and advanced, confident in his spired helmet and close-meshed mail. Conan met him half-way in a blinding whirl of swords. The curved blades ground together, sprang apart, circled in glittering arcs that blurred the sight which tried to follow them. Octavia, watching, did not see the stroke, but she heard its chopping impact, and saw Jehungir fall, blood spurting from his side where the Cimmerian's steel had sundered his mail and bitten to his spine.

But Octavia's scream was not caused by the death of her former master. With a crash of bending boughs Khosatral Khel was upon them. The girl could not flee; a moaning cry escaped her as her knees gave way and pitched her grovelling to the sward.

Conan, stooping above the body of the Agha, made no move to escape. Shifting his reddened scimitar to his left hand, he drew the great half-blade of the Yuetshi. Khosatral Khel was towering above him, his arms lifted like mauls, but as the blade caught the sheen of the sun, the giant gave back suddenly.

But Conan's blood was up. He rushed in, slashing with the crescent blade. And it did not splinter. Under its edge the dusky metal of Khosatral's body gave way like common flesh beneath a cleaver. From the deep gash flowed a strange ichor, and Khosatral cried out like the dirging of a great bell. His terrible arms flailed down, but Conan, quicker than the archers who had died beneath those awful flails, avoided their strokes and struck again and yet again. Khosatral reeled and tottered; his cries were awful to hear, as if metal were given a tongue of pain, as if iron shrieked and bellowed under torment.

Then wheeling away he staggered into the forest; he reeled in his gait, crashed through bushes and caromed off trees. Yet though Conan followed him with the speed of hot passion, the walls and towers of Dagon loomed through the trees before the man came within dagger-reach of the giant.

Then Khosatral turned again, flailing the air with desperate blows, but Conan, fired to berserk fury, was not to be denied. As a panther strikes down a bull moose at bay, so he plunged under the bludgeoning arms and drove the crescent blade to the hilt under the spot where a human's heart would be.

Khosatral reeled and fell. In the shape of a man he reeled, but it was not the shape of a man that struck the loam. Where there had been the likeness of a human face, there was no face at all, and the metal limbs melted and changed . . . Conan, who had not shrunk from Khosatral living, recoiled blenching from Khosatral dead, for he had witnessed an awful transmutation; in his dying throes Khosatral Khel had become again the *thing* that had crawled up from the Abyss millenniums gone. Gagging with intolerable repugnance, Conan turned to flee the sight; and he was suddenly aware that the pinnacles of Dagon no longer glimmered through the trees. They had faded like smoke – the battlements, the crenellated towers, the great bronze gates, the velvets, the gold, the ivory, and the dark-haired women, and the men with their shaven skulls. With the passing of the inhuman intellect which had given them rebirth, they had faded back into the dust which they had been for ages uncounted. Only the stumps of broken columns rose above crumbling walls and broken paves and shattered dome. Conan again looked upon the ruins of Xapur as he remembered them.

The wild *hetman* stood like a statue for a space, dimly grasping something of the cosmic tragedy of the fitful ephemera called mankind and the hooded shapes of darkness which prey upon it. Then as he heard his name called in accents of fear, he started, as one awaking from a dream, glanced again at the thing on the ground, shuddered and turned away toward the cliffs and the girl that waited there.

She was peering fearfully under the trees, and she greeted him with a half-stifled cry of relief. He had shaken off the dim monstrous visions which had momentarily haunted him, and was his exuberant self again.

'Where is *he*?' she shuddered.

'Gone back to hell whence he crawled,' he replied cheerfully. 'Why didn't you climb the stair and make your escape in my boat?'

'I wouldn't desert—' she began, then changed her mind, and amended rather sulkily, 'I have nowhere to go. The Hyrkanians would enslave me again, and the pirates would—'

'What of the *kozaks*?' he suggested.

'Are they better than the pirates?' she asked scornfully. Conan's admiration increased to see how well she had recovered her poise after having endured such frantic terror. Her arrogance amused him.

'You seemed to think so in the camp by Ghori,' he answered. 'You were free enough with your smiles then.'

Her red lip curled in disdain. 'Do you think I was enamored of you? Do you dream that I would have shamed myself before an ale-guzzling, meat-gorging barbarian unless I had to? My master – whose body lies there – forced me to do as I did.'

'Oh!' Conan seemed rather crestfallen. Then he laughed with undiminished zest. 'No matter. You belong to me now. Give me a kiss.'

'You dare ask—' she began angrily, when she felt herself snatched off her feet and crushed to the *hetman*'s muscular breast. She fought him fiercely, with all the supple strength of her magnificent youth, but he only laughed exuberantly, drunk with his possession of this splendid creature writhing in his arms.

He crushed her struggles easily, drinking the nectar of her lips with all the unrestrained passion that was his, until the arms that strained against him melted and twined convulsively about his massive neck. Then he laughed down into the clear eyes, and said: 'Why should not a chief of the Free People be preferable to a city-bred dog of Turan?'

She shook back her tawny locks, still tingling in every nerve from the fire of his kisses. She did not loosen her arms from his neck. 'Do you deem yourself an Agha's equal?' she challenged.

He laughed and strode with her in his arms toward the stair. 'You shall judge,' he boasted. 'I'll burn Khawarizm for a torch to light your way to my tent.'

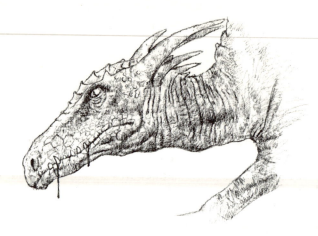

THE PEOPLE OF THE BLACK CIRCLE

1 Death Strikes a King

THE KING OF VENDHYA was dying. Through the hot, stifling night the temple gongs boomed and the conchs roared. Their clamor was a faint echo in the gold-domed chamber where Bunda Chand struggled on the velvet-cushioned dais. Beads of sweat glistened on his dark skin; his fingers twisted the gold-worked fabric beneath him. He was young; no spear had touched him, no poison lurked in his wine. But his veins stood out like blue cords on his temples, and his eyes dilated with the nearness of death. Trembling slave-girls knelt at the foot of the dais, and leaning down to him, watching him with passionate intensity, was his sister, the Devi Yasmina. With her was the *wazam*, a noble grown old in the royal court.

She threw up her head in a gusty gesture of wrath and despair as the thunder of the distant drums reached her ears.

'The priests and their clamor!' she exclaimed. 'They are no wiser than the leeches who are helpless! Nay, he dies and none can say why. He is dying now – and I stand here helpless, who would burn the whole city and spill the blood of thousands to save him.'

'Not a man of Ayodhya but would die in his place, if it might be, Devi,' answered the *wazam*. 'This poison—'

'I tell you it is not poison!' she cried. 'Since his birth he has been guarded so closely that the cleverest poisoners of the East could not reach him. Five skulls bleaching on the Tower of the Kites can testify to attempts which were made – and which failed. As you well know, there are ten men and ten women whose sole duty is to taste his food and wine, and fifty armed warriors guard his chamber as they guard it now. No, it is not poison; it is sorcery – black, ghastly magic—'

She ceased as the king spoke; his livid lips did not move, and there was no recognition in his glassy eyes. But his voice rose in an eery call, indistinct and far away, as if called to her from beyond vast, wind-blown gulfs.

'Yasmina! Yasmina! My sister, where are you? I can not find you. All is darkness, and the roaring of great winds!'

'Brother!' cried Yasmina, catching his limp hand in a convulsive grasp. 'I am here! Do you not know me—'

Her voice died at the utter vacancy of his face. A low confused moan waned from his mouth. The slave-girls at the foot of the dais whimpered with fear, and Yasmina beat her breast in anguish.

In another part of the city a man stood in a latticed balcony overlooking a long street in which torches tossed luridly, smokily revealing upturned dark faces and the whites of gleaming eyes. A long-drawn wailing rose from the multitude.

The man shrugged his broad shoulders and turned back into the arabesque chamber. He was a tall man, compactly built, and richly clad.

'The king is not yet dead, but the dirge is sounded,' he said to another man who sat cross-legged on a mat in a corner. This man was clad in a brown camel-hair robe and sandals, and a green turban was on his head. His expression was tranquil, his gaze impersonal.

'The people know he will never see another dawn,' this man answered.

The first speaker favored him with a long, searching stare.

'What I can not understand,' he said, 'is why I have had to wait so long for your masters to strike. If they have slain the king now, why could they not have slain him months ago?'

'Even the arts you call sorcery are governed by cosmic laws,' answered the man in the green turban. 'The stars direct these actions, as in other affairs. Not even my masters can alter the stars. Not until the heavens were in the proper order could they perform this necromancy.' With a long, stained fingernail he mapped the constellations on the marble-tiled floor. 'The slant of the moon presaged evil for the king of Vendhya; the stars are in turmoil, the Serpent in the House of the Elephant. During such juxtaposition, the invisible guardians are removed from the spirit of Bhunda Chand. A path is opened in the unseen realms, and once a point of contact was established, mighty powers were put in play along that path.'

'Point of contact?' inquired the other. 'Do you mean that lock of Bhunda Chand's hair?'

'Yes. All discarded portions of the human body still remain part of it, attached to it by intangible connections. The priests of Asura have a dim inkling of this truth, and so all nail trimmings, hair and other waste products of the persons of the royal family are carefully reduced to ashes and the ashes hidden. But at the urgent entreaty of the princess of Khosala, who loved Bhunda Chand vainly, he gave her a lock of his long black hair as a token of remembrance. When my masters decided upon his doom, the lock, in its golden, jewel-encrusted case, was stolen from under her pillow while she slept, and another substituted, so like the first that she never knew the difference. Then the genuine lock travelled by camel-caravan up the long, long road to Peshkhauri, thence up the Zhaibar Pass, until it reached the hands of those for whom it was intended.'

'Only a lock of hair,' murmured the nobleman.

'By which a soul is drawn from its body and across gulfs of echoing space,' returned the man on the mat.

The nobleman studied him curiously.

'I do not know if you are a man or a demon, Khemsa,' he said at last. 'Few of us are what we seem. I, whom the Kshatriyas know as Kerim Shah, a prince from Iranistan, am no greater a masquerader than most men. They are all traitors in one way or another, and half of them know not whom they serve. There at least I have no doubts; for I serve King Yezdigerd of Turan.'

'And I the Black Seers of Yimsha,' said Khemsa; 'and my masters are greater than yours, for they have accomplished by their arts what Yezdigerd could not with a hundred thousand swords.'

Outside, the moan of the tortured thousands shuddered up to the stars which crusted the sweating Vendhyan night, and the conchs bellowed like oxen in pain.

In the gardens of the palace the torches glinted on polished helmets and curved swords and gold-chased corselets. All the noble-born fighting-men of Ayodhya were gathered in the great palace or about it, and at each broad-arched gate and door fifty archers stood on guard, with bows in their hands. But Death stalked through the royal palace and none could stay his ghostly tread.

On the dais under the golden dome the king cried out again, racked by awful paroxysms. Again his voice came faintly and far away, and again the Devi bent to him, trembling with a fear that was darker than the terror of death.

'Yasmina!' Again that far, weirdly dreeing cry, from realms immeasurable. 'Aid me! I am far from my mortal house! Wizards have drawn my soul through the wind-blown darkness. They seek to snap the silver cord that binds me to my dying body. They cluster around me; their hands are taloned, their eyes are red like flame burning in darkness. *Aie*, save me, my sister! Their fingers sear me like fire! They would slay my body and damn my soul! What is this they bring before me?—*Aie!*'

At the terror in his hopeless cry Yasmina screamed uncontrollably and threw herself bodily upon him in the abandon of her anguish. He was torn by a terrible convulsion; foam flew from his contorted lips and his writhing fingers left their marks on the girl's shoulders. But the glassy blankness passed from his eyes like smoke blown from a fire, and he looked up at his sister with recognition.

'Brother!' she sobbed. 'Brother—'

'Swift!' he gasped, and his weakening voice was rational. 'I know now what brings me to the pyre. I have been on a far journey and I understand. I have been ensorcelled by the wizards of the Himelians. They drew my soul out of my body and far away, into a stone room. There they strove to break the silver cord of life, and thrust my soul into the body of a foul night-weird their sorcery summoned up from hell. Ah! I feel their pull upon me now! Your cry and the grip of your fingers brought me back, but I am going fast. My soul clings to my body, but its hold weakens. Quick – kill me, before they can trap my soul for ever!'

'I cannot!' she wailed, smiting her naked breasts.

'Swiftly, I command you!' There was the old imperious note in his failing whisper. 'You have never disobeyed me – obey my last command! Send my soul clean to Asura! Haste, lest you damn me to spend eternity as a filthy gaunt of darkness. Strike, I command you! *Strike!*'

Sobbing wildly, Yasmina plucked a jeweled dagger from her girdle and plunged it to the hilt in his breast. He stiffened and then went limp, a grim smile curving his dead lips. Yasmina hurled herself face-down on the rush-covered floor, beating the reeds with her clenched hands. Outside, the gongs and conchs brayed and thundered and the priests gashed themselves with copper knives.

2 A Barbarian from the Hills

Chunder Shan, governor of Peshkhauri, laid down his golden pen and carefully scanned that which he had written on parchment that bore his official seal. He had ruled Peshkhauri so long only because he weighed his every word, spoken or written. Danger breeds caution, and only a wary man lives long in that wild country where the hot Vendhyan plains meet the crags of the Himelians. An hour's ride westward or northward and one crossed the border and was among the Hills where men lived by the law of the knife.

The governor was alone in his chamber, seated at his ornately carven table of inlaid ebony. Through the wide window, open for the coolness, he could see a square of the blue Himelian night, dotted with great white stars. An adjacent parapet was a shadowy line, and further crenelles and embrasures were barely hinted at in the dim starlight. The governor's fortress was strong, and situated outside the walls of the city it guarded. The breeze that stirred the tapestries on the wall brought faint noises from the streets of Peshkhauri – occasional snatches of wailing song, or the thrum of a cithern.

The governor read what he had written, slowly, with his open hand shading his eyes from the bronze butterlamp, his lips moving. Absently, as he read, he heard the drum of horses' hoofs outside the barbican, the sharp staccato of the guards' challenge. He did not heed, intent upon his letter. It was addressed to the *wazam* of Vendhya, at the royal court of Ayodhya, and it stated, after the customary salutations:

> 'Let it be known to your excellency that I have faithfully carried out your excellency's instructions. The seven tribesmen are well guarded in their prison, and I have repeatedly sent word into the hills that their chief come in person to bargain for their release. But he has made no move, except to send word that unless they are freed he will burn Peshkhauri and cover his saddle with my hide, begging your excellency's indulgence. This he is quite capable of attempting, and I have tripled the numbers of the lance guards. The man is not a native of Ghulistan. I cannot with certainty predict his next move. But since it is the wish of the Devi—'

He was out of his ivory chair and on his feet facing the arched door, all in one instant. He snatched at the curved sword lying in its ornate scabbard on the table, and then checked the movement.

It was a woman who had entered unannounced, a woman whose gossamer robes did not conceal the rich garments beneath them any more than they concealed the suppleness and beauty of her tall, slender figure. A filmy veil fell below her breasts, supported by a flowing headdress bound about with a triple gold braid and adorned with a golden crescent. Her dark eyes regarded the astonished governor over the veil, and then with an imperious gesture of her white hand, she uncovered her face.

'Devi!' The governor dropped to his knees before her, surprize and confusion somewhat spoiling the stateliness of his obeisance. With a gesture she motioned him to rise, and he hastened to lead her to the ivory chair, all the while bowing level with his girdle. But his first words were of reproof.

'Your Majesty! This was most unwise! The border is unsettled. Raids from the hills are incessant. You came with a large attendance?'

'An ample retinue followed me to Peshkhauri,' she answered. 'I lodged my people there and came on to the fort with my maid, Gitara.'

Chunder Shan groaned in horror.

'Devi! You do not understand the peril. An hour's ride from this spot the hills swarm with barbarians who make a profession of murder and rapine. Women have been stolen and men stabbed between the fort and the city. Peshkhauri is not like your southern provinces—'

'But I am here, and unharmed,' she interrupted with a trace of impatience. 'I showed my signet ring to the guard at the gate, and to the one outside your door, and they admitted me unannounced, not knowing me, but supposing me to be a secret courier from Ayodhya. Let us not now waste time.

'You have received no word from the chief of the barbarians?'

'None save threats and curses, Devi. He is wary and suspicious. He deems it a trap, and perhaps he is not to be blamed. The Kshatriyas have not always kept their promises to the hill people.'

'He must be brought to terms!' broke in Yasmina, the knuckles of her clenched hands showing white.

'I do not understand.' The governor shook his head. 'When I chanced to capture these seven hillmen, I reported their capture to the *wazam*, as is the custom, and then, before I could hang them, there came an order to hold them and communicate with their chief. This I did, but the man holds aloof, as I have said. These men are of the tribe of Afghulis, but he is a foreigner from the west, and he is called Conan. I have threatened to hang them tomorrow at dawn, if he does not come.'

'Good!' exclaimed the Devi. 'You have done well. And I will tell you why I have given these orders. My brother—' she faltered, choking, and the governor bowed his head, with the customary gesture of respect for a departed sovereign.

'The king of Vendhya was destroyed by magic,' she said at last. 'I have devoted my life to the destruction of his murderers. As he died he gave me a clue, and I have followed it. I have read the *Book of Skelos*, and talked with nameless hermits in the caves below Jhelai. I learned how, and by whom, he was destroyed. His enemies were the Black Seers of Mount Yimsha.'

'Asura!' whispered Chunder Shan, paling.

Her eyes knifed him through. 'Do you fear them?'

'Who does not, Your Majesty?' he replied. 'They are black devils, haunting the uninhabited hills beyond the Zhaibar. But the sages say that they seldom interfere in the lives of mortal men.'

'Why they slew my brother I do not know,' she answered. 'But I have sworn on the altar of Asura to destroy them! And I need the aid of a man beyond the border. A Kshatriya army, unaided, would never reach Yimsha.'

'Aye,' muttered Chunder Shan. 'You speak the truth there. It would be fight every step of the way, with hairy hillmen hurling down boulders from every height, and rushing us with their long knives in every valley. The Turanians fought their way through the Himelians once, but how many returned to Khurusun? Few of those who escaped the swords of the Kshatriyas, after the king, your brother, defeated their host on the Jhumda River, ever saw Secunderam again.'

'And so I must control men across the border,' she said, 'men who know the way to Mount Yimsha—'

'But the tribes fear the Black Seers and shun the unholy mountain,' broke in the governor.

'Does the chief, Conan, fear them?' she asked.

'Well, as to that,' muttered the governor, 'I doubt if there is anything that devil fears.'

'So I have been told. Therefore he is the man I must deal with. He wishes the release of his seven men. Very well; their ransom shall be the heads of the Black Seers!' Her voice thrummed with hate as she uttered the last words, and her hands clenched at her sides. She looked an image of incarnate passion as she stood there with her head thrown high and her bosom heaving.

Again the governor knelt, for part of his wisdom was the knowledge that a woman in such an emotional tempest is as perilous as a blind cobra to any about her.

'It shall be as you wish, Your Majesty.' Then as she presented a calmer aspect, he rose and ventured to drop a word of warning. 'I can not predict what the chief Conan's action will be. The tribesmen are always turbulent, and I have reason to believe that emissaries from the Turanians are stirring them up to raid our borders. As your majesty knows, the Turanians have established themselves in Secunderam and other northern cities, though the hill tribes remain unconquered. King Yezdigerd has long looked southward with greedy lust and perhaps is seeking to gain by treachery what he could not win by force of arms. I have thought that Conan might well be one of his spies.'

'We shall see,' she answered. 'If he loves his followers, he will be at the gates at dawn, to parley. I shall spend the night in the fortress. I came in disguise to Peshkhauri, and lodged my retinue at an inn instead of the palace. Besides my people, only yourself knows of my presence here.'

'I shall escort you to your quarters, Your Majesty,' said the governor, and as they emerged from the doorway, he beckoned the warrior on guard there, and the man fell in behind them, spear held at salute.

The maid waited, veiled like her mistress, outside the door, and the group traversed a wide, winding corridor, lighted by smoky torches, and reached the quarters reserved for visiting notables – generals and viceroys, mostly; none of the royal family had ever honored the fortress before. Chunder Shan had a perturbed feeling that the suite was not suitable to such an exalted personage as the Devi, and though she sought to make him feel at ease in her presence, he was glad when she dismissed him and he bowed himself out. All the menials of the fort had been summoned to serve his royal guest – though he did not divulge her identity – and he stationed a squad of spearmen before her doors, among them the warrior who had guarded his own chamber. In his preoccupation he forgot to replace the man.

The governor had not been long gone from her when Yasmina suddenly remembered something else which she had wished to discuss with him, but had forgotten until that moment. It concerned the past actions of one Kerim Shah, a nobleman from Iranistan, who had dwelt for a while in Peshkhauri before coming on to the court at Ayodhya. A vague suspicion concerning the man had been stirred by a glimpse of him in Peshkhauri that night. She wondered if he had followed her from Ayodhya. Being a truly remarkable Devi, she did not summon the governor to her again, but hurried out into the corridor alone, and hastened toward his chamber.

Chunder Shan, entering his chamber, closed the door and went to his table. There he took the letter he had been writing and tore it to bits. Scarcely had he finished when he heard something drop softly onto the parapet adjacent to the window. He looked up to see a figure loom briefly against the stars, and then a man dropped lightly into the room. The light glinted on a long sheen of steel in his hand.

'Shhhh!' he warned. 'Don't make a noise, or I'll send the devil a henchman!'

The governor checked his motion toward the sword on the table. He was within reach of the yard-long Zhaibar knife that glittered in the intruder's fist, and he knew the desperate quickness of a hillman.

The invader was a tall man, at once strong and supple. He was dressed like a hillman, but his dark features and blazing blue eyes did not match his garb. Chunder Shan had never seen a man like him; he was not an Easterner, but some barbarian from the West. But his aspect was as untamed and formidable as any of the hairy tribesmen who haunt the hills of Ghulistan.

'You come like a thief in the night,' commented the governor, recovering some of his composure, although he remembered that there was no guard within call. Still, the hillman could not know that.

'I climbed a bastion,' snarled the intruder. 'A guard thrust his head over the battlement in time for me to rap it with my knife-hilt.'

'You are Conan?'

'Who else? You sent word into the hills that you wished for me to come and parley with you. Well, by Crom, I've come! Keep away from that table or I'll gut you.'

'I merely wish to seat myself,' answered the governor, carefully sinking into the ivory chair, which he wheeled away from the table. Conan moved restlessly before him, glancing suspiciously at the door, thumbing the razor edge of his three-foot knife. He did not walk like an Afghuli, and was bluntly direct where the East is subtle.

'You have seven of my men,' he said abruptly. 'You refused the ransom I offered. What the devil do you want?'

'Let us discuss terms,' answered Chunder Shan cautiously.

'Terms?' There was a timbre of dangerous anger in his voice. 'What do you mean? Haven't I offered you gold?'

Chunder Shan laughed.

'Gold? There is more gold in Peshkhauri than you ever saw.'

'You're a liar,' retorted Conan. 'I've seen the *suk* of the goldsmiths in Khurusun.'

'Well, more than an Afghuli ever saw,' amended Chunder Shan. 'And it is but a drop of all the treasure of Vendhya. Why should we desire gold? It would be more to our advantage to hang these seven thieves.'

Conan ripped out a sulfurous oath and the long blade quivered in his grip as the muscles rose in ridges on his brown arm.

'I'll split your head like a ripe melon!'

A wild blue flame flickered in the hillman's eyes, but Chunder Shan shrugged his shoulders, though keeping an eye on the keen steel.

'You can kill me easily, and probably escape over the wall afterward. But that would not save the seven tribesmen. My men would surely hang them. And these men are headmen among the Afghulis.'

'I know it,' snarled Conan. 'The tribe is baying like wolves at my heels because I have not procured their release. Tell me in plain words what you want, because, by Crom! if there's no other way, I'll raise a horde and lead it to the very gates of Peshkhauri!'

Looking at the man as he stood squarely, knife in fist and eyes glaring, Chunder Shan did not doubt that he was capable of it. The governor did not believe any hill-horde could take Peshkhauri, but he did not wish a devastated countryside.

'There is a mission you must perform,' he said, choosing his words with as much care as if they had been razors. 'There—'

Conan had sprung back, wheeling to face the door at the same instant, lips asnarl. His barbarian ears had caught the quick tread of soft slippers outside the door. The next instant the door was thrown open and a slim, silk-robed form entered hastily, pulling the door shut – then stopping short at sight of the hillman.

Chunder Shan sprang up, his heart jumping into his mouth.

'Devi!' he cried involuntarily, losing his head momentarily in his fright.

'*Devi!*' It was like an explosive echo from the hillman's lips. Chunder Shan saw recognition and intent flame up in the fierce blue eyes.

The governor shouted desperately and caught at his sword, but the hillman moved with the devastating speed of a hurricane. He sprang, knocked the governor sprawling with a savage blow of his knife-hilt, swept up the astounded Devi in one brawny arm and leaped for the window. Chunder Shan, struggling frantically to his feet, saw the man poise an instant on the sill in a flutter of silken skirts and white limbs that was his royal captive, and heard his fierce, exultant snarl: '*Now* dare to hang my men!' and then Conan leaped to the parapet and was gone. A wild scream floated back to the governor's ears.

'Guard! *Guard!*' screamed the governor, struggling up and running drunkenly to the door. He tore it open and reeled into the hall. His shouts re-echoed along the corridors, and warriors came running, gaping to see the governor holding his broken head, from which the blood streamed.

'Turn out the lancers!' he roared. 'There has been an abduction!' Even in his frenzy he had enough sense left to withhold the full truth. He stopped short as he heard a sudden drum of hoofs outside, a frantic scream and a wild yell of barbaric exultation.

Followed by the bewildered guardsmen, the governor raced for the stair. In the courtyard of the fort a force of lancers stood by saddled steeds, ready to ride at an instant's notice. Chunder Shan led his squadron flying after the fugitive, though his head swam so he had to hold with both hands to the saddle. He did not divulge the identity of the victim, but said merely that the noblewoman who had borne the royal signet-ring had been carried away by the chief of the Afghulis. The abductor was out of sight and hearing, but they knew the path he would strike – the road that runs straight to the mouth of the Zhaibar. There was no moon; peasant huts rose dimly in the starlight. Behind them fell away the grim bastion of the fort, and the towers of Peshkhauri. Ahead of them loomed the black walls of the Himelians.

3 Khemsa Uses Magic

In the confusion that reigned in the fortress while the guard was being turned out, no one noticed that the girl who had accompanied the Devi slipped out the great arched gate and vanished in the darkness. She ran straight for the city, her garments tucked high. She did not follow the open road, but cut straight through fields and over slopes, avoiding fences and leaping irrigation ditches as surely as if it were broad daylight, and as easily as if she were a trained masculine runner. The hoof-drum of the guardsmen had faded away up the hill before she reached the city wall. She did not go to the great gate, beneath whose arch men leaned on spears and craned their necks into the darkness, discussing the unwonted activity about the fortress. She skirted the wall until she reached a certain point where the spire of the tower was visible above the battlements. Then she placed her hands to her mouth and voiced a low weird call that carried strangely.

Almost instantly a head appeared at an embrasure and a rope came wriggling down the wall. She seized it, placed a foot in the loop at the end, and waved her arm. Then quickly and smoothly she was drawn up the sheer stone curtain. An instant later she scrambled over the merlons and stood up on a flat roof which covered a house that was built against the wall. There was an open trap there, and a man in a camel-hair robe who silently coiled the rope, not showing in any way the strain of hauling a full-grown woman up a forty-foot wall.

'Where is Kerim Shah?' she gasped, panting after her long run.

'Asleep in the house below. You have news?'

'Conan has stolen the Devi out of the fortress and carried her away into the hills!' She blurted out her news in a rush, the words stumbling over one another.

Khemsa showed no emotion, but merely nodded his turbaned head. 'Kerim Shah will be glad to hear that,' he said.

'Wait!' The girl threw her supple arms about his neck. She was panting hard, but not only from exertion. Her eyes blazed like black jewels in the starlight. Her upturned face was close to Khemsa's, but though he submitted to her embrace, he did not return it.

'Do not tell the Hyrkanian!' she panted. 'Let us use this knowledge ourselves! The governor has gone into the hills with his riders, but he might as well chase a ghost. He has not told anyone that it was the Devi who was kidnapped. None in Peshkhauri or the fort knows it except us.'

'But what good does it do us?' the man expostulated. 'My masters sent me with Kerim Shah to aid him in every way—'

'Aid yourself!' she cried fiercely. 'Shake off your yoke!'

'You mean – disobey my masters?' he gasped, and she felt his whole body turn cold under her arms.

'Aye!' she shook him in the fury of her emotion. 'You too are a magician! Why will you be a slave, using your powers only to elevate others? Use your arts for yourself!'

'That is forbidden!' He was shaking as if with an ague. 'I am not one of the Black Circle. Only by the command of the masters do I dare to use the knowledge they have taught me.'

'But you *can* use it!' she argued passionately. 'Do as I beg you! Of course Conan has taken the Devi to hold as hostage against the seven tribesmen in the governor's prison. Destroy them, so Chunder Shan can not use them to buy back the Devi. Then let us go into the mountains and take her from the Afghulis. They can not stand against your sorcery with their knives. The treasure of the Vendhyan kings will be ours as ransom – and then when we have it in our hands, we can trick them, and sell her to the king of Turan. We shall have wealth beyond our maddest dreams. With it we can buy warriors. We will take Khorbhul, oust the Turanians from the hills, and send our hosts southward; become king and queen of an empire!'

Khemsa too was panting, shaking like a leaf in her grasp; his face showed gray in the starlight, beaded with great drops of perspiration.

'I love you!' she cried fiercely, writhing her body against his, almost strangling him in her wild embrace, shaking him in her abandon. 'I will make a king of you! For love of you I betrayed my mistress; for love of me betray your masters! Why fear the Black Seers? By your love for me you have broken one of their laws already! Break the rest! You are as strong as they!'

A man of ice could not have withstood the searing heat of her passion and fury. With an inarticulate cry he crushed her to him, bending her backward and showering gasping kisses on her eyes, face and lips.

'I'll do it!' His voice was thick with laboring emotions. He staggered like a drunken man. 'The arts they have taught me shall work for me, not for my masters. We shall be rulers of the world – of the world—'

'Come then!' Twisting lithely out of his embrace, she seized his hand and led him toward the trap-door. 'First we must make sure that the governor does not exchange those seven Afghulis for the Devi.'

He moved like a man in a daze, until they had descended a ladder and she paused in the chamber below. Kerim Shah lay on a couch motionless, an arm across his face as though to shield his sleeping eyes from the soft light of a brass lamp. She plucked Khemsa's arm and made a quick gesture across her own throat. Khemsa lifted his hand; then his expression changed and he drew away.

'I have eaten his salt,' he muttered. 'Besides, he can not interfere with us.'

He led the girl through a door that opened on a winding stair. After their soft tread had faded into silence, the man on the couch sat up. Kerim Shah wiped the sweat from his face. A knife-thrust he did not dread, but he feared Khemsa as a man fears a poisonous reptile.

'People who plot on roofs should remember to lower their voices,' he muttered. 'But as Khemsa has turned against his masters, and as he was my only contact between them, I can count on their aid no longer. From now on I play the game in my own way.'

Rising to his feet he went quickly to a table, drew pen and parchment from his girdle and scribbled a few succinct lines.

> 'To Khosru Khan, governor of Secunderam: the Cimmerian Conan has carried the Devi Yasmina to the villages of the Afghulis. It is an opportunity to get the Devi into our hands, as the king has so long desired. Send three thousand horsemen at once. I will meet them in the valley of Gurashah with native guides.'

And he signed it with a name that was not in the least like Kerim Shah.

Then from a golden cage he drew forth a carrier pigeon, to whose leg he made fast the parchment, rolled into a tiny cylinder and secured with gold wire. Then he went quickly to a casement and tossed the bird into the night. It wavered on fluttering wings, balanced, and was gone like a flitting shadow. Catching up helmet, sword and cloak, Kerim Shah hurried out of the chamber and down the winding stair.

The prison quarters of Peshkhauri were separated from the rest of the city by a massive wall, in which was set a single iron-bound door under an arch. Over the arch burned a lurid red cresset, and beside the door squatted a warrior with spear and shield.

This warrior, leaning on his spear, and yawning from time to time, started suddenly to his feet. He had not thought he had dozed, but a man was standing before him, a man he had not heard approach. The man wore a camel-hair robe and a green turban. In the flickering light of the cresset his features were shadowy, but a pair of lambent eyes shone surprisingly in the lurid glow.

'Who comes?' demanded the warrior, presenting his spear. 'Who are you?'

The stranger did not seem perturbed, though the spear-point touched his bosom. His eyes held the warrior's with strange intensity.

'What are you obliged to do?' he asked, strangely.

'To guard the gate!' The warrior spoke thickly and mechanically; he stood rigid as a statue, his eyes slowly glazing.

'You lie! You are obliged to obey me! You have looked into my eyes, and your soul is no longer your own. Open that door!'

Stiffly, with the wooden features of an image, the guard wheeled about, drew a great key from his girdle, turned it in the massive lock and swung open the door. Then he stood at attention, his unseeing stare straight ahead of him.

A woman glided from the shadows and laid an eager hand on the mesmerist's arm.

'Bid him fetch us horses, Khemsa,' she whispered.

'No need of that,' answered the Rakhsha. Lifting his voice slightly he spoke to the guardsman. 'I have no more use for you. Kill yourself!'

Like a man in a trance the warrior thrust the butt of his spear against the base of the wall, and placed the keen head against his body, just below the ribs. Then slowly, stolidly, he leaned against it with all his weight, so that it transfixed his body and came out between his shoulders. Sliding down the shaft he lay still, the spear jutting above him its full length, like a horrible stalk growing out of his back.

The girl stared down at him in morbid fascination, until Khemsa took her arm and led her through the gate. Torches lighted a narrow space between the outer wall and a lower inner one, in which were arched doors at regular intervals. A warrior paced this enclosure, and when the gate opened he came sauntering up, so secure in his knowledge of the prison's strength that he was not suspicious until Khemsa and the girl emerged from the archway. Then it was too late. The Rakhsha did not waste time in hypnotism, though his action savored of magic to the girl. The guard lowered his spear threateningly, opening his mouth to shout an alarm that would bring spearmen swarming out of the guardrooms at either end of the alleyway. Khemsa flicked the spear aside with his left hand, as a man might flick a straw, and his right flashed out and back, seeming gently to caress the warrior's neck in passing. And the guard pitched on his face without a sound, his head lolling on a broken neck.

Khemsa did not glance at him, but went straight to one of the arched doors and placed his open hand against the heavy bronze lock. With a rending shudder the portal buckled inward. As the girl followed him through, she saw that the thick teakwood hung in splinters, the bronze bolts were bent and twisted from their sockets, and the great hinges broken and disjointed. A thousand-pound battering-ram with forty men to swing it could have shattered the barrier no more completely. Khemsa was drunk with freedom and the exercise of his power, glorying in his might and flinging his strength about as a young giant exercises his thews with unnecessary vigor in the exultant pride of his prowess.

The broken door let them into a small courtyard, lit by a cresset. Opposite the door was a wide grille of iron bars. A hairy hand was visible, gripping one of these bars, and in the darkness behind them glimmered the whites of eyes.

Khemsa stood silent for a space, gazing into the shadows from which those glimmering eyes gave back his stare with burning intensity. Then his hand went into his robe and came out again, and from his opening fingers a shimmering feather of sparkling dust sifted to the flags. Instantly a flare of green fire lighted the enclosure. In the brief glare the forms of seven men, standing motionless behind the bars, were limned in vivid detail; tall, hairy men in ragged hillmen's garments. They did not speak, but in their eyes blazed the fear of death, and their hairy fingers gripped the bars.

The fire died out but the glow remained, a quivering ball of lambent green that pulsed and shimmered on the flags before Khemsa's feet. The wide gaze of the tribesmen was fixed upon it. It wavered, elongated; it turned into a luminous greensmoke spiraling upward. It twisted and writhed like a great shadowy serpent, then broadened and billowed out in shining folds and whirls. It grew to a cloud moving silently over the flags – straight toward the grille. The men watched its coming with dilated eyes; the bars quivered with the grip of their desperate fingers. Bearded lips parted but no sound came forth. The green cloud rolled on the bars and blotted them from sight; like a fog it oozed through the grille and hid the men within. From the enveloping folds came a strangled gasp, as of a man plunged suddenly under the surface of water. That was all.

Khemsa touched the girl's arm, as she stood with parted lips and dilated eyes. Mechanically she turned away with him, looking back over her shoulder. Already the mist was thinning; close to the bars she saw a pair of sandalled feet, the toes turned upward – she glimpsed the indistinct outlines of seven still, prostrate shapes.

'And now for a steed swifter than the fastest horse ever bred in a mortal stable,' Khemsa was saying. 'We will be in Afghulistan before dawn.'

4 An Encounter in the Pass

Yasmina Devi could never clearly remember the details of her abduction. The unexpectedness and violence stunned her; she had only a confused impression of a whirl of happenings – the terrifying grip of a mighty arm, the blazing eyes of her abductor, and his hot breath burning on her flesh. The leap through the window to the parapet, the mad race across battlements and roofs when the fear of falling froze her, the reckless descent of a rope bound to a merlon – he went down almost at a run, his captive folded limply over his brawny shoulder – all this was a befuddled tangle in the Devi's mind. She retained a more vivid memory of him running fleetly into the shadows of the trees, carrying her like a child, and vaulting into the saddle of a fierce Bhalkhana stallion which reared and snorted. Then there was a sensation of flying, and the racing hoofs were striking sparks of fire from the flinty road as the stallion swept up the slopes.

As the girl's mind cleared, her first sensations were furious rage and shame. She was appalled. The rulers of the golden kingdoms south of the Himelians were considered little short of divine; and she was the Devi of Vendhya! Fright was submerged in regal wrath. She cried out furiously and began struggling. She, Yasmina, to be carried on the saddle-bow of a hill chief, like a common wench of the market-place! He merely hardened his massive thews slightly against her writhings, and for the first time in her life she experienced the coercion of superior physical strength. His arms felt like iron about her slender limbs. He glanced down at her and grinned hugely. His teeth glimmered whitely in the starlight. The reins lay loose on the stallion's flowing mane, and every thew and fiber of the great beast strained as he hurtled along the boulder-strewn trail. But Conan sat easily, almost carelessly, in the saddle, riding like a centaur.

'You hill-bred dog!' she panted, quivering with the impact of shame, anger, and the realization of helplessness. 'You dare – you *dare*! Your life shall pay for this! Where are you taking me?'

'To the villages of Afghulistan,' he answered, casting a glance over his shoulder.

Behind them, beyond the slopes they had traversed, torches were tossing on the walls of the fortress, and he glimpsed a flare of light that meant the great gate had been opened. And he laughed, a deep-throated boom gusty as the hill wind.

'The governor has sent his riders after us,' he laughed. 'By Crom, we will lead him a merry chase! What do you think, Devi – will they pay seven lives for a Kshatriya princess?'

'They will send an army to hang you and your spawn of devils,' she promised him with conviction.

He laughed gustily and shifted her to a more comfortable position in his arms. But she took this as a fresh outrage, and renewed her vain struggle, until she saw that her efforts were only amusing him. Besides, her light silken garments, floating on the wind, were being outrageously disarranged by her struggles. She concluded that a scornful submission was the better part of dignity, and lapsed into a smoldering quiescence.

She felt even her anger being submerged by awe as they entered the mouth of the Pass, lowering like a black well mouth in the blacker walls that rose like colossal ramparts to bar their way. It was as if a gigantic knife had cut the Zhaibar out of walls of solid rock. On either hand sheer slopes pitched up for thousands of feet, and the mouth of the Pass was dark as hate. Even Conan could not see with any accuracy, but he knew the road, even by night. And knowing that armed men were racing through the starlight after him, he did not check the stallion's speed. The great brute was not yet showing fatigue. He thundered along the road that followed the valley bed, labored up a slope, swept along a low ridge where treacherous shale on either hand lurked for the unwary, and came upon a trail that followed the lap of the left-hand wall.

Not even Conan could spy, in that darkness, an ambush set by Zhaibar tribesmen. As they swept past the black mouth of a gorge that opened into the Pass, a javelin swished through the air and thudded home behind the stallion's straining shoulder. The great beast let out his life in a shuddering sob and stumbled, going headlong in mid-stride. But Conan had recognized the flight and stroke of the javelin, and he acted with spring-steel quickness.

As the horse fell he leaped clear, holding the girl aloft to guard her from striking boulders. He lit on his feet like a cat, thrust her into a cleft of rock, and wheeled toward the outer darkness, drawing his knife.

Yasmina, confused by the rapidity of events, not quite sure just what had happened, saw a vague shape rush out of the darkness, bare feet slapping softly on the rock, ragged garments whipping on the wind of his haste. She glimpsed the flicker of steel, heard the lightning crack of stroke, parry and counter-stroke, and the crunch of bone as Conan's long knife split the other's skull.

Conan sprang back, crouching in the shelter of the rocks. Out in the night men were moving and a stentorian voice roared: 'What, you dogs! Do you flinch? In, curse you, and take them!'

Conan started, peered into the darkness and lifted his voice.

'Yar Afzal! Is it you?'

There sounded a startled imprecation, and the voice called warily.

'Conan? Is it you, Conan?'

'Aye!' the Cimmerian laughed. 'Come forth, you old war-dog. I've slain one of your men.'

There was movement among the rocks, a light flared dimly, and then a flame appeared and came bobbing toward him, and as it approached, a fierce bearded countenance grew out of the darkness. The man who carried it held it high, thrust forward, and craned his neck to peer among the boulders it lighted; the other hand gripped a great curved tulwar. Conan stepped forward, sheathing his knife, and the other roared a greeting.

'Aye, it is Conan! Come out of your rocks, dogs! It is Conan!'

Others pressed into the wavering circle of light – wild, ragged, bearded men, with eyes like wolves, and long blades in their fists. They did not see Yasmina, for she was hidden by Conan's massive body. But peeping from her covert, she knew icy fear for the first time that night. These men were more like wolves than human beings.

'What are you hunting in the Zhaibar by night, Yar Afzal?' Conan demanded of the burly chief, who grinned like a bearded ghoul.

'Who knows what might come up the Pass after dark? We Wazulis are night-hawks. But what of you, Conan?'

'I have a prisoner,' answered the Cimmerian. And moving aside he disclosed the cowering girl. Reaching a long arm into the crevice he drew her trembling forth.

Her imperious bearing was gone. She stared timidly at the ring of bearded faces that hemmed her in, and was grateful for the strong arm that clasped her possessively. The torch was thrust close to her, and there was a sucking intake of breath about the ring.

'She is my captive,' Conan warned, glancing pointedly at the feet of the man he had slain, just visible within the ring of light. 'I was taking her to Afghulistan, but now you have slain my horse, and the Kshatriyas are close behind me.'

'Come with us to my village,' suggested Yar Afzal. 'We have horses hidden in the gorge. They can never follow us in the darkness. They are close behind you, you say?'

'So close that I hear now the clink of their hoofs on the flint,' answered Conan grimly.

Instantly there was movement; the torch was dashed out and the ragged shapes melted like phantoms into the darkness. Conan swept up the Devi in his arms, and she did not resist. The rocky ground hurt her slim feet in their soft slippers and she felt very small and helpless in that brutish, primordial blackness among those colossal, nighted crags.

Feeling her shiver in the wind that moaned down the defiles, Conan jerked a ragged cloak from its owner's shoulders and wrapped it about her. He also hissed a warning in her ear, ordering her to make no sound. She did not hear the distant clink of shod hoofs on rock that warned the keen-eared hillmen; but she was far too frightened to disobey, in any event.

She could see nothing but a few faint stars far above, but she knew by the deepening darkness when they entered the gorge mouth. There was a stir about them, the uneasy movement of horses. A few muttered words, and Conan mounted the horse of the man he had killed, lifting the girl up in front of him. Like phantoms except for the click of their hoofs, the band swept away up the shadowy gorge. Behind them on the trail they left the dead horse and the dead man, which were found less than half an hour later by the riders from the fortress, who recognized the man as a Wazuli and drew their own conclusions accordingly.

Yasmina, snuggled warmly in her captor's arms, grew drowsy in spite of herself. The motion of the horse, though it was uneven, uphill and down, yet possessed a certain rhythm which combined with weariness and emotional exhaustion to force sleep upon her. She had lost all sense of time or direction. They moved in soft thick darkness, in which she sometimes glimpsed vaguely gigantic walls sweeping up like black ramparts, or great crags shouldering the stars; at times she sensed echoing depths beneath them, or felt the wind of dizzy heights blowing cold about her. Gradually these things faded into a dreamy unwakefulness in which the clink of hoofs and the creak of saddles were like the irrelevant sounds in a dream.

She was vaguely aware when the motion ceased and she was lifted down and carried a few steps. Then she was laid down on something soft and rustling, and something – a folded coat perhaps – was thrust under her head, and the cloak in which she was wrapped was carefully tucked about her. She heard Yar Afzal laugh.

'A rare prize, Conan; fit mate for a chief of the Afghulis.'

'Not for me,' came Conan's answering rumble. 'This wench will buy the lives of my seven headmen, blast their souls.'

That was the last she heard as she sank into dreamless slumber.

She slept while armed men rode through the dark hills, and the fate of kingdoms hung in the balance. Through the shadowy gorges and defiles that night there rang the hoofs of galloping horses, and the starlight glimmered on helmets and curved blades, until the ghoulish shapes that haunt the crags stared into the darkness from ravine and boulder and wondered what things were afoot.

A band of these sat gaunt horses in the black pitmouth of a gorge as the hurrying hoofs swept past. Their leader, a well-built man in a helmet and gilt-braided cloak, held up his hand warningly, until the riders had sped on. Then he laughed softly.

'They must have lost the trail! Or else they have found that Conan has already reached the Afghuli villages. It will take many riders to smoke out that hive. There will be squadrons riding up the Zhaibar by dawn.'

'If there is fighting in the hills there will be looting,' muttered a voice behind him, in the dialect of the Irakzai.

'There will be looting,' answered the man with the helmet. 'But first it is our business to reach the valley of Gurashah and await the riders that will be galloping southward from Secunderam before daylight.'

He lifted his reins and rode out of the defile, his men falling in behind him – thirty ragged phantoms in the starlight.

5 The Black Stallion

The sun was well up when Yasmina awoke. She did not start and stare blankly, wondering where she was. She awoke with full knowledge of all that had occurred. Her supple limbs were stiff from her long ride, and her firm flesh seemed to feel the contact of the muscular arm that had borne her so far.

She was lying on a sheepskin covering a pallet of leaves on a hard-beaten dirt floor. A folded sheepskin coat was under her head, and she was wrapped in a ragged cloak. She was in a large room, the walls of which were crudely but strongly built of uncut rocks, plastered with sun-baked mud. Heavy beams supported a roof of the same kind, in which showed a trap-door up to which led a ladder. There were no windows in the thick walls, only loop-holes. There was one door, a sturdy bronze affair that must have been looted from some Vendhyan border tower. Opposite it was a wide opening in the wall, with no door, but several strong wooden bars in place. Beyond them Yasmina saw a magnificent black stallion munching a pile of dried grass. The building was fort, dwelling-place and stable in one.

At the other end of the room a girl in the vest and baggy trousers of a hill-woman squatted beside a small fire, cooking strips of meat on an iron grid laid over blocks of stone. There was a sooty cleft in the wall a few feet from the floor, and some of the smoke found its way out there. The rest floated in blue wisps about the room.

The hill-girl glanced at Yasmina over her shoulder, displaying a bold, handsome face, and then continued her cooking. Voices boomed outside; then the door was kicked open, and Conan strode in. He looked more enormous than ever with the morning sunlight behind him, and Yasmina noted some details that had escaped her the night before. His garments were clean and not ragged. The broad Bakhariot girdle that supported his knife in its ornamented scabbard would have matched the robes of a prince, and there was a glint of fine Turanian mail under his shirt.

'Your captive is awake, Conan,' said the Wazuli girl, and he grunted, strode up to the fire and swept the strips of mutton off into a stone dish.

The squatting girl laughed up at him, with some spicy jest, and he grinned wolfishly, and hooking a toe under her haunches, tumbled her sprawling onto the floor. She seemed to derive considerable amusement from this bit of rough horse-play, but Conan paid no more heed to her. Producing a great hunk of bread from somewhere, with a copper jug of wine, he carried the lot to Yasmina, who had risen from her pallet and was regarding him doubtfully.

'Rough fare for a Devi, girl, but our best,' he grunted. 'It will fill your belly, at least.'

He set the platter on the floor, and she was suddenly aware of a ravenous hunger. Making no comment, she seated herself cross-legged on the floor, and taking the dish in her lap, she began to eat, using her fingers, which were all she had in the way of table utensils. After all, adaptability is one of the tests of true aristocracy. Conan stood looking down at her, his thumbs hooked in his girdle. He never sat cross-legged, after the Eastern fashion.

'Where am I?' she asked abruptly.

'In the hut of Yar Afzal, the chief of the Khurum Wazulis,' he answered. 'Afghulistan lies a good many miles farther on to the west. We'll hide here awhile. The Kshatriyas are beating up the hills for you – several of their squads have been cut up by the tribes already.'

'What are you going to do?' she asked.

'Keep you until Chunder Shan is willing to trade back my seven cow-thieves,' he grunted. 'Women of the Wazulis are crushing ink out of *shoki* leaves, and after a while you can write a letter to the governor.'

A touch of her old imperious wrath shook her, as she thought how maddeningly her plans had gone awry, leaving her captive of the very man she had plotted to get into her power. She flung down the dish, with the remnants of her meal, and sprang to her feet, tense with anger.

'I will not write a letter! If you do not take me back, they will hang your seven men, and a thousand more besides!'

The Wazuli girl laughed mockingly, Conan scowled, and then the door opened and Yar Afzal came swaggering in. The Wazuli chief was as tall as Conan, and of greater girth, but he looked fat and slow beside the hard compactness of the Cimmerian. He plucked his red-stained beard and stared meaningly at the Wazuli girl, and that wench rose and scurried out without delay. Then Yar Afzal turned to his guest.

'The damnable people murmur, Conan,' quoth he. 'They wish me to murder you and take the girl to hold for ransom. They say that anyone can tell by her garments that she is a noble lady. They say why should the Afghuli dogs profit by her, when it is the people who take the risk of guarding her?'

'Lend me your horse,' said Conan. 'I'll take her and go.'

'Pish!' boomed Yar Afzal. 'Do you think I can't handle my own people? I'll have them dancing in their shirts if they cross me! They don't love you – or any other outlander – but you saved my life once, and I will not forget. Come out, though, Conan; a scout has returned.'

Conan hitched at his girdle and followed the chief outside. They closed the door after them, and Yasmina peeped through a loop-hole. She looked out on a level space before the hut. At the farther end of that space there was a cluster of mud and stone huts, and she saw naked children playing among the boulders, and the slim erect women of the hills going about their tasks.

Directly before the chief's hut a circle of hairy, ragged men squatted, facing the door. Conan and Yar Afzal stood a few paces before the door, and between them and the ring of warriors another man sat cross-legged. This one was addressing his chief in the harsh accents of the Wazuli which Yasmina could scarcely understand, though as part of her royal education she had been taught the languages of Iranistan and the kindred tongues of Ghulistan.

'I talked with a Dagozai who saw the riders last night,' said the scout. 'He was lurking near when they came to the spot where we ambushed the lord Conan. He overheard their speech. Chunder Shan was with them. They found the dead horse, and one of the men recognized it as Conan's. Then they found the man Conan slew, and knew him for a Wazuli. It seemed to them that Conan had been slain and the girl taken by the Wazuli; so they turned aside from their purpose of following to Afghulistan. But they did not know from which village the dead man was come, and we had left no trail a Kshatriya could follow.

'So they rode to the nearest Wazuli village, which was the village of Jugra, and burnt it and slew many of the people. But the men of Khojur came upon them in darkness and slew some of them, and wounded the governor. So the survivors retired down the Zhaibar in the darkness before dawn, but they returned with reinforcements before sunrise, and there has been skirmishing and fighting in the hills all morning. It is said that a great army is being raised to sweep the hills about the Zhaibar. The tribes are whetting their knives and laying ambushes in every pass from here to Gurashah valley. Moreover, Kerim Shah has returned to the hills.'

A grunt went around the circle, and Yasmina leaned closer to the loop-hole at the name she had begun to mistrust.

'Where went he?' demanded Yar Afzal.

'The Dagozai did not know; with him were thirty Irakzai of the lower villages. They rode into the hills and disappeared.'

'These Irakzai are jackals that follow a lion for crumbs,' growled Yar Afzal. 'They have been lapping up the coins Kerim Shah scatters among the border tribes to buy men like horses. I like him not, for all he is our kinsman from Iranistan.'

'He's not even that,' said Conan. 'I know him of old. He's an Hyrkanian, a spy of Yezdigerd's. If I catch him I'll hang his hide to a tamarisk.'

'But the Kshatriyas!' clamored the men in the semicircle. 'Are we to squat on our haunches until they smoke us out? They will learn at last in which Wazuli village the wench is held. We are not loved by the Zhaibari; they will help the Kshatriyas hunt us out.'

'Let them come,' grunted Yar Afzal. 'We can hold the defiles against a host.'

One of the men leaped up and shook his fist at Conan.

'Are we to take all the risks while he reaps the rewards?' he howled. 'Are we to fight his battles for him?'

With a stride Conan reached him and bent slightly to stare full into his hairy face. The Cimmerian had not drawn his long knife, but his left hand grasped the scabbard, jutting the hilt suggestively forward.

'I ask no man to fight my battles,' he said softly. 'Draw your blade if you dare, you yapping dog!'

The Wazuli started back, snarling like a cat.

'Dare to touch me and here are fifty men to rend you apart!' he screeched.

'What!' roared Yar Afzal, his face purpling with wrath. His whiskers bristled, his belly swelled with his rage. 'Are you chief of Khurum? Do the Wazulis take orders from Yar Afzal, or from a low-bred cur?'

The man cringed before his invincible chief, and Yar Afzal, striding up to him, seized him by the throat and choked him until his face was turning black. Then he hurled the man savagely against the ground and stood over him with his tulwar in his hand.

'Is there any who questions my authority?' he roared, and his warriors looked down sullenly as his bellicose glare swept their semicircle. Yar Afzal grunted scornfully and sheathed his weapon with a gesture that was the apex of insult. Then he kicked the fallen agitator with a concentrated vindictiveness that brought howls from his victim.

'Get down the valley to the watchers on the heights and bring word if they have seen anything,' commanded Yar Afzal, and the man went, shaking with fear and grinding his teeth with fury.

Yar Afzal then seated himself ponderously on a stone, growling in his beard. Conan stood near him, legs braced apart, thumbs hooked in his girdle, narrowly watching the assembled warriors. They stared at him sullenly, not daring to brave Yar Afzal's fury, but hating the foreigner as only a hillman can hate.

'Now listen to me, you sons of nameless dogs, while I tell you what the lord Conan and I have planned to fool the Kshatriyas.' The boom of Yar Afzal's bull-like voice followed the discomfited warrior as he slunk away from the assembly.

The man passed by the cluster of huts, where women who had seen his defeat laughed at him and called stinging comments, and hastened on along the trail that wound among spurs and rocks toward the valley head.

Just as he rounded the first turn that took him out of sight of the village, he stopped short, gaping stupidly. He had not believed it possible for a stranger to enter the valley of Khurum without being detected by the hawk-eyed watchers along the heights; yet a man sat cross-legged on a low ledge beside the path – a man in a camel-hair robe and a green turban.

The Wazuli's mouth gaped for a yell, and his hand leaped to his knife-hilt. But at that instant his eyes met those of the stranger and the cry died in his throat, his fingers went limp. He stood like a statue, his own eyes glazed and vacant.

For minutes the scene held motionless; then the man on the ledge drew a cryptic symbol in the dust on the rock with his forefinger. The Wazuli did not see him place anything within the compass of that emblem, but presently something gleamed there – a round, shiny black ball that looked like polished jade. The man in the green turban took this up and tossed it to the Wazuli, who mechanically caught it.

'Carry this to Yar Afzal,' he said, and the Wazuli turned like an automaton and went back along the path, holding the black jade ball in his outstretched hand. He did not even turn his head to the renewed jeers of the women as he passed the huts. He did not seem to hear.

The man on the ledge gazed after him with a cryptic smile. A girl's head rose above the rim of the ledge and she looked at him with admiration and a touch of fear that had not been present the night before.

'Why did you do that?' she asked.

He ran his fingers through her dark locks caressingly.

'Are you still dizzy from your flight on the horse-of-air, that you doubt my wisdom?' he laughed. 'As long as Yar Afzal lives, Conan will bide safe among the Wazuli fighting-men. Their knives are sharp, and there are many of them. What I plot will be safer, even for me, than to seek to slay him and take her from among them. It takes no wizard to predict what the Wazulis will do, and what Conan will do, when my victim hands the globe of Yezud to the chief of Khurum.'

Back before the hut, Yar Afzal halted in the midst of some tirade, surprized and displeased to see the man he had sent up the valley, pushing his way through the throng.

'I bade you go to the watchers!' the chief bellowed. 'You have not had time to come from them.'

The other did not reply; he stood woodenly, staring vacantly into the chief's face, his palm outstretched holding the jade ball. Conan, looking over Yar Afzal's shoulder, murmured something and reached to touch the chief's arm, but as he did so, Yar Afzal, in a paroxysm of anger, struck the man with his clenched fist and felled him like an ox. As he fell, the jade sphere rolled to Yar Afzal's foot, and the chief, seeming to see it for the first time, bent and picked it up. The men, staring perplexedly at their senseless comrade, saw their chief bend, but they did not see what he picked up from the ground.

Yar Afzal straightened, glanced at the jade, and made a motion to thrust it into his girdle.

'Carry that fool to his hut,' he growled. 'He has the look of a lotus-eater. He returned me a blank stare. I – *aie!*'

In his right hand, moving toward his girdle, he had suddenly felt movement where movement should not be. His voice died away as he stood and glared at nothing; and inside his clenched right hand he felt the quivering of *change*, of *motion*, of *life*. He no longer held a smooth shining sphere in his fingers. And he dared not look; his tongue clove to the roof of his mouth, and he could not open his hand. His astonished warriors saw Yar Afzal's eyes distend, the color ebb from his face. Then suddenly a bellow of agony burst from his bearded lips; he swayed and fell as if struck by lightning, his right arm tossed out in front of him. Face down he lay, and from between his opening fingers crawled a spider – a hideous, black, hairy-legged monster whose body shone like black jade. The men yelled and gave back suddenly, and the creature scuttled into a crevice of the rocks and disappeared.

The warriors started up, glaring wildly, and a voice rose above their clamor, a far-carrying voice of command which came from none knew where. Afterward each man there – who still lived – denied that he had shouted, but all there heard it.

'Yar Afzal is dead! Kill the outlander!'

That shout focused their whirling minds as one. Doubt, bewilderment and fear vanished in the uproaring surge of the blood-lust. A furious yell rent the skies as the tribesmen responded instantly to the suggestion. They came headlong across the open space, cloaks flapping, eyes blazing, knives lifted.

Conan's action was as quick as theirs. As the voice shouted he sprang for the hut door. But they were closer to him than he was to the door, and with one foot on the sill he had to wheel and parry the swipe of a yard-long blade. He split the man's skull – ducked another swinging knife and gutted the wielder – felled a man with his left fist and stabbed another in the belly – and heaved back mightily against the closed door with his shoulders. Hacking blades were nicking chips out of the jambs about his ears, but the door flew open under the impact of his shoulders, and he went stumbling backward into the room. A bearded tribesman, thrusting with all his fury as Conan sprang back, overreached and pitched head-first through the doorway. Conan stopped, grasped the slack of his garments and hauled him clear, and slammed the door in the faces of the men who came surging into it. Bones snapped under the impact, and the next instant Conan slammed the bolts into place and whirled with desperate haste to meet the man who sprang from the floor and tore into action like a madman.

Yasmina cowered in a corner, staring in horror as the two men fought back and forth across the room, almost trampling her at times; the flash and clangor of their blades filled the room, and outside the mob clamored like a wolf-pack, hacking deafeningly at the bronze door with their long knives, and dashing huge rocks against it. Somebody fetched a tree trunk, and the door began to stagger under the thunderous assault. Yasmina clasped her ears, staring wildly. Violence and fury within, cataclysmic madness without. The stallion in his stall neighed and reared, thundering with his heels against the walls. He wheeled and launched his hoofs through the bars just as the tribesman, backing away from Conan's murderous swipes, stumbled against them. His spine cracked in three places like a rotten branch and he was hurled headlong against the Cimmerian, bearing him backward so that they both crashed to the beaten floor.

Yasmina cried out and ran forward; to her dazed sight it seemed that both were slain. She reached them just as Conan threw aside the corpse and rose. She caught his arm, trembling from head to foot.

'Oh, you live! I thought – I thought you were dead!'

He glanced down at her quickly, into the pale, upturned face and the wide staring dark eyes.

'Why are you trembling?' he demanded. 'Why should you care if I live or die?'

A vestige of her poise returned to her, and she drew away, making a rather pitiful attempt at playing the Devi.

'You are preferable to those wolves howling without,' she answered, gesturing toward the door, the stone sill of which was beginning to splinter away.

'That won't hold long,' he muttered, then turned and went swiftly to the stall of the stallion.

Yasmina clenched her hands and caught her breath as she saw him tear aside the splintered bars and go into the stall with the maddened beast. The stallion reared above him, neighing terribly, hoofs lifted, eyes and teeth flashing and ears laid back, but Conan leaped and caught his mane with a display of sheer strength that seemed impossible, and dragged the beast down on his forelegs. The steed snorted and quivered, but stood still while the man bridled him and clapped on the gold-worked saddle, with the wide silver stirrups.

Wheeling the beast around in the stall, Conan called quickly to Yasmina, and the girl came, sidling nervously past the stallion's heels. Conan was working at the stone wall, talking swiftly as he worked.

'A secret door in the wall here, that not even the Wazuli know about. Yar Afzal showed it to me once when he was drunk. It opens out into the mouth of the ravine behind the hut. Ha!'

As he tugged at a projection that seemed casual, a whole section of the wall slid back on oiled iron runners. Looking through, the girl saw a narrow defile opening in a sheer stone cliff within a few feet of the hut's back wall. Then Conan sprang into the saddle and hauled her up before him. Behind them the great door groaned like a living thing and crashed in, and a yell rang to the roof as the entrance was instantly flooded with hairy faces and knives in hairy fists. And then the great stallion went through the wall like a javelin from a catapult, and thundered into the defile, running low, foam flying from the bit-rings.

That move came as an absolute surprize to the Wazulis. It was a surprize, too, to those stealing down the ravine. It happened so quickly – the hurricane-like charge of the great horse – that a man in a green turban was unable to get out of the way. He went down under the frantic hoofs, and a girl screamed. Conan got one glimpse of her as they thundered by – a slim, dark girl in silk trousers and a jeweled breast-band, flattening herself against the ravine wall. Then the black horse and his riders were gone up the gorge like the spume blown before a storm, and the men who came tumbling through the wall into the defile after them met that which changed their yells of blood-lust to shrill screams of fear and death.

6 The Mountain of the Black Seers

'Where now?' Yasmina was trying to sit erect on the rocking saddle-bow, clutching her captor. She was conscious of a recognition of shame that she should not find unpleasant the feel of his muscular flesh under her fingers.

'To Afghulistan,' he answered. 'It's a perilous road, but the stallion will carry us easily, unless we fall in with some of your friends, or my tribal enemies. Now that Yar Afzal is dead, those damned Wazulis will be on our heels. I'm surprised we haven't sighted them behind us already.'

'Who was that man you rode down?' she asked.

'I don't know. I never saw him before. He's no Ghuli, that's certain. What the devil he was doing there is more than I can say. There was a girl with him, too.'

'Yes.' Her gaze was shadowed. 'I can not understand that. That girl was my maid, Gitara. Do you suppose she was coming to aid me? That the man was a friend? If so, the Wazulis have captured them both.'

'Well,' he answered, 'there's nothing we can do. If we go back, they'll skin us both. I can't understand how a girl like that could get this far into the mountains with only one man – and he a robed scholar, for that's what he looked like. There's something infernally queer in all this. That fellow Yar Afzal beat and sent away – he moved like a man walking in his sleep. I've seen the priests of Zamora perform their abominable rituals in their forbidden temples, and their victims had a stare like that man. The priests looked into their eyes and muttered incantations, and then the people became the walking dead men, with glassy eyes, doing as they were ordered.

'And then I saw what the fellow had in his hand, which Yar Afzal picked up. It was like a big black jade bead, such as the temple girls of Yezud wear when they dance before the black stone spider which is their god. Yar Afzal held it in his hand, and he didn't pick up anything else. Yet when he fell dead, a spider, like the god at Yezud, only smaller, ran out of his fingers. And then, when the Wazulis stood uncertain there, a voice cried out for them to kill me, and I know that voice didn't come from any of the warriors, nor from the women who watched by the huts. It seemed to come from *above*.'

Yasmina did not reply. She glanced at the stark outlines of the mountains all about them and shuddered. Her soul shrank from their gaunt brutality. This was a grim, naked land where anything might happen. Age-old traditions invested it with shuddery horror for anyone born in the hot, luxuriant southern plains.

The sun was high, beating down with fierce heat, yet the wind that blew in fitful gusts seemed to sweep off slopes of ice. Once she heard a strange rushing above them that was not the sweep of the wind, and from the way Conan looked up, she knew it was not a common sound to him, either. She thought that a strip of the cold blue sky was momentarily blurred, as if some all but invisible object had swept between it and herself, but she could not be sure. Neither made any comment, but Conan loosened his knife in his scabbard.

They were following a faintly marked path dipping down into ravines so deep the sun never struck bottom, laboring up steep slopes where loose shale threatened to slide from beneath their feet, and following knife-edge ridges with blue-hazed echoing depths on either hand.

The sun had passed its zenith when they crossed a narrow trail winding among the crags. Conan reined the horse aside and followed it southward, going almost at right angles to their former course.

'A Galzai village is at one end of this trail,' he explained. 'Their women follow it to a well, for water. You need new garments.'

Glancing down at her filmy attire, Yasmina agreed with him. Her cloth-of-gold slippers were in tatters, her robes and silken under-garments torn to shreds that scarcely held together decently. Garments meant for the streets of Peshkhauri were scarcely appropriate for the crags of the Himelians.

Coming to a crook in the trail, Conan dismounted, helped Yasmina down and waited. Presently he nodded, though she heard nothing.

'A woman coming along the trail,' he remarked. In sudden panic she clutched his arm.

'You will not – not kill her?'

'I don't kill women ordinarily,' he grunted; 'though some of the hill-women are she-wolves. No,' he grinned as at a huge jest. 'By Crom, I'll *pay* for her clothes! How is that?' He displayed a large handful of gold coins, and replaced all but the largest. She nodded, much relieved. It was perhaps natural for men to slay and die; her flesh crawled at the thought of watching the butchery of a woman.

Presently a woman appeared around the crook of the trail – a tall, slim Galzai girl, straight as a young sapling, bearing a great empty gourd. She stopped short and the gourd fell from her hands when she saw them; she wavered as though to run, then realized that Conan was too close to her to allow her to escape, and so stood still, staring at them with a mixed expression of fear and curiosity.

Conan displayed the gold coin.

'If you will give this woman your garments,' he said, 'I will give you this money.'

The response was instant. The girl smiled broadly with surprize and delight, and, with the disdain of a hill-woman for prudish conventions, promptly yanked off her sleeveless embroidered vest, slipped down her wide trousers and stepped out of them, twitched off her wide-sleeved shirt, and kicked off her sandals. Bundling them all in a bunch, she proffered them to Conan, who handed them to the astonished Devi.

'Get behind that rock and put these on,' he directed, further proving himself no native hill-man. 'Fold your robes up into a bundle and bring them to me when you come out.'

'The money!' clamored the hill-girl, stretching out her hands eagerly. 'The gold you promised me!'

Conan flipped the coin to her, she caught it, bit, then thrust it into her hair, bent and caught up the gourd and went on down the path, as devoid of self-consciousness as of garments. Conan waited with some impatience while the Devi, for the first time in her pampered life, dressed herself. When she stepped from behind the rock he swore in surprize, and she felt a curious rush of emotions at the unrestrained admiration burning in his fierce blue eyes. She felt shame, embarrassment, yet a stimulation of vanity she had never before experienced, and a tingling when meeting the impact of his eyes. He laid a heavy hand on her shoulder and turned her about, staring avidly at her from all angles.

'By Crom!' said he. 'In those smoky, mystic robes you were aloof and cold and far off as a star! Now you are a woman of warm flesh and blood! You went behind that rock as the Devi of Vendhya; you come out as a hill-girl – though a thousand times more beautiful than any wench of the Zhaibar! You were a goddess – now you are real!'

He spanked her resoundingly, and she, recognizing this as merely another expression of admiration, did not feel outraged. It was indeed as if the changing of her garments had wrought a change in her personality. The feelings and sensations she had suppressed rose to domination in her now, as if the queenly robes she had cast off had been material shackles and inhibitions.

But Conan, in his renewed admiration, did not forget that peril lurked all about them. The farther they drew away from the region of the Zhaibar, the less likely he was to encounter any Kshatriya troops. On the other hand he had been listening all throughout their flight for sounds that would tell him the vengeful Wazulis of Khurum were on their heels.

Swinging the Devi up, he followed her into the saddle and again reined the stallion westward. The bundle of garments she had given him, he hurled over a cliff, to fall into the depths of a thousand-foot gorge.

'Why did you do that?' she asked. 'Why did you not give them to the girl?'

'The riders from Peshkhauri are combing these hills,' he said. 'They'll be ambushed and harried at every turn, and by way of reprisal they'll destroy every village they can take. They may turn westward any time. If they found a girl wearing your garments, they'd torture her into talking, and she might put them on my trail.'

'What will she do?' asked Yasmina.

'Go back to her village and tell her people that a stranger attacked her,' he answered. 'She'll have them on our track, all right. But she had to go on and get the water first; if she dared go back without it, they'd whip the skin off her. That gives us a long start. They'll never catch us. By nightfall we'll cross the Afghuli border.'

'There are no paths or signs of human habitation in these parts,' she commented. 'Even for the Himelians this region seems singularly deserted. We have not seen a trail since we left the one where we met the Galzai woman.'

For answer he pointed to the northwest, where she glimpsed a peak in a notch of the crags.

'Yimsha,' grunted Conan. 'The tribes build their villages as far from the mountain as they can.'

She was instantly rigid with attention.

'Yimsha!' she whispered. 'The mountain of the Black Seers!'

'So they say,' he answered. 'This is as near as I ever approached it. I have swung north to avoid any Kshatriya troops that might be prowling through the hills. The regular trail from Khurum to Afghulistan lies farther south. This is an ancient one, and seldom used.'

She was staring intently at the distant peak. Her nails bit into her pink palms.

'How long would it take to reach Yimsha from this point?'

'All the rest of the day, and all night,' he answered, and grinned. 'Do you want to go there? By Crom, it's no place for an ordinary human, from what the hill-people say.'

'Why do they not gather and destroy the devils that inhabit it?' she demanded.

'Wipe out wizards with swords? Anyway, they never interfere with people, unless the people interfere with them. I never saw one of them, though I've talked with men who swore they had. They say they've glimpsed people from the tower among the crags at sunset or sunrise – tall, silent men in black robes.'

'Would you be afraid to attack them?'

'I?' The idea seemed a new one to him. 'Why, if they imposed upon me, it would be my life or theirs. But I have nothing to do with them.

I came to these mountains to raise a following of human beings, not to war with wizards.'

Yasmina did not at once reply. She stared at the peak as at a human enemy, feeling all her anger and hatred stir in her bosom anew. And another feeling began to take dim shape. She had plotted to hurl against the masters of Yimsha the man in whose arms she was now carried. Perhaps there was another way, besides the method she had planned, to accomplish her purpose. She could not mistake the look that was beginning to dawn in this wild man's eyes as they rested on her. Kingdoms have fallen when a woman's slim white hands pulled the strings of destiny. Suddenly she stiffened, pointing.

'Look!'

Just visible on the distant peak there hung a cloud of peculiar aspect. It was a frosty crimson in color, veined with sparkling gold. This cloud was in motion; it rotated, and as it whirled it contracted. It dwindled to a spinning taper that flashed in the sun. And suddenly it detached itself from the snow-tipped peak, floated out over the void like a gay-hued feather, and became invisible against the cerulean sky.

'What could that have been?' asked the girl uneasily, as a shoulder of rock shut the distant mountain from view; the phenomenon had been disturbing, even in its beauty.

'The hill-men call it Yimsha's Carpet, whatever that means,' answered Conan. 'I've seen five hundred of them running as if the devil were at their heels, to hide themselves in caves and crags, because they saw that crimson cloud float up from the peak. What in—'

They had advanced through a narrow, knife-cut gash between turreted walls and emerged upon a broad ledge, flanked by a series of rugged slopes on one hand, and a gigantic precipice on the other. The dim trail followed this ledge, bent around a shoulder and reappeared at intervals far below, working a tedious way downward. And emerging from the cut that opened upon the ledge, the black stallion halted short, snorting. Conan urged him on impatiently, and the horse snorted and threw his head up and down, quivering and straining as if against an invisible barrier.

Conan swore and swung off, lifting Yasmina down with him. He went forward, with a hand thrown out before him as if expecting to encounter unseen resistance, but there was nothing to hinder him, though when he tried to lead the horse, it neighed shrilly and jerked back. Then Yasmina cried out, and Conan wheeled, hand starting to knife-hilt.

Neither of them had seen him come, but he stood there, with his arms folded, a man in a camel-hair robe and a green turban. Conan grunted with surprize to recognize the man the stallion had spurned in the ravine outside the Wazuli village.

'Who the devil are you?' he demanded.

The man did not answer. Conan noticed that his eyes were wide, fixed, and of a peculiar luminous quality. And those eyes held his like a magnet.

Khemsa's sorcery was based on hypnotism, as is the case with most Eastern magic. The way has been prepared for the hypnotist for untold centuries of generations who have lived and died in the firm conviction of the reality and power of hypnotism, building up, by mass thought and practise, a colossal though intangible atmosphere against which the individual, steeped in the traditions of the land, finds himself helpless.

But Conan was not a son of the East. Its traditions were meaningless to him; he was the product of an utterly alien atmosphere. Hypnotism was not even a myth in Cimmeria. The heritage that prepared a native of the East for submission to the mesmerist was not his.

He was aware of what Khemsa was trying to do to him; but he felt the impact of the man's uncanny power only as a vague impulsion, a tugging and pulling that he could shake off as a man shakes spider-webs from his garments.

Aware of hostility and black magic, he ripped out his long knife and lunged, as quick on his feet as a mountain lion.

But hypnotism was not all of Khemsa's magic. Yasmina, watching, did not see by what roguery of movement or illusion the man in the green turban avoided the terrible disembowelling thrust. But the keen blade whickered between side and lifted arm, and to Yasmina it seemed that Khemsa merely brushed his open palm lightly against Conan's bull-neck. But the Cimmerian went down like a slain ox.

Yet Conan was not dead; breaking his fall with his left hand, he slashed at Khemsa's legs even as he went down, and the Rakhsha avoided the scythe-like swipe only by a most unwizardly bound backward. Then Yasmina cried out sharply as she saw a woman she recognized as Gitara glide out from among the rocks and come up to the man. The greeting died in the Devi's throat as she saw the malevolence in the girl's beautiful face.

Conan was rising slowly, shaken and dazed by the cruel craft of that blow which, delivered with an art forgotten of men before Atlantis sank, would have broken like a rotten twig the neck of a lesser man. Khemsa gazed at him cautiously and a trifle uncertainly. The Rakhsha had learned the full flood of his own power when he faced at bay the knives of the maddened Wazulis in the ravine behind Khurum village; but the Cimmerian's resistance had perhaps shaken his new-found confidence a trifle. Sorcery thrives on success, not on failure.

He stepped forward, lifting his hand – then halted as if frozen, head tilted back, eyes wide open, hand raised. In spite of himself Conan followed his gaze, and so did the women – the girl cowering by the trembling stallion, and the girl beside Khemsa.

Down the mountain slopes, like a whirl of shining dust blown before the wind, a crimson, conoid cloud came dancing. Khemsa's dark face turned ashen; his hand began to tremble, then sank to his side. The girl beside him, sensing the change in him, stared at him inquiringly.

The crimson shape left the mountain slope and came down in a long arching sweep. It struck the ledge between Conan and Khemsa, and the Rakhsha gave back with a stifled cry. He backed away, pushing the girl Gitara back with groping, fending hands.

The crimson cloud balanced like a spinning top for an instant, whirling in a dazzling sheen on its point. Then without warning it was gone, vanished as a bubble vanishes when burst. There on the ledge stood four men. It was miraculous, incredible, impossible, yet it was true. They were not ghosts or phantoms. They were four tall men, with shaven, vulture-like heads, and black robes that hid their feet. Their hands were concealed by their wide sleeves. They stood in silence, their naked heads nodding slightly in unison. They were facing Khemsa, but behind them Conan felt his own blood turning to ice in his veins. Rising, he backed stealthily away, until he could feel the stallion's shoulder trembling against his back, and the Devi crept into the shelter of his arm. There was no word spoken. Silence hung like a stifling pall.

All four of the men in black robes stared at Khemsa. Their vulture-like faces were immobile, their eyes introspective and contemplative. But Khemsa shook like a man in an ague. His feet were braced on the rock, his calves straining as if in physical combat. Sweat ran in streams down his dark face. His right hand locked on something under his brown robe so desperately that the blood ebbed from that hand and left it white. His left hand fell on the shoulder of Gitara and clutched in agony like the grasp of a drowning man. She did not flinch or whimper, though his fingers dug like talons into her firm flesh.

Conan had witnessed hundreds of battles in his wild life, but never one like this, wherein four diabolical wills sought to beat down one lesser but equally devilish will that opposed them. But he only faintly sensed the monstrous quality of that hideous struggle. With his back to the wall, driven to bay by his former masters, Khemsa was fighting for his life with all the dark power, all the frightful knowledge they had taught him through long, grim years of neophytism and vassalage.

He was stronger than even he had guessed, and the free exercise of his powers in his own behalf had tapped unsuspected reservoirs of forces. And he was nerved to super-energy by frantic fear and desperation. He reeled before the merciless impact of those hypnotic eyes, but he held his ground. His features were distorted into a bestial grin of agony, and his limbs were twisted as on a rack. It was a war of souls, of frightful brains steeped in lore forbidden to men for a million years, of mentalities which had plumbed the abysses and explored the dark stars where spawn the shadows.

Yasmina understood this better than did Conan. And she dimly understood why Khemsa could withstand the concentrated impact of those four hellish wills which might have blasted into atoms the very rock on which he stood. The reason was the girl that he clutched with the strength of his despair. She was like an anchor to his staggering soul, battered by the waves of those psychic emanations. His weakness was now his strength. His love for the girl, violent and evil though it might be, was yet a tie that bound him to the rest of humanity, providing an earthly leverage for his will, a chain that his inhuman enemies could not break; at least not break through Khemsa.

They realized that before he did. And one of them turned his gaze from the Rakhsha full upon Gitara. There was no battle there. The girl shrank and wilted like a leaf in the drought. Irresistibly impelled, she tore herself from her lover's arms before he realized what was happening. Then a hideous thing came to pass. She began to back toward the precipice, facing her tormentors, her eyes wide and blank as dark gleaming glass from behind which a lamp has been blown out. Khemsa groaned and staggered toward her, falling into the trap set for him. A divided mind could not maintain the unequal battle. He was beaten, a straw in their hands. The girl went backward, walking like an automaton, and Khemsa reeled drunkenly after her, hands vainly outstretched, groaning, slobbering in his pain, his feet moving heavily like dead things.

On the very brink she paused, standing stiffly, her heels on the edge, and he fell on his knees and crawled whimpering toward her, groping for her, to drag her back from destruction. And just before his clumsy fingers touched her, one of the wizards laughed, like the sudden, bronze note of a bell in hell. The girl reeled suddenly and, consummate climax of exquisite cruelty, reason and understanding flooded back into her eyes, which flared with awful fear. She screamed, clutched wildly at her lover's straining hand, and then, unable to save herself, fell headlong with a moaning cry.

Khemsa hauled himself to the edge and stared over, haggardly, his lips working as he mumbled to himself. Then he turned and stared for a long minute at his torturers, with wide eyes that held no human light.

And then with a cry that almost burst the rocks, he reeled up and came rushing toward them, a knife lifted in his hand.

One of the Rakhshas stepped forward and stamped his foot, and as he stamped, there came a rumbling that grew swiftly to a grinding roar. Where his foot struck, a crevice opened in the solid rock that widened instantly. Then, with a deafening crash, a whole section of the ledge gave way. There was a last glimpse of Khemsa, with arms wildly upflung, and then he vanished amidst the roar of the avalanche that thundered down into the abyss.

The four looked contemplatively at the ragged edge of rock that formed the new rim of the precipice, and then turned suddenly. Conan, thrown off his feet by the shudder of the mountain, was rising, lifting Yasmina. He seemed to move as slowly as his brain was working. He was befogged and stupid. He realized that there was a desperate need for him to lift the Devi on the black stallion and ride like the wind, but an unaccountable sluggishness weighted his every thought and action.

And now the wizards had turned toward him; they raised their arms, and to his horrified sight, he saw their outlines fading, dimming, becoming hazy and nebulous, as a crimson smoke billowed around their feet and rose about them. They were blotted out by a sudden whirling cloud – and then he realized that he too was enveloped in a blinding crimson mist – he heard Yasmina scream, and the stallion cried out like a woman in pain. The Devi was torn from his arm, and as he lashed out with his knife blindly, a terrific blow like a gust of storm wind knocked him sprawling against a rock. Dazedly he saw a crimson conoid cloud spinning up and over the mountain slopes. Yasmina was gone, and so were the four men in black. Only the terrified stallion shared the ledge with him.

7 On to Yimsha

As mists vanish before a strong wind, the cobwebs vanished from Conan's brain. With a searing curse he leaped into the saddle and the stallion reared neighing beneath him. He glared up the slopes, hesitated, and then turned down the trail in the direction he had been going when halted by Khemsa's trickery. But now he did not ride at a measured gait. He shook loose the reins and the stallion went like a thunderbolt, as if frantic to lose hysteria in violent physical exertion. Across the ledge and around the crag and down the narrow trail threading the great steep they plunged at breakneck speed. The path followed a fold of rock, winding interminably down from tier to tier of striated escarpment, and once, far below, Conan got a glimpse of the ruin that had fallen – a mighty pile of broken stone and boulders at the foot of a gigantic cliff.

The valley floor was still far below him when he reached a long and lofty ridge that led out from the slope like a natural causeway. Out upon this he rode, with an almost sheer drop on either hand. He could trace ahead of him the trail and made a great horseshoe back into the riverbed at his left hand. He cursed the necessity of traversing those miles, but it was the only way. To try to descend to the lower lap of the trail here would be to attempt the impossible. Only a bird could get to the river-bed with a whole neck.

So he urged on the wearying stallion, until a clink of hoofs reached his ears, welling up from below. Pulling up short and reining to the lip of the cliff, he stared down into the dry river-bed that wound along the foot of the ridge. Along that gorge rode a motley throng – bearded men on half-wild horses, five hundred strong, bristling with weapons. And Conan shouted suddenly, leaning over the edge of the cliff, three hundred feet above them.

At his shout they reined back, and five hundred bearded faces were tilted up towards him; a deep, clamorous roar filled the canyon. Conan did not waste words.

'I was riding for Ghor!' he roared. 'I had not hoped to meet you dogs on the trail. Follow me as fast as your nags can push! I'm going to Yimsha, and—'

'Traitor!' The howl was like a dash of ice-water in his face.

'What?' He glared down at them, jolted speechless. He saw wild eyes blazing up at him, faces contorted with fury, fists brandishing blades.

'Traitor!' they roared back, wholeheartedly. 'Where are the seven chiefs held captive in Peshkhauri?'

'Why, in the governor's prison, I suppose,' he answered.

A bloodthirsty yell from a hundred throats answered him, with such a waving of weapons and a clamor that he could not understand what they were saying. He beat down the din with a bull-like roar, and bellowed: 'What devil's play is this? Let one of you speak, so I can understand what you mean!'

A gaunt old chief elected himself to this position, shook his tulwar at Conan as a preamble, and shouted accusingly: 'You would not let us go raiding Peshkhauri to rescue our brothers!'

'No, you fools!' roared the exasperated Cimmerian. 'Even if you'd breached the wall, which is unlikely, they'd have hanged the prisoners before you could reach them.'

'And you went alone to traffic with the governor!' yelled the Afghuli, working himself into a frothing frenzy.

'Well?'

'Where are the seven chiefs?' howled the old chief, making his tulwar into a glimmering wheel of steel about his head. 'Where are they? Dead!'

'What!' Conan nearly fell off his horse in his surprise.

'Aye, dead!' five hundred bloodthirsty voices assured him.

The old chief brandished his arms and got the floor again. 'They were not hanged!' he screeched. 'A Wazuli in another cell saw them die! The governor sent a wizard to slay them by craft!'

'That must be a lie,' said Conan. 'The governor would not dare. Last night I talked with him—'

The admission was unfortunate. A yell of hate and accusation split the skies.

'Aye! You went to him alone! To betray us! It is no lie. The Wazuli escaped through the doors the wizard burst in his entry, and told the tale to our scouts whom he met in Zhaibar. They had been sent forth to search for you, when you did not return. When they heard the Wazuli's tale, they returned with all haste to Ghor, and we saddled our steeds and girt our swords!'

'And what do you fools mean to do?' demanded the Cimmerian.

'To avenge our brothers!' they howled. 'Death to the Kshatriyas! Slay him, brothers, he is a traitor!'

Arrows began to rattle around him. Conan rose in his stirrups, striving to make himself heard above the tumult, and then, with a roar of mingled rage, defiance and disgust, he wheeled and galloped back up the trail. Behind him and below him the Afghulis came pelting, mouthing their rage, too furious even to remember that the only way they could reach the height whereon he rode was to traverse the riverbed in the other direction, make the broad bend and follow the twisting trail up over the ridge. When they did remember this, and turned back, their repudiated chief had almost reached the point where the ridge joined the escarpment.

At the cliff he did not take the trail by which he had descended, but turned off on another, a mere trace along a rock-fault, where the stallion scrambled for footing. He had not ridden far when the stallion snorted and shied back from something lying in the trail. Conan stared down on the travesty of a man, a broken, shredded, bloody heap that gibbered and gnashed splintered teeth.

Impelled by some obscure reason, Conan dismounted and stood looking down at the ghastly shape, knowing that he was witness of a thing miraculous and opposed to nature. The Rakhsha lifted his gory head, and his strange eyes, glazed with agony and approaching death, rested on Conan with recognition.

'Where are they?' It was a racking croak not even remotely resembling a human voice.

'Gone back to their damnable castle on Yimsha,' grunted Conan. 'They took the Devi with them.'

'I will go!' muttered the man. 'I will follow them! They killed Gitara; I will kill them – the acolytes, the Four of the Black Circle, the Master himself! Kill – kill them all!' He strove to drag his mutilated frame along the rock, but not even his indomitable will could animate that gory mass longer, where the splintered bones hung together only by torn tissue and ruptured fibre.

'Follow them!' raved Khemsa, drooling a bloody slaver. 'Follow!'

'I'm going to,' growled Conan. 'I went to fetch my Afghulis, but they've turned on me. I'm going on to Yimsha alone. I'll have the Devi back if I have to tear down that damned mountain with my bare hands. I didn't think the governor would dare kill my headmen, when I had the Devi, but it seems he did. I'll have his head for that. She's no use to me now as a hostage, but—'

'The curse of Yizil on them!' gasped Khemsa. 'Go! I am dying. Wait – take my girdle.'

He tried to fumble with a mangled hand at his tatters, and Conan, understanding what he sought to convey, bent and drew from about his gory waist a girdle of curious aspect.

'Follow the golden vein through the abyss,' muttered Khemsa. 'Wear the girdle. I had it from a Stygian priest. It will aid you, though it failed me at last. Break the crystal globe with the four golden pomegranates. Beware of the Master's transmutations – I am going to Gitara – she is waiting for me in hell – *aie, ya Skelos yar!*' And so he died.

Conan stared down at the girdle. The hair of which it was woven was not horsehair. He was convinced that it was woven of the thick black tresses of a woman. Set in the thick mesh were tiny jewels such as he had never seen before. The buckle was strangely made, in the form of a golden serpent-head, flat, wedge-shaped and scaled with curious art. A strong shudder shook Conan as he handled it, and he turned as though to cast it over the precipice; then he hesitated, and finally buckled it about his waist, under the Bakhariot girdle. Then he mounted and pushed on.

The sun had sunk behind the crags. He climbed the trail in the vast shadow of the cliffs that was thrown out like a dark blue mantle over valleys and ridges far below. He was not far from the crest when, edging around the shoulder of a jutting crag, he heard the clink of shod hoofs ahead of him. He did not turn back. Indeed, so narrow was the path that the stallion could not have wheeled his great body upon it. He rounded the jut of the rock and came upon a portion of the path that broadened somewhat. A chorus of threatening yells broke on his ear, but his stallion pinned a terrified horse hard against the rock, and Conan caught the arm of the rider in an iron grip, checking the lifted sword in midair.

'Kerim Shah!' muttered Conan, red glints smoldering luridly in his eyes. The Turanian did not struggle; they sat their horses almost breast to breast, Conan's fingers locking the other's sword-arm. Behind Kerim Shah filed a group of lean Irakzai on gaunt horses. They glared like wolves, fingering bows and knives, but rendered uncertain because of the narrowness of the path and the perilous proximity of the abyss that yawned beneath them.

'Where is the Devi?' demanded Kerim Shah.

'What's it to you, you Hyrkanian spy?' snarled Conan.

'I know you have her,' answered Kerim Shah. 'I was on my way northward with some tribesmen when we were ambushed by enemies in Shalizah Pass. Many of my men were slain, and the rest of us harried through the hills like jackals. When we had beaten off our pursuers, we turned westward, toward Amir Jehun Pass, and this morning we came upon a Wazuli wandering through the hills. He was quite mad, but I learned much from his incoherent gibberings before he died. I learned that he was the sole survivor of a band which followed a chief of the Afghulis and a captive Kshatriya woman into a gorge behind Khurum village. He babbled much of a man in a green turban whom the Afghuli rode down, but who, when attacked by the Wazulis who pursued, smote them with a nameless doom that wiped them out as a gust of wind-driven fire wipes out a cluster of locusts.

'How that one man escaped, I do not know, nor did he; but I knew from his maunderings that Conan of Ghor had been in Khurum with his royal captive. And as we made our way through the hills, we overtook a naked Galzai girl bearing a gourd of water, who told us a tale of having been stripped and ravished by a giant foreigner in the garb of an Afghuli chief, who, she said, gave her garments to a Vendhyan woman who accompanied him. She said you rode westward.'

Kerim Shah did not consider it necessary to explain that he had been on his way to keep his rendezvous with the expected troops from Secunderam when he found his way barred by hostile tribesmen. The road to Gurashah valley through Shalizah Pass was longer than the road that wound through Amir Jehun Pass, but the latter traversed part of the Afghuli country, which Kerim Shah had been anxious to avoid until he came with an army. Barred from the Shalizah road, however, he had turned to the forbidden route, until news that Conan had not yet reached Afghulistan with his captive had caused him to turn southward and push on recklessly in the hope of overtaking the Cimmerian in the hills.

'So you had better tell me where the Devi is,' suggested Kerim Shah. 'We outnumber you—'

'Let one of your dogs nock a shaft and I'll throw you over the cliff,' Conan promised. 'It wouldn't do you any good to kill me, anyhow. Five hundred Afghulis are on my trail, and if they find you've cheated them, they'll flay you alive. Anyway, I haven't got the Devi. She's in the hands of the Black Seers of Yimsha.'

'*Tarim!*' swore Kerim Shah softly, shaken out of his poise for the first time. 'Khemsa—'

'Khemsa's dead,' grunted Conan. 'His masters sent him to hell on a landslide. And now get out of my way. I'd be glad to kill you if I had the time, but I'm on my way to Yimsha.'

'I'll go with you,' said the Turanian abruptly.

Conan laughed at him. 'Do you think I'd trust you, you Hyrkanian dog?'

'I don't ask you to,' returned Kerim Shah. 'We both want the Devi. You know my reason; King Yezdigerd desires to add her kingdom to his empire, and herself in his seraglio. And I knew you, in the days when you were a hetman of the *kozak* steppes; so I know your ambition is wholesale plunder. You want to loot Vendhya, and to twist out a huge ransom for Yasmina. Well, let us for the time being, without any illusion about each other, unite our forces, and try to rescue the Devi from the Seers. If we succeed, and live, we can fight it out to see who keeps her.'

Conan narrowly scrutinized the other for a moment, and then nodded, releasing the Turanian's arm. 'Agreed; what about your men?'

Kerim Shah turned to the silent Irakzai and spoke briefly: 'This chief and I are going to Yimsha to fight the wizards. Will you go with us, or stay here to be flayed by the Afghulis who are following this man?'

They looked at him with eyes grimly fatalistic. They were doomed and they knew it – had known it ever since the singing arrows of the ambushed Dagozai had driven them back from the pass of Shalizah. The men of the lower Zhaibar had too many reeking bloodfeuds among the crag-dwellers. They were too small a band to fight their way back through the hills to the villages of the border, without the guidance of the crafty Turanian. They counted themselves as dead already, so they made the reply that only dead men would make: 'We will go with thee and die on Yimsha.'

'Then in Crom's name let us be gone,' grunted Conan, fidgeting with impatience as he started into the blue gulfs of the deepening twilight. 'My wolves were hours behind me, but we've lost a devilish lot of time.'

Kerim Shah backed his steed from between the black stallion and the cliff, sheathed his sword and cautiously turned the horse. Presently the band was filing up the path as swiftly as they dared. They came out upon the crest nearly a mile east of the spot where Khemsa had halted the Cimmerian and the Devi. The path they had traversed was a perilous one, even for hill-men, and for that reason Conan had avoided it that day when carrying Yasmina, though Kerim Shah, following him, had taken it supposing the Cimmerian had done likewise. Even Conan sighed with relief when the horses scrambled up over the last rim. They moved like phantom riders through an enchanted realm of shadows. The soft creak of leather, the clink of steel marked their passing, then again the dark mountain slopes lay naked and silent in the starlight.

8 Yasmina Knows Stark Terror

Yasmina had time but for one scream when she felt herself enveloped in that crimson whirl and torn from her protector with appalling force. She screamed once, and then she had no breath to scream. She was blinded, deafened, rendered mute and eventually senseless by the terrific rushing of the air about her. There was a dazed consciousness of dizzy height and numbing speed, a confused impression of natural sensations gone mad, and then vertigo and oblivion.

A vestige of these sensations clung to her as she recovered consciousness; so she cried out and clutched wildly as though to stay a headlong and involuntary flight. Her fingers closed on soft fabric, and a relieving sense of stability pervaded her. She took cognizance of her surroundings.

She was lying on a dais covered with black velvet. This dais stood in a great, dim room whose walls were hung with dusky tapestries across which crawled dragons reproduced with repellent realism. Floating shadows merely hinted at the lofty ceiling, and gloom that lent itself to illusion lurked in the corners. There seemed to be neither windows nor doors in the walls, or else they were concealed by the nighted tapestries. Where the dim light came from, Yasmina could not determine. The great room was a realm of mysteries, or shadows, and shadowy shapes in which she could not have sworn to observe movement, yet which invaded her mind with a dim and formless terror.

But her gaze fixed itself on a tangible object. On another, smaller dais of jet, a few feet away, a man sat cross-legged, gazing contemplatively at her. His long black velvet robe, embroidered with gold thread, fell loosely about him, masking his figure. His hands were folded in his sleeves. There was a velvet cap upon his head. His face was calm, placid, not unhandsome, his eyes lambent and slightly oblique. He did not move a muscle as he sat regarding her, nor did his expression alter when he saw she was conscious.

Yasmina felt fear crawl like a trickle of ice-water down her supple spine. She lifted herself on her elbows and stared apprehensively at the stranger.

'Who are you?' she demanded. Her voice sounded brittle and inadequate.

'I am the Master of Yimsha.' The tone was rich and resonant, like the mellow tones of a temple bell.

'Why did you bring me here?' she demanded.

'Were you not seeking me?'

'If you are one of the Black Seers – yes!' she answered recklessly, believing that he could read her thoughts anyway.

He laughed softly, and chills crawled up and down her spine again.

'You would turn the wild children of the hills against the Seers of Yimsha!' He smiled. 'I have read it in your mind, princess. Your weak, human mind, filled with petty dreams of hate and revenge.'

'You slew my brother!' A rising tide of anger was vying with her fear; her hands were clenched, her lithe body rigid. 'Why did you persecute him? He never harmed you. The priests say the Seers are above meddling in human affairs. Why did you destroy the king of Vendhya?'

'How can an ordinary human understand the motives of a Seer?' returned the Master calmly. 'My acolytes in the temples of Turan, who are the priests behind the priests of Tarim, urged me to bestir myself in behalf of Yezdigerd. For reasons of my own, I complied. How can I explain my mystic reasons to your puny intellect? You could not understand.'

'I understand this: that my brother died!' Tears of grief and rage shook in her voice. She rose upon her knees and stared at him with wide blazing eyes, as supple and dangerous in that moment as a shepanther.

'As Yezdigerd desired,' agreed the Master calmly. 'For a while it was my whim to further his ambitions.'

'Is Yezdigerd your vassal?' Yasmina tried to keep the timbre of her voice unaltered. She had felt her knee pressing something hard and symmetrical under a fold of velvet. Subtly she shifted her position, moving her hand under the fold.

'Is the dog that licks up the offal in the temple yard the vassal of the god?' returned the Master.

He did not seem to notice the actions she sought to dissemble. Concealed by the velvet, her fingers closed on what she knew was the golden hilt of a dagger. She bent her head to hide the light of triumph in her eyes.

'I am weary of Yezdigerd,' said the Master. 'I have turned to other amusements – ha!'

With a fierce cry Yasmina sprang like a jungle cat, stabbing murderously. Then she stumbled and slid to the floor, where she cowered, staring up at the man on the dais. He had not moved; his cryptic smile was unchanged. Tremblingly she lifted her hand and stared at it with dilated eyes. There was no dagger in her fingers; they grasped a stalk of golden lotus, the crushed blossoms drooping on the bruised stem.

She dropped it as if it had been a viper, and scrambled away from the proximity of her tormenter. She returned to her own dais, because that was at least more dignified for a queen than groveling on the floor at the feet of a sorcerer, and eyed him apprehensively, expecting reprisals.

But the Master made no move.

'All substance is one to him who holds the key of the cosmos,' he said cryptically. 'To an adept nothing is immutable. At will, steel blossoms bloom in unnamed gardens, or flower-swords flash in the moonlight.'

'You are a devil,' she sobbed.

'Not I!' he laughed. 'I was born on this planet, long ago. Once I was a common man, nor have I lost all human attributes in the numberless eons of my adeptship. A human steeped in the dark arts is greater than a devil. I am of human origin, but I rule demons. You have seen the Lords of the Black Circle – it would blast your soul to hear from what far realm I summoned them and from what doom I guard them with ensorcelled crystal and golden serpents.

'But only I can rule them. My foolish Khemsa thought to make himself great – poor fool, bursting material doors and hurtling himself and his mistress through the air from hill to hill! Yet if he had not been destroyed his power might have grown to rival mine.'

He laughed again. 'And you, poor, silly thing! Plotting to send a hairy hill chief to storm Yimsha! It was such a jest that I myself could have designed, had it occurred to me, that you should fall in his hands. And I read in your childish mind an intention to seduce by your feminine wiles to attempt your purpose, anyway.

'But for all your stupidity, you are a woman fair to look upon. It is my whim to keep you for my slave.'

The daughter of a thousand proud emperors gasped with shame and fury at the word.

'You dare not!'

His mocking laughter cut her like a whip across her naked shoulders.

'The king dares not trample a worm in the road? Little fool, do you not realize that your royal pride is no more than a straw blown on the wind? I, who have known the kisses of the queens of Hell! You have seen how I deal with a rebel!'

Cowed and awed, the girl crouched on the velvet-covered dais. The light grew dimmer and more phantom-like. The features of the Master became shadowy. His voice took on a newer tone of command.

'I will never yield to you!' Her voice trembled with fear but it carried a ring of resolution.

'You will yield,' he answered with horrible conviction. 'Fear and pain shall teach you. I will lash you with horror and agony to the last quivering ounce of your endurance, until you become as melted wax to be bent and molded in my hands as I desire. You shall know such discipline as no mortal woman ever knew, until my slightest command is to you as the unalterable will of the gods. And first, to humble your pride, you shall travel back through the lost ages, and view all the shapes that have been you. *Aie, yil la khosa!*'

At these words the shadowy room swam before Yasmina's affrighted gaze. The roots of her hair prickled her scalp, and her tongue clove to her palate. Somewhere a gong sounded a deep, ominous note. The dragons on the tapestries glowed like blue fire, and then faded out. The Master on his dais was but a shapeless shadow. The dim light gave way to soft, thick darkness, almost tangible, that pulsed with strange radiations. She could no longer see the Master. She could see nothing. She had a strange sensation that the walls and ceiling had withdrawn immensely from her.

Then somewhere in the darkness a glow began, like a firefly that rhythmically dimmed and quickened. It grew to a golden ball, and as it expanded its light grew more intense, flaming whitely. It burst suddenly, showering the darkness with white sparks that did not illumine the shadows. But like an impression left in the gloom, a faint luminance remained, and revealed a slender dusky shaft shooting up from the shadowy floor. Under the girl's dilated gaze it spread, took shape; stems and broad leaves appeared, and great black poisonous blossoms that towered above her as she cringed against the velvet. A subtle perfume pervaded the atmosphere. It was the dread figure of the black lotus that had grown up as she watched, as it grows in the haunted, forbidden jungles of Khitai.

The broad leaves were murmurous with evil life. The blossoms bent toward her like sentient things, nodding serpent-like on pliant stems. Etched against soft, impenetrable darkness it loomed over her, gigantic, blackly visible in some mad way. Her brain reeled with the drugging scent and she sought to crawl from the dais. Then she clung to it as it seemed to be pitching at an impossible slant. She cried out with terror and clung to the velvet, but she felt her fingers ruthlessly torn away. There was a sensation as of all sanity and stability crumbling and vanishing. She was a quivering atom of sentiency driven through a black, roaring, icy void by a thundering wind that threatened to extinguish her feeble flicker of animate life like a candle blown out in a storm.

Then there came a period of blind impulse and movement, when the atom that was she mingled and merged with myriad other atoms of spawning life in the yeasty morass of existence, molded by formative forces until she emerged again a conscious individual, whirling down an endless spiral of lives.

In a mist of terror she relived all her former existences, recognized and *was* again all the bodies that had carried her ego throughout the changing ages. She bruised her feet again over the long, weary road of life that stretched out behind her into the immemorial past. Back beyond the dimmest dawns of Time she crouched shuddering in primordial jungles, hunted by slavering beasts of prey. Skin-clad, she waded thigh-deep in rice swamps, battling with squawking water-fowl for the precious grains. She labored with the oxen to drag the pointed stick through the stubborn soil, and she crouched endlessly over looms in peasant huts.

She saw walled cities burst into flame, and fled screaming before the slayers. She reeled naked and bleeding over burning sands, dragged at the slaver's stirrup, and she knew the grip of hot, fierce hands on her writhing flesh, the shame and agony of brutal lust. She screamed under the bite of the lash, and moaned on the rack; mad with terror she fought against the hands that forced her head inexorably down on the bloody block.

She knew the agonies of childbirth, and the bitterness of love betrayed. She suffered all the woes and wrongs and brutalities that man has inflicted on woman throughout the eons; and she endured all the spite and malice of women for woman. And like the flick of a fiery whip throughout was the consciousness she retained of her Devi-ship. She was all the women she had ever been, yet in her knowing she was Yasmina. This consciousness was not lost in the throes of reincarnation. At one and the same time she was a naked slave-wench groveling under the whip, and the proud Devi of Vendhya. And she suffered not only as the slave-girl suffered, but as Yasmina, to whose pride the whip was like a white-hot brand.

Life merged into life in flying chaos, each with its burden of woe and shame and agony, until she dimly heard her own voice screaming unbearably, like one long-drawn cry of suffering echoing down the ages.

Then she awakened on the velvet-covered dais in the mystic room.

In a ghostly gray light she saw again the dais and the cryptic robed figure seated upon it. The hooded head was bent, the high shoulders faintly etched against the uncertain dimness. She could make out no details clearly, but the hood, where the velvet cap had been, stirred a formless uneasiness in her. As she stared, there stole over her a nameless fear that froze her tongue to her palate – a feeling that it was not the Master who sat so silently on that black dais.

Then the figure moved and rose upright, towering above her. It stooped over her and the long arms in their wide black sleeves bent about her. She fought against them in speechless fright, surprized by their lean hardness. The hooded head bent down toward her averted face. And she screamed, and screamed again in poignant fear and loathing. Bony arms gripped her lithe body, and from that hood looked forth a countenance of death and decay – features like rotting parchment on a moldering skull.

She screamed again, and then, as those champing, grinning jaws bent toward her lips, she lost consciousness . . .

9 The Castle of the Wizards

The sun had risen over the white Himelian peaks. At the foot of a long slope a group of horsemen halted and stared upward. High above them a stone tower poised on the pitch of the mountainside. Beyond and above that gleamed the walls of a greater keep, near the line where the snow began that capped Yimsha's pinnacle. There was a touch of unreality about the whole – purple slopes pitching up to that fantastic castle, toy-like with distance, and above it the white glistening peak shouldering the cold blue.

'We'll leave the horses here,' grunted Conan. 'That treacherous slope is safer for a man on foot. Besides, they're done.'

He swung down from the black stallion which stood with wide-braced legs and drooping head. They had pushed hard throughout the night, gnawing at scraps from saddle-bags, and pausing only to give the horses the rests they had to have.

'That first tower is held by the acolytes of the Black Seers,' said Conan. 'Or so men say; watch-dogs for their masters – lesser sorcerers. They won't sit sucking their thumbs as we climb this slope.'

Kerim Shah glanced up the mountain, then back the way they had come; they were already far up Yimsha's side, and a vast expanse of lesser peaks and crags spread out beneath them. Among these labyrinths the Turanian sought in vain for a movement of color that would betray men. Evidently the pursuing Afghulis had lost their chief's trail in the night.

'Let us go, then.' They tied the weary horses in a clump of tamarisk and without further comment turned up the slope. There was no cover. It was a naked incline, strewn with boulders not big enough to conceal a man. But they did conceal something else.

The party had not gone fifty steps when a snarling shape burst from behind a rock. It was one of the gaunt savage dogs that infested the hill villages, and its eyes glared redly, its jaws dripped foam. Conan was leading, but it did not attack him. It dashed past him and leaped at Kerim Shah. The Turanian leaped aside, and the great dog flung itself upon the Irakzai behind him. The man yelled and threw up his arm, which was torn by the brute's fangs as it bore him backward, and the next instant half a dozen tulwars were hacking at the beast. Yet not until it was literally dismembered did the hideous creature cease its efforts to seize and rend its attackers.

Kerim Shah bound up the wounded warrior's gashed arm, looked at him narrowly, and then turned away without a word. He rejoined Conan, and they renewed the climb in silence.

Presently Kerim Shah said: 'Strange to find a village dog in this place.'

'There's no offal here,' grunted Conan.

Both turned their heads to glance back at the wounded warrior toiling after them among his companions. Sweat glistened on his dark face and his lips were drawn back from his teeth in a grimace of pain. Then both looked again at the stone tower squatting above them.

A slumberous quiet lay over the uplands. The tower showed no sign of life, nor did the strange pyramidal structure beyond it. But the men who toiled upward went with the tenseness of men walking on the edge of a crater. Kerim Shah had unslung the powerful Turanian bow that killed at five hundred paces, and the Irakzai looked to their own lighter and less lethal bows.

But they were not within bow-shot of the tower when something shot down out of the sky without warning. It passed so close to Conan that he felt the wind of rushing wings, but it was an Irakzai who staggered and fell, blood jetting from a severed jugular. A hawk with wings like burnished steel shot up again, blood dripping from the scimitar-beak, to reel against the sky as Kerim Shah's bowstring twanged. It dropped like a plummet, but no man saw where it struck the earth.

Conan bent over the victim of the attack, but the man was already dead. No one spoke; useless to comment on the fact that never before had a hawk been known to swoop on a man. Red rage began to vie with fatalistic lethargy in the wild souls of the Irakzai. Hairy fingers nocked arrows and men glared vengefully at the tower whose very silence mocked them.

But the next attack came swiftly. They all saw it – a white puffball of smoke that tumbled over the tower-rim and came drifting and rolling down the slope toward them. Others followed it. They seemed harmless, mere woolly globes of cloudy foam, but Conan stepped aside to avoid contact with the first. Behind him one of the Irakzai reached out and thrust his sword into the unstable mass. Instantly a sharp report shook the mountainside. There was a burst of blinding flame, and then the puffball had vanished, and the too-curious warrior remained only a heap of charred and blackened bones. The crisped hand still gripped the ivory sword-hilt, but the blade was gone – melted and destroyed by that awful heat. Yet men standing almost within reach of the victim had not suffered except to be dazzled and half blinded by the sudden flare.

'Steel touches it off,' grunted Conan. 'Look out – here they come!'

The slope above them was almost covered by the billowing spheres. Kerim Shah bent his bow and sent a shaft into the mass, and those touched by the arrow burst like bubbles in spurting flame. His men followed his example and for the next few minutes it was as if a thunderstorm raged on the mountain slope, with bolts of lightning striking and bursting in showers of flame. When the barrage ceased, only a few arrows were left in the quivers of the archers.

They pushed on grimly, over soil charred and blackened, where the naked rock had in places been turned to lava by the explosion of those diabolical bombs.

Now they were almost within arrow-flight of the silent tower, and they spread their line, nerves taut, ready for any horror that might descend upon them.

On the tower appeared a single figure, lifting a ten-foot bronze horn. Its strident bellow roared out across the echoing slopes, like the blare of trumpets on Judgment Day. And it began to be fearfully answered. The ground trembled under the feet of the invaders, and rumblings and grindings welled up from the subterranean depths.

The Irakzai screamed, reeling like drunken men on the shuddering slope, and Conan, eyes glaring, charged recklessly up the incline, knife in hand, straight at the door that showed in the tower-wall. Above him the great horn roared and bellowed in brutish mockery. And then Kerim Shah drew a shaft to his ear and loosed.

Only a Turanian could have made that shot. The bellowing of the horn ceased suddenly, and a high, thin scream shrilled in its place. The green-robed figure on the tower staggered, clutching at the long shaft which quivered in its bosom, and then pitched across the parapet. The great horn tumbled upon the battlement and hung precariously, and another robed figure rushed to seize it, shrieking in horror. Again the Turanian bow twanged, and again it was answered by a death-howl. The second acolyte, in falling, struck the horn with his elbow and knocked it clattering over the parapet to shatter on the rocks far below.

At such headlong speed had Conan covered the ground that before the clattering echoes of that fall had died away, he was hacking at the door. Warned by his savage instinct, he gave back suddenly as a tide of molten lead splashed down from above. But the next instant he was back again, attacking the panels with redoubled fury. He was galvanized by the fact that his enemies had resorted to earthly weapons. The sorcery of the acolytes was limited. Their necromantic resources might well be exhausted.

Kerim Shah was hurrying up the slope, his hill-men behind him in a straggling crescent. They loosed as they ran, their arrows splintering against the walls or arching over the parapet.

The heavy teak portal gave way beneath the Cimmerian's assault, and he peered inside warily, expecting anything. He was looking into a circular chamber from which a stair wound upward. On the opposite side of the chamber a door gaped open, revealing the outer slope – and the backs of half a dozen green-robed figures in full retreat.

Conan yelled, took a step into the tower, and then native caution jerked him back, just as a great block of stone fell crashing to the floor where his foot had been an instant before. Shouting to his followers, he raced around the tower.

The acolytes had evacuated their first line of defence. As Conan rounded the tower he saw their green robes twinkling up the mountain ahead of him. He gave chase, panting with earnest blood-lust, and behind him Kerim Shah and the Irakzai came pelting, the latter yelling like wolves at the flight of their enemies, their fatalism momentarily submerged by temporary triumph.

The tower stood on the lower edge of a narrow plateau whose upward slant was barely perceptible. A few hundred yards away this plateau ended abruptly in a chasm which had been invisible farther down the mountain. Into this chasm the acolytes apparently leaped without checking their speed. Their pursuers saw the green robes flutter and disappear over the edge.

A few moments later they themselves were standing on the brink of the mighty moat that cut them off from the castle of the Black Seers.

It was a sheer-walled ravine that extended in either direction as far as they could see, apparently girdling the mountain, some four hundred yards in width and five hundred feet deep. And in it, from rim to rim, a strange, translucent mist sparkled and shimmered.

Looking down, Conan grunted. Far below him, moving across the glimmering floor, which shone like burnished silver, he saw the forms of the green-robed acolytes. Their outline was wavering and indistinct, like figures seen under deep water. They walked in single file, moving toward the opposite wall.

Kerim Shah nocked an arrow and sent it singing downward. But when it struck the mist that filled the chasm it seemed to lose momentum and direction, wandering widely from its course.

'If they went down, so can we!' grunted Conan, while Kerim Shah stared after his shaft in amazement. 'I saw them last at this spot—'

Squinting down he saw something shining like a golden thread across the canyon floor far below. The acolytes seemed to be following this thread, and there suddenly came to him Khemsa's cryptic words – 'Follow the golden vein!' On the brink, under his very hand as he crouched, he found it, a thin vein of sparkling gold running from an outcropping of ore to the edge and down across the silvery floor. And he found something else, which had before been invisible to him because of the peculiar refraction of the light. The gold vein followed a narrow ramp which slanted down into the ravine, fitted with niches for hand and foot hold.

'Here's where they went down,' he grunted to Kerim Shah. 'They're no adepts, to waft themselves through the air! We'll follow them—'

It was at that instant that the man who had been bitten by the mad dog cried out horribly and leaped at Kerim Shah, foaming and gnashing his teeth. The Turanian, quick as a cat on his feet, sprang aside and the madman pitched head-first over the brink. The others rushed to the edge and glared after him in amazement. The maniac did not fall plummet-like. He floated slowly down through the rosy haze like a man sinking in deep water. His limbs moved like a man trying to swim, and his features were purple and convulsed beyond the contortions of his madness. Far down at last on the shining floor his body settled and lay still.

'There's death in that chasm,' muttered Kerim Shah, drawing back from the rosy mist that shimmered almost at his feet. 'What now, Conan?'

'On!' answered the Cimmerian grimly. 'Those acolytes are human; if the mist doesn't kill them, it won't kill me.'

He hitched his belt, and his hands touched the girdle Khemsa had given him; he scowled, then smiled bleakly. He had forgotten that girdle; yet thrice had death passed him by to strike another victim.

The acolytes had reached the farther wall and were moving up it like great green flies. Letting himself upon the ramp, he descended warily. The rosy cloud lapped about his ankles, ascending as he lowered himself. It reached his knees, his thighs, his waist, his arm-pits. He felt as one feels a thick heavy fog on a damp night. With it lapping about his chin he hesitated, and then ducked under. Instantly his breath ceased; all air was shut off from him and he felt his ribs caving in on his vitals. With a frantic effort he heaved himself up, fighting for life. His head rose above the surface and he drank air in great gulps.

Kerim Shah leaned down toward him, spoke to him, but Conan neither heard nor heeded. Stubbornly, his mind fixed on what the dying Khemsa had told him, the Cimmerian groped for the gold vein, and found that he had moved off it in his descent. Several series of hand-holds were niched in the ramp. Placing himself directly over the thread, he began climbing down once more. The rosy mist rose about him, engulfed him. Now his head was under, but he was still drinking pure air. Above him he saw his companions staring down at him, their features blurred by the haze that shimmered over his head. He gestured for them to follow, and went down swiftly, without waiting to see whether they complied or not.

Kerim Shah sheathed his sword without comment and followed, and the Irakzai, more fearful of being left alone than of the terrors that might lurk below, scrambled after him. Each man clung to the golden thread as they saw the Cimmerian do.

Down the slanting ramp they went to the ravine floor and moved out across the shining level, treading the gold vein like rope-walkers. It was as if they walked along an invisible tunnel through which air circulated freely. They felt death pressing in on them above and on either hand, but it did not touch them.

The vein crawled up a similar ramp on the other wall up which the acolytes had disappeared, and up it they went with taut nerves, not knowing what might be waiting for them among the jutting spurs of rock that fanged the lip of the precipice.

It was the green-robed acolytes who awaited them, with knives in their hands. Perhaps they had reached the limits to which they could retreat. Perhaps the Stygian girdle about Conan's waist could have told why their necromantic spells had proven so weak and so quickly exhausted. Perhaps it was knowledge of death decreed for failure that sent them leaping from among the rocks, eyes glaring and knives glittering, resorting in their desperation to material weapons.

There among the rocky fangs on the precipice lip was no war of wizard craft. It was a whirl of blades, where real steel bit and real blood spurted, where sinewy arms dealt forthright blows that severed quivering flesh, and men went down to be trodden under foot as the fight raged over them.

One of the Irakzai bled to death among the rocks, but the acolytes were down – slashed and hacked asunder or hurled over the edge to float sluggishly down to the silver floor that shone so far below.

Then the conquerors shook blood and sweat from their eyes, and looked at one another. Conan and Kerim Shah still stood upright, and four of the Irakzai.

They stood among the rocky teeth that serrated the precipice brink, and from that spot a path wound up a gentle slope to a broad stair, consisting of half a dozen steps, a hundred feet across, cut out of a green jade-like substance. They led up to a broad stage or roofless gallery of the same polished stone, and above it rose, tier upon tier, the castle of the Black Seers. It seemed to have been carved out of the sheer stone of the mountain. The architecture was faultless, but unadorned. The many casements were barred and masked with curtains within. There was no sign of life, friendly or hostile.

They went up the path in silence, and warily as men treading the lair of a serpent. The Irakzai were dumb, like men marching to a certain doom. Even Kerim Shah was silent. Only Conan seemed unaware what a monstrous dislocating and uprooting of accepted thought and action their invasion constituted, what an unprecedented violation of tradition. He was not of the East; and he came of a breed who fought devils and wizards as promptly and matter-of-factly as they battled human foes.

He strode up the shining stairs and across the wide green gallery straight toward the great golden-bound teak door that opened upon it. He cast but a single glance upward at the higher tiers of the great pyramidal structure towering above him. He reached a hand for the bronze prong that jutted like a handle from the door – then checked himself, grinning hardly. The handle was made in the shape of a serpent, head lifted on arched neck; and Conan had a suspicion that that metal head would come to grisly life under his hand.

He struck it from the door with one blow, and its bronze clink on the glassy floor did not lessen his caution. He flipped it aside with his knife-point, and again turned to the door. Utter silence reigned over the towers. Far below them the mountain slopes fell away into a purple haze of distance. The sun glittered on snow-clad peaks on either hand. High above, a vulture hung like a black dot in the cold blue of the sky. But for it, the men before the gold-bound door were the only evidence of life, tiny figures on a green jade gallery poised on the dizzy height, with that fantastic pile of stone towering above them.

A sharp wind off the snow slashed them, whipping their tatters about. Conan's long knife splintering through the teak panels roused the startled echoes. Again and again he struck, hewing through polished wood and metal bands alike. Through the sundered ruins he glared into the interior, alert and suspicious as a wolf. He saw a broad chamber, the polished stone walls untapestried, the mosaic floor uncarpeted. Square, polished ebon stools and a stone dais formed the only furnishings. The room was empty of human life. Another door showed in the opposite wall.

'Leave a man on guard outside,' grunted Conan. 'I'm going in.'

Kerim Shah designated a warrior for that duty, and the man fell back toward the middle of the gallery, bow in hand. Conan strode into the castle, followed by the Turanian and the three remaining Irakzai. The one outside spat, grumbled in his beard, and started suddenly as a low mocking laugh reached his ears.

He lifted his head and saw, on the tier above him, a tall, black-robed figure, naked head nodding slightly as he stared down. His whole attitude suggested mockery and malignity. Quick as a flash the Irakzai bent his bow and loosed, and the arrow streaked upward to strike full in the black-robed breast. The mocking smile did not alter. The Seer plucked out the missile and threw it back at the bowman, not as a weapon is hurled, but with a contemptuous gesture. The Irakzai dodged, instinctively throwing up his arm. His fingers closed on the revolving shaft.

Then he shrieked. In his hand the wooden shaft suddenly *writhed*. Its rigid outline became pliant, melting in his grasp. He tried to throw it from him, but it was too late. He held a living serpent in his naked hand, and already it had coiled about his wrist and its wicked wedge-shaped head darted at his muscular arm. He screamed again and his eyes became distended, his features purple. He went to his knees shaken by an awful convulsion, and then lay still.

The men inside had wheeled at his first cry. Conan took a swift stride toward the open doorway, and then halted short, baffled. To the men behind him it seemed that he strained against empty air. But though he could see nothing, there was a slick, smooth, hard surface under his hands, and he knew that a sheet of crystal had been let down in the doorway. Through it he saw the Irakzai lying motionless on the glassy gallery, an ordinary arrow sticking in his arm.

Conan lifted his knife and smote, and the watchers were dumbfounded to see his blow checked apparently in midair, with the loud clang of steel that meets an unyielding substance. He wasted no more effort. He knew that not even the legendary tulwar of Amir Khurum could shatter that invisible curtain.

In a few words he explained the matter to Kerim Shah, and the Turanian shrugged his shoulders. 'Well, if our exit is barred, we must find another. In the meanwhile our way lies forward, does it not?'

With a grunt the Cimmerian turned and strode across the chamber to the opposite door, with a feeling of treading on the threshold of doom. As he lifted his knife to shatter the door, it swung silently open as if of its own accord. He strode into the great hall, flanked with tall glassy columns. A hundred feet from the door began the broad jade-green steps of a stair that tapered toward the top like the side of a pyramid. What lay beyond that stair he could not tell. But between him and its shimmering foot stood a curious altar of gleaming black jade. Four great golden serpents twined their tails about this altar and reared their wedge-shaped heads in the air, facing the four quarters of the compass like the enchanted guardians of a fabled treasure. But on the altar, between the arching necks, stood only a crystal globe filled with a cloudy smoke-like substance, in which floated four golden pomegranates.

The sight stirred some dim recollection in his mind; then Conan heeded the altar no longer, for on the lower steps of the stair stood four black-robed figures. He had not seen them come. They were simply there, tall, gaunt, their vulture-heads nodding in unison, their feet and hands hidden by their flowing garments.

One lifted his arm and the sleeve fell away revealing his hand – and it was not a hand at all. Conan halted in mid-stride, compelled against his will. He had encountered a force differing subtly from Khemsa's mesmerism, and he could not advance, though he felt it in his power to retreat if he wished. His companions had likewise halted, and they seemed even more helpless than he, unable to move in either direction.

The seer whose arm was lifted beckoned to one of the Irakzai, and the man moved toward him like one in a trance, eyes staring and fixed, blade hanging in limp fingers. As he pushed past Conan, the Cimmerian threw an arm across his breast to arrest him. Conan was so much stronger than the Irakzai that in ordinary circumstances he could have broken his spine between his hands. But now the muscular arm was brushed aside like straw and the Irakzai moved toward the stair, treading jerkily and mechanically. He reached the steps and knelt stiffly, proffering his blade and bending his head. The Seer took the sword. It flashed as he swung it up and down. The Irakzai's head tumbled from his shoulders and thudded heavily on the black marble floor. An arch of blood jetted from the severed arteries and the body slumped over and lay with arms spread wide.

Again a malformed hand lifted and beckoned, and another Irakzai stumbled stiffly to his doom. The ghastly drama was re-enacted and another headless form lay beside the first.

As the third tribesman clumped his way past Conan to his death, the Cimmerian, his veins bulging in his temples with his efforts to break past the unseen barrier that held him, was suddenly aware of allied forces, unseen, but waking into life about him. This realization came without warning, but so powerfully that he could not doubt his instinct. His left hand slid involuntarily under his Bakhariot belt and closed on the Stygian girdle. And as he gripped it he felt new strength flood his numbed limbs; the will to live was a pulsing white-hot fire, matched by the intensity of his burning rage.

The third Irakzai was a decapitated corpse, and the hideous finger was lifting again when Conan felt the bursting of the invisible barrier. A fierce, involuntary cry burst from his lips as he leaped with the explosive suddenness of pent-up ferocity. His left hand gripped the sorcerer's girdle as a drowning man grips a floating log, and the long knife was a sheen of light in his right. The men on the steps did not move. They watched calmly, cynically; if they felt surprise they did not show it. Conan did not allow himself to think what might chance when he came within knife-reach of them. His blood was pounding in his temples, a mist of crimson swam before his sight. He was afire with the urge to kill – to drive his knife deep into flesh and bone, and twist the blade in blood and entrails.

Another dozen strides would carry him to the steps where the sneering demons stood. He drew his breath deep, his fury rising redly as his charge gathered momentum. He was hurtling past the altar with its golden serpents when like a levin-flash there shot across his mind again as vividly as if spoken in his external ear, the cryptic words of Khemsa: *'Break the crystal ball!'*

His reaction was almost without his own volition. Execution followed impulse so spontaneously that the greatest sorcerer of the age would not have had time to read his mind and prevent his action. Wheeling like a cat from his headlong charge, he brought his knife crashing down upon the crystal. Instantly the air vibrated with a peal of terror, whether from the stairs, the altar, or the crystal itself he could not tell. Hisses filled his ears as the golden serpents, suddenly vibrant with hideous life, writhed and smote at him. But he was fired to the speed of a maddened tiger. A whirl of steel sheared through the hideous trunks that waved toward him, and he smote the crystal sphere again and yet again. And the globe burst with a noise like a thunderclap, raining fiery shards on the black marble, and the gold pomegranates, as if released from captivity, shot upward toward the lofty roof and were gone.

A mad screaming, bestial and ghastly, was echoing through the great hall. On the steps writhed four black-robed figures, twisting in convulsions, froth dripping from their livid mouths. Then with one frenzied crescendo of inhuman ululation they stiffened and lay still, and Conan knew that they were dead. He stared down at the altar and the crystal shards. Four headless golden serpents still coiled about the altar, but no alien life now animated the dully gleaming metal.

Kerim Shah was rising slowly from his knees, whither he had been dashed by some unseen force. He shook his head to clear the ringing from his ears.

'Did you hear that crash when you struck? It was as if a thousand crystal panels shattered all over the castle as that globe burst. Were the souls of the wizards imprisoned in those golden balls? – Ha!'

Conan wheeled as Kerim Shah drew his sword and pointed.

Another figure stood at the head of the stair. His robe, too, was black, but of richly embroidered velvet, and there was a velvet cap on his head. His face was calm, and not unhandsome.

'Who the devil are you?' demanded Conan, staring up at him, knife in hand.

'I am the Master of Yimsha!' His voice was like the chime of a temple bell, but a note of cruel mirth ran through it.

'Where is Yasmina?' demanded Kerim Shah.

The Master laughed down at him.

'What is that to you, dead man? Have you so quickly forgotten my strength, once lent to you, that you come armed against me, you poor fool? I think I will take your heart, Kerim Shah!'

He held out his hand as if to receive something, and the Turanian cried out sharply like a man in mortal agony. He reeled drunkenly, and then, with a splintering of bones, a rending of flesh and muscle and a snapping of mail-links, his breast burst outward with a shower of blood, and through the ghastly aperture something red and dripping shot through the air into the Master's outstretched hand, as a bit of steel leaps to the magnet. The Turanian slumped to the floor and lay motionless, and the Master laughed and hurled the object to fall before Conan's feet – a still-quivering human heart.

With a roar and a curse Conan charged the stair. From Khemsa's girdle he felt strength and deathless hate flow into him to combat the terrible emanation of power that met him on the steps. The air filled with a shimmering steely haze through which he plunged like a swimmer, head lowered, left arm bent about his face, knife gripped low in his right hand. His half-blinded eyes, glaring over the crook of his elbow, made out the hated shape of the Seer before and above him, the outline wavering as a reflection wavers in disturbed water.

He was racked and torn by forces beyond his comprehension, but he felt a driving power outside and beyond his own lifting him inexorably upward and onward, despite the wizard's strength and his own agony.

Now he had reached the head of the stairs, and the Master's face floated in the steely haze before him, and a strange fear shadowed the inscrutable eyes. Conan waded through the mist as through a surf, and his knife lunged upward like a live thing. The keen point ripped the Master's robe as he sprang back with a low cry. Then before Conan's gaze, the wizard vanished – simply disappeared like a burst bubble, and something long and undulating darted up one of the smaller stairs that led up to left and right from the landing.

Conan charged after it, up the left-hand stair, uncertain as to just what he had seen whip up those steps, but in a berserk mood that drowned the nausea and horror whispering at the back of his consciousness.

He plunged out into a broad corridor whose uncarpeted floor and untapestried walls were of polished jade, and something long and swift whisked down the corridor ahead of him, and into a curtained door. From within the chamber rose a scream of urgent terror. The sound lent wings to Conan's flying feet and he hurtled through the curtains and headlong into the chamber within.

A frightful scene met his glare. Yasmina cowered on the farther edge of a velvet-covered dais, screaming her loathing and horror, an arm lifted as if to ward off attack, while before her swayed the hideous head of a giant serpent, shining neck arching up from dark-gleaming coils. With a choked cry Conan threw his knife.

Instantly the monster whirled and was upon him like the rush of wind through tall grass. The long knife quivered in its neck, point and a foot of blade showing on one side, and the hilt and a hand's-breadth of steel on the other, but it only seemed to madden the giant reptile. The great head towered above the man who faced it, and then darted down, the venom-dripping jaws gaping wide. But Conan had plucked a dagger from his girdle and he stabbed upward as the head dipped down. The point tore through the lower jaw and transfixed the upper, pinning them together. The next instant the great trunk had looped itself about the Cimmerian as the snake, unable to use its fangs, employed its remaining form of attack.

Conan's left arm was pinioned among the bone-crushing folds, but his right was free. Bracing his feet to keep upright, he stretched forth his hand, gripped the hilt of the long knife jutting from the serpent's neck, and tore it free in a shower of blood. As if divining his purpose with more than bestial intelligence, the snake writhed and knotted, seeking to cast its loops about his right arm. But with the speed of light the long knife rose and fell, shearing halfway through the reptile's giant trunk.

Before he could strike again, the great pliant loops fell from him and the monster dragged itself across the floor, gushing blood from its ghastly wounds. Conan sprang after it, knife lifted, but his vicious swipe cut empty air as the serpent writhed away from him and struck its blunt nose against a paneled screen of sandalwood. One of the panels gave inward and the long, bleeding barrel whipped through it and was gone.

Conan instantly attacked the screen. A few blows rent it apart and he glared into the dim alcove beyond. No horrific shape coiled there; there was blood on the marble floor, and bloody tracks led to a cryptic arched door. Those tracks were of a man's bare feet . . .

'*Conan!*' He wheeled back into the chamber just in time to catch the Devi of Vendhya in his arms as she rushed across the room and threw herself upon him, catching him about the neck with a frantic clasp, half hysterical with terror and gratitude and relief.

His wild blood had been stirred to its uttermost by all that had passed. He caught her to him in a grasp that would have made her wince at another time, and crushed her lips with his. She made no resistance; the Devi was drowned in the elemental woman. She closed her eyes and drank in his fierce, hot, lawless kisses with all the abandon of passionate thirst. She was panting with his violence when he ceased for breath, and glared down at her lying limp in his mighty arms.

'I knew you'd come for me,' she murmured. 'You would not leave me in this den of devils.'

At her words recollection of their environment came to him suddenly. He lifted his head and listened intently. Silence reigned over the castle of Yimsha, but it was a silence impregnated with menace. Peril crouched in every corner, leered invisibly from every hanging.

'We'd better go while we can,' he muttered. 'Those cuts were enough to kill any common beast – or *man* – but a wizard has a dozen lives. Wound one, and he writhes away like a crippled snake to soak up fresh venom from some source of sorcery.'

He picked up the girl and carrying her in his arms like a child, he strode out into the gleaming jade corridor and down the stairs, nerves tautly alert for any sign or sound.

'I met the Master,' she whispered, clinging to him and shuddering. 'He worked his spells on me to break my will. The most awful thing was a moldering corpse which seized me in its arms – I fainted then and lay as one dead, I do not know how long. Shortly after I regained consciousness I heard sounds of strife below, and cries, and then that snake came slithering through the curtains – ah!' She shook at the memory of that horror. 'I knew somehow that it was not an illusion, but a real serpent that sought my life.'

'It was not a shadow, at least,' answered Conan cryptically. 'He knew he was beaten, and chose to slay you rather than let you be rescued.'

'What do you mean, *he?*' she asked uneasily, and then shrank against him, crying out, and forgetting her question. She had seen the corpses at the foot of the stairs. Those of the Seers were not good to look at; as they lay twisted and contorted, their hands and feet were exposed to view, and at the sight Yasmina went livid and hid her face against Conan's powerful shoulder.

10 Yasmina and Conan

Conan passed through the hall quickly enough, traversed the outer chamber and approached the door that led upon the gallery. Then he saw the floor sprinkled with tiny, glittering shards. The crystal sheet that had covered the doorway had been shivered to bits, and he remembered the crash that had accompanied the shattering of the crystal globe. He believed that every piece of crystal in the castle had broken at that instant, and some dim instinct or memory of esoteric lore vaguely suggested the truth of the monstrous connection between the Lords of the Black Circle and the golden pomegranates. He felt the short hair bristle chilly at the back of his neck and put the matter hastily out of his mind.

He breathed a deep sigh of relief as he stepped out upon the green jade gallery. There was still the gorge to cross, but at least he could see the white peaks glistening in the sun, and the long slopes falling away into the distant blue hazes.

The Irakzai lay where he had fallen, an ugly blotch on the glassy smoothness. As Conan strode down the winding path, he was surprised to note the position of the sun. It had not yet passed its zenith; and yet it seemed to him that hours had passed since he plunged into the castle of the Black Seers.

He felt an urge to hasten, not a mere blind panic, but an instinct of peril growing behind his back. He said nothing to Yasmina, and she seemed content to nestle her dark head against his arching breast and find security in the clasp of his iron arms. He paused an instant on the brink of the chasm, frowning down. The haze which danced in the gorge was no longer rose-hued and sparkling. It was smoky, dim, ghostly, like the life-tide that flickered thinly in a wounded man. The thought came vaguely to Conan that the spells of magicians were more closely bound to their personal beings than were the actions of common men to the actors.

But far below, the floor shone like tarnished silver, and the gold thread sparkled undimmed. Conan shifted Yasmina across his shoulder, where she lay docilely, and began the descent. Hurriedly he descended the ramp, and hurriedly he fled across the echoing floor. He had a conviction that they were racing with time, that their chances of survival depended upon crossing that gorge of horrors before the wounded Master of the castle should regain enough power to loose some other doom upon them.

When he toiled up the farther ramp and came out upon the crest, he breathed a gusty sigh of relief and stood Yasmina upon her feet.

'You walk from here,' he told her; 'it's downhill all the way.'

She stole a glance at the gleaming pyramid across the chasm; it reared up against the snowy slope like the citadel of silence and immemorial evil.

'Are you a magician, that you have conquered the Black Seers of Yimsha, Conan of Ghor?' she asked, as they went down the path, with his heavy arm about her supple waist.

'It was a girdle Khemsa gave me before he died,' Conan answered. 'Yes, I found him on the trail. It is a curious one, which I'll show you when I have time. Against some spells it was weak, but against others it was strong, and a good knife is always a hearty incantation.'

'But if the girdle aided you in conquering the Master,' she argued, 'why did it not aid Khemsa?'

He shook his head. 'Who knows? But Khemsa had been the Master's slave; perhaps that weakened its magic. He had no hold on me as he had on Khemsa. Yet I can't say that I conquered him. He retreated, but I have a feeling that we haven't seen the last of him. I want to put as many miles between us and his lair as we can.'

He was further relieved to find horses tethered among the tamarisks as he had left them. He loosed them swiftly and mounted the black stallion, swinging the girl up before him. The others followed, freshened by their rest.

'And what now?' she asked. 'To Afghulistan?'

'Not just now!' He grinned hardly. 'Somebody – maybe the governor – killed my seven headmen. My idiotic followers think I had something to do with it, and unless I am able to convince them otherwise, they'll hunt me like a wounded jackal.'

'Then what of me? If the headmen are dead, I am useless to you as a hostage. Will you slay me, to avenge them?'

He looked down at her, with eyes fiercely aglow, and laughed at the suggestion.

'Then let us ride to the border,' she said. 'You'll be safe from the Afghulis there—'

'Yes, on a Vendhyan gibbet.'

'I am Queen of Vendhya,' she reminded him with a touch of her old imperiousness. 'You have saved my life. You shall be rewarded.'

She did not intend it as it sounded, but he growled in his throat, ill pleased.

'Keep your bounty for your city-bred dogs, princess! If you're a queen of the plains, I'm a chief of the hills, and not one foot toward the border will I take you!'

'But you would be safe—' she began bewilderedly.

'And you'd be the Devi again,' he broke in. 'No, girl; I prefer you as you are now – a woman of flesh and blood, riding on my saddle-bow.'

'But you can't *keep* me!' she cried. 'You can't—'

'Watch and see!' he advised grimly.

'But I will pay you a vast ransom—'

'Devil take your ransom!' he answered roughly, his arms hardening about her supple figure. 'The kingdom of Vendhya could give me nothing I desire half so much as I desire you. I took you at the risk of my neck; if your courtiers want you back, let them come up the Zhaibar and fight for you.'

'But you have no followers now!' she protested. 'You are hunted! How can you preserve your own life, much less mine?'

'I still have friends in the hills,' he answered. 'There is a chief of the Khurakzai who will keep you safely while I bicker with the Afghulis. If they will have none of me, by Crom! I will ride northward with you to the steppes of the *kozaki*. I was a hetman among the Free Companions before I rode southward. I'll make you a queen on the Zaporoska River!'

'But I can not!' she objected. 'You must not hold me—'

'If the idea's so repulsive,' he demanded, 'why did you yield your lips to me so willingly?'

'Even a queen is human,' she answered, coloring. 'But because I am a queen, I must consider my kingdom. Do not carry me away into some foreign country. Come back to Vendhya with me!'

'Would you make me your king?' he asked sardonically.

'Well, there are customs—' she stammered, and he interrupted her with a hard laugh.

'Yes, civilized customs that won't let you do as you wish. You'll marry some withered old king of the plains, and I can go my way with only the memory of a few kisses snatched from your lips. Ha!'

'But I must return to my kingdom!' she repeated helplessly.

'Why?' he demanded angrily. 'To chafe your rump on gold thrones, and listen to the plaudits of smirking, velvet-skirted fools? Where is the gain? Listen: I was born in the Cimmerian hills where the people are all barbarians. I have been a mercenary soldier, a corsair, a *kozak*, and a hundred other things. What king has roamed the countries, fought the battles, loved the women, and won the plunder that I have?

'I came into Ghulistan to raise a horde and plunder the kingdoms to the south – your own among them. Being chief of the Afghulis was only a start. If I can conciliate them, I'll have a dozen tribes following me within a year. But if I can't I'll ride back to the steppes and loot the Turanian borders with the *kozaki*. And you'll go with me. To the devil with your kingdom; they fended for themselves before you were born.'

She lay in his arms looking up at him, and she felt a tug at her spirit, a lawless, reckless urge that matched his own and was by it called into being. But a thousand generations of sovereignship rode heavy upon her.

'I can't! I can't!' she repeated helplessly.

'You haven't any choice,' he assured her. 'You – what the devil!'

They had left Yimsha some miles behind them, and were riding along a high ridge that separated two deep valleys. They had just topped a steep crest where they could gaze down into the valley on their right hand. And there was a running fight in progress. A strong wind was blowing away from them, carrying the sound from their ears, but even so the clashing of steel and thunder of hoofs welled up from far below.

They saw the glint of the sun on lance-tip and spired helmet. Three thousand mailed horsemen were driving before them a ragged band of turbaned riders, who fled snarling and striking like fleeing wolves.

'Turanians,' muttered Conan. 'Squadrons from Secunderam. What the devil are they doing here?'

'Who are the men they pursue?' asked Yasmina. 'And why do they fall back so stubbornly? They can not stand against such odds.'

'Five hundred of my mad Afghulis,' he growled, scowling down into the vale. 'They're in a trap, and they know it.'

The valley was indeed a cul-de-sac at that end. It narrowed to a high-walled gorge, opening out further into a round bowl, completely rimmed with lofty, unscalable walls.

The turbaned riders were being forced into this gorge, because there was nowhere else for them to go, and they went reluctantly, in a shower of arrows and a whirl of swords. The helmeted riders harried them, but did not press in too rashly. They knew the desperate fury of the hill tribes, and they knew too that they had their prey in a trap from which there was no escape. They had recognized the hill-men as Afghulis, and they wished to hem them in and force a surrender. They needed hostages for the purpose they had in mind.

Their emir was a man of decision and initiative. When he reached the Gurashah valley, and found neither guides nor emissary waiting for him, he pushed on, trusting to his own knowledge of the country. All the way from Secunderam there had been fighting, and tribesmen were licking their wounds in many a crag-perched village. He knew there was a good chance that neither he nor any of his helmeted spearmen would ever ride through the gates of Secunderam again, for the tribes would all be up behind him now, but he was determined to carry out his orders – which were to take Yasmina Devi from the Afghulis at all costs, and to bring her captive to Secunderam, or if confronted by impossibility, to strike off her head before he himself died.

Of all this, of course, the watchers on the ridge were not aware. But Conan fidgeted with nervousness.

'Why the devil did they get themselves trapped?' he demanded of the universe at large. 'I know what they're doing in these parts – they were hunting me, the dogs! Poking into every valley – and found themselves penned in before they knew it. The poor fools! They're making a stand in the gorge, but they can't hold out for long. When the Turanians have pushed them back into the bowl, they'll slaughter them at their leisure.'

The din welling up from below increased in volume and intensity. In the strait of the narrow gut, the Afghulis, fighting desperately, were for the time holding their own against the mailed riders, who could not throw their whole weight against them.

Conan scowled darkly, moved restlessly, fingering his hilt, and finally spoke bluntly: 'Devi, I must go down to them. I'll find a place for you to hide until I come back to you. You spoke of your kingdom – well, I don't pretend to look on those hairy devils as my children, but after all, such as they are, they're my henchmen. A chief should never desert his followers, even if they desert him first. They think they were right in kicking me out – hell, I won't be cast off! I'm still chief of the Afghulis, and I'll prove it! I can climb down on foot into the gorge.'

'But what of me?' she queried. 'You carried me away forcibly from *my* people; now will you leave me to die in the hills alone while you go down and sacrifice yourself uselessly?'

His veins swelled with the conflict of his emotions.

'That's right,' he muttered helplessly. 'Crom knows what I *can* do.'

She turned her head slightly, a curious expression dawning on her beautiful face. Then:

'Listen!' she cried. 'Listen!'

A distant fanfare of trumpets was borne faintly to their ears. They stared into the deep valley on the left, and caught a glint of steel on the farther side. A long line of lances and polished helmets moved along the vale, gleaming in the sunlight.

'The riders of Vendhya!' she cried exultingly.

'There are thousands of them!' muttered Conan. 'It has been long since a Kshatriya host has ridden this far into the hills.'

'They are searching for me!' she exclaimed. 'Give me your horse! I will ride to my warriors! The ridge is not so precipitous on the left, and I can reach the valley floor. I will lead my horsemen into the valley at the upper end and fall upon the Turanians! We will crush them in the vise! Quick, Conan! Will you sacrifice your men to your own desire?'

The burning hunger of the steppes and the wintry forests glared out of his eyes, but he shook his head and swung off the stallion, placing the reins in her hands.

'You win!' he grunted. 'Ride like the devil!'

She wheeled away down the left-hand slope and he ran swiftly along the ridge until he reached the long ragged cleft that was the defile in which the fight raged. Down the rugged wall he scrambled like an ape, clinging to projections and crevices, to fall at last, feet first, into the mêlée that raged in the mouth of the gorge. Blades were whickering and clanging about him, horses rearing and stamping, helmet plumes nodding among turbans that were stained crimson.

As he hit, he yelled like a wolf, caught a gold-worked rein, and dodging the sweep of a scimitar, drove his long knife upward through the rider's vitals. In another instant he was in the saddle, yelling ferocious orders to the Afghulis. They stared at him stupidly for an instant; then as they saw the havoc his steel was wreaking among their enemies, they fell to their work again, accepting him without comment. In that inferno of licking blades and spurting blood there was no time to ask or answer questions.

The riders in their spired helmets and gold-worked hauberks swarmed about the gorge mouth, thrusting and slashing, and the narrow defile was packed and jammed with horses and men, the warriors crushed breast to breast, stabbing with shortened blades, slashing murderously when there was an instant's room to swing a sword. When a man went down he did not get up from beneath the stamping, swirling hoofs. Weight and sheer strength counted heavily there, and the chief of the Afghulis did the work of ten. At such times accustomed habits sway men strongly, and the warriors, who were used to seeing Conan in their vanguard, were heartened mightily, despite their distrust of him.

But superior numbers counted too. The pressure of the men behind forced the horsemen of Turan deeper and deeper into the gorge, in the teeth of the flickering tulwars. Foot by foot the Afghulis were shoved back, leaving the defile-floor carpeted with dead, on which the riders trampled. As he hacked and smote like a man possessed, Conan had time for some chilling doubts – would Yasmina keep her word? She had but to join her warriors, turn southward and leave him and his band to perish.

But at last, after what seemed centuries of desperate battling, in the valley outside there rose another sound above the clash of steel and yells of slaughter. And then with a burst of trumpets that shook the walls, and rushing thunder of hoofs, five thousand riders of Vendhya smote the hosts of Secunderam.

That stroke split the Turanian squadrons asunder, shattered, tore and rent them and scattered their fragments all over the valley. In an instant the surge had ebbed back out of the gorge; there was a chaotic, confused swirl of fighting, horsemen wheeling and smiting singly and in clusters, and then the emir went down with a Kshatriya lance through his breast, and the riders in their spired helmets turned their horses down the valley, spurring like mad and seeking to slash a way through the swarms which had come upon them from the rear. As they scattered in flight, the conquerors scattered in pursuit, and all across the valley floor, and up on the slopes near the mouth and over the crests streamed the fugitives and the pursuers. The Afghulis, those left to ride, rushed out of the gorge and joined in the harrying of their foes, accepting the unexpected alliance as unquestioningly as they had accepted the return of their repudiated chief.

The sun was sinking toward the distant crags when Conan, his garments hacked to tatters and the mail under them reeking and clotted with blood, his knife dripping and crusted to the hilt, strode over the corpses to where Yasmina Devi sat her horse among her nobles on the crest of the ridge, near a lofty precipice.

'You kept your word, Devi!' he roared. 'By Crom, though, I had some bad seconds down in that gorge – *look out!*'

Down from the sky swooped a vulture of tremendous size with a thunder of wings that knocked men sprawling from their horses.

The scimitar-like beak was slashing for the Devi's soft neck, but Conan was quicker – a short run, a tigerish leap, the savage thrust of a dripping knife, and the vulture voiced a horribly human cry, pitched sideways and went tumbling down the cliffs to the rocks and river a thousand feet below. As it dropped, its black wings thrashing the air, it took on the semblance, not of a bird, but of a black-robed human body that fell, arms in wide black sleeves thrown abroad.

Conan turned to Yasmina, his red knife still in his hand, his blue eyes smoldering, blood oozing from wounds on his thickly muscled arms and thighs.

'You are the Devi again,' he said, grinning fiercely at the gold-clasped gossamer robe she had donned over her hill-girl attire, and awed not at all by the imposing array of chivalry about him. 'I have you to thank for the lives of some three hundred and fifty of my rogues, who are at least convinced that I didn't betray them. You have put my hands on the reins of conquest again.'

'I still owe you my ransom,' she said, her dark eyes glowing as they swept over him. 'Ten thousand pieces of gold I will pay you—'

He made a savage, impatient gesture, shook the blood from his knife and thrust it back in its scabbard, wiping his hands on his mail.

'I will collect your ransom in my own way, at my own time,' he said. 'I will collect it in your palace at Ayodhya, and I will come with fifty thousand men to see that the scales are fair.'

She laughed, gathering her reins into her hands. 'And I will meet you on the shores of the Jhumda with a hundred thousand!'

His eyes shone with fierce appreciation and admiration, and stepping back, he lifted his hand with a gesture that was like the assumption of kingship, indicating that her road was clear before her.

A WITCH SHALL BE BORN

1 The Blood-Red Crescent

TARAMIS, QUEEN OF KHAURAN, awakened from a dream-haunted slumber to a silence that seemed more like the stillness of nighted catacombs than the normal quiet of a sleeping place. She lay staring into the darkness, wondering why the candles in their golden candelabra had gone out. A flecking of stars marked a gold-barred casement that lent no illumination to the interior of the chamber. But as Taramis lay there, she became aware of a spot of radiance glowing in the darkness before her. She watched, puzzled. It grew and its intensity deepened as it expanded, a widening disk of lurid light hovering against the dark velvet hangings of the opposite wall. Taramis caught her breath, starting up to a sitting position. A dark object was visible in that circle of light – *a human head.*

In a sudden panic the queen opened her lips to cry out for her maids; then she checked herself. The glow was more lurid, the head more vividly limned. It was a woman's head, small, delicately molded, superbly poised, with a high-piled mass of lustrous black hair. The face grew distinct as she stared – and it was the sight of this face which froze the cry in Taramis's throat. The features were her own! She might have been looking into a mirror which subtly altered her reflection, lending it a tigerish gleam of eye, a vindictive curl of lip.

'Ishtar!' gasped Taramis. 'I am bewitched!'

Appallingly, the apparition spoke, and its voice was like honeyed venom.

'Bewitched? No, sweet sister! Here is no sorcery.'

'Sister?' stammered the bewildered girl. 'I have no sister.'

'You never had a sister?' came the sweet, poisonously mocking voice. 'Never a twin sister whose flesh was as soft as yours to caress or hurt?'

'Why, once I had a sister,' answered Taramis, still convinced that she was in the grip of some sort of nightmare. 'But she died.'

The beautiful face in the disk was convulsed with the aspect of a fury; so hellish became its expression that Taramis, cowering back, half expected to see snaky locks writhe hissing about the ivory brow.

'You lie!' The accusation was spat from between the snarling red lips. 'She did not die! Fool! Oh, enough of this mummery! Look – and let your sight be blasted!'

Light ran suddenly along the hangings like flaming serpents, and incredibly the candles in the golden sticks flared up again. Taramis crouched on her velvet couch, her lithe legs flexed beneath her, staring wide-eyed at the pantherish figure which posed mockingly before her. It was as if she gazed upon another Taramis, identical with herself in every contour of feature and limb, yet animated by an alien and evil personality. The face of this stranger waif reflected the opposite of every characteristic the countenance of the queen denoted. Lust and mystery sparkled in her scintillant eyes, cruelty lurked in the curl of her full red lips. Each movement of her supple body was subtly suggestive. Her coiffure imitated that of the queen's, on her feet were gilded sandals such as Taramis wore in her boudoir. The sleeveless, low-necked silk tunic, girdled at the waist with a cloth-of-gold cincture, was a duplicate of the queen's night-garment.

'Who are you?' gasped Taramis, an icy chill she could not explain creeping along her spine. 'Explain your presence before I call my ladies-in-waiting to summon the guard!'

'Scream until the roof beams crack,' callously answered the stranger. 'Your sluts will not wake till dawn, though the palace spring into flames about them. Your guardsmen will not hear your squeals; they have been sent out of this wing of the palace.'

'What!' exclaimed Taramis, stiffening with outraged majesty. 'Who dared give my guardsmen such a command?'

'I did, sweet sister,' sneered the other girl. 'A little while ago, before I entered. They thought it was their darling adored queen. Ha! How beautifully I acted the part! With what imperious dignity, softened by womanly sweetness, did I address the great louts who knelt in their armor and plumed helmets!'

Taramis felt as if a stifling net of bewilderment were being drawn about her.

'Who are you?' she cried desperately. 'What madness is this? Why do you come here?'

'Who am I?' There was the spite of a she-cobra's hiss in the soft response. The girl stepped to the edge of the couch, grasped the queen's white shoulders with fierce fingers, and bent to glare full into the startled eyes of Taramis. And under the spell of that hypnotic glare, the queen forgot to resent the unprecedented outrage of violent hands laid on regal flesh.

'Fool!' gritted the girl between her teeth. 'Can you ask? Can you wonder? I am Salome!'

'Salome!' Taramis breathed the word, and the hairs prickled on her scalp as she realized the incredible, numbing truth of the statement. 'I thought you died within the hour of your birth,' she said feebly.

'So thought many,' answered the woman who called herself Salome. 'They carried me into the desert to die, damn them! I, a mewing, puling babe whose life was so young it was scarcely the flicker of a candle. And do you know why they bore me forth to die?'

'I – I have heard the story—' faltered Taramis.

Salome laughed fiercely, and slapped her bosom. The low-necked tunic left the upper parts of her firm breasts bare, and between them there shone a curious mark – a crescent, red as blood.

'The mark of the witch!' cried Taramis, recoiling.

'Aye!' Salome's laughter was dagger-edged with hate. 'The curse of the kings of Khauran! Aye, they tell the tale in the market-places, with wagging beards and rolling eyes, the pious fools! They tell how the first queen of our line had traffic with a fiend of darkness and bore him a daughter who lives in foul legendry to this day. And thereafter in each century a girl baby was born into the Askhaurian dynasty, with a scarlet half-moon between her breasts, that signified her destiny.

'"Every century a witch shall be born." So ran the ancient curse. And so it has come to pass. Some were slain at birth, as they sought to slay me. Some walked the earth as witches, proud daughters of Khauran, with the moon of hell burning upon their ivory bosoms. Each was named Salome. I too am Salome. It was always Salome, the witch. It will always be Salome, the witch, even when the mountains of ice have roared down from the pole and ground the civilizations to ruin, and a new world has risen from the ashes and dust – even then there shall be Salomes to walk the earth, to trap men's hearts by their sorcery, to dance before the kings of the world, to see the heads of the wise men fall at their pleasure.'

'But – but you—' stammered Taramis.

'I?' The scintillant eyes burned like dark fires of mystery. 'They carried me into the desert far from the city, and laid me naked on the hot sand, under the flaming sun. And then they rode away and left me for the jackals and the vultures and the desert wolves.

'But the life in me was stronger than the life in common folk, for it partakes of the essence of the forces that seethe in the black gulfs beyond mortal ken. The hours passed, and the sun slashed down like the molten flames of hell, but I did not die – aye, something of that torment I remember, faintly and far away, as one remembers a dim, formless dream. Then there were camels, and yellow-skinned men who wore silk robes and spoke in a weird tongue. Strayed from the caravan road, they passed close by, and their leader saw me, and recognized the scarlet crescent on my bosom. He took me up and gave me life.

'He was a magician from far Khitai, returning to his native kingdom after a journey to Stygia. He took me with him to purple-towering Paikang, its minarets rising amid the vine-festooned jungles of bamboo, and there I grew to womanhood under his teaching. Age had steeped him deep in black wisdom, not weakened his powers of evil. Many things he taught me—'

She paused, smiling enigmatically, with wicked mystery gleaming in her dark eyes. Then she tossed her head.

'He drove me from him at last, saying that I was but a common witch in spite of his teachings, and not fit to command the mighty sorcery he would have taught me. He would have made me queen of the world and ruled the nations through me, he said, but I was only a harlot of darkness. But what of it? I could never endure to seclude myself in a golden tower, and spend the long hours staring into a crystal globe, mumbling over incantations written on serpent's skin in the blood of virgins, poring over musty volumes in forgotten languages.

'He said I was but an earthly sprite, knowing naught of the deeper gulfs of cosmic sorcery. Well, this world contains all I desire – power, and pomp, and glittering pageantry, handsome men and soft women for my paramours and my slaves. He had told me who I was, of the curse and my heritage. I have returned to take that to which I have as much right as you. Now it is mine by right of possession.'

'What do you mean?' Taramis sprang up and faced her sister, stung out of her bewilderment and fright. 'Do you imagine that by drugging a few of my maids and tricking a few of my guardsmen you have established a claim to the throne of Khauran? Do not forget that I am Queen of Khauran! I shall give you a place of honor, as my sister, but—'

Salome laughed hatefully.

'How generous of you, dear, sweet sister! But before you begin putting me in my place – perhaps you will tell me whose soldiers camp in the plain outside the city walls?'

'They are the Shemitish mercenaries of Constantius, the Kothic *voivode* of the Free Companies.'

'And what do they in Khauran?' cooed Salome.

Taramis felt that she was being subtly mocked, but she answered with an assumption of dignity which she scarcely felt.

'Constantius asked permission to pass along the borders of Khauran on his way to Turan. He himself is hostage for their good behavior as long as they are within my domains.'

'And Constantius,' pursued Salome. 'Did he not ask your hand today?'

Taramis shot her a clouded glance of suspicion.

'How did you know that?'

An insolent shrug of the slim naked shoulders was the only reply.

'You refused, dear sister?'

'Certainly I refused!' exclaimed Taramis angrily. 'Do you, an Askhaurian princess yourself, suppose that the Queen of Khauran could treat such a proposal with anything but disdain? Wed a bloody-handed adventurer, a man exiled from his own kingdom because of his crimes, and the leader of organized plunderers and hired murderers?

'I should never have allowed him to bring his black-bearded slayers into Khauran. But he is virtually a prisoner in the south tower, guarded by my soldiers. Tomorrow I shall bid him order his troops to leave the kingdom. He himself shall be kept captive until they are over the border. Meantime, my soldiers man the walls of the city, and I have warned him that he will answer for any outrages perpetrated on the villagers or shepherds by his mercenaries.'

'He is confined in the south tower?' asked Salome.

'That is what I said. Why do you ask?'

For answer Salome clapped her hands, and lifting her voice, with a gurgle of cruel mirth in it, called: 'The queen grants you an audience, Falcon!'

A gold-arabesqued door opened and a tall figure entered the chamber, at the sight of which Taramis cried out in amazement and anger.

'Constantius! You dare enter my chamber!'

'As you see, Your Majesty!' He bent his dark, hawk-like head in mock humility.

Constantius, whom men called Falcon, was tall, broad-shouldered, slim-waisted, lithe and strong as pliant steel. He was handsome in an aquiline, ruthless way. His face was burnt dark by the sun, and his hair, which grew far back from his high, narrow forehead, was black as a raven. His dark eyes were penetrating and alert, the hardness of his thin lips not softened by his thin black mustache. His boots were of Kordavan leather, his hose and doublet of plain, dark silk, tarnished with the wear of the camps and the stains of armor rust.

Twisting his mustache, he let his gaze travel up and down the shrinking queen with an effrontery that made her wince.

'By Ishtar, Taramis,' he said silkily, 'I find you more alluring in your night-tunic than in your queenly robes. Truly, this is an auspicious night!'

Fear grew in the queen's dark eyes. She was no fool; she knew that Constantius would never dare this outrage unless he was sure of himself.

'You are mad!' she said. 'If I am in your power in this chamber, you are no less in the power of my subjects, who will rend you to pieces if you touch me. Go at once, if you would live.'

Both laughed mockingly, and Salome made an impatient gesture.

'Enough of this farce; let us on to the next act in the comedy. Listen, dear sister: it was I who sent Constantius here. When I decided to take the throne of Khauran, I cast about for a man to aid me, and chose the Falcon, because of his utter lack of all characteristics men call good.'

'I am overwhelmed, princess,' murmured Constantius sardonically, with a profound bow.

'I sent him to Khauran, and, once his men were camped in the plain outside, and he was in the palace, I entered the city by that small gate in the west wall – the fools guarding it thought it was you returning from some nocturnal adventure—'

'You hell-cat!' Taramis's cheeks flamed and her resentment got the better of her regal reserve.

Salome smiled hardly.

'They were properly surprised and shocked, but admitted me without question. I entered the palace the same way, and gave the order to the surprised guards that sent them marching away, as well as the men who guarded Constantius in the south tower. Then I came here, attending to the ladies-in-waiting on the way.'

Taramis's fingers clenched and she paled.

'Well, what next?' she asked in a shaky voice.

'Listen!' Salome inclined her head. Faintly through the casement there came the clank of marching men in armor; gruff voices shouted in an alien tongue, and cries of alarm mingled with the shouts.

'The people awaken and grow fearful,' said Constantius sardonically. 'You had better go and reassure them, Salome!'

'Call me Taramis,' answered Salome. 'We must become accustomed to it.'

'What have you done?' cried Taramis. 'What have you done?'

'I have gone to the gates and ordered the soldiers to open them,' answered Salome. 'They were astounded, but they obeyed. That is the Falcon's army you hear, marching into the city.'

'You devil!' cried Taramis. 'You have betrayed my people, in my guise! You have made me seem a traitor! Oh, I shall go to them—'

With a cruel laugh Salome caught her wrist and jerked her back. The magnificent suppleness of the queen was helpless against the vindictive strength that steeled Salome's slender limbs.

'You know how to reach the dungeons from the palace, Constantius?' said the witch-girl. 'Good. Take this spitfire and lock her into the strongest cell. The jailers are all sound in drugged sleep. I saw to that. Send a man to cut their throats before they can awaken. None must ever know what has occurred tonight. Thenceforward I am Taramis, and Taramis is a nameless prisoner in an unknown dungeon.'

Constantius smiled with a glint of strong white teeth under his thin mustache.

'Very good; but you would not deny me a little – ah – amusement first?'

'Not I! Tame the scornful hussy as you will.' With a wicked laugh Salome flung her sister into the Kothian's arms, and turned away through the door that opened into the outer corridor.

Fright widened Taramis's lovely eyes, her supple figure rigid and straining against Constantius's embrace. She forgot the men marching in the streets, forgot the outrage to her queenship, in the face of the menace to her womanhood. She forgot all sensations but terror and shame as she faced the complete cynicism of Constantius's burning, mocking eyes, felt his hard arms crushing her writhing body.

Salome, hurrying along the corridor outside, smiled spitefully as a scream of despair and agony rang shuddering through the palace.

2 The Tree of Death

The young soldier's hose and shirt were smeared with dried blood, wet with sweat and gray with dust. Blood oozed from the deep gash in his thigh, from the cuts on his breast and shoulder. Perspiration glistened on his livid face and his fingers were knotted in the cover of the divan on which he lay. Yet his words reflected mental suffering that outweighed physical pain.

'She must be mad!' he repeated again and again, like one still stunned by some monstrous and incredible happening. 'It's like a nightmare! Taramis, whom all Khauran loves, betraying her people to that devil from Koth! Oh, Ishtar, why was I not slain? Better die than live to see our queen turn traitor and harlot!'

'Lie still, Valerius,' begged the girl who was washing and bandaging his wounds with trembling hands. 'Oh, please lie still, darling! You will make your wounds worse. I dared not summon a leech—'

'No,' muttered the wounded youth. 'Constantius's blue-bearded devils will be searching the quarters for wounded Khaurani; they'll hang every man who has wounds to show he fought against them. Oh, Taramis, how could you betray the people who worshipped you?' In his fierce agony he writhed, weeping in rage and shame, and the terrified girl caught him in her arms, straining his tossing head against her bosom, imploring him to be quiet.

'Better death than the black shame that has come upon Khauran this day,' he groaned. 'Did you see it, Ivga?'

'No, Valerius.' Her soft, nimble fingers were again at work, gently cleansing and closing the gaping edges of his raw wounds. 'I was awakened by the noise of fighting in the streets – I looked out a casement and saw the Shemites cutting down people; then presently I heard you calling me faintly from the alley door.'

'I had reached the limits of my strength,' he muttered. 'I fell in the alley and could not rise. I knew they'd find me soon if I lay there – I killed three of the blue-bearded beasts, by Ishtar! They'll never swagger through Khauran's streets, by the gods! The fiends are tearing their hearts in hell!'

The trembling girl crooned soothingly to him, as to a wounded child, and closed his panting lips with her own cool sweet mouth. But the fire that raged in his soul would not allow him to lie silent.

'I was not on the wall when the Shemites entered,' he burst out. 'I was asleep in the barracks, with the others not on duty. It was just before dawn when our captain entered, and his face was pale under his helmet. "The Shemites are in the city," he said. "The queen came to the southern gate and gave orders that they should be admitted. She made the men come down from the walls, where they've been on guard since Constantius entered the kingdom. I don't understand it, and neither does anyone else, but I heard her give the order, and we obeyed as we always do. We are ordered to assemble in the square before the palace. Form ranks outside the barracks and march – leave your arms and armor here. Ishtar knows what this means, but it is the queen's order."

'Well, when we came to the square the Shemites were drawn up on foot opposite the palace, ten thousand of the blue-bearded devils, fully armed, and people's heads were thrust out of every window and door on the square. The streets leading into the square were thronged by bewildered folk. Taramis was standing on the steps of the palace, alone except for Constantius, who stood stroking his mustache like a great lean cat who has just devoured a sparrow. But fifty Shemites with bows in their hands were ranged below them.

'That's where the queen's guard should have been, but they were drawn up at the foot of the palace stair, as puzzled as we, though they had come fully armed, in spite of the queen's order.

'Taramis spoke to us then, and told us that she had reconsidered the proposal made her by Constantius – why, only yesterday she threw it in his teeth in open court – and that she had decided to make him her royal consort. She did not explain why she had brought the Shemites into the city so treacherously. But she said that, as Constantius had control of a body of professional fighting-men, the army of Khauran would no longer be needed, and therefore she disbanded it, and ordered us to go quietly to our homes.

'Why, obedience to our queen is second nature to us, but we were struck dumb and found no word to answer. We broke ranks almost before we knew what we were doing, like men in a daze.

'But when the palace guard was ordered to disarm likewise and disband, the captain of the guard, Conan, interrupted. Men said he was off duty the night before, and drunk. But he was wide awake now. He shouted to the guardsmen to stand as they were until they received an order from him – and such is his dominance of his men, that they obeyed in spite of the queen. He strode up to the palace steps and glared at Taramis – and then he roared: "'This is not the queen! This isn't Taramis! It's some devil in masquerade!"

'Then hell was to pay! I don't know just what happened. I think a Shemite struck Conan, and Conan killed him. The next instant the square was a battleground. The Shemites fell on the guardsmen, and their spears and arrows struck down many soldiers who had already disbanded.

'Some of us grabbed up such weapons as we could and fought back. We hardly knew what we were fighting for, but it was against Constantius and his devils – not against Taramis, I swear it! Constantius shouted to cut the traitors down. We were not traitors!' Despair and bewilderment shook his voice. The girl murmured pityingly, not understanding it all, but aching in sympathy with her lover's suffering.

'The people did not know which side to take. It was a madhouse of confusion and bewilderment. We who fought didn't have a chance, in no formation, without armor and only half armed. The guards were fully armed and drawn up in a square, but there were only five hundred of them. They took a heavy toll before they were cut down, but there could be only one conclusion to such a battle. And while her people were being slaughtered before her, Taramis stood on the palace steps, with Constantius's arm about her waist, and laughed like a heartless, beautiful fiend! Gods, it's all mad – mad!

'I never saw a man fight as Conan fought. He put his back to the courtyard wall, and before they overpowered him the dead men were strewn in heaps thigh-deep about him. But at last they dragged him down, a hundred against one. When I saw him fall I dragged myself away feeling as if the world had burst under my very fingers. I heard Constantius call to his dogs to take the captain alive – stroking his mustache, with that hateful smile on his lips!'

That smile was on the lips of Constantius at that very moment. He sat his horse among a cluster of his men – thick-bodied Shemites with curled blue-black beards and hooked noses; the low-swinging sun struck glints from their peaked helmets and the silvered scales of their corselets. Nearly a mile behind, the walls and towers of Khauran rose sheer out of the meadowlands.

By the side of the caravan road a heavy cross had been planted, and on this grim tree a man hung, nailed there by iron spikes through his hands and feet. Naked but for a loin-cloth, the man was almost a giant in stature, and his muscles stood out in thick corded ridges on limbs and body, which the sun had long ago burned brown. The perspiration of agony beaded his face and his mighty breast, but from under the tangled black mane that fell over his low, broad forehead, his blue eyes blazed with an unquenched fire. Blood oozed sluggishly from the lacerations in his hands and feet.

Constantius saluted him mockingly.

'I am sorry, captain,' he said, 'that I cannot remain to ease your last hours, but I have duties to perform in yonder city – I must not keep your delicious queen waiting!' He laughed softly. 'So I leave you to your own devices – and those beauties!' He pointed meaningly at the black shadows which swept incessantly back and forth, high above.

'Were it not for them, I imagine that a powerful brute like yourself should live on the cross for days. Do not cherish any illusions of rescue because I am leaving you unguarded. I have had it proclaimed that anyone seeking to take your body, living or dead, from the cross, will be flayed alive together with all the members of his family, in the public square. I am so firmly established in Khauran that my order is as good as a regiment of guardsmen. I am leaving no guard, because the vultures will not approach as long as anyone is near, and I do not wish them to feel any constraint. That is also why I brought you so far from the city. These desert vultures approach the walls no closer than this spot.

'And so, brave captain, farewell! I will remember you when, in an hour, Taramis lies in my arms.'

Blood started afresh from the pierced palms as the victim's mallet-like fists clenched convulsively on the spike-heads. Knots and bunches of muscle started out of the massive arms, and Conan beat his head forward and spat savagely at Constantius's face. The *voivode* laughed coolly, wiped the saliva from his gorget and reined his horse about.

'Remember me when the vultures are tearing at your living flesh,' he called mockingly. 'The desert scavengers are a particularly voracious breed. I have seen men hang for hours on a cross, eyeless, earless, and scalpless, before the sharp beaks had eaten their way into their vitals.'

Without a backward glance he rode toward the city, a supple, erect figure, gleaming in his burnished armor, his stolid, bearded henchmen jogging beside him. A faint rising of dust from the worn trail marked their passing.

The man hanging on the cross was the one touch of sentient life in a landscape that seemed desolate and deserted in the late evening. Khauran, less than a mile away, might have been on the other side of the world, and existing in another age.

Shaking the sweat out of his eyes, Conan stared blankly at the familiar terrain. On either side of the city, and beyond it, stretched the fertile meadowlands, with cattle browsing in the distance where fields and vineyards checkered the plain. The western and northern horizons were dotted with villages, miniature in the distance. A lesser distance to the southeast a silvery gleam marked the course of a river, and beyond that river sandy desert began abruptly to stretch away and away beyond the horizon. Conan stared at that expanse of empty waste shimmering tawnily in the late sunlight as a trapped hawk stares at the open sky. A revulsion shook him when he glanced at the gleaming towers of Khauran. The city had betrayed him – trapped him into circumstances that left him hanging to a wooden cross like a hare nailed to a tree.

A red lust for vengeance swept away the thought. Curses ebbed fitfully from the man's lips. All his universe contracted, focused, became incorporated in the four iron spikes that held him from life and freedom. His great muscles quivered, knotting like iron cables. With the sweat starting out on his graying skin, he sought to gain leverage, to tear the nails from the wood. It was useless. They had been driven deep. Then he tried to tear his hands off the spikes, and it was not the knifing, abysmal agony that finally caused him to cease his efforts, but the futility of it. The spike-heads were broad and heavy; he could not drag them through the wounds. A surge of helplessness shook the giant, for the first time in his life. He hung motionless, his head resting on his breast, shutting his eyes against the aching glare of the sun.

A beat of wings caused him to look, just as a feathered shadow shot down out of the sky. A keen beak, stabbing at his eyes, cut his cheek, and he jerked his head aside, shutting his eyes involuntarily. He shouted, a croaking, desperate shout of menace, and the vultures swerved away and retreated, frightened by the sound. They resumed their wary circling above his head. Blood trickled over Conan's mouth, and he licked his lips involuntarily, spat at the salty taste.

Thirst assailed him savagely. He had drunk deeply of wine the night before, and no water had touched his lips since before the battle in the square, that dawn. And killing was thirsty, salt-sweaty work. He glared at the distant river as a man in hell glares through the opened grille. He thought of gushing freshets of white water he had breasted, laved to the shoulders in liquid jade. He remembered great horns of foaming ale, jacks of sparkling wine gulped carelessly or spilled on the tavern floor. He bit his lip to keep from bellowing in intolerable anguish as a tortured animal bellows.

The sun sank, a lurid ball in a fiery sea of blood. Against a crimson rampart that banded the horizon the towers of the city floated unreal as a dream. The very sky was tinged with blood to his misted glare. He licked his blackened lips and stared with bloodshot eyes at the distant river. It too seemed crimson with blood, and the shadows crawling up from the east seemed black as ebony.

In his dulled ears sounded the louder beat of wings. Lifting his head he watched with the burning glare of a wolf the shadows wheeling above him. He knew that his shouts would frighten them away no longer. One dipped – dipped – lower and lower. Conan drew his head back as far as he could, waiting with terrible patience. The vulture swept in with a swift roar of wings. Its beak flashed down, ripping the skin on Conan's chin as he jerked his head aside; then before the bird could flash away, Conan's head lunged forward on his mighty neck muscles, and his teeth, snapping like those of a wolf, locked on the bare, wattled neck.

Instantly the vulture exploded into squawking, flapping hysteria. Its thrashing wings blinded the man, and its talons ripped his chest. But grimly he hung on, the muscles starting out in lumps on his jaws. And the scavenger's neck-bones crunched between those powerful teeth. With a spasmodic flutter the bird hung limp. Conan let go, spat blood from his mouth. The other vultures, terrified by the fate of their companion, were in full flight to a distant tree, where they perched like black demons in conclave.

Ferocious triumph surged through Conan's numbed brain. Life beat strongly and savagely through his veins. He could still deal death; he still lived. Every twinge of sensation, even of agony, was a negation of death.

'By Mitra!' Either a voice spoke, or he suffered from hallucination. 'In all my life I have never seen such a thing!'

Shaking the sweat and blood from his eyes, Conan saw four horsemen sitting their steeds in the twilight and staring up at him. Three were lean, white-robed hawks, Zuagir tribesmen without a doubt, nomads from beyond the river. The other was dressed like them in a white, girdled *khalat* and a flowing head-dress which, banded about the temples with a triple circlet of braided camel-hair, fell to his shoulders. But he was not a Shemite. The dust was not so thick, nor Conan's hawk-like sight so clouded, that he could not perceive the man's facial characteristics.

He was as tall as Conan, though not so heavy-limbed. His shoulders were broad and his supple figure was hard as steel and whalebone. A short black beard did not altogether mask the aggressive jut of his lean jaw, and gray eyes cold and piercing as a sword gleamed from the shadow of the *kafieh*. Quieting his restless steed with a quick, sure hand, this man spoke: 'By Mitra, I should know this man!'

'Aye!' It was the guttural accents of a Zuagir. 'It is the Cimmerian who was captain of the queen's guard!'

'She must be casting off all her old favorites,' muttered the rider. 'Who'd have ever thought it of Queen Taramis? I'd rather have had a long, bloody war. It would have given us desert folk a chance to plunder. As it is we've come this close to the walls and found only this nag' – he glanced at a fine gelding led by one of the nomads – 'and this dying dog.'

Conan lifted his bloody head.

'If I could come down from this beam I'd make a dying dog out of you, you Zaporoskan thief!' he rasped through blackened lips.

'Mitra, the knave knows me!' exclaimed the other. 'How, knave, do you know me?'

'There's only one of your breed in these parts,' muttered Conan. 'You are Olgerd Vladislav, the outlaw chief.'

'Aye! and once a hetman of the *kozaki* of the Zaporoskan River, as you have guessed. Would you like to live?'

'Only a fool would ask that question,' panted Conan.

'I am a hard man,' said Olgerd, 'and toughness is the only quality I respect in a man. I shall judge if you are a man, or only a dog after all, fit only to lie here and die.'

'If we cut him down we may be seen from the walls,' objected one of the nomads.

Olgerd shook his head.

'The dusk is deep. Here, take this ax, Djebal, and cut down the cross at the base.'

'If it falls forward it will crush him,' objected Djebal. 'I can cut it so it will fall backward, but then the shock of the fall may crack his skull and tear loose all his entrails.'

'If he's worthy to ride with me he'll survive it,' answered Olgerd imperturbably. 'If not, then he doesn't deserve to live. Cut!'

The first impact of the battle-ax against the wood and its accompanying vibrations sent lances of agony through Conan's swollen feet and hands. Again and again the blade fell, and each stroke reverberated on his bruised brain, setting his tortured nerves aquiver. But he set his teeth and made no sound. The ax cut through, the cross reeled on its splintered base and toppled backward. Conan made his whole body a solid knot of iron-hard muscle, jammed his head back hard against the wood and held it rigid there. The beam struck the ground heavily and rebounded slightly. The impact tore his wounds and dazed him for an instant. He fought the rushing tide of blackness, sick and dizzy, but realized that the iron muscles that sheathed his vitals had saved him from permanent injury.

And he had made no sound, though blood oozed from his nostrils and his belly-muscles quivered with nausea. With a grunt of approval Djebal bent over him with a pair of pincers used to draw horse-shoe nails, and gripped the head of the spike in Conan's right hand, tearing the skin to get a grip on the deeply embedded head. The pincers were small for that work. Djebal sweated and tugged, swearing and wrestling with the stubborn iron, working it back and forth – in swollen flesh as well as in wood. Blood started, oozing over the Cimmerian's fingers. He lay so still he might have been dead, except for the spasmodic rise and fall of his great chest. The spike gave way, and Djebal held up the blood-stained thing with a grunt of satisfaction, then flung it away and bent over the other.

The process was repeated, and then Djebal turned his attention to Conan's skewered feet. But the Cimmerian, struggling up to a sitting posture, wrenched the pincers from his fingers and sent him staggering backward with a violent shove. Conan's hands were swollen to almost twice their normal size. His fingers felt like misshapen thumbs, and closing his hands was an agony that brought blood streaming from under his grinding teeth. But somehow, clutching the pincers clumsily with both hands, he managed to wrench out first one spike and then the other. They were not driven so deeply into the wood as the others had been.

He rose stiffly and stood upright on his swollen, lacerated feet, swaying drunkenly, the icy sweat dripping from his face and body. Cramps assailed him and he clamped his jaws against the desire to retch.

Olgerd, watching him impersonally, motioned him toward the stolen horse. Conan stumbled toward it, and every step was a stabbing, throbbing hell that flecked his lips with bloody foam. One misshapen, groping hand fell clumsily on the saddle-bow, a bloody foot somehow found the stirrup. Setting his teeth, he swung up, and he almost fainted in midair; but he came down in the saddle – and as he did so, Olgerd struck the horse sharply with his whip. The startled beast reared, and the man in the saddle swayed and slumped like a sack of sand, almost unseated. Conan had wrapped a rein about each hand, holding it in place with a clamping thumb. Drunkenly he exerted the strength of his knotted biceps, wrenching the horse down; it screamed, its jaw almost dislocated.

One of the Shemites lifted a water-flask questioningly.

Olgerd shook his head.

'Let him wait until we get to camp. It's only ten miles. If he's fit to live in the desert he'll live that long without a drink.'

The group rode like swift ghosts toward the river; among them Conan swayed like a drunken man in the saddle, bloodshot eyes glazed, foam drying on his blackened lips.

3 A Letter to Nemedia

The savant Astreas, traveling in the East in his never-tiring search for knowledge, wrote a letter to his friend and fellow-philosopher Alcemides, in his native Nemedia, which constitutes the entire knowledge of the Western nations concerning the events of that period in the East, always a hazy, half-mythical region in the minds of the Western folk.

Astreas wrote, in part: 'You can scarcely conceive, my dear old friend, of the conditions now existing in this tiny kingdom since Queen Taramis admitted Constantius and his mercenaries, an event which I briefly described in my last, hurried letter. Seven months have passed since then, during which time it seems as though the devil himself had been loosed in this unfortunate realm. Taramis seems to have gone quite mad; whereas formerly she was famed for her virtue, justice and tranquillity, she is now notorious for qualities precisely opposite to those just enumerated. Her private life is a scandal – or perhaps "private" is not the correct term, since the queen makes no attempt to conceal the debauchery of her court. She constantly indulges in the most infamous revelries, in which the unfortunate ladies of the court are forced to join, young married women as well as virgins.

'She herself has not bothered to marry her paramour, Constantius, who sits on the throne beside her and reigns as her royal consort, and his officers follow his example, and do not hesitate to debauch any woman they desire, regardless of her rank or station. The wretched kingdom groans under exorbitant taxation, the farms are stripped to the bone, and the merchants go in rags which are all that is left them by the tax-gatherers. Nay, they are lucky if they escape with a whole skin.

'I sense your incredulity, good Alcemides; you will fear that I exaggerate conditions in Khauran. Such conditions would be unthinkable in any of the Western countries, admittedly. But you must realize the vast difference that exists between West and East, especially this part of the East. In the first place, Khauran is a kingdom of no great size, one of the many principalities which at one time formed the eastern part of the empire of Koth, and which later regained the independence which was theirs at a still earlier age. This part of the world is made up of these tiny realms, diminutive in comparison with the great kingdoms of the West, or the great sultanates of the farther East, but important in their control of the caravan routes, and in the wealth concentrated in them.

'Khauran is the most southeasterly of these principalities, bordering on the very deserts of eastern Shem. The city of Khauran is the only city of any magnitude in the realm, and stands within sight of the river which separates the grasslands from the sandy desert, like a watch-tower to guard the fertile meadows behind it. The land is so rich that it yields three and four crops a year, and the plains north and west of the city are dotted with villages. To one accustomed to the great plantations and stock-farms of the West, it is strange to see these tiny fields and vineyards; yet wealth in grain and fruit pours from them as from a horn of plenty. The villagers are agriculturists, nothing else. Of a mixed, aboriginal race, they are unwarlike, unable to protect themselves, and forbidden the possession of arms. Dependent wholly upon the soldiers of the city for protection, they are helpless under the present conditions. So the savage revolt of the rural sections, which would be a certainty in any Western nation, is here impossible.

'They toil supinely under the iron hand of Constantius, and his black-bearded Shemites ride incessantly through the fields, with whips in their hands, like the slave-drivers of the black serfs who toil in the plantations of southern Zingara.

'Nor do the people of the city fare any better. Their wealth is stripped from them, their fairest daughters taken to glut the insatiable lust of Constantius and his mercenaries. These men are utterly without mercy or compassion, possessed of all the characteristics our armies learned to abhor in our wars against the Shemitish allies of Argos – inhuman cruelty, lust, and wild-beast ferocity. The people of the city are Khauran's ruling caste, predominantly Hyborian, and valorous and war-like. But the treachery of their queen delivered them into the hands of their oppressors. The Shemites are the only armed force in Khauran, and the most hellish punishment is inflicted on any Khaurani found possessing weapons. A systematic persecution to destroy the young Khaurani men able to bear arms has been savagely pursued. Many have ruthlessly been slaughtered, others sold as slaves to the Turanians. Thousands have fled the kingdom and either entered the service of other rulers, or become outlaws, lurking in numerous bands along the borders.

'At present there is some possibility of invasion from the desert, which is inhabited by tribes of Shemitish nomads. The mercenaries of Constantius are men from the Shemitish cities of the west, Pelishtim, Anakim, Akkharim, and are ardently hated by the Zuagirs and other wandering tribes. As you know, good Alcemides, the countries of these barbarians are divided into the western meadowlands which stretch to the distant ocean, and in which rise the cities of the town-dwellers, and the eastern deserts, where the lean nomads hold sway; there is incessant warfare between the dwellers of the cities and the dwellers of the desert.

'The Zuagirs have fought with and raided Khauran for centuries, without success, but they resent its conquest by their western kin. It is rumored that their natural antagonism is being fomented by the man who was formerly the captain of the queen's guard, and who, somehow escaping the hate of Constantius, who actually had him upon the cross, fled to the nomads. He is called Conan, and is himself a barbarian, one of those gloomy Cimmerians whose ferocity our soldiers have more than once learned to their bitter cost. It is rumored that he has become the right-hand man of Olgerd Vladislav, the *kozak* adventurer who wandered down from the northern steppes and made himself chief of a band of Zuagirs. There are also rumors that this band has increased vastly in the last few months, and that Olgerd, incited no doubt by this Cimmerian, is even considering a raid on Khauran.

'It can not be anything more than a raid, as the Zuagirs are without siege-machines, or the knowledge of investing a city, and it has been proven repeatedly in the past that the nomads in their loose formation, or rather lack of formation, are no match in hand-to-hand fighting for the well-disciplined, fully-armed warriors of the Shemitish cities. The natives of Khauran would perhaps welcome this conquest, since the nomads could deal with them no more harshly than their present masters, and even total extermination would be preferable to the suffering they have to endure. But they are so cowed and helpless that they could give no aid to the invaders.

'Their plight is most wretched. Taramis, apparently possessed of a demon, stops at nothing. She has abolished the worship of Ishtar, and turned the temple into a shrine of idolatry. She has destroyed the ivory image of the goddess which these eastern Hyborians worship (and which, inferior as it is to the true religion of Mitra which we Western nations recognize, is still superior to the devil-worship of the Shemites) and filled the temple of Ishtar with obscene images of every imaginable sort – gods and goddesses of the night, portrayed in all the salacious and perverse poses and with all the revolting characteristics that a degenerate brain could conceive. Many of these images are to be identified as foul deities of the Shemites, the Turanians, the Vendhyans, and the Khitans, but others are reminiscent of a hideous and half-remembered antiquity, vile shapes forgotten except in the most obscure legends. Where the queen gained the knowledge of them I dare not even hazard a guess.

'She has instituted human sacrifice, and since her mating with Constantius, no less then five hundred men, women and children have been immolated. Some of these have died on the altar she has set up in the temple, herself wielding the sacrificial dagger, but most have met a more horrible doom.

'Taramis has placed some sort of monster in a crypt in the temple. What it is, and whence it came, none knows. But shortly after she had crushed the desperate revolt of her soldiers against Constantius, she spent a night alone in the desecrated temple, alone except for a dozen bound captives, and the shuddering people saw thick, foul-smelling smoke curling up from the dome, heard all night the frenetic chanting of the queen, and the agonized cries of her tortured captives; and toward dawn another voice mingled with these sounds – a strident, inhuman croaking that froze the blood of all who heard.

'In the full dawn Taramis reeled drunkenly from the temple, her eyes blazing with demoniac triumph. The captives were never seen again, nor the croaking voice heard. But there is a room in the temple into which none ever goes but the queen, driving a human sacrifice before her. And this victim is never seen again. All know that in that grim chamber lurks some monster from the black night of ages, which devours the shrieking humans Taramis delivers up to it.

'I can no longer think of her as a mortal woman, but as a rabid she-fiend, crouching in her blood-fouled lair amongst the bones and fragments of her victims, with taloned, crimsoned fingers. That the gods allow her to pursue her awful course unchecked almost shakes my faith in divine justice.

'When I compare her present conduct with her deportment when first I came to Khauran, seven months ago, I am confused with bewilderment, and almost inclined to the belief held by many of the people – that a demon has possessed the body of Taramis. A young soldier, Valerius, had another belief. He believed that a witch had assumed a form identical with that of Khauran's adored ruler. He believed that

Taramis had been spirited away in the night, and confined in some dungeon, and that this being ruling in her place was but a female sorcerer. He swore that he would find the real queen, if she still lived, but I greatly fear that he himself has fallen victim to the cruelty of Constantius. He was implicated in the revolt of the palace guards, escaped and remained in hiding for some time, stubbornly refusing to seek safety abroad, and it was during this time that I encountered him and he told me his beliefs.

'But he has disappeared, as so many have, whose fate one dares not conjecture, and I fear he has been apprehended by the spies of Constantius.

'But I must conclude this letter and slip it out of the city by means of a swift carrier-pigeon, which will carry it to the post whence I purchased it, on the borders of Koth. By rider and camel-train it will eventually come to you. I must haste, before dawn. It is late, and the stars gleam whitely on the gardened roofs of Khauran. A shuddering silence envelops the city, in which I hear the throb of a sullen drum from the distant temple. I doubt not that Taramis is there, concocting more devilry.'

But the savant was incorrect in his conjecture concerning the whereabouts of the woman he called Taramis. The girl whom the world knew as queen of Khauran stood in a dungeon, lighted only by a flickering torch which played on her features, etching the diabolical cruelty of her beautiful countenance.

On the bare stone floor before her crouched a figure whose nakedness was scarcely covered with tattered rags.

This figure Salome touched contemptuously with the upturned toe of her gilded sandal, and smiled vindictively as her victim shrank away.

'You do not love my caresses, sweet sister?'

Taramis was still beautiful, in spite of her rags and the imprisonment and abuse of seven weary months. She did not reply to her sister's taunts, but bent her head as one grown accustomed to mockery.

This resignation did not please Salome. She bit her red lip, and stood tapping the toe of her shoe against the floor as she frowned down at the passive figure. Salome was clad in the barbaric splendor of a woman of Shushan. Jewels glittered in the torchlight on her gilded sandals, on her gold breast-plates and the slender chains that held them in place. Gold anklets clashed as she moved, jeweled bracelets weighted her bare arms. Her tall coiffure was that of a Shemitish woman, and jade pendants hung from gold hoops in her ears, flashing and sparkling with each impatient movement of her haughty head. A gem-crusted girdle supported a silk shirt so transparent that it was in the nature of a cynical mockery of convention.

Suspended from her shoulders and trailing down her back hung a darkly scarlet cloak, and this was thrown carelessly over the crook of one arm and the bundle that arm supported.

Salome stooped suddenly and with her free hand grasped her sister's dishevelled hair and forced back the girl's head to stare into her eyes. Taramis met that tigerish glare without flinching.

'You are not so ready with your tears as formerly, sweet sister,' muttered the witch-girl.

'You shall wring no more tears from me,' answered Taramis. 'Too often you have reveled in the spectacle of the queen of Khauran sobbing for mercy on her knees. I know that you have spared me only to torment me; that is why you have limited your tortures to such torments as neither slay nor permanently disfigure. But I fear you no longer; you have strained out the last vestige of hope, fright and shame from me. Slay me and be done with it, for I have shed my last tear for your enjoyment, you she-devil from hell!'

'You flatter yourself, my dear sister,' purred Salome. 'So far it is only your handsome body that I have caused to suffer, only your pride and self-esteem that I have crushed. You forget that, unlike myself, you are capable of mental torment. I have observed this when I have regaled you with narratives concerning the comedies I have enacted with some of your stupid subjects. But this time I have brought more vivid proof of these farces. Did you know that Krallides, your faithful councillor, had come skulking back from Turan and been captured?'

Taramis turned pale.

'What – what have you done to him?'

For answer Salome drew the mysterious bundle from under her cloak. She shook off the silken swathings and held it up – the head of a young man, the features frozen in a convulsion as if death had come in the midst of inhuman agony.

Taramis cried out as if a blade had pierced her heart.

'Oh, Ishtar! Krallides!'

'Aye! He was seeking to stir up the people against me, poor fool, telling them that Conan spoke the truth when he said I was not Taramis. How would the people rise against the Falcon's Shemites? With sticks and pebbles? Bah! Dogs are eating his headless body in the market-place, and this foul carrion shall be cast into the sewer to rot.

'How, sister!' She paused, smiling down at her victim. 'Have you discovered that you still have unshed tears? Good! I reserved the mental torment for the last. Hereafter I shall show you many such sights as – this!'

Standing there in the torchlight with the severed head in her hand she did not look like anything ever borne by a human woman, in spite of her awful beauty. Taramis did not look up. She lay face down on the slimy floor, her slim body shaken in sobs of agony, beating her clenched hands against the stones. Salome sauntered toward the door, her anklets clashing at each step, her ear pendants winking in the torch-glare.

A few moments later she emerged from a door under a sullen arch that led into a court which in turn opened upon a winding alley. A man standing there turned toward her – a giant Shemite, with sombre eyes and shoulders like a bull, his great black beard falling over his mighty, silver-mailed breast.

'She wept?' His rumble was like that of a bull, deep, low-pitched and stormy. He was the general of the mercenaries, one of the few even of Constantius's associates who knew the secret of the queens of Khauran.

'Aye, Khumbanigash. There are whole sections of her sensibilities that I have not touched. When one sense is dulled by continual laceration, I will discover a newer, more poignant pang. Here, dog!' A trembling, shambling figure in rags, filth and matted hair approached, one of the beggars that slept in the alleys and open courts. Salome tossed the head to him. 'Here, deaf one; cast that in the nearest sewer. Make the sign with your hands, Khumbanigash. He can not hear.'

The general complied, and the tousled head bobbed, as the man turned painfully away.

'Why do you keep up this farce?' rumbled Khumbanigash. 'You are so firmly established on the throne that nothing can unseat you. What if Khaurani fools learn the truth? They can do nothing. Proclaim yourself in your true identity! Show them their beloved ex-queen – and cut off her head in the public square!'

'Not yet, good Khumbanigash—'

The arched door slammed on the hard accents of Salome, the stormy reverberations of Khumbanigash. The mute beggar crouched in the courtyard, and there was none to see that the hands which held the severed head were quivering strongly – brown, sinewy hands, strangely incongruous with the bent body and filthy tatters.

'I knew it!' It was a fierce, vibrant whisper, scarcely audible. 'She lives! Oh, Krallides, your martyrdom was not in vain! They have her locked in that dungeon! Oh, Ishtar, if you love true men, aid me now!'

4 Wolves of the Desert

Olgerd Vladislav filled his jeweled goblet with crimson wine from a golden jug and thrust the vessel across the ebony table to Conan the Cimmerian. Olgerd's apparel would have satisfied the vanity of any Zaporoskan hetman.

His *khalat* was of white silk, with pearls sewn on the bosom. Girdled at the waist with a Bakhauriot belt, its skirts were drawn back to reveal his wide silken breeches, tucked into short boots of soft green leather, adorned with gold thread. On his head was a green silk turban, wound about a spired helmet chased with gold. His only weapon was a broad curved Cherkees knife in an ivory sheath girdled high on his left hip, *kozak* fashion. Throwing himself back in his gilded chair with its carven eagles, Olgerd spread his booted legs before him, and gulped down the sparkling wine noisily.

To his splendor the huge Cimmerian opposite him offered a strong contrast, with his square-cut black mane, brown scarred countenance and burning blue eyes. He was clad in black mesh-mail, and the only glitter about him was the broad gold buckle of the belt which supported his sword in its worn leather scabbard.

They were alone in the silk-walled tent, which was hung with gilt-worked tapestries and littered with rich carpets and velvet cushions, the loot of the caravans. From outside came a low, incessant murmur, the sound that always accompanies a great throng of men, in camp or otherwise. An occasional gust of desert wind rattled the palm-leaves.

'Today in the shadow, tomorrow in the sun,' quoth Olgerd, loosening his crimson girdle a trifle and reaching again for the wine-jug. 'That's the way of life. Once I was a hetman on the Zaporoska; now I'm a desert chief. Seven months ago you were hanging on a cross outside Khauran. Now you're lieutenant to the most powerful raider between Turan and the western meadows. You should be thankful to me!'

'For recognizing my usefulness?' Conan laughed and lifted the jug. 'When you allow the elevation of a man, one can be sure that you'll profit by his advancement. I've earned everything I've won, with my blood and sweat.' He glanced at the scars on the insides of his palms. There were scars, too, on his body, scars that had not been there seven months ago.

'You fight like a regiment of devils,' conceded Olgerd. 'But don't get to thinking that you've had anything to do with the recruits who've swarmed in to join us. It was our success at raiding, guided by my wit, that brought them in. These nomads are always looking for a successful leader to follow, and they have more faith in a foreigner than in one of their own race.

'There's no limit to what we may accomplish! We have eleven thousand men now. In another year we may have three times that number. We've contented ourselves, so far, with raids on the Turanian outposts and the city-states to the west. With thirty or forty thousand men we'll raid no longer. We'll invade and conquer and establish ourselves as rulers. I'll be emperor of all Shem yet, and you'll be my vizier, so long as you carry out my orders unquestioningly. In the meantime, I think we'll ride eastward and storm that Turanian outpost at Vezek, where the caravans pay toll.'

Conan shook his head. 'I think not.'

Olgerd glared, his quick temper irritated.

'What do you mean, *you* think not? I do the thinking for this army!'

'There are enough men in this band now for my purpose,' answered the Cimmerian. 'I'm sick of waiting. I have a score to settle.'

'Oh!' Olgerd scowled, and gulped wine, then grinned. 'Still thinking of that cross, eh? Well, I like a good hater. But that can wait.'

'You told me once you'd aid me in taking Khauran,' said Conan.

'Yes, but that was before I began to see the full possibilities of our power,' answered Olgerd. 'I was only thinking of the loot in the city. I don't want to waste our strength unprofitably. Khauran is too strong a nut for us to crack now. Maybe in a year—'

'Within the week,' answered Conan, and the *kozak* stared at the certainty in his voice.

'Listen,' said Olgerd, 'even if I were willing to throw away men on such a hare-brained attempt – what could you expect? Do you think these wolves could besiege and take a city like Khauran?'

'There'll be no siege,' answered the Cimmerian. 'I know how to draw Constantius out into the plain.'

'And what then?' cried Olgerd with an oath. 'In the arrow-play our horsemen would have the worst of it, for the armor of the *asshuri* is the better, and when it came to sword-strokes their close-marshaled ranks of trained swordsmen would cleave through our loose lines and scatter our men like chaff before the wind.'

'Not if there were three thousand desperate Hyborian horsemen fighting in a solid wedge such as I could teach them,' answered Conan.

'And where would you secure three thousand Hyborians?' asked Olgerd with vast sarcasm. 'Will you conjure them out of the air?'

'I *have* them,' answered the Cimmerian imperturbably. 'Three thousand men of Khauran camp at the oasis of Akrel awaiting my orders.'

'*What?*' Olgerd glared like a startled wolf.

'Aye. Men who had fled from the tyranny of Constantius. Most of them have been living the lives of outlaws in the deserts east of Khauran, and are gaunt and hard and desperate as man-eating tigers. One of them will be a match for any three squat mercenaries. It takes oppression and hardship to stiffen men's guts and put the fire of hell into their thews. They were broken up into small bands; all they needed was a leader. They believed the word I sent them by my riders, and assembled at the oasis and put themselves at my disposal.'

'All this without my knowledge?' A feral light began to gleam in Olgerd's eye. He hitched at his weapon-girdle.

'It was *I* they wished to follow, not *you*.'

'And what did you tell these outcasts to gain their allegiance?' There was a dangerous ring in Olgerd's voice.

'I told them that I'd use this horde of desert wolves to help them destroy Constantius and give Khauran back into the hands of its citizens.'

'You fool!' whispered Olgerd. 'Do you deem yourself chief already?'

The men were on their feet, facing each other across the ebony board, devil-lights dancing in Olgerd's cold gray eyes, a grim smile on the Cimmerian's hard lips.

'I'll have you torn between four palm-trees,' said the *kozak* calmly.

'Call the men and bid them do it!' challenged Conan. 'See if they obey you!'

Baring his teeth in a snarl, Olgerd lifted his hand – then paused. There was something about the confidence in the Cimmerian's dark face that shook him. His eyes began to burn like those of a wolf.

'You scum of the western hills,' he muttered, 'have you dared seek to undermine my power?'

'I didn't have to,' answered Conan. 'You lied when you said I had nothing to do with bringing in the new recruits. I had everything to do with it. They took your orders, but they fought for me. There is not room for two chiefs of the Zuagirs. They know I am the stronger man. I understand them better than you, and they, me; because I am a barbarian too.'

'And what will they say when you ask them to fight for Khauran?' asked Olgerd sardonically.

'They'll follow me. I'll promise them a camel-train of gold from the palace. Khauran will be willing to pay that as a guerdon for getting rid of Constantius. After that, I'll lead them against the Turanians as you have planned. They want loot, and they'd as soon fight Constantius for it as anybody.'

In Olgerd's eyes grew a recognition of defeat. In his red dreams of empire he had missed what was going on about him. Happenings and events that had seemed meaningless before now flashed into his mind, with their true significance, bringing a realization that Conan spoke no idle boast. The giant black-mailed figure before him was the real chief of the Zuagirs.

'Not if you die!' muttered Olgerd, and his hand flickered toward his hilt. But quick as the stroke of a great cat, Conan's arm shot across the table and his fingers locked on Olgerd's forearm. There was a snap of breaking bones, and for a tense instant the scene held: the men facing each other as motionless as images, perspiration starting out on Olgerd's forehead. Conan laughed, never easing his grip on the broken arm.

'Are you fit to live, Olgerd?'

His smile did not alter as the corded muscles rippled in knotting ridges along his forearm and his fingers ground into the *kozak*'s quivering flesh. There was the sound of broken bones grating together and Olgerd's face turned the color of ashes; blood oozed from his lip where his teeth sank, but he uttered no sound.

With a laugh Conan released him and drew back, and the *kozak* swayed, caught the table edge with his good hand to steady himself.

'I give you life, Olgerd, as you gave it to me,' said Conan tranquilly, 'though it was for your own ends that you took me down from the cross. It was a bitter test you gave me then; you couldn't have endured it; neither could anyone, but a western barbarian.

'Take your horse and go. It's tied behind the tent, and food and water are in the saddle-bags. None will see your going, but go quickly. There's no room for a fallen chief on the desert. If the warriors see you, maimed and deposed, they'll never let you leave the camp alive.'

Olgerd did not reply. Slowly, without a word, he turned and stalked across the tent, through the flapped opening. Unspeaking he climbed into the saddle of the great white stallion that stood tethered there in the shade of a spreading palm-tree; and unspeaking, with his broken arm thrust in the bosom of his *khalat*, he reined the steed about and rode eastward into the open desert, out of the life of the people of the Zuagir.

Inside the tent Conan emptied the wine-jug and smacked his lips with relish. Tossing the empty vessel into a corner, he braced his belt and strode out through the front opening, halting for a moment to let his gaze sweep over the lines of camel-hair tents that stretched before him, and the white-robed figures that moved among them, arguing, singing, mending bridles or whetting tulwars.

He lifted his voice in a thunder that carried to the farthest confines of the encampment: '*Aie*, you dogs, sharpen your ears and listen! Gather around here. I have a tale to tell you.'

5 The Voice from the Crystal

In a chamber in a tower near the city wall a group of men listened attentively to the words of one of their number. They were young men, but hard and sinewy, with a bearing that comes only to men rendered desperate by adversity. They were clad in mail shirts and worn leather; swords hung at their girdles.

'I knew that Conan spoke the truth when he said it was not Taramis!' the speaker exclaimed. 'For months I have haunted the outskirts of the palace, playing the part of a deaf beggar. At last I learned what I had believed – that our queen was a prisoner in the dungeons that adjoin the palace. I watched my opportunity and captured a Shemitish jailer – knocked him senseless as he left the courtyard late one night – dragged him into a cellar near by and questioned him. Before he died he told me what I have just told you, and what we have suspected all along – that the woman ruling Khauran is a witch: Salome. Taramis, he said, is imprisoned in the lowest dungeon.

'This invasion of the Zuagirs gives us the opportunity we sought. What Conan means to do, I can not say. Perhaps he merely wishes vengeance on Constantius. Perhaps he intends sacking the city and destroying it. He is a barbarian and no one can understand their minds.

'But this is what we must do: rescue Taramis while the battle rages! Constantius will march out into the plain to give battle. Even now his men are mounting. He will do this because there is not sufficient food in the city to stand a siege. Conan burst out of the desert so suddenly that there was no time to bring in supplies. And the Cimmerian is equipped for a siege. Scouts have reported that the Zuagirs have siege engines, built, undoubtedly, according to the instructions of Conan, who learned all the arts of war among the Western nations.

'Constantius does not desire a long siege; so he will march with his warriors into the plain, where he expects to scatter Conan's forces at one stroke. He will leave only a few hundred men in the city, and they will be on the walls and in the towers commanding the gates.

'The prison will be left all but unguarded. When we have freed Taramis our next actions will depend upon circumstances. If Conan wins, we must show Taramis to the people and bid them rise – they will! Oh, they will! With their bare hands they are enough to overpower the Shemites left in the city and close the gates against both the mercenaries and the nomads. Neither must get within the walls! Then we will parley with Conan. He was always loyal to Taramis. If he knows the truth, and she appeals to him, I believe he will spare the city. If, which is more probable, Constantius prevails, and Conan is routed, we must steal out of the city with the queen and seek safety in flight.

'Is all clear?'

They replied with one voice.

'Then let us loosen our blades in our scabbards, commend our souls to Ishtar, and start for the prison, for the mercenaries are already marching through the southern gate.'

This was true. The dawnlight glinted on peaked helmets pouring in a steady stream through the broad arch, on the bright housings of the chargers. This would be a battle of horsemen, such as is possible only in the lands of the East. The riders flowed through the gates like a river of steel – sombre figures in black and silver mail, with their curled beards and hooked noses, and their inexorable eyes in which glimmered the fatality of their race – the utter lack of doubt or of mercy.

The streets and the walls were lined with throngs of people who watched silently these warriors of an alien race riding forth to defend their native city. There was no sound; dully, expressionless they watched, those gaunt people in shabby garments, their caps in their hands.

In a tower that overlooked the broad street that led to the southern gate, Salome lolled on a velvet couch cynically watching Constantius as he settled his broad sword-belt about his lean hips and drew on his gauntlets. They were alone in the chamber. Outside, the rhythmical clank of harness and shuffle of horses' hoofs welled up through the gold-barred casements.

'Before nightfall,' quoth Constantius, giving a twirl to his thin mustache, 'you'll have some captives to feed to your temple-devil. Does it not grow weary of soft, city-bred flesh? Perhaps it would relish the harder thews of a desert man.'

'Take care you do not fall prey to a fiercer beast than Thaug,' warned the girl. 'Do not forget who it is that leads these desert animals.'

'I am not likely to forget,' he answered. 'That is one reason why I am advancing to meet him. The dog has fought in the West and knows the art of siege. My scouts had some trouble in approaching his columns, for his outriders have eyes like hawks; but they did get close enough to see the engines he is dragging on ox-cart wheels drawn by camels – catapults, rams, ballistas, mangonels – by Ishtar! he must have had ten thousand men working day and night for a month. Where he got the material for their construction is more than I can understand. Perhaps he has a treaty with the Turanians, and gets supplies from them.

'Anyway, they won't do him any good. I've fought these desert wolves before – an exchange of arrows for awhile, in which the armor of my warriors protects them – then a charge and my squadrons sweep through the loose swarms of the nomads, wheel and sweep back through, scattering them to the four winds. I'll ride back through the south gate before sunset, with hundreds of naked captives staggering at my horse's tail. We'll hold a fête tonight, in the great square. My soldiers delight in flaying their enemies alive – we will have a wholesale skinning, and make these weak-kneed townsfolk watch. As for Conan, it will afford me intense pleasure, if we take him alive, to impale him on the palace steps.'

'Skin as many as you like,' answered Salome indifferently. 'I would like a dress made of human hide. But at least a hundred captives you must give to me – for the altar, and for Thaug.'

'It shall be done,' answered Constantius, with his gauntleted hand brushing back the thin hair from his high bald forehead, burned dark by the sun. 'For victory and the fair honor of Taramis!' he said sardonically, and, taking his vizored helmet under his arm, he lifted a hand in salute, and strode clanking from the chamber. His voice drifted back, harshly lifted in orders to his officers.

Salome leaned back on the couch, yawned, stretched herself like a great supple cat, and called: 'Zang!'

A cat-footed priest, with features like yellowed parchment stretched over a skull, entered noiselessly.

Salome turned to an ivory pedestal on which stood two crystal globes, and taking from it the smaller, she handed the glistening sphere to the priest.

'Ride with Constantius,' she said. 'Give me the news of the battle. Go!'

The skull-faced man bowed low, and hiding the globe under his dark mantle, hurried from the chamber.

Outside in the city there was no sound, except the clank of hoofs and after a while the clang of a closing gate. Salome mounted a wide marble stair that led to the flat, canopied, marble-battlemented roof. She was above all other buildings in the city. The streets were deserted, the great square in front of the palace was empty. In normal times folk shunned the grim temple which rose on the opposite side of that square, but now the town looked like a dead city. Only on the southern wall and the roofs that overlooked it was there any sign of life. There the people massed thickly. They made no demonstration, did not know whether to hope for the victory or defeat of Constantius. Victory meant further misery under his intolerable rule; defeat probably meant the sack of the city and red massacre. No word had come from Conan.

They did not know what to expect at his hands. They remembered that he was a barbarian.

The squadrons of the mercenaries were moving out into the plain. In the distance, just this side of the river, other dark masses were moving, barely recognizable as men on horses. Objects dotted the farther bank; Conan had not brought his siege engines across the river, apparently fearing an attack in the midst of the crossing. But he had crossed with his full force of horsemen. The sun rose and struck glints of fire from the dark multitudes. The squadrons from the city broke into a gallop; a deep roar reached the ears of the people on the wall.

The rolling masses merged, intermingled; at that distance it was a tangled confusion in which no details stood out. Charge and counter-charge were not to be identified. Clouds of dust rose from the plains, under the stamping hoofs, veiling the action. Through these swirling clouds masses of riders loomed, appearing and disappearing, and spears flashed.

Salome shrugged her shoulders and descended the stair. The palace lay silent. All the slaves were on the wall, gazing vainly southward with the citizens.

She entered the chamber where she had talked with Constantius, and approached the pedestal, noting that the crystal globe was clouded, shot with bloody streaks of crimson. She bent over the ball, swearing under her breath.

'Zang!' she called. 'Zang!'

Mists swirled in the sphere, resolving themselves into billowing dust-clouds through which black figures rushed unrecognizably; steel glinted like lightning in the murk. Then the face of Zang leaped into startling distinctness; it was as if the wide eyes gazed up at Salome. Blood trickled from a gash in the skull-like head, the skin was gray with sweat-runneled dust. The lips parted, writhing; to other ears than Salome's it would have seemed that the face in the crystal contorted silently. But sound to her came as plainly from those ashen lips as if the priest had been in the same room with her, instead of miles away, shouting into the smaller crystal. Only the gods of darkness knew what unseen, magic filaments linked together those shimmering spheres.

'Salome! shrieked the bloody head. *Salome!*'

'I hear!' she cried. 'Speak! How goes the battle?'

'Doom is upon us!' screamed the skull-like apparition. 'Khauran is lost! *Aie*, my horse is down and I can not win clear! Men are falling around me! They are dying like flies, in their silvered mail!'

'Stop yammering and tell me what happened!' she cried harshly.

'We rode at the desert-dogs and they came on to meet us!' yowled the priest. 'Arrows flew in clouds between the hosts, and the nomads wavered. Constantius ordered the charge. In even ranks we thundered upon them.

'Then the masses of their horde opened to right and left, and through the cleft rushed three thousand Hyborian horsemen whose presence we had not even suspected. Men of Khauran, mad with hate! Big men in full armor on massive horses! In a solid wedge of steel they smote us like a thunderbolt. They split our ranks asunder before we knew what was upon us, and then the desert-men swarmed on us from either flank.

'They have ripped our ranks apart, broken and scattered us! It is a trick of that devil Conan! The siege engines are false – mere frames of palm trunks and painted silk, that fooled our scouts who saw them from afar. A trick to draw us out to our doom! Our warriors flee! Khumbanigash is down – Conan slew him. I do not see Constantius. The Khaurani rage through our milling masses like blood-mad lions, and the desert-men feather us with arrows. I – ahh!'

There was a flicker as of lightning, or trenchant steel, a burst of bright blood – then abruptly the image vanished, like a bursting bubble, and Salome was staring into an empty crystal ball that mirrored only her own furious features.

She stood perfectly still for a few moments, erect and staring into space. Then she clapped her hands and another skull-like priest entered, as silent and immobile as the first.

'Constantius is beaten,' she said swiftly. 'We are doomed. Conan will be crashing at our gates within the hour. If he catches me, I have no illusions as to what I can expect. But first I am going to make sure that my cursed sister never ascends the throne again. Follow me! Come what may, we shall give Thaug a feast.'

As she descended the stairs and galleries of the palace, she heard a faint rising echo from the distant walls. The people there had begun to realize that the battle was going against Constantius. Through the dust clouds masses of horsemen were visible, racing toward the city.

Palace and prison were connected by a long closed gallery, whose vaulted roof rose on gloomy arches. Hurrying along this, the false queen and her slave passed through a heavy door at the other end that let them into the dim-lit recesses of the prison. They had emerged into a wide, arched corridor at a point near where a stone stair descended into the darkness. Salome recoiled suddenly, swearing. In the gloom of the hall lay a motionless form – a Shemitish jailer, his short beard tilted toward the roof as his head hung on a half-severed neck. As panting voices from below reached the girl's ears, she shrank back into the black shadow of an arch, pushing the priest behind her, her hand groping in her girdle.

6 The Vulture's Wings

It was the smoky light of a torch which roused Taramis, Queen of Khauran, from the slumber in which she sought forgetfulness. Lifting herself on her hand she raked back her tangled hair and blinked up, expecting to meet the mocking countenance of Salome, malign with new torments. Instead a cry of pity and horror reached her ears.

'Taramis! Oh, my Queen!'

The sound was so strange to her ears that she thought she was still dreaming. Behind the torch she could make out figures now, the glint of steel, then five countenances bent toward her, not swarthy and hook-nosed, but lean, aquiline faces, browned by the sun. She crouched in her tatters, staring wildly.

One of the figures sprang forward and fell on one knee before her, arms stretched appealingly toward her.

'Oh, Taramis! Thank Ishtar we have found you! Do you not remember me, Valerius? Once with your own lips you praised me, after the battle of Korveka!'

'Valerius!' she stammered. Suddenly tears welled into her eyes. 'Oh, I dream! It is some magic of Salome's to torment me!'

'No!' The cry rang with exultation. 'It is your own true vassals come to rescue you! Yet we must hasten. Constantius fights in the plain against Conan, who has brought the Zuagirs across the river, but three hundred Shemites yet hold the city. We slew the jailer and took his keys, and have seen no other guards. But we must be gone. Come!'

The queen's legs gave way, not from weakness but from the reaction. Valerius lifted her like a child, and with the torch-bearer hurrying before them, they left the dungeon and went up a slimy stone stair. It seemed to mount endlessly, but presently they emerged into a corridor.

They were passing a dark arch when the torch was suddenly struck out, and the bearer cried out in fierce, brief agony. A burst of blue fire glared in the dark corridor, in which the furious face of Salome was limned momentarily, with a beast-like figure crouching beside her – then the eyes of the watchers were blinded by that blaze.

Valerius tried to stagger along the corridor with the queen; dazedly he heard the sound of murderous blows driven deep in flesh, accompanied by gasps of death and a bestial grunting. Then the queen was torn brutally from his arms, and a savage blow on his helmet dashed him to the floor.

Grimly he crawled to his feet, shaking his head in an effort to rid himself of the blue flame which seemed still to dance devilishly before him. When his blinded sight cleared, he found himself alone in the corridor – alone except for the dead. His four companions lay in their blood, heads and bosoms cleft and gashed. Blinded and dazed in that hell-born glare, they had died without an opportunity of defending themselves. The queen was gone.

With a bitter curse Valerius caught up his sword, tearing his cleft helmet from his head to clatter on the flags; blood ran down his cheek from a cut in his scalp.

Reeling, frantic with indecision, he heard a voice calling his name in desperate urgency: 'Valerius! *Valerius!*'

He staggered in the direction of the voice, and rounded a corner just in time to have his arms filled with a soft, supple figure which flung itself frantically at him.

'Ivga! Are you mad!'

'I had to come!' she sobbed. 'I followed you – hid in an arch of the outer court. A moment ago I saw *her* emerge with a brute who carried a woman in his arms. I knew it was Taramis, and that you had failed! Oh, you are hurt!'

'A scratch!' He put aside her clinging hands. 'Quick, Ivga, tell me which way they went!'

'They fled across the square toward the temple.'

He paled. 'Ishtar! Oh, the fiend! She means to give Taramis to the devil she worships! Quick, Ivga! Run to the south wall where the people watch the battle! Tell them that their real queen has been found – that the impostor has dragged her to the temple! Go!'

Sobbing, the girl sped away, her light sandals pattering on the cobblestones, and Valerius raced across the court, plunged into the street, dashed into the square upon which it debouched, and raced for the great structure that rose on the opposite side.

His flying feet spurned the marble as he darted up the broad stair and through the pillared portico. Evidently their prisoner had given them some trouble. Taramis, sensing the doom intended for her, was fighting against it with all the strength of her splendid young body. Once she had broken away from the brutish priest, only to be dragged down again.

The group was halfway down the broad nave, at the other end of which stood the grim altar and beyond that the great metal door, obscenely carven, through which many had gone, but from which only Salome had ever emerged. Taramis's breath came in panting gasps; her tattered garment had been torn from her in the struggle. She writhed in the grasp of her apish captor like a white, naked nymph in the arms of a satyr. Salome watched cynically, though impatiently, moving toward the carven door, and from the dusk that lurked along the lofty walls the obscene gods and gargoyles leered down, as if imbued with salacious life.

Choking with fury, Valerius rushed down the great hall, sword in hand. At a sharp cry from Salome, the skull-faced priest looked up, then released Taramis, drew a heavy knife, already smeared with blood, and ran at the oncoming Khaurani.

But cutting down men blinded by the devil's-flame loosed by Salome was different from fighting a wiry young Hyborian afire with hate and rage.

Up went the dripping knife, but before it could fall Valerius's keen narrow blade slashed through the air, and the fist that held the knife jumped from its wrist in a shower of blood. Valerius, berserk, slashed again and yet again before the crumpling figure could fall. The blade licked through flesh and bone. The skull-like head fell one way, the half-sundered torso the other.

Valerius whirled on his toes, quick and fierce as a jungle-cat, glaring about for Salome. She must have exhausted her fire-dust in the prison. She was bending over Taramis, grasping her sister's black locks in one hand, in the other lifting a dagger. Then with a fierce cry Valerius's sword was sheathed in her breast with such fury that the point sprang out between her shoulders. With an awful shriek the witch sank down, writhing in convulsions, grasping at the naked blade as it was withdrawn, smoking and dripping. Her eyes were inhuman; with a more than human vitality she clung to the life that ebbed through the wound that split the crimson crescent on her ivory bosom. She groveled on the floor, clawing and biting at the naked stones in her agony.

Sickened at the sight, Valerius stooped and lifted the half-fainting queen. Turning his back on the twisting figure on the floor, he ran toward the door, stumbling in his haste. He staggered out upon the portico, halted at the head of the steps. The square thronged with people. Some had come at Ivga's incoherent cries; others had deserted the walls in fear of the onsweeping hordes out of the desert, fleeing unreasoningly toward the centre of the city. Dumb resignation had vanished. The throng seethed and milled, yelling and screaming. About the road there sounded somewhere the splintering of stone and timbers.

A band of grim Shemites cleft the crowd – the guards of the northern gates, hurrying toward the south gate to reinforce their comrades there. They reined up short at the sight of the youth on the steps, holding the limp, naked figure in his arms. The heads of the throng turned toward the temple; the crowd gaped, a new bewilderment added to their swirling confusion.

'Here is your queen!' yelled Valerius, straining to make himself understood above the clamor. The people gave back a bewildered roar. They did not understand, and Valerius sought in vain to lift his voice above their bedlam. The Shemites rode toward the temple steps, beating a way through the crowd with their spears.

Then a new, grisly element introduced itself into the frenzy. Out of the gloom of the temple behind Valerius wavered a slim white figure, laced with crimson. The people screamed; there in the arms of Valerius hung the woman they thought their queen; yet there in the temple door staggered another figure, like a reflection of the other. Their brains reeled. Valerius felt his blood congeal as he stared at the swaying witch-girl. His sword had transfixed her, sundered her heart. She should be dead; by all laws of nature she should be dead. Yet there she swayed, on her feet, clinging horribly to life.

'Thaug!' she screamed, reeling in the doorway. '*Thaug!*' As in answer to that frightful invocation there boomed a thunderous croaking from within the temple, the snapping of wood and metal.

'That is the queen!' roared the captain of the Shemites, lifting his bow. 'Shoot down the man and other woman!'

But the roar of a roused hunting-pack rose from the people; they had guessed the truth at last, understood Valerius's frenzied appeals, knew that the girl who hung limply in his arms was their true queen. With a soul-shaking yell they surged on the Shemites, tearing and smiting with tooth and nail and naked hands, with the desperation of hard-pent fury loosed at last. Above them Salome swayed and tumbled down the marble stairs, dead at last.

Arrows flickered about him as Valerius ran back between the pillars of the portico, shielding the body of the queen with his own. Shooting and slashing ruthlessly, the mounted Shemites were holding their own with the maddened crowd. Valerius darted to the temple door – with one foot on the threshold he recoiled, crying out in horror and despair.

Out of the gloom at the other end of the great hall a vast dark form heaved up – came rushing toward him in gigantic frog-like hops. He saw the gleam of great unearthly eyes, the shimmer of fangs or talons. He fell back from the door, and then the whir of a shaft past his ear warned him that death was also behind him. He wheeled desperately. Four or five Shemites had cut their way through the throng and were spurring their horses up the steps, their bows lifted to shoot him down.

He sprang behind a pillar, on which the arrows splintered. Taramis had fainted. She hung like a dead woman in his arms.

Before the Shemites could loose again, the doorway was blocked by a gigantic shape. With affrighted yells the mercenaries wheeled and began beating a frantic way through the throng, which crushed back in sudden, galvanized horror, trampling one another in their stampede.

But the monster seemed to be watching Valerius and the girl. Squeezing its vast, unstable bulk through the door, it bounded toward him, as he ran down the steps. He felt it looming behind him, a giant shadowy thing, like a travesty of nature cut out of the heart of night, a black shapelessness in which only the staring eyes and gleaming fangs were distinct.

There came a sudden thunder of hoofs; a rout of Shemites, bloody and battered, streamed across the square from the south, plowing blindly through the packed throng. Behind them swept a horde of horsemen yelling in a familiar tongue, waving red swords – the exiles, returned! With them rode fifty black-bearded desert-riders, and at their head a giant figure in black mail.

'Conan!' shrieked Valerius. '*Conan!*'

The giant yelled a command. Without checking their headlong pace, the desert men lifted their bows, drew and loosed. A cloud of arrows sang across the square, over the seething heads of the multitudes, and sank feather-deep in the black monster. It halted, wavered, reared, a black blot against the marble pillars. Again the sharp cloud sang, and yet again, and the horror collapsed and rolled down the steps, as dead as the witch who had summoned it out of the night of ages.

Conan drew rein beside the portico, leaped off. Valerius had laid the queen on the marble, sinking beside her in utter exhaustion. The people surged about, crowding in. The Cimmerian cursed them back, lifted her dark head, pillowed it against his mailed shoulder.

'By Crom, what is this? The real Taramis! But who is that yonder?'

'The demon who wore her shape,' panted Valerius.

Conan swore heartily. Ripping a cloak from the shoulders of a soldier, he wrapped it about the naked queen. Her long dark lashes quivered on her cheeks; her eyes opened, stared up unbelievingly into the Cimmerian's scarred face.

'Conan!' Her soft fingers caught at him. 'Do I dream? *She* told me you were dead—'

'Scarcely!' He grinned hardly. 'You do not dream. You are Queen of Khauran again. I broke Constantius, out there by the river. Most of his dogs never lived to reach the walls, for I gave orders that no prisoners be taken – except Constantius. The city guard closed the gate in our faces, but we burst in with rams swung from our saddles. I left all my wolves outside, except this fifty. I didn't trust them in here, and these Khaurani lads were enough for the gate guards.'

'It has been a nightmare!' she whimpered. 'Oh, my poor people! You must help me try to repay them for all they have suffered, Conan, henceforth councilor as well as captain!'

Conan laughed, but shook his head. Rising, he set the queen upon her feet, and beckoned to a number of his Khaurani horsemen who had not continued the pursuit of the fleeing Shemites. They sprang from their horses, eager to do the bidding of their new-found queen.

'No, lass, that's over with. I'm chief of the Zuagirs now, and must lead them to plunder the Turanians, as I promised. This lad, Valerius, will make you a better captain than I. I wasn't made to dwell among marble walls, anyway. But I must leave you now, and complete what I've begun. Shemites still live in Khauran.'

As Valerius started to follow Taramis across the square towards the palace, through a lane opened by the wildly cheering multitude, he felt a soft hand slipped timidly into his sinewy fingers and turned to receive the slender body of Ivga in his arms. He crushed her to him and drank her kisses with the gratitude of a weary fighter who has attained rest at last through tribulation and storm.

But not all men seek rest and peace; some are born with the spirit of the storm in their blood, restless harbingers of violence and bloodshed, knowing no other path . . .

The sun was rising. The ancient caravan road was thronged with white-robed horsemen, in a wavering line that stretched from the walls of Khauran to a spot far out in the plain. Conan the Cimmerian sat at the head of that column, near the jagged end of a wooden beam that stuck up out of the ground. Near that stump rose a heavy cross, and on that cross a man hung by spikes through his hands and feet.

'Seven months ago, Constantius,' said Conan, 'it was I who hung there, and you who sat here.'

Constantius did not reply; he licked his gray lips and his eyes were glassy with pain and fear. Muscles writhed like cords along his lean body.

'You are more fit to inflict torture than to endure it,' said Conan tranquilly. 'I hung there on a cross as you are hanging, and I lived, thanks to circumstances and a stamina peculiar to barbarians. But you civilized men are soft; your lives are not nailed to your spines as are ours. Your fortitude consists mainly in inflicting torment, not in enduring it. You will be dead before sundown. And so, Falcon of the desert, I leave you to the companionship of another bird of the desert.'

He gestured toward the vultures whose shadows swept across the sands as they wheeled overhead. From the lips of Constantius came an inhuman cry of despair and horror.

    Conan lifted his reins and rode toward the river that shone like silver in the morning sun. Behind him the white-clad riders struck into a trot; the gaze of each, as he passed a certain spot, turned impersonally and with the desert man's lack of compassion, toward the cross and the gaunt figure that hung there, black against the sunrise. Their horses' hoofs beat out a knell in the dust. Lower and lower swept the wings of the hungry vultures.

JEWELS OF GWAHLUR

1 Paths of Intrigue

THE CLIFFS ROSE SHEER from the jungle, towering ramparts of stone that glinted jade-blue and dull crimson in the rising sun, and curved away and away to east and west above the waving emerald ocean of fronds and leaves. It looked insurmountable, that giant palisade with its sheer curtains of solid rock in which bits of quartz winked dazzlingly in the sunlight. But the man who was working his tedious way upward was already halfway to the top.

He came of a race of hillmen, accustomed to scaling forbidding crags, and he was a man of unusual strength and agility. His only garment was a pair of short red silk breeks, and his sandals were slung to his back, out of his way, as were his sword and dagger.

The man was powerfully built, supple as a panther. His skin was bronzed by the sun, his square-cut black mane confined by a silver band about his temples. His iron muscles, quick eyes and sure feet served him well here, for it was a climb to test these qualities to the utmost. A hundred and fifty feet below him waved the jungle. An equal distance above him the rim of the cliffs was etched against the morning sky.

He labored like one driven by the necessity of haste; yet he was forced to move at a snail's pace, clinging like a fly on a wall. His groping hands and feet found niches and knobs, precarious holds at best, and sometimes he virtually hung by his finger nails. Yet upward he went, clawing, squirming, fighting for every foot. At times he paused to rest his aching muscles, and, shaking the sweat out of his eyes, twisted his head to stare searchingly out over the jungle, combing the green expanse for any trace of human life or motion.

Now the summit was not far above him, and he observed, only a few feet above his head, a break in the sheer stone of the cliff. An instant later he had reached it – a small cavern, just below the edge of the rim. As his head rose above the lip of its floor, he grunted. He clung there, his elbows hooked over the lip. The cave was so tiny that it was little more than a niche cut in the stone, but held an occupant. A shriveled mummy, cross-legged, arms folded on the withered breast upon which the shrunken head was sunk, sat in the little cavern. The limbs were bound in place with rawhide thongs which had become mere rotted wisps. If the form had ever been clothed, the ravages of time had long ago reduced the garments to dust. But thrust between the crossed arms and the shrunken breast there was a roll of parchment, yellowed with age to the color of old ivory.

The climber stretched forth a long arm and wrenched away this cylinder. Without investigation he thrust it into his girdle and hauled himself up until he was standing in the opening of the niche. A spring upward and he caught the rim of the cliffs and pulled himself up and over almost with the same motion.

There he halted, panting, and stared downward.

It was like looking into the interior of a vast bowl, rimmed by a circular stone wall. The floor of the bowl was covered with trees and denser vegetation, though nowhere did the growth duplicate the jungle denseness of the outer forest. The cliffs marched around it without a break and of uniform height. It was a freak of nature, not to be paralleled, perhaps, in the whole world: a vast natural amphitheater, a circular bit of forested plain, three or four miles in diameter, cut off from the rest of the world, and confined within the ring of those palisaded cliffs.

But the man on the cliffs did not devote his thoughts to marveling at the topographical phenomenon. With tense eagerness he searched the tree-tops below him, and exhaled a gusty sigh when he caught the glint of marble domes amidst the twinkling green. It was no myth, then; below him lay the fabulous and deserted palace of Alkmeenon.

Conan the Cimmerian, late of the Baracha Isles, of the Black Coast, and of many other climes where life ran wild, had come to the kingdom of Keshan following the lure of a fabled treasure that outshone the hoard of the Turanian kings.

Keshan was a barbaric kingdom lying in the eastern hinterlands of Kush where the broad grasslands merge with the forests that roll up from the south. The people were a mixed race, a dusky nobility ruling a population that was largely pure negro. The rulers – princes and high priests – claimed descent from a white race which, in a mythical age, had ruled a kingdom whose capital city was Alkmeenon. Conflicting legends sought to explain the reason for that race's eventual downfall,

and the abandonment of the city by the survivors. Equally nebulous were the tales of the Teeth of Gwahlur, the treasure of Alkmeenon. But these misty legends had been enough to bring Conan to Keshan, over vast distances of plain, river-laced jungle, and mountains.

He had found Keshan, which in itself was considered mythical by many northern and western nations, and he had heard enough to confirm the rumors of the treasure that men called the Teeth of Gwahlur. But its hiding-place he could not learn, and he was confronted with the necessity of explaining his presence in Keshan. Unattached strangers were not welcome there.

But he was not nonplussed. With cool assurance he made his offer to the stately plumed, suspicious grandees of the barbarically magnificent court. He was a professional fighting-man. In search of employment (he said) he had come to Keshan. For a price he would train the armies of Keshan and lead them against Punt, their hereditary enemy, whose recent successes in the field had aroused the fury of Keshan's irascible king.

This proposition was not so audacious as it might seem. Conan's fame had preceded him, even into distant Keshan; his exploits as a chief of the black corsairs, those wolves of the southern coasts, had made his name known, admired and feared throughout the black kingdoms. He did not refuse tests devised by the dusky lords. Skirmishes along the borders were incessant, affording the Cimmerian plenty of opportunities to demonstrate his ability at hand-to-hand fighting. His reckless ferocity impressed the lords of Keshan, already aware of his reputation as a leader of men, and the prospects seemed favorable. All Conan secretly desired was employment to give him legitimate excuse for remaining in Keshan long enough to locate the hiding-place of the Teeth of Gwahlur. Then there came an interruption. Thutmekri came to Keshan at the head of an embassy from Zembabwei.

Thutmekri was a Stygian, an adventurer and a rogue whose wits had recommended him to the twin kings of the great hybrid trading kingdom which lay many days' march to the east. He and the Cimmerian knew each other of old, and without love. Thutmekri likewise had a proposition to make to the king of Keshan, and it also concerned the conquest of Punt – which kingdom, incidentally, lying east of Keshan, had recently expelled the Zembabwan traders and burned their fortresses.

His offer outweighed even the prestige of Conan. He pledged himself to invade Punt from the east with a host of black spearmen, Shemitish archers, and mercenary swordsmen, and to aid the king of Keshan to annex the hostile kingdom. The benevolent kings of Zembabwei desired only a monopoly of the trade of Keshan and her tributaries – and, as a pledge of good faith, some of the Teeth of Gwahlur. These would be put to no base usage. Thutmekri hastened to explain to the suspicious chieftains; they would be placed in the temple of Zembabwei beside the squat gold idols of Dagon and Derketo, sacred guests in the holy shrine of the kingdom, to seal the covenant between Keshan and Zembabwei. This statement brought a savage grin to Conan's hard lips.

The Cimmerian made no attempt to match wits and intrigue with Thutmekri and his Shemitish partner, Zargheba. He knew that if Thutmekri won his point, he would insist on the instant banishment of his rival. There was but one thing for Conan to do: find the jewels before the king of Keshan made up his mind and flee with them. But by this time he was certain that they were not hidden in Keshia, the royal city which was a swarm of thatched huts crowding about a mud wall that enclosed a palace of stone and mud and bamboo.

While he fumed with nervous impatience, the high priest Gorulga announced that before any decision could be reached, the will of the gods must be ascertained concerning the proposed alliance with Zembabwei and the pledge of objects long held holy and inviolate. The oracle of Alkmeenon must be consulted.

This was an awesome thing, and it caused tongues to wag excitedly in palace and bee-hive hut. Not for a century had the priests visited the silent city. The oracle, men said, was the Princess Yelaya, the last ruler of Alkmeenon, who had died in the full bloom of her youth and beauty, and whose body had miraculously remained unblemished throughout the ages. Of old, priests had made their way into the haunted city, and she had taught them wisdom. The last priest to seek the oracle had been a wicked man, who had sought to steal for himself the curiously cut jewels that men called the Teeth of Gwahlur. But some doom had come upon him in the deserted palace, from which his acolytes, fleeing, had told tales of horror that had for a hundred years frightened the priests from the city and the oracle.

But Gorulga, the present high priest, as one confident in his knowledge of his own integrity, announced that he would go with a handful of followers to revive the ancient custom. And in the excitement tongues buzzed indiscreetly, and Conan caught the clue for which he had sought for weeks – the overheard whisper of a lesser priest that sent the Cimmerian stealing out of Keshia the night before the dawn when the priests were to start.

Riding as hard as he dared for a night and a day and a night, he came in the early dawn to the cliffs of Alkmeenon, which stood in the southwestern corner of the kingdom, amidst uninhabited jungle which was taboo to common men. None but the priests dared approach the haunted vale within a distance of many miles. And not even a priest had entered Alkmeenon for a hundred years.

No man had ever climbed these cliffs, legends said, and none but the priests knew the secret entrance into the valley. Conan did not waste time looking for it. Steeps that balked these people, horsemen and dwellers of plain and level forest, were not impossible for a man born in the rugged hills of Cimmeria.

Now on the summit of the cliffs he looked down into the circular valley and wondered what plague, war or superstition had driven the members of that ancient race forth from their stronghold to mingle with and be absorbed by the tribes that hemmed them in.

This valley had been their citadel. There the palace stood, and there only the royal family and their court dwelt. The real city stood outside the cliffs. Those waving masses of green jungle vegetation hid its ruins. But the domes that glistened in the leaves below him were the unbroken pinnacles of the royal palace of Alkmeenon which had defied the corroding ages.

Swinging a leg over the rim he went down swiftly. The inner side of the cliffs was more broken, not quite so sheer. In less than half the time it had taken him to ascend the outer side, he dropped to the swarded valley floor.

With one hand on his sword, he looked alertly about him. There was no reason to suppose men lied when they said that Alkmeenon was empty and deserted, haunted only by the ghosts of the dead past. But it was Conan's nature to be suspicious and wary. The silence was primordial; not even a leaf quivered on a branch. When he bent to peer under the trees, he saw nothing but the marching rows of trunks, receding and receding into the blue gloom of the deep woods.

Nevertheless he went warily, sword in hand, his restless eyes combing the shadows from side to side, his springy tread making no sound on the sward. All about him he saw signs of an ancient civilization; marble fountains, voiceless and crumbling, stood in circles of slender trees whose patterns were too symmetrical to have been a chance of nature. Forest-growth and underbrush had invaded the evenly planned groves, but their outlines were still visible. Broad pavements ran away under the trees, broken, and with grass growing through the wide cracks. He glimpsed walls with ornamental copings, lattices of carven stone that might once have served as the walls of pleasure pavilions.

Ahead of him, through the trees, the domes gleamed and the bulk of the structure supporting them became more apparent as he advanced. Presently, pushing through a screen of vine-tangled branches, he came into a comparatively open space where the trees straggled, unencumbered by undergrowth, and saw before him the wide, pillared portico of the palace.

As he mounted the broad marble steps, he noted that the building was in far better state of preservation than the lesser structures he had glimpsed. The thick walls and massive pillars seemed too powerful to crumble before the assault of time and the elements. The same enchanted quiet brooded over all. The cat-like pad of his sandaled feet seemed startlingly loud in the stillness.

Somewhere in this palace lay the effigy or image which had in times past served as oracle for the priests of Keshan. And somewhere in the palace, unless that indiscreet priest had babbled a lie, was hidden the treasure of the forgotten kings of Alkmeenon.

Conan passed into a broad, lofty hall, lined with tall columns, between which arches gaped, their door long rotted away. He traversed this in a twilight dimness, and at the other end passed through great double-valved bronze doors which stood partly open, as they might have stood for centuries. He emerged into a vast domed chamber which must have served as audience hall for the kings of Alkmeenon.

It was octagonal in shape, and the great dome up to which the lofty ceiling curved obviously was cunningly pierced, for the chamber was much better lighted than the hall which led to it. At the farther side of the great room there rose a dais with broad lapsi-lazuli steps leading up to it, and on that dais there stood a massive chair with ornate arms and a high back which once doubtless supported a cloth-of-gold canopy. Conan grunted explosively and his eyes lit. The golden throne of Alkmeenon, named in immemorial legendry! He weighed it with a practised eye. It represented a fortune in itself, if he were but able to bear it away. Its richness fired his imagination concerning the treasure itself, and made him burn with eagerness. His fingers itched to plunge among the gems he had heard described by story-tellers in the market squares of Keshia, who repeated tales handed down from mouth to mouth through the centuries – jewels not to be duplicated in the world, rubies, emeralds, diamonds, bloodstones, opals, sapphires, the loot of the ancient world.

He had expected to find the oracle-effigy seated on the throne, but since it was not, it was probably placed in some other part of the palace, if, indeed, such a thing really existed. But since he had turned his face toward Keshan, so many myths had proved to be realities that he did not doubt that he would find some kind of image or god.

Behind the throne there was a narrow arched doorway which doubtless had been masked by hangings in the days of Alkmeenon's life. He glanced through it and saw that it let into an alcove, empty, and with a narrow corridor leading off from it at right angles. Turning away from it, he spied another arch to the left of the dais, and it, unlike the others, was furnished with a door. Nor was it any common door. The portal was of the same rich metal as the throne, and carved with many curious arabesques.

At his touch it swung open so readily that its hinges might recently have been oiled. Inside he halted, staring.

He was in a square chamber of no great dimensions, whose marble walls rose to an ornate ceiling, inlaid with gold. Gold friezes ran about the base and the top of the walls, and there was no door other than the one through which he had entered. But he noted these details mechanically. His whole attention was centered on the shape which lay on an ivory dais before him.

He had expected an image, probably carved with the skill of a forgotten art. But no art could mimic the perfection of the figure that lay before him.

It was no effigy of stone or metal or ivory. It was the actual body of a woman, and by what dark art the ancients had preserved that form unblemished for so many ages Conan could not even guess. The very garments she wore were intact – and Conan scowled at that, a vague uneasiness stirring at the back of his mind. The arts that preserved the body should not have affected the garments. Yet there they were – gold breast-plates set with concentric circles of small gems, gilded sandals, and a short silken skirt upheld by a jeweled girdle. Neither cloth nor metal showed any signs of decay.

Yelaya was coldly beautiful, even in death. Her body was like alabaster, slender yet voluptuous; a great crimson jewel gleamed against the darkly piled foam of her hair.

Conan stood frowning down at her, and then tapped the dais with his sword. Possibilities of a hollow containing the treasure occurred to him, but the dais rang solid. He turned and paced the chamber in some indecision. Where should he search first, in the limited time at his disposal? The priest he had overheard babbling to a courtesan had said the treasure was hidden in the palace. But that included a space of considerable vastness. He wondered if he should hide himself until the priests had come and gone, and then renew the search. But there was a strong chance that they might take the jewels with them when they returned to Keshia. For he was convinced that Thutmekri had corrupted Gorulga.

Conan could predict Thutmektri's plans from his knowledge of the man. He knew that it had been Thutmekri who had proposed the conquest of Punt to the kings of Zembabwei, which conquest was but one move toward their real goal – the capture of the Teeth of Gwahlur. Those wary kings would demand proof that the treasure really existed before they made any move. The jewels Thutmekri asked as a pledge would furnish that proof.

With positive evidence of the treasure's reality, the kings of Zembabwei would move. Punt would be invaded simultaneously from the east and the west, but the Zembabwans would see to it that the Keshani did most of the fighting, and then, when both Punt and Keshan were exhausted from the struggle the Zembabwans would crush both races, loot Keshan and take the treasure by force, if they had to destroy every building and torture every living human in the kingdom.

But there was always another possibility: if Thutmekri could get his hands on the hoard, it would be characteristic of the man to cheat his employers, steal the jewels for himself and decamp, leaving the Zembabwan emissaries holding the sack.

Conan believed that this consulting of the oracle was but a ruse to persuade the king of Keshan to accede to Thutmekri's wishes – for he never for a moment doubted that Gorulga was as subtle and devious as all the rest mixed up in this grand swindle. Conan had not approached the high priest himself, because in the game of bribery he would have no chance against Thutmekri, and to attempt it would be to play directly into the Stygian's hands. Gorulga could denounce the Cimmerian to the people, establish a reputation for integrity, and rid Thutmekri of his rival at one stroke. He wondered how Thutmekri had corrupted the high priest, and just what could be offered as a bribe to a man who had the greatest treasure in the world under his fingers.

At any rate he was sure that the oracle would be made to say that the gods willed it that Keshan should follow Thutmekri's wishes, and he was sure, too, that it would drop a few pointed remarks concerning himself. After that Keshia would be too hot for the Cimmerian, nor had Conan had any intention of returning when he rode away in the night.

The oracle chamber held no clue for him. He went forth into the great throne-room and laid his hands on the throne. It was heavy, but he could tilt it up. The floor beneath, a thick marble dais, was solid. Again he sought the alcove. His mind clung to a secret crypt near the oracle. Painstakingly he began to tap along the walls, and presently his taps rang hollow at a spot opposite the mouth of the narrow corridor. Looking more closely he saw that the crack between the marble panel at that point and the next was wider than usual. He inserted a dagger-point and pried.

Silently the panel swung open, revealing a niche in the wall, but nothing else. He swore feelingly. The aperture was empty, and it did not look as if it had ever served as a crypt for treasure. Leaning into the niche he saw a system of tiny holes in the wall, about on a level with a man's mouth. He peered through, and grunted understandingly. That was the wall that formed the partition between the alcove and the oracle chamber. Those holes had not been visible in the chamber. Conan grinned. This explained the mystery of the oracle, but it was a bit cruder than he had expected. Gorulga would plant either himself or some trusted minion in that niche, to talk through the holes, and the credulous acolytes would accept it as the veritable voice of Yelaya.

Remembering something, the Cimmerian drew forth the roll of parchment he had taken from the mummy and unrolled it carefully, as it seemed ready to fall to pieces with age. He scowled over the dim characters with which it was covered. In his roaming about the world the giant adventurer had picked up a wide smattering of knowledge, particularly including the speaking and reading of many alien tongues. Many a sheltered scholar would have been astonished at the Cimmerian's linguistic abilities, for he had experienced many adventures where knowledge of a strange language had meant the difference between life and death.

These characters were puzzling, at once familiar and unintelligible, and presently he discovered the reason. They were the characters of archaic Pelishtim, which possessed many points of difference from the modern script, with which he was familiar, and which, three centuries ago, had been modified by conquest by a nomad tribe. This older, purer script baffled him. He made out a recurrent phrase, however, which he recognized as a proper name: Bît Yakin. He gathered that it was the name of the writer.

Scowling, his lips unconsciously moving as he struggled with the task, he blundered through the manuscript, finding much of it untranslatable and most of the rest of it obscure.

He gathered that the writer, the mysterious Bît Yakin, had come from afar with his servants, and entered the valley of Alkmeenon. Much that followed was meaningless, interspersed as it was with unfamiliar phrases and characters. Such as he could translate seemed to indicate the passing of a very long period of time. The name of Yelaya was repeated frequently, and toward the last part of the manuscript it became apparent that Bît Yakin knew that death was upon him. With a slight start Conan realized that the mummy in the cavern must be the remains of the writer of the manuscript, the mysterious Pelishtim, Bît Yakin. The man had died, as he had prophesied, and his servants, obviously, had placed him in that open crypt, high up on the cliffs, according to his instructions before his death.

It was strange that Bît Yakin was not mentioned in any of the legends of Alkmeenon. Obviously he had come to the valley after it had been deserted by the original inhabitants – the manuscript indicated as much

– but it seemed peculiar that the priests who came in the old days to consult the oracle had not seen the man or his servants. Conan felt sure that the mummy and this parchment were more than a hundred years old. Bît Yakin had dwelt in the valley when the priests came of old to bow before dead Yelaya. Yet concerning him the legends were silent, telling only of a deserted city, haunted only by the dead.

Why had the man dwelt in this desolate spot, and to what unknown destination had his servants departed after disposing of their master's corpse?

Conan shrugged his shoulders and thrust the parchment back into his girdle – he started violently, the skin on the backs of his hands tingling. Startlingly, shockingly in the slumberous stillness, there had boomed the deep strident clangor of a great gong!

He wheeled, crouching like a great cat, sword in hand, glaring down the narrow corridor from which the sound had seemed to come. Had the priests of Keshia arrived? This was improbable, he knew; they would not have had time to reach the valley. But that gong was indisputable evidence of human presence.

Conan was basically a direct-actionist. Such subtlety as he possessed had been acquired through contact with the more devious races. When taken off guard by some unexpected occurrence, he reverted instinctively to type. So now, instead of hiding or slipping away in the opposite direction as the average man might have done, he ran straight down the corridor in the direction of the sound. His sandals made no more sound than the pads of a panther would have made; his eyes were slits, his lips unconsciously asnarl. Panic had momentarily touched his soul at the shock of that unexpected reverberation, and the red rage of the primitive that is wakened by threat of peril always lurked close to the surface of the Cimmerian.

He emerged presently from the winding corridor into a small open court. Something glinting in the sun caught his eye. It was the gong, a great gold disk, hanging from a gold arm extending from the crumbling wall. A brass mallet lay near, but there was no sound or sight of humanity. The surrounding arches gaped emptily. Conan crouched inside the doorway for what seemed a long time. There was no sound or movement throughout the great palace. His patience exhausted at last, he glided around the curve of the court, peering into the arches, ready to leap either way like a flash of light, or to strike right or left as a cobra strikes.

He reached the gong, stared into the arch nearest it. He saw only a dim chamber, littered with the debris of decay. Beneath the gong the polished marble flags showed no footprints, but there was a scent in the air – a faintly fetid odor he could not classify; his nostrils dilated like those of a wild beast as he sought in vain to identify it.

He turned toward the arch – with appalling suddenness the seemingly solid flags splintered and gave way under his feet. Even as he fell he spread wide his arms and caught the edges of the aperture that gaped beneath him. The edges crumbled off under his clutching fingers. Down into utter darkness he shot, into black icy water that gripped him and whirled him away with breathless speed.

2 A Goddess Awakens

The Cimmerian at first made no attempt to fight the current that was sweeping him through lightless night. He kept himself afloat, gripping between his teeth the sword, which he had not relinquished, even in his fall, and did not even seek to guess to what doom he was being borne. But suddenly a beam of light lanced the darkness ahead of him. He saw the surging, seething black surface of the water, in turmoil as if disturbed by some monster of the deep, and he saw the sheer stone walls of the channel curved up to a vault overhead. On each side ran a narrow ledge, just below the arching roof, but they were far out of his reach. At one point this roof had been broken, probably fallen in, and the light was streaming through the aperture. Beyond that shaft of light was utter blackness, and panic assailed the Cimmerian as he saw he would be swept on past that spot of light, and into the unknown blackness again.

Then he saw something else: bronze ladders extended from the ledges to the water's surface at regular intervals, and there was one just ahead of him. Instantly he struck out for it, fighting the current that would have held him to the middle of the stream. It dragged at him as with tangible, animate slimy hands, but he buffeted the rushing surge with the strength of desperation and now drew closer and closer inshore, fighting furiously for every inch. Now he was even with the ladder and with a fierce, gasping plunge he gripped the bottom rung and hung on, breathless.

A few seconds later he struggled up out of the seething water, trusting his weight dubiously to the corroded rungs. They sagged and bent, but they held, and he clambered up onto the narrow ledge which ran along the wall scarcely a man's length below the curving roof. The tall Cimmerian was forced to bend his head as he stood up. A heavy bronze door showed in the stone at a point even with the head of the ladder, but it did not give to Conan's efforts. He transferred his sword from his teeth to its scabbard, spitting blood – for the edge had cut his lips in that fierce fight with the river – and turned his attention to the broken roof.

He could reach his arms up through the crevice and grip the edge, and careful testing told him it would bear his weight. An instant later he had drawn himself up through the hole, and found himself in a wide chamber, in a state of extreme disrepair. Most of the roof had fallen in, as well as a great section of the floor, which was laid over the vault of a subterranean river. Broken arches opened into other chambers and corridors, and Conan believed he was still in the great palace. He wondered uneasily how many chambers in that palace had underground water directly under them, and when the ancient flags or tiles might give way again and precipitate him back into the current from which he had just crawled.

And he wondered just how much of an accident that fall had been. Had those rotten flags simply chanced to give way beneath his weight, or was there a more sinister explanation? One thing at least was obvious: he was not the only living thing in that palace. That gong had not sounded of its own accord, whether the noise had been meant to lure him to his death, or not. The silence of the palace became suddenly sinister, fraught with crawling menace.

Could it be someone on the same mission as himself? A sudden thought occurred to him, at the memory of the mysterious Bît-Yakin. Was it not possible that this man had found the Teeth of Gwahlur in his long residence in Alkmeenon – that his servants had taken them with them when they departed? The possibility that he might be following a will-o'-the-wisp infuriated the Cimmerian.

Choosing a corridor which he believed led back toward the part of the palace he had first entered, he hurried along it, stepping gingerly as he thought of that black river that seethed and foamed somewhere below his feet.

His speculations recurrently revolved about the oracle chamber and its cryptic occupant. Somewhere in that vicinity must be the clue to the mystery of the treasure, if indeed it still remained in its immemorial hiding-place.

The great palace lay silent as ever, disturbed only by the swift passing of his sandaled feet. The chambers and halls he traversed were crumbling into ruin, but as he advanced the ravages of decay became less apparent. He wondered briefly for what purpose the ladders had been suspended from the ledges over the subterranean river, but dismissed the matter with a shrug. He was little interested in speculating over unremunerative problems of antiquity.

He was not sure just where the oracle chamber lay, from where he was, but presently he emerged into a corridor which led back into the great throne-room under one of the arches. He had reached a decision; it was useless for him to wander aimlessly about the palace, seeking the hoard. He would conceal himself somewhere here, wait until the Keshani priests came, and then, after they had gone through the farce of consulting the oracle, he would follow them to the hiding-place of the gems, to which he was certain they would go. Perhaps they would take only a few of the jewels with them. He would content himself with the rest.

Drawn by a morbid fascination, he re-entered the oracle chamber and stared down again at the motionless figure of the princess who was worshipped as a goddess, entranced by her frigid beauty. What cryptic secret was locked in that marvelously molded form?

He started violently. The breath sucked through his teeth, the short hairs prickled at the back of his scalp. The body still lay as he had first seen it, silent, motionless, in breast-plates of jeweled gold, gilded sandals and silken shirt. But now there was a subtle difference. The lissom limbs were not rigid, a peach-bloom touched the cheeks, the lips were red—

With a panicky curse Conan ripped out his sword.

'Crom! She's alive!'

At his words the long dark lashes lifted; the eyes opened and gaped up at him inscrutably, dark, lustrous, mystical. He glared in frozen speechlessness.

She sat up with a supple ease, still holding his ensorceled stare.

He licked his dry lips and found voice.

'You – are – are you Yelaya?' he stammered.

'I am Yelaya!' The voice was rich and musical, and he stared with new wonder. 'Do not fear. I will not harm you if you do my bidding.'

'How can a dead woman come to life after all these centuries?' he demanded, as if skeptical of what his senses told him. A curious gleam was beginning to smolder in his eyes.

She lifted her arms in a mystical gesture.

'I am a goddess. A thousand years ago there descended upon me the curse of the greater gods, the gods of darkness beyond the borders of light. The mortal in me died; the goddess in me could never die. Here I have lain for so many centuries, to awaken each night at sunset and hold my court as of yore, with specters drawn from the shadows of the past. Man, if you would not view that which will blast your soul for ever, get hence quickly! I command you! Go!' The voice became imperious, and her slender arm lifted and pointed.

Conan, his eyes burning slits, slowly sheathed his sword, but he did not obey her order. He stepped closer, as if impelled by a powerful fascination – without the slightest warning he grabbed her up in a bear-like grasp. She screamed a very ungoddess-like scream, and there was a sound of ripping silk, as with one ruthless wrench he tore off her skirt.

'Goddess! Ha!' His bark was full of angry contempt. He ignored the frantic writhings of his captive. 'I thought it was strange that a princess of Alkmeenon would speak with a Corinthian accent! As soon as I'd gathered my wits I knew I'd seen you somewhere. You're Muriela, Zargheba's Corinthian dancing-girl. This crescent-shaped birthmark on your hip proves it. I saw it once when Zargheba was whipping you. Goddess! Bah!' He smacked the betraying hip contemptuously and resoundingly with his open hand, and the girl yelped piteously.

All her imperiousness had gone out of her. She was no longer a mystical figure of antiquity, but a terrified and humiliated dancing-girl, such as can be bought at almost any Shemitish market-place. She lifted up her voice and wept unashamedly. Her captor glared down at her with angry triumph.

'Goddess! Ha! So you were one of the veiled women Zargheba brought to Keshia with him. Did you think you could fool me, you little idiot? A year ago I saw you in Akbitana with that swine, Zargheba, and I don't forget faces – or women's figures. I think I'll—'

Squirming about in his grasp she threw her slender arms about his massive neck in an abandon of terror; tears coursed down her cheeks, and her sobs quivered with a note of hysteria.

'Oh, please don't hurt me! Don't! I had to do it! Zargheba brought me here to act as the oracle!'

'Why, you sacrilegious little hussy!' rumbled Conan. 'Do you not fear the gods? Crom! is there no honesty anywhere?'

'Oh, please!' she begged, quivering with abject fright. 'I couldn't disobey Zargheba. Oh, what shall I do? I shall be cursed by these heathen gods!'

'What do you think the priests will do to you if they find out you're an impostor?' he demanded.

At the thought her legs refused to support her, and she collapsed in a shuddering heap, clasping Conan's knees and mingling incoherent pleas for mercy and protection with piteous protestations of her innocence of any malign intention. It was a vivid change from her pose as the ancient princess, but not surprising. The fear that had nerved her then was now her undoing.

'Where is Zargheba?' he demanded. 'Stop yammering, damn it, and answer me.'

'Outside the palace,' she whimpered, 'watching for the priests.'

'How many men with him?'

'None. We came alone.'

'Ha!' It was much like the satisfied grunt of a hunting lion. 'You must have left Keshia a few hours after I did. Did you climb the cliffs?'

She shook her head, too choked with tears to speak coherently. With an impatient imprecation he seized her slim shoulders and shook her until she gasped for breath.

'Will you quit that blubbering and answer me? How did you get into the valley?'

'Zargheba knew the secret way,' she gasped. 'The priest Gwarunga told him, and Thutmekri. On the south side of the valley there is a broad pool lying at the foot of the cliffs. There is a cave-mouth under the surface of the water that is not visible to the casual glance. We ducked under the water and entered it. The cave slopes up out of the water swiftly and leads through the cliffs. The opening on the side of the valley is masked by heavy thickets.'

'I climbed the cliffs on the east side,' he muttered. 'Well, what then?'

'We came to the palace and Zargheba hid me among the trees while he went to look for the chamber of the oracle. I do not think he fully trusted Gwarunga. While he was gone I thought I heard a gong sound, but I was not sure. Presently Zargheba came and took me into the palace and brought me to this chamber, where the goddess Yelaya lay upon the dais. He stripped the body and clothed me in the garments and ornaments. Then he went forth to hide the body and watch for the priests. I have been afraid. When you entered I wanted to leap up and beg you to take me away from this place, but I feared Zargheba. When you discovered I was alive, I thought I could frighten you away.'

'What were you to say as the oracle?' he asked.

'I was to bid the priests to take the Teeth of Gwahlur and give some of them to Thutmekri as a pledge, as he desired, and place the rest in the palace at Keshia. I was to tell them that an awful doom threatened Keshan if they did not agree to Thutmekri's proposals. And, oh, yes, I was to tell them that you were to be skinned alive immediately.'

'Thutmekri wanted the treasure where he – or the Zembabwans – could lay hand on it easily,' muttered Conan, disregarding the remark concerning himself. 'I'll carve his liver yet – Gorulga is a party to this swindle, of course?'

'No. He believes in his gods, and is incorruptible. He knows nothing about this. He will obey the oracle. It was all Thutmekri's plan. Knowing the Keshani would consult the oracle, he had Zargheba bring me with the embassy from Zembabwei, closely veiled and secluded.'

'Well, I'm damned!' muttered Conan. 'A priest who honestly believes in his oracle, and can not be bribed. Crom! I wonder if it was Zargheba who banged that gong. Did he know I was here? Could he have known about that rotten flagging? Where is he now, girl?'

'Hiding in a thicket of lotus trees, near the ancient avenue that leads from the south wall of the cliffs to the palace,' she answered. Then she renewed her importunities. 'Oh, Conan, have pity on me! I am afraid of this evil, ancient place. I know I have heard stealthy footfalls padding about me – oh, Conan, take me away with you! Zargheba will kill me when I have served his purpose here – I know it! The priests, too, will kill me if they discover my deceit.

'He is a devil – he bought me from a slave-trader who stole me out of a caravan bound through southern Koth, and has made me the tool of his intrigues ever since. Take me away from him! You can not be as cruel as he. Don't leave me to be slain here! Please! Please!'

She was on her knees, clutching at Conan hysterically, her beautiful tear-stained face upturned to him, her dark silken hair flowing in disorder over her white shoulders. Conan picked her up and set her on his knee.

'Listen to me. I'll protect you from Zargheba. The priests shall not know of your perfidy. But you've got to do as I tell you.'

She faltered promises of explicit obedience, clasping his corded neck as if seeking security from the contact.

'Good. When the priests come, you'll act the part of Yelaya, as Zargheba planned – it'll be dark, and in the torchlight they'll never know the difference. But you'll say this to them: "It is the will of the gods that the Stygian and his Shemitish dogs be driven from Keshan. They are thieves and traitors who plot to rob the gods. Let the Teeth of Gwahlur be placed in the care of the general Conan. Let him lead the armies of Keshan. He is beloved of the gods."'

She shivered, with an expression of desperation, but acquiesced.

'But Zargheba?' she cried. 'He'll kill me!'

'Don't worry about Zargheba,' he grunted. 'I'll take care of that dog. You do as I say. Here, put up your hair again. It's fallen all over your shoulders. And the gem's fallen out of it.'

He replaced the great glowing gem himself, nodding approval.

'It's worth a room full of slaves, itself alone. Here, put your skirt back on. It's torn down the side, but the priests will never notice it. Wipe your face. A goddess doesn't cry like a whipped schoolgirl. By Crom, you do look like Yelaya, face, hair, figure and all! If you act the goddess with the priests as well as you did with me, you'll fool them easily.'

'I'll try,' she shivered.

'Good; I'm going to find Zargheba.'

At that she became panicky again.

'No! Don't leave me alone! This place is haunted!'

'There's nothing here to harm you,' he assured her impatiently. 'Nothing but Zargheba, and I'm going to look after him. I'll be back shortly. I'll be watching from close by in case anything goes wrong during the ceremony; but if you play your part properly, nothing will go wrong.'

And turning, he hastened out of the oracle chamber; behind him Muriela squeaked wretchedly at his going.

Twilight had fallen. The great rooms and halls were shadowy and indistinct; copper friezes glinted dully through the dusk. Conan strode like a silent phantom through the great halls, with a sensation of being stared at from the shadowed recesses by invisible ghosts of the past. No wonder the girl was nervous amid such surroundings.

He glided down the marble steps like a slinking panther, sword in hand. Silence reigned over the valley, and above the rim of the cliffs stars were blinking out. If the priests of Keshia had entered the valley there was not a sound, not a movement in the greenery to betray them. He made out the ancient broken-paved avenue, wandering away to the south, lost amid clustering masses of fronds and thick-leaved bushes. He followed it warily, hugging the edge of the paving where the shrubs massed their shadows thickly, until he saw ahead of him, dimly in the dusk, the clump of lotus-trees, the strange growth peculiar to the black lands of Kush. There, according to the girl, Zargheba should be lurking. Conan became stealth personified. A velvet-footed shadow, he melted into the thickets.

He approached the lotus grove by a circuitous movement, and scarcely the rustle of a leaf proclaimed his passing. At the edge of the trees he halted suddenly, crouched like a suspicious panther among the deep shrubs. Ahead of him, among the dense leaves, showed a pallid oval, dim in the uncertain light. It might have been one of the great white blossoms which shone thickly among the branches. But Conan knew that it was a man's face. And it was turned toward him. He shrank quickly deeper into the shadows. Had Zargheba seen him. The man was looking directly toward him. Seconds passed. That dim face had not moved. Conan could make out the dark tuft below that was the short black beard.

And suddenly Conan was aware of something unnatural. Zargheba, he knew, was not a tall man. Standing erect, his head would scarcely top the Cimmerian's shoulder; yet that face was on a level with Conan's own. Was the man standing on something? Conan bent and peered toward the ground below the spot where the face showed, but his vision was blocked by undergrowth and the thick boles of the trees. But he saw something else, and he stiffened. Through a slot in the underbrush he glimpsed the stem of the tree under which, apparently,

Zargheba was standing. The face was directly in line with that tree. He should have seen below that face, not the tree-trunk, but Zargheba's body – but there was no body there.

Suddenly tenser than a tiger who stalks his prey, Conan glided deeper into the thicket, and a moment later drew aside a leafy branch and glared at the face that had not moved. Nor would it ever move again, of its own volition. He looked on Zargheba's severed head, suspended from the branch of the tree by its own long black hair.

3 The Return of the Oracle

Conan wheeled supplely, sweeping the shadows with a fiercely questing stare. There was no sign of the murdered man's body; only yonder the tall lush grass was trampled and broken down and the sward was dabbled darkly and wetly. Conan stood scarcely breathing as he strained his ears into the silence. The trees and bushes with their great pallid blossoms stood dark, still and sinister, etched against the deepening dusk.

Primitive fears whispered at the back of Conan's mind. Was this the work of the priests of Keshan? If so, where were they? Was it Zargheba, after all, who had struck the gong? Again there rose the memory of Bît-Yakin and his mysterious servants. Bît-Yakin was dead, shriveled to a hulk of wrinkled leather and bound in his hollowed crypt to greet the rising sun for ever. But the servants of Bît-Yakin were unaccounted for. There was no proof they had ever left the valley.

Conan thought of the girl, Muriela, alone and unguarded in that great shadowy palace. He wheeled and ran back down the shadowed avenue, and he ran as a suspicious panther runs, poised even in full stride to whirl right or left and strike death blows.

The palace loomed through the trees, and he saw something else – the glow of fire reflecting redly from the polished marble. He melted into the bushes that lined the broken street, glided through the dense growth and reached the edge of the open space before the portico. Voices reached him; torches bobbed and their flare shone on glossy ebon shoulders. The priests of Keshan had come.

They had not advanced up the wide, overgrown avenue as Zargheba had expected them to do. Obviously there was more than one secret way into the valley of Alkmeenon.

They were filing up the broad marble steps, holding their torches high. He saw Gorulga at the head of the parade, a profile chiseled out of copper, etched in the torch glare. The rest were acolytes, giant black men from whose skins the torches struck highlights. At the end of the procession there stalked a huge negro with an unusually wicked cast of countenance, at the sight of whom Conan scowled. That was Gwarunga, whom Muriela had named as the man who had revealed the secret of the pool-entrance to Zargheba. Conan wondered how deeply the man was in the intrigues of the Stygian.

He hurried toward the portico, circling the open space to keep in the fringing shadows. They left no one to guard the entrance. The torches streamed steadily down the long dark hall. Before they reached the double-valved door at the other end, Conan had mounted the other steps and was in the hall behind them. Slinking swiftly along the column-lined wall, he reached the great door as they crossed the huge throne-room, their torches driving back the shadows. They did not look back. In single file, their ostrich plumes nodding, their leopard-skin tunics contrasting curiously with the marble and arabesqued metal of the ancient palace, they moved across the wide room and halted momentarily at the golden door to the left of the throne-dais.

Gorulga's voice boomed eerily and hollowly in the great empty space, framed in sonorous phrases unintelligible to the lurking listener; then the high priest thrust open the golden door and entered, bowing repeatedly from his waist, and behind him the torches sank and rose, showering flakes of flame, as the worshippers imitated their master. The gold door closed behind them, shutting out sound and sight, and Conan darted across the throne-chamber and into the alcove behind the throne. He made less sound than a wind blowing across the chamber.

Tiny beams of light streamed through the apertures in the wall, as he pried open the secret panel. Gliding into the niche, he peered through, Muriela sat upright on the dais, her arms folded, her head leaning back against the wall, within a few inches of his eyes. The delicate perfume of her foamy hair was in his nostrils. He could not see her face, of course, but her attitude was as if she gazed tranquilly into some far gulf of space, over and beyond the shaven heads of the black giants who knelt before her. Conan grinned with appreciation. 'The little slut's an actress,' he told himself. He knew she was shriveling with terror, but she showed no sign. In the uncertain flare of the torches she looked exactly like the goddess he had seen lying on that same dais, if one could imagine that goddess imbued with vibrant life.

Gorulga was booming forth some kind of a chant in an accent unfamiliar to Conan, and which was probably some invocation in the ancient tongue of Alkmeenon, handed down from generation to generation of high priests. It seemed interminable. Conan grew restless. The longer the thing lasted, the more terrific would be the strain on Muriela. If she snapped – he hitched his sword and dagger forward. He could not see the little trollop tortured and slain by these men.

But the chant – deep, low-pitched and indescribably ominous – came to a conclusion at last, and a shouted acclaim from the acolytes marked its period. Lifting his head and raising his arms toward the silent form on the dais, Gorulga cried in the deep, rich resonance that was the natural attribute of the Keshani priest: 'Oh, great goddess, dweller with the great one of darkness, let thy heart be melted, thy lips opened for the ears of thy slave whose head is in the dust beneath thy feet! Speak, great goddess of the holy valley! Thou knowest the paths before us; the darkness that vexes us is as the light of the midday sun to thee. Shed the radiance of thy wisdom on the paths of thy servants! Tell us, oh mouthpiece of the gods: what is their will concerning Thutmekri the Stygian?'

The high-piled burnished mass of hair that caught the torchlight in dull bronze gleams quivered slightly. A gusty sigh rose from the blacks, half in awe, half in fear. Muriela's voice came plainly to Conan's ears in the breathless silence, and it seemed, cold, detached, impersonal, though the Cimmerian winced at the Corinthian accent.

'It is the will of the gods that the Stygian and his Shemitish dogs be driven from Keshan!' She was repeating his exact words. 'They are thieves and traitors who plot to rob the gods. Let the Teeth of Gwahlur be placed in the care of the general Conan. Let him lead the armies of Keshan. He is beloved of the gods!'

There was a quiver in her voice as she ended, and Conan began to sweat, believing she was on the point of an hysterical collapse. But the blacks did not notice, any more than they identified the Corinthian accent, of which they knew nothing. They smote their palms softly together and a murmur of wonder and awe rose from them. Gorulga's eyes glittered fanatically in the torchlight.

'Yelaya has spoken!' he cried in an exalted voice. 'It is the will of the gods! Long ago, in the days of our ancestors, they were made taboo and hidden at the command of the gods, who wrenched them from the awful jaws of Gwahlur the king of darkness, in the birth of the world. At the command of the gods the teeth of Gwahlur were hidden; at their command they shall be brought forth again. Oh star-born goddess, give us your leave to go to the secret hiding-place of the Teeth to secure them for him whom the gods love!'

'You have my leave to go!' answered the false goddess, with an imperious gesture of dismissal that set Conan grinning again, and the priests backed out, ostrich plumes and torches rising and falling with the rhythm of their genuflexions.

The gold door closed and with a moan, the goddess fell back limply on the dais. 'Conan!' she whimpered faintly. 'Conan!'

'Shhh!' he hissed through the apertures, and turning, glided from the niche and closed the panel. A glimpse past the jamb of the carven door showed him the torches receding across the great throne-room, but he was at the same time aware of a radiance that did not emanate from the torches. He was startled, but the solution presented itself instantly. An early moon had risen and its light slanted through the pierced dome which by some curious workmanship intensified the light. The shining dome of Alkmeenon was no fable, then. Perhaps its interior was of the curious whitely flaming crystal found only in the hills of the black countries. The light flooded the throne-room and seeped into the chambers immediately adjoining.

But as Conan made toward the door that led into the throne-room, he was brought around suddenly by a noise that seemed to emanate from the passage that led off from the alcove. He crouched at the mouth, staring into it, remembering the clangor of the gong that had echoed from it to lure him into a snare. The light from the dome filtered only a little way into that narrow corridor, and showed him only empty space. Yet he could have sworn that he had heard the furtive pad of a foot somewhere down it.

While he hesitated, he was electrified by a woman's strangled cry from behind him. Bounding through the door behind the throne, he saw an unexpected spectacle in the crystal light.

The torches of the priests had vanished from the great hall outside – but one priest was still in the palace: Gwarunga. His wicked features were convulsed with fury, and he grasped the terrified Muriela by the throat, choking her efforts to scream and plead, shaking her brutally.

'Traitress!' Between his thick red lips his voice hissed like a cobra. 'What game are you playing? Did not Zargheba tell you what to say? Aye, Thutmekri told me! Are you betraying your master, or is he betraying his friends through you? Slut! I'll twist off your false head – but first I'll—'

A widening of his captive's lovely eyes as she stared over his shoulder warned the huge black. He released her and wheeled, just as Conan's sword lashed down. The impact of the stroke knocked him headlong backward to the marble floor, where he lay twitching, blood oozing from a ragged gash in his scalp.

Conan started toward him to finish the job – for he knew that the priest's sudden movement had caused the blade to strike flat – but Muriela threw her arms convulsively about him.

'I've done as you ordered!' she gasped hysterically. 'Take me away! Oh, please take me away!'

'We can't go yet,' he grunted. 'I want to follow the priests and see where they get the jewels. There may be more loot hidden there. But you can go with me. Where's the gem you wore in your hair?'

'It must have fallen out on the dais,' she stammered, feeling for it. 'I was so frightened – when the priests left I ran out to find you, and this big brute had stayed behind, and he grabbed me—'

'Well, go get it while I dispose of this carcass,' he commanded. 'Go on! That gem is worth a fortune itself.'

She hesitated, as if loth to return to that cryptic chamber; then, as he grasped Gwarunga's girdle and dragged him into the alcove, she turned and entered the oracle room.

Conan dumped the senseless black on the floor, and lifted his sword. The Cimmerian had lived too long in the wild places of the world to have any illusions about mercy. The only safe enemy was a headless enemy. But before he could strike, a startling scream checked the lifted blade. It came from the oracle chamber.

'Conan! Conan! She's come back!' The shriek ended in a gurgle and a scraping shuffle.

With an oath Conan dashed out of the alcove, across the throne dais and into the oracle chamber, almost before the sound had ceased. There he halted, glaring bewilderedly. To all appearances Muriela lay placidly on the dais, eyes closed as in slumber.

'What in thunder are you doing?' he demanded acidly. 'Is this any time to be playing jokes—'

His voice trailed away. His gaze ran along the ivory thigh molded in the close-fitting silk skirt. That skirt should gape from girdle to hem. He knew, because it had been his own hand that tore it as he ruthlessly stripped the garment from the dancer's writhing body. But the skirt showed no rent. A single stride brought him to the dais and he laid his hand on the ivory body – snatched it away as if it had encountered hot iron instead of the cold immobility of death.

'Crom!' he muttered, his eyes suddenly slits of bale-fire. 'It's not Muriela! It's Yelaya!'

He understood now that frantic scream that had burst from Muriela's lips when she entered the chamber. The goddess had returned. The body had been stripped by Zargheba to furnish the accouterments for the pretender. Yet now it was clad in silk and jewels as Conan had first seen it. A peculiar prickling made itself manifest among the short hairs at the base of Conan's scalp.

'Muriela!' he shouted suddenly. 'Muriela! Where the devil are you?'

The walls threw back his voice mockingly. There was no entrance that he could see except the golden door, and none could have entered or departed through that without his knowledge. This much was indisputable: Yelaya had been replaced on the dais within the few minutes that had elapsed since Muriela had first left the chamber to be seized by Gwarunga; his ears were still tingling with the echoes of Muriela's scream, yet the Corinthian girl had vanished as if into thin air. There was but one explanation that offered itself to the Cimmerian, if he rejected the darker speculation that suggested the supernatural – somewhere in the chamber there was a secret door. And even as the thought crossed his mind, he saw it.

In what had seemed a curtain of solid marble, a thin perpendicular crack showed, and in the crack hung a wisp of silk. In an instant he was bending over it. That shred was from Muriela's torn skirt. The implication was unmistakable. It had been caught in the closing door and torn off as she was borne through the opening by whatever grim beings were her captors. The bit of clothing had prevented the door from fitting perfectly into its frame.

Thrusting his dagger-point into the crack, Conan exerted leverage with a corded forearm. The blade bent, but it was of unbreakable Akbitanan steel. The marble door opened. Conan's sword was lifted as he peered into the aperture beyond, but he saw no shape of menace. Light filtering into the oracle chamber revealed a short flight of steps cut out of marble. Pulling the door back to its fullest extent, he drove his dagger into a crack in the floor, propping it open. Then he went down the steps without hesitation. He saw nothing, heard nothing. A dozen steps down, the stair ended in a narrow corridor which ran straight away into gloom.

He halted suddenly, posed like a statue at the foot of the stair, staring at the paintings which frescoed the walls, half visible in the dim light which filtered down from above. The art was unmistakably Pelishtim; he had seen frescoes of identical characteristics on the walls of Asgalun. But the scenes depicted had no connection with anything Pelishtim, except for one human figure, frequently recurrent: a lean, white-bearded old man whose racial characteristics were unmistakable. They seemed to represent various sections of the palace above. Several scenes showed a chamber he recognized as the oracle chamber with the figure of Yelaya stretched upon the ivory dais and huge black men kneeling before it. And there were other figures, too – figures that moved through the deserted palace, did the bidding of the Pelishtim, and dragged unnamable things out of the subterranean river. In the few seconds Conan stood frozen, hitherto unintelligible phrases in the parchment manuscript blazed in his brain with chilling clarity. The loose bits of the pattern clicked into place. The mystery of Bît-Yakin was a mystery no longer, nor the riddle of Bît-Yakin's servants.

Conan turned and peered into the darkness, an icy finger crawling along his spine. Then he went along the corridor, cat-footed, and without hesitation, moving deeper and deeper into the darkness as he drew farther away from the stair. The air hung heavy with the odor he had scented in the court of the gong.

Now in utter blackness he heard a sound ahead of him – the shuffle of bare feet, or the swish of loose garments against stone, he could not tell which. But an instant later his outstreched hand encountered a barrier which he identified as a massive door of carven metal. He pushed against it fruitlessly, and his sword-point sought vainly for a crack. It fitted into the sill and jambs as if molded there. He exerted all his strength, his feet straining against the door, the veins knotting in his temples. It was useless; a charge of elephants would scarcely have shaken that titanic portal.

As he leaned there he caught a sound on the other side that his ears instantly identified – it was the creak of rusty iron, like a lever scraping in its slot. Instinctively action followed recognition so spontaneously that sound, impulse and action were practically simultaneous. And as his prodigious bound carried him backward, there was the rush of a great bulk from above, and a thunderous crash filled the tunnel with deafening vibrations. Bits of flying splinters struck him – a huge block of stone, he knew from the sound, dropped on the spot he had just quitted. An instant's slower thought or action and it would have crushed him like an ant.

Conan fell back. Somewhere on the other side of that metal door Muriela was a captive, if she still lived. But he could not pass that door, and if he remained in the tunnel another block might fall, and he might not be so lucky. It would do the girl no good for him to be crushed into a purple pulp. He could not continue his search in that direction. He must get above ground and look for some other avenue of approach.

He turned and hurried toward the stair, sighing as he emerged into comparative radiance. And as he set foot on the first step, the light was blotted out, and above him the marble door rushed shut with a resounding reverberation.

Something like panic seized the Cimmerian then, trapped in that black tunnel, and he wheeled on the stair, lifting his sword and glaring murderously into the darkness behind him, expecting a rush of ghoulish assailants. But there was no sound or movement down the tunnel. Did the men beyond the door – if they were men – believe that he had been disposed of by the fall of the stone from the roof, which had undoubtedly been released by some sort of machinery?

Then why had the door been shut above him? Abandoning speculation, Conan groped his way up the steps, his skin crawling in anticipation of a knife in his back at every stride, yearning to drown his semi-panic in a barbarous burst of blood-letting.

He thrust against the door at the top, and cursed soulfully to find that it did not give to his efforts. Then as he lifted his sword with his right hand to hew at the marble, his groping left encountered a metal bolt that evidently slipped into place at the closing of the door. In an instant he had drawn this bolt, and then the door gave to his shove. He bounded into the chamber like a slit-eyed, snarling incarnation of fury, ferociously desirous to come to grips with whatever enemy was hounding him.

The dagger was gone from the floor. The chamber was empty; and so was the dais. Yelaya had again vanished.

'By Crom!' muttered the Cimmerian. 'Is she alive, after all?'

He strode out into the throne-room, baffled, and then, struck by a sudden thought, stepped behind the throne and peered into the alcove. There was blood on the smooth marble where he had cast down the senseless body of Gwarunga – that was all. The black man had vanished as completely as Yelaya.

4 The Teeth of Gwahlur

Baffled wrath confused the brain of Conan the Cimmerian. He knew no more how to go about searching for Muriela than he had known how to go about searching for the Teeth of Gwahlur. Only one thought occurred to him – to follow the priests. Perhaps at the hiding-place of the treasure some clue would be revealed to him. It was a slim chance, but better than wandering about aimlessly.

As he hurried through the great shadowy hall that led to the portico, he half expected the lurking shades to come to life behind him with rending fangs and talons. But only the beat of his own rapid heart accompanied him into the moonlight that dappled the shimmering marble.

At the foot of the wide steps he cast about in the bright moonlight for some sign to show him the direction he must go. And he found it – petals scattered on the sward told where an arm or garment had brushed against a blossom-laden branch. Grass had been pressed down under heavy feet. Conan, who had tracked wolves in his native hills, found no insurmountable difficulty in following the trail of the Keshani priests.

It led away from the palace, through masses of exotic-scented shrubbery where great pale blossoms spread their shimmering petals, through verdant, tangled bushes that showered blooms at the touch, until he came at last to a great mass of rock that jutted like a titan's castle out from the cliffs at a point closest to the palace, which, however, was almost hidden from view by vine-interlaced trees. Evidently that babbling priest in Keshia had been mistaken when he said the Teeth were hidden in the palace. This trail had led him away from the place where Muriela had disappeared, but a belief was growing in Conan that each part of the valley was connected with that palace by subterranean passages.

Crouching in the deep velvet-black shadows of the bushes, he scrutinized the great jut of rock which stood out in bold relief in the moonlight. It was covered with strange, grotesque carvings, depicting men and animals, and half-bestial creatures that might have been gods or devils. The style of art differed so strikingly from that of the rest of the valley, that Conan wondered if it did not represent a different era and race, and was itself a relic of an age lost and forgotten at whatever immeasurably distant date the people of Alkmeenon had found and entered the haunted valley.

A great door stood open in the sheer curtain of the cliff, and a gigantic dragon head was carved about it so that the open door was like the dragon's gaping mouth. The door itself was of carven bronze and looked to weigh several tons. There was no lock that he could see, but a series of bolts showing along the edge of the massive portal, as it stood open, told him that there was some system of locking and unlocking – a system doubtless known only to the priests of Keshan.

The trail showed that Gorulga and his henchmen had gone through that door. But Conan hesitated. To wait until they emerged would probably mean to see the door locked in his face, and he might not be able to solve the mystery of its unlocking. On the other hand, if he followed them in, they might emerge and lock him in the cavern.

Throwing caution to the winds, he glided silently through the great portal. Somewhere in the cavern were the priests, the Teeth of Gwahlur, and perhaps a clue to the fate of Muriela. Personal risks had never yet deterred the Cimmerian from any purpose.

Moonlight illumined, for a few yards, the wide tunnel in which he found himself. Somewhere ahead of him he saw a faint glow and heard the echo of a weird chanting. The priests were not so far ahead of him as he had thought. The tunnel debouched into a wide room before the moonlight played out, an empty cavern of no great dimensions, but with a lofty, vaulted roof, glowing with a phosphorescent encrustation, which, as Conan knew, was a common phenomenon in that part of the world. It made a ghostly half-light, in which he was able to see a bestial image squatting on a shrine and the black mouths of six or seven tunnels leading off from the chamber. Down the widest of these – the one directly behind the squat image which looked toward the outer opening – he caught the gleam of torches wavering, whereas the phosphorescent glow was fixed, and heard the chanting increase in volume.

Down it he went recklessly, and was presently peering into a larger cavern than the one he had just left. There was no phosphorus here, but the light of the torches fell on a larger altar and a more obscene and repulsive god squatting toad-like upon it. Before this repugnant deity Gorulga and his ten acolytes knelt and beat their heads upon the ground, while chanting monotonously. Conan realized why their progress had been so slow. Evidently approaching the secret crypt of the Teeth was a complicated and elaborate ritual.

He was fidgeting in nervous impatience before the chanting and bowing were over, but presently they rose and passed into the tunnel which opened behind the idol. Their torches bobbed away into the nighted vault, and he followed swiftly. Not much danger of being discovered. He glided along the shadows like a creature of the night, and the black priests were completely engrossed in their ceremonial mummery. Apparently they had not even noticed the absence of Gwarunga.

Emerging into a cavern of huge proportions, about whose upward curving walls gallery-like ledges marched in tiers, they began their worship anew before an altar which was larger, and a god which was more disgusting, than any encountered thus far.

Conan crouched in the black mouth of the tunnel, staring at the walls reflecting the lurid glow of the torches. He saw a carven stone stair winding up from tier to tier of the galleries; the roof was lost in darkness.

He started violently and the chanting broke off as the kneeling blacks flung up their heads. An inhuman voice boomed out high above them. They froze on their knees, their faces turned upward with a ghastly blue hue in the sudden glare of a weird light that burst blindingly up near the lofty roof and then burned with a throbbing glow. That glare lighted a gallery and a cry went up from the high priest, echoed shudderingly by his acolytes. In the flash there had been briefly disclosed to them a slim white figure standing upright in a sheen of silk and a glint of jewel-crusted gold. Then the blaze smoldered to a throbbing, pulsing luminosity in which nothing was distinct, and that slim shape was but a shimmering blue of ivory.

'Yelaya!' screamed Gorulga, his brown features ashen. 'Why have you followed us? What is your pleasure?'

That weird unhuman voice rolled down from the roof, re-echoing under that arching vault that magnified and altered it beyond recognition.

'Woe to the unbelievers! Woe to the false children of Keshia! Doom to them which deny their deity!'

A cry of horror went up from the priests. Gorulga looked like a shocked vulture in the glare of the torches.

'I do not understand!' he stammered. 'We are faithful. In the chamber of the oracle you told us—'

'Do not heed what you heard in the chamber of the oracle!' rolled that terrible voice, multiplied until it was as though a myriad voices thundered and muttered the same warning. 'Beware of false prophets and false gods! A demon in my guise spoke to you in the palace, giving false prophecy. Now harken and obey, for only I am the true goddess, and I give you one chance to save yourselves from doom!

'Take the Teeth of Gwahlur from the crypt where they were placed so long ago. Alkmeenon is no longer holy, because it has been desecrated by blasphemers. Give the Teeth of Gwahlur into the hands of Thutmekri, the Stygian, to place in the sanctuary of Dragon and Derketo. Only this can save Keshan from the doom the demons of the night have plotted. Take the Teeth of Gwahlur and go: return instantly to Keshia; there give the jewels to Thutmekri, and seize the foreign devil Conan and flay him alive in the great square.'

There was no hesitation in obeying. Chattering with fear the priests scrambled up and ran for the door that opened behind the bestial god. Gorulga led the flight. They jammed briefly in the doorway, yelping as wildly waving torches touched squirming black bodies; they plunged through, and the patter of their speeding feet dwindled down the tunnel.

Conan did not follow. He was consumed with a furious desire to learn the truth of this fantastic affair. Was that indeed Yelaya, as the cold sweat on the backs of his hands told him, or was it that little hussy Muriela, turned traitress after all? If it was—

Before the last torch had vanished down the black tunnel he was bounding vengefully up the stone stair. The blue glow was dying down, but he could still make out that the ivory figure stood motionless on the gallery. His blood ran cold as he approached it, but he did not hesitate. He came on with his sword lifted, and towered like a threat of death over the inscrutable shape.

'Yelaya!' he snarled. 'Dead as she's been for a thousand years! Ha!'

From the dark mouth of a tunnel behind him a dark form lunged. But the sudden, deadly rush of unshod feet had reached the Cimmerian's quick ears. He whirled like a cat and dodged the blow aimed murderously at his back. As the gleaming steel in the dark hand hissed past him, he struck back with the fury of a roused python, and the long straight blade impaled his assailant and stood out a foot and a half between his shoulders.

'So!' Conan tore his sword free as the victim sagged to the floor, gasping and gurgling. The man writhed briefly and stiffened. In the dying light Conan saw a black body and ebon countenance, hideous in the blue glare. He had killed Gwarunga.

Conan turned from the corpse to the goddess. Thongs about her knees and breast held her upright against a stone pillar, and her thick hair, fastened to the column, held her head up. At a few yards' distance these bonds were not visible in the uncertain light.

'He must have come to after I descended into the tunnel,' muttered Conan. 'He must have suspected I was down there. So he pulled out the dagger' – Conan stooped and wrenched the identical weapon from the stiffening fingers, glanced at it and replaced it in his own girdle – 'and shut the door. Then he took Yelaya to befool his brother idiots. That was he shouting a while ago. You couldn't recognize his voice, under this echoing roof. And that bursting blue flame – I thought it looked familiar. It's a trick of the Stygian priests. Thutmekri must have given some of it to Gwarunga.'

He could easily have reached this cavern ahead of his companions. Evidently familiar with the plan of the caverns by hearsay or by maps handed down in the priestcraft, he had entered the cave after the others, carrying the goddess, followed a circuitous route through the tunnels and chambers, and ensconced himself and his burden on the balcony while Gorulga and the other acolytes were engaged in their endless rituals.

The blue glare had faded, but now Conan was aware of another glow, emanating from the mouth of one of the corridors that opened on the ledge. Somewhere down that corridor there was another field of phosphorus, for he recognized the faint steady radiance. The corridor led in the direction the priests had taken, and he decided to follow it, rather than descend into the darkness of the great cavern below. Doubtless it connected with another gallery in some other chamber, which might be the destination of the priests. He hurried down it, the illumination growing stronger as he advanced, until he could make out the floor and the walls of the tunnel. Ahead of him and below he could hear the priests chanting again.

Abruptly a doorway in the left-hand wall was limned in the phosphorus glow, and to his ears came the sound of soft, hysterical sobbing. He wheeled, and glared through the door.

He was looking again into a chamber hewn out of solid rock, not a natural cavern like the others. The domed roof shone with the phosphorous light, and the walls were almost covered with arabesques of beaten gold.

Near the farther wall on a granite throne, staring for ever toward the arched doorway, sat the monstrous and obscene Pteor, the god of the Pelishtim, wrought in brass, with his exaggerated attributes reflecting the grossness of his cult. And in his lap sprawled a limp white figure.

'Well, I'll be damned!' muttered Conan. He glanced suspiciously about the chamber, seeing no other entrance or evidence of occupation, and then advanced noiselessly and looked down at the girl whose slim shoulders shook with sobs of abject misery, her face sunk in her arms. From thick bands of gold on the idol's arms slim gold chains ran to smaller bands on her wrists. He laid a hand on her naked shoulder and she started convulsively, shrieked, and twisted her tear-stained face toward him.

'Conan!' She made a spasmodic effort to go into the usual clinch, but the chains hindered her. He cut through the soft gold as close to her wrists as he could, grunting: 'You'll have to wear these bracelets until I can find a chisel or a file. Let go of me, damn it! You actresses are too damned emotional. What happened to you, anyway?'

'When I went back into the oracle chamber,' she whimpered, 'I saw the goddess lying on the dais as I'd first seen her. I called out to you and started to run to the door – then something grabbed me from behind. It clapped a hand over my mouth and carried me through a panel in the wall, and down some steps and along a dark hall. I didn't see what it was that had hold of me until we passed through a big metal door and came into a tunnel whose roof was alight, like this chamber.

'Oh, I nearly fainted when I saw! They are not humans! They are gray, hairy devils that walk like men and speak a gibberish no human could understand. They stood there and seemed to be waiting, and once I thought I heard somebody trying the door. Then one of the things pulled a metal lever in the wall, and something crashed on the other side of the door.

'Then they carried me on and on through winding tunnels and up stone stairways into this chamber, where they chained me on the knees of this abominable idol, and then they went away. Oh, Conan, what are they?'

'Servants of Bît-Yakin,' he grunted. 'I found a manuscript that told me a number of things, and then stumbled upon some frescoes that told me the rest. Bît-Yakin was a Pelishtim who wandered into the valley with his servants after the people of Alkmeenon had deserted it. He found the body of Princess Yelaya, and discovered that the priests returned from time to time to make offerings to her, for even then she was worshipped as a goddess.

'He made an oracle of her, and he was the voice of the oracle, speaking from a niche he cut in the wall behind the ivory dais. The priests never suspected, never saw him or his servants for they always hid themselves when the men came. Bît-Yakin lived and died here without ever being discovered by the priests. Crom knows how long he dwelt here, but it must have been for centuries. The wise men of the Pelishtim know how to increase the span of their lives for hundreds of years. I've seen some of them myself. Why he lived here alone, and why he played the part of oracle no ordinary human can guess, but I believe the oracle part was to keep the city inviolate and sacred, so he could remain undisturbed. He ate the food the priests brought as an offering to Yelaya, and his servants ate other things — I've always known there was a subterranean river flowing away from the lake where the people of the Puntish highlands throw their dead. That river runs under this palace. They have ladders hung over the water where they can hang and fish for the corpses that come floating through. Bît-Yakin recorded everything on parchment and painted walls.

'But he died at last, and his servants mummified him according to instructions he gave them before his death, and stuck him in a cave in the cliffs. The rest is easy to guess. His servants, who were even more nearly immortal than he, kept on dwelling here, but the next time a high priest came to consult the oracle, not having a master to restrain them, they tore him to pieces. So since then — until Gorulga — nobody came to talk to the oracle.

'It's obvious they've been renewing the garments and ornaments of the goddess, as they'd seen Bî-Yakin do. Doubtless there's a sealed chamber somewhere where the silks are kept from decay. They clothed the goddess and brought her back to the oracle room after Zargheba had stolen her. And by the way they took off Zargheba's head and hung it in a thicket.'

She shivered, yet at the same time breathed a sigh of relief.

'He'll never whip me again.'

'Not this side of hell,' agreed Conan. 'But come on. Gwarunga ruined my chances with his stolen goddess. I'm going to follow the priests and take my chance of stealing the loot from them after they get it. And you stay close to me. I can't spend all my time looking for you.'

'But the servants of Bît-Yakin!' she whispered fearfully.

'We'll have to take our chance,' he grunted. 'I don't know what's in their minds, but so far they haven't shown any disposition to come out and fight in the open. Come on.'

Taking her wrist he led her out of the chamber and down the corridor. As they advanced they heard the chanting of the priests, and mingling with the sound the low sullen rushing of waters. The light grew stronger above them as they emerged on a high-pitched gallery of a great cavern and looked down on a scene weird and fantastic.

Above them gleamed the phosphorescent roof; a hundred feet below them stretched the smooth floor of the cavern. On the far side this floor was cut by a deep, narrow stream brimming its rocky channel. Rushing out of impenetrable gloom, it swirled across the cavern and was lost again in darkness. The visible surface reflected the radiance above; the dark seething waters glinted as if flecked with living jewels, frosty blue, lurid red, shimmering green, an ever-changing iridescence.

Conan and his companion stood upon one of the gallery-like ledges that banded the curve of the lofty wall, and from this ledge a natural bridge of stone soared in a breath-taking arch over the vast gulf of the cavern to join a much smaller ledge on the opposite side, across the river. Ten feet below it another, broader arch spanned the cave. At either end a carven stair joined the extremities of these flying arches.

Conan's gaze, following the curve of the arch that swept away from the ledge on which they stood, caught a glint of light that was not the lurid phosphorus of the cavern. On that small ledge opposite them there was an opening in the cave wall through which stars were glinting.

But his full attention was drawn to the scene beneath them. The priests had reached their destination. There in a sweeping angle of the cavern wall stood a stone altar, but there was no idol upon it. Whether there was one behind it, Conan could not ascertain, because some trick of the light, or the sweep of the wall, left the space behind the altar in total darkness.

The priests had stuck their torches into holes in the stone floor, forming a semicircle of fire in front of the altar at a distance of several yards. Then the priests themselves formed a semicircle inside the crescent of torches, and Gorulga, after lifting his arms aloft in invocation, bent to the altar and laid hands on it. It lifted and tilted backward on its hinder edge, like the lid of a chest, revealing a small crypt.

Extending a long arm into the recess, Gorulga brought up a small brass chest. Lowering the altar back into place, he set the chest on it, and threw back the lid. To the eager watchers on the high gallery it seemed as if the action had released a blaze of living fire which throbbed and quivered about the opened chest. Conan's heart leaped and his hand caught at his hilt. The Teeth of Gwahlur at last! The treasure that would make its possessor the richest man in the world! His breath came fast between his clenched teeth.

Then he was suddenly aware that a new element had entered into the light of the torches and of the phosphorescent roof, rendering both void. Darkness stole around the altar, except for that glowing spot of evil radiance cast by the teeth of Gwahlur, and that grew and grew. The blacks froze into basaltic statues, their shadows streaming grotesquely and gigantically out behind them.

The altar was laved in the glow now, and the astounded features of Gorulga stood out in sharp relief. Then the mysterious space behind the altar swam into the widening illumination. And slowly with the crawling light, figures became visible, like shapes growing out of the night and silence.

At first they seemed like gray stone statues, those motionless shapes, hairy, man-like, yet hideously human; but their eyes were alive, cold sparks of gray icy fire. And as the weird glow lit their bestial countenances, Gorulga screamed and fell backward, throwing up his long arms in a gesture of frenzied horror.

But a longer arm shot across the altar and a misshapen hand locked on his throat. Screaming and fighting, the high priest was dragged back across the altar; a hammer-like fist smashed down, and Gorulga's cries were stilled. Limp and broken he sagged across the altar, his brains oozing from his crushed skull. And then the servants of Bît-Yakin surged like a bursting flood from hell on the black priests who stood like horror-blasted images.

Then there was slaughter, grim and appalling.

Conan saw black bodies tossed like chaff in the inhuman hands of the slayers, against whose horrible strength and agility the daggers and swords of the priests were ineffective. He saw men lifted bodily and their heads cracked open against the stone altar. He saw a flaming torch, grasped in a monstrous hand, thrust inexorably down the gullet of an agonized wretch who writhed in vain against the arms that pinioned him. He saw a man torn in two pieces, as one might tear a chicken, and the bloody fragments hurled clear across the cavern. The massacre was as short and devastating as the rush of a hurricane. In a burst of red abysmal ferocity it was over, except for one wretch who fled screaming back the way the priests had come, pursued by a swarm of blood-dabbled shapes of horror which reached out their red-smeared hands for him. Fugitive and pursuers vanished down the black tunnel, and the screams of the human came back dwindling and confused by the distance.

Muriela was on her knees clutching Conan's legs; her face pressed against his knee and her eyes tightly shut. She was a quaking, quivering mold of abject terror. But Conan was galvanized. A quick glance across at the aperture where the stars shone, a glance down at the chest that still blazed open on the blood-smeared altar, and he saw and seized the desperate gamble.

'I'm going after that chest!' he grated. 'Stay here!'

'Oh, Mitra, no!' In an agony of fright she fell to the floor and caught at his sandals. 'Don't! Don't! Don't leave me!'

'Lie still and keep your mouth shut!' he snapped, disengaging himself from her frantic clasp.

He disregarded the tortuous stair. He dropped from ledge to ledge with reckless haste. There was no sign of the monsters as his feet hit the floor. A few of the torches still flared in their sockets, the phosphorescent glow throbbed and quivered, and the river flowed with an almost articulate muttering, scintillant with undreamed radiances. The glow that had heralded the appearance of the servants had vanished with them. Only the light of the jewels in the brass chest shimmered and quivered.

He snatched the chest, noting its contents in one lustful glance – strange, curiously shapen stones that burned with an icy, non-terrestrial fire. He slammed the lid, thrust the chest under his arm, and ran back up the steps. He had no desire to encounter the hellish servants of Bît-Yakin. His glimpse of them in action had dispelled any illusion concerning their fighting ability. Why they had waited so long before striking at the invaders he was unable to say. What human could guess the motives or thoughts of these monstrosities? That they were possessed of craft and intelligence equal to humanity had been demonstrated. And there on the cavern floor lay crimson proof of their bestial ferocity.

The Corinthian girl still cowered on the gallery where he had left her. He caught her wrist and yanked her to her feet, grunting: 'I guess it's time to go!'

Too bemused with terror to be fully aware of what was going on, the girl suffered herself to be led across the dizzy span. It was not until they were poised over the rushing water that she looked down, voiced a startled yelp and would have fallen but for Conan's massive arm about her. Growling an objurgation in her ear, he snatched her up under his free arm and swept her, in a flutter of limply waving arms and legs, across the arch and into the aperture that opened at the other end. Without bothering to set her on her feet, he hurried through the short tunnel into which this aperture opened. An instant later they emerged upon a narrow ledge on the outer side of the cliffs that circled the valley. Less than a hundred feet below them the jungle waved in the starlight.

Looking down, Conan vented a gusty sigh of relief. He believed that he could negotiate the descent, even though burdened with the jewels and the girl; although he doubted if even he, unburdened, could have ascended at that spot. He set the chest, still smeared with Gorulga's blood and clotted with his brains, on the ledge, and was about to remove his girdle in order to tie the box to his back, when he was galvanized by a sound behind him, a sound sinister and unmistakable.

'Stay here!' he snapped at the bewildered Corinthian girl. 'Don't move!' And drawing his sword, he glided into the tunnel, glaring back into the cavern.

Halfway across the upper span he saw a gray deformed shape. One of the servants of Bît-Yakin was on his trail. There was no doubt that the brute had seen them and was following them. Conan did not hesitate. It might be easier to defend the mouth of the tunnel – but this fight must be finished quickly, before the other servants could return.

He ran out on the span, straight toward the oncoming monster. It was no ape, neither was it a man. It was some shambling horror spawned in the mysterious, nameless jungles of the south, where strange life teemed in the reeking rot without the dominance of man, and drums thundered in temples that had never known the tread of a human foot. How the ancient Pelishtim had gained lordship over them – and with it eternal exile from humanity – was a foul riddle about which Conan did not care to speculate, even if he had had opportunity.

Man and monster; they met at the highest arch of the span, where, a hundred feet below, rushed the furious black water. As the monstrous shape with its leprous gray body and the features of a carven, unhuman idol loomed over him. Conan struck as a wounded tiger strikes, with every ounce of thew and fury behind the blow. That stroke would have sheared a human body asunder; but the bones of the servant of Bît-Yakin were like tempered steel. Yet even tempered steel could not wholly have withstood that furious stroke. Ribs and shoulder-bone parted and blood spouted from the great gash.

There was no time for a second stroke. Before the Cimmerian could lift his blade again or spring clear, the sweep of a giant arm knocked him from the span as a fly is flicked from a wall. As he plunged downward the rush of the river was like a knell in his ears, but his twisted body fell halfway across the lower arch. He wavered there precariously for one blood-chilling instant, then his clutching fingers hooked over the farther edge, and he scrambled to safety, his sword still in his other hand.

As he sprang up, he saw the monster, spurting blood hideously, rush toward the cliff-end of the bridge, obviously intending to descend the stair that connected the arches and renew the feud. At the very ledge the brute paused in mid-flight – and Conan saw it too – Muriela, with the jewel chest under her arm, stood staring wildly in the mouth of the tunnel.

With a triumphant bellow the monster scooped her up under one arm, snatched the jewel chest with the other hand as she dropped it, and turning, lumbered back across the bridge. Conan cursed with passion and ran for the other side also. He doubted if he could climb the stair to the higher arch in time to catch the brute before it could plunge into the labyrinth of tunnels on the other side.

But the monster was slowing, like clockwork running down. Blood gushed from that terrible gash in his breast, and he lurched drunkenly from side to side. Suddenly he stumbled, reeled and toppled sidewise – pitched headlong from the arch and hurtled downward. Girl and jewel chest fell from his nerveless hands and Muriela's scream rang terribly above the snarl of the water below.

Conan was almost under the spot from which the creature had fallen. The monster struck the lower arch glancingly and shot off, but the writhing figure of the girl struck and clung, and the chest hit the edge of the span near her. One falling object struck on one side of Conan and one on the other. Either was within arm's length; for the fraction of a split second the chest teetered on the edge of the bridge, and Muriela clung by one arm, her face turned desperately toward Conan, her eyes dilated with the fear of death and her lips parted in a haunting cry of despair.

Conan did not hesitate, nor did he even glance toward the chest that held the wealth of an epoch. With a quickness that would have shamed the spring of a hungry jaguar, he swooped, grasped the girl's arm just as her fingers slipped from the smooth stone, and snatched her up on the span with one explosive heave. The chest toppled on over and struck the water ninety feet below, where the body of the servant of Bît-Yakin had already vanished. A splash, a jetting flash of foam marked where the Teeth of Gwahlur disappeared for ever from the sight of the man.

Conan scarcely wasted a downward glance. He darted across the span and ran up the cliff stair like a cat, carrying the limp girl as if she had been an infant. A hideous ululation caused him to glance over his shoulder as he reached the higher arch, to see the other servants streaming back into the cavern below, blood dripping from their bared fangs. They raced up the stair that wound from tier to tier, roaring vengefully; but he slung the girl unceremoniously over his shoulder, dashed through the tunnel and went down the cliffs like an ape himself, dropping and springing from hold to hold with breakneck recklessness. When the fierce countenances looked over the ledge of the aperture, it was to see the Cimmerian and the girl disappearing into the forest that surrounded the cliffs.

'Well,' said Conan, setting the girl on her feet within the sheltering screen of branches, 'we can take our time now. I don't think those brutes will follow us outside the valley. Anyway, I've got a horse tied at a water-hole close by, if the lions haven't eaten him. Crom's devils! What are you crying about now?'

She covered her tear-stained face with her hands. and her slim shoulders shook with sobs.

'I lost the jewels for you,' she wailed miserably. 'It was my fault. If I'd obeyed you and stayed out on the ledge, that brute would never have seen me. You should have caught the gems and let me drown!'

'Yes, I suppose I should,' he agreed. 'But forget it. Never worry about what's past. And stop crying, will you? That's better. Come on.'

'You mean you're going to keep me? Take me with you?' she asked hopefully.

'What else do you suppose I'd do with you?' He ran an approving glance over her figure and grinned at the torn skirt which revealed a generous expanse of tempting ivory-tinted curves. 'I can use an actress like you. There's no use going back to Keshia. There's nothing in Keshan now that I want. We'll go to Punt. The people of Punt worship an ivory woman, and they wash gold out of the rivers in wicker baskets. I'll tell them that Keshan is intriguing with Thutmekri to enslave them – which is true – and that the gods have sent me to protect them – for about a houseful of gold. If I can manage to smuggle you into their temple to exchange places with their ivory goddess, we'll skin them out of their jaw teeth before we get through with them!'

BEYOND THE BLACK RIVER

1 Conan Loses His Ax

THE STILLNESS OF THE forest trail was so primeval that the tread of a soft-booted foot was a startling disturbance. At least it seemed so to the ears of the wayfarer, though he was moving along the path with the caution that must be practised by any man who ventures beyond Thunder River. He was a young man of medium height, with an open countenance and a mop of tousled tawny hair unconfined by cap or helmet. His garb was common enough for that country – a coarse tunic, belted at the waist, short leather breeches beneath, and soft buckskin boots that came short of the knee. A knife-hilt jutted from one boot-top. The broad leather belt supported a short, heavy sword and a buckskin pouch. There was no perturbation in the wide eyes that scanned the green walls which fringed the trail. Though not tall, he was well built, and the arms that the short wide sleeves of the tunic left bare were thick with corded muscle.

He tramped imperturbably along, although the last settler's cabin lay miles behind him, and each step was carrying him nearer the grim peril that hung like a brooding shadow over the ancient forest.

He was not making as much noise as it seemed to him, though he well knew that the faint tread of his booted feet would be like a tocsin of alarm to the fierce ears that might be lurking in the treacherous green fastness. His careless attitude was not genuine; his eyes and ears were keenly alert, especially his ears, for no gaze could penetrate the leafy tangle for more than a few feet in either direction.

But it was instinct more than any warning by the external senses which brought him up suddenly, his hand on his hilt. He stood stock-still in the middle of the trail, unconsciously holding his breath, wondering what he had heard, and wondering if indeed he had heard anything. The silence seemed absolute. Not a squirrel chattered or bird chirped. Then his gaze fixed itself on a mass of bushes beside the trail a few yards ahead of him. There was no breeze, yet he had seen a branch quiver. The short hairs on his scalp prickled, and he stood for an instant undecided, certain that a move in either direction would bring death streaking at him from the bushes.

A heavy chopping crunch sounded behind the leaves. The bushes were shaken violently, and simultaneously with the sound, an arrow arched erratically from among them and vanished among the trees along the trail. The wayfarer glimpsed its flight as he sprang frantically to cover.

Crouching behind a thick stem, his sword quivering in his fingers, he saw the bushes part, and a tall figure stepped leisurely into the trail. The traveler stared in surprise. The stranger was clad like himself in regard to boots and breeks, though the latter were of silk instead of leather. But he wore a sleeveless hauberk of dark mesh-mail in place of a tunic, and a helmet perched on his black mane. That helmet held the other's gaze; it was without a crest, but adorned by short bull's horns. No civilized hand ever forged that head-piece. Nor was the face below it that of a civilized man: dark, scarred, with smoldering blue eyes, it was a face untamed as the primordial forest which formed its background. The man held a broadsword in his right hand, and the edge was smeared with crimson.

'Come on out,' he called, in an accent unfamiliar to the wayfarer. 'All's safe now. There was only one of the dogs. Come on out.'

The other emerged dubiously and stared at the stranger. He felt curiously helpless and futile as he gazed on the proportions of the forest man – the massive iron-clad breast, and the arm that bore the reddened sword, burned dark by the sun and ridged and corded with muscles. He moved with the dangerous ease of a panther; he was too fiercely supple to be a product of civilization, even of that fringe of civilization which composed the outer frontiers.

Turning, he stepped back to the bushes and pulled them apart. Still not certain just what had happened, the wayfarer from the east advanced and stared down into the bushes. A man lay there, a short, dark, thickly-muscled man, naked except for a loin-cloth, a necklace of human teeth and a brass armlet. A short sword was thrust into the girdle of the loin-cloth, and one hand still gripped a heavy black bow. The man had long black hair; that was about all the wayfarer could tell about his head, for his features were a mask of blood and brains. His skull had been split to the teeth.

'A Pict, by the gods!' exclaimed the wayfarer.

The burning blue eyes turned upon him.

'Are you surprised?'

'Why, they told me at Velitrium and again at the settlers' cabins along the road, that these devils sometimes sneaked across the border, but I didn't expect to meet one this far in the interior.'

'You're only four miles east of Black River,' the stranger informed him. 'They've been shot within a mile of Velitrium. No settler between Thunder River and Fort Tuscelan is really safe. I picked up this dog's trail three miles south of the fort this morning, and I've been following him ever since. I came up behind him just as he was drawing an arrow on you. Another instant and there'd have been a stranger in Hell. But I spoiled his aim for him.'

The wayfarer was staring wide-eyed at the larger man, dumfounded by the realization that the man had actually tracked down one of the forest-devils and slain him unsuspected. That implied woodsmanship of a quality undreamed, even for Conajohara.

'You are one of the fort's garrison?' he asked.

'I'm no soldier. I draw the pay and rations of an officer of the line, but I do my work in the woods. Valannus knows I'm of more use ranging along the river than cooped up in the fort.'

Casually the slayer shoved the body deeper into the thickets with his foot, pulled the bushes together and turned away down the trail. The other followed him.

'My name is Balthus,' he offered. 'I was at Velitrium last night. I haven't decided whether I'll take up a hide of land, or enter fort-service.'

'The best land near Thunder River is already taken,' grunted the slayer. 'Plenty of good land between Scalp Creek – you crossed it a few miles back – and the fort, but that's getting too devilish close to the river. The Picts steal over to burn and murder – as that one did. They don't always come singly. Some day they'll try to sweep the settlers out of Conajohara. And they may succeed – probably will succeed. This colonization business is mad, anyway. There's plenty of good land east of the Bossonian marches. If the Aquilonians would cut up some of the big estates of their barons, and plant wheat where now only deer are hunted, they wouldn't have to cross the border and take the land of the Picts away from them.'

'That's queer talk from a man in the service of the Governor of Conajohara,' objected Balthus.

'It's nothing to me,' the other retorted. 'I'm a mercenary. I sell my sword to the highest bidder. I never planted wheat and never will, so long as there are other harvests to be reaped with the sword. But you Hyborians have expanded as far as you'll be allowed to expand. You've crossed the marches, burned a few villages, exterminated a few clans and pushed back the frontier to Black River; but I doubt if you'll even be able to hold what you've conquered, and you'll never push the frontier any further westward. Your idiotic king doesn't understand conditions here. He won't send you enough reinforcements, and there are not enough settlers to withstand the shock of a concerted attack from across the river.'

'But the Picts are divided into small clans,' persisted Balthus. 'they'll never unite. We can whip any single clan.'

'Or any three or four clans,' admitted the slayer. 'But some day a man will rise and unite thirty or forty clans, just as was done among the Cimmerians, when the Gundermen tried to push the border northward, years ago. They tried to colonize the southern marches of Cimmeria: destroyed a few small clans, built a fort-town, Venarium – you've heard the tale.'

'So I have indeed,' replied Balthus, wincing. The memory of that red disaster was a black blot in the chronicles of a proud and war-like people. 'My uncle was at Venarium when the Cimmerians swarmed over the walls. He was one of the few who escaped that slaughter. I've heard him tell the tale, many a time. The barbarians swept out of the hills in a ravening horde, without warning, and stormed Venarium with such fury none could stand before them. Men, women and children were butchered. Venarium was reduced to a mass of charred ruins, as it is to this day. The Aquilonians were driven back across the marches, and have never since tried to colonize the Cimmerian country. But you speak of Venarium familiarly. Perhaps you were there?'

'I was,' grunted the other. 'I was one of the horde that swarmed over the hills. I hadn't yet seen fifteen snows, but already my name was repeated about the council fires.'

Balthus involuntarily recoiled, staring. It seemed incredible that the man walking tranquilly at his side should have been one of those screeching, blood-mad devils that had poured over the walls of Venarium on that long-gone day to make her streets run crimson.

'Then you, too, are a barbarian!' he exclaimed involuntarily.

The other nodded, without taking offence.

'I am Conan, a Cimmerian.'

'I've heard of you.' Fresh interest quickened Balthus' gaze. No wonder the Pict had fallen victim to his own sort of subtlety. The Cimmerians were barbarians as ferocious as the Picts, and much more intelligent. Evidently Conan had spent much time among civilized men, though that contact had obviously not softened him, nor weakened any of his primitive instincts. Balthus' apprehension turned to admiration as he marked the easy cat-like stride, the effortless silence with which the Cimmerian moved along the trail. The oiled links of his armor did not clink, and Balthus knew Conan could glide through the deepest thicket or most tangled copse as noiselessly as any naked Pict that ever lived.

'You're not a Gunderman?' It was more assertion than question.

Balthus shook his head. 'I'm from the Tauran.'

'I've seen good woodsmen from the Tauran. But the Bossonians have sheltered you Aquilonians from the outer wildernesses for too many centuries. You need hardening.'

That was true; the Bossonian marches, with their fortified villages filled with determined bowmen, had long served Aquilonia as a buffer against the outlying barbarians. Now among the settlers beyond Thunder River there was growing up a breed of forest-men capable of meeting the barbarians at their own game, but their numbers were still scanty. Most of the frontiersmen were like Balthus – more of the settler than the woodsman type.

The sun had not set, but it was no longer in sight, hidden as it was behind the dense forest wall. The shadows were lengthening, deepening back in the woods as the companions strode on down the trail.

'It will be dark before we reach the fort,' commented Conan casually; then: 'Listen!'

He stopped short, half crouching, sword ready, transformed into a savage figure of suspicion and menace, poised to spring and rend. Balthus had heard it too – a wild scream that broke at its highest note. It was the cry of a man in dire fear or agony.

Conan was off in an instant, racing down the trail, each stride widening the distance between him and his straining companion. Balthus puffed a curse. Among the settlements of the Tauran he was accounted a good runner, but Conan was leaving him behind with maddening ease. Then Balthus forgot his exasperation as his ears were outraged by the most frightful cry he had ever heard. It was not human, this one; it was a demoniacal caterwauling of hideous triumph that seemed to exult over fallen humanity and find echo in black gulfs beyond human ken.

Balthus faltered in his stride, and clammy sweat beaded his flesh. But Conan did not hesitate; he darted around a bend in the trail and disappeared, and Balthus, panicky at finding himself alone with that awful scream still shuddering through the forest in grisly echoes, put on an extra burst of speed and plunged after him.

The Aquilonian slid to a stumbling halt, almost colliding with the Cimmerian who stood in the trail over a crumpled body. But Conan was not looking at the corpse which lay there in the crimson-soaked dust. He was glaring into the deep woods on either side of the trail.

Balthus muttered a horrified oath. It was the body of a man which lay there in the trail, a short, fat man, clad in the gilt-worked boots and (despite the heat) the ermine-trimmed tunic of a wealthy merchant. His fat, pale face was set in a stare of frozen horror; his thick throat had been slashed from ear to ear as if by a razor-sharp blade. The short sword still in its scabbard seemed to indicate that he had been struck down without a chance to fight for his life.

'A Pict?' Balthus whispered, as he turned to peer into the deepening shadows of the forest.

Conan shook his head and straightened to scowl down at the dead man.

'A forest devil. This is the fifth, by Crom!'

'What do you mean?'

'Did you ever hear of a Pictish wizard called Zogar Sag?'

Balthus shook his head uneasily.

'He dwells in Gwawela, the nearest village across the river. Three months ago he hid beside this road and stole a string of pack-mules from a pack-train bound for the fort – drugged their drivers, somehow. The mules belonged to this man' – Conan casually indicated the corpse with his foot – 'Tiberias, a merchant of Velitrium. They were loaded with ale-kegs, and old Zogar stopped to guzzle before he got across the river. A woodsman named Soractus trailed him, and led Valannus and three soldiers to where he lay dead drunk in a thicket. At the importunities of Tiberias, Valannus threw Zogar Sag into a cell, which is the worst insult you can give a Pict. He managed to kill his guard and escape, and sent back word that he meant to kill Tiberias and the five men who captured him in a way that would make Aquilonians shudder for centuries to come.

'Well, Soractus and the soldiers are dead. Soractus was killed on the river, the soldiers in the very shadow of the fort. And now Tiberias is dead. No Pict killed any of them. Each victim – except Tiberias, as you see – lacked his head – which no doubt is now ornamenting the altar of Zogar Sag's particular god.'

'How do you know they weren't killed by the Picts?' demanded Balthus.

Conan pointed to the corpse of the merchant.

'You think that was done with a knife or a sword? Look closer and you'll see that only a talon could have made a gash like that. The flesh is ripped, not cut.'

'Perhaps a panther—' began Balthus, without conviction.

Conan shook his head impatiently.

'A man from the Tauran couldn't mistake the mark of a panther's claws. No. It's a forest devil summoned by Zogar Sag to carry out his revenge. Tiberias was a fool to start for Velitrium alone, and so close to dusk. But each one of the victims seemed to be smitten with madness just before doom overtook him. Look here; the signs are plain enough. Tiberias came riding along the trail on his mule, maybe with a bundle of choice otter pelts behind his saddle to sell in Velitrium, and the *thing* sprang on him from behind that bush. See where the branches are crushed down.

'Tiberias gave one scream, and then his throat was torn open and he was selling his otter skins in Hell. The mule ran away into the woods. Listen! Even now you can hear him thrashing about under the trees. The demon didn't have time to take Tiberias' head; it took fright as we came up.'

'As *you* came up,' amended Balthus. 'It must not be a very terrible creature if it flees from one armed man. But how do you know it was not a Pict with some kind of a hook that rips instead of slicing? Did you see it?'

'Tiberias was an armed man,' grunted Conan. 'If Zogar Sag can bring demons to aid him, he can tell them which men to kill and which to let alone. No, I didn't see it. I only saw the bushes shake as it left the trail. But if you want further proof, look here!'

The slayer had stepped into the pool of blood in which the dead man sprawled. Under the bushes at the edge of the path there was a footprint, made in blood on the hard loam.

'Did a man make that?' demanded Conan.

Balthus felt his scalp prickle. Neither man nor any beast that he had ever seen could have left that strange, monstrous three-toed print, that was curiously combined of the bird and the reptile, yet a true type of neither. He spread his fingers above the print, careful not to touch it, and grunted explosively. He could not span the mark.

'What is it?' he whispered. 'I never saw a beast that left a spoor like that.'

'Nor any other sane man,' answered Conan grimly. 'It's a swamp demon – they're thick as bats in the swamps beyond Black River. You can hear them howling like damned souls when the wind blows strong from the south on hot nights.'

'What shall we do?' asked the Aquilonian, peering uneasily into the deep blue shadows. The frozen fear on the dead countenance haunted him. He wondered what hideous head the wretch had seen thrust grinning from among the leaves to chill his blood with terror.

'No use to try to follow a demon,' grunted Conan, drawing a short woodsman's ax from his girdle. 'I tried tracking him after he killed Soractus. I lost his trail within a dozen steps. He might have grown himself wings and flown away, or sunk down through the earth to Hell. I don't know. I'm not going after the mule, either. It'll either wander back to the fort, or to some settler's cabin.'

As he spoke Conan was busy at the edge of the trail with his ax. With a few strokes he cut a pair of saplings nine or ten feet long, and denuded them of their branches. Then he cut a length from a serpent-like vine that crawled among the bushes near by, and making one end fast to one of the poles, a couple of feet from the end, whipped the vine over the other sapling and interlaced it back and forth. In a few moments he had a crude but strong litter.

'The demon isn't going to get Tiberias' head if I can help it,' he growled. 'We'll carry the body into the fort. It isn't more than three miles. I never liked the fat fool, but we can't have Pictish devils making so cursed free with white men's heads.'

The Picts were a white race, though swarthy, but the border men never spoke of them as such.

Balthus took the rear end of the litter, onto which Conan unceremoniously dumped the unfortunate merchant, and they moved on down the trail as swiftly as possible. Conan made no more noise laden with their grim burden than he had made when unencumbered. He had made a loop with the merchant's belt at the end of the poles, and was carrying his share of the load with one hand, while the other gripped his naked broadsword, and his restless gaze roved the sinister walls about them. The shadows were thickening. A darkening blue mist blurred the outlines of the foliage. The forest deepened in the twilight, became a blue haunt of mystery sheltering unguessed things.

They had covered more than a mile, and the muscles in Balthus' sturdy arms were beginning to ache a little, when a cry rang shuddering from the woods whose blue shadows were deepening into purple.

Conan started convulsively, and Balthus almost let go the poles.

'A woman!' cried the younger man. 'Great Mitra, a woman cried out then!'

'A settler's wife straying in the woods,' snarled Conan, setting down his end of the litter. 'Looking for a cow, probably, and – stay here!'

He dived like a hunting wolf into the leafy wall. Balthus' hair bristled.

'Stay here alone with this corpse and a devil hiding in the woods?' he yelped. 'I'm coming with you!'

And suiting action to words, he plunged after the Cimmerian. Conan glanced back at him, but made no objection, though he did not moderate his pace to accommodate the shorter legs of his companion. Balthus wasted his wind in swearing as the Cimmerian drew away from him again, like a phantom between the trees, and then Conan burst into a dim glade and halted crouching, lips snarling, sword lifted.

'What are we stopping for?' panted Balthus, dashing the sweat out of his eyes and gripping his short sword.

'That scream came from this glade, or near by,' answered Conan. 'I don't mistake the location of sounds, even in the woods. But where—'

Abruptly the sound rang out again – *behind them*; in the direction of the trail they had just quitted. It rose piercingly and pitifully, the cry of a woman in frantic terror – and then, shockingly, it changed to a yell of mocking laughter that might have burst from the lips of a fiend of lower Hell.

'What in Mitra's name—' Balthus' face was a pale blur in the gloom.

With a scorching oath Conan wheeled and dashed back the way he had come, and the Aquilonian stumbled bewilderedly after him. He blundered into the Cimmerian as the latter stopped dead, and rebounded from his brawny shoulders as though from an iron statue. Gasping from the impact, he heard Conan's breath hiss through his teeth. The Cimmerian seemed frozen in his tracks.

Looking over his shoulder, Balthus felt his hair stand up stiffly. Something was moving through the deep bushes that fringed the trail – something that neither walked nor flew, but seemed to glide like a serpent. But it was not a serpent. Its outlines were indistinct, but it was taller than a man, and not very bulky. It gave off a glimmer of weird light, like a faint blue flame. Indeed, the eery fire was the only tangible thing about it. It might have been an embodied flame moving with reason and purpose through the blackening woods.

Conan snarled a savage curse and hurled his ax with ferocious will. But the thing glided on without altering its course. Indeed it was only a few instants' fleeting glimpse they had of it – a tall, shadowy thing of misty flame floating through the thickets. Then it was gone, and the forest crouched in breathless stillness.

With a snarl Conan plunged through the intervening foliage and into the trail. His profanity, as Balthus floundered after him, was lurid and impassioned. The Cimmerian was standing over the litter on which lay the body of Tiberias. And that body no longer possessed a head.

'Tricked us with its damnable caterwauling!' raved Conan, swinging his great sword about his head in his wrath. 'I might have known! I might have guessed a trick! Now there'll be five heads to decorate Zogar's altar.'

'But what thing is it that can cry like a woman and laugh like a devil, and shines like witch-fire as it glides through the trees?' gasped Balthus, mopping the sweat from his pale face.

'A swamp devil,' responded Conan morosely. 'Grab those poles. We'll take in the body, anyway. At least our load's a bit lighter.'

With which grim philosophy he gripped the leathery loop and stalked down the trail.

2 The Wizard of Gwawela

Fort Tuscelan stood on the eastern bank of Black River, the tides of which washed the foot of the stockade. The latter was of logs, as were all the buildings within, including the donjon (to dignify it by that appellation), in which were the governor's quarters, overlooking the stockade and the sullen river. Beyond that river lay a huge forest, which approached jungle-like density along the spongy shores. Men paced the runways along the log parapet day and night, watching that dense green wall. Seldom a menacing figure appeared, but the sentries knew that they too were watched, fiercely, hungrily, with the mercilessness of ancient hate. The forest beyond the river might seem desolate and vacant of life to the ignorant eye, but life teemed there, not alone of bird and beast and reptile, but also of men, the fiercest of all the hunting beasts.

There, at the fort, civilization ended. Fort Tuscelan was the last outpost of a civilized world; it represented the westernmost thrust of the dominant Hyborian races. Beyond the river the primitive still reigned in shadowy forests, brush-thatched huts where hung the grinning skulls of men, and mud-walled enclosures where fires flickered and drums rumbled, and spears were whetted in the hands of dark, silent men with tangled black hair and the eyes of serpents. Those eyes often glared through the bushes at the fort across the river. Once dark-skinned men had built their huts where that fort stood; yes, and their huts had risen where now stood the fields and log cabins of fair-haired settlers, back beyond Velitrium, that raw, turbulent frontier town on the banks of Thunder River, to the shores of that other river that bounds the Bossonian marches. Traders had come, and priests of Mitra who walked with bare feet and empty hands, and died horribly, most of them; but soldiers had followed, and men with axes in their hands and women and children in ox-drawn wains. Back to Thunder River, and still back, beyond Black River the aborigines had been pushed, with slaughter and massacre. But the dark-skinned people did not forget that once Conajohara had been theirs.

The guard inside the eastern gate bawled a challenge. Through a barred aperture torchlight flickered, glinting on a steel head-piece and suspicious eyes beneath it.

'Open the gate,' snorted Conan. 'You see it's I, don't you?'

Military discipline put his teeth on edge.

The gate swung inward and Conan and his companion passed through. Balthus noted that the gate was flanked by a tower on each side, the summits of which rose above the stockade. He saw loopholes for arrows.

The guardsmen grunted as they saw the burden borne between the men. Their pikes jangled against each other as they thrust shut the gate, chin on shoulder, and Conan asked testily: 'Have you never seen a headless body before?'

The face of the soldiers were pallid in the torchlight.

'That's Tiberias,' blurted one. 'I recognize that fur-trimmed tunic. Valerius here owes me five lunas. I told him Tiberias had heard the loon call when he rode through the gate on his mule, with his glassy stare. I wagered he'd come back without his head.'

Conan grunted enigmatically, motioned Balthus to ease the litter to the ground, and then strode off toward the governor's quarters, with the Aquilonian at his heels. The tousle-headed youth stared about him eagerly and curiously, noting the rows of barracks along the walls, the stables, the tiny merchants' stalls, the towering blockhouse, and the other buildings, with the open square in the middle where the soldiers drilled, and where, now, fires danced and men off duty lounged. These were now hurrying to join the morbid crowd gathered about the litter at the gate. The rangy figures of Aquilonian pikemen and forest runners mingled with the shorter, stockier forms of Bossonian archers.

He was not greatly surprised that the governor received them himself. Autocratic society with its rigid caste laws lay east of the marches. Valannus was still a young man, well knit, with a finely chiseled countenance already carved into sober cast by toil and responsibility.

'You left the fort before daybreak, I was told,' he said to Conan. 'I had begun to fear that the Picts had caught you at last.'

'When they smoke my head the whole river will know it,' grunted Conan. 'They'll hear Pictish women wailing their dead as far as Velitrium – I was on a lone scout. I couldn't sleep. I kept hearing drums talking across the river.'

'They talk each night,' reminded the governor, his fine eyes shadowed, as he stared closely at Conan. He had learned the unwisdom of discounting wild men's instincts.

'There was a difference last night,' growled Conan. 'There has been ever since Zogar Sag got back across the river.'

'We should either have given him presents and sent him home, or else hanged him,' sighed the governor. 'You advised that, but—'

'But it's hard for you Hyborians to learn the ways of the outlands,' said Conan. 'Well, it can't be helped now, but there'll be no peace on the border so long as Zogar lives and remembers the cell he sweated in. I was following a warrior who slipped over to put a few white notches on his bow. After I split his head I fell in with this lad whose name is

Balthus and who's come from the Tauran to help hold the frontier.'

Valannus approvingly eyed the young man's frank countenance and strongly-knit frame.

'I am glad to welcome you, young sir. I wish more of your people would come. We need men used to forest life. Many of our soldiers and some of our settlers are from the eastern provinces and know nothing of woodcraft, or even of agricultural life.'

'Not many of that breed this side of Velitrium,' grunted Conan. 'That town's full of them, though. But listen, Valannus, we found Tiberias dead on the trail.' And in a few words he related the grisly affair.

Valannus paled. 'I did not know he had left the fort. He must have been mad!'

'He was,' answered Conan. 'Like the other four; each one, when his time came, went mad and rushed into the woods to meet his death like a hare running down the throat of a python. *Something* called to them from the deeps of the forest, something the men call a loon, for lack of a better name, but only the doomed ones could hear it. Zogar Sag has made a magic that Aquilonian civilization can't overcome.'

To this thrust Valannus made no reply; he wiped his brow with a shaky hand.

'Do the soldiers know of this?'

'We left the body by the eastern gate.'

'You should have concealed the fact, hidden the corpse somewhere in the woods. The soldiers are nervous enough already.'

'They'd have found it out some way. If I'd hidden the body, it would have been returned to the fort as the corpse of Soractus was – tied up outside the gate for the men to find in the morning.'

Valannus shuddered. Turning, he walked to a casement and stared silently out over the river, black and shiny under the glint of the stars. Beyond the river the jungle rose like an ebony wall. The distant screech of a panther broke the stillness. The night pressed in, blurring the sounds of the soldiers outside the blockhouse, dimming the fires. A wind whispered through the black branches, rippling the dusky water. On its wings came a low, rhythmic pulsing, sinister as the pad of a leopard's foot.

'After all,' said Valannus, as if speaking his thoughts aloud, 'what do we know – what does anyone know – of the things that jungle may hide? We have dim rumors of great swamps and rivers, and a forest that stretches on and on over everlasting plains and hills to end at last on the shores of the western ocean. But what things lie between this river and that ocean we dare not even guess. No white man has ever plunged deep into that fastness and returned alive to tell us what he found. We are wise in our civilized knowledge, but our knowledge extends just so far – to the western bank of that ancient river! Who knows what shapes earthly and unearthly may lurk beyond the dim circle of light our knowledge has cast?

'Who knows what gods are worshipped under the shadows of that heathen forest, or what devils crawl out of the black ooze of the swamps? Who can be sure that all the inhabitants of that black country are natural? Zogar Sag – a sage of the eastern cities would sneer at his primitive magic-making as the mummery of a fakir; yet he has driven mad and killed five men in a manner no man can explain. I wonder if he himself is wholly human.'

'If I can get within ax-throwing distance of him I'll settle that question,' growled Conan, helping himelf to the governor's wine and pushing a glass toward Balthus, who took it hesitatingly, and with an uncertain glance toward Valannus.

The governor turned toward Conan and stared at him thoughtfully.

'The soldiers, who do not believe in ghosts or devils,' he said, 'are almost in a panic of fear. You, who believe in ghosts, ghouls, goblins, and all manner of uncanny things, do not seem to fear any of the things in which you believe.'

'There's nothing in the universe cold steel won't cut,' answered Conan. 'I threw my ax at the demon, and he took no hurt, but I might have missed, in the dusk, or a branch deflected its flight. I'm not going out of my way looking for devils; but I wouldn't step out of my path to let one go by.'

Valannus lifted his head and met Conan's gaze squarely.

'Conan, more depends on you than you realize. You know the weakness of this province – a slender wedge thrust into the untamed wilderness. You know that the lives of all the people west of the marches depend on this fort. Were it to fall, red axes would be splintering the gates of Velitrium before a horseman could cross the marches. His majesty, or his majesty's advisers, have ignored my plea that more troops be sent to hold the frontier. They know nothing of border conditions, and are averse to expending any more money in this direction. The fate of the frontier depends upon the men who now hold it.

'You know that most of the army which conquered Conajohara has been withdrawn. You know the force left me is inadequate, especially since that devil Zogar Sag managed to poison our water supply, and forty men died in one day. Many of the others are sick, or have been bitten by serpents or mauled by wild beasts which seem to swarm in increasing numbers in the vicinity of the fort. The soldiers believe Zogar's boast that he could summon the forest beasts to slay his enemies.

'I have three hundred pikemen, four hundred Bossonian archers, and perhaps fifty men who, like yourself, are skilled in woodcraft. They are worth ten times their number of soldiers, but there are so few of them. Frankly, Conan, my situation is becoming precarious. The soldiers whisper of desertion; they are low-spirited, believing Zogar Sag has loosed devils on us. They fear the black plague with which he threatened us – the terrible black death of the swamplands. When I see a sick soldier I sweat with fear of seeing him turn black and shrivel and die before my eyes.

'Conan, if the plague is loosed upon us, the soldiers will desert in a body! The border will be left unguarded and nothing will check the sweep of the dark-skinned hordes to the very gates of Velitrium – maybe beyond! If we can not hold the fort, how can they hold the town?

'Conan, Zogar Sag must die, if we are to hold Conajohara. You have penetrated the unknown deeper than any other man in the fort; you know where Gwawela stands, and something of the forest trails across the river. Will you take a band of men tonight and endeavour to kill or capture him? Oh, I know it's mad. There isn't more than one chance in a thousand that any of you will come back alive. But if we don't get him, it's death for us all. You can take as many men as you wish.'

'A dozen men are better for a job like that than a regiment,' answered Conan. 'Five hundred men couldn't fight their way to Gwawela and back, but a dozen might slip in and out again. Let me pick my men. I don't want any soldiers.'

'Let me go!' eagerly exclaimed Balthus. 'I've hunted deer all my life on the Tauran.'

'All right. Valannus, we'll eat at the stall where the foresters gather, and I'll pick my men. We'll start within an hour, drop down the river in a boat to a point below the village and then steal upon it through the woods. If we live, we should be back by daybreak.'

3 The Crawlers in the Dark

The river was a vague trace between walls of ebony. The paddles that propelled the long boat creeping along in the dense shadow of the eastern bank dipped softly into the water, making no more noise than the beak of a heron. The broad shoulders of the man in front of Balthus were a blur in the dense gloom. He knew that not even the keen eyes of the man who knelt in the prow would discern anything more than a few feet ahead of them. Conan was feeling his way by instinct and an intensive familiarity with the river.

No one spoke. Balthus had had a good look at his companions in the fort before they slipped out of the stockade and down the bank into the waiting canoe. They were of a new breed growing up in the world on the raw edge of the frontier – men whom grim necessity had taught woodcraft. Aquilonians of the western provinces to a man, they had many points in common. They dressed alike – in buckskin boots, leathern breeks and deerskin shirts, with broad girdles that held axes and short swords; and they were all gaunt and scarred and hard-eyed; sinewy and taciturn.

They were wild men, of a sort, yet there was still a wide gulf between them and the Cimmerian. They were sons of civilization, reverted to a semi-barbarism. He was a barbarian of a thousand generations of barbarians. They had acquired stealth and craft, but he had been born to these things. He excelled them even in lithe economy of motion. They were wolves, but he was a tiger.

Balthus admired them and their leader and felt a pulse of pride that he was admitted into their company. He was proud that his paddle made no more noise than did theirs. In that respect at least he was their equal, though woodcraft learned in hunts on the Tauran could never equal that ground into the souls of men on the savage border.

Below the fort the river made a wide bend. The lights of the outpost were quickly lost, but the canoe held on its way for nearly a mile, avoiding snags and floating logs with almost uncanny precision.

Then a low grunt from their leader, and they swung its head about and glided toward the opposite shore. Emerging from the black shadows of the brush that fringed the bank and coming into the open of the midstream created a peculiar illusion of rash exposure. But the stars gave little light, and Balthus knew that unless one were watching for it, it would be all but impossible for the keenest eye to make out the shadowy shape of the canoe crossing the river.

They swung in under the overhanging bushes of the western shore and Balthus groped for and found a projecting root which he grasped. No word was spoken. All instructions had been given before the scouting-party left the fort. As silently as a great panther Conan slid over the side and vanished in the bushes. Equally noiseless, nine men followed him. To Balthus, grasping the root with his paddle across his knee, it seemed incredible that ten men should thus fade into the tangled forest without a sound.

He settled himself to wait. No word passed between him and the other man who had been left with him. Somewhere, a mile or so to the northwest, Zogar Sag's village stood girdled with thick woods. Balthus understood his orders; he and his companion were to wait for the return of the raiding-party. If Conan and his men had not returned by the first tinge of dawn, they were to race back up the river to the fort and report that the forest had again taken its immemorial toll of the invading race. The silence was oppressive. No sound came from the black woods, invisible beyond the ebony masses that were the overhanging bushes. Balthus no longer heard the drums. They had been silent for hours. He kept blinking, unconsciously trying to see through the deep gloom. The dank night-smells of the river and the damp forest oppressed him. Somewhere, near by, there was a sound as if a big fish had flopped and splashed the water. Balthus thought it must have leaped so close to the canoe that it had struck the side, for a slight quiver vibrated the craft. The boat's stern began to swing, slightly away from the shore. The man behind him must have let go of the projection he was gripping. Balthus twisted his head to hiss a warning, and could just make out the figure of his companion, a slightly blacker bulk in the blackness.

The man did not reply. Wondering if he had fallen asleep, Balthus reached out and grasped his shoulder. To his amazement, the man crumpled under his touch and slumped down in the canoe. Twisting his body half about, Balthus groped for him, his heart shooting into his throat. His fumbling fingers slid over the man's throat – only the youth's convulsive clenching of his jaws choked back the cry that rose to his lips. His fingers encountered a gaping, oozing wound – his companion's throat had been cut from ear to ear.

In that instant of horror and panic Balthus started up – and then a muscular arm out of the darkness locked fiercely about his throat, strangling his yell. The canoe rocked wildly. Balthus' knife was in his hand, though he did not remember jerking it out of his boot, and he stabbed fiercely and blindly. He felt the blade sink deep, and a fiendish yell rang in his ear, a yell that was horribly answered. The darkness seemed to come to life about him. A bestial clamor rose on all sides, and other arms grappled him. Borne under a mass of hurtling bodies the canoe rolled sidewise, but before he went under with it, something cracked against Balthus' head and the night was briefly illuminated by a blinding burst of fire before it gave way to a blackness where not even stars shone.

4 The Beasts of Zogar Sag

Fires dazzled Balthus again as he slowly recovered his senses. He blinked, shook his head. Their glare hurt his eyes. A confused medley of sound rose about him, growing more distinct as his senses cleared.

He lifted his head and stared stupidly about him. Black figures hemmed him in, etched against crimson tongues of flame.

Memory and understanding came in a rush. He was bound upright to a post in an open space, ringed by fierce and terrible figures. Beyond that ring fires burned, tended by naked, dark-skinned women. Beyond the fires he saw huts of mud and wattle, thatched with brush. Beyond the huts there was a stockade with a broad gate. But he saw these things only incidentally. Even the cryptic dark women with their curious coiffures were noted by him only absently. His full attention was fixed in awful fascination on the men who stood glaring at him.

Short men, broad-shouldered, deep-chested, lean-hipped, they were naked except for scanty loin-clouts. The firelight brought out the play of their swelling muscles in bold relief. Their dark faces were immobile, but their narrow eyes glittered with the fire that burns in the eyes of a stalking tiger. Their tangled manes were bound back with bands of copper. Swords and axes were in their hands. Crude bandages banded the limbs of some, and smears of blood were dried on their dark skins. There had been fighting, recent and deadly.

His eyes wavered away from the steady glare of his captors, and he repressed a cry of horror. A few feet away there rose a low, hideous pyramid: it was built of gory human heads. Dead eyes glared glassily up at the black sky. Numbly he recognized the countenances which were turned toward him. They were the heads of the men who had followed Conan into the forest. He could not tell if the Cimmerian's head were among them. Only a few faces were visible to him. It looked to him as if there must be ten or eleven heads at least. A deadly sickness assailed him. He fought a desire to retch. Beyond the heads lay the bodies of half a dozen Picts, and he was aware of a fierce exultation at the sight. The forest runners had taken toll, at least.

Twisting his head away from the ghastly spectacle, he became aware that another post stood near him – a stake painted black as was the one to which he was bound. A man sagged in his bonds there, naked except for his leathern breeks, whom Balthus recognized as one of Conan's woodsmen. Blood trickled from his mouth, oozed sluggishly from a gash in his side. Lifting his head as he licked his livid lips, he muttered, making himself heard with difficulty above the fiendish clamor of the Picts: 'So they got you, too!'

'Sneaked up in the water and cut the other fellow's throat,' groaned Balthus. 'We never heard them till they were on us. Mitra, how can anything move so silently?'

'They're devils,' mumbled the frontiersman. 'They must have been watching us from the time we left midstream. We walked into a trap.

Arrows from all sides were ripping into us before we knew it. Most of us dropped at the first fire. Three or four broke through the bushes and came to hand-grips. But there were too many. Conan might have gotten away. I haven't seen his head. Been better for you and me if they'd killed us outright. I can't blame Conan. Ordinarily we'd have gotten to the village without being discovered. They don't keep spies on the river bank as far down as we landed. We must have stumbled into a big party coming up the river from the south. Some devilment is up. Too many Picts here. These aren't all Gwaweli; men from the western tribes here and from up and down the river.'

Balthus stared at the ferocious shapes. Little as he knew of Pictish ways, he was aware that the number of men clustered about them was out of proportion to the size of the village. There were not enough huts to have accommodated them all. Then he noticed that there was a difference in the barbaric tribal designs painted on their faces and breasts.

'Some kind of devilment,' muttered the forest runner. 'They might have gathered here to watch Zogar's magic-making. He'll make some rare magic with our carcasses. Well, a border-man doesn't expect to die in bed. But I wish we'd gone out along with the rest.'

The wolfish howling of the Picts rose in volume and exultation, and from a movement in their ranks, an eager surging and crowding, Balthus deduced that someone of importance was coming. Twisting his head about, he saw that the stakes were set before a long building, larger than the other huts, decorated by human skulls dangling from the eaves. Through the door of that structure now danced a fantastic figure.

'Zogar!' muttered the woodsman, his bloody countenance set in wolfish lines as he unconsciously strained at his cords. Balthus saw a lean figure of middle height, almost hidden in ostrich plumes set on a harness of leather and copper. From amidst the plumes peered a hideous and malevolent face. The plumes puzzled Balthus. He knew their source lay half the width of a world to the south. They fluttered and rustled evilly as the shaman leaped and cavorted.

With fantastic bounds and prancings he entered the ring and whirled before his bound and silent captives. With another man it would have seemed ridiculous – a foolish savage prancing meaninglessly in a whirl of feathers. But that ferocious face glaring out from the billowing mass gave the scene a grim significance. No man with a face like that could seem ridiculous or like anything except the devil he was.

Suddenly he froze to statuesque stillness; the plumes rippled once and sank about him. The howling warriors fell silent. Zogar Sag stood erect and motionless, and he seemed to increase in height – to grow and expand. Balthus experienced the illusion that the Pict was towering above him, staring contemptuously down from a great height, though he knew the shaman was not as tall as himself. He shook off the illusion with difficulty.

The shaman was talking now, a harsh, guttural intonation that yet carried the hiss of a cobra. He thrust his head on his long neck toward the wounded man on the stake; his eyes shone red as blood in the firelight. The frontiersman spat full in his face.

With a fiendish howl Zogar bounded convulsively into the air, and the warriors gave tongue to a yell that shuddered up to the stars. They rushed toward the man on the stake, but the shaman beat them back. A snarled command sent men running to the gate. They hurled it open, turned and raced back to the circle. The ring of men split, divided with desperate haste to right and left. Balthus saw the women and naked children scurrying to the huts. They peeked out of doors and windows. A broad lane was left to the open gate, beyond which loomed the black forest, crowding sullenly in upon the clearing, unlighted by the fires.

A tense silence reigned as Zogar Sag turned toward the forest, raised on his tiptoes and sent a weird inhuman call shuddering out into the night. Somewhere, far out in the black forest, a deeper cry answered him. Balthus shuddered. From the timbre of that cry he knew it never came from a human throat. He remembered what Valannus had said – that Zogar boasted that he could summon wild beasts to do his bidding. The woodsman was livid beneath his mask of blood. He licked his lips spasmodically.

The village held its breath. Zogar Sag stood still as a statue, his plumes trembling faintly about him. But suddenly the gate was no longer empty.

A shuddering gasp swept over the village and men crowded hastily back, jamming one another between the huts. Balthus felt the short hair stir on his scalp. The creature that stood in the gate was like the embodiment of nightmare legend. Its color was of a curious pale quality which made it seem ghostly and unreal in the dim light. But there was nothing unreal about the low-hung savage head, and the great curved fangs that glistened in the firelight. On noiseless padded feet it approached like a phantom out of the past. It was a survival of an older, grimmer age, the ogre of many an ancient legend – a saber-tooth tiger. No Hyborian hunter had looked upon one of those primordial brutes for centuries. Immemorial myths lent the creatures a supernatural quality, induced by their ghostly color and their fiendish ferocity.

The beast that glided toward the men on the stakes was longer and heavier than a common, striped tiger, almost as bulky as a bear. Its shoulders and forelegs were so massive and mightily muscled as to give it a curiously top-heavy look, though its hind-quarters were more powerful than that of a lion. Its jaws were massive, but its head was brutishly shaped. Its brain capacity was small. It had room for no instincts except those of destruction. It was a freak of carnivorous development, evolution run amuck in a horror of fangs and talons.

This was the monstrosity Zogar Sag had summoned out of the forest. Balthus no longer doubted the actuality of the shaman's magic. Only the black arts could establish a domination over that tiny-brained, mighty-thewed monster. Like a whisper at the back of his consciousness rose the vague memory of the name of an ancient god of darkness and primordial fear, to whom once both men and beasts bowed and whose children – men whispered – still lurked in dark corners of the world. New horror tinged the glare he fixed on Zogar Sag.

The monster moved past the heap of bodies and the pile of gory heads without appearing to notice them. He was no scavenger. He hunted only the living, in a life dedicated solely to slaughter. An awful hunger burned greenly in the wide, unwinking eyes; the hunger not alone of belly-emptiness, but the lust of death-dealing. His gaping jaws slavered. The shaman stepped back; his hand waved toward the woodsman.

The great cat sank into a crouch, and Balthus numbly remembered tales of its appalling ferocity: of how it would spring upon an elephant and drive its sword-like fangs so deeply into the titan's skull that they could never be withdrawn, but would keep it nailed to its victim, to die by starvation. The shaman cried out shrilly, and with an ear-shattering roar the monster sprang.

Balthus had never dreamed of such a spring, such a hurtling of incarnated destruction embodied in that giant bulk of iron thews and ripping talons. Full on the woodsman's breast it struck, and the stake splintered and snapped at the base, crashing to the earth under the impact. Then the saber-tooth was gliding toward the gate, half dragging, half carrying a hideous crimson hulk that only faintly resembled a man. Balthus glared almost paralysed, his brain refusing to credit what his eyes had seen.

In that leap the great beast had not only broken off the stake, it had ripped the mangled body of its victim from the post to which it was bound. The huge talons in that instant of contact had disemboweled and partially dismembered the man, and the giant fangs had torn away the whole top of his head, shearing through the skull as easily as through flesh. Stout rawhide thongs had given way like paper; where the thongs had held, flesh and bones had not. Balthus retched suddenly. He had hunted bears and panthers, but he had never dreamed the beast lived which could make such a red ruin of a human frame in the flicker of an instant.

The saber-tooth vanished through the gate, and a few moments later a deep roar sounded through the forest, receding in the distance. But the Picts still shrank back against the huts, and the shaman still stood facing the gate that was like a black opening to let in the night.

Cold sweat burst suddenly out on Balthus' skin. What new horror would come through that gate to make carrion-meat of his body? Sick panic assailed him and he strained futilely at his thongs. The night pressed in very black and horrible outside the firelight. The fires themselves glowed lurid as the fires of hell. He felt the eyes of the Picts upon him – hundreds of hungry, cruel eyes that reflected the lust of souls utterly without humanity as he knew it. They no longer seemed men; they were devils of this black jungle, as inhuman as the creatures to which the fiend in the nodding plumes screamed through the darkness.

Zogar sent another call shuddering through the night, and it was utterly unlike the first cry. There was a hideous sibilance in it – Balthus turned cold at the implication. If a serpent could hiss that loud, it would make just such a sound.

This time there was no answer – only a period of breathless silence in which the pound of Balthus' heart strangled him; and then there sounded a swishing outside the gate, a dry rustling that sent chills down Balthus' spine. Again the firelit gate held a hideous occupant.

Again Balthus recognized the monster from ancient legends. He saw and knew the ancient and evil serpent which swayed there, its wedge-shaped head, huge as that of a horse, as high as a tall man's head, and its palely gleaming barrel rippling out behind it. A forked tongue darted in and out, and the firelight glittered on bared fangs.

Balthus became incapable of emotion. The horror of his fate paralysed him. That was the reptile that the ancients called Ghost Snake, the pale, abominable terror that of old glided into huts by night to devour whole families. Like the python it crushed its victim, but unlike other constrictors its fangs bore venom that carried madness and death. It too had long been considered extinct. But Valannus had spoken truly. No white man knew what shapes haunted the great forests beyond Black River.

It came on silently rippling over the ground, its hideous head on the same level, its neck curving back slightly for the stroke. Balthus gazed with glazed, hypnotized stare into that loathsome gullet down which he would soon be engulfed, and he was aware of no sensation except a vague nausea.

And then something that glinted in the firelight streaked from the shadows of the huts, and the great reptile whipped about and went into instant convulsions. As in a dream Balthus saw a short throwing-spear transfixing the mighty neck, just below the gaping jaws; the shaft protruded from one side, the steel head from the other.

Knotting and looping hideously, the maddened reptile rolled into the circle of men who strove back from him. The spear had not severed its spine, but merely transfixed its great neck muscles. Its furiously lashing tail mowed down a dozen men and its jaws snapped convulsively, splashing others with venom that burned like liquid fire. Howling, cursing, screaming, frantic, they scattered before it, knocking each other down in their flight, trampling the fallen, bursting through the huts. The giant snake rolled into a fire, scattering sparks and brands, and the pain lashed it to more frenzied efforts. A hut wall buckled under the ram-like impact of its flailing tail, disgorging howling people.

Men stampeded through the fires, knocking the logs right and left. The flames sprang up, then sank. A reddish dim glow was all that lighted that nightmare scene where the giant reptile whipped and rolled, and men clawed and shrieked in frantic flight.

Balthus felt something jerk at his wrists, and then, miraculously, he was free, and a strong hand dragged him behind the post. Dazedly he saw Conan, felt the forest man's iron grip on his arm.

There was blood on the Cimmerian's mail, dried blood on the sword in his right hand; he loomed dim and gigantic in the shadowy light.

'Come on! Before they get over their panic!'

Balthus felt the haft of an ax shoved into his hand. Zogar Sag had disappeared. Conan dragged Balthus after him until the youth's numb brain awoke, and his legs began to move of their own accord. Then Conan released him and ran into the building where the skulls hung. Balthus followed him. He got a glimpse of a grim stone altar, faintly lighted by the glow outside; five human heads grinned on that altar, and there was a grisly familiarity about the features of the freshest; it was the head of the merchant Tiberias. Behind the altar was an idol, dim, indistinct, bestial, yet vaguely man-like in outline. Then fresh horror choked Balthus as the shape heaved up suddenly with a rattle of chains, lifting long misshapen arms in the gloom.

Conan's sword flailed down, crunching through flesh and bone, and then the Cimmerian was dragging Balthus around the altar, past a huddled shaggy bulk on the floor, to a door at the back of the long hut. Through this they burst, out into the enclosure again. But a few yards beyond them loomed the stockade.

It was dark behind the altar-hut. The mad stampede of the Picts had not carried them in that direction. At the wall Conan halted, gripped Balthus and heaved him at arm's length into the air as he might have lifted a child. Balthus grasped the points of the upright logs set in the sun-dried mud and scrambled up on them, ignoring the havoc done his skin. He lowered a hand to the Cimmerian, when around a corner of the altar-hut sprang a fleeing Pict. He halted short, glimpsing the man on the wall in the faint glow of the fires. Conan hurled his ax with deadly aim, but the warrior's mouth was already open for a yell of warning, and it rang loud above the din, cut short as he dropped with a shattered skull.

Blinding terror had not submerged all ingrained instincts. As that wild yell rose above the clamor, there was an instant's lull, and then a hundred throats bayed ferocious answer and warriors came leaping to repel the attack presaged by the warning.

Conan leaped high, caught, not Balthus' hand but his arm near the shoulder, and swung himself up. Balthus set his teeth against the strain, and then the Cimmerian was on the wall beside him, and the fugitives dropped down on the other side.

5 The Children of Jhebbal Sag

'Which way is the river?' Balthus was confused.

'We don't dare try for the river now,' grunted Conan. 'The woods between the village and the river are swarming with warriors. Come on! We'll head in the last direction they'll expect us to go – west!'

Looking back as they entered the thick growth, Balthus beheld the wall dotted with black heads as the savages peered over. The Picts were bewildered. They had not gained the wall in time to see the fugitives take cover. They had rushed to the wall expecting to repel an attack in force. They had seen the body of the dead warrior. But no enemy was in sight.

Balthus realized that they did not yet know their prisoner had escaped. From other sounds he believed that the warriors, directed by the shrill voice of Zogar Sag, were destroying the wounded serpent with arrows. The monster was out of the shaman's control. A moment later the quality of the yells was altered. Screeches of rage rose in the night.

Conan laughed grimly. He was leading Balthus along a narrow trail that ran west under the black branches, stepping as swiftly and surely as if he trod a well-lighted thoroughfare. Balthus stumbled after him, guiding himself by feeling the dense wall on either hand.

'They'll be after us now. Zogar's discovered you're gone, and he knows my head wasn't in the pile before the altar-hut. The dog! If

I'd had another spear I'd have thrown it through him before I struck the snake. Keep to the trail. They can't track us by torchlight, and there are a score of paths leading from the village. They'll follow those leading to the river first – throw a cordon of warriors for miles along the bank, expecting us to try to break through. We won't take to the woods until we have to. We can make better time on this trail. Now buckle down to it and run as you never ran before.'

'They got over their panic cursed quick!' panted Balthus, complying with a fresh burst of speed.

'They're not afraid of anything, very long,' grunted Conan.

For a space nothing was said between them. The fugitives devoted all their attention to covering distance. They were plunging deeper and deeper into the wilderness and getting farther away from civilization at every step, but Balthus did not question Conan's wisdom. The Cimmerian presently took time to grunt: 'When we're far enough away from the village we'll swing back to the river in a big circle. No other village within miles of Gwawela. All the Picts are gathered in that vicinity. We'll circle wide around them. They can't track us until daylight. They'll pick up our path then, but before dawn we'll leave the trail and take to the woods.'

They plunged on. The yells died out behind them. Balthus' breath was whistling through his teeth. He felt a pain in his side, and running became torture. He blundered against the bushes on each side of the trail. Conan pulled up suddenly, turned and stared back down the dim path.

Somewhere the moon was rising, a dim white glow amidst a tangle of branches.

'Shall we take to the woods?' panted Balthus.

'Give me your ax,' murmured Conan softly. 'Something is close behind us.'

'Then we'd better leave the trail!' exclaimed Balthus.

Conan shook his head and drew his companion into a dense thicket. The moon rose higher, making a dim light in the path.

'We can't fight the whole tribe!' whispered Balthus.

'No human being could have found our trail so quickly, or followed us so swiftly,' muttered Conan. 'Keep silent.'

There followed a tense silence in which Balthus felt that his heart could be heard pounding for miles away. Then abruptly, without a sound to announce its coming, a savage head appeared in the dim path. Balthus' heart jumped into his throat; at first glance he feared to look upon the awful head of the saber-tooth. But this head was smaller, more narrow; it was a leopard which stood there, snarling silently and glaring down the trail. What wind there was was blowing toward the hiding men, concealing their scent. The beast lowered his head and snuffed the trail, then moved forward uncertainly. A chill played down Balthus' spine. The brute was undoubtedly trailing them.

And it was suspicious. It lifted its head, its eyes glowing like balls of fire, and growled low in its throat. And at that instant Conan hurled the ax.

All the weight of arm and shoulder was behind the throw, and the ax was a streak of silver in the dim moon. Almost before he realized what had happened, Balthus saw the leopard rolling on the ground in its death-throes, the handle of the ax standing up from its head. The head of the weapon had split its narrow skull.

Conan bounded from the bushes, wrenched his ax free and dragged the limp body in among the trees, concealing it from the casual glance.

'Now let's go, and go fast!' he grunted, leading the way southward, away from the trail. 'There'll be warriors coming after that cat. As soon as he got his wits back Zogar sent him after us. The Picts would follow him, but he'd leave them far behind. He'd circle the village until he hit our trail and then come after us like a streak. They couldn't keep up with him, but they'll have an idea as to our general direction. They'd follow, listening for his cry. Well, they won't hear that, but they'll find the blood on the trail, and look around and find the body in the brush. They'll pick up our spoor there, if they can. Walk with care.'

He avoided clinging briars and low-hanging branches effortlessly, gliding between trees without touching the stems and always planting his feet in the places calculated to show least evidence of his passing; but with Balthus it was slower, more laborious work.

No sound came from behind them. They had covered more than a mile when Balthus said: 'Does Zogar Sag catch leopard-cubs and train them for bloodhounds?'

Conan shook his head. 'That was a leopard he called out of the woods.'

'But,' Balthus persisted, 'if he can order the beasts to do his bidding, why doesn't he rouse them all and have them after us? The forest is full of leopards; why send only one after us?'

Conan did not reply for a space, and when he did it was with a curious reticence.

'He can't command all the animals. Only such as remember Jhebbal Sag.'

'Jhebbal Sag?' Balthus repeated the ancient name hesitantly. He had never heard it spoken more than three or four times in his whole life.

'Once all living things worshipped him. That was long ago, when beasts and men spoke one language. Men have forgotten him; even the beasts forget. Only a few remember. The men who remember Jhebbal Sag and the beasts who remember are brothers and speak the same tongue.'

Balthus did not reply; he had strained at a Pictish stake and seen the nighted jungle give up its fanged horrors at a shaman's call.

'Civilized men laugh,' said Conan. 'But not one can tell me how Zogar Sag can call pythons and tigers and leopards out of the wilderness and make them do his bidding. They would say it is a lie, if they dared. That's the way with civilized men. When they can't explain something by their half-baked science, they refuse to believe it.'

The people on the Tauran were closer to the primitive than most Aquilonians; superstitions persisted, whose sources were lost in antiquity. And Balthus had seen that which still prickled his flesh. He could not refute the monstrous thing which Conan's words implied.

'I've heard that there's an ancient grove sacred to Jhebbal Sag somewhere in this forest,' said Conan. 'I don't know. I've never seen it. But more beasts *remember* in this country than any I've ever seen.'

'Then others will be on our trail?'

'They are now,' was Conan's disquieting answer. 'Zogar would never leave our tracking to one beast alone.'

'What are we to do, then?' asked Balthus uneasily, grasping his ax as he stared at the gloomy arches above him. His flesh crawled with the momentary expectation of ripping talons and fangs leaping from the shadows.

'Wait!'

Conan turned, squatted and with his knife began scratching a curious symbol in the mold. Stooping to look at it over his shoulder, Balthus felt a crawling of the flesh along his spine, he knew not why. He felt no wind against his face, but there was a rustling of leaves above them and a weird moaning swept ghostily through the branches. Conan glanced up inscrutably, then rose and stood staring somberly down at the symbol he had drawn.

'What is it?' whispered Balthus. It looked archaic and meaningless to him. He supposed that it was his ignorance of artistry which prevented his identifying it as one of the conventional designs of some prevailing culture. But had he been the most erudite artist in the world, he would have been no nearer the solution.

'I saw it carved in the rock of a cave no human had visited for a million years,' muttered Conan, 'in the uninhabited mountains beyond the Sea of Vilayet, half a world away from this spot. Later I saw a black witch-finder of Kush scratch it in the sand of a nameless river. He told me part of its meaning – it's sacred to Jhebbal Sag and the creatures which worship him. Watch!'

They drew back among the dense foliage some yards away and waited in tense silence. To the east drums muttered and somewhere to north and west other drums answered. Balthus shivered, though he knew long miles of black forest separated him from the grim beaters of those drums whose dull pulsing was a sinister overture that set the dark stage for bloody drama.

Balthus found himself holding his breath. Then with a slight shaking of the leaves, the bushes parted and a magnificent panther came into view. The moonlight dappling through the leaves shone on its glossy coat rippling with the play of the great muscles beneath it.

With its head held low it glided toward them. It was smelling out their trail. Then it halted as if frozen, its muzzle almost touching the symbol cut in the mold. For a long space it crouched motionless; it flattened its long body and laid its head on the ground before the mark. And Balthus felt the short hairs stir on his scalp. For the attitude of the great carnivore was one of awe and adoration.

Then the panther rose and backed away carefully, belly almost to the ground. With his hind-quarters among the bushes he wheeled as if in sudden panic and was gone like a flash of dappled light.

Balthus mopped his brow with a trembling hand and glanced at Conan.

The barbarian's eyes were smoldering with fires that never lit the eyes of men bred to the ideas of civilization. In that instant he was all wild, and had forgotten the man at his side. In his burning gaze Balthus glimpsed and vaguely recognized pristine images and half-embodied memories, shadows from Life's dawn, forgotten and repudiated by sophisticated races – ancient, primeval fantasms unnamed and nameless.

Then the deeper fires were masked and Conan was silently leading the way deeper into the forest.

'We've no more to fear from the beasts,' he said after a while, 'but we've left a sign for men to read. They won't follow our trail very easily, and until they find that symbol they won't know for sure we've turned south. Even then it won't be easy to smell us out without the beasts to aid them. But the woods south of the trail will be full of warriors looking for us. If we keep moving after daylight, we'll be sure to run into some of them. As soon as we find a good place we'll hide and wait until another night to swing back and make the river. We've got to warn Valannus, but it won't help him any if we get ourselves killed.'

'Warn Valannus?'

'Hell, the woods along the river are swarming with Picts! That's why they got us. Zogar's brewing war-magic; no mere raid this time. He's done something no Pict has done in my memory – united as many as fifteen or sixteen clans. His magic did it; they'll follow a wizard farther than they will a war-chief. You saw the mob in the village; and there were hundreds hiding along the river bank that you didn't see. More coming, from the farther villages. He'll have at least three thousand fighting-men. I lay in the bushes and heard their talk as they went past. They mean to attack the fort; when, I don't know, but Zogar doesn't dare delay long. He's gathered them and whipped them into a frenzy. If he doesn't lead them into battle quickly, they'll fall to quarreling with one another. They're like blood-mad tigers.

'I don't know whether they can take the fort or not. Anyway, we've got to get back across the river and give the warning. The settlers on the Velitrium road must either get into the fort or back to Velitrium. While the Picts are besieging the fort, war-parties will range the road far to the east – might even cross Thunder River and raid the thickly settled country behind Velitrium.'

As he talked he was leading the way deeper and deeper into the ancient wilderness. Presently he grunted with satisfaction. They had reached a spot where the underbrush was more scattered, and an outcropping of stone was visible, wandering off southward. Balthus felt more secure as they followed it. Not even a Pict could trail them over naked rock.

'How did you get away?' he asked presently.

Conan tapped his mail-shirt and helmet.

'If more borderers would wear harness there'd be fewer skulls hanging on the altar-huts. But most men make noise if they wear armor. They were waiting on each side of the path, without moving. And when a Pict stands motionless, the very beasts of the forest pass him without seeing him. They'd seen us crossing the river and got in their places. If they'd gone into ambush after we left the bank, I'd have had some hint of it. But they were waiting, and not even a leaf trembled. The devil himself couldn't have suspected anything. The first suspicion I had was when I heard a shaft rasp against a bow as it was pulled back. I dropped and yelled for the men behind me to drop, but they were too slow, taken by surprise like that.

'Most of them fell at the first volley that raked us from both sides. Some of the arrows crossed the trail and struck Picts on the other side. I heard them howl.' He grinned with vicious satisfaction. 'Such of us as were left plunged into the woods and closed with them. When I saw the others were all down or taken, I broke through and outfooted the painted devils through the darkness. They were all around me. I ran and crawled and sneaked, and sometimes I lay on my belly under the bushes while they passed me on all sides.

'I tried for the shore and found it lined with them, waiting for just such a move. But I'd have cut my way through and taken a chance on swimming, only I heard the drums pounding in the village and knew they'd taken somebody alive.

'They were all so engrossed in Zogar's magic that I was able to climb the wall behind the altar-hut. There was a warrior supposed to be watching at that point, but he was squatting behind the hut and peering around the corner at the ceremony. I came up behind him and broke his neck with my hands before he knew what was happening. It was his spear I threw into the snake, and that's his ax you're carrying.'

'But what was that – that thing you killed in the altar-hut?' asked Balthus, with a shiver at the memory of the dim-seen horror.

'One of Zogar's gods. One of Jhebbal's children that didn't remember and had to be kept chained to the altar. A bull ape. The Picts think they're sacred to the Hairy One who lives on the moon – the gorilla-god of Gullah.

'It's getting light. Here's a good place to hide until we see how close they're on our trail. Probably have to wait until night to break back to the river.'

A low hill pitched upward, girdled and covered with thick trees and bushes. Near the crest Conan slid into a tangle of jutting rocks, crowned by dense bushes. Lying among them they could see the jungle below without being seen. It was a good place to hide or defend. Balthus did not believe that even a Pict could have trailed them over the rocky ground for the past four or five miles, but he was afraid of the beasts that obeyed Zogar Sag. His faith in the curious symbol wavered a little now. But Conan had dismissed the possibility of beasts tracking them.

A ghostly whiteness spread through the dense branches; the patches of sky visible altered in hue, grew from pink to blue. Balthus felt the gnawing of hunger, though he had slaked his thirst at a stream they had skirted. There was complete silence, except for an occasional chirp of a bird. The drums were no longer to be heard. Balthus' thoughts reverted to the grim scene before the altar-hut.

'Those were ostrich plumes Zogar Sag wore,' he said. 'I've seen them on the helmets of knights who rode from the East to visit the barons of the marches. There are no ostriches in this forest, are there?'

'They came from Kush,' answered Conan. 'West of here, many marches, lies the seashore. Ships from Zingara occasionally come and trade weapons and ornaments and wine to the coastal tribes for skins and copper ore and gold dust. Sometimes they trade ostrich plumes they got from the Stygians, who in turn got them from the black tribes of Kush, which lies south of Stygia. The Pictish shamans place great store by them. But there's much risk in such trade. The Picts are too likely to try to seize the ship. And the coast is dangerous to ships. I've sailed along it when I was with the pirates of the Barachan Isles, which lie southwest of Zingara.'

Balthus looked at his companion with admiration.

'I knew you hadn't spent your life on this frontier. You've mentioned several far places. You've traveled widely?'

'I've roamed far; farther than any other man of my race ever wandered. I've seen all the great cities of the Hyborians, the Shemites, the Stygians and the Hyrkanians. I've roamed in the unknown countries south of the black kingdoms of Kush, and east of the Sea of Vilayet. I've been a mercenary captain, a corsair, a *kozak*, a penniless vagabond, a general – hell, I've been everything except a king, and I may be that, before I die.' The fancy pleased him, and he grinned hardly. Then he shrugged his shoulders and stretched his mighty figure on the rocks. 'This is as good life as any. I don't know how long I'll stay on the frontier; a week, a month, a year. I have a roving foot. But it's as well on the border as anywhere.'

Balthus set himself to watch the forest below them. Momentarily he expected to see fierce painted faces thrust through the leaves. But as the hours passed no stealthy footfall disturbed the brooding quiet. Balthus believed the Picts had missed their trail and given up the chase. Conan grew restless.

'We should have sighted parties scouring the woods for us. If they've quit the chase, it's because they're after bigger game. They may be gathering to cross the river and storm the fort.'

'Would they come this far south if they lost the trail?'

'They've lost the trail, all right; otherwise they'd have been on our necks before now. Under ordinary circumstances they'd scour the woods for miles in every direction. Some of them should have passed within sight of this hill. They must be preparing to cross the river. We've got to take a chance and make for the river.'

Creeping down the rocks Balthus felt his flesh crawl between his shoulders as he momentarily expected a withering blast of arrows from the green masses about them. He feared that the Picts had discovered them and were lying about in ambush. But Conan was convinced no enemies were near, and the Cimmerian was right.

'We're miles to the south of the village,' grunted Conan. 'We'll hit straight through for the river. I don't know how far down the river they've spread. We'll hope to hit it below them.'

With haste that seemed reckless to Balthus they hurried eastward. The woods seemed empty of life. Conan believed that all the Picts were gathered in the vicinity of Gwawela, if indeed, they had not already crossed the river. He did not believe they would cross in the daytime, however.

'Some woodsman would be sure to see them and give the alarm. They'll cross above and below the fort, out of sight of the sentries. Then others will get in canoes and make straight across for the river wall. As soon as they attack, those hidden in the woods on the east shore will assail the fort from the other sides. They've tried that before, and got the guts shot and hacked out of them. But this time they've got enough men to make a real onslaught of it.'

They pushed on without pausing, though Balthus gazed longingly at the squirrels flitting among the branches, which he could have brought down with a cast of his ax. With a sigh he drew up his broad belt. The everlasting silence and gloom of the primitive forest was beginning to depress him. He found himself thinking of the open groves and sun-dappled meadows of the Tauran, of the bluff cheer of his father's steep-thatched, diamond-paned house, of the fat cows browsing through the deep, lush grass, and the hearty fellowship of the brawny, bare-armed plowmen and herdsmen.

He felt lonely, in spite of his companion. Conan was as much a part of this wilderness as Balthus was alien to it. The Cimmerian might have spent years among the great cities of the world; he might have walked with the rulers of civilization; he might even achieve his wild whim some day and rule as king of a civilized nation; stranger things had happened. But he was no less a barbarian. He was concerned only with the naked fundamentals of life. The warm intimacies of small, kindly things, the sentiments and delicious trivialities that make up so much of civilized men's lives were meaningless to him. A wolf was no less a wolf because a whim of chance caused him to run with the watchdogs. Bloodshed and violence and savagery were the natural elements of the life Conan knew; he could not, and would never, understand the little things that are so dear to civilized men and women.

The shadows were lengthening when they reached the river and peered through the masking bushes. They could see up and down the river for about a mile each way. The sullen stream lay bare and empty. Conan scowled across at the other shore.

'We've got to take another chance here. We've got to swim the river. We don't know whether they've crossed or not. The woods over there may be alive with them. We've got to risk it. We're about six miles south of Gwawela.'

He wheeled and ducked as a bow-string twanged. Something like a white flash of light streaked through the bushes. Balthus knew it was an arrow. Then with a tigerish bound Conan was through the bushes. Balthus caught the gleam of steel as he whirled his sword, and heard a death scream. The next instant he had broken through the bushes after the Cimmerian.

A Pict with a shattered skull lay face-down on the ground, his fingers spasmodically clawing at the grass. Half a dozen others were swarming about Conan, swords and axes lifted. They had cast away their bows, useless at such deadly close quarters. Their lower jaws were painted white, contrasting vividly with their dark faces, and the designs on their muscular breasts differed from any Balthus had ever seen.

One of them hurled his ax at Balthus and rushed after it with lifted knife. Balthus ducked and then caught the wrist that drove the knife licking at his throat. They went to the ground together, rolling over and over. The Pict was like a wild beast, his muscles hard as steel strings.

Balthus was striving to maintain his hold on the wild man's wrist and bring his own ax into play, but so fast and furious was the struggle that each attempt to strike was blocked. The Pict was wrenching furiously to free his knife hand, was clutching at Balthus' ax, and driving his knees at the youth's groin. Suddenly he attempted to shift his knife to his free hand, and in that instant Balthus, struggling up on one knee, split the painted head with a desperate blow of his ax.

He sprang up and glared wildly about for his companion, expecting to see him overwhelmed by numbers. Then he realized the full strength and ferocity of the Cimmerian. Conan bestrode two of his attackers, shorn half asunder by that terrible broadsword. As Balthus looked he saw the Cimmerian beat down a thrusting shortsword, avoid the stroke of an ax with a cat-like sidewise spring which brought him within arm's length of a squat savage stooping for a bow. Before the Pict could straighten, the red sword flailed down and clove him from shoulder to mid-breastbone, where the blade stuck. The remaining warriors rushed in, one from either side. Balthus hurled his ax with an accuracy that reduced the attackers to one, and Conan, abandoning his efforts to free his sword, wheeled and met the remaining Pict with his bare hands. The stocky warrior, a head shorter than his tall enemy, leaped in, striking with his ax, at the same time stabbing murderously with his knife. The knife broke on the Cimmerian's mail, and the ax checked in midair as Conan's fingers locked like iron on the descending arm. A bone snapped loudly, and Balthus saw the Pict wince and falter. The next instant he was swept off his feet, lifted high above the Cimmerian's head – he writhed in midair for an instant, kicking and thrashing, and then was dashed headlong to the earth with such force that he rebounded, and then lay still, his limp posture telling of splintered limbs and a broken spine.

'Come on!' Conan wrenched his sword free and snatched up an ax. 'Grab a bow and a handful of arrows, and hurry! We've got to trust to our heels again. That yell was heard. They'll be here in no time. If we tried to swim now, they'd feather us with arrows before we reached midstream!'

6 Red Axes of the Border

Conan did not plunge deeply into the forest. A few hundred yards from the river, he altered his slanting course and ran parallel with it. Balthus recognized a grim determination not to be hunted away from the river which they must cross if they were to warn the men in the fort. Behind them rose more loudly the yells of the forest men. Balthus believed the Picts had reached the glade where the bodies of the slain men lay. Then further yells seemed to indicate that the savages were streaming into the woods in pursuit. They had left a trail any Pict could follow.

Conan increased his speed, and Balthus grimly set his teeth and kept on his heels, though he felt he might collapse any time. It seemed centuries since he had eaten last. He kept going more by an effort of will than anything else. His blood was pounding so furiously in his eardrums that he was not aware when the yells died out behind them.

Conan halted suddenly. Balthus leaned against a tree and panted.

'They've quit!' grunted the Cimmerian, scowling.

'Sneaking – up – on – us!' gasped Balthus.

Conan shook his head.

'A short chase like this they'd yell every step of the way. No. They've gone back. I thought I heard somebody yelling behind them a few seconds before the noise began to get dimmer. They've been recalled. And that's good for us, but damned bad for the men in the fort. It means the warriors are being summoned out of the woods for the attack. These men we ran into were warriors from a tribe down the river. They were undoubtedly headed for Gwawela to join in the assault on the fort. Damn it, we're farther away than ever, now. We've got to get across the river.'

Turning east he hurried through the thickets with no attempt at concealment. Balthus followed him, for the first time feeling the sting of lacerations on his breast and shoulder where the Pict's savage teeth had scored him. He was pushing through the thick bushes that fringed the bank when Conan pulled him back. Then he heard a rhythmic splashing, and peering through the leaves, saw a dugout canoe coming up the river, its single occupant paddling hard against the current. He was a strongly built Pict with a white heron feather thrust in a copper band that confined his square-cut mane.

'That's a Gwawela man,' muttered Conan. 'Emissary from Zogar. White plume shows that. He's carried a peace talk to the tribes down the river and now he's trying to get back and take a hand in the slaughter.'

The lone ambassador was now almost even with their hiding-place, and suddenly Balthus almost jumped out of his skin. At his very ear had sounded the harsh gutturals of a Pict. Then he realized that Conan had called to the paddler in his own tongue. The man started, scanned the bushes and called back something, then cast a startled glance across the river, bent low and sent the canoe shooting in toward the western bank. Not understanding, Balthus saw Conan take from his hand the bow he had picked up in the glade, and notch an arrow.

The Pict had run his canoe in close to the shore, and staring up into the bushes, called out something. His answer came in the twang of the bow-string, the streaking flight of the arrow that sank to the feathers in his broad breast. With a choking gasp he slumped sidewise and rolled into the shallow water. In an instant Conan was down the bank and wading into the water to grasp the drifting canoe. Balthus stumbled after him and somewhat dazedly crawled into the canoe. Conan scrambled in, seized the paddle and sent the craft shooting toward the eastern shore. Balthus noted with envious admiration the play of the great muscles beneath the sun-burnt skin. The Cimmerian seemed an iron man, who never knew fatigue.

'What did you say to the Pict?' asked Balthus.

'Told him to pull into shore; said there was a white forest runner on the bank who was trying to get a shot at him.'

'That doesn't seem fair,' Balthus objected. 'He thought a friend was speaking to him. You mimicked a Pict perfectly—'

'We needed his boat,' grunted Conan, not pausing in his exertions. 'Only way to lure him to the bank. Which is worse – to betray a Pict who'd enjoy skinning us both alive, or betray the men across the river whose lives depend on our getting over?'

Balthus mulled over this delicate ethical question for a moment, then shrugged his shoulder and asked: 'How far are we from the fort?'

Conan pointed to a creek which flowed into Black River from the east, a few hundred yards below them.

'That's South Creek; it's ten miles from its mouth to the fort. It's the southern boundary of Conajohara. Marshes miles wide south of it. No danger of a raid from across them. Nine miles above the fort North Creek forms the other boundary. Marshes beyond that, too. That's why an attack must come from the west, across Black River. Conajohara's just like a spear, with a point nineteen miles wide, thrust into the Pictish wilderness.'

'Why don't we keep to the canoe and make the trip by water?'

'Because, considering the current we've got to brace, and the bends in the river, we can go faster afoot. Besides, remember Gwawela is south of the fort; if the Picts are crossing the river we'd run right into them.'

Dusk was gathering as they stepped upon the eastern bank. Without pause Conan pushed on northward, at a pace that made Balthus' sturdy legs ache.

'Valannus wanted a fort built at the mouths of North and South Creeks,' grunted the Cimmerian. 'Then the river could be patrolled constantly. But the Government wouldn't do it.

'Soft-bellied fools sitting on velvet cushions with naked girls offering them iced wine on their knees – I know the breed. They can't see any farther than their palace wall. Diplomacy – hell! They'd fight Picts with theories of territorial expansion. Valannus and men like him have to obey the orders of a set of damned fools. They'll never grab any more Pictish land, any more than they'll ever rebuild Venarium. The time may come when they'll see the barbarians swarming over the walls of the Eastern cities!'

A week before, Balthus would have laughed at any such preposterous suggestion. Now he made no reply. He had seen the unconquerable ferocity of the men who dwelt beyond the frontiers.

He shivered, casting glances at the sullen river, just visible through the bushes, at the arches of the trees which crowded close to its banks. He kept remembering that the Picts might have crossed the river and be lying in ambush between them and the fort. It was fast growing dark.

A slight sound ahead of them jumped his heart into his throat, and Conan's sword gleamed in the air. He lowered it when a dog, a great, gaunt, scarred beast, slunk out of the bushes and stood staring at them.

'That dog belonged to a settler who tried to build his cabin on the bank of the river a few miles south of the fort,' grunted Conan. 'The Picts slipped over and killed him, of course, and burned his cabin. We found him dead among the embers, and the dog lying senseless among three Picts he'd killed. He was almost cut to pieces. We took him to the fort and dressed his wounds, but after he recovered he took to the woods and turned wild— What now, Slasher, are you hunting the men who killed your master?'

The massive head swung from side to side and the eyes glowed greenly. He did not growl or bark. Silently as a phantom he slid in behind them.

'Let him come,' muttered Conan. 'He can smell the devils before we can see them.'

Balthus smiled and laid his hand caressingly on the dog's head.

The lips involuntarily writhed back to display the gleaming fangs; then the great beast bent his head sheepishly, and his tail moved with jerky uncertainty, as if the owner had almost forgotten the emotions of friendliness. Balthus mentally compared the great gaunt hard body with the fat sleek hounds tumbling vociferously over one another in his father's kennel yard. He sighed. The frontier was no less hard for beasts than for men. This dog had almost forgotten the meaning of kindness and friendliness.

Slasher glided ahead, and Conan let him take the lead. The last tinge of dusk faded into stark darkness. The miles fell away under their steady feet. Slasher seemed voiceless. Suddenly he halted, tense, ears lifted. An instant later the men heard it – a demoniac yelling up the river ahead of them, faint as a whisper.

Conan swore like a madman.

'They've attacked the fort! We're too late! Come on!'

He increased his pace, trusting to the dog to smell out ambushes ahead. In a flood of tense excitement Balthus forgot his hunger and weariness. The yells grew louder as they advanced, and above the devilish screaming they could hear the deep shouts of the soldiers. Just as Balthus began to fear they would run into the savages who seemed to be howling just ahead of them, Conan swung away from the river in a wide semicircle that carried them to a low rise from which they could look over the forest. They saw the fort, lighted with torches thrust over the parapets on long poles. These cast a flickering, uncertain light over the clearing, and in that light they saw throngs of naked, painted figures along the fringe of the clearing. The river swarmed with canoes. The Picts had the fort completely surrounded.

An incessant hail of arrows rained against the stockade from the woods and the river. The deep twanging of the bow-strings rose above the howling. Yelling like wolves, several hundred naked warriors with axes in their hands ran from under the trees and raced toward the eastern gate. They were within a hundred and fifty yards of their objective when a withering blast of arrows from the wall littered the ground with corpses and sent the survivors fleeing back to the trees. The men in the canoes rushed their boats toward the river-wall, and were met by another shower of clothyard shafts and a volley from the small ballistas mounted on towers on that side of the stockade. Stones and logs whirled through the air and splintered and sank half a dozen canoes, killing their occupants, and the other boats drew back out of range. A deep roar of triumph rose from the walls of the fort, answered by bestial howling from all quarters.

'Shall we try to break through?' asked Balthus, trembling with eagerness.

Conan shook his head. He stood with his arms folded, his head slightly bent, a sombre and brooding figure.

'The fort's doomed. The Picts are blood-mad, and won't stop until they're all killed. And there are too many of them for the men in the fort to kill. We couldn't break through, and if we did, we could do nothing but die with Valannus.'

'There's nothing we can do but save our own hides, then?'

'Yes. We've got to warn the settlers. Do you know why the Picts are not trying to burn the fort with fire-arrows? Because they don't want a flame that might warn the people to the east. They plan to stamp out the fort, and then sweep east before anyone knows of its fall. They may cross Thunder River and take Velitrium before the people know what's happened. At least they'll destroy every living thing between the fort and Thunder River.

'We've failed to warn the fort, and I see now it would have done no good if we had succeeded. The fort's too poorly manned. A few more charges and the Picts will be over the walls and breaking down the gates. But we can start the settlers toward Velitrium. Come on! We're outside the circle the Picts have thrown around the fort. We'll keep clear of it.'

They swung out in a wide arc, hearing the rising and falling of the volume of the yells, marking each charge and repulse. The men in the fort were holding their own; but the shrieks of the Picts did not diminish in savagery. They vibrated with a timbre that held assurance of ultimate victory.

Before Balthus realized they were close to it, they broke into the road leading east.

'Now run!' grunted Conan. Balthus set his teeth. It was nineteen miles to Velitrium, a good five to Scalp Creek beyond which began the settlements. It seemed to the Aquilonian that they had been fighting and running for centuries. But the nervous excitement that rioted through his blood stimulated him to Herculean efforts.

Slasher ran ahead of them, his head to the ground, snarling low, the first sound they had heard from him.

'Picts ahead of us!' snarled Conan, dropping to one knee and scanning the ground in the starlight. He shook his head, baffled. 'I can't tell how many. Probably only a small party. Some that couldn't wait to take the fort. They've gone ahead to butcher the settlers in their beds! Come on!'

Ahead of them presently they saw a small blaze through the trees, and heard a wild and ferocious chanting. The trail bent there, and leaving it, they cut across the bend, through the thickets. A few moments later they were looking on a hideous sight. An ox-wain stood in the road piled with meager household furnishings; it was burning; the oxen lay near with their throats cut. A man and a woman lay in the road, stripped and mutilated. Five Picts were dancing about them with fantastic leaps and bounds, waving bloody axes; one of them brandished the woman's red-smeared gown.

At the sight a red haze swam before Balthus. Lifting his bow he lined the prancing figure, black against the fire, and loosed. The slayer leaped convulsively and fell dead with the arrow through his heart. Then the two white men and the dog were upon the startled survivors. Conan was animated merely by his fighting spirit and an old, old racial hate, but Balthus was afire with wrath.

He met the first Pict to oppose him with a ferocious swipe that split the painted skull, and sprang over his falling body to grapple with the others. But Conan had already killed one of the two he had chosen, and the leap of the Aquilonian was a second late. The warrior was down with the long sword through him even as Balthus' ax was lifted. Turning toward the remaining Pict, Balthus saw Slasher rise from his victim, his great jaws dripping blood.

Balthus said nothing as he looked down at the pitiful forms in the road beside the burning wain. Both were young, the woman little more than a girl. By some whim of chance the Picts had left her face unmarred, and even in the agonies of an awful death it was beautiful. But her soft young body had been hideously slashed with many knives – a mist clouded Balthus' eyes and he swallowed chokingly. The tragedy momentarily overcame him. He felt like falling upon the ground and weeping and biting the earth.

'Some young couple just hitting out on their own,' Conan was saying as he wiped his sword unemotionally. 'On their way to the fort when the Picts met them. Maybe the boy was going to enter the service; maybe take up land on the river. Well, that's what will happen to every man, woman and child this side of Thunder River if we don't get them into Velitrium in a hurry.'

Balthus' knees trembled as he followed Conan. But there was no hint of weakness in the long easy stride of the Cimmerian. There was a kinship between him and the great gaunt brute that glided beside him. Slasher no longer growled with his head to the trail. The way was clear before them. The yelling on the river came faintly to them, but Balthus believed the fort was still holding. Conan halted suddenly, with an oath.

He showed Balthus a trail that led north from the road. It was an old trail, partly grown with new young growth, and this growth had recently been broken down. Balthus realized this fact more by feel than sight, though Conan seemed to see like a cat in the dark. The

Cimmerian showed him where broad wagon tracks turned off the main trail, deeply indented in the forest mold.

'Settlers going to the licks after salt,' he grunted. 'They're at the edges of the marsh, about nine miles from here. Blast it! They'll be cut off and butchered to a man! Listen! One man can warn the people on the road. Go ahead and wake them up and herd them into Velitrium. I'll go and get the men gathering the salt. They'll be camped by the licks. We won't come back to the road. We'll head straight through the woods.'

With no further comment Conan turned off the trail and hurried down the dim path, and Balthus, after staring after him for a few moments, set out along the road. The dog had remained with him, and glided softly at his heels. When Balthus had gone a few rods he heard the animal growl. Whirling, he glared back the way he had come, and was startled to see a vague ghostly glow vanishing into the forest in the direction Conan had taken. Slasher rumbled deep in his throat, his hackles stiff and his eyes balls of green fire. Balthus remembered the grim apparition that had taken the head of the merchant Tiberias not far from that spot, and he hesitated. The thing must be following Conan. But the giant Cimmerian had repeatedly demonstrated his ability to take care of himself, and Balthus felt his duty lay toward the helpless settlers who slumbered in the path of the red hurricane. The horror of the fiery phantom was overshadowed by the horror of those limp, violated bodies beside the burning ox-wain.

He hurried down the road, crossed Scalp Creek and came in sight of the first settler's cabin – a long, low structure of ax-hewn logs. In an instant he was pounding on the door. A sleepy voice inquired his pleasure.

'Get up! The Picts are over the river!'

That brought instant response. A low cry echoed his words and then the door was thrown open by a woman in a scanty shift. Her hair hung over her bare shoulders in disorder; she held a candle in one hand and an ax in the other. Her face was colorless, her eyes wide with terror.

'Come in!' she begged. 'We'll hold the cabin.'

'No. We must make for Velitrium. The fort can't hold them back. It may have fallen already. Don't stop to dress. Get your children and come on.'

'But my man's gone with the others after salt!' she wailed, wringing her hands. Behind her peered three tousled youngsters, blinking and bewildered.

'Conan's gone after them. He'll fetch them through safe. We must hurry up the road to warn the other cabins.'

Relief flooded her countenance.

'Mitra be thanked!' she cried. 'If the Cimmerian's gone after them, they're safe if mortal man can save them!'

In a whirlwind of activity she snatched up the smallest child and herded the others through the door ahead of her. Balthus took the candle and ground it out under his heel. He listened an instant. No sound came up the dark road.

'Have you got a horse?'

'In the stable,' she groaned. 'Oh, hurry!'

He pushed her aside as she fumbled with shaking hands at the bars. He led the horse out and lifted the children on its back, telling them to hold to its mane and to one another. They stared at him seriously, making no outcry. The woman took the horse's halter and set out up the road. She still gripped her ax and Balthus knew that if cornered she would fight with the desperate courage of a she-panther.

He held behind, listening. He was oppressed by the belief that the fort had been stormed and taken; that the dark-skinned hordes were already streaming up the road toward Velitrium, drunken on slaughter and mad for blood. They would come with the speed of starving wolves.

Presently they saw another cabin looming ahead. The woman started to shriek a warning, but Balthus stopped her. He hurried to the door and knocked. A woman's voice answered him. He repeated his warning, and soon the cabin disgorged its occupants – an old woman, two young women and four children. Like the other woman's husband, their men had gone to the salt licks the day before, unsuspecting of any danger. One of the young women seemed dazed, the other prone to hysteria. But the old woman, a stern old veteran of the frontier, quieted them harshly; she helped Balthus get out the two horses that were stabled in a pen behind the cabin and put the children on them. Balthus urged that she herself mount with them, but she shook her head and made one of the younger women ride.

'She's with child,' grunted the old woman. 'I can walk – and fight, too, if it comes to that.'

As they set out, one of the women said: 'A young couple passed along the road about dusk; we advised them to spend the night at our cabin, but they were anxious to make the fort tonight. Did – did—'

'They met the Picts,' answered Balthus briefly, and the woman sobbed in horror.

They were scarcely out of sight of the cabin when some distance behind them quavered a long high-pitched yell.

'A wolf!' exclaimed one of the women.

'A painted wolf with an ax in his hand,' muttered Balthus. 'Go! Rouse the other settlers along the road and take them with you. I'll scout along behind.'

Without a word the old woman herded her charges ahead of her. As they faded into the darkness, Balthus could see the pale ovals that were the faces of the children twisted back over their shoulders to stare toward him. He remembered his own people on the Tauran and a moment's giddy sickness swam over him. With momentary weakness he groaned and sank down in the road; his muscular arm fell over Slasher's massive neck and he felt the dog's warm moist tongue touch his face.

He lifted his head and grinned with a painful effort.

'Come on, boy,' he mumbled, rising. 'We've got work to do.'

A red glow suddenly became evident through the trees. The Picts had fired the last hut. He grinned. How Zogar Sag would froth if he knew his warriors had let their destructive natures get the better of them. The fire would warn the people farther up the road. They would be awake and alert when the fugitives reached them. But his face grew grim. The women were traveling slowly, on foot and on the overloaded horses. The swift-footed Picts would run them down within a mile, unless— he took his position behind a tangle of fallen logs beside the trail. The road west of him was lighted by the burning cabin, and when the Picts came he saw them first – black furtive figures etched against the distant glare.

Drawing a shaft to the head, he loosed and one of the figures crumpled. The rest melted into the woods on either side of the road. Slasher whimpered with the killing lust beside him. Suddenly a figure appeared on the fringe of the trail, under the trees, and began gliding toward the fallen timbers. Balthus' bow-string twanged and the Pict yelped, staggered and fell into the shadows with the arrow through his thigh. Slasher cleared the timbers with a bound and leaped into the bushes. They were violently shaken and then the dog slunk back to Balthus' side, his jaws crimson.

No more appeared in the trail; Balthus began to fear they were stealing past his position through the woods, and when he heard a faint sound to his left he loosed blindly. He cursed as he heard the shaft splinter against a tree, but Slasher glided away as silently as a phantom, and presently Balthus heard a thrashing and a gurgling; then Slasher came like a ghost through the bushes, snuggling his great, crimson-stained head against Balthus' arm. Blood oozed from a gash in his shoulder, but the sounds in the wood had ceased for ever.

The men lurking on the edges of the road evidently sensed the fate of their companion, and decided that an open charge was preferable to being dragged down in the dark by a devil-beast they could neither see nor hear. Perhaps they realized that only one man lay behind the logs. They came with a sudden rush, breaking cover from both sides of the trail. Three dropped with arrows through them – and the remaining pair hesitated. One turned and ran back down the road, but the other lunged over the breastwork, his eyes and teeth gleaming in the dim light, his ax lifted. Balthus' foot slipped as he sprang up, but the slip saved his life. The descending ax shaved a lock of hair from his head, and the Pict rolled down the logs from the force of his wasted blow. Before he could regain his feet Slasher tore his throat out.

Then followed a tense period of waiting, in which time Balthus wondered if the man who had fled had been the only survivor of the party. Obviously it had been a small band that had either left the fighting at the fort, or was scouting ahead of the main body. Each moment that passed increased the chances for safety of the women and children hurrying toward Velitrium.

Then without warning a shower of arrows whistled over his retreat. A wild howling rose from the woods along the trail. Either the survivor had gone after aid, or another party had joined the first. The burning cabin still smoldered, lending a little light. Then they were after him, gliding through the trees beside the trail. He shot three arrows and threw the bow away. As if sensing his plight, they came on, not yelling now, but in deadly silence except for a swift pad of many feet.

He fiercely hugged the head of the great dog growling at his side, muttered: 'All right, boy, give 'em hell!' and sprang to his feet, drawing his ax. Then the dark figures flooded over the breastworks and closed in a storm of flailing axes, stabbing knives and ripping fangs.

7 The Devil in the Fire

When Conan turned from the Velitrium road he expected a run of some nine miles and set himself to the task. But he had not gone four when he heard the sounds of a party of men ahead of him. From the noise they were making in their progress he knew they were not Picts. He hailed them.

'Who's there?' challenged a harsh voice. 'Stand where you are until we know you, or you'll get an arrow through you.'

'You couldn't hit an elephant in this darkness,' answered Conan impatiently. 'Come on, fool; it's I – Conan. The Picts are over the river.'

'We suspected as much,' answered the leader of the men, as they strode forward – tall, rangy men, stern-faced, with bows in their hands. 'One of our party wounded an antelope and tracked it nearly to Black River. He heard them yelling down the river and ran back to our camp. We left the salt and the wagons, turned the oxen loose and came as swiftly as we could. If the Picts are besieging the fort, war-parties will be ranging up the road toward our cabins.'

'Your families are safe,' grunted Conan. 'My companion went ahead to take them to Velitrium. If we go back to the main road we may run into the whole horde. We'll strike southeast, through the timber. Go ahead. I'll scout behind.'

A few moments later the whole band was hurrying southeastward. Conan followed more slowly, keeping just within ear-shot. He cursed the noise they were making; that many Picts or Cimmerians would have moved through the woods with no more noise than the wind makes as it blows through the black branches.

He had just crossed a small glade when he wheeled answering the conviction of his primitive instincts that he was being followed. Standing motionless among the bushes he heard the sounds of the retreating settlers fade away. Then a voice called faintly back along the way he had come: 'Conan! Conan! Wait for me, Conan!'

'Balthus!' he swore bewilderedly. Cautiously he called: 'Here I am.'

'Wait for me, Conan!' the voice came more distinctly.

Conan moved out of the shadows, scowling. 'What the devil are you doing here? – Crom!'

He half crouched, the flesh prickling along his spine. It was not Balthus who was emerging from the other side of the glade. A weird glow burned through the trees. It moved toward him, shimmering weirdly – a green witch-fire that moved with purpose and intent.

It halted some feet away and Conan glared at it, trying to distinguish its fire-misted outlines. The quivering flame had a solid core; the flame was but a green garment that masked some animate and evil entity; but the Cimmerian was unable to make out its shape or likeness. Then, shockingly, a voice spoke to him from amidst the fiery column.

'Why do you stand like a sheep waiting for the butcher, Conan?'

The voice was human but carried strange vibrations that were not human.

'Sheep?' Conan's wrath got the best of his momentary awe. 'Do you think I'm afraid of a damned Pictish swamp devil? A friend called me.'

'I called in his voice,' answered the other. 'The men you follow belong to my brother; I would not rob his knife of their blood. But you are mine. Oh, fool, you have come from the far gray hills of Cimmeria to meet your doom in the forests of Conajohara.'

'You've had your chance at me before now,' snorted Conan. 'Why didn't you kill me then, if you could?'

'My brother had not painted a skull black for you and hurled it into the fire that burns for ever on Gullah's black altar. He had not whispered your name to the black ghosts that haunt the uplands of the Dark Land. But a bat has flown over the Mountains of the Dead and drawn your image in blood on the white tiger's hide that hangs before the long hut where sleep the Four Brothers of the Night. The great serpents coil about their feet and the stars burn like fire-flies in their hair.'

'Why have the gods of darkness doomed me to death?' growled Conan.

Something – a hand, foot or talon, he could not tell which, thrust out from the fire and marked swiftly on the mold. A symbol blazed there, marked with fire, and faded, but not before he recognized it.

'You dared make the sign which only a priest of Jhebbal Sag dare make. Thunder rumbled through the black Mountain of the Dead and the altar-hut of Gullah was thrown down by a wind from the Gulf of Ghosts. The loon which is messenger to the Four Brothers of the Night flew swiftly and whispered your name in my ear. Your head will hang in the altar-hut of my brother. Your body will be eaten by the black-winged, sharp-beaked Children of Jhil.'

'Who the devil is your brother?' demanded Conan. His sword was naked in his hand, and he was subtly loosening the ax in his belt.

'Zogar Sag; a child of Jhebbal Sag who still visits his sacred groves at times. A woman of Gwawela slept in a grove holy to Jhebbal Sag. Her babe was Zogar Sag. I too am a son of Jhebbal Sag, out of a fire-being from a far realm. Zogar Sag summoned me out of the Misty Lands. With incantations and sorcery and his own blood he materialized me in the flesh of his own planet. We are one, tied together by invisible threads. His thoughts are my thoughts; if he is struck, I am bruised. If I am cut, he bleeds. But I have talked enough. Soon your ghost will talk with the ghosts of the Dark Land, and they will tell you of the old gods which are not dead, but sleep in the outer abysses, and from time to time awake.'

'I'd like to see what you look like,' muttered Conan, working his ax free, 'you who leave a track like a bird, who burn like a flame and yet speak with a human voice.'

'You shall see,' answered the voice from the flame, 'see, and carry the knowledge with you into the Dark Land.'

The flames leaped and sank, dwindling and dimming. A face began to take shadowy form. At first Conan thought it was Zogar Sag himself who stood wrapped in green fire. But the face was higher than his own and there was a demoniac aspect about it – Conan had noted various abnormalities about Zogar Sag's features – an obliqueness of the eyes, a sharpness of the ears, a wolfish thinness of the lips; these peculiarities were exaggerated in the apparition which swayed before him. The eyes were red as coals of living fire.

More details came into view: a slender torso, covered with snaky scales, which was yet man-like in shape, with man-like arms, from the waist upward; below, long crane-like legs ended in splay, three-toed feet like those of some huge bird. Along the monstrous limbs the blue fire fluttered and ran. He saw it as through a glistening mist.

Then suddenly it was towering over him, though he had not seen it move toward him. A long arm, which for the first time he noticed was armed with curving, sickle-like talons, swung high and swept down at his neck. With a fierce cry he broke the spell and bounded aside, hurling his ax. The demon avoided the cast with an unbelievably quick movement of its narrow head and was on him again with a hissing rush of leaping flames.

But fear had fought for it when it slew its other victims, and Conan was not afraid. He knew that any being clothed in material flesh can be slain by material weapons, however grisly its form may be.

One flailing talon-armed limb knocked his helmet from his head. A little lower and it would have decapitated him. But fierce joy surged through him as his savagely driven sword sank deep in the monster's groin. He bounded backward from a flailing stroke, tearing his sword free as he leaped. The talons raked his breast, ripping through maillinks as if they had been cloth. But his return spring was like that of a starving wolf. He was inside the lashing arms and driving his sword deep in the monster's belly – felt the arms lock about him and the talons ripping the mail from his back as they sought his vitals – he was lapped and dazzled by blue flame that was chill as ice – then he had torn fiercely away from the weakening arms and his sword cut the air in a tremendous swipe.

The demon staggered and fell sprawling sidewise, its head hanging only by a shred of flesh. The fires that veiled it leaped fiercely upward, now red as gushing blood, hiding the figure from view. A scent of burning flesh filled Conan's nostrils. Shaking the blood and sweat from his eyes, he wheeled and ran staggering through the woods. Blood trickled down his limbs. Somewhere, miles to the south, he saw the faint glow of flames that might mark a burning cabin. Behind him, toward the road, rose a distant howling that spurred him to greater efforts.

8 Conajohara No More

There had been fighting on Thunder River; fierce fighting before the walls of Velitrium; ax and torch had been piled up and down the bank, and many a settler's cabin lay in ashes before the painted horde was rolled back.

A strange quiet followed the storm, in which people gathered and talked in hushed voices, and men with red-stained bandages drank their ale silently in the taverns along the river bank.

There, to Conan the Cimmerian, moodily quaffing from a great wine-glass, came a gaunt forester with a bandage about his head and his arm in a sling. He was the one survivor of Fort Tuscelan.

'You went with the soldiers to the ruins of the fort?'

Conan nodded.

'I wasn't able,' murmured the other. 'There was no fighting?'

'The Picts had fallen back across the Black River. Something must have broken their nerve, though only the devil who made them knows what.'

The woodsman glanced at his bandaged arm and sighed.

'They say there were no bodies worth disposing of.'

Conan shook his head. 'Ashes. The Picts had piled them in the fort and set fire to the fort before they crossed the river. Their own dead and the men of Valannus.'

'Valannus was killed among the last – in the hand-to-hand fighting when they broke the barriers. They tried to take him alive, but he made them kill him. They took ten of the rest of us prisoners when we were so weak from fighting we could fight no more. They butchered nine of us then and there. It was when Zogar Sag died that I got my chance to break free and run for it.'

'Zogar Sag's dead?' ejaculated Conan.

'Aye. I saw him die. That's why the Picts didn't press the fight against Velitrium as fiercely as they did against the fort. It was strange. He took no wounds in battle. He was dancing among the slain, waving an ax with which he'd just brained the last of my comrades. He came at me, howling like a wolf – and then he staggered and dropped the ax, and began to reel in a circle screaming as I never heard a man or beast scream before. He fell between me and the fire they'd built to roast me, gagging and frothing at the mouth, and all at once he went rigid and the Picts shouted that he was dead. It was during the confusion that I slipped my cords and ran for the woods.

'I saw him lying in the firelight. No weapon had touched him. Yet there were red marks like the wounds of a sword in the groin, belly and neck – the last as if his head had been almost severed from his body. What do you make of that?'

Conan made no reply, and the forester, aware of the reticence of barbarians on certain matters, continued: 'He lived by magic, and somehow, he died by magic. It was the mystery of his death that took the heart out of the Picts. Not a man who saw it was in the fighting before Velitrium. They hurried back across Black River. Those that struck Thunder River were warriors who had come on before Zogar Sag died. They were not enough to take the city by themselves.

'I came along the road, behind their main force, and I know none followed me from the fort. I sneaked through their lines and got into the town. You brought the settlers through all right, but their women and children got into Velitrium just ahead of those painted devils. If the youth Balthus and old Slasher hadn't held them up awhile, they'd have butchered every woman and child in Conajohara. I passed the place where Balthus and the dog made their last stand. They were lying amid a heap of dead Picts – I counted seven, brained by his ax, or disemboweled by the dog's fangs, and there were others in the road with arrows sticking in them. Gods, what a fight that must have been!'

'He was a man,' said Conan. 'I drink to his shade, and to the shade of the dog, who knew no fear.' He quaffed part of the wine, then emptied the rest upon the floor, with a curious heathen gesture, and smashed the goblet. 'The heads of ten Picts shall pay for his, and seven heads for the dog, who was a better warrior than many a man.'

And the forester, staring into the moody, smoldering blue eyes, knew the barbaric oath would be kept.

'They'll not rebuild the fort?'

'No; Conajohara is lost to Aquilonia. The frontier has been pushed back. Thunder River will be the new border.'

The woodsman sighed and stared at his calloused hand, worn from contact with ax-haft and sword-hilt. Conan reached his long arm for the wine-jug. The forester stared at him, comparing him with the men about them, the men who had died along the lost river, comparing him with those other wild men over that river. Conan did not seem aware of his gaze.

'Barbarism is the natural state of mankind,' the borderer said, still staring somberly at the Cimmerian. 'Civilization is unnatural. It is a whim of circumstance. And barbarism must always ultimately triumph.'

SHADOWS IN ZAMBOULA

1 A Drum Begins

'PERIL HIDES IN THE house of Aram Baksh!'

The speaker's voice quivered with earnestness and his lean, black-nailed fingers clawed at Conan's mightily muscled arm as he croaked his warning. He was a wiry, sun-burnt man with a straggling black beard, and his ragged garments proclaimed him a nomad. He looked smaller and meaner than ever in contrast to the giant Cimmerian with his black brows, broad chest, and powerful limbs. They stood in a corner of the Sword-Makers' Bazar, and on either side of them flowed past the many-tongued, many-colored stream of the Zamboula streets, which is exotic, hybrid, flamboyant and clamorous.

Conan pulled his eyes back from following a bold-eyed, red-lipped Ghanara whose short skirt bared her brown thigh at each insolent step, and frowned down at his importunate companion.

'What do you mean by peril?' he demanded.

The desert man glanced furtively over his shoulder before replying, and lowered his voice.

'Who can say? But desert men and travelers *have* slept in the house of Aram Baksh, and never been seen or heard of again. What became of them? *He* swore they rose and went their way – and it is true that no citizen of the city has ever disappeared from his house. But no one saw the travelers again, and men say that goods and equipment recognized as theirs have been seen in the bazars. If Aram did not sell them, after doing away with their owners, how came they here?'

'I have no goods,' growled the Cimmerian, touching the shagreen-bound hilt of the broadsword that hung at his hip. 'I have even sold my horse.'

'But it is not always rich strangers who vanish by night from the house of Aram Baksh!' chattered the Zuagir. 'Nay, poor desert men have slept there – because his score is less than that of the other taverns – and have been seen no more. Once a chief of the Zuagirs whose son had thus vanished complained to the satrap, Jungir Khan, who ordered the house searched by soldiers.'

'And they found a cellar full of corpses?' asked Conan in good-humored derision.

'Nay! They found naught! And drove the chief from the city with threats and curses! But – ' he drew closer to Conan and shivered – 'something else was found! At the edge of the desert, beyond the houses, there is a clump of palm trees, and within that grove there is a pit. And within that pit have been found human bones, charred and blackened! Not once, but many times!'

'Which proves what?' grunted the Cimmerian.

'Aram Baksh is a demon! Nay, in this accursed city which Stygians built and which Hyrkanians rule – where white, brown and black folk mingle together to produce hybrids of all unholy hues and breeds – who can tell who is a man, and who a demon in disguise? Aram Baksh is a demon in the form of a man! At night he assumes his true guise and carries his guests off into the desert where his fellow demons from the waste meet in conclave.'

'Why does he always carry off strangers?' asked Conan skeptically.

'The people of the city would not suffer him to slay their people, but they care naught for the strangers who fall into his hands. Conan, you are of the West, and know not the secrets of this ancient land. But, since the beginning of happenings, the demons of the desert have worshipped Yog, the Lord of the Empty Abodes, with fire – fire that devours human victims.

'Be warned! You have dwelt for many moons in the tents of the Zuagirs, and you are our brother! Go not to the house of Aram Baksh!'

'Get out of sight!' Conan said suddenly. 'Yonder comes a squad of the city-watch. If they see you they may remember a horse that was stolen from the satrap's stable—'

The Zuagir gasped, and moved convulsively. He ducked between a booth and a stone horse-trough, pausing only long enough to chatter: 'Be warned, my brother! There are demons in the house of Aram Baksh!' Then he darted down a narrow alley and was gone.

Conan shifted his broad sword-belt to his liking, and calmly returned the searching stares directed at him by the squad of watchmen as they swung past. They eyed him curiously and suspiciously, for he was a man who stood out even in such a motley throng as crowded the winding streets of Zamboula. His blue eyes and alien features distinguished him from the Eastern swarms, and the straight sword at his hip added point to the racial difference.

The watchmen did not accost him, but swung on down the street, while the crowd opened a lane for them. They were Pelishtim, squat, hook-nosed, with blue-black beards sweeping their mailed breasts – mercenaries hired for work the ruling Turanians considered beneath themselves, and no less hated by the mongrel population for that reason.

Conan glanced at the sun, just beginning to dip behind the flat-topped houses on the western side of the bazar, and hitching once more at his belt, moved off in the direction of Aram Baksh's tavern.

With a hillman's stride he moved through the ever-shifting colors of the streets, where the ragged tunics of whining beggars brushed against the ermine-trimmed khalats of lordly merchants, and the pearl-sewn satin of rich courtezans. Giant black slaves slouched along, jostling blue-bearded wanderers from the Shemitish cities, ragged nomads from the surrounding deserts, traders and adventurers from all the lands of the East.

The native population was no less heterogenous. Here, centuries ago, the armies of Stygia had come, carving an empire out of the eastern desert. Zamboula was but a small trading-town then, lying amidst a ring of oases, and inhabited by descendants of nomads. The Stygians built it into a city and settled it with their own people, and with Shemite and Kushite slaves. The ceaseless caravans, threading the desert from east to west and back again, brought riches and more mingling of races. Then came the conquering Turanians, riding out of the East to thrust back the boundaries of Stygia, and now for a generation Zamboula had been Turan's westernmost outpost, ruled by a Turanian satrap.

The babel of a myriad tongues smote on the Cimmerian's ears as the restless pattern of the Zamboula streets weaved about him – cleft now and then by a squad of clattering horsemen, the tall, supple warriors of Turan, with dark hawk-faces, clinking metal and curved swords. The throng scampered from under their horses' hoofs, for they were the lords of Zamboula. But tall, somber Stygians, standing back in the shadows, glowered darkly, remembering their ancient glories. The hybrid population cared little whether the king who controlled their destinies dwelt in dark Khemi or gleaming Aghrapur. Jungir Khan ruled Zamboula, and men whispered that Nafertari, the satrap's mistress, ruled Jungir Khan; but the people went their way, flaunting their myriad colors in the streets, bargaining, disputing, gambling, swilling, loving, as the people of Zamboula have done for all the centuries its towers and minarets have lifted over the sands of the Kharamun.

Bronze lanterns, carved with leering dragons, had been lighted in the streets before Conan reached the house of Aram Baksh. The tavern was the last occupied house on the street, which ran west. A wide garden, enclosed by a wall, where date-palms grew thick, separated it from the houses farther east. To the west of the inn stood another grove of palms, through which the street, now become a road, wound out into the desert. Across the road from the tavern stood a row of deserted huts, shaded by straggling palm trees, and occupied only by bats and jackals. As Conan came down the road he wondered why the beggars, so plentiful in Zamboula, had not appropriated these empty houses for sleeping quarters. The lights ceased some distance behind him. Here were no lanterns, except the one hanging before the tavern gate: only the stars, the soft dust of the road underfoot, and the rustle of the palm leaves in the desert breeze.

Aram's gate did not open upon the road, but upon the alley which ran between the tavern and the garden of the date-palms. Conan jerked lustily at the rope which depended from the bell beside the lantern, augmenting its clamor by hammering on the iron-bound teakwork gate with the hilt of his sword. A wicket opened in the gate and a black face peered through.

'Open, blast you,' requested Conan. 'I'm a guest. I've paid Aram for a room, and a room I'll have, by Crom!'

The black craned his neck to stare into the starlit road behind Conan; but he opened the gate without comment, and closed it again behind the Cimmerian, locking and bolting it. The wall was unusually high; but there were many thieves in Zamboula, and a house on the edge of the desert might have to be defended against a nocturnal nomad raid. Conan strode through a garden where great pale blossoms nodded in the starlight, and entered the tap-room, where a Stygian with the shaven head of a student sat at a table brooding over nameless mysteries, and some nondescripts wrangled over a game of dice in a corner.

Aram Baksh came forward, walking softly, a portly man, with a black beard that swept his breast, a jutting hook-nose, and small black eyes which were never still.

'You wish food?' he asked. 'Drink?'

'I ate a joint of beef and a loaf of bread in the *suk*,' grunted Conan. 'Bring me a tankard of Ghazan wine – I've got just enough left to pay for it.' He tossed a copper coin on the wine-splashed board.

'You did not win at the gaming-tables?'

'How could I, with only a handful of silver to begin with? I paid you for the room this morning, because I knew I'd probably lose. I wanted to be sure I had a roof over my head tonight. I notice nobody sleeps in the streets in Zamboula. The very beggars hunt a niche they can barricade before dark. The city must be full of a particularly bloodthirsty brand of thieves.'

He gulped the cheap wine with relish, and then followed Aram out of the tap-room. Behind him the players halted their game to stare after him with a cryptic speculation in their eyes. They said nothing, but the Stygian laughed, a ghastly laugh of inhuman cynicism and mockery. The others lowered their eyes uneasily, avoiding one another's glance. The arts studied by a Stygian scholar are not calculated to make him share the feelings of a normal human being.

Conan followed Aram down a corridor lighted by copper lamps, and it did not please him to note his host's noiseless tread. Aram's feet were clad in soft slippers and the hallway was carpeted with thick Turanian rugs; but there was an unpleasant suggestion of stealthiness about the Zamboulan.

At the end of the winding corridor Aram halted at a door, across which a heavy iron bar rested in powerful metal brackets. This Aram lifted and showed the Cimmerian into a well-appointed chamber, the windows of which, Conan instantly noted, were small and strongly set with twisted bars of iron, tastefully gilded. There were rugs on the floor, a couch, after the Eastern fashion, and ornately carved stools. It was a much more elaborate chamber than Conan could have procured for the price nearer the center of the city – a fact that had first attracted him, when, that morning, he discovered how slim a purse his roisterings for the past few days had left him. He had ridden into Zamboula from the desert a week before.

Aram had lighted a bronze lamp, and he now called Conan's attention to the two doors. Both were provided with heavy bolts.

'You may sleep safely tonight, Cimmerian,' said Aram, blinking over his bushy beard from the inner doorway.

Conan grunted and tossed his naked broadsword on the couch.

'Your bolts and bars are strong; but I always sleep with steel by my side.'

Aram made no reply; he stood fingering his thick beard for a moment as he stared at the grim weapon. Then silently he withdrew, closing the door behind him. Conan shot the bolt into place, crossed the room, opened the opposite door and looked out. The room was on the side of the house that faced the road running west from the city. The door opened into a small court that was enclosed by a wall of its own. The end-walls, which shut it off from the rest of the tavern compound, were high and without entrances; but the wall that flanked the road was low, and there was no lock on the gate.

Conan stood for a moment in the door, the glow of the bronze lamp behind him, looking down the road to where it vanished among the dense palms. Their leaves rustled together in the faint breeze; beyond them lay the naked desert. Far up the street, in the other direction, lights gleamed and the noises of the city came faintly to him. Here was only starlight, the whispering of the palm leaves, and beyond that low wall, the dust of the road and the deserted huts thrusting their flat roofs against the low stars. Somewhere beyond the palm groves a drum began.

The garbled warnings of the Zuagir returned to him, seeming somehow less fantastic than they had seemed in the crowded, sunlit streets. He wondered again at the riddle of those empty huts. Why did the beggars shun them? He turned back into the chamber, shut the door and bolted it.

The light began to flicker, and he investigated, swearing when he found the palm oil in the lamp was almost exhausted. He started to shout for Aram, then shrugged his shoulders and blew out the light. In the soft darkness he stretched himself fully clad on the couch, his sinewy hand by instinct searching for and closing on the hilt of his broadsword. Glancing idly at the stars framed in the barred windows, with the murmur of the breeze through the palms in his ears, he sank into slumber with a vague consciousness of the muttering drum, out on the desert – the low rumble and mutter of a leather-covered drum, beaten with soft, rhythmic strokes of an open black hand . . .

2 The Night Skulkers

It was the stealthy opening of a door which awakened the Cimmerian. He did not awake as civilized men do, drowsy and drugged and stupid. He awoke instantly, with a clear mind, recognizing the sound that had interrupted his sleep. Lying there tensely in the dark he saw the outer door slowly open. In a widening crack of starlit sky he saw framed a great black bulk, broad, stooping shoulders and a misshapen head blocked out against the stars.

Conan felt the skin crawl between his shoulders. He had bolted that door securely. How could it be opening now, save by supernatural agency? And how could a human being possess a head like that outlined against the stars? All the tales he had heard in the Zuagir tents of devils and goblins came back to bead his flesh with clammy sweat. Now the monster slid noiselessly into the room, with a crouching posture and a shambling gait; and a familiar scent assailed the Cimmerian's nostrils, but did not reassure him, since Zuagir legendry represented demons as smelling like that.

Noiselessly Conan coiled his long legs under him; his naked sword was in his right hand, and when he struck it was as suddenly and murderously as a tiger lunging out of the dark. Not even a demon could have avoided that catapulting charge. His sword met and clove through flesh and bone, and something went heavily to the floor with a strangling cry. Conan crouched in the dark above it, sword dripping in his hand. Devil or beast or man, the thing was dead there on the floor. He sensed death as any wild thing senses it. He glared through the half-open door into the starlit court beyond. The gate stood open, but the court was empty.

Conan shut the door but did not bolt it. Groping in the darkness he found the lamp and lighted it. There was enough oil in it to burn for a minute or so. An instant later he was bending over the figure that sprawled on the floor in a pool of blood.

It was a gigantic black man, naked but for a loin-cloth. One hand still grasped a knotty-headed bludgeon. The fellow's kinky wool was built up into horn-like spindles with twigs and dried mud. This barbaric coiffure had given the head its misshapen appearance in the starlight. Provided with a clue to the riddle, Conan pushed back the thick red lips, and grunted as he stared down at teeth filed to points.

He understood now the mystery of the strangers who had disappeared from the house of Aram Baksh; the riddle of the black drum thrumming out there beyond the palm groves, and of that pit of charred bones – that pit where strange meat might be roasted under the stars, while black beasts squatted about to glut a hideous hunger. The man on the floor was a cannibal slave from Darfar.

There were many of his kind in the city. Cannibalism was not tolerated openly in Zamboula. But Conan knew now why people locked themselves in so securely at night, and why even beggars shunned the open alleys and doorless ruins. He grunted in disgust as he visualized brutish black shadows skulking up and down the nighted streets, seeking human prey – and such men as Aram Baksh to open the doors to them. The innkeeper was not a demon; he was worse. The slaves from Darfar were notorious thieves; there was no doubt that some of their pilfered loot found its way into the hands of Aram Baksh. And in return he sold them human flesh.

Conan blew out the light, stepped to the door and opened it, and ran his hand over the ornaments on the outer side. One of them was movable and worked the bolt inside. The room was a trap to catch human prey like rabbits. But this time instead of a rabbit it had caught a saber-toothed tiger.

Conan returned to the other door, lifted the bolt and pressed against it. It was immovable and he remembered the bolt on the other side.

Aram was taking no chances either with his victims or the men with whom he dealt. Buckling on his sword-belt, the Cimmerian strode out into the court, closing the door behind him. He had no intention of delaying the settlement of his reckoning with Aram Baksh. He wondered how many poor devils had been bludgeoned in their sleep and dragged out of that room and down the road that ran through the shadowed palm groves to the roasting-pit.

He halted in the court. The drum was still muttering, and he caught the reflection of a leaping red glare through the groves. Cannibalism was more than a perverted appetite with the black men of Darfar; it was an integral element of their ghastly cult. The black vultures were already in conclave. But whatever flesh filled their bellies that night, it would not be his.

To reach Aram Baksh he must climb one of the walls which separated the small enclosure from the main compound. They were high, meant to keep out the man-eaters; but Conan was no swamp-bred black man; his thews had been steeled in boyhood on the sheer cliffs of his native hills. He was standing at the foot of the nearer wall when a cry echoed under the trees.

In an instant Conan was crouching at the gate, glaring down the road. The sound had come from the shadows of the huts across the road. He heard a frantic choking and gurgling such as might result from a desperate attempt to shriek, with a black hand fastened over the victim's mouth. A close-knit clump of figures emerged from the shadows beyond the huts, and started down the road – three huge black men carrying a slender, struggling figure between them. Conan caught the glimmer of pale limbs writhing in the starlight, even as, with a convulsive wrench, the captive slipped from the grasp of the brutal fingers and came flying up the road, a supple young woman, naked as the day she was born. Conan saw her plainly before she ran out of the road and into the shadows between the huts. The blacks were at her heels, and back in the shadows the figures merged and an intolerable scream of anguish and horror rang out.

Stirred to red rage by the ghoulishness of the episode, Conan raced across the road.

Neither victim nor abductors were aware of his presence until the soft swish of the dust about his feet brought them about, and then he was almost upon them, coming with the gusty fury of a hill wind. Two of the blacks turned to meet him, lifting their bludgeons. But they failed to estimate properly the speed at which he was coming. One of them was down, disemboweled, before he could strike, and wheeling cat-like, Conan evaded the stroke of the other's cudgel and lashed in a whistling counter-cut. The black's head flew into the air; the headless body took three staggering steps, spurting blood and clawing horribly at the air with groping hands, and then slumped to the dust.

The remaining cannibal gave back with a strangled yell, hurling his captive from him. She tripped and rolled in the dust, and the black fled in blind panic toward the city. Conan was at his heels. Fear winged the black feet, but before they reached the easternmost hut, he sensed death at his back, and bellowed like an ox in the slaughter-yards.

'Black dog of hell!' Conan drove his sword between the dusky shoulders with such vengeful fury that the broad blade stood out half its length from the black breast. With a choking cry the black stumbled headlong, and Conan braced his feet and dragged out his sword as his victim fell.

Only the breeze disturbed the leaves. Conan shook his head as a lion shakes its mane and growled his unsatiated blood-lust. But no more shapes slunk from the shadows, and before the huts the starlit road stretched empty. He whirled at the quick patter of feet behind him, but it was only the girl, rushing to throw herself on him and clasp his neck in a desperate grasp, frantic from terror of the abominable fate she had just escaped.

'Easy, girl,' he grunted. 'You're all right. How did they catch you?'

She sobbed something unintelligible. He forgot all about Aram Baksh as he scrutinized her by the light of the stars. She was white, though a very definite brunette, obviously one of Zamboula's many mixed breeds. She was tall, with a slender, supple form, as he was in a good position to observe. Admiration burned in his fierce eyes as he looked down on her splendid bosom and her lithe limbs, which still quivered from fright and exertion. He passed an arm around her flexible waist and said, reassuringly: 'Stop shaking, wench; you're safe enough.'

His touch seemed to restore her shaken sanity. She tossed back her thick, glossy locks and cast a fearful glance over her shoulder, while she pressed closer to the Cimmerian as if seeking security in the contact.

'They caught me in the streets,' she muttered, shuddering. 'Lying in wait, beneath a dark arch – black men, like great, hulking apes! Set have mercy on me! I shall dream of it!'

'What were you doing out on the streets this time of night?' he inquired, fascinated by the satiny feel of her sleek skin under his questing fingers.

She raked back her hair and stared blankly up into his face. She did not seem aware of his caresses.

'My lover,' she said. 'My lover drove me into the streets. He went mad and tried to kill me. As I fled from him I was seized by those beasts.'

'Beauty like yours might drive a man mad,' quoth Conan, running his fingers experimentally through her glossy tresses.

She shook her head, like one emerging from a daze. She no longer trembled, and her voice was steady.

'It was the spite of a priest – of Totrasmek, the high priest of Hanuman, who desires me for himself – the dog!'

'No need to curse him for that,' grinned Conan. 'The old hyena has better taste than I thought.'

She ignored the bluff compliment. She was regaining her poise swiftly.

'My lover is a – a young Turanian soldier. To spite me, Totrasmek gave him a drug that drove him mad. Tonight he snatched up a sword and came at me to slay me in his madness, but I fled from him into the streets. The negroes seized me and brought me to this – *what was that?*'

Conan had already moved. Soundlessly as a shadow he drew her behind the nearest hut, beneath the straggling palms. They stood in tense stillness, while the low mutterings both had heard grew louder until voices were distinguishable. A group of negroes, some nine or ten, were coming along the road from the direction of the city. The girl clutched Conan's arm and he felt the terrified quivering of her supple body against his.

Now they could understand the gutturals of the black men.

'Our brothers have already assembled at the pit,' said one. 'We have had no luck. I hope they have enough for us.'

'Aram promised us a man,' muttered another, and Conan mentally promised Aram something.

'Aram keeps his word,' grunted yet another. 'Many a man we have taken from his tavern. But we pay him well. I myself have given him ten bales of silk I stole from my master. It was good silk, by Set!'

The blacks shuffled past, bare splay feet scuffing up the dust, and their voices dwindled down the road.

'Well for us those corpses are lying behind these huts,' muttered Conan. 'If they look in Aram's death-room they'll find another. Let's begone.'

'Yes, let us hasten!' begged the girl, almost hysterical again. 'My lover is wandering somewhere in the streets alone. The negroes may take him.'

'A devil of a custom this is!' growled Conan, as he led the way toward the city, paralleling the road but keeping behind the huts and straggling trees. 'Why don't the citizens clean out these black dogs?'

'They are valuable slaves,' murmured the girl. 'There are so many of them they might revolt if they were denied the flesh for which they lust. The people of Zamboula know they skulk the streets at night, and all are careful to remain within locked doors, except when something unforeseen happens, as it did to me. The blacks prey on anything they catch, but they seldom catch anybody but strangers. The people of Zamboula are not concerned with the strangers that pass through the city.

'Such men as Aram Baksh sell these strangers to the blacks. He would not dare attempt such a thing with a citizen.'

Conan spat in disgust, and a moment later led his companion out into the road which was becoming a street, with still, unlighted houses on each side. Slinking in the shadows was not congenial to his nature.

'Where do you want to go?' he asked. The girl did not seem to object to his arm about her waist.

'To my house, to rouse my servants,' she answered. 'To bid them search for my lover. I do not wish the city – the priests – anyone – to know of his madness. He – he is a young officer with a promising future. Perhaps we can drive this madness from him if we can find him.'

'If *we* find him?' rumbled Conan. 'What makes you think I want to spend the night scouring the streets for a lunatic?'

She cast a quick glance into his face, and properly interpreted the gleam in his blue eyes. Any woman could have known that he would follow her wherever she led – for a while, at least. But being a woman, she concealed her knowledge of that fact.

'Please,' she began with a hint of tears in her voice, 'I have no one else to ask for help – you have been kind—'

'All right!' he grunted. 'All right! What's the young reprobate's name?'

'Why – Alafdhal. I am Zabibi, a dancing-girl. I have danced often before the satrap, Jungir Khan, and his mistress Nafertari, and before all the lords and royal ladies of Zamboula. Totrasmek desired me, and because I repulsed him, he made me the innocent tool of his vengeance against Alafdhal. I asked a love potion of Totrasmek, not suspecting the depth of his guile and hate. He gave me a drug to mix with my lover's wine, and he swore that when Alafdhal drank it, he would love me even more madly than ever, and grant my every wish. I mixed the drug secretly with my lover's wine. But having drunk, my lover went raving mad and things came about as I have told you. Curse Totrasmek, the hybrid snake – ahhh!'

She caught his arm convulsively and both stopped short. They had come into a district of shops and stalls, all deserted and unlighted, for the hour was late. They were passing an alley, and in its mouth a man was standing, motionless and silent. His head was lowered, but Conan caught the weird gleam of eery eyes regarding them unblinkingly. His skin crawled, not with fear of the sword in the man's hand, but because of the uncanny suggestion of his posture and silence. They suggested madness. Conan pushed the girl aside and drew his sword.

'Don't kill him!' she begged. 'In the name of Set, do not slay him! You are strong – overpower him!'

'We'll see,' he muttered, grasping his sword in his right hand and clenching his left into a mallet-like fist.

He took a wary step toward the alley – and with a horrible moaning laugh the Turanian charged. As he came he swung his sword, rising on his toes as he put all the power of his body behind the blows. Sparks flashed blue as Conan parried the blade, and the next instant the madman was stretched senseless in the dust from a thundering buffet of Conan's left fist.

The girl ran forward.

'Oh, he is not – he is not—'

Conan bent swiftly, turned the man on his side and ran quick fingers over him.

'He's not hurt much,' he grunted. 'Bleeding at the nose, but anybody's likely to do that, after a clout on the jaw. He'll come to after a bit, and maybe his mind will be right. In the meantime I'll tie his wrists with his sword-belt – so. Now where do you want me to take him?'

'Wait!' She knelt beside the senseless figure, seized the bound hands and scanned them avidly. Then, shaking her head as if in baffled disappointment, she rose. She came close to the giant Cimmerian, and laid her slender hands on his arching breast. Her dark eyes, like wet black jewels in the starlight, gazed up into his.

'You are a man! Help me! Totrasmek must die! Slay him for me!'

'And put my neck into a Turanian noose?' he grunted.

'Nay!' The slender arms, strong as pliant steel, were around his corded neck. Her supple body throbbed against his. 'The Hyrkanians have no love for Totrasmek. The priests of Set fear him. He is a mongrel, who rules men by fear and superstition. I worship Set, and the Turanians bow to Erlik, but Totrasmek sacrifices to Hanuman the accursed! The Turanian lords fear his black arts and his power over the hybrid population, and they hate him. If he were slain in his temple at night, they would not seek his slayer very closely.'

'And what of his magic?' rumbled the Cimmerian.

'You are a fighting-man,' she answered. 'To risk your life is part of your profession.'

'For a price,' he admitted.

'There will be a price!' she breathed, rising on tiptoe, to gaze into his eyes.

The nearness of her vibrant body drove a flame through his veins.

The perfume of her breath mounted to his brain. But as his arms closed about her supple figure she avoided them with a lithe movement, saying: 'Wait! First serve me in this matter.'

'Name your price.' He spoke with some difficulty.

'Pick up my lover,' she directed, and the Cimmerian stooped and swung the tall form easily to his broad shoulder. At the moment he felt as if he could have toppled over Jungir Khan's palace with equal ease. The girl murmured an endearment to the unconscious man, and there was no hypocrisy in her attitude. She obviously loved Alafdhal sincerely. Whatever business arrangement she made with Conan would have no bearing on her relationship with Alafdhal. Women are more practical about these things than men.

'Follow me!' She hurried along the street, while the Cimmerian strode easily after her, in no way discomforted by his limp burden. He kept a wary eye out for black shadows skulking under arches, but saw nothing suspicious. Doubtless the men of Darfar were all gathered at the roasting-pit. The girl turned down a narrow side street, and presently knocked cautiously at an arched door.

Almost instantly a wicket opened in the upper panel, and a black face glanced out. She bent close to the opening, whispering swiftly. Bolts creaked in their sockets, and the door opened. A giant black man stood framed against the soft glow of a copper lamp. A quick glance showed Conan the man was not from Darfar. His teeth were unfiled and his kinky hair was cropped close to his skull. He was from the Wadai.

At a word from Zabibi, Conan gave the limp body into the black's arms, and saw the young officer laid on a velvet divan. He showed no signs of returning consciousness. The blow that had rendered him senseless might have felled an ox. Zabibi bent over him for an instant, her fingers nervously twining and twisting. Then she straightened and beckoned the Cimmerian.

The door closed softly, the locks clicked behind them, and the closing wicket shut off the glow of the lamps. In the starlight of the street Zabibi took Conan's hand. Her own hand trembled a little.

'You will not fail me?'

He shook his maned head, massive against the stars.

'Then follow me to Hanuman's shrine, and the gods have mercy on our souls!'

Along the silent streets they moved like phantoms of antiquity. They went in silence. Perhaps the girl was thinking of her lover lying senseless on the divan under the copper lamps; or was shrinking with fear of what lay ahead of them in the demon-haunted shrine of Hanuman. The barbarian was thinking only of the woman moving so supplely beside him. The perfume of her scented hair was in his nostrils, the sensuous aura of her presence filled his brain and left room for no other thoughts.

Once they heard the clank of brass-shod feet, and drew into the shadows of a gloomy arch while a squad of Pelishtim watchmen swung past. There were fifteen of them; they marched in close formation, pikes at the ready, and the rearmost men had their broad brass shields slung on their backs, to protect them from a knife-stroke from behind. The skulking menace of the black man-eaters was a threat even to armed men.

As soon as the clang of their sandals had receded up the street, Conan and the girl emerged from their hiding-place and hurried on. A few moments later they saw the squat, flat-topped edifice they sought looming ahead of them.

The temple of Hanuman stood alone in the midst of a broad square, which lay silent and deserted beneath the stars. A marble wall surrounded the shrine, with a broad opening directly before the portico. This opening had no gate or any sort of barrier.

'Why don't the blacks seek their prey here?' muttered Conan. 'There's nothing to keep them out of the temple.'

He could feel the trembling of Zabibi's body as she pressed close to him.

'They fear Totrasmek, as all in Zamboula fear him, even Jungir Khan and Nafertari. Come! Come quickly, before my courage flows from me like water!'

The girl's fear was evident, but she did not falter. Conan drew his sword and strode ahead of her as they advanced through the open gateway. He knew the hideous habits of the priests of the East, and was aware that an invader of Hanuman's shrine might expect to encounter almost any sort of nightmare horror. He knew there was a good chance that neither he nor the girl would ever leave the shrine alive, but he had risked his life too many times before to devote much thought to that consideration.

They entered a court paved with marble which gleamed whitely in the starlight. A short flight of broad marble steps led up to the pillared portico. The great bronze doors stood wide open as they had stood for centuries. But no worshippers burnt incense within. In the day men and women might come timidly into the shrine and place offerings to the ape-god on the black altar. At night the people shunned the temple of Hanuman as hares shun the lair of the serpent.

Burning censers bathed the interior in a soft weird glow that created an illusion of unreality. Near the rear wall, behind the black stone altar, sat the god with his gaze fixed for ever on the open door, through which for centuries his victims had come, dragged by chains of roses.

A faint groove ran from the sill to the altar, and when Conan's foot felt it, he stepped away as quickly as if he had trodden upon a snake. That groove had been worn by the faltering feet of the multitude of those who had died screaming on that grim altar.

Bestial in the uncertain light Hanuman leered with his carven mask. He sat, not as an ape would crouch, but cross-legged as a man would sit, but his aspect was no less simian for that reason. He was carved from black marble, but his eyes were rubies, which glowed red and lustful as the coals of hell's deepest pits. His great hands lay upon his lap, palms upward, taloned fingers spread and grasping. In the gross emphasis of his attributes, in the leer of his satyr-countenance, was reflected the abominable cynicism of the degenerate cult which deified him.

The girl moved around the image, making toward the back wall, and when her sleek flank brushed against a carven knee, she shrank aside and shuddered as if a reptile had touched her. There was a space of several feet between the broad back of the idol and the marble wall with its frieze of gold leaves. On either hand, flanking the idol, an ivory door under a gold arch was set in the wall.

'Those doors open into each end of a hair-pin shaped corridor,' she said hurriedly. 'Once I was in the interior of the shrine – once!' She shivered and twitched her slim shoulders at a memory both terrifying and obscene. 'The corridor is bent like a horseshoe, with each horn opening into this room. Totrasmek's chambers are enclosed within the curve of the corridor and open into it. But there is a secret door in this wall which opens directly into an inner chamber—'

She began to run her hands over the smooth surface, where no crack or crevice showed. Conan stood beside her, sword in hand, glancing warily about him. The silence, the emptiness of the shrine, with imagination picturing what might lie behind that wall, made him feel like a wild beast nosing a trap.

'Ah!' The girl had found a hidden spring at last; a square opening gaped blackly in the wall. 'Set!' she screamed, and even as Conan leaped toward her, he saw that a great misshapen hand had fastened itself in her hair. She was snatched off her feet and jerked headfirst through the opening. Conan, grabbing ineffectually at her, felt his fingers slip from a naked limb, and in an instant she had vanished and the wall showed blank as before. Only from beyond it came briefly the muffled sounds of a struggle, a scream, faintly heard, and a low laugh that made Conan's blood congeal in his veins.

3 Black Hands Gripping

With an oath the Cimmerian smote the wall a terrific blow with the pommel of his sword, and the marble cracked and chipped. But the hidden door did not give way, and reason told him that doubtless it had been bolted on the other side of the wall. Turning, he sprang across the chamber to one of the ivory doors.

He lifted his sword to shatter the panels, but on a venture tried the door first with his left hand. It swung open easily, and he glared into a long corridor that curved away into dimness under the weird light of censers similar to those in the shrine. A heavy gold bolt showed on the jamb of the door, and he touched it lightly with his finger tips. The faint warmness of the metal could have been detected only by a man whose faculties were akin to those of a wolf. That bolt had been touched – and therefore drawn – within the last few seconds. The affair was taking on more and more of the aspect of a baited trap. He might have known Totrasmek would know when anyone entered the temple.

To enter the corridor would undoubtedly be to walk into whatever trap the priest had set for him. But Conan did not hesitate. Somewhere in that dim-lit interior Zabibi was a captive, and, from what he knew of the characteristics of Hanuman's priests, he was sure that she needed help badly. Conan stalked into the corridor with a pantherish tread, poised to strike right or left.

On his left, ivory, arched doors opened into the corridor, and he tried each in turn. All were locked. He had gone perhaps seventy-five feet when the corridor bent sharply to the left, describing the curve the girl had mentioned. A door opened into this curve, and it gave under his hand.

He was looking into a broad, square chamber, somewhat more clearly lighted than the corridor. Its walls were of white marble, the floor of ivory, the ceiling of fretted silver. He saw divans of rich satin, gold-worked footstools of ivory, a disk-shaped table of some massive, metal-like substance. On one of the divans a man was reclining, looking toward the door. He laughed as he met the Cimmerian's startled glare.

This man was naked except for a loin-cloth and high-strapped sandals. He was brown-skinned, with close-cropped black hair and restless black eyes that set off a broad, arrogant face. In girth and breadth he was enormous, with huge limbs on which the great muscles swelled and rippled at each slightest movement. His hands were the largest Conan had ever seen. The assurance of gigantic physical strength colored his every action and inflection.

'Why not enter, barbarian?' he called mockingly, with an exaggerated gesture of invitation.

Conan's eyes began to smolder ominously, but he trod warily into the chamber, his sword ready.

'Who the devil are you?' he growled.

'I am Baal-pteor,' the man answered. 'Once, long ago and in another land, I had another name. But this is a good name, and why Totrasmek gave it to me, any temple wench can tell you.'

'So you're his dog!' grunted Conan. 'Well, curse your brown hide, Baal-pteor, where's the wench you jerked through the wall?'

'My master entertains her!' laughed Baal-pteor. 'Listen!'

From beyond a door opposite the one by which Conan had entered there sounded a woman's scream, faint and muffled in the distance.

'Blast your soul!' Conan took a stride toward the door, then wheeled with his skin tingling. Baal-pteor was laughing at him, and that laugh was edged with menace that made the hackles rise on Conan's neck and sent a red wave of murder-lust driving across his vision.

He started toward Baal-pteor, the knuckles on his sword-hand showing white. With a swift motion the brown man threw something at him – a shining crystal sphere that glistened in the weird light.

Conan dodged instinctively, but, miraculously, the globe stopped short in midair, a few feet from his face. It did not fall to the floor. It hung suspended, as if by invisible filaments, some five feet above the floor. And as he glared in amazement, it began to rotate with growing speed. And as it revolved it grew, expanded, became nebulous. It filled the chamber. It enveloped him. It blotted out furniture, walls, the smiling countenance of Baal-pteor. He was lost in the midst of a blinding bluish blur of whirling speed. Terrific winds screamed past Conan, tugging, tearing at him, striving to wrench him from his feet, to drag him into the vortex that spun madly before him.

With a choking cry Conan lurched backward, reeled, felt the solid wall against his back. At the contact the illusion ceased to be. The whirling, titanic sphere vanished like a bursting bubble. Conan reeled upright in the silver-ceilinged room, with a gray mist coiling about his feet, and saw Baal-pteor lolling on the divan, shaking with silent laughter.

'Son of a slut!' Conan lunged at him. But the mist swirled up from the floor, blotting out that giant brown form. Groping in a rolling cloud that blinded him, Conan felt a rending sensation of dislocation – and then room and mist and brown man were gone together. He was standing alone among the high reeds of a marshy fen, and a buffalo was lunging at him, head down. He leaped aside from the ripping scimitar-curved horns, and drove his sword in behind the foreleg, through ribs and heart. And then it was not a buffalo dying there in the mud, but the brown-skinned Baal-pteor. With a curse Conan struck off his head; and the head soared from the ground and snapped beast-like tusks into his throat. For all his mighty strength he could not tear it loose – he was choking – strangling; then there was a rush and roar through space, the dislocating shock of an immeasurable impact, and he was back in the chamber with Baal-pteor, whose head was once more set firmly on his shoulders, and who laughed silently at him from the divan.

'Mesmerism!' muttered Conan, crouching and digging his toes hard against the marble.

His eyes blazed. This brown dog was playing with him, making sport of him! But this mummery, this child's play of mists and shadows of thought, it could not harm him. He had but to leap and strike and the brown acolyte would be a mangled corpse under his heel. This time he would not be fooled by shadows of illusion – but he was.

A blood-curdling snarl sounded behind him, and he wheeled and struck in a flash at the panther crouching to spring on him from the metal-colored table. Even as he struck, the apparition vanished and his blade clashed deafeningly on the adamantine surface. Instantly he sensed something abnormal. The blade stuck to the table! He wrenched at it savagely. It did not give. This was no mesmeristic trick. The table was a giant magnet. He gripped the hilt with both hands, when a voice at his shoulder brought him about, to face the brown man, who had at last risen from the divan.

Slightly taller than Conan, and much heavier, Baal-pteor loomed before him, a daunting image of muscular development. His mighty arms were unnaturally long, and his great hands opened and closed, twitching convulsively. Conan released the hilt of his imprisoned sword and fell silent, watching his enemy through slitted lids.

'Your head, Cimmerian!' taunted Baal-pteor. 'I shall take it with my bare hands, twisting it from your shoulders as the head of a fowl is twisted! Thus the sons of Kosala offer sacrifice to Yajur. Barbarian, you look upon a strangler of Yota-pong. I was chosen by the priests of Yajur in my infancy, and throughout childhood, boyhood and youth I trained in the art of slaying with the naked hands – for only thus are the sacrifices enacted. Yajur loves blood, and we waste not a drop from the victim's veins. When I was a child they gave me infants to throttle; when I was a boy I strangled young girls; as a youth, women, old men and young boys. Not until I reached my full manhood was I given a strong man to slay on the altar of Yota-pong.

'For years I offered the sacrifices to Yajur. Hundreds of necks have snapped between these fingers—' he worked them before the

Cimmerian's angry eyes. 'Why I fled from Yota-pong to become Totrasmek's servant is no concern of yours. In a moment you will be beyond curiosity. The priests of Kosala, the stranglers of Yajur, are strong beyond the belief of men. And I was stronger than any. With my hands, barbarian, I shall break your neck!'

And like the stroke of twin cobras, the great hands closed on Conan's throat. The Cimmerian made no attempt to dodge or fend them away, but his own hands darted to the Kosalan's bull-neck. Baal-pteor's black eyes widened as he felt the thick cords of muscles that protected the barbarian's throat. With a snarl he exerted his inhuman strength, and knots and lumps and ropes of thews rose along his massive arms. And then a choking gasp burst from him as Conan's fingers locked on his throat. For an instant they stood there like statues, their faces masks of effort, veins beginning to stand out purply on their temples. Conan's thin lips drew back from his teeth in a grinning snarl. Baal-pteor's eyes were distended; in them grew an awful surprize and the glimmer of fear. Both men stood motionless as images, except for the expanding of their muscles on rigid arms and braced legs, but strength beyond common conception was warring there – strength that might have uprooted trees and crushed the skulls of bullocks.

The wind whistled suddenly from between Baal-pteor's parted teeth. His face was growing purple. Fear flooded his eyes. His thews seemed ready to burst from his arms and shoulders, yet the muscles of the Cimmerian's thick neck did not give; t3hey felt like masses of woven iron cords under his desperate fingers. But his own flesh was giving way under the iron fingers of the Cimmerian which ground deeper and deeper into the yielding throat-muscles, crushing them in upon jugular and windpipe.

The statuesque immobility of the group gave way to sudden, frenzied motion, as the Kosalan began to wrench and heave, seeking to throw himself backward. He let go of Conan's throat and grasped his wrists, trying to tear away those inexorable fingers.

With a sudden lunge Conan bore him backward until the small of his back crashed against the table. And still farther over its edge Conan bent him, back and back, until his spine was ready to snap.

Conan's low laugh was merciless as the ring of steel.

'You fool!' he all but whispered. 'I think you never saw a man from the West before. Did you deem yourself strong, because you were able to twist the heads off civilized folk, poor weaklings with muscles like rotten string? Hell! Break the neck of a wild Cimmerian bull before you call yourself strong. I did that, before I was a full-grown man – like this!'

And with a savage wrench he twisted Baal-pteor's head around until the ghastly face leered over the left shoulder, and the vertebrae snapped like a rotten branch.

Conan hurled the flopping corpse to the floor, turned to the sword again and gripped the hilt with both hands, bracing his feet against the floor. Blood trickled down his broad breast from the wounds Baal-pteor's finger nails had torn in the skin of his neck. His black hair was damp, sweat ran down his face, and his chest heaved. For all his vocal scorn of Baal-pteor's strength, he had almost met his match in the inhuman Kosalan. But without pausing to catch his breath, he exerted all his strength in a mighty wrench that tore the sword from the magnet where it clung.

Another instant and he had pushed open the door from behind which the scream had sounded, and was looking down a long straight corridor, lined with ivory doors. The other end was masked by a rich velvet curtain, and from beyond that curtain came the devilish strains of such music as Conan had never heard, not even in nightmares. It made the short hairs bristle on the back of his neck. Mingled with it was the panting, hysterical sobbing of a woman. Grasping his sword firmly, he glided down the corridor.

4 Dance, Girl, Dance!

When Zabibi was jerked head-first through the aperture which opened in the wall behind the idol, her first, dizzy, disconnected thought was that her time had come. She instinctively shut her eyes and waited for the blow to fall. But instead she felt herself dumped unceremoniously onto the smooth marble floor, which bruised her knees and hip. Opening her eyes she stared fearfully around her, just as a muffled impact sounded from beyond the wall. She saw a brown-skinned giant in a loin-cloth standing over her, and, across the chamber into which she had come, a man sat on a divan, with his back to a rich velvet curtain, a broad, fleshy man, with fat white hands and snaky eyes. And her flesh crawled, for this man was Totrasmek, the priest of Hanuman, who for years had spun his slimy webs of power throughout the city of Zamboula.

'The barbarian seeks to batter his way through the wall,' said Totrasmek sardonically, 'but the bolt will hold.'

The girl saw that a heavy golden bolt had been shot across the hidden door, which was plainly discernible from this side of the wall. The bolt and its sockets would have resisted the charge of an elephant.

'Go open one of the doors for him, Baal-pteor,' ordered Totrasmek. 'Slay him in the square chamber at the other end of the corridor.'

The Kosalan salaamed and departed by the way of a door in the side wall of the chamber. Zabibi rose, staring fearfully at the priest, whose eyes ran avidly over her splendid figure. To this she was indifferent. A dancer of Zamboula was accustomed to nakedness. But the cruelty in his eyes started her limbs to quivering.

'Again you come to me in my retreat, beautiful one,' he purred with cynical hypocrisy. 'It is an unexpected honor. You seemed to enjoy your former visit so little, that I dared not hope for you to repeat it. Yet I did all in my power to provide you with an interesting experience.'

For a Zamboulan dancer to blush would be an impossibility, but a smolder of anger mingled with the fear in Zabibi's dilated eyes.

'Fat pig! You know I did not come here for love of you.'

'No,' laughed Totrasmek, 'you came like a fool, creeping through the night with a stupid barbarian to cut my throat. Why should you seek my life?'

'You know why!' she cried, knowing the futility of trying to dissemble.

'You are thinking of your lover,' he laughed. 'The fact that you are here seeking my life shows that he quaffed the drug I gave you. Well, did you not ask for it? And did I not send what you asked for, out of the love I bear you?'

'I asked you for a drug that would make him slumber harmlessly for a few hours,' she said bitterly. 'And you – you sent your servant with a drug that drove him mad! I was a fool ever to trust you. I might have known your protestations of friendship were lies, to disguise your hate and spite.'

'Why did you wish your lover to sleep?' he retorted. 'So you could steal from him the only thing he would never give you – the ring with the jewel men call the Star of Khorala – the star stolen from the Queen of Ophir, who would pay a roomful of gold for its return. He would not give it to you willingly, because he knew that it holds a magic which, when properly controlled, will enslave the hearts of any of the opposite sex. You wished to steal it from him, fearing that his magicians would discover the key to that magic and he would forget you in his conquests of the queens of the world. You would sell it back to the queen of Ophir, who understands its power and would use it to enslave men, as she did before it was stolen.'

'And why did *you* want it?' she demanded sulkily.

'I understand its powers. It would increase the power of my arts.'

'Well,' she snapped, 'you have it now!'

'*I* have the Star of Khorala? Nay, you err.'

'Why bother to lie?' she retorted bitterly. 'He had it on his finger when he drove me into the streets. He did not have it when I found him again. Your servant must have been watching the house, and have taken it from him, after I escaped him. To the devil with it! I want my lover back sane and whole. You have the ring; you have punished us both. Why do you not restore his mind to him? Can you?'

'I could,' he assured her, in evident enjoyment of her distress. He drew a phial from among his robes. 'This contains the juice of the golden lotus. If your lover drank it he would be sane again. Yes, I will be merciful. You have both thwarted and flouted me, not once but many times; he has constantly opposed my wishes. But I will be merciful. Come and take the phial from my hand.'

She stared at Totrasmek, trembling with eagerness to seize it, but fearing it was but some cruel jest. She advanced timidly, with a hand extended, and he laughed heartlessly and drew back out of her reach. Even as her lips parted to curse him, some instinct snatched her eyes upward. From the gilded ceiling four jade-hued vessels were falling. She dodged, but they did not strike her. They crashed to the floor about her, forming the four corners of a square. And she screamed, and screamed again. For out of each ruin reared the hooded head of a cobra, and one struck at her bare leg. Her convulsive movement to evade it brought her within reach of the one on the other side and again she had to shift like lightning to avoid the flash of its hideous head.

She was caught in a frightful trap. All four serpents were swaying and striking at foot, ankle, calf, knee, thigh, hip, whatever portion of her voluptuous body chanced to be nearest to them, and she could not spring over them or pass between them to safety. She could only whirl and spring aside and twist her body to avoid the strokes, and each time she moved to dodge one snake, the motion brought her within range of another, so that she had to keep shifting with the speed of light. She could move only a short space in any direction, and the fearful hooded crests were menacing her every second. Only a dancer of Zamboula could have lived in that grisly square.

She became, herself, a blur of bewildering motion. The heads missed her by hair's breadths, but they missed, as she pitted her twinkling feet, flickering limbs and perfect eye against the blinding speed of the scaly demons her enemy had conjured out of thin air.

Somewhere a thin whining music struck up, mingling with the hissing of the serpents, like an evil night-wind blowing through the empty sockets of a skull. Even in the flying speed of her urgent haste she realized that the darting of the serpents was no longer at random. They obeyed the grisly piping of the eery music. They struck with a horrible rhythm, and perforce her swaying, writhing, spinning body attuned itself to their rhythm. Her frantic motions melted into the measures of a dance compared to which the most obscene tarantella of Zamora would have seemed sane and restrained. Sick with shame and terror Zabibi heard the hateful mirth of her merciless tormentor.

'The Dance of the Cobras, my lovely one!' laughed Totrasmek. 'So maidens danced in the sacrifice to Hanuman centuries ago – but never with such beauty and suppleness. Dance, girl, dance! How long can you avoid the fangs of the Poison People? Minutes? Hours? You will weary at last. Your swift, sure feet will stumble, your legs falter, your hips slow in their rotations. Then the fangs will begin to sink deep into your ivory flesh—'

Behind him the curtain shook as if struck by a gust of wind, and Totrasmek screamed. His eyes dilated and his hands caught convulsively at the length of bright steel which jutted suddenly from his breast.

The music broke off short. The girl swayed dizzily in her dance, crying out in dreadful anticipation of the flickering fangs – and then only four wisps of harmless blue smoke curled up from the floor about her, as Totrasmek sprawled headlong from the divan.

Conan came from behind the curtain, wiping his broad blade. Looking through the hangings he had seen the girl dancing desperately between four swaying spirals of smoke, but he had guessed that their appearance was very different to her. He knew he had killed Totrasmek.

Zabibi sank down on the floor, panting, but even as Conan started toward her, she staggered up again, though her legs trembled with exhaustion.

'The phial!' she gasped. 'The phial!'

Totrasmek still grasped it in his stiffening hand. Ruthlessly she tore it from his locked fingers, and then began frantically to ransack his garments.

'What the devil are you looking for?' Conan demanded.

'A ring – he stole it from Alafdhal. He must have, while my lover walked in madness through the streets. Set's devils!'

She had convinced herself that it was not on the person of Totrasmek. She began to cast about the chamber, tearing up divan-covers and hangings, and upsetting vessels.

She paused and raked a damp lock of hair out of her eyes.

'I forgot Baal-pteor!'

'He's in hell with his neck broken,' Conan assured her.

She expressed vindictive gratification at the news, but an instant later swore expressively.

'We can't stay here. It's not many hours until dawn. Lesser priests are likely to visit the temple at any hour of the night, and if we're discovered here with his corpse, the people will tear us to pieces. The Turanians could not save us.'

She lifted the bolt on the secret door, and a few moments later they were in the streets and hurrying away from the silent square where brooded the age-old shrine of Hanuman.

In a winding street a short distance away Conan halted and checked his companion with a heavy hand on her naked shoulder.

'Don't forget there was a price—'

'I have not forgotten!' She twisted free. 'But we must go to – to Alafdhal first!'

A few minutes later the black slave let them through the wicket door. The young Turanian lay upon the divan, his arms and legs bound with heavy velvet ropes. His eyes were open, but they were like those of a mad dog, and foam was thick on his lips. Zabibi shuddered.

'Force his jaws open!' she commanded, and Conan's iron fingers accomplished the task.

Zabibi emptied the phial down the maniac's gullet. The effect was like magic. Instantly he became quiet. The glare faded from his eyes; he stared up at the girl in a puzzled way, but with recognition and intelligence. Then he fell into a normal slumber.

'When he awakes he will be quite sane,' she whispered, motioning to the silent slave.

With a deep bow he gave into her hands a small leathern bag, and drew about her shoulders a silken cloak. Her manner had subtly changed when she beckoned Conan to follow her out of the chamber.

In an arch that opened on the street, she turned to him, drawing herself up with a new regality.

'I must now tell you the truth,' she said. 'I am not Zabibi. I am Nafertari. And *he* is not Alafdhal, a poor captain of the guardsmen. He is Jungir Khan, satrap of Zamboula.'

Conan made no comment; his scarred dark countenance was immobile.

'I lied to you because I dared not divulge the truth to anyone,' she said. 'We were alone when Jungir Khan went mad. None knew of it but myself. Had it been known that the satrap of Zamboula was a madman, there would have been instant revolt and rioting, even as Totrasmek planned, who plotted our destruction.

'You see now how impossible is the reward for which you hoped. The satrap's mistress is not – cannot be for you. But you shall not go unrewarded. Here is a sack of gold.'

She gave him the bag she had received from the slave.

'Go, now, and when the sun is come up to the palace, I will have Jungir Khan make you captain of his guard. But you will take your orders from me, secretly. Your first duty will be to march a squad to the shrine of Hanuman, ostensibly to search for clues of the priest's slayer; in reality to search for the Star of Khorala. It must be hidden there somewhere. When you find it, bring it to me. You have my leave to go now.'

He nodded, still silent, and strode away. The girl, watching the swing of his broad shoulders, was piqued to note that there was nothing in his bearing to show that he was in any way chagrined or abashed.

When he had rounded a corner, he glanced back, and then changed his direction and quickened his pace. A few moments later he was in the quarter of the city containing the Horse Market. There he smote on a door until from the window above a bearded head was thrust to demand the reason for the disturbance.

'A horse,' demanded Conan. 'The swiftest steed you have.'

'I open no gates at this time of night,' grumbled the horse-trader.

Conan rattled his coins.

'Dog's son knave! Don't you see I'm white, and alone? Come down, before I smash your door!'

Presently, on a bay stallion, Conan was riding toward the house of Aram Baksh.

He turned off the road into the alley that lay between the tavern compound and the date-palm garden, but he did not pause at the gate. He rode on to the northeast corner of the wall, then turned and rode along the north wall, to halt within a few paces of the northwest angle. No trees grew near the wall, but there were some low bushes. To one of these he tied his horse, and was about to climb into the saddle again, when he heard a low muttering of voices beyond the corner of the wall.

Drawing his foot from the stirrup he stole to the angle and peered around it. Three men were moving down the road toward the palm groves, and from their slouching gait he knew they were negroes. They halted at his low call, bunching themselves as he strode toward them, his sword in his hand. Their eyes gleamed whitely in the starlight. Their brutish lust shone in their ebony faces, but they knew their three cudgels could not prevail against his sword, just as he knew it.

'Where are you going?' he challenged.

'To bid our brothers put out the fire in the pit beyond the groves,' was the sullen, guttural reply. 'Aram Baksh promised us a man, but he lied. We found one of our brothers dead in the trap-chamber. We go hungry this night.'

'I think not,' smiled Conan. 'Aram Baksh will give you a man. Do you see that door?'

He pointed to a small, iron-bound portal set in the midst of the western wall.

'Wait there. Aram Baksh will give you a man.'

Backing warily away until he was out of reach of a sudden bludgeon blow, he turned and melted around the northwest angle of the wall. Reaching his horse he paused to ascertain that the blacks were not sneaking after him, and then he climbed into the saddle and stood upright on it, quieting the uneasy steed with a low word. He reached up, grasped the coping of the wall and drew himself up and over. There he studied the grounds for an instant. The tavern was built in the southwest corner of the enclosure, the remaining space of which was occupied by groves and gardens. He saw no one in the grounds. The tavern was dark and silent, and he knew all the doors and windows were barred and bolted.

Conan knew that Aram Baksh slept in a chamber that opened into a cypress-bordered path that led to the door in the western wall. Like a shadow he glided among the trees and a few moments later he rapped lightly on the chamber door.

'What is it?' asked a rumbling voice within.

'Aram Baksh!' hissed Conan. 'The blacks are stealing over the wall!'

Almost instantly the door opened, framing the tavern-keeper, naked but for his shirt, with a dagger in his hand.

He craned his neck to stare into the Cimmerian's face.

'What tale is this – *you*!'

Conan's vengeful fingers strangled the yell in his throat. They went to the floor together and Conan wrenched the dagger from his enemy's hand. The blade glinted in the starlight, and blood spurted. Aram Baksh made hideous noises, gasping and gagging on a mouthful of blood. Conan dragged him to his feet and again the dagger slashed, and most of the curly beard fell to the floor.

Still gripping his captive's throat – for a man can scream incoherently even with his tongue slit – Conan dragged him out of the dark chamber and down the cypress-shadowed path, to the iron-bound door in the outer wall. With one hand he lifted the bolt and threw the door open, disclosing the three shadowy figures which waited like black vultures outside. Into their eager arms Conan thrust the innkeeper.

A horrible, blood-choked scream rose from the Zamboulan's throat, but there was no response from the silent tavern. The people there were used to screams outside the wall. Aram Baksh fought like a wild man, his distended eyes turned frantically on the Cimmerian's face. He found no mercy there. Conan was thinking of the scores of wretches who owed their bloody doom to this man's greed.

In glee the negroes dragged him down the road, mocking his frenzied gibberings. How could they recognize Aram Baksh in this half-naked, bloodstained figure, with the grotesquely shorn beard and unintelligible babblings? The sounds of the struggle came back to Conan, standing beside the gate, even after the clump of figures had vanished among the palms.

Closing the door behind him, Conan returned to his horse, mounted and turned westward, toward the open desert, swinging wide to skirt the sinister belt of palm groves. As he rode, he drew from his belt a ring in which gleamed a jewel that snared the starlight in a shimmering iridescence. He held it up to admire it, turning it this way and that. The compact bag of gold pieces clinked gently at his saddle-bow, like a promise of the greater riches to come.

'I wonder what she'd say if she knew I recognized her as Nafertari and him as Jungir Khan the instant I saw them,' he mused. 'I knew the Star of Khorala, too. There'll be a fine scene if she ever guesses that I slipped it off his finger while I was tying him with his sword-belt. But they'll never catch me, with the start I'm getting.'

He glanced back at the shadowy palm groves, among which a red glare was mounting. A chanting rose to the night, vibrating with savage exultation. And another sound mingled with it, a mad, incoherent screaming, a frenzied gibbering in which no words could be distinguished. The noise followed Conan as he rode westward beneath the paling stars.

RED NAILS

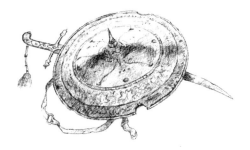

1 The Skull on the Crag

THE WOMAN ON THE horse reined in her weary steed. It stood with its legs wide-braced, its head drooping, as if it found even the weight of the gold-tassled, red-leather bridle too heavy. The woman drew a booted foot out of the silver stirrup and swung down from the gilt-worked saddle. She made the reins fast to the fork of a sapling, and turned about, hands on her hips, to survey her surroundings.

They were not inviting. Giant trees hemmed in the small pool where her horse had just drunk. Clumps of undergrowth limited the vision that quested under the somber twilight of the lofty arches formed by intertwining branches. The woman shivered with a twitch of her magnificent shoulders, and then cursed.

She was tall, full-bosomed and large-limbed, with compact shoulders. Her whole figure reflected an unusual strength, without detracting from the femininity of her appearance. She was all woman, in spite of her bearing and her garments. The latter were incongruous, a view of her present environs. Instead of a skirt she wore short, wide-legged silk breeches, which ceased a hand's breadth short of her knees, and were upheld by a wide silken sash worn as a girdle. Flaring-topped boots of soft leather came almost to her knees, and a low-necked, wide-collared, wide-sleeved silk shirt completed her costume. On one shapely hip she wore a straight double-edged sword, and on the other a long dirk. Her unruly golden hair, cut square at her shoulders, was confined by a band of crimson satin.

Against the background of somber, primitive forest she posed with an unconscious picturesqueness, bizarre and out of place. She should have been posed against a background of sea-clouds, painted masts and wheeling gulls. There was the color of the sea in her wide eyes. And that was as it should have been, because this was Valeria of the Red Brotherhood, whose deeds are celebrated in song and ballad wherever seafarers gather.

She strove to pierce the sullen green roof of the arched branches and see the sky which presumably lay about it, but presently gave it up with a muttered oath.

Leaving her horse tied she strode off toward the east, glancing back toward the pool from time to time in order to fix her route in her mind. The silence of the forest depressed her. No birds sang in the lofty boughs, nor did any rustling in the bushes indicate the presence of any small animals. For leagues she had traveled in a realm of brooding stillness, broken only by the sounds of her own flight.

She had slaked her thirst at the pool, but she felt the gnawings of hunger and began looking about for some of the fruit on which she had sustained herself since exhausting the food she had brought in her saddlebags.

Ahead of her, presently, she saw an outcropping of dark, flint-like rock that sloped upward into what looked like a rugged crag rising among the trees. Its summit was lost to view amidst a cloud of encircling leaves. Perhaps its peak rose above the tree-tops, and from it she could see what lay beyond – if, indeed, anything lay beyond but more of this apparently illimitable forest through which she had ridden for so many days.

A narrow ridge formed a natural ramp that led up the steep face of the crag. After she had ascended some fifty feet she came to the belt of leaves that surrounded the rock. The trunks of the trees did not crowd close to the crag, but the ends of their lower branches extended about it, veiling it with their foliage. She groped on in leafy obscurity, not able to see either above or below her; but presently she glimpsed blue sky, and a moment later came out in the clear, hot sunlight and saw the forest roof stretching away under her feet.

She was standing on a broad shelf which was about even with the tree-tops, and from it rose a spire-like jut that was the ultimate peak of the crag she had climbed. But something else caught her attention in the litter of blown dead leaves which carpeted the shelf. She kicked them aside and looked down on the skeleton of a man. She ran an experienced eye over the bleached frame, but saw no broken bones nor any sign of violence. The man must have died a natural death; though why he should have climbed a tall crag to die she could not imagine.

She scrambled up to the summit of the spire and looked toward the horizons. The forest roof – which looked like a floor from her vantage-point – was just as impenetrable as from below. She could

not even see the pool by which she had left her horse. She glanced northward, in the direction from which she had come. She saw only the rolling green ocean stretching away and away, with only a vague blue line in the distance to hint of the hill-range she had crossed days before, to plunge into this leafy waste.

West and east the view was the same; though the blue hill-line was lacking in those directions. But when she turned her eyes southward she stiffened and caught her breath. A mile away in that direction the forest thinned out and ceased abruptly, giving way to a cactus-dotted plain. And in the midst of that plain rose the walls and towers of a city. Valeria swore in amazement. This passed belief. She would not have been surprised to sight human habitations of another sort – the beehive-shaped huts of the black people, or the cliff-dwellings of the mysterious brown race which legends declared inhabited some country of this unexplored region. But it was a startling experience to come upon a walled city here so many long weeks' march from the nearest outposts of any sort of civilization.

Her hands tiring from clinging to the spire-like pinnacle, she let herself down on the shelf, frowning in indecision. She had come far – from the camp of the mercenaries by the border town of Sukhmet amidst the level grasslands, where desperate adventurers of many races guard the Stygian frontier against the raids that come up like a red wave from Darfar. Her flight had been blind, into a country of which she was wholly ignorant. And now she wavered between an urge to ride directly to that city in the plain, and the instinct of caution which prompted her to skirt it widely and continue her solitary flight.

Her thoughts were scattered by the rustling of the leaves below her. She wheeled cat-like, snatched at her sword; and then she froze motionless, staring wide-eyed at the man before her.

He was almost a giant in stature, muscles rippling smoothly under his skin which the sun had burned brown. His garb was similar to hers, except that he wore a broad leather belt instead of a girdle. Broadsword and poniard hung from this belt.

'Conan, the Cimmerian!' ejaculated the woman. 'What are *you* doing on my trail?'

He grinned hardly, and his fierce blue eyes burned with a light any woman could understand as they ran over her magnificent figure, lingering on the swell of her splendid breasts beneath the light shirt, and the clear white flesh displayed between breeches and boot-tops.

'Don't you know?' he laughed. 'Haven't I made my admiration for you plain ever since I first saw you?'

'A stallion could have made it no plainer,' she answered disdainfully. 'But I never expected to encounter you so far from the ale-barrels and meat-pots of Sukhmet. Did you really follow me from Zarallo's camp, or were you whipped forth for a rogue?'

He laughed at her insolence and flexed his mighty biceps.

'You know Zarallo didn't have enough knaves to whip me out of camp,' he grinned. 'Of course I followed you. Lucky thing for you, too, wench! When you knifed that Stygian officer, you forfeited Zarallo's favor and protection, and you outlawed yourself with the Stygians.'

'I know it,' she replied sullenly. 'But what else could I do? You know what my provocation was.'

'Sure,' he agreed. 'If I'd been there, I'd have knifed him myself. But if a woman must live in the war-camps of men, she can expect such things.'

Valeria stamped her booted foot and swore.

'Why won't men let me live a man's life?'

'That's obvious!' Again his eager eyes devoured her. 'But you were wise to run away. The Stygians would have had you skinned. That officer's brother followed you; faster than you thought, I don't doubt. He wasn't far behind you when I caught up with him. His horse was better than yours. He'd have caught you and cut your throat within a few more miles.'

'Well?' she demanded.

'Well what?' He seemed puzzled.

'What of the Stygian?'

'Why, what do you suppose?' he returned impatiently. 'I killed him, of course, and left his carcass for the vultures. That delayed me, though, and I almost lost your trail when you crossed the rocky spurs of the hills. Otherwise I'd have caught up with you long ago.'

'And now you think you'll drag me back to Zarallo's camp?' she sneered.

'Don't talk like a fool,' he grunted. 'Come, girl, don't be such a spitfire. I'm not like that Stygian you knifed, and you know it.'

'A penniless vagabond,' she taunted.

He laughed at her.

'What do you call yourself? You haven't enough money to buy a new seat for your breeches. Your disdain doesn't deceive me. You know I've commanded bigger ships and more men than you ever did in your life. As for being penniless – what rover isn't, most of the time? I've squandered enough gold in the sea-ports of the world to fill a galleon. You know that, too.'

'Where are the fine ships and the bold lads you commanded, now?' she sneered.

'At the bottom of the sea, mostly,' he replied cheerfully. 'The Zingarans sank my last ship off the Shemite shore – that's why I joined

Zarallo's Free Companions. But I saw I'd been stung when we marched to the Darfar border. The pay was poor and the wine was sour, and I don't like black women. And that's the only kind that came to our camp at Sukhmet – rings in their noses and their teeth filed – bah! Why did you join Zarallo's? Sukhmet's a long way from salt water.'

'Red Ortho wanted to make me his mistress,' she answered sullenly. 'I jumped overboard one night and swam ashore when we were anchored off the Kushite coast. Off Zabhela, it was. There a Shemite trader told me that Zarallo had brought his Free Companies south to guard the Darfar border. No better employment offered. I joined an eastbound caravan and eventually came to Sukhmet.'

'It was madness to plunge southward as you did,' commented Conan, 'but it was wise, too, for Zarallo's patrols never thought to look for you in this direction. Only the brother of the man you killed happened to strike your trail.'

'And now what do you intend doing?' she demanded.

'Turn west,' he answered. 'I've been this far south, but not this far east. Many days' traveling to the west will bring us to the open savannas, where the black tribes graze their cattle. I have friends among them. We'll get to the coast and find a ship. I'm sick of the jungle.'

'Then be on your way,' she advised. 'I have other plans.'

'Don't be a fool!' He showed irritation for the first time. 'You can't keep on wandering through this forest.'

'I can if I choose.'

'But what do you intend doing?'

'That's none of your affair,' she snapped.

'Yes, it is,' he answered calmly. 'Do you think I've followed you this far, to turn around and ride off empty-handed? Be sensible, wench. I'm not going to harm you.'

He stepped toward her, and she sprang back, whipping out her sword.

'Keep back, you barbarian dog! I'll spit you like a roast pig!'

He halted, reluctantly, and demanded: 'Do you want me to take that toy away from you and spank you with it?'

'Words! Nothing but words!' she mocked, lights like the gleam of the sun on blue water dancing in her reckless eyes.

He knew it was the truth. No living man could disarm Valeria of the Brotherhood with his bare hands. He scowled, his sensations a tangle of conflicting emotions. He was angry, yet he was amused and filled with admiration for her spirit. He burned with eagerness to seize that splendid figure and crush it in his iron arms, yet he greatly desired not to hurt the girl. He was torn between a desire to shake her soundly, and a desire to caress her. He knew if he came any nearer her sword would be sheathed in his heart. He had seen Valeria kill too many men in border forays and tavern brawls to have any illusions about her. He knew she was as quick and ferocious as a tigress. He could draw his broadsword and disarm her, beat the blade out of her hand, but the thought of drawing a sword on a woman, even without intent of injury, was extremely repugnant to him.

'Blast your soul, you hussy!' he exclaimed in exasperation. 'I'm going to take off your—'

He started toward her, his angry passion making him reckless, and she poised herself for a deadly thrust. Then came a startling interruption to a scene at once ludicrous and perilous.

'*What's that?*'

It was Valeria who exclaimed, but they both started violently, and Conan wheeled like a cat, his great sword flashing into his hand. Back in the forest had burst forth an appalling medley of screams – the screams of horses in terror and agony. Mingled with their screams there came the snap of splintering bones.

'Lions are slaying the horses!' cried Valeria.

'Lions, nothing!' snorted Conan, his eyes blazing. 'Did you hear a lion roar? Neither did I! Listen at those bones snap – not even a lion could make that much noise killing a horse.'

He hurried down the natural ramp and she followed, their personal feud forgotten in the adventurers' instinct to unite against common peril. The screams had ceased when they worked their way downward through the green veil of leaves that brushed the rock.

'I found your horse tied by the pool back there,' he muttered, treading so noiselessly that she no longer wondered how he had surprised her on the crag. 'I tied mine beside it and followed the tracks of your boots. Watch, now!'

They had emerged from the belt of leaves, and stared down into the lower reaches of the forest. Above them the green roof spread its dusky canopy. Below them the sunlight filtered in just enough to make a jade-tinted twilight. The giant trunks of trees less than a hundred yards away looked dim and ghostly.

'The horses should be beyond that thicket, over there,' whispered Conan, and his voice might have been a breeze moving through the branches. 'Listen!'

Valeria had already heard, and a chill crept through her veins; so she unconsciously laid her white hand on her companion's muscular brown arm. From beyond the thicket came the noisy crunching of bones and the loud rending of flesh, together with the grinding, slobbering sounds of a horrible feast.

'Lions wouldn't make that noise,' whispered Conan. 'Something's eating our horses, but it's not a lion – Crom!'

The noise stopped suddenly, and Conan swore softly. A suddenly risen breeze was blowing from them directly toward the spot where the unseen slayer was hidden.

'Here it comes!' muttered Conan, half lifting his sword.

The thicket was violently agitated, and Valeria clutched Conan's arm hard. Ignorant of jungle-lore she yet knew that no animal she had ever seen could have shaken the tall brush like that.

'It must be as big as an elephant,' muttered Conan, echoing her thought. 'What the devil—' His voice trailed away in stunned silence.

Through the thicket was thrust a head of nightmare and lunacy. Grinning jaws bared rows of dripping yellow tusks; above the yawning mouth wrinkled a saurian-like snout. Huge eyes, like those of a python a thousand times magnified, stared unwinkingly at the petrified humans clinging to the rock above it. Blood smeared the scaly, flabby lips and dripped from the huge mouth.

The head, bigger than that of a crocodile, was further extended on a long scaled neck on which stood up rows of serrated spikes, and after it, crushing down the briars and saplings, waddled the body of a titan, a gigantic, barrel-bellied torso on absurdly short legs. The whitish belly almost raked the ground, while the serrated back-bone rose higher than Conan could have reached on tiptoe. A long spiked tail, like that of a gargantuan scorpion, trailed out behind.

'Back up the crag, quick!' snapped Conan, thrusting the girl behind him. 'I don't think he can climb, but he can stand on his hind-legs and reach us—'

With a snapping and rending of bushes and saplings the monster came hurtling through the thickets, and they fled up the rock before him like leaves blown before a wind. As Valeria plunged into the leafy screen a backward glance showed her the Titan rearing up fearsomely on his massive hinder legs, even as Conan had predicted. The sight sent panic racing through her. As he reared, the beast seemed more gigantic than ever; his snouted head towered among the trees. Then Conan's iron hand closed on her wrist and she was jerked headlong into the blinding welter of the leaves, and out again into the hot sunshine above, just as the monster fell forward with his front feet on the crag with an impact that made the rock vibrate.

Behind the fugitives the huge head crashed through the twigs, and they looked down for a horrifying instant at the nightmare visage framed among the green leaves, eyes flaming, jaws gaping. Then the giant tusks clashed together futilely, and after that the head was withdrawn, vanishing from their sight as if it had sunk in a pool.

Peering down through broken branches that scraped the rock, they saw it squatting on its haunches at the foot of the crag, staring unblinkingly up at them.

Valeria shuddered.

'How long do you suppose he'll crouch there?'

Conan kicked the skull on the leaf-strewn shelf.

'That fellow must have climbed up here to escape him, or one like him. He must have died of starvation. There are no bones broken. That thing must be a dragon, such as the black people speak of in their legends. If so, it won't leave here until we're both dead.'

Valeria looked at him blankly, her resentment forgotten. She fought down a surging of panic. She had proved her reckless courage a thousand times in wild battles on sea and land, on the blood-slippery decks of burning war-ships, in the storming of walled cities, and on the trampled sandy beaches where the desperate men of the Red Brotherhood bathed their knives in one another's blood in their fights for leadership. But the prospect now confronting her congealed her blood. A cutlass stroke in the heat of battle was nothing; but to sit idle and helpless on a bare rock until she perished of starvation, besieged by a monstrous survival of an elder age – the thought sent panic throbbing through her brain.

'He must leave to eat and drink,' she said helplessly.

'He won't have to go far to do either,' Conan pointed out. 'He's just gorged on horsemeat, and like a real snake, he can go for a long time without eating or drinking again. But he doesn't sleep after eating, like a real snake, it seems. Anyway, he can't climb this crag.'

Conan spoke imperturbably. He was a barbarian, and the terrible patience of the wilderness and its children was as much a part of him as his lusts and rages. He could endure a situation like this with a coolness impossible to a civilized person.

'Can't we get into the trees and get away, traveling like apes through the branches?' she asked desperately.

He shook his head. 'I thought of that. The branches that touch the crag down there are too light. They'd break with our weight. Besides, I have an idea that devil could tear up any tree around here by its roots.'

'Well, are we going to sit here on our rumps until we starve, like that?' she cried furiously, kicking the skull clattering across the ledge. 'I won't do it! I'll go down there and cut his damned head off—'

Conan had seated himself on a rocky projection at the foot of the spire. He looked up with a glint of admiration at her blazing eyes and tense, quivering figure, but, realizing that she was in just the mood for any madness, he let none of his admiration sound in his voice.

'Sit down,' he grunted, catching her by her wrist and pulling her down on his knee. She was too surprised to resist as he took her sword from her hand and shoved it back in its sheath. 'Sit still and calm down. You'd only break your steel on his scales. He'd gobble you up in one gulp, or smash you like an egg with that spiked tail of his. We'll get out of his jam some way, but we shan't do it by getting chewed up and swallowed.'

She made no reply, nor did she seek to repulse his arm from about her waist. She was frightened, and the sensation was new to Valeria of the Red Brotherhood. So she sat on her companion's – or captor's – knee with a docility that would have amazed Zarallo, who had anathematized her as a she-devil out of hell's seraglio.

Conan played idly with her curly yellow locks, seemingly intent only upon his conquest. Neither the skeleton at his feet nor the monster crouching below disturbed his mind or dulled the edge of his interest.

The girl's restless eyes, roving the leaves below them, discovered splashes of color among the green. It was fruit, large, darkly crimson globes suspended from the boughs of a tree whose broad leaves were a peculiarly rich and vivid green. She became aware of both thirst and hunger, though thirst had not assailed her until she knew she could not descend from the crag to find food and water.

'We need not starve,' she said. 'There is fruit we can reach.'

Conan glanced where she pointed.

'If we ate that we wouldn't need the bite of a dragon,' he grunted. 'That's what the black people of Kush call the Apples of Derketa. Derketa is the Queen of the Dead. Drink a little of the juice, or spill it on your flesh, and you'd be dead before you could tumble to the foot of this crag.'

'Oh!'

She lapsed into dismayed silence. There seemed no way out of their predicament, she reflected gloomily. She saw no way of escape, and Conan seemed to be concerned only with her supple waist and curly tresses. If he was trying to formulate a plan of escape he did not show it.

'If you'll take your hands off me long enough to climb up on that peak,' she said presently, 'you'll see something that will surprise you.'

He cast her a questioning glance, then obeyed with a shrug of his massive shoulders. Clinging to the spire-like pinnacle, he stared out over the forest roof.

He stood a long moment in silence, posed like a bronze statue on the rock.

'It's a walled city, right enough,' he muttered presently. 'Was that where you were going, when you tried to send me off alone to the coast?'

'I saw it before you came. I knew nothing of it when I left Sukhmet.'

'Who'd have thought to find a city here? I don't believe the Stygians ever penetrated this far. Could black people build a city like that? I see no herds on the plain, no signs of cultivation, or people moving about.'

'How could you hope to see all that, at this distance?' she demanded.

He shrugged his shoulders and dropped down on the shelf.

'Well, the folk of the city can't help us just now. And they might not, if they could. The people of the Black Countries are generally hostile to strangers. Probably stick us full of spears—'

He stopped short and stood silent, as if he had forgotten what he was saying, frowning down at the crimson spheres gleaming among the leaves.

'Spears!' he muttered. 'What a blasted fool I am not to have thought of that before! That shows what a pretty woman does to a man's mind.'

'What are you talking about?' she inquired.

Without answering her question, he descended to the belt of leaves and looked down through them. The great brute squatted below, watching the crag with the frightful patience of the reptile folk. So might one of his breed have glared up at their troglodyte ancestors, treed on a high-flung rock, in the dim dawn ages. Conan cursed him without heat, and began cutting branches, reaching out and severing them as far from the end as he could reach. The agitation of the leaves made the monster restless. He rose from his haunches and lashed his hideous tail, snapping off saplings as if they had been toothpicks. Conan watched him warily from the corner of his eye, and just as Valeria believed the dragon was about to hurl himself up the crag again, the Cimmerian drew back and climbed up to the ledge with the branches he had cut. There were three of these, slender shafts about seven feet long, but not larger than his thumb. He had also cut several strands of tough, thin vine.

'Branches too light for spear-hafts, and creepers no thicker than cords,' he remarked, indicating the foliage about the crag. 'It won't hold our weight – but there's strength in union. That's what the Aquilonian renegades used to tell us Cimmerians when they came into the hills to raise an army to invade their own country. But we always fight by clans and tribes.'

'What the devil has that got to do with those sticks?' she demanded.

'You wait and see.'

Gathering the sticks in a compact bundle, he wedged his poniard hilt between them at one end. Then with the vines he bound them together, and when he had completed his task, he had a spear of no small strength, with a sturdy shaft seven feet in length.

'What good will that do?' she demanded. 'You told me that a blade couldn't pierce his scales—'

'He hasn't got scales all over him,' answered Conan. 'There's more than one way of skinning a panther.'

Moving down to the edge of the leaves, he reached the spear up and carefully thrust the blade through one of the Apples of Derketa, drawing aside to avoid the darkly purple drops that dripped from the pierced fruit. Presently he withdrew the blade and showed her the blue steel stained with a dull purplish crimson.

'I don't know whether it will do the job or not,' quoth he. 'There's enough poison there to kill an elephant, but – well, we'll see.'

Valeria was close behind him as he let himself down among the leaves. Cautiously holding the poisoned pike away from him, he thrust his head through the branches and addressed the monster.

'What are you waiting down there for, you misbegotten offspring of questionable parents?' was one of his more printable queries. 'Stick your ugly head up here again, you long-necked brute – or do you want me to come down there and kick you loose from your illegitimate spine?'

There was more of it – some of it couched in eloquence that made Valeria stare, in spite of her profane education among the seafarers. And it had its effect on the monster. Just as the incessant yapping of a dog worries and enrages more constitutionally silent animals, so the clamorous voice of a man rouses fear in some bestial bosoms and insane rage in others. Suddenly and with appalling quickness, the mastodonic brute reared up on its mighty hind legs and elongated its neck and body in a furious effort to reach this vociferous pigmy whose clamor was disturbing the primeval silence of its ancient realm.

But Conan had judged his distance with precision. Some five feet below him the mighty head crashed terribly but futilely through the leaves. And as the monstrous mouth gaped like that of a great snake, Conan drove his spear into the red angle of the jawbone hinge. He struck downward with all the strength of both arms, driving the long poniard blade to the hilt in flesh, sinew and bone.

Instantly the jaws clashed convulsively together, severing the triple-pieced shaft and almost precipitating Conan from his perch. He would have fallen but for the girl behind him, who caught his sword-belt in a desperate grasp. He clutched at a rocky projection, and grinned his thanks back to her.

Down on the ground the monster was wallowing like a dog with pepper in its eyes. He shook his head from side to side, pawed at it, and opened his mouth repeatedly to its widest extent. Presently he got a huge front foot on the stump of the shaft and managed to tear the blade out. Then he threw up his head, jaws wide and spouting blood, and glared up at the crag with such concentrated and intelligent fury that Valeria trembled and drew her sword. The scales along his back and flanks turned from rusty brown to a dull lurid red. Most horribly the monster's silence was broken. The sounds that issued from his blood-streaming jaws did not sound like anything that could have been produced by an earthly creation.

With harsh, grating roars, the dragon hurled himself at the crag that was the citadel of his enemies. Again and again his mighty head crashed upward through the branches, snapping vainly on empty air. He hurled his full ponderous weight against the rock until it vibrated from base to crest. And rearing upright he gripped it with his front legs like a man and tried to tear it up by the roots, as if it had been a tree.

This exhibition of primordial fury chilled the blood in Valeria's veins, but Conan was too close to the primitive himself to feel anything but a comprehending interest. To the barbarian, no such gulf existed between himself and other men, and the animals, as existed in the conception of Valeria. The monster below them, to Conan, was merely a form of life differing from himself mainly in physical shape. He attributed to it characteristics similar to his own, and saw in its wrath a counterpart of his rages, in its roars and bellowings merely reptilian equivalents to the curses he had bestowed upon it. Feeling a kinship with all wild things, even dragons, it was impossible for him to experience the sick horror which assailed Valeria at the sight of the brute's ferocity.

He sat watching it tranquilly, and pointed out the various changes that were taking place in its voice and actions.

'The poison's taking hold,' he said with conviction.

'I don't believe it.' To Valeria it seemed preposterous to suppose that anything, however lethal, could have any effect on that mountain of muscle and fury.

'There's pain in his voice,' declared Conan. 'First he was merely angry because of the stinging in his jaw. Now he feels the bite of the poison. Look! He's staggering. He'll be blind in a few more minutes. What did I tell you?'

For suddenly the dragon had lurched about and went crashing off through the bushes.

'Is he running away?' inquired Valeria uneasily.

'He's making for the pool!' Conan sprang up, galvanized into swift activity. 'The poison makes him thirsty. Come on! He'll be blind in a few moments, but he can smell his way back to the foot of the crag, and if our scent's here still, he'll sit there until he dies. And others of his kind may come at his cries. Let's go!'

'Down there?' Valeria was aghast.

'Sure! We'll make for the city! They may cut our heads off there, but it's our only chance. We may run into a thousand more dragons on the way, but it's sure death to stay here. If we wait until he dies, we may have a dozen more to deal with. After me, in a hurry!'

He went down the ramp as swiftly as an ape, pausing only to aid his less agile companion, who, until she saw the Cimmerian climb, had fancied herself the equal of any man in the rigging of a ship or on the sheer face of a cliff.

They descended into the gloom below the branches and slid to the ground silently, though Valeria felt as if the pounding of her heart must surely be heard from far away. A noisy gurgling and lapping beyond the dense thicket indicated that the dragon was drinking at the pool.

'As soon as his belly is full he'll be back,' muttered Conan. 'It may take hours for the poison to kill him – if it does at all.'

Somewhere beyond the forest the sun was sinking to the horizon. The forest was a misty twilight place of black shadows and dim vistas. Conan gripped Valeria's wrist and glided away from the foot of the crag. He made less noise than a breeze blowing among the tree-trunks, but Valeria felt as if her soft boots were betraying their flight to all the forest.

'I don't think he can follow a trail,' muttered Conan. 'But if a wind blew our body-scent to him, he could smell us out.'

'Mitra grant that the wind blow not!' Valeria breathed.

Her face was a pallid oval in the gloom. She gripped her sword in her free hand, but the feel of the shagreen-bound hilt inspired only a feeling of helplessness in her.

They were still some distance from the edge of the forest when they heard a snapping and crashing behind them. Valeria bit her lip to check a cry.

'He's on our trail!' she whispered fiercely.

Conan shook his head.

'He didn't smell us at the rock, and he's blundering about through the forest trying to pick up our scent. Come on! It's the city or nothing now! He could tear down any tree we'd climb. If only the wind stays down—'

They stole on until the trees began to thin out ahead of them. Behind them the forest was a black impenetrable ocean of shadows. The ominous crackling still sounded behind them, as the dragon blundered in his erratic course.

'There's the plain ahead,' breathed Valeria. 'A little more and we'll—'

'Crom!' swore Conan.

'Mitra!' whispered Valeria.

Out of the south a wind had sprung up.

It blew over them directly into the black forest behind them. Instantly a horrible roar shook the woods. The aimless snapping and crackling of the bushes changed to a sustained crashing as the dragon came like a hurricane straight toward the spot from which the scent of his enemies was wafted.

'Run!' snarled Conan, his eyes blazing like those of a trapped wolf. 'It's all we can do!'

Sailors' boots are not made for sprinting, and the life of a pirate does not train one for a runner. Within a hundred yards Valeria was panting and reeling in her gait, and behind them the crashing gave way to a rolling thunder as the monster broke out of the thickets and into the more open ground.

Conan's iron arm about the woman's waist half lifted her; her feet scarcely touched the earth as she was borne along at a speed she could never have attained herself. If he could keep out of the beast's way for a bit, perhaps that betraying wind would shift – but the wind held, and a quick glance over his shoulder showed Conan that the monster was almost upon them, coming like a war-galley in front of a hurricane. He thrust Valeria from him with a force that sent her reeling a dozen feet to fall in a crumpled heap at the foot of the nearest tree, and the Cimmerian wheeled in the path of the thundering titan.

Convinced that his death was upon him, the Cimmerian acted according to his instinct, and hurled himself full at the awful face that was bearing down on him. He leaped, slashing like a wildcat, felt his sword cut deep into the scales that sheathed the mighty snout – and then a terrific impact knocked him rolling and tumbling for fifty feet with all the wind and half the life battered out of him.

How the stunned Cimmerian regained his feet, not even he could have ever told. But the only thought that filled his brain was of the woman lying dazed and helpless almost in the path of the hurtling fiend, and before the breath came whistling back into his gullet he was standing over her with his sword in his hand.

She lay where he had thrown her, but she was struggling to a sitting posture. Neither tearing tusks nor trampling feet had touched her. It had been a shoulder or front leg that struck Conan, and the blind monster rushed on, forgetting the victims whose scent it had been following, in the sudden agony of its death throes. Headlong on its course it thundered until its low-hung head crashed into a gigantic tree in its path. The impact tore the tree up by the roots and must have dashed the brains from the misshapen skull. Tree and monster fell together, and the dazed humans saw the branches and leaves shaken by the convulsions of the creature they covered – and then grow quiet.

Conan lifted Valeria to her feet and together they started away at a reeling run. A few moments later they emerged into the still twilight of the treeless plain.

Conan paused an instant and glanced back at the ebon fastness behind them. Not a leaf stirred, nor a bird chirped. It stood as silent as it must have stood before Man was created.

'Come on,' muttered Conan, taking his companion's hand. 'It's touch and go now. If more dragons come out of the woods after us—'

He did not have to finish the sentence.

The city looked very far away across the plain, farther than it had looked from the crag. Valeria's heart hammered until she felt as if it would strangle her. At every step she expected to hear the crashing of the bushes and see another colossal nightmare bearing down upon them. But nothing disturbed the silence of the thickets.

With the first mile between them and the woods, Valeria breathed more easily. Her buoyant self-confidence began to thaw out again. The sun had set and darkness was gathering over the plain, lightened a little by the stars that made stunted ghosts out of the cactus growths.

'No cattle, no plowed fields,' muttered Conan. 'How do these people live?'

'Perhaps the cattle are in pens for the night,' suggested Valeria, 'and the fields and grazing pastures are on the other side of the city.'

'Maybe,' he grunted. 'I didn't see any from the crag, though.'

The moon came up behind the city, etching walls and towers blackly in the yellow glow. Valeria shivered. Black against the moon the strange city had a somber, sinister look.

Perhaps something of the same feeling occurred to Conan, for he stopped, glanced about him, and grunted: 'We stop here, No use coming to their gates in the night. They probably wouldn't let us in. Besides, we need rest, and we don't know how they'll receive us. A few hours' sleep will put us in better shape to fight or run.'

He led the way to a bed of cactus which grew in a circle – a phenomenon common to the southern desert. With his sword he chopped an opening, and motioned Valeria to enter.

'We'll be safe from snakes here, anyhow.'

She glanced fearfully back toward the black line that indicated the forest some six miles away.

'Suppose a dragon comes out of the woods?'

'We'll keep watch,' he answered, though he made no suggestion as to what they would do in such an event. He was staring at the city, a few miles away. Not a light shone from spire or tower. A great black mass of mystery, it reared cryptically against the moonlit sky.

'Lie down and sleep. I'll keep the first watch.'

She hesitated, glancing at him uncertainly, but he sat down cross-legged in the opening, facing toward the plain, his sword across his knees, his back to her. Without further comment she lay down on the sand inside the spiky circle.

'Wake me when the moon is at its zenith,' she directed.

He did not reply nor look toward her. Her last impression, as she sank into slumber, was of his muscular figure, immobile as a statue hewn out of bronze, outlined against the low-hanging stars.

2 By the Blaze of the Fire Jewels

Valeria awoke with a start, to the realization that a gray dawn was stealing over the plain.

She sat up, rubbing her eyes. Conan squatted beside the cactus, cutting off the thick pears and dexterously twitching out the spikes.

'You didn't awake me,' she accused. 'You let me sleep all night!'

'You were tired,' he answered. 'Your posterior must have been sore, too, after that long ride. You pirates aren't used to horseback.'

'What about yourself?' she retorted.

'I was a *kozak* before I was a pirate,' he answered. 'They live in the saddle. I snatch naps like a panther watching beside the trail for a deer to come by. My ears keep watch while my eyes sleep.'

And indeed the giant barbarian seemed as much refreshed as if he had slept the whole night on a golden bed. Having removed the thorns, and peeled off the tough skin, he handed the girl a thick, juicy cactus leaf.

'Skin your teeth in that pear. It's food and drink to a desert man. I was a chief of the Zuagirs once – desert men who live by plundering the caravans.'

'Is there anything you haven't been?' inquired the girl, half in derision and half in fascination.

'I've never been king of an Hyborian kingdom,' he grinned, taking an enormous mouthful of cactus. 'But I've dreamed of being even that. I may be too, some day. Why shouldn't I?'

She shook her head in wonder at his calm audacity, and fell to devouring her pear. She found it not unpleasing to the palate, and full of cool and thirst-satisfying juice. Finishing his meal, Conan wiped his hands in the sand, rose, ran his fingers through his thick black mane, hitched at his sword-belt and said:

'Well, let's go. If the people in that city are going to cut our throats they may as well do it now, before the heat of the day begins.'

His grim humor was unconscious, but Valeria reflected that it might be prophetic. She too hitched her sword belt as she rose. Her terrors of the night were past. The roaring dragons of the distant forest were like a dim dream. There was a swagger in her stride as she moved off beside the Cimmerian. Whatever perils lay ahead of them, their foes would be men. And Valeria of the Red Brotherhood had never seen the face of the man she feared.

Conan glanced down at her as she strode along beside him with her swinging stride that matched his own.

'You walk more like a hillman than a sailor,' he said. 'You must be an Aquilonian. The suns of Darfar never burnt your white skin brown. Many a princess would envy you.'

'I am from Aquilonia,' she replied. His compliments no longer irritated her. His evident admiration pleased her. For another man to have kept her watch while she slept would have angered her; she had always fiercely resented any man's attempting to shield or protect her because of her sex. But she found a secret pleasure in the fact that this man had done so. And he had not taken advantage of her fright and the weakness resulting from it. After all, she reflected, her companion was no common man.

The sun rose behind the city, turning the towers to a sinister crimson.

'Black last night against the moon,' grunted Conan, his eyes clouding with the abysmal superstition of the barbarian. 'Blood-red as a threat of blood against the sun this dawn. I do not like this city.'

But they went on, and as they went Conan pointed out the fact that no road ran to the city from the north.

'No cattle have trampled the plain on this side of the city,' said he. 'No plowshare has touched the earth for years, maybe centuries. But look: once this plain was cultivated.'

Valeria saw the ancient irrigation ditches he indicated, half filled in places, and overgrown with cactus. She frowned with perplexity as her eyes swept over the plain that stretched on all sides of the city to the forest edge, which marched in a vast, dim ring. Vision did not extend beyond that ring.

She looked uneasily at the city. No helmets or spear-heads gleamed on battlements, no trumpets sounded, no challenge rang from the towers. A silence as absolute as that of the forest brooded over the walls and minarets.

The sun was high above the eastern horizon when they stood before the great gate in the northern wall, in the shadow of the lofty rampart. Rust flecked the iron bracings of the mighty bronze portal. Spiderwebs glistened thickly on hinge and sill and bolted panel.

'It hasn't been opened for years!' exclaimed Valeria.

'A dead city,' grunted Conan. 'That's why the ditches were broken and the plain untouched.'

'But who built it? Who dwelt here? Where did they go? Why did they abandon it?'

'Who can say? Maybe an exiled clan of Stygians built it. Maybe not. It doesn't look like Stygian architecture. Maybe the people were wiped out by enemies, or a plague exterminated them.'

'In that case their treasures may still be gathering dust and cobwebs in there,' suggested Valeria, the acquisitive instincts of her profession waking in her; prodded, too, by feminine curiosity. 'Can we open the gate? Let's go in and explore a bit.'

Conan eyed the heavy portal dubiously, but placed his massive shoulder against it and thrust with all the power of his muscular calves and thighs. With a rasping screech of rusty hinges the gate moved ponderously inward, and Conan straightened and drew his sword. Valeria stared over his shoulder, and made a sound indicative of surprise.

They were not looking into an open street or court as one would have expected. The opened gate, or door, gave directly into a long, broad hall which ran away and away until its vista grew indistinct in the distance. It was of heroic proportions, and the floor of a curious red stone, cut in square tiles, that seemed to smolder as if with reflection of flames. The walls were of a shiny green material.

'Jade, or I'm a Shemite!' swore Conan.

'Not in such quantity!' protested Valeria.

'I've looted enough from the Khitan caravans to know what I'm talking about,' he asserted. 'That's jade!'

The vaulted ceiling was of lapis lazuli, adorned with clusters of great green stones that gleamed with a poisonous radiance.

'Green fire-stones,' growled Conan. 'That's what the people of Punt call them. They're supposed to be the petrified eyes of those prehistoric snakes the ancients called Golden Serpents. They glow like a cat's eyes in the dark. At night this hall would be lighted by them, but it would be a hellishly weird illumination. Let's look around. We might find a cache of jewels.'

'Shut the door,' advised Valeria. 'I'd hate to have to outrun a dragon down this hall.'

Conan grinned, and replied: 'I don't believe the dragons ever leave the forest.'

But he complied, and pointed out the broken bolt on the inner side.

'I thought I heard something snap when I shoved against it. That bolt's freshly broken. Rust has eaten nearly through it. If the people ran away, why should it have been bolted on the inside?'

'They undoubtedly left by another door,' suggested Valeria.

She wondered how many centuries had passed since the light of outer day had filtered into that great hall through the open door. Sunlight was finding its way somehow into the hall, and they quickly saw the source. High up in the vaulted ceiling skylights were set in slot-like openings – translucent sheets of some crystalline substance. In the splotches of shadow between them, the green jewels winked like the eyes of angry cats. Beneath their feet the dully lurid floor smoldered with changing hues and colors of flame. It was like treading the floors of hell with evil stars blinking overhead.

Three balustraded galleries ran along on each side of the hall, one above the other.

'A four-storied house,' grunted Conan, 'and this hall extends to the roof. It's long as a street. I seem to see a door at the other end.'

Valeria shrugged her white shoulders.

'Your eyes are better than mine, then, though I'm accounted sharp-eyed among the sea-rovers.'

They turned into an open door at random, and traversed a series of empty chambers, floored like the hall, and with walls of the same green jade, or of marble or ivory or chalcedony, adorned with friezes of bronze, gold or silver. In the ceilings the green fire-gems were set, and their light was as ghostly and illusive as Conan had predicted. Under the witch-fire glow the intruders moved like specters.

Some of the chambers lacked this illumination, and their doorways showed black as the mouth of the Pit. These Conan and Valeria avoided, keeping always to the lighted chambers.

Cobwebs hung in the corners, but there was no perceptible accumulation of dust on the floor, or on the tables and seats of marble, jade or carnelian which occupied the chambers. Here and there were rugs of that silk known as Khitan which is practically indestructible. Nowhere did they find any windows, or doors opening into streets or courts. Each door merely opened into another chamber or hall.

'Why don't we come to a street?' grumbled Valeria. 'This place or whatever we're in must be as big as the king of Turan's seraglio.'

'They must not have perished of plague,' said Conan, meditating upon the mystery of the empty city. 'Otherwise we'd find skeletons. Maybe it became haunted, and everybody got up and left. Maybe—'

'Maybe, hell!' broke in Valeria rudely. 'We'll never know. Look at these friezes. They portray men. What race do they belong to?'

Conan scanned them and shook his head.

'I never saw people exactly like them. But there's the smack of the East about them – Vendhya, maybe, or Kosala.'

'Were you a king in Kosala?' she asked, masking her keen curiosity with derision.

'No. But I was a war-chief of the Afghulis who live in the Himelian mountains above the borders of Vendhya. These people favor the Kosalans. But why should Kosalans be building a city this far to west?'

The figures portrayed were those of slender, olive-skinned men and women, with finely chiseled, exotic features. They wore filmy robes and many delicate jeweled ornaments, and were depicted mostly in attitudes of feasting, dancing or love-making.

'Easterners, all right,' grunted Conan, 'but from where I don't know. They must have lived a disgustingly peaceful life, though, or they'd have scenes of wars and fights. Let's go up that stair.'

It was an ivory spiral that wound up from the chamber in which they were standing. They mounted three flights and came into a broad chamber on the fourth floor, which seemed to be the highest tier in the building. Skylights in the ceiling illuminated the room, in which light the fire-gems winked pallidly. Glancing through the doors they saw, except on one side, a series of similarly lighted chambers. This other door opened upon a balustraded gallery that overhung a hall much smaller than the one they had recently explored on the lower floor.

'Hell!' Valeria sat down disgustedly on a jade bench. 'The people who deserted this city must have taken all their treasures with them. I'm tired of wandering through these bare rooms at random.'

'All these upper chambers seem to be lighted,' said Conan. 'I wish we could find a window that overlooked the city. Let's have a look through that door over there.'

'You have a look,' advised Valeria. 'I'm going to sit here and rest my feet.'

Conan disappeared through the door opposite that one opening upon the gallery, and Valeria leaned back with her hands clasped behind her head, and thrust her booted legs out in front of her. These silent rooms and halls with their gleaming green clusters of ornaments and burning crimson floors were beginning to depress her. She wished they could find their way out of the maze into which they had wandered and emerge into a street. She wondered idly what furtive, dark feet had glided over those flaming floors in past centuries, how many deeds of cruelty and mystery those winking ceiling-gems had blazed down upon.

It was a faint noise that brought her out of her reflections. She was on her feet with her sword in her hand before she realized what had disturbed her. Conan had not returned, and she knew it was not he that she had heard.

The sound had come from somewhere beyond the door that opened on to the gallery. Soundlessly in her soft leather boots she glided through it, crept across the balcony and peered down between the heavy balustrades.

A man was stealing along the hall.

The sight of a human being in this supposedly deserted city was a startling shock. Crouching down behind the stone balusters, with every nerve tingling, Valeria glared down at the stealthy figure.

The man in no way resembled the figures depicted on the friezes. He was slightly above middle height, very dark, though not negroid. He was naked but for a scanty silk clout that only partly covered his muscular hips, and a leather girdle, a hand's breadth broad, about his lean waist. His long black hair hung in lank strands about his shoulders, giving him a wild appearance. He was gaunt, but knots and cords of muscles stood out on his arms and legs, without that fleshy padding that presents a pleasing symmetry of contour. He was built with an economy that was almost repellent.

Yet it was not so much his physical appearance as his attitude that impressed the woman who watched him. He slunk along, stooped in a semi-crouch, his head turning from side to side. He grasped a wide-tipped blade in his right hand, and she saw it shake with the intensity of the emotion that gripped him. He was afraid, trembling in the grip of some dire terror. When he turned his head she caught the blaze of wild eyes among the lank strands of black hair.

He did not see her. On tiptoe he glided across the hall and vanished through an open door. A moment later she heard a choking cry, and then silence fell again.

Consumed with curiosity, Valeria glided along the gallery until she came to a door above the one through which the man had passed. It opened into another, smaller gallery that encircled a large chamber.

This chamber was on the third floor, and its ceiling was not so high as that of the hall. It was lighted only by the fire-stones, and their weird green glow left the spaces under the balcony in shadows.

Valeria's eyes widened. The man she had seen was still in the chamber.

He lay face down on a dark crimson carpet in the middle of the room. His body was limp, his arms spread wide. His curved sword lay near him.

She wondered why he should lie there so motionless. Then her eyes narrowed as she stared down at the rug on which he lay. Beneath and about him the fabric showed a slightly different color, a deeper, brighter crimson.

Shivering slightly, she crouched down closer behind the balustrade, intently scanning the shadows under the overhanging gallery. They gave up no secret.

Suddenly another figure entered the grim drama. He was a man similar to the first, and he came in by a door opposite that which gave upon the hall.

His eyes glared at the sight of the man on the floor, and he spoke something in a staccato voice that sounded like 'Chicmec!' The other did not move.

The man stepped quickly across the floor, bent, gripped the fallen man's shoulder and turned him over. A choking cry escaped him as the head fell back limply, disclosing a throat that had been severed from ear to ear.

The man let the corpse fall back upon the blood-stained carpet, and sprang to his feet, shaking like a wind-blown leaf. His face was an ashy mask of fear. But with one knee flexed for flight, he froze suddenly, became as immobile as an image, staring across the chamber with dilated eyes.

In the shadows beneath the balcony a ghostly light began to glow and grow, a light that was not part of the fire-stone gleam. Valeria felt her hair stir as she watched it; for, dimly visible in the throbbing radiance, there floated a human skull, and it was from this skull – human yet appallingly misshapen – that the spectral light seemed to emanate. It hung there like a disembodied head, conjured out of night and the shadows, growing more and more distinct; human, and yet not human as she knew humanity.

The man stood motionless, an embodiment of paralysed horror, staring fixedly at the apparition. The thing moved out from the wall and a grotesque shadow moved with it. Slowly the shadow became visible as a man-like figure whose naked torso and limbs shone whitely, with the hue of bleached bones. The bare skull on its shoulders grinned eyelessly, in the midst of its unholy nimbus, and the man confronting it seemed unable to take his eyes from it. He stood still, his sword dangling from nerveless fingers, on his face the expression of a man bound by the spells of a mesmerist.

Valeria realized that it was not fear alone that paralysed him. Some hellish quality of that throbbing glow had robbed him of his power to think and act. She herself, safely above the scene, felt the subtle impact of a nameless emanation that was a threat to sanity.

The horror swept toward its victim and he moved at last, but only to drop his sword and sink to his knees, covering his eyes with his hands. Dumbly he awaited the stroke of the blade that now gleamed in the apparition's hand as it reared above him like Death triumphant over mankind.

Valeria acted according to the first impulse of her wayward nature. With one tigerish movement she was over the balustrade and dropping to the floor behind the awful shape. It wheeled at the thud of her soft boots on the floor, but even as it turned, her keen blade lashed down, and a fierce exultation swept her as she felt the edge cleave solid flesh and mortal bone.

The apparition cried out gurglingly and went down, severed through shoulder, breast-bone and spine, and as it fell the burning skull rolled clear, revealing a lank mop of black hair and a dark face twisted in the convulsions of death. Beneath the horrific masquerade there was a human being, a man similar to the one kneeling supinely on the floor.

The latter looked up at the sound of the blow and the cry, and now he glared in wild-eyed amazement at the white-skinned woman who stood over the corpse with a dripping sword in her hand.

He staggered up, yammering as if the sight had almost unseated his reason. She was amazed to realize that she understood him. He was gibbering in the Stygian tongue, though in a dialect unfamiliar to her.

'Who are you? Whence come you? What do you in Xuchotl?' Then rushing on, without waiting for her to reply: 'But you are a friend – goddess or devil, it makes no difference! You have slain the Burning Skull! It was but a man beneath it, after all! We deemed it a demon *they* conjured up out of the catacombs! *Listen!*'

He stopped short in his ravings and stiffened, straining his ears with painful intensity. The girl heard nothing.

'We must hasten!' he whispered. '*They* are west of the Great Hall! They may be all around us here! They may be creeping upon us even now!'

He seized her wrist in a convulsive grasp she found hard to break.

'Whom do you mean by "they"?' she demanded.

He stared at her uncomprehendingly for an instant, as if he found her ignorance hard to understand.

'They?' he stammered vaguely. 'Why – why, the people of Xotalanc! The clan of the man you slew. They who dwell by the eastern gate.'

'You mean to say this city is inhabited?' she exclaimed.

'Aye! Aye!' He was writhing in the impatience of apprehension. 'Come away! Come quick! We must return to Tecuhltli!'

'Where is that?' she demanded.

'The quarter by the western gate!' He had her wrist again and was pulling her toward the door through which he had first come. Great beads of perspiration dripped from his dark forehead, and his eyes blazed with terror.

'Wait a minute!' she growled, flinging off his hand. 'Keep your hands off me, or I'll split your skull. What's all this about? Who are you? Where would you take me?'

He took a firm grip on himself, casting glances to all sides, and began speaking so fast his words tripped over each other.

'My name is Techotl. I am of Tecuhltli. I and this man who lies with his throat cut came into the Halls of Silence to try and ambush some of the Xotalancas. But we became separated and I returned here to find him with his gullet slit. The Burning Skull did it, I know, just as he would have slain me had you not killed him. But perhaps he was not alone. Others may be stealing from Xotalanc! The gods themselves blench at the fate of those they take alive!'

At the thought he shook as with an ague and his dark skin grew ashy. Valeria frowned puzzledly at him. She sensed intelligence behind this rigmarole, but it was meaningless to her.

She turned toward the skull, which still glowed and pulsed on the floor, and was reaching a booted toe tentatively toward it, when the man who called himself Techotl sprang forward with a cry.

'Do not touch it! Do not even look at it! Madness and death lurk in it. The wizards of Xotalanc understand its secret – they found it in the catacombs, where lie the bones of terrible kings who ruled in Xuchotl in the black centuries of the past. To gaze upon it freezes the blood and withers the brain of a man who understands not its mystery. To touch it causes madness and destruction.'

She scowled at him uncertainly. He was not a reassuring figure, with his lean, muscle-knotted frame, and snaky locks. In his eyes, behind the glow of terror, lurked a weird light she had never seen in the eyes of a man wholly sane. Yet he seemed sincere in his protestations.

'Come!' he begged, reaching for her hand, and then recoiling as he remembered her warning. 'You are a stranger. How you came here I do not know, but if you were a goddess or a demon, come to aid Tecuhltli, you would know all the things you have asked me. You must be from beyond the great forest, whence our ancestors came. But you are our friend, or you would not have slain my enemy. Come quickly, before the Xotalancas find us and slay us!'

From his repellent, impassioned face she glanced to the sinister skull, smoldering and glowing on the floor near the dead man. It was like a skull seen in a dream, undeniably human, yet with disturbing distortions and malformations of contour and outline. In life the wearer of that skull must have presented an alien and monstrous aspect. Life? It seemed to possess some sort of life of its own. Its jaws yawned at her and snapped together. Its radiance grew brighter, more vivid, yet the impression of nightmare grew too; it was a dream; all life was a dream – it was Techotl's urgent voice which snapped Valeria back from the dim gulfs whither she was drifting.

'Do not look at the skull! Do not look at the skull!' It was a far cry across unreckoned voids.

Valeria shook herself like a lion shaking his mane. Her vision cleared. Techotl was chattering: 'In life it housed the awful brain of a king of magicians! It holds still the life and fire of magic drawn from outer spaces!'

With a curse Valeria leaped, lithe as a panther, and the skull crashed to flaming bits under her swinging sword. Somewhere in the room, or in the void, or in the dim reaches of her consciousness, an inhuman voice cried out in pain and rage.

Techotl's hand was plucking at her arm and he was gibbering: 'You have broken it! You have destroyed it! Not all the black arts of Xotalanc can rebuild it! Come away! Come away quickly, now!'

'But I can't go,' she protested. 'I have a friend somewhere near by—'

The flare of his eyes cut her short as he stared past her with an expression grown ghastly. She wheeled just as four men rushed through as many doors, converging on the pair in the center of the chamber.

They were like the others she had seen, the same knotted muscles bulging on otherwise gaunt limbs, the same lank blue-black hair, the same mad glare in their wide eyes. They were armed and clad like Techotl, but on the breast of each was painted a white skull.

There were no challenges or war-cries. Like blood-mad tigers the men of Xotalanc sprang at the throats of their enemies. Techotl met them with the fury of desperation, ducked the swipe of a wide-headed blade, and grappled with the wielder, and bore him to the floor where they rolled and wrestled in murderous silence.

The other three swarmed on Valeria, their weird eyes red as the eyes of mad dogs.

She killed the first who came within reach before he could strike a blow, her long straight blade splitting his skull even as his own sword lifted for a stroke. She side-stepped a thrust, even as she parried a slash. Her eyes danced and her lips smiled without mercy. Again she was Valeria of the Red Brotherhood, and the hum of her steel was like a bridal song in her ears.

Her sword darted past a blade that sought to parry, and sheathed six inches of its point in a leather-guarded midriff. The man gasped agonizedly and went to his knees, but his tall mate lunged in, in ferocious silence, raining blow on blow so furiously that Valeria had no opportunity to counter. She stepped back coolly, parrying the strokes and watching for her chance to thrust home. He could not long keep up that flailing whirlwind. His arm would tire, his wind would fail; he would weaken, falter, and then her blade would slide smoothly into his heart. A sidelong glance showed her Techotl kneeling on the breast of his antagonist and striving to break the other's hold on his wrist and to drive home a dagger.

Sweat beaded the forehead of the man facing her, and his eyes were like burning coals. Smite as he would, he could not break past nor beat down her guard. His breath came in gusty gulps, his blows began to fall erratically. She stepped back to draw him out – and felt her thighs locked in an iron grip. She had forgotten the wounded man on the floor.

Crouching on his knees, he held her with both arms locked about her legs, and his mate croaked in triumph and began working his way around to come at her from the left side. Valeria wrenched and tore savagely, but in vain. She could free herself of this clinging menace with a downward flick of her sword, but in that instant the curved blade of the tall warrior would crash through her skull. The wounded man began to worry at her bare thigh with his teeth like a wild beast.

She reached down with her left hand and gripped his long hair, forcing his head back so that his white teeth and rolling eyes gleamed up at her. The tall Xotalanc cried out fiercely and leaped in, smiting with all the fury of his arm. Awkwardly she parried the stroke, and it beat the flat of her blade down on her head so that she saw sparks flash before her eyes, and staggered. Up went the sword again, with a low, beast-like cry of triumph – and then a giant form loomed behind the Xotalanc and steel flashed like a jet of blue lightning. The cry of the warrior broke short and he went down like an ox beneath the pole-ax, his brains gushing from his skull that had been split to the throat.

'Conan!' gasped Valeria. In a gust of passion she turned on the Xotalanc whose long hair she still gripped in her left hand. 'Dog of hell!' Her blade swished as it cut the air in an upswinging arc with a blur in the middle, and the headless body slumped down, spurting blood. She hurled the severed head across the room.

'What the devil's going on here?' Conan bestrode the corpse of the man he had killed, broadsword in hand, glaring about him in amazement.

Techotl was rising from the twitching figure of the last Xotalanc, shaking red drops from his dagger. He was bleeding from the stab deep in the thigh. He stared at Conan with dilated eyes.

'What is all this?' Conan demanded again, not yet recovered from the stunning surprise of finding Valeria engaged in a savage battle with these fantastic figures in a city he had thought empty and uninhabited. Returning from an aimless exploration of the upper chambers to find Valeria missing from the room where he had left her, he had followed the sounds of strife that burst on his dumfounded ears.

'Five dead dogs!' exclaimed Techotl, his flaming eyes reflecting a ghastly exultation. 'Five slain! Five crimson nails for the black pillar! The gods of blood be thanked!'

He lifted quivering hands on high, and then, with the face of a fiend, he spat on the corpses and stamped on their faces, dancing in his ghoulish glee. His recent allies eyed him in amazement, and Conan asked, in the Aquilonian tongue: 'Who is this madman?'

Valeria shrugged her shoulders.

'He says his name's Techotl. From his babblings I gather that his people live at one end of this crazy city, and these others at the other end. Maybe we'd better go with him. He seems friendly, and it's easy to see that the other clan isn't.'

Techotl had ceased his dancing and was listening again, his head tilted sidewise, dog-like, triumph struggling with fear in his repellent countenance.

'Come away, now!' he whispered. 'We have done enough! Five dead dogs! My people will welcome you! They will honor you! But come! It is far to Tecuhltli. At any moment the Xotalancs may come on us in numbers too great even for your swords.'

'Lead the way,' grunted Conan.

Techotl instantly mounted a stair leading up to the gallery, beckoning them to follow him, which they did, moving rapidly to keep on his heels. Having reached the gallery, he plunged into a door that opened toward the west, and hurried through chamber after chamber, each lighted by skylights or green fire-jewels.

'What sort of a place can this be?' muttered Valeria under her breath.

'Crom knows!' answered Conan. 'I've seen *his* kind before, though. They live on the shores of Lake Zuad, near the border of Kush. They're a sort of mongrel Stygians, mixed with another race that wandered into Stygia from the east some centuries ago and were absorbed by them. They're called Tlazitlans. I'm willing to bet it wasn't they who built this city, though.'

Techotl's fear did not seem to diminish as they drew away from the chamber where the dead men lay. He kept twisting his head on his shoulder to listen for sounds of pursuit, and stared with burning intensity into every doorway they passed.

Valeria shivered in spite of herself. She feared no man. But the weird floor beneath her feet, the uncanny jewels over her head, dividing the lurking shadows among them, the stealth and terror of their guide, impressed her with a nameless apprehension, a sensation of lurking, inhuman peril.

'They may be between us and Tecuhltli!' he whispered once. 'We must beware lest they be lying in wait!'

'Why don't we get out of this infernal palace, and take to the streets?' demanded Valeria.

'There are no streets in Xuchotl,' he answered. 'No squares nor open courts. The whole city is built like one giant palace under one great roof. The nearest approach to a street is the Great Hall which traverses the city from the north gate to the south gate. The only doors opening into the outer world are the city gates, through which no living man has passed for fifty years.'

'How long have you dwelt here?' asked Conan.

'I was born in the castle of Tecuhltli thirty-five years ago. I have never set foot outside the city. For the love of the gods, let us go silently! These halls may be full of lurking devils. Olmec shall tell you all when we reach Tecuhltli.'

So in silence they glided on with the green fire-stones blinking overhead and the flaming floors smoldering under their feet, and it seemed to Valeria as if they fled through hell, guided by a dark-faced lank-haired goblin.

Yet it was Conan who halted them as they were crossing an unusually wide chamber. His wilderness-bred ears were keener even than the ears of Techotl whetted though these were by a lifetime of warfare in those silent corridors.

'You think some of your enemies may be ahead of us, lying in ambush?'

'They prowl through these rooms at all hours,' answered Techotl, 'as do we. The halls and chambers between Tecuhltli and Xotalanc are a disputed region, owned by no man. We call it the Halls of Silence. Why do you ask?'

'Because men are in the chambers ahead of us,' answered Conan. 'I heard steel clink against stone.'

Again a shaking seized Techotl, and he clenched his teeth to keep them from chattering.

'Perhaps they are your friends,' suggested Valeria.

'We dare not chance it,' he panted, and moved with frenzied activity. He turned aside and glided through a doorway on the left which led into a chamber from which an ivory staircase wound down into darkness.

'This leads to an unlighted corridor below us!' he hissed, great beads of perspiration standing out on his brow. 'They may be lurking there, too. It may all be a trick to draw us into it. But we must take the chance that they have laid their ambush in the rooms above. Come swiftly, now!'

Softly as phantoms they descended the stair and came to the mouth of a corridor black as night. They crouched there for a moment, listening, and then melted into it. As they moved along, Valeria's flesh crawled between her shoulders in momentary expectation of a sword-thrust in the dark. But for Conan's iron fingers gripping her arm she had no physical cognizance of her companions. Neither made as much noise as a cat would have made. The darkness was absolute. One hand, outstretched, touched a wall, and occasionally she felt a door under her fingers. The hallway seemed interminable.

Suddenly they were galvanized by a sound behind them. Valeria's flesh crawled anew, for she recognized it as the soft opening of a door. Men had come into the corridor behind them. Even with the thought she stumbled over something that felt like a human skull. It rolled across the floor with an appalling clatter.

'Run!' yelped Techotl, a note of hysteria in his voice, and was away down the corridor like a flying ghost.

Again Valeria felt Conan's hand bearing her up and sweeping her along as they raced after their guide. Conan could see in the dark no better than she, but he possessed a sort of instinct that made his course unerring. Without his support and guidance she would have fallen or stumbled against the wall. Down the corridor they sped, while the swift patter of flying feet drew closer and closer, and then suddenly Techotl panted: 'Here is the stair! After me, quick! Oh, quick!'

His hand came out of the dark and caught Valeria's wrist as she stumbled blindly on the steps. She felt herself half dragged, half lifted up the winding stair, while Conan released her and turned on the steps, his ears and instincts telling him their foes were hard at their backs. *And the sounds were not all those of human feet.*

Something came writhing up the steps, something that slithered and rustled and brought a chill in the air with it. Conan lashed down with his great sword and felt the blade shear through something that might have been flesh and bone, and cut deep into the stair beneath. Something touched his foot that chilled like the touch of frost, and then the darkness beneath him was disturbed by a frightful thrashing and lashing, and a man cried out in agony.

The next moment Conan was racing up the winding staircase, and through a door that stood open at the head.

Valeria and Techotl were already through, and Techotl slammed the door and shot a bolt across it – the first Conan had seen since they left the outer gate.

Then he turned and ran across the well-lighted chamber into which they had come, and as they passed through the farther door, Conan glanced back and saw the door groaning and straining under heavy pressure violently applied from the other side.

Though Techotl did not abate either his speed or his caution, he seemed more confident now. He had the air of a man who has come into familiar territory, within call of friends.

But Conan renewed his terror by asking: 'What was that thing that I fought on the stair?'

'The men of Xotalanc,' answered Techotl, without looking back. 'I told you the halls were full of them.'

'This wasn't a man,' grunted Conan. 'It was something that crawled, and it was as cold as ice to the touch. I think I cut it asunder. It fell back on the men who were following us, and must have killed one of them in its death throes.'

Techotl's head jerked back, his face ashy again. Convulsively he quickened his pace.

'It was the Crawler! A monster *they* have brought out of the catacombs to aid them! What it is, we do not know, but we have found our people hideously slain by it. In Set's name, hasten! If they put it on our trail, it will follow us to the very doors of Tecuhltli!'

'I doubt it,' grunted Conan. 'That was a shrewd cut I dealt it on the stair.'

'Hasten! Hasten!' groaned Techotl.

They ran through a series of green-lit chambers, traversed a broad hall, and halted before a giant bronze door.

Techotl said: 'This is Tecuhltli!'

3 The People of the Feud

Techotl smote on the bronze door with his clenched hand, and then turned sidewise, so that he could watch back along the hall.

'Men have been smitten down before this door, when they thought they were safe,' he said.

'Why don't they open the door?' asked Conan.

'They are looking at us through the Eye,' answered Techotl. 'They are puzzled at the sight of you.' He lifted his voice and called: 'Open the door, Xecelan! It is I, Techotl, with friends from the great world beyond the forest! – They will open,' he assured his allies.

'They'd better do it in a hurry, then,' said Conan grimly. 'I hear something crawling along the floor beyond the wall.'

Techotl went ashy again and attacked the door with his fists, screaming: 'Open, you fools, open! The Crawler is at our heels!'

Even as he beat and shouted, the great bronze door swung noiselessly back, revealing a heavy chain across the entrance, over which spearheads bristled and fierce countenances regarded them intently for an instant. Then the chain was dropped and Techotl grasped the arms of his friends in a nervous frenzy and fairly dragged them over the threshold. A glance over his shoulder just as the door was closing showed Conan the long dim vista of the hall, and dimly framed at the other end an ophidian shape that writhed slowly and painfully into view, flowing in a dull-hued length from a chamber door, its hideous blood-stained head wagging drunkenly. Then the closing door shut off the view.

Inside the square chamber into which they had come heavy bolts were drawn across the door, and the chain locked into place. The door was made to stand the battering of a siege. Four men stood on guard, of the same lank-haired, dark-skinned breed as Techotl, with spears in their hands and swords at their hips. In the wall near the door there was a complicated contrivance of mirrors which Conan guessed was the Eye Techotl had mentioned, so arranged that a narrow, crystal-paned slot in the wall could be looked through from within without being discernible from without. The four guardsmen stared at the strangers with wonder, but asked no question, nor did Techotl vouchsafe any information. He moved with easy confidence now, as if he had shed his cloak of indecision and fear the instant he crossed the threshold.

'Come!' he urged his new-found friends, but Conan glanced toward the door.

'What about those fellows who were following us? Won't they try to storm that door?'

Techotl shook his head.

'They know they cannot break down the Door of the Eagle. They will flee back to Xotalanc, with their crawling fiend. Come! I will take you to the rulers of Tecuhltli.'

One of the four guards opened the door opposite the one by which they had entered, and they passed through into a hallway which, like most of the rooms on that level, was lighted by both the slot-like skylights and the clusters of winking fire-gems. But unlike the other rooms they had traversed, this hall showed evidences of occupation. Velvet tapestries adorned the glossy jade walls, rich rugs were on the crimson floors and the ivory seats, benches and divans were littered with satin cushions.

The hall ended in an ornate door, before which stood no guard. Without ceremony Techotl thrust the door open and ushered his friends into a broad chamber, where some thirty dark-skinned men and women lounging on satin-covered couches sprang up with exclamations of amazement.

The men, all except one, were of the same type as Techotl, and the women were equally dark and strange-eyed, though not unbeautiful in a weird dark way. They wore sandals, golden breast-plates, and scanty silk shirts supported by gem-crusted girdles, and their black manes, cut square at their naked shoulders, were bound with silver circlets.

On a wide ivory seat on a jade dais sat a man and a woman who differed subtly from the others. He was a giant, with an enormous sweep of breast and the shoulders of a bull. Unlike the others, he was bearded, with a thick, blue-black beard which fell almost to his broad girdle. He wore a robe of purple silk which reflected changing sheens of color with his every movement, and one wide sleeve, drawn back to his elbow, revealed a forearm massive with corded muscles. The band which confined his blue-black locks was set with glittering jewels.

The woman beside him sprang to her feet with a startled exclamation as the strangers entered, and her eyes, passing over Conan, fixed themselves with burning intensity on Valeria. She was tall and lithe, by far the most beautiful woman in the room. She was clad more scantily even than the others; for instead of a skirt she wore merely a broad strip of gilt-worked purple cloth fastened to the middle of her girdle which fell below her knees. Another strip at the back of her girdle completed that part of her costume, which she wore with a cynical indifference. Her breast-plates and the circlet about her temples were adorned with gems. In her eyes alone of all the dark-skinned people there lurked no brooding gleam of madness. She spoke no word after her first exclamation; she stood tensely, her hands clenched, staring at Valeria.

The man on the ivory seat had not risen.

'Prince Olmec,' spoke Techotl, bowing low, with arms outspread and the palms of his hands turned upward, 'I bring allies from the world beyond the forest. In the Chamber of Tezcoti the Burning Skull slew Chicmec, my companion—'

'The Burning Skull!' It was a shuddering whisper of fear from the people of Tecuhltli.

'Aye! Then came I, and found Chicmec lying with his throat cut. Before I could flee, the Burning Skull came upon me, and when I looked upon it my blood became as ice and the marrow of my bones melted. I could neither fight nor run. I could only await the stroke. Then came this white-skinned woman and struck him down with her sword; and lo, it was only a dog of Xotalanc with white paint upon his skin and the living skull of an ancient wizard upon his head! Now that skull lies in many pieces, and the dog who wore it is a dead man!'

An indescribably fierce exultation edged the last sentence, and was echoed in the low, savage exclamations from the crowding listeners.

'But wait!' exclaimed Techotl. 'There is more! While I talked with the woman, four Xotalancs came upon us! One I slew – there is the stab in my thigh to prove how desperate was the fight. Two the woman killed. But we were hard pressed when this man came into the fray and split the skull of the fourth! Aye! Five crimson nails there are to be driven into the pillar of vengeance!'

He pointed at a black column of ebony which stood behind the dais. Hundreds of red dots scarred its polished surface – the bright scarlet heads of heavy copper nails driven into the black wood.

'Five red nails for five Xotalanca lives!' exulted Techotl, and the horrible exultation in the faces of the listeners made them inhuman.

'Who are these people?' asked Olmec, and his voice was like the low, deep rumble of a distant bull. None of the people of Xuchotl spoke loudly. It was as if they had absorbed into their souls the silence of the empty halls and deserted chambers.

'I am Conan, a Cimmerian,' answered the barbarian briefly. 'This woman is Valeria of the Red Brotherhood, an Aquilonian pirate. We are deserters from an army on the Darfar border, far to the north, and are trying to reach the coast.'

The woman on the dais spoke loudly, her words tripping in her haste.

'You can never reach the coast! There is no escape from Xuchotl! You will spend the rest of your lives in this city!'

'What do you mean?' growled Conan, clapping his hand to his hilt and stepping about so as to face both the dais and the rest of the room. 'Are you telling us we're prisoners?'

'She did not mean that,' interposed Olmec. 'We are your friends. We would not restrain you against your will. But I fear other circumstances will make it impossible for you to leave Xuchotl.'

His eyes flickered to Valeria, and he lowered them quickly.

'This woman is Tascela,' he said. 'She is a princess of Tecuhltli. But let food and drink be brought our guests. Doubtless they are hungry, and weary from their long travels.'

He indicated an ivory table, and after an exchange of glances, the adventurers seated themselves. The Cimmerian was suspicious. His fierce blue eyes roved about the chamber, and he kept his sword close to his hand. But an invitation to eat and drink never found him backward. His eyes kept wandering to Tascela, but the princess had eyes only for his white-skinned companion.

Techotl, who had bound a strip of silk about his wounded thigh, placed himself at the table to attend to the wants of his friends, seeming to consider it a privilege and honor to see after their needs. He inspected the food and drink the others brought in gold vessels and dishes, and tasted each before he placed it before his guests. While they ate, Olmec sat in silence on his ivory seat, watching them from under his broad black brows. Tascela sat beside him, chin cupped in her hands and her elbows resting on her knees. Her dark, enigmatic eyes, burning with a mysterious light, never left Valeria's supple figure. Behind her seat a sullen handsome girl waved an ostrich-plume fan with a slow rhythm.

The food was fruit of an exotic kind unfamiliar to the wanderers, but very palatable, and the drink was a light crimson wine that carried a heady tang.

'You have come from afar,' said Olmec at last. 'I have read the books of our fathers. Aquilonia lies beyond the lands of the Stygians and the Shemites, beyond Argos and Zingara; and Cimmeria lies beyond Aquilonia.'

'We have each a roving foot,' answered Conan carelessly.

'How you won through the forest is a wonder to me,' quoth Olmec. 'In bygone days a thousand fighting-men scarcely were able to carve a road through it perils.'

'We encountered a bench-legged monstrosity about the size of a mastodon,' said Conan casually, holding out his wine goblet which Techotl filled with evident pleasure. 'But when we'd killed it we had no further trouble.'

The wine vessel slipped from Techotl's hand to crash on the floor. His dusky skin went ashy. Olmec started to his feet, an image of stunned amazement, and a low gasp of awe or terror breathed up from the others. Some slipped to their knees as if their legs would not support them. Only Tascela seemed not to have heard. Conan glared about him bewilderedly.

'What's the matter? What are you gaping about?'

'You – you slew the dragon-god?'

'God? I killed a dragon. Why not? It was trying to gobble us up.'

'But dragons are immortal!' exclaimed Olmec. 'They slay each other, but no man ever killed a dragon! The thousand fighting-men of our ancestors who fought their way to Xuchotl could not prevail against them! Their swords broke like twigs against their scales!'

'If your ancestors had thought to dip their spears in the poisonous juice of Derketa's Apples,' quoth Conan, with his mouth full, 'and jab them in the eyes or mouth or somewhere like that, they'd have seen that dragons are not more immortal than any other chunk of beef. The carcass lies at the edge of the trees, just within the forest. If you don't believe me, go and look for yourself.'

Olmec shook his head, not in disbelief but in wonder.

'It was because of the dragons that our ancestors took refuge in Xuchotl,' said he. 'They dared not pass through the plain and plunge into the forest beyond. Scores of them were seized and devoured by the monsters before they could reach the city.'

'Then your ancestors didn't build Xuchotl?' asked Valeria.

'It was ancient when they first came into the land. How long it had stood here, not even its degenerate inhabitants knew.'

'Your people came from Lake Zuad?' questioned Conan.

'Aye. More than half a century ago a tribe of the Tlazitlans rebelled against the Stygian king, and, being defeated in battle, fled southward. For many weeks they wandered over grasslands, desert hills, and at last they came into the great forest, a thousand fighting-men with their women and children.

'It was in the forest that the dragons fell upon them, and tore many to pieces; so the people fled in a frenzy of fear before them, and at last came into the plain and saw the city of Xuchotl in the midst of it.

'They camped before the city, not daring to leave the plain, for the night was made hideous with the noise of the battling monsters throughout the forest. They made war incessantly upon one another. Yet they came not into the plain.

'The people of the city shut their gates and shot arrows at our people from the walls. The Tlazitlans were imprisoned on the plain, as if the ring of the forest had been a great wall; for to venture into the woods would have been madness.

'That night there came secretly to their camp a slave from the city, one of their own blood, who with a band of exploring soldiers had wandered into the forest long before, when he was a young man. The dragons had devoured all his companions, but he had been taken into the city to dwell in servitude. His name was Tolkemec.' A flame lighted the dark eyes at a mention of the name, and some of the people muttered obscenely and spat. 'He promised to open the gates to the warriors. He asked only that all captives taken be delivered into his hands.

'At dawn he opened the gates. The warriors swarmed in and the halls of Xuchotl ran red. Only a few hundred folk dwelt there, decaying remnants of a once great race. Tolkemec said they came from the east, long ago, from Old Kosala, when the ancestors of those who now dwell in Kosala came up from the south and drove forth the original inhabitants of the land. They wandered far westward and finally found this forest-girdled plain, inhabited then by a tribe of black people.

'These they enslaved and set to building a city. From the hills to the east they brought jade and marble and lapis lazuli, and gold, silver and copper. Herds of elephants provided them with ivory. When their city was completed, they slew all the black slaves. And their magicians made a terrible magic to guard the city; for by their necromantic arts they re-created the dragons which had once dwelt in this lost land, and whose monstrous bones they found in the forest. Those bones they clothed in flesh and life, and the living beasts walked the earth as they walked it when Time was young. But the wizards wove a spell that kept them in the forest and they came not into the plain.

'So for many centuries the people of Xuchotl dwelt in their city, cultivating the fertile plain, until their wise men learned how to grow fruit within the city – fruit which is not planted in soil, but obtains its nourishment out of the air – and then they let the irrigation ditches run dry, and dwelt more and more in luxurious sloth, until decay seized them. They were a dying race when our ancestors broke through the forest and came into the plain. Their wizards had died, and the people had forgot their ancient necromancy. They could fight neither by sorcery nor the sword.

'Well, our fathers slew the people of Xuchotl, all except a hundred which were given living into the hands of Tolkemec, who had been their slave; and for many days and nights the halls re-echoed to their screams under the agony of his tortures.

'So the Tlazitlans dwelt here, for a while in peace, ruled by the brothers Tecuhltli and Xotalanc, and by Tolkemec. Tolkemec took a girl of the tribe to wife, and because he had opened the gates, and because he knew many of the arts of the Xuchotlans, he shared the rule of the tribe with the brothers who had led the rebellion and the flight.

'For a few years, then, they dwelt at peace within the city, doing little but eating, drinking and making love, and raising children. There was no necessity to till the plain, for Tolkemec taught them how to cultivate the air-devouring fruits. Besides, the slaying of the Xuchotlans broke the spell that held the dragons in the forest, and they came nightly and bellowed about the gates of the city. The plain ran red with the blood of their eternal warfare, and it was then that—' He bit his tongue in the midst of the sentence, then presently continued, but Valeria and Conan felt that he had checked an admission he had considered unwise.

'Five years they dwelt in peace. Then' – Olmec's eyes rested briefly on the silent woman at his side – 'Xotalanc took a woman to wife, a woman whom both Tecuhltli and old Tolkemec desired. In his madness, Tecuhltli stole her from her husband. Aye, she went willingly enough. Tolkemec, to spite Xotalanc, aided Tecuhltli. Xotalanc demanded that she be given back to him, and the council of the tribe decided that the matter should be left to the woman. She chose to remain with Tecuhltli. In wrath Xotalanc sought to take her back by force, and the retainers of the brothers came to blows in the Great Hall.

'There was much bitterness. Blood was shed on both sides. The quarrel became a feud, the feud an open war. From the welter three factions emerged – Tecuhltli, Xotalanc, and Tolkemec. Already, in the days of peace, they had divided the city between them. Tecuhltli dwelt in the western quarter of the city, Xotalanc in the eastern, and Tolkemec with his family by the southern gate.

'Anger and resentment and jealousy blossomed into bloodshed and rape and murder. Once the sword was drawn there was no turning back; for blood called for blood, and vengeance followed swift on the heels of atrocity. Tecuhltli fought with Xotalanc, and Tolkemec aided first one and then the other, betraying each faction as it fitted his purpose. Tecuhltli and his people withdrew into the quarter of the western gate, where we now sit. Xuchotl is built in the shape of an oval. Tecuhltli, which took its name from its prince, occupies the western end of the oval. The people blocked up all doors connecting the quarter with the rest of the city, except one on each floor, which could be defended easily. They went into the pits below the city and built a wall cutting off the western end of the catacombs, where lie the bodies of the ancient Xuchotlans, and of those Tlazitlans slain in the feud. They dwelt as in a besieged castle, making sorties and forays on their enemies.

'The people of Xotalanc likewise fortified the eastern quarter of the city, and Tolkemec did likewise with the quarter by the southern gate. The central part of the city was left bare and uninhabited. Those empty halls and chambers became a battleground, and a region of brooding terror.

'Tolkemec warred on both clans. He was a fiend in the form of a human, worse than Xotalanc. He knew many secrets of the city he never told the others. From the crypts of the catacombs he plundered the dead of their grisly secrets – secrets of ancient kings and wizards, long forgotten by the degenerate Xuchotlans our ancestors slew. But all his magic did not aid him the night we of Tecuhltli stormed his castle and butchered all his people. Tolkemec we tortured for many days.'

His voice sank to a caressing slur, and a faraway look grew in his eyes, as if he looked back over the years to a scene which caused him intense pleasure.

'Aye, we kept the life in him until he screamed for death as for a bride.

At last we took him living from the torture chamber and cast him into a dungeon for the rats to gnaw as he died. From that dungeon, somehow, he managed to escape, and dragged himself into the catacombs. There without doubt he died, for the only way out of the catacombs beneath Tecuhltli is through Tecuhltli, and he never emerged by that way. His bones were never found, and the superstitious among our people swear that his ghost haunts the crypts to this day, wailing among the bones of the dead. Twelve years ago we butchered the people of Tolkemec, but the feud raged on between Tecuhltli and Xotalanc, as it will rage until the last man, the last woman is dead.

'It was fifty years ago that Tecuhltli stole the wife of Xotalanc. Half a century the feud has endured. I was born in it. All in this chamber, except Tascela, were born in it. We expect to die in it.

'We are a dying race, even as those Xuchotlans our ancestors slew. When the feud began there were hundreds in each faction. Now we of Tecuhltli number only these you see before you, and the men who guard the four doors: forty in all. How many Xotalancas there are we do not know, but I doubt if they are much more numerous than we. For fifteen years no children have been born to us, and we have seen none among the Xotalancas.

'We are dying, but before we die we will slay as many of the men of Xotalanc as the gods permit.'

And with his weird eyes blazing, Olmec spoke long of that grisly feud, fought out in silent chambers and dim halls under the blaze of the green fire-jewels, on floors smoldering with the flames of hell and splashed with deeper crimson from severed veins. In that long butchery a whole generation had perished. Xotalanc was dead, long ago, slain in a grim battle on an ivory stair. Tecuhltli was dead, flayed alive by the maddened Xotalancas who had captured him.

Without emotion Olmec told of hideous battles fought in black corridors, of ambushes on twisting stairs, and red butcheries. With a redder, more abysmal gleam in his deep dark eyes he told of men and women flayed alive, mutilated and dismembered, of captives howling under tortures so ghastly that even the barbarous Cimmerian grunted. No wonder Techotl had trembled with the terror of capture. Yet he had gone forth to slay if he could, driven by hate that was stronger than his fear. Olmec spoke further, of dark and mysterious matters, of black magic and wizardry conjured out of the black night of the catacombs, of weird creatures invoked out of darkness for horrible allies. In these things the Xotalancas had the advantage, for it was in the eastern catacombs where lay the bones of the greatest wizards of the ancient Xuchotlans, with their immemorial secrets.

Valeria listened with morbid fascination. The feud had become a terrible elemental power driving the people of Xuchotl inexorably on to doom and extinction. It filled their whole lives. They were born in it, and they expected to die in it. They never left their barricaded castle except to steal forth into the Halls of Silence that lay between the opposing fortresses, to slay and be slain. Sometimes the raiders returned with frantic captives, or with grim tokens of victory in fight. Sometimes they did not return at all, or returned only as severed limbs cast down before the bolted bronze doors. It was a ghastly, unreal nightmare existence these people lived, shut off from the rest of the world, caught together like rabid rats in the same trap, butchering one another through the years, crouching and creeping through the sunless corridors to maim and torture and murder.

While Olmec talked, Valeria felt the blazing eyes of Tascela fixed upon her. The princess seemed not to hear what Olmec was saying. Her expression, as he narrated victories or defeats, did not mirror the wild rage or fiendish exultation that alternated on the faces of the other Tecuhltli. The feud that was an obsession to her clansmen seemed meaningless to her. Valeria found her indifferent callousness more repugnant than Olmec's naked ferocity.

'And we can never leave the city,' said Olmec. 'For fifty years no one has left it except those—' Again he checked himself.

'Even without the peril of the dragons,' he continued, 'we who were born and raised in the city would not dare leave it. We have never set foot outside the walls. We are not accustomed to the open sky and the naked sun. No; we were born in Xuchotl, and in Xuchotl we shall die.'

'Well,' said Conan, 'with your leave we'll take our chances with the dragons. This feud is none of our business. If you'll show us to the west gate we'll be on our way.'

Tascela's hands clenched, and she started to speak, but Olmec interrupted her: 'It is nearly nightfall. If you wander forth into the plain by night, you will certainly fall prey to the dragons.'

'We crossed it last night, and slept in the open without seeing any,' returned Conan.

Tascela smiled mirthlessly. 'You dare not leave Xuchotl!'

Conan glared at her with instinctive antagonism; she was not looking at him, but at the woman opposite him.

'I think they dare,' retorted Olmec. 'But look you, Conan and Valeria, the gods must have sent you to us, to cast victory into the laps of the Tecuhltli! You are professional fighters – why not fight for us? We have wealth in abundance – precious jewels are as common in Xuchotl as cobblestones are in the cities of the world. Some the Xuchotlans brought with them from Kosala. Some, like the firestones, they found in the hills to the east. Aid us to wipe out the Xotalancas, and we will give you all the jewels you can carry.'

'And will you help us destroy the dragons?' asked Valeria. 'With bows and poisoned arrows thirty men could slay all the dragons in the forest.'

'Aye!' replied Olmec promptly. 'We have forgotten the use of the bow, in years of hand-to-hand fighting, but we can learn again.'

'What do you say?' Valeria inquired of Conan.

'We're both penniless vagabonds,' he grinned hardily. 'I'd as soon kill Xotalancas as anybody.'

'Then you agree?' exclaimed Olmec, while Techotl fairly hugged himself with delight.

'Aye. And now suppose you show us chambers where we can sleep, so we can be fresh tomorrow for the beginning of the slaying.'

Olmec nodded, and waved a hand, and Techotl and a woman led the adventurers into a corridor which led through a door off to the left of the jade dais. A glance back showed Valeria Olmec sitting on his throne, chin on knotted fist, staring after them. His eyes burned with a weird flame. Tascela leaned back in her seat, whispering to the sullen-faced maid, Yasala, who leaned over her shoulder, her ear to the princess' moving lips.

The hallway was not so broad as most they had traversed, but it was long. Presently the woman halted, opened a door, and drew aside for Valeria to enter.

'Wait a minute,' growled Conan. 'Where do I sleep?'

Techotl pointed to a chamber across the hallway, but one door farther down. Conan hesitated, and seemed inclined to raise an objection, but Valeria smiled spitefully at him and shut the door in his face. He muttered something uncomplimentary about women in general, and strode off down the corridor after Techotl.

In the ornate chamber where he was to sleep, he glanced up at the slot-like skylights. Some were wide enough to admit the body of a slender man, supposing the glass were broken.

'Why don't the Xotalancas come over the roofs and shatter those skylights?' he asked.

'They cannot be broken,' answered Techotl. 'Besides, the roofs would be hard to clamber over. They are mostly spires and domes and steep ridges.'

He volunteered more information about the 'castle' of Tecuhltli. Like the rest of the city it contained four stories, or tiers of chambers, with towers jutting up from the roof. Each tier was named; indeed, the people of Xuchotl had a name for each chamber, hall and stair in the city, as people of more normal cities designate streets and quarters. In

Tecuhltli the floors were named The Eagle's Tier, the Ape's Tier, The Tiger's Tier and The Serpent's Tier, in the order as enumerated, The Eagle's Tier being the highest, or fourth, floor.

'Who is Tascela?' asked Conan. 'Olmec's wife?'

Techotl shuddered and glanced furtively about him before answering.

'No. She is – Tascela! She was the wife of Xotalanc – the woman Tecuhltli stole, to start the feud.'

'What are you talking about?' demanded Conan. 'That woman is beautiful and young. Are you trying to tell me that she was a wife fifty years ago?'

'Aye! I swear it! She was a full-grown woman when the Tlazitlans journeyed from Lake Zuad. It was because the king of Stygia desired her for a concubine that Xotalanc and his brother rebelled and fled into the wilderness. She is a witch, who possesses the secret of perpetual youth.'

'What's that?' asked Conan.

Techotl shuddered again.

'Ask me not! I dare not speak. It is too grisly, even for Xuchotl!'

And touching his finger to his lips, he glided from the chamber.

4 Scent of Black Lotus

Valeria unbuckled her sword-belt and laid it with the sheathed weapon on the couch where she meant to sleep. She noted that the doors were supplied with bolts, and asked where they led.

'Those lead into adjoining chambers,' answered the woman, indicating the doors on right and left. 'That one' – pointing to a copper-bound door opposite that which opened into the corridor – 'leads to a corridor which runs to a stair that descends into the catacombs. Do not fear; naught can harm you here.'

'Who spoke of fear?' snapped Valeria. 'I just like to know what sort of harbor I'm dropping anchor in. No, I don't want you to sleep at the foot of my couch. I'm not accustomed to being waited on – not by women, anyway. You have my leave to go.'

Alone in the room, the pirate shot the bolts on all the doors, kicked off her boots and stretched luxuriously out on the couch. She imagined Conan similarly situated across the corridor, but her feminine vanity prompted her to visualize him as scowling and muttering with chagrin as he cast himself on his solitary couch, and she grinned with gleeful malice as she prepared herself for slumber.

Outside, night had fallen. In the halls of Xuchotl the green fire-jewels blazed like the eyes of prehistoric cats. Somewhere among the dark towers a night wind moaned like a restless spirit. Through the dim passages stealthy figures began stealing, like disembodied shadows.

Valeria awoke suddenly on her couch. In the dusky emerald glow of the fire-gems she saw a shadowy figure bending over her. For a bemused instant the apparition seemed part of the dream she had been dreaming. She had seemed to lie on the couch in the chamber as she was actually lying, while over her pulsed and throbbed a gigantic black blossom so enormous that it hid the ceiling. Its exotic perfume pervaded her being, inducing a delicious, sensuous langour that was something more and less than sleep. She was sinking into scented billows of insensible bliss, when something touched her face. So supersensitive were her drugged senses, that the light touch was like a dislocating impact, jolting her rudely into full wakefulness. Then it was that she saw, not a gargantuan blossom, but a dark-skinned woman standing above her.

With the realization came anger and instant action. The woman turned lithely, but before she could run Valeria was on her feet and had caught her arm. She fought like a wildcat for an instant, and then subsided as she felt herself crushed by the superior strength of her captor. The pirate wrenched the woman around to face her, caught her chin with her free hand and forced her captive to meet her gaze. It was the sullen Yasala, Tascela's maid.

'What the devil were you doing bending over me? What's that in your hand?'

The woman made no reply, but sought to cast away the object. Valeria twisted her arm around in front of her, and the thing fell to the floor – a great black exotic blossom on a jade-green stem, large as a woman's head, to be sure, but tiny beside the exaggerated vision she had seen.

'The black lotus!' said Valeria between her teeth. 'The blossom whose scent brings deep sleep. You were trying to drug me! If you hadn't accidentally touched my face with the petals, you'd have – why did you do it? What's your game?'

Yasala maintained a sulky silence, and with an oath Valeria whirled her around, forced her to her knees and twisted her arm up behind her back.

'Tell me, or I'll tear your arm out of its socket!'

Yasala squirmed in anguish as her arm was forced excruciatingly up between her shoulder-blades, but a violent shaking of her head was the only answer she made.

'Slut!' Valeria cast her from her to sprawl on the floor. The pirate glared at the prostrate figure with blazing eyes. Fear and the memory of Tascela's burning eyes stirred in her, rousing all her tigerish instincts of self-preservation. These people were decadent; any sort of perversity might be expected to be encountered among them. But Valeria sensed here something that moved behind the scenes, some secret terror fouler than common degeneracy. Fear and revulsion of this weird city swept her. These people were neither sane nor normal; she began to doubt if they were even human. Madness smoldered in the eyes of them all – all except the cruel, cryptic eyes of Tascela, which held secrets and mysteries more abysmal than madness.

She lifted her head and listened intently. The halls of Xuchotl were as silent as if it were in reality a dead city. The green jewels bathed the chamber in a nightmare glow, in which the eyes of the woman on the floor glittered eerily up at her. A thrill of panic throbbed through Valeria, driving the last vestige of mercy from her fierce soul.

'Why did you try to drug me?' she muttered, grasping the woman's black hair, and forcing her head back to glare into her sullen, long-lashed eyes. 'Did Tascela send you?'

No answer. Valeria cursed venomously and slapped the woman first on one cheek and then the other. The blows resounded through the room, but Yasala made no outcry.

'Why don't you scream?' demanded Valeria savagely. 'Do you fear someone will hear you? Whom do you fear? Tascela? Olmec? Conan?'

Yasala made no reply. She crouched, watching her captor with eyes baleful as those of a basilisk. Stubborn silence always fans anger. Valeria turned and tore a handful of cords from a nearby hanging.

'You sulky slut!' she said between her teeth. 'I'm going to strip you stark naked and tie you across that couch and whip you until you tell me what you were doing here, and who sent you!'

Yasala made no verbal protest, nor did she offer any resistance, as Valeria carried out the first part of her threat with a fury that her captive's obstinacy only sharpened. Then for a space there was no sound in the chamber except the whistle and crackle of hard-woven silken cords on naked flesh. Yasala could not move her fast-bound hands or feet. Her body writhed and quivered under the chastisement, her head swayed from side to side in rhythm with the blows. Her teeth were sunk into her lower lip and a trickle of blood began as the punishment continued. But she did not cry out.

The pliant cords made no great sound as they encountered the quivering body of the captive; only a sharp crackling snap, but each cord left a red streak across Yasala's dark flesh. Valeria inflicted the punishment with all the strength of her war-hardened arm, with all the mercilessness acquired during a life where pain and torment were daily happenings, and with all the cynical ingenuity which only a woman displays towards a woman. Yasala suffered more, physically and mentally, than she would have suffered under a lash wielded by a man, however strong.

It was the application of this feminine cynicism which at last tamed Yasala.

A low whimper escaped from her lips, and Valeria paused, arm lifted, and raked back a damp yellow lock. 'Well, are you going to talk?' she demanded. 'I can keep this up all night, if necessary!'

'Mercy!' whispered the woman. 'I will tell.'

Valeria cut the cords from her wrists and ankles, and pulled to her feet. Yasala sank down on the couch, half reclining on one bare hip, supporting herself on her arm, and writhing at the contact of her smarting flesh with the couch. She was trembling in every limb.

'Wine!' she begged, dry-lipped, indicating with a quivering hand a gold vessel on an ivory table. 'Let me drink. I am weak with pain. Then I will tell you all.'

Valeria picked up the vessel, and Yasala rose unsteadily to receive it. She took it, raised it toward her lips – then dashed the contents full into the Aquilonian's face. Valeria reeled backward, shaking and clawing the stinging liquid out of her eyes. Through a smarting mist she saw Yasala dart across the room, fling back a bolt, throw open the copper-bound door and run down the hall. The pirate was after her instantly, sword out and murder in her heart.

But Yasala had the start, and she ran with the nervous agility of a woman who has just been whipped to the point of hysterical frenzy. She rounded a corner in the corridor, yards ahead of Valeria, and when the pirate turned it, she saw only an empty hall, and at the other end a door that gaped blackly. A damp moldy scent reeked up from it, and Valeria shivered. That must be the door that led to the catacombs. Yasala had taken refuge among the dead.

Valeria advanced to the door and looked down a flight of stone steps that vanished quickly into utter blackness. Evidently it was a shaft that led straight to the pits below the city, without opening upon any of the lower floors. She shivered slightly at the thought of the thousands of corpses lying in their stone crypts down there, wrapped in their moldering cloths. She had no intention of groping her way down those stone steps. Yasala doubtless knew every turn and twist of the subterranean tunnels.

She was turning back, baffled and furious, when a sobbing cry welled up from the blackness. It seemed to come from a great depth, but human words were faintly distinguishable, and the voice was that of a woman. 'Oh, help! Help, in Set's name! Ahhh!' It trailed away, and Valeria thought she caught the echo of a ghostly tittering.

Valeria felt her skin crawl. What had happened to Yasala down there in the thick blackness? There was no doubt that it had been she who had cried out. But what peril could have befallen her? Was a Xotalanca lurking down there? Olmec had assured them that the catacombs below Tecuhltli were walled off from the rest, too securely for their enemies to break through. Besides, that tittering had not sounded like a human being at all.

Valeria hurried back down the corridor, not stopping to close the door that opened on the stair. Regaining her chamber, she closed the door and shot the bolt behind her. She pulled on her boots and buckled her sword-belt about her. She was determined to make her way to Conan's room and urge him, if he still lived, to join her in an attempt to fight their way out of that city of devils.

But even as she reached the door that opened into the corridor, a long-drawn scream of agony rang through the halls, followed by the stamp of running feet and the loud clangor of swords.

5 Twenty Red Nails

Two warriors lounged in the guardroom on the floor known as the Tier of the Eagle. Their attitude was casual, though habitually alert. An attack on the great bronze door from without was always a possibility, but for many years no such assault had been attempted on either side.

'The strangers are strong allies,' said one. 'Olmec will move against the enemy tomorrow, I believe.'

He spoke as a soldier in a war might have spoken. In the miniature world of Xuchotl each handful of feudists was an army, and the empty halls between the castles was the country over which they campaigned.

The other meditated for a space.

'Suppose with their aid we destroy Xotalanc,' he said. 'What then, Xatmec?'

'Why,' returned Xatmec, 'we will drive red nails for them all. The captives we will burn and flay and quarter.'

'But afterward?' pursued the other. 'After we have slain them all? Will it not seem strange, to have no foes to fight? All my life I have fought and hated the Xotalancas. With the feud ended, what is left?'

Xatmec shrugged his shoulders. His thoughts had never gone beyond the destruction of their foes. They could not go beyond that.

Suddenly both men stiffened at a noise outside the door.

'To the door, Xatmec!' hissed the last speaker. 'I shall look through the Eye—'

Xatmec, sword in hand, leaned against the bronze door, straining his ear to hear through the metal. His mate looked into the mirror. He started convulsively. Men were clustered thickly outside the door; grim, dark-faced men with swords gripped in their teeth – *and their fingers thrust into their ears*. One who wore a feathered headdress had a set of pipes which he set to his lips, and even as the Tecuhltli started to shout a warning, the pipes began to skirl.

The cry died in the guard's throat as the thin, weird piping penetrated the metal door and smote on his ears. Xatmec leaned frozen against the door, as if paralysed in that position. His face was that of a wooden image, his expression one of horrified listening. The other guard, farther removed from the source of the sound, yet sensed the horror of what was taking place, the grisly threat that lay in that demoniac fifing. He felt the weird strains plucking like unseen fingers at the tissues of his brain, filling him with alien emotions and impulses of madness. But with a soul-tearing effort he broke the spell, and shrieked a warning in a voice he did not recognize as his own.

But even as he cried out, the music changed to an unbearable shrilling that was like a knife in the eardrums. Xatmec screamed in sudden agony, and all the sanity went out of his face like a flame blown out in a wind. Like a madman he ripped loose the chain, tore open the door and rushed out into the hall, sword lifted before his mate could stop him. A dozen blades struck him down, and over his mangled body the Xotalancas surged into the guardroom, with a long-drawn, blood-mad yell that sent the unwonted echoes reverberating.

His brain reeling from the shock of it all, the remaining guard leaped to meet them with goring spear. The horror of the sorcery he had just witnessed was submerged in the stunning realization that the enemy were in Tecuhltli. And as his spearhead ripped through a dark-skinned belly he knew no more, for a swinging sword crushed his skull, even as wild-eyed warriors came pouring in from the chambers behind the guardroom.

It was the yelling of men and the clanging of steel that brought Conan bounding from his couch, wide awake and broadsword in hand. In an instant he had reached the door and flung it open, and was glaring out into the corridor just as Techotl rushed up it, eyes blazing madly.

'The Xotalancas!' he screamed, in a voice hardly human. '*They are within the door.*'

Conan ran down the corridor, even as Valeria emerged from her chamber.

'What the devil is it?' she called.

'Techotl says the Xotalancas are in,' he answered hurriedly. 'That racket sounds like it.'

With the Tecuhltli on their heels they burst into the throneroom and were confronted by a scene beyond the most frantic dream of blood and fury. Twenty men and women, their black hair streaming, and the white skulls gleaming on their breasts, were locked in combat with the people of Tecuhltli. The women on both sides fought as madly as the men, and already the room and the hall beyond were strewn with corpses.

Olmec, naked but for a breech-clout, was fighting before his throne, and as the adventurers entered, Tascela ran from an inner chamber with a sword in her hand.

Xatmec and his mate were dead, so there was none to tell the Tecuhltli how their foes had found their way into their citadel. Nor was there any to say what had prompted that mad attempt. But the losses of the Xotalancas had been greater, their position more desperate, than the Tecuhltli had known. The maiming of their scaly ally, the destruction of the Burning Skull, and the news, gasped by a dying man, that mysterious white-skin allies had joined their enemies, had driven them to the frenzy of desperation and the wild determination to die dealing death to their ancient foes.

The Tecuhltli, recovering from the first stunning shock of the surprise that had swept them back into the throneroom and littered the floor with their corpses, fought back with an equally desperate fury, while the door-guards from the lower floors came racing to hurl themselves into the fray. It was the death-fight of rabid wolves, blind, panting, merciless. Back and forth it surged, from door to dais, blades whickering and striking into flesh, blood spurting, feet stamping the crimson floor where redder pools were forming. Ivory tables crashed over, seats were splintered, velvet hangings torn down were stained red. It was the bloody climax of a bloody half-century, and every man there sensed it.

But the conclusion was inevitable. The Tecuhltli outnumbered the invaders almost two to one, and they were heartened by that fact and by the entrance into the mêlée of their light-skinned allies.

These crashed into the fray with the devastating effect of a hurricane plowing through a grove of saplings. In sheer strength no three Tlazitlans were a match for Conan, and in spite of his weight he was quicker on his feet than any of them. He moved through the whirling, eddying mass with the surety and destructiveness of a gray wolf amidst a pack of alley curs, and he strode over a wake of crumpled figures.

Valeria fought beside him, her lips smiling and her eyes blazing. She was stronger than the average man, and far quicker and more ferocious. Her sword was like a living thing in her hand. Where Conan beat down opposition by the sheer weight and power of his blows, breaking spears, splitting skulls and cleaving bosoms to the breastbone, Valeria brought into action a finesse of swordplay that dazzled and bewildered her antagonists before it slew them. Again and again a warrior, heaving high his heavy blade, found her point in his jugular before he could strike. Conan, towering above the field, strode through the welter smiting right and left, but Valeria moved like an illusive phantom, constantly shifting, and thrusting and slashing as she shifted. Swords missed her again and again as the wielders flailed the empty air and died with her point in their hearts or throats, and her mocking laughter in their ears.

Neither sex nor condition was considered by the maddened combatants. The five women of the Xotalancas were down with their throats cut before Conan and Valeria entered the fray, and when a man or woman went down under the stamping feet, there was always a knife ready for the helpless throat, or a sandaled foot eager to crush the prostrate skull.

From wall to wall, from door to door rolled the waves of combat, spilling over into adjoining chambers. And presently only Tecuhltli and their white-skinned allies stood upright in the great throneroom. The survivors stared bleakly and blankly at each other, like survivors after Judgment Day or the destruction of the world. On legs wide-braced, hands gripping notched and dripping swords, blood trickling down their arms, they stared at one another across the mangled corpses of friends and foes. They had no breath left to shout, but a bestial mad howling rose from their lips. It was not a human cry of triumph. It was the howling of a rabid wolf-pack stalking among the bodies of its victims.

Conan caught Valeria's arm and turned her about.

'You've got a stab in the calf of your leg,' he growled.

She glanced down, for the first time aware of a stinging in the muscles of her leg. Some dying man on the floor had fleshed his dagger with his last effort.

'You look like a butcher yourself,' she laughed.

He shook a red shower from his hands.

'Not mine. Oh, a scratch here and there. Nothing to bother about. But that calf ought to be bandaged.'

Olmec came through the litter, looking like a ghoul with his naked massive shoulders splashed with blood, and his black beard dabbled in crimson. His eyes were red, like the reflection of flame on black water.

'We have won!' he croaked dazedly. 'The feud is ended! The dogs of Xotalanc lie dead! Oh, for a captive to flay alive! Yet it is good to look upon their dead faces. Twenty dead dogs! Twenty red nails for the black column!'

'You'd best see to your wounded,' grunted Conan, turning away from him. 'Here, girl, let me see that leg.'

'Wait a minute!' she shook him off impatiently. The fire of fighting still burned brightly in her soul. 'How do we know these are all of them? These might have come on a raid of their own.'

'They would not split the clan on a foray like this,' said Olmec, shaking his head, and regaining some of his ordinary intelligence. Without his purple robe the man seemed less like a prince than some repellent beast of prey. 'I will stake my head upon it that we have slain them all. There were less of them than I dreamed, and they must have been desperate. But how came they in Tecuhltli?'

Tascela came forward, wiping her sword on her naked thigh, and holding in her other hand an object she had taken from the body of the feathered leader of the Xotalancas.

'The pipes of madness,' she said. 'A warrior tells me that Xatmec opened the door to the Xotalancas and was cut down as they stormed into the guardroom. This warrior came to the guardroom from the inner hall just in time to see it happen and to hear the last of a weird strain of music which froze his very soul. Tolkemec used to talk of these pipes, which the Xuchotlans swore were hidden somewhere in the catacombs with the bones of the ancient wizard who used them in his lifetime. Somehow the dogs of Xotalanc found them and learned their secret.'

'Somebody ought to go to Xotalanc and see if any remain alive,' said Conan. 'I'll go if somebody will guide me.'

Olmec glanced at the remants of his people. There were only twenty left alive, and of these several lay groaning on the floor. Tascela was the only one of the Tecuhltli who had escaped without a wound. The princess was untouched, though she had fought as savagely as any.

'Who will go with Conan to Xotalanc?' asked Olmec.

Techotl limped forward. The wound in his thigh had started bleeding afresh, and he had another gash across his ribs.

'I will go!'

'No, you won't,' vetoed Conan. 'And you're not going either, Valeria. In a little while that leg will be getting stiff.'

'I will go,' volunteered a warrior, who was knotting a bandage about a slashed forearm.

'Very well, Yanath. Go with the Cimmerian. And you, too, Topal.' Olmec indicated another man whose injuries were slight. 'But first aid us to lift the badly wounded on these couches where we may bandage their hurts.'

This was done quickly. As they stooped to pick up a woman who had been stunned by a war-club, Olmec's beard brushed Topal's ear.

Conan thought the prince muttered something to the warrior, but he could not be sure. A few moments later he was leading his companions down the hall.

Conan glanced back as he went out the door, at that shambles where the dead lay on the smoldering floor, blood-stained dark limbs knotted in attitudes of fierce muscular effort, dark faces frozen in masks of hate, glassy eyes glaring up at the green fire-jewels which bathed the ghastly scene in a dusky emerald witch-light. Among the dead the living moved aimlessly, like people moving in a trance. Conan heard Olmec call a woman and direct her to bandage Valeria's leg. The pirate followed the woman into an adjoining chamber, already beginning to limp slightly.

Warily the two Tecuhltli led Conan along the hall beyond the bronze door, and through chamber after chamber shimmering in the green fire. They saw no one, heard no sound. After they crossed the Great Hall which bisected the city from north to south, their caution was increased by the realization of their nearness to enemy territory. But chambers and halls lay empty to their wary gaze, and they came at last along a broad dim hallway and halted before a bronze door similar to the Eagle Door of Tecuhltli. Gingerly they tried it, and it opened silently under their fingers. Awed, they stared into the green-lit chambers beyond. For fifty years no Tecuhltli had entered those halls save as a prisoner going to a hideous doom. To go to Xotalanc had been the ultimate horror that could befall a man of the western castle. The terror of it had stalked through their dreams since earliest childhood. To Yanath and Topal that bronze door was like the portal of hell.

They cringed back, unreasoning horror in their eyes, and Conan pushed past them and strode into Xotalanc.

Timidly they followed him. As each man set foot over the threshold he stared and glared wildly about him. But only their quick, hurried breathing disturbed the silence.

They had come into a sqaure guardroom, like that behind the Eagle Door of Tecuhltli, and, similarly, a hall ran away from it to a broad chamber that was a counterpart of Olmec's throneroom.

Conan glanced down the hall with its rugs and divans and hangings, and stood listening intently. He heard no noise, and the rooms had an empty feel. He did not believe there were any Xotalancas left alive in Xuchotl.

'Come on,' he muttered, and started down the hall.

He had not gone far when he was aware that only Yanath was following him. He wheeled back to see Topal standing in an attitude of horror, one arm out as if to fend off some threatening peril, his distended eyes fixed with hypnotic intensity on something protruding from behind a divan.

'What the devil?' Then Conan saw what Topal was staring at, and he felt a faint twitching of the skin between his giant shoulders. A monstrous head protruded from behind the divan, a reptilian head, broad as the head of a crocodile, with down-curving fangs that projected over the lower jaw. But there was an unnatural limpness about the thing, and the hideous eyes were glazed.

Conan peered behind the couch. It was a great serpent which lay there limp in death, but such a serpent as he had never seen in his wanderings. The reek and chill of the deep black earth were about it, and its color was an indeterminable hue which changed with each new angle from which he surveyed it. A great wound in the neck showed what had caused its death.

'It is the Crawler!' whispered Yanath.

'It's the thing I slashed on the stair,' grunted Conan. 'After it trailed us to the Eagle Door, it dragged itself here to die. How could the Xotalancas control such a brute?'

The Tecuhltli shivered and shook their heads.

'They brought it up from the black tunnels below the catacombs. They discovered secrets unknown to Tecuhltli.'

'Well, it's dead, and if they'd had any more of them, they'd have brought them along when they came to Tecuhltli. Come on.'

They crowded close at his heels as he strode down the hall and thrust on the silver-worked door at the other end.

'If we don't find anybody on this floor,' he said, 'we'll descend into the lower floors. We'll explore Xotalanc from the roof to the catacombs. If Xotalanc is like Tecuhltli, all the rooms and halls in this tier will be lighted – what the devil!'

They had come into the broad throne-chamber, so similar to that one in Tecuhltli. There were the same jade dais and ivory seat, the same divans, rugs and hangings on the walls. No black, red-scarred column stood behind the throne-dais, but evidences of the grim feud were not lacking.

Ranged along the wall behind the dais were rows of glass-covered shelves. And on those shelves hundreds of human heads, perfectly preserved, stared at the startled watchers with emotionless eyes, as they had stared for only the gods knew how many months and years.

Topal muttered a curse, but Yanath stood silent, the mad light growing in his wide eyes. Conan frowned, knowing that Tlazitlan sanity was hung on a hair-trigger.

Suddenly Yanath pointed to the ghastly relics with a twitching finger.

'There is my brother's head!' he murmured. 'And there is my father's younger brother! And there beyond them is my sister's eldest son!'

Suddenly he began to weep, dry-eyed, with harsh, loud sobs that shook his frame. He did not take his eyes from the heads. His sobs grew shriller, changed to frightful, high-pitched laughter, and that in turn became an unbearable screaming. Yanath was stark mad.

Conan laid a hand on his shoulder, and as if the touch had released all the frenzy in his soul, Yanath screamed and whirled, striking at the Cimmerian with his sword. Conan parried the blow, and Topal tried to catch Yanath's arm. But the madman avoided him and with froth flying from his lips, he drove his sword deep into Topal's body. Topal sank down with a groan, and Yanath whirled for an instant like a crazy dervish; then he ran at the shelves and began hacking at the glass with his sword, screeching blasphemously.

Conan sprang at him from behind, trying to catch him unaware and disarm him, but the madman wheeled and lunged at him, screaming like a lost soul. Realizing that the warrior was hopelessly insane, the Cimmerian side-stepped, and as the maniac went past, he swung a cut that severed the shoulder-bone and breast, and dropped the man dead beside his dying victim.

Conan bent over Topal, seeing that the man was at his last gasp. It was useless to seek to stanch the blood gushing from the horrible wound.

'You're done for, Topal,' grunted Conan. 'Any word you want to send to your people?'

'Bend closer,' gasped Topal, and Conan complied – and an instant later caught the man's wrist as Topal struck at his breast with a dagger.

'Crom!' swore Conan. 'Are you mad, too?'

'Olmec ordered it!' gasped the dying man. 'I know not why. As we lifted the wounded upon the couches he whispered to me, bidding me to slay you as we returned to Tecuhltli—' And with the name of his clan on his lips, Topal died.

Conan scowled down at him in puzzlement. This whole affair had an aspect of lunacy. Was Olmec mad, too? Were all the Tecuhltli madder than he had realized? With a shrug of his shoulders he strode down the hall and out of the bronze door, leaving the dead Tecuhltli lying before the staring dead eyes of their kinsmen's heads.

Conan needed no guide back through the labyrinth they had traversed. His primitive instinct of direction led him unerringly along the route they had come. He traversed it as warily as he had before, his sword in his hand, and his eyes fiercely searching each shadowed nook and corner; for it was his former allies he feared now, not the ghosts of the slain Xotalancas.

He had crossed the Great Hall and entered the chambers beyond when he heard something moving ahead of him – something which gasped and panted, and moved with a strange, floundering, scrambling noise. A moment later Conan saw a man crawling over the flaming floor toward him – a man whose progress left a broad bloody smear on the smoldering surface. It was Techotl and his eyes were already glazing; from a deep gash in his breast blood gushed steadily between the fingers of his clutching hand. With the other he clawed and hitched himself along.

'Conan,' he cried chokingly, 'Conan! Olmec has taken the yellow-haired woman!'

'So that's why he told Topal to kill me!' murmured Conan, dropping to his knee beside the man, who his experienced eye told him was dying. 'Olmec isn't so mad as I thought.'

Techotl's groping fingers plucked at Conan's arm. In the cold, loveless and altogether hideous life of the Tecuhltli his admiration and affection for the invaders from the outer world formed a warm, human oasis, constituted a tie that connected him with a more natural humanity that was totally lacking in his fellows, whose only emotions were hate, lust and the urge of sadistic cruelty.

'I sought to oppose him,' gurgled Techotl, blood bubbling frothily to his lips. 'But he struck me down. He thought he had slain me, but I crawled away. Ah, Set, how far I have crawled in my own blood! Beware, Conan! Olmec may have set an ambush for your return! Slay Olmec! He is a beast. Take Valeria and flee! Fear not to traverse the forest. Olmec and Tascela lied about the dragons. They slew each other years ago, all save the strongest. For a dozen years there has been only one dragon. If you have slain him, there is naught in the forest to harm you. He was the god Olmec worshipped; and Olmec fed human sacrifices to him, the very old and the very young, bound and hurled from the wall. Hasten! Olmec has taken Valeria to the Chamber of the—'

His head slumped down and he was dead before it came to rest on the floor.

Conan sprang up, his eyes like live coals. So that was Olmec's game, having first used the strangers to destroy his foes! He should have known that something of the sort would be going on in that black-bearded degenerate's mind.

The Cimmerian started toward Tecuhltli with reckless speed. Rapidly he reckoned the numbers of his former allies. Only twenty-one, counting Olmec, had survived that fiendish battle in the throneroom. Three had died since, which left seventeen enemies with which to reckon. In his rage Conan felt capable of accounting for the whole clan single-handed.

But the innate craft of the wilderness rose to guide his berserk rage. He remembered Techotl's warning of an ambush. It was quite probable that the prince would make such provisions, on the chance that Topal might have failed to carry out his order. Olmec would be expecting him to return by the same route he had followed in going to Xotalanc.

Conan glanced up at the skylight under which he was passing and caught the blurred glimmer of stars. They had not yet begun to pale for dawn. The events of the night had been crowded into a comparatively short space of time.

He turned aside from his direct course and descended a winding staircase to the floor below. He did not know where the door was to be found that let into the castle on that level, but he knew he could find it. How he was to force the locks he did not know; he believed that the doors of Tecuhltli would all be locked and bolted, if for no other reason than the habits of half a century. But there was nothing else but to attempt it.

Sword in hand, he hurried noiselessly on through a maze of green-lit or shadowy rooms and halls. He knew he must be near Tecuhltli, when a sound brought him up short. He recognized it for what it was – a human being trying to cry out through a stifling gag. It came from somewhere ahead of him, and to the left. In those deathly-still chambers a small sound carried a long way.

Conan turned aside and went seeking after the sound, which continued to be repeated. Presently he was glaring through a doorway upon a weird scene. In the room into which he was looking a low rack-like frame of iron lay on the floor, and a giant figure was bound prostrate upon it. His head rested on a bed of iron spikes, which were already crimson-pointed with blood where they had pierced his scalp. A peculiar harness-like contrivance was fastened about his head, though in such a manner that the leather band did not protect his scalp from the spikes. This harness was connected by a slender chain to the mechanism that upheld a huge iron ball which was suspended above the captive's hairy breast. As long as the man could force himself to remain motionless the iron ball hung in its place. But when the pain of the iron points caused him to lift his head, the ball lurched downwards a few inches. Presently his aching neck muscles would no longer support his head in its unnatural position and it would fall back on the spikes again. It was obvious that eventually the ball would crush him to a pulp, slowly and inexorably. The victim was gagged, and above the gag his great black ox-eyes rolled wildly toward the man in the doorway, who stood in silent amazement. The man on the rack was Olmec, prince of Tecuhltli.

6 The Eyes of Tascela

'Why did you bring me into this chamber to bandage my leg?' demanded Valeria. 'Couldn't you have done it just as well in the throneroom?'

She sat on a couch with her wounded leg extended upon it, and the Tecuhltli woman had just bound it with silk bandages. Valeria's red-stained sword lay on the couch beside her.

She frowned as she spoke. The woman had done her task silently and efficiently, but Valeria liked neither the lingering, caressing touch of her slim fingers nor the expression in her eyes.

'They have taken the rest of the wounded into the other chambers,' answered the woman in the soft speech of the Tecuhltli women, which somehow did not suggest either softness or gentleness in the speakers. A little while before, Valeria had seen this same woman stab a Xotalanca woman through the breast and stamp the eyeballs out of a wounded Xotalanca man.

'They will be carrying the corpses of the dead down into the catacombs,' she added, 'lest the ghosts escape into the chambers and dwell there.'

'Do you believe in ghosts?' asked Valeria.

'I know the ghost of Tolkemec dwells in the catacombs,' she answered with a shiver. 'Once I saw it, as I crouched in a crypt among the bones of a dead queen. It passed by in the form of an ancient man with flowing white beard and locks, and luminous eyes that blazed in the darkness. It was Tolkemec; I saw him living when I was a child and he was being tortured.'

Her voice sank to a fearful whisper: 'Olmec laughs, but I know Tolkemec's ghost dwells in the catacombs! They say it is rats which gnaw the flesh from the bones of the newly dead – but ghosts eat flesh. Who knows but that—'

She glanced up quickly as a shadow fell across the couch. Valeria looked up to see Olmec gazing down at her. The prince had cleansed his hands, torso and beard of the blood that had splashed them; but he had not donned his robe, and his great dark-skinned hairless body and limbs renewed the impression of strength bestial in its nature. His deep black eyes burned with a more elemental light, and there was the suggestion of a twitching in the fingers that tugged at his thick blue-black beard.

He stared fixedly at the woman, and she rose and glided from the chamber. As she passed through the door she cast a look over her shoulder at Valeria, a glance full of cynical derision and obscene mockery.

'She has done a clumsy job,' criticized the prince, coming to the divan and bending over the bandage. 'Let me see—'

With a quickness amazing in one of his bulk he snatched her sword and threw it across the chamber. His next move was to catch her in his giant arms.

Quick and unexpected as the move was, she almost matched it; for even as he grabbed her, her dirk was in her hand and she stabbed murderously at his throat. More by luck than skill he caught her wrist, and then began a savage wrestling-match. She fought him with fists, feet, knees, teeth and nails, with all the strength of her magnificent body and all the knowledge of hand-to-hand fighting she had acquired in her years of roving and fighting on sea and land. It availed her nothing against his brute strength. She lost her dirk in the first moment of contact, and thereafter found herself powerless to inflict any appreciable pain on her giant attacker.

The blaze in his weird black eyes did not alter, and their expression filled her with fury, fanned by the sardonic smile that seemed carved upon his bearded lips. Those eyes and that smile contained all the cruel cynicism that seethes below the surface of a sophisticated and degenerate race, and for the first time in her life Valeria experienced fear of a man. It was like struggling against some huge elemental force; his iron arms thwarted her efforts with an ease that sent panic racing through her limbs. He seemed impervious to any pain she could inflict. Only once, when she sank her white teeth savagely into his wrist so that the blood started, did he react. And that was to buffet her brutally upon the side of the head with his open hand, so that stars flashed before her eyes and her head rolled on her shoulders.

Her shirt had been torn open in the struggle, and with cynical cruelty he rasped his thick beard across her bare breasts, bringing the blood to suffuse the fair skin, and fetching a cry of pain and outraged fury from her. Her convulsive resistance was useless; she was crushed down on a couch, disarmed and panting, her eyes blazing up at him like the eyes of a trapped tigress.

A moment later he was hurrying from the chamber, carrying her in his arms. She made no resistance, but the smoldering of her eyes showed that she was not unconquered in spirit, at least. She had not cried out. She knew that Conan was not within call, and it did not occur to her that any in Tecuhltli would oppose their prince. But she noticed that Olmec went stealthily, with his head on one side as if listening for sounds of pursuit, and he did not return to the throne-chamber. He carried her through a door that stood opposite that through which he had entered, crossed another room and began stealing down a hall. As she became convinced that he feared some opposition to the abduction, she threw back her head and screamed at the top of her lusty voice.

She was rewarded by a slap that half stunned her, and Olmec quickened his pace to a shambling run.

But her cry had been echoed, and twisting her head about, Valeria, through the tears and stars that partly blinded her, saw Techotl limping after them.

Olmec turned with a snarl, shifting the woman to an uncomfortable and certainly undignified position under one huge arm, where he held her writhing and kicking vainly, like a child.

'Olmec!' protested Techotl. 'You cannot be such a dog as to do this thing! She is Conan's woman! She helped us slay the Xotalancas, and—'

Without a word Olmec balled his free hand into a huge fist and stretched the wounded warrior senseless at his feet. Stooping, and hindered not at all by the struggles and imprecations of his captive, he drew Techotl's sword from its sheath and stabbed the warrior in the breast. Then casting aside the weapon he fled on along the corridor. He did not see a woman's dark face peer cautiously after him from behind a hanging. It vanished, and presently Techotl groaned and stirred, rose dazedly and staggered drunkenly away, calling Conan's name.

Olmec hurried on down the corridor, and descended a winding ivory staircase. He crossed several corridors and halted at last in a broad chamber whose doors were veiled with heavy tapestries, with one exception – a heavy bronze door similar to the Door of the Eagle on the upper floor.

He was moved to rumble, pointing to it: 'That is one of the outer doors of Tecuhltli. For the first time in fifty years it is unguarded. We need not guard it now, for Xotalanc is no more.'

'Thanks to Conan and me, you bloody rogue!' sneered Valeria, trembling with fury and the shame of physical coercion. 'You treacherous dog! Conan will cut your throat for this!'

Olmec did not bother to voice his belief that Conan's own gullet had already been severed according to his whispered command. He was too utterly cynical to be at all interested in her thoughts or opinions. His flame-lit eyes devoured her, dwelling burningly on the generous expanse of clear white flesh exposed where her shirt and breeches had been torn in the struggle.

'Forget Conan,' he said thickly. 'Olmec is lord of Xuchotl. Xotalanc is no more. There will be no more fighting. We shall spend our lives in drinking and lovemaking. First let us drink!'

He seated himself on an ivory table and pulled her down on his knees, like a dark-skinned satyr with a white nymph in his arms. Ignoring her unnymphlike profanity, he held her helpless with one great arm about her waist while the other reached across the table and secured a vessel of wine.

'Drink!' he commanded, forcing it to her lips, as she writhed her head away.

The liquor slopped over, stinging her lips, splashing down on her naked breasts.

'Your guest does not like your wine, Olmec,' spoke a cool, sardonic voice.

Olmec stiffened; fear grew in his flaming eyes. Slowly he swung his great head about and stared at Tascela who posed negligently in the curtained doorway, one hand on her smooth hip. Valeria twisted herself about in his iron grip, and when she met the burning eyes of Tascela, a chill tingled along her supple spine. New experiences were flooding Valeria's proud soul that night. Recently she had learned to fear a man; now she knew what it was to fear a woman.

Olmec sat motionless, a gray pallor growing under his swarthy skin. Tascela brought her other hand from behind her and displayed a small gold vessel.

'I feared she would not like your wine, Olmec,' purred the princess, 'so I brought some of mine, some I brought with me long ago from the shores of Lake Zuad – do you understand, Olmec?'

Beads of sweat stood out suddenly on Olmec's brow. His muscles relaxed, and Valeria broke away and put the table between them. But though reason told her to dart from the room, some fascination she could not understand held her rigid, watching the scene.

Tascela came toward the seated prince with a swaying, undulating walk that was mockery in itself. Her voice was soft, slurringly caressing, but her eyes gleamed. Her slim fingers stroked his beard lightly.

'You are selfish, Olmec,' she crooned, smiling. 'You would keep our handsome guest to yourself, though you knew I wished to entertain her. You are much at fault, Olmec!'

The mask dropped for an instant; her eyes flashed, her face was contorted and with an appalling show of strength her hand locked convulsively in his beard and tore out a great handful. This evidence of unnatural strength was no more terrifying than the momentary baring of the hellish fury that raged under her bland exterior.

Olmec lurched up with a roar, and stood swaying like a bear, his mighty hands clenching and unclenching.

'Slut!' His booming voice filled the room. 'Witch! She-devil! Tecuhltli should have slain you fifty years ago! Begone! I have endured too much from you! This white-skinned wench is mine! Get hence before I slay you!'

The princess laughed and dashed the blood-stained strands into his face. Her laughter was less merciful than the ring of flint on steel.

'Once you spoke otherwise, Olmec,' she taunted. 'Once, in your youth, you spoke words of love. Aye, you were my lover once, years ago, and because you loved me, you slept in my arms beneath the enchanted lotus – and thereby put into my hands the chains that enslaved you. You know you cannot withstand me. You know I have but to gaze into your eyes, with the mystic power a priest of Stygia taught me, long ago, and you are powerless. You remember the night beneath the black lotus that waved above us, stirred by no worldly breeze; you scent again the unearthly perfumes that stole and rose like a cloud about you to enslave you. You cannot fight against me. You are my slave as you were that night – as you shall be so long as you shall live, Olmec of Xuchotl!'

Her voice had sunk to a murmur like the rippling of a stream running through starlit darkness. She leaned close to the prince and spread her long tapering fingers upon his giant breast. His eyes glazed, his great hands fell limply to his sides.

With a smile of cruel malice, Tascela lifted the vessel and placed it to his lips.

'Drink!'

Mechanically the prince obeyed. And instantly the glaze passed from his eyes and they were flooded with fury, comprehension and an awful fear. His mouth gaped, but no sound issued. For an instant he reeled on buckling knees, and then fell in a sodden heap on the floor.

His fall jolted Valeria out of her paralysis. She turned and sprang toward the door, but with a movement that would have shamed a leaping panther, Tascela was before her. Valeria struck at her with her clenched fist, and all the power of her supple body behind the blow. It would have stretched a man senseless on the floor. But with a lithe twist of her torso, Tascela avoided the blow and caught the pirate's wrist. The next instant Valeria's left hand was imprisoned, and holding her wrists together with one hand, Tascela calmly bound them with a cord she drew from her girdle. Valeria thought she had tasted the ultimate in humiliation already that night, but her shame at being manhandled by Olmec was nothing to the sensations that now shook her supple frame. Valeria had always been inclined to despise the other members of her sex; and it was overwhelming to encounter another woman who could handle her like a child. She scarcely resisted at all when Tascela forced her into a chair and drawing her bound wrists down between her knees, fastened them to the chair.

Casually stepping over Olmec, Tascela walked to the bronze door and shot the bolt and threw it open, revealing a hallway without.

'Opening upon this hall,' she remarked, speaking to her feminine captive for the first time, 'there is a chamber which in old times was used as a torture room. When we retired into Tecuhltli, we brought most of the apparatus with us, but there was one piece too heavy to move. It is still in working order. I think it will be quite convenient now.'

An understanding flame of terror rose in Olmec's eyes. Tascela strode back to him, bent and gripped him by the hair.

'He is only paralysed temporarily,' she remarked conversationally. 'He can hear, think, and feel – aye, he can feel very well indeed!'

With which sinister observation she started toward the door, dragging the giant bulk with an ease that made the pirate's eyes dilate. She passed into the hall and moved down it without hesitation, presently disappearing with her captive into a chamber that opened into it, and whence shortly thereafter issued the clank of iron.

Valeria swore softly and tugged vainly, with her legs braced against the chair. The cords that confined her were apparently unbreakable.

Tascela presently returned alone; behind her a muffled groaning issued from the chamber. She closed the door but did not bolt it. Tascela was beyond the grip of habit, as she was beyond the touch of other human instincts and emotions.

Valeria sat dumbly, watching the woman in whose slim hands, the pirate realized, her destiny now rested.

Tascela grasped her yellow locks and forced back her head, looking impersonally down into her face. But the glitter in her dark eyes was not impersonal.

'I have chosen you for a great honor,' she said. 'You shall restore the youth of Tascela. Oh, you stare at that! My appearance is that of youth, but through my veins creeps the sluggish chill of approaching age, as I have felt it a thousand times before. I am old, so old I do not remember my childhood. But I was a girl once, and a priest of Stygia loved me, and gave me the secret of immortality and youth everlasting. He died, then – some said by poison. But I dwelt in my palace by the shores of Lake Zuad and the passing years touched me not. So at last a king of Stygia desired me, and my people rebelled and brought me to this land. Olmec called me a princess. I am not of royal blood. I am greater than a princess. I am Tascela, whose youth your own glorious youth shall restore.'

Valeria's tongue clove to the roof of her mouth. She sensed here a mystery darker than the degeneracy she had anticipated.

The taller woman unbound the Aquilonian's wrists and pulled her to her feet. It was not fear of the dominant strength that lurked in the princess' limbs that made Valeria a helpless, quivering captive in her hands. It was the burning, hypnotic, terrible eyes of Tascela.

7 He Comes from the Dark

'Well, I'm a Kushite!'

Conan glared down at the man on the iron rack.

'What the devil are you doing on that thing?'

Incoherent sounds issued from behind the gag and Conan bent and tore it away, evoking a bellow of fear from the captive; for his action caused the iron ball to lurch down until it nearly touched the broad breast.

'Be careful, for Set's sake!' begged Olmec.

'What for?' demanded Conan. 'Do you think I care what happens to you? I only wish I had time to stay here and watch that chunk of iron grind your guts out. But I'm in a hurry. Where's Valeria?'

'Loose me!' urged Olmec. 'I will tell you all!'

'Tell me first.'

'Never!' The prince's heavy jaws set stubbornly.

'All right.' Conan seated himself on a near-by bench. 'I'll find her myself, after you've been reduced to a jelly. I believe I can speed up that process by twisting my sword-point around in your ear,' he added, extending the weapon experimentally.

'Wait!' Words came in a rush from the captive's ashy lips. 'Tascela took her from me. I've never been anything but a puppet in Tascela's hands.'

'Tascela?' snorted Conan, and spat. 'Why, the filthy—'

'No, no!' panted Olmec. 'It's worse than you think. Tascela is old – centuries old. She renews her life and her youth by the sacrifice of beautiful young women. That's one thing that has reduced the clan to its present state. She will draw the essence of Valeria's life into her own body, and bloom with fresh vigor and beauty.'

'Are the doors locked?' asked Conan, thumbing his sword edge.

'Aye! But I know a way to get into Tecuhltli. Only Tascela and I know, and she thinks me helpless and you slain. Free me and I swear I will help you rescue Valeria. Without my help you cannot win into Techultli; for even if you tortured me into revealing the secret, you couldn't work it. Let me go and we will steal on Tascela and kill her before she can work magic – before she can fix her eyes on us. A knife thrown from behind will do the work. I should have killed her thus long ago, but I feared that without her to aid us the Xotalancas would overcome us. She needed my help, too; that's the only reason she let me live this long. Now neither needs the other, and one must die. I swear that when we have slain the witch, you and Valeria shall go free without harm. My people will obey me when Tascela is dead.'

Conan stooped and cut the ropes that held the prince, and Olmec slid cautiously from under the great ball and rose, shaking his head like a bull and muttering imprecations as he fingered his lacerated scalp. Standing shoulder to shoulder the two men presented a formidable picture of primitive power. Olmec was as tall as Conan, and heavier; but there was something repellent about the Tlazitlan, something abysmal and monstrous that contrasted unfavorably with the clean-cut, compact hardness of the Cimmerian. Conan had discarded the remnants of his tattered, blood-soaked shirt, and stood with his remarkable muscular development impressively revealed. His great shoulders were as broad as those of Olmec, and more cleanly outlined, and his huge breast arched with a more impressive sweep to a hard waist that lacked the paunchy thickness of Olmec's midsection. He might have been an image of primal strength cut out of bronze. Olmec was darker, but not from the burning of the sun. If Conan was a figure out of the dawn of Time, Olmec was a shambling, somber shape from the darkness of Time's pre-dawn.

'Lead on,' demanded Conan. 'And keep ahead of me. I don't trust you any farther than I can throw a bull by the tail.'

Olmec turned and stalked on ahead of him, one hand twitching slightly as it plucked at his matted beard.

Olmec did not lead Conan back to the bronze door, which the prince naturally supposed Tascela had locked, but to a certain chamber on the border of Tecuhltli.

'This secret has been guarded for half a century,' he said. 'Not even our own clan knew of it, and the Xotalancas never learned. Tecuhltli himself built this secret entrance, afterward slaying the slaves who did the work; for he feared that he might find himself locked out of his own kingdom some day because of the spite of Tascela, whose passion for him soon changed to hate. But she discovered the secret, and barred the hidden door against him one day as he fled back from an unsuccessful raid, and the Xotalancas took him and flayed him. But once, spying upon her, I saw her enter Tecuhltli by this route, and so learned the secret.'

He pressed upon a gold ornament in the wall, and a panel swung inward, disclosing an ivory stair leading upward.

'This stair is built within the wall,' said Olmec. 'It leads up to a tower upon the roof, and thence other stairs wind down to the various chambers. Hasten!'

'After you, comrade!' retorted Conan satirically, swaying his broad-sword as he spoke, and Olmec shrugged his shoulders and stepped onto the staircase. Conan instantly followed him, and the door shut behind them. Far above a cluster of fire-jewels made the staircase a well of dusky dragon-light.

They mounted until Conan estimated that they were above the level of the fourth floor, and then came out into a cylindrical tower, in the domed roof of which was set the bunch of fire-jewels that lighted the stair. Through gold-barred windows, set with unbreakable crystal panes, the first windows he had seen in Xuchotl, Conan got a glimpse of high ridges, domes and more towers, looming darkly against the stars. He was looking across the roofs of Xuchotl.

Olmec did not look through the windows. He hurried down one of the several stairs that wound down from the tower, and when they had descended a few feet, this stair changed into a narrow corridor that wound tortuously on for some distance. It ceased at a steep flight of steps leading downward. There Olmec paused.

Up from below, muffled, but unmistakable, welled a woman's scream, edged with fright, fury and shame. And Conan recognized Valeria's voice.

In the swift rage roused by that cry, and the amazement of wondering what peril could wring such a shriek from Valeria's reckless lips, Conan forgot Olmec. He pushed past the prince and started down the stair. Awakening instinct brought him about again, just as Olmec struck with his great mallet-like fist. The blow, fierce and silent, was aimed at the base of Conan's brain. But the Cimmerian wheeled in time to receive the buffet on the side of his neck instead. The impact would have snapped the vertebrae of a lesser man. As it was, Conan swayed backward, but even as he reeled he dropped his sword, useless at such close quarters, and grasped Olmec's extended arm, dragging the prince with him as he fell. Headlong they went down the steps together, in a revolving whirl of limbs and heads and bodies. And as they went Conan's iron fingers found and locked in Olmec's bull-throat.

The barbarian's neck and shoulder felt numb from the sledge-like impact of Olmec's huge fist, which had carried all the strength of the massive forearm, thick triceps and great shoulder. But this did not affect his ferocity to any appreciable extent. Like a bulldog he hung on grimly, shaken and battered and beaten against the steps as they rolled, until at last they struck an ivory panel-door at the bottom with such an impact that they splintered it its full length and crashed through its ruins. But Olmec was already dead, for those iron fingers had crushed out his life and broken his neck as they fell.

Conan rose, shaking the splinters from his great shoulder, blinking blood and dust out of his eyes.

He was in the great throneroom. There were fifteen people in that room besides himself. The first person he saw was Valeria. A curious black altar stood before the throne-dais. Ranged about it, seven black candles in golden candlesticks sent up oozing spirals of thick green smoke, disturbingly scented. These spirals united in a cloud near the ceiling, forming a smoky arch above the altar. On that altar lay Valeria, stark naked, her white flesh gleaming in shocking contrast to the glistening ebon stone. She was not bound. She lay at full length, her arms stretched out above her head to their fullest extent. At the head of the altar knelt a young man, holding her wrists firmly. A young woman knelt at the other end of the altar, grasping her ankles. Between them she could neither rise nor move.

Eleven men and women of Tecuhltli knelt dumbly in a semicircle, watching the scene with hot, lustful eyes.

On the ivory throne-seat Tascela lolled. Bronze bowls of incense rolled their spirals about her; the wisps of smoke curled about her naked limbs like caressing fingers. She could not sit still; she squirmed and shifted about with sensuous abandon, as if finding pleasure in the contact of the smooth ivory with her sleek flesh.

The crash of the door as it broke beneath the impact of the hurtling bodies caused no change in the scene. The kneeling men and women merely glanced incuriously at the corpse of their prince and at the man who rose from the ruins of the door, then swung their eyes greedily back to the writhing white shape on the black altar. Tascela looked insolently at him, and sprawled back on her seat, laughing mockingly.

'Slut!' Conan saw red. His hands clenched into iron hammers as he started for her. With his first step something clanged loudly and steel bit savagely into his leg. He stumbled and almost fell, checked in his headlong stride. The jaws of an iron trap had closed on his leg, with teeth that sank deep and held. Only the ridged muscles of his calf saved the bone from being splintered. The accursed thing had sprung out of the smoldering floor without warning. He saw the slots now, in the floor where the jaws had lain, perfectly camouflaged.

'Fool!' laughed Tascela. 'Did you think I would not guard against your possible return? Every door in this chamber is guarded by such traps. Stand there and watch now, while I fulfill the destiny of your handsome friend! Then I will decide your own.'

Conan's hand instinctively sought his belt, only to encounter an empty scabbard. His sword was on the stair behind him. His poniard was lying back in the forest, where the dragon had torn it from his jaw. The steel teeth in his leg were like burning coals, but the pain was not as savage as the fury that seethed in his soul. He was trapped, like a wolf. If he had had his sword he would have hewn off his leg and crawled across the floor to slay Tascela. Valeria's eyes rolled toward him with mute appeal, and his own helplessness sent red waves of madness surging through his brain.

Dropping on the knee of his free leg, he strove to get his fingers between the jaws of the trap, to tear them apart by sheer strength. Blood started from beneath his finger nails, but the jaws fitted close about his leg in a circle whose segments jointed perfectly, contracted until there was no space between his mangled flesh and the fanged iron. The sight of Valeria's naked body added flame to the fire of his rage.

Tascela ignored him. Rising languidly from her seat she swept the ranks of her subjects with a searching glance, and asked: 'Where are Xamec, Zlanath and Tachic?'

'They did not return from the catacombs, princess,' answered a man. 'Like the rest of us, they bore the bodies of the slain into the crypts, but they have not returned. Perhaps the ghost of Tolkemec took them.'

'Be silent, fool!' she ordered harshly. 'The ghost is a myth.'

She came down from her dais, playing with a thin gold-hilted dagger. Her eyes burned like nothing on the hither side of hell. She paused beside the altar and spoke in the tense stillness.

'Your life shall make me young, white woman!' she said. 'I shall lean upon your bosom and place my lips over yours, and slowly – ah, slowly! – sink this blade through your heart, so that your life, fleeing your stiffening body, shall enter mine, making me bloom again with youth and with life everlasting!'

Slowly, like a serpent arching toward its victim, she bent down through the writhing smoke, closer and closer over the now motionless woman who stared up into her glowing dark eyes – eyes that grew larger and deeper, blazing like black moons in the swirling smoke.

The kneeling people gripped their hands and held their breath, tense for the bloody climax, and the only sound was Conan's fierce panting as he strove to tear his leg from the trap.

All eyes were glued to the altar and the white figure there; the crash of a thunderbolt could hardly have broken the spell, yet it was only a low cry that shattered the fixity of the scene and brought all whirling about – a low cry, yet one to make the hair stand up stiffly on the scalp. They looked, and they saw.

Framed in the door to the left of the dais stood a nightmare figure. It was a man, with a tangle of white hair and a matted white beard that fell over his breast. Rags only partly covered his gaunt frame, revealing half-naked limbs strangely unnatural in appearance. The skin was not like that of a normal human. There was a suggestion of *scaliness* about it, as if the owner had dwelt long under conditions almost antithetical to those conditions under which human life ordinarily thrives. And there was nothing at all human about the eyes that blazed from the tangle of white hair. They were great gleaming disks that stared unwinkingly, luminous, whitish, and without a hint of normal emotion or sanity. The mouth gaped, but no coherent words issued – only a high-pitched tittering.

'Tolkemec!' whispered Tascela, livid, while the others crouched in speechless horror. 'No myth, then, no ghost! Set! You have dwelt for twelve years in darkness! Twelve years among the bones of the dead! What grisly food did you find? What mad travesty of life did you live, in the stark blackness of that eternal night? I see now why Xamec and Zlanath and Tachic did not return from the catacombs – and never will return. But why have you waited so long to strike? Were you seeking something, in the pits? Some secret weapon you knew was hidden there? And have you found it at last?'

That hideous tittering was Tolkemec's only reply, as he bounded into the room with a long leap that carried him over the secret trap before the door – by chance, or by some faint recollection of the ways of Xuchotl. He was not mad, as a man is mad. He had dwelt apart from humanity so long that he was no longer human. Only an unbroken thread of memory embodied in hate and the urge for vengeance had connected him with the humanity from which he had been cut off, and held him lurking near the people he hated. Only that thin string had kept him from racing and prancing off for ever into the black corridors and realms of the subterranean world he had discovered, long ago.

'You sought something hidden!' whispered Tascela, cringing back. 'And you have found it! You remember the feud! After all these years of blackness, you remember!'

For in the lean hand of Tolkemec now waved a curious jade-hued wand, on the end of which glowed a knob of crimson shaped like a pomegranate. She sprang aside as he thrust it out like a spear, and a beam of crimson fire lanced from the pomegranate. It missed Tascela, but the woman holding Valeria's ankles was in the way. It smote between her shoulders. There was a sharp crackling sound and the ray of fire flashed from her bosom and struck the black altar, with a snapping of blue sparks. The woman toppled sidewise, shriveling and withering like a mummy even as she fell.

Valeria rolled from the altar on the other side, and started for the opposite wall on all fours. For hell had burst loose in the throneroom of dead Olmec.

The man who had held Valeria's hands was the next to die. He turned to run, but before he had taken half a dozen steps, Tolkemec, with an agility appalling in such a frame, bounded around to a position that placed the man between him and the altar. Again the red fire-beam flashed and the Tecuhltli rolled lifeless to the floor as the beam completed its course with a burst of blue sparks against the altar.

Then began slaughter. Screaming insanely the people rushed about the chamber, caroming from one another, stumbling and falling. And among them Tolkemec capered and pranced, dealing death. They could not escape by the doors; for apparently the metal of the portals served like the metal-veined stone altar to complete the circuit for whatever hellish power flashed like thunderbolts from the witch-wand the ancient waved in his hand. When he caught a man or a woman between him and a door or the altar, that one died instantly. He chose no special victim. He took them as they came, with his rags flapping about his wildly gyrating limbs, and the gusty echoes of his tittering sweeping the room above the screams. And bodies fell like falling leaves about the altar and at the doors. One warrior in desperation rushed at him, lifting a dagger, only to fall before he could strike. But the rest were like crazed cattle, with no thought for resistance, and no chance of escape.

The last Tecuhltli except Tascela had fallen when the princess reached the Cimmerian and the girl who had taken refuge beside him. Tascela bent and touched the floor, pressing a design upon it. Instantly the iron jaws released the bleeding limb and sank back into the floor.

'Slay him if you can!' she panted, and pressed a heavy knife into his hand. 'I have no magic to withstand him!'

With a grunt he sprang before the women, not heeding his lacerated leg in the heat of the fighting-lust. Tolkemec was coming toward him, his weird eyes ablaze, but he hesitated at the gleam of the knife in Conan's hand. Then began a grim game, as Tolkemec sought to circle about Conan and get the barbarian between him and the altar or a metal door, while Conan sought to avoid this and drive home his knife. The women watched tensely, holding their breath.

There was no sound except the rustle and scrape of quick-shifting feet. Tolkemec pranced and capered no more. He realized that grimmer game confronted him than the people who had died screaming and fleeing. In the elemental blaze of the barbarian's eyes he read an intent deadly as his own. Back and forth they weaved, and when one moved the other moved as if invisible threads bound them together. But all the time Conan was getting closer and closer to his enemy. Already the coiled muscles of his thighs were beginning to flex for a spring, when Valeria cried out. For a fleeting instant a bronze door was in line with Conan's moving body. The red line leaped, searing Conan's flank as he twisted aside, and even as he shifted he hurled the knife. Old Tolkemec went down, truly slain at last, the hilt vibrating on his breast.

Tascela sprang – not toward Conan, but toward the wand where it shimmered like a live thing on the floor. But as she leaped, so did Valeria, with a dagger snatched from a dead man, and the blade, driven with all the power of the pirate's muscles, impaled the princess of Tecuhltli so that the point stood out between her breasts. Tascela screamed once and fell dead, and Valeria spurned the body with her heel as it fell.

'I had to do that much, for my own self-respect!' panted Valeria, facing Conan across the limp corpse.

'Well, this cleans up the feud,' he grunted. 'It's been a hell of a night! Where did these people keep their food? I'm hungry.'

'You need a bandage on that leg,' Valeria ripped a length of silk from a hanging and knotted it about her waist, then tore off some smaller strips which she bound efficiently about the barbarian's lacerated limb.

'I can walk on it,' he assured her. 'Let's begone. It's dawn, outside this infernal city. I've had enough of Xuchotl. It's well the breed exterminated itself. I don't want any of their accursed jewels. They might be haunted.'

'There is enough clean loot in the world for you and me,' she said, straightening to stand tall and splendid before him.

The old blaze came back in his eyes, and this time she did not resist as he caught her fiercely in his arms.

'It's a long way to the coast,' she said presently, withdrawing her lips from his.

'What matter?' he laughed. 'There's nothing we can't conquer. We'll have our feet on a ship's deck before the Stygians open their ports for the trading season. And then we'll show the world what plundering means!'

THE HOUR OF THE DRAGON

The Lion Banner sways and falls in the horror-haunted gloom;
A scarlet Dragon rustles by, borne on winds of doom.
In heaps the shining horsemen lie, where the thrusting lances break,
And deep in the haunted mountains, the lost, black gods awake.
Dead hands grope in the shadows, the stars turn pale with fright,
For this is the Dragon's Hour, the triumph of Fear and Night.

THE HOUR OF THE DRAGON

1 O Sleeper, Awake!

THE LONG TAPERS FLICKERED, sending the black shadows wavering along the walls, and the velvet tapestries rippled. Yet there was no wind in the chamber. Four men stood about the ebony table on which lay the green sarcophagus that gleamed like carven jade. In the upraised right hand of each man a curious black candle burned with a weird greenish light. Outside was night and a lost wind moaning among the black trees.

Inside the chamber was tense silence, and the wavering of the shadows, while four pairs of eyes, burning with intensity, were fixed on the long green case across which cryptic hieroglyphics writhed, as if lent life and movement by the unsteady light. The man at the foot of the sarcophagus leaned over it and moved his candle as if he were writing with a pen, inscribing a mystic symbol in the air. Then he set down the candle in its black gold stick at the foot of the case, and, mumbling some formula unintelligible to his companions, he thrust a broad white hand into his fur-trimmed robe. When he brought it forth again it was as if he cupped in his palm a ball of living fire.

The other three drew in their breath sharply, and the dark, powerful man who stood at the head of the sarcophagus whispered: 'The Heart of Ahriman!' The other lifted a quick hand for silence. Somewhere a dog began howling dolefully, and a stealthy step padded outside the barred and bolted door. But none looked aside from the mummy-case over which the man in the ermine-trimmed robe was now moving the great flaming jewel while he muttered an incantation that was old when Atlantis sank. The glare of the gem dazzled their eyes, so that they could not be sure of what they saw; but with a splintering crash, the carven lid of the sarcophagus burst outward as if from some irresistible pressure applied from within, and the four men, bending eagerly forward, saw the occupant – a huddled, withered, wizened shape, with dried brown limbs like dead wood showing through moldering bandages.

'Bring that thing *back*?' muttered the small dark man who stood on the right, with a short sardonic laugh. 'It is ready to crumble at a touch. We are fools—'

'Shhh!' It was an urgent hiss of command from the large man who held the jewel. Perspiration stood upon his broad white forehead and his eyes were dilated. He leaned forward, and, without touching the thing with his hand, laid on the breast of the mummy the blazing jewel. Then he drew back and watched with fierce intensity, his lips moving in soundless invocation.

It was as if a globe of living fire flickered and burned on the dead, withered bosom. And breath sucked in, hissing, through the clenched teeth of the watchers. For as they watched, an awful transmutation became apparent. The withered shape in the sarcophagus was expanding, was growing, lengthening. The bandages burst and fell into brown dust. The shriveled limbs swelled, straightened. Their dusky hue began to fade.

'By Mitra!' whispered the tall, yellow-haired man on the left. 'He was *not* a Stygian. That part at least was true.'

Again a trembling finger warned for silence. The hound outside was no longer howling. He whimpered, as with an evil dream, and then that sound, too, died away in silence, in which the yellow-haired man plainly heard the straining of the heavy door, as if something outside pushed powerfully upon it. He half turned, his hand at his sword, but the man in the ermine robe hissed an urgent warning: 'Stay! Do not break the chain! And on your life do not go to the door!'

The yellow-haired man shrugged and turned back, and then he stopped short, staring. In the jade sarcophagus lay a living man: a tall, lusty man, naked, white of skin, and dark of hair and beard. He lay motionless, his eyes wide open, and blank and unknowing as a newborn babe's. On his breast the great jewel smoldered and sparkled.

The man in ermine reeled as if from some let-down of extreme tension.

'Ishtar!' he gasped. 'It is Xaltotun! – *and he lives!* Valerius! Tarascus! Amalric! Do you see? Do you see? You doubted me – but I have not failed! We have been close to the open gates of hell this night, and the shapes of darkness have gathered close about us – aye, they followed *him* to the very door – but we have brought the great magician back to life.'

'And damned our souls to purgatories everlasting, I doubt not,' muttered the small, dark man, Tarascus.

The yellow-haired man, Valerius, laughed harshly.

'What purgatory can be worse than life itself? So we are all damned together from birth. Besides, who would not sell his miserable soul for a throne?'

'There is no intelligence in his stare, Orastes,' said the large man.

'He has long been dead,' answered Orastes. 'He is as one newly awakened. His mind is empty after the long sleep – nay, he was *dead*, not sleeping. We brought his spirit back over the voids and gulfs of night and oblivion. I will speak to him.'

He bent over the foot of the sarcophagus, and fixing his gaze on the wide dark eyes of the man within, he said, slowly: 'Awake, Xaltotun!'

The lips of the man moved mechanically. 'Xaltotun!' he repeated in a groping whisper.

'*You* are Xaltotun!' exclaimed Orastes, like a hypnotist driving home his suggestions. 'You are Xaltotun of Python, in Acheron.'

A dim flame flickered in the dark eyes.

'I was Xaltotun,' he whispered. 'I am dead.'

'You *are* Xaltotun!' cried Orastes. 'You are not dead! You live!'

'I am Xaltotun,' came the eery whisper. 'But I am dead. In my house in Khemi, in Stygia, there I died.'

'And the priests who poisoned you mummified your body with their dark arts, keeping all your organs intact!' exclaimed Orastes. 'But now you live again! The Heart of Ahriman has restored your life, drawn your spirit back from space and eternity.'

'The Heart of Ahriman!' The flame of remembrance grew stronger. 'The barbarians stole it from me!'

'He remembers,' muttered Orastes. 'Lift him from the case.'

The others obeyed hesitantly, as if reluctant to touch the man they had recreated, and they seemed not easier in their minds when they felt firm muscular flesh, vibrant with blood and life, beneath their fingers. But they lifted him upon the table, and Orastes clothed him in a curious dark velvet robe, splashed with gold stars and crescent moons, and fastened a cloth-of-gold fillet about his temples, confining the black wavy locks that fell to his shoulders. He let them do as they would, saying nothing, not even when they set him in a carven throne-like chair with a high ebony back and wide silver arms, and feet like golden claws. He sat there motionless, and slowly intelligence grew in his dark eyes and made them deep and strange and luminous. It was as if long-sunken witchlights floated slowly up through midnight pools of darkness.

Orastes cast a furtive glance at his companions, who stood staring in morbid fascination at their strange guest. Their iron nerves had withstood an ordeal that might have driven weaker men mad. He knew it was with no weaklings that he conspired, but men whose courage was as profound as their lawless ambitions and capacity for evil. He turned his attention to the figure in the ebon-black chair. And this one spoke at last.

'I remember,' he said in a strong, resonant voice, speaking Nemedian with a curious, archaic accent. 'I am Xaltotun, who was high priest of Set in Python, which was in Acheron. The Heart of Ahriman – I dreamed I had found it again – where is it?'

Orastes placed it in his hand, and he drew breath deeply as he gazed into the depths of the terrible jewel burning in his grasp.

'They stole it from me, long ago,' he said. 'The red heart of the night it is, strong to save or to damn. It came from afar, and from long ago. While I held it, none could stand before me. But it was stolen from me, and Acheron fell, and I fled an exile into dark Stygia. Much I remember, but much I have forgotten. I have been in a far land, across misty voids and gulfs and unlit oceans. What is the year?'

Orastes answered him. 'It is the waning of the Year of the Lion, three thousand years after the fall of Acheron.'

'Three thousand years!' murmured the other. 'So long? Who are you?'

'I am Orastes, once a priest of Mitra. This man is Amalric, baron of Tor, in Nemedia; this other is Tarascus, younger brother of the king of Nemedia; and this tall man is Valerius, rightful heir of the throne of Aquilonia.'

'Why have you given me life?' demanded Xaltotun. 'What do you require of me?'

The man was now fully alive and awake, his keen eyes reflecting the working of an unclouded brain. There was no hesitation or uncertainty in his manner. He came directly to the point, as one who knows that no man gives something for nothing. Orastes met him with equal candor.

'We have opened the doors of hell this night to free your soul and return it to your body because we need your aid. We wish to place Tarascus on the throne of Nemedia, and to win for Valerius the crown of Aquilonia. With your necromancy you can aid us.'

Xaltotun's mind was devious and full of unexpected slants.

'You must be deep in the arts yourself, Orastes, to have been able to restore my life. How is it that a priest of Mitra knows of the Heart of Ahriman, and the incantations of Skelos?'

'I am no longer a priest of Mitra,' answered Orastes. 'I was cast forth from my order because of my delving in black magic. But for Amalric there I might have been burned as a magician.

'But that left me free to pursue my studies. I journeyed in Zamora, in Vendhya, in Stygia, and among the haunted jungles of Khitai. I read the iron-bound books of Skelos, and talked with unseen creatures in deep wells, and faceless shapes in black reeking jungles. I obtained a glimpse of your sarcophagus in the demon-haunted crypts below the black giant-walled temple of Set in the hinterlands of Stygia, and I learned of the arts that would bring back life to your shriveled corpse. From moldering manuscripts I learned of the Heart of Ahriman. Then for a year I sought its hiding-place, and at last I found it.'

'Then why trouble to bring me back to life?' demanded Xaltotun, with his piercing gaze fixed on the priest. 'Why did you not employ the Heart to further your own power?'

'Because no man today knows the secrets of the Heart,' answered Orastes. 'Not even in legends live the arts by which to loose its full powers. I knew it could restore life; of its deeper secrets I am ignorant. I merely used it to bring you back to life. It is the use of your knowledge we seek. As for the Heart, you alone know its awful secrets.'

Xaltotun shook his head, staring broodingly into the flaming depths.

'My necromantic knowledge is greater than the sum of all the knowledge of other men,' he said; 'yet I do not know the full power of the jewel. I did not invoke it in the old days; I guarded it lest it be used against me. At last it was stolen, and in the hands of a feathered shaman of the barbarians it defeated all my mighty sorcery. Then it vanished, and I was poisoned by the jealous priests of Stygia before I could learn where it was hidden.'

'It was hidden in a cavern below the temple of Mitra, in Tarantia,' said Orastes. 'By devious ways I discovered this, after I had located your remains in Set's subterranean temple in Stygia.

'Zamorian thieves, partly protected by spells I learned from sources better left unmentioned, stole your mummy-case from under the very talons of those which guarded it in the dark, and by camel-caravan and galley and ox-wagon it came at last to this city.

'Those same thieves – or rather those of them who still lived after their frightful quest – stole the Heart of Ahriman from its haunted cavern below the temple of Mitra, and all the skill of men and the spells of sorcerers nearly failed. One man of them lived long enough to reach me and give the jewel into my hands, before he died slavering and gibbering of what he had seen in that accursed crypt. The thieves of Zamora are the most faithful of men to their trust. Even with my conjurements, none but they could have stolen the Heart from where it has lain in demon-guarded darkness since the fall of Acheron, three thousand years ago.'

Xaltotun lifted his lion-like head and stared far off into space, as if plumbing the lost centuries.

'Three thousand years!' he muttered. 'Set! Tell me what has chanced in the world.'

'The barbarians who overthrew Acheron set up new kingdoms,' quoted Orastes. 'Where the empire had stretched now rose realms called Aquilonia, and Nemedia, and Argos, from the tribes that founded them. The older kingdoms of Ophir, Corinthia and western Koth, which had been subject to the kings of Acheron, regained their independence with the fall of the empire.'

'And what of the people of Acheron?' demanded Xaltotun. 'When I fled into Stygia, Python was in ruins, and all the great, purple-towered cities of Acheron fouled with blood and trampled by the sandals of the barbarians.'

'In the hills small groups of folk still boast descent from Acheron,' answered Orastes. 'For the rest, the tide of my barbarian ancestors rolled over them and wiped them out. They – my ancestors – had suffered much from the kings of Acheron.'

A grim and terrible smile curled the Pythonian's lips.

'Aye! Many a barbarian, both man and woman, died screaming on the altar under this hand. I have seen their heads piled to make a pyramid in the great square in Python when the kings returned from the west with their spoils and naked captives.'

'Aye. And when the day of reckoning came, the sword was not spared. So Acheron ceased to be, and purple-towered Python became a memory of forgotten days. But the younger kingdoms rose on the imperial ruins and waxed great. And now we have brought you back to aid us to rule these kingdoms, which, if less strange and wonderful than Acheron of old, are yet rich and powerful, well worth fighting for. Look!' Orastes unrolled before the stranger a map drawn cunningly on vellum.

Xaltotun regarded it, and then shook his head, baffled.

'The very outlines of the land are changed. It is like some familiar thing seen in a dream, fantastically distorted.'

'Howbeit,' answered Orastes, tracing with his forefinger, 'here is Belverus, the capital of Nemedia, in which we now are. Here run the boundaries of the land of Nemedia. To the south and southeast are Ophir and Corinthia, to the east Brythunia, to the west Aquilonia.'

'It is the map of a world I do not know,' said Xaltotun softly, but Orastes did not miss the lurid fire of hate that flickered in his dark eyes.

'It is a map you shall help us change,' answered Orastes. 'It is our desire first to set Tarascus on the throne of Nemedia. We wish to accomplish this without strife, and in such a way that no suspicion will rest on Tarascus. We do not wish the land to be torn by civil wars, but to reserve all our power for the conquest of Aquilonia.

'Should King Nimed and his sons die naturally, in a plague for instance, Tarascus would mount the throne as the next heir, peacefully and unopposed.'

Xaltotun nodded, without replying, and Orastes continued.

'The other task will be more difficult. We cannot set Valerius on the Aquilonian throne without a war, and that kingdom is a formidable foe. Its people are a hardy, war-like race, toughened by continual wars with the Picts, Zingarians and Cimmerians. For five hundred years Aquilonia and Nemedia have intermittently waged war, and the ultimate advantage has always lain with the Aquilonians.

'Their present king is the most renowned warrior among the western nations. He is an outlander, an adventurer who seized the crown by force during a time of civil strife, strangling King Namedides with his own hands, upon the very throne. His name is Conan, and no man can stand before him in battle.

'Valerius is now the rightful heir of the throne. He had been driven into exile by his royal kinsman, Namedides, and has been away from his native realm for years, but he is of the blood of the old dynasty, and many of the barons would secretly hail the overthrow of Conan, who is a nobody without royal or even noble blood. But the common people are loyal to him, and the nobility of the outlying provinces. Yet if his forces were overthrown in the battle that must first take place, and Conan himself slain, I think it would not be difficult to put Valerius on the throne. Indeed, with Conan slain, the only center of the government would be gone. He is not part of a dynasty, but only a lone adventurer.'

'I wish that I might see this king,' mused Xaltotun, glancing toward a silvery mirror which formed one of the panels of the wall. This mirror cast no reflection, but Xaltotun's expression showed that he understood its purpose, and Orastes nodded with the pride a good craftsman takes in the recognition of his accomplishments by a master of his craft.

'I will try to show him to you,' he said. And seating himself before the mirror, he gazed hypnotically into its depths, where presently a dim shadow began to take shape.

It was uncanny, but those watching knew it was no more than the reflected image of Orastes' thought, embodied in that mirror as a wizard's thoughts are embodied in a magic crystal. It floated hazily, then leaped into startling clarity – a tall man, mightily shouldered and deep of chest, with a massive corded neck and heavily muscled limbs. He was clad in silk and velvet, with the royal lions of Aquilonia worked in gold upon his rich jupon, and the crown of Aquilonia shone on his square-cut black mane; but the great sword at his side seemed more natural to him than the regal accouterments. His brow was low and broad, his eyes a volcanic blue that smoldered as if with some inner fire. His dark, scarred, almost sinister face was that of a fighting-man, and his velvet garments could not conceal the hard, dangerous lines of his limbs.

'That man is no Hyborian!' exclaimed Xaltotun.

'No; he is a Cimmerian, one of those wild tribesmen who dwell in the gray hills of the north.'

'I fought his ancestors of old,' muttered Xaltotun. 'Not even the kings of Acheron could conquer them.'

'They still remain a terror to the nations of the south,' answered Orastes. 'He is a true son of that savage race, and has proved himself, thus far, unconquerable.'

Xaltotun did not reply; he sat staring down at the pool of living fire that shimmered in his hand. Outside, the hound howled again, long and shudderingly.

2 A Black Wind Blows

The year of the dragon had birth in war and pestilence and unrest. The black plague stalked through the streets of Belverus, striking down the merchant in his stall, the serf in his kennel, the knight at his banquet board. Before it the arts of the leeches were helpless. Men said it had been sent from hell as punishment for the sins of pride and lust. It was swift and deadly as the stroke of an adder. The victim's body turned purple and then black, and within a few minutes he sank down dying, and the stench of his own putrefaction was in his nostrils even before death wrenched his soul from his rotting body. A hot, roaring wind blew incessantly from the south, and the crops withered in the fields, the cattle sank and died in their tracks.

Men cried out on Mitra, and muttered against the king; for somehow, throughout the kingdom, the word was whispered that the king was secretly addicted to loathsome practises and foul debauches in the seclusion of his nighted palace. And then in that palace death stalked grinning on feet about which swirled the monstrous vapors of the plague. In one night the king died with his three sons, and the drums that thundered their dirge drowned the grim and ominous bells that rang from the carts that lumbered through the streets gathering up the rotting dead.

That night, just before dawn, the hot wind that had blown for weeks ceased to rustle evilly through the silken window curtains. Out of the north rose a great wind that roared among the towers, and there was cataclysmic thunder, and blinding sheets of lightning, and driving rain. But the dawn shone clean and green and clear; the scorched ground veiled itself in grass, the thirsty crops sprang up anew, and the plague was gone – its miasma swept clean out of the land by the mighty wind.

Men said the gods were satisfied because the evil king and his spawn were slain, and when his young brother Tarascus was crowned in the great coronation hall, the populace cheered until the towers rocked, acclaiming the monarch on whom the gods smiled.

Such a wave of enthusiasm and rejoicing as swept the land is frequently the signal for a war of conquest. So no one was surprised when it was announced that King Tarascus had declared the truce made by the late king with their western neighbors void, and was gathering his hosts to invade Aquilonia. His reason was candid; his motives, loudly proclaimed, gilded his actions with something of the glamor of a crusade. He espoused the cause of Valerius, 'rightful heir to the throne'; he came, he proclaimed, not as an enemy of Aquilonia, but as a friend, to free the people from the tyranny of a usurper and a foreigner.

If there were cynical smiles in certain quarters, and whispers concerning the king's good friend Amalric, whose vast personal wealth seemed to be flowing into the rather depleted royal treasury, they were unheeded in the general wave of fervor and zeal of Tarascus' popularity. If any shrewd individuals suspected that Amalric was the real ruler of Nemedia, behind the scenes, they were careful not to voice such heresy. And the war went forward with enthusiasm.

The king and his allies moved westward at the head of fifty thousand men – knights in shining armor with their pennons streaming above their helmets, pikemen in steel caps and brigandines, crossbowmen in leather jerkins. They crossed the border, took a frontier castle and burned three mountain villages, and then, in the valley of the Valkia, ten miles west of the boundary line, they met the hosts of Conan, king of Aquilonia – forty-five thousand knights, archers and men-at-arms, the flower of Aquilonian strength and chivalry. Only the knights of Poitain, under Prospero, had not yet arrived, for they had far to ride up from the southwestern corner of the kingdom. Tarascus had struck without warning. His invasion had come on the heels of his proclamation, without formal declaration of war.

The two hosts confronted each other across a wide, shallow valley, with rugged cliffs, and a shallow stream winding through masses of reeds and willows down the middle of the vale. The camp-followers of both hosts came down to this stream for water, and shouted insults and hurled stones across at one another. The last glints of the sun shone on the golden banner of Nemedia with the scarlet dragon, unfurled in the breeze above the pavilion of King Tarascus on an eminence near the eastern cliffs. But the shadow of the western cliffs fell like a vast purple pall across the tents and the army of Aquilonia, and upon the black banner with its golden lion that floated above King Conan's pavilion.

All night the fires flared the length of the valley, and the wind brought the call of trumpets, the clangor of arms, and the sharp challenges of the sentries who paced their horses along either edge of the willow-grown stream.

It was in the darkness before dawn that King Conan stirred on his couch, which was no more than a pile of silks and furs thrown on a dais, and awakened. He started up, crying out sharply and clutching at his sword. Pallantides, his commander, rushing in at the cry, saw his king sitting upright, his hand on his hilt, and perspiration dripping from his strangely pale face.

'Your Majesty!' exclaimed Pallantides. 'Is aught amiss?'

'What of the camp?' demanded Conan. 'Are the guards out?'

'Five hundred horsemen patrol the stream, Your Majesty,' answered the general. 'The Nemedians have not offered to move against us in the night. They wait for dawn, even as we.'

'By Crom,' muttered Conan. 'I awoke with a feeling that doom was creeping on me in the night.'

He stared up at the great golden lamp which shed a soft glow over the velvet hangings and carpets of the great tent. They were alone; not even a slave or a page slept on the carpeted floor; but Conan's eyes blazed as they were wont to blaze in the teeth of great peril, and the sword quivered in his hand. Pallantides watched him uneasily. Conan seemed to be listening.

'Listen!' hissed the king. 'Did you hear it? A furtive step!'

'Seven knights guard your tent, Your Majesty,' said Pallantides. 'None could approach it unchallenged.'

'Not outside,' growled Conan. 'It seemed to sound inside the tent.'

Pallantides cast a swift, startled look around. The velvet hangings merged with shadows in the corners, but if there had been anyone in the pavilion besides themselves, the general would have seen him. Again he shook his head.

'There is no one here, sire. You sleep in the midst of your host.'

'I have seen death strike a king in the midst of thousands,' muttered Conan. 'Something that walks on invisible feet and is not seen—'

'Perhaps you were dreaming, Your Majesty,' said Pallantides, somewhat perturbed.

'So I was,' grunted Conan. 'A devilish dream it was, too. I trod again all the long, weary roads I traveled on my way to the kingship.'

He fell silent, and Pallantides stared at him unspeaking. The king was an enigma to the general, as to most of his civilized subjects. Pallantides knew that Conan had walked many strange roads in his wild, eventful life, and had been many things before a twist of Fate set him on the throne of Aquilonia.

'I saw again the battlefield whereon I was born,' said Conan, resting his chin moodily on a massive fist. 'I saw myself in a pantherskin loin-clout, throwing my spear at the mountain beasts. I was a mercenary swordsman again, a hetman of the *kozaki* who dwell along the Zaporoska River, a corsair looting the coasts of Kush, a pirate of the Barachan Isles, a chief of the Himelian hillmen. All these things I've been, and of all these things I dreamed; all the shapes that have been I passed like an endless procession, and their feet beat out a dirge in the sounding dust.

'But throughout my dreams moved strange, veiled figures and ghostly shadows, and a faraway voice mocked me. And toward the last I seemed to see myself lying on this dais in my tent, and a shape bent over me, robed and hooded. I lay unable to move, and then the hood fell away and a moldering skull grinned down at me. Then it was that I awoke.'

'This is an evil dream, Your Majesty,' said Pallantides, suppressing a shudder. 'But no more.'

Conan shook his head, more in doubt than in denial. He came of a barbaric race, and the superstitions and instincts of his heritage lurked close beneath the surface of his consciousness.

'I've dreamed many evil dreams,' he said, 'and most of them were meaningless. But by Crom, this was not like most dreams! I wish this battle were fought and won, for I've had a grisly premonition ever since King Nimed died in the black plague. Why did it cease when he died?'

'Men say he sinned—'

'Men are fools, as always,' grunted Conan. 'If the plague struck all who sinned, then by Crom there wouldn't be enough left to count the living! Why should the gods – who the priests tell me are just – slay five hundred peasants and merchants and nobles before they slew the king, if the whole pestilence were aimed at him? Were the gods smiting blindly, like swordsmen in a fog? By Mitra, if I aimed my strokes no straighter, Aquilonia would have had a new king long ago.

'No! The black plague's no common pestilence. It lurks in Stygian tombs, and is called forth into being only by wizards. I was a swordsman in Prince Almuric's army that invaded Stygia, and of his thirty thousand, fifteen thousand perished by Stygian arrows, and the rest by the black plague that rolled on us like a wind out of the south. I was the only man who lived.'

'Yet only five hundred died in Nemedia,' argued Pallantides.

'Whoever called it into being knew how to cut it short at will,' answered Conan. 'So I know there was something planned and diabolical about it. Someone called it forth, someone banished it when the work was completed – when Tarascus was safe on the throne and being hailed as the deliverer of the people from the wrath of the gods. By Crom, I sense a black, subtle brain behind all this. What of this stranger who men say gives counsel to Tarascus?'

'He wears a veil,' answered Pallantides; 'they say he is a foreigner; a stranger from Stygia.'

'A stranger from Stygia!' repeated Conan scowling. 'A stranger from hell, more like! – Ha! What is that?'

'The trumpets of the Nemedians!' exclaimed Pallantides. 'And hark, how our own blare upon their heels! Dawn is breaking, and the captains are marshaling the hosts for the onset! Mitra be with them, for many will not see the sun go down behind the crags.'

'Send my squires to me!' exclaimed Conan, rising with alacrity and casting off his velvet night-garment; he seemed to have forgotten his forebodings at the prospect of action. 'Go to the captains and see that all is in readiness. I will be with you as soon as I don my armor.'

Many of Conan's ways were inexplicable to the civilized people he ruled, and one of them was his insistence on sleeping alone in his chamber or tent. Pallantides hastened from the pavilion, clanking in the armor he had donned at midnight after a few hours' sleep. He cast a swift glance over the camp, which was beginning to swarm with activity, mail clinking and men moving about dimly in the uncertain light, among the long lines of tents. Stars still glimmered palely in the western sky, but long pink streamers stretched along the eastern horizon, and against them the dragon banner of Nemedia flung out its billowing silken folds.

Pallantides turned toward a smaller tent near by, where slept the royal squires. These were tumbling out already, roused by the trumpets. And as Pallantides called to them to hasten, he was frozen speechless by a deep fierce shout and the impact of a heavy blow inside the king's tent, followed by the heart-stopping crash of a falling body. There sounded a low laugh that turned the general's blood to ice.

Echoing the cry, Pallantides wheeled and rushed back into the pavilion. He cried out again as he saw Conan's powerful frame stretched out on the carpet. The king's great two-handed sword lay near his hand, and a shattered tent-pole seemed to show where his stroke had fallen. Pallantides' sword was out, and he glared about the tent, but nothing met his gaze. Save for the king and himself it was empty, as it had been when he left it.

'Your Majesty!' Pallantides threw himself on his knee beside the fallen giant.

Conan's eyes were open; they blazed up at him with full intelligence and recognition. His lips writhed, but no sound came forth. He seemed unable to move.

Voices sounded without. Pallantides rose swiftly and stepped to the door. The royal squires and one of the knights who guarded the tent stood there.

'We heard a sound within,' said the knight apologetically. 'Is all well with the king?'

Pallantides regarded him searchingly.

'None has entered or left the pavilion this night?'

'None save yourself, my lord,' answered the knight, and Pallantides could not doubt his honesty.

'The king stumbled and dropped his sword,' said Pallantides briefly. 'Return to your post.'

As the knight turned away, the general covertly motioned to the five royal squires, and when they had followed him in, he drew the flap closely. They turned pale at the sight of the king stretched upon the carpet, but Pallantides' quick gesture checked their exclamations.

The general bent over him again, and again Conan made an effort to speak. The veins in his temples and the cords in his neck swelled with his efforts, and he lifted his head clear of the ground. Voice came at last, mumbling and half intelligible.

'*The thing – the thing in the corner!*'

Pallantides lifted his head and looked fearfully about him. He saw the pale faces of the squires in the lamplight, the velvet shadows that lurked along the walls of the pavilion. That was all.

'There is nothing here, Your Majesty,' he said.

'It was there, in the corner,' muttered the king, tossing his lion-maned head from side to side in his efforts to rise. 'A man – at least he looked like a man – wrapped in rags like a mummy's bandages, with a moldering cloak drawn about him, and a hood. All I could see was his eyes, as he crouched there in the shadows. I thought he was a shadow himself, until I saw his eyes. They were like black jewels.

'I made at him and swung my sword, but I missed him clean – how, Crom knows – and splintered that pole instead. He caught my wrist as I staggered off balance, and his fingers burned like hot iron. All the strength went out of me, and the floor rose and struck me like a club. Then he was gone, and I was down, and – curse him! – I can't move! I'm paralysed!'

Pallantides lifted the giant's hand, and his flesh crawled. On the king's wrist showed the blue marks of long, lean fingers. What hand could grip so hard as to leave its print on that thick wrist? Pallantides remembered that low laugh he had heard as he rushed into the tent, and cold perspiration beaded his skin. It had not been Conan who laughed.

'This is a thing diabolical!' whispered a trembling squire. 'Men say the children of darkness war for Tarascus!'

'Be silent!' ordered Pallantides sternly.

Outside, the dawn was dimming the stars. A light wind sprang up from the peaks, and brought the fanfare of a thousand trumpets. At the sound a convulsive shudder ran through the king's mighty form. Again the veins in his temples knotted as he strove to break the invisible shackles which crushed him down.

'Put my harness on me and tie me into my saddle,' he whispered. 'I'll lead the charge yet!'

Pallantides shook his head, and a squire plucked his skirt.

'My lord, we are lost if the host learns the king has been smitten! Only he could have led us to victory this day.'

'Help me lift him on the dais,' answered the general.

They obeyed, and laid the helpless giant on the furs, and spread a silken cloak over him. Pallantides turned to the five squires and searched their pale faces long before he spoke.

'Our lips must be sealed for ever as to what happens in this tent,' he said at last. 'The kingdom of Aquilonia depends upon it. One of you go and fetch me the officer Valannus, who is a captain of the Pellian spearmen.'

The squire indicated bowed and hastened from the tent, and Pallantides stood staring down at the stricken king, while outside trumpets blared, drums thundered, and the roar of the multitudes rose in the growing dawn. Presently the squire returned with the officer Pallantides had named – a tall man, broad and powerful, built much like the king. Like him, also, he had thick black hair. But his eyes were gray and he did not resemble Conan in his features.

'The king is stricken by a strange malady,' said Pallantides briefly. 'A great honor is yours; you are to wear his armor and ride at the head of the host today. None must know that it is not the king who rides.'

'It is an honor for which a man might gladly give up his life,' stammered the captain, overcome by the suggestion. 'Mitra grant that I do not fail of this mighty trust!'

And while the fallen king stared with burning eyes that reflected the bitter rage and humiliation that ate his heart, the squires stripped Valannus of mail shirt, burganet and leg-pieces, and clad him in Conan's armor of black plate-mail, with the vizored salade, and the dark plumes nodding over the wivern crest. Over all they put the silken surcoat with the royal lion worked in gold upon the breast, and they girt him with a broad gold-buckled belt which supported a jewel-hilted broadsword in a cloth-of-gold scabbard. While they worked, trumpets clamored outside, arms clanged, and across the river rose a deep-throated roar as squadron after squadron swung into place.

Full-armed, Valannus dropped to his knee and bent his plumes before the figure that lay on the dais.

'Lord king, Mitra grant that I do not dishonor the harness I wear this day!'

'Bring me Tarascus' head and I'll make you a baron!' In the stress of his anguish Conan's veneer of civilization had fallen from him. His eyes flamed, he ground his teeth in fury and blood-lust, as barbaric as any tribesmen in the Cimmerian hills.

3 The Cliffs Reel

The Aquilonian host was drawn up, long serried lines of pikemen and horsemen in gleaming steel, when a giant figure in black armor emerged from the royal pavilion, and as he swung up into the saddle of the black stallion held by four squires, a roar that shook the mountains went up from the host. They shook their blades and thundered forth their acclaim of their warrior king – knights in gold-chased armor, pikemen in mail coats and basinets, archers in their leather jerkins, with their longbows in their left hand.

The host on the opposite side of the valley was in motion, trotting down the long gentle slope toward the river; their steel shone through the mists of morning that swirled about their horses' feet.

The Aquilonian host moved leisurely to meet them. The measured tramp of the armored horses made the ground tremble. Banners flung out long silken folds in the morning wind; lances swayed like a bristling forest, dipped and sank, their pennons fluttering about them.

Ten men-at-arms, grim, taciturn veterans who could hold their tongues, guarded the royal pavilion. One squire stood in the tent, peering out through a slit in the doorway. But for the handful in the secret, no one else in the vast host knew that it was not Conan who rode on the great stallion at the head of the army.

The Aquilonian host had assumed the customary formation: the strongest part was the center, composed entirely of heavily armed knights; the wings were made up of smaller bodies of horsemen, mounted men-at-arms, mostly, supported by pikemen and archers. The latter were Bossonians from the western marches, strongly built men of medium stature, in leathern jackets and iron head-pieces.

The Nemedian army came on in similar formation, and the two hosts moved toward the river, the wings in advance of the centers. In the center of the Aquilonian host the great lion banner streamed its billowing black folds over the steel-clad figure on the black stallion.

But on his dais in the royal pavilion Conan groaned in anguish of spirit, and cursed with strange heathen oaths.

'The hosts move together,' quoth the squire, watching from the door. 'Hear the trumpets peal! Ha! The rising sun strikes fire from lance-heads and helmets until I am dazzled. It turns the river crimson – aye, it will be truly crimson before this day is done!

'The foe have reached the river. Now arrows fly between the hosts like stinging clouds that hide the sun. Ha! Well loosed, bowmen! The Bossonians have the better of it! Hark to them shout!'

Faintly in the ears of the king, above the din of trumpets and clanging steel, came the deep fierce shout of the Bossonians as they drew and loosed in perfect unison.

'Their archers seek to hold ours in play while their knights ride into the river,' said the squire. 'the banks are not steep; they slope to the water's edge. The knights come on, they crash through the willows. By Mitra, the clothyard shafts find every crevice of their harness! Horses and men go down, struggling and thrashing in the water. It is not deep, nor is the current swift, but men are drowning there, dragged under by their armor, and trampled by the frantic horses. Now the knights of Aquilonia advance. They ride into the water and engage the knights of Nemedia. The water swirls about their horses' bellies and the clang of sword against sword is deafening.'

'Crom!' burst in agony from Conan's lips. Life was coursing sluggishly back into his veins, but still he could not lift his mighty frame from the dais.

'The wings close in,' said the squire. 'Pikemen and swordsmen fight hand to hand in the stream, and behind them the bowmen ply their shafts.

'By Mitra, the Nemedian arbalesters are sorely harried, and the Bossonians arch their arrows to drop amid the rear ranks. Their center gains not a foot, and their wings are pushed back up from the stream again.'

'Crom, Ymir, and Mitra!' raged Conan. 'Gods and devils, could I but reach the fighting, if but to die at the first blow!'

Outside through the long hot day the battle stormed and thundered. The valley shook to charge and counter-charge, to the whistling of shafts, and the crash of rending shields and splintering lances. But the hosts of Aquilonia held fast. Once they were forced back from the bank, but a counter-charge, with the black banner flowing over the black stallion, regained the lost ground. And like an iron rampart they held the right bank of the stream, and at last the squire gave Conan the news that the Nemedians were falling back from the river.

'Their wings are in confusion!' he cried. 'Their knights reel back from the sword-play. But what is this? Your banner is in motion – the center sweeps into the stream! By Mitra, Valannus is leading the host across the river!'

'Fool!' groaned Conan. 'It may be a trick. He should hold his position; by dawn Prospero will be here with the Poitanian levies.'

'The knights ride into a hail of arrows!' cried the squire. 'But they do not falter! They sweep on – they have crossed! They charge up the slope! Pallantides has hurled the wings across the river to their support! It is all he can do. The lion banner dips and staggers above the mêlée.

'The knights of Nemedia make a stand. They are broken! They fall back! Their left wing is in full flight, and our pikemen cut them down as they run! I see Valannus, riding and smiting like a madman. He is carried beyond himself by the fighting-lust. Men no longer look to Pallantides. They follow Valannus, deeming him Conan as he rides with closed vizor.

'But look! There is method in his madness! He swings wide of the Nemedian front, with five thousand knights, the pick of the army. The main host of the Nemedians is in confusion – and look! Their flank is protected by the cliffs, but there is a defile left unguarded! It is like a great cleft in the wall that opens again behind the Nemedian lines. By Mitra, Valannus sees and seizes the opportunity! He has driven their wing before him, and he leads his knights toward that defile. They swing wide of the main battle; they cut through a line of spearmen, they charge into the defile!'

'An ambush!' cried Conan, striving to struggle upright.

'*No!*' shouted the squire exultantly. 'The whole Nemedian host is in full sight! They have forgotten the defile! They never expected to be pushed back that far. Oh, fool, fool, Tarascus, to make such a blunder! Ah, I see lances and pennons pouring from the farther mouth of the defile, beyond the Nemedian lines. They will smite those ranks from the rear and crumple them. *Mitra, what is this?*'

He staggered as the walls of the tent swayed drunkenly. Afar over the thunder of the fight rose a deep bellowing roar, indescribably ominous.

'The cliffs reel!' shrieked the squire. 'Ah, gods, what is this? The river foams out of its channel, and the peaks are crumbling! The ground shakes and horses and riders in armor are overthrown! The cliffs! The cliffs are falling!'

With his words there came a grinding rumble and a thunderous concussion, and the ground trembled. Over the roar of the battle sounded screams of mad terror.

'The cliffs have crumbled!' cried the livid squire. 'They have thundered down into the defile and crushed every living creature in it! I saw the lion banner wave an instant amid the dust and falling stones, and then it vanished! Ha, the Nemedians shout with triumph! Well may they shout, for the fall of the cliffs has wiped out five thousand of our bravest knights – Hark!'

To Conan's ears came a vast torrent of sound, rising and rising in frenzy: 'The king is dead! *The king is dead! Flee! Flee! The king is dead!*'

'Liars!' panted Conan. 'Dogs! Knaves! Cowards! Oh, Crom, if I could but stand – but crawl to the river with my sword in my teeth! How, boy, do they flee?'

'Aye!' sobbed the squire. 'They spur for the river; they are broken, hurled on like spume before a storm. I see Pallantides striving to stem the torrent – he is down, and the horses trample him! They rush into the river, knights, bowmen, pikemen, all mixed and mingled in one mad torrent of destruction. The Nemedians are on their heels, cutting them down like corn.'

'But they will make a stand on this side of the river!' cried the king. With an effort that brought the sweat dripping from his temples, he heaved himself up on his elbows.

'Nay!' cried the squire. 'They cannot! They are broken! Routed! Oh gods, that I should live to see this day!'

Then he remembered his duty and shouted to the men-at-arms who stood stolidly watching the flight of their comrades. 'Get a horse, swiftly, and help me lift the king upon it. We dare not bide here.'

But before they could do his bidding, the first drift of the storm was upon them. Knights and spearmen and archers fled among the tents, stumbling over ropes and baggage, and mingled with them were Nemedian riders, who smote right and left at all alien figures. Tent-ropes were cut, fire sprang up in a hundred places, and the plundering had already begun. The grim guardsmen about Conan's tent died where they stood, smiting and thrusting, and over their mangled corpses beat the hoofs of the conquerors.

But the squire had drawn the flap close, and in the confused madness of the slaughter none realized that the pavilion held an occupant. So the flight and the pursuit swept past, and roared away up the valley, and the squire looked out presently to see a cluster of men approaching the royal tent with evident purpose.

'Here comes the king of Nemedia with four companions and his squire,' quoth he. 'He will accept your surrender, my fair lord—'

'Surrender the devil's heart!' gritted the king.

He had forced himself up to a sitting posture. He swung his legs painfully off the dais, and staggered upright, reeling drunkenly. The squire ran to assist him, but Conan pushed him away.

'Give me that bow!' he gritted, indicating a longbow and quiver that hung from a tent-pole.

'But Your Majesty!' cried the squire in great perturbation. 'The battle is lost! It were the part of majesty to yield with the dignity becoming one of royal blood!'

'I have no royal blood,' ground Conan. 'I am a barbarian and the son of a blacksmith.'

Wrenching away the bow and an arrow he staggered toward the opening of the pavilion. So formidable was his appearance, naked but for short leather breeks and sleeveless shirt, open to reveal his great, hairy chest, with his huge limbs and his blue eyes blazing under his tangled black mane, that the squire shrank back, more afraid of his king than of the whole Nemedian host.

Reeling on wide-braced legs Conan drunkenly tore the door-flap open and staggered out under the canopy. The king of Nemedia and his companions had dismounted, and they halted short, staring in wonder at the apparition confronting them.

'Here I am, you jackals!' roared the Cimmerian. 'I am the king! Death to you, dog-brothers!'

He jerked the arrow to its head and loosed, and the shaft feathered itself in the breast of the knight who stood beside Tarascus. Conan hurled the bow at the king of Nemedia.

'Curse my shaky hand! Come in and take me if you dare!'

Reeling backward on unsteady legs, he fell with his shoulders against a tent-pole, and propped upright, he lifted his great sword with both hands.

'By Mitra, it *is* the king!' swore Tarascus. He cast a swift look about him, and laughed. 'That other was a jackal in his harness! In, dogs, and take his head!'

The three soldiers – men-at-arms wearing the emblem of the royal guards – rushed at the king, and one felled the squire with a blow of a mace. The other two fared less well. As the first rushed in, lifting his sword, Conan met him with a sweeping stroke that severed mail-links like cloth, and sheared the Nemedian's arm and shoulder clean from his body. His corpse, pitching backward, fell across his companion's legs. The man stumbled, and before he could recover, the great sword was through him.

Conan wrenched out his steel with a racking gasp, and staggered back against the tent-pole. His great limbs trembled, his chest heaved, and sweat poured down his face and neck. But his eyes flamed with exultant savagery and he panted: 'Why do you stand afar off, dog of Belverus? I can't reach you; come in and die!'

Tarascus hesitated, glanced at the remaining man-at-arms, and his squire, a gaunt, saturnine man in black mail, and took a step forward. He was far inferior in size and strength to the giant Cimmerian, but he was in full armor, and was famed in all the western nations as a swordsman. But his squire caught his arm.

'Nay, Your Majesty, do not throw away your life. I will summon archers to shoot this barbarian, as we shoot lions.'

Neither of them had noticed that a chariot had approached while the fight was going on, and now came to a halt before them. But Conan saw, looking over their shoulders, and a queer chill sensation crawled along his spine. There was something vaguely unnatural about the appearance of the black horses that drew the vehicle, but it was the occupant of the chariot that arrested the king's attention.

He was a tall man, superbly built, clad in a long unadorned silk robe. He wore a Shemitish headdress, and its lower folds hid his features, except for the dark, magnetic eyes. The hands that grasped the reins, pulling the rearing horses back on their haunches, were white but strong. Conan glared at the stranger, all his primitive instincts roused. He sensed an aura of menace and power that exuded from this veiled figure, a menace as definite as the windless waving of tall grass that marks the path of the serpent.

'Hail, Xaltotun!' exclaimed Tarascus. 'Here is the king of Aquilonia! He did not die in the landslide as we thought.'

'I know,' answered the other, without bothering to say how he knew. 'What is your present intention?'

'I will summon the archers to slay him,' answered the Nemedian. 'As long as he lives he will be dangerous to us.'

'Yet even a dog has uses,' answered Xaltotun. 'Take him alive.'

Conan laughed raspingly. 'Come in and try!' he challenged. 'But for my treacherous legs I'd hew you out of that chariot like a woodman hewing a tree. But you'll never take me alive, damn you!'

'He speaks the truth, I fear,' said Tarascus. 'The man is a barbarian, with the senseless ferocity of a wounded tiger. Let me summon the archers.'

'Watch me and learn wisdom,' advised Xaltotun.

His hand dipped into his robe and came out with something shining – a glistening sphere. This he threw suddenly at Conan. The Cimmerian contemptuously struck it aside with his sword – at the instant of contact there was a sharp explosion, a flare of white, blinding flame, and Conan pitched senseless to the ground.

'He is dead?' Tarascus' tone was more assertion than inquiry.

'No. He is but senseless. He will recover his senses in a few hours. Bid your men bind his arms and legs and lift him into my chariot.'

With a gesture Tarascus did so, and they heaved the senseless king into the chariot, grunting with their burden. Xaltotun threw a velvet cloak over his body, completely covering him from any who might peer in. He gathered the reins in his hands.

'I'm for Belverus,' he said. 'Tell Amalric that I will be with him if he needs me. But with Conan out of the way, and his army broken, lance and sword should suffice for the rest of the conquest. Prospero cannot be bringing more than ten thousand men to the field, and will doubtless fall back to Tarantia when he hears the news of the battle. Say nothing to Amalric or Valerius or anyone about our capture. Let them think Conan died in the fall of the cliffs.'

He looked at the man-at-arms for a long space, until the guardsman moved restlessly, nervous under the scrutiny.

'What is that about your waist?' Xaltotun demanded.

'Why, my girdle, may it please you, my lord!' stuttered the amazed guardsman.

'You lie!' Xaltotun's laugh was merciless as a sword-edge. 'It is a poisonous serpent! What a fool you are, to wear a reptile about your waist!'

With distended eyes the man looked down; and to his utter horror he saw the buckle of his girdle rear up at him. It was a snake's head! He saw the evil eyes and the dripping fangs, heard the hiss and felt the loathsome contact of the thing about his body. He screamed hideously and struck at it with his naked hand, felt its fangs flesh themselves in that hand – and then he stiffened and fell heavily. Tarascus looked down at him without expression. He saw only the leathern girdle and the buckle, the pointed tongue of which was stuck in the guardsman's palm. Xaltotun turned his hypnotic gaze on Tarascus' squire, and the man turned ashen and began to tremble, but the king interposed: 'Nay, we can trust him.'

The sorcerer tautened the reins and swung the horses around.

'See that this piece of work remains secret. If I am needed, let Altaro, Orastes' servant, summon me as I have taught him. I will be in your palace at Belverus.'

Tarascus lifted his hand in salutation, but his expression was not pleasant to see as he looked after the departing mesmerist.

'Why should he spare the Cimmerian?' whispered the frightened squire.

'That I am wondering myself,' grunted Tarascus.

Behind the rumbling chariot the dull roar of battle and pursuit faded in the distance; the setting sun rimmed the cliffs with scarlet flame, and the chariot moved into the vast blue shadows floating up out of the east.

4 'From What Hell Have You Crawled?'

Of that long ride in the chariot of Xaltotun, Conan knew nothing. He lay like a dead man while the bronze wheels clashed over the stones of mountain roads and swished through the deep grass of fertile valleys, and finally dropping down from the rugged heights, rumbled rhythmically along the broad white road that winds through the rich meadowlands to the walls of Belverus.

Just before dawn some faint reviving of life touched him. He heard a mumble of voices, the groan of ponderous hinges. Through a slit in the cloak that covered him he saw, faintly in the lurid glare of torches, the great black arch of a gateway, and the bearded faces of men-at-arms, the torches striking fire from their spearheads and helmets.

'How went the battle, my fair lord?' spoke an eager voice, in the Nemedian tongue.

'Well indeed,' was the curt reply. 'The king of Aquilonia lies slain and his host is broken.'

A babble of excited voices rose, drowned the next instant by the whirling wheels of the chariot on the flags. Sparks flashed from under the revolving rims as Xaltotun lashed his steeds through the arch. But Conan heard one of the guardsmen mutter: 'From beyond the border to Belverus between sunset and dawn! And the horses scarcely sweating! By Mitra, they—' Then silence drank the voices, and there was only the clatter of hoofs and wheels along the shadowy street.

What he had heard registered itself on Conan's brain but suggested nothing to him. He was like a mindless automaton that hears and sees, but does not understand. Sights and sounds flowed meaninglessly about him. He lapsed again into a deep lethargy, and was only dimly aware when the chariot halted in a deep, high-walled court, and he was lifted from it by many hands and borne up a winding stone stair, and down a long dim corridor. Whispers, stealthy footsteps, unrelated sounds surged or rustled about him, irrelevant and far away.

Yet his ultimate awakening was abrupt and crystal-clear. He possessed full knowledge of the battle in the mountains and its sequences, and he had a good idea of where he was.

He lay on a velvet couch, clad as he was the day before, but with his limbs loaded with chains not even he could break. The room in which he lay was furnished with somber magnificence, the walls covered with black velvet tapestries, the floor with heavy purple carpets. There was no sign of door or window, and one curiously carven gold lamp, swinging from the fretted ceiling, shed a lurid light over all.

In that light the figure seated in a silver, throne-like chair before him seemed unreal and fantastic, with an illusiveness of outline that was heightened by a filmy silken robe. But the features were distinct – unnaturally so in that uncertain light. It was almost as if a weird nimbus played about the man's head, casting the bearded face into bold relief, so that it was the only definite and distinct reality in that mystic, ghostly chamber.

It was a magnificent face, with strongly chiseled features of classical beauty. There was, indeed, something disquieting about the calm tranquility of its aspect, a suggestion of more than human knowledge, of a profound certitude beyond human assurance. Also an uneasy sensation of familiarity twitched at the back of Conan's consciousness. He had never seen this man's face before, he well knew; yet those features reminded him of something or someone. It was like encountering in the flesh some dream-image that had haunted one in nightmares.

'Who are you?' demanded the king belligerently, struggling to a sitting position in spite of his chains.

'Men call me Xaltotun,' was the reply, in a strong, golden voice.

'What place is this?' the Cimmerian next demanded.

'A chamber in the palace of King Tarascus, in Belverus.'

Conan was not surprised. Belverus, the capital, was at the same time the largest Nemedian city so near the border.

'And where's Tarascus?'

'With the army.'

'Well,' growled Conan, 'if you mean to murder me, why don't you do it and get it over with?'

'I did not save you from the king's archers to murder you in Belverus,' answered Xaltotun.

'What the devil did you do to me?' demanded Conan.

'I blasted your consciousness,' answered Xaltotun. 'How, you would not understand. Call it black magic, if you will.'

Conan had already reached that conclusion, and was mulling over something else.

'I think I understand why you spared my life,' he rumbled. 'Amalric wants to keep me as a check on Valerius, in case the impossible happens and he becomes king of Aquilonia. It's well known that the baron of Tor is behind this move to seat Valerius on my throne. And if I know Amalric, he doesn't intend that Valerius shall be anything more than a figurehead, as Tarascus is now.'

'Amalric knows nothing of your capture,' answered Xaltotun. 'Neither does Valerius. Both think you died at Valkia.'

Conan's eyes narrowed as he stared at the man in silence.

'I sensed a brain behind all this,' he muttered, 'but I thought it was Amalric's. Are Amalric, Tarascus and Valerius all but puppets dancing on your string? Who are you?'

'What does it matter? If I told you, you would not believe me. What if I told you I might set you back on the throne of Aquilonia?'

Conan's eyes burned on him like a wolf.

'What's your price?'

'Obedience to me.'

'Go to hell with your offer!' snarled Conan. 'I'm no figurehead. I won my crown with my sword. Besides, it's beyond your power to buy and sell the throne of Aquilonia at your will. The kingdom's not conquered; one battle doesn't decide a war.'

'You war against more than swords,' answered Xaltotun. 'Was it a mortal's sword that felled you in your tent before the fight? Nay, it was a child of the dark, a waif of outer space, whose fingers were afire with the frozen coldness of the black gulfs, which froze the blood in your veins and the marrow of your thews. Coldness so cold it burned your flesh like white-hot iron!

'Was it chance that led the man who wore your harness to lead his knights into the defile? – chance that brought the cliffs crashing down upon them?'

Conan glared at him unspeaking, feeling a chill along his spine. Wizards and sorcerers abounded in his barbaric mythology, and any fool could tell that this was no common man. Conan sensed an inexplicable something about him that set him apart – an alien aura of Time and Space, a sense of tremendous and sinister antiquity. But his stubborn spirit refused to flinch.

'The fall of the cliffs was chance,' he muttered truculently. 'The charge into the defile was what any man would have done.'

'Not so. You would not have led a charge into it. You would have suspected a trap. You would never have crossed the river in the first place, until you were sure the Nemedian rout was real. Hypnotic suggestions would not have invaded your mind, even in the madness of battle, to make you mad, and rush blindly into the trap laid for you, as it did the lesser man who masqueraded as you.'

'Then if this was all planned,' Conan grunted skeptically, 'all a plot to trap my host, why did not the "child of darkness" kill me in my tent?'

'Because I wished to take you alive. It took no wizardry to predict that Pallantides would send another man out in your harness. I wanted you alive and unhurt. You may fit into my scheme of things. There is a vital power about you greater than the craft and cunning of my allies. You are a bad enemy, but might make a fine vassal.'

Conan spat savagely at the word, and Xaltotun, ignoring his fury, took a crystal globe from a near-by table and placed it before him. He did not support it in any way, nor place it on anything, but it hung motionless in midair, as solidly as if it rested on an iron pedestal. Conan snorted at this bit of necromancy, but he was nevertheless impressed.

'Would you know of what goes on in Aquilonia?' he asked.

Conan did not reply, but the sudden rigidity of his form betrayed his interest.

Xaltotun stared into the cloudy depths, and spoke: 'It is now the evening of the day after the battle of Valkia. Last night the main body of the army camped by Valkia, while squadrons of knights harried the fleeing Aquilonians. At dawn the host broke camp and pushed westward through the mountains. Prospero, with ten thousand Poitanians, was miles from the battlefield when he met the fleeing survivors in the early dawn. He had pushed on all night, hoping to reach the field before the battle joined. Unable to rally the remnants of the broken host, he fell back toward Tarantia. Riding hard, replacing his wearied horses with steeds seized from the countryside, he approaches Tarantia.

'I see his weary knights, their armor gray with dust, their pennons drooping as they push their tired horses through the plain. I see, also, the streets of Tarantia. The city is in turmoil. Somehow word has reached the people of the defeat and the death of King Conan. The mob is mad with fear, crying out that the king is dead, and there is none to lead them against the Nemedians. Giant shadows rush on Aquilonia from the east, and the sky is black with vultures.'

Conan cursed deeply.

'What are these but words? The raggedest beggar in the street might prophesy as much. If you say you saw all that in the glass ball, then you're a liar as well as a knave, of which last there's no doubt! Prospero will hold Tarantia, and the barons will rally to him. Count Trocero of Poitain commands the kingdom in my absence, and he'll drive these Nemedian dogs howling back to their kennels. What are fifty thousand Nemedians? Aquilonia will swallow them up. They'll never see Belverus again. It's not Aquilonia which was conquered at Valkia; it was only Conan.'

'Aquilonia is doomed,' answered Xaltotun, unmoved. 'Lance and ax and torch shall conquer her; or if they fail, powers from the dark of ages shall march against her. As the cliffs fell at Valkia, so shall walled cities and mountains fall, if the need arise, and rivers roar from their channels to drown whole provinces.'

'Better if steel and bowstring prevail without further aid from the *arts*, for the constant use of mighty spells sometimes sets forces in motion that might rock the universe.'

'From what hell have you crawled, you nighted dog?' muttered Conan, staring at the man. The Cimmerian involuntarily shivered; he sensed something incredibly ancient, incredibly evil.

Xaltotun lifted his head, as if listening to whispers across the void. He seemed to have forgotten his prisoner. Then he shook his head impatiently, and glanced impersonally at Conan.

'What? Why, if I told you, you would not believe me. But I am wearied of conversation with you; it is less fatiguing to destroy a walled city than it is to frame my thoughts in words a brainless barbarian can understand.'

'If my hands were free,' opined Conan, 'I'd soon make a brainless corpse out of you.'

'I do not doubt it, if I were fool enough to give you the opportunity,' answered Xaltotun, clapping his hands.

His manner had changed; there was impatience in his tone, and a certain nervousness in his manner, though Conan did not think this attitude was in any way connected with himself.

'Consider what I have told you, barbarian,' said Xaltotun. 'You will have plenty of leisure. I have not yet decided what I shall do with you. It depends on circumstances yet unborn. But let this be impressed upon you: that if I decide to use you in my game, it will be better to submit without resistance than to suffer my wrath.'

Conan spat a curse at him, just as hangings that masked a door swung apart and four giant negroes entered. Each was clad only in a silken breech-clout supported by a girdle, from which hung a great key.

Xaltotun gestured impatiently toward the king and turned away, as if dismissing the matter entirely from his mind. His fingers twitched queerly. From a carven green jade box he took a handful of shimmering black dust, and placed it in a brazier which stood on a golden tripod at his elbow. The crystal globe, which he seemed to have forgotten, fell suddenly to the floor, as if its invisible support had been removed.

Then the blacks had lifted Conan – for so loaded with chains was he that he could not walk – and carried him from the chamber. A glance back, before the heavy, gold-bound teak door was closed, showed him Xaltotun leaning back in his throne-like chair, his arms folded, while a thin wisp of smoke curled up from the brazier. Conan's scalp prickled. In Stygia, that ancient and evil kingdom that lay far to the south, he had seen such black dust before. It was the pollen of the black lotus, which creates death-like sleep and monstrous dreams; and he knew that only the grisly wizards of the Black Ring, which is the nadir of evil, voluntarily seek the scarlet nightmares of the black lotus, to revive their necromantic powers.

The Black Ring was a fable and a lie to most folk of the western world, but Conan knew of its ghastly reality, and its grim votaries who practise their abominable sorceries amid the black vaults of Stygia and the nighted domes of accursed Sabatea.

He glanced back at the cryptic, gold-bound door, shuddering at what it hid.

Whether it was day or night the king could not tell. The palace of King Tarascus seemed a shadowy, nighted place, that shunned natural illumination. The spirit of darkness and shadow hovered over it, and that spirit, Conan felt, was embodied in the stranger Xaltotun. The negroes carried the king along a winding corridor so dimly lighted that they moved through it like black ghosts bearing a dead man, and down a stone stair that wound endlessly. A torch in the hand of one cast the great deformed shadows streaming along the wall; it was like the descent into hell of a corpse borne by dusky demons.

At last they reached the foot of the stair, and then they traversed a long straight corridor, with a blank wall on one hand pierced by an occasional arched doorway with a stair leading up behind it, and on the other hand another wall showing heavy barred doors at regular intervals of a few feet.

Halting before one of these doors, one of the blacks produced the key that hung at his girdle, and turned it in the lock. Then, pushing open the grille, they entered with their captive. They were in a small dungeon with heavy stone walls, floor and ceiling, and in the opposite wall there was another grilled door. What lay beyond that door Conan could not tell, but he did not believe it was another corridor. The glimmering light of the torch, flickering through the bars, hinted at shadowy spaciousness and echoing depths.

In one corner of the dungeon, near the door through which they had entered, a cluster of rusty chains hung from a great iron ring set in the stone. In these chains a skeleton dangled. Conan glared at it with some curiosity, noticing the state of the bare bones, most of which were splintered and broken; the skull which had fallen from the vertebrae, was crushed as if by some savage blow of tremendous force.

Stolidly one of the blacks, not the one who had opened the door, removed the chains from the ring, using his key on the massive lock, and dragged the mass of rusty metal and shattered bones over to one side. Then they fastened Conan's chains to that ring, and the third black turned his key in the lock of the farther door, grunting when he had assured himself that it was properly fastened.

Then they regarded Conan cryptically, slit-eyed ebony giants, the torch striking highlights from their glossy skin.

He who held the key to the nearer door was moved to remark, gutturally: 'This your palace now, white dog-king! None but master and we know. All palace sleep. We keep secret. You live and die here, maybe. Like him!' He contemptuously kicked the shattered skull and sent it clattering across the stone floor.

Conan did not deign to reply to the taunt, and the black, galled perhaps by his prisoner's silence, muttered a curse, stooped and spat full in the king's face. It was an unfortunate move for the black. Conan was seated on the floor, the chains about his waist; ankles and wrists locked to the ring in the wall. He could neither rise, nor move more than a yard out from the wall. But there was considerable slack in the chains that shackled his wrists, and before the bullet-shaped head could be withdrawn out of reach, the king gathered this slack in his mighty hand and smote the black on the head. The man fell like a butchered ox, and his comrades stared to see him lying with his scalp laid open, and blood oozing from his nose and ears.

But they attempted no reprisal, nor did they accept Conan's urgent invitation to approach within reach of the bloody chain in his hand. Presently, grunting in their ape-like speech, they lifted the senseless black and bore him out like a sack of wheat, arms and legs dangling. They used his key to lock the door behind them, but did not remove it from the gold chain that fastened it to his girdle. They took the torch with them, and as they moved up the corridor the darkness slunk behind them like an animate thing. Their soft padding footsteps died away, with the glimmer of their torch, and darkness and silence remained unchallenged.

5 The Haunter of the Pits

Conan lay still, enduring the weight of his chains and the despair of his position with the stoicism of the wilds that had bred him. He did not move, because the jangle of his chains, when he shifted his body, sounded startlingly loud in the darkness and stillness, and it was his instinct, born of a thousand wilderness-bred ancestors, not to betray his position in his helplessness. This did not result from a logical reasoning process; he did not lie quiet because he reasoned that the darkness hid lurking dangers that might discover him in his helplessness. Xaltotun had assured him that he was not to be harmed, and Conan believed that it was in the man's interest to preserve him, at least for the time being. But the instincts of the wild were there, that had caused him in his childhood to lie hidden and silent while wild beasts prowled about his covert.

Even his keen eyes could not pierce the solid darkness. Yet after a while, after a period of time he had no way of estimating, a faint glow became apparent, a sort of slanting gray beam, by which Conan could see, vaguely, the bars of the door at his elbow, and even make out the skeleton of the other grille. This puzzled him, until at last he realized the explanation. He was far below ground, in the pits below the palace; yet for some reason a shaft had been constructed from somewhere above. Outside, the moon had risen to a point where its light slanted dimly down the shaft. He reflected that in this manner he could tell the passing of the days and nights. Perhaps the sun, too, would shine down that shaft, though on the other hand it might be closed by day. Perhaps it was a subtle method of torture, allowing a prisoner but a glimpse of daylight or moonlight.

His gaze fell on the broken bones in the farther corner, glimmering dimly. He did not tax his brain with futile speculation as to who the wretch had been and for what reason he had been doomed, but he wondered at the shattered condition of the bones. They had not been broken on a rack. Then, as he looked, another unsavory detail made itself evident. The shin-bones were split lengthwise, and there was but one explanation; they had been broken in that manner in order to obtain the marrow. Yet what creature but man breaks bones for their marrow? Perhaps those remnants were mute evidence of a horrible, cannibalistic feast, of some wretch driven to madness by starvation. Conan wondered if his own bones would be found at some future date, hanging in their rusty chains. He fought down the unreasoning panic of a trapped wolf.

The Cimmerian did not curse, scream, weep or rave as a civilized man might have done. But the pain and turmoil in his bosom were none the less fierce. His great limbs quivered with the intensity of his emotions. Somewhere, far to the westward, the Nemedian host was slashing and burning its way through the heart of his kingdom. The small host of the Poitanians could not stand before them. Prospero might be able to hold Tarantia for weeks, or months; but eventually, if not relieved, he must surrender to greater numbers. Surely the barons would rally to him against the invaders. But in the meanwhile he, Conan, must lie helpless in a darkened cell, while others led his spears and fought for his kingdom. The king ground his powerful teeth in red rage.

Then he stiffened as outside the farther door he heard a stealthy step. Straining his eyes he made out a bent, indistinct figure outside the grille. There was a rasp of metal against metal, and he heard the clink of tumblers, as if a key had been turned in the lock. Then the figure moved silently out of his range of vision. Some guard, he supposed, trying the lock. After a while he heard the sound repeated faintly somewhere farther on, and that was followed by the soft opening of a door, and then a swift scurry of softly shod feet retreated in the distance. Then silence fell again.

Conan listened for what seemed a long time, but which could not have been, for the moon still shone down the hidden shaft, but he heard no further sound. He shifted his position at last, and his chains clanked. Then he heard another, lighter footfall – a soft step outside the nearer door, the door through which he had entered the cell. An instant later a slender figure was etched dimly in the gray light.

'King Conan!' a soft voice intoned urgently. 'Oh, my lord, are you there?'

'Where else?' he answered guardedly, twisting his head about to stare at the apparition.

It was a girl who stood grasping the bars with her slender fingers. The dim glow behind her outlined her supple figure through the wisp of silk twisted about her loins, and shone vaguely on jeweled breast-plates. Her dark eyes gleamed in the shadows, her white limbs glistened softly, like alabaster. Her hair was a mass of dark foam, at the burnished luster of which the dim light only hinted.

'The keys to your shackles and to the farther door!' she whispered, and a slim white hand came through the bars and dropped three objects with a clink to the flags beside him.

'What game is this?' he demanded. 'You speak in the Nemedian tongue, and I have no friends in Nemedia. What deviltry is your master up to now? Has he sent you here to mock me?'

'It is no mockery!' The girl was trembling violently. Her bracelets and breast-plates clinked against the bars she grasped. 'I swear by Mitra! I stole the keys from the black jailers. They are the keepers of the pits, and each bears a key which will open only one set of locks. I made them drunk. The one whose head you broke was carried away to a leech, and I could not get his key. But the others I stole. Oh, please do not loiter! Beyond these dungeons lie the pits which are the doors to hell.'

Somewhat impressed, Conan tried the keys dubiously, expecting to meet only failure and a burst of mocking laughter. But he was galvanized to discover that one, indeed, loosed him of his shackles, fitting not only the lock that held them to the ring, but the locks on his limbs as well. A few seconds later he stood upright, exulting fiercely in his comparative freedom. A quick stride carried him to the grille, and his fingers closed about a bar and the slender wrist that was pressed against it, imprisoning the owner, who lifted her face bravely to his fierce gaze.

'Who are you, girl?' he demanded. 'Why do you do this?'

'I am only Zenobia,' she murmured, with a catch of breathlessness, as if in fright; 'only a girl of the king's seraglio.'

'Unless this is some cursed trick,' muttered Conan, 'I cannot see why you bring me these keys.'

She bowed her dark head, and then lifted it and looked full into his suspicious eyes. Tears sparkled like jewels on her long dark lashes.

'I am only a girl of the king's seraglio,' she said, with a certain proud humility. 'He has never glanced at me, and probably never will. I am less than one of the dogs that gnaw the bones in his banquet hall.

'But I am no painted toy; I am of flesh and blood. I breathe, hate, fear, rejoice and love. And I have loved you, King Conan, ever since I saw you riding at the head of your knights along the streets of Belverus when you visited King Nimed, years ago. My heart tugged at its strings to leap from my bosom and fall in the dust of the street under your horse's hoofs.'

Color flooded her countenance as she spoke, but her dark eyes did not waver. Conan did not at once reply; wild and passionate and untamed he was, yet any but the most brutish of men must be touched with a certain awe or wonder at the baring of a woman's naked soul.

She bent her head then, and pressed her red lips to the fingers that imprisoned her slim wrist. Then she flung up her head as if in sudden recollection of their position, and terror flared in her dark eyes.

'Haste!' she whispered urgently. 'It is past midnight. You must be gone.'

'But won't they skin you alive for stealing these keys?'

'They'll never know. If the black men remember in the morning who gave them the wine, they will not dare admit the keys were stolen from them while they were drunk. The key that I could not obtain is the one that unlocks this door. You must make your way to freedom through the pits. What awful perils lurk beyond that door I cannot even guess. But greater danger lurks for you if you remain in this cell.

'King Tarascus has returned—'

'What? Tarascus?'

'Aye! He has returned, in great secrecy, and not long ago he descended into the pits and then came out again, pale and shaking, like a man who had dared a great hazard. I heard him whisper to his squire, Arideus, that despite Xaltotun you should die.'

'What of Xaltotun?' murmured Conan.

He felt her shudder.

'Do not speak of him!' she whispered. 'Demons are often summoned by the sound of their names. The slaves say that he lies in his chamber, behind a bolted door, dreaming the dreams of the black lotus. I believe that even Tarascus secretly fears him, or he would slay you openly. But he has been in the pits tonight, and what he did here, only Mitra knows.'

'I wonder if that could have been Tarascus who fumbled at my cell door awhile ago?' muttered Conan.

'Here is a dagger!' she whispered, pressing something through the bars. His eager fingers closed on an object familiar to their touch. 'Go quickly through yonder door, turn to the left and make your way along the cells until you come to a stone stair. On your life do not stray from the line of the cells! Climb the stair and open the door at the top; one of the keys will fit it. If it be the will of Mitra, I will await you there.' Then she was gone, with a patter of light slippered feet.

Conan shrugged his shoulders, and turned toward the farther grille. This might be some diabolical trap planned by Tarascus, but plunging headlong into a snare was less abhorrent to Conan's temperament than sitting meekly to await his doom. He inspected the weapon the girl had given him, and smiled grimly. Whatever else she might be, she was proven by that dagger to be a person of practical intelligence. It was no slender stiletto, selected because of a jeweled hilt or gold guard, fitted only for dainty murder in milady's boudoir; it was a forthright poniard, a warrior's weapon, broad-bladed, fifteen inches in length, tapering to a diamond-sharp point.

He grunted with satisfaction. The feel of the hilt cheered him and gave him a glow of confidence. Whatever webs of conspiracy were drawn about him, whatever trickery and treachery ensnared him, this knife was real. The great muscles of his right arm swelled in anticipation of murderous blows.

He tried the farther door, fumbling with the keys as he did so. It was not locked. Yet he remembered the black man locking it. That furtive, bent figure, then, had been no jailer seeing that the bolts were in place. He had unlocked the door, instead. There was a sinister suggestion about that unlocked door. But Conan did not hesitate. He pushed upon the grille and stepped from the dungeon into the outer darkness.

As he had thought, the door did not open into another corridor. The flagged floor stretched away under his feet, and the line of cells ran away to the right and left behind him, but he could not make out the other limits of the place into which he had come. He could see neither the roof nor any other wall. The moonlight filtered into that vastness only through the grilles of the cells, and was almost lost in the darkness. Less keen eyes than his could scarcely have discerned the dim gray patches that floated before each cell door.

Turning to the left, he moved swiftly and noiselessly along the line of dungeons, his bare feet making no sound on the flags. He glanced briefly into each dungeon as he passed it. They were all empty, but locked. In some he caught the glimmer of naked white bones. These pits were a relic of a grimmer age, constructed long ago when Belverus was a fortress rather than a city. But evidently their more recent use had been more extensive than the world guessed.

Ahead of him, presently, he saw the dim outline of a stair sloping sharply upward, and knew it must be the stair he sought. Then he whirled suddenly, crouching in the deep shadows at its foot.

Somewhere behind him something was moving – something bulky and stealthy that padded on feet which were not human feet. He was looking down the long row of cells, before each one of which lay a square of dim gray light that was little more than a patch of less dense darkness. But he saw something moving along these squares. What it was he could not tell, but it was heavy and huge, and yet it moved with more than human ease and swiftness. He glimpsed it as it moved across the squares of gray, then lost it as it merged in the expanses of shadow between. It was uncanny, in its stealthy advance, appearing and disappearing like a blur of the vision.

He heard the bars rattle as it tried each door in turn. Now it had reached the cell he had so recently quitted, and the door swung open as it tugged. He saw a great bulky shape limned faintly and briefly in the gray doorway, and then the thing had vanished into the dungeon. Sweat beaded Conan's face and hands. Now he knew why Tarascus had come so subtly to his door, and later had fled so swiftly. The king had unlocked his door, and, somewhere in these hellish pits, had opened a cell or cage that held some grim monstrosity.

Now the thing was emerging from the cell and was again advancing up the corridor, its misshapen head close to the ground. It paid no more heed to the locked doors. It was smelling out his trail. He saw it more plainly now; the gray light limned a giant anthropomorphic body, but vaster of bulk and girth than any man. It went on two legs, though it stooped forward, and it was grayish and shaggy, its thick coat shot with silver. Its head was a grisly travesty of the human, its long arms hung nearly to the ground.

Conan knew it at last – understood the meaning of those crushed and broken bones in the dungeon, and recognized the haunter of the pits. It was a gray ape, one of the grisly man-eaters from the forests that wave on the mountainous eastern shores of the Sea of Vilayet. Half mythical and altogether horrible, these apes were the goblins of Hyborian legendry, and were in reality ogres of the natural world, cannibals and murderers of the nighted forests.

He knew it scented his presence, for it was coming swiftly now, rolling its barrel-like body rapidly along on its short, mighty bowed legs. He cast a quick glance up the long stair, but knew that the thing would be on his back before he could mount to the distant door. He chose to meet it face to face.

Conan stepped out into the nearest square of moonlight, so as to have all the advantage of illumination that he could; for the beast, he knew, could see better than himself in the dark. Instantly the brute saw him; its great yellow tusks gleamed in the shadows, but it made no sound. Creatures of night and the silence, the gray apes of Vilayet were voiceless. But in its dim, hideous features, which were a bestial travesty of a human face, showed ghastly exultation.

Conan stood poised, watching the oncoming monster without a quiver. He knew he must stake his life on one thrust; there would be no chance for another; nor would there be time to strike and spring away. The first blow must kill, and kill instantly, if he hoped to survive that awful grapple. He swept his gaze over the short, squat throat, the hairy swagbelly, and the mighty breast, swelling in giant arches like twin shields. It must be the heart; better to risk the blade being deflected by the heavy ribs than to strike in where a stroke was not instantly fatal. With full realization of the odds, Conan matched his speed of eye and hand and his muscular power against the brute might and ferocity of the man-eater. He must meet the brute breast to breast, strike a death-blow, and then trust to the ruggedness of his frame to survive the instant of manhandling that was certain to be his.

As the ape came rolling in on him, swinging wide its terrible arms, he plunged in between them and struck with all his desperate power. He felt the blade sink to the hilt in the hairy breast, and instantly, releasing it, he ducked his head and bunched his whole body into one compact mass of knotted muscles, and as he did so he grasped the closing arms and drove his knee fiercely into the monster's belly, bracing himself against that crushing grapple.

For one dizzy instant he felt as if he were being dismembered in the grip of an earthquake; then suddenly he was free, sprawling on the floor, and the monster was gasping out its life beneath him, its red eyes turned upward, the hilt of the poniard quivering in its breast. His desperate stab had gone home.

Conan was panting as if after long conflict, trembling in every limb. Some of his joints felt as if they had been dislocated, and blood dripped from scratches on his skin where the monster's talons had ripped; his muscles and tendons had been savagely wrenched and twisted. If the beast had lived a second longer, it would surely have dismembered him. But the Cimmerian's mighty strength had resisted, for the fleeting instant it had endured, the dying convulsion of the ape that would have torn a lesser man limb from limb.

6 The Thrust of a Knife

Conan stooped and tore the knife from the monster's breast. Then he went swiftly up the stair. What other shapes of fear the darkness held he could not guess, but he had no desire to encounter any more. This touch-and-go sort of battling was too strenuous even for the giant Cimmerian. The moonlight was fading from the floor, the darkness closing in, and something like panic pursued him up the stair. He breathed a gusty sigh of relief when he reached the head, and felt the third key turn in the lock. He opened the door slightly, and craned his neck to peer through, half expecting an attack from some human or bestial enemy.

He looked into a bare stone corridor, dimly lighted, and a slender, supple figure stood before the door.

'Your Majesty!' It was a low, vibrant cry, half in relief and half in fear. The girl sprang to his side, then hesitated as if abashed.

'You bleed,' she said. 'You have been hurt!'

He brushed aside the implication with an impatient hand.

'Scratches that wouldn't hurt a baby. Your skewer came in handy, though. But for it Tarascus' monkey would be cracking my shin-bones for the marrow right now. But what now?'

'Follow me,' she whispered. 'I will lead you outside the city wall. I have a horse concealed there.'

She turned to lead the way down the corridor, but he laid a heavy hand on her naked shoulder.

'Walk beside me,' he instructed her softly, passing his massive arm about her lithe waist. 'You've played me fair so far, and I'm inclined to believe in you; but I've lived this long only because I've trusted no one too far, man or woman. So! Now if you play me false you won't live to enjoy the jest.'

She did not flinch at sight of the reddened poniard or the contact of his hard muscles about her supple body.

'Cut me down without mercy if I play you false,' she answered. 'The very feel of your arm about me, even in menace, is as the fulfillment of a dream.'

The vaulted corridor ended at a door, which she opened. Outside lay another black man, a giant in turban and silk loincloth, with a curved sword lying on the flags near his hand. He did not move.

'I drugged his wine,' she whispered, swerving to avoid the recumbent figure. 'He is the last, and outer, guard of the pits. None ever escaped from them before, and none has ever wished to seek them; so only these black men guard them. Only these of all the servants knew it was King Conan that Xaltotun brought a prisoner in his chariot. I was watching, sleepless, from an upper casement that opened into the court, while the other girls slept; for I knew that a battle was being fought, or had been fought, in the west, and I feared for you …

'I saw the blacks carry you up the stair, and I recognized you in the torchlight. I slipped into this wing of the palace tonight, in time to see them carry you to the pits. I had not dared come here before nightfall. You must have lain in drugged senselessness all day in Xaltotun's chamber.

'Oh, let us be wary! Strange things are afoot in the palace tonight. The slaves said that Xaltotun slept as he often sleeps, drugged by the lotus of Stygia, but Tarascus is in the palace. He entered secretly, through the postern, wrapped in his cloak which was dusty as with long travel, and attended only by his squire, the lean silent Arideus. I cannot understand, but I am afraid.'

They came out at the foot of a narrow, winding stair, and mounting it, passed through a narrow panel which she slid aside. When they had passed through, she slipped it back in place, and it became merely a portion of the ornate wall. They were in a more spacious corridor, carpeted and tapestried, over which hanging lamps shed a golden glow.

Conan listened intently, but he heard no sound throughout the palace. He did not know in what part of the palace he was, or in which direction lay the chamber of Xaltotun. The girl was trembling as she drew him along the corridor, to halt presently beside an alcove masked with satin tapestry. Drawing this aside, she motioned for him to step into the niche, and whispered: 'Wait here! Beyond that door at the end of the corridor we are likely to meet slaves or eunuchs at any time of the day or night. I will go and see if the way is clear, before we essay it.'

Instantly his hair-trigger suspicions were aroused.

'Are you leading me into a trap?'

Tears sprang into her dark eyes. She sank to her knees and seized his muscular hand.

'Oh, my king, do not mistrust me now!' Her voice shook with desperate urgency. 'If you doubt and hesitate, we are lost! Why should I bring you up out of the pits to betray you now?'

'All right,' he muttered. 'I'll trust you; though, by Crom, the habits of a lifetime are not easily put aside. Yet I wouldn't harm you now, if you brought all the swordsmen in Nemedia upon me. But for you Tarascus' cursed ape would have come upon me in chains and unarmed. Do as you wish, girl.'

Kissing his hands, she sprang lithely up and ran down the corridor, to vanish through a heavy double door.

He glanced after her, wondering if he was a fool to trust her; then he shrugged his mighty shoulders and pulled the satin hangings together, masking his refuge. It was not strange that a passionate young beauty should be risking her life to aid him; such things had happened often enough in his life. Many women had looked on him with favor, in the days of his wanderings, and in the time of his kingship.

Yet he did not remain motionless in the alcove, waiting for her return. Following his instincts, he explored the niche for another exit, and presently found one – the opening of a narrow passage, masked by the tapestries, that ran to an ornately carved door, barely visible in the dim light that filtered in from the outer corridor. And as he stared into it, somewhere beyond that carven door he heard the sound of another door opening and shutting, and then a low mumble of voices. The familiar sound of one of those voices caused a sinister expression to cross his dark face. Without hesitation he glided down the passage, and crouched like a stalking panther beside the door. It was not locked, and manipulating it delicately, he pushed it open a crack, with a reckless disregard for possible consequences that only he could have explained or defended.

It was masked on the other side by tapestries, but through a thin slit in the velvet he looked into a chamber lit by a candle on an ebony table. There were two men in that chamber. One was a scarred, sinister-looking ruffian in leather breeks and ragged cloak; the other was Tarascus, king of Nemedia.

Tarascus seemed ill at ease. He was slightly pale, and he kept starting and glancing about him, as if expecting and fearing to hear some sound or footstep.

'Go swiftly and at once,' he was saying. 'He is deep in drugged slumber, but I know not when he may awaken.'

'Strange to hear words of fear issuing from the lips of Tarascus,' rumbled the other in a harsh, deep voice.

The king frowned.

'I fear no common man, as you well know. But when I saw the cliffs fall at Valkia I knew that this devil we had resurrected was no charlatan. I fear his powers, because I do not know the full extent of them. But I know that somehow they are connected with this accursed thing which I have stolen from him. It brought him back to life; so it must be the source of his sorcery.

'He had it hidden well; but following my secret order a slave spied on him and saw him place it in a golden chest, and saw where he hid the chest. Even so, I would not have dared steal it had Xaltotun himself not been sunk in lotus slumber.

'I believe it is the secret of his power. With it Orastes brought him back to life. With it he will make us all slaves, if we are not wary. So take it and cast it into the sea as I have bidden you. And be sure you are so far from land that neither tide nor storm can wash it up on the beach. You have been paid.'

'So I have,' grunted the ruffian. 'And I owe more than gold to you, king; I owe you a debt of gratitude. Even thieves can be grateful.'

'Whatever debt you may feel you owe me,' answered Tarascus, 'will be paid when you have hurled this thing into the sea.'

'I'll ride for Zingara and take ship from Kordava,' promised the other. 'I dare not show my head in Argos, because of the matter of a murder or so—'

'I care not, so it is done. Here it is; a horse awaits you in the court. Go, and go swiftly!'

Something passed between them, something that flamed like living fire. Conan had only a brief glimpse of it; and then the ruffian pulled a slouch hat over his eyes, drew his cloak about his shoulder, and hurried from the chamber. And as the door closed behind him, Conan moved with the devastating fury of unchained blood-lust. He had held himself in check so long as he could. The sight of his enemy so near him set his wild blood seething and swept away all caution and restraint.

Tarascus was turning toward an inner door when Conan tore aside the hangings and leaped like a blood-mad panther into the room. Tarascus wheeled, but even before he could recognize his attacker, Conan's poniard ripped into him.

But the blow was not mortal, as Conan knew the instant he struck. His foot had caught in a fold of the curtains and tripped him as he leaped. The point fleshed itself in Tarascus' shoulder and plowed down along his ribs, and the king of Nemedia screamed.

The impact of the blow and Conan's lunging body hurled him back against the table and it toppled and the candle went out. They were both carried to the floor by the violence of Conan's rush, and the foot of the tapestry hampered them both in its folds. Conan was stabbing blindly in the dark, Tarascus screaming in a frenzy of panicky terror. As if fear lent him superhuman energy, Tarascus tore free and blundered away in the darkness, shrieking: 'Help! Guards! Arideus! Orastes! Orastes!'

Conan rose, kicking himself free of the tangling tapestries and the broken table, cursing with the bitterness of his blood-thirsty disappointment. He was confused, and ignorant of the plan of the palace. The yells of Tarascus were still resounding in the distance, and a wild outcry was bursting forth in answer. The Nemedian had escaped him in the darkness, and Conan did not know which way he had gone. The Cimmerian's rash stroke for vengeance had failed, and there remained only the task of saving his own hide if he could.

Swearing luridly, Conan ran back down the passage and into the alcove, glaring out into the lighted corridor, just as Zenobia came running up it, her dark eyes dilated with terror.

'Oh, what has happened?' she cried. 'The palace is roused! I swear I have not betrayed you—'

'No, it was I who stirred up this hornet's nest,' he grunted. 'I tried to pay off a score. What's the shortest way out of this?'

She caught his wrist and ran fleetly down the corridor. But before they reached the heavy door at the other end, muffled shouts arose from behind it and the portals began to shake under an assault from the other side. Zenobia wrung her hands and whimpered.

'We are cut off! I locked that door as I returned through it. But they will burst it in a moment. The way to the postern gate lies through it.'

Conan wheeled. Up the corridor, though still out of sight, he heard a rising clamor that told him his foes were behind as well as before him.

'Quick! Into this door!' the girl cried desperately, running across the corridor and throwing open the door of a chamber.

Conan followed her through, and then threw the gold catch behind them. They stood in an ornately furnished chamber, empty but for themselves, and she drew him to a gold-barred window, through which he saw trees and shrubbery.

'You are strong,' she panted. 'If you can tear these bars away, you may yet escape. The garden is full of guards, but the shrubs are thick, and you may avoid them. The southern wall is also the outer wall of the city. Once over that, you have a chance to get away. A horse is hidden for you in a thicket beside the road that runs westward, a few hundred paces to the south of the fountain of Thrallos. You know where it is?'

'Aye! But what of you? I had meant to take you with me.'

A flood of joy lighted her beautiful face.

'Then my cup of happiness is brimming! But I will not hamper your escape. Burdened with me you would fail. Nay, do not fear for me. They will never suspect that I aided you willingly. Go! What you have just said will glorify my life throughout the long years.'

He caught her up in his iron arms, crushed her slim, vibrant figure to him and kissed her fiercely on eyes, cheeks, throat and lips, until she lay panting in his embrace; gusty and tempestuous as a storm-wind, even his love-making was violent.

'I'll go,' he muttered. 'But by Crom, I'll come for you some day!'

Wheeling, he gripped the gold bars and tore them from their sockets with one tremendous wrench; threw a leg over the sill and went down swiftly, clinging to the ornaments on the wall. He hit the ground running and melted like a shadow into the maze of towering rose-bushes and spreading trees. The one look he cast back over his shoulder showed him Zenobia leaning over the window-sill, her arms stretched after him in mute farewell and renunciation.

Guards were running through the garden, all converging toward the palace, where the clamor momentarily grew louder – tall men in burnished cuirasses and crested helmets of polished bronze. The starlight struck glints from their gleaming armor, among the trees, betraying their every movement; but the sound of their coming ran far before them. To Conan, wilderness-bred, their rush through the shrubbery was like the blundering stampede of cattle. Some of them passed within a few feet of where he lay flat in a thick cluster of bushes, and never guessed his presence. With the palace as their goal, they were oblivious to all else about them. When they had gone shouting on, he rose and fled through the garden with no more noise than a panther would have made.

So quickly he came to the southern wall, and mounted the steps that led to the parapet. The wall was made to keep people out, not in. No sentry patrolling the battlements was in sight. Crouching by an embrasure he glanced back at the great palace rearing above the cypresses behind him. Lights blazed from every window, and he could see figures flitting back and forth across them like puppets on invisible strings. He grinned hardly, shook his fist in a gesture of farewell and menace, and let himself over the outer rim of the parapet.

A low tree, a few yards below the parapet, received Conan's weight, as he dropped noiselessly into the branches. An instant later he was racing through the shadows with the swinging hillman's stride that eats up long miles.

Gardens and pleasure villas surrounded the walls of Belverus. Drowsy slaves, sleeping by their watchman's pikes, did not see the swift and furtive figure that scaled walls, crossed alleys made by the arching branches of trees, and threaded a noiseless way through orchards and vineyards. Watchdogs woke and lifted their deep-booming clamor at a gliding shadow, half scented, half sensed, and then it was gone.

In a chamber of the palace Tarascus writhed and cursed on a blood-spattered couch, under the deft, quick fingers of Orastes. The palace was thronged with wide-eyed, trembling servitors, but the chamber where the king lay was empty save for himself and the renegade priest.

'Are you sure he still sleeps?' Tarascus demanded again, setting his teeth against the bite of the herb juices with which Orastes was bandaging the long, ragged gash in his shoulder and ribs. 'Ishtar, Mitra and Set! That burns like molten pitch of hell!'

'Which you would be experiencing even now, but for your good fortune,' remarked Orastes. 'Whoever wielded that knife struck to kill. Yes, I have told you that Xaltotun still sleeps. Why are you so urgent upon that point? What has he to do with this?'

'You know nothing of what has passed in the palace tonight?' Tarascus searched the priest's countenance with burning intensity.

'Nothing. As you know, I have been employed in translating manuscripts for Xaltotun, for some months now, transcribing esoteric volumes written in the younger languages into script he can read. He was well versed in all the tongues and scripts of his day, but he has not yet learned all the newer languages, and to save time he has me translate these works for him, to learn if any new knowledge has been discovered since his time. I did not know that he had returned last night until he sent for me and told me of the battle. Then I returned to my studies, nor did I know that you had returned until the clamor in the palace brought me out of my cell.'

'Then you do not know that Xaltotun brought the king of Aquilonia a captive to this palace?'

Orastes shook his head, without particular surprise.

'Xaltotun merely said that Conan would oppose us no more. I supposed that he had fallen, but did not ask the details.'

'Xaltotun saved his life when I would have slain him,' snarled Tarascus. 'I saw his purpose instantly. He would hold Conan captive to use as a club against us – against Amalric, against Valerius, and against myself. So long as Conan lives he is a threat, a unifying factor for Aquilonia, that might be used to compel us into courses we would not otherwise follow. I mistrust this undead Pythonian. Of late I have begun to fear him.

'I followed him, some hours after he had departed eastward. I wished to learn what he intended doing with Conan. I found that he had imprisoned him in the pits. I intended to see that the barbarian died, in spite of Xaltotun. And I accomplished—'

A cautious knock sounded at the door.

'That's Arideus,' grunted Tarascus. 'Let him in.'

The saturnine squire entered, his eyes blazing with suppressed excitement.

'How, Arideus?' exclaimed Tarascus. 'Have you found the man who attacked me?'

'You did not see him, my lord?' asked Arideus, as one who would assure himself of a fact he already knows to exist. 'You did not recognize him?'

'No. It happened so quick, and the candle was out – all I could think of was that it was some devil loosed on me by Xaltotun's magic—'

'The Pythonian sleeps in his barred and bolted room. But I have been in the pits.' Arideus twitched his lean shoulders excitedly.

'Well, speak, man!' exclaimed Tarascus impatiently. 'What did you find there?'

'An empty dungeon,' whispered the squire. 'The corpse of the great ape!'

'*What?*' Tarascus started upright, and blood gushed from his opened wound.

'Aye! The man-eater is dead – stabbed through the heart – and Conan is gone!'

Tarascus was gray of face as he mechanically allowed Orastes to force him prostrate again and the priest renewed work upon his mangled flesh.

'Conan!' he repeated. 'Not a crushed corpse – escaped! Mitra! He is no man; but a devil himself! I thought Xaltotun was behind this wound. I see now. Gods and devils! It was Conan who stabbed me! Arideus!'

'Aye, your Majesty!'

'Search every nook in the palace. He may be skulking through the dark corridors now like a hungry tiger. Let no niche escape your scrutiny, and beware. It is not a civilized man you hunt, but a blood-mad barbarian whose strength and ferocity are those of a wild beast. Scour the palace-grounds and the city. Throw a cordon about the walls. If you find he has escaped from the city, as he may well do, take a troop of horsemen and follow him. Once past the walls it will be like hunting a wolf through the hills. But haste, and you may yet catch him.'

'This is a matter which requires more than ordinary human wits,' said Orastes. 'Perhaps we should seek Xaltotun's advice.'

'No!' exclaimed Tarascus violently. 'Let the troopers pursue Conan and slay him. Xaltotun can hold no grudge against us if we kill a prisoner to prevent his escape.'

'Well,' said Orastes, 'I am no Acheronian, but I am versed in some of the arts, and the control of certain spirits which have cloaked themselves in material substance. Perhaps I can aid you in this matter.'

The fountain of Thrallos stood in a clustered ring of oaks beside the road a mile from the walls of the city. Its musical tinkle reached Conan's ears through the silence of the starlight. He drank deep of its icy stream, and then hurried southward toward a small, dense thicket he saw there. Rounding it, he saw a great white horse tied among the bushes. Heaving a deep gusty sigh he reached it with one stride – a mocking laugh brought him about, glaring.

A dully glinting, mail-clad figure moved out of the shadows into the starlight. This was no plumed and burnished palace guardsman. It was a tall man in morion and gray chain-mail – one of the Adventurers, a class of warriors peculiar to Nemedia; men who had not attained to the wealth and position of knighthood, or had fallen from that estate; hard-bitten fighters, dedicating their lives to war and adventure. They constituted a class of their own, sometimes commanding troops, but themselves accountable to no man but the king. Conan knew that he could have been discovered by no more dangerous a foeman.

A quick glance among the shadows convinced him that the man was alone, and he expanded his great chest slightly, digging his toes into the turf, as his thews coiled tensely.

'I was riding for Belverus on Amalric's business,' said the Adventurer, advancing warily. The starlight was a long sheen on the great two-handed sword he bore naked in his hand. 'A horse whinnied to mine from the thicket. I investigated and thought it strange a steed should be tethered here. I waited – and lo, I have caught a rare prize!'

The Adventurers lived by their swords.

'I know you,' muttered the Nemedian. 'You are Conan, king of Aquilonia. I thought I saw you die in the valley of the Valkia, but—'

Conan sprang as a dying tiger springs. Practised fighter though the Adventurer was, he did not realize the desperate quickness that lurks in barbaric sinews. He was caught off guard, his heavy sword half lifted. Before he could either strike or parry, the king's poniard sheathed itself in his throat, above the gorget, slanting downward into his heart. With a choked gurgle he reeled and went down, and Conan ruthlessly tore his blade free as his victim fell. The white horse snorted violently and shied at the sight and scent of blood on the sword.

Glaring down at his lifeless enemy, dripping poniard in hand, sweat glistening on his broad breast, Conan poised like a statue, listening intently. In the woods about there was no sound, save for the sleepy cheep of awakened birds. But in the city, a mile away, he heard the strident blare of a trumpet.

Hastily he bent over the fallen man. A few seconds' search convinced him that whatever message the man might have borne was intended to be conveyed by word of mouth. But he did not pause in his task. It was not many hours until dawn. A few minutes later the white horse was galloping westward along the white road, and the rider wore the gray mail of a Nemedian Adventurer.

7 The Rending of the Veil

Conan knew his only chance of escape lay in speed. He did not even consider hiding somewhere near Belverus until the chase passed on; he was certain that the uncanny ally of Tarascus would be able to ferret him out. Besides, he was not one to skulk and hide; an open fight or an open chase, either suited his temperament better. He had a long start, he knew. He would lead them a grinding race for the border.

Zenobia had chosen well in selecting the white horse. His speed, toughness and endurance were obvious. The girl knew weapons and horses, and, Conan reflected with some satisfaction, she knew men. He rode westward at a gait that ate up the miles.

It was a sleeping land through which he rode, past grove-sheltered villages and white-walled villas amid spacious fields and orchards that grew sparser as he fared westward. As the villages thinned, the land grew more rugged, and the keeps that frowned from eminences told of centuries of border war. But none rode down from those castles to challenge or halt him. The lords of the keeps were following the banner of Amalric; the pennons that were wont to wave over these towers were now floating over the Aquilonian plains.

When the last huddled village fell behind him, Conan left the road, which was beginning to bend toward the northwest, toward the distant passes. To keep to the road would mean to pass by border towers, still garrisoned with armed men who would not allow him to pass unquestioned. He knew there would be no patrols riding the border marches on either side, as in ordinary times, but there were those towers, and with dawn there would probably be cavalcades of returning soldiers with wounded men in ox-carts.

This road from Belverus was the only road that crossed the border for fifty miles from north to south. It followed a series of passes through the hills, and on either hand lay a wide expanse of wild, sparsely inhabited mountains. He maintained his due westerly direction, intending to cross the border deep in the wilds of the hills that lay to the south of the passes. It was a shorter route, more arduous, but safer for a hunted fugitive. One man on a horse could traverse country an army would find impassable.

But at dawn he had not reached the hills; they were a long, low, blue rampart stretching along the horizon ahead of him. Here there were neither farms nor villages, no white-walled villas looming among clustering trees. The dawn wind stirred the tall stiff grass, and there was nothing but the long rolling swells of brown earth, covered with dry grass, and in the distance the gaunt walls of a stronghold on a low hill. Too many Aquilonian raiders had crossed the mountains in not too distant days for the countryside to be thickly settled as it was farther to the east.

Dawn ran like a prairie fire across the grasslands, and high overhead sounded a weird crying as a straggling wedge of wild geese winged swiftly southward. In a grassy swale Conan halted and unsaddled his mount. Its sides were heaving, its coat plastered with sweat. He had pushed it unmercifully through the hours before dawn.

While it munched the brittle grass and rolled, he lay at the crest of the low slope, staring eastward. Far away to the northward he could see the road he had left, streaming like a white ribbon over a distant rise. No black dots moved along that glistening ribbon. There was no sign about the castle in the distance to indicate that the keepers had noticed the lone wayfarer.

An hour later the land still stretched bare. The only sign of life was a glint of steel on the far-off battlements, a raven in the sky that wheeled backward and forward, dipping and rising as if seeking something. Conan saddled and rode westward at a more leisurely gait.

As he topped the farther crest of the slope, a raucous screaming burst out over his head, and looking up, he saw the raven flapping high above him, cawing incessantly. As he rode on, it followed him, maintaining its position and making the morning hideous with its strident cries, heedless of his efforts to drive it away.

This kept up for hours, until Conan's teeth were on edge, and he felt that he would give half his kingdom to be allowed to wring that black neck.

'Devils of hell!' he roared in futile rage, shaking his mailed fist at the frantic bird. 'Why do you harry me with your squawking? Begone, you black spawn of perdition, and peck for wheat in the farmer's fields!'

He was ascending the first pitch of the hills, and he seemed to hear an echo of the bird's clamor far behind him. Turning in his saddle, he presently made out another black dot hanging in the blue. Beyond that again he caught the glint of the afternoon sun on steel. That could mean only one thing: armed men. And they were not riding along the beaten road, which was out of his sight beyond the horizon. They were following him.

His face grew grim and he shivered slightly as he stared at the raven that wheeled high above him.

'So it is more than the whim of a brainless beast?' he muttered. 'Those riders cannot see you, spawn of hell; but the other bird can see you, and they can see him. You follow me, he follows you, and they follow him. Are you only a craftily trained feathered creature, or some devil in the form of a bird? Did Xaltotun set you on my trail? Are *you* Xaltotun?'

Only a strident screech answered him, a screech vibrating with harsh mockery.

Conan wasted no more breath on his dusky betrayer. Grimly he settled to the long grind of the hills. He dared not push the horse too hard; the rest he had allowed it had not been enough to freshen it. He was still far ahead of his pursuers, but they would cut down that lead steadily. It was almost a certainty that their horses were fresher than his, for they had undoubtedly changed mounts at that castle he had passed.

The going grew rougher, the scenery more rugged, steep grassy slopes pitching up to densely timbered mountainsides. Here, he knew, he might elude his hunters, but for that hellish bird that squalled incessantly above him. He could no longer see them in this broken country, but he was certain that they still followed him, guided unerringly by their feathered allies. That black shape became like a demoniac incubus, hounding him through measureless hells. The stones he hurled with a curse went wide or fell harmless, though in his youth he had felled hawks on the wing.

The horse was tiring fast. Conan recognized the grim finality of his position. He sensed an inexorable driving fate behind all this. He could not escape. He was as much a captive as he had been in the pits of Belverus. But he was no son of the Orient to yield passively to what seemed inevitable. If he could not escape, he would at least take some of his foes into eternity with him. He turned into a wide thicket of larches that masked a slope, looking for a place to turn at bay.

Then ahead of him there rang a strange, shrill scream, human yet weirdly timbred. An instant later he had pushed through a screen of branches, and saw the source of that eldritch cry. In a small glade below him four soldiers in Nemedian chain-mail were binding a noose about the neck of a gaunt old woman in peasant garb. A heap of fagots, bound with cord on the ground near by, showed what her occupation had been when surprised by these stragglers.

Conan felt slow fury swell his heart as he looked silently down and saw the ruffians dragging her toward a tree whose low-spreading branches were obviously intended to act as a gibbet. He had crossed the frontier an hour ago. He was standing on his own soil, watching the murder of one of his own subjects. The old woman was struggling with surprising strength and energy, and as he watched, she lifted her head and voiced again the strange, weird, far-carrying call he had heard before. It was echoed as if in mockery by the raven flapping above the trees. The soldiers laughed roughly, and one struck her in the mouth.

Conan swung from his weary steed and dropped down the face of the rocks, landing with a clang of mail on the grass. The four men wheeled at the sound and drew their swords, gaping at the mailed giant who faced them, sword in hand.

Conan laughed harshly. His eyes were bleak as flint.

'Dogs!' he said without passion and without mercy. 'Do Nemedian jackals set themselves up as executioners and hang my subjects at will? First you must take the head of their king. Here I stand, awaiting your lordly pleasure!'

The soldiers stared at him uncertainly as he strode toward them.

'Who is this madman?' growled a bearded ruffian. 'He wears Nemedian mail, but speaks with an Aquilonian accent.'

'No matter,' quoth another. 'Cut him down, and then we'll hang the old hag.'

And so saying he ran at Conan, lifting his sword. But before he could strike, the king's great blade lashed down, splitting helmet and skull. The man fell before him, but the others were hardy rogues. They gave tongue like wolves and surged about the lone figure in the gray mail, and the clamor and din of steel drowned the cries of the circling raven.

Conan did not shout. His eyes coals of blue fire and his lips smiling bleakly, he lashed right and left with his two-handed sword. For all his size he was quick as a cat on his feet, and he was constantly in motion, presenting a moving target so that thrusts and swings cut empty air oftener than not. Yet when he struck he was perfectly balanced, and his blows fell with devastating power. Three of the four were down, dying in their own blood, and the fourth was bleeding from half a dozen wounds, stumbling in headlong retreat as he parried frantically, when Conan's spur caught in the surcoat of one of the fallen men.

The king stumbled, and before he could catch himself the Nemedian, with the frenzy of desperation, rushed him so savagely that Conan staggered and fell sprawling over the corpse. The Nemedian croaked in triumph and sprang forward, lifting his great sword with both hands over his right shoulder, as he braced his legs wide for the stroke – and then, over the prostrate king, something huge and hairy shot like a thunderbolt full on the soldier's breast, and his yelp of triumph changed to a shriek of death.

Conan, scrambling up, saw the man lying dead with his throat torn out, and a great gray wolf stood over him, head sunk as it smelled the blood that formed a pool on the grass.

The king turned as the old woman spoke to him. She stood straight and tall before him, and in spite of her ragged garb, her features, clear-cut and aquiline, and her keen black eyes, were not those of a common peasant woman. She called to the wolf and it trotted to her side like a great dog and rubbed its giant shoulder against her knee, while it gazed at Conan with great green lambent eyes. Absently she laid her hand upon its mighty neck, and so the two stood regarding the king of Aquilonia. He found their steady gaze disquieting, though there was no hostility in it.

'Men say King Conan died beneath the stones and dirt when the cliffs crumbled by Valkia,' she said in a deep, strong, resonant voice.

'So they say,' he growled. He was in no mood for controversy, and he thought of those armored riders who were pushing nearer every moment. The raven above him cawed stridently, and he cast an involuntary glare upward, grinding his teeth in a spasm of nervous irritation.

Up on the ledge the white horse stood with drooping head. The old woman looked at it, and then at the raven; and then she lifted a strange weird cry as she had before. As if recognizing the call, the raven wheeled, suddenly mute, and raced eastward. But before it had got out of sight, the shadow of mighty wings fell across it. An eagle soared up from the tangle of trees, and rising above it, swooped and struck the black messenger to the earth. The strident voice of betrayal was stilled for ever.

'Crom!' muttered Conan, staring at the old woman. 'Are you a magician, too?'

'I am Zelata,' she said. 'The people of the valleys call me a witch. Was that child of the night guiding armed men on your trail?'

'Aye.' She did not seem to think the answer fantastic. 'They cannot be far behind me.'

'Lead your horse and follow me, King Conan,' she said briefly.

Without comment he mounted the rocks and brought his horse down to the glade by a circuitous path. As he came he saw the eagle reappear, dropping lazily down from the sky, and rest an instant on Zelata's shoulder, spreading its great wings lightly so as not to crush her with its weight.

Without a word she led the way, the great wolf trotting at her side, the eagle soaring above her. Through deep thickets and along tortuous ledges poised over deep ravines she led him, and finally along a narrow precipice-edged path to a curious dwelling of stone, half hut, half cavern, beneath a cliff hidden among the gorges and crags. The eagle flew to the pinnacle of this cliff, and perched there like a motionless sentinel.

Still silent, Zelata stabled the horse in a near-by cave, with leaves and grass piled high for provender, and a tiny spring bubbling in the dim recesses.

In the hut she seated the king on a rude, hide-covered bench, and she herself sat upon a low stool before the tiny fireplace, while she made a fire of tamarisk chunks and prepared a frugal meal. The great wolf drowsed beside her, facing the fire, his huge head sunk on his paws, his ears twitching in his dreams.

'You do not fear to sit in the hut of a witch?' she asked, breaking her silence at last.

An impatient shrug of his gray-mailed shoulders was her guest's only reply. She gave into his hands a wooden dish heaped with dried fruits, cheese and barley bread, and a great pot of the heady upland beer, brewed from barley grown in the high valleys.

'I have found the brooding silence of the glens more pleasing than the babble of city streets,' she said. 'The children of the wild are kinder than the children of men.' Her hand briefly stroked the ruff of the sleeping wolf. 'My children were afar from me today, or I had not needed your sword, my king. They were coming at my call.'

'What grudge had those Nemedian dogs against you?' Conan demanded.

'Skulkers from the invading army straggle all over the countryside, from the frontier to Tarantia,' she answered. 'The foolish villagers in the valleys told them that I had a store of gold hidden away, so as to divert their attentions from their villages. They demanded treasure from me, and my answers angered them. But neither skulkers nor the men who pursue you, nor any raven will find you here.'

He shook his head, eating ravenously.

'I'm for Tarantia.'

She shook her head.

'You thrust your head into the dragon's jaws. Best seek refuge abroad. The heart is gone from your kingdom.'

'What do you mean?' he demanded. 'Battles have been lost before, yet wars won. A kingdom is not lost by a single defeat.'

'And you will go to Tarantia?'

'Aye. Prospero will be holding it against Amalric.'

'Are you sure?'

'Hell's devils, woman!' he exclaimed wrathfully. 'What else?'

She shook her head. 'I feel that it is otherwise. Let us see. Not lightly is the veil rent; yet I will rend it a little, and show you your capital city.'

Conan did not see what she cast upon the fire, but the wolf whimpered in his dreams, and a green smoke gathered and billowed up into the hut. And as he watched, the walls and ceiling of the hut seemed to widen, to grow remote and vanish, merging with infinite immensities; the smoke rolled about him, blotting out everything. And in it forms moved and faded, and stood out in startling clarity.

He stared at the familiar towers and streets of Tarantia, where a mob seethed and screamed, and at the same time he was somehow able to see the banners of Nemedia moving inexorably westward through the smoke and flame of a pillaged land. In the great square of Tarantia the frantic throng milled and yammered, screaming that the king was dead, that the barons were girding themselves to divide the land between them, and that the rule of a king, even of Valerius, was better than anarchy. Prospero, shining in his armor, rode among them, trying to pacify them, bidding them trust Count Trocero, urging them to man the wall and aid his knights in defending the city. They turned on him, shrieking with fear and unreasoning rage, howling that he was Trocero's butcher, a more evil foe than Amalric himself. Offal and stones were hurled at his knights.

A slight blurring of the picture, that might have denoted a passing of time, and then Conan saw Prospero and his knights filing out of the gates and spurring southward. Behind him the city was in an uproar.

'Fools!' muttered Conan thickly. 'Fools! Why could they not trust Prospero? Zelata, if you are making game of me, with some trickery—'

'This has passed,' answered Zelata imperturbably, though somberly. 'It was the evening of the day that has passed when Prospero rode out of Tarantia, with the hosts of Amalric almost within sight. From the walls men saw the flame of their pillaging. So I read it in the smoke. At sunset the Nemedians rode into Tarantia, unopposed. Look! Even now, in the royal hall of Tarantia—'

Abruptly Conan was looking into the great coronation hall. Valerius stood on the regal dais, clad in ermine robes, and Amalric, still in his dusty, bloodstained armor, placed a rich and gleaming circlet on his yellow locks – the crown of Aquilonia! The people cheered; long lines of steel-clad Nemedian warriors looked grimly on, and nobles long in disfavor at Conan's court strutted and swaggered with the emblem of Valerius on their sleeves.

'Crom!' It was an explosive imprecation from Conan's lips as he started up, his great fists clenched into hammers, his veins on his temples knotting, his features convulsed. 'A Nemedian placing the crown of Aquilonia on that renegade – in the royal hall of Tarantia!'

As if dispelled by his violence, the smoke faded, and he saw Zelata's black eyes gleaming at him through the mist.

'You have seen – the people of your capital have forfeited the freedom you won for them by sweat and blood; they have sold themselves to the slavers and the butchers. They have shown that they do not trust their destiny. Can you rely upon them for the winning back of your kingdom?'

'They thought I was dead,' he grunted, recovering some of his poise. 'I have no son. Men can't be governed by a memory. What if the Nemedians have taken Tarantia? There still remain the provinces, the barons, and the people of the countrysides. Valerius has won an empty glory.'

'You are stubborn, as befits a fighter. I cannot show you the future, I cannot show you all the past. Nay, *I* show you nothing. I merely make you see windows opened in the veil by powers unguessed. Would you look into the past for a clue of the present?'

'Aye.' He seated himself abruptly.

Again the green smoke rose and billowed. Again images unfolded before him, this time alien and seemingly irrelevant. He saw great towering black walls, pedestals half hidden in the shadows upholding images of hideous, half-bestial gods. Men moved in the shadows, dark, wiry men, clad in red, silken loincloths. They were bearing a green jade sarcophagus along a gigantic black corridor. But before he could tell much about what he saw, the scene shifted. He saw a cavern, dim, shadowy and haunted with a strange intangible horror. On an altar of black stone stood a curious golden vessel, shaped like the shell of a scallop. Into this cavern came some of the same dark, wiry men who had borne the mummy-case. They seized the golden vessel, and then the shadows swirled around them and what happened he could not say. But he saw a glimmer in a whorl of darkness, like a ball of living fire. Then the smoke was only smoke, drifting up from the fire of tamarisk chunks, thinning and fading.

'But what does this portend?' he demanded, bewildered. 'What I saw in Tarantia I can understand. But what means this glimpse of Zamorian thieves sneaking through a subterranean temple of Set, in Stygia? And that cavern – I've never seen or heard of anything like it, in all my wanderings. If you can show me that much, these shreds of vision which mean nothing, disjointed, why can you not show me all that is to occur?'

Zelata stirred the fire without replying.

'These things are governed by immutable laws,' she said at last. 'I can not make you understand; I do not altogether understand myself, though I have sought wisdom in the silences of the high places for more years than I can remember. I cannot save you, though I would if I might. Man must, at last, work out his own salvation. Yet perhaps wisdom may come to me in dreams, and in the morn I may be able to give you the clue to the enigma.'

'What enigma?' he demanded.

'The mystery that confronts you, whereby you have lost a kingdom,' she answered. And then she spread a sheepskin upon the floor before the hearth. 'Sleep,' she said briefly.

Without a word he stretched himself upon it, and sank into restless but deep sleep through which phantoms moved silently and monstrous shapeless shadows crept. Once, limned against a purple sunless horizon, he saw the mighty walls and towers of a great city such as rose nowhere on the waking earth he knew. Its colossal pylons and purple minarets lifted toward the stars, and over it, floating like a giant mirage, hovered the bearded countenance of the man Xaltotun.

Conan woke in the chill whiteness of early dawn, to see Zelata crouched beside the tiny fire. He had not awakened once in the night, and the sound of the great wolf leaving or entering should have roused him. Yet the wolf was there, beside the hearth, with its shaggy coat wet with dew, and with more than dew. Blood glistened wetly amid the thick fell, and there was a cut upon his shoulder.

Zelata nodded, without looking around, as if reading the thoughts of her royal guest.

'He has hunted before dawn, and red was the hunting. I think the man who hunted a king will hunt no more, neither man nor beast.'

Conan stared at the great beast with strange fascination as he moved to take the food Zelata offered him.

'When I come to my throne again I won't forget,' he said briefly. 'You've befriended me – by Crom, I can't remember when I've lain down and slept at the mercy of man or woman as I did last night. But what of the riddle you would read me this morn?'

A long silence ensued, in which the crackle of the tamarisks was loud on the hearth.

'Find the heart of your kingdom,' she said at last. 'There lies your defeat and your power. You fight more than mortal man. You will not press the throne again unless you find the heart of your kingdom.'

'Do you mean the city of Tarantia?'

She shook her head. 'I am but an oracle, through whose lips the gods speak. My lips are sealed by them lest I speak too much. You must find the heart of your kingdom. I can say no more. My lips are opened and sealed by the gods.'

Dawn was still white on the peaks when Conan rode westward. A glance back showed him Zelata standing in the door of her hut, inscrutable as ever, the great wolf beside her.

A gray sky arched overhead, and a moaning wind was chill with a promise of winter. Brown leaves fluttered slowly down from the bare branches, sifting upon his mailed shoulders.

All day he pushed through the hills, avoiding roads and villages. Toward nightfall he began to drop down from the heights, tier by tier, and saw the broad plains of Aquilonia spread out beneath him.

Villages and farms lay close to the foot of the hills on the western side of the mountains, for, for half a century, most of the raiding across the frontier had been done by the Aquilonians. But now only embers and ashes showed where farm huts and villas had stood.

In the gathering darkness Conan rode slowly on. There was little fear of discovery, which he dreaded from friend as well as from foe. The Nemedians had remembered old scores on their westward drive, and Valerius had made no attempt to restrain his allies. He did not count on winning the love of the common people. A vast swath of desolation had been cut through the country from the foothills westward. Conan cursed as he rode over blackened expanses that had been rich fields, and saw the gaunt gable-ends of burned houses jutting against the sky. He moved through an empty and deserted land, like a ghost out of a forgotten and outworn past.

The speed with which the army had traversed the land showed what little resistance it had encountered. Yet had Conan been leading his Aquilonians the invading army would have been forced to buy every foot they gained with their blood. The bitter realization permeated his soul; he was not the representative of a dynasty. He was only a lone adventurer. Even the drop of dynastic blood Valerius boasted had more hold on the minds of men than the memory of Conan and the freedom and power he had given the kingdom.

No pursuers followed him down out of the hills. He watched for wandering or returning Nemedian troops, but met none. Skulkers gave him a wide path, supposing him to be one of the conquerors, what of his harness. Groves and rivers were far more plentiful on the western side of the mountains, and coverts for concealment were not lacking.

So he moved across the pillaged land, halting only to rest his horse, eating frugally of the food Zelata had given him, until, on a dawn when he lay hidden on a river bank where willows and oaks grew thickly, he glimpsed, afar, across the rolling plains dotted with rich groves, the blue and golden towers of Tarantia.

He was no longer in a deserted land, but one teeming with varied life. His progress thenceforth was slow and cautious, through thick woods and unfrequented byways. It was dusk when he reached the plantation of Servius Galannus.

8 Dying Embers

The countryside about Tarantia had escaped the fearful ravaging of the more easterly provinces. There were evidences of the march of a conquering army in broken hedges, plundered fields and looted granaries, but torch and steel had not been loosed wholesale.

There was but one grim splotch on the landscape – a charred expanse of ashes and blackened stone, where, Conan knew, had once stood the stately villa of one of his staunchest supporters.

The king dared not openly approach the Galannus farm, which lay only a few miles from the city. In the twilight he rode through an extensive woodland, until he sighted a keeper's lodge through the trees. Dismounting and tying his horse, he approached the thick, arched door with the intention of sending the keeper after Servius. He did not know what enemies the manor house might be sheltering. He had seen no troops, but they might be quartered all over the countryside. But as he drew near, he saw the door open and a compact figure in silk hose and richly embroidered doublet stride forth and turn up a path that wound away through the woods.

'Servius!'

At the low call the master of the plantation wheeled with a startled exclamation. His hand flew to the short hunting-sword at his hip, and he recoiled from the tall gray steel figure standing in the dusk before him.

'Who are you?' he demanded. 'What is your – *Mitra!*'

His breath hissed inward and his ruddy face paled. 'Avaunt!' he ejaculated. 'Why have you come back from the gray lands of death to terrify me? I was always your true liegeman in your lifetime—'

'As I still expect you to be,' answered Conan. 'Stop trembling, man; I'm flesh and blood.'

Sweating with uncertainty Servius approached and stared into the face of the mail-clad giant, and then, convinced of the reality of what he saw, he dropped to one knee and doffed his plumed cap.

'Your Majesty! Truly, this is a miracle passing belief! The great bell in the citadel has tolled your dirge, days agone. Men said you died at Valkia, crushed under a million tons of earth and broken granite.'

'It was another in my harness,' grunted Conan. 'But let us talk later. If there is such a thing as a joint of beef on your board—'

'Forgive me, my lord!' cried Servius, springing to his feet. 'The dust of travel is gray on your mail, and I keep you standing here without rest or sup! Mitra! I see well enough now that you are alive, but I swear, when I turned and saw you standing all gray and dim in the twilight, the marrow of my knees turned to water. It is an ill thing to meet a man you thought dead in the woodland at dusk.'

'Bid the keeper see to my steed which is tied behind yonder oak,' requested Conan, and Servius nodded, drawing the king up the path. The patrician, recovering from his supernatural fright, had become extremely nervous.

'I will send a servant from the manor,' he said. 'The keeper is in his lodge – but I dare not trust even my servants in these days. It is better that only I know of your presence.'

Approaching the great house that glimmered dimly through the trees, he turned aside into a little-used path that ran between close-set oaks whose intertwining branches formed a vault overhead, shutting out the dim light of the gathering dusk. Servius hurried on through the darkness without speaking, and with something resembling panic in his manner, and presently led Conan through a small side-door into a narrow, dimly illuminated corridor. They traversed this in haste and silence, and Servius brought the king into a spacious chamber with a high, oak-beamed ceiling and richly paneled walls. Logs flamed in the wide fireplace, for there was a frosty edge to the air, and a great meat pasty in a stone platter stood smoking on a broad mahogany board. Servius locked the massive door and extinguished the candles that stood in a silver candlestick on the table, leaving the chamber illuminated only by the fire on the hearth.

'Your pardon, your Majesty,' he apologized. 'These are perilous times; spies lurk everywhere. It were better that none be able to peer through the windows and recognize you. This pasty, however, is just from the oven, as I intended supping on my return from talk with my keeper. If your Majesty would deign—'

'The light is sufficient,' grunted Conan, seating himself with scant ceremony, and drawing his poniard.

He dug ravenously into the luscious dish, and washed it down with great gulps of wine from grapes grown in Servius' vineyards. He seemed oblivious to any sense of peril, but Servius shifted uneasily on his settle by the fire, nervously fingering the heavy gold chain about his neck. He glanced continually at the diamond-panes of the casement, gleaming dimly in the firelight, and cocked his ear toward the door, as if half expecting to hear the pad of furtive feet in the corridor without.

Finishing his meal, Conan rose and seated himself on another settle before the fire.

'I won't jeopardize you long by my presence, Servius,' he said abruptly. 'Dawn will find me far from your plantation.'

'My lord—' Servius lifted his hands in expostulation, but Conan waved his protests aside.

'I know your loyalty and your courage. Both are above reproach. But if Valerius has usurped my throne, it would be death for you to shelter me, if you were discovered.'

'I am not strong enough to defy him openly,' admitted Servius. 'The fifty men-at-arms I could lead to battle would be but a handful of straws. You saw the ruins of Emilius Scavonus' plantation?'

Conan nodded, frowning darkly.

'He was the strongest partician in this province, as you know. He refused to give his allegiance to Valerius. The Nemedians burned him in the ruins of his own villa. After that the rest of us saw the futility of resistance, especially as the people of Tarantia refused to fight. We submitted and Valerius spared our lives, though he levied a tax upon us that will ruin many. But what could we do? We thought you were dead. Many of the barons had been slain, others taken prisoner. The army was shattered and scattered. You have no heir to take the crown. There was no one to lead us—'

'Was there not Count Trocero of Poitain?' demanded Conan harshly.

Servius spread his hands helplessly.

'It is true that his general Prospero was in the field with a small army. Retreating before Amalric, he urged men to rally to his banner. But with your Majesty dead, men remembered old wars and civil brawls, and how Trocero and his Poitanians once rode through these provinces even as Amalric was riding now, with torch and sword. The barons were jealous of Trocero. Some men – spies of Valerius perhaps – shouted that the Count of Poitain intended seizing the crown for himself. Old sectional hates flared up again. If we had had one man with dynastic blood in his veins we would have crowned and followed him against Nemedia. But we had none.

'The barons who followed you loyally would not follow one of their own number, each holding himself as good as his neighbor, each fearing the ambitions of the others. You were the cord that held the fagots together. When the cord was cut, the fagots fell apart. If you had had a son, the barons would have rallied loyally to him. But there was no point for their patriotism to focus upon.

'The merchants and commoners, dreading anarchy and a return of feudal days when each baron was his own law, cried out that any king was better than none, even Valerius, who was at least of the blood of the old dynasty. There was no one to oppose him when he rode up at the head of his steel-clad hosts, with the scarlet dragon of Nemedia floating over him, and rang his lance against the gates of Tarantia.

'Nay, the people threw open the gates and knelt in the dust before him. They had refused to aid Prospero in holding the city. They said they had rather be ruled by Valerius than by Trocero. They said – truthfully – that the barons would not rally to Trocero, but that many would accept Valerius. They said that by yielding to Valerius they would escape the devastation of civil war, and the fury of the Nemedians. Prospero rode southward with his ten thousand knights, and the horsemen of the Nemedians entered the city a few hours later. They did not follow him. They remained to see that Valerius was crowned in Tarantia.'

'Then the old witch's smoke showed the truth,' muttered Conan, feeling a queer chill along his spine. 'Amalric crowned Valerius?'

'Aye, in the coronation hall, with the blood of slaughter scarcely dried on his hands.'

'And do the people thrive under his benevolent rule?' asked Conan with angry irony.

'He lives like a foreign prince in the midst of a conquered land,' answered Servius bitterly. 'His court is filled with Nemedians, the palace troops are of the same breed, and a large garrison of them occupy the citadel. Aye, the hour of the Dragon has come at last.

'Nemedians swagger like lords through the streets. Women are outraged and merchants plundered daily, and Valerius either can, or will, make no attempt to curb them. Nay, he is but their puppet, their figurehead. Men of sense knew he would be, and the people are beginning to find it out.

'Amalric has ridden forth with a strong army to reduce the outlying provinces where some of the barons have defied him. But there is no unity among them. Their jealousy of each other is stronger than their fear of Amalric. He will crush them one by one. Many castles and cities, realizing that, have sent in their submission. Those who resist fare miserably. The Nemedians are glutting their long hatred. And their ranks are swelled by Aquilonians whom fear, gold, or necessity of occupation are forcing into their armies. It is a natural consequence.'

Conan nodded somberly, staring at the red reflections of the firelight on the richly carved oaken panels.

'Aquilonia has a king instead of the anarchy they feared,' said Servius at last. 'Valerius does not protect his subjects against his allies. Hundreds who could not pay the ransom imposed upon them have been sold to the Kothic slave-traders.'

Conan's head jerked up and a lethal flame lit his blue eyes. He swore gustily, his mighty hands knotting into iron hammers.

'Aye, white men sell white men and white women, as it was in the feudal days. In the palaces of Shem and of Turan they will live out the lives of slaves. Valerius is king, but the unity for which the people looked, even though of the sword, is not complete.

'Gunderland in the north and Poitain in the south are yet unconquered, and there are unsubdued provinces in the west, where the border barons have the backing of the Bossonian bowmen. Yet these outlying provinces are no real menace to Valerius. They must remain on the defensive, and will be lucky if they are able to keep their independence. Here Valerius and his foreign knights are supreme.'

'Let him make the best of it then,' said Conan grimly. 'His time is short. The people will rise when they learn that I'm alive. We'll take Tarantia back before Amalric can return with his army. Then we'll sweep these dogs from the kingdom.'

Servius was silent. The crackle of the fire was loud in the stillness.

'Well,' exclaimed Conan impatiently, 'why do you sit with your head bent, staring at the hearth? Do you doubt what I have said?'

Servius avoided the king's eye.

'What mortal man can do, you will do, your Majesty,' he answered. 'I have ridden behind you in battle, and I know that no mortal being can stand before your sword.'

'What, then?'

Servius drew his fur-trimmed jupon closer about him, and shivered in spite of the flame.

'Men say your fall was occasioned by sorcery,' he said presently.

'What then?'

'What mortal can fight against sorcery? Who is this veiled man who communes at midnight with Valerius and his allies, as men say, who appears and disappears so mysteriously? Men say in whispers that he is a great magician who died thousands of years ago, but has returned from death's gray lands to overthrow the king of Aquilonia and restore the dynasty of which Valerius is heir.'

'What matter?' exclaimed Conan angrily. 'I escaped from the devil-haunted pits of Belverus, and from diabolism in the mountains. If the people rise—'

Servius shook his head.

'Your staunchest supporters in the eastern and central provinces are dead, fled or imprisoned. Gunderland is far to the north, Poitain far to the south. The Bossonians have retired to their marches far to the west. It would take weeks to gather and concentrate these forces, and before that could be done, each levy would be attacked separately by Amalric and destroyed.'

'But an uprising in the central provinces would tip the scales for us!' exclaimed Conan. 'We could seize Tarantia and hold it against Amalric until the Gundermen and Poitanians could get here.'

Servius hesitated, and his voice sank to a whisper.

'Men say you died accursed. Men say this veiled stranger cast a spell upon you to slay you and break your army. The great bell has tolled your dirge. Men believe you to be dead. And the central provinces would not rise, even if they knew you lived. They would not dare. Sorcery defeated you at Valkia. Sorcery brought the news to Tarantia, for that very night men were shouting of it in the streets.

'A Nemedian priest loosed black magic again in the streets of Tarantia to slay men who still were loyal to your memory. I myself saw it. Armed men dropped like flies and died in the streets in a manner no man could understand. And the lean priest laughed and said: 'I am only Altaro, only an acolyte of Orastes, who is but an acolyte of him who wears the veil; not mine is the power; the power but works through me.'

'Well,' said Conan harshly, 'is it not better to die honorably than to live in infamy? Is death worse than oppression, slavery and ultimate destruction?'

'When the fear of sorcery is in, reason is out,' replied Servius. 'The fear of the central provinces is too great to allow them to rise for you. The outlying provinces would fight for you – but the same sorcery that smote your army at Valkia would smite you again. The Nemedians hold the broadest, richest and most thickly populated sections of Aquilonia, and they cannot be defeated by the forces which might still be at your command. You would be sacrificing your loyal subjects uselessly. In sorrow I say it, but it is true: King Conan, you are a king without a kingdom.'

Conan stared into the fire without replying. A smoldering log crashed down among the flames without a bursting shower of sparks. It might have been the crashing ruin of his kingdom.

Again Conan felt the presence of a grim reality behind the veil of material illusion. He sensed again the inexorable drive of a ruthless fate. A feeling of furious panic tugged at his soul, a sense of being trapped, and a red rage that burned to destroy and kill.

'Where are the officials of my court?' he demanded at last.

'Pallantides was sorely wounded at Valkia, was ransomed by his family, and now lies in his castle in Attalus. He will be fortunate if he ever rides again. Publius, the chancellor, has fled the kingdom in disguise, no man knows whither. The council has been disbanded. Some were imprisoned, some banished. Many of your loyal subjects have been put to death. Tonight, for instance, the Countess Albiona dies under the headsman's ax.'

Conan started and stared at Servius with such anger smoldering in his blue eyes that the patrician shrank back.

'Why?'

'Because she would not become the mistress of Valerius. Her hands are forfeit, her henchmen sold into slavery, and at midnight, in the Iron Tower, her head must fall. Be advised, my king – to me you will ever be my king – and flee before you are discovered. In these days none is safe. Spies and informers creep among us, betraying the slightest deed or word of discontent as treason and rebellion. If you make yourself known to your subjects it will only end in your capture and death.

'My horses and all the men that I can trust are at your disposal. Before dawn we can be far from Tarantia, and well on our way toward the border. If I cannot aid you to recover your kingdom, I can at least follow you into exile.'

Conan shook his head. Servius glanced uneasily at him as he sat staring into the fire, his chin propped on his mighty fist. The firelight gleamed redly on his steel mail, on his baleful eyes. They burned in the firelight like the eyes of a wolf. Servius was again aware, as in the past, and now more strongly than ever, of something alien about the king. That great frame under the mail mesh was too hard and supple for a civilized man; the elemental fire of the primitive burned in those smoldering eyes. Now the barbaric suggestion about the king was more pronounced, as if in his extremity the outward aspects of civilization were stripped away, to reveal the primordial core. Conan was reverting to his pristine type. He did not act as a civilized man would act under the same conditions, nor did his thoughts run in the same channels. He was unpredictable. It was only a stride from the king of Aquilonia to the skin-clad slayer of the Cimmerian hills.

'I'll ride to Poitain, if it may be,' Conan said at last. 'But I'll ride alone. And I have one last duty to perform as king of Aquilonia.'

'What do you mean, your Majesty?' asked Servius, shaken by a premonition.

'I'm going into Tarantia after Albiona tonight,' answered the king. 'I've failed all my other loyal subjects, it seems – if they take her head, they can have mine too.'

'This is madness!' cried Servius, staggering up and clutching his throat, as if he already felt the noose closing about it.

'There are secrets to the Tower which few know,' said Conan. 'Anyway, I'd be a dog to leave Albiona to die because of her loyalty to me. I may be a king without a kingdom, but I'm not a man without honor.'

'It will ruin us all!' whispered Servius.

'It will ruin no one but me if I fail. You've risked enough. I ride alone tonight. This is all I want you to do: procure me a patch for my eye, a staff for my hand, and garments such as travelers wear.'

9 'It is the King or His Ghost!'

Many men passed through the great arched gates of Tarantia between sunset and midnight – belated travelers, merchants from afar with heavily laden mules, free workmen from the surrounding farms and vineyards. Now that Valerius was supreme in the central provinces, there was no rigid scrutiny of the folk who flowed in a steady stream through the wide gates. Discipline had been relaxed. The Nemedian soldiers who stood on guard were half drunk, and much too busy watching for handsome peasant girls and rich merchants who could be bullied to notice workmen or dusty travelers, even one tall wayfarer whose worn cloak could not conceal the hard lines of his powerful frame.

This man carried himself with an erect, aggressive bearing that was too natural for him to realize it himself, much less dissemble it. A great patch covered one eye, and his leather coif, drawn low over his brows, shadowed his features. With a long thick staff in his muscular brown hand, he strode leisurely through the arch where the torches flared and guttered, and, ignored by the tipsy guardsmen, emerged upon the wide streets of Tarantia.

Upon these well-lighted thoroughfares the usual throngs went about their business, and shops and stalls stood open, with their wares displayed. One thread ran a constant theme through the pattern. Nemedian soldiers, singly or in clumps, swaggered through the throngs, shouldering their way with studied arrogance. Women scurried from their path, and men stepped aside with darkened brows and clenched fists. The Aquilonians were a proud race, and these were their hereditary enemies.

The knuckles of the tall traveler knotted on his staff, but, like the others, he stepped aside to let the men in armor have the way. Among the motley and varied crowd he did not attract much attention in his drab, dusty garments. But once, as he passed a sword-seller's stall and the light that streamed from its wide door fell full upon him, he thought he felt an intense stare upon him, and turning quickly, saw a man in the brown jerkin of a free workman regarding him fixedly. This man turned away with undue haste, and vanished in the shifting throng. But Conan turned into a narrow by-street and quickened his pace. It might have been mere idle curiosity; but he could take no chances.

The grim Iron Tower stood apart from the citadel, amid a maze of narrow streets and crowding houses where the meaner structures, appropriating a space from which the more fastidious shrank, had invaded a portion of the city ordinarily alien to them. The Tower was in reality a castle, an ancient, formidable pile of heavy stone and black iron, which had itself served as the citadel in an earlier, ruder century.

Not a long distance from it, lost in a tangle of partly deserted tenements and warehouses, stood an ancient watchtower, so old and forgotten that it did not appear on the maps of the city for a hundred years back. Its original purpose had been forgotten, and nobody, of such as saw it at all, noticed that the apparently ancient lock which kept it from being appropriated as sleeping-quarters by beggars and thieves, was in reality comparatively new and extremely powerful, cunningly disguised into an appearance of rusty antiquity. Not half a dozen men in the kingdom had ever known the secret of that tower.

No keyhole showed in the massive, green-crusted lock. But Conan's practised fingers, stealing over it, pressed here and there knobs invisible to the casual eye. The door silently opened inward and he entered solid blackness, pushing the door shut behind him. A light would have showed the tower empty, a bare, cylindrical shaft of massive stone.

Groping in a corner with the sureness of familiarity, he found the projections for which he was feeling on a slab of the stone that composed the floor. Quickly he lifted it, and without hesitation lowered himself into the aperture beneath. His feet felt stone steps leading downward into what he knew was a narrow tunnel that ran straight toward the foundations of the Iron Tower, three streets away.

The Bell on the citadel, which tolled only at the midnight hour or for the death of a king, boomed suddenly. In a dimly lighted chamber in the Iron Tower a door opened and a form emerged into a corridor. The interior of the Tower was as forbidding as its external appearance. Its massive stone walls were rough, unadorned. The flags of the floor were worn deep by generations of faltering feet, and the vault of the ceiling was gloomy in the dim light of torches set in niches.

The man who trudged down that grim corridor was in appearance in keeping with his surroundings. He was a tall, powerfully built man, clad in close-fitting black silk. Over his head was drawn a black hood which fell about his shoulders, having two holes for his eyes. From his shoulders hung a loose black cloak, and over one shoulder he bore a heavy ax, the shape of which was that of neither tool nor weapon.

As he went down the corridor, a figure came hobbling up it, a bent, surly old man, stooping under the weight of his pike and a lantern he bore in one hand.

'You are not as prompt as your predecessor, master headsman,' he grumbled. 'Midnight has just struck, and masked men have gone to milady's cell. They await you.'

'The tones of the bell still echo among the towers,' answered the executioner. 'If I am not so quick to leap and run at the beck of Aquilonians as was the dog who held this office before me, they shall find my arm no less ready. Get you to your duties, old watchman, and leave me to mine. I think mine is the sweeter trade, by Mitra, for you tramp cold corridors and peer at rusty dungeon doors, while I lop off the fairest head in Tarantia this night.'

The watchman limped on down the corridor, still grumbling, and the headsman resumed his leisurely way. A few strides carried him around a turn in the corridor, and he absently noted that at his left a door stood partly open. If he had thought, he would have known that that door had been opened since the watchman passed; but thinking was not his trade. He was passing the unlocked door before he realized that aught was amiss, and then it was too late.

A soft tigerish step and the rustle of a cloak warned him, but before he could turn, a heavy arm hooked about his throat from behind, crushing the cry before it could reach his lips. In the brief instant that was allowed him he realized with a surge of panic the strength of his attacker, against which his own brawny thews were helpless. He sensed without seeing the poised dagger.

'Nemedian dog!' muttered a voice thick with passion in his ear. 'You've cut off your last Aquilonian head!'

And that was the last thing he ever heard.

In a dank dungeon, lighted only by a guttering torch, three men stood about a young woman who knelt on the rush-strewn flags staring wildly up at them. She was clad only in a scanty shift; her golden hair fell in lustrous ripples about her white shoulders, and her wrists were bound behind her. Even in the uncertain torchlight, and in spite of her disheveled condition and pallor of fear, her beauty was striking. She knelt mutely, staring with wide eyes up at her tormenters. The men were closely masked and cloaked. Such a deed as this needed masks, even in a conquered land. She knew them all nevertheless; but what she knew would harm no one – after that night.

'Our merciful sovereign offers you one more chance, Countess,' said the tallest of the three, and he spoke Aquilonian without an accent. 'He bids me say that if you soften your proud, rebellious spirit, he will still open his arms to you. If not—' he gestured toward a grim wooden block in the center of the cell. It was blackly stained, and showed many deep nicks as if a keen edge, cutting through some yielding substance, had sunk into the wood.

Albiona shuddered and turned pale, shrinking back. Every fiber in her vigorous young body quivered with the urge of life. Valerius was young, too, and handsome. Many women loved him, she told herself, fighting with herself for life. But she could not speak the word that would ransom her soft young body from the block and the dripping ax. She could not reason the matter. She only knew that when she thought of the clasp of Valerius' arms, her flesh crawled with an abhorrence greater than the fear of death. She shook her head helplessly, compelled by an impulse more irresistible than the instinct to live.

'Then there is no more to be said!' exclaimed one of the others impatiently, and he spoke with a Nemedian accent. 'Where is the headsman?'

As if summoned by the word, the dungeon door opened silently, and a great figure stood framed in it, like a black shadow from the underworld.

Albiona voiced a low, involuntary cry at the sight of that grim shape, and the others stared silently for a moment, perhaps themselves daunted with superstitious awe at the silent, hooded figure. Through the coif the eyes blazed like coals of blue fire, and as these eyes rested on each man in turn, he felt a curious chill travel down his spine.

Then the tall Aquilonian roughly seized the girl and dragged her to the block. She screamed uncontrollably and fought hopelessly against him, frantic with terror, but he ruthlessly forced her to her knees, and bent her yellow head down to the bloody block.

'Why do you delay, headsman?' he exclaimed angrily. 'Perform your task!'

He was answered by a short, gusty boom of laughter that was indescribably menacing. All in the dungeon froze in their places, staring at the hooded shape – the two cloaked figures, the masked man bending over the girl, the girl herself on her knees, twisting her imprisoned head to look upward.

'What means this unseemly mirth, dog?' demanded the Aquilonian uneasily.

The man in the black garb tore his hood from his head and flung it to the ground; he set his back to the closed door and lifted the headsman's ax.

'Do you know me, dogs?' he rumbled. 'Do you know me?'

The breathless silence was broken by a scream.

'The king!' shrieked Albiona, wrenching herself free from the slackened grasp of her captor. 'Oh, Mitra, the king!'

The three men stood like statues, and then the Aquilonian started and spoke, like a man who doubts his own senses.

'Conan!' he ejaculated. 'It is the king, or his ghost! What devil's work is this?'

'Devil's work to match devils!' mocked Conan, his lips laughing but hell flaming in his eyes. 'Come, fall to, my gentlemen. You have your swords, and I this cleaver. Nay, I think this butcher's tool fits the work at hand, my fair lords!'

'At him!' muttered the Aquilonian, drawing his sword. 'It is Conan and we must kill or be killed!'

And like men waking from a trance, the Nemedians drew their blades and rushed on the king.

The headsman's ax was not made for such work, but the king wielded the heavy, clumsy weapon as lightly as a hatchet, and his quickness of foot, as he constantly shifted his position, defeated their purpose of engaging him all three at once.

He caught the sword of the first man on his ax-head and crushed in the wielder's breast with a murderous counterstroke before he could step back or parry. The remaining Nemedian, missing a savage swipe, had his brains dashed out before he could recover his balance, and an instant later the Aquilonian was backed into a corner, desperately parrying the crashing strokes that rained about him, lacking opportunity even to scream for help.

Suddenly Conan's long left arm shot out and ripped the mask from the man's head, disclosing the pallid features.

'Dog!' grated the king. 'I thought I knew you. Traitor! Damned renegade! Even this base steel is too honorable for your foul head. Nay, die as thieves die!'

The ax fell in a devastating arch, and the Aquilonian cried out and went to his knees, grasping the severed stump of his right arm from which blood spouted. It had been shorn away at the elbow, and the ax, unchecked in its descent, had gashed deeply into his side, so that his entrails bulged out.

'Lie there and bleed to death,' grunted Conan, casting the ax away disgustedly. 'Come, Countess!'

Stooping, he slashed the cords that bound her wrists and lifting her as if she had been a child, strode from the dungeon. She was sobbing hysterically, with her arms thrown about his corded neck in a frenzied embrace.

'Easy all,' he muttered. 'We're not out of this yet. If we can reach the dungeon where the secret door opens on stairs that lead to the tunnel – devil take it, they've heard that noise, even through these walls.'

Down the corridor arms clanged and the tramp and shouting of men echoed under the vaulted roof. A bent figure came hobbling swiftly along, lantern held high, and its light shone full on Conan and the girl. With a curse the Cimmerian sprang toward him, but the old watchman, abandoning both lantern and pike, scuttled away down the corridor, screeching for help at the top of his cracked voice. Deeper shouts answered him.

Conan turned swiftly and ran the other way. He was cut off from the dungeon with the secret lock and the hidden door through which he had entered the Tower, and by which he had hoped to leave, but he knew this grim building well. Before he was king he had been imprisoned in it.

He turned off into a side passage and quickly emerged into another, broader corridor, which ran parallel to the one down which he had come, and which was at the moment deserted. He followed this only a few yards, when he again turned back, down another side passage. This brought him back into the corridor he had left, but at a strategic point. A few feet farther up the corridor there was a heavy bolted door, and before it stood a bearded Nemedian in corselet and helmet, his back to Conan as he peered up the corridor in the direction of the growing tumult and wildly waving lanterns.

Conan did not hesitate. Slipping the girl to the ground, he ran at the guard swiftly and silently, sword in hand. The man turned just as the king reached him, bawled in surprise and fright and lifted his pike; but before he could bring the clumsy weapon into play, Conan brought down his sword on the fellow's helmet with a force that would have felled an ox. Helmet and skull gave way together and the guard crumpled to the floor.

In an instant Conan had drawn the massive bolt that barred the door – too heavy for one ordinary man to have manipulated – and called hastily to Albiona, who ran staggering to him. Catching her up unceremoniously with one arm, he bore her through the door and into the outer darkness.

They had come into a narrow alley, black as pitch, walled by the side of the Tower on one hand, and the sheer stone back of a row of buildings on the other. Conan, hurrying through the darkness as swiftly as he dared, felt the latter wall for doors or windows, but found none.

The great door clanged open behind them, and men poured out, with torches gleaming on breastplates and naked swords. They glared about, bellowing, unable to penetrate the darkness which their torches served to illuminate for only a few feet in any direction, and then rushed down the alley at random – heading in the direction opposite to that taken by Conan and Albiona.

'They'll learn their mistake quick enough,' he muttered, increasing his pace. If we ever find a crack in this infernal wall – damn! The street watch!'

Ahead of them a faint glow became apparent, where the alley opened into a narrow street, and he saw dim figures looming against it with a glimmer of steel. It was indeed the street watch, investigating the noise they had heard echoing down the alley.

'Who goes there?' they shouted, and Conan grit his teeth at the hated Nemedian accent.

'Keep behind me,' he ordered the girl. 'We've got to cut our way through before the prison guards come back and pin us between them.'

And grasping his sword, he ran straight at the oncoming figures. The advantage of surprise was his. He could see them, limned against the distant glow, and they could not see him coming at them out of the black depths of the alley. He was among them before they knew it, smiting with the silent fury of a wounded lion.

His one chance lay in hacking through before they could gather their wits. But there were half a score of them, in full mail, hard-bitten veterans of the border wars, in whom the instinct for battle could take the place of bemused wits. Three of them were down before they realized that it was only one man who was attacking them, but even so their reaction was instantaneous. The clangor of steel rose deafeningly, and sparks flew as Conan's sword crashed on basinet and hauberk. He could see better than they, and in the dim light his swiftly moving figure was an uncertain mark. Flailing swords cut empty air or glanced from his blade, and when he struck it was with the fury and certainty of a hurricane.

But behind him sounded the shouts of the prison guards, returning up the alley at a run, and still the mailed figures before him barred his way with a bristling wall of steel. In an instant the guards would be on his back – in desperation he redoubled his strokes, flailing like a smith on an anvil, and then was suddenly aware of a diversion. Out of nowhere behind the watchmen rose a score of black figures and there was a sound of blows, murderously driven. Steel glinted in the gloom, and men cried out, struck mortally from behind. In an instant the alley was littered with writhing forms. A dark, cloaked shape sprang toward Conan, who heaved up his sword, catching a gleam of steel in the right hand. But the other was extended to him empty and a voice hissed urgently: 'This way, your Majesty! Quickly!'

With a muttered oath of surprise, Conan caught up Albiona in one massive arm, and followed his unknown befriender. He was not inclined to hesitate, with thirty prison guardsmen closing in behind him.

Surrounded by mysterious figures he hurried down the alley, carrying the countess as if she had been a child. He could tell nothing of his rescuers except that they wore dark cloaks and hoods. Doubt and suspicion crossed his mind, but at least they had struck down his enemies, and he saw no better course than to follow them.

As if sensing his doubt, the leader touched his arm lightly and said: 'Fear not, King Conan; we are your loyal subjects.' The voice was not familiar, but the accent was Aquilonian of the central provinces.

Behind them the guards were yelling as they stumbled over the shambles in the mud, and they came pelting vengefully down the alley, seeing the vague dark mass moving between them and the light of the distant street. But the hooded men turned suddenly toward the seemingly blank wall, and Conan saw a door gape there. He muttered a curse. He had traversed that alley by day, in times past, and had never noticed a door there. But through it they went, and the door closed behind them with the click of a lock. The sound was not reassuring, but his guides were hurrying him on, moving with the precision of familiarity, guiding Conan with a hand at either elbow. It was like traversing a tunnel, and Conan felt Albiona's lithe limbs trembling in his arms. Then somewhere ahead of them an opening was faintly visible, merely a somewhat less black arch in the blackness, and through this they filed.

After that there was a bewildering succession of dim courts and shadowy alleys and winding corridors, all traversed in utter silence, until at last they emerged into a broad lighted chamber, the location of which Conan could not even guess, for their devious route had confused even his primitive sense of direction.

10 A Coin from Acheron

Not all his guides entered the chamber. When the door closed, Conan saw only one man standing before him – a slim figure, masked in a black cloak with a hood. This the man threw back, disclosing a pale oval of a face, with calm, delicately chiseled features.

The king set Albiona on her feet, but she still clung to him and stared apprehensively about her. The chamber was a large one, with marble walls partly covered with black velvet hangings and thick rich carpets on the mosaic floor, laved in the soft golden glow of bronze lamps.

Conan instinctively laid a hand on his hilt. There was blood on his hand, blood clotted about the mouth of his scabbard, for he had sheathed his blade without cleansing it.

'Where are we?' he demanded.

The stranger answered with a low, profound bow in which the suspicious king could detect no trace of irony.

'In the temple of Asura, your Majesty.'

Albiona cried out faintly and clung closer to Conan, staring fearfully at the black, arched doors, as if expecting the entry of some grisly shape of darkness.

'Fear not, my lady,' said their guide. 'There is nothing here to harm you, vulgar superstition to the contrary. If your monarch was sufficiently convinced of the innocence of our religion to protect us from the persecution of the ignorant, then certainly one of his subjects need have no apprehensions.'

'Who are you?' demanded Conan.

'I am Hadrathus, priest of Asura. One of my followers recognized you when you entered the city, and brought the word to me.'

Conan grunted profanely.

'Do not fear that others discovered your identity,' Hadrathus assured him. 'Your disguise would have deceived any but a follower of Asura, whose cult it is to seek below the aspect of illusion. You were followed to the watch tower, and some of my people went into the tunnel to aid you if you returned by that route. Others, myself among them, surrounded the tower. And now, King Conan, it is yours to command. Here in the temple of Asura you are still king.'

'Why should you risk your lives for me?' asked the king.

'You were our friend when you sat upon your throne,' answered Hadrathus. 'You protected us when the priests of Mitra sought to scourge us out of the land.'

Conan looked about him curiously. He had never before visited the temple of Asura, had not certainly known that there was such a temple in Tarantia. The priests of the religion had a habit of hiding their temples in a remarkable fashion. The worship of Mitra was overwhelmingly predominant in the Hyborian nations, but the cult of Asura persisted, in spite of official ban and popular antagonism. Conan had been told dark tales of hidden temples where intense smoke drifted up incessantly from black altars where kidnapped humans were sacrificed before a great coiled serpent, whose fearsome head swayed for ever in the haunted shadows.

Persecution caused the followers of Asura to hide their temples with cunning art, and to veil their rituals in obscurity; and this secrecy, in turn, evoked more monstrous suspicions and tales of evil.

But Conan's was the broad tolerance of the barbarian, and he had refused to persecute the followers of Asura or to allow the people to do so on no better evidence than was presented against them, rumors and accusations that could not be proven. 'If they are black magicians,' he had said, 'how will they suffer you to harry them? If they are not, there is no evil in them. Crom's devils! Let men worship what gods they will.'

At a respectful invitation from Hadrathus he seated himself on an ivory chair, and motioned Albiona to another, but she preferred to sit on a golden stool at his feet, pressing close against his thigh, as if seeking security in the contact. Like most orthodox followers of Mitra, she had an intuitive horror of the followers and cult of Asura, instilled in her infancy and childhood by wild tales of human sacrifice and anthropomorphic gods shambling through shadowy temples.

Hadrathus stood before them, his uncovered head bowed.

'What is your wish, your Majesty?'

'Food first,' he grunted, and the priest smote a golden gong with a silver wand.

Scarcely had the mellow notes ceased echoing when four hooded figures came through a curtained doorway bearing a great four-legged silver platter of smoking dishes and crystal vessels. This they set before Conan, bowing low, and the king wiped his hands on the damask, and smacked his lips with unconcealed relish.

'Beware, your Majesty!' whispered Albiona. 'These folk eat human flesh!'

'I'll stake my kingdom that this is nothing but honest roast beef,' answered Conan. 'Come, lass, fall to! You must be hungry after the prison fare.'

Thus advised, and with the example before her of one whose word was the ultimate law to her, the countess complied, and ate ravenously though daintily, while her liege lord tore into the meat joints and guzzled the wine with as much gusto as if he had not already eaten once that night.

'You priests are shrewd, Hadrathus,' he said, with a great beef-bone in his hands and his mouth full of meat. 'I'd welcome your service in my campaign to regain my kingdom.'

Slowly Hadrathus shook his head, and Conan slammed the beef-bone down on the table in a gust of impatient wrath.

'Crom's devils! What ails the men of Aquilonia? First Servius – now you! Can you do nothing but wag your idiotic heads when I speak of ousting these dogs?'

Hadrathus sighed and answered slowly: 'My lord, it is ill to say, and

I fain would say otherwise. But the freedom of Aquilonia is at an end. Nay, the freedom of the whole world may be at an end! Age follows age in the history of the world, and now we enter an age of horror and slavery, as it was long ago.'

'What do you mean?' demanded the king uneasily.

Hadrathus dropped into a chair and rested his elbows on his thighs, staring at the floor.

'It is not alone the rebellious lords of Aquilonia and the armies of Nemedia which are arrayed against you,' answered Hadrathus. 'It is sorcery – grisly black magic from the grim youth of the world. An awful shape has risen out of the shades of the Past, and none can stand before it.'

'What do you mean?' Conan repeated.

'I speak of Xaltotun of Acheron, who died three thousand years ago, yet walks the earth today.'

Conan was silent, while in his mind floated an image – the image of a bearded face of calm inhuman beauty. Again he was haunted by a sense of uneasy familiarity. Acheron – the sound of the word roused instinctive vibrations of memory and associations in his mind.

'Acheron,' he repeated. 'Xaltotun of Acheron – man, are you mad? Acheron has been a myth for more centuries than I can remember. I've often wondered if it ever existed at all.'

'It was a black reality,' answered Hadrathus, 'an empire of black magicians, steeped in evil now long forgotten. It was finally overthrown by the Hyborian tribes of the west. The wizards of Acheron practised foul necromancy, thaumaturgy of the most evil kind, grisly magic taught them by devils. And of all the sorcerers of that accursed kingdom, none was so great as Xaltotun of Python.'

'Then how was he ever overthrown?' asked Conan skeptically.

'By some means a source of cosmic power which he jealously guarded was stolen and turned against him. That source has been returned to him, and he is invincible.'

Albiona, hugging the headsman's black cloak about her, stared from the priest to the king, not understanding the conversation. Conan shook his head angrily.

'You are making game of me,' he growled. 'If Xaltotun has been dead three thousand years, how can this man be he? It's some rogue who's taken the old one's name.'

Hadrathus leaned to an ivory table and opened a small gold chest which stood there. From it he took something which glinted dully in the mellow light – a broad gold coin of antique minting.

'You have seen Xaltotun unveiled? Then look upon this. It is a coin which was stamped in ancient Acheron, before its fall. So pervaded with sorcery was that black empire, that even this coin has its uses in making magic.'

Conan took it and scowled down at it. There was no mistaking its great antiquity. Conan had handled many coins in the years of his plunderings, and had a good practical knowledge of them. The edges were worn and the inscription almost obliterated. But the countenance stamped on one side was still clear-cut and distinct. And Conan's breath sucked in between his clenched teeth. It was not cool in the chamber, but he felt a prickling of his scalp, an icy contraction of his flesh. The countenance was that of a bearded man, inscrutable, with a calm inhuman beauty.

'By Crom! It's he!' muttered Conan. He understood, now, the sense of familiarity that the sight of the bearded man had roused in him from the first. He had seen a coin like this once before, long ago in a far land.

With a shake of his shoulders he growled: 'The likeness is only a coincidence – or if he's shrewd enough to assume a forgotten wizard's name, he's shrewd enough to assume his likeness.' But he spoke without conviction. The sight of that coin had shaken the foundations of his universe. He felt that reality and stability were crumbing into an abyss of illusion and sorcery. A wizard was understandable; but this was diabolism beyond sanity.

'We cannot doubt that it is indeed Xaltotun of Python,' said Hadrathus. 'He it was who shook down the cliffs at Valkia, by his spells that enthrall the elementals of the earth – he it was who sent the creature of darkness into your tent before dawn.'

Conan scowled at him. 'How did you know that?'

'The followers of Asura have secret channels of knowledge. That does not matter. But do you realize the futility of sacrificing your subjects in a vain attempt to regain your crown?'

Conan rested his chin on his fist, and stared grimly into nothing. Albiona watched him anxiously, her mind groping bewildered in the mazes of the problem that confronted him.

'Is there no wizard in the world who could make magic to fight Xaltotun's magic?' he asked at last.

Hadrathus shook his head. 'If there were, we of Asura would know of him. Men say our cult is a survival of the ancient Stygian serpent-worship. That is a lie. Our ancestors came from Vendhya, beyond the Sea of Vilayet and the blue Himelian mountains. We are sons of the East, not the South, and we have knowledge of all the wizards of the East, who are greater than the wizards of the West. And not one of them but would be a straw in the wind before the black might of Xaltotun.'

'But he was conquered once,' persisted Conan.

'Aye; a cosmic source was turned against him. But now that source is again in his hands, and he will see that it is not stolen again.'

'And what is this damnable source?' demanded Conan irritably.

'It is called the Heart of Ahriman. When Acheron was overthrown, the primitive priest who had stolen it and turned it against Xaltotun hid it in a haunted cavern and built a small temple over the cavern. Thrice thereafter the temple was rebuilt, each time greater and more elaborately than before, but always on the site of the original shrine, though men forgot the reason therefor. Memory of the hidden symbol faded from the minds of common men, and was preserved only in priestly books and esoteric volumes. Whence it came no one knows. Some say it is the veritable heart of a god, others that it is a star that fell from the skies long ago. Until it was stolen, none had looked upon it for three thousand years.

'When the magic of the Mitran priests failed against the magic of Xaltotun's acolyte, Altaro, they remembered the ancient legend of the heart, and the high priest and an acolyte went down into the dark and terrible crypt below the temple into which no priest had descended for three thousand years. In the ancient iron-bound volumes which speak of the Heart in their cryptic symbolism, it is also told of a creature of darkness left by the ancient priest to guard it.

'Far down in a square chamber with arched doorways leading off into immeasurable blackness, the priest and his acolytes found a black stone altar that glowed dimly with inexplicable radiance.

'On that altar lay a curious gold vessel like a double-valved sea-shell which clung to the stone like a barnacle. But it gaped open and empty. The Heart of Ahriman was gone. While they stared in horror, the keeper of the crypt, the creature of darkness, came upon them and mangled the high priest so that he died. But the acolyte fought off the being – a mindless, soulless waif of the pits brought long ago to guard the Heart – and escaped up the long black narrow stairs carrying the dying priest, who before he died, gasped out the news to his followers, bade them submit to a power they could not overcome, and commanded secrecy. But the word has been whispered about among the priests, and we of Asura learned of it.'

'And Xaltotun draws his power from this symbol?' asked Conan, still skeptical.

'No. His power is drawn from the black gulf. But the Heart of Ahriman came from some far universe of flaming light, and against it the powers of darkness cannot stand, when it is in the hands of an adept. It is like a sword that might smite at him, not a sword with which he can smite. It restores life, and can destroy life. He has stolen it, not to use against his enemies, but to keep them from using it against him.'

'A shell-shaped bowl of gold on a black altar in a deep cavern,' Conan muttered, frowning as he sought to capture the illusive image. 'That reminds me of something I have heard or seen. But what, in Crom's name, is this notable Heart?'

'It is in the form of a great jewel, like a ruby, but pulsing with blinding fire with which no ruby ever burned. It glows like living flame—'

But Conan sprang suddenly up and smote his right fist into his left palm like a thunderclap.

'Crom!' he roared, 'What a fool I've been! The Heart of Ahriman! The heart of my kingdom! Find the heart of my kingdom, Zelata said. By Ymir, it was the jewel I saw in the green smoke, the jewel which Tarascus stole from Xaltotun while he lay in the sleep of the black lotus!'

Hadrathus was also on his feet, his calm dropped from him like a garment.

'What are you saying? The Heart stolen from Xaltotun?'

'Aye!' Conan boomed. 'Tarascus feared Xaltotun and wanted to cripple his power, which he thought resided in the Heart. Maybe he thought the wizard would die if the Heart was lost. By Crom – ahhh!' With a savage grimace of disappointment and disgust he dropped his clenched hand to his side.

'I forgot. Tarascus gave it to a thief to throw into the sea. By this time the fellow must be almost to Kordava. Before I can follow him he'll take ship and consign the Heart to the bottom of the ocean.'

'The sea will not hold it!' exclaimed Hadrathus, quivering with excitement. 'Xaltotun would himself have cast it into the ocean long ago, had he not known that the first storm would carry it ashore. But on what unknown beach might it not land!'

'Well,' Conan was recovering some of his resilient confidence, 'there's no assurance that the thief will throw it away. If I know thieves – and I should, for I was a thief in Zamora in my early youth – he won't throw it away. He'll sell it to some rich trader. By Crom!' he strode back and forth in his growing excitement. 'It's worth looking for! Zelata bade me find the heart of my kingdom, and all else she showed me proved to be truth. Can it be that the power to conquer Xaltotun lurks in that crimson bauble?'

'Aye! My head upon it!' cried Hadrathus, his face lightened with fervor, his eyes blazing, his fists clenched. 'With it in our hands we can dare the powers of Xaltotun! I swear it! If we can recover it, we have an even chance of recovering your crown and driving the invaders from our portals. It is not the swords of Nemedia that Aquilonia fears, but the black arts of Xaltotun.'

Conan looked at him for a space, impressed by the priest's fire.

'It's like a quest in a nightmare,' he said at last. 'Yet your words echo the thought of Zelata, and all else she said was truth. I'll seek for this jewel.'

'It holds the destiny of Aquilonia,' said Hadrathus with conviction. 'I will send men with you—'

'Nay!' exclaimed the king impatiently, not caring to be hampered by priests on his quest, however skilled in esoteric arts. 'This is a task for a fighting man. I go alone. First to Poitain, where I'll leave Albiona with Trocero. Then to Kordava, and to the sea beyond, if necessary. It may be that, even if the thief intends carrying out Tarascus' order, he'll have some difficulty finding an outbound ship at this time of the year.'

'And if you find the Heart,' cried Hadrathus, 'I will prepare the way for your conquest. Before you return to Aquilonia I will spread the word through secret channels that you live and are returning with a magic stronger than Xaltotun's. I will have men ready to rise on your return. They will rise, if they have assurance that they will be protected from the black arts of Xaltotun.

'And I will aid you on your journey.'

He rose and struck a gong.

'A secret tunnel leads from beneath this temple to a place outside the city wall. You shall go to Poitain on a pilgrim's boat. None will dare molest you.'

'As you will.' With a definite purpose in mind Conan was afire with impatience and dynamic energy. 'Only let it be done swiftly.'

In the meantime events were moving not slowly elsewhere in the city. A breathless messenger had burst into the palace where Valerius was amusing himself with his dancing-girls, and throwing himself on his knee, gasped out a garbled story of a bloody prison break and the escape of a lovely captive. He bore also the news that Count Thespius, to whom the execution of Albiona's sentence had been entrusted, was dying and begging for a word with Valerius before he passed.

Hurriedly cloaking himself, Valerius accompanied the man through various winding ways, and came to a chamber where Thespius lay. There was no doubt that the count was dying; bloody froth bubbled from his lips at each shuddering gasp. His severed arm had been bound to stop the flow of blood, but even without that, the gash in his side was mortal.

Alone in the chamber with the dying man, Valerius swore softly.

'By Mitra, I had believed that only one man ever lived who could strike such a blow.'

'Valerius!' gasped the dying man. 'He lives! Conan lives!'

'What are you saying?' ejaculated the other.

'I swear by Mitra!' gurgled Thespius, gagging on the blood that gushed to his lips. 'It was he who carried off Albiona! He is not dead – no phantom come back from hell to haunt us. He is flesh and blood, and more terrible than ever. The alley behind the tower is full of dead men. Beware, Valerius – he has come back – to slay us all—'

A strong shudder shook the blood-smeared figure, and Count Thespius went limp.

Valerius frowned down at the dead man, cast a swift glance about the empty chamber, and stepping swiftly to the door, cast it open suddenly. The messenger and a group of Nemedian guardsmen stood several paces down the corridor. Valerius muttered something that might have indicated satisfaction.

'Have all the gates been closed?' he demanded.

'Yes, your Majesty.'

'Triple the guards at each. Let no one enter or leave the city without strictest investigation. Set men scouring the streets and searching the quarters. A very valuable prisoner has escaped, with the aid of an Aquilonian rebel. Did any of you recognize the man?'

'No, your Majesty. The old watchman had a glimpse of him, but could only say that he was a giant, clad in the black garb of the executioner, whose naked body we found in an empty cell.'

'He is a dangerous man,' said Valerius. 'Take no chances with him. You all know the Countess Albiona. Search for her, and if you find her, kill her and her companion instantly. Do not try to take them alive.'

Returning to his palace chamber, Valerius summoned before him four men of curious and alien aspect. They were tall, gaunt, of yellowish skin, and immobile countenances. They were very similar in appearance, clad alike in long black robes beneath which their sandaled feet were just visible. Their features were shadowed by their hoods. They stood before Valerius with their hands in their wide sleeves; their arms folded. Valerius looked at them without pleasure. In his far journeyings he had encountered many strange races.

'When I found you starving in the Khitan jungles,' he said abruptly, 'exiles from your kingdom, you swore to serve me. You have served me well enough, in your abominable way. One more service I require, and then I set you free of your oath.

'Conan the Cimmerian, king of Aquilonia, still lives, in spite of Xaltotun's sorcery – or perhaps because of it. I know not. The dark mind of that resurrected devil is too devious and subtle for a mortal man to fathom. But while Conan lives I am not safe. The people accepted me as the lesser of two evils, when they thought he was dead. Let him reappear and the throne will be rocking under my feet in revolution before I can lift my hand.

'Perhaps my allies mean to use him to replace me, if they decide I have served my purpose. I do not know. I do know that this planet is too small for two kings of Aquilonia. Seek the Cimmerian. Use your uncanny talents to ferret him out wherever he hides or runs. He has many friends in Tarantia. He had aid when he carried off Albiona. It took more than one man, even such a man as Conan, to wreak all that slaughter in the alley outside the tower. But no more. Take your staffs and strike his trail. Where that trail will lead you, I know not. But find him! And when you find him, slay him!'

The four Khitans bowed together, and still unspeaking, turned and padded noiselessly from the chamber.

11 Swords of the South

Dawn that rose over the distant hills shone on the sails of a small craft that dropped down the river which curves to within a mile of the walls of Tarantia, and loops southward like a great shining serpent. This boat differed from the ordinary craft plying the broad Khorotas – fishermen and merchant barges loaded with rich goods. It was long and slender, with a high, curving prow, and was black as ebony, with white skulls painted along the gunwales. Amidships rose a small cabin, the windows closely masked. Other craft gave the ominously painted boat a wide berth; for it was obviously one of those 'pilgrim boats' that carried a lifeless follower of Asura on his last mysterious pilgrimage southward to where, far beyond the Poitanian mountains, a river flowed at last into the blue ocean. In that cabin undoubtedly lay the corpse of the departed worshipper. All men were familiar with the sight of those gloomy craft; and the most fanatical votary of Mitra would not dare touch or interfere with their somber voyages.

Where the ultimate destination lay, men did not know. Some said Stygia; some a nameless island lying beyond the horizon; others said it was in the glamorous and mysterious land of Vendhya where the dead came home at last. But none knew certainly. They only knew that when a follower of Asura died, the corpse went southward down the great river, in a black boat rowed by a giant slave, and neither boat nor corpse nor slave was ever seen again; unless, indeed, certain dark tales were true, and it was always the same slave who rowed the boats southward.

The man who propelled this particular boat was as huge and brown as the others, though closer scrutiny might have revealed the fact that the hue was the result of carefully applied pigments. He was clad in leather loin-clout and sandals, and he handled the long sweep and oars with unusual skill and power. But none approached the grim boat closely, for it was well known that the followers of Asura were accursed, and that these pilgrim boats were loaded with dark magic. So men swung their boats wide and muttered an incantation as the dark craft slid past, and they never dreamed that they were thus assisting in the flight of their king and the Countess Albiona.

It was a strange journey, in that black, slim craft down the great river for nearly two hundred miles to where the Khorotas swings eastward, skirting the Poitanian mountains. Like a dream the ever-changing panorama glided past. During the day Albiona lay patiently in the little cabin, as quietly as the corpse she pretended to be. Only late at night, after the pleasure boats with their fair occupants lounging on silken cushions in the flare of torches held by slaves had left the river, before dawn brought the hurrying fisherboats, did the girl venture out. Then she held the long sweep, cunningly bound in place by ropes to aid her, while Conan snatched a few hours of sleep. But the king needed little rest. The fire of his desire drove him relentlessly; and his powerful frame was equal to the grinding test. Without halt or pause they drove southward.

So down the river they fled, through nights when the flowing current mirrored the million stars, and through days of golden sunlight, leaving winter behind them as they sped southward. They passed cities in the night, above which throbbed and pulsed the reflection of the myriad lights, lordly river villas and fertile groves. So at last the blue mountains of Poitain rose above them, tier above tier, like ramparts of the gods, and the great river, swerving from those turreted cliffs, swept thunderously through the marching hills with many a rapid and foaming cataract.

Conan scanned the shore-line closely, and finally swung the long sweep and headed inshore at a point where a neck of land jutted into the water, and fir trees grew in a curiously symmetrical ring about a gray, strangely shaped rock.

'How these boats ride those falls we hear roaring ahead of us is more than I can see,' he grunted. 'Hadrathus said they did – but here's where we halt. He said a man would be waiting for us with horses, but I don't see anyone. How word of our coming could have preceded us I don't know anyway.'

He drove inshore and bound the prow to an arching root in the low bank, and then, plunging into the water, washed the brown paint from his skin and emerged dripping, and in his natural color. From the cabin he brought forth a suit of Aquilonian ring-mail which Hadrathus had procured for him, and his sword. These he donned while Albiona put on garments suitable for mountain travel. And when Conan was fully armed, and turned to look toward the shore, he started and his hand went to his sword. For on the shore, under the trees, stood a black-cloaked figure holding the reins of a white palfrey and a bay war-horse.

'Who are you?' demanded the king.

The other bowed low.

'A follower of Asura. A command came. I obeyed.'

'How, "came"?' inquired Conan, but the other merely bowed again.

'I have come to guide you through the mountains to the first Poitanian stronghold.'

'I don't need a guide,' answered Conan. 'I know these hills well. I thank you for the horses, but the countess and I will attract less attention alone than if we were accompanied by an acolyte of Asura.'

The man bowed profoundly, and giving the reins into Conan's hands, stepped into the boat. Casting off, he floated down the swift current, toward the distant roar of the unseen rapids. With a baffled shake of his head, Conan lifted the countess into the palfrey's saddle, and then mounted the war-horse and reined toward the summits that castellated the sky.

The rolling country at the foot of the towering mountains was now a borderland, in a state of turmoil, where the barons reverted to feudal practises, and bands of outlaws roamed unhindered. Poitain had not formally declared her separation from Aquilonia, but she was now, to all intents, a self-contained kingdom, ruled by her hereditary count, Trocero. The rolling south country had submitted nominally to Valerius, but he had not attempted to force the passes guarded by strongholds where the crimson leopard banner of Poitain waved defiantly.

The king and his fair companion rode up the long blue slopes in the soft evening. As they mounted higher, the rolling country spread out like a vast purple mantle far beneath them, shot with the shine of rivers and lakes, the yellow glint of broad fields, and the white gleam of distant towers. Ahead of them and far above, they glimpsed the first of the Poitanian holds – a strong fortress dominating a narrow pass, the crimson banner streaming against the clear blue sky.

Before they reached it, a band of knights in burnished armor rode from among the trees, and their leader sternly ordered the travelers to halt. They were tall men, with the dark eyes and raven locks of the south.

'Halt, sir, and state your business, and why you ride toward Poitain.'

'Is Poitain in revolt then,' asked Conan, watching the other closely, 'that a man in Aquilonian harness is halted and questioned like a foreigner?'

'Many rogues ride out of Aquilonia these days,' answered the other coldy. 'As for revolt, if you mean the repudiation of a usurper, then Poitain is in revolt. We had rather serve the memory of a dead man than the scepter of a living dog.'

Conan swept off his helmet, and shaking back his black mane, stared full at the speaker. The Poitanian stared violently and went livid.

'Saints of heaven!' he gasped. 'It is the king – alive!'

The others stared wildly, then a roar of wonder and joy burst from them. They swarmed about Conan, shouting their war-cries and brandishing their swords in their extreme emotion. The acclaim of Poitanian warriors was a thing to terrify a timid man.

'Oh, but Trocero will weep tears of joy to see you, sire!' cried one.

'Aye, and Prospero!' shouted another. 'The general has been like one wrapped in a mantle of melancholy, and curses himself night and day that he did not reach the Valkia in time to die beside his king!'

'Now we will strike for empery!' yelled another, whirling his great sword about his head. 'Hail, Conan, king of Poitain!'

The clangor of bright steel about him and the thunder of their acclaim frightened the birds that rose in gay-hued clouds from the surrounding trees. The hot southern blood was afire, and they desired nothing but for their new-found sovereign to lead them to battle and pillage.

'What is your command, sire?' they cried. 'Let one of us ride ahead and bear the news of your coming into Poitain! Banners will wave from every tower, roses will carpet the road before your horse's feet, and all the beauty and chivalry of the south will give you the honor due you—'

Conan shook his head.

'Who could doubt your loyalty? But winds blow over these mountains into the countries of my enemies, and I would rather these didn't know that I lived – yet. Take me to Trocero, and keep my identity a secret.'

So what the knights would have made a triumphal procession was more in the nature of a secret flight. They traveled in haste, speaking to no one, except for a whisper to the captain on duty at each pass; and Conan rode among them with his vizor lowered.

The mountains were uninhabited save by outlaws and garrisons of soldiers who guarded the passes. The pleasure-loving Poitanians had no need nor desire to wrest a hard and scanty living from their stern breasts. South of the ranges the rich and beautiful plains of Poitain stretched to the river Alimane; but beyond the river lay the land of Zingara.

Even now, when winter was crisping the leaves beyond the mountains, the tall rich grass waved upon the plains where grazed the horses and cattle for which Poitain was famed. Palm trees and orange groves smiled in the sun, and the gorgeous purple and gold and crimson towers of castles and cities reflected the golden light. It was a land of warmth and plenty, of beautiful men and ferocious warriors. It is not only the hard lands that breed hard men. Poitain was surrounded by covetous neighbors and her sons learned hardihood in incessant wars. To the north the land was guarded by the mountains, but to the south only the Alimane separated the plains of Poitain from the plains of Zingara, and not once but a thousand times had that river run red. To the east lay Argos and beyond that Ophir, proud kingdoms and avaricious. The knights of Poitain held their lands by the weight and edge of their swords, and little of ease and idleness they knew.

So Conan came presently to the castle of Count Trocero . . .

Conan sat on a silken divan in a rich chamber whose filmy curtains the warm breeze billowed. Trocero paced the floor like a panther, a lithe, restless man with the waist of a woman and the shoulders of a swordsman, who carried his years lightly.

'Let us proclaim you king of Poitain!' urged the count. 'Let those northern pigs wear the yoke to which they have bent their necks. The south is still yours. Dwell here and rule us, amid the flowers and the palms.'

But Conan shook his head. 'There is no nobler land on earth than Poitain. But it cannot stand alone, bold as are its sons.'

'It *did* stand alone for generations,' retorted Trocero, with the quick jealous pride of his breed. 'We were not always a part of Aquilonia.'

'I know. But conditions are not as they were then, when all kingdoms were broken into principalities which warred with each other. The days of dukedoms and free cities are past, the days of empires are upon us. Rulers are dreaming imperial dreams, and only in unity is there strength.'

'Then let us unite Zingara with Poitain,' argued Trocero. 'Half a dozen princes strive against each other, and the country is torn asunder by civil wars. We will conquer it, province by province, and add it to your dominions. Then with the aid of the Zingarans we will conquer Argos and Ophir. We will build an empire—'

Again Conan shook his head. 'Let others dream imperial dreams. I but wish to hold what is mine. I have no desire to rule an empire welded together by blood and fire. It's one thing to seize a throne with the aid of its subjects and rule them with their consent. It's another to subjugate a foreign realm and rule it by fear. I don't wish to be another Valerius. No, Trocero, I'll rule all Aquilonia and no more, or I'll rule nothing.'

'Then lead us over the mountains and we will smite the Nemedians.'

Conan's fierce eyes glowed with appreciation.

'No, Trocero. It would be a vain sacrifice. I've told you what I must do to regain my kingdom. I must find the Heart of Ahriman.'

'But this is madness!' protested Trocero, 'The maunderings of a heretical priest, the mumblings of a mad witch-woman.'

'You were not in my tent before Valkia,' answered Conan grimly, involuntarily glancing at his right wrist, on which blue marks still showed faintly. 'You didn't see the cliffs thunder down to crush the flower of my army. No, Trocero, I've been convinced. Xaltotun's no mortal man, and only with the Heart of Ahriman can I stand against him. So I'm riding to Kordava, alone.'

'But that is dangerous,' protested Trocero.

'Life is dangerous,' rumbled the king. 'I won't go as king of Aquilonia, or even as a knight of Poitain, but as a wandering mercenary, as I rode in Zingara in the old days. Oh, I have enemies enough south of the Alimane, in the lands and the waters of the south. Many who won't know me as king of Aquilonia will remember me as Conan of the Barachan pirates, or Amra of the black corsairs. But I have friends, too, and men who'll aid me for their own private reasons.' A faintly reminiscent grin touched his lips.

Trocero dropped his hands helplessly and glanced at Albiona, who sat on a near-by divan.

'I understand your doubts, my lord,' said she. 'But I too saw the coin in the temple of Asura, and look you, Hadrathus said it was dated five hundred years *before* the fall of Acheron. If Xaltotun, then, is the man pictured on the coin, as his Majesty swears he is, that means he was no common wizard, even in his other life, for the years of his life were numbered by centuries, not as the lives of other men are numbered.'

Before Trocero could reply, a respectful rap was heard on the door and a voice called: 'My lord, we have caught a man skulking about the castle, who says he wishes to speak with your guest. I await your orders.'

'A spy from Aquilonia!' hissed Trocero, catching at his dagger, but Conan lifted his voice and called: 'Open the door and let me see him.'

The door was opened and a man was framed in it, grasped on either hand by stern-looking men-at-arms. He was a slender man, clad in a dark hooded robe.

'Are you a follower of Asura?' asked Conan.

The man nodded, and the stalwart men-at-arms looked shocked and glanced hesitantly at Trocero.

'The word came southward,' said the man. 'Beyond the Alimane we can not aid you, for our sect goes no farther southward, but stretches eastward with the Khorotas. But this I have learned: the thief who took the Heart of Ahriman from Tarascus never reached Kordava. In the mountains of Poitain he was slain by robbers. The jewel fell into the hands of their chief, who, not knowing its true nature, and being harried after the destruction of his band by Poitanian knights, sold it to the Kothic merchant Zorathus.'

'Ha!' Conan was on his feet, galvanized. 'And what of Zorathus?'

'Four days ago he crossed the Alimane, headed for Argos, with a small band of armed servants.

'He's a fool to cross Zingara in such times,' said Trocero.

'Aye, times are troublous across the river. But Zorathus is a bold man, and reckless in his way. He is in great haste to reach Messantia, where he hopes to find a buyer for the jewel. Perhaps he hopes to sell it finally in Stygia. Perhaps he guesses at its true nature. At any rate, instead of following the long road that winds along the borders of Poitain and so at last comes into Argos far from Messantia, he has struck straight across eastern Zingara, following the shorter and more direct route.'

Conan smote the table with his clenched fist so that the great board quivered.

'Then, by Crom, fortune has at last thrown the dice for me! A horse, Trocero, and the harness of a Free Companion! Zorathus has a long start, but not too long for me to overtake him, if I follow him to the end of the world!'

12 The Fang of the Dragon

At dawn Conan waded his horse across the shallows of the Alimane and struck the wide caravan trail which ran southeastward, and behind him, on the farther bank, Trocero sat his horse silently at the head of his steel-clad knights, with the crimson leopard of Poitain floating its long folds over him in the morning breeze. Silently they sat, those dark-haired men in shining steel, until the figure of their king had vanished in the blue of distance that whitened toward sunrise.

Conan rode a great black stallion, the gift of Trocero. He no longer wore the armor of Aquilonia. His harness proclaimed him a veteran of the Free Companies, who were of all races. His headpiece was a plain morion, dented and battered. The leather and mail-mesh of his hauberk were worn and shiny as if by many campaigns, and the scarlet cloak flowing carelessly from his mailed shoulders was tattered and stained. He looked the part of the hired fighting-man, who had known all vicissitudes of fortune, plunder and wealth one day, an empty purse and a close-drawn belt the next.

And more than looking the part, he felt the part; the awakening of old memories, the resurge of the wild, mad, glorious days of old before his feet were set on the imperial path when he was a wandering mercenary, roistering, brawling, guzzling, adventuring, with no thought for the morrow, and no desire save sparkling ale, red lips, and a keen sword to swing on all the battlefields of the world.

Unconsciously he reverted to the old ways; a new swagger became evident in his bearing, in the way he sat his horse; half-forgotten oaths rose naturally to his lips, and as he rode he hummed old songs that he had roared in chorus with his reckless companions in many a tavern and on many a dusty road or bloody field.

It was an unquiet land through which he rode. The companies of cavalry which usually patrolled the river, alert for raids out of Poitain, were nowhere in evidence. Internal strife had left the borders unguarded. The long white road stretched bare from horizon to horizon. No laden camel trains or rumbling wagons or lowing herds moved along it now; only occasional groups of horsemen in leather and steel, hawk-faced, hard-eyed men, who kept together and rode warily. These swept Conan with their searching gaze but rode on, for the solitary rider's harness promised no plunder, but only hard strokes.

Villages lay in ashes and deserted, the fields and meadows idle. Only the boldest would ride the roads these days, and the native population had been decimated in the civil wars, and by raids from across the river. In more peaceful times the road was thronged with merchants riding Poitain to Messantia in Argos, or back. But now these found it wiser to follow the road that led east through Poitain, and then turned south down across Argos. It was longer, but safer. Only an extremely reckless man would risk his life and goods on this road through Zingara.

The southern horizon was fringed with flame by night, and in the day straggling pillars of smoke drifted upward; in the cities and plains to the south men were dying, thrones were toppling and castles going up in flames. Conan felt the old tug of the professional fighting-man, to turn his horse and plunge into the fighting, the pillaging and the looting as in the days of old. Why should he toil to regain the rule of a people which had already forgotten him? – why chase a will-o'-the-wisp, why pursue a crown that was lost for ever? Why should he not seek forgetfulness, lose himself in the red tides of war and rapine that had engulfed him so often before? Could he not, indeed, carve out another kingdom for himself? The world was entering an age of iron, an age of war and imperialistic ambition; some strong man might well rise above the ruins of nations as a supreme conqueror. Why should it not be himself? So his familiar devil whispered in his ear, and the phantoms of his lawless and bloody past crowded upon him. But he did not turn aside; he rode onward, following a quest that grew dimmer and dimmer as he advanced, until sometimes it seemed that he pursued a dream that never was.

He pushed the black stallion as hard as he dared, but the long white road lay bare before him, from horizon to horizon. It was a long start Zorathus had, but Conan rode steadily on, knowing that he was traveling faster than the burdened merchants could travel. And so he came to the castle of Count Valbroso, perched like a vulture's eyrie on a bare hill overlooking the road.

Valbroso rode down with his men-at-arms, a lean, dark man with glittering eyes and a predatory beak of a nose. He wore black plate-armor and was followed by thirty spearmen, black-mustached hawks of the border wars, as avaricious and ruthless as himself. Of late the toll of the caravans had been slim, and Valbroso cursed the civil wars that stripped the roads of their fat traffic, even while he blessed them for the free hand they allowed him with his neighbors.

He had not hoped much from the solitary rider he had glimpsed from his tower, but all was grist that came to his mill. With a practised eye he took in Conan's worn mail and dark, scarred face, and his conclusions were the same as those of the riders who had passed the Cimmerian on the road – an empty purse and a ready blade.

'Who are you, knave?' he demanded.

'A mercenary, riding for Argos,' answered Conan. 'What matter names?'

'You are riding in the wrong direction for a Free Companion,' grunted Valbroso. 'Southward the fighting is good and also the plundering. Join my company. You won't go hungry. The road remains bare of fat merchants to strip, but I mean to take my rogues and fare southward to sell our swords to whichever side seems strongest.'

Conan did not at once reply, knowing that if he refused outright, he might be instantly attacked by Valbroso's men-at-arms. Before he could make up his mind, the Zingaran spoke again:

'You rogues of the Free Companies always know tricks to make men talk. I have a prisoner – the last merchant I caught, by Mitra, and the only one I've seen for a week – and the knave is stubborn. He has an iron box, the secret of which defies us, and I've been unable to persuade him to open it. By Ishtar, I thought I knew all the modes of persuasion there are, but perhaps you, as a veteran Free Companion, know some that I do not. At any rate come with me and see what you may do.'

Valbroso's words instantly decided Conan. That sounded a great deal like Zorathus. Conan did not know the merchant, but any man who was stubborn enough to try to traverse the Zingaran road in times like these would very probably be stubborn enough to defy torture.

He fell in beside Valbroso and rode up the straggling road to the top of the hill where the gaunt castle stood. As a man-at-arms he should have ridden behind the count, but force of habit made him careless and Valbroso paid no heed. Years of life on the border had taught the count that the frontier is not the royal court. He was aware of the independence of the mercenaries, behind whose swords many a king had trodden the throne-path.

There was a dry moat, half filled with debris in some places. They clattered across the drawbridge and through the arch of the gate. Behind them the portcullis fell with a sullen clang. They came into a bare courtyard, grown with straggling grass, and with a well in the middle. Shacks for the men-at-arms straggled about the bailey wall, and women, slatternly or decked in gaudy finery, looked from the doors. Fighting-men in rusty mail tossed dice on the flags under the arches. It was more like a bandit's hold than the castle of a nobleman.

Valbroso dismounted and motioned Conan to follow him. They went through a doorway and along a vaulted corridor, where they were met by a scarred, hard-looking man in mail descending a stone staircase – evidently the captain of the guard.

'How, Beloso,' quoth Valbroso; 'has he spoken?'

'He is stubborn,' muttered Beloso, shooting a glance of suspicion at Conan.

Valbroso ripped out an oath and stamped furiously up the winding stair, followed by Conan and the captain. As they mounted, the groans of a man in mortal agony became audible. Valbroso's torture-room was high above the court, instead of in a dungeon below. In that chamber, where a gaunt, hairy beast of a man in leather breeks squatted gnawing a beef-bone voraciously, stood the machines of torture – racks, boots, hooks and all the implements that the human mind devises to tear flesh, break bones and rend and rupture veins and l igaments.

On a rack a man was stretched naked, and a glance told Conan that he was dying. The unnatural elongation of his limbs and body told of unhinged joints and unnamable ruptures. He was a dark man, with an intelligent, aquiline face and quick dark eyes. They were glazed and bloodshot now with pain, and the dew of agony glistened on his face. His lips were drawn back from blackened gums.

'There is the box.' Viciously Valbroso kicked a small but heavy iron chest that stood on the floor near by. It was intricately carved, with tiny skulls and writhing dragons curiously intertwined, but Conan saw no catch or hasp that might serve to unlock the lid. The marks of fire, of ax and sledge and chisel showed on it but as scratches.

'This is the dog's treasure box,' said Valbroso angrily. 'All men of the south know of Zorathus and his iron chest. Mitra knows what is in it. But he will not give up its secret.'

Zorathus! It was true, then; the man he sought lay before him. Conan's heart beat suffocatingly as he leaned over the writhing form, though he exhibited no evidence of his painful eagerness.

'Ease those ropes, knave!' he ordered the torturer harshly, and Valbroso and his captain stared. In the forgetfulness of the moment Conan had used his imperial tone, and the brute in leather instinctively obeyed the knife-edge of command in that voice. He eased away gradually, for else the slackening of the ropes had been as great a torment to the torn joints as further stretching.

Catching up a vessel of wine that stood near by, Conan placed the rim to the wretch's lips. Zorathus gulped spasmodically, the liquid slopping over on his heaving breast.

Into the bloodshot eyes came a gleam of recognition, and the froth-smeared lips parted. From them issued a racking whimper in the Kothic tongue.

'Is this death, then? Is the long agony ended? For this is King Conan who died at Valkia, and I am among the dead.'

'You're not dead,' said Conan. 'But you're dying. You'll be tortured no more. I'll see to that. But I can't help you further. Yet before you die, tell me how to open your iron box!'

'My iron box,' mumbled Zorathus in delirious disjointed phrases. 'The chest forged in unholy fires among the flaming mountains of Khrosha; the metal no chisel can cut. How many treasures has it borne, across the width and the breadth of the world! But no such treasure as it now holds.'

'Tell me how to open it,' urged Conan. 'It can do you no good, and it may aid me.'

'Aye, you are Conan,' muttered the Kothian. 'I have seen you sitting on your throne in the great public hall of Tarantia, with your crown on your head and the scepter in your hand. But you are dead; you died at Valkia. And so I know my own end is at hand.'

'What does the dog say?' demanded Valbroso impatiently, not understanding Kothic. 'Will he tell us how to open the box?'

As if the voice roused a spark of life in the twisted breast Zorathus rolled his bloodshot eyes toward the speaker.

'Only Valbroso will I tell,' he gasped in Zingaran. 'Death is upon me. Lean close to me, Valbroso!'

The count did so, his dark face lit with avarice; behind him his saturnine captain, Beloso, crowded closer.

'Press the seven skulls on the rim, one after another,' gasped Zorathus. 'Press then the head of the dragon that writhes across the lid. Then press the sphere in the dragon's claws. That will release the secret catch.'

'Quick, the box!' cried Valbroso with an oath.

Conan lifted it and set it on a dais, and Valbroso shouldered him aside.

'Let me open it!' cried Beloso, starting forward.

Valbroso cursed him back, his greed blazing in his black eyes.

'None but me shall open it!' he cried.

Conan, whose hand had instinctively gone to his hilt, glanced at Zorathus. The man's eyes were glazed and bloodshot, but they were fixed on Valbroso with burning intensity; and was there the shadow of a grim twisted smile on the dying man's lips? Not until the merchant knew he was dying had he given up the secret. Conan turned to watch Valbroso, even as the dying man watched him.

Along the rim of the lid seven skulls were carved among intertwining branches of strange trees. An inlaid dragon writhed its way across the top of the lid amid ornate arabesques. Valbroso pressed the skulls in fumbling haste, and as he jammed his thumb down on the carved head of the dragon he swore sharply and snatched his hand away, shaking it in irritation.

'A sharp point on the carvings,' he snarled. 'I've pricked my thumb.'

He pressed the gold ball clutched in the dragon's talons, and the lid flew abruptly open. Their eyes were dazzled by a golden flame. It seemed to their dazed minds that the carven box was full of glowing fire that spilled over the rim and dripped through the air in quivering flakes. Beloso cried out and Valbroso sucked in his breath. Conan stood speechless, his brain snared by the blaze.

'Mitra, what a jewel!' Valbroso's hand dived into the chest, came out with a great pulsing crimson sphere that filled the room with a lambent glow. In its glare Valbroso looked like a corpse. And the dying man on the loosened rack laughed wildly and suddenly.

'Fool!' he screamed. 'The jewel is yours! I give you death with it! The scratch on your thumb – look at the dragon's head, Valbroso!'

They all wheeled, stared. Something tiny and dully gleaming stood up from the gaping, carved mouth.

'The dragon's fang!' shrieked Zorathus. 'Steeped in the venom of the black Stygian scorpion! Fool, fool to open the box of Zorathus with your naked hand! Death! You are a dead man now!'

And with bloody foam on his lips he died.

Valbroso staggered, crying out. 'Ah, Mitra, I burn!' he shrieked. 'My veins race with liquid fire! My joints are bursting asunder! Death! Death!' And he reeled and crashed headlong. There was an instant of awful convulsions, in which the limbs were twisted into hideous and unnatural positions, and then in that posture the man froze, his glassy eyes staring sightlessly upward, his lips drawn back from blackened gums.

'Dead!' muttered Conan, stooping to pick up the jewel where it rolled on the floor from Valbroso's rigid hand. It lay on the floor like a quivering pool of sunset fire.

'Dead!' muttered Beloso, with madness in his eyes. And then he moved.

Conan was caught off guard, his eyes dazzled, his brain dazed by the blaze of the great gem. He did not realize Beloso's intention until something crashed with terrible force upon his helmet. The glow of the jewel was splashed with redder flame, and he went to his knees under the blow.

He heard a rush of feet, a bellow of ox-like agony. He was stunned but not wholly senseless, and realized that Beloso had caught up the iron box and crashed it down on his head as he stooped. Only his basinet had saved his skull. He staggered up, drawing his sword, trying to shake the dimness out of his eyes. The room swam to his dizzy gaze. But the door was open and fleet footsteps were dwindling down the winding stair. On the floor the brutish torturer was gasping out his life with a great gash under his breast. And the Heart of Ahriman was gone.

Conan reeled out of the chamber, sword in hand, blood streaming down his face from under his burganet. He ran drunkenly down the steps, hearing a clang of steel in the courtyard below, shouts, then the frantic drum of hoofs. Rushing into the bailey he saw the men-at-arms milling about confusedly, while women screeched. The postern gate stood open and a soldier lay across his pike with his head split. Horses, still bridled and saddled, ran neighing about the court, Conan's black stallion among them.

'He's mad!' howled a woman, wringing her hands as she rushed brainlessly about. 'He came out of the castle like a mad dog, hewing right and left! Beloso's mad! Where's Lord Valbroso?'

'Which way did he go?' roared Conan.

All turned and stared at the stranger's blood-stained face and naked sword.

'Through the postern!' shrilled a woman, pointing eastward, and another bawled: 'Who is this rogue?'

'Beloso has killed Valbroso!' yelled Conan, leaping and seizing the stallion's mane, as the men-at-arms advanced uncertainly on him. A wild outcry burst forth at his news, but their reaction was exactly as he had anticipated. Instead of closing the gates to take him prisoner, or pursuing the fleeing slayer to avenge their lord, they were thrown into even greater confusion by his words. Wolves bound together only by fear of Valbroso, they owed no allegiance to the castle or to each other.

Swords began to clash in the courtyard, and women screamed. And in the midst of it all, none noticed Conan as he shot through the postern gate and thundered down the hill. The wide plain spread before him, and beyond the hill the caravan road divided: one branch ran south, the other east. And on the eastern road he saw another rider, bending low and spurring hard. The plain swam to Conan's gaze, the sunlight was a thick red haze and he reeled in his saddle, grasping the flowing mane with his hand. Blood rained on his mail, but grimly he urged the stallion on.

Behind him smoke began to pour out of the castle on the hill where the count's body lay forgotten and unheeded beside that of his prisoner. The sun was setting; against a lurid red sky the two black figures fled.

The stallion was not fresh, but neither was the horse ridden by Beloso. But the great beast responded mightily, calling on deep reservoirs of reserve vitality. Why the Zingaran fled from one pursuer Conan did not tax his bruised brain to guess. Perhaps unreasoning panic rode Beloso, born of the madness that lurked in that blazing jewel. The sun was gone; the white road was a dim glimmer through a ghostly twilight fading into purple gloom far ahead of him.

The stallion panted, laboring hard. The country was changing, in the gathering dusk. Bare plains gave way to clumps of oaks and alders. Low hills mounted up in the distance. Stars began to blink out. The stallion gasped and reeled in his course. But ahead rose a dense wood that stretched to the hills on the horizon, and between it and himself Conan glimpsed the dim form of the fugitive. He urged on the distressed stallion, for he saw that he was overtaking his prey, yard by yard. Above the pound of the hoofs a strange cry rose from the shadows, but neither pursuer nor pursued gave heed.

As they swept in under the branches that overhung the road, they were almost side by side. A fierce cry rose from Conan's lips as his sword went up; a pale oval of a face was turned toward him, a sword gleamed in a half-seen hand, and Beloso echoed the cry – and then the weary stallion, with a lurch and a groan, missed his footing in the shadows and went heels over head, hurling his dazed rider from the saddle. Conan's throbbing head crashed against a stone, and the stars were blotted out in a thicker night.

How long Conan lay senseless he never knew. His first sensation of returning consciousness was that of being dragged by one arm over rough and stony ground and through dense underbrush. Then he was thrown carelessly down, and perhaps the jolt brought back his senses.

His helmet was gone, his head ached abominably, he felt a qualm of nausea, and blood was clotted thickly among his black locks. But with the vitality of a wild thing life and consciousness surged back into him, and he became aware of his surroundings.

A broad red moon was shining through the trees, by which he knew that it was long after midnight. He had lain senseless for hours, long enough to have recovered from that terrible blow Beloso had dealt him, as well as the fall which had rendered him senseless. His brain felt clearer than it had felt during that mad ride after the fugitive.

He was not lying beside the white road, he noticed with a start of surprise, as his surroundings began to record themselves on his perceptions. The road was nowhere in sight. He lay on the grassy earth, in a small glade hemmed in by a black wall of tree stems and tangled branches. His face and hands were scratched and lacerated as if he had been dragged through brambles. Shifting his body he looked about him. And then he started violently – something was squatting over him . . .

At first Conan doubted his consciousness, thought it was but a figment of delirium. Surely it could not be real, that strange, motionless gray being that squatted on its haunches and stared down at him with unblinking soulless eyes.

Conan lay and stared, half expecting it to vanish like a figure of a dream, and then a chill of recollection crept along his spine. Half-forgotten memories surged back, of grisly tales whispered of the shapes that haunted these uninhabited forests at the foot of the hills that mark the Zingaran-Argossean border. Ghouls, men called them, eaters of human flesh, spawn of darkness, children of unholy matings of a lost and forgotten race with the demons of the underworld. Somewhere in these primitive forests were the ruins of an ancient, accursed city, men whispered, and among its tombs slunk gray, anthropomorphic shadows – Conan shuddered strongly.

He lay staring at the malformed head that rose dimly above him, and cautiously he extended a hand toward the sword at his hip. With a horrible cry that the man involuntarily echoed, the monster was at his throat.

Conan threw up his right arm, and the dog-like jaws closed on it, driving the mail links into the hard flesh. The misshapen yet man-like hands clutched for his throat, but he evaded them with a heave and roll of his whole body, at the same time drawing his dagger with his left hand.

They tumbled over and over on the grass, smiting and tearing. The muscles coiling under that gray corpse-like skin were stringy and hard as steel wires, exceeding the strength of a man. But Conan's thews were iron too, and his mail saved him from the gnashing fangs and ripping claws long enough for him to drive home his dagger, again and again and again. The horrible vitality of the semi-human monstrosity seemed inexhaustible, and the king's skin crawled at the feel of that slick, clammy flesh. He put all his loathing and savage revulsion behind the plunging blade, and suddenly the monster heaved up convulsively beneath him as the point found its grisly heart, and then lay still.

Conan rose, shaken with nausea. He stood in the center of the glade uncertainly, sword in one hand and dagger in the other. He had not lost his instinctive sense of direction, as far as the points of the compass were concerned, but he did not know in which direction the road lay. He had no way of knowing in which direction the ghoul had dragged him. Conan glared at the silent, black, moon-dappled woods which ringed him, and felt cold moisture bead his flesh. He was without a horse and lost in these haunted woods, and that staring deformed thing at his feet was a mute evidence of the horrors that lurked in the forest. He stood almost holding his breath in his painful intensity, straining his ears for some crack of twig or rustle of grass.

When a sound did come he started violently. Suddenly out on the night air broke the scream of a terrified horse. His stallion! There were panthers in the wood – or – ghouls ate beasts as well as men.

He broke savagely through the brush in the direction of the sound, whistling shrilly as he ran, his fear drowned in berserk rage. If his horse was killed, there went his last chance of following Beloso and recovering the jewel. Again the stallion screamed with fear and fury, somewhere nearer. There was a sound of lashing heels, and something that was struck heavily and gave way.

Conan burst out into the wide white road without warning, and saw the stallion plunging and rearing in the moonlight, his ears laid back, his eyes and teeth flashing wickedly. He lashed out with his heels at a slinking shadow that ducked and bobbed about him – and then about Conan other shadows moved: gray, furtive shadows that closed in on all sides. A hideous charnel-house scent reeked up in the night air.

With a curse the king hewed right and left with his broadsword, thrust and ripped with his dagger. Dripping fangs flashed in the moonlight, foul paws caught at him, but he hacked his way through to the stallion, caught the rein, leaped into the saddle. His sword rose and fell, a frosty arc in the moon, showering blood as it split misshapen heads, clove shambling bodies. The stallion reared, biting and kicking. They burst through and thundered down the road. On either hand, for a short space, flitted gray abhorrent shadows. Then these fell behind, and Conan, topping a wooded crest, saw a vast expanse of bare slopes sweeping up and away before him.

13 'A Ghost Out of the Past'

Soon after sunrise Conan crossed the Argossean border. Of Beloso he had seen no trace. Either the captain had made good his escape while the king lay senseless, or had fallen prey to the grim man-eaters of the Zingaran forest. But Conan had seen no signs to indicate the latter possibility. The fact that he had lain unmolested for so long seemed to indicate that the monsters had been engrossed in futile pursuit of the captain. And if the man lived, Conan felt certain that he was riding along the road somewhere ahead of him. Unless he had intended going into Argos he would never have taken the eastward road in the first place.

The helmeted guards at the frontier did not question the Cimmerian. A single wandering mercenary required no passport nor safe-conduct, especially when his unadorned mail showed him to be in the service of no lord. Through the low, grassy hills where streams murmured and oak groves dappled the sward with lights and shadows he rode, following the long road that rose and fell away ahead of him over dales and rises in the blue distance. It was an old, old road, this highway from Poitain to the sea.

Argos was at peace; laden ox-wains rumbled along the road, and men with bare, brown, brawny arms toiled in orchards and fields that smiled away under the branches of the roadside trees. Old men on settles before inns under spreading oak branches called greetings to the wayfarer.

From the men that worked the fields, from the garrulous old men in the inns where he slaked his thirst with great leathern jacks of foaming ale, from the sharp-eyed silk-clad merchants he met upon the road, Conan sought for news of Beloso.

Stories were conflicting, but this much Conan learned: that a lean, wiry Zingaran with the dangerous black eyes and mustaches of the western folk was somewhere on the road ahead of him, and apparently making for Messantia. It was a logical destination; all the sea-ports of Argos were cosmopolitan, in strong contrast with the inland provinces, and Messantia was the most polyglot of all. Craft of all the maritime nations rode in its harbor, and refugees and fugitives from many lands gathered there. Laws were lax; for Messantia thrived on the trade of the sea, and her citizens found it profitable to be somewhat blind on their dealings with seamen. It was not only legitimate trade that flowed into Messantia; smugglers and buccaneers played their part. All this Conan knew well, for had he not, in the days of old when he was a Barachan pirate, sailed by night into the harbor of Messantia to discharge strange cargoes? Most of the pirates of the Barachan Isles – small islands off the southwestern coast of Zingara – were Argossean sailors, and as long as they confined their attentions to the shipping of other nations, the authorities of Argos were not too strict in their interpretation of sea-laws.

But Conan had not limited his activities to those of the Barachans. He had also sailed with the Zingaran buccaneers, and even with those wild black corsairs that swept up from the far south to harry the northern coasts, and this put him beyond the pale of any law. If he were recognized in any of the ports of Argos it would cost him his head. But without hesitation he rode on to Messantia, halting day or night only to rest the stallion and to snatch a few winks of sleep for himself.

He entered the city unquestioned, merging himself with the throngs that poured continually in and out of this great commercial center. No walls surrounded Messantia. The sea and the ships of the sea guarded the great southern trading city.

It was evening when Conan rode leisurely through the streets that marched down to the waterfront. At the ends of these streets he saw the wharves and the masts and sails of ships. He smelled salt water for the first time in years, heard the thrum of cordage and the creak of spars in the breeze that was kicking up whitecaps out beyond the headlands. Again the urge of far wandering tugged at his heart.

But he did not go on to the wharves. He reined aside and rode up a steep flight of wide, worn stone steps, to a broad street where ornate white mansions overlooked the waterfront and the harbor below. Here dwelt the men who had grown rich from the hard-won fat of the seas – a few old sea-captains who had found treasure afar, many traders and merchants who never trod the naked decks nor knew the roar of tempest or sea-fight.

Conan turned in his horse at a certain gold-worked gate, and rode into a court where a fountain tinkled and pigeons fluttered from marble coping to marble flagging. A page in jagged silken jupon and hose came forward inquiringly. The merchants of Messantia dealt with many strange and rough characters but most of these smacked of the sea. It was strange that a mercenary trooper should so freely ride into the court of a lord of commerce.

'The merchant Publio dwells here?' It was more statement than question, and something in the timbre of the voice caused the page to doff his feather chaperon as he bowed and replied: 'Aye, so he does, my captain.'

Conan dismounted and the page called a servitor, who came running to receive the stallion's rein.

'Your master is within?' Conan drew off his gauntlets and slapped the dust of the road from cloak and mail.

'Aye, my captain. Whom shall I announce?'

'I'll announce myself,' grunted Conan. 'I know the way well enough. Bide you here.'

And obeying that peremptory command the page stood still, staring after Conan as the latter climbed a short flight of marble steps, and wondering what connection his master might have with this giant fighting-man who had the aspect of a northern barbarian.

Menials at their tasks halted and gaped open-mouthed as Conan crossed a wide, cool balcony overlooking the court and entered a broad corridor through which the sea-breeze swept. Halfway down this he heard a quill scratching, and turned into a broad room whose many wide casements overlooked the harbor.

Publio sat at a carved teakwood desk writing on rich parchment with a golden quill. He was a short man, with a massive head and quick dark eyes. His blue robe was of the finest watered silk, trimmed with cloth-of-gold, and from his thick white throat hung a heavy gold chain.

As the Cimmerian entered, the merchant looked up with a gesture of annoyance. He froze in the midst of his gesture. His mouth opened; he stared as at a ghost out of the past. Unbelief and fear glimmered in his wide eyes.

'Well,' said Conan, 'have you no word of greeting, Publio?'

Publio moistened his lips.

'Conan!' he whispered incredulously. 'Mitra! Conan! *Amra!*'

'Who else?' The Cimmerian unclasped his cloak and threw it with his gauntlets down upon the desk. 'How man?' he exclaimed irritably. 'Can't you at least offer me a beaker of wine? My throat's caked with the dust of the highway.'

'Aye, wine!' echoed Publio mechanically. Instinctively his hand reached for a gong, then recoiled as from a hot coal, and he shuddered.

While Conan watched him with a flicker of grim amusement in his eyes, the merchant rose and hurriedly shut the door, first craning his neck up and down the corridor to be sure that no slave was loitering about. Then, returning, he took a gold vessel of wine from a near-by table and was about to fill a slender goblet when Conan impatiently took the vessel from him and lifting it with both hands, drank deep and with gusto.

'Aye, it's Conan, right enough,' muttered Publio. 'Man, are you mad?'

'By Crom, Publio,' said Conan, lowering the vessel but retaining it in his hands, 'you dwell in different quarters than of old. It takes an Argossean merchant to wring wealth out of a little waterfront shop that stank of rotten fish and cheap wine.'

'The old days are past,' muttered Publio, drawing his robe about him with a slight involuntary shudder. 'I have put off the past like a worn-out cloak.'

'Well,' retorted Conan, 'you can't put *me* off like an old cloak. It isn't much I want of you, but that much I do want. And you can't refuse me. We had too many dealings in the old days. Am I such a fool that I'm not aware that this fine mansion was built on my sweat and blood? How many cargoes from my galleys passed through your shop?'

'All merchants of Messantia have dealt with the sea-rovers at one time or another,' mumbled Publio nervously.

'But not with the black corsairs,' answered Conan grimly.

'For Mitra's sake, be silent!' ejaculated Publio, sweat starting out on his brow. His fingers jerked at the gilt-worked edge of his robe.

'Well, I only wished to recall it to your mind,' answered Conan. 'Don't be so fearful. You took plenty of risks in the past, when you were struggling for life and wealth in that lousy little shop down by the wharves, and were hand-and-glove with every buccaneer and smuggler and pirate from here to the Barachan Isles. Prosperity must have softened you.'

'I am respectable,' began Publio.

'Meaning you're rich as hell,' snorted Conan. 'Why? Why did you grow wealthy so much quicker than your competitors? Was it because you did a big business in ivory and ostrich feathers, copper and skins and pearls and hammered gold ornaments, and other things from the coast of Kush? And where did you get them so cheaply, while other merchants were paying their weight in silver to the Stygians for them? I'll tell you, in case you've forgotten: you bought them from me, at considerably less than their value, and I took them from the tribes of the Black Coast, and from the ships of the Stygians – I, and the black corsairs.'

'In Mitra's name, cease!' begged Publio. 'I have not forgotten. But what are you doing here? I am the only man in Argos who knew that the king of Aquilonia was once Conan the buccaneer, in the old days. But word has come southward of the overthrow of Aquilonia and the death of the king.'

'My enemies have killed me a hundred times by rumors,' grunted Conan. 'Yet here I sit and guzzle wine of Kyros.' And he suited the action to the word.

Lowering the vessel, which was now nearly empty, he said: 'It's but a small thing I ask of you, Publio. I know that you're aware of everything that goes on in Messantia. I want to know if a Zingaran named Beloso, or he might call himself anything, is in this city. He's tall and lean and dark like all his race, and it's likely he'll seek to sell a very rare jewel.'

Publio shook his head.

'I have not heard of such a man. But thousands come and go in Messantia. If he is here my agents will discover him.'

'Good. Send them to look for him. And in the meantime have my horse cared for, and have food served me here in this room.'

Publio assented volubly, and Conan emptied the wine vessel, tossed it carelessly into a corner, and strode to a near-by casement, involuntarily expanding his chest as he breathed deep of the salt air. He was looking down upon the meandering waterfront streets. He swept the ships in the harbor with an appreciative glance, then lifted his head and stared beyond the bay, far into the blue haze of the distance where sea met sky. And his memory sped beyond that horizon, to the golden seas of the south, under flaming suns, where laws were not and life ran hotly. Some vagrant scent of spice or palm woke clear-etched images of strange coasts where mangroves grew and drums thundered, of ships locked in battle and decks running blood, of smoke and flame and the crying of slaughter ... Lost in his thoughts he scarcely noticed when Publio stole from the chamber.

Gathering up his robe, the merchant hurried along the corridors until he came to a certain chamber where a tall, gaunt man with a scar upon his temple wrote continually upon parchment. There was something about this man which made his clerkly occupation seem incongruous. To him Publio spoke abruptly:

'Conan has returned!'

'Conan?' The gaunt man started up and the quill fell from his fingers. 'The corsair?'

'Aye!'

The gaunt man went livid. 'Is he mad? If he is discovered here we are ruined! They will hang a man who shelters or trades with a corsair as quickly as they'll hang the corsair himself! What if the governor should learn of our past connections with him?'

'He will not learn,' answered Publio grimly. 'Send your men into the markets and wharfside dives and learn if one Beloso, a Zingaran, is in Messantia. Conan said he had a gem, which he will probably seek to dispose of. The jewel merchants should know of him, if any do. And here is another task for you: pick up a dozen or so desperate villains who can be trusted to do away with a man and hold their tongues afterward. You understand me?'

'I understand.' The other nodded slowly and somberly.

'I have not stolen, cheated, lied and fought my way up from the gutter to be undone now by a ghost out of my past,' muttered Publio, and the sinister darkness of his countenance at that moment would have surprised the wealthy nobles and ladies who bought their silks and pearls from his many stalls. But when he returned to Conan a short time later, bearing in his own hands a platter of fruit and meats, he presented a placid face to his unwelcome guest.

Conan still stood at the casement, staring down into the harbor at the purple and crimson and vermilion and scarlet sails of galleons and caracks and galleys and dromonds.

'There's a Stygian galley, if I'm not blind,' he remarked, pointing to a long, low, slim black ship lying apart from the others, anchored off the low broad sandy beach that curved round to the distant headland. 'Is there peace, then, between Stygia and Argos?'

'The same sort that has existed before,' answered Publio, setting the platter on the table wth a sigh of relief, for it was heavily laden; he knew his guest of old. 'Stygian ports are temporarily open to our ships, as ours to theirs. But may no craft of mine meet their cursed galleys out of sight of land! That galley crept into the bay last night. What its masters wish I do not know. So far they have neither bought nor sold. I distrust those dark-skinned devils. Treachery had its birth in that dusky land.'

'I've made them howl,' said Conan carelessly, turning from the window. 'In my galley manned by black corsairs I crept to the very bastions of the sea-washed castles of black-walled Khemi by night, and burned the galleons anchored there. And speaking of treachery, mine host, suppose you taste these viands and sip a bit of this wine, just to show me that your heart is on the right side.'

Publio complied so readily that Conan's suspicions were lulled, and without further hesitation he sat down and devoured enough for three men.

And while he ate, men moved through the markets and along the waterfront, searching for a Zingaran who had a jewel to sell or who sought for a ship to carry him to foreign ports. And a tall gaunt man with a scar on his temple sat with his elbows on a wine-stained table in a squalid cellar with a brass lantern hanging from a smoke-blackened beam overhead, and held converse with ten desperate rogues whose sinister countenances and ragged garments proclaimed their profession.

And as the first stars blinked out, they shone on a strange band spurring their mounts along the white road that led to Messantia from the west. They were four men, tall, gaunt, clad in black, hooded robes, and they did not speak. They forced their steeds mercilessly onward, and those steeds were gaunt as themselves, and sweat-stained and weary as if from long travel and far wandering.

14 The Black Hand of Set

Conan woke from a sound sleep as quickly and instantly as a cat. And like a cat he was on his feet with his sword out before the man who had touched him could so much as draw back.

'What word, Publio?' demanded Conan, recognizing his host. The gold lamp burned low, casting a mellow glow over the thick tapestries and the rich coverings of the couch whereon he had been reposing.

Publio, recovering from the start given him by the sudden action of his awakening guest, replied: 'The Zingaran has been located. He arrived yesterday, at dawn. Only a few hours ago he sought to sell a huge, strange jewel to a Shemitish merchant, but the Shemite would have naught to do with it. Men say he turned pale beneath his black beard at the sight of it, and closing his stall, fled as from a thing accursed.'

'It must be Beloso,' muttered Conan, feeling the pulse in his temples pounding with impatient eagerness. 'Where is he now?'

'He sleeps in the house of Servio.'

'I know that dive of old,' grunted Conan. 'I'd better hasten before some of these waterfront thieves cut his throat for the jewel.'

He took up his cloak and flung it over his shoulders, then donned a helmet Publio had procured for him.

'Have my steed saddled and ready in the court,' said he. 'I may return in haste. I shall not forget this night's work, Publio.'

A few moments later Publio, standing at a small outer door, watched the king's tall figure receding down the shadowy street.

'Farewell to you, corsair,' muttered the merchant. 'This must be a notable jewel, to be sought by a man who has just lost a kingdom. I wish I had told my knaves to let him secure it before they did their work. But then, something might have gone awry. Let Argos forget Amra, and let my dealings with him be lost in the dust of the past. In the alley behind the house of Servio – that is where Conan will cease to be a peril to me.'

Servio's house, a dingy, ill-famed den, was located close to the wharves, facing the waterfront. It was a shambling building of stone and heavy ship-beams, and a long narrow alley wandered up alongside it. Conan made his way along the alley, and as he approached the house he had an uneasy feeling that he was being spied upon. He stared hard into the shadows of the squalid buildings, but saw nothing, though once he caught the faint rasp of cloth or leather against flesh. But that was nothing unusual. Thieves and beggars prowled these alleys all night, and they were not likely to attack him, after one look at his size and harness.

But suddenly a door opened in the wall ahead of him, and he slipped into the shadow of an arch. A figure emerged from the open door and moved along the alley, not furtively, but with a natural noiselessness, like that of a jungle beast. Enough starlight filtered into the alley to silhouette the man's profile dimly as he passed the doorway where Conan lurked. The stranger was a Stygian. There was no mistaking that hawk-faced, shaven head, even in the starlight, nor the mantle over the broad shoulders. He passed on down the alley in the direction of the beach, and once Conan thought he must be carrying a lantern among his garments, for he caught a flash of lambent light, just as the man vanished.

But the Cimmerian forgot the stranger as he noticed that the door through which he had emerged still stood open. Conan had intended entering by the main entrance and forcing Servio to show him the room where the Zingaran slept. But if he could get into the house without attacting anyone's attention, so much the better.

A few long strides brought him to the door, and as his hand fell on the lock he stifled an involuntary grunt. His practised fingers, skilled among the thieves of Zamora long ago, told him that the lock had been forced, apparently by some terrific pressure from the outside that had twisted and bent the heavy iron bolts, tearing the very sockets loose from the jambs. How such damage could have been wrought so violently without awakening everyone in the neighborhood Conan could not imagine, but he felt sure that it had been done that night. A broken lock, if discovered, would not go unmended in the house of Servio, in this neighborhood of thieves and cutthroats.

Conan entered stealthily, poniard in hand, wondering how he was to find the chamber of the Zingaran. Groping in total darkness he halted suddenly. He sensed death in that room, as a wild beast senses it – not as peril threatening him, but a dead thing, something freshly slain. In the darkness his foot hit and recoiled from something heavy and yielding. With a sudden premonition he groped along the wall until he found the shelf that supported the brass lamp, with its flint, steel and tinder beside it. A few seconds later a flickering, uncertain light sprang up, and he stared narrowly about him.

A bunk built against the rough stone wall, a bare table and a bench completed the furnishings of the squalid chamber. An inner door stood closed and bolted. And on the hard-beaten dirt floor lay Beloso. On his back he lay, with his head drawn back between his shoulders so that he seemed to stare with his wide glassy eyes at the sooty beams of the cobwebbed ceiling. His lips were drawn back from his teeth in a frozen grin of agony. His sword lay near him, still in its scabbard. His shirt was torn open, and on his brown, muscular breast was the print of a black hand, thumb and four fingers plainly distinct.

Conan glared in silence, feeling the short hairs bristle at the back of his neck.

'Crom!' he muttered. 'The black hand of Set!'

He had seen that mark of old, the death-mark of the black priests of Set, the grim cult that ruled in dark Stygia. And suddenly he remembered that curious flash he had seen emanating from the mysterious Stygian who had emerged from this chamber.

'The Heart, by Crom!' he muttered. 'He was carrying it under his mantle. He stole it. He burst that door by his magic, and slew Beloso. He was a priest of Set.'

A quick investigation confirmed at least part of his suspicions. The jewel was not on the Zingaran's body. An uneasy feeling rose in Conan that this had not happened by chance, or without design; a conviction that the mysterious Stygian galley had come into the harbor of Messantia on a definite mission. How could the priests of Set know that the Heart had come southward? Yet the thought was no more fantastic than the necromancy that could slay an armed man by the touch of an open, empty hand.

A stealthy footfall outside the door brought him round like a great cat. With one motion he extinguished the lamp and drew his sword. His ears told him that men were out there in the darkness, were closing in on the doorway. As his eyes became accustomed to the sudden darkness, he could make out dim figures ringing the entrance. He could not guess their identity, but as always he took the initiative – leaping suddenly forth from the doorway without awaiting the attack.

His unexpected movement took the skulkers by surprise. He sensed and heard men close about him, saw a dim masked figure in the starlight before him; then his sword crunched home, and he was fleeting away down the alley before the slower-thinking and slower-acting attackers could intercept him.

As he ran he heard, somewhere ahead of him, a faint creak of oarlocks, and he forgot the men behind him. A boat was moving out into the bay! Gritting his teeth he increased his speed, but before he reached the beach he heard the rasp and creak of ropes, and the grind of the great sweep in its socket.

Thick clouds, rolling up from the sea, obscured the stars. In thick darkness Conan came upon the strand, straining his eyes out across the black restless water. Something was moving out there – a long, low, black shape that receded in the darkness, gathering momentum as it went. To his ears came the rhythmical clack of long oars. He ground his teeth in helpless fury. It was the Stygian galley and she was racing out to sea, bearing with her the jewel that meant to him the throne of Aquilonia.

With a savage curse he took a step toward the waves that lapped against the sands, catching at his hauberk and intending to rip it off and swim after the vanishing ship. Then the crunch of a heel in the sand brought him about. He had forgotten his pursuers.

Dark figures closed in on him with a rush of feet through the sands. The first went down beneath the Cimmerian's flailing sword, but the others did not falter. Blades whickered dimly about him in the darkness or rasped on his mail. Blood and entrails spilled over his hand and someone screamed as he ripped murderously upward. A muttered voice spurred on the attack, and that voice sounded vaguely familiar. Conan plowed through the clinging, hacking shapes toward the voice. A faint light gleaming momentarily through the drifting clouds showed him a tall gaunt man with a great livid scar on his temple. Conan's sword sheared through his skull as through a ripe melon.

Then an ax, swung blindly in the dark, crashed on the king's basinet, filling his eyes with sparks of fire. He lurched and lunged, felt his sword sink deep and heard a shriek of agony. Then he stumbled over a corpse, and a bludgeon knocked the dented helmet from his head; the next instant the club fell full on his unprotected skull.

The king of Aquilonia crumpled into the wet sands. Over him wolfish figures panted in the gloom.

'Strike off his head,' muttered one.

'Let him lie,' grunted another. 'Help me tie up my wounds before I bleed to death. The tide will wash him into the bay. See, he fell at the water's edge. His skull's split; no man could live after such blows.'

'Help me strip him,' urged another. 'His harness will fetch a few pieces of silver. And haste. Tiberio is dead, and I hear seamen singing as they reel along the strand. Let us be gone.'

There followed hurried activity in the darkness, and then the sound of quickly receding footsteps. The tipsy singing of the seamen grew louder.

In his chamber Publio, nervously pacing back and forth before a window that overlooked the shadowed bay, whirled suddenly, his nerves tingling. To the best of his knowledge the door had been bolted from within; but now it stood open and four men filed into the chamber. At the sight of them his flesh crawled. Many strange beings Publio had seen in his lifetime, but none before like these. They were tall and gaunt, black-robed, and their faces were dim yellow ovals in the shadows of their coifs. He could not tell much about their features and was unreasoningly glad that he could not. Each bore a long, curiously mottled staff.

'Who are you?' he demanded, and his voice sounded brittle and hollow. 'What do you wish here?'

'Where is Conan, he who was king of Aquilonia?' demanded the tallest of the four in a passionless monotone that made Publio shudder. It was like the hollow tone of a Khitan temple bell.

'I do not know what you mean,' stammered the merchant, his customary poise shaken by the uncanny aspect of his visitors. 'I know no such man.'

'He has been here,' returned the other with no change of inflection. 'His horse is in the courtyard. Tell us where he is before we do you an injury.'

'Gebal!' shouted Publio frantically, recoiling until he crouched against the wall. '*Gebal!*'

The four Khitans watched him without emotion or change of expression.

'If you summon your slave he will die,' warned one of them, which only served to terrify Publio more than ever.

'Gebal!' he screamed. 'Where are you, curse you? Thieves are murdering your master!'

Swift footsteps padded in the corridor outside, and Gebal burst into the chamber – a Shemite, of medium height and mightily muscled build, his curled blue-black beard bristling, and a short leaf-shaped sword in his hand.

He stared in stupid amazement at the four invaders, unable to understand their presence; dimly remembering that he had drowsed unexplainably on the stair he was guarding and up which they must have come. He had never slept on duty before. But his master was shrieking with a note of hysteria in his voice, and the Shemite drove like a bull at the strangers, his thickly muscled arm drawing back for the disemboweling thrust. But the stroke was never dealt.

A black-sleeved arm shot out, extending the long staff. Its end but touched the Shemite's brawny breast and was instantly withdrawn. The stroke was horribly like the dart and recovery of a serpent's head.

Gebal halted short in his headlong plunge, as if he had encountered a solid barrier. His bull head toppled forward on his breast, the sword slipped from his fingers, and then he melted slowly to the floor. It was as if all the bones of his frame had suddenly become flabby. Publio turned sick.

'Do not shout again,' advised the tallest Khitan. 'Your servants sleep soundly, but if you awaken them they will die, and you with them. Where is Conan?'

'He is gone to the house of Servio, near the waterfront, to search for the Zingaran Beloso,' gasped Publio, all his power of resistance gone out of him. The merchant did not lack courage; but these uncanny visitors turned his marrow to water. He started convulsively at a sudden noise of footsteps hurrying up the stair outside, loud in the ominous stillness.

'Your servant?' asked the Khitan.

Publio shook his head mutely, his tongue frozen to his palate. He could not speak.

One of the Khitans caught up a silken cover from a couch and threw it over the corpse. Then they melted behind the tapestry, but before the tallest man disappeared, he murmured: 'Talk to this man who comes, and send him away quickly. If you betray us, neither he nor you will live to reach that door. Make no sign to show him you are not alone.' And lifting his staff suggestively, the yellow man faded behind the hangings.

Publio shuddered and choked down a desire to retch. It might have been a trick of the light, but it seemed to him that occasionally those staffs moved slightly of their own accord, as if possessed of an unspeakable life of their own.

He pulled himself together with a mighty effort, and presented a composed aspect to the ragged ruffian who burst into the chamber.

'We have done as you wished, my lord,' this man exclaimed. 'The barbarian lies dead on the sands at the water's edge.'

Publio felt a movement in the arras behind him, and almost burst from fright. The man swept heedlessly on.

'Your secretary, Tiberio, is dead. The barbarian slew him, and four of my companions. We bore their bodies to the rendezvous. There was nothing of value on the barbarian except a few silver coins. Are there any further orders?'

'None!' gasped Publio, white about the lips. 'Go!'

The desperado bowed and hurried out, with a vague feeling that Publio was both a man of weak stomach and few words.

The four Khitans came from behind the arras.

'Of whom did this man speak?' the taller demanded.

'Of a wandering stranger who did me an injury,' panted Publio.

'You lie,' said the Khitan calmly. 'He spoke of the king of Aquilonia. I read it in your expression. Sit upon that divan and do not move or speak. I will remain with you while my three companions go search for the body.'

So Publio sat and shook with terror of the silent, inscrutable figure which watched him, until the three Khitans filed back into the room, with the news that Conan's body did not lie upon the sands. Publio did not know whether to be glad or sorry.

'We found the spot where the fight was fought,' they said. 'Blood was on the sand. But the king was gone.'

The fourth Khitan drew imaginary symbols upon the carpet with his staff, which glistened scalily in the lamplight.

'Did you read naught from the sands?' he asked.

'Aye,' they answered. 'The king lives, and he has gone southward in a ship.'

The tall Khitan lifted his head and gazed at Publio, so that the merchant broke into a profuse sweat.

'What do you wish of me?' he stuttered.

'A ship,' answered the Khitan. 'A ship well manned for a very long voyage.'

'For how long a voyage?' stammered Publio, never thinking of refusing.

'To the ends of the world, perhaps,' answered the Khitan, 'or to the molten seas of hell that lie beyond the sunrise.'

15 The Return of the Corsair

Conan's first sensation of returning consciousness was that of motion; under him was no solidity, but a ceaseless heaving and plunging. Then he heard wind humming through cords and spars, and knew he was aboard a ship even before his blurred sight cleared. He heard a mutter of voices and then a dash of water deluged him, jerking him sharply into full animation. He heaved up with a sulphurous curse, braced his legs and glared about him, with a burst of coarse guffaws in his ears and the reek of unwashed bodies in his nostrils.

He was standing on the poopdeck of a long galley which was running before the wind that whipped down from the north, her striped sail bellying against the taut sheets. The sun was just rising, in a dazzling blaze of gold and blue and green. To the left of the shoreline was a dim purple shadow. To the right stretched the open ocean. This much Conan saw at a glance that likewise included the ship itself.

It was long and narrow, a typical trading-ship of the southern coasts, high of poop and stern, with cabins at either extremity. Conan looked down into the open waist, whence wafted that sickening abominable odor. He knew it of old. It was the body-scent of the oarsmen, chained to their benches. They were all negroes, forty men to each side, each confined by a chain locked about his waist, with the other end welded to a heavy ring set deep in the solid runway beam that ran between the benches from stem to stern. The life of a slave aboard an Argossean galley was a hell unfathomable. Most of these were Kushites, but some thirty of the blacks who now rested on their idle oars and stared up at the stranger with dull curiosity were from the far southern isles, the homelands of the corsairs. Conan recognized them by their straighter features and hair, their rangier, cleaner-limbed build. And he saw among them men who had followed him of old.

But all this he saw and recognized in one swift, all-embracing glance as he rose, before he turned his attention to the figures about him. Reeling momentarily on braced legs, his fists clenched wrathfully, he glared at the figures clustered about him. The sailor who had drenched him stood grinning, the empty bucket still poised in his hand, and Conan cursed him with venom, instinctively reaching for his hilt. Then he discovered that he was weaponless and naked except for his short leather breeks.

'What lousy tub is this?' he roared. 'How did I come aboard here?'

The sailors laughed jeeringly – stocky, bearded Argosseans to a man – and one, whose richer dress and air of command proclaimed him captain, folded his arms and said domineeringly: 'We found you lying on the sands. Somebody had rapped you on the pate and taken your clothes. Needing an extra man, we brought you aboard.'

'What ship is this?' Conan demanded.

'The *Venturer*, out of Messantia, with a cargo of mirrors, scarlet silk cloaks, shields, gilded helmets and swords to trade to the Shemites for copper and gold ore. I am Demetrio, captain of this vessel and your master henceforward.'

'Then I'm headed in the direction I wanted to go, after all,' muttered

Conan, heedless of that last remark. They were racing southeastward, following the long curve of the Argossean coast. These trading-ships never ventured far from the shoreline. Somewhere ahead of him he knew that low dark Stygian galley was speeding southward.

'Have you sighted a Stygian galley—' began Conan, but the beard of the burly, brutal-faced captain bristled. He was not in the least interested in any question his prisoner might wish to ask, and felt it high time he reduced this independent wastrel to his proper place.

'Get for'ard!' he roared. 'I've wasted time enough with you! I've done you the honor of having you brought to the poop to be revived, and answered enough of your infernal questions. Get off this poop! You'll work your way aboard this galley—'

'I'll buy your ship—' began Conan, before he remembered that he was a penniless wanderer.

A roar of rough mirth greeted these words, and the captain turned purple, thinking he sensed ridicule.

'You mutinous swine!' he bellowed, taking a threatening step forward, while his hand closed on the knife at his belt. 'Get for'ard before I have you flogged! You'll keep a civil tongue in your jaws, or by Mitra, I'll have you chained among the blacks to tug an oar!'

Conan's volcanic temper, never long at best, burst into explosion. Not in years, even before he was king, had a man spoken to him thus and lived.

'Don't lift your voice to me, you tar-breeched dog!' he roared in a voice as gusty as the sea-wind, while the sailors gaped dumfounded. 'Draw that toy and I'll feed you to the fishes!'

'Who do you think you are?' gasped the captain.

'I'll show you!' roared the maddened Cimmerian, and he wheeled and bounded toward the rail, where weapons hung in their brackets.

The captain drew his knife and ran at him bellowing, but before he could strike, Conan gripped his wrist with a wrench that tore the arm clean out of the socket. The captain bellowed like an ox in agony, and then rolled clear across the deck as he was hurled contemptuously from his attacker. Conan ripped a heavy ax from the rail and wheeled cat-like to meet the rush of the sailors. They ran in, giving tongue like hounds, clumsy-footed and awkward in comparison to the pantherish Cimmerian. Before they could reach him with their knives he sprang among them, striking right and left too quickly for the eye to follow, and blood and brains spattered as two corpses struck the deck.

Knives flailed the air wildly as Conan broke through the stumbling, gasping mob and bounded to the narrow bridge that spanned the waist from poop to forecastle, just out of reach of the slaves below. Behind him the handful of sailors on the poop were floundering after him, daunted by the destruction of their fellows, and the rest of the crew – some thirty in all – came running across the bridge toward him, with weapons in their hands.

Conan bounded out on the bridge and stood poised above the upturned black faces, ax lifted, black mane blown in the wind.

'Who am I?' he yelled. 'Look, you dogs! Look, Ajonga, Yasunga, Laranga! *Who am I?*'

And from the waist rose a shout that swelled to a mighty roar: 'Amra! It is Amra! The Lion has returned!'

The sailors who caught and understood the burden of that awesome shout paled and shrank back, staring in sudden fear at the wild figure on the bridge. Was this in truth that bloodthirsty ogre of the southern seas who had so mysteriously vanished years ago, but who still lived in gory legends? The blacks were frothing crazy now, shaking and tearing at their chains and shrieking the name of Amra like an invocation. Kushites who had never seen Conan before took up the yell. The slaves in the pen under the after-cabin began to batter at the walls, shrieking like the damned.

Demetrio, hitching himself along the deck on one hand and his knees, livid with the agony of his dislocated arm, screamed: 'In and kill him, dogs, before the slaves break loose!'

Fired to desperation by that word, the most dread to all galleymen, the sailors charged on to the bridge from both ends. But with a lionlike bound Conan left the bridge and hit like a cat on his feet on the runway between the benches.

'Death to the masters!' he thundered, and his ax rose and fell crashingly full on a shackle-chain, severing it like matchwood. In an instant a shrieking slave was free, splintering his oar for a bludgeon. Men were racing frantically along the bridge above, and all hell and bedlam broke loose on the *Venturer*. Conan's ax rose and fell without pause, and with every stroke a frothing, screaming black giant broke free, mad with hate and the fury of freedom and vengeance.

Sailors leaping down into the waist to grapple or smite at the naked white giant hewing like one possessed at the shackles, found themselves dragged down by the hands of slaves yet unfreed, while others, their broken chains whipping and snapping about their limbs, came up out of the waist like a blind, black torrent, screaming like fiends, smiting with broken oars and pieces of iron, tearing and rending with talons and teeth. In the midst of the mêlée the slaves in the pen broke down the walls and came surging up on the decks, and with fifty blacks freed of their benches Conan abandoned his iron-hewing and bounded up on the bridge to add his notched ax to the bludgeons of his partisans.

Then it was massacre. The Argosseans were strong, sturdy, fearless like all their race, trained in the brutal school of the sea. But they could not stand against these maddened giants, led by the tigerish barbarian. Blows and abuse and hellish suffering were avenged in one red gust of fury that raged like a typhoon from one end of the ship to the other, and when it had blown itself out, but one white man lived aboard the Venturer, and that was the blood-stained giant about whom the chanting blacks thronged to cast themselves prostrate on the bloody deck and beat their heads against the boards in an ecstasy of hero-worship.

Conan, his mighty chest heaving and glistening with sweat, the red ax gripped in his blood-smeared hand, glared about him as the first chief of men might have glared in some primordial dawn, and shook back his black mane. In that moment he was not king of Aquilonia; he was again lord of the black corsairs, who had hacked his way to lordship through flame and blood.

'Amra! Amra!' chanted the delirious blacks, those who were left to chant. 'The Lion has returned! Now will the Stygians howl like dogs in the night, and the black dogs of Kush will howl! Now will villages burst in flames and ships founder! Aie, there will be wailing of women and the thunder of the spears!'

'Cease this yammering, dogs!' Conan roared in a voice that drowned the clap of the sail in the wind. 'Ten of you go below and free the oarsmen who are yet chained. The rest of you man the sweeps and bend to oars and halyards. Crom's devils, don't you see we've drifted inshore during the fight? Do you want to run aground and be retaken by the Argosseans? Throw these carcasses overboard. Jump to it, you rogues, or I'll notch your hides for you!'

With shouts and laughter and wild singing they leaped to do his commands. The corpses, white and black, were hurled overboard, where triangular fins were already cutting the water.

Conan stood on the poop, frowning down at the black men who watched him expectantly. His heavy brown arms were folded, his black hair, grown long in his wanderings, blew in the wind. A wilder and more barbaric figure never trod the bridge of a ship, and in this ferocious corsair few of the courtiers of Aquilonia would have recognized their king.

'There's food in the hold!' he roared. 'Weapons in plenty for you, for this ship carried blades and harness to the Shemites who dwell along the coast. There are enough of us to work ship, aye, and to fight! You rowed in chains for the Argossean dogs: will you row as free men for Amra?'

'*Aye!*' they roared. 'We are thy children! Lead us where you will!'

'Then fall to and clean out that waist,' he commanded. 'Free men don't labor in such filth. Three of you come with me and break out food from the after-cabin. By Crom, I'll pad out your ribs before this cruise is done.'

Another yell of approbation answered him, as the half-starved blacks scurried to do his bidding. The sail bellied as the wind swept over the waves with renewed force, and the white crests danced along the sweep of the wind. Conan planted his feet to the heave of the deck, breathed deep and spread his mighty arms. King of Aquilonia he might no longer be; king of the blue ocean he was still.

16 Black-Walled Khemi

The *Venturer* swept southward like a living thing, her oars pulled now by free and willing hands. She had been transformed from a peaceful trader into a war-galley, insofar as the transformation was possible. Men sat at the benches now with swords at their sides and gilded helmets on their kinky heads. Shields were hung along the rails, and sheafs of spears, bows and arrows adorned the mast. Even the elements seemed to work for Conan now; the broad purple sail bellied to a stiff breeze that held day by day, needing little aid from the oars.

But though Conan kept a man on the masthead day and night, they did not sight a long, low, black galley fleeing southward ahead of them. Day by day the blue waters rolled empty to their view, broken only by fishing-craft which fled like frightened birds before them, at sight of the shields hung along the rail. The season for trading was practically over for the year, and they sighted no other ships.

When the lookout did sight a sail, it was to the north, not the south. Far on the skyline behind them appeared a racing-galley, with full spread of purple sail. The blacks urged Conan to turn and plunder it, but he shook his head. Somewhere south of him a slim black galley was racing toward the ports of Stygia. That night, before darkness shut down, the lookout's last glimpse showed him the racing-galley on the horizon, and at dawn it was still hanging on their tail, afar off, tiny in the distance. Conan wondered if it was following him, though he could think of no logical reason for such a supposition. But he paid little heed.

Each day that carried him farther southward filled him with fiercer impatience. Doubts never assailed him. As he believed in the rise and set of the sun he believed that a priest of Set had stolen the Heart of Ahriman. And where would a priest of Set carry it but to Stygia? The blacks sensed his eagerness, and toiled as they had never toiled under the lash, though ignorant of his goal. They anticipated a red career of pillage and plunder and were content. The men of the southern isles knew no other trade; and the Kushites of the crew joined whole-heartedly in the prospect of looting their own people, with the callousness of their race. Blood-ties meant little; a victorious chieftain and personal gain everything.

Soon the character of the coastline changed. No longer they sailed past steep cliffs with blue hills marching behind them. Now the shore was the edge of broad meadowlands which barely rose above the water's edge and swept away and away into the hazy distance. Here were few harbors and fewer ports, but the green plain was dotted with the cities of the Shemites; green sea, lapping the rim of the green plains, and the ziggurats of the cities gleaming whitely in the sun, some small in the distance.

Through the grazing-lands moved the herds of cattle, and squat, broad riders with cylindrical helmets and curled blue-black beards, with bows in their hands. This was the shore of the lands of Shem, where there was no law save as each city-state could enforce its own. Far to the eastward, Conan knew, the meadowlands gave way to desert, where there were no cities and the nomadic tribes roamed unhindered.

Still as they plied southward, past the changeless panorama of city-dotted meadowland, at last the scenery again began to alter. Clumps of tamarind appeared, the palm groves grew denser. The shoreline became more broken, a marching rampart of green fronds and trees, and behind them rose bare, sandy hills. Streams poured into the sea, and along their moist banks vegetation grew thick and of vast variety.

So at last they passed the mouth of a broad river that mingled its flow with the ocean, and saw the great black walls and towers of Khemi rise against the southern horizon.

The river was the Styx, the real border of Stygia. Khemi was Stygia's greatest port, and at that time her most important city. The king dwelt at more ancient Luxur, but in Khemi reigned the priestcraft; though men said the center of their dark religion lay far inland, in a mysterious, deserted city near the bank of the Styx. This river, springing from some nameless source far in the unknown lands south of Stygia, ran northward for a thousand miles before it turned and flowed westward for some hundreds of miles, to empty at last into the ocean.

The Venturer, showing no lights, stole past the port in the night, and before dawn discovered her, anchored in a small bay a few miles south of the city. It was surrounded by marsh, a green tangle of mangroves, palms and lianas, swarming with crocodiles and serpents. Discovery was extremely unlikely. Conan knew the place of old; he had hidden there before, in his corsair days.

As they slid silently past the city whose great black bastions rose on the jutting prongs of land which locked the harbor, torches gleamed and smoldered luridly, and to their ears came the low thunder of drums. The port was not crowded with ships, as were the harbors of Argos. The Stygians did not base their glory and power upon ships and fleets. Trading-vessels and war-galleys, indeed, they had, but not in proportion to their inland strength. Many of their craft plied up and down the great river, rather than along the sea-coasts.

The Stygians were an ancient race, a dark, inscrutable people, powerful and merciless. Long ago their rule had stretched far north of the Styx, beyond the meadowlands of Shem, and into the fertile uplands now inhabited by the peoples of Koth and Ophir and Argos. Their borders had marched with those of ancient Acheron. But Acheron had fallen, and the barbaric ancestors of the Hyborians had swept southward in wolfskins and horned helmets, driving the ancient rulers of the land before them. The Stygians had not forgotten.

All day the *Venturer* lay at anchor in the tiny bay, walled in with green branches and tangled vines through which flitted gay-plumed, harsh-voiced birds, and among which glided bright-scaled, silent reptiles. Toward sundown a small boat crept out and down along the shore, seeking and finding that which Conan desired – a Stygian fisherman in his shallow, flat-prowed boat.

They brought him to the deck of the *Venturer* – a tall, dark, rangily built man, ashy with fear of his captors, who were ogres of that coast. He was naked except for his silken breeks, for, like the Hyrkanians, even the commoners and slaves of Stygia wore silk; and in his boat was a wide mantle such as these fishermen flung about their shoulders against the chill of the night.

He fell to his knees before Conan, expecting torture and death.

'Stand on your legs, man, and quit trembling,' said the Cimmerian impatiently, who found it difficult to understand abject terror. 'You won't be harmed. Tell me but this: has a galley, a black racing-galley returning from Argos, put into Khemi within the last few days?'

'Aye, my lord,' answered the fisherman. 'Only yesterday at dawn the priest Thutothmes returned from a voyage far to the north. Men say he has been to Messantia.'

'What did he bring from Messantia?'

'Alas, my lord, I know not.'

'Why did he go to Messantia?' demanded Conan.

'Nay, my lord, I am but a common man. Who am I to know the minds of the priests of Set? I can only speak what I have seen and what I have heard men whisper along the wharves. Men say that news of great import came southward, though of what none knows; and it is well known that the lord Thutothmes put off in his black galley in great haste. Now he is returned, but what he did in Argos, or what cargo he brought back, none knows, not even the seamen who manned his galley. Men say that he has opposed Thoth-Amon, who is the master of all priests of Set, and dwells in Luxur, and that Thutothmes seeks hidden power to overthrow the Great One. But who am I to say? When priests war with one another a common man can but lie on his belly and hope neither treads upon him.'

Conan snarled in nervous exasperation at this servile philosophy, and turned to his men. 'I'm going alone into Khemi to find this thief Thutothmes. Keep this man prisoner, but see that you do him no hurt. Crom's devils, stop your yowling! Do you think we can sail into the harbor and take the city by storm? I must go alone.'

Silencing the clamor of protests, he doffed his own garments and donned the prisoner's silk breeches and sandals, and the band from the man's hair, but scorned the short fisherman's knife. The common men of Stygia were not allowed to wear swords, and the mantle was not voluminous enough to hide the Cimmerian's long blade, but Conan buckled to his hip a Ghanata knife, a weapon borne by the fierce desert men who dwelt to the south of the Stygians, a broad, heavy, slightly curved blade of fine steel, edged like a razor and long enough to dismember a man.

Then, leaving the Stygian guarded by the corsairs, Conan climbed into the fisher's boat.

'Wait for me until dawn,' he said. 'If I haven't come then, I'll never come, so hasten southward to your own homes.'

As he clambered over the rail, they set up a doleful wail at his going, until he thrust his head back into sight to curse them into silence. Then, dropping into the boat, he grasped the oars and sent the tiny craft shooting over the waves more swiftly than its owner had ever propelled it.

17 'He Has Slain the Sacred Son of Set!'

The harbor of Khemi lay between two great jutting points of land that ran into the ocean. He rounded the southern point, where the great black castles rose like a man-made hill, and entered the harbor just at dusk, when there was still enough light for the watchers to recognize the fisherman's boat and mantle, but not enough to permit recognition of betraying details. Unchallenged he threaded his way among the great black war galleys lying silent and unlighted at anchor, and drew up to a flight of wide stone steps which mounted up from the water's edge. There he made his boat fast to an iron ring set in the stone, as numerous similar craft were tied. There was nothing strange in a fisherman leaving his boat there. None but a fisherman could find a use for such a craft, and they did not steal from one another.

No one cast him more than a casual glance as he mounted the long steps, unobtrusively avoiding the torches that flared at intervals above the lapping black water. He seemed but an ordinary, empty-handed fisherman, returning after a fruitless day along the coast. If one had observed him closely, it might have seemed that his step was somewhat too springy and sure, his carriage somewhat too erect and confident for a lowly fisherman. But he passed quickly, keeping in the shadows, and the commoners of Stygia were no more given to analysis than were the commoners of the less exotic races.

In build he was not unlike the warrior casts of the Stygians, who were a tall, muscular race. Bronzed by the sun, he was nearly as dark as many of them. His black hair, square-cut and confined by a copper band, increased the resemblance. The characteristics which set him apart from them were the subtle difference in his walk, and his alien features and blue eyes.

But the mantle was a good disguise, and he kept as much in the shadows as possible, turning away his head when a native passed him too closely.

But it was a desperate game, and he knew he could not long keep up the deception. Khemi was not like the seaports of the Hyborians, where types of every race swarmed. The only aliens here were negro and Shemite slaves; and he resembled neither even as much as he resembled the Stygians themselves. Strangers were not welcome in the cities of Stygia; tolerated only when they came as ambassadors or licensed traders. But even then the latter were not allowed ashore after dark. And now there were no Hyborian ships in the harbor at all. A strange restlessness ran through the city, a stirring of ancient ambitions, a whispering none could define except those who whispered. This Conan felt rather than knew, his whetted primitive instincts sensing unrest about him.

If he were discovered his fate would be ghastly. They would slay him merely for being a stranger; if he were recognized as Amra, the corsair chief who had swept their coasts with steel and flame – an involuntary shudder twitched Conan's broad shoulders. Human foes he did not fear, nor any death by steel or fire. But this was a black land of sorcery and nameless horror. Set the Old Serpent, men said, banished long ago from the Hyborian races, yet lurked in the shadows of the cryptic temples, and awful and mysterious were the deeds done in the nighted shrines.

He had drawn away from the waterfront streets with their broad steps leading down to the water, and was entering the long shadowy streets of the main part of the city. There was no such scene as was offered by any Hyborian city – no blaze of lamps and cressets, with gay-clad people laughing and strolling along the pavements, and shops and stalls wide open and displaying their wares.

Here the stalls were closed at dusk. The only lights along the streets were torches, flaring smokily at wide intervals. People walking the streets were comparatively few; they went hurriedly and unspeaking, and their numbers decreased with the lateness of the hour. Conan found the scene gloomy and unreal; the silence of the people, their furtive haste, the great black stone walls that rose on each side of the streets. There was a grim massiveness about Stygian architecture that was overpowering and oppressive.

Few lights showed anywhere except in the upper parts of the buildings. Conan knew that most of the people lay on the flat roofs, among the palms of artificial gardens under the stars. There was a murmur of weird music from somewhere. Occasionally a bronze chariot rumbled along the flags, and there was a brief glimpse of a tall, hawk-faced noble, with a silk cloak wrapped about him, and a gold band with a rearing serpent-head emblem confining his black mane; of the ebon, naked charioteer bracing his knotty legs against the straining of the fierce Stygian horses.

But the people who yet traversed the streets on foot were commoners, slaves, tradesmen, harlots, toilers, and they became fewer as he progressed. He was making toward the temple of Set, where he knew he would be likely to find the priest he sought. He believed he would know Thutothmes if he saw him, though his one glance had been in the semi-darkness of the Messantian alley. That the man he had seen there had been the priest he was certain. Only occultists high in the mazes of the hideous Black Ring possessed the power of the black hand that dealt death by its touch; and only such a man would dare defy Thoth-Amon, whom the western world knew only as a figure of terror and myth.

The street broadened, and Conan was aware that he was getting into the part of the city dedicated to the temples. The great structures reared their black bulks against the dim stars, grim, indescribably menacing in the flare of the few torches. And suddenly he heard a low scream from a woman on the other side of the street and somewhat ahead of him – a naked courtesan wearing the tall plumed head-dress of her class. She was shrinking back against the wall, staring across at something he could not yet see. At her cry the few people on the street halted suddenly as if frozen. At the same instant Conan was aware of a sinister slithering ahead of him. Then about the dark corner of the building he was approaching poked a hideous, wedge-shaped head, and after it flowed coil after coil of rippling, darkly glistening trunk.

The Cimmerian recoiled, remembering tales he had heard – serpents were sacred to Set, god of Stygia, who men said was himself a serpent. Monsters such as this were kept in the temples of Set, and when they hungered, were allowed to crawl forth into the streets to take what prey they wished. Their ghastly feasts were considered a sacrifice to the scaly god.

The Stygians within Conan's sight fell to their knees, men and women, and passively awaited their fate. One the great serpent would select, would lap in scaly coils, crush to a red pulp and swallow as a rat-snake swallows a mouse. The others would live. That was the will of the gods.

But it was not Conan's will. The python glided toward him, its attention probably attracted by the fact that he was the only human in sight still standing erect. Gripping his great knife under his mantle, Conan hoped the slimy brute would pass him by. But it halted before him and reared up horrifically in the flickering torchlight, its forked tongue flickering in and out, its cold eyes glittering with the ancient cruelty of the serpent-folk. Its neck arched, but before it could dart, Conan whipped his knife from under his mantle and struck like a flicker of lightning. The broad blade split that wedge-shaped head and sheared deep into the thick neck.

Conan wrenched his knife free and sprang clear as the great body knotted and looped and whipped terrifically in its death throes. In the moment that he stood staring in morbid fascination, the only sound was the thud and swish of the snake's tail against the stones.

Then from the shocked votaries burst a terrible cry: 'Blasphemer! He has slain the sacred son of Set! Slay him! Slay! Slay!'

Stones whizzed about him and the crazed Stygians rushed at him, shrieking hysterically, while from all sides others emerged from their houses and took up the cry. With a curse Conan wheeled and darted into the black mouth of an alley. He heard the patter of bare feet on the flags behind him as he ran more by feel than by sight, and the walls resounded to the vengeful yells of the pursuers. Then his left hand found a break in the wall, and he turned sharply into another, narrower alley. On both sides rose sheer black stone walls. High above him he could see a thin line of stars. These giant walls, he knew, were the walls of temples. He heard, behind him, the pack sweep past the dark mouth in full cry. Their shouts grew distant, faded away. They had missed the smaller alley and run straight on in the blackness. He too kept straight ahead, though the thought of encountering another of Set's 'sons' in the darkness brought a shudder from him.

Then somewhere ahead of him he caught a moving glow, like that of a crawling glow-worm. He halted, flattened himself against the wall and gripped his knife. He knew what it was: a man approaching with a torch. Now it was so close he could make out the dark hand that gripped it, and the dim oval of a dark face. A few more steps and the man would certainly see him. He sank into a tigerish crouch – the torch halted. A door was briefly etched in the glow, while the torch-bearer fumbled with it. Then it opened, the tall figure vanished through it, and darkness closed again on the alley. There was a sinister suggestion of furtiveness about that slinking figure, entering the alley-door in darkness; a priest, perhaps, returning from some dark errand.

But Conan groped toward the door. If one man came up that alley with a torch, others might come at any time. To retreat the way he had come might mean to run full into the mob from which he was fleeing. At any moment they might return, find the narrower alley and come howling down it. He felt hemmed in by those sheer, unscalable walls, desirous of escape, even if escape meant invading some unknown building.

The heavy bronze door was not locked. It opened under his fingers and he peered through the crack. He was looking into a great square chamber of massive black stone. A torch smoldered in a niche in the wall. The chamber was empty. He glided through the lacquered door and closed it behind him.

His sandaled feet made no sound as he crossed the black marble floor. A teak door stood partly open, and gliding through this, knife in hand, he came out into a great, dim, shadowy place whose lofty ceiling was only a hint of darkness high above him, toward which the black walls swept upward. On all sides black-arched doorways opened into the great still hall. It was lit by curious bronze lamps that gave a dim weird light. On the other side of the great hall a broad black marble stairway, without a railing, marched upward to lose itself in gloom, and above him on all sides dim galleries hung like black stone ledges.

Conan shivered; he was in a temple of some Stygian god, if not Set himself, then someone barely less grim. And the shrine did not lack an occupant. In the midst of the great hall stood a black stone altar, massive, somber, without carvings or ornament, and upon it coiled one of the great sacred serpents, its iridescent scales shimmering in the lamplight. It did not move, and Conan remembered stories that the priests kept these creatures drugged part of the time. The Cimmerian took an uncertain step out from the door, then shrank back suddenly, not into the room he had just quitted, but into a velvet-curtained recess. He had heard a soft step somewhere near by.

From one of the black arches emerged a tall, powerful figure in sandals and silken loin-cloth, with a wide mantle trailing from his shoulders. But face and head were hidden by a monstrous mask, a half-bestial, half-human countenance, from the crest of which floated a mass of ostrich plumes.

In certain ceremonies the Stygian priests went masked. Conan hoped the man would not discover him, but some instinct warned the Stygian. He turned abruptly from his destination, which apparently was the stair, and stepped straight to the recess. As he jerked aside the velvet hanging, a hand darted from the shadows, crushed the cry in his throat and jerked him headlong into the alcove, and the knife impaled him.

Conan's next move was the obvious one suggested by logic. He lifted off the grinning mask and drew it over his own head. The fisherman's mantle he flung over the body of the priest, which he concealed behind the hangings, and drew the priestly mantle about his own brawny shoulders. Fate had given him a disguise. All Khemi might well be searching now for the blasphemer who dared defend himself against a sacred snake; but who would dream of looking for him under the mask of a priest?

He strode boldly from the alcove and headed for one of the arched doorways at random; but he had not taken a dozen strides when he wheeled again, all his senses edged for peril.

A band of masked figures filed down the stair, appareled exactly as he was. He hesitated, caught in the open, and stood still, trusting to his disguise, though cold sweat gathered on his forehead and the backs of his hands. No word was spoken. Like phantoms they descended into the great hall and moved past him toward a black arch. The leader carried an ebon staff which supported a grinning white skull, and Conan knew it was one of the ritualistic processions so inexplicable to a foreigner, but which played a strong – and often sinister – part in the Stygian religion. The last figure turned his head slightly toward the motionless Cimmerian, as if expecting him to follow. Not to do what was obviously expected of him would rouse instant suspicion. Conan fell in behind the last man and suited his gait to their measured pace.

They traversed a long, dark, vaulted corridor in which, Conan noticed uneasily, the skull on the staff glowed phosphorescently. He felt a surge of unreasoning, wild animal panic that urged him to rip out his knife and slash right and left at these uncanny figures, to flee madly from the grim, dark temple. But he held himself in check, fighting down the dim monstrous intuitions that rose in the back of his mind and peopled the gloom with shadowy shapes of horror; and presently he barely stifled a sigh of relief as they filed through a great double-valved door which was three times higher than a man, and emerged into the starlight.

Conan wondered if he dared fade into some dark alley; but hesitated, uncertain, and down the long dark street they padded silently, while such folk as they met turned their heads away and fled from them. The procession kept far out from the walls; to turn and bolt into any of the alleys they passed would be too conspicuous. While he mentally fumed and cursed, they came to a low-arched gateway in the southern wall, and through this they filed. Ahead of them and about them lay clusters of low, flat-topped mud houses, and palm-groves, shadowy in the starlight. Now if ever, thought Conan, was his time to escape his silent companions.

But the moment the gate was left behind them those companions were no longer silent. They began to mutter excitedly among themselves. The measured, ritualistic gait was abandoned, the staff with its skull was tucked unceremoniously under the leader's arm, and the whole group broke ranks and hurried onward. And Conan hurried with them. For in the low murmur of speech he had caught a word that galvanized him. The word was: '*Thutothmes!*'

18 'I Am the Woman Who Never Died'

Conan stared with burning interest at his masked companions. One of them was Thutothmes, or else the destination of the band was a rendezvous with the man he sought. And he knew what that destination was, when beyond the palms he glimpsed a black triangular bulk looming against the shadowy sky.

They passed through the belt of huts and groves, and if any man saw them he was careful not to show himself. The huts were dark. Behind them the black towers of Khemi rose gloomily against the stars that were mirrored in the waters of the harbor; ahead of them the desert stretched away in dim darkness; somewhere a jackal yapped. The quick-passing sandals of the silent neophytes made no noise in the sand. They might have been ghosts, moving toward that colossal pyramid that rose out of the murk of the desert. There was no sound over all the sleeping land.

Conan's heart beat quicker as he gazed at the grim black wedge that stood etched against the stars, and his impatience to close with Thutothmes in whatever conflict the meeting might mean was not unmixed with a fear of the unknown. No man could approach one of those somber piles of black stone without apprehension. The very name was a symbol of repellent horror among the northern nations, and legends hinted that the Stygians did not build them; that they were in the land at whatever immeasurably ancient date the dark-skinned people came into the land of the great river.

As they approached the pyramid he glimpsed a dim glow near the base which presently resolved itself into a doorway, on either side of which brooded stone lions with the heads of women, cryptic, inscrutable, nightmares crystalized in stone. The leader of the band made straight for the doorway, in the deep well of which Conan saw a shadowy figure.

The leader paused an instant beside this dim figure, and then vanished into the dark interior, and one by one the others followed. As each masked priest passed through the gloomy portal he was halted briefly by the mysterious guardian and something passed between them, some word or gesture Conan could not make out. Seeing this, the Cimmerian purposely lagged behind, and stooping, pretended to be fumbling with the fastening of his sandal. Not until the last of the masked figures had disappeared did he straighten and approach the portal.

He was uneasily wondering if the guardian of the temple were human, remembering some tales he had heard. But his doubts were set at rest. A dim bronze cresset glowing just within the door lighted a long narrow corridor that ran away into blackness, and a man standing silent in the mouth of it, wrapped in a wide black cloak. No one else was in sight. Obviously the masked priests had disappeared down the corridor.

Over the cloak that was drawn about his lower features, the Stygian's piercing eyes regarded Conan sharply. With his left hand he made a curious gesture. On a venture Conan imitated it. But evidently another gesture was expected; the Stygian's right hand came from under his cloak with a gleam of steel and his murderous stab would have pierced the heart of an ordinary man.

But he was dealing with one whose thews were nerved to the quickness of a jungle cat. Even as the dagger flashed in the dim light, Conan caught the dusky wrist and smashed his clenched right fist against the Stygian's jaw. The man's head went back against the stone wall with a dull crunch that told of a fractured skull.

Standing for an instant above him, Conan listened intently. The cresset burned low, casting vague shadows about the door. Nothing stirred in the blackness beyond, though far away and below him, as it seemed, he caught the faint, muffled note of a gong.

He stooped and dragged the body behind the great bronze door which stood wide, opened inward, and then the Cimmerian went warily but swiftly down the corridor, toward what doom he did not even try to guess.

He had not gone far when he halted, baffled. The corridor split in two branches, and he had no way of knowing which the masked priests had taken. At a venture he chose the left. The floor slanted slightly downward and was worn smooth as by many feet. Here and there a dim cresset cast a faint nightmarish twilight. Conan wondered uneasily for what purpose these colossal piles had been reared, in what forgotten age. This was an ancient, ancient land. No man knew how many ages the black temples of Stygia had looked against the stars.

Narrow black arches opened occasionally to right and left, but he kept to the main corridor, although a conviction that he had taken the wrong branch was growing in him. Even with their start on him, he should have overtaken the priests by this time. He was growing nervous. The silence was like a tangible thing, and yet he had a feeling that he was not alone. More than once, passing a nighted arch he seemed to feel the glare of unseen eyes fixed upon him. He paused, half minded to turn back to where the corridor had first branched. He wheeled abruptly, knife lifted, every nerve tingling.

A girl stood at the mouth of a smaller tunnel, staring fixedly at him. Her ivory skin showed her to be Stygian of some ancient noble family, and like all such women she was tall, lithe, voluptuously figured, her hair a great pile of black foam, among which gleamed a sparkling ruby. But for her velvet sandals and broad jewel-crusted girdle about her supple waist she was quite nude.

'What do you here?' she demanded.

To answer would betray his alien origin. He remained motionless, a grim, somber figure in the hideous mask with the plumes floating over him. His alert gaze sought the shadows behind her and found them empty. But there might be hordes of fighting-men within her call.

She advanced toward him, apparently without apprehension though with suspicion.

'You are not a priest,' she said. 'You are a fighting-man. Even with that mask that is plain. There is as much difference between you and a priest as there is between a man and a woman. By Set!' she exclaimed, halting suddenly, her eyes flaring wide. 'I do not believe you are even a Stygian!'

With a movement too quick for the eye to follow, his hand closed about her round throat, lightly as a caress.

'Not a sound out of you!' he muttered.

Her smooth ivory flesh was cold as marble, yet there was no fear in the wide, dark, marvelous eyes which regarded him.

'Do not fear,' she answered calmly. 'I will not betray you. But are you mad to come, a stranger and a foreigner, to the forbidden temple of Set?'

'I'm looking for the priest Thutothmes,' he answered. 'Is he in this temple?'

'Why do you seek him?' she parried.

'He has something of mine which was stolen.'

'I will lead you to him,' she volunteered so promptly that his suspicions were instantly roused.

'Don't play with me, girl,' he growled.

'I do not play with you. I have no love for Thutothmes.'

He hesitated, then made up his mind; after all, he was as much in her power as she was in his.

'Walk beside me,' he commanded, shifting his grasp from her throat to her wrist. 'But walk with care. If you make a suspicious move—'

She led him down the slanting corridor, down and down, until there were no more cressets, and he groped his way in darkness, aware less by sight than by feel and sense of the woman at his side. Once when he spoke to her, she turned her head toward him and he was startled to see her eyes glowing like golden fire in the dark. Dim doubts and vague monstrous suspicions haunted his mind, but he followed her, through a labyrinthine maze of black corridors that confused even his primitive sense of direction. He mentally cursed himself for a fool, allowing himself to be led into that black abode of mystery; but it was too late to turn back now. Again he felt life and movement in the darkness about him, sensed peril and hunger burning impatiently in the blackness. Unless his ears deceived him he caught a faint sliding noise that ceased and receded at a muttered command from the girl.

She led him at last into a chamber lighted by a curious seven-branched candelabrum in which black candles burned weirdly. He knew they were far below the earth. The chamber was square, with walls and ceiling of polished black marble and furnished after the manner of the ancient Stygians; there was a couch of ebony, covered with black velvet, and on a black stone dais lay a carven mummy-case.

Conan stood waiting expectantly, staring at the various black arches which opened into the chamber. But the girl made no move to go farther. Stretching herself on the couch with feline suppleness, she intertwined her fingers behind her sleek head and regarded him from under long drooping lashes.

'Well?' he demanded impatiently. 'What are you doing? Where's Thutothmes?'

'There is no haste,' she answered lazily. 'What is an hour – or a day, or a year, or a century, for that matter? Take off your mask. Let me see your features.'

With a grunt of annoyance Conan dragged off the bulky headpiece, and the girl nodded as if in approval as she scanned his dark scarred face and blazing eyes.

'There is strength in you – great strength; you could strangle a bullock.'

He moved restlessly, his suspicion growing. With his hand on his hilt he peered into the gloomy arches.

'If you've brought me into a trap,' he said, 'you won't live to enjoy your handiwork. Are you going to get off that couch and do as you promised, or do I have to—'

His voice trailed away. He was staring at the mummy-case, on which the countenance of the occupant was carved in ivory with the startling vividness of a forgotten art. There was a disquieting familiarity about that carven mask, and with something of a shock he realized what it was; there was a startling resemblance between it and the face of the girl lolling on the ebon couch. She might have been the model from which it was carved, but he knew the portrait was at least centuries old. Archaic hieroglyphics were scrawled across the lacquered lid, and, seeking back into his mind for tag-ends of learning, picked up here and there as incidentals of an adventurous life, he spelled them out, and said aloud: 'Akivasha!'

'You have heard of Princess Akivasha?' inquired the girl on the couch.

'Who hasn't?' he grunted. The name of that ancient, evil, beautiful princess still lived the world over in song and legend, though ten thousand years had rolled their cycles since the daughter of Tuthamon had reveled in purple feasts amid the black halls of ancient Luxur.

'Her only sin was that she loved life and all the meanings of life,' said the Stygian girl. 'To win life she courted death. She could not bear to think of growing old and shriveled and worn, and dying at last as hags die. She wooed Darkness like a lover and his gift was life – life that, not being life as mortals know it, can never grow old and fade. She went into the shadows to cheat age and death—'

Conan glared at her with eyes that were suddenly burning slits. And he wheeled and tore the lid from the sarcophagus. It was empty. Behind him the girl was laughing and the sound froze the blood in his veins. He whirled back to her, the short hairs on his neck bristling.

'You are Akivasha!' he grated.

She laughed and shook back her burnished locks, spread her arms sensuously.

'I am Akivasha! I am the woman who never died, who never grew old! Who fools say was lifted from the earth by the gods, in the full bloom of her youth and beauty, to queen it for ever in some celestial clime! Nay, it is in the shadows that mortals find immortality! Ten thousand years ago I died to live for ever! Give me your lips, strong man!'

Rising lithely she came to him, rose on tiptoe and flung her arms about his massive neck. Scowling down into her upturned, beautiful countenance he was aware of a fearful fascination and an icy fear.

'Love me!' she whispered, her head thrown back, eyes closed and lips parted. 'Give me of your blood to renew my youth and perpetuate my everlasting life! I will make you, too, immortal! I will teach you the wisdom of all the ages, all the secrets that have lasted out the eons in the blackness beneath these dark temples. I will make you king of that shadowy horde which revels among the tombs of the ancients when night veils the desert and bats flit across the moon. I am weary of priests and magicians, and captive girls dragged screaming through the portals of death. I desire a man. Love me, barbarian!'

She pressed her dark head down against his mighty breast, and he felt a sharp pang at the base of his throat. With a curse he tore her away and flung her sprawling across the couch.

'Damned vampire!' Blood was trickling from a tiny wound in his throat.

She reared up on the couch like a serpent poised to strike, all the golden fires of hell blazing in her wide eyes. Her lips drew back, revealing white pointed teeth.

'Fool!' she shrieked. 'Do you think to escape me? You will live and die in darkness! I have brought you far below the temple. You can never find your way out alone. You can never cut your way through those which guard the tunnels. But for my protection the sons of Set would long ago have taken you into their bellies. Fool, I shall yet drink your blood!'

'Keep away from me or I'll slash you asunder,' he grunted, his flesh crawling with revulsion. 'You may be immortal, but steel will dismember you.'

As he backed toward the arch through which he had entered, the light went out suddenly. All the candles were extinguished at once, though he did not know how; for Akivasha had not touched them. But the vampire's laugh rose mockingly behind him, poison-sweet as the viols of hell, and he sweated as he groped in the darkness for the arch in a near-panic. His fingers encountered an opening and he plunged through it. Whether it was the arch through which he had entered he did not know, nor did he very much care. His one thought was to get out of the haunted chamber which had housed that beautiful, hideous, undead fiend for so many centuries.

His wanderings through those black, winding tunnels were a sweating nightmare. Behind him and about him he heard faint slitherings and glidings, and once the echo of that sweet, hellish laughter he had heard in the chamber of Akivasha. He slashed ferociously at sounds and movements he heard or imagined he heard in the darkness near him, and once his sword cut through some yielding tenuous substance that might have been cobwebs. He had a desperate feeling that he was being played with, lured deeper and deeper into ultimate night, before being set upon by demoniac talon and fang.

And through his fear ran the sickening revulson of his discovery. The legend of Akivasha was so old, and among the evil tales told of her ran a thread of beauty and idealism, of everlasting youth. To so many dreamers and poets and lovers she was not alone the evil princess of Stygian legend, but the symbol of eternal youth and beauty, shining for ever in some far realm of the gods. And this was the hideous reality. This foul perversion was the truth of that everlasting life. Through his physical revulsion ran the sense of a shattered dream of man's idolatry, its glittering gold proved slime and cosmic filth. A wave of futility swept over him, a dim fear of the falseness of all men's dreams and idolatries.

And now he knew that his ears were not playing him tricks. He was being followed, and his pursuers were closing in on him. In the darkness sounded shufflings and slidings that were never made by human feet; no, nor by the feet of any normal animal. The underworld had its bestial life too, perhaps. They were behind him. He turned to face them, though he could see nothing, and slowly backed away. Then the sounds ceased, even before he turned his head and saw, somewhere down the long corridor, a glow of light.

19 In the Hall of the Dead

Conan moved cautiously in the direction of the light he had seen, his ear cocked over his shoulder, but there was no further sound of pursuit, though he *felt* the darkness pregnant with sentient life.

The glow was not stationary; it moved, bobbing grotesquely along. Then he saw the source. The tunnel he was traversing crossed another, wider corridor some distance ahead of him. And along this latter tunnel filed a bizarre procession – four tall, gaunt men in black, hooded robes, leaning on staffs. The leader held a torch above his head – a torch that burned with a curious steady glow. Like phantoms they passed across his limited range of vision and vanished, with only a fading glow to tell of their passing. Their appearance was indescribably eldritch. They were not Stygians, not like anything Conan had ever seen. He doubted if they were even humans. They were like black ghosts, stalking ghoulishly along the haunted tunnels.

But his position could be no more desperate than it was. Before the inhuman feet behind him could resume their slithering advance at the fading of the distant illumination, Conan was running down the corridor. He plunged into the other tunnel and saw, far down it, small in the distance, the weird procession moving in the glowing sphere. He stole noiselessly after them, then shrank suddenly back against the wall as he saw them halt and cluster together as if conferring on some matter. They turned as if to retrace their steps, and he slipped into the nearest archway. Groping in the darkness to which he had become so accustomed that he could all but see through it, he discovered that the tunnel did not run straight, but meandered, and he fell back beyond the first turn, so that the light of the strangers should not fall on him as they passed.

But as he stood there, he was aware of a low hum of sound from somewhere behind him, like the murmur of human voices. Moving down the corridor in that direction, he confirmed his first suspicion. Abandoning his original intention of following the ghoulish travelers to whatever destination might be theirs, he set out in the direction of the voices.

Presently he saw a glint of light ahead of him, and turning into the corridor from which it issued, saw a broad arch filled with a dim glow at the other end. On his left a narrow stone stair went upward, and instinctive caution prompted him to turn and mount the stair. The voices he heard were coming from beyond that flame-filled arch.

The sounds fell away beneath him as he climbed, and presently he came out through a low arched door into a vast open space glowing with a weird radiance.

He was standing on a shadowy gallery from which he looked down into a broad dim-lit hall of colossal proportions. It was a hall of the dead, which few ever see but the silent priests of Stygia. Along the black walls rose tier above tier of carven, painted sarcophagi. Each stood in a niche in the dusky stone, and the tiers mounted up and up to be lost in the gloom above. Thousands of carven masks stared impassively down upon the group in the midst of the hall, rendered futile and insignificant by that vast array of the dead.

Of this group ten were priests, and though they had discarded their masks Conan knew they were the priests he had accompanied to the pyramid. They stood before a tall, hawk-faced man beside a black altar on which lay a mummy in rotting swathings. And the altar seemed to stand in the heart of a living fire which pulsed and shimmered, dripping flakes of quivering golden flame on the black stones about it. This dazzling glow emanated from a great red jewel which lay upon the altar, and in the reflection of which the faces of the priests looked ashy and corpse-like. As he looked, Conan felt the pressure of all the weary leagues and the weary nights and days of his long quest, and he trembled with the mad urge to rush among those silent priests, clear his way with mighty blows of naked steel, and grasp the red gem with passion-taut fingers. But he gripped himself with iron control, and crouched down in the shadow of the stone balustrade. A glance showed him that a stair led down into the hall from the gallery, hugging the wall and half hidden in the shadows. He glared into the dimness of the vast place, seeking other priests or votaries, but saw only the group about the altar.

In that great emptiness the voice of the man beside the altar sounded hollow and ghostly:

'. . . And so the word came southward. The night wind whispered it, the ravens croaked of it as they flew, and the grim bats told it to the owls and the serpents that lurk in hoary ruins. Werewolf and vampire knew, and the ebon-bodied demons that prowl by night. The sleeping Night of the World stirred and shook its heavy mane, and there began a throbbing of drums in deep darkness, and the echoes of far weird cries frightened men who walked by dusk. For the Heart of Ahriman had come again into the world to fulfill its cryptic destiny.

'Ask me not how I, Thutothmes of Khemi and the Night, heard the word before Thoth-Amon who calls himself prince of all wizards. There are secrets not meet for such ears even as yours, and Thoth-Amon is not the only lord of the Black Ring.

'I knew, and I went to meet the Heart which came southward. It was like a magnet which drew me, unerringly. From death to death it came, riding on a river of human blood. Blood feeds it, blood draws it. Its power is greatest when there is blood on the hands that grasp it, when it is wrested by slaughter from its holder. Wherever it gleams, blood is spilt and kingdoms totter, and the forces of nature are put in turmoil.

'And here I stand, the master of the Heart, and have summoned you to come secretly, who are faithful to me, to share in the black kingdom that shall be. Tonight you shall witness the breaking of Thoth-Amon's chains which enslave us, and the birth of empire.

'Who am I, even I, Thutothmes, to know what powers lurk and dream in those crimson deeps? It holds secrets forgotten for three thousand years. But I shall learn. These shall tell me!'

He waved his hand toward the silent shapes that lined the hall.

'See how they sleep, staring through their carven masks! Kings, queens, generals, priests, wizards, the dynasties and the nobility of Stygia for ten thousand years! The touch of the heart will awaken them from their long slumber. Long, long the Heart throbbed and pulsed in ancient Stygia. Here was its home in the centuries before it journeyed to Acheron. The ancients knew its full power, and they will tell me when by its magic I restore them to life to labor for me.

'I will rouse them, will waken them, will learn their forgotten wisdom, the knowledge locked in those withered skulls. By the lore of the dead we shall enslave the living! Aye, kings and generals and wizards of eld shall be our helpers and our slaves. Who shall stand before us?

'Look! This dried, shriveled thing on the altar was once Thothmekri, a high priest of Set, who died three thousand years ago. He was an adept of the Black Ring. He knew of the Heart. He will tell us of its powers.'

Lifting the great jewel, the speaker laid it on the withered breast of the mummy, and lifted his hand as he began an incantation. But the incantation was never finished. With his hand lifted and his lips parted he froze, glaring past his acolytes, and they wheeled to stare in the direction in which he was looking.

Through the black arch of a door four gaunt, black-robed shapes had filed into the great hall. Their faces were dim yellow ovals in the shadow of their hoods.

'Who are you?' ejaculated Thutothmes in a voice as pregnant with danger as the hiss of a cobra. 'Are you mad, to invade the holy shrine of Set?'

The tallest of the strangers spoke, and his voice was toneless as a Khitan temple bell.

'We follow Conan of Aquilonia.'

'He is not here,' answered Thutothmes, shaking back his mantle from his right hand with a curious menacing gesture, like a panther unsheathing his talons.

'You lie. He is in this temple. We tracked him from a corpse behind the bronze door of the outer portal through a maze of corridors. We were following his devious trail when we became aware of this conclave. We go now to take it up again. But first give us the Heart of Ahriman.'

'Death is the portion of madmen,' murmured Thutothmes, moving nearer the speaker. His priests closed in on cat-like feet, but the strangers did not appear to heed.

'Who can look upon it without desire?' said the Khitan. 'In Khitai we have heard of it. It will give us power over the people which cast us out. Glory and wonder dream in its crimson deeps. Give it to us, before we slay you.'

A fierce cry rang out as a priest leaped with a flicker of steel. Before he could strike, a scaly staff licked out and touched his breast, and he fell as a dead man falls. In an instant the mummies were staring down on a scene of blood and horror. Curved knives flashed and crimsoned, snaky staffs licked in and out, and whenever they touched a man, that man screamed and died.

At the first stroke Conan had bounded up and was racing down the stairs. He caught only glimpses of that brief, fiendish fight – saw men swaying, locked in battle and streaming blood; saw one Khitan, fairly hacked to pieces, yet still on his feet and dealing death, when Thutothmes smote him on the breast with his open empty hand, and he dropped dead, though naked steel had not been enough to destroy his uncanny vitality.

By the time Conan's hurtling feet left the stair, the fight was all but over. Three of the Khitans were down, slashed and cut to ribbons and disemboweled, but of the Stygians only Thutothmes remained on his feet.

He rushed at the remaining Khitan, his empty hand lifted like a weapon, and that hand was black as that of a negro. But before he could strike, the staff in the tall Khitan's hand licked out, seeming to elongate itself as the yellow man thrust. The point touched the bosom of Thutothmes and he staggered; again and yet again the staff licked out, and Thutothmes reeled and fell dead, his features blotted out in a rush of blackness that made the whole of him the same hue as his enchanted hand.

The Khitan turned toward the jewel that burned on the breast of the mummy, but Conan was before him.

In a tense stillness the two faced each other, amid that shambles, with the carven mummies staring down upon them.

'Far have I followed you, oh king of Aquilonia,' said the Khitan calmly. 'Down the long river, and over the mountains, across Poitain and Zingara and through the hills of Argos and down the coast. Not easily did we pick up your trail from Tarantia, for the priests of Asura are crafty. We lost it in Zingara, but we found your helmet in the forest below the border hills, where you had fought with the ghouls of the forests. Almost we lost the trail again tonight among these labyrinths.'

Conan reflected that he had been fortunate in returning from the vampire's chamber by another route than that by which he had been led to it. Otherwise he would have run full into these yellow fiends instead of sighting them from afar as they smelled out his spoor like human bloodhounds, with whatever uncanny gift was theirs.

The Khitan shook his head slightly, as if reading his mind.

'That is meaningless; the long trail ends here.'

'Why have you hounded me?' demanded Conan, poised to move in any direction with the celerity of a hair-trigger.

'It was a debt to pay,' answered the Khitan. 'To you who are about to die, I will not withhold knowledge. We were vassals of the king of Aquilonia, Valerius. Long we served him, but of that service we are free now – my brothers by death, and I by the fulfilment of obligation. I shall return to Aquilonia with two hearts; for myself the Heart of Ahriman; for Valerius the heart of Conan. A kiss of the staff that was cut from the living Tree of Death—'

The staff licked out like the dart of a viper, but the slash of Conan's knife was quicker. The staff fell in writhing halves, there was another flicker of the keen steel like a jet of lightning, and the head of the Khitan rolled to the floor.

Conan wheeled and extended his hand toward the jewel – then he shrank back, his hair bristling, his blood congealing icily.

For no longer a withered brown thing lay on the altar. The jewel shimmered on the full, arching breast of a naked, living man who lay among the moldering bandges. Living? Conan could not decide. The eyes were like dark murky glass under which shone inhuman somber fires.

Slowly the man rose, taking the jewel in his hand. He towered beside the altar, dusky, naked, with a face like a carven image. Mutely he extended his hand toward Conan, with the jewel throbbing like a living heart within it. Conan took it, with an eery sensation of receiving gifts from the hand of the dead. He somehow realized that the proper incantations had not been made – the conjurement had not been completed – life had not been fully restored to his corpse.

'Who are you?' demanded the Cimmerian.

The answer came in a toneless monotone, like the dripping of water from stalactites in subterranean caverns. 'I was Thothmekri; I am dead.'

'Well, lead me out of this accursed temple, will you?' Conan requested, his flesh crawling.

With measured, mechanical steps the dead man moved toward a black arch. Conan followed him. A glance back showed him once again the vast, shadowy hall with its tiers of sarcophagi, the dead men sprawled about the altar; the head of the Khitan he had slain stared sightless up at the sweeping shadows.

The glow of the jewel illuminated the black tunnels like an ensorceled lamp, dripping golden fire. Once Conan caught a glimpse of ivory flesh in the shadows, believed he saw the vampire that was Akivasha shrinking back from the glow of the jewel; and with her, other less human shapes scuttled or shambled into the darkness.

The dead man strode straight on, looking neither to right nor left, his pace as changeless as the tramp of doom. Cold sweat gathered thick on Conan's flesh. Icy doubts assailed him. How could he know that this terrible figure out of the past was leading him to freedom? But he knew that, left to himself, he could never untangle this bewitched maze of corridors and tunnels. He followed his awful guide through blackness that loomed before and behind them and was filled with skulking shapes of horror and lunacy that cringed from the blinding glow of the Heart.

Then the bronze doorway was before him, and Conan felt the night wind blowing across the desert, and saw the stars, and the starlit desert across which streamed the great black shadow of the pyramid. Thothmekri pointed silently into the desert, and then turned and stalked soundlessly back in the darkness. Conan stared after that silent figure that receded into the blackness on soundless, inexorable feet as one that moves to a known and inevitable doom, or returns to everlasting sleep.

With a curse the Cimmerian leaped from the doorway and fled into the desert as if pursued by demons. He did not look back toward the pyramid, or toward the black towers of Khemi looming dimly across the sands. He headed southward toward the coast, and he ran as a man runs in ungovernable panic. The violent exertion shook his brain free of black cobwebs; the clean desert wind blew the nightmares from his soul and his revulsion changed to a wild tide of exultation before the desert gave way to a tangle of swampy growth through which he saw the black water lying before him, and the *Venturer* at anchor.

He plunged through the undergrowth, hip-deep in the marshes; dived headlong into the deep water, heedless of sharks or crocodiles, and swam to the galley and was clambering up the chain on to the deck, dripping and exultant, before the watch saw him.

'Awake, you dogs!' roared Conan, knocking aside the spear the startled lookout thrust at his breast. 'Heave up the anchor! Lay to the doors! Give that fisherman a helmet full of gold and put him ashore! Dawn will soon be breaking, and before sunrise we must be racing for the nearest port of Zingara!'

He whirled about his head the great jewel, which threw off splashes of light that spotted the deck with golden fire.

20 Out of the Dust Shall Acheron Arise

Winter had passed from Aquilonia. Leaves sprang out on the limbs of trees, and the fresh grass smiled to the touch of the warm southern breezes. But many a field lay idle and empty, many a charred heap of ashes marked the spot where proud villas or prosperous towns had stood. Wolves prowled openly along the grass-grown highways, and bands of gaunt, masterless men slunk through the forests. Only in Tarantia was feasting and wealth and pageantry.

Valerius ruled like one touched with madness. Even many of the barons who had welcomed his return cried out at last against him. His tax-gatherers crushed rich and poor alike; the wealth of a looted kingdom poured into Tarantia, which became less like the capital of a realm than the garrison of conquerors in a conquered land. Its merchants waxed rich, but it was a precarious prosperity; for none knew when he might be accused of treason on a trumped-up charge, and his property confiscated, himself cast into prison or brought to the bloody block.

Valerius made no attempt to conciliate his subjects. He maintained himself by means of the Nemedian soldiery and by desperate mercenaries. He knew himself to be a puppet of Amalric. He knew that he ruled only on the sufferance of the Nemedian. He knew that he could never hope to unite Aquilonia under his rule and cast off the yoke of his masters, for the outland provinces would resist him to the last drop of blood. And for that matter the Nemedians would cast him from his throne if he made any attempt to consolidate his kingdom. He was caught in his own vise. The gall of defeated pride corroded his soul, and he threw himself into a reign of debauchery, as one who lives from day to day, without thought or care for tomorrow.

Yet there was subtlety in his madness, so deep that not even Amalric guessed it. Perhaps the wild, chaotic years of wandering as an exile had bred in him a bitterness beyond common conception. Perhaps his loathing of his present position increased this bitterness to a kind of madness. At any event he lived with one desire: to cause the ruin of all who associated with him.

He knew that his rule would be over the instant he had served Amalric's purpose; he knew, too, that so long as he continued to oppress his native kingdom the Nemedian would suffer him to reign, for Amalric wished to crush Aquilonia into ultimate submission, to destroy its last shred of independence, and then at last to seize it himself, rebuild it after his own fashion with his vast wealth, and use its men and natural resources to wrest the crown of Nemedia from Tarascus. For the throne of an emperor was Amalric's ultimate ambition, and

Valerius knew it. Valerius did not know whether Tarascus suspected this, but he knew that the king of Nemedia approved of his ruthless course. Tarascus hated Aquilonia, with a hate born of old wars. He desired only the destruction of the western kingdom.

And Valerius intended to ruin the country so utterly that not even Amalric's wealth could ever rebuild it. He hated the baron quite as much as he hated the Aquilonians, and hoped only to live to see the day when Aquilonia lay in utter ruin, and Tarascus and Amalric were locked in hopeless civil war that would as completely destroy Nemedia.

He believed that the conquest of the still defiant provinces of Gunderland and Poitain and the Bossonian marches would mark his end as king. He would then have served Amalric's purpose, and could be discarded. So he delayed the conquest of these provinces, confining his activities to objectless raids and forays, meeting Amalric's urges for action with all sorts of plausible objections and postponements.

His life was a series of feasts and wild debauches. He filled his palace with the fairest girls of the kingdom, willing or unwilling. He blasphemed the gods and sprawled drunken on the floor of the banquet hall wearing the golden crown, and staining his royal purple robes with the wine he spilled. In gusts of blood-lust he festooned the gallows in the market square with dangling corpses, glutted the axes of the headsmen and sent his Nemedian horsemen thundering through the land pillaging and burning. Driven to madness, the land was in a constant upheaval of frantic revolt, savagely suppressed. Valerius plundered and raped and looted and destroyed until even Amalric protested, warning him that he would beggar the kingdom beyond repair, not knowing that such was his fixed determination.

But while in both Aquilonia and Nemedia men talked of the madness of the king, in Nemedia men talked much of Xaltotun, the masked one. Yet few saw him on the streets of Belverus. Men said he spent much time in the hills, in curious conclaves with surviving remnants of an old race: dark, silent folk who claimed descent from an ancient kingdom. Men whispered of drums beating far up in the dreaming hills, of fires glowing in the darkness, and strange chantings borne on the winds, chantings and rituals forgotten centuries ago except as meaningless formulas mumbled beside mountain hearths in villages whose inhabitants differed strangely from the people of the valleys.

The reason for these conclaves none knew, unless it was Orastes, who frequently accompanied the Pythonian, and on whose countenance a haggard shadow was growing.

But in the full flood of spring a sudden whisper passed over the sinking kingdom that woke the land to eager life. It came like a murmurous wind drifting up from the south, waking men sunk in the apathy of despair. Yet how it first came none could truly say. Some spoke of a strange, grim old woman who came down from the mountains with her hair flowing in the wind, and a great gray wolf following her like a dog. Others whispered of the priests of Asura who stole like furtive phantoms from Gunderland to the marches of Poitain, and to the forest villages of the Bossonians.

However the word came, revolt ran like a flame along the borders. Outlying Nemedian garrisons were stormed and put to the sword, foraging parties were cut to pieces; the west was up in arms, and there was a different air about the rising, a fierce resolution and inspired wrath rather than the frantic despair that had motivated the preceding revolts. It was not only the common people; barons were fortifying their castles and hurling defiance at the governors of the provinces. Bands of Bossonians were seen moving along the edges of the marches: stocky, resolute men in brigandines and steel caps, with longbows in their hands. From the inert stagnation of dissolution and ruin the realm was suddenly alive, vibrant and dangerous. So Amalric sent in haste for Tarascus, who came with an army.

In the royal palace in Tarantia the two kings and Amalric discussed the rising. They had not sent for Xaltotun, immersed in his cryptic studies in the Nemedian hills. Not since that bloody day in the valley of the Valkia had they called upon him for aid of his magic, and he had drawn apart, communing but little with them, apparently indifferent to their intrigues.

Nor had they sent for Orastes, but he came, and he was white as spume blown before the storm. He stood in the gold-domed chamber where the kings held conclave and they beheld in amazement his haggard stare, the fear they had never guessed the mind of Orastes could hold.

'You are weary, Orastes,' said Amalric. 'Sit upon this divan and I will have a slave fetch you wine. You have ridden hard—'

Orastes waved aside the invitation.

'I have killed three horses on the road from Belverus. I cannot drink wine, I cannot rest, until I have said what I have to say.'

He paced back and forth as if some inner fire would not let him stand motionless, and halting before his wondering companions:

'When we employed the Heart of Ahriman to bring a dead man back to life,' Orastes said abruptly, 'we did not weigh the consequences of tampering in the black dust of the past. The fault is mine, and the sin. We thought only of our ambitions, forgetting what ambitions this man might himself have. And we have loosed a demon upon the earth, a fiend inexplicable to common humanity. I have plumbed deep in evil, but there is a limit to which I, or any man of my race and age, can go. My ancestors were clean men, without any demoniacal taint; it is only I who have sunk into the pits, and I can sin only to the extent of my personal individuality. But behind Xaltotun lie a thousand centuries of black magic and diabolism, an ancient tradition of evil. He is beyond our conception not only because he is a wizard himself, but also because he is the son of a race of wizards.

'I have seen things that have blasted my soul. In the heart of the slumbering hills I have watched Xaltotun commune with the souls of the damned, and invoke the ancient demons of forgotten Acheron. I have seen the accursed descendants of that accursed empire worship him and hail him as their arch-priest. I have seen what he plots – and I tell you it is no less than the restoration of the ancient, black, grisly kingdom of Acheron!'

'What do you mean?' demanded Amalric. 'Acheron is dust. There are not enough survivals to make an empire. Not even Xaltotun can reshape the dust of three thousand years.'

'You know little of his black powers,' answered Orastes grimly. 'I have seen the very hills take on an alien and ancient aspect under the spell of his incantations. I have glimpsed, like shadows behind the realities, the dim shapes and outlines of valleys, forests, mountains and lakes that are not as they are today, but as they were in that dim yesterday – have even sensed, rather than glimpsed, the purple towers of forgotten Python shimmering like figures of mist in the dusk.

'And in the last conclave to which I accompanied him, understanding of his sorcery came to me at last, while the drums beat and the beast-like worshippers howled with their heads in the dust. I tell you he would restore Acheron by his magic, by the sorcery of a gigantic blood-sacrifice such as the world has never seen. He would enslave the world, and with a deluge of blood *wash away the present and restore the past!*'

'You are mad!' exclaimed Tarascus.

'Mad?' Orastes turned a haggard stare upon him. 'Can any man see what I have seen and remain wholly sane? Yet I speak the truth. He plots the return of Acheron, with its towers and wizards and kings and horrors, as it was in the long ago. The descendants of Acheron will serve him as a nucleus upon which to build, but it is the blood and the bodies of the people of the world today that will furnish the mortar and the stones for the rebuilding. I cannot tell you how. My own brain reels when I try to understand. *But I have seen!* Acheron will be Acheron again, and even the hills, the forests and the rivers will resume their ancient aspect. Why not? If I, with my tiny store of knowledge, could bring to life a man dead three thousand years, why cannot the greatest wizard of the world bring back to life a kingdom dead three thousand years? Out of the dust shall Acheron arise at his bidding.'

'How can we thwart him?' asked Tarascus, impressed.

'There is but one way,' answered Orastes. 'We must steal the Heart of Ahriman!'

'But I—' began Tarascus involuntarily, then closed his mouth quickly.

None had noticed him, and Orastes was continuing.

'It is a power that can be used against him. With it in my hands I might defy him. But how shall we steal it? He has it hidden in some secret place, from which not even a Zamorian thief might filch it. I cannot learn its hiding-place. If he would only sleep again the sleep of the black lotus – but the last time he slept thus was after the battle of the Valkia, when he was weary because of the great magic he had performed, and—'

The door was locked and bolted, but it swung silently open and Xaltotun stood before them, calm, tranquil, stroking his patriarchal beard; but the lambent lights of hell flickered in his eyes.

'I have taught you too much,' he said calmly, pointing a finger like an index of doom at Orastes. And before any could move, he had cast a handful of dust on the floor near the feet of the priest, who stood like a man turned to marble. It flamed, smoldered; a blue serpentine of smoke rose and swayed upward about Orastes in a slender spiral. And when it had risen above his shoulders it curled about his neck with a whipping suddenness like the stroke of a snake. Orastes' scream was choked to a gurgle. His hands flew to his neck, his eyes were distended, his tongue protruded. The smoke was like a blue rope about his neck; then it faded and was gone, and Orastes slumped to the floor a dead man.

Xaltotun smote his hands together and two men entered, men often observed accompanying him – small, repulsively dark, with red, oblique eyes and pointed, rat-like teeth. They did not speak. Lifting the corpse, they bore it away.

Dismissing the matter with a wave of his hand, Xaltotun seated himself at the ivory table about which sat the pale kings.

'Why are you in conclave?' he demanded.

'The Aquilonians have risen in the west,' answered Amalric, recovering from the grisly jolt the death of Orastes had given him. 'The fools believe that Conan is alive, and coming at the head of a Poitanian army to reclaim his kingdom. If he had reappeared immediately after Valkia, or if a rumor had been circulated that he lived, the central provinces would not have risen under him, they feared your powers so. But they have become so desperate under Valerius' misrule that they are ready to follow any man who can unite them against us, and prefer sudden death to torture and continual misery.

'Of course the tale has lingered stubbornly in the land that Conan was not really slain at Valkia, but not until recently have the masses accepted it. But Pallantides is back from exile in Ophir, swearing that the king was ill in his tent that day, and that a man-at-arms wore his harness, and a squire who but recently recovered from the stroke of a mace received at Valkia confirms his tale – or pretends to.

'An old woman with a pet wolf has wandered up and down the land, proclaiming that King Conan yet lives, and will return some day to reclaim the crown. And of late the cursed priests of Asura sing the same song. They claim that word has come to them by some mysterious means that Conan is returning to reconquer his domain. I cannot catch either her or them. This is, of course, a trick of Trocero's. My spies tell me there is indisputable evidence that the Poitanians are gathering to invade Aquilonia. I believe that Trocero will bring forward some pretender who he will claim is King Conan.'

Tarascus laughed, but there was no conviction in his laughter. He surreptitiously felt of a scar beneath his jupon, and remembered ravens that cawed on the trail of a fugitive; remembered the body of his squire, Arideus, brought back from the border mountains horribly mangled, by a great gray wolf, his terrified soldiers said. But he also remembered a red jewel stolen from a golden chest while a wizard slept, and he said nothing.

And Valerius remembered a dying nobleman who gasped out a tale of fear, and he remembered four Khitans who disappeared into the mazes of the south and never returned. But he held his tongue, for hatred and suspicion of his allies ate at him like a worm, and he desired nothing so much as to see both rebels and Nemedians go down locked in the death grip.

But Amalric exclaimed: 'It is absurd to dream that Conan lives!'

For answer Xaltotun cast a roll of parchment on the table.

Amalric caught it up, glared at it. From his lips burst a furious, incoherent cry. He read:

To Xaltotun, grand fakir of Nemedia: Dog of Acheron, I am returning to my kingdom, and I mean to hang your hide on a bramble.
Conan

'A forgery!' exclaimed Amalric.

Xaltotun shook his head.

'It is genuine. I have compared it with the signature on the royal documents on record in the libraries of the court. None could imitate that bold scrawl.'

'Then if Conan lives,' muttered Amalric, 'this uprising will not be like the others, for he is the only man living who can unite the Aquilonians. But,' he protested, 'this is not like Conan. Why should he put us on our guard with his boasting? One would think that he would strike without warning, after the fashion of the barbarians.'

'We are already warned,' pointed out Xaltotun. 'Our spies have told us of preparations for war in Poitain. He could not cross the mountains without our knowledge; so he sends me his defiance in characteristic manner.'

'Why to you?' demanded Valerius. 'Why not to me, or to Tarascus?'

Xaltotun turned his inscrutable gaze upon the king.

'Conan is wiser than you,' he said at last. 'He already knows what you kings have yet to learn – that it is not Tarascus, nor Valerius, no, nor Amalric, but Xaltotun who is the real master of the western nations.'

They did not reply; they sat staring at him, assailed by a numbing realization of the truth of his assertion.

'There is no road for me but the imperial highway,' said Xaltotun. 'But first we must crush Conan. I do not know how he escaped me at Belverus, for knowledge of what happened while I lay in the slumber of the black lotus is denied me. But he is in the south, gathering an army. It is his last, desperate blow, made possible only by the desperation of the people who have suffered under Valerius. Let them rise; I hold them all in the palm of my hand. We will wait until he moves against us, and then we will crush him once and for all.

'Then we shall crush Poitain and Gunderland and the stupid Bossonians. After them Ophir, Argos, Zingara, Koth – all the nations of the world we shall weld into one vast empire. You shall rule as my satraps, and as my captains shall be greater than kings are now. I am unconquerable, for the Heart of Ahriman is hidden where no man can ever wield it against me again.'

Tarascus averted his gaze, lest Xaltotun read his thoughts. He knew the wizard had not looked into the golden chest with its carven serpents that had seemed to sleep, since he laid the Heart therein. Strange as it seemed, Xaltotun did not know that the heart had been stolen; the strange jewel was beyond or outside the ring of his dark wisdom; his uncanny talents did not warn him that the chest was empty. Tarascus did not believe that Xaltotun knew the full extent of Orastes' revelations, for the Pythonian had not mentioned the restoration of Acheron, but only the building of a new, earthly empire. Tarascus did not believe that Xaltotun was yet quite sure of his power; if they needed his aid in their ambitions, no less he needed theirs. Magic depended, to a certain extent after all, on sword strokes and lance thrusts. The king read meaning in Amalric's furtive glance; let the wizard use his arts to help them defeat their most dangerous enemy. Time enough then to turn against him. There might yet be a way to cheat this dark power they had raised.

21 Drums of Peril

Confirmation of the war came when the army of Poitain, ten thousand strong, marched through the southern passes with waving banners and shimmer of steel. And at their head, the spies swore, rode a giant figure in black armor, with the royal lion of Aquilonia worked in gold upon the breast of his rich silken surcoat. Conan lived! The king lived! There was no doubt of it in men's minds now, whether friend or foe.

With the news of the invasion from the south there also came word, brought by hard-riding couriers, that a host of Gundermen was moving southward, reinforced by the barons of the northwest and the northern Bossonians. Tarascus marched with thirty-one thousand men to Galparan, on the river Shirki, which the Gundermen must cross to strike at the towns still held by the Nemedians. The Shirki was a swift, turbulent river rushing southwestward through rocky gorges and canyons, and there were few places where an army could cross at that time of the year, when the stream was almost bank-full with the melting of the snows. All the country east of the Shirki was in the hands of the Nemedians, and it was logical to assume that the Gundermen would attempt to cross either at Galparan, or at Tanasul, which lay to the south of Galparan. Reinforcements were daily expected from Nemedia, until word came that the king of Ophir was making hostile demonstrations on Nemedia's southern border, and to spare any more troops would be to expose Nemedia to the risk of an invasion from the south.

Amalric and Valerius moved out from Tarantia with twenty-five thousand men, leaving as large a garrison as they dared to discourage revolts in the cities during their absence. They wished to meet and crush Conan before he could be joined by the rebellious forces of the kingdom.

The king and his Poitanians had crossed the mountains, but there had been no actual clash of arms, no attack on towns or fortresses. Conan had appeared and disappeared. Apparently he had turned westward through the wild, thinly settled hill country, and entered the Bossonian marches, gathering recruits as he went. Amalric and Valerius with their host, Nemedians, Aquilonian renegades, and ferocious mercenaries, moved through the land in baffled wrath, looking for a foe which did not appear.

Amalric found it impossible to obtain more than vague general tidings about Conan's movements. Scouting-parties had a way of riding out and never returning, and it was not uncommon to find a spy crucified to an oak. The countryside was up and striking as peasants and country-folk strike – savagely, murderously and secretly. All that Amalric knew certainly was that a large force of Gundermen and northern Bossonians was somewhere to the north of him, beyond the Shirki, and that Conan with a smaller force of Poitanians and southern Bossonians was somewhere to the southwest of him.

He began to grow fearful that if he and Valerius advanced further into the wild country, Conan might elude them entirely, march around them and invade the central provinces behind them. Amalric fell back from the Shirki valley and camped in a plain a day's ride from Tanasul. There he waited. Tarascus maintained his position at Galparan, for he feared that Conan's maneuvers were intended to draw him southward, and so let the Gundermen into the kingdom at the northern crossing.

To Amalric's camp came Xaltotun in his chariot drawn by the uncanny horses that never tired, and he entered Amalric's tent where the baron conferred with Valerius over a map spread on an ivory camp table.

This map Xaltotun crumpled and flung aside.

'What your scouts cannot learn for you,' quoth he, 'my spies tell me, though their information is strangely blurred and imperfect, as if unseen forces were working against me.

'Conan is advancing along the Shirki river with ten thousand Poitanians, three thousand southern Bossonians, and barons of the west and south with their retainers to the number of five thousand. An army of thirty thousand Gundermen and northern Bossonians is pushing southward to join him. They have established contact by means of secret communications used by the cursed priests of Asura, who seem to be opposing me, and whom I will feed to a serpent when the battle is over – I swear it by Set!

'Both armies are headed for the crossing at Tanasul, but I do not believe that the Gundermen will cross the river. I believe that Conan will cross, instead, and join them.'

'Why should Conan cross the river?'

'Because it is to his advantage to delay the battle. The longer he waits, the stronger he will become, the more precarious our position. The hills on the other side of the river swarm with people passionately loyal to his cause – broken men, refugees, fugitives from Valerius' cruelty. From all over the kingdom men are hurrying to join his army, singly and by companies. Daily, parties from our armies are ambushed and cut to pieces by the country-folk. Revolt grows in the central provinces, and will soon burst into open rebellion. The garrisons we left there are not sufficient, and we can hope for no reinforcements from Nemedia for the time being. I see the hand of Pallantides in this brawling on the Ophirean frontier. He has kin in Ophir.

'If we do not catch and crush Conan quickly the provinces will be in blaze of revolt behind us. We shall have to fall back to Tarantia to defend what we have taken; and we may have to fight our way through a country in rebellion, with Conan's whole force at our heels, and then stand siege in the city itself, with enemies within as well as without. No, we cannot wait. We must crush Conan before his army grows too great, before the central provinces rise. With his head hanging above the gate at Tarantia you will see how quickly the rebellion will fall apart.'

'Why do you not put a spell on his army to slay them all?' asked Valerius, half in mockery.

Xaltotun stared at the Aquilonian as if he read the full extent of the mocking madness that lurked in those wayward eyes.

'Do not worry,' he said at last. 'My arts shall crush Conan finally like a lizard under the heel. But even sorcery is aided by pikes and swords.'

'If he crosses the river and takes up his position in the Goralian hills he may be hard to dislodge,' said Amalric. 'But if we catch him in the valley on this side of the river we can wipe him out. How far is Conan from Tanasul?'

'At the rate he is marching he should reach the crossing sometime tomorrow night. His men are rugged and he is pushing them hard. He should arrive there at least a day before the Gundermen.'

'Good!' Amalric smote the table with his clenched fist. 'I can reach Tanasul before he can. I'll send a rider to Tarascus, bidding him follow me to Tanasul. By the time he arrives I will have cut Conan off from the crossing and destroyed him. Then our combined force can cross the river and deal with the Gundermen.'

Xaltotun shook his head impatiently.

'A good enough plan if you were dealing with anyone but Conan. But your twenty-five thousand men are not enough to destroy his eighteen thousand before the Gundermen come up. They will fight with the desperation of wounded panthers. And suppose the Gundermen come up while the hosts are locked in battle? You will be caught between two fires and destroyed before Tarascus can arrive. He will reach Tanasul too late to aid you.'

'What then?' demanded Amalric.

'Move with your whole strength against Conan,' answered the man from Acheron. 'Send a rider bidding Tarascus join us here. We will wait his coming. Then we will march together to Tanasul.'

'But while we wait,' protested Amalric, 'Conan will cross the river and join the Gundermen.'

'Conan will not cross the river,' answered Xaltotun

Amalric's head jerked up and he stared into the cryptic dark eyes.

'What do you mean?'

'Suppose there were torrential rains far to the north, at the head of the Shirki? Suppose the river came down in such flood as to render the crossing at Tanasul impassable? Could we not then bring up our entire force at our leisure, catch Conan on this side of the river and crush him, and then, when the flood subsided, which I think it would do the next day, could we not cross the river and destroy the Gundermen? Thus we could use our full strength against each of these smaller forces in turn.'

Valerius laughed as he always laughed at the prospect of the ruin of either friend or foe, and drew a restless hand jerkily through his unruly yellow locks. Amalric stared at the man from Acheron with mingled fear and admiration.

'If we caught Conan in Shirki valley with the hill ridges to his right and the river in flood to his left,' he admitted, 'with our whole force we could annihilate him. Do you think – are you sure – do you believe such rains will fall?'

'I go to my tent,' answered Xaltotun, rising. 'Necromancy is not accomplished by the waving of a wand. Send a rider to Tarascus. And let none approach my tent.'

That last command was unnecessary. No man in that host could have been bribed to approach that mysterious black silken pavilion, the door-flaps of which were always closely drawn. None but Xaltotun ever entered it, yet voices were often heard issuing from it; its walls billowed sometimes without a wind, and weird music came from it. Sometimes, deep in midnight, its silken walls were lit red by flames flickering within, limning misshapen silhouettes that passed to and fro.

Lying in his own tent that night, Amalric heard the steady rumble of a drum in Xaltotun's tent; through the darkness it boomed steadily, and occasionally the Nemedian could have sworn that a deep, croaking voice mingled with the pulse of the drum. And he shuddered, for he knew that voice was not the voice of Xaltotun. The drum rustled and muttered on like deep thunder, heard afar off, and before dawn Amalric glancing from his tent, caught the red flicker of lightning afar on the northern horizon. In all other parts of the sky the great stars blazed whitely. But the distant lightning flickered incessantly, like the crimson glint of firelight on a tiny, turning blade.

At sunset of the next day Tarascus came up with his host, dusty and weary from hard marching, the footmen straggling hours behind the horsemen. They camped in the plain near Amalric's camp, and at dawn the combined army moved westward.

Ahead of him roved a swarm of scouts, and Amalric waited impatiently for them to return and tell of the Poitanians trapped beside a furious flood. But when the scouts met the column it was with the news that Conan had crossed the river!

'What?' exclaimed Amalric. 'Did he cross before the flood?'

'There was no flood,' answered the scouts, puzzled. 'Late last night he came up to Tanasul and flung his army across.'

'No flood?' exclaimed Xaltotun, taken aback for the first time in Amalric's knowledge. 'Impossible! There were mighty rains upon the headwaters of the Shirki last night and the night before that!'

'That may be your lordship,' answered the scout. 'It is true the water was muddy, and the people of Tanasul said that the river rose perhaps a foot yesterday; but that was not enough to prevent Conan's crossing.'

Xaltotun's sorcery had failed! The thought hammered in Amalric's brain. His horror of this strange man out of the past had grown steadily since that night in Belverus when he had seen a brown, shriveled mummy swell and grow into a living man. And the death of Orastes had changed lurking horror into active fear. In his heart was a grisly conviction that the man – or devil – was invincible. Yet now he had undeniable proof of his failure.

Yet even the greatest of necromancers might fail occasionally, thought the baron. At any rate, he dared not oppose the man from Acheron – yet. Orastes was dead, writhing in Mitra only knew what nameless hell, and Amalric knew his sword would scarcely prevail where the black wisdom of the renegade priest had failed. What grisly abomination Xaltotun plotted lay in the unpredictable future. Conan and his host were a present menace against which Xaltotun's wizardry might well be needed before the play was all played.

They came to Tanasul, a small fortified village at the spot where a reef of rocks made a natural bridge across the river, passable always except in times of greatest flood. Scouts brought in the news that Conan had taken up his position in the Goralian hills, which began to rise a few miles beyond the river. And just before sundown the Gundermen had arrived in his camp.

Amalric looked at Xaltotun, inscrutable and alien in the light of the flaring torches. Night had fallen.

'What now? Your magic has failed. Conan confronts us with an army nearly as strong as our own, and he has the advantage of position. We have a choice of two evils: to camp here and await his attack, or to fall back toward Tarantia and await reinforcements.'

'We are ruined if we wait,' answered Xaltotun. 'Cross the river and camp on the plain. We will attack at dawn.'

'But his position is too strong!' exclaimed Amalric.

'Fool!' A gust of passion broke the veneer of the wizard's calm. 'Have you forgotten Valkia? Because some obscure elemental principle prevented the flood do you deem me helpless? I had intended that your spears should exterminate our enemies; but do not fear: it is my arts shall crush their host. Conan is in a trap. He will never see another sun set. Cross the river!'

They crossed by the flare of torches. The hoofs of the horses clinked on the rocky bridge, splashed through the shallows. The glint of the torches on shields and breast-plates was reflected redly in the black water. The rock bridge was broad on which they crossed, but even so it was past midnight before the host was camped in the plain beyond. Above them they could see fires winking redly in the distance. Conan had turned at bay in the Goralian hills, which had more than once before served as the last stand of an Aquilonian king.

Amalric left his pavilion and strode restlessly through the camp. A weird glow flickered in Xaltotun's tent, and from time to time a demoniacal cry slashed the silence, and there was a low sinister muttering of a drum that rustled rather than rumbled.

Amalric, his instincts whetted by the night and the circumstances, felt that Xaltotun was opposed by more than physical force. Doubts of the wizard's power assailed him. He glanced at the fires high above him, and his face set in grim lines. He and his army were deep in the midst of a hostile country. Up there among those hills lurked thousands of wolfish figures out of whose hearts and souls all emotion and hope had been scourged except a frenzied hate for their conquerors, a mad lust for vengeance. Defeat meant annihilation, retreat through a land swarming with blood-mad enemies. And on the morrow he must hurl his host against the grimmest fighter in the western nations, and his desperate horde. If Xaltotun failed them now—

Half a dozen men-at-arms strode out of the shadows. The firelight glinted on their breast-plates and helmet crests. Among them they half led, half dragged a gaunt figure in tattered rags.

Saluting, they spoke: 'My lord, this man came to the outposts and said he desired word with King Valerius. He is an Aquilonian.'

He looked more like a wolf – a wolf the traps had scarred. Old sores that only fetters make showed on his wrists and ankles. A great brand, the mark of hot iron, disfigured his face. His eyes glared through the tangle of his matted hair as he half crouched before the baron.

'Who are you, you filthy dog?' demanded the Nemedian.

'Call me Tiberias,' answered the man, and his teeth clicked in an involuntary spasm. 'I have come to tell you how to trap Conan.'

'A traitor, eh?' rumbled the baron.

'Men say you have gold,' mouthed the man, shivering under his rags. 'Give some to me! Give me gold and I will show you how to defeat the king!' His eyes glazed widely, his outstretched, upturned hands were spread like quivering claws.

Amalric shrugged his shoulder in distaste. But no tool was too base for his use.

'If you speak the truth you shall have more gold than you can carry,' he said. 'If you are a liar and a spy I will have you crucified head-down. Bring him along.'

In the tent of Valerius, the baron pointed to the man who crouched shivering before them, huddling his rags about him.

'He says he knows a way to aid us on the morrow. We will need aid, if Xaltotun's plan is no better than it has proved so far. Speak on, dog.'

The man's body writhed in strange convulsions. Words came in a stumbling rush:

'Conan camps at the head of the Valley of Lions. It is shaped like a fan, with steep hills on either side. If you attack him tomorrow you will have to march straight up the valley. You cannot climb the hills on either side. But if King Valerius will deign to accept my service, I will guide him through the hills and show him how he can come upon King Conan from behind. But if it is to be done at all, we must start soon. It is many hours' riding, for one must go miles to the west, then miles to the north, then turn eastward and so come into the Valley of Lions from behind, as the Gundermen came.'

Amalric hesitated, tugging his chin. In these chaotic times it was not rare to find men willing to sell their souls for a few gold pieces.

'If you lead me astray you will die,' said Valerius. 'You are aware of that, are you not?'

The man shivered, but his wide eyes did not waver.

'If I betray you, slay me!'

'Conan will not dare divide his force,' mused Amalric. 'He will need all his men to repel our attack. He cannot spare any to lay ambushes in the hills. Besides, this fellow knows his hide depends on his leading you as he promised. Would a dog like him sacrifice himself? Nonsense! No, Valerius, I believe the man is honest.'

'Or a greater thief than most, for he would sell his liberator,' laughed Valerius. 'Very well. I will follow the dog. How many men can you spare me?'

'Five thousand should be enough,' answered Amalric. 'A surprise attack on their rear will throw them into confusion, and that will be enough. I shall expect your attack about noon.'

'You will know when I strike,' answered Valerius.

As Amalric returned to his pavilion he noted with gratification that Xaltotun was still in his tent, to judge from the blood-freezing cries that shuddered forth into the night air from time to time. When presently he heard the clink of steel and the jingle of bridles in the outer darkness, he smiled grimly. Valerius had about served his purpose. The baron knew that Conan was like a wounded lion that rends and tears even in his death-throes. When Valerius struck from the rear, the desperate strokes of the Cimmerian might well wipe his rival out of existence before he himself succumbed. So much the better. Amalric felt he could well dispense with Valerius, once he had paved the way for a Nemedian victory.

The five thousand horsemen who accompanied Valerius were hard-bitten Aquilonian renegades for the most part. In the still starlight they moved out of the sleeping camp, following the westward trend of the great black masses that rose against the stars ahead of them. Valerius rode at their head, and beside him rode Tiberias, a leather thong about his wrist gripped by a man-at-arms who rode on the other side of him. Others kept close behind with drawn swords.

'Play us false and you die instantly,' Valerius pointed out. 'I do not know every sheep-path in these hills, but I know enough about the general configuration of the country to know the directions we must take to come in behind the Valley of Lions. See that you do not lead us astray.'

The man ducked his head and his teeth chattered as he volubly assured his captor of his loyalty, staring up stupidly at the banner that floated over him, the golden serpent of the old dynasty.

Skirting the extremities of the hills that locked the Valley of Lions, they swung wide to the west. An hour's ride and they turned north, forging through wild and rugged hills, following dim trails and tortuous paths. Sunrise found them some miles northwest of Conan's position, and here the guide turned eastward and led them through a maze of labyrinths and crags. Valerius nodded, judging their position by various peaks thrusting up above the others. He had kept his bearings in a general way, and he knew they were still headed in the right direction.

But now, without warning, a gray fleecy mass came billowing down from the north, veiling the slopes, spreading out through the valleys. It blotted out the sun; the world became a blind gray void in which visibility was limited to a matter of yards. Advance became a stumbling, groping muddle. Valerius cursed. He could no longer see the peaks that had served him as guide-posts. He must depend wholly upon the traitorous guide. The golden serpent drooped in the windless air.

Presently Tiberias seemed himself confused; he halted, stared about uncertainly.

'Are you lost, dog?' demanded Valerius harshly.

'Listen!'

Somewhere ahead of them a faint vibration began, the rhythmic rumble of a drum.

'Conan's drum!' exclaimed the Aquilonian.

'If we are close enough to hear the drum,' said Valerius, 'why do we not hear the shouts and the clang of arms? Surely battle has joined.'

'The gorges and the winds play strange tricks,' answered Tiberias, his teeth chattering with the ague that is frequently the lot of men who have spent much time in damp underground dungeons. Listen!'

Faintly to their ears came a low muffled roar.

'They are fighting down in the valley!' cried Tiberias. 'The drum is beating on the heights. Let us hasten!'

He rode straight on toward the sound of the distant drum as one who knows his ground at last. Valerius followed, cursing the fog. Then it occurred to him that it would mask his advance. Conan could not see him coming. He would be at the Cimmerian's back before the noonday sun dispelled the mists.

Just now he could not tell what lay on either hand, whether cliffs, thickets or gorges. The drum throbbed unceasingly, growing louder as they advanced, but they heard no more of the battle. Valerius had no idea toward what point of the compass they were headed. He started as he saw gray rock walls looming through the smoky drifts on either hand, and realized that they were riding through a narrow defile. But the guide showed no sign of nervousness, and Valerius hove a sigh of relief when the walls widened out and became invisible in the fog. They were through the defile; if an ambush had been planned, it would have been made in that pass.

But now Tiberias halted again. The drum was rumbling louder, and Valerius could not determine from what direction the sound was coming. Now it seemed ahead of him, now behind, now on one hand or the other. Valerius glared about him impatiently, sitting on his war-horse with wisps of mist curling about him and the moisture gleaming on his armor. Behind him the long lines of steel-clad riders faded away and away like phantoms into the mist.

'Why do you tarry, dog?' he demanded.

The man seemed to be listening to the ghostly drum. Slowly he straightened in his saddle, turned his head and faced Valerius, and the smile on his lips was terrible to see.

'The fog is thinning, Valerius,' he said in a new voice, pointing a bony finger. 'Look!'

The drum was silent. The fog was fading away. First the crests of cliffs came in sight above the gray clouds, tall and spectral. Lower and lower crawled the mists, shrinking, fading. Valerius started up in his stirrups with a cry that the horsemen echoed behind him. On all sides of them the cliffs towered. They were not in a wide, open valley as he had supposed. They were in a blind gorge walled by sheer cliffs hundreds of feet high. The only entrance or exit was that narrow defile through which they had ridden.

'Dog!' Valerius struck Tiberias full in the mouth with his clenched mailed hand. 'What devil's trick is this?'

Tiberias spat out a mouthful of blood and shook with fearful laughter.

'A trick that shall rid the world of a beast! Look, dog!'

Again Valerius cried out, more in fury than in fear.

The defile was blocked by a wild and terrible band of men who stood silent as images – ragged, shock-headed men with spears in their hands – hundreds of them. And up on the cliffs appeared other faces – thousands of faces – wild, gaunt, ferocious faces, marked by fire and steel and starvation.

'A trick of Conan's!' raged Valerius.

'Conan knows nothing of it,' laughed Tiberias. 'It was the plot of broken men, of men you ruined and turned to beasts. Amalric was right. Conan has not divided his army. We are the rabble who followed him, the wolves who skulked in these hills, the homeless men, the hopeless men. This was our plan, and the priests of Asura aided us with their mist. Look at them, Valerius! Each bears the mark of your hand, on his body or on his heart!

'Look at me! You do not know me, do you, what of this scar your hangman burned upon me? Once you knew me. Once I was lord of Amilius, the man whose sons you murdered, whose daughter your mercenaries ravished and slew. You said I would not sacrifice myself to trap you? Almighty gods, if I had a thousand lives I would give them all to buy your doom!

'And I have bought it! Look on the men you broke, dead men who once played the king! Their hour has come! This gorge is your tomb.

Try to climb the cliffs: they are steep, they are high. Try to fight your way back through the defile: spears will block your path, boulders will crush you from above! Dog! I will be waiting for you in hell!'

Throwing back his head he laughed until the rocks rang. Valerius leaned from his saddle and slashed down with his great sword, severing shoulder-bone and breast. Tiberias sank to the earth, still laughing ghastlily through a gurgle of gushing blood.

The drums had begun again, encircling the gorge with guttural thunder; boulders came crashing down; above the screams of dying men shrilled the arrows in blinding clouds from the cliffs.

22 The Road to Acheron

Dawn was just whitening the east when Amalric drew up his hosts in the mouth of the Valley of Lions. This valley was flanked by low, rolling but steep hills, and the floor pitched upward in a series of irregular natural terraces. On the uppermost of these terraces Conan's army held its position, awaiting the attack. The host that had joined him, marching down from Gunderland, had not been composed exclusively of spearmen. With them had come seven thousand Bossonian archers, and four thousand barons and their retainers of the north and west, swelling the ranks of his cavalry.

The pikemen were drawn up in a compact wedge-shaped formation at the narrow head of the valley. There were nineteen thousand of them, mostly Gundermen, though some four thousand were Aquilonians of other provinces. They were flanked on either hand by five thousand Bossonian archers. Behind the ranks of the pikemen the knights sat their steeds motionless, lances raised: ten thousand knights of Poitain, nine thousand Aquilonians, barons and their retainers.

It was a strong positon. His flanks could not be turned, for that would mean climbing the steep, wooded hills in the teeth of the arrows and swords of the Bossonians. His camp lay directly behind him, in a narrow, steep-walled valley which was indeed merely a continuation of the Valley of Lions, pitching up at a higher level. He did not fear a surprise from the rear, because the hills behind him were full of refugees and broken men whose loyalty to him was beyond question.

But if his position was hard to shake, it was equally hard to escape from. It was a trap as well as a fortress for the defenders, a desperate last stand of men who did not expect to survive unless they were victorious. The only line of retreat possible was through the narrow valley at their rear.

*

Xaltotun mounted a hill on the left side of the valley, near the wide mouth. This hill rose higher than the others, and was known as the King's Altar, for a reason long forgotten. Only Xaltotun knew, and his memory dated back three thousand years.

He was not alone. His two familiars, silent, hairy, furtive and dark, were with him, and they bore a young Aquilonian girl, bound hand and foot. They laid her on an ancient stone, which was curiously like an altar, and which crowned the summit of the hill. For long centuries it had stood there, worn by the elements until many doubted that it was anything but a curiously shapen natural rock. But what it was, and why it stood there, Xaltotun remembered from of old. The familiars went away, with their bent backs like silent gnomes, and Xaltotun stood alone beside the altar, his dark beard blown in the wind, overlooking the valley.

He could see clear back to the winding Shirki, and up into the hills beyond the head of the valley. He could see the gleaming wedge of steel drawn up at the head of the terraces, the burganets of the archers glinting among the rocks and bushes, the silent knights motionless on their steeds, their pennons flowing above their helmets, their lances rising in a bristling thicket.

Looking in the other direction he could see the long serried lines of the Nemedians moving in ranks of shining steel into the mouth of the valley. Behind them the gay pavilions of the lords and knights and the drab tents of the common soldiers stretched back almost to the river.

Like a river of molten steel the Nemedian host flowed into the valley, the great scarlet dragon rippling over it. First marched the bowmen, in even ranks, arbalests half raised, bolts nocked, fingers on triggers. After them came the pikemen, and behind them the real strength of the army – the mounted knights, their banners unfurled to the wind, their lances lifted, walking their great steeds forward as if they rode to a banquet.

And higher up on the slopes the smaller Aquilonian host stood grimly silent.

There were thirty thousand Nemedian knights, and, as in most Hyborian nations, it was the chivalry which was the sword of the army. The footmen were used only to clear the way for a charge of the armored knights. There were twenty-one thousand of these, pikemen and archers.

The bowmen began loosing as they advanced, without breaking ranks, launching their quarrels with a whir and tang. But the bolts fell short or rattled harmlessly from the overlapping shields of the Gundermen. And before the arbalesters could come within killing range, the arching shafts of the Bossonians were wreaking havoc in their ranks.

A little of this, a futile attempt at exchanging fire, and the Nemedian bowmen began falling back in disorder. Their armor was light, their weapons no match for the Bossonian longbows. The western archers were sheltered by bushes and rocks. Moreover, the Nemedian footmen lacked something of the morale of the horsemen, knowing as they did that they were being used merely to clear the way for the knights.

The crossbowmen fell back, and between their opening lines the pikemen advanced. These were largely mercenaries, and their masters had no compunction about sacrificing them. They were intended to mask the advance of the knights until the latter were within smiting distance. So while the arbalesters plied their bolts from either flank at long range, the pikemen marched into the teeth of the blast from above, and behind them the knights came on.

When the pikemen began to falter beneath the savage hail of death that whistled down the slopes among them, a trumpet blew, their companies divided to right and left, and through them the mailed knights thundered.

They ran full into a cloud of stinging death. The clothyard shafts found every crevice in their armor and the housings of the steeds. Horses scrambling up the grassy terraces reared and plunged backward, bearing their riders with them. Steel-clad forms littered the slopes. The charge wavered and ebbed back.

Back down in the valley Amalric reformed his ranks. Tarascus was fighting with drawn sword under the scarlet dragon, but it was the baron of Tor who commanded that day. Amalric swore as he glanced at the forest of lance-tips visible above and beyond the head-pieces of the Gundermen. He had hoped his retirement would draw the knights out in a charge down the slopes after him, to be raked from either flank by his bowmen and swamped by the numbers of his horsemen. But they had not moved. Camp-servants brought skins of water from the river. Knights doffed their helmets and drenched their sweating heads. The wounded on the slopes screamed vainly for water. In the upper valley, springs supplied the defenders. They did not thirst that long, hot spring day.

On the King's Altar, beside the ancient, carven stone, Xaltotun watched the steel tide ebb and flow. On came the knights, with waving plumes and dipping lances. Through a whistling cloud of arrows they plowed to break like a thundering wave on the bristling wall of spears and shields. Axes rose and fell above the plumed helmets, spears thrust upward, bringing down horses and riders. The pride of the Gundermen was no less fierce than that of the knights. They were not spear-fodder, to be sacrificed for the glory of better men. They were the finest infantry in the world, with a tradition that made their morale unshakable. The kings of Aquilonia had long learned the worth of unbreakable infantry. They held their formation unshaken; over their gleaming ranks flowed the great lion banner, and at the tip of the wedge a giant figure in black armor roared and smote like a hurricane, with a dripping ax that split steel and bone alike.

The Nemedians fought as gallantly as their traditions of high courage demanded. But they could not break the iron wedge, and from the wooded knolls on either hand arrows raked their close-packed ranks mercilessly. Their own bowmen were useless, their pikemen unable to climb the heights and come to grips with the Bossonians. Slowly, stubbornly, sullenly, the grim knights fell back, counting their empty saddles. Above them the Gundermen made no outcry of triumph. They closed their ranks, locking up the gaps made by the fallen. Sweat ran into their eyes from under their steel caps. They gripped their spears and waited, their fierce hearts swelling with pride that a king should fight on foot with them. Behind them the Aquilonian knights had not moved. They sat their steeds, grimly immobile.

A knight spurred a sweating horse up the hill called the King's Altar, and glared at Xaltotun with bitter eyes.

'Amalric bids me say that it is time to use your magic, wizard,' he said. 'We are dying like flies down there in the valley. We cannot break their ranks.'

Xaltotun seemed to expand, to grow tall and awesome and terrible.

'Return to Amalric,' he said. 'Tell him to reform his ranks for a charge, but to await my signal. Before that signal is given he will see a sight that he will remember until he lies dying!'

The knight saluted as if compelled against his will, and thundered down the hill at breakneck pace.

Xaltotun stood beside the dark altarstone and stared across the valley, at the dead and wounded men on the terraces, at the grim, blood-stained band at the head of the slopes, at the dusty, steel-clad ranks reforming in the vale below. He glanced up at the sky, and he glanced down at the slim white figure on the dark stone. And lifting a dagger inlaid with archaic hieroglyphs, he intoned an immemorial invocation:

'Set, god of darkness, scaly lord of the shadows, by the blood of a virgin and the sevenfold symbol I call to your sons below the black earth! Children of the deeps, below the red earth, under the black earth, awaken and shake your awful manes! Let the hills rock and the stones topple upon my enemies! Let the sky grow dark above them, the earth unstable beneath their feet! Let a wind from the deep black earth curl up beneath their feet, and blacken and shrivel them—'

He halted short, dagger lifted. In the tense silence the roar of the hosts rose beneath him, borne on the wind.

On the other side of the altar stood a man in a black hooded robe, whose coif shadowed pale delicate features and dark eyes calm and meditative.

'Dog of Asura!' whispered Xaltotun, his voice was like the hiss of an angered serpent. 'Are you mad, that you seek your doom? Ho, Baal! Chiron!'

'Call again, dog of Acheron!' said the other, and laughed. 'Summon them loudly. They will not hear, unless your shouts reverberate in hell.'

From a thicket on the edge of the crest came a somber old woman in peasant garb, her hair flowing over her shoulders, a great gray wolf following at her heels.

'Witch, priest and wolf,' muttered Xaltotun grimly, and laughed. 'Fools, to pit your charlatan's mummery against my arts! With a wave of my hand I brush you from my path!'

'Your arts are straws in the wind, dog of Python,' answered the Asurian. 'Have you wondered why the Shirki did not come down in flood and trap Conan on the other bank? When I saw the lightning in the night I guessed your plan, and my spells dispersed the clouds you had summoned before they could empty their torrents. You did not even know that your rain-making wizardry had failed.'

'You lie!' cried Xaltotun, but the confidence in his voice was shaken. 'I have felt the impact of a powerful sorcery against mine – but no man on earth could undo the rain-magic, once made, unless he possessed the very heart of sorcery.'

'But the flood you plotted did not come to pass,' answered the priest. 'Look at your allies in the valley, Pythonian! You have led them to the slaughter! They are caught in the fangs of the trap, and you cannot aid them. Look!'

He pointed. Out of the narrow gorge of the upper valley, behind the Poitanians, a horseman came flying, whirling something about his head that flashed in the sun. Recklessly he hurtled down the slopes, through the ranks of the Gundermen, who sent up a deep-throated roar and clashed their spears and shields like thunder in the hills. On the terraces between the hosts the sweat-soaked horse reared and plunged, and his wild rider yelled and brandished the thing in his hands like one demented. It was the torn remnant of a scarlet banner, and the sun struck dazzlingly on the golden scales of a serpent that writhed thereon.

'Valerius is dead!' cried Hadrathus ringingly. 'A fog and a drum lured him to his doom! I gathered that fog, dog of Python, and I dispersed it! I, with my magic which is greater than your magic!'

'What matters it?' roared Xaltotun, a terrible sight, his eyes blazing, his features convulsed. 'Valerius was a fool. I do not need him. I can crush Conan without human aid!'

'Why have you delayed?' mocked Hadrathus. 'Why have you allowed so many of your allies to fall pierced by arrows and spitted on spears?'

'Because blood aids great sorcery!' thundered Xaltotun, in a voice that made the rocks quiver. A lurid nimbus played about his awful head. 'Because no wizard wastes his strength thoughtlessly. Because I would conserve my powers for the great days to be, rather than employ them in a hill-country brawl. But now, by Set, I shall loose them to the uttermost! Watch, dog of Asura, false priest of an outworn god, and see a sight that shall blast your reason for evermore!'

Hadrathus threw back his head and laughed, and hell was in his laughter.

'Look, black devil of Python!'

His hand came from under his robe holding something that flamed and burned in the sun, changing the light to a pulsing golden glow in which the flesh of Xaltotun looked like the flesh of a corpse.

Xaltotun cried out as if he had been stabbed.

'The Heart! The Heart of Ahriman!'

'Aye! The one power that is greater than your power!'

Xaltotun seemed to shrivel, to grow old. Suddenly his beard was shot with snow, his locks flecked with gray.

'The Heart!' he mumbled. 'You stole it! Dog! Thief!'

'Not I! It has been on a long journey far to the southward. But now it is in my hands, and your black arts cannot stand against it. As it resurrected you, so shall it hurl you back into the night whence it drew you. You shall go down the dark road to Acheron, which is the road of silence and the night. The dark empire, unreborn, shall remain a legend and a black memory. Conan shall reign again. And the Heart of Ahriman shall go back into the cavern below the temple of Mitra, to burn as a symbol of the power of Aquilonia for a thousand years!'

Xaltotun screamed inhumanly and rushed around the altar, dagger lifted; but from somewhere – out of the sky, perhaps, or the great jewel that blazed in the hand of Hadrathus – shot a jetting beam of blinding blue light. Full against the breast of Xaltotun it flashed, and the hills re-echoed the concussion. The wizard of Acheron went down as though struck by a thunderbolt, and before he touched the ground he was fearfully altered. Beside the altar-stone lay no fresh-slain corpse, but a shriveled mummy, a brown, dry, unrecognizable carcass sprawling among moldering swathings.

Somberly old Zelata looked down.

'He was not a living man,' she said. 'The Heart lent him a false aspect of life, that deceived even himself. I never saw him as other than a mummy.'

Hadrathus bent to unbind the swooning girl on the altar, when from among the trees appeared a strange apparition – Xaltotun's chariot drawn by the weird horses. Silently they advanced to the altar and halted, with the chariot wheel almost touching the brown withered thing on the grass. Hadrathus lifted the body of the wizard and placed it in the chariot. And without hesitation the uncanny steeds turned and moved off southward, down the hill. And Hadrathus and Zelata and the gray wolf watched them go – down the long road to Acheron which is beyond the ken of men.

Down in the valley Amalric had stiffened in his saddle when he saw that wild horseman curvetting and caracoling on the slopes while he brandished that blood-stained serpent-banner. Then some instinct jerked his head about, toward the hill known as the King's Altar. And his lips parted. Every man in the valley saw it – an arching shaft of dazzling light that towered up from the summit of the hill, showering golden fire. High above the hosts it burst in a blinding blaze that momentarily paled the sun.

'That's not Xaltotun's signal!' roared the baron.

'No!' shouted Tarascus. 'It's a signal to the Aquilonians! Look!'

Above them the immobile ranks were moving at last, and a deep-throated roar thundered across the vale.

'Xaltotun has failed us!' bellowed Amalric furiously. 'Valerius has failed us! We have been led into a trap! Mitra's curse on Xaltotun who led us here! Sound the retreat!'

'*Too late!*' yelled Tarascus. '*Look!*'

Up on the slopes the forest of lances dipped, leveled. The ranks of the Gundermen rolled back to right and left like a parting curtain. And with a thunder like the rising roar of a hurricane, the knights of Aquilonia crashed down the slopes.

The impetus of that charge was irresistible. Bolts driven by the demoralized arbalesters glanced from their shields, their bent helmets. Their plumes and pennons streaming out behind them, their lances lowered, they swept over the wavering lines of pikemen and roared down the slopes like a wave.

Amalric yelled an order to charge, and the Nemedians with desperate courage spurred their horses at the slopes. They still outnumbered the attackers.

But they were weary men on tired horses, charging uphill. The onrushing knights had not struck a blow that day. Their horses were fresh. They were coming downhill and they came like a thunderbolt. And like a thunderbolt they smote the struggling ranks of the Nemedians – smote them, split them apart, ripped them asunder and dashed the remnants headlong down the slopes.

After them on foot came the Gundermen, blood-mad, and the Bossonians were swarming down the hills, loosing as they ran at every foe that still moved.

Down the slopes washed the tide of battle, the dazed Nemedians swept on the crest of the wave. Their archers had thrown down their arbalests and were fleeing. Such pikemen as had survived the blasting charge of the knights were cut to pieces by the ruthless Gundermen.

In a wild confusion the battle swept through the wide mouth of the valley and into the plain beyond. All over the plain swarmed the warriors, fleeing and pursuing, broken into single combat and clumps of smiting, hacking knights on rearing, wheeling horses. But the Nemedians were smashed, broken, unable to re-form or make a stand. By the hundreds they broke away, spurring for the river. Many reached it, rushed across and rode eastward. The countryside was up behind them; the people hunted them like wolves. Few ever reached Tarantia.

The final break did not come until the fall of Amalric. The baron, striving in vain to rally his men, rode straight at the clump of knights that followed the giant in black armor whose surcoat bore the royal lion, and over whose head floated the golden lion banner with the scarlet leopard of Poitain beside it. A tall warrior in gleaming armor couched his lance and charged to meet the lord of Tor. They met like a thunderclap. The Nemedian's lance, striking his foe's helmet, snapped bolts and rivets and tore off the casque, revealing the features of Pallantides. But the Aquilonian's lance-head crashed through shield and breast-plate to transfix the baron's heart.

A roar went up as Amalric was hurled from his saddle, snapping the lance that impaled him, and the Nemedians gave way as a barrier bursts under the surging impact of a tidal wave. They rode for the river in a blind stampede that swept the plain like a whirlwind. The hour of the Dragon had passed.

Tarascus did not flee. Amalric was dead, the color-bearer slain, and the royal Nemedian banner trampled in the blood and dust. Most of his knights were fleeing and the Aquilonians were riding them down; Tarascus knew the day was lost, but with a handful of faithful followers he raged through the mêlée, conscious of but one desire – to meet Conan, the Cimmerian. And at last he met him.

Formations had been destroyed utterly, close-knit bands broken asunder and swept apart. The crest of Trocero gleamed in one part of the plain, those of Prospero and Pallantides in others. Conan was alone. The house-troops of Tarascus had fallen one by one. The two kings met man to man.

Even as they rode at each other, the horse of Tarascus sobbed and sank under him. Conan leaped from his own steed and ran at him, as the king of Nemedia disengaged himself and rose. Steel flashed blindingly in the sun, clashed loudly, and blue sparks flew; then a clang of armor as Tarascus measured his full length on the earth beneath a thunderous stroke of Conan's broadsword.

The Cimmerian placed a mail-shod foot on his enemy's breast, and lifted his sword. His helmet was gone; he shook back his black mane and his blue eyes blazed with their old fire.

'Do you yield?'

'Will you give me quarter?' demanded the Nemedian.

'Aye. Better than you'd have given me, you dog. Life for you and all your men who throw down their arms. Though I ought to split your head for an infernal thief,' the Cimmerian added.

Tarascus twisted his neck and glared over the plain. The remnants of the Nemedian host were flying across the stone bridge with swarms of victorious Aquilonians at their heels, smiting with fury of glutted vengeance. Bossonians and Gundermen were swarming through the camp of their enemies, tearing the tents to pieces in search of plunder, seizing prisoners, ripping open the baggage and upsetting the wagons.

Tarascus cursed fervently, and then shrugged his shoulders, as well as he could, under the circumstances.

'Very well. I have no choice. What are your demands?'

'Surrender to me all your present holdings in Aquilonia. Order your garrisons to march out of the castles and towns they hold, without their arms, and get your infernal armies out of Aquilonia as quickly as possible. In addition you shall return all Aquilonians sold as slaves, and pay an indemnity to be designated later, when the damage your occupation of the country has caused has been properly estimated. You will remain as hostage until these terms have been carried out.'

'Very well,' surrendered Tarascus. 'I will surrender all the castles and towns now held by my garrisons without resistance, and all the other things shall be done. What ransom for my body?'

Conan laughed and removed his foot from his foe's steel-clad breast, grasped his shoulder and heaved him to his feet. He started to speak, then turned to see Hadrathus approaching him. The priest was as calm and self-possessed as ever, picking his way between rows of dead men and horses.

Conan wiped the sweat-smeared dust from his face with a bloodstained hand. He had fought all through the day, first on foot with the pikemen, then in the saddle, leading the charge. His surcoat was gone, his armor splashed with blood and battered with strokes of sword, mace and ax. He loomed gigantically against a background of blood and slaughter, like some grim pagan hero of mythology.

'Well done, Hadrathus!' quoth he gustily. 'By Crom, I am glad to see your signal! My knights were almost mad with impatience and eating their hearts out to be at sword-strokes. I could not have held them much longer. What of the wizard?'

'He has gone down the dim road to Acheron,' answered Hadrathus. 'And I – I am for Tarantia. My work is done here, and I have a task to perform at the temple of Mitra. All our work is done here. On this field we have saved Aquilonia – and more than Aquilonia. Your ride to your capital will be a triumphal procession through a kingdom mad with joy. All Aquilonia will be cheering the return of their king. And so, until we meet again in the great royal hall – farewell!'

Conan stood silently watching the priest as he went. From various parts of the field knights were hurrying toward him. He saw Pallantides, Trocero, Prospero, Servius Galannus, their armor splashed with crimson. The thunder of battle was giving way to a roar of triumph and acclaim. All eyes, hot with strife and shining with exultation, were turned toward the great black figure of the king; mailed arms brandished red-stained swords. A confused torrent of sound rose, deep and thunderous as the sea-surf: '*Hail, Conan, king of Aquilonia!*'

Tarascus spoke.

'You have not yet named my ransom.'

Conan laughed and slapped his sword home in its scabbard. He flexed his mighty arms, and ran his blood-stained fingers through his thick black locks, as if feeling there his re-won crown.

'There is a girl in your seraglio named Zenobia.'

'Why, yes, so there is.'

'Very well.' The king smiled as at an exceedingly pleasant memory. 'She shall be your ransom, and naught else. I will come to Belverus for her as I promised. She was a slave in Nemedia, but I will make her queen of Aquilonia!'

THE GOD IN THE BOWL

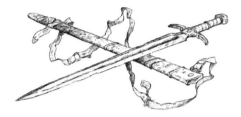

A RUS THE WATCHMAN GRASPED his crossbow with shaky hands, and he felt beads of clammy perspiration on his skin as he stared at the unlovely corpse sprawling on the polished floor before him. It is not pleasant to come upon Death in a lonely place at midnight.

Arus stood in a vast corridor, lighted by huge candles in niches along the walls. These walls were hung with black velvet tapestries, and between the tapestries hung shields and crossed weapons of fantastic make. Here and there, too, stood figures of curious gods – images carved of stone or rare wood, or cast of bronze, iron or silver – mirrored in the gleaming black mahogany floor.

Arus shuddered; he had never become used to the place, although he had worked there as watchman for some months. It was a fantastic establishment, the great museum and antique house which men called Kallian Publico's Temple, with its rarities from all over the world – and now, in the lonesomeness of midnight, Arus stood in the great silent hall and stared at the sprawling corpse that had been the rich and powerful owner of the Temple.

It entered even the dull brain of the watchman that the man looked strangely different now, than when he rode along the Palian Way in his golden chariot, arrogant and dominant, with his dark eyes glinting with magnetic vitality. Men who had hated and feared Kallian Publico would scarcely have recognized him now as he lay like a disintegrated tun of fat, his rich robe half torn from him, and his purple tunic awry. His face was blackened, his eyes almost starting from his head, and his tongue lolled blackly from his gaping mouth. His fat hands were thrown out as in a gesture of curious futility. On the thick fingers gems glittered.

'Why didn't they take his rings?' muttered the watchman uneasily, then he started and glared, the short hairs prickling at the nape of his neck. Through the dark silken hangings that masked one of the many doorways opening into the hallway, came a figure.

Arus saw a tall powerfully built youth, naked but for a loin-cloth, and sandals strapped high about his ankles. His skin was burned brown as by the suns of the wastelands, and Arus glanced nervously at the broad shoulders, massive chest and heavy arms. A single look at the moody, broad-browed features told the watchman that the man was no Nemedian. From under a mop of unruly black hair smoldered a pair of dangerous blue eyes. A long sword hung in a leather scabbard at his girdle.

Arus felt his skin crawl, and he fingered his crossbow tensely, of half a mind to drive a bolt through the stranger's body without parley, yet fearful of what might happen if he failed to inflict death at the first shot.

The stranger looked at the body on the floor more in curiosity than surprise.

'Why did you kill him?' asked Arus nervously.

The other shook his tousled head.

'I didn't kill him,' he answered, speaking Nemedian with a barbaric accent. 'Who is he?'

'Kallian Publico,' replied Arus, edging back.

A flicker of interest showed in the moody blue eyes.

'The owner of the house?'

'Aye.' Arus had edged his way to the wall, and now he took hold of a thick velvet rope which swung there, and jerked it violently. From the street outside sounded the strident clang of the bell that hung before all shops and establishments to summon the watch.

The stranger started.

'Why did you do that?' he asked. 'It will fetch the watchman.'

'I am the watchman, knave,' answered Arus, bracing his rocking courage. 'Stand where you are; don't move or I'll loose a bolt through you.'

His finger was on the trigger of his arbalest, the wicked square head of the quarrel leveled full on the other's broad breast. The stranger scowled, and his dark face was lowering. He showed no fear, but seemed to be hesitating in his mind as to whether he should obey the command or chance a sudden break of some kind. Arus licked his lips and his blood turned cold as he plainly saw indecision struggle with a murderous intent in the foreigner's cloudy eyes.

Then he heard a door crash open, and a medley of voices, and he drew a deep breath of amazed thankfulness. The stranger tensed and glared worriedly, like a startled hunting beast, as half a dozen men entered the hall. All but one wore the scarlet tunic of the Numalian police, were girt with stabbing swords and carried bills – long-shafted weapons, half pike, half axe.

'What devil's work is this?' exclaimed the foremost man, whose cold gray eyes and lean keen features, no less than his civilian garments, set him apart from his burly companions.

'By Mitra, Demetrio!' exclaimed Arus thankfully. 'Fortune is assuredly with me tonight. I had no hope that the watch would answer the summons so swiftly – or that you would be with them!'

'I was making the rounds with Dionus,' answered Demetrio. 'We were just passing the Temple when the watch-bell clanged. But who is this? Mitra! The master of the Temple himself!'

'No other,' replied Arus. 'And foully murdered. It is my duty to walk about the building steadily all night, because, as you know, there is an immense amount of wealth stored here. Kallian Publico had rich patrons – scholars, princes and wealthy collectors of rarities. Well, only a few minutes ago I tried the door which opens on the portico, and found it to be only bolted. The door is provided with a bolt, which works both from within or without, and a great lock which can be worked only from without. Only Kallian Publico had a key to that, the key which you see now hanging at his girdle.

'Naturally my suspicions were roused, for Kallian Publico always locks the door with the great lock when he closes the Temple; and I had not seen him return since he left earlier in the evening for his villa in the eastern suburbs of the city. I have a key that works the bolt; I entered and found the body lying as you see. I have not touched it.'

'So,' Demetrio's keen eyes swept the somber stranger. 'And who is this?'

'The murderer, without doubt!' cried Arus. 'He came from that door yonder. He is a northern barbarian of some sort – a Hyperborean or a Bossonian, perhaps.'

'Who are you?' asked Demetrio.

'I am Conan,' answered the barbarian. 'I am a Cimmerian.'

'Did you kill this man?'

The Cimmerian shook his head.

'Answer me!' snapped the questioner.

An angry glint rose in the moody blue eyes.

'I am no dog,' he replied resentfully.

'Oh, an insolent fellow!' sneered Demetrio's companion, a big man wearing the insignia of prefect of police. 'An independent cur! One of these citizens with rights, eh? I'll soon knock it out of him! Here, you! Come clean! Why did you murder—'

'Just a moment, Dionus,' ordered Demetrio curtly. 'Fellow, I am chief of the Inquisitorial Council of the city of Numalia. You had best tell me why you are here, and if you are not the murderer, prove it.'

The Cimmerian hesitated. He was not afraid, but slightly bewildered, as a barbarian always is when confronted by the evidence of civilized networks and systems, the workings of which are so baffling and mysterious to him.

'While he's thinking it over,' rapped Demetrio, turning to Arus, 'tell me – did you see Kallian Publico leave the Temple this evening?'

'No, he's usually gone when I arrive to begin my sentry-go. But the great door was bolted and locked.'

'Could he have entered the building again without your having seen him?'

'Why, it's possible, but hardly probable. The Temple is large, and I walk clear around it in a few minutes. If he had returned from his villa, he would of course have come in his chariot, for it is a long way – and who ever heard of Kallian Publico travelling otherwise? Even if I had been on the other side of the Temple, I'd have heard the wheels of the chariot on the cobblestones, and I've heard no such thing, nor seen any chariots, except those which always pass along the streets just at dusk.'

'And the door was locked earlier in the night?'

'I'll swear to it. I try all doors several times during the night. The door was locked on the outside until perhaps half an hour ago – that was the last time I tried it, until I found it unlocked.'

'You heard no cries or struggles?'

'No. But that's not strange. The walls of the Temple are so thick, they're practically sound-proof – an effect increased by the heavy hangings.'

'Why go to all this trouble of questions and speculations?' complained the burly prefect. 'It's much easier to beat a confession out of a suspect. Here's our man, no doubt about it. Let's take him to the Court of Justice – I'll get a statement if I have to smash his bones to pulp.'

Demetrio looked at the barbarian.

'You understand what he said?' asked the Inquisitor. 'What have you to say?'

'That any man who touches me will quickly be greeting his ancestors in hell,' the Cimmerian ground between his powerful teeth, his eyes glinting quick flames of dangerous anger.

'Why did you come here, if not to kill this man?' pursued Demetrio.

'I came to steal,' sullenly answered the other.

'To steal what?' rapped the Inquisitor.

'Food,' the reply came after an instant's hesitation.

'That's a lie!' snapped Demetrio. 'You knew there was no food here. Don't lie to me. Tell me the truth or—'

The Cimmerian laid his hand on his sword hilt, and the gesture was as fraught with menace as the lifting of a tiger's lip to bare his fangs.

'Save your bullying for the fools who fear you,' he growled, blue fires smoldering in his eyes. 'I'm no city-bred Nemedian to cringe before your hired dogs. I've killed better men than you for less than this.'

Dionus, who had opened his mouth to bellow in wrath, closed it suddenly. The watchmen shifted their bills uncertainly and glanced at Demetrio for orders. They were struck speechless at hearing the all-powerful police thus bearded and expected a command to seize the barbarian. But Demetrio did not give it. He knew, if the others were too stupid to know, the steel-trap muscles and blinding quickness of men raised beyond civilization's frontiers where life was a continual battle for existence, and he had no desire to loose the barbaric frenzy of the Cimmerian if it could be avoided. Besides, there was a doubt in his mind.

'I have not accused you of killing Kallian,' he snapped. 'But you must admit the appearances are against you. How did you enter the Temple?'

'I hid in the shadows of the warehouse which stands behind this building,' Conan answered grudgingly. 'When this dog –' jerking a thumb at Arus – 'passed by and rounded the corner, I ran quickly to the wall and scaled it—'

'A lie!' broke in Arus. 'No man could climb that straight wall!'

'Did you ever see a Cimmerian scale a sheer cliff?' asked Demetrio impatiently. 'I am conducting this investigation. Go on, Conan.'

'The corner is decorated with carvings,' said the Cimmerian. 'It was easy to climb. I gained the roof before this dog came around the building again. I went across the roof until I came upon a trap-door which was fastened with an iron bolt that went through it and was locked on the inside. I was forced to hew the bolt in twain with my sword—'

Arus, remembering the thickness of that bolt, gulped involuntarily and moved further back from the barbarian, who scowled abstractedly at him, and continued.

'I feared the noise might wake somebody, but it was a chance I had to take. I passed through the trap-door and came into an upper chamber. I didn't pause there, but came straightway to the stair—'

'How did you know where the stair was?' snapped the Inquisitor. 'I know that only Kallian's servants and his rich patrons were ever allowed in those upper rooms.'

A dogged stubbornness shadowed Conan's eyes and he remained silent.

'What did you do after you reached the stair?' demanded Demetrio.

'I came straight down it,' muttered the Cimmerian. 'It let into the chamber behind yonder curtained door. As I came down the stairs I heard the noise of a door being opened. When I looked through the hangings I saw this dog standing over the dead man.'

'Why did you come from your hiding place?'

'It was dark when I saw the watchman outside the Temple. When I saw him here I thought he was a thief too. It was not until he jerked the watch-bell rope and lifted his bow that I knew he was the watchman.'

'But even so,' persisted the Inquisitor, 'why did you reveal yourself?'

'I thought perhaps he had come to steal what—' the Cimmerian checked himself suddenly as if he had said too much.

'—What you had come after, yourself!' finished Demetrio. 'You have told me more than you intended! You came here with a definite purpose. You did not, by your own admission, tarry in the upper rooms, where the richest goods are generally stored. You knew the plan of the building – you were sent here by someone who knows the Temple well to steal some special thing!'

'And to kill Kallian Publico!' exclaimed Dionus. 'By Mitra, we've hit it! Grab him, men! We'll have a confession before morning!'

With a heathen curse Conan leaped back, whipping out his sword with a viciousness that made the keen blade hum.

'Back, if you value your dog-lives!' he snarled, his blue eyes blazing. 'Because you dare to torture shopkeepers and strip and beat harlots to make them talk, don't think you can lay your fat paws on a hillman! I'll take some of you to hell with me! Fumble with your bow, watchman – I'll burst your guts with my heel before this night's work is over!'

'Wait!' interposed Demetrio. 'Call your dogs off, Dionus. I'm not convinced that he is the murderer. You fool,' he added in a whisper, 'wait until we can summon more men, or trick him into laying down his sword.' Demetrio did not wish to forgo the advantage of his civilized mind by allowing matters to change to a physical basis, where the wild beast ferocity of the barbarian might even balance the odds against him.

'Very well,' grunted Dionus grudgingly. 'Fall back, men, but keep an eye on him.'

'Give me your sword,' said Demetrio.

'Take it if you can,' snarled Conan. Demetrio shrugged his shoulders.

'Very well. But don't try to escape. Four men with crossbows watch the house on the outside. We always throw a cordon about a house before we enter it.'

The barbarian lowered his blade, though he only slightly relaxed the tense watchfulness of his attitude. Demetrio turned again to the corpse.

'Strangled,' he muttered. 'Why strangle him when a sword-stroke is so much quicker and surer? These Cimmerians are a bloody race, born with a sword in their hand, as it were; I never heard of them killing a man in this manner.'

'Perhaps to divert suspicion,' muttered Dionus.

'Possibly.' He felt the body with experienced hands. 'Dead possibly half an hour,' he muttered. 'If Conan tells the truth about when he entered the Temple he would hardly have had time to commit the murder before Arus entered. But he may be lying – he might have broken in earlier.'

'I climbed the wall after Arus made the last round,' Conan growled.

'So *you* say.' Demetrio brooded for a space over the dead man's throat, which had been literally crushed to a pulp of purplish flesh. The head sagged awry on splintered vertebrae. Demetrio shook his head in doubt.

'Why should a murderer use a pliant cable apparently thicker than a man's arm?' he muttered. 'And what terrible constriction was applied to so crush the man's heavy neck.'

He rose and walked to the nearest door opening into the corridor.

'Here is a bust knocked from a stand near the door,' he said, 'and here the polished floor is scratched and the hangings in the doorway are pulled awry as if a clutching hand had grasped them – perhaps for support. Kallian Publico must have been attacked in that room. Perhaps he broke away from the assailant, or dragged the fellow with him as he fled. Anyway, he ran staggeringly out into the corridor where the murderer must have followed and finished him.'

'And if this heathen isn't the murderer, where is he?' demanded the prefect.

'I haven't exonerated the Cimmerian yet,' snapped the Inquisitor. 'But we'll investigate that room and—'

He halted and wheeled, listening. From the street had sounded a sudden rattle of chariot wheels, which approached rapidly, then ceased abruptly.

'Dionus!' snapped the Inquisitor. 'Send two men to find that chariot. Bring the driver here.'

'From the sound,' said Arus, who was familiar with all the noises of the street, 'I'd say it stopped in front of Promero's house, just on the other side of the silk-merchant's shop.'

'Who is Promero?' asked Demetrio.

'Kallian Publico's chief clerk.'

'Bring him here with the chariot driver,' snapped Demetrio. 'We'll wait until they come before we examine that room.'

Two guardsmen clomped away. Demetrio still studied the body; Dionus, Arus and the remaining policemen watched Conan, who stood, sword in hand, like a bronze figure of brooding menace. Presently sandalled feet re-echoed outside, and the two guardsmen entered with a strongly built, dark-skinned man in the helmet and tunic of a charioteer, with a whip in his hand; and a small, timid-looking individual, typical of that class which, risen from the ranks of artisans, supplies righthand men for wealthy merchants and traders.

This one recoiled with a cry from the sprawling bulk on the floor.

'Oh, I knew evil would come of this!'

'You are Promero, the clerk, I suppose. And you?'

'Enaro, Kallian Publico's charioteer.'

'You do not seem overly moved at the sight of his corpse,' observed Demetrio.

'Why should I be moved?' the dark eyes flashed. 'Someone has only done what I dared not, but longed to do.'

'So!' murmured the Inquisitor. 'Are you a free man?'

Enaro's eyes were bitter as he drew aside his tunic, showing the brand of the debtor-slave on his shoulder.

'Did you know your master was coming here tonight?'

'No. I brought the chariot to the Temple this evening for him as usual. He entered it and I drove toward his villa. But before we came to the Palian Way, he ordered me to turn and drive him back. He seemed much agitated in his mind.'

'And did you drive him back to the Temple?'

'No. He bade me stop at Promero's house. There he dismissed me, ordering me to return there for him shortly after midnight.'

'What time was this?'

'Shortly after dusk. The streets were almost deserted.'

'What did you do then?'

'I returned to the slave quarters where I remained until it was time to return to Promero's house. I drove straight there, and your men seized me as I talked with Promero in his door.'

'You have no idea why Kallian went to Promero's house?'

'He didn't speak of his business to his slaves.'

Demetrio turned to Promero. 'What do you know about this?'

'Nothing.' The clerk's teeth chattered as he spoke.

'Did Kallian Publico come to your house as the charioteer says?'

'Yes.'

'How long did he stay?'

'Only a few minutes. Then he left.'

'Did he come from your house to the Temple?'

'I don't know!' The clerk's voice was shrill with taut nerves.

'Why did he come to your house?'

'To – to talk matters of business with me.'

'You're lying,' snapped Demetrio. *'Why did he come to your house?'*

'I don't know! I don't know anything!' Promero was growing hysterical. 'I had nothing to do with it—'

'Make him talk, Dionus,' snapped Demetrio, and Dionus grunted and nodded to one of his men who, grinning savagely, moved toward the two captives.

'Do you know who I am?' he growled, thrusting his head forward and staring domineeringly at his shrinking prey.

'You're Posthumo,' answered the charioteer sullenly. 'You gouged out a girl's eye in the Court of Justice because she wouldn't give you information incriminating her lover.'

'I always get what I go after!' bellowed the guardsman, the veins in his thick neck swelling, and his face growing purple, as he seized the wretched clerk by the collar of his tunic, twisting it so the man was half strangled.

'Speak up, you rat!' he growled. 'Answer the Inquisitor.'

'Oh Mitra, mercy!' screamed the wretch. 'I swear that—'

Posthumo slapped him terrifically first on one side of the face and then on the other, and continued the interrogation by flinging him to the floor and kicking him with vicious accuracy.

'Mercy!' moaned the victim. 'I'll tell – I'll tell anything—'

'Then get up, you cur!' roared Posthumo, swelling with self-importance. 'Don't lie there whining.'

Dionus cast a quick glance at Conan to see if he were properly impressed.

'You see what happens to those who cross the police,' he said.

The Cimmerian spat with a sneer of cruel contempt for the moaning clerk.

'He's a weakling and a fool,' he growled. 'Let one of you touch me and I'll spill his guts on the floor.'

'Are you ready to talk?' asked Demetrio tiredly. He found these scenes wearyingly monotonous.

'All I know,' sobbed the clerk, dragging himself to his feet and whimpering like a beaten dog in his pain, 'is that Kallian came to my house shortly after I arrived – I left the Temple at the same time he did – and sent his chariot away. He threatened me with discharge if I ever spoke of it. I am a poor man, without friends or favor. Without my position with him, I would starve.'

'What's that to me?' snapped Demetrio. 'How long did he remain at your house?'

'Until perhaps half an hour before midnight. Then he left, saying that he was going to the Temple, and would return after he had done what he wished to do there.'

'What was he going to do there?'

Promero hesitated at revealing the secrets of his dreaded employer, then a shuddering glance at Posthumo, who was grinning evilly as he doubled his huge fist, opened his lips quickly.

'There was something in the Temple he wished to examine.'

'But why should he come here alone in so much secrecy?'

'Because it was not his property. It arrived in a caravan from the south, at dawn. The men of the caravan knew nothing of it, except that it had been placed with them by the men of a caravan from Stygia, and was meant for Kalanthes of Hanumar, priest of Ibis. The master of the caravan had been paid by these other men to deliver it directly to Kalanthes, but he's a rascal by nature, and wished to proceed directly to Aquilonia, on the road to which Hanumar does not lie. So he asked if he might leave it in the Temple until Kalanthes could send for it.

'Kallian agreed, and told him he himself would send a runner to inform Kalanthes. But after the men had gone, and I spoke of the runner, Kallian forbade me to send him. He sat brooding over what the men had left.'

'And what was that?'

'A sort of sarcophagus, such as is found in ancient Stygian tombs, but this one was round, like a covered metal bowl. Its composition was something like copper, but much harder, and it was carved with hieroglyphics, like those found on the more ancient menhirs in southern Stygia. The lid was made fast to the body by carven copper-like bands.'

'What was in it?'

'The men of the caravan did not know. They only said that the men who gave it to them told them that it was a priceless relic, found among the tombs far beneath the pyramids and sent to Kalanthes "because of the love the sender bore the priest of Ibis". Kallian Publico believed that it contained the diadem of the giant-kings, of the people who dwelt in that dark land before the ancestors of the Stygians came there. He showed me a design carved on the lid, which he swore was the shape of the diadem which legend tells us the monster-kings wore.

'He determined to open the Bowl and see what it contained. He was like a madman when he thought of the fabled diadem, which myths say was set with the strange jewels known only to that ancient race, a single one of which is worth more than all the jewels of the modern world.

'I warned him against it. But he stayed at my house as I have said, and a short time before midnight, he came along to the Temple, hiding in the shadows until the watchman had passed to the other side of the building, then letting himself in with his belt key. I watched him from the shadows of the silk shop, saw him enter the Temple, and then returned to my own house. If the diadem was in the Bowl, or anything else of great value, he intended hiding it somewhere in the Temple and slipping out again. Then on the morrow he would raise a great hue and cry, saying that thieves had broken into his house and stolen Kalanthes's property. None would know of his prowlings but the charioteer and I, and neither of us would betray him.'

'But the watchman?' objected Demetrio.

'Kallian did not intend being seen by him; he planned to have him crucified as an accomplice of the thieves,' answered Promero. Arus gulped and turned pale as this duplicity of his employer came home to him.

'Where is this sarcophagus?' asked Demetrio. Promero pointed, and the Inquisitor grunted. 'So! The very room in which Kallian must have been attacked.'

Promero turned pale and twisted his thin hands.

'Why should a man in Stygia send Kalanthes a gift? Ancient gods and queer mummies have come up the caravan roads before, but who loves the priest of Ibis so well in Stygia, where they still worship the arch-demon Set who coils among the tombs in the darkness? The god Ibis has fought Set since the first dawn of the earth, and Kalanthes has fought Set's priests all his life. There is something dark and hidden here.'

'Show us this sarcophagus,' commanded Demetrio, and Promero hesitantly led the way. All followed, including Conan, who was apparently heedless of the wary eye the guardsmen kept on him, and seemed merely curious. They passed through the torn hangings and entered the room, which was rather more dimly lighted than the corridor. Doors on each side gave into other chambers, and the walls were lined with fantastic images, gods of strange lands and far peoples. And Promero cried out sharply.

'Look! The Bowl! It's open – and empty!'

In the center of the room stood a strange black cylinder, nearly four feet in height, and perhaps three feet in diameter at its widest circumference, which was halfway between the top and bottom. The heavy carven lid lay on the floor, and beside it a hammer and a chisel. Demetrio looked inside, puzzled an instant over the dim hieroglyphs, and turned to Conan.

'Is this what you came to steal?'

The barbarian shook his head.

'How could I bear it away? It is too big for one man to carry.'

'The bands were cut with this chisel,' mused Demetrio, 'and in haste. There are marks where misstrokes of the hammer dented the metal. We may assume that Kallian opened the Bowl. Someone was hiding nearby – possibly in the hangings in the doorway. When Kallian had the Bowl open, the murderer sprang on him – or he might have killed Kallian and opened the Bowl himself.'

'This is a grisly thing,' shuddered the clerk. 'It's too ancient to be holy. Who ever saw metal like it in a sane world? It seems less destructible than Aquilonian steel, yet see how it is corroded and eaten away in spots. Look at the bits of black mold clinging in the grooves of the hieroglyphics; they smell as earth smells from far below the surface. And look – here on the lid!' The clerk pointed with a shaky finger. 'What would you say it is?'

Demetrio bent closer to the carven design.

'I'd say it represents a crown of some sort,' he grunted.

'No!' exclaimed Promero. 'I warned Kallian, but he would not believe me! It is a scaled serpent coiled with its tail in its mouth. It is the sign of Set, the Old Serpent, the god of the Stygians! This Bowl is too old for a human world – it is a relic of the time when Set walked the earth in the form of a man! The race which sprang from his loins laid the bones of their kings away in such cases as these, perhaps!'

'And you'll say that those moldering bones rose up and strangled Kallian Publico and then walked away, perhaps,' derided Demetrio.

'It was no man who was laid to rest in that bowl,' whispered the clerk, his eyes wide and staring. 'What human could lie in it?'

Demetrio swore disgustedly.

'If Conan is not the murderer,' he snapped, 'the slayer is still somewhere in this building. Dionus and Arus, remain here with me, and you three prisoners stay here too. The rest of you search the building. The murderer could only have escaped – if he got away before Arus found the body – by the way Conan used in entering, and in that case the barbarian would have seen him, if he's telling the truth.'

'I saw no one but this dog,' growled Conan, indicating Arus.

'Of course not, because you're the murderer,' said Dionus. 'We're wasting time, but we'll search the building as a formality. And if we find no one, I promise you shall burn! Remember the law, my black-haired savage – you go to the mines for killing a commoner, you hang for killing a tradesman, and for murdering a rich man, you burn!'

Conan answered with a wicked lift of his lip, baring his teeth, and the men began their search. The listeners in the chamber heard them stamping upstairs and down, moving objects, opening doors and bellowing to one another through the rooms.

'Conan,' said Demetrio, 'you know what it means if they find no one?'

'I didn't kill him,' snarled the Cimmerian. 'If he had sought to hinder me I'd have split his skull. But I did not see him until I saw his corpse.'

'I know that someone sent you here tonight, to steal at least,' said Demetrio. 'By your silence you incriminate yourself in this murder as well. You had best speak. The mere fact of your being here is sufficient to send you to the mines for ten years, anyhow, whether you admit your guilt or not. But if you tell the whole tale, you may save yourself from the stake.'

'Well,' answered the barbarian grudgingly, 'I came here to steal the Zamorian diamond goblet. A man gave me a diagram of the Temple and told me where to look for it. It is kept in that room –' Conan pointed – 'in a niche in the floor under a copper Shemitish god.'

'He speaks truth there,' said Promero. 'I'd thought that not half a dozen men in the world knew the secret of that hiding place.'

'And if you had secured it,' asked Dionus sneeringly, 'would you really have taken it to the man who hired you? Or would you have kept it for yourself?'

Again the smoldering eyes flashed resentment.

'I am no dog,' the barbarian muttered. 'I keep my word.'

'Who sent you here?' Demetrio demanded, but Conan kept a sullen silence.

The guardsmen were straggling back from their search.

'There's no man hiding in this building,' they growled. 'We've ransacked the place. We found the trap-door in the roof through which the barbarian entered, and the bolt he cut in half. A man escaping that way would have been seen by the guards we posted about the building, unless he fled before we came. Then, besides, he would have had to stack tables or chairs or cases upon each other to reach it from below, and that has not been done. Why couldn't he have gone out the front door just before Arus came around the building?'

'Because the door was bolted on the inside, and the only keys which will work that bolt are the one belonging to Arus and the one which still hangs on the girdle of Kallian Publico.'

'I've found the cable the murderer used,' one of them announced. 'A black cable, thicker than a man's arm, and curiously splotched.'

'Then where is it, fool?' exclaimed Dionus.

'In the chamber adjoining this one,' answered the guard. 'It's wrapped about a marble pillar, where no doubt the murderer thought it would be safe from detection. I couldn't reach it. But it must be the right one.'

He led the way into a room filled with marble statuary, and pointed to a tall column, one of several which served a purpose more of ornament to set off the statues, than of utility. And then he halted and stared.

'It's gone!' he cried.

'It never was there!' snorted Dionus.

'By Mitra, it was!' swore the guardsman. 'Coiled about the pillar just above those carven leaves. It's so shadowy up there near the ceiling I couldn't tell much about it – but it was there.'

'You're drunk,' snapped Demetrio, turning away. 'That's too high for a man to reach; and nothing but a snake could climb that smooth pillar.'

'A Cimmerian could,' muttered one of the men.

'Possibly. Say that Conan strangled Kallian, tied the cable about the pillar, crossed the corridor and hid in the room where the stair is. How then, could he have removed it after you saw it? He has been among us ever since Arus found the body. No, I tell you Conan didn't commit the murder. I believe the real murderer killed Kallian to secure whatever was in the Bowl, and is hiding now in some secret nook in the Temple. If we can't find him, we'll have to put the blame on the barbarian to satisfy Justice, but – where is Promero?'

They had returned to the silent body in the corridor. Dionus bellowed threateningly for Promero, and the clerk came suddenly from the room in which stood the empty Bowl. He was shaking and his face was white.

'What now, man?' exclaimed Demetrio irritably.

'I found a symbol on the bottom of the Bowl!' chattered Promero. 'Not an ancient hieroglyphic, but a symbol recently carved! The mark of Thoth-amon, the Stygian sorcerer, Kalanthes's deadly foe! He found it in some grisly cavern below the haunted pyramids! The gods of old times did not die, as men died – they fell into long sleeps and their worshippers locked them in sarcophagi so that no alien hand might break their slumbers. Thoth-amon sent death to Kalanthes – Kallian's greed caused him to loose the horror – and it is lurking somewhere near us – even now it may be creeping upon us—'

'You gibbering fool!' roared Dionus disgustedly, striking him heavily across the mouth. Dionus was a materialist, with scant patience for eery speculations.

'Well, Demetrio,' he said, turning to the Inquisitor, 'I see nothing else to do other than to arrest this barbarian—'

The Cimmerian cried out suddenly and they wheeled. He was glaring toward the door of a chamber that adjoined the room of statues.

'Look!' he exclaimed. 'I saw something move in that room – I saw it through the hangings. Something that crossed the floor like a long dark shadow!'

'Bah!' snorted Posthumo. 'We searched that room—'

'He saw something!' Promero's voice shrilled and cracked with hysterical excitement. 'This place is accursed! Something came out of the sarcophagus and killed Kallian Publico! It hid from you where no human could hide, and now it is in that room! Mitra defend us from the powers of Darkness! I tell you it was one of Set's children in that grisly Bowl!' He caught Dionus's sleeve with claw-like fingers. 'You must search that room again!'

The prefect shook him off disgustedly, and Posthumo was inspired to a flight of humor.

'You shall search it yourself, clerk!' he said, grasping Promero by neck and girdle, and propelling the screaming wretch forcibly toward the door, outside of which he paused and hurled him into the room so violently the clerk fell and lay half stunned.

'Enough of this,' growled Dionus, eyeing the silent Cimmerian. The prefect lifted his hand, Conan's eyes began to burn bluely, and a tension crackled in the air, when an interruption came. A guardsman entered, dragging a slender, richly dressed figure.

'I saw him slinking about the back of the Temple,' quoth the guard, looking for commendation. Instead he received curses that lifted his hair.

'Release that gentleman, you bungling fool!' swore the prefect. 'Don't you know Aztrias Petanius, the nephew of the city's governor?'

The abashed guard fell away and the foppish young nobleman brushed his embroidered sleeve fastidiously.

'Save your apologies, good Dionus,' he lisped affectedly. 'All in line of duty, I know. I was returning from a late revel and walking to rid my brain of the wine fumes. What have we here? By Mitra, is it murder?'

'Murder it is, my lord,' answered the prefect. 'But we have a man who, though Demetrio seems to have doubts on the matter, will doubtless go to the stake for it.'

'A vicious looking brute,' murmured the young aristocrat. 'How can any doubt his guilt? I have never seen such a villainous countenance before.'

'Yes, you have, you scented dog,' snarled the Cimmerian, 'when you hired me to steal the Zamorian goblet for you. Revels, eh? Bah! You were waiting in the shadows for me to hand you the goblet. I would not have revealed your name if you had given me fair words. Now tell these dogs that you saw me climb the wall after the watchman made the last round, so that they'll know I didn't have time to kill this fat swine before Arus entered and found the body.'

Demetrio looked quickly at Aztrias, who did not change color.

'If what he says is true, my lord,' said the Inquisitor, 'it clears him of the murder, and we can easily hush up the matter of attempted theft. He is due ten years at hard labor for house-breaking, but if you say the word, we'll arrange for him to escape and none but us will ever know anything about it. I understand – you wouldn't be the first young nobleman who had to resort to such things to pay gambling debts and the like. You can rely on our discretion.'

Conan looked at the young nobleman expectantly, but Aztrias shrugged his slender shoulders and covered a yawn with a delicate white hand.

'I know him not,' he answered. 'He is mad to say I hired him. Let him take his just desserts. He has a strong back and the toil in the mines will be well for him.'

Conan's eyes blazed and he started as if stung; the guards tensed, grasping their bills, then relaxed as he dropped his head suddenly, as if in sullen resignation, and not even Demetrio could tell that he was watching them from under his heavy black brows, with eyes that were slits of blue bale-fire.

He struck with no more warning than a striking cobra; his sword flashed in the candlelight. Aztrias shrieked and his head flew from his shoulders in a shower of blood, the features frozen in a white mask of horror. Cat-like, Conan wheeled and thrust murderously for Demetrio's groin. The Inquisitor's instinctive recoil barely deflected the point which sank into his thigh, glanced from the bone and ploughed out through the outer side of the leg. Demetrio went to his knee with a groan, unnerved and nauseated with agony.

Conan had not paused. The bill which Dionus flung up saved the prefect's skull from the whistling blade which turned slightly as it cut through the shaft, and sheared his ear cleanly from his head. The blinding speed of the barbarian paralyzed the senses of the police and made their actions futile gestures. Caught flat-footed and dazed by his quickness and ferocity, half of them would have been down before they had a chance to fight back, except that Posthumo, more by luck than skill, threw his arms about the Cimmerian, pinioning his sword-arm. Conan's left hand leaped to the guard's head, and Posthumo fell away and writhed shrieking on the floor, clutching a gaping red socket where an eye had been.

Conan bounded back from the waving bills and his leap carried him outside the ring of his foes, to where Arus stood fumbling at his crossbow. A savage kick in the belly dropped him, green-faced and gagging, and Conan's sandalled heel crunched square in the watchman's mouth. The wretch screamed through a ruin of splintered teeth, blowing bloody froth from his mangled lips.

Then all were frozen in their tracks by the soul-shaking horror of a scream which rose from the chamber into which Posthumo had hurled Promero, and from the velvet-hung door the clerk came reeling, and stood there, shaking with great silent sobs, tears running down his pasty face and dripping off his loose sagging lips, like an idiot-babe weeping.

All halted to stare at him aghast – Conan with his dripping sword, the police with their lifted bills, Demetrio crouching on the floor and striving to staunch the blood that jetted from the great gash in his thigh, Dionus clutching the bleeding stump of his severed ear, Arus weeping and spitting out fragments of broken teeth – even Posthumo ceased his howls and blinked whimpering through the bloody mist that veiled his half-sight.

Promero came reeling out into the corridor and fell stiffly before them. Screeching in an unbearable high-pitched laughter of madness, he cried shrilly, 'The god has a long neck! Ha! ha! ha! Oh, a long, a cursed long neck!' And then with a frightful convulsion he stiffened and lay grinning vacantly at the shadowy ceiling.

'He's dead!' whispered Dionus, awedly, forgetting his own hurt, and the barbarian who stood with his dripping sword so near him. He bent over the body, then straightened, his eyes flaring. 'He's not wounded – *in Mitra's name what is in that chamber?*'

Then horror swept over them and they ran screaming for the outer door, jammed there in a clawing shrieking mob, and burst through like madmen. Arus followed and the half-blind Posthumo struggled up and blundered blindly after his fellows, squealing like a wounded pig and begging them not to leave him behind. He fell among them and they knocked him down and trampled him, screaming in their fear. But he crawled after them, and after him came Demetrio. The Inquisitor had the courage to face the unknown, but he was unnerved and wounded, and the sword that had struck him down was still near him. Grasping his blood-spurting thigh, he limped after his companions. Police, charioteer and watchman, wounded or whole, they burst screaming into the street, where the men watching the building took panic and joined in the flight, not waiting to ask why. Conan stood in the great corridor alone, save for the corpses on the floor.

The barbarian shifted his grip on his sword and strode into the chamber. It was hung with rich silken tapestries; silken cushions and couches lay strewn about in careless profusion; and over a heavy gilded screen a face looked at the Cimmerian.

Conan stared in wonder at the cold classic beauty of that countenance, whose like he had never seen among the sons of men. Neither weakness nor mercy nor cruelty nor kindness, nor any other human emotion was in those features. They might have been the marble mask of a god, carved by a master hand, except for the unmistakable life in them – life cold and strange, such as the Cimmerian had never known and could not understand. He thought fleetingly of the marble perfection of the body which the screen concealed – it must be perfect, he thought, since the face was so inhumanly beautiful. But he could see only the god-like face, the finely molded head which swayed curiously from side to side. The full lips opened and spoke a single word in a rich vibrant tone that was like the golden chimes that ring in the jungle-lost temples of Khitai. It was an unknown tongue, forgotten before the kingdoms of man arose, but Conan knew that it meant, 'Come!'

And the Cimmerian came, with a desperate leap and a humming slash of his sword. The beautiful head rolled from the top of the screen in a jet of dark blood and fell at his feet, and he gave back, fearing to touch it. Then his skin crawled, for the screen shook and heaved with the convulsions of something behind. Conan had seen and heard men die by the scores, and never had he heard a human being make such sounds in the death-throes. There was a thrashing, floundering noise, as if a great cable were being lashed violently about.

At last the movements ceased and Conan looked gingerly behind the screen. Then the full horror of it all rushed over the Cimmerian, and he fled, nor did he slacken his headlong flight until the spires of Numalia faded into the dawn behind him. The thought of Set was like a nightmare, and the children of Set who once ruled the earth and who now sleep in their nighted caverns far below the black pyramids. Behind that gilded screen there had been no human body – only the shimmering, headless coils of a gigantic serpent.

THE BLACK STRANGER

1 The Painted Men

ONE MOMENT THE GLADE lay empty; the next, a man stood poised warily at the edge of the bushes. There had been no sound to warn the grey squirrels of his coming. But the gay-hued birds that flitted about in the sunshine of the open space took fright at his sudden appearance and rose in a clamoring cloud. The man scowled and glanced quickly back the way he had come, as if fearing their flight had betrayed his position to some one unseen. Then he stalked across the glade, placing his feet with care. For all his massive, muscular build he moved with the supple certitude of a panther. He was naked except for a rag twisted about his loins, and his limbs were criss-crossed with scratches from briars, and caked with dried mud. A brown-crusted bandage was knotted about his thickly-muscled left arm. Under his matted black mane his face was drawn and gaunt, and his eyes burned like the eyes of a wounded panther. He limped slightly as he followed the dim path that led across the open space.

Halfway across the glade he stopped short and whirled, catlike, facing back the way he had come, as a long-drawn call quavered out across the forest. To another man it would have seemed merely the howl of a wolf. But this man knew it was no wolf. He was a Cimmerian and understood the voices of the wilderness as a city-bred man understands the voices of his friends.

Rage burned redly in his bloodshot eyes as he turned once more and hurried along the path, which, as it left the glade, ran along the edge of a dense thicket that rose in a solid clump of greenery among the trees and bushes. A massive log, deeply embedded in the grassy earth, paralleled the fringe of the thicket, lying between it and the path. When the Cimmerian saw this log he halted and looked back across the glade. To the average eye there were no signs to show that he had passed; but there was evidence visible to his wilderness-sharpened eyes, and therefore to the equally keen eyes of those who pursued him. He snarled silently, the red rage growing in his eyes – the berserk fury of a hunted beast which is ready to turn at bay.

He walked down the trail with comparative carelessness, here and there crushing a grass-blade beneath his foot. Then, when he had reached the further end of the great log, he sprang upon it, turned and ran lightly back along it. The bark had long been worn away by the elements. He left no sign to show the keenest forest-eyes that he had doubled on his trail. When he reached the densest point of the thicket he faded into it like a shadow, with hardly the quiver of a leaf to mark his passing.

The minutes dragged. The grey squirrels chattered again on the branches – then flattened their bodies and were suddenly mute. Again the glade was invaded. As silently as the first man had appeared, three other men materialized out of the eastern edge of the clearing. They were dark-skinned men of short stature, with thickly-muscled chests and arms. They wore beaded buckskin loin-cloths, and an eagle's feather was thrust into each black mane. They were painted in hideous designs, and heavily armed.

They had scanned the glade carefully before showing themselves in the open, for they moved out of the bushes without hesitation, in close single file, treading as softly as leopards, and bending down to stare at the path. They were following the trail of the Cimmerian, but it was no easy task even for these human bloodhounds. They moved slowly across the glade, and then one stiffened, grunted and pointed with his broad-bladed stabbing spear at a crushed grass-blade where the path entered the forest again. All halted instantly and their beady black eyes quested the forest walls. But their quarry was well hidden; they saw nothing to awake their suspicion, and presently they moved on, more rapidly, following the faint marks that seemed to indicate their prey was growing careless through weakness or They had just passed the spot where the thicket crowded desperation.

closest to the ancient trail when the Cimmerian bounded into the path behind them and plunged his knife between the shoulders of the last man. The attack was so quick and unexpected the Pict had no chance to save himself. The blade was in his heart before he knew he was in peril. The other two whirled with the instant, steel-trap quickness of savages, but even as his knife sank home, the Cimmerian struck a tremendous blow with the war-axe in his right hand. The second Pict was in the act of turning as the axe fell. It split his skull to the teeth.

The remaining Pict, a chief by the scarlet tip of his eagle-feather, came savagely to the attack. He was stabbing at the Cimmerian's breast even as the killer wrenched his axe from the dead man's head. The Cimmerian hurled the body against the chief and followed with an attack as furious and desperate as the charge of a wounded tiger. The Pict, staggering under the impact of the corpse against him, made no attempt to parry the dripping axe; the instinct to slay submerging even the instinct to live, he drove his spear ferociously at his enemy's broad breast. The Cimmerian had the advantage of a greater intelligence, and a weapon in each hand. The hatchet, checking its downward sweep, struck the spear aside, and the knife in the Cimmerian's left hand ripped upward into the painted belly.

An awful howl burst from the Pict's lips as he crumpled, disembowelled – a cry not of fear or of pain, but of baffled, bestial fury, the death-screech of a panther. It was answered by a wild chorus of yells some distance east of the glade. The Cimmerian started convulsively, wheeled, crouching like a wild thing at bay, lips asnarl, shaking the sweat from his face. Blood trickled down his forearm from under the bandage.

With a gasping, incoherent imprecation he turned and fled westward. He did not pick his way now, but ran with all the speed of his long legs, calling on the deep and all but inexhaustible reservoirs of endurance which are Nature's compensation for a barbaric existence. Behind him for a space the woods were silent, then a demoniacal howling burst out at the spot he had recently left, and he knew his pursuers had found the bodies of his victims. He had no breath for cursing the blood-drops that kept spilling to the ground from his freshly opened wound, leaving a trail a child could follow. He had thought that perhaps these three Picts were all that still pursued him of the war-party which had followed him for over a hundred miles. But he might have known these human wolves never quit a blood-trail.

The woods were silent again, and that meant they were racing after him, marking his path by the betraying blood-drops he could not check. A wind out of the west blew against his face, laden with a salty dampness he recognized. Dully he was amazed. If he was that close to the sea the long chase had been even longer than he had realized. But it was nearly over. Even his wolfish vitality was ebbing under the terrible strain. He gasped for breath and there was a sharp pain in his side. His legs trembled with weariness and the lame one ached like the cut of a knife in the tendons each time he set the foot to earth. He had followed the instincts of the wilderness which bred him, straining every nerve and sinew, exhausting every subtlety and artifice to survive. Now in his extremity he was obeying another instinct, looking for a place to turn at bay and sell his life at a bloody price.

He did not leave the trail for the tangled depths on either hand. He knew that it was futile to hope to evade his pursuers now. He ran on down the trail while the blood pounded louder and louder in his ears and each breath he drew was a racking, dry-lipped gulp. Behind him a mad baying broke out, token that they were close on his heels and expected to overhaul their prey swiftly. They would come as fleet as starving wolves now, howling at every leap.

Abruptly he burst from the denseness of the trees and saw, ahead of him, the ground pitching upward, and the ancient trail winding up rocky ledges between jagged boulders. All swam before him in a dizzy red mist, but it was a hill he had come to, a rugged crag rising abruptly from the forest about its foot. And the dim trail wound up to a broad ledge near the summit.

That ledge would be as good a place to die as any. He limped up the trail, going on hands and knees in the steeper places, his knife between his teeth. He had not yet reached the jutting ledge when some forty painted savages broke from among the trees, howling like wolves. At the sight of their prey their screams rose to a devil's crescendo, and they raced toward the foot of the crag, loosing arrows as they came. The shafts showered about the man who doggedly climbed upward, and one stuck in the calf of his leg. Without pausing in his climb he tore it out and threw it aside, heedless of the less accurate missiles which splintered on the rocks about him. Grimly he hauled himself over the rim of the ledge and turned about, drawing his hatchet and shifting knife to hand. He lay glaring down at his pursuers over the rim, only his shock of hair and blazing eyes visible. His chest heaved as he drank in the air in great shuddering gasps, and he clenched his teeth against a tendency toward nausea.

Only a few arrows whistled up at him. The horde knew its prey was cornered. The warriors came on howling, leaping agilely over the rocks at the foot of the hill, war-axes in their hand. The first to reach the crag was a brawny brave whose eagle feather was stained scarlet as a token of chieftainship. He halted briefly, one foot on the sloping trail, arrow notched and drawn halfway back, head thrown back and lips parted for an exultant yell. But the shaft was never loosed. He froze into motionlessness and the blood-lust in his black eyes gave way to a look of startled recognition. With a whoop he gave back, throwing his arms wide to check the rush of his howling braves. The man crouching on the ledge above them understood the Pictish tongue, but he was too far away to catch the significance of the staccato phrases snapped at the warriors by the crimson-feathered chief.

But all ceased their yelping, and stood mutely staring up – not at the man on the ledge, it seemed to him, but at the hill itself. Then without further hesitation, they unstrung their bows and thrust them into buckskin cases at their girdles; turned their backs and trotted across the open space, to melt into the forest without a backward look.

The Cimmerian glared in amazement. He knew the Pictish nature too well not to recognize the finality expressed in the departure. He knew they would not come back. They were heading for their villages, a hundred miles to the east.

But he could not understand it. What was there about his refuge that would cause a Pictish war-party to abandon a chase it had followed so long with all the passion of hungry wolves? He knew there were sacred places, spots set aside as sanctuaries by the various clans, and that a fugitive, taking refuge in one of these sanctuaries, was safe from the clan which raised it. But the different tribes seldom respected sanctuaries of other tribes; and the men who had pursued him certainly had no sacred spots of their own in this region. They were the men of the Eagle, whose villages lay far to the east, adjoining the country of the Wolf-Picts.

It was the Wolves who had captured him, in a foray against the Aquilonian settlements along Thunder River, and they had given him to the Eagles in return for a captured Wolf chief. The Eaglemen had a red score against the giant Cimmerian, and now it was redder still, for his escape had cost the life of a noted war-chief. That was why they had followed him so relentlessly, over broad rivers and hills and through the long leagues of gloomy forest, the hunting grounds of hostile tribes. And now the survivors of that long chase turned back when their enemy was run to earth and trapped. He shook his head, unable to understand it.

He rose gingerly, dizzy from the long grind, and scarcely able to realize that it was over. His limbs were stiff, his wounds ached. He spat dryly and cursed, rubbing his burning, bloodshot eyes with the back of his thick wrist. He blinked and took stock of his surroundings. Below him the green wilderness waved and billowed away and away in a solid mass, and above its western rim a steel-blue haze he knew hung over the ocean. The wind stirred his black mane, and the salt tang of the atmosphere revived him. He expanded his enormous chest and drank it in.

Then he turned stiffly and painfully about, growling at the twinge in his bleeding calf, and investigated the ledge whereon he stood. Behind it rose a sheer rocky cliff to the crest of the crag, some thirty feet above him. A narrow ladder-like stair of hand-holds had been niched into the rock. And a few feet from its foot there was a cleft in the wall, wide enough and tall enough for a man to enter.

He limped to the cleft, peered in, and grunted. The sun, hanging high above the western forest, slanted into the cleft, revealing a tunnel-like cavern beyond, and rested a revealing beam on the arch at which this tunnel ended. In that arch was set a heavy iron-bound oaken door!

This was amazing. This country was howling wilderness. The Cimmerian knew that for a thousand miles this western coast ran bare and uninhabited except by the villages of the ferocious sea-land tribes, who were even less civilized than their forest-dwelling brothers.

The nearest outposts of civilization were the frontier settlements along Thunder River, hundreds of miles to the east. The Cimmerian knew he was the only white man ever to cross the wilderness that lay between that river and the coast. Yet that door was no work of Picts.

Being unexplainable, it was an object of suspicion, and suspiciously he approached it, ax and knife ready. Then as his bloodshot eyes became more accustomed to the soft gloom that lurked on either side of the narrow shaft of sunlight, he noticed something else – thick iron-bound chests ranged along the walls. A blaze of comprehension came into his eyes. He bent over one, but the lid resisted his efforts. He lifted his hatchet to shatter the ancient lock then changed his mind and limped toward the arched door. His bearing was more confident now, his weapons hung at his sides. He pushed against the ornately carven door and it swung inward without resistance.

Then his manner changed again, with lightning-like abruptness; he recoiled with a startled curse, knife and hatchet flashing as they leaped to positions of defense. An instant he poised there, like a statue of fierce menace, craning his massive neck to glare through the door. It was darker in the large natural chamber into which he was looking, but a dim glow emanated from the great jewel which stood on a tiny ivory pedestal in the center of the great ebony table about which sat those silent shapes whose appearance had so startled the intruder.

They did not move, they did not turn their heads toward him.

'Well,' he said harshly; 'are you all drunk?'

There was no reply. He was not a man easily abashed, yet now he felt disconcerted.

'You might offer me a glass of that wine you're swigging,' he growled, his natural truculence roused by the awkwardness of the situation. 'By Crom, you show damned poor courtesy to a man who's been one of your own brotherhood. Are you going to—' his voice trailed into silence, and in silence he stood and stared awhile at those bizarre figures sitting so silently about the great ebon table.

'They're not drunk,' he muttered presently. 'They're not even drinking. What devil's game is this?' He stepped across the threshold and was instantly fighting for his life against the murderous, unseen fingers that clutched his throat.

2 Men from the Sea

Belesa idly stirred a sea-shell with a daintily slippered toe, mentally comparing its delicate pink edges to the first pink haze of dawn that rose over the misty beaches. It was not dawn now, but the sun was not long up, and the light, pearl-grey clouds which drifted over the waters had not yet been dispelled.

Belesa lifted her splendidly shaped head and stared out over a scene alien and repellent to her, yet drearily familiar in every detail. From her dainty feet the tawny sands ran to meet the softly lapping waves which stretched westward to be lost in the blue haze of the horizon. She was standing on the southern curve of the wide bay, and south of her the land sloped upward to the low ridge which formed one horn of that bay. From that ridge, she knew, one could look southward across the bare waters – into infinities of distance as absolute as the view to the westward and to the northward.

Glancing listlessly landward, she absently scanned the fortress which had been her home for the past year. Against a vague pearl and cerulean morning sky floated the golden and scarlet flag of her house – an ensign which awakened no enthusiasm in her youthful bosom, though it had flown trimphantly over many a bloody field in the far South. She made out the figures of men toiling in the gardens and fields that huddled near the fort, seeming to shrink from the gloomy rampart of the forest which fringed the open belt on the east, stretching north and south as far as she could see. She feared that forest, and that fear was shared by every one in that tiny settlement. Nor was it an idle fear – death lurked in those whispering depths, death swift and terrible, death slow and hideous, hidden, painted, tireless, unrelenting.

She sighed and moved listlessly toward the water's edge, with no set purpose in mind. The dragging days were all of one color, and the world of cities and courts and gaiety seemed not only thousands of miles but long ages away. Again she sought in vain for the reason that had caused a Count of Zingara to flee with his retainers to this wild coast, a thousand miles from the land that bore him, exchanging the castle of his ancestors for a hut of logs.

Her eyes softened at the light patter of small bare feet across the sands. A young girl came running over the low sandy ridge, quite naked, her slight body dripping, and her flaxen hair plastered wetly on her small head. Her wistful eyes were wide with excitement.

'Lady Belesa!' she cried, rendering the Zingaran words with a soft Ophirean accent. 'Oh, Lady Belesa!'

Breathless from her scamper, she stammered and made incoherent gestures with her hands. Belesa smiled and put an arm about the child, not minding that her silken dress came in contact with the damp, warm body. In her lonely, isolated life Belesa bestowed the tenderness of a naturally affectionate nature on the pitiful waif she had taken away from a brutal master encountered on that long voyage up from the southern coasts.

'What are you trying to tell me, Tina? Get your breath, child.'

'A ship!' cried the girl, pointing southward. 'I was swimming in a pool that the sea-tide left in the sand, on the other side of the ridge, and I saw it! A ship sailing up out of the south!'

She tugged timidly at Belesa's hand, her slender body all aquiver, and Belesa felt her own heart beat faster at the mere thought of an unknown visitor. They had seen no sail since coming to that barren shore.

Tina flitted ahead of her over the yellow sands, skirting the tiny pools the outgoing tide had left in shallow depressions. They mounted the low undulating ridge, and Tina poised there, a slender white figure against the clearing sky, her wet flaxen hair blowing about her thin face, a frail quivering arm outstretched.

'Look, my Lady!'

Belesa had already seen it – a billowing white sail, filled with the freshening south wind, beating up along the coast, a few miles from the point. Her heart skipped a beat. A small thing can loom large in colorless and isolated lives; but Belesa felt a premonition of strange and violent events. She felt that it was not by chance that this sail was beating up this lonely coast. There was no harbor town to the north, though one sailed to the ultimate shores of ice; and the nearest port to the south was a thousand miles away. What brought this stranger to lonely Korvela Bay?

Tina pressed close to her mistress, apprehension pinching her thin features.

'Who can it be, my Lady?' she stammered, the wind whipping color to her pale cheeks. 'Is it the man the Count fears?'

Belesa looked down at her, her brow shadowed.

'Why do you say that, child? How do you know my uncle fears anyone?'

'He must,' returned Tina naïvely, 'or he would never have come to hide in this lonely spot. Look, my Lady, how fast it comes!'

'We must go and inform my uncle,' murmured Belesa. 'The fishing boats have not yet gone out, and none of the men have seen that sail. Get your clothes, Tina. Hurry!'

The child scampered down the low slope to the pool where she had been bathing when she sighted the craft, and snatched up the slippers, tunic and girdle she had left lying on the sand. She skipped back up the ridge, hopping grotesquely as she donned her scanty garments in mid-flight.

Belesa, anxiously watching the approaching sail, caught her hand, and they hurried toward the fort. A few moments after they had entered the gate of the log palisade which enclosed the building, the strident blare of the trumpet startled the workers in the gardens, and the men just opening the boat-house doors to push the fishing boats down their rollers to the water's edge.

Every man outside the fort dropped his tool or abandoned whatever he was doing and ran for the stockade without pausing to look about for the cause of the alarm. The straggling lines of fleeing men converged on the opened gate, and every head was twisted over its shoulder to gaze fearfully at the dark line of woodland to the east. Not one looked seaward.

They thronged through the gate, shouting questions at the sentries who patrolled the firing-ledges built below the up-jutting points of the upright palisade logs.

'What is it? Why are we called in? Are the Picts coming?'

For answer one taciturn man-at-arms in worn leathers and rusty steel pointed southward. From his vantage-point the sail was now visible. Men began to climb up on the ledges, staring toward the sea.

On a small lookout tower on the roof of the manor house, which was built of logs like the other buildings, Count Valenso watched the onsweeping sail as it rounded the point of the southern horn. The Count was a lean, wiry man of medium height and late middle age. He was dark, somber of expression. Trunk-hose and doublet were of black silk, the only color about his costume the jewels that twinkled on his sword hilt, and the wine-colored cloak thrown carelessly over his shoulder. He twisted his thin black mustache nervously, and turned his gloomy eyes on his seneschal – a leather-featured man in steel and satin.

'What do you make of it, Galbro?'

'A carack,' answered the seneschal. 'It is a carack trimmed and rigged like a craft of the Barachan pirates – look there!'

A chorus of cries below them echoed his ejaculation; the ship had cleared the point and was slanting inward across the bay. And all saw the flag that suddenly broke forth from the masthead – a black flag, with a scarlet skull gleaming in the sun.

The people within the stockade stared wildly at that dread emblem; then all eyes turned up toward the tower, where the master of the fort stood somberly, his cloak whipping about him in the wind.

'It's a Barachan, all right,' grunted Galbro. 'And unless I am mad, it's Strom's *Red Hand*. What is he doing on this naked coast?'

'He can mean no good for us,' growled the Count. A glance below showed him that the massive gates had been closed, and that the captain of his men-at-arms, gleaming in steel, was directing his men to their stations, some to the ledges, some to the tower loop-holes. He was massing his main strength along the western wall, in the midst of which was the gate.

Valenso had been followed into exile by a hundred men: soldiers, vassals and serfs. Of these some forty were men-at-arms, wearing helmets and suits of mail, armed with swords, axes and crossbows. The rest were toilers, without armor save for shirts of toughened leather, but they were brawny stalwarts, and skilled in the use of their hunting bows, woodsmen's axes, and boar-spears. They took their places, scowling at their hereditary enemies. The pirates of the Barachan Isles, a tiny archipelago off the southwestern coast of Zingara, had preyed on the people of the mainland for more than a century.

The men on the stockade gripped their bows or boar-spears and stared somberly at the carack which swung inshore, its brass work flashing in the sun. They could see the figures swarming on the deck, and hear the lusty yells of the seamen. Steel twinkled along the rail.

The Count had retired from the tower, shooing his niece and her eager protégée before him, and having donned helmet and cuirass, he betook himself to the palisade to direct the defense. His subjects watched him with moody fatalism. They intended to sell their lives as dearly as they could, but they had scant hope of victory, in spite of their strong position. They were oppressed by a conviction of doom. A year on that naked coast, with the brooding threat of that devil-haunted forest looming for ever at their backs, had shadowed their souls with gloomy forebodings. Their women stood silently in the doorways of their huts, built inside the stockade, and quieted the clamor of their children.

Belesa and Tina watched eagerly from an upper window in the manor house, and Belesa felt the child's tense little body all aquiver within the crook of her protecting arm.

'They will cast anchor near the boat-house,' murmured Belesa. 'Yes! There goes their anchor, a hundred yards off-shore. Do not tremble so, child! They can not take the fort. Perhaps they wish only fresh water and supplies. Perhaps a storm blew them into these seas.'

'They are coming ashore in long boats!' exclaimed the child. 'Oh, my Lady, I am afraid! They are big men in armor! Look how the sun strikes fire from their pikes and burgonets! Will they eat us?'

Belesa burst into laughter in spite of her apprehension.

'Of course not! Who put that idea into your head?'

'Zingelito told me the Barachans eat women.'

'He was teasing you. The Barachans are cruel, but they are no worse than the Zingaran renegades who call themselves buccaneers. Zingelito was a buccaneer once.'

'He was cruel,' muttered the child. 'I'm glad the Picts cut his head off.'

'Hush, child.' Belesa shuddered slightly. 'You must not speak that way. Look, the pirates have reached the shore. They line the beach, and one of them is coming toward the fort. That must be Strom.'

'Ahoy, the fort there!' came a hail in a voice gusty as the wind. 'I come under a flag of truce!'

The Count's helmeted head appeared over the points of the palisade; his stern face, framed in steel, surveyed the pirate somberly. Strom had halted just within good earshot. He was a big man, bare-headed, his tawny hair blowing in the wind. Of all the sea-rovers who haunted the Barachans, none was more framed for deviltry than he.

'Speak!' commanded Valenso. 'I have scant desire to converse with one of your breed.'

Strom laughed with his lips, not with his eyes.

'When your galleon escaped me in that squall off the Trallibes last year I never thought to meet you again on the Pictish Coast, Valenso!' said he. 'Although at the time I wondered what your destination might be. By Mitra, had I known, I would have followed you then! I got the start of my life a little while ago when I saw your scarlet falcon floating over a fortress where I had thought to see naught but bare beach. You have found it, of course?'

'Found what?' snapped the Count impatiently.

'Don't try to dissemble with me!' The pirate's stormy nature showed itself momentarily in a flash of impatience. 'I know why you came here – and I have come for the same reason. I don't intend to be balked. Where is your ship?'

'That is none of your affair.'

'You have none,' confidently asserted the pirate. 'I see pieces of a galleon's masts in that stockade. It must have been wrecked, somehow, after you landed here. If you'd had a ship you'd have sailed away with your plunder long ago.'

'What are you talking about, damn you?' yelled the Count. 'My plunder? Am I a Barachan to burn and loot? Even so, what would I loot on this naked coast?'

'That which you came to find,' answered the pirate coolly. 'The same thing I'm after – and mean to have. But I'll be easy to deal with – just give me the loot and I'll go my way and leave you in peace.'

'You must be mad,' snarled Valenso. 'I came here to find solitude and seclusion, which I enjoyed until you crawled out of the sea, you yellow-headed dog. Begone! I did not ask for a parley, and I weary of this empty talk. Take your rogues and go your ways.'

'When I go I'll leave that hovel in ashes!' roared the pirate in a transport of rage. 'For the last time – will you give me the loot in return for your lives? I have you hemmed in here, and a hundred and fifty men ready to cut your throats at my word.'

For answer the Count made a quick gesture with his hand below the points of the palisade. Almost instantly a shaft hummed venomously through a loop-hole and splintered on Strom's breastplate. The pirate yelled ferociously, bounded back and ran toward the beach, with arrows whistling all about him. His men roared and came on like a wave, blades gleaming in the sun.

'Curse you, dog!' raved the Count, felling the offending archer with his iron-clad fist. 'Why did you not strike his throat above the gorget? Ready with your bows, men – here they come!'

But Strom had reached his men, checked their headlong rush. The pirates spread out in a long line that overlapped the extremities of the western wall, and advanced warily, loosing their shafts as they came. Their weapon was the longbow, and their archery was superior to that of the Zingarans. But the latter were protected by their barrier. The long arrows arched over the stockade and quivered upright in the earth. One struck the window-sill over which Belesa watched, wringing a cry of fear from Tina, who cringed back, her wide eyes fixed on the venomous vibrating shaft.

The Zingarans sent their bolts and hunting arrows in return, aiming and loosing without undue haste. The women had herded the children into their huts and now stoically awaited whatever fate the gods had in store for them.

The Barachans were famed for their furious and headlong style of battling, but they were weary as they were ferocious, and did not intend to waste their strength vainly in direct charges against the ramparts. They maintained their wide-spread formation, creeping along and taking advantage of every natural depression and bit of vegetation – which was not much, for the ground had been cleared on all sides of the fort against the threat of Pictish raids.

A few bodies lay prone on the sandy earth, back-pieces glinting in the sun, quarrel shafts standing up from arm-pit or neck. But the pirates were quick as cats, always shifting their position, and were protected by their light armor. Their constant raking fire was a continual menace to the men in the stockade. Still, it was evident that as long as the battle remained an exchange of archery, the advantage must remain with the sheltered Zingarans.

But down at the boat-house on the beach, men were at work with axes. The Count cursed sulphurously when he saw the havoc they were making among his boats, which had been built laboriously of planks sawn out of solid logs.

'They're making a mantlet, curse them!' he raged. 'A sally now, before they complete it – while they're scattered—'

Galbro shook his head, glancing at the bare-armed henchmen with their clumsy pikes.

'Their arrows would riddle us, and we'd be no match for them in hand-to-hand fighting. We must keep behind our walls and trust to our archers.'

'Well enough,' growled Valenso. 'If we can keep *them* outside our walls.'

Presently the intention of the pirates became apparent to all, as a group of some thirty men advanced, pushing before them a great shield made out of the planks from the boats, and the timbers of the boat-house itself. They had found an ox-cart, and mounted the mantlet on the wheels, great solid disks of oak. As they rolled it ponderously before them it hid them from the sight of the defenders except for glimpses of their moving feet.

It rolled toward the gate, and the straggling line of archers converged toward it, shooting as they ran.

'Shoot!' yelled Valenso, going livid. 'Stop them before they reach the gate!'

A storm of arrows whistled across the palisade, and feathered themselves harmlessly in the thick wood. A derisive yell answered the volley. Shafts were finding loop-holes now, as the rest of the pirates drew nearer, and a soldier reeled and fell from the ledge, gasping and choking, with a clothyard shaft through his throat.

'Shoot at their feet!' screamed Valenso; and then – 'Forty men at the gate with pikes and axes! The rest hold the wall!'

Bolts ripped into the sand before the moving shield. A blood-thirsty howl announced that one had found its target beneath the edge, and a man staggered into view, cursing and hopping as he strove to withdraw the quarrel that skewered his foot. In an instant he was feathered by a dozen hunting arrows.

But, with a deep-throated shout, the mantlet was pushed to the wall, and a heavy, iron-tipped boom, thrust through an aperture in the center of the shield, began to thunder on the gate, driven by arms knotted with brawny muscles and backed with blood-thirsty fury. The massive gate groaned and staggered, while from the stockade bolts poured in a steady hail and some struck home. But the wild men of the sea were afire with the fighting-lust.

With deep shouts they swung the ram, and from all sides the others closed in, braving the weakened fire from the walls, and shooting fast and hard.

Cursing like a madman, the Count sprang from the wall and ran to the gate, drawing his sword. A clump of desperate men-at-arms closed in behind him, gripping their spears. In another moment the gate would cave in and they must stop the gap with their living bodies.

Then a new note entered the clamor of the mêlée. It was a trumpet, blaring stridently from the ship. On the cross-trees a figure waved his arms and gesticulated wildly.

That sound registered on Strom's ears, even as he lent his strength to the swinging ram. Exerting his mighty thews he resisted the surge of the other arms, bracing his legs to halt the ram on its backward swing. He turned his head, sweat dripping from his face.

'Wait!' he roared. 'Wait, damn you! *Listen!*'

In the silence that followed that bull's bellow, the blare of the trumpet was plainly heard, and a voice that shouted something unintelligible to the people inside the stockade.

But Strom understood, for his voice was lifted again in profane command. The ram was released, and the mantlet began to recede from the gate as swiftly as it had advanced.

'Look!' cried Tina at her window, jumping up and down in her wild excitement. 'They are running! All of them! They are running to the beach! Look! They have abandoned the shield just out of range! They are leaping into the boats and rowing for the ship! Oh, my Lady, have we won?'

'I think not!' Belesa was staring sea-ward. 'Look!'

She threw the curtains aside and leaned from the window. Her clear young voice rose above the amazed shouts of the defenders, turned their heads in the direction she pointed. They sent up a deep yell as they saw another ship swinging majestically around the southern point. Even as they looked she broke out the royal golden flag of Zingara.

Strom's pirates were swarming up the sides of their carack, heaving up the anchor. Before the stranger had progressed half-way across the bay, the *Red Hand* was vanishing around the point of the northern horn.

3 The Coming of the Black Man

'Out, quick!' snapped the Count, tearing at the bars of the gate. 'Destroy that mantlet before these strangers can land!'

'But Strom has fled,' expostulated Galbro, 'and yonder ship is Zingaran.'

'Do as I order!' roared Valenso. 'My enemies are not all foreigners! Out, dogs! Thirty of you, with axes, and make kindling wood of that mantlet. Bring the wheels into the stockade.'

Thirty axemen raced down toward the beach, brawny men in sleeveless tunics, their axes gleaming in the sun. The manner of their lord had suggested a possibility of peril in that oncoming ship, and there was panic in their haste. The splintering of the timbers under their flying axes came plainly to the people inside the fort, and the axemen were racing back across the sands, trundling the great oaken wheels with them, before the Zingaran ship had dropped anchor where the pirate ship had stood.

'Why does not the Count open the gate and go down to meet them?' wondered Tina. 'Is he afraid that the man he fears might be on that ship?'

'What do you mean, Tina?' Belesa demanded uneasily. The Count had never vouchsafed a reason for this self-exile. He was not the sort of a man to run from an enemy, though he had many. But this conviction of Tina's was disquieting; almost uncanny.

Tina seemed not to have heard her question.

'The axemen are back in the stockade,' she said. 'The gate is closed again and barred. The men still keep their places along the wall. If that ship was chasing Strom, why did it not pursue him? But it is not a war-ship. It is a carack, like the other. Look, a boat is coming ashore. I see a man in the bow, wrapped in a dark cloak.'

The boat having grounded, this man came pacing leisurely up the sands, followed by three others. He was a tall, wiry man, clad in black silk and polished steel.

'Halt!' roared the Count. 'I will parley with your leader alone!'

The taller stranger removed his morion and made a sweeping bow. His companions halted, drawing their wide cloaks about them, and behind them the sailors leaned on their oars and stared at the flag floating over the palisade.

When he came within easy call of the gate: 'Why surely,' said he, 'there should be no suspicion between gentlemen in these naked seas!'

Valenso stared at him suspiciously. The stranger was dark, with a lean, predatory face, and a thin black mustache. A bunch of lace was gathered at his throat, and there was lace on his wrists.

'I know you,' said Valenso slowly. 'You are Black Zarono, the buccaneer.'

Again the stranger bowed with stately elegance.

'And none could fail to recognize the red falcon of the Korzettas!'

'It seems this coast has become the rendezvous of all the rogues of the southern seas,' growled Valenso. 'What do you wish?'

'Come, come, sir!' remonstrated Zarono. 'This is a churlish greeting to one who has just rendered you a service. Was not that Argossean dog, Strom, just thundering at your gate? And did he not take to his sea-heels when he saw me round the point?'

'True,' grunted the Count grudgingly. 'Though there is little to choose between a pirate and a renegade.'

Zarono laughed without resentment and twirled his mustache.

'You are blunt in speech, my Lord. But I desire only leave to anchor in your bay, to let my men hunt for meat and water in your woods, and perhaps, to drink a glass of wine myself at your board.'

'I see not how I can stop you,' growled Valenso. 'But understand this, Zarono: no man of your crew comes within this palisade. If one approaches closer than a hundred feet, he will presently find an arrow through his gizzard. And I charge you do no harm to my gardens or the cattle in the pens. Three steers you may have for fresh meat, but no more. And we can hold this fort against your ruffians, in case you think otherwise.'

'You were not holding it very successfully against Strom,' the buccaneer pointed out with a mocking smile.

'You'll find no wood to build mantlets unless you chop down trees, or strip it from your own ship,' assured the Count grimly. 'And your men are not Barachan archers; they're no better bowmen than mine. Besides, what little loot you'd find in this castle would not be worth the price.'

'Who speaks of loot and warfare?' protested Zarono. 'Nay, my men are sick to stretch their legs ashore, and nigh to scurvy from chewing salt pork. I guarantee their good conduct. May they come ashore?'

Valenso grudgingly signified his content, and Zarono bowed, a thought sardonically, and retired with a tread as measured and stately as if he trod the polished crystal floor of the Kordava royal court, where indeed, unless rumor lied, he had once been a familiar figure.

'Let no man leave the stockade,' Valenso ordered Galibro. 'I do not trust that renegade dog. Because he drove Strom from our gate is no guarantee that he would not cut our throats.'

Galbro nodded. He was well aware of the enmity which existed between the pirates and the Zingaran buccaneers. The pirates were mainly Argossean sailors, turned outlaw; to the ancient feud between Argos and Zingara was added, in the case of the freebooters, the rivalry of opposing interests. Both breeds preyed on the shipping and the coastal towns; and they preyed on one another with equal rapacity.

So no one stirred from the palisade while the buccaneers came ashore, dark-faced men in flaming silk and polished steel, with scarfs bound about their heads and gold hoops in their ears. They camped on the beach, a hundred and seventy-odd of them, and Valenso noticed that Zarono posted lookouts on both points. They did not molest the gardens, and only the three beeves designated by Valenso, shouting from the palisade, were driven forth and slaughtered. Fires were kindled on the strand, and a wattled cask of ale was brought ashore and broached.

Other kegs were filled with water from the spring that rose a short distance south of the fort, and men began to straggle toward the woods, crossbows in their hands. Seeing this, Valenso was moved to shout to Zarono, striding back and forth through the camp: 'Don't let your men go into the forest. Take another steer from the pens if you haven't enough meat. If they go trampling into the woods they may fall foul of the Picts.

'Whole tribes of the painted devils live back in the forest. We beat off an attack shortly after we landed, and since then six of my men have been murdered in the forest, at one time or another. There's peace between us just now, but it hangs by a thread. Don't risk stirring them up.'

Zarono shot a startled glance at the lowering woods, as if he expected to see hordes of savage figures lurking there. Then he bowed and said: 'I thank you for the warning, my Lord.' And he shouted for his men to come back, in a rasping voice that contrasted strangely with his courtly accents when addressing the Count.

If Zarono could have penetrated the leafy mask he would have been more apprehensive, if he could have seen the sinister figure that lurked there, watching the strangers with inscrutable black eyes – a hideously painted warrior, naked but for a doe-skin breech-clout, with a toucan feather drooping over his left ear.

As evening drew on, a thin skim of gray crawled up from the sea-rim and overcast the sky. The sun sank in a wallow of crimson, touching the tips of the black waves with blood. Fog crawled out of the sea and lapped at the feet of the forest, curling about the stockade in smoky wisps. The fires on the beach shone dull crimson through the mist, and the singing of the buccaneers seemed deadened and far away. They had brought old sail-canvas from the carack and made them shelters along the strand, where beef was still roasting, and the ale granted them by their captain was doled out sparingly.

The great gate was shut and barred. Soldiers stolidly tramped the ledges of the palisade, pike on shoulder, beads of moisture glistening on their steel caps. They glanced uneasily at the fires on the beach, stared with greater fixity toward the forest, now a vague dark line in the crawling fog. The compound lay empty of life, a bare, darkened space. Candles gleamed feebly through the crack of the huts, and light streamed from the windows of the manor. There was silence except for the tread of the sentries, the drip of water from the eaves, and the distant singing of the buccaneers.

Some faint echo of this singing penetrated into the great hall where Valenso sat at wine with his unsolicited guest.

'Your men make merry, sir,' grunted the Count.

'They are glad to feel the sand under their feet again,' answered Zarono. 'It has been a wearisome voyage – yes, a long, stern chase.' He lifted his goblet gallantly to the unresponsive girl who sat on his host's right, and drank ceremoniously.

Impassive attendants ranged the walls, soldiers with pikes and helmets, servants in satin coats. Valenso's household in this wild land was a shadowy reflection of the court he had kept in Kordava.

The manor house, as he insisted on calling it, was a marvel for that coast. A hundred men had worked night and day for months building it. Its log-walled exterior was devoid of ornamentation, but, within, it was as nearly a copy of Korzetta Castle as was possible. The logs that composed the walls of the hall were hidden with heavy silk tapestries, worked in gold. Ship beams, stained and polished, formed the beams of the lofty ceiling. The floor was covered with rich carpets. The broad stair that led up from the hall was likewise carpeted, and its massive balustrade had once been a galleon's rail.

A fire in the wide stone fireplace dispelled the dampness of the night. Candles in the great silver candelabrum in the center of the broad mahogany board lit the hall, throwing long shadows on the stair. Count Valenso sat at the head of that table, presiding over a company composed of his niece, his piratical guest, Galbro, and the captain of the guard. The smallness of the company emphasized the proportions of the vast board, where fifty guests might have sat at ease.

'You followed Strom?' asked Valenso. 'You drove him this far afield?'

'I followed Strom,' laughed Zarono, 'but he was not fleeing from me. Strom is not the man to flee from anyone. No; he came seeking for something; something I too desire.'

'What could tempt a pirate or a buccaneer to this naked land?' muttered Valenso, staring into the sparkling contents of his goblet.

'What could tempt a count of Kordava?' retorted Zarono, and an avid light burned an instant in his eyes.

'The rottenness of a royal court might sicken a man of honor,' remarked Valenso.

'Korzettas of honor have endured its rottenness with tranquillity for several generations,' said Zarono bluntly. 'My Lord, indulge my curiosity – why did you sell your lands, load your galleon with the furnishings of your castle and sail over the horizon out of the knowledge of the king and the nobles of Zingara? And why settle here, when your sword and your name might carve out a place for you in any civilized land?'

Valenso toyed with the golden seal-chain about his neck.

'As to why I left Zingara,' he said, 'that is my own affair. But it was chance that left me stranded here. I had brought all my people ashore, and much of the furnishings you mentioned, intending to build a temporary habitation. But my ship, anchored out there in the bay, was driven against the cliffs of the north point and wrecked by a sudden storm out of the west. Such storms are common enough at certain times of the year. After that there was naught to do but remain and make the best of it.'

'Then you would return to civilization, if you could?'

'Not to Kordava. But perhaps to some far clime – to Vendhya, or Khitai—'

'Do you not find it tedious here, my Lady?' asked Zarono, for the first time addressing himself directly to Belesa.

Hunger to see a new face and hear a new voice had brought the girl to the great hall that night. But now she wished she had remained in her chamber with Tina. There was no mistaking the meaning in the glance Zarono turned on her. His speech was decorous and formal, his expression sober and respectful; but it was but a mask through which gleamed the violent and sinister spirit of the man. He could not keep the burning desire out of his eyes when he looked at the aristocratic young beauty in her low-necked satin gown and jeweled girdle.

'There is little diversity here,' she answered in a low voice.

'If you had a ship,' Zarono bluntly asked his host, 'you would abandon this settlement?'

'Perhaps,' admitted the Count.

'I have a ship,' said Zarono. 'If we could reach an agreement—'

'What sort of an agreement?' Valenso lifted his head to stare suspiciously at his guest.

'Share and share alike,' said Zarono, laying his hand on the board with the fingers spread wide. The gesture was curiously reminiscent of a great spider. But the fingers quivered with curious tension, and the buccaneer's eyes burned with a new light.

'Share what?' Valenso stared at him in evident bewilderment. 'The gold I brought with me went down in my ship, and unlike the broken timbers, it did not wash ashore.'

'Not that!' Zarono made an impatient gesture. 'Let us be frank, my Lord. Can you pretend it was chance which caused you to land at this particular spot, with a thousand miles of coast from which to choose?'

'There is no need for me to pretend,' answered Valenso coldly. 'My ship's master was one Zingelito, formerly a buccaneer. He had sailed this coast, and persuaded me to land here, telling me he had a reason he would later disclose. But this reason he never divulged, because the day after we landed he disappeared into the woods, and his headless body was found later by a hunting party. Obviously he was ambushed and slain by the Picts.'

Zarono stared fixedly at Valenso for a space.

'Sink me,' quoth he at last, 'I believe you, my Lord. A Korzetta has no skill at lying, regardless of his other accomplishments. And I will make you a proposal. I will admit when I anchored out there in the bay I had other plans in mind. Supposing you to have already secured the treasure, I meant to take this fort by strategy and cut all your throats. But circumstances have caused me to change my mind—' He cast a glance at Belesa that brought the color into her face, and made her lift her head indignantly.

'I have a ship to carry you out of exile,' said the buccaneer, 'with your household and such of your retainers as you shall choose. The rest can fend for themselves.'

The attendants along the walls shot uneasy glances sidelong at each other. Zarono went on, too brutally cynical to conceal his intentions.

'But first you must help me secure the treasure for which I've sailed a thousand miles.'

'What treasure, in Mitra's name?' demanded the Count angrily. 'You are yammering like that dog Strom, now.'

'Did you ever hear of Bloody Tranicos, the greatest of the Barachan pirates?' asked Zarono.

'Who has not? It was he who stormed the island castle of the exiled prince Tothmekri of Stygia, put the people to the sword and bore off the treasure the prince had brought with him when he fled from Khemi.'

'Aye! And the tale of that treasure brought the men of the Red Brotherhood swarming like vultures after carrion – pirates, buccaneers, even the black corsairs from the South. Fearing betrayal by his captains, he fled northward with one ship, and vanished from the knowledge of men. That was nearly a hundred years ago.

'But the tale persists that one man survived that last voyage, and returned to the Barachans, only to be captured by a Zingaran war-ship. Before he was hanged he told his story and drew a map in his own blood, on parchment, which he smuggled somehow out of his captor's reach. This was the tale he told: Tranicos had sailed far beyond the paths of shipping, until he came to a bay on a lonely coast, and there he anchored. He went ashore, taking his treasure and eleven of his most trusted captains who had accompanied him on his ship. Following his orders, the ship sailed away, to return in a week's time, and pick up their admiral and his captains. In the meantime Tranicos meant to hide the treasure somewhere in the vicinity of the bay. The ship returned at the appointed time, but there was no trace of Tranicos and his eleven captains, except the rude dwelling they had built on the beach.

'This had been demolished, and there were tracks of naked feet about it, but no sign to show there had been any fighting. Nor was there any trace of the treasure, or any sign to show where it was hidden. The pirates plunged into the forest to search for their chief and his captains, but were attacked by wild Picts and driven back to their ship. In despair they heaved anchor and sailed away, but before they raised the Barachans, a terrific storm wrecked the ship and only that one man survived.

'That is the tale of the Treasure of Tranicos, which men have sought in vain for nearly a century. That the map exists is known, but its whereabouts have remained a mystery.

'I have had one glimpse of that map. Strom and Zingelito were with me, and a Nemedian who sailed with the Barachans. We looked upon it in a hovel in a certain Zingaran sea-port town, where we were skulking in disguise. Somebody knocked over the lamp, and somebody howled in the dark, and when we got the light on again, the old miser who owned the map was dead with a dirk in his heart, and the map was gone, and the night-watch was clattering down the street with their pikes to investigate the clamor. We scattered, and each went his own way.

'For years thereafter Strom and I watched one another, each supposing the other had the map. Well, as it turned out, neither had it, but recently word came to me that Strom had departed northward, so I followed him. You saw the end of that chase.

'I had but a glimpse at the map as it lay on the old miser's table, and could tell nothing about it. But Strom's actions show that he knows this is the bay where Tranicos anchored. I believe that they hid the treasure somewhere in that forest and returning, were attacked and slain by the Picts. The Picts did not get the treasure. Men have traded up and down this coast a little, knowing nothing of the treasure, and no gold ornament or rare jewel has ever been seen in the possession of the coastal tribes.

'This is my proposal: let us combine our forces. Strom is somewhere within striking distance. He fled because he feared to be pinned between us, but he will return. But allied, we can laugh at him. We can work out from the fort, leaving enough men here to hold it if he attacks. I believe the treasure is hidden near by. Twelve men could not have conveyed it far. We will find it, load it in my ship, and sail for some foreign port where I can cover my past with gold. I am sick of this life. I want to go back to a civilized land, and live like a noble, with riches, and slaves, and a castle – and a wife of noble blood.'

'Well?' demanded the Count, slit-eyed with suspicion.

'Give me your niece for my wife,' demanded the buccaneer bluntly.

Belesa cried out sharply and started to her feet. Valenso likewise rose, livid, his fingers knotting convulsively about his goblet as if he contemplated hurling it at his guest. Zarono did not move; he sat still, one arm on the table and the fingers hooked like talons. His eyes smoldered with passion, and a deep menace.

'You dare!' ejaculated Valenso.

'You seem to forget you have fallen from your high estate, Count Valenso,' growled Zarono. 'We are not at the Kordavan court, my Lord. On this naked coast nobility is measured by the power of men and arms. And there I rank you. Strangers tread Korzetta Castle, and the Korzetta fortune is at the bottom of the sea. You will die here, an exile, unless I give you the use of my ship.

'You will have no cause to regret the union of our houses. With a new name and a new fortune you will find that Black Zarono can take his place among the aristocrats of the world and make a son-in-law of which not even a Korzetta need be ashamed.'

'You are mad to think of it!' exclaimed the Count violently. 'You— who is that?'

A patter of soft-slippered feet distracted his attention. Tina came hurriedly into the hall, hesitated when she saw the Count's eyes fixed angrily on her, curtsied deeply, and sidled around the table to thrust her small hands into Belesa's fingers. She was panting slightly, her slippers were damp, and her flaxen hair was plastered down on her head.

'Tina!' exclaimed Belesa anxiously. 'Where have you been? I thought you were in your chamber, hours ago.'

'I was,' answered the child breathlessly, 'but I missed my coral necklace you gave me—' She held it up, a trivial trinket, but prized beyond all her other possessions because it had been Belesa's first gift to her. 'I was afraid you wouldn't let me go if you knew – a soldier's wife helped me out of the stockade and back again – please, my Lady, don't make me tell who she was, because I promised not to. I found my necklace by the pool where I bathed this morning. Please punish me if I have done wrong.'

'Tina!' groaned Belesa, clasping the child to her. 'I'm not going to punish you. But you should not have gone outside the palisade, with these buccaneers camped on the beach, and always a chance of Picts skulking about. Let me take you to your chamber and change these damp clothes—'

'Yes, my Lady,' murmured Tina, 'but first let me tell you about the black man—'

'*What?*' The startling interruption was a cry that burst from Valenso's lips. His goblet clattered to the floor as he caught the table with both hands. If a thunderbolt had struck him, the lord of the castle's bearing could not have been more subtly or horrifyingly altered. His face was livid, his eyes almost starting from his head.

'What did you say?' he panted, glaring wildly at the child who shrank back against Belesa in bewilderment. 'What did you say, wench?'

'A black man, my Lord,' she stammered, while Belesa, Zarono and the attendants stared at him in amazement. 'When I went down to the pool to get my necklace, I saw him. There was a strange moaning in the wind, and the sea whimpered like a thing in fear, and then he came. I was afraid, and hid behind a little ridge of sand. He came from the sea in a strange black boat with blue fire playing all about it, but there was no torch. He drew his boat up on the sands below the south point, and strode toward the forest, looking like a giant in the fog – a great, tall man, black like a Kushite—'

Valenso reeled as if he had received a mortal blow. He clutched at his throat, snapping the golden chain in his violence. With the face of a madman he lurched about the table and tore the child screaming from Belesa's arms.

'You little slut,' he panted. 'You lie! You have heard me mumbling in my sleep and have told this lie to torment me! Say you lie before I tear the skin from your back!'

'Uncle!' cried Belesa, in outraged bewilderment, trying to free Tina from his grasp. 'Are you mad? What are you about?'

With a snarl he tore her hand from his arm and spun her staggering into the arms of Galbro who received her with a leer he made little effort to disguise.

'Mercy, my Lord!' sobbed Tina. 'I did not lie!'

'I said you lied!' roared Valenso. 'Gebbrelo!'

The stolid serving man seized the trembling youngster and stripped her with one brutal wrench that tore her scanty garments from her body. Wheeling, he drew her slender arms over his shoulders, lifting her writhing feet clear of the floor.

'Uncle! shrieked Belesa, writhing vainly in Galbro's lustful grasp. 'You are mad! You can not – oh, you can not—!' The voice choked in her throat as Valenso caught up a jewel-hilted riding whip and brought it down across the child's frail body with a savage force that left a red weal across her naked shoulders.

Belesa moaned, sick with the anguish in Tina's shriek. The world had suddenly gone mad. As in a nightmare she saw the stolid faces of the soldiers and servants, beast-faces, the faces of oxen, reflecting neither pity nor sympathy. Zarono's faintly sneering face was part of the nightmare. Nothing in that crimson haze was real except Tina's naked white body, criss-crossed with red welts from shoulders to knees; no sound real except the child's sharp cries of agony, and the panting gasps of Valenso as he lashed away with the staring eyes of a madman, shrieking: 'You lie! You lie! Curse you, you lie! Admit your guilt, or I will flay your stubborn body! *He* could not have followed me here—'

'Oh, have mercy, my Lord!' screamed the child, writhing vainly on the brawny servant's back, too frantic with fear and pain to have the wit to save herself by a lie. Blood trickled in crimson beads down her quivering thighs. 'I saw him! I do not lie! Mercy! Please! Ahhhh!'

'You fool! *You fool!*' screamed Belesa, almost beside herself. 'Do you not see she is telling the truth? Oh, you beast! Beast! Beast!'

Suddenly some shred of sanity seemed to return to the brain of Count Valenso Korzetta. Dropping the whip he reeled back and fell up against the table, clutching blindly at its edge. He shook as with an ague. His hair was plastered across his brow in dank strands, and sweat dripped from his livid countenance which was like a carven mask of Fear. Tina, released by Gebbrelo, slipped to the floor in a whimpering heap. Belesa tore free from Galbro, rushed to her, sobbing, and fell on her knees, gathering the pitiful waif into her arms. She lifted a terrible face to her uncle, to pour upon him the full vials of her wrath – but he was not looking at her. He seemed to have forgotten both her and his victim. In a daze of incredulity, she heard him say to the buccaneer: 'I accept your offer, Zarono; in Mitra's name, let us find this accursed treasure and begone from this damned coast!'

At this the fire of her fury sank to sick ashes. In stunned silence she lifted the sobbing child in her arms and carried her up the stair. A glance backward showed Valenso crouching rather than sitting at the table, gulping wine from a huge goblet he gripped in both shaking hands, while Zarono towered over him like a somber predatory bird

– puzzled at the turn of events, but quick to take advantage of the shocking change that had come over the Count. He was talking in a low, decisive voice, and Valenso nodded mute agreement, like one who scarcely heeds what is being said. Galbro stood back in the shadows, chin pinched between forefinger and thumb, and the attendants along the walls glanced furtively at each other, bewildered by their lord's collapse.

Up in her chamber Belesa laid the half-fainting girl on the bed and set herself to wash and apply soothing ointments to the weals and cuts on her tender skin. Tina gave herself up in complete submission to her mistress's hands, moaning faintly. Belesa felt as if her world had fallen about her ears. She was sick and bewildered, overwrought, her nerves quivering from the brutal shock of what she had witnessed. Fear of and hatred for her uncle grew in her soul. She had never loved him; he was harsh and apparently without natural affection, grasping and avid. But she had considered him just, and fearless. Revulsion shook her at the memory of his staring eyes and bloodless face. It was some terrible fear which had roused this frenzy; and because of this fear Valenso had brutalized the only creature she had to love and cherish; because of that fear he was selling her, his niece, to an infamous outlaw. What was behind this madness? Who was the black man Tina had seen?

The child muttered in semi-delirium.

'I did not lie, my Lady! Indeed I did not! It was a black man, in a black boat that burned like blue fire on the water! A tall man, black as a negro, and wrapped in a black cloak! I was afraid when I saw him, and my blood ran cold. He left his boat on the sands and went into the forest. Why did the Count whip me for seeing him?'

'Hush, Tina,' soothed Belesa. 'Lie quiet. The smarting will soon pass.'

The door opened behind her and she whirled, snatching up a jeweled dagger. The Count stood in the door, and her flesh crawled at the sight. He looked years older; his face was grey and drawn, and his eyes stared in a way that roused fear in her bosom. She had never been close to him; now she felt as though a gulf separated them. He was not her uncle who stood there, but a stranger come to menace her.

She lifted the dagger.

'If you touch her again,' she whispered from dry lips, 'I swear before Mitra I will sink this blade in your breast.'

He did not heed her.

'I have posted a strong guard about the manor,' he said. 'Zarono brings his men into the stockade tomorrow. He will not sail until he has found the treasure. When he finds it we shall sail at once for some port not yet decided upon.'

'And you will sell me to him?' she whispered. 'In Mitra's name—'

He fixed upon her a gloomy gaze in which all considerations but his own self-interest had been crowded out. She shrank before it, seeing in it the frantic cruelty that possessed the man in his mysterious fear.

'You will do as I command,' he said presently, with no more human feeling in his voice than there is in the ring of flint on steel. And turning, he left the chamber. Blinded by a sudden rush of horror, Belesa fell fainting beside the couch where Tina lay.

4 A Black Drum Droning

Belesa never knew how long she lay crushed and senseless. She was first aware of Tina's arms about her and the sobbing of the child in her ear. Mechanically she straightened herself and drew the girl into her arms; and she sat there, dry-eyed, staring unseeingly at the flickering candle. There was no sound in the castle. The singing of the buccaneers on the strand had ceased. Dully, almost impersonally she reviewed her problem.

Valenso was mad, driven frantic by the story of the mysterious black man. It was to escape this stranger that he wished to abandon the settlement and flee with Zarono. That much was obvious. Equally obvious was the fact that he was ready to sacrifice her in exchange for that opportunity to escape. In the blackness of spirit which surrounded her she saw no glint of light. The serving men were dull or callous brutes, their women stupid and apathetic. They would neither dare nor care to help her. She was utterly helpless.

Tina lifted her tear-stained face as if she were listening to the prompting of some inner voice. The child's understanding of Belesa's inmost thoughts was almost uncanny, as was her recognition of the inexorable drive of Fate and the only alternative left to the weak.

'We must go, my Lady!' she whispered. 'Zarono shall not have you. Let us go far away into the forest. We shall go until we can go no further, and then we shall lie down and die together.'

The tragic strength that is the last refuge of the weak entered Belesa's soul. It was the only escape from the shadows that had been closing in upon her since that day when they fled from Zingara.

'We shall go, child.'

She rose and was fumbling for a cloak, when an exclamation from Tina brought her about. The girl was on her feet, a finger pressed to her lips, her eyes wide and bright with terror.

'What is it, Tina?' The child's expression of fright induced Belesa to pitch her voice to a whisper, and a nameless apprehension crawled over her.

'Someone outside in the hall,' whispered Tina, clutching her arm convulsively. 'He stopped at our door, and then went on, toward the Count's chamber at the other end.'

'Your ears are keener than mine,' murmured Belesa. 'But there is nothing strange in that. It was the Count himself, perchance, or Galbro.' She moved to open the door, but Tina threw her arms frantically about her neck, and Belesa felt the wild beating of her heart.

'No, no, my Lady! Do not open the door! I am afraid! I do not know why, but I feel that some evil thing is skulking near us!'

Impressed, Belesa patted her reassuringly, and reached a hand toward the gold disk that masked the tiny peep-hole in the center of the door.

'He is coming back!' shivered the girl. 'I hear him!'

Belesa heard something too – a curious stealthy pad which she knew, with a chill of nameless fear, was not the step of anyone she knew. Nor was it the step of Zarono, or any booted man. Could it be the buccaneer gliding along the hallway on bare, stealthy feet, to slay his host while he slept? She remembered the soldiers who would be on guard below. If the buccaneer had remained in the manor for the night, a man-at-arms would be posted before his chamber door. But who was that sneaking along the corridor? None slept upstairs besides herself, Tina and the Count, except Galbro.

With a quick motion she extinguished the candle so it would not shine through the hole in the door, and pushed aside the gold disk. All the lights were out in the hall, which was ordinarily lighted by candles. Someone was moving along the darkened corridor. She sensed rather than saw a dim bulk moving past her doorway, but she could make nothing of its shape except that it was man-like. But a chill wave of terror swept over her; so she crouched dumb, incapable of the scream that froze behind her lips. It was not such terror as her uncle now inspired in her, or fear like her fear of Zarono, or even of the brooding forest. It was blind unreasoning terror that laid an icy hand on her soul and froze her tongue to her palate.

The figure passed on to the stairhead, where it was limned momentarily against the faint glow that came up from below, and at the glimpse of that vague black image against the red, she almost fainted.

She crouched there in the darkness, awaiting the outcry that would announce that the soldiers in the great hall had seen the intruder. But the manor remained silent; somewhere a wind wailed shrilly. That was all.

Belesa's hands were moist with perspiration as she groped to relight the candle. She was still shaken with horror, though she could not decide just what there had been about that black figure etched against the red glow that had roused this frantic loathing in her soul. It was man-like in shape, but the outline was strangely alien – abnormal – though she could not clearly define that abnormality. But she knew that it was no human being that she had seen, and she knew that the sight had robbed her of all her new-found resolution. She was demoralized, incapable of action.

The candle flared up, limning Tina's white face in the yellow glow.

'It was the black man!' whispered Tina. 'I know! My blood turned cold, just as it did when I saw him on the beach. There are soldiers downstairs; why did they not see him? Shall we go and inform the Count?'

Belesa shook her head. She did not care to repeat the scene that had ensued upon Tina's first mention of the black man. At any event, she dared not venture out into that darkened hallway.

'We dare not go into the forest!' shuddered Tina. 'He will be lurking there—'

Belesa did not ask the girl how she knew the black man would be in the forest; it was the logical hiding-place for any evil thing, man or devil. And she knew Tina was right; they dared not leave the fort now. Her determination, which had not faltered at the prospect of certain death, gave way at the thought of traversing those gloomy woods with that black shambling creature at large among them. Helplessly she sat down and sank her face in her hands.

Tina slept, presently, on the couch, whimpering occasionally in her sleep. Tears sparkled on her long lashes. She moved her smarting body uneasily in her restless slumber. Toward dawn Belesa was aware of a stifling quality in the atmosphere. She heard a low rumble of thunder somewhere off to sea-ward. Extinguishing the candle, which had burned to its socket, she went to a window whence she could see both the ocean and a belt of the forest behind the fort.

The fog had disappeared, but out to sea a dusky mass was rising from the horizon. From it lightning flickered and the low thunder growled. An answering rumble came from the black woods. Startled, she turned and stared at the forest, a brooding black rampart. A strange rhythmic pulsing came to her ears – a droning reverberation that was not the roll of a Pictish drum.

'The drum!' sobbed Tina, spasmodically opening and closing her fingers in her sleep. 'The black man – beating on a black drum – in the black woods! Oh, save us—!'

Belesa shuddered. Along the eastern horizon ran a thin white line that presaged dawn. But that black cloud on the western rim writhed and billowed, swelling and expanding. She stared in amazement, for storms were practically unknown on that coast at that time of the year, and she had never seen a cloud like that one.

It came pouring up over the world-rim in great boiling masses of blackness, veined with fire. It rolled and billowed with the wind in its belly. Its thundering made the air vibrate. And another sound mingled awesomely with the reverberations of the thunder – the voice of the wind, that raced before its coming. The inky horizon was torn and convulsed in the lightning flashes; afar to sea she saw the white-capped waves racing before the wind. She heard its droning roar, increasing in volume as it swept shoreward. But as yet no wind stirred on the land. The air was hot, breathless. There was a sensation of unreality about the contrast: out there wind and thunder and chaos sweeping inland; but here stifling stillness. Somewhere below her a shutter slammed, startling in the tense silence, and a woman's voice was lifted, shrill with alarm. But most of the people of the fort seemed sleeping, unaware of the oncoming hurricane.

She realized that she still heard that mysterious droning drum-beat and she stared toward the black forest, her flesh crawling. She could see nothing, but some obscure instinct or intuition prompted her to visualize a black hideous figure squatting under black branches and enacting a nameless incantation on something that sounded like a drum—

Desperately she shook off the ghoulish conviction, and looked seaward, as a blaze of lightning fairly split the sky. Outlined against its glare she saw the masts of Zarono's ship; she saw the tents of the buccaneers on the beach, the sandy ridges of the south point and the rock cliffs of the north point as plainly as by midday sun. Louder and louder rose the roar of the wind, and now the manor was awake. Feet came pounding up the stair, and Zarono's voice yelled, edged with fright.

Doors slammed and Valenso answered him, shouting to be heard above the roar of the elements.

'Why didn't you warn me of a storm from the west?' howled the buccaneer. 'If the anchors don't hold—'

'A storm never came from the west before, at this time of year!' shrieked Valenso, rushing from his chamber in his night-shirt, his face livid and his hair standing stiffly on end. 'This is the work of—' His words were drowned as he raced madly up the ladder that led to the lookout tower, followed by the swearing buccaneer.

Belesa crouched at her window, awed and deafened. Louder and louder rose the wind, until it drowned all other sound – all except that maddening droning that now rose like an inhuman chant of triumph. It roared inshore, driving before it a foaming league-long crest of white – and then all hell and destruction was loosed on that coast. Rain fell in driving torrents, sweeping the beaches with blind frenzy. The wind hit like a thunder-clap, making the timbers of the fort quiver. The surf roared over the sands, drowning the coals of the fires the seamen had built. In the glare of lightning Belesa saw, through the curtain of the slashing rain, the tents of the buccaneers whipped to ribbons and washed away, saw the men themselves staggering toward the fort, beaten almost to the sands by the fury of torrent and blast.

And limned against the blue glare she saw Zarono's ship, ripped loose from her moorings, driven headlong against the jagged cliffs that jutted up to receive her . . .

5 A Man from the Wilderness

The storm had spent its fury. Full dawn rose in a clear blue rain-washed sky. As the sun rose in a blaze of fresh gold, bright-hued birds lifted a swelling chorus from the trees on whose broad leaves beads of water sparkled like diamonds, quivering in the gentle morning breeze.

At a small stream which wound over the sands to join the sea, hidden beyond a fringe of trees and bushes, a man bent to lave his hands and face. He performed his ablutions after the manner of his race, grunting lustily and splashing like a buffalo. But in the midst of these splashing he lifted his head suddenly, his tawny hair dripping and water running in rivulets over his brawny shoulders. He crouched in a listening attitude for a split second, then was on his feet and facing inland, sword in hand, all in one motion. And there he froze, glaring wide-mouthed.

A man as big as himself was striding toward him over the sands, making no attempt at stealth; and the pirate's eyes widened as he stared at the close-fitting silk breeches, high flaring-topped boots, wide-skirted coat and head-gear of a hundred years ago. There was a broad cutlass in the stranger's hand and unmistakable purpose in his approach.

The pirate went pale, as recognition blazed in his eyes.

'You!' he ejaculated unbelievingly. 'By Mitra! *You!*'

Oaths streamed from his lips as he heaved up his cutlass. The birds rose in flaming showers from the trees as the clang of steel interrupted their song. Blue sparks flew from the hacking blades, and the sand grated and ground under the stamping boot heels. Then the clash of steel ended in a chopping crunch, and one man went to his knees with a choking gasp. The hilt escaped his nerveless hand and he slid full-length on the sand which reddened with his blood. With a dying effort he fumbled at his girdle and drew something from it, tried to lift it to his mouth, and then stiffened convulsively and went limp.

The conqueror bent and ruthlessly tore the stiffening fingers from the object they crumpled in their desperate grasp.

Zarono and Valenso stood on the beach, staring at the driftwood their men were gathering – spars, pieces of masts, broken timbers. So savagely had the storm hammered Zarono's ship against the low cliffs that most of the salvage was match-wood. A short distance behind them stood Belesa, listening to their conversation, one arm about Tina. The girl was pale and listless, apathetic to whatever Fate held in store for her. She heard what the men said, but with little interest. She was crushed by the realization that she was but a pawn in the game, however it was to be played out – whether it was to be a wretched life dragged out on that desolate coast, or a return, effected somehow, to some civilized land.

Zarono cursed venomously, but Valenso seemed dazed.

'This is not the time of year for storms from the west,' he muttered, staring with haggard eyes at the men dragging the wreckage up on the beach. 'It was not chance that brought that storm out of the deep to splinter the ship in which I meant to escape. Escape? I am caught like a rat in a trap, as it was meant. Nay, we are all trapped rats—'

'I don't know what you're talking about,' snarled Zarono, giving a vicious yank at his mustache. 'I've been unable to get any sense out of you since that flaxen-haired slut upset you last night with her wild tale of black men coming out of the sea. But I do know that I'm not going to spend my life on this cursed coast. Ten of my men went to hell in the ship, but I've got a hundred and sixty more. You've got a hundred. There are tools in your fort, and plenty of trees in yonder forest. We'll build a ship. I'll set men to cutting down trees as soon as they get this drift dragged up out of the reach of the waves.'

'It will take months,' muttered Valenso.

'Well, is there any better way in which we could employ our time? We're here – and unless we build a ship we'll never get away. We'll have to rig up some kind of a sawmill, but I've never encountered anything yet that balked me long. I hope that storm smashed Strom to bits – the Argossean dog! While we're building the ship we'll hunt for old Tranicos' loot.'

'We will never complete your ship,' said Valenso somberly.

'You fear the Picts? We have enough men to defy them.'

'I do not speak of the Picts. I speak of a black man.'

Zarono turned on him angrily. 'Will you talk sense? Who is this accursed black man?'

'Accursed indeed,' said Valenso, staring sea-ward. 'A shadow of mine own red-stained past risen up to hound me to hell. Because of him I fled Zingara, hoping to lose my trail in the great ocean. But I should have known he would smell me out at last.'

'If such a man came ashore he must be hiding in the woods,' growled Zarono. 'We'll rake the forest and hunt him out.'

Valenso laughed harshly.

'Seek for a shadow that drifts before a cloud that hides the moon; grope in the dark for a cobra; follow a mist that steals out the swamp at midnight.'

Zarono cast him an uncertain look, obviously doubting his sanity.

'Who is this man? Have done with ambiguity.'

'The shadow of my own mad cruelty and ambition; a horror came out of the lost ages; no man of mortal flesh and blood, but—'

'Sail ho!' bawled the lookout on the north point.

Zarono wheeled and his voice slashed the wind.

'Do you know her?'

'Aye!' the reply came back faintly. 'It's the *Red Hand*!'

Zarono cursed like a wild man.

'Strom! The devil takes care of his own! How could he ride out that blow?' The buccaneer's voice rose to a yell that carried up and down the strand. 'Back to the fort, you dogs!'

Before the *Red Hand*, somewhat battered in appearance, nosed around the point, the beach was bare of human life, the palisade bristling with helmets and scarf-bound heads. The buccaneers accepted the alliance with the easy adaptability of adventurers, the henchmen with the apathy of serfs.

Zarono ground his teeth as a longboat swung leisurely in to the beach, and he sighted the tawny head of his rival in the bow. The boat grounded, and Strom strode toward the fort alone.

Some distance away he halted and shouted in a bull's bellow that carried clearly in the still morning. 'Ahoy, the fort! I want to parley!'

'Well, why in hell don't you?' snarled Zarono.

'The last time I approached under a flag of truce an arrow broke on my brisket!' roared the pirate. 'I want a promise it won't happen again!'

'You have my promise!' called Zarono sardonically.

'Damn your promise, you Zingaran dog! I want Valenso's word.'

A measure of dignity remained to the Count. There was an edge of authority to his voice as he answered: 'Advance, but keep your men back. You will not be fired upon.'

'That's enough for me,' said Strom instantly. 'Whatever a Korzetta's sins, once his word is given, you can trust him.'

He strode forward and halted under the gate, laughing at the hate-darkened visage Zarono thrust over at him.

'Well, Zarono,' he taunted, 'you are a ship shorter than you were when I last I saw you! But you Zingarans never were sailors.'

'How did you save your ship, you Messantian gutter-scum?' snarled the buccaneer.

'There's a cove some miles to the north protected by a high-ridged arm of land that broke the force of the gale,' answered Strom. 'I was anchored behind it. My anchors dragged, but they held me off the shore.'

Zarono scowled blackly. Valenso said nothing. He had not known of that cove. He had done scant exploring of his domain. Fear of the Picts and lack of curiosity had kept him and his men near the fort. The Zingarans were by nature neither explorers nor colonists.

'I come to make a trade,' said Strom, easily.

'We've naught to trade with you save sword-strokes,' growled Zarono.

'I think otherwise,' grinned Strom, thin-lipped. 'You tipped your hand when you murdered Galacus, my first mate, and robbed him. Until this morning I supposed that Valenso had Tranicos' treasure. But if either of you had it, you wouldn't have gone to the trouble of following me and killing my mate to get the map.'

'The map?' Zarono ejaculated, stiffening.

'Oh, don't dissemble!' laughed Strom, but anger blazed blue in his eyes. 'I know you have it. Picts don't wear boots!'

'But—' began the Count, nonplussed, but fell silent as Zarono nudged him.

'And if we have the map,' said Zarono, 'what have you to trade that we might require?'

'Let me come into the fort,' suggested Strom. 'There we can talk.'

He was not so obvious as to glance at the men peering at them from along the wall, but his two listeners understood. And so did the men. Strom had a ship. That fact would figure in any bargaining, or battle. But it would carry just so many, regardless of who commanded; whoever sailed away in it, there would be some left behind. A wave of tense speculation ran along the silent throng at the palisade.

'Your men will stay where they are,' warned Zarono, indicating both the boat drawn up on the beach, and the ship anchored out in the bay.

'Aye. But don't get the idea that you can seize me and hold me for a hostage!' He laughed grimly. 'I want Valenso's word that I'll be allowed to leave the fort alive and unhurt within the hour, whether we come to terms or not.'

'You have my pledge,' answered the Count.

'All right, then. Open that gate and let's talk plainly.'

The gate opened and closed, the leaders vanished from sight, and the common men of both parties resumed their silent surveillance of each other: the men on the palisade, and the men squatting beside their boat, with a broad stretch of sand between; and beyond a strip of blue water, the carack, with steel caps glinting all along her rail.

On the broad stair, above the great hall, Belesa and Tina crouched, ignored by the men below. These sat about the broad table: Valenso, Galbro, Zarono and Strom. But for them the hall was empty.

Strom gulped wine and set the empty goblet on the table. The frankness suggested by his bluff countenance was belied by the dancing lights of cruelty and treachery in his wide eyes. But he spoke bluntly enough.

'We all want the treasure old Tranicos hid somewhere near this bay,' he said abruptly. 'Each has something the others need. Valenso has laborers, supplies, and a stockade to shelter us from the Picts. You, Zarono, have my map. I have a ship.'

'What I'd like to know,' remarked Zarono, 'is this: if you've had that map all these years, why haven't you come after the loot sooner?'

'I didn't have it. It was that dog, Zingelito, who knifed the old miser in the dark and stole the map. But he had neither ship nor crew, and it took him more than a year to get them. When he did come after the treasure, the Picts prevented his landing, and his men mutinied and made him sail back to Zingara. One of them stole the map from him, and recently sold it to me.'

'That was why Zingelito recognized the bay,' muttered Valenso.

'Did that dog lead you here, Count? I might have guessed it. Where is he?'

'Doubtless in hell, since he was once a buccaneer. The Picts slew him, evidently while he was searching in the woods for the treasure.'

'Good!' approved Strom heartily. 'Well, I don't know how you knew my mate was carrying the map. I trusted him, and the men trusted him more than they did me, so I let him keep it. But this morning he wandered inland with some of the others, got separated from them, and we found him sworded to death near the beach, and the map gone. The men were ready to accuse me of killing him, but I showed the fools the tracks left by his slayer, and proved to them that my feet wouldn't fit them. And I knew it wasn't any one of the crew, because none of them wear boots that make that sort of track. And Picts don't wear boots at all. So it had to be a Zingaran.

'Well, you've got the map, but you haven't got the treasure. If you had it, you wouldn't have let me inside the stockade. I've got you penned up in this fort. You can't get out to look for the loot, and even if you did get it, you have no ship to get away in.

'Now here's my proposal: Zarono, give me the map. And you, Valenso, give me fresh meat and other supplies. My men are nigh to scurvy after the long voyage. In return I'll take you three men, the Lady Belesa and her girl, and set you ashore within reach of some Zingaran port – or I'll put Zarono ashore near some buccaneer rendezvous if he prefers, since doubtless a noose awaits him in Zingara. And to clinch the bargain I'll give each of you a handsome share in the treasure.'

The buccaneer tugged his mustache meditatively. He knew that Strom would not keep any such pact, if made. Nor did Zarono even consider agreeing to his proposal. But to refuse bluntly would be to force the issue into a clash of arms. He sought his agile brain for a plan to outwit the pirate. He wanted Strom's ship as avidly as he desired the lost treasure.

'What's to prevent us from holding you captive and forcing your men to give us your ship in exchange for you?' he asked.

Strom laughed at him.

'Do you think I'm a fool? My men have orders to heave up the anchors and sail hence if I don't reappear within the hour, or if they suspect treachery. They wouldn't give you the ship, if you skinned me alive on the beach. Besides, I have the Count's word.'

'My pledge is not straw,' said Valenso somberly. 'Have done with threats, Zarono.'

Zarono did not reply, his mind wholly absorbed in the problem of getting possession of Strom's ship; of continuing the parley without betraying the fact that he did not have the map. He wondered who in Mitra's name did have the accursed map.

'Let me take my men away with me on your ship when we sail,' he said. 'I can not desert my faithful followers—'

Strom snorted.

'Why don't you ask for my cutlass to slit my gullet with? Desert your faithful – bah! You'd desert your brother to the devil if you could gain anything by it. No! You're not going to bring enough men aboard to give you a chance to mutiny and take my ship.'

'Give us a day to think it over,' urged Zarono, fighting for time.

Strom's heavy fist banged on the table, making the wine dance in the glasses.

'No, by Mitra! Give me my answer now!'

Zarono was on his feet, his black rage submerging his craftiness.

'You Barachan dog! I'll give you your answer – in your guts—'

He tore aside his cloak, caught at his sword-hilt. Strom heaved up with a roar, his chair crashing backward to the floor. Valenso sprang up, spreading his arms between them as they faced one another across the board, jutting jaws close together, blades half drawn, faces convulsed.

'Gentlemen, have done! Zarono, he has my pledge—'

'The foul fiends gnaw your pledge!' snarled Zarono.

'Stand from between us, my Lord,' growled the pirate, his voice thick with the killing lust. 'Your word was that I should not be treacherously treated. It shall be considered no violation of your pledge for this dog and me to cross swords in equal play.'

'Well spoken, Strom!' It was a deep, powerful voice behind them, vibrant with grim amusement. All wheeled and glared, open-mouthed. Up on the stair Belesa started up with an involuntary exclamation.

A man strode out from the hangings that masked a chamber door, and advanced toward the table without haste or hesitation. Instantly he dominated the group, and all felt the situation subtly charged with a new, dynamic atmosphere.

The stranger was as tall as either of the freebooters, and more powerfully built than either, yet for all his size he moved with pantherish suppleness in his high, flaring-topped boots. His thighs were cased in close-fitting breeches of white silk, his wide-skirted sky-blue coat open to reveal an open-necked white silken shirt beneath, and the scarlet sash that girdled his waist. There were silver acorn-shaped buttons on the coat, and it was adorned with gilt-worked cuffs and pocket-flaps, and a satin collar. A lacquered hat completed a costume obsolete by nearly a hundred years. A heavy cutlass hung at the wearer's hip.

'Conan!' ejaculated both freebooters together, and Valenso and Galbro caught their breath at that name.

'Who else?' The giant strode up to the table, laughing sardonically at their amazement.

'What – what do you here?' stuttered the seneschal. 'How come you here, uninvited and unannounced?'

'I climbed the palisade on the east side while you fools were arguing at the gate,' Conan answered. 'Every man in the fort was craning his neck westward. I entered the manor while Strom was being let in at the gate. I've been in that chamber there ever since, eavesdropping.'

'I thought you were dead,' said Zarono slowly. 'Three years ago the shattered hull of your ship was sighted off a reefy coast, and you were heard of on the Main no more.'

'I didn't drown with my crew,' answered Conan. 'It'll take a bigger ocean than that one to drown me.'

Up on the stair Tina was clutching Belesa in her excitement and staring through the balustrades with all her eyes.

'Conan! My Lady, it is Conan! Look! Oh, look!'

Belesa was looking; it was like encountering a legendary character in the flesh. Who of all the sea-folk had not heard the wild, bloody tales told of Conan, the wild rover who had once been a captain of the Barachan pirates, and one of the greatest scourges of the sea? A score of ballads celebrated his ferocious and audacious exploits. The man could not be ignored; irresistibly he had stalked into the scene, to form another, dominant element in the tangled plot. And in the midst of her frightened fascination, Belesa's feminine instinct prompted the speculation as to Conan's attitude toward her – would it be like Strom's brutal indifference, or Zarono's violent desire?

Valenso was recovering from the shock of finding a stranger within his very hall. He knew Conan was a Cimmerian, born and bred in the wastes of the far north, and therefore not amenable to the physical limitations which controlled civilized men. It was not so strange that he had been able to enter the fort undetected, but Valenso flinched at the reflection that other barbarians might duplicate that feat – the dark, silent Picts, for instance.

'What do you want here?' he demanded. 'Did you come from the sea?'

'I came from the woods.' The Cimmerian jerked his head toward the east.

'You have been living with the Picts?' Valenso asked coldly.

A momentary anger flickered bluely in the giant's eyes.

'Even a Zingaran ought to know there's never been peace between Picts and Cimmerians, and never will be,' he retorted with an oath. 'Our feud with them is older than the world. If you'd said that to one of my wilder brothers, you'd have found yourself with a split head. But I've lived among you civilized men long enough to understand your ignorance and lack of common courtesy – the churlishness that demands his business of a man who appears at your door out of a thousand-mile wilderness. Never mind that.' He turned to the two freebooters who stood staring glumly at him.

'From what I overheard,' quoth he, 'I gather there is some dissension over a map!'

'That is none of your affair,' growled Strom.

'Is this it?' Conan grinned wickedly and drew from his pocket a crumpled object – a square of parchment, marked with crimson lines.

Strom stared violently, paling.

'My map!' he ejaculated. 'Where did you get it?'

'From your mate, Galacus, when I killed him,' answered Conan with grim enjoyment.

'You dog!' raved Strom, turning on Zarono. 'You never had the map! You lied—'

'I didn't say I had it,' snarled Zarono. 'You deceived yourself. Don't be a fool. Conan is alone. If he had a crew he'd have already cut our throats. We'll take the map from him—'

'You'll never touch it!' Conan laughed fiercely.

Both men sprang at him, cursing. Stepping back he crumpled the parchment and cast it into the glowing coals of the fireplace. With an incoherent bellow Strom lunged past him, to be met with a buffet under the ear that stretched him half-senseless on the floor. Zarono whipped out his sword but before he could thrust, Conan's cutlass beat it out of his hand.

Zarono staggered against the table, with all hell in his eyes. Strom dragged himself erect, his eyes glazed, blood dripping from his bruised ear. Conan leaned slightly over the table, his outstretched cutlass just touched the breast of Count Valenso.

'Don't call for your soldiers, Count,' said the Cimmerian softly. 'Not a sound out of you – or from you, either, dog-face!' His name for Galbro, who showed no intention of braving his wrath. 'The map's burned to ashes, and it'll do no good to spill blood. Sit down, all of you.'

Strom hesitated, made an abortive gesture toward his hilt, then shrugged his shoulders and sank sullenly into a chair. The others followed suit. Conan remained standing, towering over the table, while his enemies watched him with bitter eyes of hate.

'You were bargaining,' he said. 'That's all I've come to do.'

'And what have you to trade?' sneered Zarono.

'*The treasure of Tranicos!*'

'*What?*' All four men were on their feet, leaning toward him.

'Sit down!' he roared, banging his broad blade on the table. They sank back, tense and white with excitement.

He grinned in huge enjoyment of the sensation his words had caused.

'Yes! I found it before I got the map. That's why I burned the map. I don't need it. And now nobody will ever find it, unless I show him where it is.'

They stared at him with murder in their eyes.

'You're lying,' said Zarono without conviction. 'You've told us one lie already. You said you came from the woods, yet you say you haven't been living with the Picts. All men know this country is a wilderness, inhabited only by savages. The nearest outposts of civilization are the Aquilonian settlements on Thunder River, hundreds of miles to eastward.'

'That's where I came from,' replied Conan imperturbably. 'I believe I'm the first white man to cross the Pictish Wilderness. I crossed Thunder River to follow a raiding party that had been harrying the frontier. I followed them deep into the wilderness, and killed their chief, but was knocked senseless by a stone from a sling during the mêlée, and the dogs captured me alive. They were Wolfmen, but they traded me to the Eagle clan in return for a chief of theirs the Eagles had captured. The Eagles carried me nearly a hundred miles westward to burn me in their chief village, but I killed their war-chief and three or four others one night, and broke away.

'I couldn't turn back. They were behind me, and kept herding me westward. A few days ago I shook them off, and by Crom, the place where I took refuge turned out to be the treasure trove of old Tranicos! I found it all: chests of garments and weapons – that's where I got these clothes and this blade – heaps of coins and gems and gold ornaments, and in the midst of all, the jewels of Tothmekri gleaming like frozen starlight! And old Tranicos and his eleven captains sitting about an ebon table and staring at the board, as they've stared for a hundred years!'

'What?'

'Aye!' he laughed. 'Tranicos died in the midst of his treasure, and all with him! Their bodies have not rotted nor shriveled. They sit there in their high boots and skirted coats and lacquered hats, with their wineglasses in their stiff hands, just as they have sat for a century!'

'That's an unchancy thing!' muttered Strom uneasily, but Zarono snarled: 'What boots it? It's the treasure we want. Go on, Conan.'

Conan seated himself at the board, filled a goblet and quaffed it before he answered.

'The first wine I've drunk since I left Conawaga, by Crom! Those cursed Eagles hunted me so closely through the forest I had hardly time to munch the nuts and roots I found. Sometimes I caught frogs and ate them raw because I dared not light a fire.'

His impatient hearers informed him profanely that they were not interested in his adventures prior to finding the treasure.

He grinned hardly and resumed: 'Well, after I stumbled onto the trove I lay up and rested a few days, and made snares to catch rabbits, and let my wounds heal. I saw smoke against the western sky, but thought it some Pictish village on the beach. I lay close, but as it happens, the loot's hidden in a place the Picts shun. If any spied on me, they didn't show themselves.

'Last night I started westward, intending to strike the beach some miles north of the spot where I'd seen the smoke. I wasn't far from the shore when that storm hit. I took shelter under the lee of a rock and waited until it had blown itself out. Then I climbed a tree to look for Picts, and from it I saw your carack at anchor, Strom, and your men coming in to shore. I was making my way toward your camp on the beach when I met Galacus. I shoved a sword through him because there was an old feud between us. I wouldn't have known he had a map, if he hadn't tried to eat it before he died.

'I recognized it for what it was, of course, and was considering what use I could make of it, when the rest of you dogs came up and found the body. I was lying in a thicket not a dozen yards from you while you were arguing with your men over the matter. I judged the time wasn't ripe for me to show myself then!'

He laughed at the rage and chagrin displayed in Strom's face.

'Well, while I lay there, listening to your talk, I got a drift of the situation, and learned, from the things you let fall, that Zarono and Valenso were a few miles south of the beach. So when I heard you say that Zarono must have done the killing and taken the map, and that you meant to go and parley with him, seeking an opportunity to murder him and get it back—'

'Dog!' snarled Zarono. Strom was livid, but he laughed mirthlessly.

'Do you think I'd play fairly with a treacherous dog like you? – Go on, Conan.'

The Cimmerian grinned. It was evident that he was deliberately fanning the fires of hate between the two men.

'Nothing much, then. I came straight through the woods while you tacked along the coast, and raised the fort before you did. Your guess that the storm had destroyed Zarono's ship was a good one – but then, you knew the configuration of this bay.

'Well, there's the story. I have the treasure, Strom has a ship. Valenso has supplies. By Crom, Zarono, I don't see where you fit into the scheme, but to avoid strife I'll include you. My proposal is simple enough.

'We'll split the treasure four ways. Strom and I will sail away with our shares aboard the *Red Hand*. You and Valenso take yours and remain lords of the wilderness, or build a ship out of tree trunks, as you wish.'

Valenso blenched and Zarono swore, while Strom grinned quietly.

'Are you fool enough to go aboard the *Red Hand* alone with Strom?' snarled Zarono. 'He'll cut your throat before you're out of sight of land!'

Conan laughed with genuine enjoyment.

'This is like the problem of the sheep, the wolf and the cabbage,' he admitted. 'How to get them across the river without their devouring each other!'

'And that appeals to your Cimmerian sense of humor,' complained Zarono.

'I will not stay here!' cried Valenso, a wild gleam in his dark eyes. 'Treasure or no treasure, I must go!'

Conan gave him a slit-eyed glance of speculation.

'Well, then,' said he, 'how about this plan: we divide the loot as I suggested. Then Strom sails away with Zarono, Valenso, and such members of the Count's household as he may select, leaving me in command of the fort and the rest of Valenso's men, and all of Zarono's. I'll build my own ship.'

Zarono looked slightly sick.

'I have the choice of remaining here in exile, or abandoning my crew and going alone on the *Red Hand* to have my throat cut?'

Conan's laughter rang gustily through the hall, and he smote Zarono jovially on the back, ignoring the black murder in the buccaneer's glare.

'That's it, Zarono!' quoth he. 'Stay here while Strom and I sail away, or sail away with Strom, leaving your men with me.'

'I'd rather have Zarono,' said Strom frankly. 'You'd turn my own men against me, Conan, and cut my throat before I raised the Barachans.'

Sweat dripped from Zarono's livid face.

'Neither I, the Count, nor his niece will ever reach the land alive if we ship with that devil,' said he. 'You are both in my power in this hall. My men surround it. What's to prevent me cutting you both down?'

'Not a thing,' Conan admitted cheerfully. 'Except the fact that if you do Strom's men will sail away and leave you stranded on this coast where the Picts will presently cut all your throats; and the fact that with me dead you'll never find the treasure; and the fact that I'll split your skull down to your chin if you try to summon your men.'

Conan laughed as he spoke, as if at some whimsical situation, but even Belesa sensed that he meant what he said. His naked cutlass lay across his knees, and Zarono's sword was under the table, out of the buccaneer's reach. Galbro was not a fighting man, and Valenso seemed incapable of decision or action.

'Aye!' said Strom with an oath. 'You'd find the two of us no easy prey. I'm agreeable to Conan's proposal. What do you say, Valenso?'

'I must leave this coast!' whispered Valenso, staring blankly. 'I must hasten – I must go – go far – quickly!'

Strom frowned, puzzled at the Count's stranger manner and turned to Zarono, grinning wickedly: 'And you Zarono?'

'What can I say?' snarled Zarono. 'Let me take my three officers and forty men aboard the *Red Hand*, and the bargain's made.'

'The officers and thirty men!'

'Very well.'

'Done!'

There was no shaking of hands, or ceremonial drinking of wine to seal the pact. The two captains glared at each other like hungry wolves. The Count plucked his mustache with a trembling hand, rapt in his own somber thoughts. Conan stretched like a great cat, drank wine, and grinned on the assemblage, but it was the sinister grin of a stalking tiger. Belesa sensed the murderous purposes that reigned there, the treacherous intent that dominated each man's mind. Not one had any intention of keeping his part of the pact, Valenso possibly excluded. Each of the freebooters intended to possess both the ship and the entire treasure. Neither would be satisfied with less. But how? What was going on in each crafty mind? Belesa felt oppressed and stifled by the atmosphere of hatred and treachery. The Cimmerian, for all his ferocious frankness, was no less subtle than the others – and even fiercer. His domination of the situation was not physical alone, though his gigantic shoulders and massive limbs seemed too big even for the great hall. There was an iron vitality about the man that overshadowed even the hard vigor of the other freebooters.

'Lead us to the treasure!' Zarono demanded.

'Wait a bit,' answered Conan. 'We must keep our power evenly balanced, so one can't take advantage of the others. We'll work it this way: Strom's men will come ashore, all but half a dozen or so, and camp on the beach. Zarono's men will come out of the fort, and likewise camp on the strand, within easy sight of them. Then each crew can keep a check on the other, to see that nobody slips after us who go after the treasure, to ambush any of us. Those left aboard the Red Hand will take her out into the bay out of reach of either party. Valenso's men will stay in the fort, but will leave the gate open. Will you come with us, Count?'

'Go into that forest?' Valenso shuddered, and drew his cloak about his shoulders. 'Not for all the gold of Tranicos!'

'All right. It'll take about thirty men to carry the loot. We'll take fifteen from each crew and start as soon as possible.'

Belesa, keenly alert to every angle of the drama being played out beneath her, saw Zarono and Strom shoot furtive glaces at one another, then lower their gaze quickly as they lifted their glasses to hide the murky intent in their eyes. Belesa saw the fatal weakness in Conan's plan, and wondered how he could have overlooked it. Perhaps he was too arrogantly confident in his personal prowess. But she knew that he would never come out of that forest alive. Once the treasure was in their grasp, the others would form a rogues' alliance long enough to rid themselves of the man both hated. She shuddered, staring morbidly at the man she knew was doomed; strange to see that powerful fighting man sitting there, laughing and swilling wine, in full prime and power, and to know that he was already doomed to a bloody death.

The whole situation was pregnant with dark and bloody portents. Zarono would trick and kill Strom if he could, and she knew that Strom had already marked Zarono for death, and doubtless, also, her uncle and herself. If Zarono won the final battle of cruel wits, their lives were safe – but looking at the buccaneer as he sat there chewing his mustache, with all the stark evil of his nature showing naked in his dark face, she could not decide which was more abhorrent – death or Zarono.

'How far is it?' demanded Strom.

'If we start within the hour we can be back before midnight,' answered Conan. He emptied his glass, rose, adjusted his girdle, and glanced at the Count.

'Valenso,' he said, 'are you mad, to kill a Pict in his hunting paint?'

Valenso started.

'What do you mean?'

'Do you mean to say you don't know that your men killed a Pict hunter in the woods last night?'

The Count shook his head.

'None of my men was in the woods last night.'

'Well, somebody was,' grunted the Cimmerian, fumbling in a pocket. 'I saw his head nailed to a tree near the edge of the forest. He wasn't painted for war. I didn't find any boot-tracks, from which I judged that it had been nailed up there before the storm. But there were plenty of other signs – moccasin tracks on the wet ground. Picts have been there and seen that head. They were men of some other clan, or they'd have taken it down. If they happen to be at peace with the clan the dead man belonged to, they'll make tracks to his village to tell his tribe.'

'Perhaps they killed him,' suggested Valenso.

'No, they didn't. But they know who did, for the same reason that I know. This chain was knotted about the stump of the severed neck. You must have been utterly mad, to identify your handiwork like that.'

He drew forth something and tossed it on the table before the Count, who lurched up, choking, as his hand flew to his throat. It was the gold seal-chain he habitually wore about his neck.

'I recognized the Korzetta seal,' said Conan. 'The presence of that chain would tell any Pict it was the work of a foreigner.'

Valenso did not reply. He sat staring at the chain as if at a venomous serpent.

Conan scowled at him, and glanced questioningly at the others. Zarono made a quick gesture to indicate the Count was not quite right in the head.

Conan sheathed his cutlass and donned his lacquered hat.

'All right; let's go.'

The captains gulped down their wine and rose, hitching at their sword-hilts. Zarono laid a hand on Valenso's arm and shook him slightly. The Count started and stared about him, then followed the others out, like a man in a daze, the chain dangling from his fingers. But not all left the hall.

Belesa and Tina, forgotten on the stair, peeping between the balusters, saw Galbro fall behind the others, loitering until the heavy door closed after them. Then he hurried to the fireplace and raked carefully at the smoldering coals. He sank to his knees and peered closely at something for a long space. Then he straightened, and with a furtive air stole out of the hall by another door.

'What did Galbro find in the fire?' whispered Tina. Belesa shook her head, then, obeying the promptings of her curiosity, rose and went down to the empty hall. An instant later she was kneeling where the seneschal had knelt, and she saw what he had seen.

It was the charred remnant of the map Conan had thrown into the fire. It was ready to crumble at a touch, but faint lines and bits of writing were still discernible upon it. She could not read the writing, but she could trace the outlines of what seemed to be the picture of a hill or crag, surrounded by marks evidently representing dense trees. She could make nothing of it, but from Galbro's actions, she believed he recognized it as portraying some scene or topographical feature familiar to him. She knew the seneschal had penetrated inland further than any other man of the settlement.

6 The Plunder of the Dead

Belesa came down the stair and paused at the sight of Count Valenso seated at the table, turning the broken chain about in his hands. She looked at him without love, and with more than a little fear. The change that had come over him was appalling; he seemed to be locked up in a grim world all of his own, with a fear that flogged all human characteristics out of him.

The fortress stood strangely quiet in the noonday heat that had followed the storm of the dawn. Voices of people within the stockade sounded subdued, muffled. The same drowsy stillness reigned on the beach outside where the rival crews lay in armed suspicion, separated by a few hundred yards of bare sand. Far out in the bay the *Red Hand* lay at anchor with a handful of men aboard her, ready to snatch her out of reach at the slightest indication of treachery. The carack was Strom's trump card, his best guarantee against the trickery of his associates.

Conan had plotted shrewdly to eliminate the chances of an ambush in the forest by either party. But as far as Belesa could see, he had failed utterly to safeguard himself against the treachery of his companions. He had disappeared into the woods, leading the two captains and their thirty men, and the Zingaran girl was positive that she would never see him alive again.

Presently she spoke, and her voice was strained and harsh to her own ear.

'The barbarian has led the captains into the forest. When they have the gold in their hands, they'll kill him. But when they return with the treasure, what then? Are we to go aboard the ship? Can we trust Strom?'

Valenso shook his head absently.

'Strom would murder us all for our shares of the loot. But Zarono whispered his intentions to me secretly. We will not go aboard the *Red Hand* save as her masters. Zarono will see that night overtakes the treasure-party, so they are forced to camp in the forest. He will find a way to kill Strom and his men in their sleep. Then the buccaneers will come on stealthily to the beach. Just before dawn I will send some of my fishermen secretly from the fort to swim out to the ship and seize her. Strom never thought of that, neither did Conan. Zarono and his men will come out of the forest and with the buccaneers encamped on the beach, fall upon the pirates in the dark, while I lead my men-at-arms from the fort to complete the rout. Without their captain they will be demoralized, and outnumbered, fall easy prey to Zarono and me. Then we will sail in Strom's ship with all the treasure.'

'And what of me?' she asked with dry lips.

'I have promised you to Zarono,' he answered harshly. 'But for my promise he would not take us off.'

'I will never marry him,' she said helplessly.

'You will,' he responded gloomily, and without the slightest touch of sympathy. He lifted the chain so it caught the gleam of the sun, slanting through a window. 'I must have dropped it on the sand,' he muttered. '*He* has been that near – on the beach—'

'You did not drop it on the strand,' said Belesa, in a voice as devoid of mercy as his own; her soul seemed turned to stone. 'You tore it from your throat, by accident, last night in this hall, when you flogged Tina. I saw it gleaming on the floor before I left the hall.'

He looked up, his face grey with a terrible fear.

She laughed bitterly, sensing the mute question in his dilated eyes.

'Yes! the black man! He was here! In this hall! He must have found the chain on the floor. The guardsmen did not see him. But he was at your door last night. I saw him, padding along the upper hallway.'

For an instant she thought he would drop dead of sheer terror. He sank back in his chair, the chain slipping from his nerveless fingers and clinking on the table.

'In the manor!' he whispered. 'I thought bolts and bars and armed guards could keep him out, fool that I was! I can no more guard against him than I can escape him! At my door! At my door!' The thought overwhelmed him with horror. 'Why did he not enter?' he shrieked, tearing at the lace upon his collar as though it strangled him. 'Why did he not end it? I have dreamed of waking in my darkened chamber to see him squatting above me and the blue hell-fire playing about his horned head! Why—'

The paroxysm passed, leaving him faint and trembling.

'I understand!' he panted. 'He is playing with me, as a cat with a mouse. To have slain me last night in my chamber were too easy, too merciful. So he destroyed the ship in which I might have escaped him, and he slew that wretched Pict and left my chain upon him, so that the savages might believe I had slain him – they have seen that chain upon my neck many a time.

'But why? What subtle deviltry has he in mind, what devious purpose no human mind can grasp or understand?'

'Who is this black man?' asked Belesa, chill fear crawling along her spine.

'A demon loosed by my greed and lust to plague me throughout eternity!' he whispered. He spread his long thin fingers on the table before him, and stared at her with hollow, weirdly luminous eyes that seemed to see her not at all, but to look through her and far beyond to some dim doom.

'In my youth I had an enemy at court,' he said, as if speaking more to himself than to her. 'A powerful man who stood between me and my ambition. In my lust for wealth and power I sought aid from the people of the black arts – a black magician, who, at my desire, raised up a fiend from the outer gulfs of existence and clothed it in the form of a man. It crushed and slew my enemy; I grew great and wealthy and none could stand before me. But I thought to cheat my fiend of the price a mortal must pay who calls *the black folk* to do his bidding.

'By his grim arts the magician tricked the soulless waif of darkness and bound him in hell where he howled in vain – I supposed for eternity. But because the sorcerer had given the fiend the form of a man, he could never break the link that bound it to the material world; never completely close the cosmic corridors by which it had gained access to this planet.

'A year ago in Kordava word came to me that the magician, now an ancient man, had been slain in his castle, with marks of demon fingers on his throat. Then I knew that the black one had escaped from the hell where the magician had bound him, and that he would seek vengeance upon me. One night I saw his demon face leering at me from the shadows in my castle hall—

'It was not his material body, but his spirit sent to plague me – his spirit which could not follow me over the windy waters. Before he could reach Kordava in the flesh, I sailed to put broad seas between me and him. He has his limitations. To follow me across the seas he must remain in his man-like body of flesh. But that flesh is not human flesh. He can be slain, I think, by fire, though the magician, having raised him up, was powerless to slay him – such are the limits set upon the powers of sorcerers.

'But the black one is too crafty to be trapped or slain. When he hides himself no man can find him. He steals like a shadow through the night, making naught of bolts and bars. He blinds the eyes of guardsmen with sleep. He can raise storms and command the serpents of the deep, and the fiends of the night. I hoped to drown my trail in the blue rolling wastes – but he has tracked me down to claim his grim forfeit.'

The weird eyes lit palely as he gazed beyond the tapestried walls to far, invisible horizons.

'I'll trick him yet,' he whispered. 'Let him delay to strike this night – dawn will find me with a ship under my heels and again I will cast an ocean between me and his vengeance.'

'Hell's fire!'

Conan stopped short, glaring upward. Behind him the seamen halted – two compact clumps of them, bows in their hands, and suspicion in their attitude. They were following an old path made by Pictish hunters which led due east, and though they had progressed only some thirty yards, the beach was no longer visible.

'What is it?' demanded Strom suspiciously. 'What are you stopping for?'

'Are you blind? Look there!'

From the thick limb of a tree that overhung the trail a head grinned down at them – a dark painted face, framed in thick black hair, in which a toucan feather drooped over the left ear.

'I took that head down and hid it in the bushes,' growled Conan, scanning the woods about them narrowly. 'What fool could have stuck it back up there? It looks as if somebody was trying his damnedest to bring the Picts down on the settlement.'

Men glanced at each other darkly, a new element of suspicion added to the already seething caldron.

Conan climbed the tree, secured the head and carried it into the bushes, where he tossed it into a stream and saw it sink.

'The Picts whose tracks are about this tree weren't Toucans,' he growled, returning through the thicket. 'I've sailed these coasts enough to know something about the sea-land tribes. If I read the prints of their moccasins right, they were Cormorants. I hope they're having a war with the Toucans. If they're at peace, they'll head straight for the Toucan village, and there'll be hell to pay. I don't know how far away that village is – but as soon as they learn of this murder, they'll come through the forest like starving wolves. That's the worst insult possible to a Pict – kill a man not in war-paint and stick his head up in a tree for the vultures to eat. Damn peculiar things going on along this coast. But that's always the way when civilized men come into the wilderness. They're all crazy as hell. Come on.'

Men loosened blades in their scabbards and shafts in their quivers as they strode deeper into the forest. Men of the sea, accustomed to the rolling expanses of grey water, they were ill at ease with the green mysterious walls of trees and vines hemming them in. The path wound and twisted until most of them quickly lost their sense of direction, and did not even know in which direction the beach lay.

Conan was uneasy for another reason. He kept scanning the trail, and finally grunted: 'Somebody's passed along here recently – not more than an hour ahead of us. Somebody in boots, with no woods-craft. Was he the fool who found that Pict's head and stuck it back up in that tree? No, it couldn't have been him. I didn't find his tracks under the tree. But who was it? I didn't find any tracks there, except those of the Picts I'd seen already. And who's this fellow hurrying ahead of us? Did either of you bastards send a man ahead of us for any reason?'

Both Strom and Zarono loudly disclaimed any such act, glaring at each other with mutual disbelief. Neither man could see the signs Conan pointed out; the faint prints which he saw on the grassless, hard-beaten trail were invisible to their untrained eyes.

Conan quickened his pace and they hurried after him, fresh coals of suspicion added to the smoldering fire of distrust. Presently the path veered northward, and Conan left it, and began threading his way through the dense trees in a southeasterly direction. Strom stole an uneasy glance at Zarono. This might force a change in their plans. Within a few hundred feet from the trail both were hopelessly lost, and convinced of their inability to find their way back to the path. They were shaken by the fear that, after all, the Cimmerian had a force at his command, and was leading them into an ambush.

This suspicion grew as they advanced, and had almost reached panic proportions when they emerged from the thick woods and saw just ahead of them a gaunt crag that jutted up from the forest floor. A dim path leading out of the woods from the east ran among a cluster of boulders and wound up the crag on a ladder of stony shelves to a flat ledge near the summit.

Conan halted, a bizarre figure in his piratical finery.

'That trail is the one I followed, running from the Eagle-Picts,' he said. 'It leads up to a cave behind that ledge. In that cave are the bodies of Tranicos and his captains, and the treasure he plundered from Tothmekri. But a word before we go up after it: if you kill me here, you'll never find your way back to the trail we followed from the beach. I know you sea-faring men. You're helpless in the deep woods. Of course the beach lies due west, but if you have to make your way through the tangled woods, burdened with the plunder, it'll take you not hours, but days. And I don't think these woods will be very safe for white men, when the Toucans learn about their hunter.' He laughed at the ghastly, mirthless smiles with which they greeted his recognition of their intentions regarding him. And he also comprehended the thought that sprang in the mind of each: let the barbarian secure the loot for them, and lead them back to the beach-trail before they killed him.

'All of you stay here except Strom and Zarono,' said Conan. 'We three are enough to pack the treasure down from the cave.'

Strom grinned mirthlessly.

'Go up there alone with you and Zarono? Do you take me for a fool? One man at least comes with me!' And he designated his boatswain, a brawny, hard-faced giant, naked to his broad leather belt, with gold hoops in his ears, and a crimson scarf knotted about his head.

'And my executioner comes with me!' growled Zarono. He beckoned to a lean sea-thief with a face like a parchment-covered skull, who carried a two-handed scimitar naked over his bony shoulder.

Conan shrugged his shoulders. 'Very well. Follow me.'

They were close on his heels as he strode up the winding path and mounted the ledge. They crowded him close as he passed through the cleft in the wall behind it, and their breath sucked greedily between their teeth as he called their attention to the iron-bound chests on either side of the short tunnel-like cavern.

'A rich cargo there,' he said carelessly. 'Silks, laces, garments, ornaments, weapons – the loot of the southern seas. But the real treasure lies beyond that door.'

The massive door stood partly open. Conan frowned. He remembered closing that door before he left the cavern. But he said nothing of the matter to his eager companions as he drew aside to let them look through.

They looked into a wide cavern, lit by a strange blue glow that glimmered through a smoky mist-like haze. A great ebon table stood in the midst of the cavern, and in a carved chair with a high back and broad arms, that might once have stood in the castle of some Zingaran baron, sat a giant figure, fabulous and fantastic – there sat Bloody Tranicos, his great head sunk on his bosom, one brawny hand still gripping a jeweled goblet in which wine still sparkled; Tranicos, in his lacquered hat, his gilt-embroidered coat with jeweled buttons that winked in the blue flame, his flaring boots and gold-worked baldric that upheld a jewel-hilted sword in a golden sheath.

And ranging the board, each with his chin resting on his lace-bedecked crest, sat the eleven captains. The blue fire played weirdly on them and on their giant admiral, as it flowed from the enormous jewel on the tiny ivory pedestal, striking glints of frozen fire from the heaps of fantastically cut gems which shone before the place of Tranicos – the plunder of Khemi, the jewels of Tothmekri! The stones whose value was greater than the value of all the rest of the known jewels in the world put together!

The faces of Zarono and Strom showed pallid in the blue glow; over their shoulders their men gaped stupidly.

'Go in and take them,' invited Conan, drawing aside, and Zarono and Strom crowded avidly past him, jostling one another in their haste. Their followers were treading on their heels. Zarono kicked the door wide open – and halted with one foot on the threshold at the sight of a figure on the floor, previously hidden from view by the partly-closed door. It was a man, prone and contorted, head drawn back between his shoulders, white face twisted in a grin of mortal agony, gripping his own throat with clawed fingers.

'Galbro!' ejaculated Zarono. 'Dead! What—' With sudden suspicion he thrust his head over the threshold, into the bluish mist that filled the inner cavern. And he screamed, chokingly: 'There is death in the smoke!'

Even as he screamed, Conan hurled his weight against the four men bunched in the doorway, sending them staggering – but not headlong into the mist-filled cavern as he had planned. They were recoiling at the sight of the dead man and the realization of the trap, and his violent push, while it threw them off their feet, yet failed of the result he desired. Strom and Zarono sprawled half over the threshold on their knees, the boatswain tumbling over their legs, and the executioner caromed against the wall. Before Conan could follow up his ruthless intention of kicking the fallen men into the cavern and holding the door against them until the poisonous mist did its deadly work, he had to turn and defend himself against the frothing onslaught of the executioner who was the first to regain his balance and his wits.

The buccaneer missed a tremendous swipe with his headsman's sword as the Cimmerian ducked, and the great blade banged against the stone wall, spattering blue sparks. The next instant his skull-faced head rolled on the cavern-floor under the bite of Conan's cutlass.

In the split seconds this swift action consumed, the boatswain regained his feet and fell on the Cimmerian raining blows with a cutlass that would have overwhelmed a lesser man. Cutlass met cutlass with a ring of steel that was deafening in the narrow cavern. The two captains rolled back across the threshold, gagging and gasping, purple in the face and too near strangled to shout, and Conan redoubled his efforts, in an endeavor to dispose of his antagonist and cut down his rivals before they could recover from the effects of the poison. The boatswain dripped blood at each step, as he was driven back before the ferocious onslaught, and he began desperately to bellow for his companions. But before Conan could deal the finishing stroke the two chiefs, gasping but murderous, came at him with swords in their hands, croaking for their men.

The Cimmerian bounded back and leaped out onto the ledge. He felt himself a match for all three men, though each was a famed swordsman, but he did not wish to be trapped by the crews which would come charging up the path at the sound of the battle.

These were not coming with as much celerity as he expected, however. They were bewildered at the sounds and muffled shouts issuing from the cavern above them but no man dared start up the path for fear of a sword in the back. Each band faced the other tensely, grasping their weapons but incapable of decision, and when they saw the Cimmerian bound out on the ledge, they still hesitated. While they stood with their arrows nocked he ran up the ladder of handholds niched in the rock near the cleft, and threw himself prone on the summit of the crag, out of their sight.

The captains stormed out on the ledge, raving and brandishing their swords, and their men, seeing their leaders were not at sword-strokes, ceased menacing each other, and gaped bewilderedly.

'Dog!' screamed Zarono. 'You planned to poison us! Traitor!'

Conan mocked them from above.

'Well, what did you expect? You two were planning to cut my throat as soon as I got the plunder for you. If it hadn't been for that fool Galbro I'd have trapped the four of you, and explained to your men how you rushed in heedless to your doom.'

'And with us both dead, you'd have taken my ship, and all the loot too!' frothed Strom.

'Aye! And the pick of each crew! I've been wanting to get back on the Main for months, and this was a good opportunity!

'It was Galbro's foot-prints I saw on the trail. I wonder how the fool learned of this cave, or how he expected to lug away the loot by himself.'

'But for the sight of his body we'd have walked into that death-trap,' muttered Zarono, his swarthy face still ashy. 'That blue smoke was like unseen fingers crushing my throat.'

'Well, what are you going to do?' their unseen tormentor yelled sardonically.

'What *are* we to do?' Zarono asked Strom. 'The treasure-cavern is filled with that poisonous mist, though for some reason it does not flow across the threshold.'

'You can't get the treasure,' Conan assured them with satisfaction from his aerie. 'That smoke will strangle you. It nearly got me, when I stepped in there. Listen, and I'll tell you a tale the Picts tell in their huts when the fires burn low! Once, long ago, twelve strange men came out of the sea, and found a cave and heaped it with gold and and jewels; but a Pictish *shaman* made magic and the earth shook, and smoke came out of the earth and strangled them where they sat at wine. The smoke, which was the smoke of hell's fire, was confined within the cavern by the magic of the wizard. The tale was told from tribe to tribe, and all the clans shun the accursed spot.

'When I crawled in there to escape the Eagle-Picts, I realized that the old legend was true, and referred to old Tranicos and his men. An earthquake cracked the rock floor of the cavern while he and his captains sat at wine, and let the mist out of the depths of the earth – doubtless out of hell, as the Picts say. Death guards old Tranicos' treasure!'

'Bring up the men!' frothed Strom. 'We'll climb up and hew him down!'

'Don't be a fool,' snarled Zarono. 'Do you think any man on earth could climb those hand-holds in the teeth of his sword? We'll have the men up here, right enough, to feather him with shafts if he dares show himself. But we'll get those gems yet. He had some plan of obtaining the loot, or he wouldn't have brought thirty men to bear it back. If he could get it, so can we. We'll bend a cutlass-blade to make a hook, tie it to a rope and cast it about the leg of that table, then drag it to the door.'

'Well thought, Zarono!' came down Conan's mocking voice. 'Exactly what I had in mind. But how will you find your way back to the beach-path? It'll be dark long before you reach the beach, if you have to feel your way through the woods, and I'll follow you and kill you one by one in the dark.'

'It's no empty boast,' muttered Strom. 'He can move and strike in the dark as subtly and silently as a ghost. If he hunts us back through the forest, few of us will live to see the beach.'

'Then we'll kill him here,' gritted Zarono. 'Some of us will shoot at him while the rest climb the crag. If he is not struck by arrows, some of us will reach him with our swords. Listen! Why does he laugh?'

'To hear dead men making plots,' came Conan's grimly amused voice.

'Heed him not,' scowled Zarono, and lifting his voice, shouted for the men below to join him and Strom on the ledge.

The sailors started up the slanting trail, and one started to shout a question. Simultaneously there sounded a hum like that of an angry bee, ending in a sharp thud. The buccaneer gasped and blood gushed from his open mouth. He sank to his knees, clutching the black shaft that quivered in his breast. A yell of alarm went up from his companions.

'What's the matter?' shouted Strom.

'*Picts!*' bawled a pirate, lifting his bow and loosing blindly. At his side a man moaned and went down with an arrow through his throat.

'Take cover, you fools!' shrieked Zarono. From his vantage-point he glimpsed painted figures moving in the bushes. One of the men on the winding path fell back dying. The rest scrambled hastily down among the rocks about the foot of the crag. They took cover clumsily, not used to this kind of fighting. Arrows flickered from bushes, splintering on the boulders. The men on the ledge lay prone at full length.

'We're trapped!' Strom's face was pale. Bold enough with a deck under his feet, this silent, savage warfare shook his ruthless nerves.

'Conan said they feared this crag,' said Zarono. 'When night falls the men must climb up here. We'll hold the crag. The Picts won't rush us.'

'Aye!' mocked Conan above them. 'They won't climb the crag to get at you, that's true. They'll merely surround it and keep you here until you all die of thirst and starvation.'

'He speaks truth,' said Zarono helplessly. 'What shall we do?'

'Make a truce with him,' muttered Strom. 'If any man can get us out of this jam, he can. Time enough to cut his throat later.' Lifting his voice he called: 'Conan, let's forget our feud for the time being. You're in this fix as much as we are. Come down and help us out of it.'

'How do you figure that?' retorted the Cimmerian. 'I have but to wait until dark, climb down the other side of this crag and melt into the forest. I can crawl through the line the Picts have thrown around this hill, and return to the fort to report you all slain by the savages – which will shortly be truth!'

Zarono and Strom stared at each other in pallid silence.

'But I'm not going to do that!' Conan roared. 'Not because I have any love for you dogs, but because a white man doesn't leave white men, even his enemies, to be butchered by Picts.'

The Cimmerian's tousled black head appeared over the crest of the crag.

'Now listen closely: that's only a small band down there. I saw them sneaking through the brush when I laughed, a while ago. Anyway, if there had been many of them, every man at the foot of the crag would be dead already. I think that's a band of fleet-footed young men sent ahead of the main war-party to cut us off from the beach. I'm certain a big war-band is heading in our direction from somewhere.

'They've thrown a cordon around the west side of the crag, but I don't think there are any on the east side. I'm going down on that side and get in the forest and work around behind them. Meanwhile, you crawl down the path and join your men among the rocks. Tell them to sling their bows and draw their swords. When you hear me yell, rush the trees on the west side of the clearing.'

'What of the treasure?'

'To hell with the treasure! We'll be lucky if we get out of here with our heads on our shoulders.'

The black-maned head vanished. They listened for sounds to indicate that Conan had crawled to the almost sheer eastern wall and was working his way down, but they heard nothing. Nor was there any sound in the forest. No more arrows broke against the rocks where the sailors were hidden. But all knew that fierce black eyes were watching with murderous patience. Gingerly Strom, Zarono and the boatswain started down the winding path. They were halfway down when the black shafts began to whisper around them. The boatswain groaned and toppled limply down the slope, shot through the heart. Arrows shivered on the helmets and breastplates of the chiefs as they tumbled in frantic haste down the steep trail. They reached the foot in a scrambling rush and lay panting among the boulders, swearing breathlessly.

'Is this more of Conan's trickery?' wondered Zarono profanely.

'We can trust him in this matter,' asserted Strom. 'These barbarians live by their own particular code of honor, and Conan would never desert men of his own complexion to be slaughtered by people of another race. He'll help us against the Picts, even though he plans to murder us himself – *hark!*'

A blood-freezing yell knifed the silence. It came from the woods to the west, and simultaneously an object arched out of the trees, struck the ground and rolled bouncingly towards the rocks – a severed human head, the hideously painted face frozen in a snarl of death.

'Conan's signal!' roared Strom, and the desperate freebooters rose like a wave from the rocks and rushed headlong toward the woods.

Arrows whirred out of the bushes, but their flight was hurried and erratic, only three men fell. Then the wild men of the sea plunged through the fringe of foliage and fell on the naked painted figures that rose out of the gloom before them. There was a murderous instant of panting, ferocious effort, hand-to-hand, cutlasses beating down war-axes, booted feet trampling naked bodies, and then bare feet were rattling through the bushes in headlong flight as the survivors of that brief carnage quit the fray, leaving seven still, painted figures stretched on the blood-stained leaves that littered the earth. Further back in the thickets sounded a thrashing and heaving, and then it ceased and Conan strode into view, his lacquered hat gone, his coat torn, his cutlass dripping in his hand.

'What now?' panted Zarono. He knew the charge had succeeded only because Conan's unexpected attack on the rear of the Picts had demoralized the painted men, and prevented them from falling back before the rush. But he exploded into curses as Conan passed his cutlass through a buccaneer who writhed on the ground with a shattered hip.

'We can't carry him with us,' grunted Conan. 'It wouldn't be any kindness to leave him to be taken alive by the Picts. Come on!'

They crowded close at his heels as he trotted through the trees. Alone they would have sweated and blundered among the thickets for hours before they found the beach-trail – if they had ever found it. The Cimmerian led them as unerringly as if he had been following a blazed path, and the rovers shouted with hysterical relief as they burst suddenly upon the trail that ran westward.

'Fool!' Conan clapped a hand on the shoulder of a pirate who started to break into a run, and hurled him back among his companions. 'You'll burst your heart and fall within a thousand yards. We're miles from the beach. Take an easy gait. We may have to sprint the last mile. Save some of your wind for it. Come on, now.'

He set off down the trail at a steady jog-trot; the seamen followed him, suiting their pace to his.

The sun was touching the waves of the western ocean. Tina stood at the window from which Belesa had watched the storm.

'The setting sun turns the ocean to blood,' she said. 'The carack's sail is a white fleck on the crimson waters. The woods are already darkened with clustering shadows.'

'What of the seamen on the beach?' asked Belesa languidly. She reclined on a couch, her eyes closed, her hands clasped behind her head.

'Both camps are preparing their supper,' said Tina. 'They gather driftwood and build fires. I can hear them shouting to one another – *what is that?*'

The sudden tenseness in the girl's tone brought Belesa upright on the couch. Tina grasped the window-sill, her face white.

'Listen! A howling, far off, like many wolves!'

'Wolves?' Belesa sprang up, fear clutching her heart. 'Wolves do not hunt in packs at this time of the year—'

'Oh, look!' shrilled the girl, pointing. 'Men are running out of the forest!'

In an instant Belesa was beside her, staring wide-eyed at the figures, small in the distance, streaming out of the woods.

'The sailors!' she gasped. 'Empty-handed! I see Zarono – Strom—'

'Where is Conan?' whispered the girl.

Belesa shook her head.

'Listen! Oh, listen!' whimpered the child, clinging to her. 'The Picts!'

All in the fort could hear it now – a vast ululation of mad exultation and blood-lust, from the depths of the dark forest.

That sound spurred on the panting men reeling toward the palisade.

'Hasten!' gasped Strom, his face a drawn mask of exhausted effort. 'They are almost at our heels. My ship—'

'She is too far out for us to reach,' panted Zarono. 'Make for the stockade. See, the men camped on the beach have seen us!' He waved his arms in breathless pantomime, but the men on the strand understood, and they recognized the significance of that wild howling, rising to a triumphant crescendo. The sailors abandoned their fires and cooking-pots and fled for the stockade gate. They were pouring through it as the fugitives from the forest rounded the south angle and reeled into the gate, a heaving, frantic mob, half-dead from exhaustion. The gate was slammed with frenzied haste, and sailors began to climb the firing-ledge, to join the men-at-arms already there.

Belesa confronted Zarono.

'Where is Conan?'

The buccaneer jerked a thumb toward the blackening woods; his chest heaved; sweat poured down his face. 'Their scouts were at our heels before we gained the beach. He paused to slay a few and give us time to get away.'

He staggered away to take his place on the firing-ledge, whither Strom had already mounted. Valenso stood there, a somber, cloak-wrapped figure, strangely silent and aloof. He was like a man bewitched.

'Look!' yelped a pirate, above the deafening howling of the yet unseen horde.

A man emerged from the forest and raced fleetly across the open belt.

'Conan!'

Zarono grinned wolfishly.

'We're safe in the stockade; we know where the treasure is. No reason why we shouldn't feather him with arrows now.'

'Nay!' Strom caught his arm. 'We'll need his sword! Look!'

Behind the fleet-footed Cimmerian a wild horde burst from the forest, howling as they ran – naked Picts, hundreds and hundreds of them. Their arrows rained about the Cimmerian. A few strides more and Conan reached the eastern wall of the stockade, bounded high, seized the points of the logs and heaved himself up and over, his cutlass in his teeth. Arrows thudded venomously into the logs where his body had just been. His resplendent coat was gone, his white silk shirt torn and blood-stained.

'Stop them!' he roared as his feet hit the ground inside. 'If they get on the wall, we're done for!'

Pirates, buccaneers and men-at-arms responded instantly, and a storm of arrows and quarrels tore into the oncoming horde.

Conan saw Belesa, with Tina clinging to her hand, and his language was picturesque.

'Get into the manor,' he commanded in conclusion. 'Their shafts will arch over the wall – what did I tell you?' As a black shaft cut into the earth at Belesa's feet and quivered like a serpent-head, Conan caught up a longbow and leaped to the firing-ledge. 'Some of you fellows prepare torches!' he roared, above the rising clamor of the battle. 'We can't fight them in the dark!'

The sun had sunk in a welter of blood; out in the bay the men aboard the carack had cut the anchor chain and the *Red Hand* was rapidly receding on the crimson horizon.

7 Men of the Woods

Night had fallen, but torches streamed across the strand, casting the mad scene into lurid revealment. Naked men in paint swarmed the beach; like waves they came against the palisade, bared teeth and blazing eyes gleaming in the glare of the torches thrust over the wall. Toucan feathers waved in black manes, and the feathers of the cormorant and the sea-falcon. A few warriors, the wildest and most barbaric of them all, wore shark's teeth woven in their tangled locks. The sea-land tribes had gathered from up and down the coast in all directions to rid their country of the white-skinned invaders.

They surged against the palisade, driving a storm of arrows before them, fighting into the teeth of the shafts and bolts that tore into their masses from the stockade. Sometimes they came so close to the wall they were hewing at the gate with their war-axes and thrusting their spears through the loop-holes. But each time the tide ebbed back without flowing over the palisade, leaving its drift of dead. At this kind of fighting the freebooters of the sea were at their stoutest; their arrows and bolts tore holes in the charging horde, their cutlasses hewed the wild men from the palisades they strove to scale.

Yet again and again the men of the woods returned to the onslaught with all the stubborn ferocity that had been roused in their fierce hearts.

'They are like mad dogs!' gasped Zarono, hacking downward at the dark hands that grasped at the palisade points, the dark faces that snarled up at him.

'If we can hold the fort until dawn they'll lose heart,' grunted Conan, splitting a feathered skull with professional precision. 'They won't maintain a long siege. Look, they're falling back.'

The charge rolled back and the men on the wall shook the sweat out of their eyes, counted their dead and took a fresh grasp on the blood-slippery hilts of their swords. Like blood-hungry wolves, grudgingly driven from a cornered prey, the Picts skulked back beyond the ring of torches. Only the bodies of the slain lay before the palisade.

'Have they gone?' Strom shook back his wet, tawny locks. The cutlass in his fist was notched and red, his brawny bare arm was splashed with blood.

'They're still out there,' Conan nodded toward the outer darkness which ringed the circle of torches, made more intense by their light. He glimpsed movements in the shadows; glitter of eyes and the dull sheen of steel.

'They've drawn off for a bit, though,' he said. 'Put sentries on the wall, and let the rest drink and eat. It's past midnight. We've been fighting for hours without much interval.'

The chiefs clambered down from the ledges, calling their men from the walls. A sentry was posted in the middle of each wall, east, west, north and south, and a clump of men-at-arms were left at the gate. The Picts, to reach the wall, would have to charge across a wide, torchlit space, and the defenders could resume their places long before the attackers could reach the palisade.

'Where's Valenso?' demanded Conan, gnawing a huge beef-bone as he stood beside the fire the men had built in the center of the compound. Pirates, buccaneers and henchmen mingled with each other, wolfing the meat and ale the women brought them, and allowing their wounds to be bandaged.

'He disappeared an hour ago,' grunted Strom. 'He was fighting on the wall beside me, when suddenly he stopped short and glared out into the darkness as if he saw a ghost. "Look!" he croaked. "The black devil! I see him! Out there in the night!" Well, I could swear I saw a figure moving among the shadows that was too tall for a Pict. But it was just a glimpse and it was gone. But Valenso jumped down from the firing-ledge and staggered into the manor like a man with a mortal wound. I haven't seen him since.'

'He probably saw a forest-devil,' said Conan tranquilly. 'The Picts say this coast is lousy with them. What I'm more afraid of is fire-arrows. The Picts are likely to start shooting them at any time. What's that? It sounded like a cry for help?'

When the lull came in the fighting, Belesa and Tina had crept to their window, from which they had been driven by the danger of flying arrows. Silently they watched the men gather about the fire.

'There are not enough men on the stockade,' said Tina.

In spite of her nausea at the sight of the corpses sprawled about the palisade, Belesa was forced to laugh.

'Do you think you know more about wars and sieges than the free-booters?' she chided gently.

'There should be more men on the walls,' insisted the child, shivering. 'Suppose the black man came back?'

Belesa shuddered at the thought.

'I am afraid,' murmured Tina. 'I hope Strom and Zarono are killed.'

'And not Conan?' asked Belesa curiously.

'Conan would not harm us,' said the child, confidently. 'He lives up to his barbaric code of honor, but they are men who have lost all honor.'

'You are wise beyond your years, Tina,' said Belesa, with the vague uneasiness the precocity of the girl frequently roused in her.

'Look!' Tina stiffened. 'The sentry is gone from the south wall! I saw him on the ledge a moment ago; now he has vanished.'

From their window the palisade points of the south wall were just visible over the slanting roofs of a row of huts which paralleled that wall almost its entire length. A sort of open-topped corridor, three or four yards wide, was framed by the stockade and the back of the huts, which were built in a solid row. These huts were occupied by the serfs.

'Where could the sentry have gone?' whispered Tina uneasily.

Belesa was watching one end of the hut-row which was not far from a side door of the manor. She could have sworn she saw a shadowy figure glide from behind the huts and disappear at the door. Was that the vanished sentry? Why had he left the wall, and why should he steal so subtly into the manor? She did not believe it was the sentry she had seen, and a nameless fear congealed her blood.

'Where is the Count, Tina?' she asked.

'In the great hall, my Lady. He sits alone at the table, wrapped in his cloak and drinking wine, with a face gray as death.'

'Go and tell him what we have seen. I will keep watch from this window, lest the Picts steal to the unguarded wall.'

Tina scampered away. Belesa heard her slippered feet pattering along the corridor, receding down the stair. Then abruptly, terribly, there rang out a scream of such poignant fear that Belesa's heart almost stopped with the shock of it. She was out of the chamber and flying down the corridor before she was aware that her limbs were in motion. She ran down the stair – and halted as if turned to stone.

She did not scream as Tina had screamed. She was incapable of sound or motion. She saw Tina, was aware of the reality of small hands grasping her frantically. But these were the only sane realities in a scene of black nightmare and lunacy and death, dominated by the monstrous, anthropomorphic shadow which spread awful arms against a lurid, hell-fire glare.

Out in the stockade Strom shook his head at Conan's question.

'I heard nothing.'

'I did!' Conan's wild instincts were roused; he was tensed, his eyes blazing. 'It came from the south wall, behind those huts!'

Drawing his cutlass he strode toward the palisade. From the compound the wall on the south and the sentry posted there were not visible, being hidden behind the huts. Strom followed, impressed by the Cimmerian's manner.

At the mouth of the open space between the huts and wall Conan halted, warily. The space was dimly lighted by torches flaring at either corner of the stockade. And about mid-way of that natural corridor a crumpled shape sprawled on the ground.

'Bracus!' swore Strom, running forward and dropping on one knee beside the figure. 'By Mitra, his throat's been cut from ear to ear!'

Conan swept the space with a quick glance, finding it empty save for himself, Strom and the dead man. He peered through a loop-hole. No living man moved within the ring of torch-light outside the fort.

'Who could have done this?' he wondered.

'Zarono!' Strom sprang up, spitting fury like a wildcat, his hair bristling, his face convulsed. 'He has set his thieves to stabbing my men in the back! He plans to wipe me out by treachery! Devils! I am leagued within and without!'

'Wait!' Conan reached a restraining hand. 'I don't believe Zarono—'

But the maddened pirate jerked away and rushed around the end of the hut-row, breathing blasphemies. Conan ran after him, swearing. Strom made straight toward the fire by which Zarono's tall lean form was visible as the buccaneer chief quaffed a jack of ale.

His amazement was supreme when the jack was dashed violently from his hand, spattering his breastplate with foam, and he was jerked around to confront the passion-distorted face of the pirate captain.

'You murdering dog!' roared Strom. 'Will you slay my men behind my back while they fight for your filthy hide as well as for mine?'

Conan was hurrying toward them and on all sides men ceased eating and drinking to stare in amazement.

'What do you mean?' sputtered Zarono.

'You've set your men to stabbing mine at their posts!' screamed the maddened Barachan.

'You lie!' Smoldering hate burst into sudden flame.

With an incoherent howl Strom heaved up his cutlass and cut at the buccaneer's head. Zarono caught the blow on his armored left arm and sparks flew as he staggered back, ripping out his own sword.

In an instant the captains were fighting like madmen, their blades flaming and flashing in the firelight. Their crews reacted instantly and blindly. A deep roar went up as pirates and buccaneers drew their swords and fell upon each other. The men left on the walls abandoned their posts and leaped down into the stockade, blades in hand. In an instant the compound was a battle-ground, where knotting, writhing groups of men smote and slew in a blind frenzy. Some of the men-at-arms and serfs were drawn into the mêlée, and the soldiers at the gate turned and stared down in amazement, forgetting the enemy which lurked outside.

It had all happened so quickly – smoldering passions exploding into sudden battle – that men were fighting all over the compound before Conan could reach the maddened chiefs. Ignoring their swords he tore them apart with such violence that they staggered backward, and Zarono tripped and fell headlong.

'You cursed fools, will you throw away all our lives?'

Strom was frothing mad and Zarono was bawling for assistance. A buccaneer ran at Conan from behind and cut at his head. The Cimmerian half turned and caught his arm, checking the stroke in mid-air.

'Look, you fools!' he roared, pointing with his sword. Something in his tone caught the attention of the battle-crazed mob; men froze in their places, with lifted swords, Zarono on one knee, and twisted their heads to stare. Conan was pointing at a soldier on the firing-ledge. The man was reeling, arms clawing the air, choking as he tried to shout. Suddenly he pitched headlong to the ground and all saw the black arrow standing up between his shoulders.

A cry of alarm rose from the compound. On the heels of the shout came a clamor of blood-freezing screams, the shattering impact of axes on the gate. Flaming arrows arched over the wall and stuck in logs, and thin wisps of blue smoke curled upward. Then from behind the huts that ranged the south wall came swift and furtive figures racing across the compound.

'The Picts are in!' roared Conan.

Bedlam followed his shout. The freebooters ceased their feud, some turned to meet the savages, some to spring to the wall. Savages were pouring from behind the huts and they streamed over the compound; their axes flashed against the cutlasses of the sailors.

Zarono was struggling to his feet when a painted savage rushed upon him from behind and brained him with a war-ax.

Conan with a clump of sailors behind him was battling with the Picts inside the stockade, and Strom, with most of his men, was climbing up on the firing-ledges, slashing at the dark figures already swarming over the wall. The Picts, who had crept up unobserved and surrounded the fort while the defenders were fighting among themselves, were attacking from all sides. Valenso's soldiers were clustered at the gate, trying to hold it against a howling swarm of exultant demons.

More and more savages streamed from behind the huts, having scaled the undefended south wall. Strom and his pirates were beaten back from the other sides of the palisade and in an instant the compound was swarming with naked warriors. They dragged down the defenders like wolves; the battle revolved into swirling whirlpools of painted figures surging about small groups of desperate white men. Picts, sailors and henchmen littered the earth, stamped underfoot by the heedless feet. Blood-smeared braves dived howling into huts and the shrieks that rose from the interiors where women and children died beneath the red axes rose above the din of the battle. The men-at-arms abandoned the gate when they heard those pitiful cries, and in an instant the Picts had burst it and were pouring into the palisade at that point also. Huts began to go up in flames.

'Make for the manor!' roared Conan, and a dozen men surged in behind him as he hewed an inexorable way through the snarling pack.

Strom was at his side, wielding his red cutlass like a flail.

'We can't hold the manor,' grunted the pirate.

'Why not?' Conan was too busy with his crimson work to spare a glance.

'Because—uh!' A knife in a dark hand sank deep in the Barachan's back. 'Devil eat you, bastard!' Strom turned staggeringly and split the savage's head to his teeth. The pirate reeled and fell to his knees, blood starting from his lips.

'The manor's burning!' he croaked, and slumped over in the dust.

Conan cast a swift look about him. The men who had followed him were all down in their blood. The Pict gasping out his life under the Cimmerian's feet was the last of the group which had barred his way. All about him battle was swirling and surging, but for the moment he stood alone. He was not far from the south wall. A few strides and he could leap to the ledge, swing over and be gone through the night. But he remembered the helpless girls in the manor – from which, now, smoke was rolling in billowing masses. He ran toward the manor.

A feathered chief wheeled from the door, lifting a war-ax, and behind the racing Cimmerian lines of fleet-footed braves were converging upon him. He did not check his stride. His downward sweeping cutlass met and deflected the ax and split the skull of the wielder. An instant later Conan was through the door and had slammed and bolted it against the axes that splintered into the wood.

The great hall was full of drifting wisps of smoke through which he groped, half-blinded. Somewhere a woman was whimpering, little, catchy, hysterical sobs of nerve-shattering horror. He emerged from a whorl of smoke and stopped dead in his tracks, glaring down the hall.

The hall was dim and shadowy with drifting smoke; the silver candelabrum was overturned, the candles extinguished; the only illumination was a lurid glow from the great fireplace and the wall in which it was set, where the flames licked from burning floor to smoking roof-beams. And limned against that lurid glare Conan saw a human form swinging slowly at the end of a rope. The dead face turned toward him as the body swung, and it was distorted beyond recognition. But Conan knew it was Count Valenso, hanged to his own roof-beam.

But there was something else in the hall. Conan saw it through the drifting smoke – a monstrous black figure, outlined against the hell-fire glare. That outline was vaguely human; but the shadow thrown on the burning wall was not human at all.

'Crom!' muttered Conan aghast, paralysed by the realization that he was confronted by a being against which his sword was helpless. He saw Belesa and Tina, clutched in each other's arms, crouching at the bottom of the stair.

The black monster reared up, looming gigantic against the flame, great arms spread wide; a dim face leered through the drifting smoke, semi-human, demonic, altogether terrible – Conan glimpsed the close-set horns, the gaping mouth, the peaked ears – it was lumbering toward him through the smoke, and an old memory woke with desperation.

Near the Cimmerian stood a massive silver bench, ornately carven, once part of the splendor of Korzetta castle. Conan grasped it, heaved it high above his head.

'Silver and fire!' he roared in a voice like a clap of wind, and hurled the bench with all the power of his iron muscles. Full on the great black breast it crashed, a hundred pounds of silver winged with terrific velocity. Not even the black one could stand before such a missile. He was carried off his feet – hurtled backward headlong into the open fireplace which was a roaring mouth of flame. A horrible scream shook the hall, the cry of an unearthly thing gripped suddenly by earthly death. The mantel cracked and stones fell from the great chimney; half-hiding the black writhing limbs at which the flames were eating in elemental fury. Burning beams crashed down from the roof and thundered on the stones, and the whole heap was enveloped by a roaring burst of fire.

Flames were racing down the stair when Conan reached it. He caught up the fainting child under one arm and dragged Belesa to her feet. Through the crackle and snap of the fire sounded the splintering of the door under war-axes.

He glared about, sighted a door opposite the stair-landing, and hurried through it, carrying Tina and half-dragging Belesa, who seemed dazed. As they came into the chamber beyond, a reverberation behind them announced that the roof was falling in the hall. Through a strangling wall of smoke Conan saw an open, outer door on the other side of the chamber. As he lugged his charges through it, he saw it sagged on broken hinges, lock and bolt snapped and splintered as if by some terrific force.

'The black man came in by this door!' Belesa sobbed hysterically. 'I saw him – but I did not know—'

They emerged into the fire-lit compound, a few feet from the hut-row that lined the south wall. A Pict was skulking toward the door, eyes red in the firelight, ax lifted. Turning the girl on his arm away from the blow, Conan drove his cutlass through the savage's breast, and then, sweeping Belesa off her feet, ran toward the south wall, carrying both girls.

The compound was full of billowing smoke clouds that hid half the red work going on there; but the fugitives had been seen. Naked figures, black against the dull glare, pranced out of the smoke, brandishing gleaming axes. They were still yards behind him when Conan ducked into the space between the huts and the wall. At the other end of the corridor he saw other howling shapes, running to cut him off. Halting short he tossed Belesa bodily to the fire-ledge and leaped after her. Swinging her over the palisade he dropped her into the sand outside, and dropped Tina after her. A thrown ax crashed into a log by his shoulder, and then he too was over the wall and gathering up his dazed and helpless charges. When the Picts reached the wall the space before the palisade was empty of all except the dead.

8 A Pirate Returns to the Sea

Dawn was tingeing the dim waters with an old rose hue. Far out across the tinted waters a fleck of white grew out of the mist – a sail that seemed to hang suspended in the pearly sky. On a bushy headland Conan the Cimmerian held a ragged cloak over a fire of green wood. As he manipulated the cloak, puffs of smoke rose upward, quivered against the dawn and vanished.

Belesa crouched near him, one arm about Tina.

'Do you think they'll see it and understand?'

'They'll see it, right enough,' he assured her. 'They've been hanging off and on this coast all night, hoping to sight some survivors. They're scared stiff. There's only half a dozen of them, and not one can navigate well enough to sail from here to the Barachan Isles. They'll understand my signals; it's the pirate code. I'm telling them that the captains are dead and all the sailors, and for them to come inshore and take us aboard. They know I can navigate, and they'll be glad to ship under me; they'll have to. I'm the only captain left.'

'But suppose the Picts see the smoke?' She shuddered, glancing back over the misty sands and bushes to where, miles to the north, a column of smoke stood up in the still air.

'They're not likely to see it. After I hid you in the woods I crept back and saw them dragging barrels of wine and ale out of the storehouses. Already most of them were reeling. They'll all be lying around too drunk to move by this time. If I had a hundred men I could wipe out the whole horde. Look! There goes a rocket from the *Red Hand*! That means they're coming to take us off!'

Conan stamped out the fire, handed the cloak back to Belesa and stretched like a great lazy cat. Belesa watched him in wonder. His unperturbed manner was not assumed; the night of fire and blood and slaughter, and the flight through the black woods afterward, had left his nerves untouched. He was as calm as if he had spent the night in feast and revel. Belesa did not fear him; she felt safer than she had felt since she landed on that wild coast. He was not like the freebooters, civilized men who had repudiated all standards of honor, and lived without any. Conan, on the other hand, lived according to the code of his people, which was barbaric and bloody, but at least upheld its own peculiar standards of honor.

'Do you think he is dead?' she asked, with seeming irrelevancy.

He did not ask her to whom she referred.

'I believe so. Silver and fire are both deadly to evil spirits, and he got a belly-full of both.'

Neither spoke of that subject again; Belesa's mind shrank from the task of conjuring up the scene when a black figure skulked into the great hall and a long-delayed vengeance was horribly consummated.

'What will you do when you get back to Zingara?' Conan asked.

She shook her head helplessly. 'I do not know. I have neither money nor friends. I am not trained to earn my living. Perhaps it would have been better had one of those arrows struck my heart.'

'Do not say that, my Lady!' begged Tina. 'I will work for us both!'

Conan drew a small leather bag from inside his girdle.

'I didn't get Tothmekri's jewels,' he rumbled. 'But here are some baubles I found in the chest where I got the clothes I'm wearing.' He spilled a handful of flaming rubies into his palm. 'They're worth a fortune, themselves.' He dumped them back into the bag and handed it to her.

'But I can't take these—' she began.

'Of course you'll take them. I might as well leave you for the Picts to scalp as to take you back to Zingara to starve,' said he. 'I know what it is to be penniless in a Hyborian land. Now in my country sometimes there are famines; but people are hungry only when there's no food in the land at all. But in civilized countries I've seen people sick of gluttony while others were starving. Aye, I've seen men fall and die of hunger against the walls of shops and storehouses crammed with food.

'Sometimes I was hungry, too, but then I took what I wanted at sword's-point. But you can't do that. So you take these rubies. You can sell them and buy a castle, and slaves and fine clothes, and with them it won't be hard to get a husband, because civilized men all desire wives with these possessions.'

'But what of you?'

Conan grinned and indicated the *Red Hand* drawing swiftly inshore.

'A ship and a crew are all I want. As soon as I set foot on that deck, I'll have a ship, and as soon as I can raise the Barachans I'll have a crew. The lads of the Red Brotherhood are eager to ship with me, because I always lead them to rare loot. And as soon as I've set you and the girl ashore on the Zingaran coast, I'll show the dogs some looting! Nay,

nay, no thanks! What are a handful of gems to me, when all the loot of the southern seas will be mine for the grasping?'

THE FROST-GIANT'S DAUGHTER

THE CLANGOR OF THE swords had died away, the shouting of the slaughter was hushed; silence lay on the red-stained snow. The bleak pale sun that glittered so blindingly from the ice-fields and the snow-covered plains struck sheens of silver from rent corselet and broken blade, where the dead lay as they had fallen. The nerveless hand yet gripped the broken hilt; helmeted heads, back-drawn in the death throes, tilted red beards and golden beards grimly upward, as if in last invocation to Ymir the frost-giant, god of a warrior-race.

Across the red drifts and mail-clad forms, two figures glared at each other. In that utter desolation only they moved. The frosty sky was over them, the white illimitable plain around them, the dead men at their feet. Slowly through the corpses they came, as ghosts might come to a tryst through the shambles of a dead world. In the brooding silence they stood face to face.

Both were tall men, built like tigers. Their shields were gone, their corselets battered and dented. Blood dried on their mail; their swords were stained red. Their horned helmets showed the marks of fierce strokes. One was beardless and black-maned. The locks and beard of the other were red as the blood on the sunlit snow.

'Man,' said he, 'tell me your name, so that my brothers in Vanaheim may know who was the last of Wulfhere's band to fall before the sword of Heimdul.'

'Not in Vanaheim,' growled the black-haired warrior, 'but in Valhalla will you tell your brothers that you met Conan of Cimmeria.'

Heimdul roared and leaped, and his sword flashed in a deathly arc. Conan staggered and his vision was filled with red sparks as the singing blade crashed on his helmet, shivering into bits of blue fire. But as he reeled he thrust with all the power of his broad shoulders behind the humming blade. The sharp point tore through brass scales and bones and heart, and the red-haired warrior died at Conan's feet.

The Cimmerian stood upright, trailing his sword, a sudden sick weariness assailing him. The glare of the sun on the snow cut his eyes like a knife and the sky seemed shrunken and strangely apart. He turned away from the trampled expanses where yellow-bearded warriors lay locked with red-haired slayers in the embrace of death. A few steps he took, and the glare of the snow-fields was suddenly dimmed. A rushing wave of blindness engulfed him and he sank down into the snow, supporting himself on one mailed arm, seeking to shake the blindness out of his eyes as a lion might shake his mane.

A silvery laugh cut through his dizziness, and his sight cleared slowly. He looked up; there was a strangeness about all the landscape that he could not place or define – an unfamiliar tinge to earth and sky. But he did not think long of this. Before him, swaying like a sapling in the wind, stood a woman. Her body was like ivory to his dazed eyes, and save for a light veil of gossamer, she was naked as the day. Her slender bare feet were whiter than the snow they spurned. She laughed down at the bewildered warrior. Her laughter was sweeter than the rippling of silvery fountains, and poisonous with cruel mockery.

'Who are you?' asked the Cimmerian. 'Whence come you?'

'What matter?' Her voice was more musical than a silver-stringed harp, but it was edged with cruelty.

'Call up your men,' said he, grasping his sword. 'Yet though my strength fail me, they shall not take me alive. I see that you are of the Vanir.'

'Have I said so?'

His gaze went again to her unruly locks, which at first glance he had thought to be red. Now he saw that they were neither red nor yellow, but a glorious compound of both colors. He gazed spellbound. Her hair was like elfin-gold; the sun struck it so dazzlingly that he could scarcely bear to look upon it. Her eyes were likewise neither wholly blue nor wholly grey, but of shifting colors and dancing lights and clouds of colors he could not define. Her full red lips smiled, and from her slender feet to the blinding crown of her billowy hair, her ivory body was as perfect as the dream of a god. Conan's pulse hammered in his temples.

'I cannot tell,' said he, 'whether you are of Vanaheim and mine enemy, or of Asgard and my friend. Far have I wandered, but a woman like you I have never seen. Your locks blind me with their brightness. Never have I seen such hair, not even among the fairest daughters of the Æsir. By Ymir—'

'Who are you to swear by Ymir?' she mocked. 'What know you of the gods of ice and snow, you who have come up from the south to adventure among an alien people?'

'By the dark gods of my own race!' he cried in anger. 'Though I am not of the golden-haired Æsir, none has been more forward in sword-play! This day I have seen four score men fall, and I alone have survived the field where Wulfhere's reavers met the wolves of Bragi. Tell me, woman, have you seen the flash of mail out across the snow-plains, or seen armed men moving upon the ice?'

'I have seen the hoar-frost glittering in the sun,' she answered. 'I have heard the wind whispering across the everlasting snows.'

He shook his head with a sigh.

'Niord should have come up with us before the battle was joined. I fear he and his fighting-men have been ambushed. Wulfhere and his warriors lie dead.'

'I had thought there was no village within many leagues of this spot, for the war carried us far, but you cannot have come a great distance over these snows, naked as you are. Lead me to your tribe, if you are of Asgard, for I am faint with blows and the weariness of strife.'

'My village is further than you can walk, Conan of Cimmeria,' she laughed. Spreading her arms wide, she swayed before him, her golden head lolling sensuously, her scintillant eyes half shadowed beneath their long silken lashes. 'Am I not beautiful, oh man?'

'Like Dawn running naked on the snows,' he muttered, his eyes burning like those of a wolf.

'Then why do you not rise and follow me? Who is the strong warrior who falls down before me?' she chanted in maddening mockery. 'Lie down and die in the snow with the other fools, Conan of the black hair. You cannot follow where I would lead.'

With an oath the Cimmerian heaved himself up on his feet, his blue eyes blazing, his dark scarred face contorted. Rage shook his soul, but desire for the taunting figure before him hammered at his temples and drove his wild blood fiercely through his veins. Passion fierce as physical agony flooded his whole being, so that earth and sky swam red to his dizzy gaze. In the madness that swept upon him, weariness and faintness were swept away.

He spoke no word as he drove at her, fingers spread to grip her soft flesh. With a shriek of laughter she leaped back and ran, laughing at him over her white shoulder. With a low growl Conan followed. He had forgotten the fight, forgotten the mailed warriors who lay in their blood, forgotten Niord and the reavers who had failed to reach the fight. He had thought only for the slender white shape which seemed to float rather than run before him.

Out across the white blinding plain the chase led. The trampled red field fell out of sight behind him, but still Conan kept on with the silent tenacity of his race. His mailed feet broke through the frozen crust; he sank deep in the drifts and forged through them by sheer strength. But the girl danced across the snow light as a feather floating across a pool; her naked feet barely left their imprint on the hoar-frost that overlaid the crust. In spite of the fire in his veins, the cold bit through the warrior's mail and fur-lined tunic; but the girl in her gossamer veil ran as lightly and as gaily as if she danced through the palm and rose gardens of Poitain.

On and on she led, and Conan followed. Black curses drooled through the Cimmerian's parched lips. The great veins in his temples swelled and throbbed and his teeth gnashed.

'You cannot escape me!' he roared. 'Lead me into a trap and I'll pile the heads of your kinsmen at your feet! Hide from me and I'll tear apart the mountains to find you! I'll follow you to hell!'

Her maddening laughter floated back to him, and foam flew from the barbarian's lips. Further and further into the wastes she led him. The land changed; the wide plains gave way to low hills, marching upward in broken ranges. Far to the north he caught a glimpse of towering mountains, blue with the distance, or white with the eternal snows. Above these mountains shone the flaring rays of the borealis. They spread fan-wise into the sky, frosty blades of cold flaming light, changing in color, growing and brightening.

Above him the skies glowed and crackled with strange lights and gleams. The snow shone weirdly, now frosty blue, now icy crimson, now cold silver. Through a shimmering icy realm of enchantment Conan plunged doggedly onward, in a crystalline maze where the only reality was the white body dancing across the glittering snow beyond his reach – ever beyond his reach.

He did not wonder at the strangeness of it all, not even when two gigantic figures rose up to bar his way. The scales of their mail were white with hoar-frost; their helmets and their axes were covered with ice. Snow sprinkled their locks; in their beards were spikes of icicles; their eyes were cold as the lights that streamed above them.

'Brothers!' cried the girl, dancing between them. 'Look who follows! I have brought you a man to slay! Take his heart that we may lay it smoking on our father's board!'

The giants answered with roars like the grinding of icebergs on a frozen shore and heaved up their shining axes as the maddened Cimmerian hurled himself upon them. A frosty blade flashed before his eyes, blinding him with its brightness, and he gave back a terrible stroke that sheared through his foe's thigh. With a groan the victim fell, and at the instant Conan was dashed into the snow, his left shoulder numb from the blow of the survivor, from which the Cimmerian's mail had barely saved his life. Conan saw the remaining giant looming high above him like a colossus carved of ice, etched against the cold glowing sky. The axe fell, to sink through the snow and deep into the frozen earth as Conan hurled himself aside and leaped to his feet. The giant roared and wrenched his axe free, but even as he did, Conan's sword sang down. The giant's knees bent and he sank slowly into the snow, which turned crimson with the blood that gushed from his half-severed neck.

Conan wheeled, to see the girl standing a short distance away, staring at him in wide-eyed horror, all the mockery gone from her face. He cried out fiercely and the blood-drops flew from his sword as his hand shook in the intensity of his passion.

'Call the rest of your brothers!' he cried. 'I'll give their hearts to the wolves! You cannot escape me—'

With a cry of fright she turned and ran fleetly. She did not laugh now, nor mock him over her white shoulder. She ran as for her life, and though he strained every nerve and thew until his temples were like to burst and the snow swam red to his gaze, she drew away from him, dwindling in the witch-fire of the skies, until she was a figure no bigger than a child, then a dancing white flame on the snow, then a dim blur in the distance. But grinding his teeth until the blood started from his gums, he reeled on, and he saw the blur grow to a dancing white flame, and the flame to a figure big as a child; and then she was running less than a hundred paces ahead of him, and slowly the space narrowed, foot by foot.

She was running with effort now, her golden locks blowing free; he heard the quick panting of her breath, and saw a flash of fear in the look she cast over her white shoulder. The grim endurance of the barbarian had served him well. The speed ebbed from her flashing white legs; she reeled in her gait. In his untamed soul leaped up the fires of hell she had fanned so well. With an inhuman roar he closed in on her, just as she wheeled with a haunting cry and flung out her arms to fend him off.

His sword fell into the snow as he crushed her to him. Her lithe body bent backward as she fought with desperate frenzy in his iron arms. Her golden hair blew about his face, blinding him with its sheen; the feel of her slender body twisting in his mailed arms drove him to blinder madness. His strong fingers sank deep into her smooth flesh; and that flesh was cold as ice. It was as if he embraced not a woman of human flesh and blood, but a woman of flaming ice. She writhed her golden head aside, striving to avoid the fierce kisses that bruised her red lips.

'You are cold as the snows,' he mumbled dazedly. 'I will warm you with the fire in my own blood—'

With a scream and a desperate wrench she slipped from his arms, leaving her single gossamer garment in his grasp. She sprang back and faced him, her golden locks in wild disarray, her white bosom heaving, her beautiful eyes blazing with terror. For an instant he stood frozen, awed by her terrible beauty as she posed naked against the snows.

And in that instant she flung her arms toward the lights that glowed in the skies above her and cried out in a voice that rang in Conan's ears forever after: 'Ymir! Oh, my father, save me!'

Conan was leaping forward, arms spread to seize her, when with a crack like the breaking of an ice mountain, the whole sky leaped into icy fire. The girl's ivory body was suddenly enveloped in a cold blue flame so blinding that the Cimmerian threw up his hands to shield his eyes from the intolerable blaze. For a fleeting instant, sky and snowy hills were bathed in crackling white flames, blue darts of icy light, and frozen crimson fires. Then Conan staggered and cried out. The girl was gone. The glowing snow lay empty and bare; high above his head the witch-lights flashed and played in a frosty sky gone mad, and among the distant blue mountains there sounded a rolling thunder as of a gigantic war-chariot rushing behind steeds whose frantic hoofs struck lightning from the snows and echoes from the skies.

Then suddenly the borealis, the snow-clad hills and the blazing heavens reeled drunkenly to Conan's sight; thousands of fire-balls burst with showers of sparks, and the sky itself became a titanic wheel which rained stars as it spun. Under his feet the snowy hills heaved up like a wave, and the Cimmerian crumpled into the snows to lie motionless.

In a cold dark universe, whose sun was extinguished eons ago, Conan felt the movement of life, alien and unguessed. An earthquake had him in its grip and was shaking him to and fro, at the same time chafing his hands and feet until he yelled in pain and fury and groped for his sword.

'He's coming to, Horsa,' said a voice. 'Haste – we must rub the frost out of his limbs if he's ever to wield sword again.'

'He won't open his left hand,' growled another. 'He's clutching something—'

Conan opened his eyes and stared into the bearded faces that bent over him. He was surrounded by tall golden-haired warriors in mail and furs.

'Conan! You live!'

'By Crom, Niord,' gasped the Cimmerian. 'Am I alive, or are we all dead and in Valhalla?'

'We live,' grunted the Æsir, busy over Conan's half-frozen feet. 'We had to fight our way through an ambush, or we had come up with you before the battle was joined. The corpses were scarce cold when we came upon the field. We did not find you among the dead, so we followed your spoor. In Ymir's name, Conan, why did you wander off into the wastes of the north? We have followed your tracks in the snow for hours. Had a blizzard come up and hidden them, we had never found you, by Ymir!'

'Swear not so often by Ymir,' uneasily muttered a warrior, glancing at the distant mountains. 'This is his land and the god bides among yonder mountains the legends say.'

'I saw a woman,' Conan answered hazily. 'We met Bragi's men in the plains. I know not how long we fought. I alone lived. I was dizzy and faint. The land lay like a dream before me. Only now do all things seem natural and familiar. The woman came and taunted me. She was beautiful as a frozen flame from hell. A strange madness fell upon me when I looked at her, so I forgot all else in the world. I followed her. Did you not find her tracks? Or the giants in icy mail I slew?'

Niord shook his head.

'We found only your tracks in the snow, Conan.'

'Then it may be I am mad,' said Conan dazedly. 'Yet you yourself are no more real to me than was the golden-locked witch who fled naked across the snows before me. Yet from under my very hands she vanished in icy flame.'

'He is delirious,' whispered a warrior.

'Not so!' cried the older man, whose eyes were wild and weird. 'It was Atali, the daughter of Ymir, the frost-giant! To fields of the dead she comes, and shows herself to the dying! Myself when a boy I saw her, when I lay half-slain on the bloody field of Wolraven. I saw her walk among the dead in the snows, her naked body gleaming like ivory and her golden hair unbearably bright in the moonlight. I lay and howled like a dying dog because I could not crawl after her. She lures men from stricken fields into the wastelands to be slain by her brothers the ice-giants, who lay men's red hearts smoking on Ymir's

THE FROST-GIANT'S DAUGHTER

board. The Cimmerian has seen Atali, the frost-giant's daughter.'

'Bah!' grunted Horsa. 'Old Gorm's mind was touched in his youth by a sword cut on the head. Conan was delirious from the fury of battle – look how his helmet is dented. Any of those blows might have addled his brain. It was an hallucination he followed into the wastes. He is from the south; what does he know of Atali?'

'You speak truth, perhaps,' muttered Conan. 'It was all strange and weird – by Crom!'

He broke off, glaring at the object that still dangled from his clenched left fist; the others gaped silently at the veil he held up – a wisp of gossamer that was never spun by human distaff.

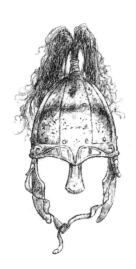

DRUMS OF TOMBALKU

(Draft)

I

THREE MEN SQUATTED BESIDE the water hole, beneath the sunset sky that painted the desert umber and red. Two were Ghanatas, desert warriors, their tatters scarcely concealing their wiry dark frames. Men called them Gobir and Saidu; they looked like vultures as they crouched beside the water hole. The third was yellow-haired and gray-eyed; he was called Amalric.

Nearby a camel ground its cud noisily, and a pair of weary horses vainly nuzzled the bare sand. The men munched dried dates cheerlessly, the desert men intent only on the working of their jaws, Amalric occasionally glancing at the dull red sky, or out across the level monotony where the shadows were gathering and deepening. He was first to see the horseman who rode up and drew rein with a jerk that set the steed rearing.

The rider was a dark-skinned giant. His wide silk pantaloons were gathered in about his bare ankles. They were supported by a broad girdle wrapped repeatedly about his huge belly; that girdle also supported a flaring-tipped scimitar few men could wield with one hand. With that scimitar the man was famed wherever the sons of the desert rode. He was Tilutan, the pride of the Ghanata.

Across his saddle bow a limp shape lay, or rather hung. Breath hissed through the teeth of the Ghanatas as they caught the gleam of smooth, white limbs. A girl hung across Tilutan's saddle bow, face down, her loose hair flowing over his stirrup in a rippling black wave. The giant grinned with a glint of white teeth, and cast her casually onto the sand, where she lay laxly, unconscious. Instinctively Gobir and Saidu turned toward Amalric, and Tilutan watched him from his saddle. Three Ghanatas and an outlander. The entrance of a woman into the scene wrought a subtle change in the atmosphere.

Almaric was the only one who was apparently oblivious to the tenseness. He raked back his rebellious yellow locks absently, and glanced indifferently at the girl's limp figure. If there was a momentary gleam in his grey eyes, the others did not catch it.

Tilutan swung down from his saddle, contemptuously tossing the rein to Amalric.

'Tend my horse,' he said. 'By Jhil, I did not find a desert antelope, but I found this little filly. She was reeling through the sands, and she fell just as I approached. I think she fainted from weariness and thirst. Get away from there, you jackals, and let me give her a drink.'

The big man stretched her out beside the water hole and began laving her face and wrists, trickling a few drops between her parched lips. She moaned presently and stirred vaguely. Gobir and Saidu crouched with their hands on their knees, staring at her over Tilutan's burly shoulder. Amalric stood a little apart from them, his interest seeming only casual.

'She is coming to,' announced Gobir.

Saidu said nothing, but he licked his lips involuntarily, animal-like.

Amalric's gaze travelled impersonally over the prostrate form, from the torn sandals to the loose crown of glossy black hair. Her only garment was a silk kirtle, girdled at the waist. It left her arms, neck and part of her bosom bare, and the skirt ended several inches above her knees. On the parts revealed rested the gaze of the Ghanatas with devouring intensity, taking in the soft contours, childish in their white tenderness, yet rounded with budding womanhood.

Amalric shrugged his shoulders.

'After Tilutan, who?' he asked carelessly.

A pair of lean heads turned toward him, bloodshot eyes rolled at the question, then the Ghanatas turned and mutually stared at one another. Sudden rivalry crackled electrically between them.

'Cast the dice,' urged Amalric. 'No need to fight.' His hand came from under his worn tunic, and he threw down a pair of dice before them. A claw-like hand seized them.

'Aye!' agreed Gobir. 'We cast – after Tilutan, the winner!'

Amalric cast a glance toward the giant who still bent above his captive, bringing life back into her exhausted body. As he looked, her long-lashed lids parted. Deep violet eyes stared up into the leering face bewilderedly. An explosive exclamation of gratification escaped the thick lips of Tilutan. Wrenching a flask from his girdle, he put it to her mouth. She drank the wine mechanically. Amalric avoided her wandering gaze. He was one man and the three Ghanatas were all his match.

Gobir and Saidu bent above the dice; Saidu cupped them in his palm, breathed on them for luck, shook and threw. Two vulture-like heads bent over the spinning cubes in the dim light. And Amalric drew and struck with the same motion. The edge sliced through a thick neck, severing the windpipe, and Gobir fell across the dice, spurting blood, his head hanging by a shred.

Simultaneously, Saidu, with the desperate quickness of a desert man, shot to his feet and hacked ferociously at the slayer's head. Amalric barely had time to catch the stroke on his lifted sword. The whistling scimitar beat the straight blade down on Amalric's head, staggering him. He released his sword and threw both arms about Saidu, dragging him into close quarters where his scimitar was useless. Under the desert man's rags, the wiry frame was like steel cords.

Tilutan, comprehending the matter instantly, had cast the girl down and risen with a roar. He rushed toward the struggling pair like a charging bull, his great scimitar flaming in his hand. Amalric saw him coming, and his flesh turned cold. Saidu was jerking and wrenching, handicapped by the scimitar he was still seeking futilely to turn against his antagonist. Their feet twisted and stamped in the sand, their bodies ground against one another. Amalric smashed his sandal heel down on the Ghanata's bare instep, feeling bones give way. Saidu howled and plunged convulsively, and Amalric gave a desperate heave. The pair lurched drunkenly about, just as Tilutan struck with a rolling drive of his broad shoulders. Amalric felt the steel rasp the under part of his arm, and chug deep into Saidu's body. The Ghanata gave an agonized scream, and his convulsive start tore himself free of Amalric's grasp. Tilutan roared a ferocious oath and, wrenching his steel free, hurled the dying man aside. Before he could srike again, Amalric, his skin crawling with the fear of that great curved blade, had grappled with him.

Despair swept over him as he felt the strength of the warrior. Tilutan was wiser than Saidu. He dropped the scimitar and with a bellow, caught Amalric's throat with both hands. The great fingers locked like iron, and Amalric, striving vainly to break their grip, was borne down, with the Ghanata's great weight pinning him to the earth. The smaller man was shaken like a rat in the jaws of a dog. His head was smashed savagely against the sandy earth. As in a red mist he saw the furious face of his opponent, lips writhed back in a bestial grin of hate, teeth glistening. An inhuman snarling slavered from his thick throat.

'You want her, you dog!' the Ghanata mouthed, insane with rage and lust. 'Arrrrghhh! I break your back! I tear out your throat! I – my scimitar! I cut off your head and make her kiss it!'

A final ferocious smash of Amalric's head against the hardpacked sand, and Tilutan half-lifted him and hurled him down in an excess of bestial passion. Rising, the man ran, stooping like an ape, and caught up his scimitar where it lay like a broad crescent of steel in the sand. Yelling in ferocious exultation, he turned and charged back, brandishing the blade on high. Amalric rose slowly to meet him, dazed, shaken, sick from the manhandling he had received.

Tilutan's girdle had become unwound in the fight, and now the end dangled about his feet. He tripped, stumbled, fell headlong, throwing out his arms to save himself. The scimitar flew from his hand.

Amalric, galvanized, caught up the scimitar and took a reeling step forward. The desert swam darkly to his gaze. In the dusk before him he saw Tilutan's face suddenly ashy. The wide mouth gaped, the whites of the eyeballs rolled up. The giant froze on one knee and a hand, as if incapable of further motion. Then the scimitar fell, cleaving the round, shaven head to the chin, where its downward course was checked with a sickening jerk. Amalric had a dim impression of a face divided by a widening red line, fading in the thickening shadows. Then darkness caught him with a rush.

Something soft and cool was touching Amalric's face with gentle persistence. He groped blindly and his hand closed on something warm, firm and resilient. Then his sight cleared and he looked into a soft oval face, framed in lustrous black hair. As in a trance he gazed unspeaking, hungrily dwelling on each detail of the full red lips, dark violet eyes, and alabaster throat. With a start he realized the vision was speaking in a soft musical voice. The words were strange, yet possessed an illusive familiarity. A small white hand holding a dripping bunch of silk was passed gently over his throbbing head and face. He sat up dizzily.

It was night, under the star-splashed skies. The camel still munched its cud; a horse whinnied restlessly. Not far away lay a hulking dark figure with its cleft head in a horrible puddle of blood and brains. Amalric looked up at the girl who knelt beside him, talking in her gentle, unknown tongue. As the mists cleared from his brain, he began to understand her. Harking back into half-forgotten tongues he had learned and spoken in the past, he remembered a language used by a scholarly class in a southern province of Koth.

'Who are you, girl?' he demanded, prisoning a small hand in his own hardened fingers.

'I am Lissa.' The name was spoken with almost the suggestion of a lisp. It was like the rippling of a slender stream.

'I am glad you are conscious. I feared you were not alive.'

'A little more and I wouldn't have been,' he muttered, glancing at the grisly sprawl that had been Tilutan. She paled, refusing to follow his gaze. Her hand trembled, and in their nearness, Amalric thought he could feel the quick throb of her heart.

'It was horrible,' she faltered. 'Like an awful dream. Anger – and blows – and blood—'

'It might have been worse,' he growled.

She seemed sensitive to every changing inflection of his voice or mood. Her free hand stole timidly to his arm.

'I did not mean to offend you. It was very brave for you to risk your life for a stranger. You are noble as the knights about which I have read.'

He cast a quick glance at her. Her wide clear eyes met his, reflecting only the thought she had spoken. He started to speak, then changed his mind and said another thing.

'What are you doing in the desert?'

'I came from Gazal,' she answered. 'I – I was running away. I could not stand it any longer. But it was hot and lonely and weary, and I saw only sand, sand – and the blazing blue sky. The sands burned my feet, and my sandals were worn out quickly. I was so thirsty, my canteen was soon empty. And then I wished to return to Gazal, but one direction looked like another. I did not know which way to go. I was terribly afraid, and started running in the direction in which I thought Gazal to be. I do not remember much after that. I ran until I could run no further, and I must have lain in the burning sand for a while. I remember rising and staggering on, and toward the last I thought I heard someone shouting, and saw a huge man on a black horse riding toward me, and then I knew no more until I awoke and found myself lying with my head in that man's lap, while he gave me wine to drink. Then there was shouting and fighting—' She shuddered. 'When it was all over, I crept to where you lay like a dead man, and I tried to bring you to—'

'Why?' he demanded.

She seemed at a loss. 'Why,' she floundered, 'why, you were hurt – and – why, it is what anyone would do. Besides, I realized that you were fighting to protect me from these men. The people of Gazal have always said that the desert people were wicked and would harm the helpless.'

'That's no exclusive characteristic,' muttered Amalric. 'Where is this Gazal?'

'It can not be far,' she answered. 'I walked a whole day – and then I do not know how far the warrior carried me after he found me. But he must have discovered me about sunset, so he could not have come far.'

'In what direction?' he demanded.

'I do not know. I travelled eastward when I left the city.'

'City?' he muttered. 'A day's travel from this spot? I had thought there was only desert for a thousand miles.'

'Gazal is in the desert,' she answered. 'It is built amidst the palms of an oasis.'

Putting her aside, he got to his feet, swearing softly as he fingered his throat, the skin of which was bruised and lacerated. He examined the three Ghanatas in turn, finding no sign of life in them. Then, one by one, he dragged them a short distance out into the desert. Somewhere the jackals were yelping. Returning to the water hole where the girl squatted patiently, he cursed to find only the black stallion of Tilutan with the camel. The other horses had broken their tethers and bolted during the fight.

Amalric went to the girl and proffered her a handful of dried dates. She nibbled at them eagerly, while the other sat and watched her, his chin on his fists, an increasing impatience throbbing in his veins.

'Why did you run away?' he asked abruptly. 'Are you a slave?'

'We have no slaves in Gazal,' she answered. 'Oh, I was weary – so weary of the eternal monotony. I wished to see something of the outer world. Tell me, from what land do you come?'

'I was born in the western hills of Aquilonia,' he answered.

She clapped her hands like a delighted child.

'I know where it is! I have seen it on the maps. It is the western-most country of the Hyborians, and its king is Epeus the Sword-wielder!'

Amalric experienced a distinct shock. His head jerked up and he stared at his fair companion.

'Epeus? Why, Epeus has been dead for nine hundred years. The king's name is Vilerus.'

'Oh, of course,' she said, rather embarrassedly. 'I am foolish. Of course, Epeus was king nine centuries ago, as you say. But tell me – tell me all about the world!'

'Why, that is a big order,' he answered nonplussed. 'You have not travelled?'

'This is the very first time that I have ever been out of sight of the walls of Gazal,' she admitted to him.

His gaze was fixed on the curve of her white bosom. He was not interested in her adventures at the moment, and Gazal might have been Hell for all he cared.

He started to speak, then changing his mind caught her roughly in his arms, his muscles tensing for the struggle he expected. But he encountered no resistance. Her soft, yielding body lay across his knees, and she looked up at him somewhat in surprize, but without fear or embarrassment. She might have been a child submitting to a new kind of play. Something about her direct gaze confused him. If she had screamed, wept, fought, or smiled knowingly, he would have known how to deal with her.

'Who in Mitra's name are you, girl?' he asked roughly. 'You are neither touched with the sun, nor playing a game with me. Your speech shows you to be no ignorant country lass, innocent in ignorance. Yet you seem to know nothing of the world and its ways.'

'I am a daughter of Gazal,' she answered helplessly. 'If you saw Gazal, perhaps you would understand.'

He lifted her and placed her on the sand. Rising, he brought a saddle blanket and set it out for her.

'Sleep, Lissa,' he said, his voice harsh with conflicting emotions. 'Tomorrow I mean to see Gazal.'

At dawn they started westward. Amalric had lifted Lissa onto the camel, showing her how to maintain her balance. She clung to the seat with both hands, showing no knowledge whatever of camels, which again surprized the young Aquilonian. A girl raised in the desert, she had never before been on a camel, nor, until the preceding night, had she ever ridden or been carried on a horse. Amalric had manufactured a sort of cloak for her, and she wore it without question, not asking whence it came, accepting it as she accepted all things he did for her, gratefully but blindly, without asking the reason. Amalric did not tell her that the silk that shielded her from the sun had once covered the skin of her abductor.

As they rode she again begged him to tell her something of the world, like a child asking for a story.

'I know Aquilonia is far from this desert,' she said. 'Stygia lies between, and the Lands of Shem, and other countries. How is it that you are here, so far from your homeland?'

He rode for a space in silence, his hand on the camel's guide-rope.

'Argos and Stygia were at war,' he said abruptly. 'Koth became embroiled. The Kothians urged a simultaneous invasion of Stygia. Argos raised an army of mercenaries, which went into ships and sailed southward along the coast. At the same time, a Kothic army was to invade Stygia by land. I was one of that mercenary army. We met the Stygian fleet and defeated it, driving it back into Khemi. We should have landed, looted the city, and advanced along the course of the Styx – but our admiral was cautious. Our leader was Prince Zapayo da Kova, a Zingaran. We cruised southward until we reached the jungle-clad coasts of Kush. There we landed, and the ships anchored, while the army pushed eastward along the Stygian frontier, burning and pillaging as we went. It was our intention to turn northward at a certain point and strike into the heart of Stygia to form a juncture with the Kothic host which was supposed to be pushing down from the north. Then word came that we were betrayed. Koth had concluded a separate peace with the Stygians. A Stygian army was pushing southward to intercept us, while another already had cut us off from the coast.

'Prince Zapayo, in desperation, conceived the mad idea of marching eastward, hoping to skirt the Stygian border and eventually reach the eastern lands of Shem. But the army from the north overtook us. We turned and fought. All day we fought, and finally they gave before us, their retreat turning into rout. But the next day the pursuing army came up from the west, and crushed between the hosts, our army ceased to be. We were broken, annihilated, destroyed. There were few left to flee. But when night fell, I broke away with my companion, a Cimmerian named Conan, a brute of a man with the strength of a bull.

'We rode southward into the desert, because there was no other direction in which we might go. Conan had been in this part of the world before, and he believed we had a chance to survive. Far to the south we found an oasis, but Stygian riders harried us, and we fled again, from oasis to oasis, fleeing, starving, thirsting, until we found ourselves in a barren, unknown land of blazing and empty sand. We rode until our horses were reeling, and we were half delirious. Then one night we saw fires and rode up to them, taking a desperate chance that we might make friends. As soon as we came within range, a shower of arrows greeted us. Conan's horse was hit and it reared, throwing its rider. His neck must have broken like a twig, for he never moved. I got away in the darkness, somehow, though my horse died under me. I had only a glance at the attackers. They were tall, lean brown men, wearing strange, barbaric garments. I wandered on foot through the desert, and fell in with those three vultures you saw yesterday. They were jackals – Ghanatas – members of a robber tribe of mixed blood. The only reason they didn't murder me was because I had nothing they wished. For a month I have been wandering and thieving with them because there was nothing else I could do.'

'I did not know it was like that,' Lissa murmured faintly. 'They said there were wars and cruelty out in the world, but it seemed like a dream and far away. Listening to you speak of treachery and battle seems almost like seeing it.'

'Do no enemies ever come against Gazal?' he demanded.

She shook her head. 'Men ride wide of Gazal. Sometimes I have seen black dots moving in lines along the horizon, and the old men said they were armies moving to war. But they never come near to Gazal.'

Amalric felt a dim stirring of uneasiness. This desert, seemingly empty of life, nevertheless contained some of the fiercest tribes on earth – the Ghanatas, who ranged far to the east; the masked Tibu, whom he believed dwelt further to the south; and somewhere off to the southwest lay the semi-mythical empire of Tombalku, ruled by a wild and barbaric race. It was strange that a city in the midst of this savage land should be left so completely alone that one of its inhabitants did not even know the meaning of war.

When he turned his gaze elsewhere, strange thoughts assailed him. Was the girl touched by the sun? Was she a demon in womanly form come out of the desert to lure him to some cryptic doom? A glance at her clinging childishly to the high peak of the camel saddle was sufficient to dispel these broodings. Then again doubt assailed him. Was he bewitched? Had she cast a spell on him?

Westward they forged steadily, halting only to nibble dates and drink water at midday. Amalric fashioned a frail shelter out of his sword and sheath and the saddle blankets to shield her from the burning sun. Weary and stiff from the tossing, bucking gait of the camel, she had to be lifted down in his arms. As he felt again the voluptuous sweetness of her soft body, he felt a hot throb of passion sear through him, and he stood momentarily motionless, intoxicated with the nearness of her, before he laid her down in the shade of the makeshift tent.

He felt a touch of almost anger at the clear gaze with which she met his, at the docility with which she yielded her young body to his hands. It was as if she were unaware of things which might harm her; her innocent trust shamed him and pent a helpless wrath within him.

As they ate, he did not taste the dates he munched; his eyes burned on her, avidly drinking in every detail of her lithe young figure. She seemed as unaware of his intentness as a child. When he lifted her to place her again on the camel, and her arms went instinctively about his neck, he shuddered. But he lifted her up on her mount, and they took up the journey once more.

It was just before sundown when Lissa pointed and cried out: 'Look! The towers of Gazal!'

On the desert rim he saw them – spires and minarets, rising in a jade-green cluster against the blue sky. But for the girl, he would have thought it the phantom city of a mirage. He glanced at Lissa curiously. She showed no signs of eager joy at her homecoming. Instead, she sighed, and her slim shoulders seemed to droop.

As they approached, the details swam more plainly into view. Sheer from the desert sands rose the wall which enclosed the towers. And

Amalric saw that the wall was crumbling in many places. The towers, too, he saw, were much in disrepair. Roofs sagged, broken battlements gaped, spires leaned drunkenly. Panic assailed him; was it a city of the dead to which he rode, guided by a vampire? A quick glance at the girl reassured him. No demon could lurk in that divinely molded exterior. She glanced at him with a strange and wistful questioning in her deep eyes, turned resolutely toward the desert, then, with a deep sigh, set her face toward the city, as if gripped by a subtle and fatalistic despair.

Now through the gaps of the jade-green wall, Amalric saw figures moving within the city. No one hailed them as they rode through a broad breach in the wall, and came out into a broad street. Close at hand, limned in the sinking sun, the decay was more apparent. Grass grew rank in the streets, pushing through shattered paving; grass grew rank in the small plazas. Streets and courts likewise were littered with rubbish of masonry and fallen stones.

Domes rose, cracked and discolored. Portals gaped, vacant of doors. Everywhere ruin had laid his hand. Then Amalric saw one spire untouched; a shining red cylindrical tower which rose in the extreme southeastern corner of the city.

It shone among the ruins, and Amalric pointed to it.

'Why is that tower less in ruins than the others?' he asked. Lissa turned pale; she trembled and caught his hand convulsively.

'Do not speak of it!' she whispered. 'Do not look toward it – do not even *think* of it!'

Amalric scowled; the nameless implication of her words somehow changed the aspect of the mysterious tower. Now it seemed like a serpent's head rearing among ruin and desolation.

The young Aquilonian looked warily about him. After all, he had no assurance that the people of Gazal would receive him in a friendly manner. He saw people moving leisurely about the streets. They halted and stared at him, and for some reason his flesh crawled. They were men and women with kindly features, and their looks were mild. But their interest seemed so slight – so vague and impersonal. They made no movement to approach him or to speak to him. It might have been the most common thing in the world for an armed horseman to ride into their city from the desert; yet Amalric knew that was not the case, and the casual manner in which the people of Gazal received him caused a faint uneasiness in his bosom.

Lissa spoke to them, indicating Amalric, whose hand she lifted like an affectionate child. 'This is Amalric of Aquilonia, who rescued me from the desert people and has brought me home.'

A polite murmur of welcome rose from the people, and several of them approached to extend their hands. Amalric thought he had never seen such vague, kindly faces. Their eyes were soft and mild, without fear and without wonder. Yet they were not the eyes of stupid oxen; rather, they were the eyes of people wrapped in dreams.

Their stare gave him a feeling of unreality; he hardly knew what was said to him. His mind was occupied by the strangeness of it all; these quiet, dreamy people in their silken tunics and soft sandals, moving with aimless vagueness among the discolored ruins. A lotus paradise of illusion? Somehow, the thought of that sinister red tower struck a discordant note.

One of the men, his face smooth and unlined, but his hair silver, was saying: 'Aquilonia? There was an invasion – we heard – King Bragorus of Nemedia – how went the war?'

'He was driven back,' answered Amalric briefly, resisting a shudder. Nine hundred years had passed since Bragorus led his spearmen across the marches of Aquilonia.

His questioner did not press him further; the people drifted away, and Lissa tugged at his hand. He turned, feasted his eyes upon her; in a realm of illusion and dream, her soft firm body anchored his wandering conjectures. She was no dream; she was real; her body was sweet and tangible as cream and honey.

'Come, let us go to rest and eat.'

'What of the people?' he demurred. 'Will you not tell them of your experiences?'

'They would not heed, except for a few minutes,' she answered. 'They would listen a little, and then drift away. They hardly know I have been gone. Come!'

Amalric led the horse and camel into an enclosed court where the grass grew high, and water seeped from a broken fountain into a marble trough. There he tethered them, and then turned to Lissa. Taking his hand, she led him across the court into an arched doorway. Night had fallen. In the open space above the court, the stars were clustering, etching the jagged pinnacles. Through a series of dark chambers Lissa went, moving with the sureness of long practice. Amalric groped after her, guided by her little hand in his. He found it no pleasant adventure. The scent of dust and decay hung in the thick darkness. At times, what felt like broken tiles underfoot caused him to move carefully. At other times there was the softness of worn carpets. His free hand touched the fretted arches of doorways. Then the stars gleamed through a broken roof, showing him a dim, winding hallway hung with rotting tapestries. They rustled in a faint wind, and their noise was like the whispering of witches, causing the hair to stir next his scalp.

Then they came into a chamber dimly lighted by the starshine streaming through open windows. Lissa released his hand, fumbled an instant, and produced a faint light of some sort. It was a glassy knob which glowed with a golden radiance. She set it on a marble table and indicated that Amalric should recline on a couch thickly littered with silks. Groping into some mysterious recess, she produced a gold vessel of wine and others containing food unfamiliar to Amalric. There were dates, but the other food, which he did not recognize, was pallid and insipid to his taste. The wine was pleasant to the palate, but no more heady than dish water.

Seated on a marble seat opposite him, Lissa nibbled daintily.

'What sort of place is this?' he demanded. 'You are like these people – yet strangely unlike.'

'They say I am like our ancestors,' answered Lissa. 'Long ago they came into the desert and built this city over a great oasis which was in reality only a series of springs. The stone they took from the ruins of a much older city – only the red tower—' her voice dropped and she glanced nervously at the star-framed windows – 'only the red tower stood there. It was empty – then.

'Our ancestors, who were called Gazali, once dwelt in the southern part of Koth. They were noted for their scholarly wisdom. But they sought to revive the worship of Mitra which the Kothians had long ago abandoned, and the king drove them from his kingdom. They came southward, many of them, priests, scholars, teachers, scientists, along with their Shemitish slaves.

'They reared Gazal in the desert; but the slaves revolted almost as soon as the city was built and, fleeing, mixed with the wild tribes of the desert. They were not treated badly, but word came to them in the night – a word which sent them fleeing madly from the city into the desert.

'My people dwelt here, learning to manufacture their food and drink from such material as was at hand. Their learning was a marvel. When the slaves fled, they took with them every camel, horse and donkey in the city. There was no communication with the outer world. There are whole chambers in Gazal that are filled with maps and books and chronicles. But they are all nine hundred years old, at the least, for it was nine hundred years ago that my people fled from Koth. Since then, no man of the outside world has set forth in Gazal. And the people are slowly vanishing. They have become so dreamy and introspective that they have neither human passions nor ambitions. The city falls into ruins and none moves hand to repair it. Horror—' she choked, and shuddered, 'when horror came upon them, they could neither flee nor fight.'

'What do you mean?' he whispered, a cold wind blowing on his spine. The rustling of rotten hangings down nameless black corridors stirred dim fear in his soul.

She shook her head, rose, and came around the marble table. She laid hands on his shoulders. Her eyes were wet and shone with horror and a desperate yearning that caught at his throat. Instinctively, his arm went around her lithe form, and he felt her tremble.

'Hold me!' she begged. 'I am afraid! Oh, I have dreamed of such a man as you. I am not like my people; they are dead men walking forgotten streets; but I am alive. I am warm and sentient. I hunger and thirst and yearn for life. I cannot abide the silent streets and ruined halls and dim people of Gazal, though I have never known anything else. That is why I ran away – I yearned for life—'

She was sobbing uncontrollably in his arms. Her hair streamed over his face; her fragrance made him dizzy. Her firm body strained against him. She was lying across his knees, her arms locked about his neck. Straining her to his breast, he crushed her lips with his. Eyes, lips, cheeks, hair, throat, breasts, he showered with hot kisses, until her sobs changed to panting gasps. The passion that slumbered in her woke in one overpowering wave. The glowing gold ball, struck by his groping fingers, tumbled to the floor and was extinguished. Only the starshine gleamed through the windows.

Lying in Amalric's arms on the silk-heaped couch, Lissa opened her heart and whispered her dreams and hopes and aspirations, childish, pathetic, terrible.

'I'll take you away,' he muttered. 'Tomorrow. You are right. Gazal is a city of the dead; we will seek life and the outer world. It is violent, rough, and cruel, but it is better than this living death—'

The night was broken by a shuddering cry of agony, horror and despair. Its timbre brought out cold sweat on Amalric's skin. He started upright from the couch, but Lissa clung to him desperately.

'No, no!' she begged in a frantic whisper. 'Do not go! Stay!'

'But murder is being done!' he exclaimed, fumbling for his sword. The cries seemed to come from across an outer court. Mingled with them there was an indescribable tearing, rending sound. They rose higher and thinner, unbearable in their hopeless agony, then sank away in a long, shuddering sob.

'I have heard men dying on the rack cry out like that!' muttered Amalric, shaking with horror. 'What devil's work is this?'

Lissa was trembling violently in a frenzy of terror. He felt the wild pounding of her heart.

'It is the Horror of which I spoke!' she whispered. 'The Horror which dwells in the red tower. Long ago it came – and some say it dwelt there in the lost years and returned after the building of Gazal. It devours human beings. What it is, no one knows, since none have seen it and lived to tell. It is a god or a devil. That is why the slaves fled; why the desert people shun Gazal. Many of us have gone into its awful belly. Eventually, all will have gone, and it will rule over an empty city, as men say it ruled over the ruins from which Gazal was reared.'

'Why have the people stayed to be devoured?' he demanded.

'I do not know,' she whimpered; 'they dream—'

'Hypnosis,' muttered Amalric; 'hypnosis coupled with decay. I saw it in their eyes. This devil has them mesmerized. Mitra, what a foul secret!'

Lissa pressed her face against his bosom and clung to him.

'But what are we to do?' he asked uneasily.

'There is nothing to do,' she whispered. 'Your sword would be helpless. Perhaps it will not harm us. It has taken a victim tonight. We must wait like sheep for the butcher.'

'I'll be damned if I will!' Amalric exclaimed, galvanized. 'We will not wait for morning. We'll go tonight. Make a bundle of food and drink. I'll get the horse and camel and bring them to the court outside. Meet me there!'

Since the unknown monster had already struck, Amalric felt that he was safe in leaving the girl alone for a few minutes. But his flesh crawled as he groped his way down the winding corridor and through the black chambers where the swinging tapestries whispered. He found the beasts huddled nervously together in the court where he had left them. The stallion whinnied anxiously and nuzzled him, as if sensing peril in the breathless night.

He saddled and bridled and hurriedly led them through the narrow opening onto the street. A few minutes later he was standing in the starlit court. And even as he reached it; he was electrified by an awful scream which rang shudderingly upon the air. It came from the chamber where he had left Lissa.

He answered that piteous cry with a wild yell; drawing his sword, he rushed across the court and hurled himself through the window. The golden ball was glowing again, carving out black shadows in the shrinking corners. Silks lay scattered on the floor. The marble seat was upset. But the chamber was empty.

A sick weakness overcame Amalric and he staggered against the marble table, the dim light waving dizzily to his sight. Then he was swept by a mad rage. The red tower! There the fiend would bear his victim!

He darted across the court, found the streets and raced toward the tower which glowed with an unholy light under the stars. The streets did not run straight. He cut through silent black buildings and crossed courts whose rank grass waved in the night wind.

Ahead of him, clustered about the crimson tower, rose a heap of ruins where decay had eaten more savagely than at the rest of the city. Apparently none dwelt among them. They reeled and tumbled, a crumbling mass of quaking masonry, with the red tower rearing up among them like a poisonous red flower from charnel-house ruin.

To reach the tower he would be forced to traverse the ruins. Recklessly, he plunged into the black mass, groping for a door. He found one and entered, thrusting his sword ahead of him. Then he saw such a vista as men sometimes see in fantastic dreams. Far ahead of him stretched a long corridor, visible in a faint, unhallowed glow, its black walls hung with strange shuddersome tapestries. Far down it he saw a receding figure – a white, naked, stooped figure, lurching along, dragging something the sight of which filled him with sweating horror. Then the apparition vanished from his sight, and with it vanished the eery glow. Amalric stood in the soundless dark, seeing nothing, hearing nothing; thinking only of that stooped white figure that dragged a limp human being down a long, black corridor.

As he groped onward, a vague memory stirred in his brain – the memory of a grisly tale mumbled to him over a dying fire in the skull-heaped, devil-devil hut of a black witchman – a tale of a god which dwelt in a crimson house in a ruined city and which was worshipped by darksome cults in dank jungles and along sullen dusky rivers. And there stirred, too, in his mind an incantation whispered in his ear in awed and shuddering tones, while the night had held its breath, the lions had ceased to roar along the river, and the very fronds had ceased their scraping one against the other.

Ollam-onga, whispered a dark wind down the sightless corridor. *Ollam-onga* whispered the dust that ground beneath his stealthy feet. Sweat stood on his skin and the sword shook in his hand. He stole through the house of a god, and fear held him by its bony hand. *The house of the god* – the full horror of the phrase filled his mind. All the ancestral fears and the fears that reached beyond ancestry and primordial race-memory crowded upon him; horror cosmic and unhuman sickened him. His weak humanity crushed him in its realization as he went through the house of darkness that was the house of a god.

About him shimmered a glow so faint that it was scarcely discernible; he knew that he was approaching the tower itself. Another instant and he groped his way through an arched door and stumbled upon strangely spaced steps. Up them he went and, as he climbed, that blind fury which is mankind's last defence against diabolism and all the hostile forces of the universe, surged in him, and he forgot his fear. Burning with terrible eagerness, he climbed up and up through the thick, evil darkness until he came into a chamber lit by a weird glow.

And before him stood a white, naked figure. Amalric halted, his tongue cleaving to his palate. It was a naked white man, to all appearance, who stood there, gazing at him with mighty arms folded on an alabaster breast. The features were classic, cleanly carven, with more than human beauty. But the eyes were balls of luminous fire, such as never looked from any human head. In those eyes, Amalric glimpsed the frozen fires of the ultimate hells, touched by awful shadows.

Then before him the form began to grow dim in outline – to waver. With a terrible effort, the Aquilonian burst the bonds of silence and spoke a cryptic and awful incantation. And as the frightful words cut the silence, the white giant halted – froze – again his outlines stood out clear and bold against the golden background.

'Now fall on, damn you!' cried Amalric hysterically. 'I have bound you into your human shape! The black wizard spoke truly! It was the master word he gave me! Fall on, *Ollam-onga* – till you break the spell by feasting on my heart, you are no more than a man like me!'

With a roar that was like the gust of a whirlwind, the creature charged. Amalric sprang aside from the clutch of those hands whose strength was more than that of a giant. A single taloned finger, spread wide and catching in his tunic, ripped the garment from him like a rotten rag as the monster plunged by. But Amalric, nerved to more than human quickness by the horror of the fight, wheeled and drove his sword through the thing's back, so that the point stood out a foot from the broad breast.

A fiendish howl of agony shook the tower; the monster whirled and rushed at Amalric, but the youth sprang aside and raced up the stairs to the dais. There he wheeled and, catching up a marble seat, hurled it down upon the horror that was lumbering up the stairs. Full in the face the massive missile struck, carrying the fiend back down the steps. He rose, an awful sight, streaming blood and again essayed the stairs. In desperation, Amalric lifted a jade bench whose weight wrenched a groan of effort from him, and hurled it.

Beneath the impact of the hurtling bulk, Ollam-onga pitched back down the stair and lay among the marble shards, which were flooded with his blood. With a last, desperate effort, he heaved himself up on his hands, eyes glazing, and throwing back his bloody head, voiced an awful cry. Amalric shuddered and recoiled from the abysmal horror of that scream. *And it was answered.* From somewhere in the air above the tower a faint medley of fiendish cries came back like an echo. Then the mangled white figure went limp among the blood-stained shards.

And Amalric knew that one of the gods of Kush was no more. With the thought came blind, unreasoning horror.

In a fog of terror he rushed down the stair, shrinking from the thing that lay staring on the floor. The night seemed to cry out against him, aghast at the sacrilege. Reason, exultant over his triumph, was submerged in a flood of cosmic fear.

As he put foot on the head of the steps, he halted short. Up from the darkness Lissa came to him, her white arms outstretched, her eyes pools of horror and revulsion.

'Amalric!' It was a haunting cry. He crushed her in his arms.

'I saw *It*,' she whimpered – 'dragging a dead man through the corridor. I screamed and fled; then when I returned, I heard you cry out and knew you had gone to search for me in the red tower—'

'And you came to share my fate,' his voice was almost inarticulate. Then, as she tried to peer in trembling fascination past him, he covered her eyes with his hands and turned her about. Better that she should not see what lay on the crimson floor. As he half led, half carried her down the shadowed stairs, a glance over his shoulder showed him that a naked white figure lay no longer among the broken marble. The incantation had bound Ollam-onga into his human form in life, but not in death. Blindness momentarily assailed Amalric; then, galvanized into frantic haste, he hurried Lissa down the stairs and through the dark ruins.

He did not slacken pace until they reached the street where the camel and stallion huddled against one another. Quickly he placed the girl on the camel and swung up on the stallion. Taking the lead-line, he headed straight for the broken wall. A few minutes later he breathed gustily. The open air of the desert cooled his blood; it was free of the scent of decay and hideous antiquity.

There was a small water-pouch hanging from his saddle bow. They had no food, and his sword was in the chamber of the red tower. He had not dared touch it. Without food and unarmed, they faced the desert, but its peril seemed less grim than the horror of the city behind them.

Without speaking they rode. Amalric headed south; somewhere in that direction there was a water hole. Just at dawn, as they mounted a crest of sand, he looked back toward Gazal, unreal in the pink light. And he stiffened as Lissa, sharing his vision, cried out. From a breach in the wall rode seven horsemen; their steeds were black, and the riders were cloaked in black from head to foot. Horror swept over Amalric as he realized there had been no horses in Gazal. Turning, he urged their mounts on.

The sun rose, red, and then gold, and then a ball of white-beaten flame. On and on the fugitives pressed, reeling with heat and fatigue, blinded by the glare. They moistened their lips with water from time to time, and behind them, at an even pace, rode seven black dots. Evening began to fall, and the sun reddened and lurched toward the desert rim. And a cold hand clutched at Amalric's heart. The riders were closing in. As darkness came on, so came the black riders. Amalric glanced at Lissa, and a groan burst from him. His stallion stumbled and fell. The sun had gone down, the moon was blotted out suddenly by a bat-shaped shadow. In the utter darkness the stars glowed red, and behind him Amalric heard a rising rush as of an approaching wind. A black, speeding clump bulked against the night, in which glinted sparks of awful light.

'Ride girl!' he cried despairingly. 'Go on – save yourself; it is me they want!'

For answer she slid down from the camel and threw her arms about him.

'I will die with you!'

Seven black shapes loomed against the stars, racing like the wind. Under the hoods shone balls of evil fire. Jaw bones seemed to clack together. Suddenly, a horse swept past Amalric, a vague bulk in the unnatural darkness. There was the sound of an impact as the unknown steed caromed among the oncoming shapes. A horse screamed in frenzy, and a bull-like voice bellowed in a strange tongue. From somewhere in the night a clamor of yells answered.

Some sort of violent action was taking place. Horse's hoofs stamped and clattered. There was the impact of savage blows, and the same stentorian voice was cursing lustily. Then the moon abruptly came out and lit a fantastic scene.

A man on a giant horse whirled, slashed and smote apparently at thin air, and from another direction swept a wild horde of riders, their curved swords flashing in the moonlight. Away over the crest of a rise, seven black figures were vanishing, their cloaks floating out like the wings of bats.

Amalric was swamped by wild men who leaped from their horses and swarmed around him. Sinewy, naked arms pinioned him; fierce brown, hawk-like faces snarled at him. Lissa screamed. Then the attackers were thrust right and left as the man on the great horse reined through the crowd. He bent from his saddle and glared closely at Amalric.

'The devil!' he roared. 'Amalric the Aquilonian!'

'Conan!' Amalric exclaimed bewilderedly. 'Conan! Alive!'

'More alive than you seem to be,' answered the other. 'By Crom, man, you look as if all the devils in this desert had been hunting you through the night. What things were those pursuing you? I was riding around the camp my men had pitched to make sure no enemies were in hiding, when the moon went out like a candle, and then I heard sounds of flight. I rode towards the sounds and, by Crom, I was among those devils before I knew what was happening. I had my sword in my hand and I laid about me – by Crom, their eyes blazed like fire in the dark! I know my edge bit them, but when the moon came out, they were gone like a puff of wind. Were they men or fiends?'

'Ghouls sent up from Hell,' shuddered Amalric. 'Ask me no more; there are some things that cannot be discussed.'

Conan did not press the matter, nor did he look incredulous. His beliefs included night fiends, ghosts, hobgoblins and dwarfs.

'Trust you to find a woman, even in a desert,' he said, glancing at Lissa, who had crept to Amalric and was clinging close to him, glancing fearfully at the wild figures which hemmed them in.

'Wine!' roared Conan. 'Bring flasks! Here!' He seized a leather flask from those who thrust it out to him, and placed it in Amalric's hand. 'Give the girl a swig and drink some yourself,' he advised. 'Then we'll put you on horses and take you to the camp. You need food, rest and sleep. I can see that.'

A richly caparisoned horse was brought, rearing and prancing, and willing hands helped Amalric into the saddle. Then the girl was handed up to him, and they moved off southward, surrounded by the wiry brown riders in their picturesque semi-nakedness. Conan rode ahead, humming a riding song of the mercenaries.

'Who is he?' whispered Lissa, her arms about her lover's neck; he was holding her on the saddle in front of him.

'Conan, the Cimmerian,' muttered Amalric. 'The man I wandered with in the desert after the defeat of the mercenaries. These are the men who struck him down. I left him lying under their spears, apparently dead. Now we meet him obviously in command of, and respected by them.'

'He is a terrible man,' she whispered.

He smiled. 'You never saw a white-skinned barbarian before. He is a wanderer and a plunderer and a slayer, but he has his own code of morals. I don't think we have anything to fear from him.'

In his heart he was not sure. In a way, it might be said that he had forfeited Conan's comradeship when he had ridden away into the desert, leaving the Cimmerian senseless on the ground. But he had not known that Conan was alive. Doubt haunted Amalric. Savagely loyal to his companions, the Cimmerian's wild nature saw no reason why the rest of the world should not be plundered. He lived by the sword. And Amalric suppressed a shudder as he thought of what might chance did Conan desire Lissa.

Later on, having eaten and drunk in the camp of the riders, Amalric sat by a small fire in front of Conan's tent; Lissa, covered with a silken cloak, slumbered with her curly head on his knees. And across from him the firelight played on Conan's face, interchanging lights and shadows.

'Who are these men?' asked the young Aquilonian.

'The riders of Tombalku,' answered the Cimmerian.

'Tombalku!' exclaimed Amalric. 'Then it is no myth.'

'Far from it!' agreed Conan. 'When my accursed steed fell with me, I was knocked senseless, and when I recovered consciousness the devils had me bound hand and foot. This angered me, so I snapped several of the cords they had tied me with, but they rebound them as fast as I could break them – never did I get a hand entirely free. But to them my strength seemed remarkable—'

Amalric gazed at Conan unspeaking. The man was tall and broad as Tilutan had been, without the dead man's surplus flesh. He could have broken the Ghanata's neck with his naked hands.

'They decided to carry me to their city instead of killing me out of hand,' Conan went on. 'They thought a man like me should be a long time in dying by torture, and so give them sport. Well, they bound me on a horse without a saddle, and we went to Tombalku.

'There were two kings of Tombalku. They took me before them – one a lean, brown-skinned devil named Zehbeh, the other a big, hulking black who dozed on his ivory-tusk throne. They spoke a dialect I could understand a little, it being much like that of the western Mandingo who dwell on the coast. Zehbeh asked one of his priests what should be done with me, and the priest cast dice made of sheep bone, and said I should be flayed alive before the altar of Jhil. Everyone cheered and that woke the other king.

'I spat at the priest and cursed him roundly, and the kings as well, telling them that if I were to be skinned, by Crom, I wanted a good belly-full of wine before they began. Then I damned them for thieves and cowards and sons of harlots.

'At this the black king roused and sat up to stare at me. Then he rose and shouted: "Amra!" and I knew him – Sakumbe, a Suba from the Black Coast, a fat adventurer I had known well in the days when I was a corsair along the coast. He trafficked in ivory, gold dust and slaves, and would cheat the devil out of his eye-teeth. Well, he knew me and descended from his throne and embraced me for joy – the fat, smelly devil – and took my cords off with his own hands. Then he announced that I was Amra, the Lion, his friend, and that no harm should come to me. Then followed much discussion because Zehbeh and his priest, Daura, wanted my life. But Sakumbe yelled for his witch-finder, Askia, and he came, all feathers and bells and snake-skins – a wizard of the Black Coast, and a son of the devil if there ever was one.

'Askia pranced and made incantations, and announced that Sakumbe was the chosen of Ajujo, the Dark One, and all the black people of Tombalku shouted, and Zehbeh backed down.

'The blacks in Tombalku are the real power. Several centuries ago, the Aphaki, a Shemitish race, pushed into the southern desert and established the kingdom of Tombalku. They mixed with the desert blacks and the result was a brown, straight-haired race. They are the dominant caste in Tombalku, but they are in the minority, and Sakumbe is the real ruler of Tombalku. The Aphaki worship Jhil, but the blacks worship Ajujo the Dark One, and his kin. Askia came to Tombalku with Sakumbe and revived the worship of Ajujo, which was crumbling because of the Aphaki priests. Askia made black magic which defeated the wizardry of the Aphaki, and the blacks hailed him as a prophet sent by the dark gods. Sakumbe and Askia wax as Zehbeh and Daura wane.

'Well, as I am Sakumbe's friend, and Askia spoke for me, the blacks received me with great applause. Sakumbe had Kordofo, the general of the horsemen, poisoned, and gave me his place, which delighted the blacks and exasperated the Aphaki.

'You will like Tombalku! It was made for men like us to loot! There are half a dozen powerful factions plotting and intriguing against each other – there are continual brawls in the taverns and streets, secret murders, mutilations and executions. And there are women, gold, wine – all that a mercenary wants! By Crom, Amalric, you could not have come at a better time! I am high in favor and power! Why, what's the matter? You do not seem as enthusiastic as I remember you having once been in such matters.'

'I crave your pardon, Conan,' apologized Amalric. 'I do not lack interest, but weariness and want of sleep overcomes me.'

But it was not of gold, women and intrigue that the Aquilonian was thinking, but of the girl who slumbered on his lap. There was no joy in the thought of taking her into such a welter of intrigue and blood as Conan had described. A subtle change had come over Amalric, almost without his knowledge.

THE VALE OF LOST WOMEN

1

THE THUNDER OF THE drums and the great elephant-tusk horns was deafening, but in Livia's ears the clamor seemed but a confused muttering dull and far away. As she lay on the *angareb* in the great hut, her state bordered between delirium and semi-unconsciousness. Outward sounds and movements scarcely impinged upon her senses. Her whole mental vision, though dazed and chaotic, was yet centered with hideous certitude on the naked, writhing figure of her brother, blood streaming down his quivering thighs. Against a dim nightmare background of dusky interweaving shapes and shadows, that white form was limned in merciless and awful clarity. The air seemed still to pulsate with an agonized screaming, mingled and interwoven obscenely with a rustle of fiendish laughter.

She was not conscious of sensation as an individual, separate and distinct from the rest of the cosmos. She was drowned in a great gulf of pain – was herself but pain crystalized and manifested in flesh. So she lay without conscious thought or motion, while outside the drums bellowed, the horns clamored, and barbaric voices lifted hideous chants, keeping time to naked feet slapping the hard earth and open palms smiting one another softly.

But through her frozen mentality individual consciousness at last began to seep. A dull wonder that she was still bodily unharmed first made itself manifest. She accepted the miracle without thanksgiving. The matter seemed meaningless. Acting mechanically, she sat up on the *angareb* and stared dully about her. Her extremities made feeble beginnings of motions, as if responding to blindly awakening nerve centers. Her naked feet scruffed nervously at the hard-beaten dirt floor.

Her fingers twitched convulsively at the skirt of the scanty undertunic which constituted her only garment. Impersonally she remembered that once, it seemed long, long ago, rude hands had torn her other garments from her body, and she had wept with fright and shame. It seemed strange, now, that so small a wrong should have caused her so much woe. The magnitude of outrage and indignity was only relative, after all, like everything else.

The hut door opened, and a black woman entered – a lithe pantherish creature, whose supple body gleamed like polished ebony, adorned only by a wisp of silk twisted about her strutting loins. The white of her eyeballs reflected the firelight outside, as she rolled them with wicked meaning.

She bore a bamboo dish of food – smoking meat, roasted yams, mealies, unwieldy ingots of native bread – and a vessel of hammered gold, filled with *yarati* beer. These she set down on the *angareb*, but Livia paid no heed; she sat staring dully at the opposite wall, hung with mats woven of bamboo shoots. The young black woman laughed evilly, with a flash of dark eyes and white teeth, and with a hiss of spiteful obscenity and a mocking caress that was more gross than her language, she turned and swaggered out of the hut, expressing more taunting insolence with the motions of her hips than any civilized woman could with spoken insults.

Neither the wench's words nor her actions had stirred the surface of Livia's consciousness. All her sensations were still turned inward. Still the vividness of her mental pictures made the visible world seem like an unreal panorama of ghosts and shadows. Mechanically she ate the food and drank the liquor without tasting either.

It was still mechanically that at last she rose and walked unsteadily across the hut, to peer out through a crack between the bamboos. It was an abrupt change in the timbre of the drums and horns that reacted upon some obscure part of her mind and made her seek the cause, without sensible volition.

At first she could make out nothing of what she saw; all was chaotic and shadowy, shapes moving and mingling, writhing and twisting, black formless blocks hewed out starkly against a setting of blood-red that dulled and glowed. Then actions and objects assumed their proper proportions, and she made out men and women moving about the fires. The red light glinted on silver and ivory ornaments; white plumes nodded against the glare; naked black figures strutted and posed, silhouettes carved out of darkness and limned in crimson.

On an ivory stool, flanked by giants in plumed headpieces and leopardskin girdles, sat a fat, squat shape, abysmal, repulsive, a toad-like

chunk of blackness, reeking of the dank rotting jungle and the nighted swamps. The creature's pudgy hands rested on the sleek arch of his belly; his nape was a roll of sooty fat that seemed to thrust his bullet-head forward. His eyes gleamed in the firelight, like live coals in a dead black stump. Their appalling vitality belied the inert suggestion of the gross body.

As the girl's gaze rested on that repellant figure her body stiffened and tensed as frantic life surged through her again. From a mindless automaton, she changed suddenly to a sentient mold of live, quivering flesh, stinging and burning. Pain was drowned in hate, so intense it in turn became pain; she felt hard and brittle, as if her body were turning to steel. She felt her hate flow almost tangibly out along the line of her vision; so it seemed to her that the object of her emotion should fall dead from his carven stool because of its force.

But if Bajujh, king of Bakalah, felt any psychic discomfort because of the concentration of his captive, he did not show it. He continued to cram his frog-like mouth to capacity with handfuls of mealies scooped up from a vessel held up to him by a kneeling woman, and to stare down a broad lane which was being formed by the action of his subjects in pressing back on either hand.

Down this lane, walled with sweaty black humanity, Livia vaguely realized some important personage would come, judging from the strident clamor of drum and horn. And as she watched, one came.

A column of fighting-men, marching three abreast, advanced toward the ivory stool, a thick line of waving plumes and glinting spears meandering through the motley crowd. At the head of the ebon spearmen strode a figure at the sight of which Livia started violently; her heart seemed to stop, then began to pound again, suffocatingly. Against that dusky background, this man stood out with vivid distinctness. He was clad like his followers in leopardskin loin-cloth and plumed headpiece, but he was a white man.

It was not in the manner of a supplicant or a subordinate that he strode up to the ivory stool, and sudden silence fell over the throng as he halted before the squatting figure. Livia felt the tenseness, though she only dimly knew what it portended. For a moment Bajujh sat, craning his short neck upward, like a great frog; then, as if pulled against his will by the other's steady glare, he shambled up off his stool, and stood grotesquely bobbing his shaven head.

Instantly the tension was broken. A tremendous shout went up from the massed villagers, and at a gesture from the stranger, his warriors lifted their spears and boomed a salute royale for King Bajujh. Whoever he was, Livia knew the man must indeed be powerful in that wild land, if Bajujh of Bakalah rose to greet him. And power meant military prestige – violence was the only thing respected by those ferocious races.

Thereafter Livia stood with her eyes glued to the crack in the hut wall, watching the white stranger. His warriors mingled with the Bakalas, dancing, feasting, swigging beer. He himself, with a few of his chiefs, sat with Bajujh and the headmen of Bakalah, cross-legged on mats, gorging and guzzling. She saw his hands dipped deep into the cooking-pots with the others, saw his muzzle thrust into the beer vessel out of which Bajujh also drank. But she noticed, nevertheless, that he was accorded the respect due to a king. Since he had no stool, Bajujh renounced his also, and sat on the mats with his guest. When a new pot of beer was brought, the king of Bakalah barely sipped it before he passed it to the white man. Power! All this ceremonial courtesy pointed to power – strength – prestige! Livia trembled in excitement as a breathless plan began to form in her mind.

So she watched the white man with painful intensity, noting every detail of his appearance. He was tall; neither in height nor in massiveness was he exceeded by many of the giant blacks. He moved with the lithe suppleness of a great panther. When the firelight caught his eyes, they burned like blue fire. High-strapped sandals guarded his feet, and from his broad girdle hung a sword in a leather scabbard. His appearance was alien and unfamiliar. Livia had never seen his like, but she made no effort to classify his position among the races of mankind. It was enough that his skin was white.

The hours passed, and gradually the roar of revelry lessened, as men and women sank into drunken sleep. At last Bajujh rose tottering, and lifted his hands, less a sign to end the feast, than a token of surrender in the contest of gorging and guzzling, and stumbling, was caught by his warriors, who bore him to his hut. The white man rose, apparently none the worse for the incredible amount of beer he had quaffed, and was escorted to the guest hut by such of the Bakalah headmen as were able to reel along. He disappeared into the hut, and Livia noticed that a dozen of his own spearmen took their places about the structure, spears ready. Evidently the stranger was taking no chances on Bajujh's friendship.

Livia cast her glance about the village, which faintly resembled a dusky Night of Judgment, what with the straggling streets strewn with drunken shapes. She knew that men in full possession of their faculties guarded the outer boma, but the only wakeful men she saw inside the village were the spearmen about the white man's hut –

and some of these were beginning to nod and lean on their spears.

With her heart beating hammer-like, she glided to the back of her prison hut and out the door, passing the snoring guard Bajujh had set over her. Like an ivory shadow she glided across the space between her hut and that occupied by the stranger. On her hands and knees she crawled up to the back of that hut. A black giant squatted here, his plumed head sunk on his knees. She wriggled past him to the wall of the hut. She had first been imprisoned in that hut, and a narrow aperture in the wall, hidden inside by a hanging mat, represented her weak and pathetic attempt at escape. She found the opening, turned sidewise and wriggled her lithe body through, thrusting the inner mat aside.

Firelight from without faintly illumined the interior of the hut. Even as she thrust back the mat, she heard a muttered curse, felt a vise-like grasp in her hair, and was dragged bodily through the aperture and plumped down on her feet.

Staggering with the suddenness of it, she gathered her scattered wits together, and raked her disordered tresses out of her eyes to stare up into the face of the white man who towered over her, amazement written on his dark scarred face. His sword was naked in his hand, and his eyes blazed like bale-fire, whether with anger, suspicion or surprize she could not judge. He spoke in a language she could not understand – a tongue which was not a negro guttural, yet did not have a civilized sound.

'Oh, please!' she begged. 'Not so loud. *They* will hear . . .'

'Who are you?' he demanded, speaking Ophirean with a barbarous accent. 'By Crom, I never thought to find a white girl in this hellish land!'

'My name is Livia,' she answered. 'I am Bajujh's captive. Oh, listen, please listen to me! I cannot stay here long. I must return before they miss me from my hut.

'My brother . . .' a sob choked her, then she continued: 'My brother was Theteles, and we were of the house of Chelkus, scientists and noblemen of Ophir. By special permission of the king of Stygia, my brother was allowed to go to Kheshatta, the city of magicians, to study their arts, and I accompanied him. He was only a boy – younger than myself . . .' her voice faltered and broke. The stranger said nothing, but stood watching her with burning eyes, his face frowning and unreadable. There was something wild and untamable about him that frightened her and made her nervous and uncertain.

'The black Kushites raided Kheshatta,' she continued hurriedly. 'We were approaching the city in a camel caravan. Our guards fled and the raiders carried us away with them. But they did us no harm, and let us know that they would parley with the Stygians and accept a ransom for our return. But one of the chiefs desired all the ransom for himself, and he and his followers stole us out of the camp one night, and fled far to the southeast with us, to the very borders of Kush. There they were attacked and cut down by a band of Bakalah raiders. Theteles and I were dragged into this den of beasts . . .' she sobbed convulsively. '. . . This morning my brother was mutilated and butchered before me . . .' She gagged and went momentarily blind at the memory. 'They fed his body to the jackals. How long I lay in a faint I do not know . . .'

Words failing her, she lifted her eyes to the scowling face of the stranger. A mad fury swept over her; she lifted her fists and beat futilely on his mighty breast, which he heeded no more than the buzzing of a fly.

'How can you stand there like a dumb brute?' she screamed in a ghastly whisper. 'Are you but a beast like these others? Ah, Mitra, once I thought there was honor in men. Now I know each has his price. You – what do you know of honor – or of mercy or decency? You are a barbarian like these others – only your skin is white; your soul is black as theirs. You care naught that a man of your own colour has been foully done to death by these black dogs – that a white woman is their slave! Very well.'

She fell back from him, panting, transfigured by her passion.

'I will give you a price,' she raved, tearing away her tunic from her ivory breasts. 'Am I not fair? Am I not more desirable than these soot-coloured wenches? Am I not a worthy reward for blood-letting? Is not a fair-skinned virgin a price worth slaying for?

'Kill that black dog Bajujh! Let me see his cursed head roll in the bloody dust! Kill him! *Kill him!*' She beat her clenched fists together in the agony of her intensity. 'Then take me and do as you wish with me. I will be your slave!'

He did not speak for an instant, but stood like a giant brooding figure of slaughter and destruction, fingering his hilt.

'You speak as if you were free to give yourself at your pleasure,' he said, 'as if the gift of your body had power to swing kingdoms. Why should I kill Bajujh to obtain you? Women are cheap as plantains in this land, and their willingness or unwillingness matters as little. You value yourself too highly. If I wanted you, I wouldn't have to fight Bajujh to take you. He would rather give you to me than to fight me.'

Livia gasped. All the fire went out of her, the hut reeled dizzily before her eyes. She staggered and sank in a crumpled heap on an *angareb*. Dazed bitterness crushed her soul as the realization of her utter helplessness was thrust brutally upon her. The human mind clings unconsciously to familiar values and ideas, even among surroundings and conditions alien and unrelated to those environs to which such values and ideas are adapted. In spite of all Livia had experienced, she had still instinctively supposed a woman's consent the pivotal point of such a game as she proposed to play. She was stunned by the realization that nothing hinged upon her at all. She could not move men as pawns in a game; she herself was the helpless pawn.

'I see the absurdity of supposing that any man in this corner of the world would act according to rules and customs existent in another corner of the planet,' she murmured weakly, scarcely conscious of what she was saying, which was indeed only the vocal framing of the thought which overcame her. Stunned by that newest twist of fate, she lay motionless, until the white barbarian's iron fingers closed on her shoulder and lifted her again to her feet.

'You said I was a barbarian,' he said harshly, 'and that is true, Crom be thanked. If you had had men of the outlands guarding you instead of soft gutted civilized weaklings, you would not be the slave of a black pig this night. I am Conan, a Cimmerian, and I live by the sword's edge. But I am not such a dog as to leave a white woman in the clutches of a black man; and though your kind call me a robber, I never forced a woman against her consent. Customs differ in various countries, but if a man is strong enough, he can enforce a few of his native customs anywhere. And no man ever called me a weakling!

'If you were old and ugly as the devil's pet vulture, I'd take you away from Bajujh, simply because of the colour of your hide. But you are young and beautiful, and I have looked at black sluts until I am sick at the guts. I'll play this game your way, simply because some of your instincts correspond with some of mine. Get back to your hut, Bajujh's too drunk to come to you tonight, and I'll see that he's occupied tomorrow. And tomorrow night it will be Conan's bed you'll warm, not Bajujh's.'

'How will it be accomplished?' She was trembling with mingled emotions. 'Are these all your warriors?'

'They're enough,' he grunted. 'Bamulas, every one of them, and suckled at the teats of war. I came here at Bajujh's request. He wants me to join him in an attack on Jihiji. Tonight we feasted. Tomorrow we hold council. When I get through with him, he'll be holding council in Hell.'

'You will break the truce?'

'Truces in this land are made to be broken,' he answered grimly. 'He would break his truce with Jihiji. And after we'd looted the town together, he'd wipe me out the first time he caught me off guard. What would be blackest treachery in another land, is wisdom here. I have not fought my way alone to the position of war-chief of the Bamulas without learning all the lessons the black country teaches. Now go back to your hut and sleep, knowing that it is not for Bajujh but for Conan that you preserve your beauty!'

2

Through the crack in the bamboo wall, Livia watched, her nerves taut and trembling. All day, since their late waking, bleary and sodden from their debauch of the night before, the black people had prepared the feast for the coming night. All day Conan the Cimmerian had sat in the hut of Bajujh, and what had passed between them, Livia could not know. She had fought to hide her excitement from the only person who entered her hut – the vindictive black girl who brought her food and drink. But that ribald wench had been too groggy from her libations of the previous night to notice the change in her captive's demeanor.

Now night had fallen again, fires lighted the village, and once more the chiefs left the king's hut and squatted down in the open space between the huts to feast and hold a final, ceremonious council. This time there was not so much beer-guzzling. Livia noticed the Bamulas casually converging toward the circle where sat the chief men. She saw Bajujh, and sitting opposite him across the eating pots, Conan, laughing and conversing with the giant Aja, Bajujh's war-chief.

The Cimmerian was gnawing a great beef-bone, and as she watched, she saw him cast a glance across his shoulder. As if it were a signal for which they had been waiting, the Bamulas all turned their gaze toward their chief. Conan rose, still smiling, as if to reach into a near-by cooking pot; then quick as a cat he struck Aja a terrible blow with the heavy bone. The Bakalah war-chief slumped over, his skull crushed in, and instantly a frightful yell rent the skies as the Bamulas went into action like blood-mad panthers.

Cooking pots overturned, scalding the squatting women, bamboo walls buckled to the impact of plunging bodies, screams of agony ripped the night, and over all rose the exultant '*Yee! yee! yee!*' of maddened Bamulas, the flame of spears that crimsoned in the lurid glow.

Bakalah was a madhouse that reddened into a shambles. The action of the invaders paralyzed the luckless villagers by its unexpected suddenness. No thought of attack by their guests had ever entered their woolly pates. Most of the spears were stacked in the huts, many of the warriors already half drunk. The fall of Aja was a signal that plunged the gleaming blades of the Bamulas into a hundred unsuspecting bodies; after that it was massacre.

At her peep-hole Livia stood frozen, white as a statue, her golden locks drawn back and grasped in a knotted cluster with both hands at her temples. Her eyes were dilated, her whole body rigid. The yells of pain and fury smote her tortured nerves like a physical impact, the writhing, slashing forms blurred before her, then sprang out again with horrifying distinctness. She saw spears sink into writhing black bodies, spilling red. She saw clubs swing and descend with brutal force on kinky heads. Brands were kicked out of the fires, scattering sparks; hut-thatches smoldered and blazed up. A fresh stridency of anguish cut through the cries, as living victims were hurled head-first into the blazing structures. The scent of scorched flesh began to sicken the air, already rank with reeking sweat and fresh blood.

Livia's overwrought nerves gave way. She cried out again and again, shrill screams of torment, lost in the roar of flames and slaughter. She beat her temples with her clenched fists. Her reason tottered, changing her cries to more awful peals of hysterical laughter. In vain she sought to keep before her the fact that it was her enemies who were dying thus horribly – that this was as she had madly hoped and plotted – that this ghastly sacrifice was a just repayment for the wrongs done her and hers. Frantic terror held her in its unreasoning grasp.

She was aware of no pity for the victims who were dying, wholesale under the dripping spears. Her only emotion was blind, stark, mad, unreasoning fear. She saw Conan, his white form contrasting with the blacks. She saw his sword flash, and men went down around him. Now a struggling knot swept around a fire, and she glimpsed a fat squat shape writhing in its midst. Conan ploughed through and was hidden from view by the twisting black figures. From the midst a thin squealing rose unbearably. The press split for an instant, and she had one awful glimpse of a reeling desperate squat figure, streaming blood. Then the throng crowded in again, and steel flashed in the mob like a beam of lightning through the dusk.

A beast-like baying rose, terrifying in its primitive exultation. Through the mob Conan's tall form pushed its way. He was striding toward the hut where the girl cowered, and in his hand he bore a ghastly relic – the firelight gleamed redly on King Bajujh's severed head. The black eyes, glassy now instead of vital, rolled up, revealing only the whites; the jaw hung slack as if in a grin of idiocy; red drops showered thickly along the ground.

Livia gave back with a moaning cry. Conan had paid the price and was coming to claim her, bearing the awful token of his payment. He would grasp her with his hot bloody fingers, crush her lips with mouth still panting from the slaughter. With the thought came delirium.

With a scream Livia ran across the hut, threw herself against the door in the back wall. It fell open, and she darted across the open space, a flitting white ghost in a realm of black shadows and red flame.

Some obscure instinct led her to the pen where the horses were kept. A warrior was just taking down the bars that separated the horse-pen from the main boma, and he yelled in amazement as she darted past him. A dusky hand clutched at her, closed on the neck of her tunic. With a frantic jerk she tore away leaving the garment in his hand. The horses snorted and stampeded past her, rolling the black warrior in the dust – lean, wiry steeds of the Kushite breed, already frantic with the fire and the scent of blood.

Blindly she caught at a flying mane, was jerked off her feet, struck the ground again on her toes, sprang high, pulled and scrambled herself upon the horse's straining back. Mad with fear the herd plunged through the fires, their small hoofs knocking sparks in a blinding shower. The startled black people had a wild glimpse of the girl clinging naked to the mane of a beast that raced like the wind that streamed out his rider's loose yellow hair. Then straight for the boma the steed bolted, soared breathtakingly into the air, and was gone into the night.

3

Livia could make no attempt to guide her steed, nor did she feel any need of so doing. The yells and the glow of the fires were fading out behind her; the wind tossed her hair and caressed her naked limbs. She was aware only of a dazed need to hold to the flowing mane and ride, ride, ride over the rim of the world and away from all agony and grief and horror.

And for hours the wiry steed raced, until, topping a starlit crest, he stumbled and hurled his rider headlong.

She struck on soft cushioning sward, and lay for an instant half stunned, dimly hearing her mount trot away. When she staggered up, the first thing that impressed her was the silence. It was an almost tangible thing – soft, darkly velvet – after the incessant blare of barbaric horns and drums which had maddened her for days. She stared up at the great white stars clustered thickly in the dark blue sky. There was no moon, yet the starlight illuminated the land, though illusively, with unexpected clusterings of shadow. She stood on a swarded eminence from which the gently molded slopes ran away, soft as velvet under the starlight. Far away in one direction she discerned a dense dark line of trees which marked the distant forest. Here there was only night and trance-like stillness and a faint breeze blowing through the stars.

The land seemed vast and slumbering. The warm caress of the breeze made her aware of her nakedness, and she wriggled uneasily, spreading her hands over her body. Then she felt the loneliness of the night, and the unbrokenness of the solitude. She was alone; she stood naked on the summit of the land and there was none to see; nothing but night and the whispering wind.

She was suddenly glad of the night and the loneliness. There was none to threaten her, or to seize her with rude violent hands. She looked before her and saw the slope falling away into a broad valley; there fronds waved thickly and the starlight reflected whitely on many small objects scattered throughout the vale. She thought they were great white blossoms and the thought gave rise to vague memory; she thought of a valley of which the blacks had spoken with fear; a valley to which had fled the young women of a strange brown-skinned race which had inhabited the land before the coming of the ancestors of the Bakalahs. There, men said, they had turned into white flowers, had been transformed by the old gods to escape their ravishers. There no black man dared go.

But into that valley Livia dared go. She would go down those grassy slopes which were like velvet under her tender feet; she would dwell there among the nodding white blossoms and no man would ever come to lay hot, rude hands on her. Conan had said that pacts were made to be broken; she would break her pact with him. She would go into the vale of the lost women; she would lose herself in solitude and stillness ... even as these dreamy and disjointed thoughts floated through her consciousness, she was descending the gentle slopes, and the tiers of the valley walls were rising higher on each hand.

But so gentle were their slopes that when she stood on the valley floor she did not have the feeling of being imprisoned by rugged walls. All about her floated seas of shadow, and great white blossoms nodded and whispered to her. She wandered at random, parting the fronds with her small hands, listening to the whisper of the wind through the leaves, finding a childish pleasure in the gurgling of an unseen stream. She moved as in a dream, in the grasp of a strange unreality. One thought reiterated itself continually: there she was safe from the brutality of men. She wept, but the tears were of joy. She lay full-length upon the sward and clutched the soft grass as if she would crush her new-found refuge to her breast and hold it there for ever.

*

She plucked the petals of the blossoms and fashioned them into a chaplet for her golden hair. Their perfume was in keeping with all other things in the valley, dreamy, subtle, enchanting.

So she came at last to a glade in the midst of the valley, and saw there a great stone, hewn as if by human hands, and adorned with ferns and blossoms and chains of flowers. She stood staring at it, and then there was movement and life about her. Turning, she saw figures stealing from the denser shadows – slender brown women, lithe, naked, with blossoms in their night-black hair. Like creatures of a dream they came about her, and they did not speak. But suddenly terror seized her as she looked into their eyes. Those eyes were luminous, radiant in the starshine, but they were not human eyes. The forms were human but in the souls a strange change had been wrought; a change reflected in their glowing eyes. Fear descended on Livia in a wave. The serpent reared its grisly head in her new-found Paradise.

But she could not flee. The lithe brown women were all about her. One, lovelier than the rest, came silently up to the trembling girl, and enfolded her with supple brown arms. Her breath was scented with the same perfume that stole from the white blossoms that waved in the starshine. Her lips pressed Livia's in a long terrible kiss. The Ophirean felt coldness, running through her veins; her limbs turned brittle; like a white statue of marble she lay in the arms of her captress, incapable of speech or movement.

Quick soft hands lifted her and laid her on the altar-stone amidst a bed of flowers. The brown women joined hands in a ring and moved supplely about the altar, dancing a strange dark measure. Never the sun or the moon looked on such a dance, and the great white stars grew whiter and glowed with a more luminous light as if its dark witchery struck response in things cosmic and elemental.

And a low chant arose, that was less human than the gurgling of the distant stream; a rustle of voices like the whispering of the great white blossoms that waved beneath the stars. Livia lay, conscious but without power of movement. It did not occur to her to doubt her sanity. She sought not to reason or analyze; she *was* and these strange beings dancing about her *were*; a dumb realization of existence and recognition of the actuality of nightmare possessed her as she lay helplessly gazing up at the star-clustered sky, whence, she somehow knew with more than mortal knowledge, some*thing* would come to her, as it had come long ago to make these naked brown women the soulless beings they now were.

First, high above her, she saw a black dot among the stars, which grew and expanded; it neared her; it swelled to a bat; and still it grew, though its shape did not alter further to any great extent. It hovered over her in the stars, dropping plummet-like earthward, its great wings spread over her; she lay in its tenebrous shadow. And all about her the chant rose higher, to a soft paean of soulless joy, a welcome to the god which came to claim a fresh sacrifice, fresh and rose-pink as a flower in the dew of dawn.

Now it hung directly over her, and her soul shriveled and grew chill and small at the sight. Its wings were bat-like; but its body and the dim face that gazed down upon her were like nothing of sea or earth or air; she knew she looked upon ultimate horror, upon black cosmic foulness born in night-black gulfs beyond the reach of a madman's wildest dreams.

Breaking the unseen bonds that held her dumb, she screamed awfully. Her cry was answered by a deep menacing shout. She heard the pounding of rushing feet; all about her there was a swirl as of swift waters; the white blossoms tossed wildly, and the brown women were gone. Over her hovered the great black shadow, and she saw a tall white figure, with plumes nodding in the stars, rushing toward her.

'Conan!' The cry broke involuntarily from her lips. With a fierce inarticulate yell, the barbarian sprang into the air, lashing upward with his sword that flamed in the starlight.

The great black wings rose and fell. Livia, dumb with horror, saw the Cimmerian enveloped in the black shadow that hung over him. The man's breath came pantingly; his feet stamped the beaten earth, crushing the white blossoms into the dirt. The rending impact of his blows echoed through the night. He was hurled back and forth like a rat in the grip of a hound, blood splashed thickly on the sward, mingling with the white petals that lay strewn like a carpet.

And then the girl, watching that devilish battle as in a nightmare, saw the black-winged thing waver and stagger in mid-air; there was a threshing beat of crippled wings and the monster had torn clear and was soaring upward to mingle and vanish among the stars. Its conqueror staggered dizzily, sword poised, legs wide-braced, staring upward stupidly amazed at victory, but ready to take up again the ghastly battle.

An instant later, Conan approached the altar, panting, dripping blood at every step. His massive chest heaved, glistening with perspiration. Blood ran down his arms in streams from his neck and shoulders. As he touched her, the spell on the girl was broken and she scrambled up and slid from the altar, recoiling from his hand. He leaned against the stone, looking down at her, where she cowered at his feet.

'Men saw you ride out of the village,' he said. 'I followed as soon as

I could, and picked up your track, though it was no easy task following it by torchlight. I tracked you to the place where your horse threw you, and though the torches were exhausted by then, and I could not find the prints of your bare feet on the sward, I felt sure you had descended into the valley. My men would not follow me, so I came alone on foot. What vale of devils is this? What was that thing?'

'A god,' she whispered. 'The black people spoke of it – a god from far away and long ago!'

'A devil from the Outer Dark,' he grunted. 'Oh, they're nothing uncommon. They lurk as thick as fleas outside the belt of light which surrounds this world. I've heard the wise men of Zamora talk of them. Some find their way to Earth, but when they do they have to take on Earthly form and flesh of some sort. A man like myself, with a sword, is a match for any amount of fangs and talons, infernal or terrestrial. Come; my men await me beyond the ridge of the valley.'

She crouched motionless, unable to find words, while he frowned down at her. Then she spoke: 'I ran away from you. I planned to dupe you. I was not going to keep my promise to you; I was yours by the bargain we made but I would have escaped from you if I could. Punish me as you will.'

He shook the sweat and blood from his locks, and sheathed his sword.

'Get up,' he grunted. 'It was a foul bargain I made. I do not regret that black dog Bajujh, but you are no wench to be bought and sold. The ways of men vary in different lands, but a man need not be a swine, wherever he is. After I thought awhile, I saw that to hold you to your bargain would be the same as if I had forced you. Besides, you are not tough enough for this land. You are a child of cities and books and civilized ways – which isn't your fault, but you'd die quickly following the life I thrive on. A dead woman would be no good to me. I will take you to the Stygian borders. The Stygians will send you home to Ophir.'

She stared up at him as if she had not heard aright. 'Home?' she repeated mechanically. 'Home? Ophir? My people? Cities, towers, peace, my *home*?' Suddenly tears welled into her eyes, and sinking to her knees, she embraced his knees in her arms.

'Crom, girl,' grunted Conan, embarrassed. 'Don't do that; you'd think I was doing you a favor by kicking you out of this country; haven't I explained that you're not the proper woman for the war-chief of the Bamulas?'

WOLVES BEYOND THE BORDER

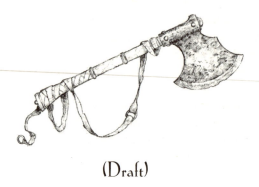

(Draft)

1

It was the mutter of a drum that awakened me. I lay still amidst the bushes where I had taken refuge, straining my ears to locate it, for such sounds are illusive in the deep forest. In the dense woods about me there was no sound. Above me the tangled vines and brambles bent close to form a massed roof, and above them there loomed the higher, gloomier arch of the branches of the great trees. Not a star shone through that leafy vault. Low-hanging clouds seemed to press down upon the very tree-tops. There was no moon. The night was dark as a witch's hate.

The better for me. If I could not see my enemies, neither could they see me. But the whisper of that ominous drum stole through the night: *thrum! thrum! thrum!*, a steady monotone that grunted and growled of nameless secrets. I could not mistake the sound. Only one drum in the world makes just that deep, menacing, sullen thunder: a Pictish war-drum, in the hands of those wild painted savages who haunted the Wilderness beyond the border of the Westermarck.

And I was beyond that border, alone, and concealed in a brambly covert in the midst of the great forest where those naked fiends have reigned since Time's earliest dawns.

Now I located the sound; the drum was beating westward of my position and I believed at no great distance. Quickly I girt my belt more firmly, settled war-ax and knife in their beaded sheaths, strung my heavy bow and made sure that my quiver was in place at my left hip – groping with my fingers in the yutter darkness – and then I crawled from the thicket and went warily toward the sound of the drum.

That it personally concerned me I did not believe. If the forest-men had discovered me, their discovery would have been announced by a sudden knife in my throat, not by a drum beating in the distance. But the throb of the war-drum had a significance no forest-runner could ignore. It was a warning and a threat, a promise of doom for those white-skinned invaders whose lonely cabins and ax-marked clearings menaced the immemorial solitude of the wilderness. It meant fire and torture, flaming arrows dropping like falling stars through the darkness, and the red ax crunching through skulls of men and women and children.

So through the blackness of the nighted forest I went, feeling my way delicately among the mighty boles, sometimes creeping on hands and knees, and now and then my heart in my throat when a creeper brushed across my face or groping hand. For there are huge serpents in that forest which sometimes hang by their tails from branches and so snare their prey. But the creatures I sought were more terrible than any serpent, and as the drum grew louder I went as cautiously as if I trod on naked swords. And presently I glimpsed a red gleam among the trees, and heard a mutter of barbaric voices mingling with the snarl of the drum.

Whatever weird ceremony might be taking place yonder under the black trees, it was likely that they had outposts scattered about the place, and I knew how silent and motionless a Pict could stand, merging with the natural forest growth even in dim light, and unsuspected until his blade was through his victim's heart. My flesh crawled at the thought of colliding with one such grim sentry in the darkness, and I drew my knife and held it extended before me. But I knew not even a Pict could see me in that blackness of tangled forest-roof and the cloud-massed sky.

The light revealed itself as a fire before which black silhouettes moved like black devils against the red fires of hell, and presently I crouched close among the dense tamarack and looked into a black-walled glade and the figures that moved therein.

There were forty or fifty Picts, naked but for loin-cloths, and hideously painted, who squatted in a wide semi-circle, facing the fire, with their backs to me. By the hawk feathers in their thick black manes, I knew them to be of the Hawk Clan, or Onayaga. In the midst of the glade there was a crude altar made of rough stones heaped together, and at the sight of this my flesh crawled anew. For I had seen these Pictish altars before, all charred with fire and stained with blood, in empty forest glades, and though I had never witnessed the rituals wherein these things were used, I had heard the tales told about them by men who had been captives among the Picts, or spied upon them even as I was spying.

A feathered shaman was dancing between the fire and the altar, a slow, shuffling dance indescribably grotesque, which caused his plumes to swing and sway about him: his features were hidden by a grinning scarlet mask that looked like a forest-devil's face.

In the midst of the semi-circle of warriors squatted one with the great drum between his knees and as he smote it with his clenched fist it gave forth that low, growling rumble which is like the mutter of distant thunder.

Between the warriors and the dancing shaman stood one who was no Pict. For he was tall as I, and his skin was light in the play of the fire. But he was clad only in doeskin loin-clout and moccasins, and his body was painted, and there was a hawk-feather in his hair, so I knew he must be a Ligurean, one of those light-skinned savages who dwell in small clans in the great forest, generally at war with the Picts, but sometimes at peace and allied with them. Their skins are white as an Aquilonian's. The Picts are a white race too, in that they are not black nor brown nor yellow, but they are black-eyed and black-haired and dark of skin, and neither they nor the Ligureans are spoken of as 'white' by the people of Westermarck, who only designate thus a man of Hyborian blood.

Now as I watched I saw three warriors drag a man into the ring of the firelight – another Pict, naked and bloodstained, who still wore in his tangled mane a feather that identified him as a member of the Raven Clan, with whom the Hawkmen were ever at war. His captors cast him down upon the altar, bound hand and foot, and I saw his muscles swell and writhe in the firelight as he sought in vain to break the rawhide thongs which prisoned him.

Then the shaman began dancing again, weaving intricate patterns about the altar, and the man upon it, and he who beat the drum wrought himself into a fine frenzy, thundering away like one possessed of a devil. And suddenly, down from an overhanging branch dropped one of those great serpents of which I have spoken. The firelight glistened on its scales as it writhed toward the altar, its beady eyes glittered, and its forked tongue darted in and out, but the warriors showed no fear, though it passed within a few feet of some of them. And that was strange, for ordinarily these serpents are the only living creatures a Pict fears.

The monster reared its head up on arched neck above the altar, and it and the shaman faced one another across the prone body of the prisoner. The shaman danced with a writhing of body and arms, scarcely moving his feet, and as he danced, the great serpent danced with him, weaving and swaying as though mesmerized, and from the mask of the shaman rose a weird wailing that shuddered like the wind through the dry reeds along the sea-marshes. And slowly the great reptile reared higher and higher, and began looping itself about the altar and the man upon it, until his body was hidden by its shimmering folds, and only his head was visible with that other terrible head swaying close above it.

The shrilling of the shaman rose to a crescendo of infernal triumph, and he cast something into the fire. A great green cloud of smoke billowed up and rolled about the altar, so that it almost hid the pair upon it, making their outlines indistinct and illusive. But in the midst of that cloud I saw a hideous writhing and *changing* – those outlines melted and flowed together horribly, and for a moment I could not tell which was the serpent and which the man. A shuddering sigh swept over the assembled Picts like a wind moaning through nighted branches.

Then the smoke cleared and man and snake lay limply on the altar, and I thought both were dead. But the shaman seized the neck and let the great reptile ooze to the ground, and he tumbled the body of the man from the stones to fall beside the monster, and cut the rawhide thongs that bound wrist and ankle.

Then he began a weaving dance about them, chanting as he danced and swaying his arms in mad gestures. And presently the man moved. But he did not rise. His head swayed from side to side, and I saw his tongue dart out and in again. And Mitra, he began to *wriggle* away from the fire, squirming along on his belly, as a snake crawls!

And the serpent was suddenly shaken with convulsions and arched its neck and reared up almost its full length, and then fell back, loop on loop and reared up again vainly, horribly like a man trying to rise and stand and walk upright after being deprived of his limbs.

The wild howling of the Picts shook the night, and I was sick where I crouched among the bushes, and fought an urge to retch. I understood the meaning of this ghastly ceremony now. I had heard tales of it. By black, primordial sorcery that spawned and throve in the depths of this black primal forest, that painted shaman had transferred the soul of a captured enemy into the foul body of a serpent. It was the revenge of a fiend. And the screaming of the blood-mad Picts was like the yelling of all Hell's demons.

And the victims writhed and agonized side by side, the man and the serpent, until a sword flashed in the hand of the shaman and both heads fell together – and gods, it was the serpent's trunk which but quivered and jerked a little and then lay still, and the man's body which rolled and knotted and thrashed like a beheaded snake. A deathly faintness and weakness took hold of me, for what white man could watch such black diabolism unmoved? And these painted savages, smeared with war-paint howling and posturing and triumphing over the ghastly doom of a foe, seemed not humans at all to me, but foul fiends of the black world whom it was a duty and an obligation to slay.

The shaman sprang up and faced the ring of warriors, and, ripping off his mask, threw up his head and howled like a wolf. And as the firelight fell full on his face, I recognized him, and with that recognition all horror and revulsion gave place to red rage, and all thought of personal peril and the recollection of my mission, which was my first obligation, was swept away. For that shaman was old Teyanoga of the South Hawks, he who burnt alive my friend, Jon Galter's son.

In the lust of my hate I acted almost instinctively – whipped up my bow, notched an arrow and loosed, all in an instant. The firelight was uncertain, but the range was not great, and we of the Westermarck live by twang of bow. Old Teyanoga yowled like a cat and reeled back and his warriors howled with amazement to see a shaft quivering suddenly in his breast. The tall, light-skinned warrior wheeled, and for the first time I saw his face – and Mitra, he was a white man!

The horrid shock of that surprise held me paralysed for a moment and had almost undone me. For the Picts instantly sprang up and rushed into the forest, like panthers, seeking the foe who fired that arrow. They had reached the first fringe of bushes when I jerked out of my spell of amaze and horror, and sprang up and raced away in the darkness, ducking and dodging among trees which I avoided more by instinct than otherwise, for it was dark as ever. But I knew the Picts could not strike my trail, but must hunt as blindly as I fled. And presently, as I ran northward, behind me I heard a hideous howling whose blood-mad fury was enough to freeze the blood even of a forest-runner. And I believed that they had plucked my arrow from the shaman's breast and discovered it to be a white man's shaft. That would bring them after me with fiercer blood-lust than ever.

I fled on, my heart pounding from fear and excitement, and the horror of the nightmare I had witnessed. And that a white man, a Hyborian, should have stood there as a welcome and evidently honored guest – for he was armed – I had seen knife and hatchet at his belt – was so monstrous I wondered if, after all, the whole thing were a nightmare. For never before had a white man observed The Dance of the Changing Serpent save as a prisoner, or a spy, as I had. And what monstrous thing it portended I knew not, but I was shaken with foreboding and horror at the thought.

And because of my horror I went more carelessly than is my wont, seeking haste at the expense of stealth, and occasionally blundering into a tree I could have avoided had I taken more care. And I doubt not it was the noise of this blundering progress which brought the Pict upon me, for he could not have seen me in that pitch-darkness.

Behind me sounded no more yells, but I knew that the Picts were ranging like fire-eyed wolves through the forest, spreading in a vast semi-circle and combing it as they ran. That they had not picked up my trail was evidenced by their silence, for they never yell except when they believe only a short dash is ahead of them, and feel sure of their prey.

The warrior who heard the sounds of my flight could not have been one of that party, for he was too far ahead of them. He must have been a scout ranging the forest to guard against his comrades being surprised from the north.

At any rate he heard me running close to him, and came like a devil of the black night. I knew of him first only by the swift faint pad of his naked feet, and when I wheeled I could not even make out the dim bulk of him, but only heard the soft thudding of those inexorable feet coming to me unseen in the darkness.

They see like cats in the dark, and I know he saw well enough to locate me, though doubtless I was only a dim blur in the darkness. But my blindly upswung hatchet met his falling knife and he impaled himself on my knife as he lunged in, his death-yell ringing like a peal of doom under the forest-roof. And it was answered by a ferocious clamor to the south, only a few hundred yards away, and then they were racing through the bushes giving tongue like wolves, certain of their quarry.

I ran for it in good earnest now, abandoning stealth entirely for the sake of speed, and trusting to luck that I would not dash out my brains against a tree-stem in the darkness.

But here the forest opened up somewhat; there was no underbrush, and something almost like light filtered in through the branches, for the clouds were clearing a little. And through this forest I fled like a damned soul pursued by demons, hearing the yells at first rising higher and higher in blood-thirsty triumph, then edged with anger and rage as they grew fainter and fell away behind me, for in a straight-away race no Pict can match the long legs of a white forest-runner. The desperate risk was that there were other scouts or war-parties ahead of me who could easily cut me off, hearing my flight; but it was a risk I had to take. But no painted figures started up like phantoms out of the shadows ahead of me, and presently, through the thickening growth that betokened the nearness of a creek, I saw a glimmer through the trees far ahead of me and knew it was the light of Fort Kwanyara, the southernmost outpost of Schohira.

2

Perhaps, before continuing with this chronicle of the bloody years, it might be well were I to give an account of myself, and the reason why I traversed the Pictish Wilderness, by night and alone.

My name is Gault Hagar's son. I was born in the province of Conajohara. But when I was ten years of age, the Picts broke over Black River and stormed Fort Tuscelan and slew all within save one man, and drove all the settlers of the province east of Thunder River. Conajohara became again part of the Wilderness, haunted only by wild beasts and wild men. The people of Conajohara scattered throughout the Westermarck, in Schohira, Conawaga, or Oriskawny, but many of them went southward and settled near Fort Thandara, an isolated outpost on the Warhorse River, my family among them. There they were later joined by other settlers for whom the older provinces were too thickly inhabited, and presently there grew up the district known as the Free Province of Thandara, because it was not like the other provinces, royal grants to great lords east of the marches and settled by them, but cut out of the wilderness by the pioneers themselves without aid of the Aquilonian nobility. We paid no taxes to any baron. Our governor was not appointed by any lord, but we elected him ourselves, from our own people, and he was responsible only to the king. We manned and built our forts ourselves, and sustained ourselves in war as in peace. And Mitra knows war was a constant state of affairs, for there was never peace between us and our savage neighbors, the wild Panther, Alligator and Otter tribes of Picts.

But we throve, and seldom questioned what went on east of the marches in the kingdom whence our grandsires had come. But at last events in Aquilonia did touch upon us in the wilderness. Word came of civil war, and a fighting man risen to wrest the throne from the ancient dynasty. And sparks from that conflagration set the frontier ablaze, and turned neighbor against neighbor and brother against brother. And it was because knights in their gleaming steel were fighting and slaying on the plains of Aquilonia that I was hastening alone through the stretch of wilderness that separated Thandara from Schohira, with news that might well change the destiny of all the Westermarck.

Fort Kwanyara was a small outpost, a square fortress of hewn logs with a palisade on the bank of Knife Creek. I saw its banner streaming against the pale rose of the morning sky, and noted that only the ensign of the province floated there. The royal standard that should have risen above it, flaunting the golden serpent, was not in evidence. That might mean much, or nothing. We of the frontier are careless about the delicate punctilios of custom and etiquette which mean so much to the knights beyond the marches.

I crossed Knife Creek in the early dawn, wading through the shallows, and was challenged by a picket on the other bank, a tall man in the buckskins of a ranger. When he knew I was from Thandara: 'By Mitra!' quoth he, 'your business must be urgent, that you cross the wilderness instead of taking the longer road.'

For Thandara was separated from the other provinces, as I have said, and the Little Wilderness lay between it and the Bossonian marches; but a safe road ran through it into the marches and thence to the other provinces but it was a long and tedious road.

Then he asked for news from Thandara, but I told him I knew little of the latest events, having just returned from a long scout into the country of the Ottermen, which was a lie, but I had no way of knowing Schohira's political color, and was not inclined to betray my own until I knew. Then I asked him if Hakon Strom's son was in Fort Kwanyara, and he told me that the man I sought was not in the fort, but was at the town of Schondara, which lay a few miles east of the fort.

'I hope Thandara declares for Conan,' said he with an oath, 'for I tell you plainly it is our political complexion. And it is my cursed luck which keeps me here with the handful of rangers who watch the border for raiding Picts. I would give my bow and hunting shirt to be with your army which lies even now at Thenitea on Ogaha Creek waiting the onslaught of Brocas of Torh with his damned renegades.'

I said naught but was astounded. This was news indeed. For the Baron of Torh was lord of Conawaga, not Schohira, whose patron was Lord Thasperas of Kormon.

'Where is Thasperas?' I asked, and the ranger answered, a thought shortly: 'Away in Aquilonia, fighting for Conan.' And he looked at me narrowly as if he had begun to wonder if I were a spy.

'Is there a man in Schohira,' I began, 'who has such connections with the Picts that he dwells, naked and painted among them, and attends their ceremonies of blood-feast and—'

I checked myself at the fury that contorted the Schohiran's features.

'Damn you,' says he, choking with passion, 'what is your purpose in coming here to insult us thus?'

And indeed, to call a man a renegade was the direst insult that could be offered along the Westermarck, though I had not meant it in that way. But I saw the man was ignorant of any knowledge concerning the renegade I had seen, and not wishing to give out information, I merely told him that he misunderstood my meaning.

'I understand it well enough,' said he, shaking with passion. 'But for your dark skin and southern accent I would deem you a spy from Conawaga. But spy or no, you cannot insult the men of Schohira in such manner. Were I not on military duty I would lay down my weapon-belt and show you what manner of men we breed in Schohira.'

'I want no quarrel,' said I. 'But I am going to Schondara, where it will not be hard for you to find me, if you so desire.'

'I will be there anon,' quoth he grimly. 'I am Storm Grom's son and they know me in Schohira.'

I left him striding his post along the bank, and fingering his knife hilt and hatchet as if he itched to try their edge on my head, and I swung wide of the small fort to avoid other scouts or pickets. For in these troublous times suspicion might fall on me as a spy very easily. Nay, this Storm Grom's son was beginning to turn such thoughts in his thick noddle when they were swept away by his personal resentment at what he mistook for a slur. And having quarreled with me, his sense of personal honor would not allow him to arrest me on suspicion of being a spy – even had he thought of it. In ordinary times none would think of halting or questioning a white man crossing the border – but everything was in a mad whirl now – it must be, if the patroon of Conawaga was invading the domain of his neighbors.

The forest had been cleared about the fort for a few hundred yards in each direction, forming a solid green wall. I kept within this wall as I skirted the clearing, and met no one, even when I crossed several paths leading from the fort. I avoided clearings and farms. I headed eastward and the sun was not high in the heavens when I sighted the roofs of Schondara.

The forest ran to within less than half a mile of the town, which was a handsome one for a frontier village, with neat houses mostly of squared logs, some painted, but also some fine frame buildings which is something we have not in Thandara. But there was not so much as a ditch or a palisade about the village, which was strange to me. For we of Thandara build our dwelling places for defense as much as shelter, and while there is not a village in the width and breadth of the province, yet every cabin is like a tiny fort.

Off to the right of the village stood a fort, in the midst of a meadow, with palisade and ditch, somewhat larger than Fort Kwanyara, but I saw few heads moving above the parapet, either helmeted or capped. And only the spreading winged hawk of Schohira flapped on the standard. And I wondered why, if Schohira were for Conan, they did not fly the banner he had chosen – the golden lion on a black field, the standard of the regiment he commanded as a mercenary general of Aquilonia.

Away to the left, at the edge of the forest I saw a large house of stone set amid gardens and orchards, and knew it for the estate of Lord

Valerian, the richest land-owner in western Schohira. I had never seen the man, but knew he was wealthy and powerful. But now the Hall, as it was called, seemed deserted.

The town seemed curiously deserted, likewise; at least of men, though there were women and children in plenty, and it seemed to me that the men had assembled their families here for safety. I saw few able-bodied men. As I went up the street many eyes followed me suspiciously, but none spoke except to reply briefly to my questions.

At the tavern only a few old men and cripples huddled about the ale-stained tables and conversed in low tones, all conversation ceasing as I loomed in the doorway in my worn buck-skins, and all turned to stare at me silently.

More significant silence when I asked for Hakon Strom's son, and the host told me that Hakon was ridden to Thenitea shortly after sun-up, where the militia-army lay encamped, but would return shortly. So being hungry and weary, I ate a meal in the taproom, aware of those questioning eyes fixed on me, and then lay down in a corner on a bear skin the host fetched for me, and slept. And was so slumbering when Hakon Strom's son returned, close upon sunset.

He was a tall man, rangy and broad-shouldered, like most West-landers, and clad in buckskin hunting shirt and fringed leggins and moccasins like myself. Half a dozen rangers were with him, and they sat them down at a board close to the door and watched him and me over the rims of their ale jacks.

When I named myself and told him I had word for him, he looked at me closely, and bade me sit with him at a table in the corner where mine host brought us ale foaming in leathern jacks.

'Has no word come through of the state of affairs in Thandara?' I asked.

'No sure word; only rumors.'

'Very well,' I said. 'I bring you word from Brant Drago's son, governor of Thandara, and the council of captains, and by this sign you shall know me for a true man.' And so saying I dipped my finger in the foamy ale and with it drew a symbol on the table, and instantly erased it. He nodded, his eyes blazing with interest.

'This is the word I bring you,' quoth I; 'Thandara has declared for Conan and stands ready to aid his friends and defy his enemies.'

At that he smiled joyfully and grasped my brown hand warmly with his own rugged fingers.

'Good!' he exclaimed. 'But it is no more than I expected.'

'What man of Thandara could forget Conan?' said I. 'Nay, I was but a child in Conajohara, but I remember him when he was a forest-runner and a scout there. When his rider came into Thandara telling us that Poitain was in revolt, with Conan striking for the throne, and asking our support – he asked no volunteers for his army, merely our loyalty – we sent him one word: "We have not forgotten Conajohara." Then came the Baron Attelius over the marches against us, but we ambushed him in the Little Wilderness and cut his army to pieces. And now I think we need fear no invasion in Thandara.'

'I would I could say as much for Schohira,' he said grimly. 'Baron Thasperas sent us word that we could do as we chose – he has declared for Conan and joined the rebel army. But he did not demand western levies. Nay, both he and Conan know the Westermarck needs every man it has to guard the border.

'He removed his troops from the forts, however, and we manned them with our own foresters. There was some little skirmishing among ourselves, especially in the towns like Goyaga, where dwell the land-holders, for some of them held to Namedides – well, these loyalists either fled away to Conawaga with their retainers, or else surrendered and gave their pledge to remain neutral in their castles, like Lord Valerian of Schondara. The loyalists who fled swore to return and cut all our throats. And presently Lord Brocas marched over the border.

'In Conawaga the land-owners and Brocas are for Namedides, and we have heard pitiful tales of their treatment of the common people who favor Conan.'

I nodded, not surprised. Conawaga was the largest, richest and most thickly settled province in all the Westermarck, and it had a comparatively large, and very powerful class of titled land-holders – which we have not in Thandara, and by the favor of Mitra, never shall.

'It is an open invasion for conquest,' said Hakon. 'Brocas commanded us to swear loyalty to Namedides – the dog. I think the black-jowled fool plots to subdue all the Westermarck and rule it as Namedides' viceroy. With an army of Aquilonian men-at-arms, Bossonian archers, Conawaga loyalists, and Schohira renegades, he lies at Coyaga, ten miles beyond Ogaha Creek. Thenitea is full of refugees from the eastern country he has devastated.

'We do not fear him, though we are outnumbered. He must cross Ogaha Creek to strike us, and we have fortified the west bank and blocked the road against his cavalry.'

'That touches upon my mission,' I said. 'I am authorized to offer the services of a hundred and fifty Thandaran rangers. We are all of one mind in Thandara and fight no internal wars; and we can spare that many men from our war with the Panther Picts.'

'That will be good news for the commandant of Fort Kwanyara!'

'What?' quoth I. 'Are you not the commandant?'

'Nay,' said he, 'it is my brother Dirk Strom's son.'

'Had I known that I would have given my message to him,' I said. 'Brant Drago's son thought you commanded Kwanyara. However, it does not matter.'

'Another jack of ale,' quoth Hakon, 'and we'll start for the fort so that Dirk shall hear your news first-hand. A plague on commanding a fort. A party of scouts is good enough for me.'

And in truth Hakon was not the man to command an outpost or any large body of men, for he was too reckless and hasty, though a brave man and a gay rogue.

'You have but a skeleton force left to watch the border,' I said. 'What of the Picts?'

'They keep the peace to which they swore,' answered he. 'For some months there has been peace along the border, except for the usual skirmishing between individuals of both races.'

'Valerian Hall seemed deserted.'

'Lord Valerian dwells there alone except for a few servants. Where his fighting men have gone, none knows. But he has sent them off. If he had not given his pledge we would have felt it necessary to place him under guard, for he is one of the few white men to whom the Picts give heed. If it had entered his head to stir them up against our borders we might be hard put to it to defend ourselves against them on one side and Brocas on the other.

'The Hawks, Wildcats and Turtles listen when Valerian speaks, and he has even visited the towns of the Wolf Picts and come away alive.'

If that were true that were strange indeed, for all men knew the ferocity of the great confederacy of allied clans known as the Wolf tribe which dwelt in the west beyond the hunting grounds of the three lesser tribes he had named. Mostly they held aloof from the frontier, but the threat of their hatred was ever a menace along the borders of Schohira.

Hakon looked up as a tall man in trunk-hose, boots and scarlet cloak entered the taproom.

'There is Lord Valerian now,' he said.

I stared, started and was on my feet instantly.

'That man?' I ejaculated. 'I saw that man last night beyond the border, in a camp of the Hawks, watching the Dance of the Changing Snake!'

Valerian heard me and he whirled, going pale. His eyes blazed like those of a panther.

Hakon sprang up too.

'What are you saying?' he cried. 'Lord Valerian gave his pledge—'

'I care not!' I exclaimed fiercely, striding forward to confront the tall noble. 'I saw him where I lay hidden among the tamarack. I could not mistake that hawk-like face. I tell you he was there, naked and painted like a Pict—'

'You lie, damn you!' cried Valerian, and whipping aside his cloak he caught at the hilt of his sword. But before he could draw it I closed with him and bore him to the floor, where he caught at my throat with both hands, blaspheming like a madman. Then there was a swift stamp of feet, and men were dragging us apart, grasping my lord firmly, who stood white and panting with fury, still clutching my neckcloth which had been torn away from my throat in the struggle.

'Loose me, you dogs!' he raved. 'Take your peasant hands from me! I'll cleave this liar to the chin—'

'Here is no lie,' I said more calmly. 'I lay in the tamarack last night and watched while old Teyanoga dragged a Raven chief's soul from his body and forced it into that of a tree-serpent. It was my arrow which struck down the shaman. And I saw you there – you, a white man, naked and painted, accepted as one of the clan.'

'If this be true—' began Hakon.

'It is true, and there is your proof!' I exclaimed. 'Look there! On his bosom!'

His doublet and shirt had been torn open in the scuffle, and there, dim on his naked breast, showed the outline of the white skull which the Picts paint only when they mean war against the whites. He had sought to wash it off his skin, but Pictish paint stains strongly.

'Disarm him,' said Hakon, white to the lips.

'Give me my neckcloth,' I demanded, but his lordship spat at me, and thrust the cloth inside his shirt.

'When it is returned to you it shall be knotted in a hangman's noose about your rebel neck,' he snarled.

Hakon seemed undecided.

'Let us take him to the fort,' I said. 'Give him in custody of the commander. It was for no good purpose he took part in the Dance of the Snake. Those Picts were painted for battle. That symbol on his breast means he intended to take part in the war for which they danced.'

'But great Mitra, this is incredible!' exclaimed Hakon. 'A white man, loosing those painted devils on his friends and neighbors?'

My lord said naught. He stood there between the men who grasped his arms, livid, his thin lips drawn back in a snarl that bared his teeth, but all hell burned like yellow fire in his eyes where I seemed to sense lights of madness.

But Hakon was uncertain. He dared not release Valerian, and he feared what the effect might be on the people if they saw the lord being led a captive to the fort.

'They will demand the reason,' he argued, 'and when they learn he has been dealing with the Picts in their war-paint, a panic might well ensue. Let us lock him into the gaol until we can bring Dirk here to question him.'

'It is dangerous to compromise with a situation like this,' I answered bluntly. 'But it is for you to decide. You are in command here.'

So we took his lordship out the back door, secretly, and it being dusk by that time, reached the gaol without being noticed by the people, who indeed stayed indoors mostly. The gaol was a small affair of logs, somewhat apart from the town, with four cells, and one only occupied, that by a fat rogue who had been imprisoned overnight for drunkenness and fighting in the street. He stared to see our prisoner. Not a word said Lord Valerian as Hakon locked the grilled door upon him, and detailed one of the men to stand guard. But a demon fire burned in his dark eyes as if behind the mask of his pale face he were laughing at us with fiendish triumph.

'You place only one man on guard?' I asked Hakon.

'Why more?' said he. 'Valerian cannot break out, and there is no one to rescue him.'

It seemed to me that Hakon was prone to take too much for granted, but after all, it was none of my affair, so I said no more.

Then Hakon and I went to the fort, and there I talked with Dirk Strom's son, the commander, who was in command of the town, in the absence of Jon Storm's son, the governor appointed by Lord Thasperas, who was now in command of the militia-army which lay at Thenitea. He looked sober indeed when he heard my tale, and said he would come to the gaol and question Lord Valerian as soon as his duties permitted, though he had little belief that my lord would talk, for he came of a stubborn and haughty breed. He was glad to hear of the men Thandara offered him, and told me that he could find a man to return to Thandara accepting the offer, if I wished to remain in Schohira awhile, which I did. Then I returned to the tavern with Hakon, for it was our purpose to sleep there that night, and set out for Thenitea in the morning. Scouts kept the Schohirans posted on the movements of Brocas, and Hakon, who had been in their camp that day, said Brocas showed no signs of moving against us, which made me believe that he was waiting for Valerian to lead his Picts against the border. But Hakon still doubted, in spite of all I had told him, believing Valerian had but visited the Picts through friendliness as he often did. But I pointed out that no white man, however friendly to the Picts, was ever allowed to witness such a ceremony as the Dance of the Snake; he would have to be a blood-member of the clan.

3

I awakened suddenly and sat up in bed. My window was open, both shutters and pane, for coolness, for it was an upstairs room, and there was no tree near by which a thief might gain access. But some noise had awakened me, and now as I stared at the window, I saw the star-lit sky blotted out by a bulky, misshapen figure. I swung my legs around off the bed, demanding to know who it was, and groping for my hatchet, but the thing was on me with frightful speed and before I could even rise something was around my neck, choking and strangling me. Thrust almost against my face there was a dim frightful visage, but all I could make out in the darkness was a pair of flaming red eyes, and a peaked head. My nostrils were filled with a bestial reek.

I caught one of the thing's wrists and it was hairy as an ape's, and thick with iron muscles. But then I had found the haft of my hatchet and I lifted it and split that misshapen skull with one blow. It fell clear of me and I sprang up, gagging and gasping, and quivering in every limb. I found flint, steel and tinder, and struck a light and lit a candle, and glared wildly at the creature lying on the floor.

In form it was like a man, gnarled and misshapen, covered with thick hair. Its nails were long and black, like the talons of a beast, and its chinless, low-browed head was like that of an ape. The thing was a Chakan, one of those semi-human beings which dwell deep in the forests.

There came a knocking on my door and Hakon's voice called to know what the trouble was, so I bade him enter. He rushed in, ax in hand, his eyes widened at the sight of the thing on the floor.

'A *Chakan!*' he whispered. 'I have seen them, far to the west, smelling out trails through the forests – the damned bloodhounds! What is that in his fingers?'

A chill of horror crept along my spine as I saw the creature still clutched a neckcloth in his fingers – the cloth which he had tried to knot like a hangman's noose about my neck.

'I have heard that Pictish shamans catch these creatures and tame them and use them to smell out their enemies,' he said slowly. 'But how could Lord Valerian so use one?'

'I know not,' I answered. 'But that neck cloth was given to the beast, and according to its nature it smelled my trail out and sought to break my neck. Let us go to the gaol, and quickly.'

Hakon roused his rangers and we hurried there, and found the guard lying before the open door of Valerian's empty cell with his throat cut. Hakon stood like one turned to stone, and then a faint call made us turn and we saw the white face of the drunkard peering at us from the next cell.

'He's gone,' quoth he; 'Lord Valerian's gone. Hark'ee; an hour agone while I lay on my bunk, I was awakened by a sound outside, and saw a strange dark woman come out of the shadows and walk up to the guard. He lifted his bow and bade her halt, but she laughed at him, staring into his eyes and he became as one in a trance. He stood staring stupidly – and Mitra, he took his own knife from his girdle and cut his throat, and he fell down and died. Then she took the keys from his belt and opened the door, and Valerian came out, and laughed like a devil out of hell, and kissed the wench, and she laughed with him. And she was not alone, for *something* lurked in the shadows behind her – some vague, monstrous being that never came into the light of the lanthorn hanging over the door.

'I heard her say best to kill the fat drunkard in the next cell, and by Mitra I was so nigh dead of fright I knew not if I were even alive. But Valerian said I was dead drunk, and I could have kissed him for that word. So they went away and as they went he said he would send her companion on a mission, and then they would go to a cabin on Lynx Creek, and there meet his retainers who had been hiding in the forest ever since he sent them from Valerian Hall. He said that Teyanoga would come to them there and they would cross the border and go among the Picts, and bring them back to cut all our throats.'

Hakon looked livid in the lanthorn light.

'Who is this woman?' I asked curiously.

'His half-breed Pictish mistress,' he said. 'Half Hawk-Pict and half-Ligurean. I have heard of her. They call her the witch of Skandaga. I have never seen her, never before credited the tales whispered of her and Lord Valerian. But it is the truth.'

'I thought I had slain old Teyanoga,' I muttered. 'The old fiend must bear a charmed life – I saw my shaft quivering in his breast. What now?'

'We must go to the hut on Lynx Creek and slay them all,' said Hakon. 'If they loose the Picts on the border hell will be to pay. We can spare no men from the fort or the town. We are enough. I know not how many men there will be on Lynx Creek, and I do not care. We will take them by surprise.'

We set out at once through the starlight. The land lay silent, lights twinkling dimly in the houses. To the westward loomed the black forest, silent, primordial, a brooding threat to the people who dared it.

We went in single file, bows strung and held in our left hands, hatchets swinging in our right hands. Our moccasins made no sound in the dew-wet grass. We melted into the woods and struck a trail that wound among oaks and alders. Here we strung out with some fifteen feet between each man, Hakon leading, and presently we dipped down into a grassy hollow and saw light streaming faintly from the cracks of shutters that covered a cabin's windows.

Hakon halted us and whispered for the men to wait, while we crept forward and spied upon them. We stole forward and surprised the sentry – a Schohiran renegade, who must have heard our stealthy approach but for the wine which staled his breath. I shall never forget the fierce hiss of satisfaction that breathed between Hakon's clenched teeth as he drove his knife into the villain's heart. We left the body hidden in the tall rank grass and stole up to the very wall of the cabin and dared to peer in at a crack. There was Valerian, with his fierce eyes blazing, and a dark, wildly beautiful girl in doeskin loin-clout and beaded moccasins, and her blackly burnished hair bound back by a gold band, curiously wrought. And there were half a dozen Schohiran renegades, sullen rogues in the woollen breeches and jerkins of farmers, with cutlasses at their belts, three forest-runners in buckskins, wild-looking men, and half a dozen Gundermen guards, compactly-built men with yellow hair cut square and confined under steel caps, corselets of chain mail, and polished leg-pieces. They were girt with swords and daggers – yellow-haired men with fair complexions and steely eyes and an accent differing greatly from the natives of the Westermarck. They were sturdy fighters, ruthless and well-disciplined, and very popular as guardsmen among the land-owners of the frontier.

Listening there we heard them all laughing and conversing, Valerian boastful of his escape and swearing that he had sent a visitor to that cursed Thandaran that should do his proper business for him; the renegades sullen and full of oaths and curses for their former friends; the forest-runners silent and attentive; the Gundermen careless and jovial, which joviality thinly masked their utterly ruthless natures. And the half-breed girl, whom they called Kwarada, laughed, and plagued Valerian, who seemed grimly amused. And Hakon trembled with fury as we listened to him boasting how he meant to rouse the Picts and lead them across the border to smite the Schohirans in the back while Brocas attacked from Coyaga.

Then we heard a light patter of feet and hugged the wall close, and saw the door open, and seven painted Picts entered, horrific figures in paint and feathers. They were led by old Teyanoga, whose breast-muscles were bandaged, whereby I knew my shaft had but fleshed itself in those heavy muscles. And wondered if the old demon were really a werewolf which could not be killed by mortal weapons as he boasted and many believed.

We lay close there, Hakon and I, and heard Teyanoga say that the Hawks, Wildcats and Turtles dared not strike across the border unless an alliance with the powerful Wolfmen could be struck up, for they feared that the Wolves might ravage their country while they fought the Schohirans. Teyonoga said that the three lesser tribes met the Wolves on the edge of Ghost Swamp for a council; and that the Wolves would abide by the counsel of the Wizard of the Swamp.

So Valerian said they would go to the Ghost Swamp and see if they could not persuade the Wizard to induce the Wolves to join the others. At that Hakon told me to crawl back and get the others, and I saw it was in his mind that we should attack, outnumbered as we were, but so fired was I by the infamous plot to which we had listened that I was as eager as he. I stole back and brought the others, and as soon as he heard us coming, he sprang up and ran at the door to beat it in with his war-ax.

At the same instant others of us burst in the shutters and poured arrows into the room, striking down some and set the cabin on fire.

They were thrown into confusion, and made no attempt to hold the cabin. The candles were upset and went out, but the fire lent a dim glow. They rushed the door and some were slain then, and others as we grappled with them. But presently all fled into the woods except those we slew, Gundermen, renegades and painted Picts, but Valerian and the girl were still in the cabin. Then they came forth and she laughed and hurled something on the ground that burst and blinded us with a foul smoke, through which they escaped.

All but four of our men had been slain in the desperate fighting, but we started instantly in pursuit, sending back one of the wounded men to warn the town.

The trail led into the wilderness.

We followed, and in fights and skirmishes slew several others, and presently all our men were slain except Hakon and I. We trailed Valerian across the border and into a camp of the war-tribes near Ghost Swamp, where the chiefs were going to consult the Wizard, a pre-Pictish shaman.

We trailed Valerian into the swamp, he going secretly to give the shamans instructions, and Hakon waited on the trail to slay Valerian while I stole into the swamp to slay the Wizard. But both of us were captured by the Wizard, who gave his consent to the war and gave them a ghastly magic to use against the white men, and the tribes went howling toward the border. But Hakon and I escaped and slew the Wizard and followed, in time to turn their magic against them, and rout them.

THE SNOUT IN THE DARK

(Draft)

1

AMBOOLA AWAKENED SLOWLY, HIS senses still sluggish from the wine he had guzzled the night before. For a muddled moment he could not remember where he was; the moonlight, streaming through the barred window, shone on unfamiliar surroundings. Then he remembered that he was lying in the upper cell of the prison where the anger of Tananda, sister to the king of Kush, had consigned him. It was no ordinary cell, for even Tananda had not dared to go too far in her punishment of the commander of the black spearmen which were the strength of Kush's army. There were carpets and tapestries and silk-covered couches, and jugs of wine – he remembered that he had been awakened and wondered why.

His gaze wandered to the square of barred moonlight that was the window, and he saw something that partially sobered him, and straightened his blurred gaze. The bars of that window were bent and buckled and twisted back. It must have been the noise of their rending that had awakened him. But what could have bent them? And where was whatever had so bent them? Suddenly he was completely sober, and an icy sensation wandered up his spine. *Something* had entered through that window, something was in the room with him.

With a low cry he started up on his couch and stared about him; and he froze at the sight of the motionless figure that stood at the head of his couch. An icy hand clutched the heart of Amboola which had never known fear. That silent, greyish shape did not move nor speak; it stood there in the shadowy moonlight, misshapen, deformed, its outline outside the bounds of sanity. Staring wildly, Amboola made out a pig-like head, snouted, covered with coarse bristles – but the thing stood upright and its thick hair-covered arms ended in rudimentary hands –

Amboola shrieked and sprang up – and then the motionless thing moved, with the paralyzing speed of a monster in a nightmare. The black man had one frenzied vision of champing, foaming jaws, of great chisel-like tusks flashing in the moonlight . . . presently the moonlight fell on a black shape sprawled amidst the dabbled coverings of the couch on the floor; a grayish, shambling form moved silently across the chamber toward the window whose broken bars leaned out against the stars.

2

'Tuthmes!' The voice was urgent, urgent as the fist that hammered on the teak door of the chamber where slept Shumballa's most ambitious nobleman. 'Tuthmes! Let me in! The devil is loose in Shumballa!'

The door was opened, and the speaker burst into the room – a lean, wiry man in a white djebbeh, dark-skinned, the whites of his eyes gleaming. He was met by Tuthmes, tall, slender, dusky, with the straight features of his caste.

'What are you saying, Afari?'

Afari closed the door before he answered; he was panting as if from a long run. He was shorter than Tuthmes, and the negroid was more predominant in his features.

'Amboola! He is dead! In the Red Tower!'

'What?' exclaimed Tuthmes. 'Tananda dared execute him?'

'No! No, no! She would not be such a fool, surely. He was not executed, but murdered. Something broke through the bars of his cell and tore his throat out, and stamped in his ribs, and broke his skull – Set, I have seen many dead men, but never one less lovely in his death than Amboola! Tuthmes, it is the work of some demon! His throat was bitten out, and the prints of the teeth were not like those of a lion or an ape. It was as if they had been made by chisels, sharp as razors!'

'When was this done?'

'Sometime about midnight. Guards in the lower part of the tower, watching the stair that leads up to the cell in which he was imprisoned, heard him cry out, and rushing up the stairs, burst into the cell and found him lying as I have said. I was sleeping in the lower part of the tower as you bade me, and having seen, I came straight here, bidding the guards say naught to anyone.'

Tuthmes smiled and his smile was not pleasant to see.

'Gods and demons work for a bold man,' he said. 'I do not think Tananda was fool enough to have Amboola murdered, however she desired it. The blacks have been sullen, ever since she cast him into prison. She could not have kept him imprisoned much longer.

'But this matter puts a weapon into our hands. If the Gallahs *think* she did it, so much the better. Each resentment against the dynasty is a weapon for us. Go, now, and strike before the king can learn of it. First, take a detachment of black spearmen to the Red Tower and execute the guards for sleeping at their duty. Be sure you take care to do it by my orders. That will show the Gallahs that I have avenged their commander, and remove a weapon from Tananda's hands. Kill them before she can have it done.

'Then go into Punt and find old Ageera, the witch-finder. Do not tell him flatly that Tananda had this deed done, but hint at it.'

Afari shuddered visibly.

'How can a common man lie to that black devil? His eyes are like coals of red fire that look into depths unnameable. I have seen him make corpses rise and walk, and skulls champ and grind their naked jaws.'

'Don't lie,' answered Tuthmes. 'Simply hint to him your own suspicions. After all, even if a demon *did* slay Amboola, some human summoned it out of the night. Perhaps Tananda is behind this, after all!'

When Afari had left, mulling intensely over what his patron had told him, Tuthmes drew a silken cloak about his otherwise naked limbs and mounting a short, wide staircase of polished mahogany, he came out upon the flat roof of his palace.

Looking over the parapet, he saw below him the silent streets of the inner city of Shumballa, the palaces and gardens, and the great square, into which, at an instant's notice, a thousand black horsemen could ride, from the courts of adjoining barracks.

Looking further, he saw the great bronze gates, and beyond them, the outer city that men called Punt, to distinguish it from El Shebbeh, the inner city. Shumballa stood in the midst of a great plain, of rolling grass lands that stretched to the horizons, broken only by occasional low hills. A narrow, deep river, meandering across the grass lands, touched the straggling edges of the city. El Shebbeh was separated from Punt by a tall and massive wall, which enclosed the palaces of the ruling caste, descendants of those Stygians who centuries ago had come southward to hack out a black empire, and to mix their proud blood with the blood of their dusky subjects. El Shebbeh was well laid out, with regular streets and squares, stone buildings and gardens; Punt was a sprawling wilderness of mud huts; the streets straggled into squares that were squares in name only. The black people of Kush, the Gallahs, the original inhabitants of the country, lived in Punt; none but the ruling caste, the Chagas, dwelt in El Shebbeh, except for their servants, and the black horsemen who served as their guardsmen.

Tuthmes glanced out over that vast expanse of huts. Fires glowed in the ragged squares, torches swayed to and fro in the wandering streets, and from time to time he caught a snatch of song, a barbaric chanting that thrummed with an undertone of wrath or bloodlust. Tuthmes drew his cloak closer about him and shivered.

Advancing across the roof, he halted by a figure which slept in the shadow of a palm growing in the artifical garden. When stirred by Tuthmes's toe, this man awoke and sprang up.

'There is no need for speech,' cautioned Tuthmes. 'The deed is done. Amboola is dead, and before dawn, all Punt will know he was murdered by Tananda.'

'And the – the devil?' whispered the man, shivering.

'Shh! Gone back into the darkness whence it was invoked. Harken, Shubba, it is time you were gone. Search among the Shemites until you find a woman suitable – a white woman. Bring her here speedily. If you return within the moon, I will give you her weight in silver. If you fail, I will hang your head from that palm tree.'

Shubba prostrated himself and touched his head to the dust. Then rising, he hurried from the roof. Tuthmes glanced again into Punt. The fires seemed to glow more fiercely, somehow, and a drum had begun an ominous monotone. A sudden clamor of bestial yells welled up to his ears.

'They have heard that Amboola is dead,' he muttered, and again he was shaken by a strong shudder.

3

Life flowed on its accustomed course in the filth-littered streets of Punt. Giant black men squatted in the doorways of their thatched huts, or lolled on the ground in their shade. Black women went up and down the streets with water-gourds or baskets of food on their heads. Children played or fought in the dust, laughing or squalling shrilly. In the squares the black folk chaffered and bargained over plantains, beer and hammered brass ornaments. Smiths crouched over tiny charcoal fires, laboriously beating out spear blades. The hot sun beat down on all, the sweat, mirth, anger, nakedness and squalor of the black people.

Suddenly there came a change in the pattern, a new note in the timbre. With a clatter of hoofs a group of horsemen rode by, half a dozen men, and a woman. It was the woman who dominated the group. Her skin was dusky, her hair, a thick black mass, caught back and confined by a gold fillet. Her only garment, besides the sandals on her feet, was a short silk skirt girdled at the waist. Gold plates, crusted with jewels, partially covered her dusky breasts. Her features were straight, her bold, scintillant eyes full of challenge and sureness. She rode and handled her steed with ease and certitude, the slim Kushite horse, with the jeweled bridle, the reins of scarlet leather, as broad as a man's palm and worked with gilt, and her sandalled feet in the wide silver stirrups.

As she rode by, work and chatter ceased suddenly. The black faces grew sullen, and the murky eyes burned redly. The blacks turned their heads to whisper in each other's ears, and the whispers grew to a sullen, audible murmur.

The youth who rode at the woman's stirrup grew nervous. He glanced ahead, along the winding street, measured the distance to the bronze gates, not yet in view along the flat-topped houses, and whispered: 'The people grow ugly, Tananda; it was foolish to ride in Punt.'

'All the black dogs in Kush shall not keep me from my hunting,' answered the woman. 'If any seem threatening, ride them down.'

'Easier said than done,' muttered the youth, scanning the silent throng. 'They are coming from their houses and massing thick along the street – look there!'

They were entering a broad, ragged square, where the black folk swarmed. On one side of this square stood a house of mud and rough-hewn beams, larger than its neighbors, with a cluster of skulls above the wide doorway. This was the temple of Jullah, which the black folk worshipped in opposition to Set, the Serpent-god worshipped by the Chagas in imitation of their Stygian ancestors. The black folk were thronged in this square, sullenly staring at the horsemen. There was a distinct menace in their attitude, and Tananda, for the first time feeling a slight nervousness, did not notice another rider approaching the square along another street. This rider would have attracted attention in ordinary times, for he was neither Chaga nor Gallah, but a white man, a powerful figure in chain-mail and helmet, with a scarlet cloak whipping its folds about him.

'These dogs mean mischief,' muttered the youth at Tananda's side, half drawing his curved sword. The others, guardsmen, black men like the folk about them, drew closer about her, but did not draw their blades. A low sullen muttering rose louder, though no movement was made.

'Push through them,' ordered Tananda, reining her horse forward.

The blacks gave back sullenly before her advance, and suddenly, from the devil-devil house came a lean black figure. It was old Ageera, clad only in a loin-cloth. Pointing his finger at Tananda, he yelled: 'There she rides, she whose hands are dipped in blood! She who murdered Amboola!'

His yell was the spark that set off the explosion. A vast roar rose from the mob, and they surged forward, yelling: 'Death to Tananda!' In an instant a hundred black hands were clawing at the legs of the riders. The youth reined between Tananda and the mob, but a stone, cast from a black hand, shattered his skull. The guardsmen, slashing and hacking, were torn from their steeds and beaten, stamped and stabbed to death. Tananda, beset at last with terror, screamed as her horse reared. A score of wild black figures, men and women, were clawing at her.

A giant grasped her thigh and plucked her from her saddle, full into the eager and furious hands which awaited her. Her skirt was ripped from her body and waved in the air above her, while a bellow of primitive laughter went up from the surging mob. A woman spat in her face and tore off her breastplates, scratching her breasts with her fingernails. A stone hurled at her grazed her head. She screamed in frantic fear; a score of brutal hands were tearing at her, threatening to dismember her. She saw a stone clenched in a black hand, while the owner sought to reach her in the press and brain her. Daggers glinted. Only the hindering numbers of the jammed mass kept them from doing her to death instantly. 'To the devil-devil house!' went up a roar, followed by a responsive clamor, and Tananda felt herself half carried, half dragged along with the surging mob, grasped by her hair, arms, legs, wherever a black hand could grip. Blows aimed at her in the press were blocked or diverted by the mass; and then there came a shock under which the whole throng staggered as a horseman on a powerful steed crashed full into the press.

Men went down screaming, to be crushed under the flailing hoofs; Tananda got a dizzy glimpse of a figure towering above the press, of a dark scarred face under a steel helmet, of a scarlet cloak unfurled from mighty mailed shoulders, and a great sword lashing up and down, spattering crimson splashes. But from somewhere in the press a spear licked upward, disembowelling the steed. It screamed, plunged and went down, but the rider landed on his feet, smiting right and left. Wildly driven spears and knives glanced from his helmet or the shield on his left arm, while his broadsword cleft flesh and bone, split skulls, scattered brains and spilled entrails into the bloody dust.

Flesh and blood could not stand before it. Clearing a space he stooped, caught up the terrified girl and, covering her with his shield, fell back, cutting a ruthless way. He backed into the angle of a wall and, dropping her behind him, stood before her, beating back the frothing, screaming onslaught.

Then there was a clatter of hoofs and a regiment of the guardsmen swept into the square, driving the rioters before them. The captain approached, a giant negro resplendent in crimson silk and gold-worked harness.

'You were long in coming,' said Tananda, who had risen and regained much of her poise. The captain turned ashy, but before he could turn, Tananda had made a sign that was caught by his men behind him. One of them grasped his spear with both hands and drove it between his captain's shoulders with such force that the point started out from his breast. The captain sank to his knees, and thrusts from half a dozen more spears finished the task.

Tananda shook back her long black disheveled hair and faced her rescuer. She was bleeding from a score of scratches on her breasts and thighs, her locks fell in confusion down her back, and she was as naked as the day she was born; but she stared at him without perturbation or uncertainty, and he gave back her stare, frank admiration in his expression of her cool bearing, and the ripeness of her brown limbs.

'Who are you?' she demanded.

'Conan, a Cimmerian,' he answered.

'What are you doing in Shumballa?'

'I came here to seek my fortune. I was formerly a corsair.'

'Oh!' New interest shone in her dark eyes; she gathered her hair back in her hands. 'We have heard tales of you, whom men call Amra the Lion. But if you are no longer a corsair, what are you now?'

'A penniless wanderer.'

She shook her head. 'No, by Set! You are captain of the royal guard.'

He glanced casually at the sprawling figure in silk and steel, and the sight did not alter the zest of his sudden grin.

4

Shubba returned to Shumballa, and coming to Tuthmes in his chamber where leopard skins carpeted the marble floor, he said: 'I have found the woman you desired. A Nemedian girl, captured from a trading vessel of Argos. I paid the Shemitish slave-trader many broad gold pieces.'

'Let me see her,' commanded Tuthmes, and Shubba left the room, returning a moment later leading a girl by the wrist. She was supple, her white skin almost dazzling in contrast with the brown and black bodies to which Tuthmes was accustomed. Her hair fell in a curly rippling gold stream over her white shoulders. She was clad only in a tattered shift. This Shubba removed, leaving her shrinking in complete nudity.

Tuthmes nodded, impersonally.

'She is a fine bit of merchandise. If I were not gambling for a throne, I might be tempted to keep her for myself. Have you taught her Kushite, as I commanded?'

'Aye; in the city of the Shemites, and later daily on the caravan trail, I taught her, and impressed upon her the need of learning by means of a slipper, after the Shemite fashion. Her name is Diana.'

Tuthmes seated himself on a couch, and indicated that the girl should sit cross-legged on the floor at his feet, which she did.

'I am going to give you to the king of Kush as a present,' he said. 'You will nominally be his slave, but actually you will belong to me. You will receive your orders regularly, and you will not fail to carry them out. The king is degenerate, slothful, dissipated. It should not be hard for you to achieve complete dominance over him. But lest you might be tempted to disobey, when you fancy yourself out of my reach in the palace of the king, I will demonstrate my power to you.'

He took her hand and led her through a corridor, down a flight of stone stairs and into a long chamber, dimly lighted. The chamber was divided in equal halves by a wall of crystal, clear as water though some three feet in thickness and of such strength as to have resisted the lunge of a bull elephant. He led her to this wall and made her stand, facing it, while he stepped back. Abruptly the light went out. She stood there in darkness, her slender limbs trembling with an unreasoning panic, then light began to float in the darkness. She saw a hideous malformed head grow out of the blackness; she saw a bestial snout, chisel-like teeth, bristles – turned and ran, frantic with fear, and forgetful of the sheet of crystal that kept the brute from her. She ran full into the arms of Tuthmes in the darkness, and heard his hiss in her ear: 'You have seen my servant; do not fail me, for if you do he will search you out wherever you may be, and you cannot hide from him.' And when he hissed something else into the quivering ear of the Nemedian girl, she promptly fainted.

Tuthmes carried her up the stairs and gave her into the hands of a black wench with instructions to revive her, to see that she had food and wine, and to bathe, comb, perfume and dress her for her presentation to the king.

THE HALL OF THE DEAD

(Synopsis)

A SQUAD OF ZAMORIAN soldiers, led by the officer Nestor, a Gunderman mercenary, were marching down a narrow gorge, in pursuit of a thief, Conan the Cimmerian, whose thefts from rich merchants and nobles had infuriated the government of the nearest Zamorian city. Conan had left the city and been followed into the mountains. The walls of the gorge were steep and the gorge floor grown thickly with high rich grass. Striding through this grass at the head of his men, Nestor tripped over something and fell heavily. It was a rawhide rope stretched there by Conan, and it tripped a spring-pole which started a sudden avalanche that overwhelmed all the soldiers except Nestor, who escaped, bruised, and with his armor scratched and dented. Enraged, he followed the trail alone, and emerging into an upland plateau, came into the deserted city of the ancients, where he met Conan. He instantly attacked the Cimmerian, who, after a desperate battle, knocked him senseless with a sword-stroke on his helmet, and went on into the deserted city, thinking him dead. Nestor recovered and followed the Cimmerian. Conan, meanwhile, had entered the city, clambering over the walls, the gates being locked, and had encountered the monstrous being which haunted the city. This he slew by casting great blocks of stone upon it from an elevation, and then descending and hacking it to pieces with his sword. He had made his way to the great palace which was hewn out of a single monstrous hill of stone in the center of the city. He was seeking an entrance, when Nestor came upon him again, sword in hand, having followed him over the wall. Conan disgustedly advised him to aid him in securing the vast fabulous treasure instead of fighting. After some argument the Gunderman agreed, and they made their way into the palace, eventually coming to the great

THE HALL OF THE DEAD

treasure chamber, where warriors of a by-gone age lay about in life-like positions. The companions made up packages of gold and precious stones, and threw dice to decide which should take a set of perfectly matched uncanny gems which adorned an altar, on which lay a jade serpent, apparently a god. Conan won the toss, and gave all the gold and the other jewels to Nestor. He himself swept up the altar-gems and the jade serpent – but when he lifted it off the altar, the ancient warriors came terrifically to life, and a terrible battle ensued, in which the thieves barely managed to escape with their lives. Hewing their way out of the palace, they were followed by the giant warriors who, upon coming into the sunlight, crumpled into dust. A terrific earthquake shook down the deserted city, and the companions were separated. Conan made his way back to the city, and entering a tavern, where his light-of-love was guzzling wine, spilled the jewels out on the ale-splashed table, in the Maul. To his amazement, they had turned to green dust. He then prepared to examine the jade serpent, who was still in the leather sack. The girl lifted the sack and dropped it with a scream, swearing that something moved inside it. At this instant a magistrate entered with a number of soldiers and arrested Conan, who set his back to a wall, and drew his sword. Before the soldiers could close in, the magistrate thrust his hand into the sack. Nestor had regained the city, with the coins which had not crumpled, and drunk, had told of the exploit. They had sought to arrest him, but drunk though he was, he had cut his way through and escaped. Now as the magistrate thrust his fat hand into the sack, he shrieked and jerked it forth, a living serpent fast to his fingers. The turmoil which followed gave Conan and the girl an opportunity to escape.

THE HAND OF NERGAL

(Fragment)

1

THE BATTLEFIELD STRETCHED SILENT, crimson pools among the still sprawling figures seeming to reflect the lurid red-streamered sunset sky. Furtive figures slunk from the tall grass; birds of prey dropped down on mangled heaps with a rustle of dusky wings. Like harbingers of Fate a wavering line of herons flapped slowly away toward the reed-grown banks of the river. No rumble of chariot wheel or peal of trumpet disturbed the unseeing stillness. The silence of death followed the thundering of battle.

Yet one figure moved through that wide-strewn field of ruin – pygmy-like against the vast dully crimson sky. The fellow was a Cimmerian, a giant with a black mane and smoldering blue eyes. His girdled loin-cloth and high-strapped sandals were splashed with blood. The great sword he trailed in his right hand was stained to the cross-piece. There was a ghastly wound in his thigh, which caused him to limp as he walked. Carefully yet impatiently he moved among the dead, limping from corpse to corpse, and swearing wrathfully as he did so. Others had been before him; not a bracelet, gemmed dagger, or silver breastplate rewarded his search. He was a wolf who had lingered too long at the blood-letting while jackals stripped the prey.

Glaring out across the littered plains, he saw no body unstripped or moving. The knives of the mercenaries and camp-followers had been at work. Straightening up from his fruitless quest, he glanced uncertainly afar off across the deepening plain, to where the towers of the city gleamed faintly in the sunset. Then he turned quickly as a low tortured cry reached his ears. That meant a wounded man, living, therefore presumably unlooted. He limped quickly toward the sound, and coming to the edge of the plain, parted the first straggling reeds and glared down at the figure which writhed feebly at his feet.

It was a girl that lay there. She was naked, her white limbs cut and bruised. Blood was clotted in her long dark hair. There was unseeing agony in her dark eyes and she moaned in delirium.

The Cimmerian stood looking down at her, and his eyes were momentarily clouded by what would have been an expression of pity in another man. He lifted his sword to put the girl out of her misery, and as the blade hovered above her, she whimpered again like a child in pain. The great sword halted in midair, and the Cimmerian stood for an instant like a bronze statue. Then sheathing the blade with sudden decision, he bent and lifted the girl in his mighty arms. She struggled blindly but weakly. Carrying her carefully, he limped toward the reed-masked riverbank some distance away.

2

In the city of Yaralet, when night came on, the people barred windows and bolted doors, and sat behind their barriers shuddering, with candles burning before their household gods until dawn etched the minarets. No watchmen walked the streets, no painted wenches beckoned from the shadows, no thieves stole nimbly through the winding alleys. Rogues, like honest people, shunned the shadowed ways, gathering in foul-smelling dens, or candle-lighted taverns. From dusk to dawn Yaralet was a city of silence, her streets empty and desolate.

Exactly what they feared, the people did not know. But they had ample evidence that it was no empty dream they bolted their doors against. Men whispered of slinking shadows, glimpsed from barred windows – of hurrying shapes alien to humanity and sanity. They told of doorways splintering in the night, and the cries and shrieks of humans followed by significant silence; and they told of the rising sun etching broken doors that swung in empty houses, whose occupants were seen no more.

Even stranger, they told of the swift rumble of phantom chariot wheels along the empty streets in the darkness before dawn, when those who heard dared not look forth. One child looked forth, once, but he was instantly stricken mad and died screaming and frothing, without telling what he saw when he peered from his darkened window.

On a certain night, then, while the people of Yaralet shivered in their bolted houses, a strange conclave was taking place in the small velvet-hung taper-lighted chamber of Atalis, whom some called a philosopher and others a rogue. Atalis was a slender man of medium height, with a splendid head and the features of a shrewd merchant. He was clad in a plain robe of rich fabric, and his head was shaven to denote devotion to study and the arts. As he talked he unconsciously gestured with his left hand. His right arm lay across his lap at an unnatural angle. From time to time a spasm of pain contorted his features, at which time his right foot, hidden under the long robe, would twist back excruciatingly upon his ankle.

He was talking to one whom the city of Yaralet knew, and praised, as Prince Than. The prince was a tall lithe man, young and undeniably handsome. The firm outline of his limbs and the steely quality of his grey eyes belied the slightly effeminate suggestion of his curled black locks, and feathered velvet cap.

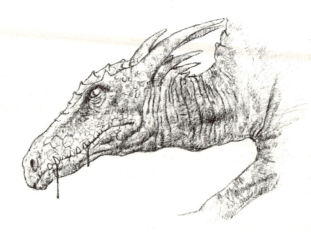

NOTES ON VARIOUS PEOPLES OF THE HYBORIAN AGE

Aquilonians

This was a more or less pure-blooded race, though modified by contact with the Zingarans in the south and, much less extensively, with the Bossonians of the west and north. Aquilonia, as the westernmost of the Hyborian kingdoms, retained frontier traditions equalled only by the more ancient kingdom of Hyperborea and the Border Kingdom. Its most important provinces were Poitain in the south, Gunderland in the north, and Attalus in the southeast. The Aquilonians were a tall race, averaging five feet, ten and three-fourths inches in height, and were generally inclined to be rangy, though in the last generations the city dwellers inclined towards portliness. They varied in complexion largely according to locality. Thus the people of Gunderland were uniformly tawny-haired and gray-eyed, while the people of Poitain were almost uniformly dark as their neighbors the Zingarans. All were inclined to be dolichocephalic, except a sprinkling of peasantry along the Bossonian border, whose type had been modified by admixture with the latter race, and here and there in the more primitive parts of the kingdom where remnants of unclassified aboriginal races still existed, absorbed into the surrounding population. The people of Attalus boasted the greatest advances in commerce and culture, though the whole level of Aquilonian civilization was enviable. Their language was much like the other Hyborian tongues and their chief god was Mitra. At the height of their power their religion was of a refined and imaginative type, and they did not practise human sacrifice. In war they relied largely upon their cavalry, heavily armed knights. Their pikemen and spearmen were mainly Gundermen, while their archers were supplied from the Bossonian Marches.

Gundermen

Gunderland was once a separate kingdom, but was brought into the larger kingdom, less by conquest than agreement. Its people never considered themselves exactly Aquilonians, and after the fall of the great kingdom, Gunderland existed for several generations in its former state as a separate principality. Their ways were ruder and more primitively Hyborian than those of the Aquilonians, and their main concession to the ways of their more civilized southern neighbors was the adoption of the god Mitra in place of the primitive Bori – a worship to which they returned, however, upon the fall of Aquilonia. They were, next to the Hyperboreans, the tallest of the Hyborian races. They were fine soldiers, and inclined to wander far. Gunderland mercenaries were to be found in all the armies of the Hyborian kingdoms, and in Zamora and the more powerful kingdoms of Shem.

Cimmerians

These people were descendants of the ancient Atlanteans, though they themselves were unaware of their descent, having evolved by their own efforts from the ape-men to which their ancient ancestors had sunk. They were a tall, powerful race, averaging six feet in height. They were black-haired, and gray- or blue-eyed. They were dolichocephalic, and dark-skinned, though not so dark as either the Zingarans, Zamorians or Picts. They were barbaric and warlike, and were never conquered, although, at the end of the Hyborian Age, the southward-drifting Nordics drove them from their country. They were a moody, brooding race, whose gods were Crom and his brood. They did not practise human sacrifice, for it was their belief that their gods were indifferent to the fate of men. They fought on foot, mainly, and made savage raids on their neighbors to the east, north, and south.

The Westermarck

Located between the Bossonian Marches and the Pictish Wilderness. Provinces: Thandara, Conawaga, Oriskonie, Schohira. Political situation: Oriskonie, Conawaga, and Schohira were ruled by royal patent. Each was under the jurisdiction of a baron of the western marches, which lie just east of the Bossonian Marches. These barons were accountable only to the king of Aquilonia. Theoretically they owned the land, and received a certain percentage of the gain. In return they supplied troops to protect the frontier against the Picts, built fortresses and towns, and appointed judges and other officials. Actually their power was not nearly so absolute as it seemed. There was a sort of supreme court located in the largest town of Conawaga, Scanaga, presided over by a judge appointed directly by the king of Aquilonia, and it was a defendant's privilege, under certain circumstances, to appeal to this court. Thandara was the southernmost province, Oriskonie the northernmost and the most thinly settled. Conawaga lay south of Oriskonie, and south of Conawaga lay Schohira, the smallest of the provinces. Conawaga was the largest, richest and most thickly settled, and the only one in which landed patricians had settled to any extent. Thandara was the most purely pioneer province. Originally it had only been a fortress by that name, on Warhorse River, built by direct order of the king of Aquilonia, and commanded by royal troops. After the conquest of the province of Conajohara by the Picts, the settlers from that province moved southward and settled the country in the vicinity of the fortress. They held their land by force of arms, and neither received nor needed any patent. They acknowledged no baron as overlord. Their governor was merely a military commander, elected from among themselves, their choice being always submitted to and approved by the king of Aquilonia as a matter of form. No troops were ever sent to Thandara. They built forts, or rather blockhouses, and manned them themselves, and formed companies of military bodies called Rangers. They were incessantly at war with the Picts. When the word came that Aquilonia was being torn by civil war, and that the Cimmerian Conan was striking for the crown, Thandara instantly declared for Conan, renounced their allegiance to King Namedides and sent word asking Conan to endorse their elected governor, which the Cimmerian instantly did. This enraged the commander of a fort in the Bossonian Marches, and he marched with his host to ravage Thandara. But the frontiersmen met him at their borders and gave him a savage defeat, after which there was no attempt to meddle with Thandara. But the province was isolated, separated from Schohira by a stretch of uninhabited wilderness, and behind them lay the Bossonian country, where most of the people were loyalists. The baron of Schohira declared for Conan, and marched to join his army, but asked no levies of Schohira where indeed every man was needed to guard the frontier. But in Conawaga were many loyalists, and the baron of Conawaga rode in person into Scandaga and demanded that the people supply him with a force to ride and aid King Namedides. There was civil war in Conawaga, and the baron planned to crush all other provinces and make himself governor of them all. Meantime, in Oriskonie, the people had driven out the governor appointed by their baron and were savagely fighting such loyalists as skulked among them.

AFTERWORD: ROBERT E. HOWARD AND CONAN

By Stephen Jones

ROBERT ERVIN HOWARD was born in the fading ex-cowtown of Peaster, Texas, about forty-five miles west of Fort Worth, on January 22, 1906. He was the only son of Dr Isaac Mordecai Howard and Hester Jane (Ervin) Howard. The couple met while living in Mineral Wells, in Palo Pinto County, and were married on January 24, 1904.

Named after his great-grandfather, Robert Ervin, Howard later revealed in a 1931 biographical sketch: 'I come of old pioneer American stock. By nationality I am predominantly Gaelic, in spite of my English name – some three-fourths Irish, while the rest is a mixture of English, Highland Scotch [sic], and Danish . . . Practically all my life has been spent in the country and small towns, outside of a few brief sojourns in New Orleans and some of the Texas cities.'

After moving around the state and living briefly in a number of different locales, in September 1919 the family finally settled in the small oil boom town of Cross Plains, in Callahan County, Texas, where Howard would spend the rest of his life.

'As my father had his practice and did not attempt to run a farm, I had more leisure time that the average country kid,' Howard later recalled. 'I lived pretty much the average life of the time and place. Then (as now) I had more enemies than friends, but I did not lack companionship of my own age. I played the rough and savage games popular in those parts then, wrestled, hunted a little, fished a little, trapped a little, stole watermelons, went swimming, and spent more time than all in wandering about over the countryside on foot or on horseback.'

Suffering from poor health (probably rheumatic fever) as a child, he once told his father, 'Dad, when I was in school, I had to take a lot because I was alone and no one to take my part, so I intend to build my body until when anyone crosses me up, I can with my bare hands tear him to pieces, double him up, and break his back with my hands alone.'

Although he started attending school when he was eight, Howard was mostly self-educated and read voraciously, revealing in one letter: 'In my passionate quest for reading material, nothing could have halted me but a bullet through the head.'

Despite hating 'the clock-like regularity' of school, in 1923 he graduated at the age of seventeen from Brownwood High School and, not being able to afford college, attended the Commercial School at Howard Payne College in Brownwood, where he studied non-credit courses in shorthand, typing, book-keeping and commercial law.

In her 1986 memoir about Howard, *One Who Walked Alone*, former Cross Plains high school teacher Novalyne Price Ellis described her first meeting with the author, in the late spring of 1933: 'He was not dressed as I thought a writer should dress. His cap was pulled down low on his forehead. He had on a dingy white shirt and some loose-fitting brown pants that only came to his ankles and the top of his high-buttoned shoes. He took off his cap and I saw that his hair was dark brown, short, almost clipped. He ran his hand over his head.'

E. Hoffman Price was one of the few writers and fellow correspondents who actually visited Howard. In 1934 he drove down to Cross Plains and recalled years later meeting a 'broad, towering man with a bluff, tanned face and a big, hearty hand, and a voice which was surprisingly soft and easy, instead of the bull-bellow one would expect of the creator of Conan and those other swashbucklers . . . Robert Howard was packed with whimsy and poetry which rang out in his letters, and blazed up in much of his published fiction but, as is usually the case with writers, his appearance belied him. His face was boyish, not yet having squared off into angles; his blue eyes, slightly prominent, had a wide-openness which did not suggest anything of the man's keen wit and agile fancy. That first picture persists – a powerful, solid, round-faced fellow, kindly and somewhat stolid.'

However, Price also discovered that there was a darker side to Howard while his host was driving Price and his new wife, Wanda, to the nearby town of Brownwood for a shopping and sight-seeing trip: 'Suddenly he took his foot off the throttle, cocked his head, idled down. We were approaching a clump of vegetation which was near the roadside. He reached across us, to the side pocket. He took out a pistol, sized up the terrain, put the weapon back again, and resumed speed. He explained, in a matter-of-fact tone, "I have a lot of enemies, everyone has around here. Wasn't that I figured we were running into anything but I had to make sure.'"

Some time later Howard confided to Novalyne Price Ellis that a man with as many enemies as he had needed to be careful. 'Anybody who is not your friend is your enemy,' he explained pleasantly to her.

Howard had written his first story – a historical adventure about a Viking named Boealf – at the age of nine or ten, and he was fifteen when he began writing professionally. 'I took up writing simply because it seemed to promise an easier mode of work, more money, and more freedom than any job I'd tried. I wouldn't write otherwise.' He sent off his first effort to *Adventure*, but it was rejected, and it was another three years before Howard made his professional début in the pulp magazine *Weird Tales*.

Originally selling for just twenty-five cents on newsstands, and printed on low-grade 'pulp' paper, *Weird Tales* was the first magazine devoted exclusively to weird and fantastic fiction. It ran for 279 issues, starting in March 1923 and finally giving up the ghost in September 1954. Although just one title amongst many hundreds being published at that time, it carried the subtitle 'The Unique Magazine', and during its original thirty-two-year-run (the title has been revived – unsuccessfully – on several occasions since) it presented all types of fantasy fiction, from supernatural stories to Gothic horror, sword and sorcery to science fiction. Among some of its most famous contributors were H.P. Lovecraft, Ray Bradbury, Clark Ashton Smith, Robert Bloch, Seabury Quinn, C.L. Moore, Henry Kuttner, Manly Wade Wellman, Jack Williamson, Henry S. Whitehead, and even Tennessee Williams.

At the time Howard began submitting manuscripts, Farnsworth Wright had replaced Edwin F. Baird as editor of the Chicago-based magazine, after founder and owner J.C. Henneberger was forced to reorganise the title because of debts. From the November 1924 issue onwards, *Weird Tales* began to flourish under Wright's guidance, and he edited 179 copies before retiring after the March 1940 edition. He died as a result of Parkinson's disease in June that same year.

Written when Howard was just eighteen, 'Spear and Fang' was a story about the struggles faced by prehistoric man. Wright published it in the July 1925 issue and paid its teenage author a fee of $16.00, or half a cent a word. Even in pre-Depression Texas that didn't go far, and Howard quickly realised that he would have to work at a variety of jobs to supplement his meagre income from writing. These included picking cotton, branding cattle, hauling garbage, working in a grocery store and a law office, jerking soda in a drug store, trying to be a public stenographer, packing a surveyor's rod and working up oil field news for some Texas and Oklahoma papers. However, by his own admission, he 'wasn't a success at any of them'.

In his 1931 biographical sketch he told Wright: 'Pounding out a living at the writing game is no snap – but the average man's life is no snap, whatever he does. I'm merely one of a huge army, all of whom are bucking the line one way or another for meat for their bellies – which is the main basic principle and reason and eventual goal of Life. Every now and then one of us finds the going too hard and blows his brains out, but it's all in the game, I reckon.'

Thanks to Wright and *Weird Tales*, things soon began to change for Howard. In just three years his income from writing jumped from $772.50 to $1,500.26. The prolific author also began to sell other types of fiction – Westerns, sports stories, horror tales, true confessions, historical adventures and detective thrillers – to pulp markets besides *Weird Tales*, while at the same time he began to develop a series of characters with whom he would forever be identified with: the English Puritan swordsman Solomon Kane (actually created while he was still in high school); the king of fabled Valusia, King Kull; Pictish chieftain Bran Mak Morn; prize-fighter Sailor Steve Costigan; Celtic warrior Turlogh O'Brien; soldier of fortune Francis X. Gordon, also known as 'El Borak'; humorous hillbilly Breckenridge Elkins; and of course the mighty barbarian, Conan.

Conan quickly became Howard's most popular character. Howard set his savage exploits in the Hyborian Age, a fictional period of pre-history 'which men have forgotten, but which remains in classical names, and distorted myths.' He detailed Conan's world in a pseudo-historical essay entitled 'The Hyborian Age', which ran as a serial in Donald A. Wollheim's amateur magazine *The Phantagraph* in the issues dated February, August and October-November 1936. However, the fanzine only published the first half of the essay, and it finally appeared in its complete form as a mimeographed booklet in 1938.

According to his creator, Conan 'was born on a battle field, during a fight between his tribe and a horde of raiding Vanir. The country claimed by and roved over by his clan lay in the northwest of Cimmeria, but Conan was of mixed blood, although a pure-bred Cimmerian. His grandfather was a member of a southern tribe who had fled from his own people because of a blood-feud and after long wanderings, eventually taken refuge with the people of the north. He had taken part in many raids into the Hyborian nations in his youth, before his flight, and perhaps it was the tales he told of those softer countries which roused in Conan, as a child, a desire to see them.

'There are many things concerning Conan's life of which I am not certain myself. I do not know, for instance, when he got his first sight of civilised people. It might have been at Vanarium, or he might have made a peaceable visit to some frontier town before that. At Vanarium he was already a formidable antagonist, though only fifteen. He stood six feet and weighed 180 pounds, though he lacked much of having his full growth.'

However, despite what Howard would claim later, the mighty-thewed barbarian did not leap fully-formed into his creator's mind. The June 1932 issue of *Strange Stories* contained Howard's story 'People of the Dark', whose hero was a warrior named Conan the reaver, who was physically similar to the later Conan; he too swore 'by Crom'.

The first published Conan story, 'The Phoenix on the Sword', is one of the final adventures in Conan's chronology, set after he had become king of Aquilonia. Wright conditionally accepted it in a letter dated March 10, 1932, describing it as having 'points of real excellence. I hope you will see your way clear to touch it up and resubmit it.' It eventually appeared in the December 1932 issue of *Weird Tales* and was an instant hit, as indicated in the February 1933 edition of the letters column, 'The Eyrie', where readers and writers alike were invited to air their comments and opinions about the magazine: '"The Phoenix on the Sword" fairly took my breath away with its fine intrigue and excellent action and description,' exclaimed a reader from Denver, Colorado, adding: 'It was a magnificent story. Mr Howard never writes but that he produces a masterpiece.' In fact, the story was a reworking of an unsold King Kull tale entitled 'By This Axe I Rule!', which finally saw print in its original form in the 1967 collection *King Kull*.

Still king of Aquilonia, Conan was ambushed and shackled in a dungeon, where he encountered an enormous serpent in 'The Scarlet Citadel', published in the January 1933 *Weird Tales*. Although Howard had already been awarded the coveted cover spot on previous issues of the magazine (his first had been for 'Wolfshead' back in April 1926), the covers for the December and January issues were two out of the four which J. Allen St John produced consecutively for Otis Adelbert Kline's serial 'Buccaneers of Venus'.

Howard also missed out on the cover for the March 1933 issue, which contained 'The Tower of the Elephant'. As Howard later explained in a letter written to P. Schuyler Miller, 'Conan was about seventeen when he was introduced to the public in 'The Tower of the Elephant'. While not fully matured, he was riper than the average civilised youth at that age.' The author apparently borrowed the setting for the Zamorian thieves' quarter from one of his favourite movies, the 1923 version of *The Hunchback of Notre Dame*.

Conan led an army against a revived wizard in 'Black Colossus', his fourth adventure in *Weird Tales*, in the June 1933 issue. It also marked the first of nine cover appearances Howard's Conan series would make on the magazine.

Margaret Brundage's paintings were featured on most of the Weird Tales covers during the mid-1930s, and her cover for 'Black Colossus' depicted the naked Yasmela reaching out to touch the seated stone idol. A former Chicago fashion artist, Brundage was paid $90 per cover and usually worked in delicate pastel chalks on canvas. Wright admitted in the magazine that they had to be careful handling the artist's work: 'The originals are so delicate that we are afraid even to sneeze when we have a cover design in our possession, for fear the picture will disappear in a cloud of dust.'

'They were so impressed by the cover that they brought it to the best engraver in Chicago,' Brundage later recalled. 'Wright later told me that it generated the most mail ever for a cover for *Weird Tales*.'

That was probably because her depictions of nude or diaphanously draped women, often in risqué or blatant bondage positions, provoked many outraged letters to 'The Eyrie'. However, Farnsworth Wright was a smart enough editor and businessman to note that issues which featured a Brundage nude on the cover invariably sold more copies on the newsstands.

In a letter to Clark Ashton Smith postmarked July 22, 1933, Howard told his fellow *Weird Tales* writer: 'Thanks, too, for the kind things you said about Conan. I enjoy writing about him more than any character I have ever created. He almost seems to write himself. I find stories dealing with him roll out much easier than any others.'

Originally titled 'Xuthal of the Dusk', 'The Slithering Shadow' in the September 1933 *Weird Tales* found Conan in yet another lost city battling an evil Stygian witch and the toad-like god, Thog. The story was also featured on the cover with one of Brundage's most infamous 'whipping' scenes. Future author Henry Kuttner commented in 'The Eyrie': 'Allow me to pan you for your charmingly sadistic cover illustrating 'The Slithering Shadow'. I haven't the slightest objection to the female nude in art, but it seems rather a pity that it is possible to find such pictures in any sex magazine, while *Weird Tales* is about the only type of magazine which can run fantastic and weird cover illustrations and doesn't.'

Conan joined up with a group of buccaneers in search of a treasure island in 'The Pool of the Black One' in the October 1933 issue of *Weird Tales*. In another letter to Clark Ashton Smith, postmarked December 14, 1933, Howard gave some more background to the creation of his most memorable character: 'I'm rather of the opinion myself that widespread myths and legends are based on some fact, though the fact may be distorted out of all recognition in the telling . . . I know that for months I had been absolutely barren of ideas, completely unable to work up anything sellable. Then the man Conan seemed suddenly to grow up in my mind without much labour on my part and immediately a stream of stories flowed off my pen – or rather, off my type-writer – almost without effort on my part. I did not seem to be creating, but rather relating events that had occurred. Episode crowded on episode so fast that I could scarcely keep up with them. For weeks I did nothing but write of the adventures of Conan. The character took complete possession of my mind and crowded out everything else in the way of story-writing. When I deliberately tried to write something else, I couldn't do it.'

By now Howard's stories in the magazine were bringing him the same kind of popularity that such authors as Seabury Quinn and H.P. Lovecraft were also receiving in the letters column. In fact, except for Quinn's exploits of the psychic detective Jules de Grandin, Conan was the most popular character to ever appear in *Weird Tales*.

'Rogues in the House', which appeared in the January 1934 *Weird Tales*, was another of those Conan stories which seemed to write itself. This time, the young barbarian thief was saved from a dungeon by a nobleman seeking revenge. As Howard recalled: 'I didn't rewrite it even once. As I remember I only erased and changed one word in it, and then sent it in just as it was written.'

Perhaps that was why, in a letter to P. Schuyler Miller written in 1936, Howard admitted that even he was not absolutely certain of the background to his own story: 'I am not sure that the adventure chronicled in "Rogues in the House" occurred in Zamora. The presence of opposing factions of politics would seem to indicate otherwise, since Zamora was an absolute despotism where differing political opinions were not tolerated. I am of the opinion that the city was one of the small city-states lying just west of Zamora, and into which Conan had wandered after leaving Zamora. Shortly after this he returned for a brief period to Cimmeria, and there were other returns to his native land from time to time.'

Another Conan story, 'The Frost King's Daughter', had originally been submitted to *Weird Tales* back in 1932 along with 'The Phoenix on the Sword'. However, Wright had rejected it in a letter dated March 10, in which he declared simply: 'I do not much care for it'. Retaining its Hyborian Age setting, Howard re-wrote the tale, replacing Conan with a similar hero named Amra of Akbitana. The Amra version finally appeared in Charles D. Hornig's amateur journal *The Fantasy Fan* for March 1934 under the title 'Gods of the North'. The Conan version didn't see publication until many years after Howard's death, and then under the title 'The Frost-Giant's Daughter'.

'Shadows in the Moonlight' in the April 1934 *Weird Tales* was originally titled 'Iron Shadows in the Moon' by Howard. This time Conan and his female companion escaped from a battlefield slaughter, only to find themselves menaced by iron statues imbued with life by the rays of the full moon. According to one reader from Rockdale, Texas, in the June 1934 issue: 'As usual Conan provided some real thrills in Robert E. Howard's story, 'Shadows in the Moonlight'. In my humble opinion Conan is the greatest of *WT*'s famous characters.'

Conan fell in love with the female pirate Bêlit, leader of the Black Corsairs, in his next adventure. After keeping Conan off the cover for several issues, Wright used a Margaret Brundage painting for 'Queen of the Black Coast' on the May 1934 *Weird Tales*. It featured a delicate-looking Conan with a diaphanously draped damsel throwing her arms around his neck as he warded off a flying attacker with an ineffectual knife.

Meanwhile, the Brundage debate continued to rage in 'The Eyrie': 'I do not think it would be at all an easy task to find anything to compare with Brundage's representations of sheer feminine loveliness without the touch of vulgarity and suggestiveness which usually accompany nudes in magazines,' commented a male reader from El Paso, Texas, in the June 1934 issue, adding: 'The cover illustrating "Black Colossus" was about as beautiful a piece of art as I have seen in a long time.'

However, in the same issue, a female reader from Oregon declared: 'I do enjoy *Weird Tales* and usually manage to acquire one each month, even though I do tear off the cover immediately and stick it in the nearest receptacle for trash. Are such covers absolutely necessary?'

Like Wright, Howard also knew his markets, and he knew how much he could get past his editor and still be certain of an eye-catching cover: 'Another problem is how far you can go without shocking the readers into distaste for your stuff – and therefore cutting down sales . . . I don't know how much slaughter and butchery the readers will endure. Their capacity for grisly details seems unlimited, when the cruelty is the torturing of some naked girl. The torture of a naked writhing wretch, utterly helpless – and especially when of the feminine sex amid voluptuous surroundings – seems to excite keen pleasure in some people who have a distaste for wholesale butchery in the heat and fury of a battlefield.'

Conan was the leader of a band of outlaws who battled a giant god of living metal in 'The Devil in Iron' in the August 1934 issue. It was the tenth Conan story to appear in *Weird Tales* and was voted by the readers as the best in that issue, despite another feeble Brundage cover depicting an unlikely-looking Conan entrapped by the coils of a giant green serpent while a semi-naked blonde looked on.

A much better Brundage cover was used for the first instalment of 'The People of the Black Circle', a three-part serial set in exotic northwest Asia which ran in the September, October and November 1934 editions of the magazine. This time the artist ignored Conan in favour of the beautiful princess Yasmina being held in the clutches of an evil sorcerer.

This is how Wright introduced the serial to his readers: 'Rough, and at times uncouth, Conan is a primitive man, who will brave almost certain death against terrific odds to rescue a damsel in distress; yet he will just as quickly give her a resounding slap on the posterior or drop her into a cesspool if she displeases him. But rude though he is, he possesses a sort of primordial chivalry and an innate reverence for womanhood that make him wholly fascinating.'

Obviously the readers agreed, as this short novel was again voted the best story in the magazine and editor Wright revealed that 'Robert E. Howard's spectacular and original hero, Conan the barbarian adventurer and fighting-man, has captured the fancy of our readers by his brilliant exploits and his utter humanness.'

However, not everyone was so enamoured with the mighty Cimmerian. In the November 1934 *Weird Tales*, the following letter appeared in 'The Eyrie': 'I am awfully tired of poor old Conan the Cluck, who for the past fifteen issues has every month slain a new wizard, tackled a new monster, come to a violent and sudden end that was averted (incredibly enough!) in just the nick of time, and won a new girlfriend, each of whose penchant for nudism won her place of honour, either on the cover or on the interior illustration . . . I cry: "Enough of this brute and his iron-thewed sword-thrusts – may he be sent to Valhalla to cut out paper dolls."' The author of this anti-Conan diatribe was none other than seventeen-year-old Robert Bloch, later to find lasting fame as the author of *Psycho*, whose own first story would be appearing in the January 1935 edition of 'The Unique Magazine'.

When 'A Witch Shall Be Born', with its memorable crucifixion scene, was published in the December 1934 issue of *Weird Tales*, Brundage instead went for another of her suggestive 'whipping' scenes on the cover, this time involving two near-naked women and a cat-o'-nine-tails.

Editor Farnsworth Wright's lengthy introduction announced that since Howard's first publication in the magazine back in 1925, 'he has had forty stories in *Weird Tales* alone, and has gained an enormous following among the readers of this magazine. Many thousands of readers eagerly buy any magazines that feature one of Mr Howard's stories . . . He has the faculty of making real characters of his heroes, not mere automatons who act as they do merely because the author pulls the strings.'

In early 1935 Howard's mother Hester underwent a serious operation, remaining in hospital for a month before returning home. Novalyne Price Ellis later recalled meeting her: 'Mrs Howard was sitting on the end of a divan. Her hair was nearly white, short, and parted on one side, not stylish. It looked as if she just combed it quickly to get it over with, not to make her look better. She got up with a great effort and stood leaning slightly to one side.' Hester Howard never fully recovered her health; she spent the remainder of her life in and out of various hospitals and sanatoriums when not being cared for at home by her husband and son.

Meanwhile, 'Jewels of Gwahlur' appeared in the March 1935 *Weird Tales*. It was a minor Conan tale, about the stealing of a cursed treasure from yet another lost city, which Howard had originally titled 'Teeth of Gwahlur'. But there was nothing minor about 'Beyond the Black River', the second of Conan's four serial-length appearances in *Weird Tales*, published in the May and June issues for 1935. Drawing upon its author's Texas background, it was a variation on the American frontier saga, with Howard's fictional Picts standing in for Native American warriors. It was also in this story that Howard had one of his characters famously observe: 'Barbarism is the natural state of mankind. Civilisation is unnatural. It is a whim of circumstance. And barbarism must always triumph.' There is little doubt that the author was expressing his own views directly to the reader.

With 'Beyond the Black River' Howard was still experimenting with the series, as he revealed in a letter to H.P. Lovecraft: 'I wanted to see if I could write an interesting Conan yarn without sex interest... I've attempted a new style of setting entirely – abandoned the exotic settings of lost cities, decaying civilisations, golden domes, marble palaces, silk-clad dancing girls, &c., and thrown my story against a background of forests and rivers, log cabins, frontier outposts, buckskin-clad settlers, and painted tribesmen.'

It was around this time that Howard also wrote but failed to sell 'Wolves Beyond the Border', which was set in the same milieu as 'Beyond the Black River' but did not feature Conan directly.

The May 1935 *Weird Tales* also included another letter from Robert Bloch, whose story 'The Secret of the Tomb' ran in the same issue: 'I have been highly interested in the comments anent my so-called "attack" on Howard in the Eyrie... At no time have I ever, directly or indirectly, maligned Mr Howard's fine and obviously talented abilities as a writer; I confined myself solely to a criticism of Conan's career.'

Meanwhile, the cost of Mrs Howard's continued medical treatment and the effect it was having on his own practice was draining

Dr Howard's finances, and the family was in need of urgent cash. At the time, *Weird Tales* still owed Howard more than $800 for stories which had already appeared and were supposed to have been paid for upon publication. In frustration, Howard wrote to editor Farnsworth Wright on May 6: 'For some time now I have been receiving a check regularly each month from *Weird Tales* – half checks, it is true, but by practicing the most rigid economy I have managed to keep my head above the water; that I was able to do so was largely because of, not the size but the regularity of the checks. I came to depend upon them and to expect them, as I felt justified in so doing. But this month, at the very time when I need money so desperately bad, I did not receive a check. Somehow, some way, my family and I have struggled along this far, but if you cut off my monthly checks now, I don't know what in God's name we'll do . . .'

In an autobiographical sketch in the July 1935 issue of Julius Schwartz's amateur *Fantasy Magazine*, Howard told the readers: 'Conan simply grew up in my mind a few years ago when I was stopping in a little border town on the lower Rio Grande. I did not create him by any conscious process. He simply stalked full grown out of oblivion and set me at work recording the saga of his adventures.'

In a letter that same month to Clark Ashton Smith, Howard continued: 'It may sound fantastic to link the term "realism" with Conan; but as a matter of fact – his supernatural adventures aside – he is the most realistic character I ever evolved. He is simply a combination of a number of men I have known, and I think that's why he seemed to step full-grown into my consciousness when I wrote the first yarn of the series. Some mechanism in my subconsciousness took the dominant characteristics of various prize-fighters, gunmen, bootleggers, oil field bullies, gamblers, and honest workmen I had come in contact with, and combining them all, produced the amalgamation I call Conan the Cimmerian.'

Between the early months of 1932 and July 1935, Robert E. Howard wrote twenty-one adventures of Conan the barbarian. These tales varied in length from around 3,500 words to the almost novel-length of 75,000 words, and seventeen of them were published in *Weird Tales*.

As the author explained: 'Literature is a business to me – a business at which I was making an ample living when the Depression knocked the guts out of the markets. My sole desire in writing is to make a reasonable living. I may cling to many illusions, but I am not ridden by the illusion that I have anything wonderful or magical to say, or that it would amount to anything particularly if I did say it. I have no quarrel with art-for-art's-sakers. On the contrary, I admire their work. But my pet delusions tend in other directions.'

Although Howard's writing career was improving again, his mother's fragile health was not. She had terminal tuberculosis. As Novalyne Price Ellis later observed: 'His mother had him so completely in her power that he hovered over her, even in a store. She was, of course, the only woman in his life.' Howard's idolisation of his mother would be his downfall. What neither knew was that time was quickly running out for both of them.

Despite enjoying an all-time high in sales during 1935, to such diverse pulp magazines as *Action Stories, Argosy, Dime Sports Magazine, Spicy-Adventure Stories, Star Western, Thrilling Adventures, Thrilling Mystery, Top-Notch, Western Aces* and, of course, *Weird Tales,* Howard had started talking about taking his own life when it appeared that his mother was

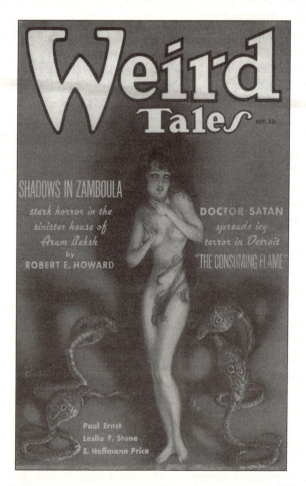

'Shadows in Zamboula' appeared in the November 1935 issue of Weird Tales *with a cover illustration by Margaret Brundage.*

dying. As his father, Dr I.M. Howard later recalled: 'Last March a year ago, again when his mother was very low in the King's Daughters Hospital in Temple, Texas, Dr McCelvey expressed a fear that she would not recover; he began to talk to me about his business, and I at once understood what it meant. I began to talk to him, trying to dissuade him from such a course, but his mother began to improve. Immediately she began to improve, he became cheerful and no more was said.'

Howard was ignored or simply dismissed as eccentric by most of the inhabitants of his hometown of Cross Plains, Texas, but he began to exhibit even more bizarre behaviour. He had told writer E. Hoffman Price the previous year: 'Nobody thinks I amount to much, so I am proud to show these people that a successful writer thinks enough of me to drive a thousand miles to hell and gone out of his way to visit me.' Howard now decided to grow a long walrus moustache and walk around town dressed somewhat unconventionally.

As Novalyne Price Ellis described in her memoir *One Who Walked Alone*: 'The first thing that startled me was the black sombrero he had on. It was a real Mexican sombrero with little balls dangling from its rim. The chin strap was a thin little strip of leather attached to the hat. It came down and was tied under his chin. The vaqueros used the chin strap to keep their hats from being blown off by the incessant winds that swept the plains. But the flat crown and chin strap made Bob's face look rounder than ever . . . The red bandana around his neck was tied in the back. He didn't have on those old short, brown pants. Not this year! He had on short, *black* pants that came to the top of his black shoes.'

In 'Shadows in Zamboula', which was published in the November 1935 issue of *Weird Tales*, Conan found himself staying in a city filled with intrigue and cannibalism. Howard's original title for the story had been 'The Man-Eaters of Zamboula'. The issue once again featured a Conan cover by Margaret Brundage, with a naked Nafertari surrounded by four hissing cobras. However, the story was closely beaten in the readers' poll by 'The Way Home' by Paul Frederick Stern (a pen-name for writer Paul Ernst).

At around 75,000 words, Howard's next entry in the series was twice as long as any other Conan story, and Howard's only completed novel. Written over four months in the spring of 1934, he cannibalised and expanded a number of his earlier Conan stories – specifically 'The Scarlet Citadel', 'Black Colossus' and 'The Devil in Iron' – to create one of his finest and most mature works. According to the author, 'Conan was about forty when he seized the crown of Aquilonia, and was about forty-four or forty-five at the time of *The Hour of the Dragon*.

Conan's first British publication was 'Rogues in the House' in the 1934 anthology Terror by Night *edited by Christine Campbell Thomson.*

He had no male heir at that time, because he had never bothered to formally make some woman his queen, and the sons of concubines, of which he had a goodly number, were not recognised as heirs to the throne.'

Howard had already had several stories reprinted between hardcovers in Britain in the *Not at Night* series of horror anthologies edited by Christine Campbell Thomson (including the Conan story 'Rogues in the House', which appeared in the 1934 volume *Terror at Night*). *The Hour of the Dragon* was submitted to British publisher Denis Archer in May 1934. The year before, Archer had turned down a collection of Howard's stories (which featured two Conan tales) with the suggestion that 'any time you find yourself able to produce a full-length novel of about 70,000-75,000 words along the lines of the stories, my allied Company, Pawling & Ness Ltd, who deal with the lending libraries, and are able to sell a first edition of 5,000 copies, will be very willing to publish it.'

In fact, Archer accepted *The Hour of the Dragon*, but the publisher went bankrupt and his assets, including Howard's novel, were put into the hands of the official receiver. The book was never published, and the story finally appeared as a five-part serial running in *Weird Tales* from December 1935 to April 1936 (with chapter 20 apparently misnumbered as chapter 21).

Despite Margaret Brundage's cover depicting her most pathetic-looking Conan ever, chained in a cell while a scantily clad Zenobia hands him the keys, readers reacted favourably to the serial in 'The Eyrie': 'If "The Hour of the Dragon" ends as good as it began I shall vote Mr Howard your ace writer,' promised a reader from Sioux City, Iowa. 'Robert E. Howard's "Hour of the Dragon" is vividly written, as are all Mr Howard's stories,' praised a reader from Hazleton, Pennsylvania, who continued: 'Conan is at his bloodthirsty worst, killing off his enemies left and right; lovely damozels walk about in scanty shifts and pine to be held in his muscular arms – so what more could one want, I ask you?'

However, the Brundage controversy continued to rage: 'I was greatly pleased with the stories in the December *WT*, but at the same time greatly disappointed with Mrs. Brundage's illustration of Conan,' complained a reader from Washington DC. 'From Howard's stories I have always pictured Conan as a rough, muscular, scarred figure of giant stature with thick, wiry, black hair covering his massive chest, powerful arms, and muscular legs; and a face that's as rugged as the weather-beaten face of an old sea captain.'

Howard expressed his own opinion of Brundage's work in a letter in the June 1936 issue: 'Enthusiasm impels me to pause from burning spines off cactus for my drouth-bedeviled goats long enough to give three slightly dust-choked cheers for the April cover illustration . . . altogether I think it's the best thing Mrs Brundage has done since she illustrated my "Black Colossus". And that's no depreciation of the covers done between these master-pictures.'

'Howard was my favourite author,' Brundage recalled many years later, admitting, 'I always liked his stories best.'

In terms of Conan's history, *The Hour of the Dragon* (which was later reprinted under the title *Conan the Conqueror*) is the final story in the sequence. It was also the last Conan story Howard himself would ever see published.

Howard was still upset over his mother's failing health, as his father later revealed: 'Again this year, in February, while his mother was very sick and not expected to live but a few days, at that time she was in the Shannon Hospital in San Angelo, Texas. San Angelo is something like one hundred miles from here. He was driving back and forth daily from San Angelo to home. One evening he told me I would find his business, what little there was to it, all carefully written up and in a large envelope in his desk.'

In a letter to Novalyne Price Ellis dated February 14, 1936, Howard admitted: 'You ask how my mother is getting along. I hardly know what to say. Some days she seems to be improving a little, and other days she seems to be worse. I frankly don't know.'

Conan's final appearance in *Weird Tales* was the three-part serial 'Red Nails' in the July, August-September and October 1936 issues. Howard described it as 'the grimmest, bloodiest and most merciless story of the series so far. Too much raw meat, maybe, but I merely portrayed what I honestly believe would be the reactions of certain types of people in the situations on which the plot of the story hung.'

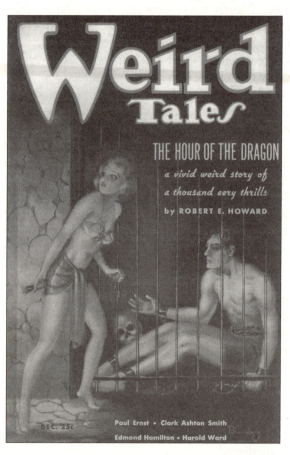

'The Hour of the Dragon' began its serialisation in Weird Tales *with the December 1935 issue, featuring another cover illustration by Margaret Brundage.*

In a letter dated December 5, 1935, he called it 'the bloodiest and most sexy weird story I ever wrote. I have been dissatisfied with my handling of decaying races in stories, for the reason that degeneracy is so prevalent in such races that even in fiction it can not be ignored as a motive and as a fact if the fiction is to have any claim to realism. I have ignored it in all other stories, as one of the taboos, but I did not ignore it in this story. When, or if, you ever read it, I'd like to know how you like my handling of the subject of lesbianism.'

In fact, there is only the slightest suggestion of lesbianism in the published version of the story, in which Conan and beautiful Aquilonian mercenary Valeria discovered yet another lost city and battled a monster reptile.

Introducing 'Red Nails' in the July 1936 issue, editor Farnsworth Wright recalled: 'Nearly four years ago, *Weird Tales* published a story called 'The Phoenix on the Sword' built around a barbarian adventurer named Conan, who had become king of a country by sheer force of valour and brute strength . . . The stories of Conan were speedily acclaimed by our readers, and the barbarian's weird adventures became immensely popular. The story presented herewith is one of the most powerful and eery [sic] weird tales yet written about Conan. We commend this story to you, for we know you will enjoy it through and through.'

Margaret Brundage's suggestive cover depicted a naked Valeria about to be sacrificed on an altar by three seductive slave girls. It was the last illustration Brundage would do for a Howard story and with the next issue of *Weird Tales* she ended her continuous run of thirty-nine covers for 'The Unique Magazine'. (She would still occasionally make an appearance on the cover over the next nine years, and her final original painting – her sixty-sixth – appeared on the January 1945 issue.)

Written in July 1935, 'Red Nails' was the final Conan story – and the final fantasy story – which Howard would complete. With his mother's hospital bills escalating and *Weird Tales* (supposedly) paying on publication some of the lowest rates in the pulp field, he began to look around for better and more dependable markets. As Howard revealed in a letter dated February 15, 1936, to E. Hoffman Price: 'For myself, I haven't submitted anything to *Weird Tales* for many months, though I would, if payments could be made a little more promptly. I reckon the boys have their troubles, same as me, but my needs are urgent and immediate.'

Price observed that during his 1934 visit to Cross Plains: 'I had often got the impression that Robert was a parent to his parents; that while he could have done the gypsying which other authors permitted themselves, solicitude for his father and mother kept him fairly close to home.'

Novalyne Price Ellis agreed: 'I do think Bob has tried to take over his parents' lives. He said once that parents and children change places in life. When parents become old and sick, you take care of them as you would a child.'

During the spring of 1936, Hester Howard appeared to grow stronger, much to the relief of her son, as Dr Howard later explained: 'He accepted her condition as one of permanent improvement and one that would continue. I knew well that it would not, but I kept it from him.'

In a letter written to young Wisconsin writer August Derleth, dated May 9, 1936, Howard offered his own thoughts after recent deaths in Derleth's family: 'Death to the old is inevitable, and yet somehow I often feel that it is a greater tragedy than death to the young. When a man dies young he misses much suffering, but the old have only life as a possession and somehow to me the tearing of a pitiful remnant from weak old fingers is more tragic than the looting of a life in its full rich plume. I don't want to live to be old. I want to die when my time comes, quickly and suddenly, in the full tide of my strength and health.'

In a letter dated May 13, he also confided to his old correspondent and fellow *Weird Tales* writer H.P. Lovecraft that he did not know whether his mother would: 'live or not. She is very weak and weighs only 109 pounds – 150 pounds is her normal weight – and very few kinds of food agree with her; but if she does live, she will owe her life to my father's efforts.'

For three weeks Robert E. Howard continued to maintain an almost constant vigil at his beloved mother's bedside as her condition began to decline rapidly. Atypically, his mood became almost cheerful, as if he had finally made up his mind about something.

On the morning of June 11, 1936, Howard learned from one of two trained nurses attending Mrs Howard that his mother had entered a terminal coma and that she would probably never recognise him again. He rose from beside her sickbed, slipped out of the house, climbed into his 1935 Chevrolet sedan, which was parked in front of the garage, and rolled up the windows. At a few minutes past eight o'clock in the morning, he fired a single bullet from a borrowed Colt .380 automatic into his right temple. He had come to the decision that he would not see his mother die.

The bullet passed through his brain and he survived for eight hours in a coma. He was thirty years old. His mother died shortly after ten o'clock on the evening of the following day, without ever regaining consciousness. She was sixty-six (although she had always claimed to be several years younger). They were buried in adjacent graves in identical caskets at Brownwood's Greenleaf Cemetery.

A strip of paper was discovered after Howard shot himself. It contained two typewritten lines taken from Viola Garvin's poem 'The House of Cæsar':

> *All fled – all done, so lift me on the pyre –*
> *The Feast is over and the lamps expire.*

Having pretty much ignored him for most of his life, on the day of his death the local newspaper reprinted one of Howard's last Western stories, along with a 6,000-word article and an obituary – more space than any citizen of Cross Plains had ever received.

On June 24, 1936, Howard's beloved library of some three hundred books and file copies of all the magazines which contained his stories were donated by his father to Howard Payne College to form The Robert E. Howard Memorial Collection. Nine months later Dr Howard reclaimed all his son's magazines because they were falling apart.

In a letter dated June 29, 1936, Dr Howard wrote to H.P. Lovecraft: 'Robert was a great admirer of you. I have often heard him say that you were the best weird writer in the world, and he keenly enjoyed corresponding with you. He often expressed hope that you might visit in our home some day, so that he, his mother and I might see and know you personally. Robert greatly admired all weird writers, often heard him speak of each separately and express the highest admiration of all. He said they were a bunch of great men and he admired all of them very much.'

Lovecraft's own 'Robert Ervin Howard: A Memoriam' was published in the September 1936 issue of Julius Schwartz's *Fantasy Magazine*: 'The character and attainments of Mr Howard were wholly unique. He was, above everything else, a lover of the simpler, older world of barbarian and pioneer days, when courage and strength took the place of subtlety and stratagem, and when a hardy, fearless race battled and bled, and asked no quarter from hostile nature. All his stories reflect this philosophy, and derive from it a vitality found in few of his contemporaries. No one could write more convincingly of violence and gore than he, and his battle passages reveal an instinctive aptitude for military tactics which would have brought him distinction in times of war. His real gifts were even higher than the readers of his published works would suspect, and had he lived, would have helped him to make his mark in serious literature with some folk epic of his beloved south

> # Funeral Notice
>
> ### Mrs. I. M. Howard
>
> Born July 11, 1874
> Died June 12, 1936
> Age 61 Years, 11 Months and One Day.
>
> ### Robert E. Howard
>
> Born January 22, 1906
> Died June 11, 1936
> Age 30 Years, 4 Months and 19 Days.
>
> Funeral Services Promptly at 10 A. M. Sunday
> Morning, June 14, at Baptist Tabernacle,
> Cross Plains.
> Interment In Greenleaf Cemetary, Brownwood, Texas
> 1 P. M. June 14, 1936

Robert and Hester Jane Howard's Funeral Notice, June 1936.

west... Always a disciple of hearty and strenuous living, he suggested more than casually his own famous character – the intrepid warrior, adventurer, and seizer of thrones, Conan the Cimmerian. His loss at the age of thirty is a tragedy of the first magnitude, and a blow from which fantasy fiction will not soon recover.'

While writing those words, Lovecraft could hardly have realised that the world of fantasy fiction would soon be mourning the impact of his own premature death, at the age of forty-seven, little more than nine months later.

Howard's father continued to correspond with E. Hoffman Price until he died, a lonely old man suffering from diabetes and cataracts in both eyes, on November 12, 1944. As Price later recalled: 'Whenever I think of Dr Howard, well into his seventy-fourth year, and with failing eyesight, having for these past eight years faced alone and single handed a home and a world from which both wife and son were taken in one day, I can not help but say, "I wish Robert had had more of his father's courage."'

The notice of Howard's death appeared in the August-September issue of *Weird Tales*: 'As this issue goes to press, we are saddened by the news of the sudden death of Robert E. Howard of Cross Plains, Texas. Mr Howard for years has been one of the most popular magazine authors in the country . . . It was in *Weird Tales* that the cream of his writing appeared. Mr Howard was one of our literary discoveries . . . Prolific though he was, his genius shone through everything he wrote and he did not lower his high literary standards for the sake of mere volume.' At the time, the magazine still owed Howard $1,350 for stories it had already published.

Regular *Weird Tales* cover artist Margaret Brundage remembered how she learned of the author's death: 'I came into the offices one day and Wright informed me of Howard's suicide. We both just sat around and cried for most of the day. He was always my personal favourite.'

Robert Bloch, who had previously criticised Howard in the magazine wrote: 'Robert E. Howard's death is quite a shock – and a severe blow to *WT*. Despite my standing opinion of Conan, the fact always remains that Howard was one of *WT*'s finest contributors.'

Although it is true that Robert E. Howard neither wrote nor published the Conan stories in any particular sequence, in a letter dated March 10, 1936, to science fiction writer P. Schuyler Miller, the author responded to an attempt by Miller and chemist Dr John D. Clark to put the Conan series into chronological order with his own concept of Conan's eventual fate: 'Frankly I can't predict it. In writing these yarns I've always felt less as creating them than as if I were simply chronicling his adventures as he told them to me. That's why they skip about so much, without following a regular order. The average adventurer, telling tales of a wild life at random, seldom follows any ordered plan, but narrates episodes widely separated by space and years, as they occur to him.'

The Cimmerian's adventures appeared as the author imagined them – consequently the first two stories published, 'The Phoenix on the Sword' and 'The Scarlet Citadel', feature an older Conan who has already been crowned king of Aquilonia, while the character appears as a teenage thief in the third published tale, 'The Tower of the Elephant'.

One explanation for this apparently random chronology appears in a letter postmarked December 14, 1933, to Clark Ashton Smith, in which Howard hinted at a possible preternatural power behind the creation of his character: ' While I don't go so far as to believe that stories are inspired by actually existent spirits or powers (though I am rather opposed to flatly denying anything) I have sometimes wondered if it were possible that unrecognised forces of the past or present – or even the future – work through the thoughts and actions of living men. This occurred to me when I was writing the first stories of the Conan series especially . . . I do not attempt to explain this by esoteric or occult means, but the facts remain. I still write of Conan more powerfully and with more understanding than any of my other characters. But the time will probably come when I will suddenly find myself unable to write convincingly of him at all. That has happened in the past with nearly all my rather numerous characters; suddenly I would find myself out of contact with the conception, as if the man himself had been standing at my shoulder directing my efforts, and had suddenly turned and gone away, leaving me to search for another character.'

Robert E. Howard's death did not mark the end of Conan. The unpublished manuscripts of four completed Conan stories, which had been rejected by *Weird Tales* editor Farnsworth Wright, were discovered amongst the author's papers many years after his death. The first of these, 'The God in the Bowl', appeared in the September 1952 issue of *Space Science Fiction*. A combination of murder mystery and magic, it was revised considerably for publication by writer L. Sprague de Camp, who produced yet another version of the story, closer to the original manuscript, for paperback publication fifteen years later.

Another greatly abridged version by de Camp of Howard's story 'The Black Stranger' appeared in the first issue of *Fantasy Magazine* for February-March, 1953. 'It was quite an event to discover that a full novelette by [Howard] had never been published,' wrote editor Lester Del Rey, 'and we finally got it. It isn't the sort of a tale you'll usually find in this magazine – because nobody else can quite recapture the pre-mythical past.'

This 33,000-word short novel had been written around the same time as 'Beyond the Black River' and 'Wolves Beyond the Border' and mixed Conan with Picts and pirates. When he could not sell it as a Conan adventure, Howard had attempted to rescue the story by turning the hero into the swashbuckling pirate Black Vulmea, but it remained unpublished until 1976, when it appeared in the collection *Black Vulmea's Vengeance* under the title 'Swords of the Red Brotherhood'. The Conan treatment was subsequently republished under the title 'The Treasure of Tranicos', and the complete version finally saw print, exactly as Howard wrote it, in Karl Edward Wagner's 1987 anthology *Echoes of Valor*.

Originally rejected by Wright in 1932, Howard had submitted a

'The Black Stranger' appeared in the first issue of Fantasy Magazine for February-March, 1953. Cover by Hannes Bok.

revised draft of 'The Frost King's Daughter', featuring the Conan-like hero Amra of Akbitana, to the amateur journal *The Fantasy Fan*, which had published the story in the March 1934 issue as 'Gods of the North'. When Howard's Conan version appeared in the August 1953 issue of *Fantasy Fiction* as 'The Frost-Giant's Daughter', it had been extensively rewritten by de Camp, and it was not until 1976 that the author's original manuscript finally saw print. Although *Fantasy Fiction* had claimed, 'Here, for the last time in an original story, the barbarian hero stalks through the strange, magic-ridden lands of the Hyperborean [*sic*] Age', another Conan story, 'The Vale of Lost Women', eventually appeared in the Spring 1967 issue of Robert A.W. Lowndes' *Magazine of Horror*. This story was probably rejected by Wright because of scenes where an older Conan massacred an entire village and the heroine had to barter her virginity in order to be rescued. Reaction to its publication was decidedly mixed: 'The so-called "Conan" story with its fantasy domino slightly askew is a thinly-masked "porny" of the cheapest sado-sexual variety and doesn't belong in your pages,' wrote one reader to the magazine's letters column, while another was of the opinion: 'I cannot imagine why "The Vale of Lost Women" was not published during Howard's lifetime... It is certainly one of Howard's better works.'

Howard also left behind a number of fragments and brief outlines for never-completed adventures which various authors, including L. Sprague de Camp and Lin Carter, completed and added to in an attempt to fill in the gaps in Conan's career. Some of these manuscripts were Oriental adventures that the writers then converted into Conan stories by changing names, deleting anachronisms and introducing a supernatural element.

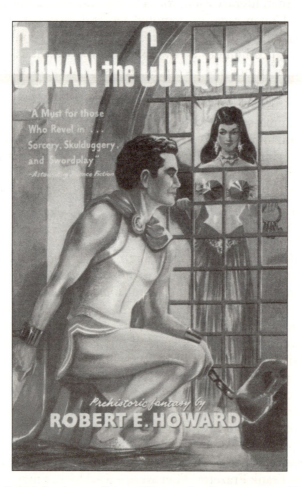

The British hardcover edition of Conan the Conqueror, *published by T. V. Boardman & Co. of London in 1954.*

AFTERWORD: ROBERT E. HOWARD AND CONAN

In 1953, Ace Books issued Howard's novel *Conan the Conqueror* as an 'Ace Double' paperback, bound back-to-back with *The Sword of Rhiannon* by Leigh Brackett, and the following year the book finally made its British début, exactly twenty years after it had first been submitted by Howard, in a hardcover edition from T.V. Boardman & Co. of London. Unfortunately, the uncredited dust-jacket artist decided to illustrate the same scene that Margaret Brundage had used for her cover of the December 1935 *Weird Tales*, with equally wretched results.

Between 1950-57 New York's Gnome Press published seven hardcover volumes of Conan stories, which included several tales either edited by or in collaboration with de Camp, who later explained: 'Late in 1951, I stumbled upon a cache of Howard's manuscripts in the apartment of the then literary agent for Howard's estate . . . The incomplete state of the Conan saga has tempted me and others to add to it, as Howard might have done had he lived . . . The reader must judge how successful our posthumous collaboration with Howard has been.'

However, as author and editor Karl Edward Wagner wrote in 1977, 'The only man who could write a Robert E. Howard story was Robert E. Howard. It is far more than a matter of imitating adjective usage or analysing comma-splices. It is a matter of spirit. Pastiche-Conan is not the same Conan as portrayed by Robert E. Howard. Read such, as it pleases you – but don't delude yourself into thinking that this is any more Robert E. Howard's Conan than a Conan story you decided to write yourself. It is this editor's belief that a Conan collection should contain *only* Robert E. Howard's Conan tales, and that *no* editorial emendations should alter the authenticity of Howard's creation.' And this came from one of the better writers of Howard pastiches.

In fact, *Weird Tales* editor Farnsworth Wright had told his readers much the same thing four decades earlier: 'Sorry to deny your request for some other author to carry on the Conan stories of the late Robert E. Howard. His work was touched with genius, and he had a distinctive style of writing that put the stamp of his personality on every story he wrote. It would hardly be fair to his memory if we allowed Conan to be recreated by another hand, no matter how skilful.'

Amateur publications such as Glenn Lord's *The Howard Collector*, George H. Scithers' *Amra* and The Robert E. Howard United Press Association (REHupa) rekindled interest in Howard's fiction during the 1960s and '70s, and beginning in 1966 Lancer Books in America, and later Sphere Books in Britain, collected the Conan stories into a series of twelve paperbacks, many of which featured distinctive cover paintings by Frank Frazetta. They were edited by L. Sprague de Camp, and once again Howard's original texts were altered: the series included revisions, posthumous collaborations, fixed-up novels and totally new pastiches. Over a million copies of the Lancer editions were sold during the first few years of publication, ranking Howard second only to J.R.R. Tolkien in the field of fantasy fiction.

In 1957 a Swedish fan named Björn Nyberg had collaborated with L. Sprague de Camp on a new novel entitled *The Return of Conan*, and with Howard's renewed popularity, soon other authors were adding original novels to the Conan canon. These included Karl Edward Wagner, Poul Anderson, Andrew J. Offutt, Robert Jordan, John Maddox Roberts, Steve Perry, Roland Green, Leonard Carpenter and John C. Hocking.

Thirty-five years after his creator's death, Howard's mighty Cimmerian had turned into a money-spinning franchise.

In October 1970, Marvel Comics Group launched its hugely successful *Conan the Barbarian* title, written by Roy Thomas and initially illustrated by artist Barry (Windsor-)Smith. Many issues adapted or were based on Howard's original stories, and there was even a two-issue cross-over with Michael Moorcock's character Elric of Melniboné. The following year, Marvel introduced another series of Conan adaptations by Thomas in *Savage Tales*. *Conan the Barbarian King-Size* appeared in 1973, and it was followed over the years by such titles as *The Savage Sword of Conan*, *King Conan*, *Conan the Destroyer* and *The Conan Saga*.

In 1982 director John Milius and co-writer Oliver Stone turned *Conan the Barbarian* into a multi-million dollar fantasy movie. Austrian bodybuilder and former Mr Universe Arnold Schwarzenegger was cast as the sword-wielding hero, pitted against James Earl Jones' evil shape-changing sorcerer, Thulsa Doom. Two years later Schwarzenegger returned to the screen in *Conan the Destroyer* for veteran director Richard Fleischer. This time Sarah Douglas' treacherous Queen Taramis sent Conan and his companions on a quest for a magical key to unlock the secret of a mystical horn. Filmed on a lower budget in Mexico, this pulpy sequel was slightly more faithful to the spirit of Howard's characters, probably because it was based on a story by comic-book writers Roy Thomas and Gerry Conway.

Schwarzenegger returned as Conan-like warrior Kalidor in Fleischer's woeful *Red Sonja* (1985), which starred Brigitte Nielsen as the eponymous swordswoman in a film that barely had any connection to Howard's work. John Nicolella's *Kull the Conqueror* (1997) featured Kevin Sorbo as the future king of Valusia. It was apparently derived from a 1991 script for the third *Conan* film, a loose adaptation of 'The Hour of the Dragon'.

Robert E. Howard was not even credited on the 1992-93 half-hour children's cartoon series *Conan the Adventurer*, in which the brawny barbarian and his comrades set out to undo the spell of living stone cast upon Conan's family by driving the evil serpent men back into another dimension. German weightlifter Ralph Moeller took over the role for the 1997-98 live-action television series Conan, produced by Brian Yuzna. The pilot film, *The Heart of the Elephant*, was loosely based on Howard's story 'The Tower of the Elephant' and featured a bizarre computer-created image of the late Richard Burton as the Cimmerian god Crom.

Even more unexpected was director Dan Ireland's little 1996 independent film *The Whole Wide World*, based on Novalyne Price Ellis' book *One Who Walked Alone*. Filmed on location in Texas, René Zellweger portrayed the young schoolteacher who befriended eccentric pulp magazine writer Robert E. Howard, played by Vincent D'Onofrio. It is difficult to imagine a more perfect film biography of Howard's final years.

Howard himself had already hinted in letters that he was planning to move away from fantasy fiction, and there has been much conjecture over the years that, had he lived, he would have made his name as a regional writer, with more mainstream stories or histories set in his native Southwest.

In his Foreword to the 1946 Arkham House collection of Howard's short fiction, *Skull-Face and Others*, editor August Derleth supports this view: 'The late Robert E. Howard was a writer of pulp fiction. He was also more than that. He had in him the promise of becoming an important American regionist, and to that end he had been assimilating the lore and legend, the history and culture patterns of his own corner of Texas.'

We shall never know how Robert E. Howard might have developed as a writer, but had he continued to work in the fantastic field, we can only speculate as to where Howard himself might have taken Conan. In his 1936 letter to P. Schuyler Miller he left behind a number of clues: 'He was, I think, king of Aquilonia for many years, in a turbulent and unquiet reign, when the Hyborian civilisation had reached its most magnificent high-tide, and every king had imperial ambitions. At first he fought on the defensive, but I am of the opinion that at last he was forced into wars of aggression as matter of self-preservation. Whether he succeeded in conquering a world-wide empire, or perished in the attempt, I do not know.

'He travelled widely, not only before his kingship, but after he was king. He travelled to Khitai and Hyrkania, and to the even less known regions north of the latter and south of the former. He even visited a nameless continent in the western hemisphere, and roamed among the islands adjacent to it. How much of this roaming will get into print, I can not foretell with any accuracy.'

Tragically, because of Howard's suicide, none of it ever did.

As we celebrate the centenary of Robert E. Howard's birth, it is worth noting that these stories – often written for less than a cent per word and published in disposable magazines printed on cheap pulp paper – have remained with us over the decades. Today, through films, television and comic books, Howard's name is more widely known than it ever was during his lifetime. His most famous creation, Conan the Cimmerian, has outlived his creator and, with the exception of Edgar Rice Burroughs' Tarzan, is possibly the best-known character in modern fantasy fiction.

In 1998, independent British publishing imprint Wandering Star began an ambitious programme of reprinting Howard's fiction in beautifully designed and illustrated limited editions aimed at the collector's market. The publisher began issuing a series of complete Conan stories in 2003, lovingly illustrated by artists such as Mark Schultz and Gary Gianni.

That same year, Dark Horse Books started *The Chronicles of Conan*, a series of graphic volumes reprinting the original Marvel Comics series from the 1970s with fascinating new Afterwords by writer/editor Roy Thomas and remastered artwork from Barry Windsor-Smith, John Buscema, Neal Adams and others. In 2004, Dark Horse launched its own *Conan* comic, billed as 'A faithful return to Robert E. Howard's original version' and featuring adaptations of 'The Frost-Giant's Daughter', 'The God in the Bowl' and 'The Jewels of Gwahlur'.

Towards the end of 2000, it was announced that Marvel Comics' Stan Lee had purchased the film rights to Conan. However, the project became stalled when Lee's company suspended operations less than three months later, after bridging financing fell through. An attempt by Wachowski brothers Larry and Andy (*The Matrix*, etc.) to develop a movie entitled *King Conan* for Warner Bros., with John Milius once again attached to write and direct, also collapsed in early 2004 over creative differences. The rights to the character are currently held by a Swedish media company, but any talk about a new Conan movie appears premature at this time.

However, those who only know the barbarian through his media incarnations have not experienced the *real* Conan. At his best, Robert E. Howard could sweep the reader away on a red tide of bloodlust to lost cities, unexplored jungles and savage pirate galleons, where all a brave man needed was a sharp sword in his hand and a beautiful woman by his side to face whatever hideous horror or supernatural menace confronted him.

These, then, are the original tales of Conan, as fresh, atmospheric and vibrant today as when they were first published around seventy years ago in the pages of *Weird Tales* and elsewhere.

As H.P. Lovecraft accurately observed: 'It is hard to describe precisely what made Mr Howard's stories stand out so sharply; but the real secret is that he himself is in every one of them . . . He was greater than any profit-making policy he could adopt – for even when he outwardly made concessions to Mammon-guided editors and commercial critics, he had an internal force and sincerity which broke through the surface and put the imprint of his personality on everything he wrote. Before he concluded with it, it always took on some tinge of vitality and reality in spite of popular editorial policy – always drew something from his own experience and knowledge of life instead of from the sterile herbarium of desiccated pulpish standby. Not only did he excel in pictures of strife and slaughter, but he was almost alone in his ability to create real emotions of spectral fear and dread suspense. No author – even in the humblest fields – can truly excel unless he takes his work very seriously; and Mr Howard did just that even in cases where he consciously thought he did not.'

For the discerning reader of fantasy fiction, Robert E. Howard's talent and tragedy will continue to live on through these authentic adventures of his greatest creation, Conan the Cimmerian.

Stephen Jones
London, England

ROBERT E. HOWARD was born and raised in rural Texas, where he lived all his life. The son of a pioneer physician, he began writing professionally at fifteen, and three years later sold his first story to *Weird Tales*. A prolific and proficient author, he published westerns, sports stories, horror tales, true confessions, historical adventures and detective thrillers, all the while developing a series of heroic characters with whom he would forever be identified with: Solomon Kane, King Kull, Bran Mak Morn and, of course, Conan the Cimmerian. Between 1932 and 1935, Howard wrote twenty-one sword and sorcery adventures of Conan, ranging in length from 3,500-word short stories to novel-length tales of 75,000 words. He committed suicide at the age of thirty, in June 1936. For more information about Robert E. Howard and Conan visit the REHupa website at http://www.rehupa.com

STEPHEN JONES is one of Britain's most acclaimed anthologists of horror and dark fantasy. He has more than eighty books to his credit, and has won numerous awards. You can visit his website at http://www.herebedragons.co.uk/jones

LES EDWARDS is an award-winning artist who has established himself as a stalwart of the British fantasy, horror and science fiction illustration scene in a career spanning thirty years. You can visit his website at http://www.lesedwards.com